ARAGORN

J. R. R. Tolkien's Undervalued Hero

"I see on his breast a green stone, and from that his true name shall come and his chief renown: for he shall be a healer and a renewer"

(The History of Middle-earth XII. Foreword)

Angela P. Nicholas

Academia Lunare

Second Edition, by Luna Press Publishing™, Edinburgh, 2017
First published, by Bright Pen, Sandy, 2012

Text Copyright © 2012 Angela P Nicholas
Cover photograph: bespoke jewellery owned by the author
Cover design © 2017 Jay Johnstone

Aragorn. JRR Tolkien's Undervalued Hero ©2017. All rights reserved. No part of this publication may be reproduced, stored in a retrieval system, or transmitted in any form or by any means, electronic, mechanical, photocopy, recording or otherwise, without prior written permission of the publisher. Nor can it be circulated in any form of binding or cover other than that in which it is published and without similar condition including this condition being imposed on a subsequent purchaser.

www.lunapresspublishing.com

ISBN-13: 978-1-911143-13-0

CONTENTS

ABBREVIATIONS	ii
FOREWORD	v
PREFACE	1

PART ONE

BIOGRAPHY, CHARACTER AND SIGNIFICANCE — 5

Chapter 1.0 - Introduction	7
Chapter 1.1 - Ancestry	8
Chapter 1.2 - Prophecies	10
Chapter 1.3 - Childhood	15
Chapter 1.4 - Adulthood Prior To *LotR*	18
Chapter 1.5 - *LotR*: An "Aragorn-Centric" View	27
Chapter 1.6 - The Palantír Confrontation	60
Chapter 1.7 - King Elessar	75
Chapter 1.8 - Death	85
Chapter 1.9 - Names and Titles	88
Chapter 1.10 - Appearance	99

PART TWO

RELATIONSHIPS — 109

Chapter 2.0 - Introduction	111
Chapter 2.1 - Elves	112
Chapter 2.2 - Dúnedain	137
Chapter 2.3 - Istari	148
Chapter 2.4 - Legolas and Gimli	180
Chapter 2.5 - Hobbits	208
Chapter 2.6 - Gondorians	251
Chapter 2.7 - Rohirrim	298
Chapter 2.8 - Ancestors, The Ring and Gollum	337
Chapter 2.9 - Miscellaneous Relationships	363
CONCLUSION	407

APPENDICES

GENEALOGICAL TABLES	412
THE SILMARILLION: CHIEF NAMES AND CONCEPTS USED	420
BIBLIOGRAPHY	422
INDEX	425

Abbreviations

The Lord of the Rings	*LotR*
The Lord of the Rings Appendices	App
The Hobbit	*TH*
The Silmarillion	*TSil*
The Silmarillion Valaquenta	*Val*
The Silmarillion Akallabêth	*Ak*
The Silmarillion Rings of Power	*RoP*
Unfinished Tales of Númenor and Middle-earth	*UT*
The History of Middle-earth	*HoM-e*
Second Age	SA
Third Age	TA
Fourth Age	FA

Acknowledgements

I wish to thank the following people for their help
and support during the writing of this book:
All members - past and present - of the Southampton UK Tolkien Reading Group,
Lynn Forest-Hill, and last, but not least, my husband Chris Mac Arthur.

FOREWORD

Although I bought the first edition of *Aragorn: J.R.R. Tolkien's Undervalued Hero* as soon as it was published, it stood for almost a year on a long shelf of books waiting its turn to be read. As a specialist in Tolkien studies I try to keep up with new critical writings in the field. When I began to read and collect Tolkien seriously in the early 1980s, it was a good year when only two or three books about him were published; and if they were not all of the first rank, their authors generally had good knowledge of the subject and its literature, wrote largely without jargon or 'theory', and increased rather than dulled one's enjoyment of Tolkien's creations. Now it is a much harder business, because of the enormous quantity of products issuing from the mill of Tolkien scholarship and because of their widely varying quality.

Jaded, perhaps, when at last I picked up Ms. Nicholas' book it was without any special promise or expectation. But I had not gone far into it before finding it the most enjoyable work on Tolkien I had read in many years, so much so, in fact, that I slowed my reading to prolong the pleasure. In her study of Aragorn, Ms. Nicholas has used all of Tolkien's Middle-earth writings, as well as *Letters*, and has given *The Lord of the Rings* what she describes in her preface as 'the "fine-tooth comb" treatment'. It is not that she reveals unknown facts or makes some new interpretation, but rather, in an admirably readable and thorough manner, by means of a careful and detailed analysis of Tolkien's text as it relates to Aragorn, his interaction with others, and his response to events, she uncovers aspects of the character which may not be immediately apparent to readers. Only rarely does Tolkien let us see into Aragorn's mind, and some points become clear only after one has read *The Lord of the Rings* complete, including 'A Part of the Tale of Aragorn and Arwen' in Appendix A. Ms. Nicholas' book therefore is welcome, and valuable.

Christina Scull

PREFACE

Aragorn, Strider, Dúnadan, Elfstone, King Elessar...

We encounter Aragorn by all these names (and a few more) in *The Lord of the Rings*[1], as well as by various titles, for example "heir of Isildur" and "Chieftain of the Dúnedain", to cite just two of them.

So who is Aragorn?

Paul Kocher says: *"Aragorn is rather more difficult to know truly than any other important person in the story."*[2] This certainly seems to be the case.

Aragorn first appears in the Prancing Pony Inn at Bree, (*LotR* 1.9) a complete mystery to Frodo and his friends, and to the reader. He is heavily cloaked and hooded, grim, travel-worn, an object of suspicion to the inn-keeper, *"He is one of the wandering folk - Rangers we call them"*[3] and known only by a nick-name given to him by the locals. He was even unknown to Tolkien himself at first. In a letter to W. H. Auden of June 7th 1955 describing the writing of *LotR* Tolkien said: *"Strider sitting in the corner at the inn was a shock, and I had no more idea who he was than had Frodo."*[4] Likewise the first-time reader is similarly in the dark, uncertain as to whether this sinister-looking stranger twice the height of the Hobbits is really trying to help them or whether he is in league with the terrifying "Black Riders" who have been pursuing them.

Something of Aragorn's ancestry and significance comes to light at the Council of Elrond (*LotR* 2.2) where he is revealed to be the hidden heir to the kingships of Arnor and Gondor, and also the heir of Isildur, the Man who had robbed Sauron of the One Ring three thousand years earlier. In Lothlórien (*LotR* 2.8) Galadriel presents him with a kingly jewel and addresses him by the name he has been prophesied to bear as King. During Books 3, 4 and 5 of *LotR* he is firmly established as King-in-waiting. However he and the Hobbits have been separated since the end of Book 2 and although there are brief reunions with Merry and Pippin, the latter at any rate still has no idea who Aragorn really is, as is clear from his conversation with Gandalf in *LotR* 5.1 *" 'Kingship?' said Pippin amazed."*.[5] As far as Frodo and Sam are concerned it is not until their meeting with their royal healer on the Field of Cormallen that "the penny drops" and they fully realise the identity of the mysterious protector they met in Bree.

If we study the Appendices to *LotR* we find out that even Aragorn himself did not know who he was until he was twenty, and that he spent most of the next seventy years of his life disguised or incognito. We can also read the full account of the deep and long-standing love between him and Arwen, of which there are only the barest of hints in the main narrative - easily missed by both Hobbits and reader.

In short it is only with the hindsight of second and subsequent readings of *LotR* (assuming these take place) and perusal of the Appendices (ditto), that we begin to get any proper idea of who Aragorn is or any sort of appreciation of his significance in the history of Middle-earth in general and, more specifically, in the struggle to destroy the One Ring. I have long felt that he is underestimated, with his achievements, qualities and struggles often ignored, misunderstood or unappreciated. In addition I believe that his contribution to the "Ring Quest" is at least equal to that of Frodo, Sam, Gandalf and Gollum.

*

---

1. J.R.R. Tolkien, *The Lord of the Rings*, London, HarperCollins Publishers, 2007, 2nd edition, based on the 50th Anniversary Edition of 2004.
2. P. Kocher, *Master of Middle-earth: The Achievement of J. R. R. Tolkien*, London, Pimlico, 2002, first published in Great Britain by Thames & Hudson 1973, Chapter 6, p. 131.
3. Op. cit, [1], *LotR* p. 156.
4. H. Carpenter (ed.), *The Letters of J.R.R. Tolkien*, with the assistance of Christopher Tolkien, London, HarperCollins Publishers, 1995. First published in Great Britain by George Allen & Unwin, 1981, Letter. 163, p. 216.
5. Op. cit [1], *LotR* p. 754.

This book unofficially began during the year 2001 when I re-read *LotR* (after neglecting it for a few years) in preparation for the release of Peter Jackson's films. I hadn't visited a cinema for fifteen years but that was about to change as I found that I couldn't get enough of the films, so fascinated was I by seeing Middle-earth and its characters brought to life. However, much as I enjoyed Viggo Mortensen's portrayal of Aragorn, it was obvious that this was not the Aragorn I had come to know and love on my first reading of the book in 1973 and during the years/re-readings since. Also, with the proliferation of "Tolkien" and "Lord of the Rings" web-sites following the films, I became aware of worrying interpretations of Aragorn's character in on-line forums and articles, perhaps the result of a superficial reading of the book or the influence of the film interpretation. Some examples are accusations of arrogance (try typing "Aragorn" and "arrogant" into a search-engine) and a lack of any sense of humour, along with the view that "film" Aragorn is more human than "book" Aragorn. None of these are true in my opinion.

It was important to me that I rediscover the Aragorn created by Tolkien, so I turned to the book again with a vengeance, studying the narrative and Aragorn in depth, making notes on anything significant. This was accompanied by a growing disillusionment with the films which came to a head on the release of "The Return of the King" in 2003.

As well as *LotR* I re-read *The Hobbit*, *The Silmarillion* and *Unfinished Tales* and purchased all twelve volumes of *The History of Middle-earth* (edited by Christopher Tolkien) through which I laboriously ploughed my way searching for anything of relevance. I also discovered Paul Kocher's *Master of Middle-earth: The Achievement of J. R. R. Tolkien* which had just been reprinted and which contained a considerable amount about Aragorn including some views and ideas similar to my own. I was particularly struck by his statement that Aragorn is *"probably the least written about, least valued and most misunderstood"*[6] of all the major characters in *LotR*. Although I didn't read this until 2003 I saw that the comment had originally been made in 1972 when Kocher's book was first published. In 2006 I read an article about Aragorn by Håken Arvidsson in which he quoted these words of Paul Kocher then went on to express similar views about the lack of recognition given to Aragorn, thus implying that attitudes to him had not changed over more than thirty years.[7]

Concurrently with my reading I took up three additional activities:
- I discovered a web-site where people were posting *LotR* "fan-fiction" - a term I hadn't come across before - and after a few months I decided to have a go myself. My efforts seemed to be appreciated and the writing of fan-fiction became an absorbing and enjoyable hobby over the next few years until I ran out of ideas.
- I joined the Tolkien Society and contributed the occasional article to its *Amon Hen* bulletin.
- I also joined the Southampton UK Tolkien Reading Group (or Southfarthing Smial) run by Dr. Lynn Forest-Hill and found the discussions very stimulating.

For copyright reasons my fan-fiction could obviously go no further, and articles for *Amon Hen* had to be limited in length. Both were in fact vehicles for exploring my views on Aragorn and it was clear to me from the volume of notes I had made that a much bigger project was needed. On account of the comments of Kocher and Arvidsson my first idea was to do some sort of analysis of what the critics had said about Aragorn over the years. However my notes were in fact emerging as the basis of a study of Aragorn's character, importance and relationships, and I soon came to feel that pursuing and developing this aspect would be the best way forward. As a result the book was officially "born" in the summer of 2008.

The book is in two parts. Part One covers Aragorn's biography, character and significance, while Part Two deals with his interactions and relationships with the other individuals and races of Middle-earth. There are also eight genealogical tables. My overall aims are:
- To raise his profile by focusing on aspects of him, his roles and deeds which are not always obvious.
- To address the issues relating to misconceptions about his character and behaviour referred to above, mainly by default through my analysis of him, but sometimes by tackling specific episodes which tend

---

6. Op. cit. [2], Kocher, Chapter 6, p. 130.
7. H. Arvidsson, 'Aragorn: Tales of the heir of Isildur, Part 1 - The Evolution of the man', *Mallorn*, 44, 2006, pp. 47-59.

to be misinterpreted.
- To attempt to "see into his mind". This phrase is used by Wayne G. Hammond and Christina Scull[8] in a comment on Aragorn's speech shortly after the Fellowship of the Ring paddled their boats past the Argonath. He said to himself: *"Would that Gandalf were here! How my heart yearns for Minas Anor and the walls of my own city! But whither now shall I go?"*.[9] His words reflected the difficult choice he was facing between following his heart and going to Minas Tirith, or accepting that he might have to accompany Frodo to Mordor, thus prompting Hammond and Scull to observe: *"Only rarely does Tolkien let us see into Aragorn's mind."*

Although all Tolkien's "Middle-earth" writings, along with his Letters, have been important sources for my work, *LotR* in particular has been given the "fine-tooth comb" treatment. This has involved:
- Analysis of individual words, facial expressions, circumstances, etc. For example: Is the situation formal or informal? Are words spoken with a smile or seriously?
- Looking beneath the surface or at the wider context, such as examination of concurrent events, or a character's background - historical, educational and personal. For example: It is important to know what Aragorn was doing while Frodo was in Ithilien, and to understand why the Dunlendings were hostile to the Dúnedain and the Rohirrim.
- Picking out the not-so-obvious as well as the obvious. For example: Aragorn's weariness and fear of the Nazgûl during the journey to Rivendell are less obvious than the weariness and fear experienced by the Hobbits, but are there nevertheless.
- Repeated re-readings of the text to pick up minor points previously overlooked and identify new depths in the characters: a process emphasised by Rosemary Cass-Beggs in a paper presented at Oxonmoot (the annual gathering of the Tolkien Society) in September 2008.[10] I had been following the same method without realising it.

Although my emphasis is obviously on analysing the contents of the actual text, I have also used some other techniques:
- Speculation. For example: I speculate on the background of Halbarad, about which we learn very little from the text.
- Inference. For example: We know that the young Aragorn, serving incognito in Rohan, knew Théoden's father and encountered Théoden as a youth, so we can infer that he probably also met Théoden's mother and four sisters.
- Implication. For example: The fact that Halbarad brought a very personal verbal message to Aragorn from Arwen implies that he was a trusted friend to her as well as to Aragorn.
- Analysis of evidence where situations are open-ended, ambiguous, contradictory or insufficiently documented. For example: This technique is needed when working out Aragorn's activities during the spring and summer of TA 3018 prior to meeting Frodo.

*

There now follow some issues of which the reader needs to be aware.

Repetition
Because the book examines Aragorn from many different angles and in many different contexts, some repetition of episodes, ideas and quotations is unavoidable if each chapter is to be comprehensive in itself. To give an example: Appendix A.I.v to *LotR* states that Elrond came to love Aragorn as his own son. I refer to this in the account of Aragorn's early years given in Part One in order to make the point that his childhood was spent in a loving environment. I also use it in the chapter on Aragorn's relationship with the Elves in Part Two,

---
8. W.G. Hammond and C. Scull, *The Lord of the Rings: a Reader's Companion*, London, HarperCollins Publishers, 2005, p. 348.
9. Op. cit. [1], *LotR* 2.9, p. 393.
10. R. Cass-Beggs, 'They're only characters in a book - why do they seem so real?', Handout for Paper presented at Oxonmoot 2008.

in order to emphasise the poignancy of the fact that Elrond is very fond of the man who will be responsible for parting him permanently from his beloved daughter.

Fourth Age Dates

LotR App B states that, in Gondor, the end of the Third Age and beginning of the Fourth Age occurred on March 25th 3021. However, the official end of the Third Age is given as September 29th 3021, namely the date of the sailing of the Ring-bearers (Frodo, Bilbo, Galadriel, Elrond and Gandalf) over Sea. Meanwhile the Shire continued to use its own dating system and the Fourth Age was held to have started at the beginning of 1422 in Shire Reckoning (i.e. Third Age 3022). I have followed the Gondor reckoning and regard the Fourth Age as starting on March 25th 3021. For simplicity I assume that Third Age 3021 is also Fourth Age 1.

Christopher Tolkien's twelve-volume *The History of Middle-earth*

Several of these volumes provide great detail on the history and development of the *LotR* narrative between 1938 and its actual publication in 1954-5. The character of Aragorn went through many changes during this period, his first incarnation being as a strange-looking Hobbit called Trotter. Since my purpose is to examine the "final" Aragorn, not to trace the various stages of his development, I only refer to the earlier versions when I feel that some feature is particularly relevant to him as he is in the published *LotR*. However, some volumes of *HoM-e* provide new material which I have found very useful: for example the unused *Epilogue*[11] to *LotR* and *Athrabeth Finrod ah Andreth*.[12]

The Silmarillion

As it is impossible to write about Aragorn's ancestry, heritage and destiny without referring to people and places from *The Silmarillion*[13] I have added a brief list of the chief names and concepts I have used, in case some readers are unfamiliar with them, thus avoiding unwieldy explanations in the text. [See "*The Silmarillion*: Chief Names and Concepts Used" at the end of the book.] However, in general I have assumed some familiarity with *The Hobbit*, *The Lord of the Rings* (including the Appendices), *The Silmarillion* and *Unfinished Tales*[14], and some awareness of *The History of Middle-earth*.

Conventions Used

I have used initial capital letters throughout when referring to the various races in Tolkien's works: Hobbits, Elves, Dwarves, Orcs, etc. "Men" indicates the specific race of Men, while "men" means males in a general sense.

Sauron's nine wraith servants are referred to by several names in *LotR*. I use Black Riders, Nazgûl or The Nine depending on context. I refer to their leader as the Witch-king of Angmar, the Witch-king, or the Lord of the Nazgûl - again depending on context.

The Palantíri are also known as Seeing-stones or simply Stones. A single Palantír is described by its location, for example the Palantír of Orthanc or the Orthanc-stone. All these terms are used, mainly to avoid undue repetition of a particular one.

Quotations from the works of Tolkien and others are in italics.

Text in square brackets is my own asides.

---

11. C. Tolkien (ed.), *The History of Middle-earth*, vol. IX, *Sauron Defeated*, London HarperColllins Publishers, 2002, first published in Great Britain by HarperCollins Publishers 1992.
12. C. Tolkien (ed.), *The History of Middle-earth*, vol. X, *Morgoth's Ring*, London HarperColllins Publishers, 2002, first published in Great Britain by HarperCollins Publishers 1993.
13. C. Tolkien (ed.), *The Silmarillion*, London, HarperCollins Publishers, 1999, first published in Great Britain by George Allen & Unwin 1977.
14. C. Tolkien (ed.), *Unfinished Tales of Númenor and Middle-earth*, London, HarperCollins Publishers, 1998, first published in Great Britain by George Allen & Unwin 1980.

PART ONE

BIOGRAPHY, CHARACTER AND SIGNIFICANCE

CHAPTER 1.0 - INTRODUCTION

Part 1 of this book (Chapters 1.0-1.10) uses a narrative and biographical approach beginning with Aragorn's ancestry and the prophecies concerning him, followed by the different stages of his life from his birth in TA 2931 until his death in FA 120. It also examines his deeds, struggles, motives, roles, names and appearance. Events in Middle-earth during these years are considered from his point of view, looking at the various qualities he displayed, showing how he dealt with the difficulties he encountered, and emphasising the mental, as well as the physical, aspect of his struggles.

I do not give any detailed treatment of his relationships with the other characters in the story as these are fully covered in Part 2 (Chapters 2.0-2.9). The one exception to this approach is Sauron. The need to defeat Sauron was Aragorn's *raison d'être* and so fundamental to his story, thus making a separate "relationship" analysis unnecessary.

CHAPTER 1.1 - ANCESTRY

Although Aragorn is frequently referred to as the heir of Isildur or the heir of Elendil (from whom he was descended in direct line, father to son, for thirty-nine and forty generations respectively) his full pedigree is still more impressive. Genealogical Tables 1, 2 and 3 show the relationships described in this chapter. *The Silmarillion* **is the main source of information on Aragorn's First and Second Age ancestry.**

Aragorn was in fact descended from the Maia Melian and the Elf-king Elwë Thingol (referred to as Thingol from now on), one of the first Elves to awake in Middle-earth. Their daughter was Lúthien Tinúviel, the Elf-X-Maia who wedded the mortal Man, (and First-Age hero) Beren - thereby becoming mortal herself. Lúthien's and Beren's son Dior wedded the Elf Nimloth, the union resulting in a daughter, Elwing, who wedded Eärendil, himself the product of the Elf/mortal union of Idril Celebrindal and the Man Tuor (another First-Age hero). Eärendil and Elwing were the parents of two sons, Elrond and Elros. At the end of the First Age these "Half-elven" brothers were allowed, by the Vala Manwë, to choose whether to belong to the race of Elves or the race of Men. Elrond chose to be numbered among the Elves while Elros chose to be mortal and became the first King of Númenor from whom Elendil's line (and therefore Aragorn himself) was descended.

Thus Aragorn had Elf blood in him, plus a streak of Maia from Melian. He was also - though many generations removed - a nephew of Elrond and a cousin of Elladan, Elrohir and Arwen. In addition he could claim distant kinship with Galadriel whose mother Eärwen was the daughter of Thingol's brother Olwë, and possibly with Celeborn also who was, according to one of the versions of Galadriel's and Celeborn's story in *UT 2.4*, the grandson of Elmo, another brother of Thingol.[1] A different version of Celeborn's ancestry makes him, like Galadriel, a grandchild of Olwë rather than Elmo. Celebrían, daughter of Galadriel and Celeborn and wife of Elrond, would therefore also have been a distant relation to Aragorn. As well as the Elf blood from Thingol, who was of the kindred of the Teleri, Aragorn could also claim Elf blood from the kindreds of the Noldor and the Vanyar, via Idril Celebrindal who was the great-granddaughter of Finwë (first King of the Noldor) and his wife Indis, who was a Vanya. Thus Aragorn had three strains of Elf blood. He was also descended from all three of the first Houses of Men: from the House of Bëor through Beren, and from the House of the Haladin and the House of Hador through Tuor who had a parent from each of these two Houses.

In Genealogical Table 1, note that:
- I have shown Celeborn as Elmo's grandson, not Olwë's, as this version is given precedence in *UT 2.4*.
- Thingol and Elmo, although of the Telerin kindred, became known as Sindar (the Grey Elves) which was the name given to those members of the Teleri who chose to stay in Beleriand instead of sailing to Valinor. Their brother Olwë did go to Valinor.
- The choice of race given to Elrond and Elros was also given to their parents, Eärendil and Elwing,[2] and to Elrond's children (App. A.I.i.).[3] According to *HoM-e* V the choice was a special dispensation from the Vala Manwë. The actual rule for these Elf/mortal beings stated that "... *all those who have the blood of mortal Men, in whatever part, great or small, are mortal,* **unless other doom be granted to them**."[4] [my emphasis]. Hence Christopher Tolkien's observation, in his commentary on this passage, that Dior

---

1. C. Tolkien (ed.), *Unfinished Tales of Númenor and Middle-earth*, London, HarperCollins Publishers, 1998, first published in Great Britain by George Allen & Unwin 1980.
2. C. Tolkien (ed.), *The Silmarillion*, London, HarperCollins Publishers, 1999, first published in Great Britain by George Allen & Unwin 1977, *TSil* Chapter 24, pp. 299-300.
3. J.R.R. Tolkien, *The Lord of the Rings,* London, HarperCollins Publishers, 2007, 2nd edition, based on the 50th Anniversary Edition of 2004, App A.I.i, p. 1035.
4. C. Tolkien (ed.), *The History of Middle-earth*, vol. V, *The Lost Road*, London HarperColllins Publishers, 2002, first published in Great Britain by Unwin Hyman 1987, *HoM-e* V Part 2, Chapter 6, p. 326.

was therefore automatically mortal as there is no reference to him being offered a choice. [Perhaps this was because Lúthien had become mortal before she gave birth to him - he was thus the child of two mortals even though by blood he was half mortal, a quarter Maia and a quarter Elf. Since he married Nimloth, a pure Elf, they were presumably parted eternally after Dior's death.]
- Nimloth is shown as the niece of Celeborn as per *UT* 2.4. However in *HoM-e* XI.5[5] Christopher Tolkien refers to the possibility that she may have been Celeborn's sister - something he had failed to mention in *UT*. His father appeared to have been undecided about the relationship.
- Towards the end of his life Tolkien considered changing the history of Celeborn, making him a Telerin Elf who had sailed to Valinor, rather than a Sindarin Elf of Beleriand (*UT* 2.4). I have left him as a Sinda as depicted in *LotR* and *TSil*.
- *TSil* refers to the belief that Tuor acquired Elvish immortality.[6]

As already stated, Aragorn was descended from the Kings of Númenor. This island was created at the beginning of the Second Age to be a home for the Men who had supported the Elves in their battles against Morgoth in the First Age. Númenóreans, although mortal, had a greatly increased lifespan compared with other Men, their Kings living for approximately four hundred years in the early days of Númenor, but dwindling to something over two hundred as the Númenóreans became corrupted by Sauron and grew increasingly arrogant and resentful of the immortality of the Elves. Eventually, in *SA* 3319 King Ar-Pharazôn sailed to Valinor with a great fleet intending to demand immortality from the Valar, with the result that Ilúvatar himself caused the fleet and the island of Númenor to be swallowed up by the sea. Elendil, a kinsman of the royal line who had resisted corruption, managed to escape the drowning, along with his family and followers, and his ships were eventually washed up in Middle-earth where he established the kingdoms of Arnor and Gondor, ruling Arnor himself and committing the rule of Gondor to his sons Isildur and Anárion. Just over a hundred years later the Last Alliance of Elves and Men defeated Sauron's forces in battle and besieged Barad-dûr. Eventually Sauron appeared in person and was wrestled to the ground by Elendil and the Elf Gil-galad who were both killed in the process, with Elendil's sword Narsil being broken in two. Isildur then seized its hilt shard and cut the One Ring from Sauron's hand thus reducing him to a spiritual form which fled into hiding. Anárion too had died during the siege and Isildur, after committing the rule of Gondor to Anárion's son Meneldil, set off northwards, with the Ring in his possession, to take on his father's role in Arnor. On the way he, his three eldest sons, and most of his men were killed by Orcs in the Gladden Fields. One of the survivors managed to convey the Shards of Narsil to Rivendell where Isildur's youngest son (and now his heir) Valandil was living. From then on Isildur's line ruled in Arnor while Anárion's line ruled in Gondor. The Númenórean race in exile were known as the Dúnedain, Men of the West.

By the time of Aragorn's birth at the end of the third millennium of the Third Age, Gondor had been ruled by Stewards (themselves Dúnedain of a more junior branch) for nine hundred years as the direct male line of Anárion had died out. Meanwhile the northern kingdom of Arnor had been split into three in TA 861 due to dissension among the King's sons, with the line of Isildur continuing in Arthedain, the largest of the three sub-kingdoms. From TA 1409 there was intermittent war with the Witch-king of Angmar, who was in fact the Lord of the Nazgûl sent by Sauron to destroy the descendants of Isildur. The war eventually ended with the destruction of the North Kingdom and the death of the last king, Arvedui, in 1975. However Isildur's line still survived unbroken and Arvedui's descendants took the title of "Chieftain". The Dúnedain, now a wandering and much-diminished race, continued to enjoy an extended lifespan, with most Chieftains who died naturally, living to between a hundred and fifty and a hundred and sixty. (See the dates given in *HoM-e* XII).[7] Aragorn was the sixteenth Chieftain of the Dúnedain.

---

5. C. Tolkien (ed.), *The History of Middle-earth*, vol. XI, *The War of the Jewels*, London HarperColllins Publishers, 2002, first published in Great Britain by HarperCollins Publishers 1994, *HoM-e* XI Part 3, Chapter 5, p. 350.
6. Op. cit. [2], *TSil* Chapter 23, p. 294.
7. C. Tolkien (ed.), *The History of Middle-earth*, vol. XII, *The Peoples of Middle-earth*, London HarperColllins Publishers, 2002, first published in Great Britain by HarperCollins Publishers 1996, *HoM-e* XII Part 1, Chapter 7, p. 196.

CHAPTER 1.2 - PROPHECIES

Before looking in detail at Aragorn's life I examine the many prophecies concerning his coming, some of which dated from three thousand years before his birth.

The most significant prophecy relates to the green stone set in a silver eagle-shaped brooch which Galadriel gave to Aragorn when the Fellowship passed through Lothlórien (*LotR* 2.8).[1] The stone was known as the Elfstone, or (in Quenya) the Elessar. "Elessar" subsequently became Aragorn's official name as King, with "Elfstone" being used more informally. In *UT* 2.4,[2] there are two versions of the history of the Elessar. According to one, it was made during the First Age for Idril Celebrindal, daughter of the Elf-king Turgon of Gondolin. Idril gave it to her son Eärendil and it was subsequently taken to Valinor by him where it remained until the sailing of Olórin (Gandalf) to Middle-earth around *TA* 1000-1100. He brought the Elessar with him and at some point gave it to Galadriel to bring healing to the fading grass and trees in her land, saying "*... it is not for you to possess. You shall hand it on when the time comes. For before you ... forsake Middle-earth one shall come who is to receive it, and his name shall be that of the stone: Elessar he shall be called.*".[3] The second version of the Elessar story states that the original stone remained in Valinor and that the Elf Celebrimbor (the creator of the Three Elven Rings) made a copy for Galadriel and set it in a silver eagle-shaped brooch. As Celebrimbor was killed in SA 1697 (App B.1083) the copy must have been made prior to that date.

Both versions have some relevance to Aragorn's story as can be seen by referring to the gift-giving scene in Lothlórien mentioned above. Galadriel's words as she gave the Elessar to Aragorn were: "*In this hour take the name that was foretold for you, Elessar, the Elfstone of the House of Elendil!*"[4] This reflects the prophecy of Gandalf in the first version of the Elessar story; on the other hand the stone being set in a silver, eagle-shaped brooch reflects the second version. Whatever the case, it is clear from Galadriel's words that a prophecy had been made. She also told Aragorn that she had given the stone to her daughter Celebrían who had in turn given it to her own daughter Arwen. Arwen had subsequently left it in Galadriel's care so that she could give it to Aragorn when the Fellowship reached Lothlórien. In addition to the prophecy itself there was clearly a great deal of foresight at play here, on the part of both Galadriel and Arwen - and possibly Celebrían too. Since Celebrían sailed to Valinor in TA 2510 (App B.1087), the date of Galadriel's original receipt of the stone (and thus of the prophecy) must have been prior to that, possibly as early as Gandalf's arrival in Middle-earth. It is clear from *LotR* 2.1.237 that Aragorn himself was aware of the existence of the Elessar - and maybe of the prophecy too - from his insistence that Bilbo's song about Eärendil should contain a reference to a green stone.

Another prophecy concerning the Elessar (though the gem is not actually named), appears in *HoM-e* XII, where Christopher Tolkien refers to a brief text written by his father on the back of a rejected manuscript, describing Aragorn's naming ceremony as a baby.[5] The child had been given the name Aragorn by his father, but his maternal grandmother Ivorwen said, "*... I see on his breast a green stone, and from that his true name shall come and his chief renown: for he shall be a healer and a renewer.*". The others present did not know what she meant as no-one else could see the green stone she referred to. This account was not included in the published version of *LotR* but Ivorwen's prophecy is reflected in *LotR* 5.8 after Aragorn had spent many hours saving the lives of people affected by the Black Breath of the Nazgûl: "*And word went through the City: 'The King is come again indeed.' And they named him Elfstone, because of the green stone that he wore, and so*

---

1 J.R.R. Tolkien, *The Lord of the Rings,* London, HarperCollins Publishers, 2007, 2nd edition, based on the 50th Anniversary Edition of 2004.
2. C. Tolkien (ed.), *Unfinished Tales of Númenor and Middle-earth*, London, HarperCollins Publishers, 1998, first published in Great Britain by George Allen & Unwin 1980.
3. Op. cit., *UT* p. 323.
4. Op. cit [1], *LotR* p. 375.
5. C. Tolkien (ed.), *The History of Middle-earth*, vol. XII, *The Peoples of Middle-earth*, London HarperColllins Publishers, 2002, first published in Great Britain by HarperCollins Publishers 1996, Foreword, p. xii.

*the name **which it was foretold at his birth** that he should bear was chosen for him by his own people."*.[6] [my emphasis]. Ivorwen's second prediction that the child would be a renewer is also echoed in *LotR* 5.8 when Aragorn referred to himself as *"Envinyatar, the Renewer"*.[7] I have not found any reference to an actual **birth** prophecy concerning Aragorn's name in Tolkien's works apart from these words of Ivorwen at his naming ceremony. The prophecy of Gandalf to Galadriel, as already noted, would have been made at least four hundred and twenty years earlier and possibly even two thousand years earlier. Likewise I have been unable to find any other reference to Aragorn being called a Renewer. This is why I have included the passage in this account even though it was actually rejected for publication. I refer to it again in later chapters.

Another example of Ivorwen's foresight did make it into the published version of the Appendices to *LotR*, where she persuaded her husband to allow the marriage of their daughter Gilraen to Arathorn by prophesying that *"... if these two wed now, hope may be born for our people"*.[8] Subsequently, during Aragorn's childhood in Rivendell, Elrond gave him the name Estel (meaning Hope) as a reflection of the prophecy and in order to hide his true identity and lineage. In *RoP* it is stated that Elrond gave sanctuary to the heirs of Isildur in childhood and old age, partly because of their kinship to himself and partly because *"... he knew in his wisdom that one should come of their line to whom a great part was appointed in the last deeds of that Age. And until that time came the shards of Elendil's sword were given into the keeping of Elrond, when the days of the Dúnedain darkened and they became a wandering people."*.[9] Ivorwen's prophecy of hope echoed the one made in the First Age by the Vala Ulmo to Turgon King of Gondolin. He told Turgon that someone would come to warn him of peril, and that *"from him beyond ruin and fire hope shall be born for Elves and Men"*.[10] This "someone" was Aragorn's ancestor, the Man Tuor, who would marry Turgon's daughter Idril. It was their son Eärendil who sailed to Valinor to plead with the Valar to take pity on Elves and Men in their war against Morgoth. His plea was successful: the Valar sent their armies to Middle-earth and Morgoth was defeated and cast out into the Void. *UT* also refers to the prophecy, describing Ulmo's meeting with Tuor when he told him *"... it is not for thy valour only that I send thee, but to bring into the world a hope beyond thy sight, and a light that shall pierce the darkness."*.[11] Compare the line in the poem *The Riddle of Strider* composed for Aragorn by Bilbo: *"A light from the shadow shall spring."*.[12]

There is a more veiled (and retrospective) reference to the advent of Aragorn in *UT* in the account of the deaths of Isildur and his three eldest sons: *"So perished Elendur [Isildur's heir], **who should afterwards have been King**, and as all foretold who knew him, in his strength and wisdom, and his majesty without pride, one of the greatest, **the fairest of the seed of Elendil, most like to his grandsire.**"*[13] [my emphasis]. A note to this passage says, *"It is said that in later days those (such as Elrond) whose memories recalled him [Elendur] were struck by the great likeness to him, in body and mind, of King Elessar..."*.[14] Further to this, in *RoP* Aragorn, in spite of existing thirty-nine generations later, is described as being *"... more like to Elendil than any before him."*.[15] These words are echoed again in a conversation between Elrond and the young Aragorn in App A.I.v, where Elrond told him, *"A great doom awaits you, either to rise above the height of all your fathers since the days of Elendil, or to fall into darkness..."*.[16] One could almost read into these passages that the advent of a king like Aragorn was delayed for over three thousand years due to the weakness of Isildur in succumbing to the lure of the Ring and bringing himself and his promising eldest son to an untimely death. This is illustrated by subsequent prophecies of Elrond and Gandalf recorded in *RoP*. When the Shards of Narsil were brought to Rivendell, Elrond foretold that the sword would not be reforged *"until the Ruling Ring should be found again*

---

6. Op. cit. [1], *LotR* 5.8, p. 871.
7. Op. cit., *LotR* 5.8, p. 863.
8. Op. cit., App A.I.v., p. 1057.
9. C. Tolkien (ed.), *The Silmarillion*, London, HarperCollins Publishers, 1999, first published in Great Britain by George Allen & Unwin 1977, *RoP* p. 357.
10. Op. cit., *TSil* Chapter 15, p. 144.
11. Op. cit. [2], *UT* Part 1, Chapter 1, p. 39.
12. Op. cit. [1], *LotR* 2.2, p. 247.
13. Op. cit. [2], *UT* Part 3, Chapter 1, p. 355.
14. Op. cit., *UT* Part 3, Chapter 1, p. 367.
15. Op. cit. [9], *RoP* p. 364.
16. Op. cit. [1], App A.I.v., p. 1059.

and Sauron should return.".[17] Later, in the third millennium of the Third Age, Gandalf reported to Elrond that Sauron had established himself at Dol Guldur (in the south of Mirkwood Forest) and that he "... *seeks ever for news of the One, and of the Heirs of Isildur, if they live still on earth.*". Elrond replied "... *In the hour that Isildur took the Ring and would not surrender it, this doom was wrought, that Sauron should return.*".[18] The Northern Dúnedain, by this time, had diminished to a wandering, anonymous people, whose ancestry was forgotten. Nevertheless their line remained unbroken from father to son since Isildur, with each heir regarding the Shards of Narsil as a cherished heirloom. The prophecy of the sword appears again in *LotR* in the prophetic dream of Faramir and Boromir ("*Seek for the sword that was broken*"),[19] and in *The Riddle of Strider* ("*Renewed shall be blade that was broken*" and "*The crownless again shall be king*".).[20]

It was due to the foresight of Elrond, as illustrated by the examples given above, that various heirlooms of Elendil's House were kept in the safety of Rivendell until the time came for the prophecies to be fulfilled. These were:
- The Shards of Narsil already referred to.
- The Ring of Barahir. This had been given to the Man Barahir in the First Age by the Elf Finrod Felagund whose life he had saved during the war with Morgoth. The ring was to be a pledge of Finrod's help to Barahir's family in the future. When Barahir was killed by Orcs his son Beren retrieved the ring from his father's body and was subsequently helped by Finrod in his quest to obtain one of the Silmarils from the crown of Morgoth. The ring remained with Beren's line and came into the possession of his descendants of the royal House of Númenor from whom Elendil's line was descended. In the middle of the Third Age it was given by Arvedui, the last king of Arnor, to the Lossoth people from Forochel in gratitude for their help following his defeat in battle with the Witch-king of Angmar. The Dúnedain later ransomed it and it was subsequently kept in Rivendell until Elrond presented it to Aragorn. I reached this conclusion based on the entry in App B.1086 for TA 1976 which states that Arvedui's son became Chieftain of the Dúnedain (as opposed to being King) and that the heirlooms of Arnor were given into the keeping of Elrond. As the Dúnedain were now living secretive lives and hiding the fact that there was still an heir of Isildur in existence, it seems unlikely that their Chieftains would have worn an identifying ring.
- The Sceptre of Annúminas. This had been the chief mark of royalty in the North Kingdom having been saved from the drowning of Númenor by Elendil.
- The Elendilmir: also called the Star of the North Kingdom, the Star of the North and the Star of Elendil. It was a jewel worn on the brow, instead of a crown, by the Kings in the North.
- I also include the silver horn used by Aragorn to summon the Dead although it is not actually referred to as an heirloom. It was given to him by Elrohir when he came south with the Grey Company (*LotR* 5.2.789) so had presumably been kept in Rivendell prior to that.

A further prophecy concerning Aragorn, though it does not actually name him, was made by Isildur himself,[21] and then subsequently reiterated by the seer Malbeth[22] during the reign of Arvedui. It referred to the Men of Dunharrow who had sworn an oath to Isildur promising to aid him against Sauron. When they subsequently refused this aid, Isildur cursed them, so that their ghosts haunted the Paths of the Dead in the Haunted Mountain, never to rest until their oath should be fulfilled. Both versions of the prophecy indicate that the Dead Men would be summoned again and given the chance to redeem their treachery, with Malbeth's version explicitly stating that the summoner would be an heir of Isildur. It is clear that the prophecy was known to both Galadriel (*LotR* 3.5.503) and Elrond (*LotR* 5.2.775), as well as to Aragorn himself who recited both versions to Legolas and Gimli (*LotR* 5.2.781-2).

---

17. Op. cit. [9], *RoP* pp. 354-5
18. Op.cit., *RoP* p. 361.
19. Op. cit. [1], *LotR* 2.2, p. 246.
20. Op. cit., *LotR* 2.2, p. 247.
21. Op. cit., *LotR* 5.2, pp. 781-2.
22. Op. cit., *LotR* 5.2, pp. 781-2.

Some years earlier Malbeth had made another prophecy (App A.I.iv), principally concerning King Arvedui but also indirectly related to Aragorn. At Arvedui's birth it was Malbeth who gave him his name (meaning "Last King") as he foresaw the ending of the North Kingdom. However he also foresaw that the Dúnedain would be given an opportunity to reverse the prophecy and enable Arvedui to become *"king of a great realm"*[23]. The opportunity was missed: eighty years later when Arvedui claimed the throne of Gondor in addition to being heir to the North Kingdom, his claim was rejected and the original prophecy was fulfilled. The Dúnedain of the North and South would not be reunited for another thousand and seventy-five years when Aragorn claimed the kingships of Arnor and Gondor. In the words of Malbeth "... *much sorrow and many lives of men shall pass, until the Dúnedain arise and are united again.*"[24].

Finally, Frodo, Sam, Merry and Pippin saw a vision of Aragorn before they actually met him, and without realising who it was they were seeing. This occurred after Tom Bombadil had rescued them from the Barrow-wight and was recounting the history of the knives he had selected for them to use as swords. He told them how the Men of Westernesse (the Dúnedain) were overcome by the evil king of Angmar, but went on to say that some of them still survived, "... *sons of forgotten kings walking in loneliness, guarding from evil things folk that are heedless.*".[25] As he talked, the Hobbits had a vision "... *as it were of a great expanse of years behind them...*"[26] seeing the shapes of the Dúnadan chieftains through the ages, the last one wearing a star on his brow (namely the Elendilmir worn instead of a crown by the kings of the North Kingdom).

*

A further prophecy needs to be discussed here, namely that of Tar-Palantir concerning the White Tree of Gondor (*Ak* 321-2, 326-7). Though it did not concern Aragorn specifically, it was linked to the kingship in general and is therefore relevant in this study. The following chart shows the early history of the White Tree.

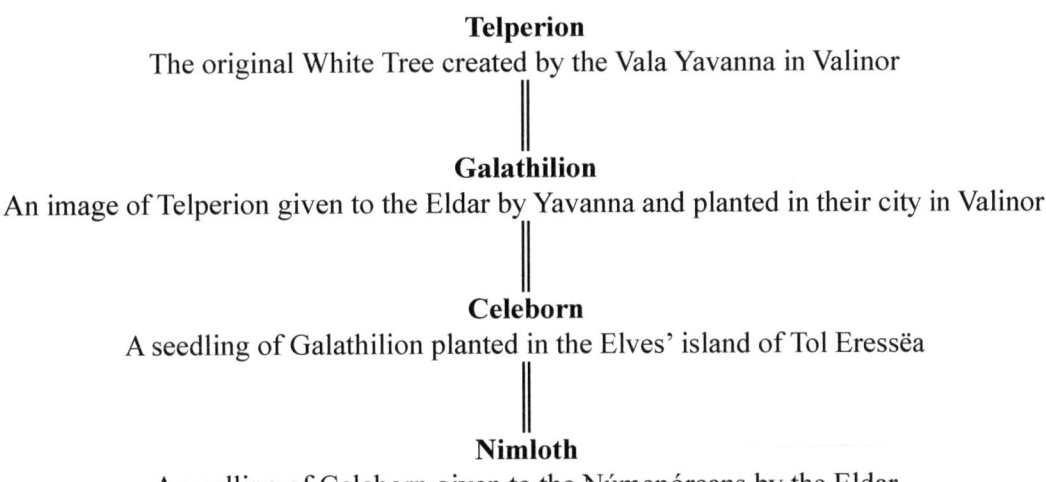

Telperion
The original White Tree created by the Vala Yavanna in Valinor
‖
Galathilion
An image of Telperion given to the Eldar by Yavanna and planted in their city in Valinor
‖
Celeborn
A seedling of Galathilion planted in the Elves' island of Tol Eressëa
‖
Nimloth
A seedling of Celeborn given to the Númenóreans by the Eldar

During the later years of Númenor when the Kings became corrupted by the Shadow of Morgoth and the influence of Sauron, they stopped reverencing the White Tree, Nimloth, due to its connection with the Eldar and the Valar. However Tar-Palantir, the very foresighted penultimate King, repented. Nimloth was tended and respected again during his reign and he prophesied that if the White Tree failed, the line of the Kings would perish. When he was succeeded by Ar-Pharazôn, who came totally under the sway of Sauron, Isildur, one of those faithful to the Valar, realised the risk to the tree and managed to take a fruit from it before Sauron destroyed it. Thus the line of the Tree continued to survive after the Downfall of Númenor when Elendil and his sons established their kingdoms in Middle-earth. Tar-Palantir's prophecy would be remembered throughout

---

23. Op. cit. [1], App A.I.iv, p. 1050.
24. Op. cit., App A.I.iv, p. 1050.
25. Op. cit., *LotR* 1.8, p. 146.
26. Op. cit., *LotR* 1.8, p. 146.

the Third Age.

App A.I.iv tells us that after the failure of the line of kings in Gondor "... *many in Gondor still believed that a king would indeed return in some time to come*"[27], and when the White Tree died in Minas Tirith in 2872 during the stewardship of Belecthor II it was left in its place "*until the King returns*"[28], because no sapling could be found to replace it. Perhaps it was more wishful thinking than expectation. *UT* 3.2.iii refers to the granting of the land of Calenardhon (later called Rohan) to Eorl the Young by the Steward Cirion in TA 2510. Cirion's proclamation stated that he acted with the authority of the Steward "... *until the Great King returns*" while Eorl addressed him as "*Lord Steward of the Great King*".[29] A note to this passage indicates that this was standard practice in such a pronouncement even though few still believed that the Kings would return. However even the Steward Denethor II, who could by no means be described as favourable to the idea of a returning king, believed that a Steward of Gondor could never assume the kingship even if ten thousand years had passed since a king last reigned. This view was quoted to Frodo and Sam by Faramir, who went on to tell them, "*For myself I would see the White Tree in flower again ... and the Silver Crown return...*".[30]

Thus it can be seen that an exceptional Chieftain of the Dúnedain, capable of wielding the sword of Elendil and withstanding Sauron, and destined to regain the kingships of Arnor and Gondor, had long been awaited, expected, and in some cases yearned for, by the likes of Elrond, Galadriel, Gandalf, and the Northern Dúnedain themselves, as well as by some in Gondor. Defeating Sauron meant destroying the One Ring as well as facing him in battle, hence the stipulation in the prophecies that the sword of Elendil (which had robbed Sauron of the Ring) would only be reforged when the Ring was found. Aragorn's destiny, life and struggles would be driven by these prophecies.

---

27. Op. cit. [1], App A.I.iv, pp. 1052-3.
28. Op. cit., App A.I.iv, p. 1054.
29. Op. cit. [2], *UT* pp. 392-3, 408.
30. Op. cit. [1], *LotR* 4.5, p. 671.

CHAPTER 1.3 - CHILDHOOD

The main *LotR* narrative covers approximately one and a half years of Aragorn's life. For information on the years before and after that, it is necessary to turn to App B and App A, in particular App A.I.v entitled "Here follows a part of the Tale of Aragorn and Arwen". Some further detail is contained in *UT* and *TSil*.

Aragorn was born on March 1st TA 2931 (ten years before the events recounted in *The Hobbit*), the only child of Arathorn II and Gilraen the Fair. Arathorn was the thirty-eighth heir in direct line from Isildur, while Gilraen was herself descended (through her father) from a more junior branch of the same line. Gilraen's parents were both foresighted and her father Dírhael had been opposed to his daughter's marriage to Arathorn, partly on account of her youth (she was twenty-two which was younger than the normal age of marriage for Dúnadan women), but also because he predicted that Arathorn would be short-lived. However his wife Ivorwen persuaded him to agree to the marriage with her prophecy that *"if these two wed now, hope may be born for our people, but if they delay, it will not come while this age lasts."*.[1]

The foresight of both Dírhael and Ivorwen was proved to be accurate during the next four years. Arathorn succeeded his father Arador as Chieftain of the Dúnedain in 2930, a year after his marriage, and a year before the birth of Aragorn. When he was killed by Orcs in 2933, the two-year old child became Chieftain of the Dúnedain (as Aragorn II) and the heir of Isildur. At this point he and Gilraen were taken to live in Rivendell, where Aragorn was given the name "Estel" (meaning "Hope"), due to Elrond's insistence that his real name and lineage should be kept secret, and also to indicate the hope which he represented. It is not clear in App A.I.v whether this name was given to him by Elrond or Gilraen, or by general agreement between the two of them. However the entry for TA 2933 in App B specifically states that Elrond received him as foster-son and gave him the name "Estel".[2]

Aragorn was to live in Rivendell for the next eighteen years. During June 2941 (when he was ten years old) Gandalf, Bilbo Baggins, and a party of Dwarves led by Thorin Oakenshield visited Rivendell for two weeks on their way to the Lonely Mountain, to win back treasure stolen by the dragon Smaug and to regain the Dwarf kingdom there. The following year, Gandalf and Bilbo visited again for a week in May on their journey back to Hobbiton. In *TH* we are told that on the day of their arrival, *"there were many eager ears that evening to hear the tale of their adventures."*.[3] It is tempting to wonder if Gilraen and the young Estel were among the listeners. At any rate they must have encountered the visitors at some point during their stay, though nothing of such a meeting is recorded in *TH*, for the simple reason that when Tolkien wrote it neither Aragorn nor *LotR* had been thought of, and even Gandalf and Elrond at this stage would have been unaware of the full repercussions of Bilbo's activities. App B, written with the hindsight of *TH*, also refers to the two visits of Gandalf in 2941-2, but again there is no reference to any encounter between him and Aragorn. In addition it is stated that Sauron returned secretly to Mordor (from Dol Guldur) during the year of Bilbo's return visit to Rivendell and that Gollum left the Misty Mountains to look for his "Precious" two years later in 2944. Meanwhile Saruman had been conducting his own investigation into the whereabouts of the One Ring, but deceiving the White Council about his findings.

In *LotR* Aragorn is shown to be a very educated and cultured man, with a knowledge of music, poetry, languages, history and lore, and he would have had an excellent grounding in these subjects in Rivendell as well as in the military and survival skills which would be vital to him later on: e.g. weapons, horse-riding, tracking,

---

1. Which I referred to in Chapter 1.2, footnote 8.
2. J.R.R. Tolkien, *The Lord of the Rings,* London, HarperCollins Publishers, 2007, 2nd edition, based on the 50th Anniversary Edition of 2004, App B, p. 1089.
3. J.R.R. Tolkien, *The Hobbit*, 3rd edition, London, Allen & Unwin, 1966, 1975 printing, *TH* Chapter 19, p. 309.

navigation, herb lore, healing, and "reading" nature - even to the extent of understanding the languages of birds and animals (*LotR* 1.9.149).

Though it was the custom for the Chieftains of the Dúnedain to be fostered in Rivendell during childhood, this particular one stood out from the others through being fatherless at the time of his fostering and therefore actually holding the title of Chieftain (as opposed to only being the son/heir of the Chieftain). There is no indication in App A.I.ii or in *HoM-e* XII.7[4] (which lists the Chieftains and their dates) of any other Chieftains succeeding as minors. In addition to the significance of the alias given to him, we are told that "*Elrond took the place of his father and **came to love him as a son of his own**.*"[5] [my emphasis]. Thus it was clear that Elrond not only anticipated the promise of this child, but also had a deep affection for him. Estel/Aragorn matured early and by 2951 had grown into a noble and personable twenty-year-old who had distinguished himself when out on exploits with Elrond's sons. We are told that Elrond chose this time to reveal his identity and lineage to him, and to give him some of his family heirlooms, namely the Shards of Narsil and the Ring of Barahir. A third heirloom was the Sceptre of Annúminas which Elrond withheld from Aragorn at this stage as he had yet to show himself worthy of it.

The day after this conversation with Elrond Aragorn met, and fell immediately in love with, Arwen newly-returned from an extended visit to her grandparents in Lothlórien. This event was followed, "*before the fall of the year*", by his departure from Rivendell to take up his role as Chieftain of the Dúnedain (App A.I.v.1059). Thus in the space of a few months he had received some astounding revelations about himself and his identity, had met and fallen in love with a beautiful woman, and had exchanged a life of luxury and protection for one of hardship and danger. Although the last-mentioned event was due to occur anyway its actual timing seems to have been directly prompted by Elrond's disapproval of Aragorn's feelings for Arwen.

I believe that one of the aspects of Aragorn which is unappreciated is the intense emotional and psychological (in addition to physical) pressures he must have been under for most of his life, and it seems likely that this would have begun in childhood. Due to the necessity of keeping Sauron in ignorance of the fact that Isildur's line was still flourishing, one can understand Elrond's insistence on keeping quiet about the identity of his young fosterling - particularly as the child was destined to be involved in the destruction of Sauron. However, it comes as something of a shock to realise that this information had also been withheld from Aragorn himself. Until he was twenty he did not even know who he was, let alone have any appreciation of the sheer enormity of what would be expected of him in life.

This decision to keep him ignorant of his real identity prompts many questions and issues:
- It is difficult to see how this deception could have been achieved without Elrond, Gilraen and the whole household lying elaborately to him, and if we assume that Aragorn was totally unsuspecting, then an element of shock when he found out the truth must have been inevitable, even if delayed.
- Alternatively, he may have guessed that information was being withheld from him, in which case perhaps the revelations were not wholly surprising. If he did suspect Elrond, Gilraen and others of being less than honest with him about his background the effect must have been very unsettling, unless of course he was mature enough to realise that there was good reason for it and trusted that all would be revealed in due course. This does not in fact seem to have been the case considering the excitement he showed when informed of his true identity.
- Elrond's decision to enlighten Aragorn when he did was due to his foster-son's early physical maturity, but was it also influenced by concern that Aragorn might suspect the truth or learn of it from others?
- Wouldn't a child as gifted as Aragorn have had an enquiring mind and asked questions about his real father? Did he wonder if there was something discreditable in his background which was being kept from him?
- Wouldn't he have wondered why he was being brought up in a community of Elves, as opposed to among his own kind?

---

4. C. Tolkien (ed.), *The History of Middle-earth*, vol. XII, *The Peoples of Middle-earth*, London HarperColllins Publishers, 2002, first published in Great Britain by HarperCollins Publishers 1996, *HoM-e* XII, Part 1, Chapter 7, p. 196.
5. Op. cit. [2], App,A.I.ii, p. 1057.

- "*Law and Customs among the Eldar*" in *HoM-e* X.3[6], refers to the similarity between Elf and mortal children at some stages of their growth. This begs the question as to whether Aragorn actually knew he was a mortal, or whether he thought he was an Elf or a Half-elf, since he seems to have been elvish in appearance. Did he think Elrond really was his father?
- There is evidence of confusion in his reaction to Arwen's youthful looks. He must have known that her brothers had Elvish life-spans, having lived with them and been trained by them for eighteen years, yet he initially assumed she was a young girl of his own age even **after** she had told him she was Elrond's daughter.
- Looking at the matter from another perspective, Helen Armstrong suggests that Arwen may initially have believed Aragorn to be an Elf.[7]

Considering these factors it seems perfectly possible that Aragorn was totally confused as to who/what he was. Following Elrond's revelations he announced excitedly to Arwen, "*Estel I was **called** but I **am** Aragorn, Arathorn's son...*"[8] [my emphasis]. He now knew who and what he was, as opposed to what he had been called up to then. His mind must have been in a whirl during those few days.

This confusion surrounding his background and identity would not have been helped by his emotional immaturity - in contrast to his physical maturity. This was particularly evident from his inappropriate reaction to Elrond's revelations. He had been presented with Elendil's sword - a weapon which had been in pieces for the last three thousand years - with Elrond actually predicting its reforging during his (Aragorn's) lifetime and warning of a long and hard struggle before he would be deemed worthy of the royal Sceptre of Annúminas - a struggle which might end in failure or death. He must have learnt enough of the history of Middle-earth to be under no illusion about the significance of this heritage which had been suddenly sprung upon him, about the lethal nature of what lay ahead, and of the absolute necessity of continuing to keep his identity secret indefinitely. And yet, we are told he reacted with excitement, his heart "*high within him*",[9] full of hope, and rejoicing in his high lineage. His immaturity was further illustrated by his inability to hide his feelings about Arwen, even though his mother had made it clear that Elf/mortal relationships were generally regarded as inappropriate and that this one in particular would arouse Elrond's disapproval, possibly jeopardising the protection which the Dúnedain had come to rely on. However it must be admitted that hiding such feelings from a being like Elrond would undoubtedly have proved difficult even for a mature person. Thus when Aragorn left Rivendell towards the end of 2951, he carried the emotional burden of forbidden and (apparently) unrequited love and also the knowledge that Elrond seemed to regard him as unworthy of Arwen: "*She is too far above you*"[10].

Another factor which would influence his mental state in his new life, would be the need to live with fear. Elrond and his sons, along with his own study of Middle-earth's history, would undoubtedly have taught him that the Dark Lord and his servants were to be feared, but this element of fear would have been greatly intensified now that he was going out into the Wild possessed of the chilling knowledge that Sauron was growing in strength and scouring Middle-earth to see if he, the heir of Isildur, existed. As if to emphasise the point, this was the same year that Sauron declared his presence in Mordor and started rebuilding Barad-dûr. Aragorn's departure from Rivendell also coincided with the reoccupation of Dol Guldur (in the south of Mirkwood Forest) by three of the Nazgûl, and the commencement of Gollum's journey towards Mordor.

In the years to come Aragorn's increasing danger, along with the resulting strain of keeping his identity secret, would subject him to a depth of pressure not experienced by his predecessors.

---

6. C. Tolkien (ed.), *The History of Middle-earth*, vol. X, *Morgoth's Ring*, London HarperColllins Publishers, 2002, first published in Great Britain by HarperCollins Publishers 1993, HoM-e X, Part 3, Section 2, pp. 209-210.
7. H. Armstrong, 'There are Two People in this Marriage', *Mallorn*, 36, 1998, pp. 5-12.
8. Op. cit. [2], App A.I.v, p. 1058.
9. Op. cit., App A.I.v, p. 1058.
10. Op. cit., App A.I.v, p. 1059.

CHAPTER 1.4 - ADULTHOOD PRIOR TO *LOTR*

Aragorn's life-story between his departure from Rivendell in TA 2951 and the events of *LotR* in 3018-9, occupies a mere four pages in App A.I.iv and A.I.v, augmented by roughly the same amount of space in *UT*. However there is sufficient information to show that his achievements in these years were impressive, and App B enables his activities to be put in context with other events taking place at the time. I also consider the identity and role issues which affected Aragorn during these years.

This period is split into two sections, namely before and after his betrothal to Arwen which took place in 2980.

2951-2980

From App A.I.v we learn that during these twenty-nine years Aragorn "*laboured in the cause against Sauron*".[1] Five years after leaving Rivendell, in 2956, he made the acquaintance of Gandalf, gaining much knowledge and wisdom from him, as well as accompanying him on perilous journeys as a prelude to making similar journeys on his own in disguise and under assumed names. He rode with the Rohirrim, and he fought for Gondor by land and sea. He also travelled alone "*... far into the East and deep into the South...*"[2] to spy on Sauron and his servants and to gauge the views and feelings of the people in these lands. From comments made by him later at the Council of Elrond (*LotR* 2.2.248), we know that his travels took him far enough east and south for the stars to be unfamiliar. He learnt the crafts and lore of the places he visited too - in addition to the languages where necessary. Due to the need to hide his identity and purpose, he became adept at adopting the language and style of speech of those around him (App F.II.1133-4).

It has already been made clear that Aragorn, at twenty years old, was considered physically equipped to become a Ranger and take up his duties as Chieftain. In addition his excitement after Elrond told him of his identity and destiny implied that he would have approached the future with enthusiasm and commitment. However I believe that the psychological and emotional aspects of leaving Rivendell and taking up his new role must have been a huge burden to him in the early days:

- He had lived, since babyhood, in a refuge largely inhabited by Elves, with other races (such as the Dúnedain) mainly going there for counsel, protection and healing. During his forays from this haven he would have been accompanied and protected by Elladan and Elrohir, who as children of Elrond had the lifespan of the Elves and had, by this time, nearly three thousand years' experience of dealing with the evils in Middle-earth, with the last four hundred in particular being spent relentlessly pursuing Orcs with the Dúnedain, in revenge for the capture, wounding and torment (possibly including rape) of their mother Celebrían in 2509. No doubt his foster brothers and senior Rangers were there to offer support during the period immediately after leaving his childhood home, but this would not have compensated for the extreme change in circumstances which he was experiencing.
- In Rivendell he had been a son, younger brother and pupil to Elrond, Elladan and Elrohir. Now, as a Chieftain, he found himself having to adapt to a position of authority at extremely short notice and at a tender age so that many of his subordinates would certainly have been much older than he was. A study of the lifespans of the Chieftains of the Dúnedain in *HoM-e* XII.7[3] shows that, while Araglas was thirty-one when he succeeded to the Chieftainship and Arathorn II fifty-seven, all the others were

---

1. J.R.R. Tolkien, *The Lord of the Rings,* London, HarperCollins Publishers, 2007, 2nd edition, based on the 50th Anniversary Edition of 2004, App A.I.v, p. 1060.
2. Op. cit., App A.I.v, p. 1060.
3. C. Tolkien (ed.), *The History of Middle-earth*, vol. XII, *The Peoples of Middle-earth*, London HarperColllins Publishers, 2002, first published in Great Britain by HarperCollins Publishers 1996, HoM-e XII, Part 1, Chapter 7, p. 196.

in their nineties. As Men, these people were of a different race from most of Aragorn's companions to date. Thus the unsettling nature of the sudden change from subordinate to leader would have been aggravated by age differences and culture shock.
- The burden of his heritage, the predictions of Elrond, and the need to keep his identity secret may have seemed exciting when he was safely ensconced in Rivendell, but would no doubt have taken on a completely different complexion in the context of the "real world" in which Sauron searched relentlessly for Isildur's heir. The concept of fear would have taken on a new dimension. Sauron wasn't the only threat either, as App B.1089 records that as early as 2953 Saruman was already spying on Gandalf and planting agents in Bree and the Southfarthing of the Shire - though these activities would not of course come to light until much later.
- In addition to these issues specific to him, there would have been the inevitable health problems and homesickness which must have faced all new Rangers, though perhaps the parting from his mother would have had an extra poignancy for Aragorn given the short time they had been together since he had become aware of who they really were.
- Overall there was his new, and seemingly hopeless, love for Arwen along with the feeling that he was not considered worthy of her.

As the years went by, the pressures would have changed but not lessened as he journeyed further and further afield, often alone. Though this would have given him the advantage of having only his own safety and welfare to think of, solitariness would have brought with it an additional set of "stress factors", such as:
- The need for total self-sufficiency as regards to obtaining food and dealing with illness and injury.
- Having to be constantly alert, resulting in insufficient opportunity for sleeping and other bodily needs.
- Relying on disguise, camouflage, concealment and trickery (e.g. speaking in feigned voices to deceive a foe) in dangerous situations, rather than on confrontation and weapons.
- Problems of communication: with Gandalf, Rivendell, Rangers, etc.
- The psychological effects of isolation and having no-one to talk to for possibly weeks/months on end.

App A.I.v.1060 tells of Aragorn's long and hard journeys and the extreme hardiness he developed as a result. Not surprisingly his sufferings and the weight of his "*doom*" were reflected in his grim appearance and sad and stern face, a striking contrast to the "*fair and noble*" twenty-year-old encountered earlier. An additional factor which would have taken its toll was the need to mask his true nature and loyalties when associating with folk who were under the sway of Sauron, e.g. Haradrim and Easterlings. What is perhaps surprising is that "*hope dwelt ever in the depths of his heart, from which mirth would arise at times...*".[4] Maybe his innate Dúnadan foresight and his knowledge of the prophecies helped him to believe in a favourable outcome and buoyed him up. This would be helped by his perseverance, and his dogged endurance - both physical and mental - of long-term danger, hardship, homelessness, loneliness, hunger, sleep-deprivation, and the stress of being permanently a "*hunted man*", as he described himself to the Hobbits in *LotR* 1.10.170, never able to let his guard slip for a moment. The text goes on to describe other qualities which made him stand out: a presence - perhaps an innate authority - which made people honour him (when he wasn't concealing his true character), his elven wisdom, his ability to understand the thoughts and motives of the people he encountered, and the "*light in his eyes that when they were kindled few could endure.*".[5]

*

Aragorn's "*great journeys and errantries*" are stated to have taken place during the years 2957-80 (App B.1090). From the information available it is clear that the time would have been divided between journeys with Gandalf and on his own, service in Rohan under Thengel King, service in Gondor under the Steward Ecthelion II, and journeys to the South and East. According to App A.I.iv.1055 it was in Gondor that people

---
4. Op. cit. [1], App A.I.v, p. 1060.
5. Op. cit., App A.I.v, p. 1060.

gave him the Elvish (Sindarin) name "Thorongil" (meaning the Eagle of the Star) because he was swift and keen-eyed like an eagle and wore a star-shaped brooch on his cloak. There is no reference to the alias he used in Rohan, though in App B.1090 the entry for 2957-80 implies that he was known as "Thorongil" there as well.

Regarding the journeys with Gandalf, by the time Aragorn met him he had been *de facto* (as well as *de jure*) Chieftain of the Dúnedain for five years. During that time, and in his earlier travels with Elladan and Elrohir, he would probably have travelled fairly widely between the Misty Mountains in the east, the Blue Mountains in the west, the North Downs in the north and possibly as far as Tharbad in the south, but not any further afield. [These were Rangers of the **North**. In *LotR* 5.2.774 it is clear that Halbarad and the Grey Company had not been to Rohan before.] The process by which his horizons were extended, first in the company of Gandalf and then on his own, must have taken several years. These journeys would perhaps have involved crossing the Misty Mountains to the Anduin and Mirkwood Forest, or travelling further south along the mountain range. Also Gandalf may well have accompanied him to Rohan - presumably some sort of introduction to Thengel would have been required.

In App A.I.iv Aragorn, during his time in Gondor, is referred to as "*a great leader of men, by land or by sea*".[6] He would certainly have developed general leadership ability as Chieftain of the Dúnedain prior to coming south, though it would no doubt have required his stint in Rohan to hone his military skills, both on foot and on horseback. App A.II.1069 also records that Saruman was secretly starting to support Rohan's enemies during Thengel's reign, so there would have been troubles with Dunlendings and Orcs. Regarding naval prowess, it is difficult to see where he could have obtained this, apart from in Gondor. Indeed to achieve the high level of attainment mentioned in all these areas he must have spent a substantial time in both Rohan and Gondor - probably the largest portion of the period 2957-80. It is stated that he had a very close relationship with Ecthelion who regarded him with affection and respect and placed great reliance on his counsel. Such a relationship was unlikely to have been formed overnight.

Aragorn's most renowned deed in Gondor was his recognition of the deadly threat posed to the southern fiefs by the Corsairs of Umbar if Sauron were to wage open war. He therefore persuaded Ecthelion to let him take a small fleet to attack the enemy ships. He did this by night taking the Corsairs by surprise and after destroying a large number of their ships he overthrew the Captain in battle on the quays, his own fleet suffering only small losses. This episode was right at the end of his service in Gondor so he must presumably have acquired a lot of seafaring experience in the years leading up to it to be capable of leading a fleet. App A.I.iv.1044-5 shows that there had been several sea-kings ruling in Gondor during the Third Age, starting with Tarannon Falastur (the 12th king) who built navies and extended Gondor's power along the coasts west and south of the mouth of the Anduin. He was followed by Eärnil I, Ciryandil and Ciryaher Hyarmendacil. In addition Aragorn's Númenórean ancestors, including Elendil, had been great mariners. It was therefore logical that he would aspire to becoming proficient in this line of leadership. However following his naval victory over the Corsairs he refused to return to Minas Tirith. Instead he crossed the Anduin at Pelargir and set off alone towards the Mountains of Shadow, sending a message to Ecthelion: "*Other tasks now call me, lord, and much time and many perils must pass, ere I come again to Gondor, if that be my fate.*"[7] [There must have been a sense of *déjà vu* for Aragorn when he met the black fleet in the War of the Ring. Also this early experience was clearly the reason why, when he obtained the Palantír of Orthanc in *LotR* 5.2.780-1 he looked for evidence of such an attack being planned].

From the information given I would suggest that a possible breakdown of this period of "*great journeys and errantries*" would be that Aragorn stayed nearer to home up until about 2960 and then travelled further afield, first to Rohan and then Gondor where the bulk of his time would have been spent, leaving only one or two years for travelling South and East. The question of the eastern and southern journeys is dealt with in more detail in Section 2 of this chapter.

*

---

6. Op. cit. [1], App A.I.iv, p. 1055.
7. Op. cit., App A.I.iv, p. 1055.

During the years Aragorn spent incognito in Rohan and Gondor, he would have met a number of the characters who appear in *LotR*. Some of these associations are specifically documented while others can be inferred.

In Rohan he served Thengel the father of Théoden. Théoden was seventeen years younger than Aragorn so would probably have been somewhere in his teens at this period. In *LotR* 3.2.438 at his first meeting with Éomer, Aragorn specifically mentioned being in Rohan before and knowing not only Théoden, but also Éomer's father Éomund (Éomer himself was not yet born at the time).

In Gondor, during his service to the Steward Ecthelion II, he also worked closely with his son Denethor - a year his senior and the future Steward Denethor II whom we meet in *LotR*. App A.I.iv.1055-6 records the jealousy of Denethor towards Thorongil on account of the favour shown to the stranger by his father. There are also hints that Denethor had worked out Thorongil's true identity. During this period Aragorn would probably have come into contact with Denethor's wife Finduilas and possibly also with their infant son Boromir (Faramir was not born until after Thorongil had left Gondor.). In addition, the Princes of Dol Amroth were high in the counsels of the Stewards of Gondor, the ruling Prince at this period being Angelimir (grandfather of Imrahil whom we know from *LotR*) until he was succeeded by his son Adrahil in 2977 (see *HoM-e* XII.1.7.223). Imrahil himself was twenty-four years younger than Aragorn so would have been in his teens to early twenties during Thorongil's service.

All these relationships, actual and potential, are discussed in more detail in the "Relationship" chapters in Part Two of this book.

2980-3017

Whatever the breakdown of Aragorn's early travels, the year 2980 found him heading to Rivendell to recuperate from an exhausting journey on the confines of Mordor "*... ere he journeyed into the far countries*".[8] It is not clear whether he was returning from the South or East **via** the borders of Mordor or whether he had been specifically reconnoitring a border area such as the Morgul Vale. In any event, instead of going directly to Rivendell, he found himself drawn into Lothlórien and a second meeting with Arwen Undómiel. After a courtship in this home of Arwen's grandparents, the two of them plighted their troth on the hill of Cerin Amroth, with Arwen renouncing her elvish immortality to pledge herself to a mortal. Aragorn was now forty-nine. Elrond's reaction to his daughter's betrothal was to accept her choice but to stipulate that no wedding would take place unless Aragorn first regained the kingship of both Gondor and Arnor. He and Aragorn discussed this in person, so it seems that after his time in Lothlórien Aragorn followed up his original intention of visiting Rivendell.

After that there is very little detail in App A.I.v. of Aragorn's life between the age of forty-nine and eighty-seven, though he would presumably have embarked on the next stage of his travels as indicated by "*... ere he journeyed into the far countries*" quoted above. This phrase implies that he made further journeys East and South. The earlier period of his travels seems to have been very full considering his activities in Rohan and Gondor, with not very much time available for exhaustive reconnaissance of places such as Harad, Khand and the areas east of Mordor and the Sea of Rhûn. After his departure from Gondor - in 2980 or shortly before - it seems very unlikely that he returned there, or to Rohan, until 3019. Éomer was born in 2991, so if Aragorn had gone back to Rohan after that date he would have been aware of his existence, and at their meeting in 3019 he specifically said he did not remember him, implying that this was due to Éomer's youth. His farewell message to Ecthelion quoted earlier seemed, in itself, to preclude any return to Gondor in the near future - if at all. Ecthelion died in 2984 (only four or five years after Thorongil's departure) to be succeeded by Denethor, so Aragorn was hardly likely to entertain the idea of going to Gondor with him as Steward unless - as eventually happened - he was actually intending to make a claim for the kingship. Also, in the light of Denethor's suspicions (mentioned earlier), such a visit may have caused Aragorn's identity to be revealed prematurely with all the attendant risks of Sauron finding out. It is perhaps feasible that he visited Rohan again prior to the birth of Éomer.

---

8. Op. cit. [1], App A.I.v, p. 1060.

Whatever the destinations of his later journeys, Aragorn's life was basically more of the same ("*danger and toil*") only more so as the power of Sauron grew, with little opportunity for spending time with Arwen. He must have been involved in the ongoing watch over the Shire (and also Bree), especially as Gandalf's suspicions about the nature of Bilbo's ring deepened. We know that his mother died prematurely (for a Dúnadan), in 3007, a victim of the fear, darkness and despair which Sauron caused to infiltrate Middle-earth, and that this event was clearly a cause of grief for Aragorn. It is recorded that he had visited her at her home in Eriador a few months before her death, the implication being that his presence in the North was exceptional rather than the norm.

App B throws some light on other events taking place during this period. For example, nine years after Aragorn's betrothal (i.e. 2989) Balin re-established the Dwarf colony in Moria only for it to be destroyed five years later, though the latter event would not actually be known for certain until the arrival of the Fellowship in 3019. Glóin was clearly unaware of it at the Council of Elrond. This raises the question of Aragorn's first visit to Moria, referred to in *LotR*, when Gandalf was trying to persuade the Fellowship that they should go via that route after the abortive attempt on the pass of Caradhras. Aragorn made the comment that he had been to Moria before, via the Dimrill Gate (the east entrance), and that the memory was "*very evil*".[9] This visit (or imprisonment?) must have been made prior to Balin's attempted recolonisation, as if it had taken place afterwards, Aragorn would have been able to provide Glóin with definite information at the Council of Elrond: either that there were Dwarves there, or that there were no Dwarves. Why did he describe the memory as evil? No doubt both he and Gandalf would have known the tales of Durin's Bane, but it was apparent in *LotR* that neither were aware of the actual nature of it. Once the Fellowship encountered the Balrog, Gandalf recognised its identity immediately, but from Aragorn's conversation with Celeborn when the party reached Lothlórien (*LotR* 2.7.356) it was clear that he had not known what it was - it being left to Legolas to put a name to it. Hammond and Scull point out that a visit to Moria is referred to in earlier drafts of *LotR* where Aragorn was still "Trotter" who was captured in Moria by the forces of the Dark Lord and subsequently tortured.[10] There is no hint of such an incident in *LotR* as published, thus the reason for Aragorn being there can only be guessed. Was he taken prisoner by Orcs? Was a journey to Moria one of the perilous ones he made with Gandalf? Did he enter the mines because he felt that he should learn something about them first-hand, or because he was trying to escape from some other danger? Or did he choose that route back from Lothlórien following his betrothal? This last suggestion seems unlikely as in *LotR* 2.4.300, when the mountain pass proved impossible, Gandalf took over from Aragorn as guide because the latter did not know the area well. Also the same conversation between Gandalf and Aragorn in *LotR* 2.4.297/300 does not seem to indicate that they were together when they made their previous visit to Moria. Therefore the implication is that Aragorn was in Moria alone - or certainly without Gandalf - sometime before TA 2989 for some reason which is not explained, and that he entered and exited the Mines via the east entrance, the Dimrill Gate.

From 3000 onwards Saruman began using the Palantír of Orthanc and became ensnared by Sauron who possessed an answering Palantír, the Ithil-stone. This finally established his treachery which had been in operation at a low level throughout Aragorn's life and probably for a great deal longer - though the rest of the White Council were still ignorant of it at this stage.

Following Bilbo's birthday party in 3001, Gandalf began suspecting that the Hobbit's ring was the One Ring. As a result the guard of Rangers around the Shire was doubled and Aragorn and Gandalf began to look for Gollum, a task which they would be undertaking for the next sixteen years, albeit intermittently. For example we know from App A.I.v.1061 and App B.1090 that Aragorn was in the North at some point during 3006 as this was when his last meeting with his mother took place. The search is discussed in *LotR* 1.2.58 by Gandalf and Frodo at Bag End, and in *LotR* 2.2.251-3 by Aragorn and Gandalf at the Council of Elrond. It reached its conclusion in 3017 according to App B.1090, with Gollum's capture by Aragorn in the Dead Marshes and his

---

9. Op. cit. [1], *LotR* 2.4, p. 297.
10. W.G. Hammond and C. Scull, *The Lord of the Rings: A Reader's Companion*, London, HarperCollins Publishers, 2005, pp. 275-6. For example see also: C. Tolkien (ed.), *The History of Middle-earth*, vol. VI, *The Return of the Shadow*, London HarperColllins Publishers, 2002, first published in Great Britain by Unwin Hyman 1988, *HoM-e* VI, Chapter 24, pp. 437-8, and C. Tolkien (ed.), *The History of Middle-earth*, vol. VII, *The Treason of Isengard*, London HarperColllins Publishers, 1993, first published in Great Britain by Unwyn Hyman 1989, *HoM-e* VII, Chapter 1, p. 10.

subsequent handing-over to the Elf-king Thranduil in Mirkwood. At the Council of Elrond Gandalf told how he had been travelling back from a visit to Minas Tirith (to read the Scroll of Isildur relating to the Ring) and had received the news of Gollum's capture via messengers from Lothlórien who had been aware of Aragorn's journey. He had then made his way to Mirkwood to meet Aragorn and question Gollum.

UT 3.4.ii. gives further details of Aragorn's journey to Mirkwood with Gollum, spanning the period February 1st to March 21st.[11] However the implication in this passage is that the capture took place, not in 3017, but 3018 (only a few months before Frodo's departure from the Shire), with Gandalf hurrying to Mirkwood to question Gollum and then travelling straight to Hobbiton, arriving on April 12th 3018 after a journey of nearly eight hundred miles. In UT.Introduction.16 Christopher Tolkien refers to general date discrepancies between UT 3.4.436-459 and App B, which he attributes to the fact that the UT manuscripts involved were written after the publication of the first volume of LotR, but prior to that of Volume Three which contained the Appendices. Therefore I have followed the date in App B.1090, as being the later version, and assumed that Gollum's capture was in 3017. This probably covers Aragorn's movements well into the spring of that year, after which he and Gandalf no doubt remained in close contact.

There is plenty of evidence, as already indicated, that Aragorn's travels pre-*LotR* took him close to Mordor, for example after his naval victory against the Corsairs and during the search for Gollum. The latter journey actually covered both the Morannon and Morgul Vale approaches as illustrated by the fact that he found Gollum in the Dead Marshes and by his referral to the "*deadly flowers of Morgul Vale*"[12] which he encountered during the search. This leads to further considerations concerning this most dangerous part of his travels:

- Did he actually go to Mordor itself? Looking at the *LotR* map it appears to be accessible from the east without having to scale a mountain range.
- Was he aware of the existence of Shelob?
- Did he ever inadvertently drink water flowing from the Morgul Vale (against which Faramir warned Frodo and Sam in *LotR* 4.7.694)?
- His experiences around the Morannon/Dagorlad area must have stood him in good stead when it came to going there again at the end of the War of the Ring, not least in enabling him to understand the terror which paralysed some of the young and inexperienced soldiers in his army.
- No doubt his journeys would also have taken him near to Dol Guldur (an earlier stronghold of Sauron in the south of Mirkwood Forest now held by some of the Nazgûl). It is possible that he encountered Nazgûl in all the areas mentioned, though they would have been invisible at this stage. It was not until Sauron sent them to search for the Shire and the Ring in earnest (in the summer of 3018) that they became visible, being clothed as Black Riders. However *UT* 3.4.ii.443 states that the terror they inflicted was actually greater in their unclad state, so this would have been a new fear for Aragorn to experience and try to overcome. As a result he would have been better prepared for his Nazgûl encounters in *LotR*.

Identity and Role Issues

As has been seen, prior to the events of *LotR* Aragorn had spent sixty-seven years adopting, or being given, different identities in order to keep his real one secret from all but a trusted few. In addition he had multiple roles and levels of responsibility operating in often widely-separated places. Perhaps his words to Elrohir in *LotR*, "*Always my days have seemed to me too short to achieve my desire*",[13] give some idea of the pressure. Before moving on to the events of 3018-9 these aspects of his life need to be looked at in more detail as they shed an important light on the background and nature of the mysterious stranger whom Frodo encountered in Bree.

In Chapter 1.3 I drew attention to his response when Arwen asked him who he was. He told her he had been

---

11. C. Tolkien (ed.), *Unfinished Tales of Númenor and Middle-earth*, London, HarperCollins Publishers, 1998, first published in Great Britain by George Allen & Unwin 1980, *UT* pp. 444, 457 (Note 6).
12. Op. cit. [1], *LotR* 2.2, p. 253.
13. Op. cit., *LotR* 5.2, p. 775.

called Estel, but **was** Aragorn son of Arathorn, etc. Estel was the first of his aliases, being given to him by Elrond at the age of two. There are other references to him being 'called' a particular name. In the following examples the emphasis is mine:
- "*Thorongil men **called** him in Gondor*".[14]
- "*... he is often **called** that here*".[15] Bilbo was referring to the name Dúnadan which was used for Aragorn in Rivendell.
- "*I am **called** Strider*", he said respectively to Frodo, Pippin and to Éomer.[16]
- "*I am Aragorn son of Arathorn and am **called** Elessar, the Elfstone, Dúnadan*", to Éomer.[17] By now he had passed through Lothlórien and been given the brooch with the green stone by Galadriel along with the name he would bear as King, Elessar/Elfstone. However in the passage just quoted he seemed to regard even this as something which he was called as opposed to Aragorn, which he was. This is confirmed in *LotR* 5.8.871 except that the word 'named' is used rather than 'called': "*And they named him Elfstone, because of the green stone that he wore, and so the name which it was foretold at his birth that he should bear was chosen for him by his own people.*" The description of this birth prophecy, made by Ivorwen[18], adds a further nuance to this as it states that at his naming ceremony as a baby, his father gave him the name Aragorn (as opposed to calling him Aragorn) and Ivorwen went on to say that the green stone she could see would give him his "*true name*".

The names given here all originated in lands opposed to Sauron, but we know that Aragorn spent a great deal of time in places which were under his sway or were less than friendly for other reasons - for example the Dunlendings were hostile to Rohan. In these situations an alias could well have been accompanied by the need to assume a totally different character and personality, emulating his companions and their traits - e.g. cruelty, loyalty to Sauron, hostility to Rohan - so as to appear as one of them, or at least as a friend. The danger and concentration involved would have been extreme and there must have been many close shaves, both with personality slip-ups and inappropriate use of names, especially perhaps following a period of relative security, with his kinsfolk or with Gandalf, when he had actually been able to be himself for a while. Even in Bree he found it advantageous to be seen as a rather sinister and disreputable figure, while as far as the Shire was concerned he and his kinsmen relied on actually avoiding detection by the locals. The identity issues of his childhood were compounded as he grew older. At least during his 'Estel' years he had been none the wiser.

Linked to - and complicated by - his identity issues were his multiple roles and the various responsibilities which went with them. These will now be considered in chronological order showing Aragorn as a leader and as a subordinate:
- From two years old the child, Estel, was Chieftain of the Dúnedain, the leader of the survivors of Númenor, being the direct descendant of Elendil. However he was unaware of it and was very much a youngest son to Elrond and a little brother to Elladan and Elrohir. As well as being family he would have been a pupil with a great deal to learn. During this period there must have been some sort of "regency" in operation with a Ranger (or Rangers) acting as Chieftain, probably with help from Elladan and Elrohir and certainly with support from Elrond and possibly Gilraen.
- On leaving Rivendell in 2951, Estel was now Chieftain of the Dúnedain in practice as well as in name. He would have left Elrond's immediate influence, but some of his senior Rangers must have had a training and advisory role in the early days - presumably those who had acted as regent during his minority. Thus although he was the leader of the Northern Dúnedain he was also under supervision. As Elladan and Elrohir had always spent a lot of their time riding against Orcs with the Dúnedain, Estel would have continued to see them. However the relationship between them would have changed, not least because Aragorn now knew who he was. He could safely use his real name with them and with the

---
14. Op. cit. [1], App A.I.iv, p. 1055.
15. Op. cit., *LotR* 2.1, p. 233.
16. Op. cit., *LotR* 1.9, p. 156, *LotR* 1.10, p. 163, *LotR* 3.2, p. 432 respectively.
17. Op. cit., *LotR* 3.2, p. 433.
18. Op. cit. [3], *HoM-e* XII, Foreword, p. xii.

Dúnedain - though to avoid mishaps it is possible that the name Estel may have continued to be used.
- In 2956 Aragorn got to know Gandalf. In the early days of their acquaintance he would have been very much a pupil as we know, from App A.I.v, that Gandalf taught him much wisdom and also took him on perilous journeys as a prelude to him travelling alone. However as shown throughout *LotR*, the two of them became close friends and trusty allies in the fight against Sauron, regarding each other with mutual respect and affection. Aragorn was however the equivalent of a second-in-command to Gandalf, as the Wizard certainly out-ranked the Chieftain of the Dúnedain.
- As already discussed, Aragorn's travels took him to Rohan where he served Théoden's father Thengel using the incognito of Thorongil. Thus although he was the senior descendant of Elendil with a claim to the Kingship of Arnor and Gondor he was serving as a subordinate to a ruler who would have been his vassal if he had actually been King of Gondor.
- He was in a similar situation in Gondor itself serving Ecthelion who would have been his own Steward if he had been *de facto* monarch. Acting in a subordinate role to people who were actually **his** subordinates must have become more difficult as he grew older and more experienced. He became a much trusted counsellor to Ecthelion and when he fought the naval battle against the Corsairs at Umbar around 2979-80 he went as the leader of the fleet. As noted earlier App A.I.iv describes him as "*a great leader of men, by land or by sea*". The fact that Ecthelion thought well of him indicates that he must have been convincing and respectful in his "inferior" role. Indeed although Denethor was resentful of the favour shown to Thorongil we are told that the latter "*had never himself vied with Denethor, nor held himself higher than the servant of his* [Denethor's] *father.*".[19]

These examples illustrate the conflict which must have existed between Aragorn's role as Chieftain of the Dúnedain, his role as Gandalf's ally in the struggle to defeat Sauron, and his role in preparing for kingship. The first of these was based in the North in the old kingdom of Arnor, which he regarded as home, and where he was indisputably the leader of the Northern Dúnedain, able to assume his real identity if in the presence of his kinsfolk. The other two roles required extensive travels further south and east, using a host of different identities/disguises and often in inferior positions. We know that the search for Gollum went on for approximately sixteen years and that Aragorn's service in Rohan and Gondor would probably have occupied at least twenty years of his life. This is without taking into account time spent in places like Rhûn and Harad. Thus there were long periods when he was away from the North and therefore unable to be Chieftain in person - a situation which would not have applied to his predecessors.

Perhaps an idea of the conflict of roles can be gleaned from Aragorn's statement to Frodo in *LotR* 1.10.172 that he had often guarded the Shire for Gandalf during the preceding few years. This doesn't seem to fit in with his search for Gollum which was happening intermittently during the years 3001-3017 and required lengthy and patient scouring of lands well over a thousand miles from the Shire. Even if he was making interim journeys to the North he couldn't have handled both roles without delegation. Obviously in this situation it would have been essential to appoint a deputy to be Acting Chieftain on a semi-permanent basis. There must have been occasions when younger Rangers among the Northern Dúnedain did not even know Aragorn and were meeting him for the first time when he returned after a long absence.

Other roles of a very different kind were those of family member in various capacities, namely:
- Foster-son to Elrond.
- Foster-brother to Elladan and Elrohir.
- Son to Gilraen.
- Fiancé to Arwen - from 2980 onwards.
- Friend to members of the Dúnedain of the North - e.g. Halbarad.

All these relationships will be discussed in the "Relationship" chapters.

Aragorn's feelings about the life he was forced to lead are perhaps summed up in his heart-felt comment to

---
19. Op. cit. [1], App A.I.iv, p. 1055.

Frodo in *LotR*, "... *it is not my fate to sit in peace, even in the fair house of Elrond.*".[20]

*

By the start of the year TA 3018 the stage was set for the culmination of Aragorn's struggle to defeat Sauron, regain the kingdoms of Arnor and Gondor and win the hand of Arwen.

---

20. Op. cit. [1], *LotR* 1.12, p. 202.

CHAPTER 1.5 - *LOTR*: AN "ARAGORN-CENTRIC" VIEW

In a draft letter to Michael Straight, probably written in January or February 1956, Tolkien describes *LotR* as *"hobbito-centric"*[1], giving this as the reason why Aragorn's story before and after TA 3018-9 was confined to an appendix - albeit *"the most important of the Appendices"*. My aim in this chapter is to be "Aragorn-centric", telling the story of *LotR* from Aragorn's point of view and examining his personal struggles and motives.

I have split the account into sections as follows:

- Sarn Ford to Bree
- Bree to Rivendell
- In Rivendell
- Rivendell to Moria
- Moria to Lothlórien
- Lothlórien to Parth Galen
- Parth Galen to Fangorn
- Fangorn to Isengard
- Isengard to the Pelennor Fields
- The Houses of Healing
- Minas Tirith to the Morannon
- Coronation and Wedding

Sarn Ford to Bree

This section covers Aragorn's activities between May and September 3018 and is based on information in *LotR* 1.2-1.10, App B and *UT* 3.4. Since the Nazgûl played an important role in the events described I have compiled a chart showing their activities between June 20th and October 20th 3018. This can be found at the end of the chapter.

To put Aragorn's position during the early part of 3018 in context, it is first necessary to summarise Frodo's situation in the same period. For him the matter of the Ring began in earnest on April 12th, when Gandalf turned up at Bag End after a gap of over nine years. This visit resulted in the decision for Frodo to leave the Shire with the Ring, and by the end of April his departure date had been fixed for September 23rd. Gandalf carried on staying at Bag End until late June, at which point he left unexpectedly to investigate something which was worrying him, but promised to be back, at the latest, in time to accompany Frodo to Rivendell in September, saying *"I think after all you may need my company on the road."*[2]. Of course in the event, things were to turn out very differently due to Gandalf's imprisonment by Saruman. Frodo did indeed leave Bag End on September 23rd but without Gandalf from whom he had heard nothing. During September 24th-28th he received help from Gildor Inglorion, Farmer Maggot and Tom Bombadil before finally getting together with Aragorn/Strider in Bree on September 29th.

Unfortunately Aragorn's movements during this period are by no means so easy to pin down, since the

---

1. H. Carpenter (ed.), *The Letters of J.R.R. Tolkien*, with the assistance of Christopher Tolkien, London, HarperCollins Publishers, 1995. First published in Great Britain by George Allen & Unwin, 1981. Letter. 181, p. 237.
2. J.R.R. Tolkien, *The Lord of the Rings,* London, HarperCollins Publishers, 2007, 2nd edition, based on the 50th Anniversary Edition of 2004, *LotR* 1.3, p. 67.

account he gave to the Hobbits in the Prancing Pony (*LotR* 1.10.172) contained some vagueness and ambiguity, and to some extent contradicted the timetable given above. He told them:
- That he had been in close contact with Gandalf in recent years, often guarding the Shire when his friend was elsewhere.
- That he had come west with Gandalf that spring, his last meeting with him being on May 1st at Sarn Ford, when Gandalf had reported that his business at Bag End had gone well and that Frodo would be leaving the Shire in the last week of September.
- That he had then gone off on a journey of his own, since he knew that Gandalf was taking care of Frodo.
- That he had returned from his journey *"many days ago"* to reports that Gandalf was missing and the Nazgûl had been seen.

As Hammond and Scull point out[3], May 1st would have been in the middle of Gandalf's two-month sojourn at Bag End. They also refer to a note by Christopher Tolkien in *HoM-e* VII.4 Note 20[4] which states that there is no record of Gandalf leaving Hobbiton during his visit to Frodo. Gandalf's comment on his departure in late June, that he was going south of the Shire to get news because he had been idle longer than he should have (*LotR* 1.3.67), seems to support the suggestion that he had stayed put in Frodo's house. Due to the uncertainty, I decided to consider other possible dates for this meeting between Aragorn and Gandalf but found that nothing else would make much sense. Their meeting could not have been before Gandalf's visit to Frodo as its purpose was clearly to report on the outcome of this visit. From a study of the events as described in App B.1091 and in Gandalf's account at the Council of Elrond (*LotR* 2.2.256-264), it does not seem likely that the meeting would have taken place after he left Frodo at the end of June either. As already stated, Gandalf left Bag End because of a premonition of danger and subsequently went to the southern border of the Shire, where he received messages indicating that the Nazgûl might have appeared. He then turned east to join the Greenway (a route which would have crossed Sarn Ford), then north along the Greenway towards Bree, encountering Radagast on the way, who confirmed his fears about the Nazgûl. The conversation with Radagast occurred on Mid-Year's Day, after which Gandalf spent the night at Bree, decided he had no time to return to the Shire, then went with all speed to Isengard to consult Saruman. By July 10th he was a prisoner of Saruman and remained so until September 18th. After his escape he made his way north but did not arrive at Sarn Ford until September 28th by which time Aragorn was lying in wait on the East Road hoping to intercept Frodo. In the event Aragorn remained ignorant of Gandalf's activities until the Council of Elrond on October 25th.

The only time that a meeting could have taken place between Aragorn and Gandalf after the latter had left Hobbiton would have been during the last few days of June as Gandalf passed over Sarn Ford on the way to the Greenway. At this point Gandalf was aware of the possible Nazgûl threat, and was heading away from the Shire to find out more, leaving Frodo without support. Therefore if he had had a meeting with Aragorn, it seems highly improbable that he would have given a report which was optimistic enough for Aragorn to go off on a journey of his own! In fact Aragorn had already gone off on his journey by this point anyway; referring again to his conversation with the Hobbits in Bree, "... *plainly some news reached him, and I was not at hand to help.*"[5].

What is clear is that they must definitely have met at some point, as Aragorn was aware of Frodo's plans including his intention to leave the Shire in the last week of September, and it doesn't seem likely that he and Gandalf would have trusted such information to a physical message or an intermediary. Gandalf's later action of leaving a letter for Frodo with Barliman Butterbur was a last resort. Also Aragorn's account to Frodo in Bree was in answer to the specific question: *"When did you last see Gandalf?"*[6] [My emphasis]. Considering the evidence I am convinced that Gandalf must have interrupted his sojourn at Bag End to update Aragorn - probably just after Frodo's departure date had been decided - hence May 1st, or soon after, seems likely even though the meeting was not documented. In particular, note Aragorn's choice of words in the conversation with

---
3. W.G. Hammond and C. Scull, *The Lord of the Rings: A Reader's Companion*, London, HarperCollins Publishers, 2005, p. 162.
4. C. Tolkien (ed.), *The History of Middle-earth*, vol. VII, *The Treason of Isengard*, London HarperColllins Publishers, 1993, first published in Great Britain by Unwyn Hyman 1989, *HoM-e* VII, Chapter 4, Note 20, p. 80.
5. Op. cit. [2], *LotR* 1.10, p. 172.
6. Op. cit., *LotR* 1.10, p. 172.

the Hobbits: "***As I knew he was at your side***, *I went away on a journey of my own.*"[7] [My emphasis]. This could well be interpreted to imply that Gandalf would shortly be on his way back to Frodo. (At this point there was no indication that he was actually intending to accompany Frodo in September.). Looking at the *LotR* map, the journey from Hobbiton to Sarn Ford and back was approximately four hundred miles, a distance which would probably take at least three weeks to walk, but could perhaps be done in four or five days on horseback, especially if the rider was Gandalf. (No doubt he was in touch with other Rangers besides Aragorn, who could have arranged horses for him.). Maybe the incident was deliberately kept low-key: the Rangers were guarding the Shire secretly, so Gandalf wouldn't have given details to Frodo of where he was going or whom he was meeting. It is clear too, from his receipt of reports of danger, that he must have been out and about and in communication with various messengers (birds? Elves? Rangers?) during his stay at Hobbiton, so a meeting with Aragorn would have fallen into that category. Gandalf's comment about having been idle longer than he should (referred to above) would still be valid at the end of June given a May 1st meeting with Aragorn. Also, from the point of view of the story, the appearance of Strider in the inn at Bree was a complete surprise - to the reader as well as to the Hobbits - so this effect could have been spoiled by a veiled reference to an excursion made by Gandalf during his stay at Bag End.

There are further uncertainties in Aragorn's words to the Hobbits. He told them that he had returned from his journey "*many days ago*", and that "*The tidings had gone far and wide that Gandalf was missing and the horsemen had been seen. It was the Elven-folk of Gildor that told me this; and later they told me that you had left your home...*"[8] There is no real indication of when Aragorn returned; "*many days ago*" is vague, but it must have been after sufficient time had elapsed from the start of Gandalf's imprisonment (July 12th) for him to be regarded as missing, and not too close to Aragorn's meeting with the Hobbits. The nature of the journey is also unknown, though the implication is that it was something solitary and remote where he was unable to receive news or messages, as he knew nothing about Gandalf's disappearance or the Nazgûl sightings until he came back.

Regarding the liaison with Gildor, the question is: did Gildor tell Aragorn that the horsemen had been seen and that Gandalf was missing? Or did he just tell him that the horsemen had been seen? If the first, then Gildor's behaviour during his conversation with Frodo on September 24th (*LotR* 1.3.83-84) was a little strange as he seemed to be surprised and concerned that Frodo didn't know where Gandalf was. This doesn't really imply that he'd already told Aragorn that Gandalf was missing. However a possible interpretation could be that Gildor realised Gandalf hadn't been seen or heard of for a while, but assumed that Frodo would know of his whereabouts due to Gandalf's obvious involvement in Frodo's flight. Thus it was Gandalf's failure to meet Frodo on a pre-arranged date which worried Gildor. Aragorn's words "... *later they told me that you had left your home...*"[9] would presumably mean that Gildor spoke to him for a second time after his [Gildor's] encounter with Frodo on September 24th. (The Elf had told Frodo that he would alert the "Wandering Companies" to his journey.). This fits in with Gildor having already been in touch with Aragorn about the Nazgûl sightings (and possibly about Gandalf as well, depending on the interpretation of Gildor's conversation with Frodo). Aragorn would not necessarily be dependent on Gildor for news about Gandalf; his Rangers and the folk in Rivendell would seem to be more likely sources of information and, as quoted above, "*The tidings had gone far and wide...*"[10].

One event during this period which **is** documented with a definite date (September 22nd) is the Nazgûl attack on the guard of Rangers at Sarn Ford. However even here there is some uncertainty as App B.1091 states that it occurred in the evening of that day, while *UT* 3.4.i.441 states that the Nazgûl arrived when "*Night was waning on the twenty-second day of September*"[11] which implies that it took place in the early morning. In Chapter 1.4 I mentioned the general date discrepancies between *UT* 3.4.436-459 and App B referred to by Christopher Tolkien (*UT*.Introduction.16) attributable to the fact that some *UT* manuscripts were written prior

---

7. Op. cit. [2], *LotR* 1.10, p. 172.
8. Op. cit., *LotR* 1.10, p. 172.
9. Op. cit., *LotR* 1.10 p. 172.
10. Op. cit., *LotR* 1.10, p. 172.
11. C. Tolkien (ed.), *Unfinished Tales of Númenor and Middle-earth*, London, HarperCollins Publishers, 1998, first published in Great Britain by George Allen & Unwin 1980, *UT* p. 441.

to the finalisation of the *LotR* Appendices, so no doubt the timing of events at Sarn Ford on September 22nd is another example of this problem. In either case the account in *UT* 3.4.i.441 makes grim reading as it describes the Rangers fleeing and being killed or driven off into the wild. Even those who tried to continue barring the ford were eventually swept away by the Lord of the Nazgûl after which he and five of his companions entered the Shire at its southern border at dawn on September 23rd - the day Frodo was to leave his home. We are told that the task of facing the Nazgûl was "*beyond the power of the Dúnedain*" and that their hearts "*misgave them*"[12]. Note that the Northern Dúnedain were the toughest Men in Middle-earth, being not far short of Aragorn himself as regards courage and strength, and in a few months' time, some of them would be accompanying their Chieftain through the Paths of the Dead and on the desperate ride to Pelargir. Their defeat, with the resulting loss and trauma - along with the effects of the Black Breath - was a chilling indication of the terror the Nazgûl could instil in even the strongest people. In addition we are told that even if Aragorn had been present at the Ford, the result may not have been any different. In the event Aragorn was in fact already keeping watch on the East Road near Bree - which was why he hadn't been at the Ford. Some of the Rangers tried to track him down and give him news of the disaster. It is not stated if they succeeded or not; thus we don't know whether Aragorn first found out about the entry of the Nazgûl into the Shire from Gildor, or from his Rangers. If the Rangers were unable to contact him he would presumably have been unaware of the deaths sustained at Sarn Ford. Although the Rangers failed to withstand the Nazgûl they did succeed in delaying their progress sufficiently to enable Frodo to move out of Bag End before one of them (named Khamûl) questioned Gaffer Gamgee as to his whereabouts (*LotR* 1.3.69).

After considering all the information we have concerning Aragorn's activities prior to joining the Hobbits, I suggest that the most likely scenario would be:
- He had a meeting with Gandalf at Sarn Ford on or around May 1st, and soon afterwards went off on his unknown journey.
- On returning, perhaps sometime in August, he became concerned that there were no messages for him from Gandalf. He also realised, from his Rangers and the folk in Rivendell, that nothing had been heard of Gandalf since early July.
- Sometime between September 18th and 22nd Gildor told him that the Nazgûl had been seen (App B.1091 records them as crossing the Fords of Isen on 18th.)
- He then presumably alerted the Rangers to the threat, and strengthened the guard at Sarn Ford hoping to prevent the Nazgûl entering the Shire, before putting all his own energies into tracking down Frodo.
- Sometime after September 24th Gildor told him of his meeting with Frodo - so even if he hadn't known previously (from the Rangers who were at Sarn Ford) that the Nazgûl had entered the Shire, he would have found out from Gildor.
- On September 29th he used his finely-tuned stalking skills to eavesdrop on the Hobbits' conversation with Tom Bombadil and then to follow Frodo's party to Bree undetected.
- This timetable fits in with Barliman Butterbur's remark to Frodo that "Strider" had been in and out of the Prancing Pony quite often during the spring of that year, but that he hadn't seen him lately.

There remain two further questions:
The first is: Did Aragorn have any encounters himself with the Nazgûl in their Black Rider guise prior to meeting Frodo? It is clear from his conversation with the Hobbits that he knew that two of them had been seen in Bree during the previous two days and that he witnessed their meeting with Harry Goatleaf the gatekeeper on September 26th. Also *UT* 3.4.ii.451 mentions the deployment of some of the Nazgûl to the eastern border areas of the Shire - so Aragorn may have been aware of them, or even had close encounters with them, as he was watching the East Road himself at least from September 22nd onwards.

The second question is: Did he visit Rivendell sometime before mid-September to fetch the Shards of Narsil, in case he needed them as proof of his identity? Note that Aragorn did not know that Gandalf had provided a written introduction for him in the letter to Frodo which had been left with Barliman Butterbur.

---

12. Op. cit. [11], *UT* p. 441.

He was well aware that some of the inhabitants of Bree regarded him and his Rangers with suspicion, and realised that he might have problems getting the Hobbits to trust him. He may also have known, from his last meeting with Gandalf, that Frodo had been told something of Isildur and the Last Alliance between the Elves and the Dúnedain. I feel that there needs to be a reason for Aragorn to have been carrying the Shards of Narsil when he met the Hobbits. The broken sword of Elendil had been a cherished heirloom of the heirs of Isildur for three thousand years and it does not seem logical or sensible for Aragorn to have been taking with him something so valuable (not to mention cumbersome, and useless in an emergency!) during his sixty-seven years of travelling. Also, in the wrong company, the presence of Elendil's sword on his person could have been downright dangerous for him if he had been travelling in lands dominated by Sauron.

Whatever the finer details of Aragorn's timetable during the summer and early autumn of 3018, he had basically taken on Gandalf's role and was trying to protect the Hobbits before the Fellowship had been formed and before the Ring-bearer was even aware of his existence. It was now his responsibility to try and get the Hobbits (and the Ring) safely to Rivendell, knowing that if he failed, his long struggle would have been in vain as Sauron would get the Ring back and take over Middle-earth.

*

The disappearance of Gandalf and the sightings of the Nazgûl must have been deeply disturbing and frightening to Aragorn. In addition he must have considered the question as to whether he had made the right decision to be absent from Sarn Ford. Did he feel that if he had been there and begun his search for Frodo slightly later the Nazgûl may have been prevented from entering the Shire when they did? There was also the question of the journey he went on in May 3018 once he believed that Frodo was being looked after by Gandalf. Although, given the seriousness of the situation, he must surely have gone only with Gandalf's blessing there may nevertheless have been pangs of guilt that he had not been around to help when Gandalf heard the news of the Nazgûl. Such pangs would have been understandable. Even assuming that Gandalf would still have sought the advice of Saruman he would have been able, with the help of Aragorn, to come to a more reliable arrangement for getting messages to Frodo, or even arranged for Aragorn to guide them to Bree much earlier on - perhaps using some Elvish liaison to ensure that Frodo would readily accept the Ranger. Also Aragorn himself would have realised that something had happened to Gandalf much earlier on and the journey to Rivendell would have been accomplished without being followed by the Nazgûl - and without Frodo being wounded. [Obviously it was meant to be otherwise so that Aragorn and Frodo were left to fend for themselves instead of relying on the Wizard.]

Aragorn's worries would have been greatly increased by anticipating events at Bree when he finally caught up with the Hobbits, not least because, as he later told them, *"The Enemy has set traps for me before now"*[13] and he had to be sure that the Hobbits really were Frodo and his companions. This remark just quoted could be taken to mean that Sauron suspected Aragorn of being Isildur's heir, but in reality he probably assumed, after the depredations on the North Kingdom of the Witch-king of Angmar (actually the Lord of the Nazgûl) in TA 1409-1975, that Isildur's line was extinct - as was indeed the case in the old northern sub-kingdoms of Cardolan and Rhudaur. Sauron's servants probably tried to set traps for Dúnedain in general, hoping to find some definite proof as to whether Isildur had an heir or not. They may have honed in on Aragorn in particular as a leading member of the remnants of the Northern Dúnedain, and also as a known friend of Gandalf. Although it would later be demonstrated (in *LotR* 5.2.780) that Sauron only became finally aware of the existence of an heir of Isildur when Aragorn confronted him in the Palantír of Orthanc, Aragorn's caution was not an overreaction. There is understandably much emphasis in *LotR*, due to its *"Hobbito-centric"* nature, on what Sauron would do to Frodo if he got hold of him, but it is also worth considering what Sauron would do to Aragorn if he got hold of him and found out that he was Isildur's heir. Note that Sauron was searching for the heir of Isildur with as much intensity as for the One Ring. [Ironically the real risk at this juncture was from Saruman as some Shire Hobbits were already in his pay (*UT* 3.4.ii.449).]

---

13. Op. cit. [2], *LotR* 1.10, p. 170.

Aragorn's other concern was the uphill struggle to get the Hobbits to trust him and accept him as their guide. He must have been absolutely exasperated (not to mention frightened) by the behaviour of everyone around him at the Prancing Pony:
- Pippin's reckless chattering about Bilbo's farewell party in the crowded bar.
- Frodo putting on the Ring and disappearing.
- Sam's refusal to trust him even when his companions had been won over.
- Merry going out on his own in the dark with Nazgûl about.
- Barliman Butterbur's obstructive behaviour in refusing to let him visit the Hobbits privately beforehand (so he could advise them to lie low), and then later almost undoing the budding trust by advising the Hobbits not to take up with a Ranger.

All this must have been doubly hard to bear in the light of the thankless danger he and his people had put themselves in over the years, and with the memory of Sarn Ford still fresh. Perhaps the clearest indication of his state of mind is the whole gamut of contrasting emotions and reactions he displayed during his first encounter with the Hobbits as described in *LotR* 1.9.156-161 and then 1.10:163-6 and 168-171.
- The self-controlled whispered warnings in the initial interaction with Frodo with a touch of wry humour [something Aragorn has been accused of lacking] at his own off-putting appearance: "*There are queer folk about. Though I say it as shouldn't, you may think ...*"[14]
- Then the urgent whisper telling Frodo to interrupt Pippin's exuberance.
- His pretence of ignoring Frodo's song and disappearance. Given the drama of the situation and the fact that this would have been the first time Aragorn had seen the Ring in action his behaviour was an impressive feat of self-control.
- The calm, slightly contemptuous, reprimand of Frodo as he reappeared, designed to frighten him and bring him to his senses by using a very neat piece of humour which left no doubt that Strider knew Mr. Underhill's real name and all about the Ring: "*You have put your foot in it! Or should I say your finger?*"[15]
- The teasing about his "reward" in return for useful information, interrupted with a gentle reassurance that the reward would not be more than Frodo could afford. This reassurance was accompanied by a "*slow smile*"[16] - the first time he smiled, an indication that his true self was starting to come through.
- His appreciation and laughter when Frodo answered him back and demanded that he explain his reasons for his interest in the Hobbits.
- Further deprecating humour (including face-pulling) at his own rascally appearance - the cause of Butterbur's distrust.
- Deadly seriousness when speaking of the Nazgûl and Bill Ferny: "*his eyes were cold and hard*"[17]
- His calm understatement of the reasons for accepting him as a guide, namely long-standing experience and knowledge of the lands they'd be travelling in: "*I might prove useful*"[18] (meaning: "I'm the only person with the slightest hope of protecting you from these creatures").
- His attempt to convince the Hobbits of the true terror of the Nazgûl, which degenerated into what appeared to be some sort of traumatic flashback or vision: face drawn as if with pain, hands clenching his chair, staring with unseeing eyes, wiping his brow. Was he reliving some experience of his own? Or recalling the effect on the Rangers at Sarn Ford? Or looking back to the near-destruction of his people by the Witch king of Angmar in years gone by? Or looking ahead to possible future encounters with the Nazgûl, perhaps even foreseeing the attack on Weathertop? His use of the word "terrible" left no doubt as to the nature of these creatures.
- Immediately afterwards the tactic of referring to himself in the third person: "*Strider can take you by*

---
14. Op. cit. [2], *LotR* 1.9, p. 157.
15. Op. cit., *LotR* 1.9, p. 161.
16. Op. cit., *LotR* 1.10, p. 163.
17. Op. cit., *LotR* 1.10, p. 165.
18. Op. cit., *LotR* 1.10, p. 165.

paths that are seldom trodden. Will you have him?"[19] He almost seemed to be pleading with them, trying to encourage their trust by appearing vulnerable. He may also have been emphasising the fact that Strider was not his real name.

- His blunt follow-up statement when the Hobbits were still reluctant to trust him: *"You will never get to Rivendell now on your own, and to trust me is your only chance."*[20] He was not being bullying or boastful but merely stating the truth. This was a life and death situation and it was absolutely essential that the Hobbits were made to realise this and understand that they had to accept him as a guide if there was to be any chance at all of keeping the Ring from the Nazgûl and reaching the safety of Rivendell.
- The angry outburst at Butterbur's forgetfulness and suspicious attitude during which he called him *"A fat innkeeper who only remembers his own name because people shout it at him all day."*[21] Although rude this reaction was hardly surprising in the circumstances. Aragorn knew that the incident in the bar could have been prevented if Barliman had allowed him to speak to the Hobbits beforehand. Also Barliman had just advised the Hobbits not to take up with a Ranger right at the point when they were starting to trust him. The failure of the innkeeper to deliver Gandalf's letter on time, through pure absent-mindedness, must have been the last straw. As a result of this combination of actions and omissions the Hobbits (and Aragorn himself) were in hugely increased danger. In addition Barliman's suspicion and mistrust must have been extremely humiliating.
- His admittance that he had hoped the Hobbits would take to him for his own sake rather than because of the proof in Gandalf's letter. He seemed vulnerable and emotional at this point: *"A hunted man sometimes wearies of distrust and longs for friendship."*[22]
- His further outburst at Pippin's naïve under-estimation of the hardships he had endured in which he again referred to himself in the third person.
- His respect for Sam (*"you are a stout fellow"*[23]) even though Sam continued to distrust him.
- His pretended threat to seize the Ring. I have never regarded this incident as implying that Aragorn was in any danger of yielding to the temptation of the Ring. He was merely trying to get the Hobbits to see that their only chance of escape was to trust him by demonstrating that he could easily have killed them and taken the Ring already, but had chosen not to.
- His pledge to look after them, now using the first person, his face softened by a sudden smile: *"I am Aragorn son of Arathorn; and if by life or death I can save you, I will."*[24]
- Laughter at Frodo's implication that he **looked** foul but **felt** fair.
- Speaking of himself in the third person again: *"Strider shall be your guide."*[25]

The picture of Aragorn which emerges is of a frightened but courageous and steadfast man, who would try to protect his charges whatever the cost to himself, and who was desperately trying to make the Hobbits understand the danger of their situation: *"You fear them* [the Nazgûl], *but you do not fear them enough, yet."*[26] Most of the time he exercised great self-control, but was capable of outbursts of bitterness and anger. He also showed himself as a man of gentleness and sensitivity who yearned for friendship and affection and there is a poignancy in his desire to be accepted as a friend on his own merits. This is also the case in the scene when he used his real name and patronymic for the first time as he pledged himself to protect the Hobbits, rather than the nickname Strider given to him by others. He sensed the way Frodo's mind was working, and was not afraid to show his anxiety and fear. This must have helped the Hobbits to realise his genuineness, though Aragorn was disappointed that it took Gandalf's letter and the broken sword to complete the trust. He was well aware of the hostility his appearance and demeanour engendered and hid his hurt by laughing at himself.

---

19. Op. cit. [2], *LotR* 1.10, p. 165.
20. Op. cit., *LotR* 1.10, p. 166.
21. Op. cit., *LotR* 1.10, p. 168.
22. Op. cit., *LotR* 1.10, p. 170.
23. Op. cit., *LotR* 1.10, p. 171.
24. Op. cit., *LotR* 1.10, p. 171.
25. Op. cit., *LotR* 1.10, p. 172.
26. Op. cit., *LotR* 1.10, p. 165.

It is also evident that Aragorn knew Bree and its people well - as was the case with the other places he visited. He knew that Barliman Butterbur was trustworthy, and that Bill Ferny wasn't; he knew how frightened Harry Goatleaf had been in his encounter with some of the Nazgûl. His casual reference to witnessing the Hobbits' conversation with "*old Bombadil*"[27] implies that he must have been pretty well-acquainted with Tom. Did he know Farmer Maggot too? We know Bombadil and Maggot knew each other (*LotR* 1.7.132). Aragorn could also adapt his speech to fit the situation. When he first spoke to Frodo he used the same accent as that of the Bree folk, but as the conversation progressed Frodo noticed that his voice changed, leading to a feeling of trust in "Strider", which nevertheless was in conflict with the need to take care and "*Watch every shadow!*"[28] Aragorn's response to Frodo's voicing of this conflict was: "*... the lesson in caution has been well learned...*"[29] seemingly referring to Frodo's belated caution compared with his earlier behaviour. However an interesting alternative interpretation (offered by a member of the Southampton UK Tolkien Reading Group) is that he was referring to himself as much as to Frodo. Instead of changing his voice intentionally to encourage the Hobbits' trust, had he **accidentally** lapsed into his true accent due to his own trust of **them**, letting the Bree one "slip" prematurely?

As he took on the task of protecting and guiding the Hobbits, he must have felt that a confrontation with the Nazgûl was well-nigh inevitable, possibly with all the Nine together. The failure of the Dúnedain to withstand these creatures can only have aroused feelings of terror in him. In addition, as he voiced his concern about Gandalf's absence, he told the Hobbits that he could think of nothing apart from the Nazgûl or Sauron himself which would have been capable of delaying the Wizard. So, as well as worrying about what had happened to Gandalf, there was the further consideration that if even Gandalf might have problems withstanding the Nazgûl what hope did he have himself of doing so? He may also have known Glorfindel's view on the subject: on finding Aragorn and the Hobbits, the Elf stated "*There are few even in Rivendell that can ride openly against the Nine...*"[30] It is impossible to overstate the fear Aragorn must have felt at this juncture. The Hobbits were frightened of something they didn't really know or understand, but Aragorn was under no illusion as to the nature of what lay ahead of them. He knew "*Too much; too many dark things*"[31].

At this stage it had not occurred to Aragorn, or to anyone else, that **Saruman** might be responsible for Gandalf's disappearance.

Bree to Rivendell

Aragorn and the Hobbits left Bree on September 30th and reached Rivendell on October 20th, a journey which is described in *LotR* 1.11 and 1.12. As with the previous section the chart of Nazgûl activity is relevant.

Aragorn's role in guiding the Hobbits during this period should not be under-estimated. Even before leaving Bree his decision that they should all sleep in the parlour, rather than using the special Hobbit bedrooms, meant that Frodo and his companions were safe when two of the Nazgûl attacked the Hobbit rooms during the night. Before they slept Aragorn had built the fire up, and during the night when Frodo woke suddenly (presumably at the point of the attack) the fire had again been made up and Aragorn was sleepless, clearly aware of the ongoing attack and ready to fight off the Nazgûl if they turned their attention to the parlour. It must have been particularly galling the next morning to be beholden to Bill Ferny for an overpriced pony and then leave Bree to the sound of name-calling and insults from him - though it must be said that Aragorn was able to silence nearly everyone else merely by looking at them. Another small insight into his character at this point in the narrative was his willingness to help Nob carry the Hobbits' luggage into the parlour after the decision had been made not to sleep in their bedrooms. Thus he showed that he was happy to "get his hands dirty" and was not too proud to help a servant do a menial job.

---

27. Op. cit. [2], *LotR* 1.10, p. 163.
28. Op. cit., *LotR* 1.10, p. 164.
29. Op. cit., *LotR* 1.10, p. 166.
30. Op. cit., *LotR* 1.12, p. 210.
31. Op. cit., *LotR* 1.10, p. 163.

During the journey from Bree to the Bruinen Ford he looked after his small charges in numerous ways:
- His "Ranger" skills took them through the Chetwood avoiding pursuit by Bill Ferny and subsequently got them safely across the Midgewater Marshes.
- He sat up keeping watch while the Hobbits slept.
- He drove off the five Nazgûl who attacked them on Weathertop.
- His healing skills and knowledge of herbs helped to keep Frodo alive until Glorfindel found them.
- At the Ford he joined Glorfindel in driving the Nazgûl into the river.

In addition to these crucial actions, we are made aware that he knew alternative ways out of Bree if necessary, was capable of hunting for food in an emergency and seemed oblivious to the cold on Weathertop which had the Hobbits wrapping themselves in every garment and blanket they possessed. He also established friendly relations by joking with the Hobbits about short-cuts and the stone Troll having a bird's nest behind his ear.

He revealed his knowledge of history, legend and poetry by telling stories of the Elder Days, and chanting the lay of Tinúviel which told the story of Beren and Lúthien. It says much for his self-control that he told the Hobbits these tales on Weathertop, in order to calm their fear. Indeed it was probably his own fear he was trying to allay as well as theirs. When he told the tale of Tinúviel it almost seemed that it kept the Nazgûl at bay, and then "*Suddenly a pale light* [of the Moon] *appeared over the crown of Weathertop behind him*"[32] perhaps symbolising the white crown he would one day wear. As soon as the tale ended "*... Frodo felt a cold dread creeping over his heart, now that Strider was no longer speaking.*"[33] The Nazgûl attack occurred soon afterwards. Aragorn's own fear must have been at least as great as that of the Hobbits, especially in view of his probable assumption that Gandalf had been overcome by these creatures. He was not to know at this point that in fact Gandalf had already drawn off four of them thus leaving only five to contend with when Frodo was attacked, or that Glorfindel would subsequently drive three of them away from the Bridge of Mitheithel (thus rendering it safe to cross two days later), in the process causing two more to turn aside southwards. Aragorn fully expected to face all the Nine, and to face a second confrontation at the bridge. An additional chilling factor on Weathertop was the presence of the Lord of the Nazgûl himself whose chief aim in his war against the North Kingdom as the Witch king of Angmar had been to try and eradicate the Northern Dúnedain and Isildur's line in particular.

Following the attack on Weathertop he and the Hobbits crossed the East Road heading south to more wooded country, trembling when they heard Nazgûl cries in the distance, and as they trudged along Frodo noted that "*Even Strider seemed tired and heavy-hearted.*"[34] Some days later they were **all** exhausted after scaling a particularly steep ridge north of the road. During the period when Glorfindel was leading them, Frodo noted that "*even Strider seemed by the sag of his shoulders to be weary*"[35] and the Elf made a point of keeping watch that night. Aragorn, as well as the Hobbits, needed sleep and Glorfindel's cordial. It is significant too that, in addition to the constant fear, he had the strain of responsibility: for keeping Frodo alive, for the diminishing food supplies and for getting the wounded Hobbit and the Ring to the safety of Rivendell before it was too late. A further cause of anxiety was that there were occasions when he had to leave the Hobbits alone for a time, for example on Weathertop after Frodo's injury when he went to find the athelas, and in the area near the stone Trolls when he went to reconnoitre, having lost his bearings - probably in itself an indication of the strain he was under. (He had told the Hobbits in Bree that he knew all the lands between Bree and the Misty Mountains.) Also the constant presence and lure of the Ring must have added to the pressures on him throughout the journey. Note that this would have been the first time he had been in contact with it.

Aragorn's behaviour during this terrifying three-week journey was also affected by his desperate desire to find Gandalf. It was for this reason that he had decided to aim for Weathertop, hoping to find him there. Weathertop was a good look-out point: it had been the location of the Palantír of Amon Sûl earlier in the Third Age while there were still kings in Arnor, and was still visited by Rangers, as witnessed by their tracks and the firewood they left (*LotR* 1.11.185,189). However when the companions drew in sight of the hill, Aragorn

---

32. Op. cit. [2], *LotR* 1.11, p. 194.
33. Op. cit., *LotR* 1.11, p. 194.
34. Op. cit., *LotR* 1.12, p. 200.
35. Op. cit., *LotR* 1.12, p. 211.

became hesitant, now raising many objections to that route and admitting that the chance of finding Gandalf there was slim. As a result he decided to approach it from the north instead of making for it directly. Even though they took turns to watch that night, he himself did not sleep at all, and during the next two days he became jumpy when the Hobbits used the words "wraith" and "Mordor" during their conversations. When they finally reached Weathertop his anxiety about finding evidence of Gandalf made him careless to the extent that he, Frodo and Merry lingered too long on the hilltop, thus causing the Nazgûl who were gathering on the East Road to become aware of them. In addition, when he returned to Sam and Pippin in the dell below, he found that the Hobbits' footprints had obscured many boot-marks in the soft ground, making it now impossible to identify their origin. He openly admitted that he was to blame for these lapses and that they were due to him being so anxious to find Gandalf. By that time it was too late in the day to go anywhere else, making the lighting of a fire their only option in the hope that it could be used to drive the Nazgûl away. In Aragorn's defence, the Nazgûl could sense the presence, and smell the blood, of living things, and in addition the Ring would draw them, so an attack would have been inevitable at some point. At least they were now forewarned enough to prepare a fire. However it is clear that his anxiety about Gandalf, as well as making him careless, was also causing him to fall victim to the kind of hesitancy, indecisiveness and lack of faith in himself which were to plague him later on, particularly after the loss of Gandalf in Moria. Also his words on finding no Gandalf at Weathertop ("*we must now look after ourselves and make our own way to Rivendell, as best we can*"[36]), and his lack of any alternative to sitting it out on the hill, seem to show that he had been clinging to the hope of finding Gandalf to the extent of being in denial of the possibility that he might **not** find him.

It is worth saying something about Aragorn's healing powers at this stage in the light of their importance later on. In *LotR* 1.12.198 when he saw the weapon which the Lord of the Nazgûl had used to stab Frodo, he knew - from the fact that the blade disintegrated as he held it up - that it was a Morgul-knife. He also realised that Frodo's blade (from the Barrow-downs and made by the Dúnedain of old) could not have done any damage to the Witch-king because it was still whole and "*... all blades perish that pierce that dreadful King.*"[37] His first reaction was to tell the Hobbits that few now had the skill to deal with wounds made by such evil weapons, but that he would do his best. He then proceeded to sing in a strange tongue over the knife before speaking softly to Frodo, the others being unable to catch the words. Thus he showed that he knew the counter-spell for wounds made by Morgul-knives. Next he put the athelas leaves he had collected into boiling water and bathed Frodo's wound with the liquid, thereby reducing the pain and chill and also calming the others who inhaled the fragrance. Following the wounding of Frodo it was important that he should be kept warm and this incident stands out as being the first occasion when Aragorn actually issued orders, reflecting the urgency of the situation. He "*ordered*" the other Hobbits to lay Frodo near the fire, and then later "*ordered*"[38] Merry and Pippin to heat water in their kettles. Although Frodo's condition improved to some extent following his ministrations, Aragorn realised that ultimately the healing of the wound was beyond his skill. Glorfindel too would admit the same limitation, recognising, as did Aragorn, that Frodo's only hope lay in reaching Rivendell and the care and skills of Elrond as quickly as possible. Nevertheless there is sufficient evidence here to show that Aragorn had special powers when it came to healing. To refer again to the tale of Beren and Lúthien, Hammond and Scull point out that the healing of Frodo on Weathertop was reminiscent of Lúthien healing Beren with a herb and singing/chanting.[39]

Without Aragorn's help and protection, the Hobbits would have had little chance of even surviving the night at Bree, let alone making it to Weathertop and beyond. In the safety of Rivendell, Gandalf and Frodo both recognised that he had saved the day. As Gandalf said to the recuperating Frodo, "*For the moment we have been saved from disaster, by Aragorn*". Frodo agreed: "*it was Strider that saved us.*"[40]

---

36. Op. cit. [2], *LotR* 1.11, p. 187.
37. Op. cit., *LotR* 1.12, p. 198.
38. Op. cit., *LotR* 1.12, p. 197.
39. Op. cit. [3], Hammond and Scull, pp. 182-3, In reference to: C. Tolkien (ed.), *The Silmarillion*, London, HarperCollins Publishers, 1999, first published in Great Britain by George Allen & Unwin 1977, Chapter 19, p. 209. And C. Tolkien (ed.), *The History of Middle-earth*, vol. III, *The Lays of Beleriand*, London HarperColllins Publishers, 2002, first published in Great Britain by George Allen & Unwin (Publishers) Ltd. 1985, lines 3118-3128 in "The Lay of Leithian", p. 266.
40. Op. cit. [2], *LotR* 2.1, p. 220.

In Rivendell

Aragorn and the Hobbits arrived in Rivendell on October 20th. The Council of Elrond took place five days later, when Frodo had recovered sufficiently to participate. The Council and its aftermath are described in *LotR* 2.2 and 2.3.

Aragorn's situation at the Council was reminiscent of that in the Prancing Pony: namely, he sat alone in the corner wearing his shabby travelling clothes, doubted, insulted or unappreciated by people who should have been honouring him. In the case of the Prancing Pony, "people" means Barliman Butterbur, the Bree-folk in general and the Hobbits; in the case of the Council it means Boromir. In both situations Aragorn had to provide proof of who he was by means of the broken sword of Elendil, and in both situations someone vouched for him by confirming his identity - namely Gandalf in his letter in the Prancing Pony, and Elrond verbally at the Council. As a result the significant doubters were won over, though reluctantly in the case of Sam and Boromir. At the Council, as in Bree, Aragorn displayed a variety of reactions and emotions:

- The dramatic casting of the broken sword on to the table.
- His smile of appreciation for Bilbo for his support in the face of Boromir's obvious doubt.
- His reply to Boromir, initially conciliatory, admitting that his doubt was understandable, running himself down.
- His increasing bitterness as he explained the reasons for his haggard and shabby appearance (as opposed to the rich clothes worn by Boromir), giving the lie to Boromir's apparent insinuation that only Gondor was doing anything worthwhile to protect the West from Sauron.
- Later his almost casual reply to a further insult from Boromir about his [Aragorn's] suitability to wield the sword of Elendil.

It is notable that during his account to Boromir of the Northern Dúnedain's activities, Aragorn gave an impassioned speech about the scornful nicknames they had to endure, and about "... *one fat man who lives within a day's march of foes that would freeze his heart, or lay his little town in ruin, if he were not guarded ceaselessly.*"[41] He was obviously still harbouring anger and resentment at Barliman Butterbur's unhelpful stance when he was trying to gain the trust of the Hobbits. He explained that in contrast with Gondor's very visible opposition to Sauron, he and his Rangers operated in secret enduring insults and misunderstanding as they struggled to keep the Shire-folk and Breelanders ignorant of the horrors which existed outside their borders: "*If simple folk are free from care and fear, simple they will be, and we must be secret to keep them so.*"[42] Paul Kocher remarks that the wisdom of such a policy could be debated and it does seem reasonable to suggest that these "*simple folk*" should perhaps have been made aware of the dangers surrounding them.[43] However it could equally well be argued that by keeping them ignorant the Rangers were actually preserving their sanity as well as their physical safety, particularly now the Nazgûl had entered the equation. I have already described the terror these could instil in even the bravest of people, including the Rangers who were not ordinary Men but had extra powers of endurance and strength, both mental and physical. Also two further incidents (in *LotR* 5.10.884,886), namely Gandalf's concern for the sanity of the troops if they were to enter the Morgul Vale and the unmanning of the young soldiers on the march to the Morannon, serve to illustrate the real risk of permanent mental damage through exposure to Sauron's creatures.

At the Council, as well as his interaction with Boromir, Aragorn was involved in the discussion about the capture of Gollum. When Gandalf drew the Council's attention to the deadly perils his friend must have endured, alone, during his search for the creature, Aragorn brushed his remarks aside as irrelevant. However a few minutes later when Legolas reported that Gollum had since escaped, he lashed out angrily against the failure of Thranduil's folk to guard their captive more securely, no doubt infuriated that after all the effort he had made and the danger he had endured in his sixteen-year search, Gollum had escaped little more than a year

---

41. Op. cit. [2], *LotR* 2.2, p. 248.
42. Op. cit., *LotR* 2.2, p. 248.
43. P. Kocher, *Master of Middle-earth: The Achievement of J. R. R. Tolkien*, London, Pimlico, 2002, first published in Great Britain by Thames & Hudson 1973, Chapter 6, p. 134.

after his capture.

Aragorn's behaviour at the Council, as in the inn at Bree, showed initial calmness and a tendency to disparage himself by agreeing that his appearance was not such as to inspire confidence, but then gave way to outbursts of bitterness and resentment. It is not difficult to imagine that these feelings, bottled-up over the years, were now being given full rein, exacerbated by the stresses and strains of the recent journey to Rivendell with the Hobbits.

*

Before proceeding to events following the departure of the Fellowship from Rivendell, I wish to digress in order to discuss a comment made by Anne Petty. She says that often during a hero's quest, *"he is threatened by very subtle traps in addition to the blatant physical obstacles set in his path, **one of the most familiar motifs being the woman as temptress.**"*[44] [My emphasis]. She then goes on to accuse Aragorn of delaying the departure of the Fellowship from Rivendell for two months because of his enjoyment of being in Arwen's company. To quote her: *"The days 'slipped away'* [Tolkien's words] *as happiness and contentment settled on each member of the Company, in particular Aragorn, whose lack of motivation to muster the Fellowship may be accounted for in the presence of Arwen Evenstar."*[45] This would have been wishful thinking on the part of Aragorn who no doubt, after all he had been through, would have wanted nothing more than to rest in Elrond's house for two months (as the Hobbits did) in the company of the woman he loved. However a careful examination of *LotR* 2.1.219-2.3.282 reveals the following timetable for him:

Oct 20: Arrived in Rivendell.

Oct 21-23: Three days for recuperation, and no doubt facing discussion and questioning with Elrond and Gandalf, plus brief reunion with Arwen one assumes.

Oct 24: Frodo recovered. A feast was held, at which Arwen was present but not Aragorn because Elladan and Elrohir had returned unexpectedly out of the Wild and he felt it was important to hear their news. Brief relaxation after the feast in the company of Bilbo, and then later with Arwen (with Elrond also present!).

Oct 25: Council of Elrond, which Aragorn attended in his travelling clothes, so he could set off immediately afterwards with Elladan and Elrohir to join Elrond's scouts in scouring the land for signs of the Nazgûl. Gandalf and Bilbo told Frodo that he would have a long stay in Rivendell because the lands would be scoured for leagues around with scouts from as far as Mirkwood probably being involved. No start could be made until the scouts came back.

Sometime in December when the Hobbits had been in Rivendell nearly 2 months: The scouts started returning.

Dec 18: We know Aragorn was back in Rivendell on this date as he was present for the selection of the Fellowship members. Elrond said they must leave in seven days.

Dec 18-24: Getting sword reforged and finalising route, etc. with Gandalf (and, with hindsight, presumably arguing about whether to go via Moria or the pass of Caradhras, and whether to take a pony or not). Frodo was content to let them do most of the hard work so he could spend more time with Bilbo.

Dec 25: Fellowship left Rivendell.

The words of Tolkien which Anne Petty quotes, namely that the days '*slipped away*' in Rivendell, refer only to the Hobbits (and possibly to Boromir, Legolas and Gimli) and not to Aragorn at all.

It is clear from this timetable that Aragorn was sacrificing his own interests and desires for duty and the sake of others, and would have had very little time to spend with Arwen. The Fellowship did not even exist until a week before departure, so he could hardly have been delaying its departure even if he **had** been in Rivendell. Moreover the members were selected by Elrond, with input from Gandalf. There is a suggestion in the text that Aragorn might also have some say, but no actual indication of this. Elrond also set the departure date which was dependent on the reports of the returning scouts (who included Aragorn himself) regarding the Nazgûl. It is clear too that - with hindsight - he was also waiting for Elladan and Elrohir to report on their

---

44. A. Petty, *One Ring To Bind Them All: Tolkien's Mythology*, Tuscaloosa & London, The University of Alabama Press, 2002, first published 1979, Chapter 4, p. 59.
45. Op. cit., Chapter 4, p. 59.

journey to Lothlórien. An additional consideration is that Aragorn, along with Boromir, was only a member of the Fellowship because **their** journey (namely the one to Minas Tirith) would initially follow the same route as the journey to Mordor. It would not actually have been Aragorn's job to decide when the Fellowship should leave even if he **had** been in Rivendell for the whole two months.

Rivendell to Moria

The Fellowship of the Ring left Rivendell on December 25th 3018. This section covers the journey south, the attempt on the pass of Caradhras, and the events in Moria which culminated in the loss of Gandalf and the escape of the rest of the Company into the Dimrill Dale on January 15th 3019. The relevant chapters are *LotR* 2.3-2.5.

Although Aragorn was a member of the Fellowship his purpose, as just stated, was not to accompany Frodo all the way to Mordor, but to go to Minas Tirith with Boromir where he would use the newly-reforged sword to help in Gondor's war against Sauron. This journey would follow the same route as Frodo's for several hundred miles. We are told that he sat *"with his head bowed to his knees"*[46] before embarking on what would be the last stage of his epic struggle. This posture - silent, with face hidden - perhaps indicated more eloquently than words the depth of feeling within him.

Even though Gandalf was the official leader of the Company, Aragorn was the one actually guiding them during the first part of the journey, due to his considerable familiarity with the lands they were traversing which he knew even in the dark. This familiarity included an awareness of the animal and bird-life and mountain climate, in addition to realisation that there were hostile creatures around which were independent of Sauron. He led his companions for seventeen days, during which time they travelled down the west side of the Misty Mountains and attempted to cross the pass of Caradhras. Aragorn seemed to have more say than Gandalf at this stage. For example when he alone felt that there was something sinister about the silence and lack of birds in Eregion (Hollin), Gandalf immediately deferred to him, telling the others, *"If you bring a Ranger with you, it is well to pay attention to him, especially if the Ranger is Aragorn."*[47] Later, after the flocks of crows had flown over, Aragorn was the one giving the orders, forbidding the lighting of any more fires. It was only when the decision was made to enter Moria that Gandalf began to lead the way, with Aragorn taking over from Legolas as rearguard.

Aragorn's behaviour between the departure from Rivendell and the loss of Gandalf on the Bridge of Khazad-dûm showed protectiveness, endurance and raw courage, as illustrated by the following examples:
- Joining Sam on his watch due to his concern about the crows flying over.
- Joining Boromir in making a path through the snow drifts on Caradhras and then carrying the Hobbits to safety.
- Going without sleep so he and Gandalf could consider the next part of the journey after the pass crossing failed.
- Doing his part in the battles with the wolves, and with the Orcs in Moria.
- Reassuring the others when they were afraid that Gandalf had lost the way in Moria, by telling them that the Wizard was *"surer of finding the way home in a blind night than the cats of Queen Berúthiel"*[48], thus, as on Weathertop, using a tale to help in calming fears. [Berúthiel, the Queen of Tarannon Falastur the twelfth King of Gondor, had ten cats which she used as spies, being able to read their memories - see *UT* 4.2.519-20 Note 7.]
- Keeping quiet about his awareness of Gollum trailing them so as not to worry the others.
- His refusal (along with Boromir) to leave Gandalf on the Bridge of Khazad-dûm, until it was clear that there was nothing more they could do.
- His subsequent assumption of the leadership to get his companions to safety.

---

46. Op. cit. [2], *LotR* 2.3, p. 280.
47. Op. cit., *LotR* 2.3, p. 284.
48. Op. cit., *LotR* 2.4, p. 311.

As well as the fears and hardships shared by all of them, for Aragorn there was the additional issue of which route the Fellowship were to use to cross the Misty Mountains. It is clear from the conversations between him and Gandalf in the latter part of *LotR* 2.3.286-8 and the beginning of 2.4 .295-7,302 that the two of them had had heated discussions on the subject, going back to the days in Rivendell when they were preparing for the journey. However it was not until the Company, minus Gandalf, had escaped from Moria that the full significance of their differences of opinion became apparent as Aragorn cried, "*Farewell, Gandalf! Did I not say to you: 'if you pass the doors of Moria, beware?' Alas that I spoke true!*"[49]. It was not just that Aragorn didn't like the idea of going through Moria due to some unspecified evil experience in the past. His reluctance was due to a conviction that something bad would happen to Gandalf if he entered Moria. It was this which made him insist that they try the pass of Caradhras first - an insistence which led to considerable feelings of guilt on his part when the attempt almost proved disastrous. When it became clear that they had no other choice but to go through Moria he agreed to go with Gandalf, saying, "*You followed my lead almost to disaster in the snow, and have said no word of blame. I will follow your lead now - if this last warning does not move you. It is not of the Ring, nor of us others I am thinking now, but of you, Gandalf. And I say to you: if you pass the doors of Moria, beware!*"[50]. Gandalf, on the other hand, made it clear that he had expected to be forced to use the Moria route all along, and declared to Frodo that he would not have brought a pony with them if he had had his way, knowing that it would not be able to enter the mountain.

Aragorn's premonition had clearly been bothering him prior to the Fellowship's departure from Rivendell, and during the journey through Moria it would have preyed on his mind. At the point when Gandalf was uncertain which to choose out of three possible paths, Aragorn reassured the others that the Wizard would get them out of Moria "*... at whatever cost to himself*"[51]. This example of his foresight was entirely in keeping with what we know of him, his family and the Dúnedain in general. His mother and grandmother had been particularly gifted in this respect and Aragorn had clearly inherited their gift. He must have realised too that in the event of anything happening to Gandalf, the leadership would fall to him - again. This must have been an extremely daunting prospect in the light of his experiences on the journey to Rivendell and the knowledge that the danger would only increase as they got nearer to Mordor. His frame of mind would not have been eased by his residual guilt about the near-disaster on Caradhras, or by his growing awareness that Gollum was following them (shared by Frodo but not disclosed by either of them until the journey down the river in *LotR* 2.9.384). Small wonder that he was "*grim and silent*"[52] as he strode along in the dark at the rear of the Company anticipating some unknown and terrifying calamity.

At the moment when the Bridge of Khazad-dûm cracked and Gandalf fell into the abyss, Aragorn took on the leadership, telling the others to follow him. As they approached the East gates of the mines, his furious slaying of the Orc captain standing in his path was enough to make the remaining Orcs flee in terror, thus enabling the Company to escape and get far enough away to be able to stop and give way to their grief in relative safety. His worst fears had been realised. Not only was he facing the shock and grief of losing, in a particularly horrifying manner, the person who had been his mentor and close friend for sixty-two years, but he was once again thrust into the leadership, in an even worse situation than on the journey from Bree to Rivendell.

Moria to Lothlórien

Gandalf's fall was on January 15th 3019. After taking on the leadership Aragorn led the Fellowship to Lothlórien (as Gandalf himself had planned to do) arriving at its borders later the same day then reaching the residence of Galadriel and Celeborn at Caras Galadhon on 17th. They stayed there until February 16th. The relevant chapters are *LotR* 2.6-2.8.

From now on Aragorn entered a downward spiral of self-doubt and crippling indecision which was to culminate in him breaking down following the death of Boromir and the sundering of the Fellowship, and

---
49. Op. cit. [2], *LotR* 2.6, p. 333.
50. Op. cit., *LotR* 2.4, p. 297.
51. Op. cit., *LotR* 2.4, p. 311.
52. Op. cit., *LotR* 2.4, p. 310.

would plague him to a greater or lesser degree until his reunion with Gandalf in Fangorn on March 1st. There were many reasons for his frame of mind, namely:

- The loss of Gandalf.
- The strain of having to control his own grief for the sake of the others.
- The stress of having to take on the leadership in these circumstances. This was immediately apparent when in the urgency of their escape from Moria he failed to notice that Frodo and Sam were lagging far behind and had even forgotten that they had been hurt in the battle with the Orcs. It seems a pretty serious lapse given that Frodo's injury had initially appeared to be fatal, and it is clear from the remorse Aragorn expressed that he himself regarded it as such. An element of shock at the manner of Gandalf's loss must also be taken into account here.
- His feeling that things were hopeless without Gandalf, as evidenced by his despairing cry: *"What hope have we without you?"*[53] and his attempts to spur the others on by talk of revenge.
- Ignorance of what Gandalf had planned (if anything) for the next stages of the journey.
- Uncertainty regarding his own role/route now that Gandalf was gone. Perhaps the first indication of this conflict appeared soon after entering Lothlórien as he relived his betrothal to Arwen on Cerin Amroth telling Frodo, *"here my heart dwells ever, unless there be a light beyond the dark roads that we still must tread, you and I."*[54]. Were these *"dark roads"* a premonition of the Paths of the Dead, or was he already thinking that he might have to change his plans and go to Mordor with Frodo, instead of to Minas Tirith with Boromir as originally planned? As stated in *LotR* 2.8.368 he had regarded Faramir's dream verse to be a summons to use his newly-reforged sword against Sauron's armies: *"But in Moria the burden of Gandalf had been laid on him* [again]*; and he knew that he could not now forsake the Ring..."*[55].
- Boromir's attitude to Lothlórien and Galadriel, and to Frodo. On arrival at the borders of Lothlórien Boromir's aversion to the place first manifested itself, and it was clear from Aragorn's words to him (*"... only evil need fear it* [Lothlórien]*, or those who bring some evil with them"*)[56] that he must have been growing uneasy about Boromir's own state of mind. In addition Boromir began to harass Frodo by questioning him about Galadriel's searching of his mind, and when he openly expressed his mistrust of her, Aragorn was driven to rebuke him again, stressing that a person would only find evil in her or in Lothlórien if he brought it there himself.
- Last but not least the combination of grief, fear and sheer exhaustion which led to him saying, *"... tonight I shall sleep without fear for the first time since I left Rivendell. And may I sleep deep, and forget for a while my grief! I am weary in body and in heart."*[57].

In spite of his inner turmoil Aragorn showed many signs of the wise, knowledgeable and caring leader he was, deeply committed to protecting Frodo and the rest of his companions. Once he had been alerted to Frodo's and Sam's plight he administered first aid to them in his usual gentle and competent manner, with all the Company benefiting from inhaling the steaming athelas-water. As he removed Frodo's jacket and tunic to tend his bruises, the mithril shirt was exposed to view causing him to call the others in wonder and amusement reciting the words, *"Here's a pretty hobbit-skin to wrap an elven-princeling in!"*[58]. His laughter and amazement, shared with his companions, would have been one of those light moments which help to keep one going during times of danger and bereavement. He was also enormously relieved that Frodo had protection against injury: *"My heart is glad to know that you have such a coat."*[59] [One weight off his mind.] Aragorn's remarks about the coat also showed his knowledge of its history, as *The Hobbit* Chapter 13 describes the Dwarf-made garment

---

53. Op. cit. [2], *LotR* 2.6, p. 333.
54. Op. cit., *LotR* 2.6, p. 352.
55. Op. cit., *LotR* 2.8, pp. 368-9.
56. Op. cit., *LotR* 2.6, p. 338.
57. Op. cit., *LotR* 2.7, p. 358.
58. Op. cit., *LotR* 2.6, p. 336.
59. Op. cit., *LotR* 2.6, p. 336.

as "*wrought for some young elf-prince*".[60]

When the Fellowship met Haldir, it turned out that the Elf was aware of the fact that Aragorn was known and respected in Lothlórien. This eased the acceptance of Gimli into the forest with Aragorn and Legolas (as another Wood-elf) being trusted to answer for the Dwarf. Later Aragorn resolved the potentially explosive incident when Haldir insisted on blindfolding Gimli, with fairness, firmness and common-sense. He empathised with Gimli's indignation, gently insisted that if he was to lead the Company then they must do as he said, then declared that they should all be blindfolded so that the Dwarf would not feel singled-out.

It was during the last night in Lothlórien, at a meeting with Celeborn and Galadriel (*LotR* 2.8.367) that Aragorn's indecisiveness started to become obvious as he admitted to Celeborn that the Company had not yet (a month later) decided its course. When Boromir stated a preference for journeying via Minas Tirith but then added a pointed "*But I am not the leader of the Company*" Aragorn looked "*doubtful and troubled*"[61]. When Celeborn then decided to give them boats, Aragorn's almost pathetic gratitude was mainly because travelling by river enabled him to delay the day when he would be actually forced to decide the route: east bank or west bank. Later, as the Company discussed the subject among themselves, he was "*still divided in his mind*"[62]. He became so wrapped up in his own thoughts that he was even oblivious to Boromir's muttered implication that it would be folly to destroy the Ring.

This picture of hesitancy and self-doubt was relieved briefly by the glimpse of Aragorn as the future king when Galadriel presented him with the silver eagle-shaped brooch with the green Elessar set in it. As she did so she called him by his royal name Elessar/Elfstone for the first time, thus restating the prophecy of Olórin/Gandalf as I described in Chapter 1.2.

*

I finish this section on Lothlórien with a second digression to examine a passage by Anne Petty. Earlier in this chapter I refuted her argument that Aragorn delayed the Fellowship's departure from Rivendell because of his enjoyment of Arwen's company. She also states, "*This delay is paralleled in Lórien, when Aragorn tarries in the land of Arwen's birth .... his delay is lengthy.*"[63] This too can be refuted. At the first meeting of the Fellowship with Galadriel and Celeborn (*LotR* 2.7.355,357), Celeborn immediately recognised the ordeal they had all gone through and decided that they should have refuge until they were "*healed and refreshed*". He was the one who initiated the "delay" in Lothlórien, with the words, "*Now you shall rest, and we will not speak of your further road for a while.*" In addition, disturbed by Aragorn's appearance, he specifically told him to "*... lay aside your burden for a while!*" In the event it was Galadriel who decided on the departure date - after she had permitted Frodo and Sam to look in her mirror and after she herself had made her choice between taking possession of the One Ring or diminishing and going into the West: "*In the morning you must depart, for now we have chosen, and the tides of fate are flowing.*"[64] Anne Petty's accusation seems to hinge solely on the very brief incident of Aragorn's flashback to his betrothal and his description of Cerin Amroth as "*the heart of Elvendom on earth.*"[65] Does there have to be any reason for the month's sojourn in Lothlórien **other** than the need to recover from a severely stressful and dangerous journey, the loss of a much-loved mentor and friend in a particularly horrible fashion, the need to recoup his strength for the undoubted traumas which lay ahead and his inability to decide which course he and the Fellowship should now take?! Incidentally it seems to me unlikely that Arwen was born in Lothlórien: Elrond founded Rivendell in the middle of the Second Age and married Celebrían in TA 109 after which she presumably went to live in Rivendell with him. Elladan and Elrohir were born in TA 130 and Arwen in TA 241 (App B.1083,1085).

---

60. J.R.R. Tolkien, *The Hobbit*, 3rd edition, London, Allen & Unwin, 1966, 1975 printing, p. 252.
61. Op. cit. [2], *LotR* 2.8, p. 367.
62. Op. cit., *LotR* 2.8, p. 368.
63. Op. cit. [44], Petty, Chapter 4, p. 59.
64. Op. cit. [2], *LotR* 2.7, p. 366.
65. Op. cit., *LotR* 2.6, p. 352.

Lothlórien to Parth Galen

After leaving Lothlórien on February 16th Aragorn led the Company by boat down the Anduin to Parth Galen above the Falls of Rauros arriving there on February 25th. The following day Boromir tried to take the Ring from Frodo and the Fellowship became scattered with Boromir subsequently being killed by Orcs. These events are described in *LotR* 2.9-2.10 and 3.1.

Aragorn's worries and indecision continued to plague him during the journey down the Anduin:
- Although the Company spent many hours each day travelling, he let them drift with the stream, supposedly to preserve their strength, but probably also subconsciously postponing decision-day as long as possible.
- His frame of mind was clear from his comment, *"Time flows on to a spring of little hope."*[66].
- His unease led him to lie awake watching the birds circling overhead when he should have been sleeping.
- He misjudged the distance to the rapids at Sarn Gebir - thus leading the Company into a dangerous situation. He admitted that he was out of his reckoning, though to be fair he had said earlier that he had not actually journeyed by boat on that section of the river before. It is worth pointing out that during the Orc attack immediately after the incident with the rapids an arrow passed through Aragorn's hood. Thus he only narrowly escaped death or serious injury.
- Boromir began to hassle Frodo again, and then renewed the argument with Aragorn about the route to be taken, wanting to abandon the boats at Sarn Gebir and head to Minas Tirith, while Aragorn wished to find an old portage-way he knew of so that they could carry the boats past the rapids and then take to the river again. He wanted to continue to Parth Galen before leaving the boats, partly to postpone the decision and partly because he wanted to visit Amon Hen (the Hill of Sight) in the hope that he might see something to help him decide what to do. This hill and its companion, Amon Lhaw (the Hill of Hearing) on the opposite bank of the river, had high seats and lookout-points on the top. The discussion became heated and was only resolved when Frodo made it clear that he would follow Aragorn whatever he decided. At this point Gimli too became drawn into the argument, resentful at Boromir's implied underestimation of his ability to cope with the portage-way route.
- When the boats passed the Argonath, Aragorn appeared briefly transformed into a king returning from exile, but then *"... the light of his eyes faded, and he spoke to himself: 'Would that Gandalf were here! How my heart yearns for Minas Anor and the walls of my own city! But whither now shall I go?'"*[67]. This speech leaves no doubt that he was being torn in two between his desire to go to Minas Tirith and do his part in the war against Sauron, and what he saw as his duty to help and protect Frodo.

However, as always, the journey was greatly assisted by Aragorn's knowledge of the lands they travelled through, his protectiveness and his awareness of danger:
- He had been to Lothlórien before and understood how time seemed to pass at a different rate within its borders.
- He knew the geography of Rohan, including the dangers of trying to cross the fens around the Entwash at Rohan's northern border.
- He knew what sort of climate to expect in the different latitudes.
- When the boats reached Sarn Gebir, he remembered the old portage-way from previous journeys thus enabling the boats to be carried past the rapids.
- His constant alertness meant that he was well aware of Gollum following the Company down the river, and when Frodo drew his sword, having also spotted Gollum during his turn at night watch, Aragorn was instantly awake and insisted on taking over the watch for the rest of the night while Frodo went to sleep again.
- A similar example of his awareness occurred at Parth Galen when he sensed the proximity of Orcs even

---

66. Op. cit. [2], *LotR* 2.9, p. 389.
67. Op. cit., *LotR* 2.9, p. 393.

in his sleep.

With the arrival of the Company at Parth Galen the point was reached when a decision had to be made. It was clear that the "east bank" versus "west bank" choice was a "no-win" situation if the emphasis was on the Fellowship staying together: the former was useless for Boromir going to Minas Tirith and the latter inappropriate for the journey to Mordor. Aragorn continued to display a marked lack of faith in himself, bewailing the absence of Gandalf and clearly feeling ill-equipped to offer advice to Frodo. Thus the burden of deciding the route was placed on Frodo himself, though as Aragorn said, this may have been the case even if Gandalf had been with them, an opinion borne out by his remark that, "*I do not think that it is our part to drive him* [Frodo] *one way or the other ... There are other powers at work far stronger.*"[68]. In spite of his hesitancy, he made it clear that he would be willing to go to Mordor with Frodo.

With Boromir's attempt to take the Ring by force and Frodo's subsequent disappearance, Aragorn's problems came to a head as the Company was seized by "*... A sudden panic or madness...*"[69], ignoring his instructions and attempts to restore order. Having tracked Frodo up Amon Hen, he took the opportunity to sit in the Seat of Seeing as he had planned. However, far from seeing something which would help his indecision, he was faced with a darkened sun and a world which looked "*dim and remote*"[70], the only things he could make out being distant hills and a descending eagle far away. This was in sharp contrast to Frodo's experience shortly earlier (*LotR* 2.10.400-401). Even though Frodo had had the Ring on and thus at first saw only mist and shadow - as would be expected - these cleared as he remained in the Seat and he was then able to see all around for miles - the Misty Mountains, Mirkwood Forest, Rohan, Orthanc, the Anduin Delta and Mordor itself - along with the ongoing preparations for war in all these areas. Was Aragorn's experience perhaps a reflection of his own dark depression and despair at losing Gandalf? To make matters worse his fruitless detour to this lookout point meant that he was too far away to respond in time to Boromir's horn-call. His panic was already starting to overwhelm him ("*Alas!* **An ill fate is on me this day**, *and* **all that I do goes amiss**"[71] [My emphasis - see later]), but he mastered it sufficiently to comfort, forgive and reassure the dying Boromir, taking it on himself to go and save Minas Tirith. Legolas and Gimli found him kneeling by Boromir's body, holding his hand and weeping, overcome with grief, despair, guilt and indecision, convinced that he, rather than Boromir, was the one who had failed, and blaming himself for the disastrous turn of events. His words left no doubt as to the turmoil in his heart: "*This is a bitter end. Now the Company is all in ruin. It is I that have failed. Vain was Gandalf's trust in me. What shall I do now? Boromir has laid it on me to go to Minas Tirith, and my heart desires it; but where are the Ring and the Bearer? How shall I find them and save the Quest from disaster?*"[72]. Such was his condition that Legolas initially thought that he was fatally wounded too. The enquiries of his companions prompted another string of laments, for example, "*Boromir is dead. I am unscathed, for I was not here with him ...*" and "*I did not ask him* [Boromir] *if Frodo or Sam were with him: not until it was too late.* **All that I have done today has gone amiss.** *What is to be done now?*"[73] [My emphasis]. He blamed himself for not being there when Boromir blew the horn, rather than Boromir for trying to take the Ring from Frodo. Also there is no indication that he actually killed any of the Orcs who attacked the Company - which would only have added to his guilt. In addition there was also a sense of bitterness and fatalism in some of his words, a belief that everything had gone wrong for him that day. This is illustrated by the passages I have emphasised above, in particular "*an ill fate is on me*". Did he believe at that point that he wasn't fated to succeed? If so what power did he think had caused things to have "*gone amiss*"? Did the words of Elrond, on learning of his feelings for Arwen, come back to haunt him at that point: "*A great doom awaits you, either to rise above the height of all your fathers since the days of Elendil,* **or to fall into darkness with all that is left of your kin**"[74]? [My emphasis]. The latter outcome must have seemed a distinct possibility at that point.

---

68. Op. cit. [2], *LotR* 2.10, p. 404.
69. Op. cit., *LotR* 2.10, p. 404.
70. Op. cit., *LotR* 3.1, p. 413.
71. Op. cit., *LotR* 3.1, p. 413.
72. Op. cit., *LotR* 3.1, p. 414.
73. Op. cit., *LotR* 3.1, p. 414.
74. Op. cit., App A.I.v., p. 1059.

This collapse was undoubtedly due to a build-up of fear and stress dating back to the late summer of 3018 when he returned from his unknown journey to reports of Gandalf's disappearance and the Nazgûl sightings. He had realised then that he himself would have to be responsible for getting the Ring safely to Rivendell, knowing that if he failed, the Ring would go back to Sauron and his long struggle would have been in vain. This fear of failure was clearly with him at Parth Galen as well, along with the strain of much conscience-searching as he tried to make the right decisions. Nevertheless, in spite of his inner turmoil, Aragorn had been very much the leader since the loss of Gandalf, and - as with the journey from Bree to Rivendell - it is difficult to see how his companions would have managed without him.

Following a bit of prompting from Legolas, he recovered sufficiently to organise Boromir's river funeral, and then to do a detailed assessment of the evidence, working out the actions of Frodo and Sam, and guessing Saruman's involvement in events. He also preserved the honour of Boromir by keeping quiet about his attempt to seize the Ring. However the trauma of indecision and guilt was still with him as Legolas and Gimli waited for him to decide whether to follow Frodo and Sam or to try and rescue Merry and Pippin: "*Let me think! And now may I make a right choice, and change the evil fate of this unhappy day!*" Then, more decisively, as he chose to follow the Orcs: "*I would have guided Frodo to Mordor and gone with him to the end; but if I seek him now ... I must abandon the captives to torment and death. My heart speaks clearly at last: the fate of the Bearer is in my hands no longer.*"[75].

Aragorn's selflessness and his devotion to duty were very obvious in the making of this decision. We know that he wanted, more than anything else, to go straight to Minas Tirith as he believed that was the route which gave him the best chance of defeating Sauron, regaining his kingships and marrying Arwen. However he only considered two options - Frodo and Sam, or Merry and Pippin - and chose the one he believed to be right. Although this decision seemed to be driven primarily by his horror at the thought of Merry and Pippin being tortured, looked at more cold-bloodedly the torture of his friends would have resulted in Saruman finding out about Frodo and the Ring. Thus Aragorn's decision was a good one from the common-sense and political angles as well as the humanitarian. [With hindsight, any information gleaned by Saruman would soon have been picked up by Sauron during their Palantír "conversations" - though such a possibility would not of course have been known to Aragorn at the time.]

Parth Galen to Fangorn

Aragorn's pursuit of the Orcs with Legolas and Gimli began on the evening of February 26th, the same date the Fellowship was scattered. On February 30th the meeting with Éomer took place, followed by the reunion with Gandalf in Fangorn Forest on March 1st. These events are described in *LotR* 3.2 and 3.5.

Once Aragorn had made the decision to follow the Orcs and try to rescue Merry and Pippin his demeanour appeared to change completely. Accepting that he would now have to postpone any journey to Gondor and the fulfilment of his promise to Boromir to save Minas Tirith, he unflaggingly led his two companions on a four-day chase across Rohan, determined to carry on, with or without hope, even to the extent of being prepared to sit down and starve with Merry and Pippin if that turned out to be all that he could do for them. He was indisputably the leader, with Legolas and Gimli turning naturally to him for all decisions, which they accepted even if they didn't agree with them. They also depended on him for most of the tracking, in which, as before, he excelled, spotting Pippin's footprints leading to the dropped brooch, detecting the horses of the Rohirrim by listening to the ground, and working out the Hobbits' movements in Fangorn. His knowledge of the lands and peoples was also to the fore again, as he identified the different races of Orc among the bodies, and told his companions about the land and people of Rohan. He realised that the lack of any signs of life in this east part of Rohan was suspicious and probably due to Saruman: "*... silence that did not seem to be the quiet of peace.*"[76]. In spite of the fact that Legolas had been living for thousands of years he still respected Aragorn's experience

---

75. Op. cit. [2], *LotR* 3.1, p. 419.
76. Op. cit., *LotR* 3.2, p. 427.

and travels, and Gimli declared that "*A bent blade* [of grass] *is enough for Aragorn to read.*"[77].

Aragorn handled the meeting with Éomer with courage, confidence and diplomacy, as well as displaying an understanding of this new acquaintance through a combination of intuition, personal knowledge of the general nature of the Rohirrim, and his ability to read something of people's minds and characters. With Éomer's spear within a foot of his chest he did not bat an eyelid. He calmed a difficult and dangerous situation when Gimli and Legolas took offence at Éomer's unwitting slur on Galadriel. He took the risk of revealing his true identity to Éomer, reeling off his titles to him and sweeping out Andúril in such a manner that Legolas and Gimli were amazed at the transformation in him. He appealed to Éomer's better judgement, encouraging him to use his initiative and let the three of them go free so that they could continue the search for Merry and Pippin before honouring his promise to go to Rohan and help in the war against Saruman. At the same time he made it clear that they would put up a fight if Éomer insisted on following the law of Rohan to the letter and taking them prisoner.

His courage was no less evident in his dealings with the sinister old men they met in Fangorn, to whom he displayed courtesy and fairness in spite of the potential danger of the situation. On the first occasion he invited the man to come and warm himself at their fire, and then later at the second encounter (before he realised that this old man was Gandalf), he declared that "*We may not shoot an old man so, at unawares and unchallenged, whatever fear or doubt be on us.*"[78]. His protective instincts were as strong as ever, as shown by his advice to Gimli not to cut any living tree in Fangorn in order to feed the fire, his willingness to be woken at need, and his alertness in waking up when danger threatened.

Although we now seem to have a more confident Aragorn, a close inspection of the text shows that, under the surface, he could not so easily shake off his pessimism and lack of faith in himself. As evening approached on the second day of their chase, Legolas and Gimli insisted on him making the decision as to whether they should rest for the night or carry on in the dark. Aragorn's reaction was: "*You give the choice to an ill chooser. Since we passed through the Argonath my choices have gone amiss,*" and he later added that their chase was "*A vain pursuit from its beginning, maybe...*"[79]. He decided to rest for the night, though Legolas had advised differently and in the morning the Elf made it clear that his fears were well-founded as the Orcs were by then far ahead. They had risen while it was still dark because of the urgent need to resume the chase, yet Aragorn lay listening to the ground for so long that Gimli thought he was asleep or unconscious; it was growing light before he got up, looking pale and drawn, and troubled by the sounds of galloping horses. Later his feeling of inadequacy without Gandalf showed itself during the meeting with Éomer as he ran himself down: "*... when the great fall, the less must lead.*"[80].

As the chase continued all three became progressively more dispirited and weary, due to the increasingly hopeless nature of their task, and to the power of Saruman in the lands around them. Aragorn, as a Ranger with a clear trail to follow, did not expect to experience physical weariness, yet he described himself as being "*... weary as I have seldom been before ...*"[81], and when the Rohirrim approached, he decided that he and his companions would sit huddled up in their cloaks on the grass and wait for the Riders to approach rather than go and meet them. His tiredness was due to mental rather than physical factors: despair, the evil power of Saruman, and his own lack of self-worth. During the discussion with Éomer as to whether Merry and Pippin might still be alive, Aragorn explained that no trail had turned aside (apart from when Pippin dropped his brooch) but then followed this up with "*... unless my skill has wholly left me.*"[82]. Maybe in his current frame of mind he felt that this was a possibility. The loss of the horses lent to them by Éomer must have been the last straw.

Perhaps the episode which best illustrates Aragorn's mood during this stage of his journey occurred after the reunion with Gandalf. After listening to Aragorn's account of events at Parth Galen Gandalf said, "*Come Aragorn son of Arathorn! Do not regret your choice in the valley of the Emyn Muil, nor call it a **vain pursuit**.*

---

77. Op. cit. [2], *LotR* 3.5, p. 488.
78. Op. cit., *LotR* 3.5, pp.492-3.
79. Op. cit., *LotR* 3.2, p. 426.
80. Op. cit., *LotR* 3.2, p. 436.
81. Op. cit., *LotR* 3.2, p. 428.
82. Op. cit., *LotR* 3.2, p. 438.

You chose amid doubts the path that seemed right: the choice was just, and it has been rewarded."[83] [My emphasis]. This seems a clear indication that Aragorn was still haunted by the events surrounding the breakup of the Fellowship, and tormented by having made what he perceived to have been the wrong decision. This is demonstrated in particular by the fact that he had obviously repeated the phrase *"vain pursuit"* (used earlier to Legolas and Gimli) while giving his account to Gandalf. As well as the burden of the choice he had made to choose Merry and Pippin over Frodo and Sam, he now had two promises which he had to fulfil: in addition to the one already made to Boromir to save Minas Tirith he had now also promised Éomer that he would go to Rohan to support Théoden in the war against Saruman.

Fangorn to Isengard

After the reunion with Gandalf on March 1st, Aragorn, Legolas and Gimli went with him to Edoras where the wizard healed Théoden, and Aragorn first met Éowyn. The Battle of the Hornburg was fought overnight on March 3rd- 4th and was followed by the journey to Isengard. The reunion with Merry and Pippin and the parley with Saruman took place on March 5th. By the end of that day Aragorn was in possession of the Palantír of Orthanc. These events are described in *LotR* 3.6 - 3.11.

Aragorn's behaviour during these few days was much more self-assured, in spite of the physical weariness from the long ride to Edoras and the battle at Helm's Deep. His key traits of courage, loyalty and local knowledge were apparent, without the underlying current of self-doubt. His old friend and mentor was back and he was going to Edoras to keep his promise to Éomer to aid the Rohirrim. He was on familiar ground having fought for them in his younger days, when Théoden's father was King. On arrival at Edoras he again revealed his knowledge of the history and culture of Rohan, relating the story of Eorl and chanting a poem in the language of the Rohirrim, then translating it into the Common Speech.

An incident worthy of mention took place at the doors of Meduseld, when Háma the Doorward insisted that Gandalf and his companions should leave their weapons outside. Aragorn was very reluctant to leave his sword and questioned whether Théoden's will should prevail over that of the heir of Elendil. This attitude was purely due to the particular sword he was carrying as borne out by his statement that *"... I would do as the master of the house bade me, were this only a woodman's cot, if I bore now any sword but Andúril."*[84]. This renowned sword had been newly reforged specifically for him after being broken for three thousand years, so his reaction was only natural in the circumstances. In this case Gandalf played the role of peacemaker in much the same way as Aragorn had done with the blindfolding of Gimli in Lothlórien and with the altercation between Éomer, Legolas and Gimli regarding Galadriel. [I discuss this incident with the sword in much more detail in my analysis of the relationship between Aragorn and Théoden in Chapter 2.7.]

Once in Meduseld, following the healing of Théoden, Aragorn had his first encounter with Éowyn as she offered him wine to drink Théoden's health. Although initially he returned the smile with which she greeted him, he became troubled after perceiving her attraction to him made clear by her hand trembling against his on the cup. This relationship [also covered in detail in Chapter 2.7] was to be a source of considerable pain and guilt to him in the days to come.

During the journey to Helm's Deep he was eager for the chance to fight the enemy rather than fleeing to the refuge. In the battle itself he went round helping and encouraging wherever it was needed, repeatedly joining Éomer in rallying the men, and rushing to assist him when he was set on by Orcs. At dawn he stood unprotected above the gates raising his hand in token of parley so he could warn of the imminent arrival of Gandalf, Erkenbrand and the Huorns. The Dunlendings became uneasy at his words, sensing the *"power and royalty"*[85] in him. Then when Théoden rode out from the Hornburg against the enemy Aragorn was with him. Typically he paid no heed to his own exhaustion, at one point stumbling on the stairs up to the Hornburg and only escaping with his life due to the quick response of Legolas, and of those who rolled a boulder down on to the attacking Orcs. This appears to have shaken him considerably as specific mention is made of him wiping

---
83. Op. cit. [2], *LotR* 3.5, p. 500.
84. Op. cit., *LotR* 3.6, p. 511.
85. Op. cit., *LotR* 3.7, p. 540.

the sweat from his face after scrambling to safety. After the battle he spent the time allocated to resting (prior to the journey to Isengard) tending Gimli's head wound.

On arrival at Isengard Aragorn, Legolas and Gimli, now reunited with Merry and Pippin, had a chance to relax with the Hobbits over a meal in the ruins of Saruman's guard-house, followed by a smoke outside, while, in the words of Legolas, "*the great ones*" (namely Gandalf and Théoden's company) went to discuss "*high matters*"[86]. This was a strange description, excluding Aragorn as it did, and perhaps showed how easily he gelled with them all. Aragorn had been noticeably silent when they first encountered the Hobbits, as opposed to Legolas and Gimli who had been torn between fury and delight. Now he seemed almost casual ("*Well, well! The hunt is over, and we meet again at last, where none of us ever thought to come*")[87], perhaps guarding against a too-emotional reaction which might have embarrassed both him and the Hobbits.

Later, as they talked, it was clear that he was very aware of the power of Saruman's voice over people's minds - information gleaned perhaps from Gandalf and/or from his time in Rohan in his younger days. He took no obvious part in the parley with Saruman, which chiefly involved Gandalf and Théoden and ended with a Palantír being thrown from the tower of Orthanc by Gríma Wormtongue. In fact Aragorn remained very quiet until the time when Gandalf presented him with the Palantír following Pippin's misguided and nearly disastrous meddling with it.

On receiving the Orthanc-stone he seemed to undergo a mental transformation, becoming self-assured, and unconcerned by Gandalf's warning that it was a dangerous charge. His attitude was due to his conviction that the Stone would not be dangerous for him since it was his by right, and also to his belief that the time was approaching when he would no longer have to keep his identity secret: "*Now my hour draws near. I will take it.*"[88]. Gandalf went on to warn him in no uncertain terms about the perils of premature use of the Stone, talking at length of how he himself had been saved, by Pippin's action, from experimenting with it and thus showing himself to Sauron. Although Aragorn yielded the last word to Gandalf in the argument, he remained firm in his view that the time had in fact come when secrecy should be abandoned. Thus while Gandalf was advising that they should carry on as long as possible with the pretence that Pippin and the Palantír were in Orthanc (as Sauron would have believed), Aragorn was already planning to use the Stone to make himself known to Sauron.

Following the departure of Gandalf and Pippin for Minas Tirith, Aragorn and Merry prepared to ride back to Helm's Deep with Théoden's party. In spite of his apparent confidence, Aragorn's somewhat irritable manner to Merry at this point must have been symptomatic of an underlying uneasiness and apprehension. He rebuked the Hobbit for criticising Pippin's meddling with the Palantír, pointing out that he [Merry] might have fared even worse if he had been the one to handle it, and was clearly put out by Merry's insinuation that travelling with Gandalf had been seen as the preferred option by the Hobbits. Meanwhile, on the ride to Minas Tirith with Pippin, Gandalf was again voicing his concern that Sauron would find out about Aragorn's existence too soon.

Isengard to the Pelennor Fields

In the early hours of March 6th Aragorn used the Palantír of Orthanc to reveal himself to Sauron as Isildur's heir, showing him the reforged sword Andúril and clearly leaving the impression in Sauron's mind that he was in possession of the Ring. Thus Sauron's attention was drawn away from his own land in order to give Frodo a better chance of approaching Mordor undetected. The Palantír also revealed the threat to Gondor from the Corsairs of Umbar whose ships were gathering at Pelargir. Aragorn subsequently journeyed through the Paths of the Dead summoning the ghosts of the Dead Men of Dunharrow to fulfil the oath they had sworn to Isildur but failed to honour. He then rode to Pelargir, seized the ships from the Corsairs (aided by the fear engendered by the Dead) and sailed up the River Anduin on March 15th, arriving at the Battle of the Pelennor Fields just in time to turn defeat into victory. *LotR* 5.2 covers the Palantír episode and part of the journey to Pelargir. Aragorn's arrival at the Pelennor Fields is described at the end of *LotR* 5.6, while further description of the Paths of the Dead and

---

86. Op. cit. [2], *LotR* 3.9, p. 560.
87. Op. cit., *LotR* 3.9, p. 560.
88. Op. cit., *LotR* 3.11, p. 594.

the ride to Pelargir is covered in *LotR* 5.9 in a conversation between Legolas, Gimli, Merry and Pippin in the Houses of Healing.

I regard Aragorn's use of the Palantír to confront Sauron as his most courageous, significant and crucial achievement, and its implications are discussed at length in Chapter 1.6 which is solely devoted to this episode. Thus only the bare details are covered here as I continue to follow the *LotR* narrative from Aragorn's point of view.

As Aragorn rode back to Helm's Deep (from Isengard) with Théoden's company on the evening of March 5th, it was a momentous time for him. He had the Palantír with him which (as evidenced by his earlier conversation with Gandalf) he had clearly already made up his mind to use; but at the same time a dark uncertainty was on him about the route he should take to Minas Tirith, along with a premonition that something significant was about to happen. This conflict was summed up in his words to Legolas and Gimli: "*... it is dark before me ... I do not yet see the road. An hour long prepared approaches.*". Also: "*Many hopes will wither in this bitter spring.*"[89]

The arrival of Halbarad Dúnadan and his company of Rangers, along with Elrond's sons, as if in answer to Aragorn's thoughts and wishes, added to the sense of foreboding. Elrohir's message from his father bidding Aragorn remember the Paths of the Dead and Halbarad's message from Arwen along with the royal battle standard she had made for him only served to increase the tension. The general effect was illustrated by Aragorn looking to the north and then being unwilling (or unable?) to speak for the rest of the journey. When the company reached Helm's Deep in the early hours of March 6th, he went to a high chamber in the Hornburg taking only Halbarad with him, and used the Palantír to show himself to Sauron. The presence of his Dúnadan kinsmen seems to have reinforced his resolve to do the deed.

His non-appearance at the mid-day meal some hours later, was clearly a cause of concern for the whole party, from Merry's anxious enquiry as to his whereabouts, to Legolas's observation that "*He has neither rested nor slept ... some dark doubt or care sits on him*"[90], to Théoden's order for a message to be sent to remind him that it was time to leave. When he finally emerged with Halbarad, accompanied by Éomer, Elladan, Elrohir, Legolas and Gimli (who all appear to have felt worried enough to go and see for themselves what the problem was), his haggard, exhausted appearance left no doubt of the suffering he had endured due to the very real ordeal of the mental struggle to control the Palantír and dominate Sauron. (He would later tell Legolas and Gimli that "*The strength was enough - **barely**.*"[91] [My emphasis].) There was also the problem of his old enemy, indecision: he had not, at that point, finally made up his mind how to get to Minas Tirith, though he must have known deep down that he would have to use the Paths of the Dead. Elrond, in his message via Elrohir, had clearly been hinting that he would have to take that route, and he had already had a similar message from Galadriel - passed on to him by Gandalf at the time of their reunion in Fangorn. Nevertheless he was determined to avoid the Paths of the Dead if at all possible as indicated by his words to Elrohir earlier, "*... great indeed will be my haste ere I take that road.*"[92]. However his use of the Palantír had alerted him to the threat of the Corsairs from Umbar who were preparing to sail up the Anduin to Minas Tirith, and he now knew that speed was of the essence. When he confirmed time-scales with Théoden and Éomer and learnt that it would be four days before the Muster of Rohan would take place at Edoras, he knew that there was no time to go that way and thus finally decided to go through the Paths of the Dead. As a result of this decision "*... his face was less troubled.*"[93] A stressful meal with Legolas and Gimli followed during which he told them what he had done and why, and explained the significance of the prophecies concerning the Paths of the Dead. The result was that his two friends agreed to accompany him, along with the Grey Company (the Dúnedain) and Elrond's sons.

They reached Dunharrow (where the entrance to the Paths of the Dead was situated) on the evening of March 7, where Aragorn had to endure the additional ordeal of Éowyn, unable to hide her feelings, first begging him not to go that way and then, when he insisted, pleading on her knees to be allowed to accompany

---

89. Op. cit. [2], *LotR* 5.2, p. 773.
90. Op. cit., *LotR* 5.2, p. 776.
91. Op. cit., *LotR* 5.2, p. 780.
92. Op. cit., *LotR* 5.2, p. 775.
93. Op. cit., *LotR* 5.2, p. 779.

him. As he refused and rode away without looking back we are told that "... *only those who knew him well and were near to him saw the pain that he bore.*"[94] [I.e. Halbarad, Legolas and Elrond's sons presumably - we find out later that Gimli was only thinking of himself at this point!]

Anne Petty's interpretation of this incident prompted me to introduce a third digression. As I have already discussed, she argues that Aragorn faced a number of temptations to delay his quest because of a woman, and the Aragorn/Éowyn relationship is used as the third example of this. She states: "*But as the urgency of his newly defined hero's path presses upon him, Aragorn rejects his third temptation. The Lady Éowyn of Rohan presents him with reason to stay; unable to mask her love for Aragorn, she implores the hero to remain behind rather than take the shunned path where death waits. But the quest has been delayed too long already; thus the hero must be resolute and immediately embrace the road leading to peril and the unknown.*"[95] I find this puzzling as it is very clear that Aragorn made his decision to go through the Paths of the Dead prior to the encounter with Éowyn at Dunharrow, and had absolutely no intention of changing his mind. Also, given that he had no romantic feelings for Éowyn, why would there have been any "temptation" to stay with her?

As the Company approached the Paths of the Dead early on March 8th, Aragorn's raw courage and will-power asserted themselves. He led his companions through the Haunted Mountain ordering the Dead to follow, then on a gruelling and exhausting ride to the Stone of Erech where he formally summoned the Dead to fight for him and fulfil their oath, and finally across southern Gondor to Pelargir where he captured the Corsairs' fleet on March 13th. In *LotR* 5.2.790 we are told that only Aragorn's will held them to go on and that, among mortal Men, only the Dúnedain of the North could have endured that "*journey of greatest haste and weariness that any among them had known, save he alone...*" Later in *LotR* 5.9.874, Legolas was to tell Merry and Pippin that the Company were also held to their purpose by the love they felt for Aragorn, something which Éowyn had also realised, telling him before they set out, "*They go only because they would not be parted from thee - because they love thee.*"[96] Perhaps this is best illustrated by Halbarad's willingness to enter the Haunted Mountain even though his foresight told him that his death lay beyond it.

The horses too went into the Mountain because of the strength of Aragorn's will and because of their love for their riders. It is significant that Halbarad had brought Aragorn's own horse Roheryn for him to ride, a wise move given the problems Legolas and Gimli had getting their Rohan horse to enter the Mountain. In *UT* 2.1.218-9 we read about how the Númenóreans could summon a favourite horse at need by thought alone if horse and rider loved each other enough. Clearly this trait survived to some extent in the Dúnedain of the Third Age, with the love between Aragorn and Roheryn being enhanced by the fact that the horse had been given to him by Arwen. (See *TSil* Appendix.440, entry "*roch*".)

As well as conquering the fear of his companions on the journey through the Paths of the Dead, Aragorn also had his own fear to deal with which he could not afford to show to the others. As his remark to Elrohir (quoted earlier) showed, he regarded the route through the mountain as very much a last resort, and he told Legolas and Gimli "*... I do not go gladly; only need drives me. Therefore, only of your free will would I have you come, for you will find both toil and great fear, and maybe worse.*"[97]. As the last phrase showed there was also the fear of the unknown. When they reached the door in the mountain we are told that "*... there was not a heart among them that did not quail, unless it were the heart of Legolas...*"[98] Therefore there is no reason to believe that Aragorn was not just as frightened as everyone else. Regarding the free will of those accompanying him, he would have realised that unwilling companions would have been a liability, hence his insistence that anyone who wished to could ride with the Rohirrim instead. This point was emphasised by his statement that he would go through the Paths of the Dead alone if necessary.

During this episode there are several examples of Aragorn's foresightedness. In spite of his feelings about the Paths of the Dead he seemed to believe that he would get through them, saying to (a very disturbed) Éomer, "*... in battle we may yet meet again, though all the hosts of Mordor should stand between.*"[99] Later he

---

94. Op. cit. [2], *LotR* 5.2, p. 785.
95. Op. cit. [44], Petty, Chapter 4, pp. 59-60.
96. Op. cit. [2], *LotR* 5.2, p. 785.
97. Op. cit., *LotR* 5.2, p. 781.
98. Op. cit., *LotR* 5.2, p. 786.
99. Op. cit., *LotR* 5.2, p. 779.

told Éowyn to say to her brother, *"beyond the shadows we may meet again!"*[100] He also told her that she had no errand to the South, and then we learn that he had asked her to make sure that Merry was provided with battle gear (*LotR* 5.3.802). Was his foresight telling him that the two of them had a role in battle? Was he even thinking of the prophecy made by Glorfindel concerning the Lord of the Nazgûl, in TA 1975: *"Far off yet is his doom, and not by the hand of man will he fall."*[101]? He knew Glorfindel well and may have been aware of the prophecy and that the time was drawing near for its fulfilment.

As stated earlier, the journey through the Paths of the Dead was recounted to Merry and Pippin by Legolas and Gimli, and their comments throw further light on the episode. Legolas spoke of how even the Dead were obedient to Aragorn's will, and Gimli recognised that it didn't matter whether the weapons of the Dead still worked, because they didn't need any other weapon than fear: *"Strange and wonderful I thought it that the designs of Mordor should be overthrown by such wraiths of fear and darkness. With its own weapons was it worsted!"*[102]. He also emphasised Aragorn's compassion by noting that he sent the Dúnedain not only to free the slaves on the captured ships, but also to comfort them. Legolas then remarked on the strength of Aragorn's will and how *"great and terrible"* he could have been if he had taken the Ring himself, but then went on to point out that Aragorn was too noble to do such a thing, attributing this characteristic to his Maia/Elf ancestry.[103] [However it must be said that Isildur had shared the same ancestry!] The two of them also emphasised the urgency of the journey and Aragorn's fear that they would be too late as he seemed to realise that Minas Tirith had already been assailed. This raises the question of how he knew that. Was it due to foresight, or had he been using the Palantír again to monitor the situation? Later, at the Last Debate, Aragorn himself would refer to this urgency putting it down to the swiftness of Sauron's response to seeing him in the Palantír: *"... if I had foreseen how swift would be his onset in answer, maybe I should not have dared to show myself. Bare time was given me to come to your aid."*[104].

Aragorn's low point during these events had been between using the Palantír and actually deciding what action to take next. Once he had made up his mind to go through the Paths of the Dead, he displayed his usual tirelessness, courage and endurance which carried him and his companions through the Haunted Mountain, on the desperate five-day ride to Pelargir and the naval battle with the Corsairs, then finally down the river to the Battle of the Pelennor Fields. When the ships arrived at the Harlond, Aragorn was wearing the Star of Elendil on his brow, and the great standard bearing the symbols of Gondor and Elendil was unfurled - the gift from Arwen. Aragorn was reunited with Éomer as he had predicted, and when the battle was over, the two of them, along with Prince Imrahil, were *"... weary beyond joy or sorrow."*[105].

In spite of the fact that he had displayed the banner and tokens of kingship as he came down the river, Aragorn now removed these, and insisted on staying in his tent outside Minas Tirith, not wanting to risk hostility and unrest with his own people by entering the City and making a claim while the war with Sauron was still in the balance.

The Battle of the Pelennor Fields was over, but there was another exhausting ordeal now facing him that same day - albeit of a completely different nature.

The Houses of Healing

Having followed Aragorn's progress through *LotR* thus far it has already become clear that he had healing powers over and above standard first-aid skills. This was first demonstrated on Weathertop after Frodo was stabbed by the Lord of the Nazgûl, and then again after the Company's escape from Moria when he used the dried-up athelas leaves left over from Weathertop to relieve Sam's and Frodo's injuries. Aragorn's work in the Houses of Healing on March 15th (described in *LotR* 5.8) revealed the full extent and significance of his gift of healing and of the green jewel he wore.

---

100. Op. cit. [2], *LotR* 5.2, p. 785.
101. Op. cit., App A.I.iv., p. 1051.
102. Op. cit., *LotR* 5.9, p. 876.
103. Op. cit., *LotR* 5.9, p. 876.
104. Op. cit., *LotR* 5.9, p. 879.
105. Op. cit., *LotR* 5.6, p. 849.

During the Battle of the Pelennor Fields, the Nazgûl had been much in evidence and many people who had fought in the battle or who had been besieged in Minas Tirith were suffering from the effects of the Black Breath. There were three victims whose condition raised particular concern, namely Faramir, Éowyn and Merry. We are told that those affected by the Black Breath *"fell slowly into an ever deeper dream, and then passed to silence and a deadly cold, and so died."*[106] Gandalf and the healers were at a loss as to how to treat this new malady, until Ioreth, an elderly woman who assisted the healers, quoted a piece of old lore stating *"The hands of the king are the hands of a healer."*[107] Thus, she said, the rightful king could be identified. At these words Gandalf realised that only Aragorn had any hope of healing the afflicted, and duly sent for him. Aragorn entered the city incognito hidden in his Elf-cloak due to his unwillingness to enter as king while the war against Sauron was still ongoing.

When he saw Faramir, Éowyn and Merry, he immediately realised that he would require all the healing power and skill he possessed, and then his lack of faith in himself rose its head again with the words *"Would that Elrond were here"*[108]. This reaction was hardly surprising given what he had been through in the last ten days: the Palantír confrontation, the Paths of the Dead, the ride to Pelargir, the naval battle and most recently the Battle of the Pelennor Fields itself which had only just finished at this point. Éomer, in spite of being in the throes of grief and exhaustion himself, was concerned enough at Aragorn's obvious sorrow and weariness to suggest that he rest and eat before attempting any healing, even though one of the patients at death's door was his own sister. Aragorn, realising the urgency, refused.

The healing of Faramir, who was the most seriously ill, was a very draining experience: *"those that watched felt that some great struggle was going on"* while *"Aragorn's face grew grey with weariness"*[109]. It was clear too that Aragorn knew exactly what Faramir had been through and understood his illness more than Gandalf did, even though he had not met him before. He displayed a similar appreciation of Éowyn's sufferings. With all three healings, although it was the athelas which drew the patients back to consciousness, the main healing process was done prior to the use of the herb, by Aragorn's innate power to call the person back from the darkness, enhanced by the healing properties of the Elessar which he wore on his breast.

After an affectionate parting from the newly-healed Merry, Aragorn finally managed to get a meal, but not without a throng of people waiting at the door who *"prayed"* that he would heal their sick relatives and friends. This time, no doubt due to the numbers involved, Aragorn enlisted the help of Elladan and Elrohir for the healing. Meanwhile the word was spreading that the King had returned, and the people *"... named him Elfstone, because of the green stone that he wore..."*[110] thus reconfirming the prophecies (of Olórin and Ivorwen) that his true name would be that of the jewel. It was nearly dawn when sheer exhaustion drove him to his tent to sleep for what remained of the night.

I feel this is the appropriate place for a discussion on various aspects of Aragorn's healing, starting with some observations made on the subject by others:
- Hammond and Scull state that: *"An analysis of this chapter by a Tolkien discussion group comments: 'We felt it significant that Aragorn breathes on the athelas leaves before infusing them. Symbolically he is imparting his life-force, his mana, to the victims of the Black Breath, countering the evil breath with his own.'"*[111]
- They also refer to Katharyn W. Crabbe's suggestion that Faramir, Éowyn and Merry *"wake to impressions of those things that are most important to them."*[112] For Faramir this was a golden age [of Númenor presumably] long past, for Éowyn an image of unbreathed air and high stars representing her desire for purity after feeling that her life and race were being defiled by the behaviour of Gríma, while for Merry it was the orchards, heather, sunshine and bees in the Shire.

---

106. Op. cit. [2], *LotR* 5.8, p. 860.
107. Op. cit., *LotR* 5.8, p. 860.
108. Op. cit., *LotR* 5.8, p. 863.
109. Op. cit., *LotR* 5.8, p. 865.
110. Op. cit., *LotR* 5.8, p. 871.
111. Op. cit. [3], Hammond and Scull, pp. 581-2 quoting Rómenna Meeting Report, 26 October 1986, p.3.
112. Op. cit., pp. 581-2 quoting K.W. Crabbe, *J.R.R. Tolkien*, New York, Continuum, 1988, revised and expanded edition, pp. 95-6.

- Tolkien himself, in Letter 155, (a draft passage which was intended to be part of letter 154 to Naomi Mitchison dated September 25th 1954, but was never included) says: *"Aragorn's 'healing' might be regarded as 'magical', or at least a blend of magic with pharmacy and 'hypnotic' processes."*[113]

My own comments, which follow, reflect the content of the quoted passages along with the descriptions of relevant incidents in *LotR* - including the treatment of Frodo on Weathertop and Frodo and Sam in the Dimrill Dale:
- Regarding the breathing on the athelas leaves, this is only actually mentioned in the case of Faramir's healing, though maybe the same leaves were used also for Éowyn and Merry. There is no reference to breathing on them on Weathertop. In each of the three cases in the Houses of Healing Aragorn had already called the patients back from their death-like state **prior** to infusing the athelas - and in the case of Faramir prior to breathing on it. However the idea of him imparting his life force to his patients does explain the obviously exhausting nature of the healing.
- It has occurred to me that, after recalling Faramir from the shadow and then breathing on and steeping the athelas, Aragorn himself seemed to benefit from the result as much as his patients did. We are told that afterwards he *"... stood up as one refreshed, and his eyes smiled ..."*[114] By breathing in the vapour from the herb was he was in fact re-inhaling his own strength-giving breath with which the leaves had been imbued? [Compare the situation when hyperventilation due to stress, shock or exhaustion is counteracted by breathing into a bag thus taking in previously exhaled air in order to increase the depleted carbon dioxide levels in the body].
- After this apparent self-healing, the subsequent descriptions of him tending Éowyn and Merry make no mention of the grey-faced exhaustion he displayed with Faramir. This would follow from my previous point, though admittedly Aragorn had said that time was running out for Faramir more than for the others, so a harder struggle was to have been expected. To what extent had he himself become enmeshed in the darkness in Faramir's mind?
- Katharyn W. Crabbe's points clearly refer to the effects of the athelas.
- Tolkien's own suggestion of hypnosis is appealing. The Black Breath was a shadow of despair so Aragorn's association with hope, his strong will, the ability of his eyes to hold another's and the green jewel shining on his breast all seem to fit.
- Regarding the tending of Frodo on Weathertop, as I observed earlier Aragorn obviously knew the counter-spells for Morgul-knives. As with the three Houses of Healing cases he called Frodo back before using the athelas: *"... in a soft tone* [he] *spoke words the others could not catch."*[115] The Hobbits found the fragrance of the athelas refreshing and calming and Frodo's pain was reduced by it, as was the sensation of chill caused by the wound.
- In the Dimrill Dale after the escape from Moria the Fellowship found the herb refreshing and strengthening. The liquid from steeping it was used to clean Sam's wound - it was not infected and the cleansing would have prevented infection forming. Frodo's pain from his bruises was reduced and his breathing eased.

In *LotR* 1.12.198 Aragorn told the Hobbits that athelas was brought to Middle-earth by the Númenóreans. *UT* 3.1. states that *"the medicine and other arts of Númenor were potent and not yet forgotten."*[116] This was referring to the time of Isildur's death in TA 2. Clearly much of this knowledge was still remembered in TA 3018. In fact Aragorn's healing gifts can be traced back to Melian from whom *"... there came among both Elves and Men a strain of the Ainur who were with Ilúvatar before Eä."*[117] She was akin to the Vala Yavanna and, prior to taking up residence in Middle-earth, had served the Valier Vana and Estë, the latter being a *"healer of*

---

113. Op. cit. [1], Letter 155, p. 200.
114. Op. cit. [2], *LotR* 5.8, p. 865.
115. Op. cit., *LotR* 1.12, p. 198.
116. Op. cit. [11], *UT* Part 3, Chapter 1, p 358.
117. C. Tolkien (ed.), *The Silmarillion*, London, HarperCollins Publishers, 1999, first published in Great Britain by George Allen & Unwin 1977, *TSil* Chapter 4, p. 55.

hurts and of weariness"[118]. Melian clearly derived the gift of healing from her and this was inherited by Lúthien as shown by her healing of Beren using the leaves of a specific plant (*TSil* 19.209), and so it passed down to her descendants. This, along with the fact that Elrond, Elladan and Elrohir were also healers, shows that Aragorn's powers were part of his inheritance as well as being related to the kingship.

Minas Tirith to the Morannon

On March 16th the Last Debate was held to decide the strategy for the last stage of the War of the Ring. On March 18th the Army of the West left Minas Tirith for the Morannon with the final battle and the destruction of the Ring taking place on March 25th. These events are covered by *LotR* 5.9-5.10 and the beginning of *LotR* 6.4

After his night of healing Aragorn left the City as he had entered it, with his Elf-cloak hiding his identity, so that people wondered if the King's return had just been a dream when they woke the next morning and saw only the banner of Dol Amroth flying from the White Tower. Thus the Last Debate was held in Aragorn's tent. Apart from Aragorn himself, those who took part were Gandalf, Imrahil, Éomer, Elladan and Elrohir, the purpose being to decide the next (and final) step in the war against Sauron.

Some days earlier Gandalf had guessed that Aragorn had used the Palantír of Orthanc, perceiving his motive of drawing Sauron's attention out of Mordor in order to give the Ring-bearer a better chance of going undetected. He had also perceived that the strategy had been successful and that Sauron was now concentrating exclusively on the Captains of the West, convinced that they (or more specifically Aragorn) must have the Ring. He therefore proposed to continue this strategy ("*As Aragorn has begun, so we must go on*")[119] and send a small army to the Morannon to act as bait and draw Sauron out, thus reinforcing his belief in their possession of the Ring. Aragorn was in agreement with this, though he was still reluctant to assert his royal authority, and refused to actually command the others. However this was not a problem, because Imrahil already recognised him as his liege-lord whose wish was as good as a command, Éomer agreed because of friendship and a wish to return the help Aragorn had given him in Rohan, while Elrond's sons were bringing the self-same counsel from their father anyway.

During the discussions, Aragorn made it clear that he had been thinking ahead, as he had already made arrangements for extra forces from the south, both on foot and in boats, and in addition had taken thought for the rebuilding of the City Gate by the Dwarves of the Lonely Mountain.

When the small Army of the West left Minas Tirith on March 18th there was initially some debate as to whether the army should start by destroying Minas Morgul and then assaulting Mordor via the pass above it, but Gandalf refused to consider this due to reports from Faramir that Frodo and Sam had gone that way, and because of the possibility of the men being driven mad by the horror of the valley. Aragorn had been there in the search for Gollum so would undoubtedly have agreed with Gandalf on this. The two of them did however break the bridge there and set fire to the land around it - presumably to prevent an army coming out that way, and as another bit of distraction for Sauron.

By March 21st the Nazgûl were following their every move from high up as they headed north along the line of the Mountains of Shadow towards the Morannon. On March 23rd they reached the desolation before Cirith Gorgor where some of the young soldiers from Lossarnach and the Westfold of Rohan, to whom Mordor had previously only been some ghastly legend, were overcome by the horror of the place and unable to go on. Aragorn's reaction was typical of him: "*... there was pity in his eyes rather than wrath...*"[120] With his long experience of the horrors of Mordor, and his ability to empathise with people's fears, he would have known exactly what these men were going through. He would in addition have understood their shame in not having the courage to continue, hence his suggestion that they should go to the isle of Cair Andros (in the Anduin) instead and try to retake it from the enemy - a worthwhile task which was more suited to their capabilities. His behaviour at this juncture showed some of his finest qualities: compassion, empathy, wisdom and an ability to

---

118. Op. cit. [117], *Val* p. 19.
119. Op. cit. [2], *LotR* 5.9, p. 880.
120. Op. cit., *LotR* 5.10, p. 886.

bring out the best in people. This last-mentioned was shown by the fact that some of the men, as a result of his mercy, recovered sufficiently to go with him after all, while those who went to Cair Andros were able to keep their honour and self-respect. There is a parallel here with the journey through the Paths of the Dead when Aragorn only wanted people to go with him of their own free will - he was not willing to actually **command** them to go on such a horrendous journey. At Cirith Gorgor these terrified men would have been a liability if they had been forced to carry on, and a terror-induced madness would have been infectious. The reduction in numbers would scarcely have been an issue since the army was merely acting as bait to engage Sauron's attention - it had never had any hope of actually defeating him in battle. Aragorn's solution was a combination of mercy and common-sense, and no doubt this incident was one of the many reasons why the people of Gondor unanimously accepted him as King when the time came.

On the morning of March 25th, at the parley with the Mouth of Sauron before the Black Gate, Aragorn showed that he could outstare the Dark Lord's ambassador: *"Aragorn said naught in answer, but he took the other's eye and held it, and for a moment they strove thus; but soon, though Aragorn did not stir nor move hand to weapon, the other quailed and gave back as if menaced with a blow."*[121]. No doubt this achievement was relatively easy compared with the struggle he had had to dominate Sauron in the Palantír, and both incidents are good examples of the *"... light in his eyes that when they were kindled few could endure."*[122].

At the height of the ensuing battle *"Aragorn stood beneath his banner, silent and stern, as one lost in thought of things long past or far away; but his eyes gleamed like stars that shine the brighter as the night deepens."*[123]. He appeared briefly transformed in this scene as there is something elvish in this description of him, especially in the reference to his eyes resembling stars. Was he thinking of Elendil in the same spot at the Battle of Dagorlad three thousand years previously when the Last Alliance of Elves and Men defeated Sauron? Were his thoughts also on Arwen far away in Rivendell? Then Gandalf raised the cry of the Eagles' approach, and as the birds swooped down over the Nazgûl, the latter fled towards Mount Doom, having received the call from Sauron as Frodo put on the Ring. Was Aragorn, too, aware that something momentous was about to happen as he stood there apparently lost in his own thoughts? Had his perception and foresight increased - perhaps since using the Palantír?

It was not until Frodo actually put on the Ring that Sauron realised that for the last nineteen days his enemies had been operating a distraction strategy designed to fool him as to the whereabouts of the Ring. In the event the destruction of the Ring was a joint effort: the army at the Morannon was saved by the destruction of the Ring, but the destruction of the Ring was only made possible by the distraction strategy, as without it Frodo, Sam and Gollum would not have been able to get as far as the Cracks of Doom undetected by Sauron.

Coronation and wedding

The final stages of Aragorn's long struggle to regain the thrones of Arnor and Gondor and to win the hand of Arwen are covered in *LotR* 6.4 and 6.5, while his final appearance in the narrative proper occurs in *LotR* 6.6. App B is helpful in dating some of the events.

With the destruction of the Ring on March 25th, Gandalf immediately sought Gwaihir so that Frodo and Sam could be rescued from the slopes of Mount Doom, and we are told that he left Aragorn and the other leaders in charge of the battle. According to the account given in *LotR* 6.4.957 there was much fighting with the remnants of the Southrons and Easterlings until they were all subdued, and some of the army went into Mordor itself to destroy the fortresses in the north of that land. The latter event took place over a number of days. However Aragorn would not have had much part to play in these operations personally as, according to Gandalf's conversation with Frodo and Sam when they first awoke on April 8th, the Hobbits had been brought out of the fire to him on the same day as the Ring was destroyed (namely March 25th). This seems logical as it would certainly have been a matter of extreme urgency for Frodo and Sam to be treated, and only Aragorn would have been capable of saving them. Indeed, after the celebrations on the Field of Cormallen, Gandalf

---

121. Op. cit. [2], *LotR* 5.10, p. 889.
122. Op. cit., App A.I.v., p. 1060.
123. Op. cit., *LotR* 6.4, p. 948.

told the Hobbits that Aragorn had had to put forth all his power in order to bring them back from the brink of death and send them into a natural sleep. This must have been his greatest healing challenge yet. Thus it would seem that between March 25th and April 8th, Aragorn spent most of his time healing rather than in battle, with Frodo, Sam and probably Pippin too clearly owing their lives to him - along with many others presumably. [One hopes that he also found time to lavish some care on himself during this period!]

The meeting with Frodo and Sam on the Field of Cormallen was another incident which showed Aragorn at his best. By his acts of kneeling before them and setting them on his throne he showed his humility, and his willingness to recognise and respect other people's achievements and sufferings: "*yours has been the darkest road*"[124] he said to the Hobbits - though his own road had hardly been a bed of roses. Although he was now King - and looked it - he still happily accepted being called Strider by Sam, gently recalling how the Hobbits had not liked the look of him in Bree.

The middle weeks of April were a time of rest for those who had been hurt or who were late in returning from the fighting. During the last few days of the month, the captains and their men sailed from Cair Andros to Osgiliath, spending one day there before setting off for the Pelennor where they set up their pavilions in the fields on April 30th. Meanwhile considerable activity had been taking place in Minas Tirith since the destruction of the Ring, with the return of the women and children, and people travelling in from all parts of Gondor. Merry was sent for to join those at the Field of Cormallen, and Faramir, now recovered, formally took up his Stewardship, "*although it was only for a little while, and his duty was to prepare for one who should replace him.*"[125].

On May 1st Faramir met Aragorn outside Minas Tirith and knelt before him with the words, "*The last Steward of Gondor begs leave to surrender his office.*"[126]. Typically Aragorn handed the surrendered Steward's rod back to Faramir bestowing the office of Steward on him and his heirs for as long as his [Aragorn's] line should last. Faramir then issued a formal invitation to Aragorn to take up the kingship, citing his titles/ancestry and his qualities of military prowess and healing. This was followed by the unanimous acceptance of the people of Gondor. As Aragorn's subjects gazed in silence at their newly-crowned monarch, he appeared to them "*Tall as the sea-kings of old ... ancient of days he seemed and yet in the flower of manhood; and wisdom sat upon his brow, and strength and healing were in his hands, and a light was about him.*"[127]. In contrast to this impressive description, his behaviour on the occasion showed supreme humility, recognising that "*By the labour and valour of many I have come into my inheritance.*"[128] Instead of crowning himself as many expected, he had involved Frodo and Gandalf in the act of coronation, with Frodo bringing the crown to him and Gandalf actually putting it on his head.

The two months between Aragorn's coronation (on May 1st) and his wedding (on Mid-year's Day) were a time of anticipation and also anxiety for him. As he was now King of Arnor and Gondor, he had fulfilled Elrond's condition for his long-awaited marriage to Arwen. However the White Tree in the Court of the Fountain was dead and no sapling could be found to replace it. The lack of a sapling was a considerable source of worry due to the prophecy made by Tar-Palantir, the penultimate King of Númenor who had prophesied that if the White Tree died and no replacement could be found, the line of the Kings would perish. Two White Trees had died during the Third Age, the first in 1636 following the death of King Telemnar and his family from plague. In this case the king's successor had found and planted a seedling four years later. It was this replacement tree which had died in 2872 during the stewardship of Belecthor II and, due to the lack of a sapling or seedling, was still standing by the fountain when Aragorn became king. Aragorn must have been in a state of great uncertainty, since although he was now King and able to marry Arwen, the signs were apparently that the line of kings was about to die out. Quite apart from his personal happiness being at stake, he was anxious about the need to provide for the succession. Fortunately Gandalf was able to help him find a sapling growing in a hallowed place right on the snowline of Mount Mindolluin. He explained that the fruits of the tree were capable of lying dormant for many years, so one must have been planted there by an earlier king as a safeguard

---

124. Op. cit. [2], *LotR* 6.4, p. 954.
125. Op. cit., *LotR* 6.5, p. 964.
126. Op. cit., *LotR* 6.5, p. 967.
127. Op. cit., *LotR* 6.5, p. 968.
128. Op. cit., *LotR* 6.5, p. 967.

should the tree in the Court die: *"Here it has lain hidden on the mountain, even as the race of Elendil lay hidden in the wastes of the North."*[129]

There is some inconsistency of dates relating to this visit of Aragorn and Gandalf to the hallow on the mountain. App B.1095 records it as happening on June 25th, but the text of *LotR* 6.5.972 tells of how Aragorn replanted the sapling in the court by the fountain and *"...when the month of June entered in it was laden with blossom"*, thus implying that the sapling had been found in May. Whichever month it was, Elrond, Arwen, Galadriel and Celeborn and their parties arrived in Minas Tirith on Midsummer's Eve. According to App B.1095 the Rivendell party had set out on May 1st, the same day as Aragorn's coronation, with the departure of the full party from Lothlórien being on May 27th. Elrond now surrendered the Sceptre of Annúminas to Aragorn (as the chief mark of kingship in Arnor) and formally gave Arwen in marriage. The wedding took place the following day.

After three weeks of post-wedding celebrations, Aragorn's last travels as a member of the official Fellowship of the Ring began on July 22nd. The first stage consisted of the journey to Rohan as part of Théoden's funeral cortège, ending with the burial and wake at Edoras on August 10th. It was on this date also that the formal betrothal of Faramir and Éowyn took place. The journey continued to Helm's Deep and then to Isengard, where Treebeard gave Aragorn the keys of Orthanc, and Legolas and Gimli left the party to travel back to their own lands.

Aragorn took leave of Gandalf and the four Hobbits at sunset on August 22nd on Dol Baran, the hill near Isengard where Pippin had looked in the Orthanc-stone. When the Hobbits looked back *"they saw the King of the West sitting upon his horse with his knights about him; and the falling Sun shone upon them and made all their harness to gleam like red gold, and the white mantle of Aragorn was turned to a flame. Then Aragorn took the green stone and held it up, and there came a green fire from his hand."*[130]

Thus we have our last view of him in the main *LotR* narrative.

ACTIVITIES OF THE NAZGÛL DURING THE SUMMER AND AUTUMN OF 3018	
Based on information in: *LotR*; *UT* 3.4; *The Tale of Years* (App B); Marquette Paper 4/2/36 discussed by Hammond & Scull in *The Lord of the Rings: A Reader's Companion* (commentary on *LotR* 1.11 & 1.12). LotN=Lord of the Nazgûl; DG=Dol Guldur; S-eS=squint-eyed Southerner; ToY=Tale of Years	
JUN 20	LotN and co. attacked Gondor and took Osgiliath. As Khamûl and 1 or 2 others were in DG, they were presumably not present at the attack. Sauron then told the Nazgûl to search for the Ring. [The version in *UT* says only 1 Nazgûl was with Khamûl in DG, but probably superseded by ToY which gives 2.] On the same date the escape of Gollum was organised - he had been imprisoned by the Elves of Mirkwood Forest.
JUL 1	LotN + 5 others set out from Minas Morgul.
c. JUL 17	They reached the west bank of Anduin, then went northwards. Gandalf now a prisoner in Orthanc (since July 10).
JUL 22	They joined Khamûl and his 2 companions from DG. Khamûl reported that no halfling dwellings had been found near Anduin. The Nine then rode further north to reconnoitre, perhaps hoping to track down Gollum.
EARLY SEP	The Nine had returned south. Sauron now knew about the prophetic dream, Boromir's journey and Gandalf's capture. He sent the Nazgûl to Isengard on the assumption that Saruman might have some idea where the Ring was.
SEP 18	Gandalf escaped from Isengard. The Nazgûl crossed the Fords of Isen. Sometime between Sep 18-22 Gildor Inglorion found out about the Nazgûl and alerted Aragorn.

---

129. Op. cit. [2], *LotR* 6.5, p. 972.
130. Op. cit., *LotR* 6.6, p. 982.

SEP 20	The Nazgûl reached Isengard. Saruman feigned ignorance of the whereabouts of the Shire and suggested they pursue Gandalf for info. They met Gríma who told them how to find the Shire and made them aware that Saruman did actually know where it was. LotN now split Nazgûl into 4 pairs, he himself going ahead with the swiftest pair. They met 2 of Saruman's spies, including the S-eS from whom they obtained maps of the Shire and whom they now swore to the service of Mordor. [Another version of the story says that the Nazgûl reached Isengard while Gandalf was still prisoner. Saruman, panicking, decided to ask Gandalf for help and told the Nazgûl he was going to consult him. Gandalf escaped just before he got to him and returning to the Nazgûl Saruman delivered "Gandalf's instructions" for getting to the Shire. At this point Saruman knew of the guard of Rangers at Sarn Ford and believed the Ring was *en route* to Rivendell. He also knew of the prophetic dream and Boromir's journey. The Nazgûl met the S-eS in this version too.]
SEP 22	The Nine, now gathered together again, reached Sarn Ford in the early hours (acc. to *UT*) or in the evening (acc. to ToY). Rangers were on guard there. Some fled north hoping to let Aragorn know, but they were killed or driven off into the wild by the Nazgûl. Others continued trying to guard the Ford but were eventually swept away by LotN. Aragorn was not at Sarn Ford because he was lying in wait near the East Road to intercept Frodo.
SEP 23	Khamûl and 4 other Nazgûl entered the Shire before dawn. The others pursued the Rangers east then returned to watch the Greenway. That evening Khamûl arrived in Hobbiton as Frodo was leaving Bag End and spoke to Gaffer Gamgee. Getting no joy from him he picked up the Hobbits' trail and pursued them for the next 2 days.
SEP 24	At some point during Sep 24-26 LotN set up camp at Andrath in a defile between the Barrow-downs and the South Downs. He sent some of the Nazgûl to patrol the eastern borders of the Shire. He himself visited the Barrow-downs and stirred up the wights. He also stirred up evil things in the Old Forest. Gandalf crossed the Isen.
SEP 25	The Hobbits crossed Bucklebury Ferry leaving Khamûl stranded on the landing-stage. He summoned the other 4 Nazgûl who'd entered the Shire. One of them, a companion from DG who had communicated with him on the ridge above Woodhall, had visited Farmer Maggot with him not long before the Hobbits arrived there.
SEP 26	Khamûl and the other 4 Nazgûl all assembled early that day. Khamûl sent 1 Nazgûl to lurk near the Brandywine Bridge and 2 along the East Road to tell LotN the Ring was going East. He himself and a companion entered Buckland secretly via its North Gate (next to the Brandywine Bridge where the hedge ran to the river bank). The 2 Nazgûl who went along the East Road visited Bree and the inn *en route*. Presumably these were the ones who called on Butterbur and whom Aragorn saw speaking to Harry Goatleaf the Gatekeeper. Aragorn would also tell the Hobbits he had seen Nazgûl passing through Bree from north and south along the Greenway (see September 27). Frodo and co. were in the Old Forest at this time and about to meet Bombadil.
SEP 27	The 2 Nazgûl whom Khamûl had sent along the East Road found LotN who knew Ring-bearer was aware of pursuit and suspected he might avoid the road. He sent 3 Nazgûl eastwards separately and told them to reassemble just east of Weathertop then return towards Bree along or near the road. He knew of communication between Elves and Dúnedain (e.g. Gildor and Aragorn) and decided, with 2 others, to increase vigilance along the Greenway. Khamûl + companion were searching Buckland (not shown on Saruman's maps). Gandalf crossed the Greyflood.
SEP 28	Khamûl and companion found Crickhollow. Khamûl sent his companion to fetch the Nazgûl guarding Brandywine Bridge + horses. Thus the road between the Bridge and Bree was unguarded for a while. The 3 of them kept watch at Crickhollow for rest of that night. Hobbits captured by Barrow-wight. Gandalf reached Sarn Ford.
SEP 29	Frodo reached Bree. The 3 Nazgûl who were sent eastwards by LotN reached Bree in the evening (on their way back presumably) and heard of the events at the inn. One of them left to find LotN but was waylaid by Dúnedain. The other 2 were foiled in their attack on Merry. Gandalf visited Gaffer Gamgee.
SEP 30	The 2 Nazgûl who tried to seize Merry attacked the inn in the early hours. When that failed they set off to go to LotN to report that Ring-bearer had gone. At the same time Khamûl and his 2 companions attacked the house at Crickhollow where Fatty Bolger was. When that failed they rode down the Buckland Gate and made for Andrath where LotN was. The Nazgûl who was waylaid by Dúnedain caught up with LotN. All Nazgûl now at Andrath. LotN believed Ring-bearer to be east of Bree. He was unaware of Gandalf at this stage and knew only that a Ranger had been in the inn the previous evening (29th). He sent 4 Nazgûl across country from Andrath to Weathertop while he and the remaining 4 scoured the borders from Sarn Ford to Bree. They then rode through Bree knocking down the gates and took the East Road. Gandalf reached Bree that night and was aware of them. [Aragorn and the Hobbits had left that morning.]
OCT 1	Gandalf left Bree.
OCT 2	Possibly 1 of the 4 Nazgûl sent to Weathertop remained there while the other 3 went east on/near the road.
OCT 3	Gandalf reached Weathertop. LotN and his 4 companions aware of his approach and hid, closing in behind him. LotN realised Gandalf hadn't got the Ring. These 5 followed him to Weathertop assuming it was a trysting place. Gandalf was attacked by them that night and by the others as well according to his account at the Council of Elrond. Aragorn and Frodo saw the flashes in the distance.

OCT 4	Gandalf drove Nazgûl off and escaped north at sunrise. 4 of them followed him hoping to find out from him the whereabouts of the Ring-bearer. Then they turned back and made for the Bruinen Ford. LotN and Khamûl stayed near Weathertop.
OCT 5	LotN and Khamûl became aware of Aragorn and the Hobbits approaching Weathertop.
OCT 6	Aragorn and Frodo were spotted on Weathertop. Aragorn saw the 3 Nazgûl who had not followed Gandalf returning from a patrol to the west. Thus those 3 + LotN + Khamûl attacked their camp that night and were driven off by Aragorn. LotN now knew who the Ring-bearer was and was surprised it wasn't Aragorn. He thought Frodo would soon die. Why was their camp not watched for rest of night of 6/7? And why were they not seen when they crossed the road? Because LotN was dismayed: by Gandalf, by Frodo resisting him, by the sword from the Barrow-downs, by the mention of Elbereth, and by fear of Aragorn and Frodo. [Elbereth was the Vala who created the stars and on whom the Elves called when in danger or distress.]
OCT 7	LotN plus 4 Nazgûl who hadn't followed Gandalf north patrolled road to Bridge of Mitheithel. Aragorn and Hobbits now south of the road.
OCT 8	News reached Elrond of Hobbits' situation. Possibly knew Aragorn was with them.
OCT 9	Glorfindel sent out from Rivendell.
OCT 11	Glorfindel at Bridge of Mitheithel. He found 3 Nazgûl there one of which was Khamûl. They withdrew and he pursued them west. He came across 2 more Nazgûl, one of whom was LotN, who turned away southward. Glorfindel left green jewel on the Bridge as a token of safety.
OCT 13	Aragorn and Hobbits found the green jewel and crossed Bridge of Mitheithel.
OCT 14	The 5 Nazgûl encountered by Glorfindel reassembled. LotN and Khamûl realised Ring had crossed the Bridge.
OCT 18	Glorfindel met Aragorn and Hobbits.
OCT 19	The Nazgûl realised the Ring wasn't far ahead.
OCT 20	The 4 Nazgûl who had pursued Gandalf returned from the north and reached the Ford where they lay in wait for Frodo who was being pursued by the other 5 Nazgûl. LotN broke Frodo's sword. He and Khamûl attempted to cross the water but were overwhelmed. Glorfindel and Aragorn then drove them and the others into the river with torches. The bodies of 8 horses were found and the raiment of LotN. He probably managed to save one horse and make his way back to Mordor unclad and invisible. Sauron's fear increased seeing the power of his enemies and how fortune favoured them. The winged mounts were the next stage but withheld until the time when Sauron launched his war.

CHAPTER 1.6 - THE PALANTÍR CONFRONTATION

This chapter looks in detail at Aragorn's confrontation with Sauron in the Palantír of Orthanc on March 6th 3019 drawing attention to the nature, significance and repercussions of this deed. *LotR* **5.2 deals with the episode in context while a detailed account of the Palantíri themselves is given in** *UT* **4.3.**

I have devoted a whole chapter to this confrontation because I believe it to be the most crucial action Aragorn took in *LotR* - in fact one of the most crucial actions taken by **any** of the characters in the struggle to destroy the Ring. As well as being extremely courageous and dangerous, it was also hugely successful in diverting Sauron's attention away from Frodo. I also believe its impact is often overlooked and its significance underestimated, for example:
- The Encyclopedia of Arda (an online encyclopedia of the works of J. R. R. Tolkien) does not mention the Palantír confrontation in its entry for Aragorn.[1]
- Holly A. Crocker recognises the importance of Aragorn's military achievements in diverting Sauron's attention from Frodo but fails to mention the crux of the diversion - namely the Palantír confrontation.[2]
- Robert Foster refers to the confrontation, but only in the context of using it to gain information on the imminent naval invasion by the Corsairs of Umbar.[3]
- The episode was one of those which Peter Jackson omitted in the cinema version of the film of *The Return of the King* and while he did actually include it in the extended version he put it in the wrong place (immediately prior to the Battle of the Morannon) and also managed to give the impression that Aragorn lost the struggle with Sauron.[4]

It is in fact easy to miss the full import of this deed, partly due to the fact that it happened "off-stage" so to speak. Pippin's encounter with the Orthanc-stone is described in fairly graphic detail at the time it actually occurs while, in contrast, Aragorn's use of it is merely reported some hours after the event during a stressful meal with Legolas and Gimli. I first read *LotR* over forty years ago, so it's difficult to recall my initial impressions exactly, but I'm sure it took several readings to appreciate the true nature of what Aragorn had done and how momentous it was **in the context of the other events which were happening at the time**. The real significance is not immediately obvious and an understanding of the full impact of this heroic deed can only be achieved by a certain amount of interpretation and reading between the lines, and by studying the time-tables for all the characters involved.

Before analysing the incident in detail, it is necessary to fit it into its context in the narrative and then to establish something of the history and properties of the Palantíri.

*

Following the Battle of the Hornburg at Helm's Deep Gandalf, Théoden and their companions rode to Isengard for a parley with Saruman, arriving on March 5th. At the end of the parley Gríma Wormtongue threw a dark crystal globe with a glowing centre out of the Tower of Orthanc. That night Pippin, feeling drawn to the globe (probably because he had handled it after it fell), removed it from the arms of a sleeping Gandalf, looked into it and encountered the Eye of Sauron. From this incident, Aragorn and Gandalf realised that the globe

---
1. M. Fisher, *The Encyclopedia of Arda*, [website], 1997-2016, http://www.glyphweb.com/arda/default.asp, (accessed 1 March 2010).
2. H.A. Crocker, 'Masculinity', in R. Eaglestone (ed.), *Reading The Lord of the Rings: New Writings on Tolkien's Classic*, London, New York, Continuum, 2005, Chapter 8, pp. 111-123.
3. 'Aragorn' in R. Foster, *The Complete Guide to Middle-earth: From The Hobbit to The Silmarillion,* First published in Great Britain by George Allen & Unwin 1978, London, HarperCollins Publishers, 1993, pp. 16-18.
4. The Lord of the Rings: The Return of the King, dir. Peter Jackson, USA, Newline, 2003, [extendedDVD].

was one of the seven Palantíri (or Seeing-stones) which had been brought to Middle-earth by Elendil after the drowning of Númenor. They also now realised that this Palantír had been used as the means of communication between Saruman in Orthanc and Sauron in Barad-dûr who, evidently, also had access to a Palantír. As Aragorn was *"de jure"* King, being Elendil's heir, Gandalf accordingly presented the Orthanc-stone to him for safe-keeping, as its rightful owner, at the same time advising him to be wary about using it.

In the early hours of March 6th, as Frodo, Sam and Gollum were drawing near to Ithilien, and Gandalf and Pippin were riding to Gondor on Shadowfax, Aragorn put an end to eighty-eight years of secrecy and used the Palantír of Orthanc to reveal himself to Sauron as Isildur's heir, showing him the sword of Elendil now reforged. His chief purpose was to give Sauron something momentous to think about in order to draw his attention away from the borders of his own land where Frodo and Sam were trying to find a way in.

The seven Seeing-stones had been made in the First Age by Fëanor, the most skilled and gifted of all the Elves[5]. Later, towards the end of the Second Age, the Eldar gave them to Elendil's father Amandil in Númenor in recognition of his fidelity and his refusal to be corrupted by Sauron. Following the downfall and drowning of Númenor they were brought to Middle-earth by Elendil and his sons Isildur and Anárion. During the Third Age the Kings of Arnor and Gondor, or those authorised by them, used the Stones to view distant events and places in their kingdoms and also to communicate with users of answering Palantíri. During communication *"... thought could be 'transferred' (received as 'speech'), and visions of the things in the mind of the surveyor of one Stone could be seen by the other surveyor."*[6].

By the time of the War of the Ring, only four of the Palantíri survived: the Orthanc-stone, the Anor-stone, the Ithil-stone and the Elendil-stone. The last-mentioned was located in the Tower of Elostirion near the Grey Havens and could only look West to the Sea and the Undying Lands - it could not communicate with any other Palantír. The Ithil-stone had been seized during the capture of Minas Ithil (subsequently called Minas Morgul) by the Nazgûl in TA 2002[7], while the other two were located in Orthanc and the White Tower of Minas Tirith.

The Palantíri were originally an innocent aid to communication for the Kings. They were not considered sinister or dangerous until the possibility arose of Sauron having access to them when, as mentioned above, the Ithil-stone was seized in 2002. From that date the Kings - and subsequently the Stewards - of Gondor stopped using the two remaining Stones for fear of being drawn into an encounter with Sauron wielding the Ithil-stone. This situation continued until around 2984 when the theoretical danger from Sauron became a reality during the stewardship of Denethor II who began to use the Anor-stone for his own purposes, believing that he had the strength to resist any interference from Sauron. Also, some sixteen years later Saruman began using the Orthanc-stone (App B.1090). The results of these Palantír "liaisons" are summed up in *UT* 4.3.527: Saruman *"... fell under the domination of Sauron and desired his victory, or no longer opposed it"*, while Denethor *"remained steadfast in his rejection of Sauron, but was made to believe that his victory was inevitable, and so fell into despair"* [and into madness too in the end]. *UT* 4.3.527 also states that the Palantíri were more amenable to legitimate users: Saruman, having no right to use them, was corrupted, while Denethor, as a Steward standing in for the King, did have the right and resisted corruption, though he was still manipulated and deceived by Sauron.

When Gandalf gave the Orthanc-stone to Aragorn he expressed grave misgivings about it, calling it *"a dangerous charge"* and telling Aragorn, *"... if I may counsel you in the use of your own, do not use it - yet! Be wary!"*[8]. He was anxious that Aragorn should not act hastily after so many years of patience and waiting. He went on to say that if it hadn't been for Pippin's behaviour he may have been tempted to try and use the Stone himself - which would have been disastrous *"... until the hour comes when secrecy will avail no longer."* He also felt that he was not ready for such a confrontation and might never be. Strangely Aragorn proved unwilling to accept Gandalf's advice, declaring that the Stone would not be dangerous to him as it was his by right, and

---

5. C. Tolkien (ed.), *The Silmarillion*, London, HarperCollins Publishers, 1999, first published in Great Britain by George Allen & Unwin 1977, Chapter 6, pp. 64-5.
6. C. Tolkien (ed.), *Unfinished Tales of Númenor and Middle-earth*, London, HarperCollins Publishers, 1998, first published in Great Britain by George Allen & Unwin 1980, Chapter 4.3, Note 5, p. 532.
7. J.R.R. Tolkien, *The Lord of the Rings*, London, HarperCollins Publishers, 2007, 2nd edition, based on the 50th Anniversary Edition of 2004, App B, p. 1087.
8. Op. cit., *LotR* 3.11, pp. 594-5.

making it clear that as far as he was concerned the hour had already come when secrecy should be cast aside.

Later, on the way to Minas Tirith, Gandalf explained to Pippin the reason for his caution, telling him that the Orthanc-stone was "... *so bent towards Barad-dûr that, if any save a will of adamant now looks into it, it will bear his mind and sight swiftly thither*"[9], before expressing concern that Sauron might find out about Aragorn too soon. In addition he spoke to Pippin about the "pull" of the corrupted Stone, explaining how it made him want to test his will against Sauron's and turn the Stone to his own use, looking back in time and distance to see Fëanor at work when the Two Trees of Valinor still existed. He also referred to Saruman being "**constrained** *to come often to his glass for inspection and instruction*"[10] [My emphasis]. Pippin of course had experienced the "pull" for himself. However the situation would be different for Aragorn: he didn't look in the Stone because he was "pulled", but because he chose to - he was the **initiator** of the confrontation, not dragged into it against his will.

*

The task facing Aragorn once he had decided to use the Palantír had multiple elements to it. As well as showing Sauron that an heir of Isildur existed and that the sword of Elendil had been reforged, he had to find the mental strength to:

- Stay in control of himself physically and mentally, enduring pain and fear without crying out or losing consciousness as Pippin had done.
- Dominate Sauron in order to wrench the Stone away from his control and direct it where he wished.
- Deceive Sauron so he could fool him into believing that he [Aragorn] had the Ring.
- Ensure Sauron did not perceive any of his thoughts and knowledge - or any fear.
- Learn how to use the Stone to view Sauron's plans - i.e. to see what really was, not what Sauron wanted him to see - and thus make a decision on how to proceed.
- Find the power to withdraw himself. Note Pippin's experience ("... *it held his eyes, so that now he could not look away*")[11] and also Gandalf's concern had he tried to use it himself ("... *even if I found the power to withdraw myself...*")[12]

Knowing that the Palantíri were more amenable to legitimate users and that he had a better right to use them than anyone else in Middle-earth, Aragorn believed that he possessed the strength to do the task he had set himself. This was justified: unlike Saruman and Denethor he was not corrupted, dominated or deceived, and he achieved his objectives. However, it was a close-run thing, as demonstrated by the effect the struggle had on him.

LotR 5.2 provides plenty of comments and observations which show that the experience was nothing short of harrowing. We've seen Aragorn weary and sleepless, we've seen him tortured by indecision, guilt and fear of failure, but it's only in the hours following his use of the Palantír, that we see him completely drained, physically and mentally, from exhaustion and no doubt shock, to the extent that he apparently couldn't face the company and the mid-day meal. We are told that "*Grim was his face, grey-hued and weary*" and that he looked, in Merry's eyes, "*as if in one night many years had fallen on his head*".[13] Later (*LotR* 5.2.780) as he steeled himself to tell Legolas and Gimli what he had done, he uncharacteristically turned on Gimli when the Dwarf questioned the wisdom of his actions reminding him that "*Even Gandalf feared that encounter.*" Aragorn himself regarded the confrontation with Sauron as "*A struggle somewhat grimmer for my part than the battle of the Hornburg*"[14], a battle where he had narrowly escaped death, and in the aftermath of which he had stated, "*I feel a weariness such as I have seldom felt before.*"[15]. He went on to say "*It was a bitter struggle, and the*

---

9. Op. cit. [7], *LotR* 3.11, p. 598.
10. Op. cit., *LotR* 3.11, p. 598.
11. Op. cit., *LotR* 3.11, p. 592.
12. Op. cit., *LotR* 3.11, p. 595.
13. Op. cit., *LotR* 5.2, p. 778.
14. Op. cit., *LotR* 5.2, p. 780.
15. Op. cit., *LotR* 3.9, p. 563.

weariness is slow to pass."[16] There is also some indication that his ordeal was physically painful: Pippin had complained that Sauron hurt him - which was why he had yielded and told him he was a Hobbit - and had described Sauron's laughter as "*... like being stabbed with knives.*"[17]. Legolas and Gimli thought that Aragorn looked "*like one who has laboured in sleepless pain for many nights.*"[18]. At the end of the following day Éowyn would notice the difference in him when they met for the second time at Dunharrow: "*Greatly changed he seemed to me since I saw him first in the king's house, grimmer, older. Fey I thought him, and like one whom the Dead call.*"[19] His condition demonstrated the severity of his ordeal. He was a man who had lived rough for much of his life, self-sufficient, going on solitary and perilous journeys (even close to the Morannon and into the Morgul Vale), capable of facing up to the Nazgûl, running for four days with minimal food and sleep, giving his all in the Battle of the Hornburg and still having the strength afterwards to tend Gimli's head wound instead of resting. This is without mentioning what still lay ahead of him, such as the journey through the Paths of the Dead, the ride across the southern fiefs of Gondor to Pelargir, the Battle of the Pelennor Fields and the night spent healing the victims of the Black Breath. He had been variously described as "*the greatest traveller and huntsman of this age of the world*"[20], and "*the most hardy of living Men*"[21].

This battle of wills with Sauron involved a mortal man striving with a Maia. Yes, Aragorn did have a streak of Maia himself due to his descent from Melian, but there were sixty-seven generations between him and Melian and he was, to all intents and purposes, a mortal Man. As indicated earlier Gandalf doubted his own ability to withstand Sauron in the Palantír and he was pure Maia. Moreover Sauron had spent thousands of years terrorising, dominating, corrupting, seducing and brainwashing Elves and Men in Middle-earth and Númenor - it would thus be no small achievement to win a confrontation with such a being. In *Ak* it is told how Sauron's spirit escaped from the drowning of Númenor and made its way back to Middle-earth and Mordor. "*There he took up again his great Ring in Barad-dûr, and dwelt there, dark and silent, until he wrought himself a new guise, **an image of malice and hatred made visible; and the Eye of Sauron the Terrible few could endure.***"[22] [My emphasis]. This description is in itself sufficient to explain the traumatic and exhausting nature of Aragorn's struggle, even allowing for the fact that he had the "advantages" of physical distance and rightful ownership of the Palantír referred to by Tolkien himself in a draft letter to Mrs Eileen Elgar dated September 1963.[23] His ordeal was also exacerbated by additional factors. As he received the Orthanc-stone from Gandalf Aragorn became very self-assured - probably more so than at any other point in *LotR* thus far. He was convinced that he would have no problem using the Stone due to his undoubted superior right to do so, and in carrying out this act he disregarded the advice of Gandalf - something which one imagines he didn't do very often. When he told Legolas and Gimli about the confrontation, he said "*I am the lawful master of the Stone, and I had both the right and the strength to use it, **or so I judged**. The right cannot be doubted. The strength was enough - **barely**.*"[24]. At this point he drew a deep breath. The words I have emphasised seem to me to imply that the struggle was far more severe than he had anticipated and that he only succeeded by the skin of his teeth. That single word "barely" says a great deal. As is pointed out in *UT* 4.3.523-4 and as Gandalf clearly realised, using the Orthanc-stone once it had become corrupted by Sauron became incredibly risky for anyone, right or no right. It must have been a terrible shock to realise that he had almost failed in such a dangerous (even reckless) action - the consequences if he had failed and Sauron had read his thoughts did not bear thinking about. He went on to say that "*... **in the end I wrenched** the Stone to my own will*" [My emphasis], thus indicating the prolonged and violent mental effort required.

UT 4.3 contains further hints as to the exhausting nature of the confrontation as illustrated by two of the Notes. In Note 13 (534) attention is drawn to the mental strain of using a Palantír, "*especially on men of later*

---

16. Op. cit. [7], *LotR* 5.2, p. 780.
17. Op. cit., *LotR* 3.11, p.593.
18. Op. cit., *LotR* 5.2, p. 780.
19. Op. cit., *LotR* 5.3, p. 797.
20. Op. cit., *LotR* 1.2, p. 58.
21. Op. cit., App A.I.v, p. 1060.
22. Op. cit. [5], *Ak* p. 336.
23. H. Carpenter (ed.), *The Letters of J.R.R. Tolkien*, with the assistance of Christopher Tolkien, London, HarperCollins Publishers, 1995. First published in Great Britain by George Allen & Unwin, 1981. Letter. 246, p. 332.
24. Op. cit. [7], *LotR* 5.2, p. 780.

days not trained to the task..." This is not referring to use of a corrupted Palantír, but of a normal one. Aragorn couldn't possibly have had any training in using a Palantír as the North Kingdom ones (the Stones of Annúminas and Amon Sûl) were destroyed before he was born and he could not have had access to those in Minas Morgul, Minas Tirith or Orthanc. Note 16 (535) in *UT* 4.3 mentions that it is not recorded whether he ever used the Elendil-stone (guarded by Círdan at the Tower of Elostirion), and even if he had used it, it wouldn't have been relevant training since that particular Stone only looked West towards Tol Eressëa and couldn't communicate with other Stones. Therefore, to add to the strain of confronting Sauron, Aragorn also had to learn how to use the Orthanc-stone for its normal purpose. In addition *UT* 4.3.530-31 tells us that by concentrating on distant objects the user of a Palantír could cause them to be enlarged and appear in more detail. However this could be very tiring and exhausting, so was only done in situations of urgency. Such a situation would have arisen when Aragorn observed the ships of the Corsairs; he knew from past experience serving incognito in Gondor that the Corsairs posed a threat, so he would certainly have been concentrating on them especially.

A further comment, in Note 5 (532-3), says that "*It was only Sauron who used a Stone for the transference of his superior will, dominating the weaker surveyor and forcing him to reveal hidden thought and to submit to commands.*" However, although Aragorn did not carry out long-term dominance in the way Sauron did over Saruman and Denethor, he did actually display, in that one confrontation, a superior will to Sauron's and he did deceive Sauron and read his mind, as the following points illustrate:
- He wrenched control of the Stone from Sauron to use it for his own purposes.
- He deceived him into supposing that he himself had the Ring.
- He was able to hide his thoughts from him, thus preventing him from realising that, actually, Frodo had the Ring.
- He showed himself to Sauron "*in other guise than you see me here*" (these words were spoken to Gimli in *LotR* 5.2.780). Sauron clearly saw Aragorn as looking more regal than he actually did at the time, and later we will read of him [Sauron] brooding over his tormentor's "*bright sword*" and "*stern and kingly face*" (*LotR* 6.2.923). It occurs to me that this transformation could have been achieved by means of the Elessar. In *UT* 2.4.322 (The Elessar), we are told that "*... those who looked through this stone saw things that were withered or burned healed again or as they were in the grace of their youth...*". Also we know that when Aragorn first pinned it on his breast in Lothlórien his companions saw him as tall and kingly (*LotR* 2.8.375). If he deliberately exposed it to Sauron's view when using the Palantír then a similar effect could perhaps have been achieved.
- He also understood Sauron's thoughts and fears. In App A.I.v.1060 we are told that Aragorn spent time "*... exploring the hearts of Men, both evil and good...*" and there are many instances where he seemed able to read the thoughts and feelings of others - including those of Sauron. In a strangely empathetic speech, he told Legolas and Gimli "*... I wrenched the Stone to my own will. That alone he will find hard to endure .... To know that I lived and walked the earth was a blow to his heart, I deem; for he knew it not till now .... Now in the very hour of his great designs the heir of Isildur and the Sword are revealed... He is not so mighty yet that he is above fear; nay, doubt ever gnaws him.*"[25]

Aragorn perceived Sauron's fear and doubt and realised the effect that the sight of Isildur's heir and the reforged sword would have on him. If his confrontation with Sauron was an ordeal for himself, it was no less an ordeal for Sauron as would be made clear in the days to come.

*

Through his use of the Palantír and his ability to take control of it, Aragorn found out that the ships of the Corsairs of Umbar were gathering at Pelargir and planning an attack on Minas Tirith from the south. This was in the early morning of March 6th. The news of these ships would not reach Minas Tirith itself until the evening of March 7th (see Beregond's conversation with Pippin in *LotR* 5.1.765 and App B.1093 for March 9th [which

---
25. Op. cit. [7], *LotR* 5.2, p. 780.

was when Gandalf and Pippin reached Minas Tirith and Beregond had the conversion with Pippin in which he said that the beacons were lit 2 days ago when news of the ships was received]). When Aragorn spoke to Théoden and Éomer of the time-scale for the muster of the Rohirrim at Edoras, he realised that he would be too late to intercept the Corsairs if he went to Minas Tirith with Théoden and subsequently to Pelargir from there. As a result he finally made the reluctant decision to shorten the journey by going through the Paths of the Dead. As he would explain to Éowyn the following day, *"Only so can I see any hope of doing my part in the war against Sauron."*[26]. In addition to the time factor, if he could call on the Dead Men of Dunharrow to fulfil their oath and fight for him, he might have some chance of actually defeating the Corsairs and preventing their attack on Minas Tirith.

Thus the immediate outcome of Aragorn's action was his journey to Pelargir via the Paths of the Dead, along with the Grey Company, Elrond's sons, Legolas and Gimli. This was in itself an outstanding feat of courage and endurance, and has a higher profile than the even more traumatic, and solitary (apart from Halbarad for support and counsel only), Palantír confrontation. Through the fear engendered by the Dead he was able to take over the Corsairs' ships then sail up the Anduin to the Pelennor Fields in time to ensure a victory over Sauron's forces. Gondor was losing the battle when he arrived, in spite of the help from Rohan.

However there are other less obvious, but far-reaching and hugely significant, implications to consider, because, as Paul Kocher puts it, *"The ripples of Aragorn's open challenge spread far and wide through the remainder of the story"*[27]. [The full significance of the confrontation is also recognised by Tom A Shippey[28] and Fleming Rutledge.][29] The confrontation with Sauron took place on the morning of March 6th and the Ring was destroyed on March 25th. During this nineteen-day interval Frodo, Sam and Gollum were able to make their way alongside the Mountains of Shadow to the Cross Roads, bypass Minas Morgul, get into Mordor via Cirith Ungol, make their way along the Morgai to the Isenmouthe, walk for forty miles along the Barad-dûr road, then turn south across the plain of Gorgoroth to scale Mount Doom with Sauron first being unaware of them and then simply ignoring them. Aragorn had, **by confronting him in the Palantír**, succeeded in frightening and misleading him to the extent that all his attention was centred on Isildur's heir rather than his own land and borders. This effect is best illustrated by viewing the events between March 6th and March 25th in chronological order, examining the deeds, motives, reactions and observations of Aragorn, Frodo, Sauron (or his servants) and others in context. Only thus is it possible to grasp the true significance of Aragorn's diversion strategy.

Prior to March 6th there had indeed been factors which helped Frodo to go undetected. After three to four days of being lost in the Emyn Muil he was safely guided by Gollum for five days including on a crossing of the mist-covered Dead Marshes using a path known only to Gollum. In addition, much of Sauron's attention during this period was on Rohan and Isengard (he was sending Nazgûl there), particularly through his communication with Saruman via the Orthanc-stone - which of course ceased when Aragorn obtained the Stone. In the following account any emphasis in quoted passages is mine.

March 6th
- Aragorn looked into the Palantír early in the morning thereby making Sauron aware that his worst nightmare had come true: an heir of Isildur existed and the sword which had robbed him of the Ring had been reforged. From his own recent travels in the Emyn Muil and Dead Marshes while searching for Gollum, Aragorn was aware that, ten days since the breaking of the Fellowship, Frodo would probably be getting near to Mordor and it was therefore time that Sauron had something to distract him. This explains his conviction that it was time to abandon his incognito.
  Later that day he set out from Helm's Deep for his journey through the Paths of the Dead
- As if confirming Aragorn's estimate this was actually the day when Frodo started the journey down

---

26. Op. cit. [7], *LotR* 5.2, p. 784.
27. P. Kocher, *Master of Middle-earth: The Achievement of J. R. R. Tolkien*, London, Pimlico, 2002, first published in Great Britain by Thames & Hudson 1973, Chapter 3, p. 47.
28. T.A. Shippey, *J.R.R. Tolkien: Author of the Century*, London, HarperCollins Publishers, 2001, Chapter 2, pp. 109-110.
29. F. Rutledge, *The Battle for Middle-earth: Tolkien's Divine Design in The Lord of the Rings*, Grand Rapids Michigan and Cambridge UK, Wm. B. Eerdmans Publishing Co., 2004, Book V, pp. 259-260.

the west side of the Mountains of Shadow thus making himself more visible and running a high risk of meeting enemy troops from the south on their way to the Morannon. In fact the Hobbits had narrowly avoided a meeting with a troop of Haradrim only the previous morning (*LotR* 4.3.645-6). However, during the night of March 6th-7th, they heard no-one on the road.
- Was this the first sign of Sauron in shock, leaving his servants without proper guidance?

March 7th
- Aragorn arrived at Dunharrow and the entrance to the Paths of the Dead at nightfall.
- Frodo met Faramir and his Rangers and was thus safe when another troop of Haradrim appeared. After these had been defeated Faramir told the Hobbits "*You cannot go along the road southwards, if that was your purpose. It will be unsafe for some days, and **always more closely watched after this affray than it has been yet.***"[30]. Frodo too recognised the increased danger. However some hours later Faramir's Rangers reported that "*Of the enemy no movement could be seen; **not even an orc-spy was abroad.***"[31]
- This situation was a further indication of Sauron's shock at seeing Aragorn in the Palantír. He was ignoring his borders - even when a party of his allies had just been wiped out by Gondor's Rangers - withdrawing all his spies and troops inside Mordor while he brooded on how to deal with the new threat.

March 8th
- Aragorn went through the Paths of the Dead, then rode on to the Stone of Erech.
- As Frodo, Sam and Gollum prepared to resume their journey Faramir told them that all his scouts and watchers had returned, even those who had been watching the area around the Morannon. He went on to say "***They all find a strange thing.*** *The land is empty. Nothing is on the road ... A waiting silence broods above the Nameless Land.* ***I do not know what this portends... Hasten while you may!***"[32] Faramir urgently advised Frodo to take advantage of the strange fact that Mordor had apparently ground to a halt. Later, as he took leave of the Hobbits, he said "*The land dreams in a false peace, and for a while all evil is withdrawn.*"[33] For the rest of the day as the Hobbits journeyed "*... all about them was silence.*"[34]
- Sauron was planning his attack on Isildur's heir and ignoring everything else. Aragorn's diversion strategy was clearly working.

March 9th
- Aragorn had formally summoned the Dead at Erech, and was now riding towards Pelargir.
- Frodo found that "*... the silence seemed deeper... **as if thunder was brewing***"[35]. He reached the road to Minas Morgul.
- Sauron was building up to his attack. He began his Darkness that evening, which Gandalf would interpret as being caused by Frodo's approach to Mordor until reassured by Faramir (see March 10th).

March 10th
- Aragorn was now approximately midway between the Paths of the Dead and Pelargir.
- Frodo, Sam and Gollum were making their way up the north wall of the Morgul Vale to get to the Stairs of Cirith Ungol.
- As they did so the Lord of the Nazgûl led his host out of Minas Morgul. He paused, suddenly uneasy, but decided not to follow up his misgivings as "*... he was in haste... at his great Master's bidding he must march with war into the West .... So great an army had never issued from that vale since the days of*

---

30. Op. cit. [7], *LotR* 4.5, p. 668.
31. Op. cit., *LotR* 4.5, p. 675.
32. Op. cit., *LotR* 4.7, p. 694.
33. Op. cit., *LotR* 4.7, p. 695.
34. Op. cit., *LotR* 4.7, p. 696.
35. Op. cit., *LotR* 4.7, p. 696.

Isildur's might ..."[36]. The references to Isildur and the size of the army seem highly significant. Sauron would undoubtedly have been recalling the army of the Last Alliance of Elves and Men at the end of the Second Age when Barad-dûr was besieged and Isildur had used the shards of Elendil's sword to cut the One Ring from his hand. The size of his army in TA 3019 seems to enforce the idea that Sauron believed Aragorn had the Ring. Note that *UT* 3.4.ii states that the Nazgûl were "*entirely enslaved to their Nine Rings*" and were "*quite incapable of acting against his* [Sauron's] *will*"[37]. Thus, even though the Lord of the Nazgûl undoubtedly sensed the presence of the Ring, he did nothing about it because his master was solely intent on preparing to face Isildur's heir in battle.

- Faramir met Gandalf in Minas Tirith. He explained that the Darkness issuing from Mordor was not due to Frodo's proximity to the border, because he wouldn't have had time to get so far since he [Faramir] had parted from him on March 8th: "*... the darkness is not due to their* [i.e. Frodo, Sam and Gollum] *venture...*"[38]. Faramir thought that Sauron had long planned an assault, and its hour had already been determined "*... before ever the travellers left my keeping.*" This would fit with Aragorn's use of the Palantír on March 6th. No doubt Faramir now linked the darkness with the strange calm and lack of activity which he had noticed on March 7th and 8th.
- Gandalf, in Minas Tirith, perceived Sauron's disquiet and his disregard for what was happening under his nose. When he realised that Sauron's panic and the Darkness were not due to Frodo, he thought of Aragorn and shared his thoughts with Pippin: "*... our Enemy has opened his war at last and made the first move while Frodo was still free. So now for many days he will have his eye turned this way and that, away from his own land. And yet, Pippin,* **I feel from afar his haste and fear. He has begun sooner than he would. Something has happened to stir him. .... Ah! I wonder. Aragorn? .... He may have used the Stone and shown himself to the Enemy, challenging him, for this very purpose.**"[39]

Gandalf perceived that Sauron had acted precipitately and guessed the reason for it.

March 11th
- Aragorn reached Linhir in southern Gondor where he encountered enemy forces from Umbar and Harad.
- Frodo climbed the Stairs of Cirith Ungol.

March 12th
- Aragorn drove the enemy towards Pelargir with the assistance of the Dead Men of Dunharrow.
- Frodo was stung by Shelob.

March 13th
- Aragorn captured the Corsairs' fleet at Pelargir, again with the help of the Dead, prompting Gimli to observe "*Strange and wonderful I thought it that the designs of Mordor should be overthrown by such wraiths of fear and darkness. With its own weapons was it worsted!*"[40]. Such an occurrence must have made an equally strong impression on Sauron.
- Frodo was captured by the Orcs of Cirith Ungol.
- Sam overheard the Orc captains Shagrat (from the Tower of Cirith Ungol) and Gorbag (from Minas Morgul) talking following their discovery of the unconscious Frodo after the attack by Shelob. They were clearly aware that something was amiss and that the war was not going entirely Sauron's way. They also realised that Sauron was apparently ignoring reports of intruders on the Stairs. Their concerns are clear from the following snippets of their conversation taken from *LotR* 4.10.737-9:

   Gor: *... they can make mistakes, even the Top Ones can.*

---

36. Op. cit. [7], *LotR* 4.8, p. 707.
37. Op. cit. [6], *UT*, p. 443.
38. Op. cit. [7], *LotR* 5.4, p. 812.
39. Op. cit., *LotR* 5.4, p. 815.
40. Op. cit. *LotR* 5.9, p. 876.

Sha: *... there's no doubt about it, they're troubled about something. The Nazgûl down below are, by your account; and Lugbúrz* [Barad-dûr] *is too. Something nearly slipped.*
Gor: *I'm not easy in my mind ... the Big Bosses, ay, even the Biggest, can make mistakes ... But see here: when were you ordered out?*
Sha: *About an hour ago, just before you saw us. A message came: 'Nazgûl uneasy. Spies feared on Stairs ...' I came at once.*
Gor: *See here - our Silent Watchers were uneasy* **more than two days ago**, *that I know. But my patrol wasn't ordered out for another day, nor any message sent to Lugbúrz either: owing to the Great Signal going up, and the High Nazgûl going off to war, and all that.* [Referring to the Witch-king's failure to act on March 10th.] **And then they couldn't get Lugbúrz to pay attention for a good while, I'm told.**"
Sha: "*The Eye was busy elsewhere, I suppose. Big things going on away west, they say.*"
Gorbag then went on to lecture Shagrat about the fact that spies had got up the Stairs under his [Shagrat's] watch. Based on the injury to Shelob and the cutting of the cords she had put round Frodo, Gorbag reckoned that "*... there's someone loose hereabouts as is more dangerous than any other damned rebel that ever walked since the bad old times,* **since the Great Siege**" - another reference to the end of the Second Age. Although the "*rebel*" loose in Cirith Ungol was actually Sam, Gorbag's perceptive assessment of the danger was spot on, as was his realisation that Barad-dûr seemed to be "losing the plot".

March 14th
- Aragorn was sailing up the River Anduin towards the Pelennor Fields.
- Sam was rescuing Frodo from the Tower of Cirith Ungol.

March 15th
- On the Pelennor Fields the Lord of the Nazgûl realised that "*The darkness was breaking too soon, before the date that his Master had set for it ...*"[41]. It was being broken up by the south wind which was blowing Aragorn's ships towards the Harlond.
- Frodo and Sam too were aware of the wind changing. "*There was battle far above in the high spaces of the air. The billowing clouds of Mordor were being driven back ...*". Sam said, "*The wind's changed. Something's happening. He's not having it all his own way.*"[42]. He also recalled the Orc conversation from 13th and realised Gorbag had known then that things were going wrong for Sauron because he hadn't been paying attention to reports.
- This was the same date as Aragorn's arrival at the Pelennor as King and the same date as the demise of the Lord of the Nazgûl. These two incidents must have greatly increased Sauron's fear and would have confirmed his suspicion that Aragorn had the Ring.

March 16th
- The Last Debate took place, and Gandalf was able to verify his theory that Aragorn had looked into the Palantír:

Gan: "*... he* [Sauron] *is now in great doubt. For if we have found this thing, there are some among us with strength enough to wield it. That too he knows. For do I not guess rightly, Aragorn, that you have shown yourself to him in the Stone of Orthanc?*"
Sauron presumably thought that if Aragorn was capable of wrenching the Palantír out of his control, he was also capable of wielding the Ring. In fact it probably wouldn't even have occurred to him that a mere mortal would deliberately confront him **without** having the Ring.
Ara: "*... I deemed that the time was ripe, and that the Stone had come to me for just such a*

---
41. Op. cit. [7], *LotR* 5.6, p. 839.
42. Op. cit., *LotR* 6.2, p. 919.

purpose. It was then ten days since the Ring-bearer went east from Rauros, and the Eye of Sauron, I thought, should be drawn out from his own land."[43]

Aragorn's strategy of distracting Sauron was then adopted as the strategy for the Battle of the Morannon. Gandalf said, "*His Eye is now straining towards us, blind almost to all else that is moving...* **As Aragorn has begun, so we must go on.** *We must push Sauron to his last throw. We must call out his hidden strength...* **he will think that in such rashness he sees the pride of the new Ringlord ...**"[44]

- Meanwhile as Frodo and Sam were struggling along the Morgai, we are told that "*The Dark Power was deep in thought, and the Eye turned inward, pondering tidings of doubt and danger: a bright sword and a stern and kingly face it saw, and for a while it gave little thought to other things...*"[45]. Sauron's fear and shock from the Palantír confrontation seemed to have become an obsession.
- Later that day Frodo and Sam overheard a conversation between a tracker Orc (TO) and a fighter Orc (FO) who had been sent from Cirith Ungol to pursue them. Their words indicated further doubt and confusion among Sauron's servants. As a side-effect of putting Sauron off his guard Aragorn had also succeeded in throwing the management and communication in Mordor into chaos:

TO: "*Garn! You don't even know what you're looking for.*"
FO: "*Whose blame's that? Not mine. That comes from Higher Up. First they say it's a great Elf in bright armour, then it's a sort of small dwarf-man, then it must be a pack of rebel Uruk-hai; or maybe it's all the lot together.*"
TO: "*Ar! They've lost their heads, that's what it is. And some of the bosses are going to lose their skins too, I guess, if what I hear is true: Tower raided and all, and hundreds of your lads done in, and prisoner got away ... small wonder there's bad news from the battles.*"
FO: "*Who says there's bad news?*"
TO: "*Ar! Who says there isn't?*"[46]

It had been the Nazgûl now in charge at Cirith Ungol, not Sauron, who had instigated the pursuit of Frodo and Sam. *LotR* 6.1.900 describes Cirith Ungol as "*a last unsleeping guard against any that might pass the vigilance of Morgul and of Shelob*". Aragorn's effect on Sauron was such that even this "*last unsleeping guard*" didn't work because he didn't take the reports of the Minas Morgul and Cirith Ungol staff seriously.

March 17th
- Frodo and Sam were still journeying along the Morgai.
- Shagrat brought Frodo's cloak and mithril shirt, and Sam's sword, to Sauron (App B.1094). Hammond and Scull refer to Tolkien's manuscript time-scheme for *LotR* (Marquette MSS 4/2/18) in which he said that news of Frodo's capture and news of his escape from Cirith Ungol reached Barad-dûr at roughly the same time.[47] This would no doubt have made Sauron take the "spies on the Stairs" reports seriously, but the army of the West was preparing to set out for the Morannon, so the distraction continued. Isildur's heir was more important (because he must be the one who had the Ring). According to MSS 4/2/18 Sauron now killed Shagrat. His own negligence and failure to listen to reports were partly responsible for the prisoner escaping, so he took it out on Shagrat. This was another sign of Aragorn's effect on Mordor management! [Shagrat's panic three days earlier, as illustrated by his words to Snaga, "*News must get through to Lugbúrz, or we'll both be for the Black Pits*"[48] was clearly justified.]

---

43. Op. cit. [7], *LotR* 5.9, p. 879.
44. Op. cit., *LotR* 5.9, p. 880.
45. Op. cit., *LotR* 6.2, p. 923.
46. Op. cit., *LotR* 6.2, p. 925.
47. W.G. Hammond and C. Scull, *The Lord of the Rings: A Reader's Companion*, London, HarperCollins Publishers, 2005, p. 608.
48. Op. cit. [7], *LotR* 6.1, p. 905.

March 18th
- The Captains of the West had set out and were heading east.
- All the roads in Mordor were full of Sauron's troops speeding north towards the Morannon where Sauron (correctly) assumed Aragorn's army was intending to do battle.
- Frodo and Sam, dressed as Orcs, were spotted by one of the Orc captains and forced to march with his army.

March 19th
- "*All the land now brooded as at the coming of a great storm...*" because Aragorn and Gandalf had broken down the bridge at Minas Morgul and set fire to the land around it - another little distraction for Sauron before they turned north. "*So the desperate journey went on, as the Ring went south and the banners of the kings rode north.*"[49]
- This extra distraction coincided with the point when Frodo and Sam, having managed to escape from the Orcs in the confusion of the converging armies near the Isenmouthe, now made themselves more visible by taking to the Barad-dûr road. During their three days of travelling along it they would meet no-one.
- As for Sauron: "*... even in the fastness of his own realm he sought the secrecy of night, fearing the winds of the world that had turned against him, tearing aside his veils, and troubled with tidings of bold spies that had passed through his fences*"[50] - because he had been ignoring reports of "spies on the Stairs" and concentrating exclusively on the "*bright sword*" and "*stern and kingly face*" he had seen in the Palantír, instead of keeping a proper watch.

March 20th
- The Army of the West headed north claiming all Sauron's attention, especially as their heralds were now repeatedly proclaiming the coming of "*The King Elessar*". [During the parley on March 25th the Mouth of Sauron would show that he was aware of the significance of the Elessar. Although he treated Aragorn (and Gandalf) with contempt, addressing him as "*thou*" and referring to the jewel as "*a piece of Elvish glass*", his own glance soon quailed before Aragorn's, as his master's had in the Orthanc-stone, and he "*gave back as if menaced with a blow*".][51]
- Frodo and Sam were travelling along the Barad-dûr road.

March 21st
- The Army of the West continued north, defeating an ambush of Orcs and Easterlings as they went. From then on the Nazgûl would follow their every move (*Lotr* 6.3.885-6).
- Frodo and Sam were travelling along the Barad-dûr road.

March 22th
- The Nazgûl continued to follow the Army of the West as it travelled northwards.
- Frodo and Sam now left the Barad-dûr road and turned south across the plain of Gorgoroth towards Mount Doom.

March 23rd
- The Army of the West left Ithilien and approached the Desolation of the Morannon. Aragorn dismissed the faint-hearted, giving them the option instead, of trying to retake Cair Andros from Sauron's forces.
- Frodo and Sam were now "*... thinking no more of concealment... Of all the slaves of the Dark Lord, only the Nazgûl could have warned him [Sauron] of the peril that crept, small but indomitable, into the very heart of his guarded realm. But the Nazgûl and their black wings were ... gathered far away, shadowing*

---

49. Op. cit. [7], *LotR* 6.3, p. 935.
50. Op. cit., *LotR* 6.3, p. 935.
51. Op. cit., *LotR* 5.10, pp. 888-9.

*the march of the Captains of the West, and **thither the thought of the Dark Tower was turned**.*"[52]

March 24th
- The Army of the West camped in the Desolation of the Morannon.
- Frodo and Sam reached the foot of Mount Doom.
- The Nazgûl continued their watch on the Army of the West.

March 25th
- The parley with the Mouth of Sauron took place.
- As it was getting light Frodo and Sam both experienced a sudden feeling of urgency as if they had been called: "*Now, now, or it will be too late!*"[53]
- As Frodo and Sam joined Sauron's path from Barad-dûr to the Cracks of Doom, Frodo yielded to a compulsion to look east. At the same time the clouds cleared, briefly exposing the topmost tower of the fortress. However "**The Eye was not turned to them**: *it was gazing north to where the Captains of the West stood at bay, and thither all its malice was now bent...*"[54]
It was not until Frodo put on the Ring, that Sauron was suddenly aware of "*the magnitude of his own folly*"[55], realising that he had been well and truly duped by Aragorn and that it was one of the insignificant spies on the stairs who had had the Ring.

Perhaps, in the brief interval between Frodo claiming the Ring and Gollum destroying it, Sauron had time to reflect on a few additional shocking facts, namely that:
- Isildur's heir had had the strength to reject the Ring.
- Isildur's heir had therefore had the strength to wrest control of the Palantír from him, and to deceive him in it, **unaided**.
- The Wise had deliberately set out to destroy the Ring.

*

Given the generally low profile of Aragorn's Palantír confrontation, it is easy to attribute the strategy of distracting Sauron to Gandalf. Such attribution is based on Gandalf's proposal, at the Last Debate on March 16th, to send a small army to the Morannon as bait to draw Sauron's forces that way in the hope that the area near Mount Doom would thus be relatively unwatched enabling Frodo to go undetected. He also argued that Sauron would regard the action as a rash and arrogant move which would confirm in his mind that someone in this small army was in possession of the Ring.

However, this interpretation - as I hope I have demonstrated - falls far short of the real extent of the diversion strategy, which was actually begun by Aragorn on March 6th, against Gandalf's advice. (The small army did not set off for the Morannon until March 18th.) By using the Orthanc-stone to show himself to Sauron Aragorn provided the necessary distraction while Frodo was still in Ithilien, before he had even met Faramir. Leaving it until March 18th to actually initiate such a strategy would have meant that Frodo would have had to negotiate the length of the Mountains of Shadow as far as the Cross Roads, enter the Morgul Vale and the Stairs of Cirith Ungol, and journey along the Morgai **without** the benefit of Sauron brooding exclusively on the "*bright sword*" and the "*stern and kingly face*" he had seen in the Palantír. Aragorn used the Palantír as soon as he obtained it precisely **because** he estimated that Frodo was likely to be dangerously exposed. He also told Legolas and Gimli immediately afterwards "*We must press our Enemy, and no longer wait upon him for the move.*"[56]. By the morning of March 6th he had already made **himself** the bait by drawing the full force of Sauron's aggression, fear, hatred and attention on to Isildur's heir rather than the borders of his own

---

52. Op. cit. [7], *LotR* 6.3, p. 938.
53. Op. cit., *LotR* 6.3, p. 942.
54. Op. cit., *LotR* 6.3, p. 942.
55. Op. cit., *LotR* 6.3, p. 946.
56. Op. cit., *LotR* 5.2, p. 780.

land. Nothing could have proved a more effective distraction for Sauron than the knowledge that an heir of Isildur was alive and kicking and bearing the sword, now reforged, which had robbed him of the One Ring and brought about his downfall three thousand years earlier. Note too that Aragorn resembled Elendil, so it wasn't just that he was heir to the Man who had cut off the Ring; he would also have reminded Sauron of the Man who had joined forces with the Elf Gil-galad to defeat him physically. After that he had not been able to take on bodily form again.

That this had happened **in spite of** Sauron's seven-hundred-year deployment of the Lord of the Nazgûl (in the guise of the Witch-king of Angmar) to wage war on the North Kingdom in an attempt to destroy the Dúnedain there would only have added to the effect. Who else but Aragorn, as far as Sauron was concerned, could be in possession of the Ring? Gandalf, who had already guessed what Aragorn had done, himself gave credit to him at the Last Debate with the words "*As Aragorn has begun, so we must go on...*"[57] before recommending that this diversion policy should be continued. The sending of the small Army of the West to the Morannon was merely the final element of a strategy which had already been in operation for ten days when the Last Debate was held. It couldn't possibly have had the same impact without Aragorn's confrontation with Sauron in the Palantír. Gandalf's words, "*... there are names among us that are worth more than a thousand mail-clad knights apiece*"[58] undoubtedly referred to Aragorn above all.

The other implication of interpreting the "diversion strategy" as merely the army sent to the Morannon is that Aragorn's huge personal achievement is ignored. Paul Kocher refers to the fact that the self-sacrificial courage of Frodo and Sam receives more attention than "*the equal if less **solitary** unselfish daring*"[59] [My emphasis] of those in the army. However the earlier, and more significant, part of the "diversion strategy", namely the Palantír confrontation, was most certainly a solitary struggle on Aragorn's part - more solitary than that of Frodo as there is no indication that Halbarad actually **helped** him with the confrontation. From then on Sauron's attention was very much concentrated on Aragorn above anything/anyone else.

*

It seems appropriate at this point to identify some further issues which shed light on the attitude of Sauron and Aragorn to each other, particularly relating to Sauron's misunderstanding of Aragorn in contrast with Aragorn's ability to read **him**.

In *UT* 3.4.i.439-441 we are told that around early September 3018 Sauron became aware (presumably from his spies or via the Ithil-stone) of the prophecy in Faramir's dreams, of Boromir's journey and of Gandalf's capture by Saruman. Concluding that neither Saruman nor any other of the Wise could have the Ring, but that Saruman might have an idea as to its whereabouts, he accordingly sent the Nazgûl openly (that is, clothed rather than invisible) to Isengard to tackle him. When this proved abortive, he sent them to search for the Ring. As far as he was concerned few could withstand even one of the Nazgûl and no-one would be able to withstand them when they were all together with their captain. This view would have been reinforced in late September when even the Dúnedain of the North were put to flight by them at Sarn Ford. However Aragorn himself was able to withstand five of them (including their captain) at Weathertop and he faced all Nine at the Bruinen Ford when he and Glorfindel drove them into the river. Given that he was clearly aware of their activities in the Breeland area (*LotR* 1.10.164-5,174) he may well have had other close encounters with them around the time of his first meeting with Frodo.

As recognised by Gandalf and Aragorn, Sauron was not worried about the possibility of the Ring being destroyed because it did not occur to him that his enemies would **want** to destroy it. If he had come to believe that the Ring was not in the possession of Saruman, Gandalf, Galadriel or Elrond, then he must surely have started to dwell increasingly on the possible existence of an heir of Isildur. Assuming that Sauron would have expected an heir of Isildur who was in possession of the One Ring to be openly leading an army against him, the fact that he actually found out about Aragorn by seeing him in the Orthanc-stone must have greatly increased the element of shock. The shock would have been exacerbated by the fact that, shortly before seeing Aragorn

---

57. Op. cit. [7], *LotR* 5.9, p. 880.
58. Op. cit., *LotR* 5.9, p. 882.
59. Op. cit. [27], Kocher, Chapter 6, p. 157.

in the Stone, he had seen Pippin in it while it was still (he assumed) in the possession of Saruman. Aragorn's cock-sureness (as Sauron would have interpreted it) in initiating the encounter as opposed to submitting to the "pull" of the Stone, plus his strength in taking control of it, must have led Sauron to believe that Isildur's heir now possessed the Ring after seizing it from the Hobbit. This would have been another reason why reports of **small** spies on the Stairs of Cirith Ungol would have been ignored. Even though Sauron knew that the Ring had originally been in the possession of a Hobbit called Baggins, he would now assume that this was no longer the case. In fact Aragorn's courage and daring were the more praiseworthy because he **didn't** have the Ring when he looked in the Palantír. Basically Sauron completely underestimated and misunderstood him. The concept of Isildur's heir refusing to have anything to do with the Ring would have been totally alien to him.

From Aragorn's point of view he knew that his destiny was to defeat Sauron and he must have naturally assumed that this would be in battle. This assumption is born out by the statement in *LotR* as he agonised over whether he should give up his plan of going to Minas Tirith with Boromir and instead accompany Frodo now that Gandalf was gone: "... *he believed that the message of the dreams* [Faramir's] *was a summons, and that the hour had come at last when the heir of Elendil should come forth and strive with Sauron for the mastery.*"[60] He may even have expected Sauron to appear in battle in bodily form. Did he see himself in a physical fight with him comparable with the one involving Gil-galad and Elendil?

In the event of course he would decide to follow the Orcs across Rohan. At the reunion with Gandalf in *LotR* 3.5.496-7 he listened to the Wizard's speech regarding Sauron's attention being currently on Minas Tirith and Isengard (due to the activities of Saruman and Denethor) and his inability to comprehend that anyone would want to destroy the Ring. Aragorn took all this on board (or more likely was aware of it anyway) and when he received the Palantír of Orthanc from Gandalf he saw clearly what he had to do to fight Sauron and to give the best chance to Frodo. His **chief** battle (in my opinion) against the Dark Lord was psychological: a mental, rather than a physical, wrestling match.

In the end Sauron was defeated because Aragorn defied Gandalf and looked into the Palantír, believing (rightly) that once Sauron knew of his existence nothing else would be of any importance. He used his own judgement instead of meekly following Gandalf's advice. One of Sauron's problems was that he had so dominated his servants - especially the Nazgûl - that they obeyed him blindly even against their better judgement. If the Lord of the Nazgûl, on sensing Frodo's presence on the north wall of the Morgul Vale (*LotR* 4.8.706-7), had followed up his misgivings the Ring would have been seized there and then and taken straight to Sauron. *UT* 3.4.ii.443 confirms that any of the Nazgûl, even their captain, would have brought the Ring to Sauron in such a situation.

*

The Palantír confrontation was a momentous achievement from the point of view of the courage and mental strength required, and because it was a pivotal action in the struggle to destroy the Ring. When Aragorn looked into the Palantír the destruction of the Ring began to look as if it might be achievable, a fact illustrated by Gandalf's glimmer of hope, expressed to Pippin on realising that Sauron's darkness was not due to Frodo: "*I believe that the news that Faramir brings has some hope in it.*"[61] Just prior to this, he had been brooding on Denethor's words that Frodo's venture was "a fool's hope". (See also the entry for March 10th above). The most visible result of Aragorn's action was the journey through the Paths of the Dead which brought about the defeat of the Corsairs and the victory at the Pelennor Fields. However the true and deeper significance was the effect on Sauron's mind, which led to a brooding obsession with Isildur's heir, making him oblivious to the **real** danger posed by Frodo, Sam and Gollum, and leading to a carelessness and lack of control which enabled them to continually elude capture. This distraction operated right up until the final denouement when the small Army of the West at the Morannon was saved by the timely destruction of the Ring ... but the timely destruction of the Ring was only made possible by the diversion strategy begun by Aragorn in a chamber at the top of the Hornburg on March 6th. Frodo, Sam and Gollum between them destroyed the Ring, but Aragorn had made it

---

60. Op. cit. [7], *LotR* 2.8, p. 368.
61. Op. cit., *LotR* 5.4, p. 815.

possible for them to do so.

The final significance of the Palantír confrontation was the effect it had on Aragorn himself during the remainder of the War of the Ring. Once he had made the decision to go through the Paths of the Dead and had succeeded in obtaining the support of Legolas and Gimli for his actions, he shook off his exhaustion and became strong and decisive, to the extent that it was the strength of his will and his charisma alone that enabled him and his companions to travel safely through the Haunted Mountain, to withstand the terror of the Dead and to endure the almost impossibly gruelling ride to Pelargir followed by the voyage up the river with a major battle at the end of it. After the battle he spent most of the night healing people then took part in the Last Debate the following morning prepared to continue acting as bait for Sauron - a role he carried out until the final moment when the Ring was destroyed. He did not falter once during this period but confidently made his own decisions, courageously tackling whatever came his way. The knowledge that he had been capable of mentally deceiving and defeating Sauron gave him the necessary faith in himself.

Sauron's Ring may have been Isildur's Bane, but Isildur's heir made himself Sauron's Bane.

CHAPTER 1.7 - KING ELESSAR

On May 1st TA 3019, Aragorn was crowned King of Gondor before the gates of Minas Tirith. He was eighty-eight when he became King but, due to his Númenórean lifespan, he would still have many years ahead of him. In fact he did not die until FA 120 at the age of two hundred and ten. Thus his time as King proved to be by far the longest section of his life. I therefore felt that it deserved to be studied in detail, rather than being dismissed as a "happy ever after" conclusion to his struggles. Genealogical Tables 2-6 are relevant to this chapter.

Before looking at Aragorn's reign I want first to consider the nature of his claims to the kingship. Although most emphasis in *LotR* is on the kingship of Gondor, Aragorn was the heir to two kingdoms - Gondor in the South and Arnor in the North - which together became known as the Reunited Kingdom after the War of the Ring reflecting the situation when Elendil - and briefly Isildur - was ruler of both kingdoms. As regards the kingship in the North where Aragorn had grown up there was never any dispute about his claim: the succession had passed directly from father to eldest son from Elendil onwards, continuing during the period when Arnor became split into three smaller kingdoms with the largest (Arthedain) being ruled by the senior member of Elendil's line, and also during the following years when the heirs of Elendil and Isildur were merely Chieftains of the Dúnedain. Aragorn himself was the sixteenth Chieftain.

However the situation was different in Gondor, as can be illustrated by looking at the case of Arvedui, the last King of the North Kingdom before power became vested in the Chieftains[1]. In TA 1944, during the reign of his father King Araphant, Arvedui made a claim for the throne of Gondor on the death of its King, Ondoher, along with that of his two sons. Arvedui based his claim on his direct descent from Isildur and on the fact that he was married to Ondoher's daughter Fíriel (now the only surviving child). The claim was rejected by the Council of Gondor, led by the Steward Pelendur, the reasons given being:
- That the crown of Gondor belonged solely to the heirs of Isildur's younger brother Anárion, since Isildur had, on the deaths of Elendil and Anárion, relinquished the realm to Anárion's son Meneldil while he himself went north intending to take up Elendil's kingship in Arnor
- That Gondor only recognised inheritance through sons - thus Fíriel had no right to her father's throne and Arvedui's marriage to her was therefore irrelevant

To this Arvedui explained that Elendil - father of both Isildur and Anárion - had actually been high king of both kingdoms of the Dúnedain. For practical reasons he had ruled in the North himself, committing the rule in the South jointly to his sons, but in no way relinquishing his royalty in Gondor where his name headed the line of kings. After the deaths of Elendil and Anárion, Isildur, as the elder son, had then become high king himself, and in similar vein continued to maintain his royalty in Gondor while committing the actual rule to Anárion's son so he could go north to take on his father's role. (In fact *UT* states that Isildur "*proclaimed his sovereign lordship over all the Dúnedain in the North and in the South*".)[2] Arvedui also pointed out that Númenórean law had recognised inheritance by daughters. The law had been changed to allow this when the sixth king of Númenor had no sons but did have a daughter. Prior to that, inheritance had been only by sons. For example the fourth king had been succeeded by his only son, not by his eldest (female) child Silmarien. It is significant, though, that the male line eventually died out in Númenor, and Elendil, Isildur and Anárion were actually

---
1. J.R.R. Tolkien, *The Lord of the Rings,* London, HarperCollins Publishers, 2007, 2nd edition, based on the 50th Anniversary Edition of 2004, App A.I.iv, pp. 1049-50.
2. C. Tolkien (ed.), *Unfinished Tales of Númenor and Middle-earth*, London, HarperCollins Publishers, 1998, first published in Great Britain by George Allen & Unwin 1980, *UT* Part 3, Chapter 1, p. 351.

directly descended from Silmarien not from her younger brother.

Arvedui received no response to his arguments and the Gondorian crown was subsequently claimed by Eärnil (II) who was of a more junior branch of the royal House and had won renown in battle. Arvedui did not press his claim because he did not have the power, or the will, to oppose the choice of Gondor. As Eärnil was wise and reasonable the friendship between the two lines - initiated by Arvedui's marriage to Fíriel - continued. The fact that Gondor would not recognise Arvedui's descent through the female line in no way alters the fact that Aragorn was a direct descendant from Fíriel just as he was from Arvedui himself. In addition, of course, this also made him a direct descendant of Anárion.

Arvedui was the last king of the North Kingdom, dying in TA 1975, and his son Aranarth became the first Chieftain of the Dúnedain over a much reduced, and increasingly secretive and wandering, people following nearly seven hundred years of war with the Witch-king of Angmar. App A.I.iv.1050 states that Arvedui's name - meaning "Last King" - was given to him at his birth by Malbeth the Seer who foresaw the failing of the kingship in the North Kingdom. He also prophesied that a choice would be offered to the Dúnedain and that if they chose the less hopeful option Arvedui would change his name and become king of a great realm. Otherwise "... *much sorrow and many lives of men shall pass, until the Dúnedain arise and are united again.*"[3] This clearly refers to Gondor's failure to accept Arvedui's claim. The treatment of Arvedui by Gondor partly explains why no claim was made for the kingship by any of the Chieftains prior to Aragorn. In addition the Northern Dúnedain, being depleted and weakened, had to rely on secrecy to protect and preserve Isildur's line until the time came for the prophecies to be fulfilled - namely with the finding of the Ring, the reforging of Elendil's sword and the birth of the particular heir of Elendil who was destined to redress Isildur's failure to destroy the Ring.

The line of the kings in Gondor also came to an end less than a hundred years later with Eärnil's son Eärnur who was captured by the Lord of the Nazgûl and was presumed to have died in Minas Morgul in TA 2050. From then on Gondor was ruled by the Stewards - an office which became hereditary in the House of Húrin. However, over the years, people in Gondor still remembered Arvedui's claim and the royal line in the North "... *which it was rumoured still lived on in the shadows.* **But against such thoughts the Ruling Stewards hardened their hearts.**"[4]. The text I have emphasised here, along with the case of Arvedui, explains the reaction of the Steward Denethor II in *LotR* to a possible claimant from the North. For example he said to Gandalf "*I am Steward of the House of Anárion ... Even were his* [Aragorn's] *claim proved to me, still he comes **but of the line of Isildur.**"*[5] [My emphasis]. This attitude of the Stewards provided further discouragement to potential claimants from the North. An interesting addition to this debate is Tolkien's letter to Richard Jeffery of Dec 17th 1972 where he states that Arnor means 'royal land' as being the realm of Elendil and so taking precedence over the southern realm of Gondor.[6] Thus in rejecting Arvedui Gondor rejected a claimant from the senior kingdom who was directly descended from Elendil.

Genealogical Table 2 shows Aragorn's descent from the female line of the Númenórean royal House. Table 3 shows his descent from Isildur and Anárion illustrating the claim made by Arvedui and Fíriel. Tables 4 and 5 show the Kings of Arnor and Gondor respectively, while Table 6 gives the Steward succession in Gondor to complete the picture.

In the event Aragorn didn't have to make an official claim for the kingship of Gondor. By the time Faramir said, "*... one has come to claim the kingship again at last*"[7] everything seemed to have happened by default: the death of Denethor leaving the Stewardship to Faramir who immediately recognised Aragorn as King; the last-minute victory at Pelennor Fields when all had seemed hopeless; the friendship and support of Éomer and Imrahil; and not least the recognition of Aragorn's healing powers which had enabled him to save the lives of many of his future subjects. In fact it could almost be said that Ioreth, the elderly woman from the Houses of Healing, was the one responsible for getting him recognised as King by the people of Gondor. It was her

---

3. Op. cit. [1], App A.I.iv, p. 1050.
4. Op. cit., App A.I.iv, p. 1053.
5. Op. cit., *LotR* 5.7, p. 854.
6. H. Carpenter (ed.), *The Letters of J.R.R. Tolkien*, with the assistance of Christopher Tolkien, London, HarperCollins Publishers, 1995. First published in Great Britain by George Allen & Unwin, 1981. Letter. 347, p. 428.
7. Op. cit. [1], *LotR* 6.5, p. 967.

memory of the "old wives' tale" about the hands of the king being the hands of a healer which resulted in Gandalf sending for Aragorn to heal Faramir, Éowyn and Merry (plus many others), and she was the one who subsequently spread the word about the King's return.

*

Aragorn's coronations and the symbols of royalty will now be considered.

The custom in Gondor while the Kings ruled had been for the dying King to give the crown to his successor in person. However as there had not been a King in Gondor for nearly a thousand years Faramir had arranged for the crown to be brought from the tomb of Eärnil the last King to be laid to rest in the House of the Kings. According to a note in App A.I.iii.1043 the crown of Gondor was originally a plain Númenórean war-helm which was said to have been actually worn by Isildur at the Battle of Dagorlad at the end of the Second Age. However during the reign of Atanatar Alcarin who died in TA 1226 (App A.I.ii.1038) it was replaced by the jewelled helm with which Aragorn was crowned. This was white, with wings of pearl and silver, gems of adamant in its circlet and a single jewel like a flame at its summit. The wings resembled those of a seagull to signify the kings who had come over the Sea (from Númenor). Even as a young man in the guise of "Thorongil" Aragorn had been recognised as "... *a great leader of men, by land **or by sea**"*[8] [My emphasis] and he saw himself as a sea-king. At his coronation, as he took the crown from Faramir, he repeated the words spoken by Elendil when he disembarked from his ship on to the shores of Middle-earth: "*Et Eärello Endorenna utúlien. Sinome maruvan ar Hildinyar tenn' Ambar-metta!*" [Translated as: "Out of the Great Sea to Middle-earth I am come. In this place will I abide, and my heirs, unto the ending of the world."][9] Aragorn too had arrived by water sailing up the Anduin from Pelargir, blown by the south wind from the sea.

In the kingdom of Arnor the chief mark of royalty was the Sceptre of Annúminas. In App A.I.iii.1043 we learn that the Kings of Númenor had had a different sceptre - the Sceptre of Númenor - which perished when Númenor was destroyed. Ar-Pharazôn was the last of the male line of the Kings and, as noted earlier, the succession passed to the line of Silmarien, the elder daughter and eldest child, of the fourth King of Númenor. Her line held the title "Lord of Andúnië", the office being marked by a silver rod; it was this rod which Elendil inherited from his father Amandil the last Lord of Andúnië, and was thus able to save from the drowning of Númenor. It subsequently became the Sceptre of Annúminas of the kingdom of Arnor. When the kings of Arnor were replaced by Chieftains, the Sceptre was kept at Rivendell along with the Shards of Narsil and the Ring of Barahir. Aragorn had been given the last two items as a young man before leaving Rivendell to become a Ranger in TA 2951, but Elrond had deliberately withheld the Sceptre of Annúminas "*for you have yet to earn it.*"[10]. It had been finally surrendered to him at the end of the War of the Ring at the same time as Elrond officially gave Arwen in marriage. The Ring of Barahir had survived because it too had belonged to the Lords of Andúnië, having been given to Silmarien by her father. As I stated in Chapter 1.2 this Ring had originally been a gift to Barahir, father of Beren, by the Elf Finrod Felagund in the First Age in return for saving his life. Aragorn gave it to Arwen when they plighted their troth in TA 2980 (App B.1090).

The Kings of Arnor did not have a crown but instead wore on their brows a white gem called the Elendilmir held in place by a silver fillet. In *LotR* it is referred to as "the Star of Elendil", "the Star of the North" and "the Star of the North Kingdom." However there is much more information in *UT*. There had in fact been two Elendilmirs, the first of which belonged to Silmarien, a "*white star of Elvish crystal upon a fillet of mithril*"[11]. Although it survived the drowning of Númenor and was brought to Middle-earth by Elendil, it was lost (supposedly for good) in the River Anduin along with Isildur's body when he was killed at the Gladden Fields while on his way back to his North Kingdom with the One Ring. During the battle the attacking Orcs avoided him, being afraid of the Elendilmir. There is a description of how even after he put the Ring on and became invisible, the Elendilmir on his brow "... *blazed forth red and wrathful as a burning star*"[12] again

---

8. Op. cit. [1], App A.I.iv, p. 1055.
9. Op. cit., *LotR* 6.5, p. 967.
10. Op. cit., App A.I.v, p. 1057.
11. Op. cit. [2], *UT* Part 3, Chapter 1, p. 359.
12. Op. cit., *UT* Part 3, Chapter 1, p. 355.

causing his enemies to avoid him. Covering his head with a hood he escaped to the Anduin and tried to swim across to the west bank. He became entangled in weeds and the Ring came off his finger rendering him visible again as he stood up in the water. This time the Elendilmir was his downfall as it shone out again frightening a few Orc watchers who loosed a few arrows at him before fleeing in terror. Isildur's three oldest sons also died at the Gladden Fields and he was succeeded by his fourth son Valandil who was living in Rivendell at the time of his father's death. The elven smiths of Rivendell made a new Elendilmir which was used by Valandil and his heirs up until the time when the Kings of the North Kingdom were replaced by Chieftains - after which it was kept in Rivendell until the War of the Ring. It was then brought to Aragorn by Elladan and Elrohir when they rode south with Halbarad and the other Dúnedain prior to the journey through the Paths of the Dead. Aragorn wore it at the Battle of the Pelennor Fields but then gave it back temporarily into the care of his foster brothers as he did not at that point want to enter Minas Tirith as King (*LotR* 5.8.861).

UT 3.1.358-9 also gives an account of the rediscovery, contrary to all expectations, of the original Elendilmir soon after Aragorn's coronation in Gondor. With the help of Gimli he was searching the Tower of Orthanc and they discovered that Saruman had been hoarding jewels and heirlooms, not only from Rohan but from burial mounds and tombs far and wide. They also found two items in a secret closet: the gold chain which had once hung round Isildur's neck bearing the One Ring, and the original Elendilmir. We are told that when Aragorn went North to take up the kingship of Arnor officially, Arwen bound the jewel on his brow rendering the onlookers silent in amazement at its splendour. Although the replacement Elendilmir was clearly inferior to the original it may still have had the ability to instil fear into the Orcs when Aragorn wore it at the Battle of the Pelennor Fields (and presumably at the Battle of the Morannon as well).

*

By the end of *LotR*, Aragorn had played his destined part in the defeat of Sauron, he had regained the kingships of Arnor and Gondor and he was married to the woman he loved after waiting for nearly seventy years. By pulling together the many scattered comments, hints and veiled references in the main text, Prologue and Appendices of *LotR*, as well as in various chapters in *UT*, it is possible to uncover a surprising amount of information on the nature, achievements, struggles, joys and sorrows of his reign. We can also try to answer questions such as: What kind of king was he? How did his subjects view him?

LotR 6.5.968-9 and App B.1095 tells of his first days as King when he received embassies from Dale and the Lonely Mountain, as well as from the East and South, the borders of Mirkwood, and Dunland. His actions showed mercy, justice and wisdom:
- He pardoned the Easterlings who had given themselves up after the Battle of the Morannon sending them away free.
- He made peace with Harad.
- He released the slaves of Mordor and made them owners of the cultivated area around Lake Núrnen in the south of that land.
- He praised and rewarded those who had shown courage in battle.
- He made Faramir Prince of Ithilien as well as making the Stewardship of Gondor hereditary in his line.

There was also the matter of passing judgement on Beregond for his treasonable act of shedding blood in the Houses of the Dead during Denethor's attempt to burn Faramir alive. Aragorn revoked the death penalty, but "punished" him by sacking him from the Citadel Guard and sending him away from Minas Tirith. However the reason for this was that Beregond was being promoted to be Captain of the Guard to Faramir in Ithilien. Thus Aragorn recognised and rewarded the courage and loyalty by which Faramir's life had been saved.

Other early events of Aragorn's reign are covered in *LotR*. During the journey with the departing guests following the wedding celebrations, the first stage was to Rohan for the funeral of Théoden. As the party entered the Drúadan Forest *en route*, Aragorn formally gave that land to Ghân-buri-Ghân and his people in perpetuity, with no-one being allowed to enter it without their leave.[13] A later stage of the journey took the (reduced) party to Isengard and a meeting with Treebeard. Here Aragorn gave the Ents free rein to plant trees in the surrounding valley in return for ensuring that no unauthorised person entered the Tower of Orthanc. The Ent Quickbeam then handed over the keys to the Tower.[14] Later, as referred to in *UT* 3.1.358, Orthanc would be restored and its Palantír set in place again. I assume that Aragorn would also have used the Palantír of Minas Tirith even though we are told in *LotR* that, following Denethor's suicide, "*... if any man looked in that Stone, unless he had a great strength of will to turn it to other purpose, he saw only two aged hands withering in flame*"[15]. Aragorn must surely have had the required "*strength of will*" to use this Palantír for his own purposes considering his feat in facing Sauron in the Orthanc-stone.

As Aragorn said to Faramir on appointing him Prince of Ithilien (*LotR* 6.5.969), further work would be required in destroying Minas Ithil/Morgul - it would be many years before the area would be wholesome enough to live in. No doubt there was much to do also in cleaning up Ithilien and Mordor itself. Another task was the restoring of Minas Tirith with Gimli's folk from the Lonely Mountain doing the building (including new gates of mithril and steel, and streets paved with white marble) and the folk of Legolas providing trees, song-birds and fountains. When Aragorn was King they moved from their original homes bringing some of their people with them, Gimli becoming Lord of the Glittering Caves of Aglarond at Helm's Deep and Legolas settling in Ithilien (App A.III.1080).

Further afield, Bard II King of Dale and Thorin III King of the Lonely Mountain had sent their ambassadors to Aragorn's coronation. They maintained a lasting friendship with Gondor, and their kingdoms came "*under the crown and protection of the King of the West.*"[16].

In *LotR* 6.7.993 Gandalf reassured Barliman Butterbur that the new King would be turning his attention to his North Kingdom, rebuilding the town of Fornost Erain and making the roads safe. App A.I.iii.1044 refers to the restoration of the town of Annúminas and the building of the King's house there. App B.1097 also records some significant events. Aragorn made the Shire a Free Land under the protection of the North Kingdom with "Big Folk" prohibited from entering it. In FA 14 Merry, Pippin and Sam were made Counsellors of the North Kingdom. Then two years later there is a record of Aragorn coming North himself. During his stay Sam's daughter Elanor was a maid of honour to Arwen, and Sam himself was awarded the Star of the Dúnedain - presumably a star-shaped brooch similar to the ones worn by the Dúnedain on their cloaks (*LotR* 5.2.778). This visit may well have been the one described in *UT* 3.1.359 (referred to earlier) when Arwen crowned Aragorn with the original Elendilmir found in Orthanc. Alternatively *HoM-e* IX.1.11 contains an Epilogue to *LotR* which refers to an earlier visit by Aragorn when Elanor was a baby[17] (she was born in TA 3021 or FA 1), so the northern coronation could have taken place then. However Tolkien eventually decided not to include the Epilogue and Christopher Tolkien states that he knows of no other mention of this earlier visit. Some years later in FA 32 the land between the Far Downs and the Tower Hills was added to the Shire as the Westmarch.

Although Aragorn had made peace with Harad following the War of the Ring, it was in fact many years before a full peace was achieved as Sauron's legacy of hatred lived on. This was true also of the lands in the East beyond the Sea of Rhûn. App A.II.1071 tells us that Éomer went riding into battle with Aragorn to subdue these lands until he [Éomer] was an old man - he was twenty-eight at the time of the War of the Ring. The Rohirrim continued to live under their own kings and laws, and Aragorn renewed the gift of the land of Rohan to them - it had originally been given to Eorl, the first King of the Mark, by the Steward Cirion in TA 2510 in recognition for his help against the Easterlings. Éomer, on his part, repeated the Oath of Eorl by which he undertook to aid Gondor against its enemies. The friendship between Gondor and Rohan was further strengthened by the marriages of Faramir and Éowyn, and Éomer and Lothíriel (Imrahil's daughter).

Aragorn continued to have a close relationship with the remaining members of the Fellowship. As already observed, Legolas and Gimli soon moved south from their original homes, while App B.1097 records that

---

13. Op. cit. [1], *LotR* 6.6, p. 976.
14. Op. cit., *LotR* 6.6, p. 980.
15. Op. cit., *LotR* 5.7, p. 854.
16. Op. cit., App B, p. 1095.
17. C. Tolkien (ed.), *The History of Middle-earth*, vol. IX, *Sauron Defeated*, London HarperColllins Publishers, 2002, first published in Great Britain by HarperCollins Publishers 1992, pp. 126, 135.

Sam, Rose and Elanor spent the year FA 22 living in Gondor. Also Merry and Pippin spent their last years there. There must have been much liaison on the cultural level too. *LotR*.Prologue.14-15 refers to the increased interest shown by the Hobbits in the history of the two kingdoms and mentions the libraries developed by the families of Merry, Pippin and Sam. Pippin in particular collected items relating to the history of Númenor and the rising of Sauron, and of Elendil and his heirs. Also Aragorn commissioned a copy of the Red Book giving Bilbo's and Frodo's accounts of the War of the Ring. This was duly made in the Shire and brought to him by Pippin on his retirement to Gondor in FA 64. A further example is the genealogical table of the Dwarves of the Lonely Mountain in App AIII.1079 which was prepared by Gimli specifically for Aragorn.

A final example of Aragorn's actions as King is given in *HoM-e* VIII.3.12. Note 45. The passage concerned was apparently written on the back of an early typescript of "The Last Debate":

> "*Then spoke Elessar: Many Guthrond would hold that your insolence merited rather punishment than answer from your king; but since you have in open malice uttered lies in the hearing of many, I will first lay bare their falsehood, so that all here may know you for what you are, and have ever been. Afterwards maybe a chance shall be given you to repent and turn from your old evil.*"[18]

This seems to describe a situation where Guthrond had made false accusations against the King - or against someone connected with him - and had challenged him to answer them. Rather than reacting by simply punishing the man Aragorn's reply showed his recognition of the need to refute the falsehood publicly, and also offered Guthrond the chance to make a new start. Aragorn, from his years of travelling incognito, would have appreciated the power of Sauron to turn folk to evil and understood the lasting legacy of the Dark Lord. However all this is pure speculation as Christopher Tolkien himself can shed no further light on this incident.

*

Having looked at the actions and events during Aragorn's reign, the questions arise as to what kind of king he was and how his subjects viewed him.

Paul Kocher says that Aragorn overcame Gondor's enemies by arms, but overcame Gondor itself by love[19]. His compassionate treatment of the faint-hearted before the Battle of the Morannon and his tireless healing during the night after the Battle of the Pelennor Fields, at a time when he himself was exhausted and grief-stricken, provide very good examples of actions which would inspire love. Ioreth's affectionate naming of him as "*our Elfstone*"[20] further illustrates Kocher's statement, as does her observation that although she found him "*not too soft in his speech*" he had "*a golden heart*". [Cf. "*All that is gold does not glitter*" in *The Riddle of Strider* poem.] Although clearly a man of great personal courage and prowess in battle - as leader and subordinate - Aragorn's chief renown had been prophesied, by his maternal grandmother Ivorwen, to be as a healer and renewer[21]. His work in renewing the glory and beauty of his kingdoms illustrates the latter, while his subjects themselves showed their acknowledgement and appreciation of his healing powers - as witnessed by the crowd which gathered, begging him to cure their loved ones following the healing of Faramir, Éowyn and Merry (*LotR* 5.8.871). Ioreth also referred to his healing hands, and the Warden of the Houses of Healing said, "*A great lord is that, and a healer; and it is a thing passing strange to me that the healing hand should also wield the sword.*"[22]. Both speakers also showed an awareness of the link between healing and the kingship in days past.

---

18. C. Tolkien (ed.), *The History of Middle-earth*, vol. VIII, *The War of the Ring*, London HarperColllins Publishers, 2002, first published in Great Britain by Unwin Hyman 1990, p. 427.
19. P. Kocher, *Master of Middle-earth: The Achievement of J. R. R. Tolkien*, London, Pimlico, 2002, first published in Great Britain by Thames & Hudson 1973, Chapter 6, p. 157.
20. Op. cit. [1], *LotR* 6.5, p. 966.
21. C. Tolkien (ed.), *The History of Middle-earth*, vol. XII, *The Peoples of Middle-earth*, London HarperColllins Publishers, 2002, first published in Great Britain by HarperCollins Publishers 1996, Foreword, p. xii.
22. Op. cit. [1], *LotR* 6.5, p. 958.

Another quotation from Paul Kocher states, *"Aragorn the man recedes from us into Aragorn the King"*, seemingly implying that Aragorn changed when he became King as he goes on to say, *"But there are still times when the regal robes are off"*.[23] He then refers to the finding of the White Tree sapling when Aragorn made it clear that he still wanted to be able to depend on Gandalf's counsel even though he knew that the Wizard's work in Middle-earth was finished. However I can find no evidence of any major change in Aragorn after he became King. His humility was certainly still present at the finding of the original Elendilmir in Orthanc when he referred even to the inferior later copy of the jewel as being *"... a thing of reverence, and above my worth."*[24]. App A.I.iii.1044 refers to Aragorn's visits to his northern kingdom. He was known to the Hobbits as *"Our King"* and we are told that everyone in the Shire was glad when he came to stay at his house in Annúminas. Because of the law that no "Big People" should enter the Shire, he would ride to the Brandywine Bridge to meet his friends and anyone else who wanted to see him. Apparently some people would *"... ride away with him and stay in his house as long as they have a mind."*[25] [Open house!] App A.I.iii emphasises that he "often" rode to the Bridge and that Pippin and Sam had stayed in his house *"many times"*. The impression given here is of a sociable, accessible and very "unstuffy" King who greatly valued his friends. Also it is typical of Aragorn that, having made a law that "Big People" couldn't enter the Shire, he abode by that law himself even though he, of all people, would certainly have been welcome there. A further example of the "common touch" is Sam's reassurance to Barliman Butterbur (appreciative of the Rangers at last) that the new King loved Bree and had a high opinion of the beer at the Prancing Pony (*LotR* 6.7.994). Perhaps another achievement of King Elessar's would have been the establishment of inns in Minas Tirith - something which Pippin had noticed as being sadly lacking in *LotR* 5.1.761! His years of wandering prior to the events of *LotR* were undoubtedly a major reason for his approachability. As well as the ruling families of the places he visited he would have met many of their subjects - the professional classes, tradespeople, farm-workers, criminals, "riff-raff", etc. - living, travelling and working with them incognito using his heightened perception to understand their motives, hopes and fears.

LotR contains the following passage immediately after the point when the newly-crowned Aragorn had officially entered Minas Tirith:

> *"In his time the City was made more fair than it had ever been, even in the days of its first glory; and it was filled with trees and with fountains, and its gates were wrought of mithril and steel, and its streets were paved with white marble;* **and the Folk of the Mountain laboured in it, and the Folk of the Wood rejoiced to come there; and all was healed and made good, and the houses were filled with men and women and the laughter of children...**"[26]

The text I have emphasised shows that Minas Tirith - like Annúminas - must have been a happy place to be, and also a very cosmopolitan city where Elves, Dwarves, Hobbits, and Men of all races felt at home. This reflected well on Aragorn and showed his success in uniting the Free Peoples as well as his commitment to his subjects' well-being. Overall he proved himself a strong ruler who combined the wisdom and dignity of kingship with friendship and humanity. He never lost that endearing common touch.

*

The final section of this chapter has a more sombre note.

In App A we are told that Aragorn and Arwen lived together as King and Queen *"for six-score years in great glory and bliss"*[27]. There can be no doubt of either the glory of the reign or of the personal happiness enjoyed by the pair. However there is a huge amount of underlying grief present in the final stage of their story, the most obvious examples being the heartbreak of Arwen's parting from her father and the rest of her Elven kin, and the bitter-sweet nature of her sacrifice of her immortality for love of Aragorn. Much is (rightly) made of

---

23. Op. cit. [19], Kocher, Chapter 6, p. 159.
24. Op. cit. [2], *UT* Part 3, Chapter 1, p. 359.
25. Op. cit. [1], App A.I.iii, p. 1044.
26. Op. cit., *LotR* 6.5, p. 968.
27. Op. cit., App A.I.v, p. 1062.

these in *LotR* and also of the sad partings at the Grey Havens when Frodo and Bilbo sailed West with Elrond, Galadriel and Gandalf.

Arwen and the Hobbits were not the only ones to endure heart-breaking separations though. Aragorn may have won Arwen at last, but he had lost just about everyone else he had been close to. Elrond had been a loving foster-father to him during his childhood and adolescence (and no doubt in later life too), providing him with protection, security, counsel, education and affection. Galadriel had done much to further his relationship with Arwen and had provided a safe haven and practical help for the Fellowship after the loss of Gandalf. Aragorn had first met Gandalf at the age of twenty-five. The wizard had been his mentor initially, but as time went on they had become mutual friends and confidants. Aragorn's grief at parting from these people must have been great. He would have suffered too from the parting with Frodo (whom he would not have seen again after the farewells at Dol Baran in *LotR* 6.6.982), and with Bilbo who had been a supportive friend for approximately sixteen years. Sadly he had not been strong enough to travel to Aragorn's wedding and their final parting would actually have been at Rivendell as the Fellowship set out. At the Battle of the Pelennor Fields Aragorn had lost his kinsman and standard-bearer Halbarad, the man who had brought thirty of the Dúnedain to his aid in Rohan, who had supported him during his Palantír confrontation with Sauron and had accompanied him through the Paths of the Dead. There may well have been other members of that party who lost their lives either at Pelennor Fields or the Morannon. His mother Gilraen had died in despair twelve years prior to Aragorn becoming King; it is not difficult to imagine that her absence, and that of Halbarad, would have been keenly felt during the celebrations which marked his coronation and marriage.

We know that Elladan, Elrohir and Celeborn remained in Middle-earth for an unspecified period after the Third Age ended (*LotR* Prologue.15-16), maybe permanently in the case of the first two, so it is possible that Aragorn and Arwen saw them again. Also there were the new friendships made during the War of the Ring, such as those with Imrahil, Éomer, Éowyn and Faramir. As stated earlier, there was much contact with Legolas and Gimli and with Merry, Pippin and Sam. However these friendships need to be seen in the context of Aragorn's Númenórean lifespan: although he became King when he was eighty-eight, he had well over half his life still ahead of him. From studying App B.1097-8 and *HoM-e* XII.1.vii.221-3 it is clear that all those mentioned were themselves long-lived: Imrahil died in FA 34 at the age of ninety-nine; Sam sailed to the West in FA 62 at the age of a hundred and two; Éomer was ninety-three when he died in FA 64 and in the same year Merry and Pippin, aged a hundred and two, and ninety-four respectively, came to spend their last years in Gondor; Faramir died in FA 83 at a hundred and twenty. I have not found any death-date for Éowyn, but she was close in age to Éomer and perhaps died between FA 60 and 70. The point is that all these people were younger than Aragorn (considerably so in most cases), yet he long outlived them: by thirty-seven years in Faramir's case, nearly sixty years in the case of Sam, Merry, Pippin and Éomer, and by well over eighty years in Imrahil's case. In *LotR* when speaking to Gandalf in the hallow on Mount Mindolluin, Aragorn referred to his Númenórean lifespan thus: "... *when those who are now in the wombs of women are born and have grown old, I too shall grow old...*"[28]. It seems to me that he must have experienced a similar sort of grief to that felt by the Elves who watched mortals whom they loved grow old and die after what seemed to them a tragically short lifespan. The feeling of loss at the time of his accession must have continued throughout his reign as the generations came and went - it may well have been that he also outlived the children of some of those mentioned. Out of all his contemporaries, old and young, during the Third Age, it was only the Elves and Gimli who survived him. [I suppose it is conceivable that some of the Northern Dúnedain who had been young people at the time of the War of the Ring could also have outlived him.]

As well as this underlying sense of loss, there must also have been an underlying sense of guilt. In App A it is stated that "... *grievous among the sorrows of that Age was the parting of Elrond and Arwen, for they were sundered by the Sea and by a doom beyond the end of the world.*"[29] The knowledge that this situation had come about because of Arwen's love for him must always have been at the back of Aragorn's mind. Arwen would have had the longing for the sea and the desire to go into the West shared by all the Elves. By winning her love Aragorn had deprived her of this essential part of her nature. The question also arises: Did Aragorn himself

---

28. Op. cit. [1], *LotR* 6.5, p. 971.
29. Op. cit., App A.I.v, p. 1062.

have a yearning for the sea and the Undying Lands? He had lived almost entirely among Elves during his childhood and continued to benefit from their friendship and counsel during later life, absorbing their values and culture along with those of Men. In addition, the account of Númenor in *Ak* states that the Númenóreans had been great mariners and that before the kings became corrupted they were revered in Middle-earth as sea-kings[30]. Indeed their original journey to take up residence in Númenor was necessarily by sea, and during peace-time their main interest was in ship-building and sea-craft. Aragorn's great ancestor Elendil (along with his father Amandil) had been a great sea-captain. Aragorn himself was clearly well used to ships as shown by the manner of his arrival at Pelennor Fields, and by his earlier exploits when serving Gondor under his alias of "Thorongil".

After the drowning of Númenor the Dúnedain, now in exile in Middle-earth, continued to yearn for the immortality which King Ar-Pharazôn had arrogantly tried to wrest from the Valar, and also retained their interest in sea-faring. *Ak*.337 describes how the Dúnedain believed that the summit of the Meneltarma (the mountain in the centre of Númenor) still existed as a lonely island from which it would be possible to glimpse the Undying Lands, and their mariners tried to find it on their voyages, but without success. *RoP* describes how one of the Palantíri was set up in the Tower of Elostirion on the Tower Hills so that it looked only to the West. It is stated that *"Thither Elendil would repair, and thence he would gaze out over the sundering seas, when the yearning of exile was upon him..."*[31] even seeing as far as Tol Eressëa. The Sea was in Aragorn's blood and it seems to me that it would have been perfectly natural for him to yearn for it and want to sail West - especially in his darkest moments during his years of wandering. App A.I.i.1035 refers to the resentment felt by the descendants of Elros, first King of Númenor, because he chose to be numbered among Men rather than Elves - Aragorn was one of these descendants. The words of Faramir in Henneth Annûn as he observed the minute's silence before supper show that Númenor and the West were still very much revered by the Dúnedain: "... *we look towards Númenor that was, and beyond to Elvenhome that is, and to that which is beyond Elvenhome and will ever be.*"[32].

Aragorn and Arwen had a son, Eldarion, and an unspecified number of daughters whose names are not recorded. These children would not have known Elrond, Galadriel or Gandalf, nor perhaps have fully appreciated the sacrifice made by their mother. The sundering from the old life at the end of the Third Age had been final and complete.

It is quite clear then that Aragorn had many and varied struggles still to face when he became King. One not yet emphasised would have been the struggle to leave a prosperous, peaceful kingdom to his successor. His reign was far from the fairy-tale ending that a casual interpretation might assume from the euphoria of the coronation and wedding in *LotR* 6.5.965-8, 972-3. The conversation between him and Gandalf on Mount Mindolluin showed his yearning to continue receiving Gandalf's counsel. Aragorn was under no illusion as to the task and burden which lay ahead.

*

It has been suggested to me that Aragorn must have found it difficult to adapt to a life of indoor luxury after living rough and outside for much of his earlier life. This remark set me wondering whether he wouldn't have been happier if his eventual resting place had been in a green barrow in Arnor rather than an elaborate tomb in Gondor. After all he came from the Northern Kingdom originally and was at one with nature and the outdoor life, with his travelling, and his knowledge of the geography of Middle-earth, plants, birds, animals, etc. - in addition to his absorption of Elvish values and culture in his formative years. On the other hand I have stated myself that his reign formed the largest portion of his life, so he had plenty of time to adapt - and maybe Paul Kocher is right and Aragorn did change in some ways when he became King. It has to be admitted too that the Fourth Age was the Age of Men and the Elves were sailing West or fading in Middle-earth. Aragorn's adaptation to luxury would perhaps have depended on how he viewed his years of wandering. Some of it

---

30. C. Tolkien (ed.), *The Silmarillion*, London, HarperCollins Publishers, 1999, first published in Great Britain by George Allen & Unwin 1977, pp. 314-5.
31. Op. cit., *Ak* p. 350.
32. Op. cit. [1], *LotR* 4.5, p. 676.

would undoubtedly have been totally traumatic: Mordor border areas, lands under Sauron's sway, periods of cold, danger, starvation, sleep-deprivation, illness, injury and loneliness. On the other hand he must have been happy during his youthful service in Rohan and Gondor - especially the latter where he was trusted, loved and successful. There was also the fascination of seeing many different lands, flora, fauna, customs, etc. as well as getting to know his future subjects. There must too have been many times of camaraderie with his fellow Dúnedain of the North. It is to be hoped that a bit of his earlier persona still survived in him to the end as the demise of Strider the Ranger would be a matter for regret.

CHAPTER 1.8 - DEATH

This chapter describes Aragorn's death explaining the manner of it in the context of his Númenórean ancestry and heritage. The main sources are App A.I.v and *Ak*.

Aragorn died on March 1st FA 120, his two hundred and tenth birthday, voluntarily giving up his life while still in possession of his faculties, and while his heir was in his prime. App A.I.v[1] tells us that "*... he felt the approach of old age and knew that the span of his life-days was drawing to an end*". A grief-stricken Arwen, knowing that he now intended to die willingly, took him to task for leaving his people before his time. He replied "*Not before my time ... For if I will not go now, then I must soon go perforce. And Eldarion our son is a man full-ripe for kingship.*" Thereupon he laid himself down on a specially prepared bed in the House of the Kings and took leave of Eldarion giving him the crown of Gondor and the Sceptre of Arnor. He tried to make Arwen see that this was preferable to him waiting until he became "*unmanned and witless*", finally telling her "*I am the last of the Númenóreans ... and to me has been given not only a span thrice that of Men of Middle-earth, but also **the grace to go at my will, and give back the gift.***" [My emphasis]. Shortly afterwards he bade farewell to Arwen and fell into sleep and then death.

To appreciate the manner and significance of Aragorn's death it is necessary to look at the history of the Númenórean Kings.

At the end of the First Age of Middle-earth, the island of Númenor was created by the Valar, between the Undying Lands and Middle-earth, and given to the races of Men who had remained loyal to the Elves during the war with Morgoth. These Men were the first Dúnedain and they settled in Númenor at the beginning of the Second Age. The Valar did not have the power to reward them by making them immortal, but they were able to grant them a much longer lifespan than other Men - three to four hundred years or more in the case of the royal line. Death was regarded as the gift of Ilúvatar to Men as it enabled them to escape from the world - as opposed to the Elves who were immortal as long as the world lasted and were thus forced to remain in it indefinitely. In the early (uncorrupted) days of Númenor its Kings and Queens did not fear death and would die willingly when they felt the first signs of old age, rather than clinging to life until they became senile and decrepit and then died in spite of themselves. Also, as they tended to marry late, their deaths were usually timed so that their heirs came to the throne when they were in their prime rather than when they were starting to age themselves.

However about half-way through the Second Age, the Númenórean Kings became corrupted by the influence of the Shadow of Morgoth and the growing power of Sauron. As a result they began to see death as something to be feared, and clung to life, regardless of its quality and their state of mind and body, rather than giving it up voluntarily with faith and trust. The final upshot of this was the voyage of King Ar-Pharazôn to Valinor with the intention of forcing the Valar to grant him immortality. This action led to the destruction of Númenor and the escape of Elendil and his sons (who had remained faithful to the Valar) to Middle-earth and exile.

The significance of Aragorn's title of the Renewer (referred to in *LotR* 5.8.863, and prophesied by Ivorwen in *HoM-e* XII Foreword[2]) was that he renewed the glory of early Númenor, both in the beauty of his restored kingdoms and in his own person with his resemblance to "*the kindly kings of the ancient days*" referred to in *Ak*[3]. As a direct descendant of the Númenórean Kings he had inherited not only their extended lifespan but also, in his own words to Arwen which I emphasised earlier, "*... the grace to go at my will, and give back the gift.*" Thus, like the Númenórean Kings before the corruption of Sauron had set in, he gave up his life willingly

---
1. J.R.R. Tolkien, *The Lord of the Rings*, London, HarperCollins Publishers, 2007, 2nd edition, based on the 50th Anniversary Edition of 2004, p. 1062.
2. C. Tolkien (ed.), *The History of Middle-earth*, vol. XII, *The Peoples of Middle-earth*, London HarperColllins Publishers, 2002, first published in Great Britain by HarperCollins Publishers 1996, p. xii.
3. C. Tolkien (ed.), *The Silmarillion*, London, HarperCollins Publishers, 1999, first published in Great Britain by George Allen & Unwin 1977, p. 328.

while his mind and body were still sound. He did not cling to life until he lost his faculties thereby depriving Eldarion of the chance to take on the kingship while he was at the height of his mental and physical strength. As stated in Tolkien's letter to Robert Murray in November 1954: "*A good Númenórean died of free will when he felt it to be time to do so.*".[4]

The subject of Aragorn's death is also raised in *Athrabeth Finrod ah Andreth* (*HoM-e* X Part Four). This piece of writing is set in the First Age and concerns a discussion between the Elf Finrod Felagund (a brother of Galadriel) and Andreth a wise-woman of the House of Bëor (she was actually the great-aunt of Beren) about the different fates of Elves and Men. The reference to Aragorn is in Author's [i.e. Tolkien's] Note 4 which talks about the special cases of mortals who were allowed to sail oversea with the Elves [i.e. Frodo, Bilbo, Sam and Gimli]. Note 4 states that this gave them the chance to die "*... according to the original plan for the unfallen: they went to a state in which they could acquire greater knowledge and peace of mind, and being healed of all hurts both of mind and body, could at last surrender themselves: die of free will, and even of desire, in 'estel'. A thing which Aragorn achieved without any such aid.*"[5] [My emphasis]. This achievement was impressive: it is true that Aragorn did not actually bear the Ring, but the Ring - and the need to resist it - had dominated his life for nearly seventy years by the time he became King. It was **because** of the Ring that he had been the subject of a relentless search by Sauron for the heir of Isildur. He had also seen many of the horrors of Mordor at first hand, travelling in the Morgul Vale on at least two occasions, withstanding Nazgûl and of course confronting and overcoming Sauron in the Palantír. He may even have been to Mordor itself. His life had included more than enough close contact with the Shadow to justify the reward of a sojourn in the Undying Lands - but he was able to die in peace without that.

Regarding the word "estel" in the passage just quoted: this is defined earlier in the *Athrabeth* as hope based on trust in the unknown, as opposed to hope which has some foundation in actual knowledge. Aragorn had no fear of death because he hoped and trusted that there was something good to come afterwards. His last words (spoken to Arwen) were, "*In sorrow we must go, but not in despair.* **Behold!** *we are not bound for ever to the circles of the world, and beyond them is more than memory. Farewell!*"[6] [My emphasis]. At first glance this speech seems to reflect his belief in a good outcome. However another interpretation is possible, based on the word 'behold'. 'Behold' means seeing or perceiving via the visual (or sometimes mental) faculty. Did Aragorn, at the point of passing from life to death, actually perceive that there was indeed something more than memory ahead for them? His words following "Behold!" seem to be a statement of fact. To explore this idea a bit more I looked at occurrences of 'behold' in the main text of *LotR* and identified three main ways of using the word, namely:

As an exhortation to look at something, for example:
- "**Behold** *Isildur's Bane!*"[7]. Elrond when Frodo held up the Ring for the Council to see.
- "**Behold** *the King!*"[8]. Faramir to the crowd at Aragorn's coronation.

Meaning simply to see or look at, for example:
- "They were terrible to **behold**!"[9]. Frodo to Gandalf referring to the Nazgûl.
- "*... I was grieved to* **behold** *it.*"[10]. Legolas speaking of the parting between Aragorn and Éowyn at Dunharrow.

However in twenty-one out of the forty occurrences I found in the main text of *LotR*, the word 'behold' is followed immediately by an exclamation-mark and then a reference to something momentous or revealing, sometimes with an element of shock or realisation. For example:
- "**And behold!** *when he washed the mud away, there in his hand lay a beautiful golden ring ...*"[11].

---

4. H. Carpenter (ed.), *The Letters of J.R.R. Tolkien*, with the assistance of Christopher Tolkien, London, HarperCollins Publishers, 1995. First published in Great Britain by George Allen & Unwin, 1981. Letter. 156, p. 205.
5. C. Tolkien (ed.), *The History of Middle-earth*, vol. X, *Morgoth's Ring*, London HarperColllins Publishers, 2002, first published in Great Britain by HarperCollins Publishers 1993, p. 341.
6. Op. cit. [1], App A.I.v, p. 1063.
7. Op. cit., *LotR* 2.2, p. 247.
8. Op. cit., *LotR* 6.5, p. 968.
9. Op. cit., *LotR* 2.1, p. 222.
10. Op. cit., *LotR* 5.9, p. 874.
11. Op. cit., *LotR* 1.2, p. 53.

Gandalf to Frodo relating the story of how Déagol found the One Ring in the River Anduin.
- "... *and behold! it was brought within my grasp.*"[12]. Galadriel when Frodo offered her the Ring after she had spent long years wondering what she would do in such a situation.
- "... *and behold! he had a kingly crown; and yet upon no head visible was it set.*"[13]. Referring to the Lord of the Nazgûl as he threw back his hood at the gates of Minas Tirith.
- "... *and behold! a little mist was laid on it ...*"[14]. Referring to Éowyn's breath on Imrahil's vambrace thus supporting his view that she was still alive.
- "... *and behold! upon the foremost ship a great standard broke ...*"[15]. Referring to the raising of Arwen's standard as Aragorn arrived at the Pelennor Fields in the ships of the Corsairs.
- "... *behold! their enemies were flying ...*"[16]. At the Battle of the Morannon after the Ring had been destroyed.

There is a further example of such use in App A when the young Aragorn, newly aware of his true identity, was wandering in the woods of Rivendell singing of Lúthien and Beren: "*And behold! there Lúthien walked before his eyes in Rivendell ...*"[17] He was of course seeing Arwen for the first time.

This study of the use of 'behold' followed by an exclamation-mark convinced me that Aragorn's dying words fit the same pattern, with him experiencing a sudden realisation that his faith was to be rewarded. A similar interpretation has in fact been suggested by Richard C. West who states "*Tolkien normally uses the word 'behold' only when there is something real to be seen ...*"[18].

*

In *Ak* it is stated that the Númenóreans went to great effort to find methods of recalling life, or at least of prolonging it. They failed but they did achieve "*... the art of preserving incorrupt the dead flesh of Men*"[19]. It is evident from the words of Denethor in *LotR*, prior to cremating himself, that this process was the norm in Gondor too: "*To my pyre! ... No tomb! No long slow sleep of death embalmed.*"[20] A little later as Pippin accompanied him and the wounded Faramir into the Houses of the Dead he saw marble tables each bearing a sleeping form with hands folded and head pillowed on stone. The words "sleeping form" imply that these were not stone effigies but the actual embalmed bodies. In App A.I.iv.1052 we are told that during the years when Gondor was ruled by the Stewards, the crown remained in the lap of King Eärnil who was the last King to be laid to rest in the Houses of the Dead prior to the Stewards' rule. Again the implication is that it was Eärnil's embalmed body which held the crown and from which it would be retrieved by Faramir for Aragorn's coronation nearly a thousand years later. App B records that Merry and Pippin were laid in the Houses of the Dead when they died, being regarded as "*... among the Great of Gondor*"[21]. After Aragorn's death their beds were placed beside his.

---

12. Op. cit. [1], *LotR* 2.7, p. 365.
13. Op. cit., *LotR* 5.4, p. 829.
14. Op. cit., *LotR* 5.6, p. 845.
15. Op. cit., *LotR* 5.6, p. 847.
16. Op. cit., *LotR* 6.4, p. 949.
17. Op. cit., App A.I.v, p. 1058.
18. R.C. West, "'*Her Choice was made and her Doom appointed*': Tragedy and Divine Comedy in the Tale of Aragorn and Arwen', in W.G. Hammond and C. Scull (eds.), *The Lord of the Rings 1954-2004: Scholarship in Honor of Richard E. Blackwelder*, Milwaukee, Marquette University Press, 2006, pp.317-329. To support his view West refers to the examples of the word "behold" given in Richard E. Blackwelder's A Tolkien Thesaurus, pp. 326, 329.
19. Op. cit. [3], *Ak* p. 318.
20. Op. cit. [1], *LotR* 5.4, p. 825.
21. Op. cit., App B p. 1098.

CHAPTER 1.9 - NAMES AND TITLES

This chapter has two purposes:
- To list Aragorn's names and titles along with their origin, meaning and use
- To look at the process whereby his true identity was revealed during the course of the events of TA 3018-9

LotR 2.1 contains the following conversation:
"Suddenly Bilbo looked up. 'Ah, there you are at last, *Dúnadan!*' he cried.
'Strider!' said Frodo. 'You seem to have a lot of names.'"[1]
Note that at this point in the narrative Frodo had already come across the name "Aragorn" for his friend as well - on receipt of Gandalf's letter in Bree.

Many people in *LotR* have multiple names and titles, but Aragorn must hold the record. His situation is also particularly complex for a number of reasons:
- Some of his names exist in two different languages, for example Elvish (either Quenya or Sindarin) and Common Speech.
- Some of his names are the subject of prophecies. These prophecies will only be mentioned briefly in context as I have treated them in much more detail in Chapter 1.2.
- In some cases a name also gives rise to one or more titles.
- Some of his titles contain a reference to one of his ancestors, for example Isildur.

*

Aragorn's names are now listed with brief explanations of their language, origin and meaning as appropriate. They are given in alphabetical order, except where it is necessary to keep related forms together. Where a name gives rise to a title, or titles, these are also discussed. Titles which are not directly linked to one of Aragorn's names are listed separately.

Aragorn
This was a Sindarin name and was given to him at his birth. It was often combined with his patronymic, hence "Aragorn son of Arathorn" or "Aragorn, Arathorn's son". In Rohan, after Gandalf had informed people of Aragorn's identity, he was usually referred to as "Lord Aragorn" or "The Lord Aragorn" though Théoden addressed him as "son of Arathorn" at one point (*LotR* 3.7.539) as did Éomer (*LotR* 3.2.436).
In *HoM-e* XII Foreword Christopher Tolkien refers to a letter he received from Christopher Gilson (a leading member of the Elvish Linguistic Fellowship) informing him of a passage relating to *The Tale of Aragorn and Arwen* which he had seen in a text at Marquette University[2]. Part of this passage states: "... *and his father gave him the name* **Aragorn**, *a name used in the House of the Chieftains. But Ivorwen* [Aragorn's maternal grandmother] *at his naming stood by, and said* '**Kingly Valour**' *(for so that name is interpreted)*..." [My emphasis]. Christopher Gilson had gone on to observe that this seemed to be the only place where the name Aragorn is translated, referring to a letter Tolkien wrote to Richard Jeffery on December 17th 1972 to back this up: "*The names in the line of Arthedain are peculiar in several ways; and several, though S.* [Sindarin] *in form,*

---
1. J.R.R. Tolkien, *The Lord of the Rings,* London, HarperCollins Publishers, 2007, 2nd edition, based on the 50th Anniversary Edition of 2004, *LotR* 2.1, p. 232.
2. C. Tolkien (ed.), *The History of Middle-earth*, vol. XII, *The Peoples of Middle-earth*, London HarperColllins Publishers, 2002, first published in Great Britain by HarperCollins Publishers 1996, Foreword, p. xii.

are not readily interpretable. But it would need more historical records and linguistic records of S. [Sindarin] *than exist (sc. than I have found time or need to invent!) to explain them.*"[3] Elizabeth M. Stephen refers to an alternative meaning of the name[4] in Tolkien's commentary, *Words, Phrases and Passages in various tongues in the Lord of the Rings*, published by Gilson in Parma Eldalamberon XVII (a journal of the Elvish Linguistic Fellowship). Here the meaning of "gorn" is given as "dread", "reverence" or "awe", thus giving the meaning "revered king" when combined with "ara".[5]

Dúnadan

This name, the singular form of Dúnedain, was Sindarin meaning "*Man of the West*", that is a Númenórean. As Bilbo explained to Frodo, the people in Rivendell often called Aragorn that - or even "***The Dúnadan***"[6]. Bilbo himself used it, and so did Glorfindel at his meeting with Aragorn on the way to the Bruinen Ford: "*Ai na vedui Dúnadan!*"[7]

Aragorn was the sixteenth Chieftain of the Dúnedain, the Men descended from the Númenóreans. This title actually applied only to the Northern Dúnedain and when Elrond introduced him to Boromir he called him "*Chief of the Dúnedain in the North*".[8] Similarly when Faramir announced Aragorn's titles at his coronation he called him "*chieftain of the Dúnedain of Arnor*".[9] As Aragorn arrived at the Houses of Healing, he declared that he wanted to be known as "*Captain of the Dúnedain of Arnor*" at this stage, rather than being acknowledged as King while the war with Sauron was still being fought.[10] "Captain" here is a more military title and is frequently used of Faramir in a battle context.

In App A.I.v.1058-9 Elrond, after informing the twenty-year-old Aragorn of his true identity called him "***Lord** of the Dúnedain*" [My emphasis] thus perhaps indicating respect for his young foster-son's high rank and noble descent. Aragorn himself used the same title when introducing himself to Arwen at their first meeting.

Elessar/Elfstone

The Quenya "Elessar" along with its Common Speech equivalent "Elfstone" was the name of the green jewel which Aragorn received from Galadriel when the Fellowship visited Lothlórien (*LotR* 2.8.375). He wore it on his breast thereafter and "Elessar/Elfstone" subsequently became his name as King, being given to him by the people of Gondor on account of the jewel and its association with healing. Galadriel had addressed him by both versions of the name as she presented it to him: "*Elessar, the Elfstone of the House of Elendil!*".[11] "Elfstone" was also used by Arwen in her message to Aragorn which was delivered by Halbarad: "*Fare well, Elfstone!*"[12] She used it again when she presented her white gem to Frodo: "*... wear this now in memory of Elfstone and Evenstar...*"[13]

Other uses of these two names include:
- "*the Elfstone*" and "*Elessar of the line of Valandil, Isildur's son, Elendil's son of Númenor*" by Faramir at Aragorn's coronation.[14]
- "*the Lord Elfstone*" by Bergil[15] and Ioreth[16].
- "*our Elfstone*" by Ioreth[17].

---

3. H. Carpenter (ed.), *The Letters of J.R.R. Tolkien*, with the assistance of Christopher Tolkien, London, HarperCollins Publishers, 1995. First published in Great Britain by George Allen & Unwin, 1981. Letter. 347, p. 426.
4. E.M. Stephen, *Hobbit to Hero: The Making of Tolkien's King*, Moreton in Marsh, ADC Publications Ltd., 2012, Chapter 2, pp. 53-4.
5. C. Gilson (ed.), *Words, Phrases and Passages in various tongues in 'The Lord of the Rings'*, Mountain View, CA: Parma Eldalamberon XVII, 2007.
6. Op. cit. [1], *LotR* 2.1, p. 233.
7. Op. cit., *LotR* 1.12, p. 209.
8. Op. cit., *LotR* 2.2, p. 246.
9. Op. cit., *LotR* 6.5, p. 967.
10. Op. cit., *LotR* 5.8, p. 862.
11. Op. cit., *LotR* 2.8, p. 375.
12. Op. cit., *LotR* 5.2, p. 775.
13. Op. cit., *LotR* 6.6, p. 975.
14. Op. cit., *LotR* 6.5, p. 967.
15. Op. cit., *LotR* 5.10, p. 884.
16. Op. cit., *LotR* 6.5, p. 966.
17. Op. cit., *LotR* 6.5, p. 966.

- "*The King Elessar*" by the heralds of the Army of the West[18].
- "*in Aragorn Elessar the dignity of the kings of old was renewed*"[19]

These names were also the subject of prophecies: by Gandalf - under his name Olórin - in *UT*[20] 2.4 (*The Elessar*) and by Ivorwen in *HoM-e* XII xii Foreword. In each case it was foreseen that someone would come in the future and take the name of a green stone as his own name, with Olórin's prophecy actually specifying the name "Elessar" and Ivorwen's emphasising the healing properties of the jewel. See *LotR* 5.8 where it is stated "*... and so the name which it was foretold at his birth that he should bear was chosen for him by his own people.*"[21]

Envinyatar

This was a Quenya name meaning "The Renewer" and both versions were used by Aragorn himself in *LotR* 5.8.863 when he explained some of his titles to Prince Imrahil. Aragorn's role as a renewer was also part of Ivorwen's "green stone" prophecy.

Estel

This name was Sindarin for "hope" and was used during Aragorn's childhood in Rivendell because "*his true name and lineage were kept secret at the bidding of Elrond*"[22]. It reflected Ivorwen's prophetic words: "*If these two* [Gilraen and Arathorn] *wed now,* **hope** *may be born for our people...*"[23] [My emphasis]. Gilraen clearly carried on using this name for her son as she addressed him as "Estel" in her last meeting with him before her death, seventy-four years after the name had been given to him. In addition her last recorded words to him were, "*I gave Hope to the Dúnedain, I have kept no hope for myself.*"[24] The initial capital in the first occurrence of "Hope" must indicate Aragorn himself. Arwen too continued to use this name, addressing Aragorn as "Estel" at their betrothal, and as her last words to him as he died, "*Estel, Estel!*"[25]. Thus although the name was originally an incognito to prevent Aragorn's existence being discovered by Sauron it was used until the end by the two women in his life.

Longshanks

The only use of this name is by the Breelander Bill Ferny in *LotR* 1.11.181. As he was particularly hostile to Aragorn, it was clearly intended as an insult.

Strider/Telcontar

In *LotR* Aragorn told Bilbo "*They call me that in Bree*", referring to the name "Strider" which Bilbo had not come across before.[26] As Frodo and his companions first met Aragorn in Bree they too knew him by that name, continuing to use it long after they knew his real name. For example Pippin startled Prince Imrahil by calling Aragorn "*Strider*"[27], while Merry inadvertently used it while in the company of Théoden and Éomer before hastily changing it to "*the Lord Aragorn*"[28] and Sam even addressed him as "*Strider*" on the Field of Cormallen[29]. Bill Ferny, not content with just "Longshanks" to express his contempt, coined the variation "*Stick-at-naught Strider*" following this up with the comment that he had heard "*other names not so pretty*".[30]

As Aragorn made clear at the Council of Elrond (*LotR* 2.2.248) he initially regarded "Strider" as a scornful nickname, but due to his growing friendship with the Hobbits he came to feel sufficient affection for it to adopt its Quenya translation "Telcontar" as the name of his Royal House after he became King. Like "Elfstone", "Strider" too was technically a name chosen for him by his own people - namely the Bree-folk - though for

---

18. Op. cit. [1], *LotR* 5.10, p. 885.
19. Op. cit., App A.I.iii, p. 1044.
20. C. Tolkien (ed.), *Unfinished Tales of Númenor and Middle-earth*, London, HarperCollins Publishers, 1998, first published in Great Britain by George Allen & Unwin 1980, p. 323.
21. Op. cit. [1], *LotR* 5.8, p. 871.
22. Op. cit., App A.I.v, p. 1057.
23. Op. cit., App A.I.v, p. 1057.
24. Op. cit., App A.I.v, p. 1061.
25. Op. cit., App A.I.v, p. 1063.
26. Op. cit., *LotR* 2.1, p. 232.
27. Op. cit., *LotR* 5.8, p. 863.
28. Op. cit., *LotR* 5.3, p. 797.
29. Op. cit., *LotR* 6.4, p. 953.
30. Op. cit., *LotR* 1.11, p. 181.

different reasons.

Thorongil

This name, which was Sindarin and composed of two elements meaning "eagle" and "star", was used by people in Gondor during Aragorn's youthful service there, incognito, on account of the star he wore on his cloak and his eagle-like swiftness and keen eyes. It may also have been used by the Rohirrim during a similar period of service prior to his time in Gondor.

Wingfoot

When Éomer first met Aragorn in *LotR* 3.2.436 he was so impressed by his achievement of leading Legolas and Gimli on the four-day pursuit of the Orcs across Rohan - a distance of a hundred and thirty-five miles - that he gave him the name "Wingfoot". This is the only occurrence of it.

*

Aragorn's titles are now listed in alphabetical order with brief explanations.

Bearer of the Star of the North

Included in Faramir's list of titles at the coronation. "Star of the North" refers to the Elendilmir, the jewel used instead of a crown in the North Kingdom.

Captain of the Host of the West

Included in Faramir's list of titles at the coronation. It recognised Aragorn's leadership of the host which set out from Minas Tirith to the Morannon as the final diversion for Sauron, to draw his attention away from Frodo.

Heir of Elendil

Used when it was necessary to stress Aragorn's descent from Elendil. This topic is expanded below and also discussed more fully in Chapter 2.8.

Heir of Isildur

Used when it was necessary to stress Aragorn's descent from Isildur. This topic is expanded below and also discussed more fully in Chapter 2.8.

Heir of Kings

Used by Gandalf in *LotR* 3.6.509 when introducing Aragorn to the guards who greeted them on their arrival at the gates of Edoras in Rohan.

Heir of Valandil

Used when it was necessary to stress Aragorn's descent from Valandil. This topic is expanded below and also discussed more fully in Chapter 2.8.

King of Gondor

Used by the heralds when the Army of the West arrived at the Morannon (*LotR* 5.10.888), and by Gandalf in *LotR* 6.4.952 when speaking to Frodo and Sam of the king who had healed them.

King of the Dead

Used ambiguously by the locals in *LotR* 5.2 as the Grey Company rode towards the Stone of Erech after the summoning of the Dead Men of Dunharrow. The title ostensibly applied to the ghost King of the Dead but could also have applied to Aragorn as the heir of the king (Isildur) who had originally summoned the Dead Men to fight for him. In fact it is not clear whether those who used the title knew the difference when they cried out "*The King of the Dead is come upon us!*"[31]

King of the Elder Days

Used by Aragorn on his death-bed - referring to his descent from the Númenórean kings - as he explained the manner of his death to Arwen. See also the following title.

King of the Númenóreans

Used by Arwen as Aragorn prepared to die. See also the previous title.

---

31. Op. cit. [1], *LotR* 5.2, p. 789.

King of the Reunited Kingdom
This applied after Aragorn formally took up his kingships. He was the first king since Isildur to be ruler of both the North Kingdom of Arnor and the South Kingdom of Gondor.

King of the West
This title was also used after Aragorn became King.

Lord of the Western Lands
Used by Gandalf in *LotR* 6.4.952 when speaking to Frodo and Sam of the king who had healed them.

Lord of the White Tree
Legolas expressed his wish to be involved in the last stage of the war with Sauron, one of his reasons being *"for the love of the Lord of the White Tree"* thus showing his deep regard and affection for Aragorn.[32] There is no other occurrence of it in *LotR*.

Our King
Used by the Shire Hobbits after Aragorn became King.

Wielder of the Sword Reforged
Included in Faramir's list of titles at the coronation, referring to the Shards of Narsil reforged as Andúril and subsequently used by Aragorn.

No doubt Aragorn picked up additional names and titles on his travels into the East and South.

*

For completion I now include the names used in Aragorn's various earlier incarnations in *HoM-e* VI[33], VII[34], IX[35] and XII[36]. He was actually first conceived by Tolkien as a Hobbit known as "Trotter" who wore wooden shoes, had shaggy dark hair and grinned a lot! The names are given in alphabetical, rather than chronological, order (volume and page number within brackets):

Amin
Precursor of "Estel", but still meaning Hope (XII.9.ii.269-70)

Aragorn Elfstone son of Arathorn Tarkil
Used in an early version of the meeting with Éomer (VII.22.393)

Aragorn son of Aramir (VII.1.7, 3.63)
Aragorn son of Celegorn (VII.3.50-51, 3.63, 4.77, 6.113, 6.120)
Aragorn son of Kelegorn (VII.4.77, 4.80, 5.82, 5.105, 7.146, 17.361)
Du-finnion Trotter's Elvish name used by Glorfindel and Gandalf (VI.21.361, 23.392)
Eldakar (VII.14.276)
Eldamir (VII.14.276, 14.280, 14.293-4, 17.360, 17.366)
Eldavel (VII.14.276, 17.366)
Eledon (VII.14.276)
Elf-friend (VII.14.277)
Elfmere (VII.14.277)
Elfspear (VII.14.277)
Elfstan (VII.14.276)
Elfstone son of Elfhelm (VII.7.146, 14.276, 17.360-61)

---

32. Op. cit. [1], *LotR* 5.9, p. 878.
33. C. Tolkien (ed.), *The History of Middle-earth*, vol. VI, *The Return of the Shadow*, London HarperColllins Publishers, 2002, first published in Great Britain by Unwin Hyman 1988.
34. C. Tolkien (ed.), *The History of Middle-earth*, vol. VII, *The Treason of Isengard*, London HarperColllins Publishers, 1993, first published in Great Britain by Unwyn Hyman 1989.
35. C. Tolkien (ed.), *The History of Middle-earth*, vol. IX, *Sauron Defeated*, London HarperColllins Publishers, 2002, first published in Great Britain by HarperCollins Publishers 1992.
36. Op. cit. [2], *HoM-e* XII.

Elfwold (VII.17.366)
Erkenbrand (VII.4.80)
Ethelion Trotter's Elvish name used by Glorfindel and Gandalf (VI.23.392, 23.395)
Ingold (VII.4.80, 12-14.236-293 *passim*, 17.360, 19.381)
Ingold son of Ingrim (VII.13.246, 13.256, 13.262, 14.277)
Padathir Trotter's Elvish name used by Glorfindel and Gandalf (VI.11.194-5, 11.198, 12.217, 21.361)
Qendemir (VII.14.276)
Rimbedir Trotter's Elvish name used by Glorfindel and Gandalf (VI.11.198, 12.207, 12.217)
Tarantar Seemed to be the precursor of "Telcontar" but a translation of "Trotter" rather than "Strider" (IX.11.121)
Torfir Trotter's Elvish name used by Glorfindel and Gandalf (VII.3.61)
Trotter Precursor of "Strider" as the name by which the mysterious character encountered in the Prancing Pony was known. Superseded by "Strider" once it had been decided that "Trotter" was definitely a Man rather than a Hobbit. (VI.8-13.133-229 *passim*, VI.20-25.331-467 *passim*, VII.1-21.5-410 *passim*)

Finally *HoM-e* VI.20.351 Note 10 contains a suggestion that "Aragorn" could be used as the name of Gandalf's horse!

*

One of the misconceptions about Aragorn is that he was continually announcing his names and titles to all and sundry in a manner which was boastful and arrogant. Rachel C. A. M. Hawes accuses him of continually "*enumerating his titles*", "*showing off*" and never losing an opportunity "*to thrust his position down the throats of any assembled company*".[37] In answer to this Valerie M. Sleith, purporting to write in defence of Aragorn, stresses that his behaviour is due to his character being based on the tradition of the pre-Christian or Celtic hero "*whose ethos permits, indeed compels him to broadcast his feats and lineage to everyone he meets, and to repeat them frequently*". She carries on to state that Aragorn "*lacks humility*" and "*trumpets his achievements endlessly*", thus in fact seeming to agree with Hawes as to the nature of his behaviour, if not the reason for it.[38] These two articles were written over thirty years ago, but more recent examples of a belief in Aragorn's arrogance can be found in Web discussion forums by searching for "Aragorn" and "arrogant".[39]

In fact there were usually extremely good reasons for the announcement of Aragorn's names and titles in *LotR* and on many occasions they were actually made by someone **other** than Aragorn.

In Chapter 1.4, while discussing his early adulthood, I emphasised the need to use aliases in order to keep his identity secret. However in 3018-9 his long struggle to defeat Sauron and regain his kingships was reaching its climax and the time was approaching when secrecy would have to be cast aside. The gradual exposure of Aragorn's role and identity is a clear thread in *LotR* and is achieved mainly by the strategic use of name and title announcements the content of which is specified to a nicety. This thread will now be studied chronologically assessing the significance, purpose and impact of such announcements, and refuting the arrogance accusations where applicable.

App A.I.v.1058-9. At his first meeting with Arwen, Aragorn proudly told her "*... I am Aragorn, Arathorn's son, Isildur's Heir, Lord of the Dúnedain.*" To put this in context: he was twenty years old; he had only just found out, the previous day, that he was the possessor of these grand titles; he was excited; he had just met a lovely "young girl" whom he had fallen for and naturally wanted to impress. Even in the act of introducing

---

37. R.C.A.M. Hawes, 'Aragorn: Not a Laudable Lord', *Amon Hen*, no. 60, February 1983, p. 17.
38. V.M. Sleith, 'In Defence of Aragorn', *Amon Hen*, no 62, July 1983, pp. 14-15.
39. For example: *The One Ring*, [website], 1999, http://newboards.theonering.net/forum/gforum/perl/gforum.cgi?do=post_view_printable;post=211882;guest=9442070, (accessed 1 August 2010); *The Tolkien Forum*, [website], 2010, http://www.thetolkienforum.com/archive/index.php/t-15346.html, (accessed 1 August 2010); *The Hall of Fire*, [website], http://www.thehalloffire.net/forum/viewtopic.php?t=1680&postdays=0&postorder=asc&start=80, (accessed 1 August 2010); *Parablemania*, [website], http://parablemania.ektopos.com/archives/2004/01/thoughts_on_lot.html#comment-136, (accessed 1 August 2010).

himself he became overawed by Arwen's beauty and then grew deeply embarrassed at his failure to perceive her elvishness. This hardly constitutes an example of arrogance. Soon afterwards when Elrond spoke to Aragorn about his feelings for Arwen he showed his foster son the respect of addressing him by his name, patronymic and rank: "*Aragorn, Arathorn's son, Lord of the Dúnedain*". These episodes marked the beginning of the process of Aragorn's true identity coming to light, with Aragorn himself now finding out who he was and what would be expected of him in life.

***LotR* 1.2.58.** As Gandalf and Frodo sat in the study at Bag End in April 3018 discussing the nature of Bilbo's Ring and the search for Gollum, Gandalf referred briefly to his friend Aragorn. Although the name escaped Frodo's notice at the time, Gandalf had made the decision to use Aragorn's real name. In fact this is the first mention of him in the main text of *LotR*.

***LotR* 1.10.171.** At his first meeting with Frodo and his companions in the inn at Bree Aragorn told them "*I am Aragorn son of Arathorn; and if by life or death I can save you, I will*". Frodo had just read a letter from Gandalf telling him to look out for a friend of his known as Strider, but whose real name was Aragorn. Gandalf had again given Frodo information about Aragorn. However Sam was raising doubts as to whether they were talking to "*the real Strider*" or an imposter. Aragorn's words just quoted followed a display of power in which he tried to get the Hobbits to see that if he hadn't been the real Strider he would have killed them already and taken the Ring. His face was then softened by a smile as he pledged himself to look after them. The point of his words and behaviour was to make the Hobbits understand the danger they were in and to persuade them of his genuineness and the need to trust him in what was a "life and death" situation. There was no arrogance involved - it was just of paramount importance that the Hobbits should be in no doubt as to who he was. This episode is significant for being the first time in the *LotR* narrative that Aragorn himself gave his real name.

***LotR* 1.11.186,** ***LotR* 2.1.232-3, 237,** ***LotR* 2.2.247-8.** These chapters show that Aragorn and Bilbo knew each other and in fact had been friends for some time, probably about seventeen years. It is also clear that Bilbo had known Aragorn's identity from the start of their acquaintance and was thus the first Hobbit to be aware of who he was. [The relationship between Bilbo and Aragorn is discussed in Chapter 2.5.]

***LotR* 2.2.246.** At the Council of Elrond Boromir, doubtfully and not very respectfully, asked the lean shabby Ranger with the broken sword who he was, particularly wanting to know his connection with Minas Tirith. It was Elrond, not Aragorn, who answered, introducing his foster-son thus: "*He is Aragorn son of Arathorn ... descended through many fathers from **Isildur** Elendil's son **of Minas Ithil**. He is the Chief of the Dúnedain in the North...*" The text I have emphasised shows that Elrond was making a point of stressing Isildur's link with Gondor by mentioning Minas Ithil, his home during his time as king there. [Elrond would certainly have been aware of the reluctance of Gondor to consider a claimant of Isildur's line in the past.] Thus the heir of the Steward of Gondor now knew that the senior branch of Elendil's line still survived and that there was thus a claimant to the kingship among the Northern Dúnedain. At the same time this information was being imparted to Legolas, son of the king of the Mirkwood Elves, and to Glóin and Gimli, Dwarves of the Lonely Mountain. Elrond's revelation may also have been news to Círdan's representative Galdor, though Círdan himself, being one of the inner circle of the Wise and a member of the White Council, may already have been aware that Isildur's line survived.

***LotR* 2.8.375.** When Galadriel presented Aragorn with the Elessar brooch she said "*In this hour take the name that was foretold for you, Elessar, the Elfstone of the House of Elendil!*" This marked the first time that Aragorn was called by the name he would later bear as King.

***LotR* 2.9.393.** As the Fellowship passed the Argonath during their voyage down the River Anduin, Aragorn referred to Isildur and Anárion (represented by the statues) as "*my sires of old*", then proclaimed himself "*Elessar, the Elfstone son of Arathorn of the House of Valandil Isildur's son, heir of Elendil*". These words were not spoken in arrogance but were part of a speech in which he was trying to calm a seriously frightened

Frodo and Sam by making the point that it was safe to pass the Argonath - the old northern boundary of Gondor - because of who he was. The statues themselves were intimidating and the river at this point was exceptionally narrow and fast with the cliffs rising sheer to a terrifying height causing darkness, roaring water and screaming wind. Aragorn was now entering his kingdom of Gondor for the first time as himself, rather than as a disguised wanderer under an assumed name, and fittingly he appeared briefly transformed as Frodo looked at him.

LotR 3.2.433. The meeting with Éomer provides a further example of Aragorn's identity-revelation process, as well as unfortunately another opportunity for an "arrogance" accusation. Initially, when asked who he was, he told Éomer he was called Strider then, at Éomer's insistence, he revealed his true identity by proclaiming his titles ("*I am Aragorn son of Arathorn, and am called Elessar, the Elfstone, Dúnadan, the heir of Isildur Elendil's son of Gondor*") while simultaneously sweeping out his sword Andúril. It is significant that Legolas and Gimli were amazed by his behaviour "*... for they had not seen him in this mood before,*" thus hardly implying that he was always acting like that. At this point Aragorn and his companions were in danger either of being taken prisoner by the Rohirrim which would prevent them continuing the search for Merry and Pippin, or of being killed while trying to escape. Aragorn had decided that he trusted Éomer and therefore took the risk of telling him who he really was. By his declaration he drew attention not only to his descent from Isildur and Elendil but also to the prophecy foretelling the name he would take as King (Elessar/Elfstone), and to his Númenórean ancestry (Dúnadan). His manner of doing this was necessary in order to make enough of an impact and show of authority to get Éomer to go against Théoden's orders and let him and his companions go free, and also to emphasise the importance of the search for the Hobbits. The situation was handled impeccably in the only manner which would have achieved the required result. It also gained him Éomer's lasting regard and affection. The episode marked a further stage in the dropping of Aragorn's aliases, with a member of the royal House of Rohan now being aware of who he was.

LotR 3.6.509-11. Two days later Aragorn, Legolas and Gimli, now accompanied by Gandalf, arrived at Edoras. It was actually the Wizard who introduced Aragorn to the guards calling him "*Aragorn son of Arathorn, the heir of Kings*" who was on his way to Minas Tirith, thus impressing on them that these were folk to be reckoned with, not just tired scruffy strangers. At the entrance to Meduseld, the Doorward Háma insisted on the companions leaving their weapons outside. Being reluctant to let the sword of Elendil out of his sight, Aragorn became embroiled in an altercation with Háma as to whether Théoden's will should take precedence over the will of "*Aragorn son of Arathorn, Elendil's heir of Gondor.*" His apparent arrogance here was only due to the particular sword he was carrying as illustrated by his statement that he would obey the owner of the house and leave any sword but Andúril outside if Meduseld was only a woodman's cottage. Andúril was a cherished heirloom with a significant history, and also as it happened an equally significant future - both in battle and as proof of identity (e.g. in the Palantír confrontation and on the journey through the Paths of the Dead). Also as Aragorn was now revealed as the potential King of Gondor he must have found it deeply insulting to be told to leave his weapon outside - Théoden was his vassal. In addition due to Saruman's influence on Théoden none of them knew what sort of danger they were likely to meet inside the hall. After being persuaded by Gandalf to comply he told Háma the sword's history - how it was "*the Blade that was Broken*", forged in the First Age by the Dwarf smith Telchar, and carrying a spell or prophecy that "*Death shall come to any man that draws Elendil's sword save Elendil's heir.*" Háma - like Éomer two days previously - now became awestruck and respectful, as a result of which Aragorn was able to persuade him to disobey orders and allow Gandalf's staff to be taken into the hall - the really crucial requirement as it turned out. Note that Gandalf and Legolas also spoke out about the origin of their weapons - it wasn't a case of just Aragorn flaunting his ownership of a particular sword. [I analyse this incident in much more detail in Chapter 2.7.]

LotR 3.9.563. As Aragorn, Legolas and Gimli relaxed in the ruins of Isengard with Merry and Pippin, Aragorn wrapped his cloak around him hiding his mail shirt and causing Pippin to exclaim "*Look! Strider the Ranger has come back.*" In reply Aragorn stated, "*He has never been away. I am Strider and Dúnadan too, and I belong both to Gondor and the North.*" This was an informal situation with friends in which Aragorn was reassuring Pippin that he was still the same old Strider in spite of his battle gear, his Númenórean descent and his claim to both kingdoms.

***LotR* 4.5.663-4.** Frodo told Faramir and his Rangers of the existence of Aragorn as the descendant of Isildur and the bearer of the sword of Elendil. Thus the Steward's younger son now also knew that there was a claimant to the throne of Gondor among the Dúnedain of the North.

***LotR* 5.2.774.** As Aragorn rode from Isengard to Helm's Deep with Théoden's company he had the Palantír of Orthanc in his possession and had made up his mind to use it to confront Sauron. On the arrival of the Grey Company Halbarad asked for him as *"Aragorn son of Arathorn"*, the first time this had happened as Fleming Rutledge points out.[40] Halbarad too, clearly knew that the time for secrecy was past. Some hours later Aragorn revealed his identity to Sauron as Isildur's heir wielding Elendil's sword. He had shaken off his disguises and incognitos and his life would no longer be dominated by the need to prevent Sauron from finding out that he existed. By this confrontation he had put an end to eighty-eight years of secrecy.

***LotR* 5.2.789, *LotR* 5.9.875-6.** The journey through the Paths of the Dead necessitated further announcements of Aragorn's titles. When he formally summoned the Dead Men of Dunharrow at the Stone of Erech, he raised Arwen's battle standard and announced himself as *"Elessar, Isildur's heir of Gondor."* This was essential to enact the prophecy and let the Dead know his identity. Similarly, during the ride to Pelargir, he bade Angbor of Lamedon gather his men and follow him saying *"At Pelargir the Heir of Isildur will have need of you."* Then after the black ships of the Corsairs had been taken with the assistance of the Dead, Aragorn dismissed them with the following words: *"Hear now the words of the Heir of Isildur! Your oath is fulfilled ... Depart and be at rest!"* This self-identification was essential in all these incidents, with the emphasis being on Aragorn's descent from Isildur. It was Isildur who had taken the One Ring from Sauron at the end of the Second Age. It was Isildur who had cursed the Dead Men of Dunharrow for not fulfilling their oath to support him against Sauron - and he had been King of Gondor at the time. It was because of Aragorn's continual statement of his identity that the Dead fulfilled their oath enabling the Battle of the Pelennor Fields to be won.

***LotR* 5.6.847, *LotR* 5.8.861,863, *LotR* 5.9.873.** A more complex situation, referred to by Rachel Hawes who accuses Aragorn of being *"inconsistent in word and action"*[41], arose during the Battle of the Pelennor Fields and its aftermath. Aragorn proclaimed himself as King in the battle by sailing up the Anduin wearing the Star of the North Kingdom on his brow and displaying the standard of the King of Gondor. Subsequently he furled the standard, took off the Star and refused to enter Minas Tirith as King. Shortly afterwards he did actually enter the City where he announced his titles. Then the following day he insisted on holding the Last Debate in his tent outside the city as he didn't want to enter it as King. Described in those terms this certainly sounds rather irrational. However a detailed consideration of the circumstances reveals a perfectly logical explanation:
- During the battle it was necessary for Aragorn to proclaim to Sauron's armies the presence of Isildur's heir, with a claim to the two kingdoms. This would complete what was begun in his confrontation with Sauron in the Palantír, and also give hope to his own side, as well as making it clear that the ships of the Corsairs did not actually contain the Enemy. Therefore as he sailed up the river he displayed the standard of Gondor and wore the Star of the North Kingdom.
- His refusal to enter Minas Tirith afterwards was because Gondor had been ruled by the Stewards for nearly a thousand years and he was afraid that *"... if I enter it unbidden, then doubt and debate may arise .... I will not enter in, nor make any claim, until it be seen whether we or Mordor shall prevail..."*. He went on to say *"... I have no mind for strife except with our Enemy..."* He knew, from his service as "Thorongil" during the stewardship of Denethor's father, that Denethor would be hostile to such a claim and he was backed up in this opinion by Prince Imrahil (Denethor's brother-in-law). Note that Aragorn and Imrahil [and Éomer] **didn't know** at this point that Denethor was dead. Aragorn may also

---

40. F. Rutledge, *The Battle for Middle-earth: Tolkien's Divine Design in The Lord of the Rings*, Grand Rapids Michigan and Cambridge UK, Wm. B. Eerdmans Publishing Co., 2004, Book V, p. 254.
41. Op. cit. [37], Hawes, p. 17.

have had in mind the history of Gondor, in particular the fighting over the succession during the War of the Kin-strife. This had begun in TA 1400s shortly before the accession of King Eldacar who was of mixed blood due to his father's marriage to a woman of the Northmen (ancestors of the Rohirrim). The opposition to Eldacar was due to the mingling of lesser blood (and thus shorter lifespan) with that of the Dúnedain, and for a while his throne was usurped by his cousin Castamir who was of pure Dúnadan blood. The ramifications of the resulting war lasted over four hundred years until Castamir's line died out. Aragorn would naturally have wanted to avoid any similar conflict. [Genealogical Table 5 shows the extent of this war.]

- When Aragorn entered the City he hid his identity by covering himself with his Elf-cloak. He was there **because Gandalf had sent for him**, recognising that he was the only one who had any chance of helping those in the Houses of Healing who had been affected by the Black Breath of the Nazgûl. He had come as a healer to save lives, not as a king, and the only token he brought was the Elessar - because of its healing properties. When he, Gandalf, Éomer and Imrahil approached the Houses of Healing they found Pippin on guard there. He and Aragorn were very glad to see each other with Pippin addressing him as "Strider" and Aragorn reacting by laughing and taking his hand. The incident was quite a shock to Prince Imrahil who asked Éomer "*Is it thus that we speak to our kings?*" then suggested that maybe Aragorn would use some other name than Strider for his "king" name. Overhearing him Aragorn briefly recited the royal names which had been prophesied for him - namely Elessar, Elfstone and Envinyatar the Renewer - followed by a statement that he would use the Quenya version of Strider, "Telcontar", to be the name of his royal House. This was not an official proclamation nor a situation where Aragorn "*boasts his title to all and sundry who care to listen*" (to quote Rachel Hawes again), but a brief, jokey interlude in a horrendous day at the meeting of two friends who were relieved and delighted to see each other again. In any case Aragorn's speech had been prompted by Imrahil's comment. I discuss this incident further in Chapter 2.5.
- Aragorn's insistence on holding the Last Debate in his tent the following day was entirely in keeping with his desire to avoid making any claim while the war with Sauron was still in the balance. Denethor was admittedly now dead and Faramir, as the new Steward, had recognised Aragorn as King, but he was still gravely ill at this point making it rather premature for Aragorn to push his claim. The reinstating of the kingship in Gondor, if it was to be done peacefully, required delicacy and diplomacy.

LotR 5.8.866. Further steps were taken in the process of revealing Aragorn's identity when the newly-healed Faramir immediately recognised him as King and then Ioreth saw to it that this news was passed around the City.

LotR 5.10.885. As the Army of the West made its way to the Morannon, the name of King Elessar was announced three times a day by the heralds. This was not at Aragorn's instigation, but was the work of Gandalf and Imrahil. Gandalf had ordered the heralds to blow their trumpets and cry "*The Lords of Gondor are come!*", but Imrahil advised that they should say "*The King Elessar*" instead because it would give Sauron more to think about. The announcement of Aragorn as King would have added to the effect of the confrontation in the Palantír. In the circumstances it made sense to keep announcing Aragorn's identity *ad nauseam*.

LotR 6.5.967. Finally Faramir proclaimed the full list of Aragorn's titles at his coronation: "*Here is Aragorn son of Arathorn, chieftain of the Dúnedain of Arnor, Captain of the Host of the West, bearer of the Star of the North, wielder of the Sword Reforged, victorious in battle, whose hands bring healing, the Elfstone, Elessar of the line of Valandil, Isildur's son, Elendil's son of Númenor.*" By this speech he showed the people that Aragorn was the rightful heir to both kingdoms by tracing his descent back to Isildur, Elendil and the kings of Númenor. He showed too that Aragorn embodied the qualities of a King: his prowess in battle as the wielder of Elendil's sword, and his role as a healer. In addition the name Elessar - along with its Common Speech equivalent Elfstone - reflected the prophecies that he should take the name of a green stone.

The process of Aragorn's revelation was now complete. Prior to the events in *LotR* he had been fighting the

battle against Sauron for nearly seventy years, going to great lengths to prevent him finding out that Isildur's line still survived. However by 3018-9:
- The Ring had been found.
- Faramir had had his prophetic dream.
- The prophecies were due to be realised.
- The sword of Elendil was reforged.
- By chance (as it seemed) a Palantír came into his possession.

This was the time when it was appropriate and necessary for him to start announcing himself. It was also the time when proof of his identity was required, hence many of the occasions when he announced himself (or others announced him) also involved the production of the sword - either broken (as in Bree and at the Council of Elrond), or reforged (as at the first meeting with Éomer, at Meduseld, and in the confrontation with Sauron). He was not being arrogant or boastful, merely doing what was required for the fulfilling of his destiny. He was after all a Chieftain, military and naval captain, healer and King-in-waiting as well as an extremely wise, perceptive, educated and knowledgeable man. In such capacities he would have displayed an innate authority which he wielded when - and only when - appropriate. App A.I.v, describing his wandering years, states that *"he seemed to Men worthy of honour, as a king that is in exile, when he did not hide his true shape."*[42] However his situation in the *LotR* years is best summed up by his words following his night of exhaustion wrestling with the Palantír: *"For me the time of stealth has passed."*[43]

---

42. Op. cit. [1], *LotR* 5.2, p. 1060.
43. Op. cit., *LotR* 5.2, p. 779.

CHAPTER 1.10 - APPEARANCE

As well as discussing Aragorn's appearance, this chapter also looks at the issues of disguise, invisibility and transformation.

Assessing Aragorn's appearance can be nearly as complex as unravelling his character and deeds. In *LotR*[1] we (and Frodo) are introduced to a man with shaggy dark hair flecked with grey, a pale stern face and keen grey eyes. Gandalf's letter to Frodo (*LotR* 1.10.169-70) added that he was tall and lean, and then went on to quote a verse which included lines such as: "*All that is gold does not glitter*" and "*The old that is strong does not wither*". These cryptic statements are reflected in the many references to Aragorn's appearance throughout the main text and Appendices of *LotR*, for example:

- He was pale and lean but nevertheless extremely strong and fit.
- His appearance was often off-putting although he came from a race renowned for its beauty.
- In spite of being grim and weather-beaten with greying hair he told the Hobbits "*I am older than I look.*"[2]. Thus he apparently nevertheless looked younger than his years.
- He sometimes switched suddenly from being weary and travel-worn to regal and commanding.
- He was capable of quelling the strongest opponent with a look, but had a smile which transformed his expression into one of gentleness and empathy.

Perhaps it is inconsistencies such as these which make it difficult to visualise what Aragorn really looked like. The two main factors which affected his appearance - namely inheritance and lifestyle - were in fact working in opposition to each other. These will now be expanded.

Regarding the inheritance factor, Aragorn counted among his ancestors a Maia, Elves, Edain (mortal Men who supported the Elves against Morgoth in the First Age) and Númenóreans. Genealogical Table 1 shows his descent from Melian, the first Elf-kings and the three Houses of the Edain (via Beren and Tuor). Many of these last-mentioned subsequently became the Númenóreans of the Second Age. In the Third Age the exiled survivors of the drowning of Númenor were known as the Dúnedain. With such forebears as these, there were a number of significant physical traits which affected the appearance of Aragorn, namely:

- Lifespan
- Features and colouring
- Physique and constitution

Lifespan

As a reward for their assistance to the Elves during the wars of the First Age the Númenóreans were granted a lifespan far surpassing that of other mortals: up to four hundred years or more in the early days of Númenor, then declining to between two and three hundred by the time of its Downfall after which it was reduced still further. However the Dúnedain, as survivors of Númenor, still had an extended life expectancy, especially those in the north of Middle-earth from whom Aragorn was descended. This, along with his small amount of Elf and Maia blood and royal blood from both his parents, explains Aragorn's great lifespan (two hundred

---

1. J.R.R. Tolkien, *The Lord of the Rings,* London, HarperCollins Publishers, 2007, 2nd edition, based on the 50th Anniversary Edition of 2004, *LotR* 1.9, p. 156.
2. Op. cit., *LotR* 1.10, p. 165.

and ten years), abnormally long even for a Dúnadan by the end of the Third Age. *UT* 2.3 Note 1[3] explains that the Númenóreans grew to maturity at the same rate as other Men, after which they enjoyed an extended period of physical and mental vigour, before declining into the *"decrepitude and senility"* of old age - this last stage taking about ten years. We know from App A.I.v.1062 that Aragorn died voluntarily when he felt the *"**approach** of old age"* [My emphasis], that is before *"decrepitude and senility"* began to take effect. Thus the implication is that his active adulthood lasted for approximately a hundred and ninety years. *HoM-e* XII.6 contains a reference to a note by Tolkien stating that *"In character Aragorn was a hardened man of say 45"*[4] at the time of his meeting with the Hobbits in Bree even though his actual age was ninety (this became eighty-seven in the published *LotR*). Also, in a draft letter to an unknown reader written around 1963 Tolkien refers to Aragorn's age pointing out that it was *"not accompanied by any physical decay"*[5]. The letter in question is discussing the unsuitability of a relationship between Aragorn and Éowyn, so again we are talking about an Aragorn in his late eighties. The issue is further exemplified in *LotR* 6.5 by his appearance at his coronation: *"... ancient of days he seemed **and yet in the flower of manhood**"*[6][My emphasis]. Such an appearance of youth was also an Elvish characteristic and the description just given bears a marked resemblance to that of Elrond, *"**V**enerable he seemed as a king crowned with many winters, and yet hale as a tried warrior in the fullness of his strength"*[7], and of Elladan and Elrohir who were *"neither young nor old"*[8].

Features and colouring

TSil, in describing the appearance of the Edain of the First Age, states that the Men of the House of Bëor had dark or brown hair and grey eyes[9], features which matched Aragorn's. An earlier version of the chapter in *HoM-e* XI adds that their faces were *"fair and shapely"* and also draws attention to their *"keen"* eyes[10]. App A.I.iv refers to Aragorn's incognito "Thorongil" stating that the "thoron" part was due to him being *"swift and keen-eyed"*[11] like an eagle. A further reference in *LotR* describes Pippin's vision of *"the keen face of Strider"*[12] bent over the Orcs' trail. During the pursuit of the Orcs across Rohan (*LotR* 3.2.430) his *"keen eyes"* enabled him to spot the Riders of Rohan when they were still far distant, while earlier in the chase, when Legolas had spotted an eagle very high up, Aragorn had said *"... not even my eyes can see him ... He must be far aloft indeed."*[13] Thus "keen" seems to mean sharp-eyed along with an ability to see a long way. However there are other uses of the word which imply something more perceptive and impressive. In *LotR* 1.9.156-7 there are two examples of Aragorn's eyes being described as *"keen"* and Frodo felt very uncomfortable under their scrutiny. The significance of eyes is further emphasised in *UT* 1.2 (*The Departure of Túrin*) which refers to those of Morwen (a woman of the House of Bëor and mother of Túrin) and the fear experienced by Brodda the Easterling when he looked into them: *" He thought that he had looked in the fell eyes of a white-fiend"*[14]. Another example, from *UT* 1.2 (*Of Mîm the Dwarf*), refers to the eyes of Túrin himself: *"He looked steadfastly in the eyes of the Dwarf, and Mîm could not endure it; few indeed could challenge the eyes of Túrin in set will*

---
3. C. Tolkien (ed.), *Unfinished Tales of Númenor and Middle-earth*, London, HarperCollins Publishers, 1998, first published in Great Britain by George Allen & Unwin 1980, *UT* Part 2, Chapter 3, p. 290.
4. C. Tolkien (ed.), *The History of Middle-earth*, vol. XII, *The Peoples of Middle-earth*, London HarperColllins Publishers, 2002, first published in Great Britain by HarperCollins Publishers 1996, p. 167.
5. H. Carpenter (ed.), *The Letters of J.R.R. Tolkien*, with the assistance of Christopher Tolkien, London, HarperCollins Publishers, 1995. First published in Great Britain by George Allen & Unwin, 1981. Letter. 244, p. 323.
6. Op. cit. [1], *LotR* 6.5, p. 968.
7. Op. cit., *LotR* 2.1, p. 227.
8. Op. cit., *LotR* 5.2, p. 778.
9. C. Tolkien (ed.), *The Silmarillion*, London, HarperCollins Publishers, 1999, first published in Great Britain by George Allen & Unwin 1977, *TSil* Chapter 17, p. 173.
10. C. Tolkien (ed.), *The History of Middle-earth*, vol. XI, *The War of the Jewels*, London HarperColllins Publishers, 2002, first published in Great Britain by HarperCollins Publishers 1994, Part 2, Chapter 14, p. 224.
11. Op. cit. [1], App A.I.iv, p. 1055.
12. Op. cit., *LotR* 3.3, p. 449.
13. Op. cit., *LotR* 3.2, p. 423.
14. Op. cit. [3], *UT* 1.2, p. 90.

or in wrath."[15] App A.I.v.1060 makes it clear that Aragorn's eyes could have the same effect, as few could withstand them when they were kindled. A very good example of this is the confrontation with the Mouth of Sauron who "*quailed and gave back as if menaced with a blow*"[16] when Aragorn stared at him. The similarity between his eyes and those of Morwen and Túrin is unmistakeable.

These features were also part of Aragorn's Elvish (via Elrond's family) and Númenórean legacy. For example in *LotR* we are told that Elrond's hair was "*dark as the shadows of twilight*" while his eyes were "*grey as a clear evening, and in them was a light like the light of stars.*"[17] Arwen's hair and eyes are similarly described in the same chapter, while Elladan and Elrohir are "*dark-haired, grey-eyed, and their faces elven-fair*"[18]. *UT* 2.2 Note 3 states that when the Númenóreans first began to sail to Middle-earth the inhabitants were "*in awe*" of them as they "*resembled rather Elvish lords than mortal Men in bearing and apparel*"[19], while a copy of a letter to Milton Waldman from - probably - late 1951 describes them as "*hardly distinguishable from the Elves*"[20] in appearance - thus implying considerable beauty. In App A.I.v.1057 Aragorn as a twenty-year-old is described as "*fair and noble*" then later, at the age of forty-nine, after Galadriel had replaced his travelling clothes with garments of silver and white, he resembled "*an Elf-lord from the Isles of the West*"[21]. This image was repeated in *LotR* when Frodo saw him standing next to Arwen's chair in Rivendell: "*... he seemed to be clad in elven-mail, and a star shone on his breast.*"[22] *Ak* states that "*The light of their* [the Númenóreans'] *eyes was like the bright stars*"[23]. There is a parallel with Aragorn's eyes in *LotR* as he stood beneath his banner at the Battle of the Morannon: "*his eyes gleamed like stars that shine the brighter as the night deepens.*"[24] Indeed initially the only facial feature of the hooded and cloaked Aragorn actually visible to Frodo in the Prancing Pony was his eyes, which gleamed as he watched the Hobbits (*LotR* 1.9.156).

Some of the traits which characterised Aragorn's appearance were also apparent in his contemporaries among the Dúnedain and therefore descriptions of these people perhaps help to give a clearer idea of what Aragorn himself looked like. App A.I.iv.1055 refers to a close resemblance between Aragorn as "Thorongil" and Denethor. Pippin noted the Steward's "*... carven face with its proud bones and skin like ivory, and the long curved nose between the dark deep eyes...*"[25] and was reminded of Aragorn. Later in the same chapter Denethor is described as looking "*... more kingly, beautiful, and powerful...*"[26] during a comparison with Gandalf. These observations could presumably have applied equally well to Aragorn, though I can find no specific reference to him having a curved nose. Pippin's first impression of Faramir, too, (in *LotR* 5.4.810) was that he reminded him of Aragorn but this time because of his air of nobility, sadness and wisdom. In *LotR*, as Frodo observed Faramir's Rangers, Mablung and Damrod, he noted that they were "*... goodly men, pale-skinned, dark of hair, with grey eyes and faces sad and proud.*"[27]

A point of uncertainty concerns the length of Aragorn's hair. Although it was definitely dark, there is no clear indication as to how long it was, though at the first meeting between him and Frodo it is described as "*shaggy*" which could imply that it was long, as well as being thick and unkempt. Also as the Fellowship sailed past the Argonath his hair is described as "*blowing in the wind*"[28] which could imply a reasonable length. The hair of Boromir (also a Dúnadan) is described as being "*shorn about his shoulders*"[29] which seems to indicate that it normally extended below his shoulders. Perhaps he had cut it shorter during his journey to make it more manageable, or alternatively after he had reached Rivendell so as to be more presentable at the Council

---

15. Op. cit. [3], *UT* 1.2, p. 127.
16. Op. cit. [1], *LotR* 5.10, p. 889.
17. Op. cit., *LotR* 2.1, p. 227.
18. Op. cit., *LotR* 5.2, p. 778.
19. Op. cit. [3], *UT* 2.2, p. 275.
20. Op. cit. [5], Letter 131, p. 154.
21. Op. cit. [1], App A.I.v, p. 1060.
22. Op. cit., *LotR* 2.1, p. 238.
23. Op. cit. [9], *Ak* p. 311.
24. Op. cit. [1], *LotR* 6.4, p. 948.
25. Op. cit., *LotR* 5.1, p. 754.
26. Op. cit., *LotR* 5.1, p. 757.
27. Op. cit., *LotR* 4.4, p. 659.
28. Op. cit., *LotR* 2.9, p. 393.
29. Op. cit., *LotR* 2.2, p. 240.

of Elrond. At his funeral in *LotR* 3.1.416 his hair is described as long. Another indication that the Dúnedain tended to have long hair is in the description of Faramir and Éowyn as they stood on the walls of Minas Tirith at the moment when the Ring was destroyed: a strong wind blew and *"their hair, raven and golden, streamed out mingling in the air."*[30]. *LotR* contains specific evidence that Elves had long hair - Glorfindel in *LotR* 1.12.209 and Celeborn in *LotR* 2.7.354 - suggesting that the Númenóreans and Dúnedain, being of Elvish appearance, may also have had long hair as the norm.

A further uncertainty about Aragorn's appearance relates to facial hair. In *UT* 2.4 (*Amroth and Nimrodel*), Christopher Tolkien says *"In a note written in December 1972 or later, and **among the last writings of my father's on the subject of Middle-earth**, there is a discussion of the Elvish strain in Men, as to its being observable in the beardlessness of those who were so descended (it was a characteristic of all Elves to be beardless)..."*[31] [My emphasis]. The description, in *LotR* 6.9.1030, of Círdan being bearded contradicts this; however *LotR* pre-dated the passage quoted, as indicated by the text I have emphasised. Thus taking into account Aragorn's Elvish ancestry and the hair-style of Boromir and Faramir as fellow Dúnedain, the likelihood is that he had long hair but no facial hair. What is not clear is whether Elves, and Men with Elvish blood, always **chose** to be beardless or whether they simply did not have facial hair in the first place.

Physique and constitution

It is stated clearly in *LotR* 2.3.292 that Aragorn was the tallest member of the Fellowship. Boromir however was only slightly shorter and in addition was broader and more heavily-built. Hammond and Scull refer to the following note written by Tolkien around 1969: *"Aragorn, direct descendant of Elendil and his son Isildur, both of whom had been seven feet tall, must nonetheless have been a very tall man (with a great stride), probably at least 6 ft. 6; and Boromir, of high Númenórean lineage, not much shorter (say 6 ft.4)"*[32].

Regarding Aragorn's slighter build, he is described as *"lean"* by Gandalf in the letter to Frodo which he left with Barliman Butterbur (*LotR* 1.10.169). This fits with another passage in *HoM-e* XI which speaks thus of the people of the House of Bëor: *"Lithe and lean in body they were long-enduring in hardship."*[33] Aragorn too had great physical strength and endurance in spite of his leanness; in fact his travels made him *"the most hardy of living Men"*[34]. This is shown particularly by his ability to do without sleep, the obvious example being his achievements during the period March 6th - 15th 3019: while still recovering from the Palantír confrontation he went on the terrifying journey through the Paths of the Dead, followed by the desperate ride to Pelargir, the Battle of the Pelennor Fields and then an exhausting night healing people. All this was done on very little sleep (or food) according to his conversation with Merry in the Houses of Healing: *"... I have not slept in such a bed as this, since I rode from Dunharrow, nor eaten since the dark before dawn."*[35]

Aragorn's Elvish and Númenórean blood also contributed to his strong constitution. Elves too seemed to be able to manage without sleep as shown by the behaviour of Legolas during the pursuit of the Orcs across Rohan. In addition the *"Drowning of Anadûnê"* texts in *HoM-e* IX Part Three state that the Númenóreans had some immunity from illness, at least in the days when they were "unfallen"[36] - that is before they became corrupted and began to fear death and yearn for the immortality of the Elves.

*

App A.I.iii.1043 relates how the Northern Dúnedain declined in numbers during the Third Age, especially after the kingship came to an end with the death of King Arvedui following over six hundred years of war against

---
30. Op. cit. [1], *LotR* 6.5, p. 963.
31. Op. cit. [3], *UT* 2.4, p. 320.
32. W.G. Hammond and C. Scull, *The Lord of the Rings: A Reader's Companion*, London, HarperCollins Publishers, 2005, referring to the Tolkien Papers, Bodleian Library, Oxford, p. 272.
33. Op. cit. [10], *HoM-e* XI, Part 2, Chapter 14, p. 224.
34. Op. cit. [1], App A.I.v, p. 1060.
35. Op. cit., *LotR* 5.8, p. 870.
36. C. Tolkien (ed.), *The History of Middle-earth*, vol. IX, *Sauron Defeated*, London HarperColllins Publishers, 2002, first published in Great Britain by HarperCollins Publishers 1992, Part 3, section ii, p. 343; Part 3, section iii, p. 361.

the Witch-king of Angmar. Unlike the situation in Gondor the line of the kings remained intact and the longer lifespans in the North seem to indicate a greater purity in the line, thus pointing to a high level of inbreeding which would have enhanced the characteristics of the race. This certainly seems to have happened in the case of Aragorn, both of whose parents were of Isildur's line. However the positive effect of this Maian, Elven and Númenórean ancestry - which passed on beauty, youthful looks and strong physique - was pitted against the rigours of his preparation for the kingship, greatly contrasting with a childhood and adolescence spent in the security and luxury of Rivendell. The two main factors which had a negative effect on his appearance were hardship and the need for disguise and secrecy.

Effects of hardship

Although some of Aragorn's early adulthood was spent serving in Rohan and Gondor, where he presumably had regular meals and reasonable living quarters, this probably only accounted for about twenty of the seventy years of his "apprenticeship". Thus approximately fifty years were spent enduring homelessness and increasing hardship and danger, necessarily disguised and/or incognito. Some of his travels would have been in the company of Gandalf or fellow Dúnedain of the North, but as time went by many of his journeys were solitary and in lands ruled by Sauron, as exemplified by his long search for Gollum near the borders of Mordor, and the time spent in the East and South secretly investigating Sauron's plots and devices.

In *LotR*, on the arrival of the Fellowship in Lothlórien, Celeborn noted the effect of Aragorn's struggles on his appearance with the observation: "*... those years lie heavy on you*"[37], referring to the thirty-eight years since he had last seen him. Later, Gimli summed up Aragorn's kinsmen, the Grey Company, thus: "*... they are grim men of face, worn like weathered rocks for the most part, even as Aragorn himself...*"[38] Also App A.I.v.1060 emphasises his grimness, and the sadness and sternness of his face during his wandering years. A description of Túrin in *UT* 1.2 (*Túrin in Doriath*) as seen by the Elf-king Thingol could easily be describing Aragorn: "*Thingol looked on Túrin in wonder, seeing suddenly before him in the place of his fosterling a Man and a stranger, tall, dark-haired, looking at him with deep eyes in a white face.*"[39] We are also told that "*... he [Túrin] cared no longer for his looks or his attire, but his hair was unkempt, and his mail covered with a grey cloak stained with the weather.*"[40] It seems safe to say that looks and clothing would not have been high on Aragorn's agenda unless there was a good political or social reason for making himself more presentable. In addition there are many occasions in *LotR* when he looks positively unwell as illustrated by the following descriptions:

- At Frodo's first meeting with him he noticed his "*pale stern face*"[41]. Also during the pursuit of the Orcs across Rohan Aragorn lay listening to the ground and when he rose Legolas and Gimli saw that his face was "*pale and drawn*"[42]. Although the Dúnedain had naturally pale skin the use of the word "pale" in these examples seems to indicate strain and suffering rather than a healthy colour. Note that in my earlier reference to Denethor's appearance his complexion is described as "ivory" rather than "pale".
- The word "lean" is used in a similar manner. Gandalf's letter to Frodo delivered by Barliman Butterbur described Aragorn as "lean". At the Council of Elrond Boromir's doubts of him were triggered by his "*lean face*" and "*weather-stained cloak*".[43] Although "lean" could be interpreted as indicating a healthy absence of excess fat, it is not used thus in *LotR*. Aragorn and Denethor were supposed to resemble each other and therefore Boromir might perhaps be expected to notice this likeness. The fact that he did not was down to Aragorn's generally worn and unhealthy looks, something recognised by Aragorn himself as he subsequently sympathised with Boromir's doubts, actually stating that his appearance was due to his long and hard life. His leanness must have been due to inadequate food as well as natural

---

37. Op. cit. [1], *LotR* 2.7, p. 355.
38. Op. cit., *LotR* 5.2, p. 776.
39. Op. cit. [3], *UT* 1.2, p. 102.
40. Op. cit., *UT* 1.2, p. 103.
41. Op. cit., [1], *LotR* 1.9, p. 156.
42. Op. cit., *LotR* 3.2, p. 426.
43. Op. cit., *LotR* 2.2, p. 246.

physique and strenuous activity. On this particular occasion it was only a few days since he had arrived in Rivendell following the traumatic journey there with the Hobbits. It is significant too that the word "lean" is also used of Gollum, a) by Aragorn at the Council of Elrond referring to him as *"one so lean and withered"*[44], b) in *LotR* 4.8 which refers to his *"lean hungry face"*[45], and c) in *LotR* 6.3 where he is referred to as *"a lean, starved, haggard thing"*[46]. In these examples "lean" clearly means starving and unhealthy thus lending weight to the assumption that the word has a similar connotation when used of Aragorn.

- In a letter to his son Christopher written on Oct 6th 1944 Tolkien wrote of a meeting with the poet Roy Campbell in the Eagle and Child public house in Oxford. Campbell, who had been sitting in a corner listening to the conversation of Tolkien and his companions, is described as *"a strange tall gaunt man"*[47] who reminded Tolkien of "Trotter" (the original name of Strider). The implication is that he envisaged Aragorn as looking "gaunt", a word which is variously defined in dictionaries as emaciated, haggard, or thin on account of illness, insufficient food or worry. Certainly the last two would have applied to Aragorn as seen by the Hobbits in the Prancing Pony and by Boromir at the Council of Elrond.

- In *LotR* when Aragorn, Legolas and Gimli carried Boromir's bier, *"they found it no easy task, for Boromir was a man both tall and strong."*[48] This is perhaps evidence of Aragorn not being in the best physical shape at this point.

- *LotR* describes Aragorn's appearance after using the Palantír of Orthanc to confront Sauron. To Merry he looked *"... as if in one night many years had fallen on his head. Grim was his face, grey-hued and weary."*[49] To Legolas and Gimli he looked *"like one who has laboured in sleepless pain for many nights."*[50] On his arrival at Dunharrow the following day Éowyn would notice that he looked grimmer, older and fey (*LotR* 5.3.797).

- *LotR* 5.8 tells how his face *"grew grey with weariness"*[51] from the effort to counteract the effects of the Black Breath on Faramir.

Aragorn was clearly capable of astounding mental and physical achievements, but the resulting suffering was reflected in his appearance. His strength was in his dogged endurance regardless of pain, fear and deprivation.

Disguise, invisibility and transformation

Aragorn's looks were also affected by his need for secrecy. In App A he is said to have seemed *"worthy of honour ... **when he did not hide his true shape**"*[52] [My emphasis]. Thus, in addition to being caused by his lifestyle, his scruffy, lean, haggard appearance was useful for concealing his identity and true character. For example Frodo saw him as someone frightening on first acquaintance (*LotR* 1.10.171), while Barliman Butterbur saw him as a vagabond (*LotR* 1.10.164) and Saruman as a cut-throat (*LotR* 3.10.583). Nevertheless his real self sometimes showed through his grim exterior. Frodo indeed quickly formed the opinion that his appearance was a deliberate disguise as illustrated by his words *"you are not really as you choose to look"*, followed by the questions *"Why the disguise? and Who are you?"*[53] Later he would explain his trust by stating his belief that a spy of Sauron would *"seem fairer and feel fouler"*[54] than Aragorn did. App A.I.v.1060 states that his grimness was dispelled when he smiled, an example of this occurring when he forcefully demonstrated to the Hobbits that he was powerful enough to take the Ring from them if he wanted to, but then looked down

---

44. Op. cit. [1], *LotR* 2.2, p. 255.
45. Op. cit., *LotR* 4.8, p. 714.
46. Op. cit., *LotR* 6.3, p. 943.
47. Op. cit. [5], Letter 83, p. 95.
48. Op. cit. [1], *LotR* 3.1, p. 416.
49. Op. cit., *LotR* 5.2, p. 778.
50. Op. cit., *LotR* 5.2, p. 780.
51. Op. cit., *LotR* 5.8, p. 865.
52. Op. cit., App A.I.v, p. 1060.
53. Op. cit., *LotR* 1.10, p. 166.
54. Op. cit., *LotR* 1.10, p. 171.

on them *"with his face softened by a sudden smile"*[55].

Another aspect of Aragorn's appearance (or more appropriately **non**-appearance) was his apparent invisibility when it suited him, due to his mastery of stealth and camouflage. As he said to Frodo in their first proper conversation, "*... though I cannot disappear ... I can usually avoid being seen, if I wish*"[56]. There are many examples in *LotR* which illustrate this:
- He went unnoticed by the Hobbits as they took leave of Tom Bombadil on the East Road - he was hiding behind the hedge at the time. He also followed them all the way to Bree - four miles - and after they had been admitted to the village by Harry Goatleaf the gatekeeper he climbed over the gate, again without being detected, and *"melted into the shadows"*[57].
- In the bar at the Prancing Pony Frodo did not notice him for some time - certainly it was well after the introductions had been made to the locals as Pippin had had time to settle in sufficiently to regale the company with the story of Will Whitfoot having the Town Hole roof collapsing on him.
- Similarly, when Frodo, Sam and Pippin were back in the parlour after Frodo's mishap with the Ring, they had built up the fire before discovering that Aragorn had come into the room with them and was calmly sitting in a chair by the door. Judging by Pippin's surprised reaction he obviously hadn't noticed him in the bar either.
- Shortly afterwards, when Barliman Butterbur came to the parlour to bring Gandalf's letter to Frodo, Aragorn moved to a dark corner of the room where he was unnoticed by Butterbur until he actually stepped forward and spoke, causing the inn-keeper to jump in surprise and accuse him of *"always popping up"*[58].
- A similar situation arose when Merry rushed in following his encounter with the Nazgûl in the street: he was startled when Aragorn spoke, having clearly failed to notice him before that.
- At the Council of Elrond (*LotR* 2.2.239, 246) Aragorn sat alone in a corner wearing his travelling clothes and Boromir did not seem to notice him until he flung the Shards of Narsil on to the table.
- In *LotR* 5.8 we are told that Gandalf arrived at the Houses of Healing accompanied by *"one cloaked in grey"*. Imrahil, clearly unaware of this person's identity, said *"Shall we not send now for the Lord Aragorn?"*, whereupon Aragorn announced himself and moved out of the shadows and into the light of a lantern.[59]

In all these examples Aragorn used a variety of techniques to achieve his objective of remaining hidden or unobtrusive for whatever reason:
- As a Ranger, when travelling, he wore green and brown clothing which acted as camouflage. He was in fact dressed like this at the Council of Elrond which possibly explained why Boromir overlooked him until he produced the Shards of Narsil. An additional suggestion, made at a meeting of the Southampton UK Tolkien Reading Group, was that Boromir was the sort of person who believed in his own importance and therefore automatically overlooked people who appeared scruffy and insignificant. His own rich clothing perhaps emphasises the point.
- A hood proved useful in hiding his face. In Bree it wasn't until he removed his hood that Frodo saw what he actually looked like. Also in the Houses of Healing incident described above, he wore his grey Elf-cloak to hide his identity until his actual arrival at the beds of the sick. If Imrahil didn't realise it was him initially, this may have been partly because he was hiding his face with the hood. At that stage he was in Minas Tirith only as a healer and wanted to avoid being seen as a potential King.
- He was adept at being unobtrusive by sitting in corners (as in the Prancing Pony and at the Council of Elrond), and by taking advantage of shadows (in the streets of Bree at night, in the parlour at the inn lit only by candlelight and firelight, and at the entrance to the Houses of Healing where he avoided

---
55. Op. cit. [1], *LotR* 1.10, p. 171.
56. Op. cit., *LotR* 1.10, p. 163.
57. Op. cit., *LotR* 1.9, p. 152.
58. Op. cit., *LotR* 1.10, p. 168.
59. Op. cit., *LotR* 5.8, p. 862.

standing near the lantern).
- He was an accomplished tracker and stalker, able to move silently and good at concealing himself. His experiences of tracking, and eventually capturing, Gollum must have made his unseen pursuit of the Hobbits to Bree remarkably easy.
- Because of the qualities just mentioned he was also a competent eavesdropper as shown by his overhearing the Hobbits' leave-taking of Tom Bombadil. This skill would have been honed during his many years of spying in the lands ruled by Sauron in the South and East. It would also have been assisted by his apparently acute hearing as illustrated by Frodo's feeling that Strider had heard his conversation with Barliman Butterbur across the crowded bar in the Prancing Pony (*LotR* 1.9.156), or maybe Frodo's alternative interpretation was true and Strider had merely guessed what was being said. This was quite possible with his exceptional powers of perception. It also seems likely that he would have been skilled in lip-reading.
- Even when camouflage wasn't necessary he still managed to achieve it unintentionally. For example as Bilbo and Frodo sat exchanging news in the Hall of Fire in Rivendell Aragorn stood looking down at them "*For many minutes*"[60] before they noticed him. Admittedly the two Hobbits were very engrossed in their conversation, but other factors were the lack of light - apart from the fire - and the fact that Aragorn was dressed in dark green.

Sometimes his appearance underwent a complete transformation, albeit briefly, as the following examples show:
- When Frodo witnessed him reliving his betrothal to Arwen on Cerin Amroth "*the grim years were removed from the face of Aragorn*" and Frodo saw him as "*a young lord tall and fair ...*"[61]. Thus we get a glimpse of Aragorn as he was thirty-eight years earlier under the healing influence of Lothlórien.
- When Galadriel gave him the Elessar brooch his companions wondered "*for they had not marked before how tall and kingly he stood, and it seemed to them that many years of toil had fallen from his shoulders*"[62]. This incident implies that Aragorn was normally somewhat bowed due to his cares and hardship.
- He underwent a similar sort of change when the Fellowship sailed past the Argonath, being described as proud and erect, his hair blowing in the wind and a light in his eye, "*a king returning from exile to his own land*"[63]. This was in startling contrast to his words to Boromir at the Council of Elrond: "*Little do I resemble the figures of Elendil and Isildur as they stand carven in their majesty in the halls of Denethor.*"[64]. The statues of the Argonath were of Isildur and Anárion, and Aragorn at this point certainly appeared comparable with them.
- This image was picked up again when he revealed his identity to Éomer. Legolas and Gimli saw "*in his living face ... a brief vision of the power and majesty of the kings of stone*"[65] with Legolas even seeing a white flame on his brow resembling a crown.
- Perhaps it was a similar image which Sauron saw in the Palantír when Aragorn confronted him. We know that he appeared "*in other guise than you see me here*"[66] as he told Legolas and Gimli.

It is on the Field of Cormallen after the destruction of the Ring that we get our first genuine view (as opposed to visions or brief transformations) of Aragorn as he was meant to look. Frodo and Sam were taken to meet the unknown "*King of Gondor and Lord of the Western Lands*"[67] who, Gandalf said, had tended them after their rescue from Mordor. As they approached the throne they saw a man who was bare-headed, dressed

---

60. Op. cit. [1], *LotR* 2.1, p. 232.
61. Op. cit., *LotR* 2.6, p. 352.
62. Op. cit., *LotR* 2.8, p. 375.
63. Op. cit., *LotR* 2.9, p. 393.
64. Op. cit., *LotR* 2.2, p. 248.
65. Op. cit., *LotR* 3.2, pp. 433-4.
66. Op. cit., *LotR* 5.2, p. 780.
67. Op. cit., *LotR* 6.4, p. 952.

in mail and with an impressive sword across his knees. He stood up as they drew near, *"And then they knew him, changed as he was, so high and glad of face, kingly, lord of Men, dark-haired with eyes of grey."*[68] There was now no need to keep his identity secret; he was no longer living rough; the risk he had taken revealing himself to Sauron had paid off; the Ring had been destroyed with Frodo and Sam surviving the ordeal; he was indisputably King of both his kingdoms thus fulfilling Elrond's conditions for marrying Arwen. All these factors were responsible for the phrase *"changed as he was"* - not forgetting the obvious effects of baths, haircut, a shave (unless his Elf blood made this unnecessary), clean clothes, regular meals and some good nights' sleep!

*

All Aragorn's adult life his appearance had been subject to the conflict between his natural beauty from his Maian, Elvish and Númenórean descent and the ravages of the unrelenting hardship of his life of wandering. I finish this chapter by quoting the description of him after his death:

> "... *a great beauty was revealed in him, so that all who after came there looked on him in wonder; for they saw that the grace of his youth, and the valour of his manhood, and the wisdom and majesty of his age were blended together. And long there he lay, an image of the splendour of the Kings of Men* [i.e. of Númenor] *in glory undimmed before the breaking of the world."*[69]

---

68. Op. cit. [1], *LotR* 6.4, p. 953.
69. Op. cit., App A.I.v, p. 1063.

PART TWO

RELATIONSHIPS

CHAPTER 2.0 - INTRODUCTION

Having studied Aragorn's story it can be seen that he was an extremely complex character. In *LotR*[1] he appears as a creature of contrasts, see-sawing between hope and despair, decisiveness and uncertainty, self-confidence and vulnerability, endless patience and outbursts of anger or bitterness. Much of this contradictory behaviour arose from being in stressful and dangerous situations where he felt out of his depth, or overwhelmed by guilt, or was being torn between several courses of action and striving to make the right choice. In addition to these characteristics however there are many qualities which are consistently present: courage, compassion, protectiveness, loyalty, sense of duty, integrity, humility and dogged persistence. He was someone who took a lot on himself, physically and mentally. He possessed the gifts of healing, perceptiveness, elven wisdom, empathy and foresightedness. Legolas said of him, "*... all those who come to know him come to love him after their own fashion ...*"[2] This was no doubt explained by some of the qualities mentioned above, along with his ability to forge relationships of affection and trust with many different kinds of people: Hobbits, Elves, Dwarves and the various races of Men, not to mention Gandalf.

Aragorn's relationships are very significant in a study of him and the aim in the following chapters is to round out the picture obtained from the generally biographical approach adopted up until now by examining his interactions with those who affected and influenced his life. In practice this covers most of the characters and races in *LotR*.

As well as showing how others viewed him this approach leads to increased emphasis on Aragorn's strengths, weaknesses, motives and personal struggles, particularly the psychological and emotional issues affecting him which were touched on in Part One. In addition there are a number of recurring themes, such as guilt, hope, pity, foresight and love. The element of hope is reflected in his childhood name as well as in the foresight of the Elves and Dúnedain who shaped his upbringing. As I have already observed in Chapter 1.7, Paul Kocher says that Aragorn overcame Gondor's enemies by arms, but overcame Gondor itself by love[3]. As well as inspiring devotion he had a great capacity for giving love and affection. Often his interactions with others brought out the best in him and the best in them. This trait was part of the reason for him achieving his goals, yet it was also spontaneous and empathetic - part of his nature.

Chapters 2.1-2.9 contain detailed studies of Aragorn's relationships as depicted in *LotR* (chiefly) and elsewhere. This inevitably involves a fair amount of analysis of the other characters as well.

I also look at the influence on him of some of his ancestors.

---

1. J.R.R. Tolkien, *The Lord of the Rings,* London, HarperCollins Publishers, 2007, 2nd edition, based on the 50th Anniversary Edition of 2004.
2. Op. cit., *LotR* 5.9, p. 874.
3. P. Kocher, *Master of Middle-earth: The Achievement of J. R. R. Tolkien*, London, Pimlico, 2002, first published in Great Britain by Thames & Hudson 1973, Chapter 6, p. 157.

CHAPTER 2.1 - ELVES

The chief purpose of this chapter is to carry out a detailed analysis of Aragorn's relationships with Arwen, Elrond, Galadriel, Celeborn, Elladan and Elrohir - both individually and as a family. Genealogical Table 1 is relevant. In addition I address the questions as to how well acquainted he was with Glorfindel, Gildor Inglorion, and Círdan and his people. I have deliberately omitted Legolas (and by extension the Elves of Mirkwood in general) from the discussion as I feel that the unique threesome of Aragorn, Legolas and Gimli merits a chapter of its own.

Although Aragorn was of the race of Men, he had a small amount of Elf blood in him from his Elven and Half-elven ancestors, in addition to a tiny streak of divinity from Melian. More than sixty generations had elapsed between him and his Maian/Elven forebears - nevertheless their influence was apparent as demonstrated by the extent of his foresight, healing powers, Elven wisdom, ability to quell a person with his gaze, and his perception of the minds and feelings of others - even Sauron. These qualities, in essence the result of his Númenórean inheritance, were enhanced by his Elf and Maia blood. His upbringing in Rivendell among Elves, being tutored by Elrond and his sons would have further developed these characteristics, as well as steeping him in Elvish culture and behaviour. A couple of examples from *LotR*[1] serve to illustrate the Elvish influences on him. In Lothlórien (*LotR* 2.7.357) as Galadriel searched the minds of the Fellowship, Aragorn was the only one (apart from the Elf Legolas) who could withstand her gaze for any length of time. She and Celeborn had stood up to greet their guests *"after the manner of Elves, even those who were accounted mighty kings."*[2] Likewise in *LotR* 6.6.974 Aragorn and Arwen, as King and Queen, stood up to greet Frodo when he went to see them.

I now look in detail at the relationship between Aragorn and Arwen and study the roles and significance of Elrond, Galadriel, Celeborn, Elladan and Elrohir with regard to the romance between the pair and in relation to Aragorn's struggles and destiny. Love, foresight, hope, death and immortality are important elements throughout.

ARWEN

There were three marriages between Eldar and Edain. Two of these unions took place in the First Age - those of Lúthien Tinúviel with Beren and Idril Celebrindal with Tuor - while the marriage of Arwen and Aragorn took place at the end of the Third Age. App A.I.i states that the last-mentioned union reunited the *"long-sundered branches of the Half-elven"*[3], meaning the line of Elrond Half-elven, Arwen's father, and the line of his mortal brother Elros Half-elven, first King of Númenor, from whom Aragorn was sixty-third in descent. There are some similarities between the Beren/Lúthien and Aragorn/Arwen relationships which will be referred to where relevant. The case of Idril and Tuor bears less resemblance to that of Aragorn and Arwen since there was no question of Idril sacrificing her Elvish immortality and Tuor appears to have been been allowed to sail to the Undying Lands with her - possibly because of his affinity with the sea and his role as messenger of Ulmo, the Vala of the Sea and other waters.[4]

There are few references to Arwen in the main narrative of *LotR* (she was a very late addition to the story), and most of the hints which **are** available prior to her marriage are fairly meaningless to a first-time reader of

---

1. J.R.R. Tolkien, *The Lord of the Rings,* London, HarperCollins Publishers, 2007, 2nd edition, based on the 50th Anniversary Edition of 2004.
2. Op. cit., *LotR* 2.7, p. 354.
3. Op. cit., App A.I.i, p. 1034.
4. C. Tolkien (ed.), *The Silmarillion*, London, HarperCollins Publishers, 1999, first published in Great Britain by George Allen & Unwin 1977, *TSil* Chapter 23, pp. 293-4.

the book, as they were to Frodo and his friends. However in the present context they are certainly worthy of study:

- When Aragorn and the Hobbits were preparing to spend the night in the dell on Weathertop, Aragorn told them about Beren and Lúthien, starting by chanting the verses which described their meeting and then narrating the rest of their story, including the fact that Lúthien alone of the Elf-kindred had actually died and left the world. With hindsight we know that another member of that kindred will soon be following in her footsteps. Aragorn's emotion as he told the tale was clear from his shining eyes and *"strange eager face"* while the fire burned and the moon climbed up the sky behind him.[5]
- A week later in *LotR* 1.12.202, he told Frodo that his heart was in Rivendell - Arwen's home and where he had first met her.
- Once in Rivendell (*LotR* 2.1.233, 238) two hints were made about the relationship between Aragorn and Arwen. Bilbo pointedly asked Aragorn why he hadn't gone to the feast particularly as Arwen had been there. Later the same evening Frodo saw them talking together as a couple, Aragorn clothed in elven-mail and wearing a star on his breast. Frodo was surprised so he obviously hadn't picked up the significance of Bilbo's question earlier on.
- *LotR* relates the episode on Cerin Amroth where Frodo found Aragorn, momentarily resembling a young Elf-lord, *"wrapped in some fair memory"* and speaking in Elvish to someone whom Frodo couldn't see.[6] Arwen's name was one of the words he spoke and he was reliving his betrothal to her which had taken place in that spot nearly forty years earlier. Again he told Frodo *"... here my heart dwells ever..."*.[7] Lothlórien was as deeply associated with Arwen as Rivendell.
- In *LotR* 2.8.375 as the Fellowship prepared to leave Lothlórien to begin their journey down the Anduin Galadriel gave Aragorn the Elessar set in its silver eagle-shaped brooch. During the ensuing conversation it was made clear that Arwen had left it with Galadriel so she could pass it on to him. Arwen's name was actually mentioned in their conversation. Apart from the significance of the Elessar for Aragorn's royal claim, Galadriel hoped it would be a comfort to him in his yearning for Arwen.
- Halbarad's delivery of Arwen's gift was another very emotionally-charged incident. Referring to her as the Lady of Rivendell he repeated the message she had sent, at which point Aragorn realised that her gift was the royal battle-standard she had been making in secret. He turned and looked to the north, *"then he fell silent and spoke no more while the night's journey lasted."*[8] His silence spoke volumes.
- The following day as he prepared to go through the Paths of the Dead he made a desperate attempt to make Éowyn see that he was already committed to a woman, telling her that if he were to go where his heart dwelt he would now be in Rivendell not in Dunharrow (*LotR* 5.2.784).
- In *LotR* 6.5.971 after Aragorn had been crowned King, we are told how Gandalf took him to the hallow on Mount Mindolluin and guided him to a sapling of the White Tree growing at the snow-line. This would be used to replace the dead tree which had stood in the Court of the Citadel for nearly a hundred and fifty years. Owing to the prophecy of Tar-Palantir, that the line of Kings would die out if the White Tree were to fail, one can understand the acute anxiety Aragorn expressed to Gandalf. He had played his part in the defeat of Sauron and had regained his kingdoms, thus fulfilling Elrond's conditions for marrying Arwen. Was it all about to fall apart at the last moment?

It is only with hindsight that it is possible to appreciate the significance of these incidents and the emotions connected with them. However a study of these hints in conjunction with the excerpt from *The Tale of Aragorn and Arwen* in App A.I.v.1057-1063 leaves no doubt as to Arwen's importance to Aragorn. Paul Kocher describes his longing for her during his years of struggle as being *"... a torment, a joy, a despair, a comfort... in a time of little hope."*[9]

*

---

5. Op. cit. [1], *LotR* 1.11, p. 194.
6. Op. cit., *LotR* 2.6, p. 352.
7. Op. cit., *LotR* 2.6, p. 352.
8. Op. cit., *LotR* 5.2, p. 775.
9. P. Kocher, *Master of Middle-earth: The Achievement of J. R. R. Tolkien*, London, Pimlico, 2002, first published in Great Britain by Thames & Hudson 1973, Chapter 6, p. 137.

Arwen was born to Elrond and Celebrían in the year TA 241 (App B.1085) and was thus not far short of three thousand years old at the time of Aragorn's birth. As well as being the daughter of Elrond and the grand-daughter of Galadriel and Celeborn she was the great great grand-daughter of Lúthien who was half Elf and half Maia. As is clear in *TSil* 19.206, 212-3, 220, Lúthien's divine blood gave her gifts of healing and enchantment including the ability to bring down the walls of Sauron's tower with a spell and, with the power of her singing, to overcome Morgoth himself and to arouse pity in Mandos, the Vala who judged the spirits of the dead. Arwen's similarity to Lúthien is emphasised in App A.I.v.1058 as she resembled her in appearance and shared her fate by sacrificing her immortality in order to marry a mortal. A relationship which receives less attention is Arwen's descent from Idril Celebrindal (daughter of Turgon the Elf-King of Gondolin) whose wisdom, courage and foresight played a significant part in the escape of the remnant of the people of Gondolin (including the child Eärendil) following the onslaught of Morgoth. Idril was actually a closer relation to Arwen than Lúthien, being her great-grandmother.

A superficial interpretation of Arwen shows her as a rather pale copy of her impressive ancestors, doing little for Aragorn except look beautiful and embroider a banner. In examining her relationships with Aragorn and Elrond I hope to dispel this image of her. App A.I.v.1057-1063 provides most of the material for the following discussion.

The first meeting between Aragorn and Arwen occurred in Rivendell - to which Arwen had just returned after a long absence (by mortal standards) in Lothlórien visiting her grandparents. The twenty-year-old Aragorn had just been told, by Elrond, of his true identity and destiny. He was emotionally immature and inexperienced, and childishly excited at his newly-discovered status. As he wandered through the birch trees, singing about Lúthien Tinúviel, he encountered Arwen whom he initially assumed to be Lúthien herself, believing that he was dreaming, or else that he had suddenly been granted the elven gift of actually seeing images from his song. Being corrected on these points by Arwen herself, he then made the further mistake of assuming she was a girl of his own age, becoming acutely embarrassed when the elven-light and wisdom in her eyes, plus her gentle reminder that "*the children of Elrond have the life of the Eldar*"[10], made him aware of the reality. As far as Aragorn was concerned it was love at first sight and he was never to waver from this love. However it was not an auspicious beginning: Aragorn was not able to hide his feelings from Elrond who made it very clear to him that any marriage was out of the question at this stage in his life, let alone one with his daughter. Apart from the difference in race, age and maturity which made him a mere child compared with Arwen, there would also be the matter of Arwen having to lose her elvish immortality if she were to marry a mortal - as Lúthien had had to do on marrying Beren. This would result in her dying as a mortal and being parted - prematurely and most likely for ever - from her father and the rest of her race who would live as long as the world lasted. Almost immediately after his conversation with Elrond Aragorn departed from Rivendell to take up the lonely and dangerous life of a Ranger.

Regarding Arwen's feelings and behaviour at this first encounter, she seemed friendly, perhaps rather amused initially - as she might have been on meeting an appealing child. However when Aragorn told her he had thought she was Lúthien she became serious, making a significant and seemingly prophetic speech: "*... her [i.e.Luthien's] name is not mine.* **Though maybe my doom will be not unlike hers.**"[11] [My emphasis]. The implication seems to be that Arwen suspected from the first that she and this mortal boy might have a future together. On looking into his eyes she perceived his bewilderment at the apparent contradiction between her youthful appearance and her long absence [at least eighteen years] from her father's home. On their second meeting, in Lothlórien, when Aragorn was a mature man of forty-nine, it is noted that although Arwen had hardly aged at all, "*... her face was more grave, and her laughter now seldom was heard.*"[12] This could imply that Aragorn - and the doom of Lúthien - had remained in her thoughts during their years apart, an interpretation strengthened by the fact that on meeting him again "*... her choice was made and her doom appointed.*"[13] It was almost as if she had fallen in love at their initial meeting - not with Aragorn as he was then, but with the man she knew he would become.

---

10. Op. cit. [1], App A.I.v, p. 1058.
11. Op. cit., App A.I.v, p. 1058.
12. Op. cit., App A.I.v, p. 1060.
13. Op. cit., App A.I.v, p. 1060.

Her words at their betrothal showed both foresight and hope: *"Dark is the Shadow, and yet my heart rejoices; for you, Estel, shall be among the great whose valour will destroy it."*[14] Aragorn's eventual victory against Sauron seemed to be a certainty as far as she was concerned. Also she addressed him by his childhood name of Estel/Hope. His reply showed that although he didn't have her degree of foresight, he was steadfast in his rejection of the Shadow and clung to the hope that she felt: *"Yet with your hope I will hope."*[15] He then gently reminded her of the reality of their situation, of the necessity for her to renounce a future in the Undying Lands with her people. For his own peace of mind he would have wanted to be sure that she realised exactly what she was doing by pledging herself to him. At this point she stood still looking into the West, *"... **and at last** she said: 'I will cleave to you, Dúnadan, and turn from the Twilight. Yet there lies the land of my people and the long home of all my kin.' She loved her father dearly."*[16] [My emphasis]. Her words and the use of "at last", while illustrating the depth of her love for Aragorn, also showed that her decision was not made lightly or easily. There was a great deal at stake whatever she chose to do.

Her hope and foresight were further illustrated in *LotR* 2.8.375 when Galadriel gave the Elessar brooch to Aragorn indicating that it had been left in her care by Arwen in case he should pass through Lothlórien. Galadriel referred to the Elessar as a token of hope and called Aragorn by his royal name Elessar/Elfstone for the first time. In App B.1090 it is stated that in TA 3009, due to increasing danger in the Misty Mountains, Elrond had sent for Arwen to return to Rivendell (from Lothlórien). Therefore she must have left the brooch with Galadriel at that point - ten years before the Fellowship went that way - believing that she herself would not be going to Lothlórien again before Aragorn went there, and believing also that he would be visiting it on the way to claiming the kingship. This implies a marked degree of foresight.

Due to Elrond's stipulation that his daughter should wed no less a person than the King of Arnor and Gondor, another thirty-nine years were still to elapse after their betrothal before Arwen and Aragorn would be able to marry. These were years of increasing danger and hardship as far as Aragorn was concerned and opportunities of being with Arwen were few and far between. It is stated that during his absences she watched over him in thought. It is difficult to interpret this statement exactly, but it must surely mean much more than merely keeping him in her thoughts. I take it to mean that she had some sort of awareness of Aragorn's sufferings and danger and was able to communicate support, comfort and even possibly protection from afar. Perhaps some hint as to the nature of her gift can be obtained from considering Galadriel. There is an incident in *LotR* 6.2.918, 920 where Frodo and Sam were struggling north along the Morgai and Sam said that if he could speak to Galadriel he would tell her that they needed water and light. Shortly afterwards light appeared in the sky and Sam found a trickle of water. In an earlier incident, in Shelob's lair (*LotR* 4.9.719-20), he saw a vision of Galadriel which reminded him of the Phial she had given to Frodo, prompting them both to use it as protection against Shelob. In addition there are references to the magical qualities of the Lothlórien rope (which detached itself thus enabling it to be retrieved after use), of the cloaks worn by the Fellowship, and also of the sheath given to Aragorn by Galadriel which would prevent his sword being stained or broken. Given the significant amount of Maian blood in Arwen and the fact that she was Galadriel's grand-daughter it seems quite conceivable that she could have given similar support to Aragorn, both psychologically and by use of physical objects. Was she, among other things, able to help sustain his will to resist the Ring, and to overrule Sauron during the Palantír confrontation? The white jewel she gave to Frodo after the War of the Ring was clearly much more than mere adornment as its purpose was to alleviate his pain when the memory of his sufferings threatened to overwhelm him. This begs the question of the Elessar: as stated above, this had been in Arwen's possession until 3009 when she left it in Galadriel's care. She had originally received it from her mother and as Celebrían had departed from Middle-earth in TA 2510 Arwen must have possessed it at least since then if not for longer. Did the Elessar enable her to protect Aragorn in some way, if not from a distance, at least for healing when she was with him, if his travels and hardship pressed particularly heavily on him? If this was the case then Aragorn would have been familiar with the gem prior to actually receiving it. That it had healing properties was demonstrated by Galadriel's original desire for it to beautify her land, and later by Aragorn's use of it in the Houses of Healing. Arwen is never referred to as a healer but she would undoubtedly have inherited

---

14. Op. cit. [1], App A.I.v, p. 1061.
15. Op. cit., App A.I.v, p. 1061.
16. Op. cit., App A.I.v, p. 1061.

this ability (as her brothers did) which would have been enhanced by the Elessar. [The Elessar is discussed in more detail later in this chapter.]

In addition to her mental strivings Arwen also occupied herself with making the royal standard which would be brought to Aragorn by Halbarad when the Dúnedain came to him in Rohan during the War of the Ring. This standard was made in secret (according to Halbarad) and was a further indication of Arwen's hope and foresight. As well as the standard itself hidden in a black cloth, Halbarad delivered a verbal message from her: "*The days now are short. Either our hope cometh, or all hope's end. Therefore I send thee what I have made for thee. Fare well, Elfstone!*"[17]. Note that she used the name he would bear as King - as Galadriel had done when the Fellowship were in Lothlórien. At this speech Aragorn realised what it was that Halbarad was carrying and became silent for the rest of the journey to the Hornburg. The standard obviously wasn't a secret as far as he was concerned. This was a crucial time for him - he had just acquired the Palantír of Orthanc and was considering whether to cast secrecy aside and reveal himself to Sauron. The presence of Halbarad and his companions, and the message and standard from Arwen removed any lingering doubt as to what he should do.

The standard is worthy of consideration in its own right. It was first unfurled at the Stone of Erech as Aragorn summoned the Dead Men of Dunharrow : "*... **and behold!** it was black, and if there was any device upon it, it was hidden in the darkness.*"[18] [My emphasis]. Nevertheless it had the desired effect on the Dead who heeded the call to redeem their oath, clearly satisfied that this was indeed the heir of Isildur. The standard was unfurled again by Halbarad at the Battle of the Pelennor Fields in the light of day : "***and behold!*** *upon the foremost ship a great standard broke...*"[19] [My emphasis]. In contrast it now appeared as a work of great splendour and intricacy with the White Tree of Gondor and the Seven Stars and crown of Elendil depicted in gems, mithril and gold. During the battle Halbarad was killed, but the standard survived to be displayed again at the Battle of the Morannon (where it flew "*fair and desperate*"[20]) and then at the honouring of the Ring-bearers on the Field of Cormallen (*LotR* 6.4.953). The next time it was used was in Minas Tirith as King Elessar entered the city after his coronation. Note that "behold" followed by an exclamation-mark (used many times in *LotR* to denote some momentous occurrence) precedes the first two unfurlings of the standard. It was clearly something out of the ordinary. Is it fanciful to suggest that the cloth itself was partly woven from Arwen's own hair (in imitation of the enchanted cloak of Lúthien in *TSil* 19.202), thus incorporating a protective spell in it?

Another significant gift from Arwen was the horse Roheryn, brought south by the Dúnedain. In *TSil* Appendix.440, this name is interpreted as meaning "horse of the lady", with Roheryn being so named because he was given to Aragorn by Arwen. In *LotR* 5.2.778 Roheryn is simply described as Aragorn's own horse, thus implying that the gift had been made sometime before. As a result of his presence Aragorn was able to ride him through the Paths of the Dead instead of the horse of Rohan he had been using up until then. Arwen must have been aware of Elrond's advice to Aragorn about using the Paths of the Dead and would have been keen to ensure that the horse he rode was capable of withstanding the horrors of that journey.

A further aspect of Arwen's support for Aragorn's struggles was her care for the welfare of the Ring-bearers. This is evident, with hindsight, from the incident in *LotR* 2.1.238 when Frodo saw her talking with Aragorn in Rivendell and then became aware of her attention being focused on himself. This seems to me to mark the moment when Arwen perceived the extent of Frodo's current and future sufferings on account of the Ring, and the beginning of her idea of Frodo being allowed to sail West, instead of her, if she were to marry Aragorn. The idea came to fruition in *LotR* 6.6.974-5 when, as Aragorn's wife, she offered Frodo the chance to take ship in her place if his memories and pain became unbearable. Meanwhile she gave him her jewel to wear, as a comfort and "*... in memory of Elfstone and Evenstar with whom your life has been woven!*"[21] In addition she showed perception of Bilbo's suffering as a result of the Ring, explaining to Frodo that it was hardly surprising that his kinsman hadn't been strong enough to come south for the wedding due to his age (artificially extended by the Ring) and the length of time he had possessed the Ring. Arwen had known Bilbo for about ten years so would have had plenty of opportunity to observe him. In her observation that "*... all that was done by that*

---

17. Op. cit. [1], *LotR* 5.2, p. 775.
18. Op. cit., *LotR* 5.2, p. 789.
19. Op. cit., *LotR* 5.6, p. 847.
20. Op. cit., *LotR* 5.10, p. 891.
21. Op. cit., *LotR* 6.6, p. 975.

power [i.e. the Ring] is now passing away"[22] she included Bilbo's long lifespan telling Frodo, "*... he will not again make any long journey save one.*"[23] This could be interpreted as being either death or his journey to the Undying Lands. It is not clear whether she knew about the latter.

Continuing with the events described in *LotR* 6.6: as Arwen sat with Aragorn by the fountain we are told that she "*... sang a song of Valinor, while the Tree grew and blossomed.*"[24] The implication here seems to be that her song encouraged the White Tree to grow, thereby strengthening not only the Tree, but the kingship itself. In *TSil* 4.54 it is stated that Melian was akin to the Vala Yavanna who sang the original White Tree into existence in Valinor - so there would technically be a streak of Yavanna in Arwen. The description of Yavanna's singing in *TSil* ("*Under her song the saplings grew and became fair and tall, and came to flower...*"[25]) is remarkably similar to that of Arwen's. Compare also the song of Galadriel in *LotR* : "*I sang of leaves, of leaves of gold, and leaves of gold there grew*"[26]. Arwen is impressive in this chapter - as she is elsewhere if one reads between the lines.

It is clear that during her long courtship Arwen had shown both the depth of her love and great courage by forsaking her own people and her immortal life for what must have been, to her, a very brief period of happiness. (She was married to Aragorn for approximately one twenty-fifth of a life which was curtailed due to the mortality she took on herself.) It is clear too that even if she hadn't been able to be with Aragorn in person during his struggles, her support of him had been enormous, with her unshakable hope and her deep faith in him, as well as that elvish/semi-divine ability to watch over him from afar. The fact that Aragorn was usually able to keep his own hopes up must have been in large part due to Arwen. She and Aragorn are said to have lived in glory and bliss during their reign as King and Queen of the Reunited Kingdom. With her elvish wisdom, foresight and perception she would undoubtedly have excelled in her role, as well as producing heirs with a strong elvish strain.

However this happiness was over all too soon and Elrond's prediction, "*I fear that to Arwen the Doom of Men may seem hard at the ending*"[27], was realised. During Aragorn's death scene, he was the one trying to instil hope and faith into her as grief and bitterness overwhelmed her. Although she had accepted this fate on committing herself to Aragorn she had perhaps underestimated just how traumatic the end would be. Certainly she understood for the first time the motives of the corrupted kings of Númenor who had tried to wrest immortality from the Valar, admitting that she now felt pity for them rather than scorn, and calling the gift of death "*bitter to receive*"[28]. Seeing her grief Aragorn gave her his blessing, even at this late stage, to repent her decision and take ship into the West where their love would endure for the lifetime of the world - but only as a memory. On the other hand if she were to accept a mortal death in hope and trust ("*In sorrow we must go, but not in despair*"[29]) then they would escape from the world to something that was perhaps more than just memory. It seems strange that Aragorn offered her such a choice as it was not in his power to do so. In addition her fate had surely been irrevocably sealed from the time of her marriage and the departure of her father from Middle-earth. That Arwen herself realised this is confirmed by her words, "*... that choice is long over*" followed by "*There is now no ship that would bear me hence*".[30] It is not explained whether this was because she would not be allowed to board a ship or whether there were no more ships sailing. [Legolas did in fact build his own ship after Aragorn's death though he did not sail from the Grey Havens.]

Arwen's last words to Aragorn as he died were "*Estel, Estel!*"[31] - the childhood name of hope by which she had first known him, and also the name by which she had addressed him at their betrothal. However her condition after Aragorn's death seemed to indicate a loss of hope along with her elvishness and her foresight. Aragorn had clearly failed to make her believe, as he did, that something better than Elvish immortality lay

---

22. Op. cit. [1], *LotR* 6.6, p. 974.
23. Op. cit., *LotR* 6.6, p. 974.
24. Op. cit., *LotR* 6.6, p. 974.
25. Op. cit. [4], *TSil* Chapter 1, p. 31.
26. Op. cit. [1], *LotR* 2.8, p. 372.
27. Op. cit., App A.I.v, p. 1061.
28. Op. cit., App A.I.v, p. 1063.
29. Op. cit., App A.I.v, p. 1063.
30. Op. cit., App A.I.v, p. 1063.
31. Op. cit., App A.I.v, p. 1063.

ahead for them. It was almost as though she were already dead, and her body an empty shell. She appeared "*cold and grey*", and we are told that she bade farewell to her children "*and to all whom she **had** loved*" [My emphasis - the past tense is used][32]. Most tellingly "*the light of her eyes was quenched*"[33] - in contrast to the elven-light Aragorn saw in them at their first meeting. Her sacrifice had been made for Aragorn alone and her life was totally meaningless without him. Even the family they had raised together now seemed to mean nothing to her. The sadness of her situation was compounded by the fact that, still thinking and feeling as an Elf, she was not ready to leave her life so soon. Thus, unlike Lúthien and Beren, she and Aragorn died separately. Hammond and Scull refer to an unpublished letter to Eileen Elgar begun on September 22nd 1963 where Tolkien suggests that Arwen could have surrendered her life at the same time as Aragorn, but was not yet prepared to do so.[34] Ironically one of the reasons for Aragorn's ability to achieve sufficient mental healing to embrace death with willingness and trust, without having a sojourn in the Undying Lands first, was undoubtedly the peace and serenity he gained from his marriage to Arwen - along with his own superb mental strength. [I have also discussed this in Chapter 1.8.]

Arwen's solitary death and burial on Cerin Amroth in Lothlórien, the place of their betrothal, occurred approximately a year later and we are told that the elanor and niphredil flowers bloomed no more outside the Undying Lands. Niphredil had first appeared at the birth of Lúthien in the Forest of Doriath three ages before. Later it had grown in Lothlórien (presumably brought there by Galadriel), being present in profusion at the time of Aragorn's and Arwen's betrothal and at the time of the Fellowship's visit (*LotR* 2.6.350). It now disappeared from Middle-earth with the death of Lúthien's descendant, the Evenstar of her people who shared Lúthien's fate.

It is not clear whether Arwen came to share Aragorn's faith in the end and died voluntarily, or whether she just wasted away and died from grief, though Hammond and Scull's reference to the Eileen Elgar letter suggests the former. Denis Bridoux believes that Aragorn, by his last words, was "*showing [Arwen] the way*", and "*inviting her to follow him*".[35] There is also a ray of hope in the last two paragraphs of *LotR* 2.6 in the incident where Frodo climbed Cerin Amroth and witnessed Aragorn reliving his betrothal. After speaking a few words to Frodo "*... he left the hill of Cerin Amroth and came there never again **as living man.**"*[36] [My emphasis]. The implication is surely that although he did not come there again when living, he did come there again after death, thus indicating a spiritual reunion with Arwen. I cannot see why the last three words would be needed if this sentence simply meant that Aragorn never went to Cerin Amroth again. A similar quotation about Frodo in *LotR* 2.8 makes no such distinction, just simply states "*To that fair land Frodo never came again*"[37]. The last lines of the Tale of Tinúviel which Aragorn had chanted to Frodo and his friends on Weathertop also give cause for optimism: "*And long ago they passed away/In the forest singing sorrowless.*"[38]. One can only hope that a similar "sorrowless" fate was in store for Aragorn and Arwen.

*

In a letter to his son Michael of 6-8 March 1941 Tolkien states: "*... only the rarest good fortune brings together the man and woman who are really as it were 'destined' for one another, and capable of a very great and splendid love .... In such great inevitable love, often love at first sight, we catch a vision, I suppose, of marriage as it should have been in an unfallen world.*"[39] The relationship between Aragorn and Arwen (along with that between Lúthien and Beren) seems to me to belong in this category, with the emphasis on love at first sight - certainly on Aragorn's part and maybe on Arwen's too - in addition to the obvious depth of their feelings

---

32. Op. cit. [1], App A.I.v, p. 1063.
33. Op. cit., App A.I.v, p. 1063.
34. W.G. Hammond and C. Scull, *The Lord of the Rings: A Reader's Companion*, London, HarperCollins Publishers, 2005, p. 701.
35. D. Bridoux, 'Re-readings and Re-interpretations 1: *The Tale of Aragorn and Arwen*', *Amon Hen*, no. 250, November 2014, pp. 14-16.
36. Op. cit. [1], *LotR* 2.6, p. 352.
37. Op. cit., *LotR* 2.8, p. 378.
38. Op. cit., *LotR* 1.11, p. 193.
39. H. Carpenter (ed.), *The Letters of J.R.R. Tolkien*, with the assistance of Christopher Tolkien, London, HarperCollins Publishers, 1995. First published in Great Britain by George Allen & Unwin, 1981. Letter. 43, p. 52.

and their enduring faithfulness to each other during the long wait until they could marry. There is also, in my opinion, a purity about their relationship. It is easy to visualise the sheltered, and no doubt well-chaperoned, Arwen as being a virgin when their marriage finally took place, but what about Aragorn with his sixty-eight years of journeying in Middle-earth and his lengthy sojourns in the courts of Rohan and Gondor? On the face of it it is, perhaps, idealistic to imagine him keeping himself as pure for Arwen as she would have done for him, but on the other hand, looking at Tolkien's writings concerning the attitude of the Elves and the Númenóreans/ Dúnedain to sex and marriage, it may well be a valid interpretation of their relationship:

- In *Laws and Customs among the Eldar* (*HoM-e* X) it is stated,
  "*... seldom is any tale told of deeds of lust among them* [the Elves]"[40], and also that they were
  "*... seldom swayed by the desires of the body only, but are by nature continent and steadfast.*"[41]
- In addition it was normal for husband and wife to live apart some of the time.
- The Elvish attitude to children is illustrated by the following quotation: "*... it would seem to any of the Eldar a grievous thing if a wedded pair were sundered during the bearing of a child, or while the first years of its childhood lasted. For which reason the Eldar would beget children only in days of happiness and peace if they could.*"[42]
- In *Athrabeth Finrod ah Andreth* Finrod tells Andreth, "*This is time of war Andreth, and in such days the Elves do not wed or bear child*"[43], thus extending the delay to marriage itself as well as childbirth.
- The Númenóreans were similar to the Elves in many ways as shown by the statement in *Ak* describing them as "*... in all things more like to the Firstborn than any other of the kindreds of Men... But their numbers increased only slowly...*" and "*their children were few*".[44]
- In addition *UT* states that they "*... avoided the begetting of children if they foresaw any separation likely between husband and wife between the conception of the child and at least its very early years.*"[45]

Assuming that these customs and attitudes were also applicable to the Dúnedain of the Third Age and that intimacy inevitably meant children the concept of Aragorn's virginity on marriage to Arwen is not so far-fetched. Even if the Dúnedain were generally less sexually continent than the Elves, Aragorn would have been inspired to adopt the Elvish behaviour both for Arwen's sake and out of respect to Elrond. Also, as well as the embarrassing possibility of an illegitimate child, any pre-marital liaison would have been alien to Aragorn's nature and to his feelings for Arwen which had begun at the age of twenty at their first meeting in Rivendell.

*

Since there is no indication that Arwen's brothers married, it must be assumed that she was the only one of Elrond's children who carried on his line. This was true likewise of the line of Galadriel and Celeborn as their only child was Celebrían who of course was Arwen's mother. Thus Aragorn, through his marriage to Arwen, fathered the heirs of the Elves as well as those of the Númenórean kings. Tolkien's letter to Milton Waldman probably written in late 1951 refers to Aragorn, as the returning King "*... inheriting all that can be transmitted of Elfdom in his high marriage with Arwen daughter of Elrond, as well as the lineal royalty of Númenor.*"[46]

ELROND

The bitter-sweet nature of this story is heightened by the introduction of Elrond into the equation.

There was intense devotion between Elrond and his daughter (no doubt enhanced by the departure of Celebrían over the Sea five hundred years earlier), thus making Arwen's sacrifice the more notable. There

---

40. C. Tolkien (ed.), *The History of Middle-earth*, vol. X, *Morgoth's Ring*, London HarperColllins Publishers, 2002, first published in Great Britain by HarperCollins Publishers 1993, *HoM-e* X Part 3, Second Phase, p. 210.
41. Op. cit., *HoM-e* X Part 3, Second Phase, p. 211.
42. Op. cit., *HoM-e* X Part 3, Second Phase, p. 213.
43. Op. cit., *HoM-e* X Part 4, p. 324.
44. Op. cit. [4], *Ak* p. 311.
45. C. Tolkien (ed.), *Unfinished Tales of Númenor and Middle-earth*, London, HarperCollins Publishers, 1998, first published in Great Britain by George Allen & Unwin 1980, *UT* Part 2, Chapter 2, p. 279.
46. Op. cit. [39], Letter 131, p. 160.

was also a great deal of affection between Elrond and Aragorn. Throughout the Third Age Elrond had offered counsel and protection to the Dúnedain of the North, including caring for their Kings and Chieftains during childhood and/or old age when necessary. Aragorn, being only two years old when his father was killed and with his great destiny and resulting danger, was a particularly vulnerable charge for Elrond. As well as providing him with protection, security, training and education, Elrond recognised his potential in the alias he gave him (Estel) and also proved to be a loving foster-father to him. In fact he actually "... *came to love him as a son of his own.*"[47]. There is no doubt that this particular heir of Isildur was special in Elrond's affections as well as in having a significant destiny. This love seems to have been mutual, and endured in spite of Aragorn being the unwitting cause of Elrond's eventual heart-breaking parting from Arwen. For example on Aragorn's departure from Rivendell to become a Ranger we are told that he took leave "*lovingly*"[48] of Elrond even though his foster-father had just taken him to task about the inappropriateness of his feelings for Arwen and was sending him to a life of hardship with little hope of his love being reciprocated. Twenty-nine years later when Elrond learnt of his daughter's betrothal he still called Aragorn "*my son*" and told him that he loved him[49] - as if to soften the implications of his insistence that Aragorn must regain his kingships before a marriage could take place. This was very different from the situation in the story of Beren and Lúthien where Thingol knew nothing about Beren prior to his interest in his daughter and initially displayed extreme hostility to him even to the point of trying to bring about his death. In the case of Idril and Tuor, Idril's father Turgon supported their relationship from the start as there never seems to have been any question of his daughter having to lose her immortality. No doubt Elrond's attitude would have been different if Arwen and Aragorn had been able to go West with him.

Foresight was a dominant feature of the relationship between Aragorn and Elrond. As Elrond told Aragorn his true identity, he could foresee that his foster-son would have a long life-span and would do great deeds with the sword of Elendil "*unless evil befalls you or you fail at the test*"[50]. Shortly afterwards, having seen in Aragorn's eyes that he had fallen in love with Arwen, Elrond summoned him and foretold the many years of hardship ahead, after which he would either become as great as Elendil or be utterly destroyed along with the rest of the Dúnedain. Aragorn's own gift of foresight was awakened during the same conversation and he perceived that the time was coming when Elrond would leave Middle-earth, and his children would have to choose whether or not to accompany him. His vision of the future was incomplete/uncertain as was Elrond's in the two examples cited here.

It was at this point that Aragorn left Rivendell and, as described in App A.I.v.1060 and App B.1090, spent nearly thirty years labouring in the cause against Sauron, becoming acquainted with Gandalf and undertaking "great journeys and errantries"[51], including periods of service in Rohan and Gondor. These activities spanned the years 2951-2980 and it seems unlikely that he would have been back to Rivendell in that time or seen Elrond. Apart from his obviously fraught schedule, this assumption is borne out by the following observations:
- During the early years after his departure he would surely have kept away from Rivendell because Arwen was there, given that one of Elrond's reasons for sending him away when he did must have been to keep them apart.
- After meeting Gandalf in 2956 there would have been more than enough to occupy him - not least their extensive travels together - to preclude further visits to Rivendell. Also the matter of Arwen's presence there must still have applied.
- His time in Rohan and Gondor (and possibly even further afield) must have occupied by far the largest section of the period in question - say 2960-2980 - and the distances involved would have made a visit to Rivendell less likely. Again he might have assumed that Arwen was still there.
- When he was drawn into Lothlórien in 2980 he was actually on his way to Rivendell because he was exhausted from a journey in the border areas of Mordor and wanted to be able to rest in his childhood home. The fact that this visit is emphasised points to it being unusual. His suffering from his journey

---
47. Op. cit. [1], App A.I.v, p. 1057.
48. Op. cit., App A.I.v, p. 1060.
49. Op. cit., App A.I.v, p. 1061.
50. Op. cit., App A.I.v, p. 1057.
51. Op. cit., App B p. 1090.

must have been considerable given that shortly before this incident we are told how he had become *"the most hardy of living Men"*[52]. His need for recuperation may have been so great that he no longer cared about the propriety of visiting Rivendell when Arwen was there. It is clear from the account in App A.I.v.1060 that he had no idea that Arwen was staying in Lothlórien thus giving further indication that he had not made any recent visits to Rivendell. If he had been there he would have known where Arwen was.

- App A.I.v.1060 also makes it clear that Aragorn and Arwen only met for the second time in 2980 - note the reference to her seeing him again after their "long parting".

In the event Aragorn clearly achieved all the healing he needed in Lothlórien.

As I observed in Chapter 1.4, following his betrothal to Arwen Aragorn did carry out his original intention of going to Rivendell - presumably in 2980 or soon after. Elrond's uncertainty as to what lay ahead was still present as indicated by his words to his foster-son after learning of the betrothal, *"... years come when hope will fade, **and beyond them little is clear to me**..."*[53] [My emphasis]. However Arwen's choice was not unexpected and Elrond was beginning to accept that his loss of her might be necessary in order for the kingship of Men to be restored. Thus even a long-awaited victory against Sauron would nevertheless be a cause of grief to him. Perhaps his feelings were best expressed by his remark to Aragorn, *"And now a shadow lies between us."*[54]

The uncertainty of Elrond's and Aragorn's vision of the future was in contrast to the foresight of Arwen as she plighted her troth to Aragorn at which point she seemed to know that Aragorn would not *"fail at the test"*[55]. Similarly, her making of the royal standard, though done in hope rather than certainty, further illustrated her great faith in Aragorn's ability to overcome the evil of Sauron.

In the main narrative of *LotR*, there are not many direct references to the relationship between Aragorn and his foster-father, as the emphasis is on the Ring-bearer's danger and the need to destroy the Ring, with Elrond's role being to provide counsel and practical help to that end. This manifested itself in his organisation of the rescue of Frodo and his companions (including Aragorn) from the Nazgûl and subsequently sending out parties of scouts to scour the land. He also called a Council to decide what action should be taken about the Ring. After the departure of the Fellowship, his attention (and that of his sons) was concentrated on maintaining communication with Lothlórien and with Aragorn's people. He was thus directly involved in Aragorn's struggle as well as that of Frodo. The arrival of the Grey Company for the journey through the Paths of the Dead (*LotR* 5.2.774-6) was achieved by this Lothlórien/Rivendell/Dúnedain liaison.

With the usual reading between the lines, it is possible to throw further light on how things were between Aragorn and Elrond at this period - nearly forty years after the betrothal. During the journey from Bree with the Hobbits, Aragorn referred to his heart being in Rivendell telling them that he went there when he could, and when his companions complained about the meagreness of their food rations, he told them to look forward to the fare they would get at Elrond's house. Once in Rivendell there are many hints that this was a place where he belonged and was at ease:

- Elrond's smiling agreement to Bilbo that his friend "The Dúnadan" should be found to help him finish writing a song.
- The acceptance of Aragorn and Arwen as a couple - by Bilbo and by Elrond himself.
- At the Council, when a doubting Boromir asked Aragorn to say who he was and to explain his connection with Gondor, it was Elrond who answered, telling Boromir in no uncertain terms of Aragorn's descent from Isildur and Elendil and making clear his respect for the unimpressive-looking man with the broken sword.
- Elendil's sword was reforged by the Elvish smiths of Rivendell.
- Perhaps one of the most telling incidents was immediately prior to the departure of the Fellowship when

---

52. Op. cit. [1], App A.I.v, p. 1060.
53. Op. cit., App A.I.v, p. 1061.
54. Op. cit., App A.I.v, p. 1061.
55. Op. cit., App A.I.v, p. 1057.

Aragorn sat with bowed head and *"only Elrond knew fully what this hour meant to him."*[56]. Although one could perhaps suggest that Arwen might have had a pretty good idea too, the message is clear that Elrond empathised with Aragorn's deepest thoughts and emotions, just as he had nearly seventy years previously when he perceived his feelings for Arwen simply by looking into his eyes and realised that this was a lasting love rather than an adolescent crush.

Thus Elrond showed himself as very much the supportive father to Aragorn.

The efforts of all the Rivendell family were combined with the coming of Halbarad and his companions to Aragorn's aid in *LotR* 5.2.774-5. Being aware of the prophecy concerning the Paths of the Dead, Elrond's foresight would have told him that the time had come for it to be fulfilled and he duly sent a message to Aragorn to this effect via Elladan and Elrohir who travelled with Halbarad's party. In addition Arwen sent her own message and her royal standard via Halbarad himself. There is no doubt that a close father/son relationship had continued to exist between Elrond and Aragorn. A poignant example of this occurred as Aragorn arrived in the Houses of Healing, exhausted, sorrowful and starving and now faced with the task of healing Faramir, Éowyn and Merry. His heart-felt words, uttered with a sigh, *"Would that Elrond were here, for he is the eldest of all our race, and has the greater power"*[57], showed his yearning for his foster-father's support and his reverence for his gifts. It also showed perhaps his lack of faith in himself, his doubt that he could do this task on his own, wanting to lean on Elrond as he did on Gandalf.

Elrond's last documented action regarding Aragorn in *LotR* was his journey to Gondor after the War of the Ring to surrender the Sceptre of Annúminas to him and give Arwen in marriage. Six weeks later he left for Rivendell having seen Arwen for the last time. No-one saw their last meeting: as told in *LotR*, *"... they went up into the hills* [i.e. above Edoras] *and there spoke long together, and bitter was their parting that should endure beyond the ends of the world."*[58] What was presumably Elrond's final farewell to Aragorn would have taken place at Dol Baran where the latter took leave of the Hobbits and the rest of the party and began the journey back to Arwen in Edoras and thence to Minas Tirith. Nothing is said of this leave-taking, in contrast to that from Galadriel and Celeborn (as will be seen). Perhaps anything significant had already been said unwitnessed - or needed no saying. There is a sharp contrast between the grief of these partings and the description of Elrond's arrival back at Rivendell - minus Arwen: *"... all the house was filled with light and song for joy at Elrond's home-coming."*[59]

The parting between Elrond and Arwen as she took up her mortal life as Aragorn's Queen is described in App A as *"... grievous among the sorrows of that Age"*.[60] This echoes the moment in *TSil* when Melian realised that Lúthien had chosen mortality so she could live and die with Beren: *"... no grief of loss has been heavier than the grief of Melian the Maia in that hour."*[61] A similar passage appears in *HoM-e* XI Part One, Grey Annals, with the addition of the following phrase: *"unless only it were the grief of Elrond and Arwen"*[62].

In Chapter 1.7 I have already mentioned the underlying sense of guilt which Aragorn must always have felt knowing that through Arwen's love for him she had been parted for ever from her own people, most of all from the father she adored. From studying his relationship with Elrond it is obvious that this guilt would also have been part of his feelings towards the foster-father with whom he had shared a mutual affection. Was this guilt still playing on his mind on his death-bed when he suggested to Arwen that she could still sail into the West (and by implication be reunited with her father) even though this would mean that he himself would lose her?

When Elrond told him, on hearing of his and Arwen's betrothal, that a shadow now lay between them he spoke truly; he wasn't just referring to the immediate future but permanently.

---

56. Op. cit. [1], *LotR* 2.3, p. 280.
57. Op. cit., *LotR* 5.8, p. 863.
58. Op. cit., *LotR* 6.6, p. 978.
59. Op. cit., *LotR* 6.6, p. 985.
60. Op. cit., App A.I.v, p. 1062
61. Op. cit. [4], *TSil* Chapter 20, p. 222.
62. C. Tolkien (ed.), *The History of Middle-earth*, vol. XI, *The War of the Jewels*, London HarperColllins Publishers, 2002, first published in Great Britain by HarperCollins Publishers 1994, Part 1, Grey Annals 469, p. 71.

GALADRIEL

Galadriel's involvement in Aragorn's story actually began many years before he was born when she acquired the Elessar and learnt of the prophecy foretelling the coming of someone who would possess this jewel and also take the name Elessar himself. As I discussed in Chapter 1.2 this would certainly have happened before TA 2510 and probably much earlier. Having been born in the First Age Galadriel's situation in the Third Age was that she was the greatest Elf living in Middle-earth, the founder of the White Council, a close friend of Gandalf, mother-in-law of Elrond and grandmother of Arwen. She would therefore have been well aware of the events surrounding the defeat of Sauron at the end of the Second Age, including the failure of Isildur to destroy the One Ring leading to the inevitability of Sauron arising again. Likewise, as the Third Age progressed, she would have noted other significant events, namely the prophecy of the Elessar, the prophecy of Malbeth the Seer relating to the Paths of the Dead, the failing of the kingship in Gondor and Arnor yet with the direct line of Elendil still surviving in the North, and the increasing power of Sauron and the Nazgûl (particularly in Dol Guldur so close to Lothlórien). In TA 2929 there was the prophecy of Aragorn's grandmother about hope being born for the Dúnedain, followed two years later by the birth of a promising heir of Elendil's line in the North. From 2942 onwards there would have been growing speculation about the One Ring after Bilbo's journey with Thorin's company, with Sauron declaring himself in Mordor and beginning the rebuilding of Barad-dûr in 2951. In that year also the heir of Elendil, now come of age, met and fell in love with Arwen. Given that Galadriel was Arwen's mother-figure since the sailing of Celebrían to the Undying Lands, as well as her grandmother, and that Arwen spent a great deal of time in Lothlórien it is inconceivable that Galadriel would have been ignorant of these affairs of the heart. She would also have been aware of the choice facing the children of Elrond: whether to sail into the West with him when he eventually left Middle-earth or to stay behind and become mortal. In addition Galadriel would have been personally acquainted with Beren and Lúthien during the First Age so would be familiar with the issues surrounding Elf/Mortal unions. As far as I can see, the only question is when, rather than if, Galadriel realised what Arwen's future would hold. To put her role in Aragorn's life in context it is necessary to look in more detail at the story of Beren and Lúthien.

As related in *TSil* 19.189-221, Lúthien was the daughter of Thingol (one of the first Elf-kings) and the Maia Melian. She grew up in the Forest of Doriath which was surrounded by an invisible girdle of enchantment created by the divine Melian in order to prevent enemies - or anyone else - entering the forest without her or Thingol's permission. However, unknown to Thingol, the Man Beren did manage to break through the Girdle of Melian and enter Doriath where he met and fell in love with Lúthien - much to the fury of Thingol who had sworn that no Man would ever enter his realm, let alone have the temerity to ask for his daughter in marriage. He retaliated by agreeing to give Lúthien to Beren on condition that he first went to Morgoth's stronghold and retrieved one of the stolen Silmarils from the Dark Lord's crown - a task which would almost certainly lead to Beren's death (which was what Thingol intended). While these events were going on the young Galadriel was living in Doriath where she was a pupil and friend of Melian, from whom she learnt "*great lore and wisdom concerning Middle-earth*"[63]. Prior to Beren's entry into Doriath, Melian had spoken to Galadriel of her prediction of his coming: "*... one of Men, even of Bëor's house, shall indeed come, and the Girdle of Melian shall not restrain him, for doom greater than my power shall send him*"[64]. Melian's role during the first meeting between Thingol and Beren had been silently to encourage Beren: when he looked at her "*... it seemed to him that words were put into his mouth.*"[65]. The purpose behind Beren's entry into Doriath is summed up in *Athrabeth Finrod ah Andreth* where it is stated: "*Thus from the union of Lúthien and Beren... the infusion of a 'divine' and an Elvish strain into Mankind was to be brought about, providing a link between Mankind and the Elder World, after the establishment of the Dominion of Men.*"[66]

The similarity between Melian's situation in the First Age and Galadriel's in the Third Age is unmistakeable. The enchantment emanating from Lothlórien due to Galadriel's wielding of the Elven-ring Nenya kept the evil of Sauron's fortress of Dol Guldur at bay, and entry to the Golden Wood was strictly controlled. In *LotR*

---

63. Op. cit. [4], *TSil* Chapter 13, p. 130.
64. Op. cit., *TSil* Chapter 17, p. 167.
65. Op. cit., *TSil* Chapter 19, p. 195.
66. Op. cit. [40], *HoM-e* X Part 4, p. 340.

Treebeard told Merry and Pippin [about Lothlórien], "*I am surprised that you ever got out, **but much more surprised that you ever got in**"*[67] [My emphasis]. In fact, due to the contact between Rivendell and Lothlórien, Galadriel and Celeborn were aware of the approach of the Fellowship - hence their being allowed to enter it. Prior to that, in App A, we are told specifically that when the forty-nine year old Aragorn came to the border of Lothlórien [where Arwen happened to be staying at the time] on his way to recuperate in Rivendell, he "*... was admitted to the hidden land by the Lady Galadriel.*"[68] In *TSil*, Melian had spoken of a power greater than her own (that of Ilúvatar himself presumably) which would allow Beren into Doriath. In *LotR* it was Galadriel herself who allowed Aragorn into Lothlórien, perceiving the need to reinforce "*the infusion of a 'divine' and an Elvish strain into Mankind*" by bringing Aragorn and Arwen together again. She had seen it all before and realised that a higher power was willing this further union between Eldar and Edain and that it was not for her to interfere. She compounded her action by telling Aragorn to discard his travelling clothes and then dressing him as an Elven-lord in silver and white with a gem on his brow. When Arwen saw him again walking towards her under the trees "*... her choice was made and her doom appointed.*"[69] Note the similarity with Lúthien's doom coming upon her when seeing Beren in the enchanted forest of Doriath - as sung by Aragorn on Weathertop: "*doom fell on Tinúviel.*"[70].

Leaving aside divine purpose as a factor in Galadriel's attitude to Aragorn, there is enough evidence in *LotR* to show that personal affection and respect were also involved. In *LotR* 2.6.343 as the Fellowship entered Lothlórien, Aragorn's presence eased their acceptance by Haldir as his name was known and he was favoured by Galadriel. Aragorn was clearly at ease in Lothlórien, and with Galadriel herself, as shown by his ability to return her searching gaze. He must also have been profoundly relieved at being in a place where he felt safe enough to sleep without fear for the first time since the Fellowship had left Rivendell. His high regard for Galadriel was very evident by his rebuking of Boromir whenever he cast doubt on her motives (*LotR* 2.6.338 and 2.7.358).

The gift-giving scene too throws considerable light on their relationship. After giving Aragorn the sheath to protect his sword from being stained or broken, Galadriel asked him if there was anything else he wanted from her, the reason being that "*... it may be that we shall not meet again, unless it be far hence upon a road that has no returning.*"[71]. Aragorn's answer was, "*Lady, you know all my desire, and long held in keeping the only treasure that I seek. Yet it is not yours to give me, even if you would; and only through darkness shall I come to it*"[72], showing that he had no secrets from Galadriel who was fully aware of his feelings for Arwen and his apprehension about what lay ahead of him. Her next action, the presentation of the Elessar to him, was highly significant as it represented the fulfilment of the prophecy, confirmed by her addressing him as "*Elessar, the Elfstone of the House of Elendil!*"[73] She referred to this gift as "*a token of hope*" and made it clear that it had been left with her by Arwen.[74] As Aragorn pinned the brooch to his breast the healing properties of the gem took effect as his companions saw him as a king with the weight of his cares removed. In *UT* in a description of the Elessar, we are told that "*... those who looked through this stone saw things that were withered or burned healed again or as they were in the grace of their youth...*"[75] Galadriel's words as she gave the Elessar seemed to imply confidence and hope in Aragorn's eventual victory, in contrast to the uncertainty in her earlier remark, quoted above, that they might not meet again. It seems that by giving the Elessar to the one who had been predicted to be its eventual owner she was helping to ensure a good outcome and also foreseeing the situations where the healing gem would be needed. The passage from *UT* just quoted carries on to say that "*... the hands of one who held it brought to all that they touched healing from hurt.*"[76] Arwen's later gift of the royal standard and her message of hope showed a similar confidence - in contrast to the uncertainty of Elrond referred to

---

67. Op. cit. [1], *LotR* 3.4, p. 467.
68. Op. cit., App A.I.v, p. 1060.
69. Op. cit., App A.I.v, p. 1060.
70. Op. cit., *LotR* 1.11, p. 192.
71. Op. cit., *LotR* 2.8, p. 375.
72. Op. cit., *LotR* 2.8, p. 375.
73. Op. cit., *LotR* 2.8, p. 375.
74. Op. cit., *LotR* 2.8, p. 375.
75. Op. cit. [45], *UT* 2.4, The Elessar, p. 322.
76. Op. cit., *UT* 2.4, The Elessar, p. 322.

earlier in this chapter. [I am not clear on the significance of Galadriel's comment quoted above that she and Aragorn might not meet again "... *unless it be far hence upon a road that has no returning*". Was she referring to a time after the end of the world when possibly all the races would meet again? This is perhaps borne out by her words to Treebeard after the end of the War of the Ring when she hinted that they would not meet again "... *until the lands that lie under the wave are lifted up again. Then in the willow-meads of Tasarinan we may meet in the Spring*"[77], presumably referring to Beleriand drowned at the end of the First Age - which was where Tasarinan was.]

A further area for discussion of Galadriel's gifts is highlighted in *"Law and Customs among the Eldar"* in *HoM-e* X, in a section on marriage laws and customs where Tolkien states: *"Among the Noldor also it was a custom that the bride's mother should give to the bridegroom a jewel upon a chain or collar; and the bridegroom's father should give a like gift to the bride. These gifts were sometimes given before the* [wedding] *feast. (**Thus the gift of Galadriel to Aragorn, since she was in place of Arwen's mother, was in part a bridal gift and earnest of the wedding that was later accomplished.**)"*[78] [My emphasis].

Technically there are three possible gifts which this could refer to: the Elessar, the *"bright gem"* which Galadriel put on Aragorn's brow during his previous visit to Lothlórien (App A.I.v.1060), and the sheath for his sword. It seems to me that the sheath can be discounted as it wasn't a jewel and with its connection with war was perhaps inappropriate for a bridal gift. It could be argued (considering Galadriel's foresight) that the gem for his brow had been in *"earnest of the wedding"*, but since Aragorn and Arwen were not actually betrothed at the time it was given it would seem to be contravening custom and thus also inappropriate. The passage must therefore refer to the Elessar as by the time of *LotR* the engagement was long-standing with a wedding depending only(!) on Aragorn regaining his kingships. If the Elessar, then, was *"in part a bridal gift"* it further emphasised Galadriel's (and Arwen's) confidence in a favourable outcome - and therefore a wedding. On the assumption that it was indeed partly a bridal gift, it had to be given **prior** to the wedding in order for the conditions for the wedding to be fulfilled - namely the acceptance of Aragorn as King in Gondor under the name Elessar/Elfstone. Arwen too had been aware of the importance of the timing, having left the Elessar with Galadriel ten years previously in anticipation of just such a situation.

However, Hammond and Scull refer to the inconsistency between the passage from *HoM-e* X quoted above describing the Elessar as Galadriel's gift, and a passage in *UT* 2.4.325 which states that once Galadriel acquired the Elven-ring Nenya, she gave the Elessar to Celebrían who subsequently gave it to Arwen.[79] This is actually borne out in Galadriel's own words in *LotR*: *"This stone I gave to Celebrían my daughter, and she to hers; and now it comes to you as a token of hope,"*[80] implying that the Elessar was actually a gift from Arwen so could not have been *"in part a bridal gift"* from the bride's "mother". My feeling is that Galadriel, Celebrían and Arwen were all equally involved with the Elessar and the prophecies concerning it, so that it was perhaps immaterial which one of them actually had it in her keeping at any given time. However as Galadriel was the one with overall responsibility for handing it to the rightful recipient it would seem appropriate for Arwen to leave it with her rather than give it to Aragorn herself. It was very much a family affair with all three of them knowing they were waiting for the one who would receive the gem and take its name as his own. At what point did Galadriel realise that Arwen was destined to repeat the role of Lúthien? And did Celebrían realise, before she sailed West, that she would never be reunited with her daughter?

Although the Elessar could certainly be interpreted as *"in part a bridal gift"* its main significance seems to be as a representation of kingship with the emphasis on the healing aspect of the king's role. This ties in with the prophecy concerning the jewel. The *"bright gem"* which Galadriel gave Aragorn on his first visit to Lothlórien in TA 2980 can also be interpreted as representing kingship - thus giving a further example of Galadriel's foresight relating to Aragorn's and Arwen's destinies. The Kings of Númenor had worn a jewel on the brow instead of a crown, and so had the Kings of Arnor, the jewel in question in their case being the Elendilmir (referred to as "the Star of Elendil", "the Star of the North" and "the Star of the North Kingdom" in *LotR*). Galadriel's act of giving such a gem to Aragorn could almost be a foreshadowing of his northern

---

77. Op. cit. [1], *LotR* 6.6, p. 981.
78. Op. cit. [40], *HoM-e* X Part 3, Second Phase, p. 211.
79. Op. cit. [34], Hammond and Scull, p. 338.
80. Op. cit. [1], *LotR* 2.8, p. 375.

coronation (described in *UT* 3.1.359) when Arwen bound the Elendilmir itself on his brow.

Whatever the significance of the gifts and the extent of her foreknowledge, Galadriel continued to help Aragorn when the Fellowship had left Lothlórien. She sent him a message (via Gandalf), in the form of a verse, reminding him of the prophecy concerning the Paths of the Dead:

> *"Where now are the Dúnedain, Elessar, Elessar?*
> *Why do thy kinsfolk wander afar?*
> *Near is the hour when the Lost should come forth,*
> *And the Grey Company ride from the North.*
> *But dark is the path appointed for thee:*
> *The Dead watch the road that leads to the Sea"*[81]

She again addressed him as "Elessar", and her words show her conviction that Aragorn would indeed be making the prophesied journey. She also knew that he would need the support of his Rangers of the North. In *LotR*, on the arrival of Halbarad and the Grey Company, it is made clear that she had sent a message to Rivendell requiring their presence: *"Aragorn has need of his kindred. Let the Dúnedain ride to him in Rohan!"*[82]

In the event Aragorn and Galadriel did meet again - at his wedding. Her words to him at their final parting near Isengard seven weeks later showed affection, and pleasure in his happiness - in spite of the fact that she, like Elrond, was going to be parted for ever from Arwen as a result of the marriage. *"Elfstone, through darkness you have come to your hope, and have now all your desire. Use well the days!"*[83]

It remains to consider the question as to whether Aragorn had any inkling of Galadriel being tempted by the Ring. His words to Boromir in *LotR* that Lothlórien was *"... fair and perilous; but only evil need fear it, or those who bring some evil with them"*[84], followed later by the rebuke *"Speak no evil of the Lady Galadriel! ... There is in her and in this land no evil, unless a man bring it hither himself"*[85], seemed to rule out any doubt of Galadriel on his part. However Frodo had brought evil into Lothlórien in the shape of the Ring, and through his possession of it he was able to perceive Galadriel's wielding of the Elven Ring Nenya. In *LotR* 2.9.388, during the river journey, he referred to this, prompting a rebuke from Aragorn, since the whereabouts of the Three Elven Rings were supposed to be a closely guarded secret known only to the present and former bearers, and possibly to those close to them. (This may or may not have included Aragorn.) From Frodo's slip-up Aragorn would surely have realised that Galadriel had arranged some private meeting with the Hobbit, though with his high regard for her he would no doubt have taken it for granted that she would reject the Ring or even not be tempted by it in the first place. Another interpretation is that Aragorn, preoccupied and unsure of himself as he was at the time, may have failed to give much thought to the matter.

It must go without saying that Aragorn's feelings towards Galadriel would have been ones of reverence, and also of extreme gratitude: for enabling his relationship with Arwen to develop, for her obvious faith in him and her support, and for the generosity of her parting words.

CELEBORN

Although Galadriel's role in Aragorn's earlier life is prominent in the description of his first visit to Lothlórien which was to lead to his betrothal to Arwen (App A.I.v.1060-1), there is no mention of Celeborn's involvement until the War of the Ring years. However the evidence in the main narrative of *LotR* shows him to be, like Galadriel, very involved in Aragorn's future and personally concerned for him. This had undoubtedly been the case during Aragorn's earlier visit as well, as Celeborn's first words to him when greeting the Fellowship expressed concern at his appearance and the effect his struggles had had on him: *"It is eight and thirty years of the world outside since you came to this land; and those years lie heavy on you... Here lay aside your burden*

---

81. Op. cit. [1], *LotR* 3.5, p. 503.
82. Op. cit., *LotR* 5.2, p. 776.
83. Op. cit., *LotR* 6.6, p. 982.
84. Op. cit., *LotR* 2.6, p. 338.
85. Op. cit., *LotR* 2.7, p. 358.

for a while!"[86]. His further comment, *"... the end is near, for good or ill"*[87], showed (as with Elrond) less confidence in a good outcome than that displayed by Galadriel and Arwen.

Celeborn came into his own when preparing the Fellowship for departure from Lothlórien, clearly perceiving Aragorn's uncertainty without Gandalf and his inability to decide what route to take - hence the gift of boats, so they could travel by river and delay the point when they would have to choose between following the left or right bank. In addition he gave a great deal of practical advice about the lands they would be travelling through. He saw too from Aragorn's *"doubtful and troubled"* expression that Boromir was not making things any easier for him and became irritated on his own account when Boromir made it clear that he regarded the advice about Fangorn as old wives' tales and then launched into a speech about his journey from Minas Tirith to Rivendell, emphasising the solitariness and danger involved.[88] Celeborn, being well aware of Aragorn's own journeys and sufferings which greatly exceeded what Boromir had been through, would not have been impressed. His reply, warning Boromir not to despise lore, ended with the reminder that often *"... old wives keep in memory word of things that once were needful for the wise to know."*[89] [These words were of course prophetic as in *LotR* Ioreth, an "old wife" in the Houses of Healing, recalled the saying from "old lore" that *"The hands of the king are the hands of a healer"*.[90] This was overheard by Gandalf who immediately sent for Aragorn - thus Aragorn's healing powers were revealed leading to his recognition as King by the people of Minas Tirith.] *LotR* 2.8.368 makes it clear how grateful Aragorn was for Celeborn's gift of boats. He must also have been thankful for his implicit support against Boromir and for his lack of criticism over his indecisiveness.

Celeborn's attitude was similar to that of Elrond at the Council, namely irritation at Boromir's comments, and supportive to Aragorn. Like Elrond too he showed a fatherly affection for this man who was betrothed to his grand-daughter. This quality was particularly apparent in his parting words to him after the wedding: *"Kinsman, farewell! May your doom be other than mine, and your treasure remain with you to the end!"*[91]. Regarding the use of the word "kinsman": although Aragorn was a very distant relation of Celeborn (see Genealogical Table 1), the use of the word here emphasised the fact that he was now his kinsman due to his marriage to Arwen. In spite of his own sadness at Galadriel's imminent departure into the West before he himself was ready to leave Middle-earth, Celeborn generously expressed the hope that Aragorn would not experience such a parting and that Arwen would stay with him until his death. In referring to Arwen as Aragorn's treasure he picked up on Aragorn's own reference to her (mentioned earlier) when he told Galadriel that she long held in keeping *"... the only treasure that I seek."* Like Galadriel, Celeborn too would suffer the permanent loss of his grand-daughter due to her marriage, but displayed no ill-feeling towards Aragorn. Aragorn must have greatly appreciated his attitude.

*

Further evidence of the involvement of Lothlórien in Aragorn's affairs is given in comments by Gandalf at the Council of Elrond, during his report on Aragorn's capture of Gollum. Gandalf had been in Minas Tirith at the time, and on his way north afterwards he was intercepted by messengers from Lothlórien who told him that Aragorn had passed by with Gollum *en route* to Mirkwood. In *UT* 3.4.ii.444, 457 it is stated that after catching Gollum in the Dead Marshes, Aragorn had carefully chosen his route to Mirkwood so as to reduce the likelihood of being intercepted by Sauron's spies. Travelling via the *"eaves of Lórien"* was clearly a deliberate ploy and also a wise precaution as he and Gollum were actually followed by spies from Dol Guldur. The Lothlórien scouts could well have misled them to prevent them from catching up with Aragorn.

---

86. Op. cit. [1], *LotR* 2.7, p. 355.
87. Op. cit., *LotR* 2.7, p. 355.
88. Op. cit., *LotR* 2.8, pp. 367, 374.
89. Op. cit., *LotR* 2.8, p. 374.
90. Op. cit., *LotR* 5.8, p. 860.
91. Op. cit., *LotR* 6.6, p. 982.

ELLADAN AND ELROHIR

As with many other aspects of Aragorn's life, some time spent reading between the lines uncovers more about his relationship with Elrond's sons than is apparent at first sight. As well as being his distant cousins and foster-brothers Elladan and Elrohir also had a long-standing close relationship with the Northern Dúnedain in general, particularly since the Orc attack on their mother in TA 2509 after which they appear to have devoted most of their energies to hunting Orcs in revenge - in company with generations of Rangers. They were with Aragorn's father Arathorn when he met his death from an Orc arrow. In App A it is stated that twenty-year-old Estel/Aragorn had done "... *great deeds in the company of the sons of Elrond...*".[92] Clearly the close relationship between the Half-elven and the Dúnadan Chieftain had continued during Aragorn's minority, enhanced by the acceptance of the youngster into the family, with Elrond taking the place of his dead father. It seems very probable that most of Aragorn's childhood training in preparation for the future would have been carried out by the two brothers.

Once Aragorn had left Rivendell to take up his role as Chieftain much of his time (unlike that of his predecessors) was spent in southern and eastern lands rather than in the North. It is not stated whether Elladan and Elrohir sometimes accompanied him further afield though we know that many of his journeys were solitary or with Gandalf. However in the main narrative of *LotR* there are signs that the close relationship with his foster-brothers survived. In Rivendell in *LotR* 2.1.233 Aragorn missed the feast in spite of the fact that Arwen was present at it, because Elladan and Elrohir had returned from their travels unexpectedly and he wanted to hear their news. Later (*LotR* 2.3.273) after the Council, when Elrond's scouts departed to look for signs of the Nazgûl, Aragorn specifically set out with the brothers whose close involvement with the mission to destroy the Ring would continue throughout. From hints in *LotR* 2.3.274 and 2.6.343, 350 they appear to have been the liaison between Rivendell and Lothlórien, keeping Galadriel and Celeborn informed of events concerning the Fellowship.

However the true significance of the rapport between Aragorn and Elrond's sons becomes apparent in *LotR* 5.2.774-5 onwards, starting with the arrival of Halbarad and the Grey Company in Rohan, riding to Aragorn's aid as a result of messages from Galadriel to Elrond. Elladan and Elrohir were also with the company, "... *desiring to go to the war...*"[93]. From then on they were prominent in their support for their foster-brother:

- They had brought a personal message to Aragorn from Elrond reminding him of the option of going through the Paths of the Dead if time were pressing: "*If thou art in haste, remember the Paths of the Dead.*"[94]
- They were among those who accompanied Aragorn when he emerged from his Palantír confrontation with Sauron - concerned enough to go and investigate his absence from the mid-day meal.
- They accompanied him on the journey through the Paths of the Dead.
- They remained with him for the rest of the war: during the battle at Pelargir, the journey up the River Anduin, the Battle of the Pelennor Fields and the Battle of the Morannon.
- They had brought with them from Rivendell the Elendilmir, the symbol of kingship of the North Kingdom. Aragorn wore it as he came up the river to the Pelennor as King, then when he took it off to enter Minas Tirith as a Ranger and healer (rather than as a king) he gave it back into their care until it should be needed again.
- They were also a great support to Aragorn in the Houses of Healing. After saving the lives of Faramir, Éowyn and Merry, he was faced with a crowd of people begging him to heal their loved ones - too many for one healer - and so he enlisted the help of his foster-brothers and the three of them "... *laboured far into the night.*"[95].
- At the Last Debate the following day, they gave their support for the continuation of the strategy to distract Sauron, making the point that this was also the counsel of their father.

---

92. Op. cit. [1], App A.I.v, p. 1057.
93. Op. cit., *LotR* 5.2, p. 775.
94. Op. cit., *LotR* 5.2, p. 775.
95. Op. cit., *LotR* 5.8, p. 871.

- Their final role in the main narrative was to meet Arwen's wedding escort after it had left Lothlórien and then ride at the head of it on the final stage of her journey to Gondor.

Wishing to get past the image of these presumably twin brothers [they were born in the same year], who were frequently referred to as "the sons of Elrond" rather than by their actual names, were identical in appearance, dressed alike and seemed to go everywhere together, I decided to look at them individually and see if in fact there was any difference in their role, and in their relationship with Aragorn. This analysis showed the following:

- It was Elrohir who gave him Elrond's message about the Paths of the Dead, then, when Aragorn declared that his haste would have to be great indeed before he chose that route, made a non-committal remark and suggested that they should drop the subject while on the open road.
- Elladan was rearguard during that journey through the Paths, carrying a torch, while Aragorn led the way with another torch. There is no indication of Elrohir's position, but perhaps he was with Aragorn at the front. However, when the party stopped on the discovery of a long-dead body Elladan came forward and held both torches while Aragorn investigated.
- It was Elrohir who gave Aragorn the silver horn with which he summoned the Dead at Erech. Thus the implication is that Elrohir had brought the horn from Rivendell to accompany his message about the Paths of the Dead. Had it actually belonged to Isildur? Or had it been made specially for Aragorn in order for the prophecy to be fulfilled?
- At the Last Debate it was Elrohir who spoke for the two of them, giving Elrond's advice that they should send an army to draw Sauron's attention out of Mordor and thus away from Frodo.

Though both were obviously very supportive overall, there are clear differences in their behaviour. Elrohir was definitely the spokesperson. In fact Elladan's only recorded words in *LotR* were to Gimli during the journey through the Paths of the Dead - probably due to them being at the back together. Thus in some ways Elrohir appeared more overtly supportive of Aragorn, or perhaps more protective or emotionally closer to him. However it could also just have been that the brothers had different characters, with Elladan assessing the best course of action and quietly doing what was needed and Elrohir being naturally better fitted to do the talking.

Another aspect of Aragorn's relationship with the brothers is that they all had personal experience of family tragedy due to Sauron and thus would have shared emotions such as grief, guilt and desire for revenge. As related in App A.I.iii.1043, in TA 2509 Elladan's and Elrohir's mother, Celebrían, had been attacked by Orcs while travelling through the pass of Caradhras in the Misty Mountains on her way to Lothlórien. Elladan and Elrohir had been with her but had been unable to prevent the Orcs carrying her off. By the time they managed to rescue her she had suffered "*torment*" (the nature of which can easily be imagined) and "*a poisoned wound*".[96] Although Elrond had been able to heal her physically she was so traumatised by her ordeal that she had sailed to the Undying Lands the following year. Her sons' seemingly insatiable quest for revenge was no doubt partly driven by guilt that they had been unable to prevent her capture, as well as by grief on their own behalf and that of their father and sister - particularly Arwen's because if her marriage to a mortal were to take place she would not see her mother again. Aragorn's father had been killed by Orcs and his mother Gilraen was driven to despair and premature death due to the increasing horrors in Middle-earth as Sauron grew stronger. Although Aragorn would have had very little, if any, memory of his father, there is evidence in App A.I.v.1061 that his mother's death and the manner of it certainly distressed and grieved him. Feelings of guilt too may well have been an issue due to the infrequency of his visits to her, unavoidable though that was. [I discuss Aragorn's relationship with Gilraen in Chapter 2.2.]

HoM-e XII Part One describes the development of the *LotR* Appendices.[97] Chapters 8 and 9, dealing with Apps A and B, contain two references to Elladan and Elrohir being present at the Battle of the Field of Celebrant (in TA 2510) at which the cavalry charge of Eorl the Young enabled Gondor to defeat armies of wild men from the north-east and Orcs from the Misty Mountains. [He was subsequently rewarded by being given the land

---
96. Op. cit. [1], App A.I.iii, p. 1043.
97. C. Tolkien (ed.), *The History of Middle-earth*, vol. XII, *The Peoples of Middle-earth*, London HarperColllins Publishers, 2002, first published in Great Britain by HarperCollins Publishers 1996, pp. 3-289.

which became Rohan and becoming its first king.] The passage in Chapter 9 (*The House of Eorl*) is particularly impressive: "*In the forefront of the charge they saw two great horsemen, clad in grey, unlike all the others, and the Orcs fled before them; but when the battle was won they could not be found, and none knew whence they came or whither they went. But in Rivendell it was recorded that these were the sons of Elrond, Elladan and Elrohir.*"[98] Unfortunately neither reference was included in the published *LotR*, but the year of this battle coincided with Celebrían's departure from Middle-earth, so it is certainly feasible that this could have been the beginning of the brothers' vendetta against the Orcs on her behalf.

The nature of Aragorn's relationship with Elladan and Elrohir must have changed considerably over his lifetime. As he was only two years old when he went to live in Rivendell they must have been part of his earliest memories as older brothers then, as he grew up, as teachers and advisers. It is clear from the "*great deeds*" he had done in their company at the age of twenty that he must have been accustomed to riding against the Orcs with them for some time before that. In fact his great knowledge of Orcs [note his words to Éomer in *LotR* 3.2.433 that there were few mortals who knew more of Orcs than he did] must have been partly attributable to the teaching of Elladan and Elrohir - in addition to his own experiences.

There is no real indication as to how Elladan and Elrohir viewed Aragorn's relationship with Arwen. One hint we have is the fact that it was Halbarad rather than the brothers who carried Arwen's gift of the standard and delivered her personal message to Aragorn. This arrangement was perhaps more diplomatic as it prevented the family being involved in what was a very intimate matter between Aragorn and his betrothed. Also with Halbarad being designated standard-bearer it would have been more appropriate for him to bring the standard. Other incidents with the potential to shed light on the matter are those at Dunharrow when Éowyn's feelings for Aragorn became obvious to the Grey Company. Unfortunately there is no indication of what Elladan and Elrohir felt, so one can only speculate as to what was going through their minds.

Regarding Elladan's and Elrohir's long-standing involvement with the Dúnedain, I assume they would have been unofficial Rangers so to speak, rather than having any sort of formal role. It is not clear whether Aragorn's early forays with them were just as part of a threesome, or with other Elves, or with Rangers - though the last-mentioned is perhaps unlikely while he was still unaware of who he was. After Aragorn took over as Chieftain diplomacy would have been of great importance for the brothers due to his change of status, particularly before he found his feet. Given their staunch support of him during the War of the Ring, it is inconceivable that they weren't tactfully keeping a protective eye on him during his early years of responsibility.

By the *LotR* years the three of them were very much on an equal footing as can be seen from Aragorn's anxiety to hear their news in Rivendell (*LotR* 2.1.233) and his setting out with them after the Council of Elrond to search for traces of the Nazgûl. During the journey through the Paths of the Dead Aragorn was very much the leader, as he was during the healing of those afflicted by the Black Breath following the Battle of the Pelennor Fields. He was now the main healer and sent for them to share the load with him. The Battle of the Morannon would have been the brothers' last battle seeking revenge for their mother - apart perhaps from "mopping-up" operations. The root cause of her torment, namely Sauron, was now destroyed, due in no small part to the courage and determination of their young foster-brother.

*

As children of Elrond, Elladan and Elrohir (like Arwen) had been granted (by the Vala Manwë) the right to choose whether to be Elf or mortal. Elrond himself and his brother Elros had made their own choice at the end of the First Age, as had their parents, Eärendil and Elwing, before them. Arwen, by her decision to marry Aragorn had chosen mortality; thus her brothers were the last to face such a decision. However, as we have no definite information regarding their choice, what happened to them after the War of the Ring must be based on speculation.

It is stated in *LotR* Prologue that Elladan and Elrohir "*... long remained...*"[99] in Rivendell after Elrond had left Middle-earth, and in a passage in the (unused) Epilogue to *LotR* in *HoM-e* IX Sam told his daughter Elanor

---

98. Op. cit. [97], *HoM-e* XII Chapter 9, Section iii, p. 273.
99. Op. cit. [1], *LotR* Prologue, p. 15.

that the brothers would be present at the King's house during Aragorn's and Arwen's imminent visit North (in FA 15/16).[100] App A.I.i.1035 states that Elrond's children had the choice of either departing with him, or remaining behind and becoming mortal. Thus the implication of this passage, and that from the Prologue just quoted, is that they became mortal. However in a draft letter to Peter Hastings of September 1954 Tolkien says that the end of Elladan and Elrohir is not told and that they delayed their choice.[101] Aragorn, on his death-bed, referred to the first meeting between him and Arwen "*... under the white birches in the garden of Elrond **where none now walk***"[102] [My emphasis], seeming to imply that Rivendell was deserted - though whether that was because Elladan and Elrohir had sailed West or whether they had become mortal and died is not clear. The matter is further complicated by the question of who made Arwen's grave in Lothlórien. I have come across assumptions on the Web that it was her brothers, thus contradicting the theory that they had either died or sailed by that point. However I have never read anything by Tolkien which suggests this. It seems to me perfectly likely that Eldarion would have arranged his mother's burial - she would surely have told him where she was going when she left Minas Tirith as a widow.

It is clear that Elladan and Elrohir had a great rapport with the Dúnedain, having spent so much time travelling and fighting in their company and no doubt making many friends among them over the generations. Added to this was their obvious regard and affection for Aragorn - as well as for their sister presumably - so it is feasible that they might in the end have wanted to share their mortal fate. On the other hand they may well have wanted to be reunited with their father, and with the mother on whose account they had fought alongside the Dúnedain for so long. It must have been an agonising decision to make and it is easy to see why they might have delayed their choice. Did they actually make the same choice? Or did they follow Elrond and Elros and make different choices?

Another poignant dimension to the story of Aragorn and his adoptive family.

FAMILY ISSUES

This seems a suitable point to look more closely at two issues which involved the family as a whole, namely the first meeting of Aragorn and Arwen, and the manner of their betrothal.

Earlier in this chapter I mentioned Arwen's reference to the possibility of her doom resembling that of Lúthien. Was it some foresight on her part which had caused her to return to Rivendell at that crucial point, or was a higher power involved? If she had arrived, perhaps, only a few weeks later Aragorn might already have left to take up his role as Chieftain and they would not have met when they did. The question also arises as to whether Elrond had similar prescience or suspicions and had been hoping to prevent such a meeting. It is clear from Aragorn's amazed words to Arwen in App A ("*... though I have dwelt in this house from childhood, I have heard no word of you*"[103]) that Elrond, Elladan and Elrohir - along with Gilraen and the inhabitants of Rivendell in general - must have studiously avoided mentioning Arwen's existence to him during the eighteen years he had spent growing up as part of the family.

When Elrond first found out that Aragorn had fallen for Arwen, he made it clear to him that he was not going to be betrothed to anyone at that stage in his life - implying "and certainly not to Arwen". His actual words were "*You shall neither have wife, **nor bind any woman to you in troth**, until your time comes and you are found worthy of it.*"[104] [My emphasis]. After this conversation Aragorn left Rivendell. This was in TA 2951 and he did not meet Arwen again until 2980 in Lothlórien when they became betrothed - there is no evidence of any other meetings before that date and the text specifically implies a long separation. The betrothal seems to have taken place without any consultation with Elrond and in disregard of his stipulations just quoted. There is no indication of Aragorn having been officially "*found worthy*" by 2980 or of his "*time coming*". It was not until he took possession of the Palantír of Orthanc in 3019 that he said "*Now my hour draws near. I

---

100. C. Tolkien (ed.), *The History of Middle-earth*, vol. IX, *Sauron Defeated*, London HarperColllins Publishers, 2002, first published in Great Britain by HarperCollins Publishers 1992, *HoM-e* IX Chapter 11, p. 127.
101. Op. cit. [39], Letter 153, p. 193.
102. Op. cit. [1], App A.I.v, p. 1062.
103. Op. cit., App A.I.v, p. 1058.
104. Op. cit., App A.I.v, p. 1059.

will take it."[105]. All we are told in the account of the second meeting with Arwen is that he "... *was grown to full stature of body and mind*"[106], which would show why Arwen now unreservedly returned his feelings but wouldn't necessarily imply the worthiness which Elrond had specified. Basically Aragorn and Arwen appear to have taken the law into their own hands, aided and abetted by Galadriel, with no attempt to ask Elrond's permission. He was presented with a *fait accompli* as indicated by the words "*When Elrond learned the choice of his daughter ...*"[107].

Elrond **was** of course able to delay the actual marriage, hence his condition that Aragorn had to regain his kingships first, a task which was tied up with the defeat of Sauron. Elrond's attitude was understandable. If the War of the Ring were to end in Sauron's victory Elrond and a still unmarried Arwen would have a chance of escaping over the sea to the Undying Lands. If Arwen were to be married to Aragorn prior to a Mordor victory, then she would already be mortal and thus parted irrevocably from her father without even fully experiencing the marriage with Aragorn for which her sacrifice was made. Even a spiritual reunion after death, which Aragorn at any rate seemed to believe in, may have eluded them. It is not difficult to imagine how a victorious Sauron would have treated the wife of Isildur's heir, or indeed Isildur's heir himself if he had the misfortune to survive battle. Such considerations explain Elrond's determination that "*Arwen Undómiel shall not diminish her life's grace for less cause.*"[108] He was prepared to accept the loss of his daughter, but only as the price of victory over Sauron and the restoration of the kingship. By this stipulation he was in fact giving Aragorn the highest motivation to fulfil his destiny. Aragorn, on his part, would have had just as much regard for Arwen's welfare and happiness - hence his willingness to comply with Elrond's condition. As Paul Kocher says, the choice of Lúthien was "*an intolerable gift for any sensitive man to bestow on the woman he loves.*"[109] In the circumstances Aragorn would only have wanted Arwen to make this sacrifice in the event of a happy outcome in the war with Sauron.

Galadriel's involvement in the betrothal was - as already explained - due to her perception **and** acceptance that the relationship between Aragorn and Arwen was ordained by a higher power and was therefore not something with which she had the right to interfere. Her absorption of the wisdom of Melian in her youth along with the example of Beren and Lúthien, which she had witnessed at first-hand, showed that she herself was part of the plan to bring about these special Elf/mortal marriages. In fact she was not the only member of her family to be so fated as further consideration of her brother Finrod Felagund shows. Finrod gave his own life to save Beren's during the latter's quest to retrieve a Silmaril from Morgoth's crown, so by this sacrifice he helped to bring about the Beren/Lúthien union - and by implication subsequently the Aragorn/Arwen one. [I have given a brief history of the relationship between Finrod and Beren's father Barahir in Chapter 1.2.] In fact Finrod was something of an authority on Elf/mortal unions as shown by a further look at *Athrabeth Finrod ah Andreth* (*HoM-e* X.303-366). During his conversation with Andreth it becomes clear that this wise-woman was in love with Finrod's [and therefore Galadriel's] brother Aegnor and he with her. They would never marry and in fact Aegnor was subsequently killed in the war with Morgoth. Finrod realised that Elf/mortal unions only occurred as part of a grand plan by Ilúvatar telling Andreth "*... if any marriage can be between our kindred and thine, then it shall be for some high purpose of Doom.*"[110] His death occurred before any such marriages took place. Since Finrod was the first Elf to meet Men and always loved them, his involvement in what Tolkien described, in the draft letter to Peter Hastings referred to earlier, as "*... a Divine Plan for the ennoblement of the Human Race, from the beginning destined to replace the Elves*" was very fitting.[111]

*

At the end of the Third Age Elrond and his sons, and Galadriel and Celeborn knew that the long struggle

---

105. Op. cit. [1], *LotR* 3.11, p. 594.
106. Op. cit., App A.I.v, p. 1060.
107. Op. cit., App A.I.v, p. 1061.
108. Op. cit., App A.I.v, p. 1061.
109. Op. cit. [9], Kocher, Chapter 6, p. 138.
110. Op. cit. [40], *HoM-e* X Part 4, p. 324.
111. Op. cit. [39], Letter 153, p. 194.

against Sauron was reaching its conclusion one way or the other, and were naturally doing all in their power to bring an end to an evil which should have been cut short by Isildur three thousand years previously. As part of this struggle Aragorn, as Isildur's heir and the one whose destiny was to repair Isildur's fault, was a natural ally and would have expected to have their help and support. Nevertheless an analysis of his relationship with these people shows a mutual love and respect unrelated to the mere call of duty and allegiance. Aragorn was one of the family - by blood, by adoption, and later by marriage - and it is this which adds an extra poignancy to the story of his union with Arwen and its repercussions.

OTHER ELF RELATIONSHIPS

I round off this chapter by considering actual or possible relationships with the other Elves mentioned in *LotR* (apart from those from Mirkwood, as mentioned at the beginning of this chapter):
- Glorfindel and the Elves of Rivendell in general
- Gildor Inglorion
- Círdan and the Elves of the Grey Havens

Glorfindel and the Elves of Rivendell in general

Before looking at Glorfindel as we see him in *LotR* it is necessary to consider his actions and achievements prior to TA 3018-19.

TSil 23.291-2 describes the fall of Gondolin in the First Age including the heroic and selfless actions of a golden-haired Elf called Glorfindel who sacrificed his own life to save others (including Idril, Tuor and Eärendil) from a Balrog. The question as to whether this was the same Glorfindel who appears in *LotR* has long been debated. However Tolkien's last writings from the early 1970s, given in *HoM-e* XII.13.377-382, indicate that he was leaning towards the view that the two were the same, with Glorfindel being reincarnated by the Valar sometime after his death in Gondolin - a common occurrence in such cases especially if the Elf concerned had acted in a praiseworthy manner. He would have stayed in Valinor, becoming enhanced in wisdom and power under the influence of the Valar and of the Elves who had always lived there, then at some point returned to Middle-earth, probably sometime during the Second Age, possibly to support Elrond and Gil-galad against the growing power of Sauron. Such an interpretation of him fits the statement in *LotR* 1.12.210 that he was one of the few even in Rivendell who could ride openly against the Nazgûl. It also ties in with the conversation between Gandalf and Frodo in *LotR* when Frodo referred to the shining white figure he had seen at the crossing of the Bruinen Ford and Gandalf confirmed that it was Glorfindel: "*... you saw him for a moment as he is upon the other side: one of the mighty of the Firstborn.*"[112]

During the second millennium of the Third Age Glorfindel is mentioned, in App A.I.iv, as playing a part in the war between the Northern Dúnedain and the Witch-king of Angmar. We are told that in TA 1974-5 he led a force out of Rivendell against the Witch-king and succeeded in driving him off after he turned on Eärnur, the heir of the King of Gondor who had been sent to assist their northern kinsmen. It was at this point that Glorfindel made his famous prophecy, telling the furious Eärnur not to pursue his fleeing enemy because "*Far off yet is his doom, and not by the hand of man will he fall.*"[113] The Glorfindel in this incident is indisputably the Glorfindel from the main narrative of *LotR*. His ability to frighten away the Witch king, along with his remarkable foresight, lends further weight to the view that he was the same Elf who had been capable of fighting the Balrog in Gondolin.

Glorfindel's first appearance in *LotR* occurs in 1.12.209 when Aragorn and the Hobbits were forced to take to the East Road again on their way to the Bruinen Ford. They soon heard the noise of hoofs behind them but agreed that it did not sound like a Black Rider's horse. It was of course Glorfindel and as Aragorn spotted him from his hiding-place in the bushes he cried out and sprang back down to the road seconds after the Elf had sensed their presence and halted. Glorfindel in turn shouted out a greeting and ran to meet him. Aragorn's

---
112. Op. cit. [1], *LotR* 2.1, p. 223.
113. Op. cit., App A.I.iv, p. 1051.

reactions in this encounter resembled those in his later meeting with Halbarad in *LotR* 5.2.774 when he led the Grey Company to Rohan - the same surprise, relief and joy were evident. From Glorfindel's words, translated as "*Hail at last Dúnadan! Well-met!*", the Elf seemed to be experiencing the same sense of relief.[114] This was perhaps not surprising as it had been nine days since he had left Rivendell with the knowledge that a party of Hobbits carrying the One Ring would potentially need rescuing from the Nazgûl - if they hadn't been captured by them already. He had done what he could during that time, namely driving off three of them at the Bridge of Mitheithel and causing two more to turn away southward. He had then left a green jewel on the Bridge as a token to indicate that it was safe to cross it.

During subsequent conversations with Aragorn and Frodo he learnt the details of the attack on Weathertop and gave advice to Aragorn about being wary of handling the hilt which was all that was left of the Morgul-knife which had wounded Frodo. He then took over the leadership of the group, offering them mouthfuls of his cordial when necessary. His insistence that Frodo should ride his horse to the Ford must have been a further cause of relief to Aragorn who joined him in driving the Nazgûl into the river once Frodo was safely across (*UT* 3.4.456 Note 3).

Another important result of the meeting with Glorfindel was that Sam lost his doubts about Aragorn. While recuperating in Rivendell Frodo told Gandalf, "*Sam never quite trusted him* [Aragorn], *I think, not at any rate until we met Glorfindel.*"[115]. Glorfindel being an Elf was, in itself, sufficient reason for Sam's change of attitude, but it had also been clear that Glorfindel had been glad to see Aragorn and respected him, had had conversations with him in Elvish and had actually called him "Aragorn" at one point, thus dispelling any remaining doubts about whether he was "*the real Strider*"[116].

Glorfindel had stated at the beginning of their encounter that Elrond's decision to send some of his people to look for Frodo was prompted by news received from a group of Elves travelling in the Shire who had "*... learned that things were amiss, and sent messages as swiftly as they could.*".[117] This clearly refers to Frodo's meeting with Gildor Inglorion when the Elf had told Frodo, "*The Wandering Companies* [the Rangers] *shall know of your journey...*"[118]. Obviously as well as alerting the Rangers he had also sent word to Rivendell. We know, from Aragorn's conversation with the Hobbits in Bree, that he had been in contact with Gildor, but it is not clear whether Gildor subsequently found out that Aragorn had actually joined Frodo. If he did not then Elrond, and by implication Glorfindel, would not have known either. It must have been a relief to the latter to find that Aragorn was one of Frodo's party. Gandalf's words to Frodo in Rivendell, "*For the moment we have been saved from disaster, by Aragorn*"[119], must also have been echoed by Glorfindel and Elrond himself. It is of course possible that Gildor reported again to Rivendell saying that Aragorn was also looking for the Hobbits, in which case Elrond and Glorfindel would have been hoping that he had caught up with them.

Glorfindel's home during the Third Age was Rivendell and since Aragorn had spent his childhood and adolescence there the two of them must have known each other well. The same must also apply in the case of the other Rivendell Elves such as Erestor, introduced in *LotR* 2.2.240 as Elrond's chief counsellor, and the rather superior Lindir who commented on Bilbo's song about Eärendil in *LotR* 2.1.237. In fact in *HoM-e* XII.9.264 an earlier version of the story of Aragorn's childhood states that he was "*loved by all*" at Rivendell. Both Glorfindel and Erestor are mentioned in *LotR* 6.5.972 following behind Elladan and Elrohir in Arwen's wedding escort as it approached Minas Tirith.

Gildor Inglorion

Although Gildor Inglorion and Aragorn (and presumably the Dúnedain in general) clearly knew each other, it seems that they may have met on their travels rather than in Rivendell as Gildor told Frodo, in *LotR* 1.3.80, that **some of his kinsfolk** (namely Noldor Elves) still lived in Rivendell but made no reference to living there

---

114. Op. cit. [1], *LotR* 1.12, p. 209.
115. Op. cit., *LotR* 2.1, p. 220.
116. Op. cit., *LotR* 1.10, p. 171.
117. Op. cit., *LotR* 1.12, p. 210.
118. Op. cit., *LotR* 1.3, pp. 84-5.
119. Op. cit., *LotR* 2.1, p. 220.

himself. There is no particular indication that they lived at the Grey Havens either. Also when the Hobbits shared their meal under the stars Gildor's companions told them that the food would be better if they were at home in their "halls", a rather vague term which does not seem to fit either with Rivendell or the Grey Havens. Hammond and Scull refer to material appended to *The Road Goes Ever On: A Song Cycle* (by Tolkien and Donald Swann) in which Tolkien suggested that Gildor and his companions lived in or near Rivendell and that, when Frodo met them, they were returning from a visit to the Grey Havens to use the Palantír of the Tower Hills in the hope of being able to glimpse a vision of the Vala Elbereth (the subject of the song Frodo heard them singing).[120]

Círdan and the Elves of the Grey Havens

There is no mention in *LotR* of any meeting between Aragorn and the Elves of the Grey Havens, apart from the fact that Círdan's representative Galdor attended the Council of Elrond. They did not exchange any words and there was no indication of them knowing each other. However Aragorn was well-travelled and other meetings with Círdan's folk could well have occurred: from his own journeys, via Gandalf, or through some of the Grey Havens Elves visiting Rivendell.

Círdan himself was present at Sauron's defeat at the end of the Second Age and joined Elrond in trying to get Isildur to destroy the Ring. This was related by Elrond in person at the Council (*LotR* 2.2.243). Círdan was also involved in the war between the Northern Dúnedain and the Witch king of Angmar. App A.I.iii and A.I.iv between them cover his role, and piecing together the information it seems that the following timetable applied:

- In TA 1409 the Witch king unleashed a host from Angmar and King Arveleg I was killed. His son Araphor was helped by Círdan who sent an army from Lindon. This, combined with an army from Rivendell under the command of Elrond, resulted in the Witch king being subdued for some time.
- In the 1900s the Witch king arose again during the reigns of Araphant and then Arvedui.
- The northern capital of Fornost was captured and Arvedui escaped north towards Forochel with some of his men, while most of the other surviving Dúnedain were driven westwards towards the River Lune and the Grey Havens. This included Arvedui's heir Aranarth and his brother who, according to *HoM-e* XII.7.195, took refuge with Círdan.
- When Círdan learnt of Arvedui's whereabouts he immediately sent a ship north to rescue him, though this unfortunately sank killing Arvedui and everyone else on board including Círdan's skilled mariners. Thus Malbeth's prophecy that Arvedui would be the last king of the North Kingdom was realised, there being now too few people left to justify the term "kingdom". Aranarth took the title of Chieftain of the Dúnedain.
- It was after the death of Arvedui that Eärnil the King of Gondor was able to send assistance in the form of his heir (Eärnur) who arrived at the Grey Havens with a fleet. [Eärnil had had his own problems with invading armies and was thus unable to send help earlier.] At this point Círdan gathered an army from among the Elves of Lindon and the Men of Arnor and went to challenge the Witch king. His action coincided with the arrival of the army from Rivendell led by Glorfindel - as already mentioned - and the Witch king was defeated and driven away from the North.

Thus it can be seen that Círdan had behaved similarly to Elrond and Glorfindel in assisting the Dúnedain and it would therefore not be surprising if friendly relations were maintained between them thereafter. Hence I feel that there must have been some contact between him and Aragorn's people.

A further issue which could link Aragorn with Círdan relates to the Elendil-stone, the Palantír of the Tower Hills (referred to above). *RoP* describes how this Palantír was set up in Elostirion the tallest of the three towers located on the Tower Hills so that it looked only to the West. Unlike the other Palantíri it could not be used

---

120. Op. cit. [34], Hammond and Scull p. 100, referring to J.R.R. Tolkien, *The Road Goes Ever On: A Song Cycle*, music by D. Swann, Boston, Houghton Mifflin, 1967.

for communication. We are told that *"Thither Elendil would repair, and thence he would gaze out over the sundering seas, when the yearning of exile was upon him..."* even seeing as far as Tol Eressëa in the Undying Lands.[121] *UT* 4.3.535 Note 16 states that the Stone and the tower were maintained and guarded by Círdan and the Elves of Lindon. It also points out that *"Hereditary right to use it would no doubt still reside in the 'heir of Isildur', the recognized chieftain of the Dúnedain, and descendant of Arvedui. But it is not known whether any of them,* **including Aragorn***, ever looked into it, desiring to gaze into the lost West."*[122] [My emphasis]. App A.I.iii.1042 states that Círdan stowed the Elendil-stone on Elrond's ship when he sailed from the Grey Havens thus breaking the link which enabled the exiled Númenóreans to look into "the lost West". Perhaps Aragorn, if he had a friendly relationship with Círdan, did get a chance to use it at some point. Gandalf, with his close alliance with Círdan, could have helped to arrange it.

---

121. Op. cit. [4], *RoP* p. 350.
122. Op. cit. [45], *UT* 4.3, p. 535.

CHAPTER 2.2 - Dúnedain

The purpose of this chapter is to look at Aragorn's relationships with his contemporaries among the Dúnedain of the North, particularly his parents, Arathorn II and Gilraen, his paternal grandfather Arador, his maternal grandparents Dírhael and Ivorwen, and Halbarad, the friend, kinsman, second-in-command and standard-bearer who led the Grey Company to Aragorn's aid during the War of the Ring. Halbarad's story is recounted in the main narrative of *LotR*, but for information on Aragorn's immediate family it is necessary to refer to App A.I.v and App B. Genealogical Table 4 shows the relevant relationships.

Aragorn was a Dúnadan (or indeed "*the Dúnadan*" according to Bilbo in *LotR*[1]), a Man of the West descended from the exiled Númenóreans who had escaped to Middle-earth at the end of the Second Age under the leadership of Elendil, and established the kingdoms of Arnor and Gondor. The line of Elendil had continued in the North even though the kingdom of Arnor was no more. Long before Aragorn's time all that was left of the Northern Dúnedain (or the Rangers as they were called in Bree) was "*... a strange people wandering secretly in the wild, and other men knew not their homes nor the purpose of their journeys, and save in Imladris, in the house of Elrond, their ancestry was forgotten.*"[2]. A website referring to the "home" of the Dúnedain mentions information provided by the Tolkien linguist David Salo which suggests that they lived in woodlands between the Rivers Mitheithel and Bruinen.[3] Such a location, in the angle created by the joining of the rivers would have been within a hundred to a hundred and fifty miles of Rivendell, perhaps protected to some extent by Elrond's power over the Bruinen (see *LotR* 1.12.214-5 where it flooded at the ford during the Nazgûl's pursuit of Frodo). The area would have been approximately two hundred and fifty miles (as the crow flies) from Bree and three hundred miles from the Brandywine Bridge at the eastern border of the Shire.

Elvish characteristics, especially the gift of foresight, which were possessed to a high degree by Aragorn were also present to some extent in the Dúnedain in general, due to their Númenórean ancestry and in some cases, as with Aragorn himself, to a streak of Maian/Elven blood. The Dúnedain also had longer lifespans than other races of Men as will be seen in the following discussion. When Aragorn left Rivendell at the age of twenty to be *de facto*, as well as *de jure*, Chieftain of the Dúnedain these were the people with whom he would have been associating.

ARADOR AND ARATHORN II

Arador, Fourteenth Chieftain of the Dúnedain and heir of Isildur, was captured and killed by Trolls in the Coldfells north of Rivendell in TA 2930 and was succeeded as Chieftain by his son Arathorn II who had married Gilraen the previous year. Their son Aragorn was born in 2931, himself becoming Chieftain (as Aragorn II) and Isildur's heir only two years later, after Arathorn died as a result of an arrow in his eye while out hunting Orcs with Elladan and Elrohir. We know that Aragorn was born on March 1st but there are no precise dates for the deaths of his grandfather and father. However if Arador was killed in the second half of 2930 Aragorn would have already been conceived at the time and it is possible that Arador died knowing that his son and daughter-

---

1. J.R.R. Tolkien, *The Lord of the Rings,* London, HarperCollins Publishers, 2007, 2nd edition, based on the 50th Anniversary Edition of 2004, *LotR* 2.1, p. 233.
2. C. Tolkien (ed.), *The Silmarillion*, London, HarperCollins Publishers, 1999, first published in Great Britain by George Allen & Unwin 1977, *RoP* p. 355.
3. Actors At Work Productions, *Born of Hope*, [website], 2002-2009, http://www.bornofhope.com/QA.html, (accessed 1 February 2011). (See questions dated October 2007). The source of the information is a short but hardly legible note which Tolkien wrote for insertion into the story of Aragorn and Arwen (and which was not in the event used). Held on microfilm at Marquette University (Series 3, Box 9, Folder 3).

in-law were expecting the birth of an heir who had been prophesied to be the hope of the Dúnedain. In later life Aragorn would certainly have become aware of the manner of his grandfather's death and this may explain his statement to the Hobbits during the journey to Rivendell (*LotR* 1.12.203) when he made it clear that the Troll country to the north was little known to him and that if they were to take the north route to Rivendell it would take too long as he did not know the way. It seems likely that he had always given the area a wide berth in the light of Arador's fate. Regarding his father it is feasible that Aragorn might have had faint memories of him, particularly if Arathorn died late in 2933 when his son was nearer three than two.

DÍRHAEL AND IVORWEN

It is stated in App A.I.v.1057 that Dírhael was a descendant of Aranarth, First Chieftain of the Dúnedain [and therefore of Isildur himself], but from a more junior branch than Arador and Arathorn. In fact in an earlier version of this Appendix in *HoM-e* XII Ivorwen too is said to be descended from Isildur[4]. In either case Aragorn had royal blood from his mother's side of the family as well as his father's.

The gift of foresight is particularly relevant to this discussion, and is apparent in the behaviour of Dírhael and Ivorwen when Arathorn asked permission to marry their daughter. Dírhael's response was to object, partly because Gilraen was rather young to marry according to Dúnadan customs, and partly because he had a premonition that Arathorn would become Chieftain sooner than expected and that he would be short-lived. Maybe he did not want to see his daughter widowed - possibly pregnant or with a young child - at a tender age. Regarding the youth of Gilraen, *UT* states that Aldarion (the sixth King of Númenor) was regarded as being of "*full age*" on his 25th birthday.[5] Therefore if the Dúnedain of the Third Age followed this tradition, it seems logical that the women would delay marriage until they were of "*full age*" thus making sense of Dírhael's view that Gilraen, at twenty-two, was too young to marry. In App A.I.v as Elrond observed the twenty-year-old Aragorn he noted that he "*was **early** come to manhood*"[6] [My emphasis]. As events turned out Dírhael had foreseen both the premature death of Arador, and that of Arathorn at only sixty years of age (very young for a Dúnadan).

Ivorwen's response to her husband's objections was the prophecy from which Aragorn's childhood name resulted. It is worth quoting in full here: "*The more need of haste! The days are darkening before the storm, and great things are to come. If these two wed now, hope may be born for our people; but if they delay, it will not come while this age lasts.*"[7] As I discussed in Chapter 1.2, *HoM-e* XII Foreword.xii contains a further prophecy made by Ivorwen at Aragorn's naming ceremony in which she declared that she could see a green stone on the baby's breast, that he would take the name of this stone as his true name, and that his chief renown would be as a healer and a renewer. Admittedly Tolkien omitted this passage from the published version of App A.I.v.1057-63, but I believe it is very important nevertheless because it is the only reference I have found in Tolkien's works to a prophecy actually made at Aragorn's **birth**, as opposed to many years earlier. See *LotR* 5.8 where it is stated, after Aragorn had revealed his gift of healing, "*And they named him Elfstone, because of the green stone that he wore, and so the name **which it was foretold at his birth that he should bear** was chosen for him by his own people.*"[8] [My emphasis]. In the same chapter Aragorn stated that he was "'*Elessar', the Elfstone, and 'Envinyatar', the Renewer*"[9]. Again Ivorwen's birth prophecy is the only reference I have found to Aragorn being called a Renewer. One wonders if this far-seeing Dúnadan woman was descended from Malbeth the Seer!

A further bit of speculation relates to whether Aragorn had any sort of contact with Ivorwen and Dírhael. If Ivorwen had married in her late twenties, for example, and given birth to Gilraen a few years later, then

---

4. C. Tolkien (ed.), *The History of Middle-earth*, vol. XII, *The Peoples of Middle-earth*, London HarperColllins Publishers, 2002, first published in Great Britain by HarperCollins Publishers 1996, *HoM-e* XII Part 1, Chapter 9.ii, p. 263.
5. C. Tolkien (ed.), *Unfinished Tales of Númenor and Middle-earth*, London, HarperCollins Publishers, 1998, first published in Great Britain by George Allen & Unwin 1980, *UT* 2.2, p. 224.
6. Op. cit. [1], App A.I.v, p. 1057.
7. Op. cit., App A.I.v, p. 1057.
8. Op. cit., *LotR* 5.8, p. 871.
9. Op. cit., *LotR* 5.8, p. 863.

she would have been in her fifties at the time of Aragorn's birth and in her seventies when he left Rivendell. Allowing for the fact that the Dúnedain expected to live to well over a hundred (Gilraen died "prematurely" at that age) there was every reason why both Ivorwen and Dírhael would have still been alive at least during the first part of Aragorn's adulthood - even allowing for Dírhael being twenty or thirty years older than his wife. Did they visit their daughter and grandchild in Rivendell? And did Aragorn visit them as an adult?

GILRAEN

The first reference to Gilraen in App A calls her "*Gilraen the Fair*"[10] which I take to mean that she was considered to be beautiful rather than that she was fair-haired (unusual in the Dúnedain). Aragorn himself as a twenty-year-old is also described as "*fair*" and we know for certain that he was dark-haired. There is no indication in the published version of App A.I.v as to Gilraen's own view of Arathorn's marriage proposal, though an earlier - and in some places fuller - version in *HoM-e* XII states that she "*... did not yet desire to be a wife...*"[11] on account of her youth. Thus there was perhaps no objection to Arathorn himself, just to early marriage. He was certainly significantly older than she, being in his late fifties, but this was not old for a Dúnadan, and the same *HoM-e* reference just quoted also indicates that the heirs of Isildur "*were not accustomed to wed until they had laboured long in the world.*"[12]

Whatever her feelings on the matter the year 2933 saw Gilraen a widow at twenty-six, with a two-year-old child. In the space of four years her marriage had taken place, an heir had been born and two Chieftains had been killed. Thus the prophecies of her parents were realised. She and Aragorn now went to live in Rivendell. It was standard practice for the sons of the Chieftains to be fostered there in childhood, but the fosterling this time was actually the Chieftain himself.

The case of Gilraen and Aragorn can be compared and contrasted with those of the First Age heroes Tuor and Túrin and their mothers. As described in *TSil* both children were fostered by Elves after the loss of their fathers, Huor and Húrin respectively.[13] In the case of Tuor his mother Rían had not yet given birth to him at the time of her husband's death. She fled into the wild and was helped by the Grey Elves of Mithrim who delivered and fostered Tuor. Rían herself went to the burial mound where Huor lay and died of grief. Túrin's mother Morwen, after the capture of Húrin by Morgoth, sent her son to the Elf-king Thingol (Lúthien's father) to be fostered - on account of Thingol's friendship with Húrin and her own kinship to Beren. She herself refused to go with her son, partly from reluctance to accept Thingol's charity and partly because she was due to give birth to Túrin's sister. Her refusal persisted over the years - to the detriment of her son who was accordingly deprived of his mother at a very young age. Gilraen's behaviour was different from that of both these women as she accompanied Aragorn to Rivendell and remained with him while he grew up.

There is only one incident described in App A.I.v which throws any light on the relationship between Aragorn and his mother during the period when they were living together in Rivendell. This occurred after Aragorn, recently informed of his true identity, had met and fallen in love with Arwen. Due to his silence in the ensuing days Gilraen realised that something was on his mind and questioned him until he gave in and told her the reason, making it clear that his aim was to marry Arwen. Gilraen's reaction showed her knowledge and understanding of her people's history during the Second and Third Ages. When she told Aragorn that "*... it is not fit that mortal should wed with the Elf-kin*", he started to argue that the two of them also had Elf blood in them, but she made it clear to him that this was now very much diluted and the Dúnadan race very much diminished.[14] She also expressed her fear for the welfare of her people in the event of losing Elrond's good will - which she felt could happen if he were to find out Aragorn's intentions. Her attitude brings home the extent to which the Dúnedain in general, and her gifted and vulnerable son in particular, were dependent on Elrond's help and support: "*... I am afraid; for without the good will of Master Elrond the Heirs of Isildur will soon come*

---

10. Op. cit. [1], App A.I.v, p. 1057.
11. Op. cit. [4], *HoM-e* XII Part 1, Chapter 9.ii, p. 263.
12. Op. cit., *HoM-e* XII Part 1, Chapter 9.ii, p. 263.
13. Op. cit. [2], *TSil* Chapter 21, p. 235 and pp. 235-6 respectively.
14. Op. cit. [1], App A.I.v, p. 1059.

to an end."[15] The conversation also illustrates Gilraen's foresight. When Aragorn declared that he would spend his days in bitterness alone in the wild if there were no hope of him being able to marry Arwen she agreed that that would indeed be his fate, but then we are told that "*... she said no more to him of her foreboding...*"[16].

It is not easy to analyse the character of Gilraen. Her behaviour on the loss of her husband had compared favourably with that of Rían and Morwen as, unlike them, she had put her child's welfare before her own grief and principles. However there is ambiguity and uncertainty in the incident just described:
- Regarding the light it throws on the mother/son relationship, it perhaps indicates Gilraen's concern for her son and Aragorn's closeness to her in that he was able to open his heart to her.
- On the other hand did she actually have to bully him into telling her what was wrong ("*... at last he yielded to her questions...*"[17])?
- Was her primary concern for his emotional welfare, or was it fear for the future, or fear of Elrond's immediate displeasure? Or all these equally?
- Why did she tell Aragorn of her foreknowledge that he would wander in the wild alone? On the face of it such a remark seems callous and would surely have led him to despair rather than hope. However, there is evidence that some of the foresight experiences of the Dúnedain could come suddenly, perhaps taking them unawares. For example, during the conversation between Elrond and Aragorn about the unsuitability of the latter's attachment to Arwen, we are told that "*... **suddenly** the foresight of his [Aragorn's] kindred came to him...*"[18] [My emphasis] as he realised that the time would soon come when Arwen would have to choose between sailing West with her father and staying in Middle-earth. Likewise, the incident when Ivorwen saw the green stone on the breast of the infant Aragorn also seemed to occur unexpectedly during the child's naming ceremony so must have been sudden (*HoM-e* XII.Foreword.xii). Other instances, such as Halbarad's premonition of his own death as he stood at the door to the Paths of the Dead (*LotR* 5.2.786), and perhaps even Ivorwen's realisation that Gilraen's and Arathorn's child would be the "Hope" of the Dúnedain, also lend themselves to such an interpretation. Therefore it may be that Gilraen's awareness of Aragorn's wanderings alone in the Wild came suddenly as they spoke, so that she inadvertently gave voice to what she had seen.
- Was it the sudden realisation that she had spoken out of turn which made her say no more? Or did she suspect that Aragorn would in fact marry Arwen and feel that it was inappropriate to continue? She would obviously have been aware of the union of Beren and Lúthien, from which she and Aragorn were descended. She may also have been familiar with the story of the First-age hero Túrin and the incident described in *TSil*, where the Elf Gwindor told the Elf Finduilas, on perceiving her love for Túrin, "*It is not fitting that the Elder Children of Ilúvatar should wed with the Younger... Neither will fate suffer it, unless it be once or twice only, for some high cause of doom...*"[19] The first sentence is echoed in Gilraen's own words which I quoted on the previous page. However, given the prophecies concerning her son and the high expectations of him she may have felt that he and Arwen would in fact be one of the exceptions "*suffered by fate for some high cause of doom*".

There are other considerations which add to the difficulty of analysing the relationship between Aragorn and his mother at this early stage in his life:
- His identity had been kept secret in Rivendell and an alias used - at Elrond's insistence - and although Gilraen would have understood the need for this precaution, because of it she had been living a lie with her child for eighteen years.
- His true identity was not revealed to him until (probably) only a matter of weeks before he left Rivendell; thus by the time that Gilraen was in a position to have an honest and open relationship with him, they were due to be separated.

---

15. Op. cit. [1], App A.I.v, p. 1059.
16. Op. cit., App A.I.v, p. 1059.
17. Op. cit., App A.I.v, p. 1058.
18. Op. cit., App A.I.v, p. 1059.
19. Op. cit. [2], *TSil* Chapter 21, p. 251.

- There is also the question of what Aragorn himself felt about the deception. He may have been highly excited about his new-found rank and titles, and enthusiastic about carrying out what was expected of him, but that didn't alter the fact that the two people closest to him, as well as everyone else in Rivendell, had been deceiving him for eighteen years.
- In fact when he found out that he was Chieftain of the Dúnedain and Isildur's heir he also found out that his mother was the widow of a Chieftain so she took on a new identity too.

The period between these revelations and his departure from Rivendell must have been a highly stressful and emotional time for both of them - even without the added complication of Aragorn's love for Arwen and the fear this aroused in his mother. Their resulting conversation would have been very disturbing to them, leading as it did to the crushing of Aragorn's hopes for a union with Arwen. He clearly came to share his mother's wish for silence on the matter - as shown by his anxiety on realising that Elrond had become aware of the situation, initially thinking that this was due to Gilraen speaking of it.

We are told that Gilraen went back to live among her own people in Eriador after Aragorn's departure and that she "... *seldom saw her son again...*"[20] due to the extent and duration of his travels. However there is some uncertainty as to when she actually left Rivendell. Robert Foster states that this occurred in 2954[21] - three years after Aragorn became a Ranger - but I have found nothing in Tolkien's works to support this. App A.I.v is rather ambiguous as it deals with Aragorn's departure from Rivendell in 2951 and then goes on to describe his activities during the following twenty-nine years up until his betrothal to Arwen in 2980. The text then returns to Gilraen in a new paragraph and states that "*After a few years Gilraen took leave of Elrond and returned to her own people...*"[22] which could be interpreted to mean either that she left Rivendell a few years after Aragorn did, or that she left a few years after Aragorn's betrothal. It is not a hundred per cent clear whether the new paragraph is continuing with the time sequence of the previous paragraph or backtracking to the earlier time (2951) to bring **Gilraen**'s actions up to date. Although on balance the evidence seems to be in favour of the later departure date for her, I cannot help feeling that the earlier one, of 2954 or thereabouts, is more feasible for the following reasons:
- Aragorn would have already been away from Rivendell for three years at that point and the chances of him returning there in the near future were pretty slim, partly because he was now a Ranger, and partly because Elrond would undoubtedly have wanted him to stay away from Arwen. As it turned out Aragorn seems not to have gone to Rivendell again until after his betrothal. The meeting between him and Arwen in Lothlórien in 2980 (described in App A.I.v.1060-1) was clearly only the second to take place and it is definitely stated that Aragorn had had no idea she was there. If he had been visiting Rivendell he would have known where she was - therefore the implication is that he hadn't been back to his childhood home between 2951 and 2980.
- Gilraen herself would have felt awkward in Rivendell due to the Aragorn/Arwen situation and would probably have been anxious to avoid any further indebtedness to Elrond in the circumstances.
- She would also, surely, have wanted to live among her own people again, particularly if her parents were still alive, and with Aragorn gone there would have been nothing to keep her in Rivendell. In fact by remaining there she would have reduced her chance of seeing him, and his rare - and no doubt eagerly-awaited - visits would in any case be more straight-forward in her own home.

To conclude, I cannot see any reason why she would have carried on living in Rivendell for thirty years or more after Aragorn's departure, unless her frame of mind was such as to make her yearn for peace, safety and escape from the outside world. It may have taken the actual betrothal of Aragorn and Arwen to make her feel that it would be more diplomatic for her to leave. We know that Aragorn did actually go to Rivendell and speak to Elrond at some point after the betrothal so if Gilraen was still there they may well have discussed the idea

---

20. Op. cit. [1], App A.I.v, p. 1061.
21. 'Gilraen' in R. Foster, *The Complete Guide to Middle-earth: From The Hobbit to The Silmarillion*, London, HarperCollins Publishers, 1993, p. 162. First published in Great Britain by George Allen & Unwin 1978.
22. Op. cit. [1], App A.I.v, p. 1061.

of her moving back to live with the Dúnedain.

Gilraen was forty-four when Aragorn left Rivendell and she would live for another fifty-six years. Nothing further is recorded of her life until her final meeting with Aragorn just before her death in 3007 when she told him that this was their last parting because she would soon die. Although she was now a hundred years old she made it plain that she had aged prematurely - especially for someone of Isildur's blood - due to the burden of care she had suffered over the years and to her premonition of the horrors which were now approaching in Middle-earth. To put her distress into context:

- It was now over five years since Bilbo's farewell party. Aragorn and Gandalf knew that the One Ring had been found and were intermittently searching for Gollum.
- Aragorn was seventy-six and had thus been enduring his life of homelessness, danger and hardship for well over fifty years. She hardly ever saw him and the anxiety she must have suffered in his absence - not to mention her concern at his appearance when she did see him - would undoubtedly have sapped any positive feelings she might have about the future.
- Had she seen relations and friends suffering illness, premature death and despair due to the increasing evil?
- Also, did she herself know that the Ring had been found - either through her own foresight or because Aragorn had actually told her?
- The Nazgûl had not yet made an appearance in the North, but there may have been other creatures/spirits sent by Sauron which broke down people's strength and resistance, causing fear and hopelessness. For example note Barliman Butterbur referred to "... *dark shapes in the woods, dreadful things that it makes the blood run cold to think of.*"[23]

By the time of her last meeting with Aragorn she seemed to be consumed by despair, maybe doubting the truth of her mother's prophecies and fearing the worst for her son. The fact that she is recorded as living alone when she returned to her own people perhaps shows that this state of mind was something which afflicted her quite early on in her life. Or it may have been nothing more than ensuring that she could have Aragorn entirely to herself when he visited. It must be stressed that, due to Aragorn's ignorance of his identity as a child, it was only during his adulthood when she was separated from him for probably years at a time that she had been able to have a frank mother/son relationship with him. Perhaps another hint to Gilraen's character lies in *HoM-e* XII where she is described as "... *fearless and strong as were all the women of that kin...*"[24] In addition, as I mentioned earlier, she felt that she had married too young. These characteristics do not appear in the published *LotR*, but Tolkien clearly did see her thus at some point. Considering the dangerous and secretive lives her people led it would have been very necessary for everyone to be able to defend themselves when it came to the crunch. As far as the case of Gilraen was concerned, premature marriage and motherhood followed by early widowhood, along with dependence on Elrond's charity and goodwill, were hardly likely to lead to happiness for someone who perhaps hankered after a much more physically protective role in her community. Would she rather have been fighting Orcs?

Aragorn's grief at knowing that his mother's death was approaching is very evident in the account in App A.I.v as he tried to comfort her with the words, "*Yet there may be a light beyond the darkness; and if so, I would have you see it and be glad.*"[25] A man of his sensitivity and perception would have been under no illusion as to what she had suffered and he would naturally have wanted her to be there to share in his joy if he became king and wedded Arwen. Her last words to him before he left were, "*Ónen i-Estel Edain, ú-chebin estel anim*"[26] (translated as: "*I gave Hope to the Dúnedain, I have kept no hope for myself*"). At its first occurrence the word "Estel" begins with a capital "E", thus denoting Aragorn himself (whom she still addressed by this childhood name) as the embodiment of hope for the Dúnedain, while the second, lower-case, "estel" indicated her own personal lack of hope. It is open to interpretation how this speech was said: with sadness? bitterness? sarcasm?

---

23. Op. cit. [1], *LotR* 6.7, p. 993.
24. Op. cit. [4], *HoM-e* XII Part 1, Chapter 9.ii, p. 263.
25. Op. cit. [1], App A.I.v, p. 1061.
26. Op. cit., App A.I.v, p. 1061.

or a mixture of these?

On Aragorn's departure we are told that he *"went away heavy of heart."*[27] As well as the grief and guilt he must have felt at having spent so little time with her - unavoidable though that was - and now having to leave her in such a situation, her decline and despair must have been deeply unnerving for him knowing her gift of foresight, thus making it more difficult for him to keep his own hopes up. She died less than a year later. The fact that he was absent at the time would have only increased his distress.

Was Gilraen's death the first incident which really brought home to Aragorn the ability of Sauron to crush even the strongest people by despair? Was it a foretaste of the attack at Sarn Ford twelve years later when his Rangers were overcome by the Nazgûl? The Dúnedain were tough, but at Sarn Ford they couldn't cope with the Nazgûl, and Gilraen couldn't cope with Sauron-induced despair. Was his mother's decline - and later the Sarn Ford incident - a shock and revelation to Aragorn? Did they stir up a hatred in him for what Sauron had done to him personally, as well as to Middle-earth in general?

Gilraen must have been much missed at his coronation and wedding.

*

Some final thoughts on the foresight of Aragorn's immediate ancestors.

Given that Arathorn was sixty when he died, it can be established from App B that he would have been born the year after the death of the White Tree in Gondor. No sapling could be found at that point to replace the tree, giving rise to the fear that the line of Kings had finally died out (as indicated by the prophecy of Tar-Palantir). If Dírhael was aware of this did it perhaps lead to his premonition of a short life-span for Arathorn? And by his unwillingness to let his daughter marry him was he showing a loss of hope for the future? This was overruled by Ivorwen's greater foresight and her premonition of hope. Gilraen in the end seems to have shared her father's attitude, and thus succumbed to despair. Did Ivorwen, with her greater hope, survive them both, perhaps living to see Aragorn become King? Or did even she succumb to despair in the end?

HALBARAD

Aragorn must have encountered Rangers in Rivendell during his early years - for example those seeking counsel and help from Elrond, or family members visiting him and his mother - and perhaps also when out on forays with his foster-brothers. However it would have been his departure from his childhood home in 2951 which marked the start of his association with them on a daily basis and of his relationship with them as Chieftain with full knowledge of his own identity.

During his sixty-eight years as Chieftain of the Dúnedain Aragorn must have formed close relationships with many of his people, some perhaps being of a father-son type in the earlier years, particularly prior to his friendship with Gandalf. However we know none of these people by name except Halbarad, who does not appear in the *LotR* narrative until *Return of the King*, and then only in *The Passing of the Grey Company* (*LotR* 5.2) and (briefly) in *The Battle of the Pelennor Fields* (*LotR* 5.6). Nevertheless a significant amount about the relationship between him and Aragorn can be gleaned from these two chapters - and there is also scope for speculation.

Halbarad was Aragorn's "kinsman", and when he and his companions (the Grey Company) caught up with him in Rohan shortly after the parley with Saruman, Aragorn, suddenly realising who the "strangers" were, ran to embrace him. This embrace was more than a mere formal greeting between relatives, as evidenced by Aragorn's words, *"Halbarad! Of all joys this is the least expected!"*[28] In reply to Halbarad's statement that he had come in answer to his summons, Aragorn denied summoning him *"... save only in wish..."*[29] then went on to tell Halbarad how he had often thought of him and wished for him to come - especially on that particular night (he now had the Palantír of Orthanc in his possession and was already planning to use it to confront Sauron). His kinsmen's presence would have strengthened his resolve to abandon secrecy. Fleming Rutledge

---
27. Op. cit. [1], App A.I.v, p. 1061.
28. Op. cit., *LotR* 5.2, p. 774.
29. Op. cit., *LotR* 5.2, p. 775.

refers to this encounter as *"one of the most unexpected and most joyful meetings in the entire saga."*[30] She also emphasises the impact of the name Dúnadan (Halbarad had announced himself as *"Halbarad Dúnadan, Ranger of the North"*) and states that this was the first time Aragorn had been asked for as *"Aragorn son of Arathorn"*[31]. Halbarad too knew that the time for secrecy was past.

As the two of them briefly exchanged news Aragorn noticed that Halbarad was carrying what appeared to be a standard instead of a spear. When questioned he explained that he was bringing a gift from Arwen which she had long been making in secret. He then delivered a verbal, and very personal, message from her: *"... Either our hope cometh, or all hope's end. Therefore I send thee what I have made for thee. Fare well, Elfstone!"*[32] Now understanding the nature of the gift, Aragorn became silent from emotion and did not speak again during the journey to the Hornburg. Halbarad had witnessed Aragorn's feelings, had obviously been privy to the making of the standard, and had been entrusted with Arwen's gift and message. Thus it seems that he was very close to Arwen as well as to Aragorn and was acting as a go-between for them. He, rather than Arwen's brothers, was the bearer of her intimate message. Such a level of trust and emotional confidence could not have been reached overnight and the implication is that Halbarad's role here was long-standing.

Halbarad had also brought a riderless horse with him, namely Aragorn's own horse Roheryn which had also been a gift from Arwen - though evidently at some previous time as he is not actually referred to as her gift in *LotR*. It is not clear whether he was brought south at her instigation, Halbarad's or Elrond's, though the last-mentioned seems most likely in view of his anticipation of the journey through the Paths of the Dead which, as would be seen, required a horse of the Dúnedain familiar with its rider rather than a horse of Rohan.

Later that same night when Aragorn went to a room at the top of the Hornburg to use the Palantír, the only person who went with him was Halbarad. This made sense for a variety of reasons:
- Aragorn would have realised by now that the summons for the Northern Dúnedain to come to Rohan had been instigated by Galadriel, and would have realised too that this summons related to her message to him (delivered by Gandalf in *LotR* 3.5.503) concerning the prophecy of the Paths of the Dead - which specifically mentioned the Grey Company.
- After his Palantír confrontation, whatever the outcome, he would have to take counsel with Halbarad, particularly if the Paths of the Dead appeared to be their only option.
- Galadriel had sent Halbarad and his companions specifically to help Aragorn and they were the only ones who needed to be involved in his decision now - not Gandalf, Théoden, Éomer, Legolas and Gimli, or anyone else.
- As a senior member of the Northern Dúnedain Halbarad would surely have had knowledge of the Palantíri and of the prophecies relating to the Paths of the Dead as well.

In the event, the Palantír confrontation proved harrowing and exhausting beyond Aragorn's expectations and his kinsman was undoubtedly invaluable for moral and physical support. In fact an earlier draft of the incident in *HoM-e* VIII[33] states that Aragorn needed to lean on Halbarad as he left the Hornburg after his struggle with Sauron. A touching conversation between the pair occurred the following morning with Aragorn confiding, as they watched Théoden, Éomer and Merry ride away, *"There go three that I love, and the smallest not the least ... He knows not to what end he rides; yet if he knew, he still would go on."*[34] Halbarad immediately responded with an acknowledgement of the worth of the Shire-folk, making it clear that he felt no resentment against them for the thankless vigil the Rangers had kept over the Shire. He must, by now, surely have been aware of the reason for the vigil and must have played the main part in it in Aragorn's absence. It is interesting too that Halbarad shared Aragorn's opinion of Hobbits in general.

---

30. F. Rutledge, *The Battle for Middle-earth: Tolkien's Divine Design in The Lord of the Rings*, Grand Rapids Michigan and Cambridge UK, Wm. B. Eerdmans Publishing Co., 2004, Book V, p. 254.
31. Op. cit., Rutledge, Book V, p. 254.
32. Op. cit. [1], *LotR* 5.2, p. 775.
33. C. Tolkien (ed.), *The History of Middle-earth*, vol. VIII, *The War of the Ring*, London HarperColllins Publishers, 2002, first published in Great Britain by Unwin Hyman 1990, *HoM-e* VIII Part 3, Chapter 4, p. 299.
34. Op. cit. [1], *LotR* 5.2, p. 779.

From now on Halbarad took on the additional roles of herald and standard-bearer. As the Grey Company departed from the Hornburg, along with Legolas and Gimli, he blew a great horn, the blast of which echoed in Helm's Deep. At Dunharrow, as the Grey Company prepared for their journey through the Paths of the Dead, Aragorn had to face the additional ordeal of a desperate Éowyn pleading to be allowed to accompany him. As he rejected her request and rode off "*... only those who knew him well and were near to him saw the pain that he bore.*"[35] Halbarad would undoubtedly have been near him and empathised with his pain.

The finest aspect of Halbarad's character was revealed as the Company reached the entrance to the Paths of the Dead and he observed, "*This is an evil door, and my death lies beyond it.*"[36] He went in nevertheless. When the Dead were summoned at Erech at dead of night he raised Aragorn's standard for the first time. In the darkness it appeared black with any device hidden. However it convinced the Dead that Aragorn was Isildur's heir. Halbarad raised the standard again in the light of day as Aragorn sailed up the river to the Battle of the Pelennor Fields, revealing it in all its glory with the White Tree of Gondor and the stars and crown of Elendil depicted in gold, gems and mithril. This would have been Halbarad's finest hour. Soon afterwards he was killed in the battle thus demonstrating his foresight by his premonition of death, and his courage and loyalty by knowingly making the ultimate sacrifice for his Chieftain. Unlike Merry he **did** know to what end he rode and as Merry would have done he still went on. Note that Aragorn (by his words to Éowyn) had made it very clear that **no-one** was actually under **orders** to go through the Paths of the Dead: "*... I go on a path appointed. But those who follow me do so of their free will; and if they wish now to remain and ride with the Rohirrim, they may do so. But I shall take the Paths of the Dead, alone, if needs be.*"[37] It was Halbarad's own choice to go with him. His premonition raises several questions. Was Aragorn (and the rest of the Grey Company for that matter) aware of it? Or had Halbarad just been talking to himself rather than out loud? Was it a **sudden** premonition, or something which had been preying on his mind for some time? If Aragorn **had** been aware of it then he would have felt guilt as well as grief when it turned out to be true.

It surely goes without saying that Aragorn must have felt Halbarad's death keenly, both immediately after the battle (in the *Houses of Healing* in *LotR* 5.8.863 Éomer particularly noticed Aragorn's weariness and sorrow), and later at his coronation and wedding. A particular poignancy is added by the absence of Halbarad's name from the song of lament written later by a minstrel of Rohan to commemorate the battle and mourn the fallen heroes of Rohan and the southern fiefs of Gondor. No-one in the South would have had any idea of who Halbarad was. He basically turned up in Rohan with the Grey Company, disappeared into the Paths of the Dead, then reappeared at Pelennor Fields where he died.

The facts as given in *LotR* provide every indication of a long-standing intimacy and understanding between Aragorn and Halbarad, and it is clear that these were preserved in spite of the former's lengthy and frequent absences from the North. In fact a strong "deputy" figure such as Halbarad would have been particularly important in these circumstances. However there is much left unsaid. How old was Halbarad, and what was his relationship to Aragorn? He is described as Aragorn's "kinsman". Was he descended from Isildur with the streak of Elf blood? A cousin? An uncle? A nephew? Or was he a more distant relation? In *LotR* 5.2.774 Aragorn introduced the Grey Company to Théoden collectively as his "kin", but this could just have meant that they were all Dúnedain of the North.

Other significant unanswered questions are:
- How long had Halbarad had been in the position he held at the time of the War of the Ring when he was clearly the senior Ranger, in close contact with Rivendell, and responsible for gathering the Grey Company together? Had he been in this role for many years, or had he taken over as Aragorn's deputy more recently?
- Had he been in charge at Sarn Ford on September 22nd 3018 when the guard of Rangers tried to prevent the Nazgûl entering the Shire? Aragorn's disturbed behaviour in the Prancing Pony when talking to the Hobbits about the Nazgûl (*LotR* 1.10.165) may have been due to his awareness of this confrontation when a number of his people were killed by them (*UT* 3.4.i.441).

---

35. Op. cit. [1], *LotR* 5.2, p. 785.
36. Op. cit., *LotR* 5.2, p. 786.
37. Op. cit., *LotR* 5.2, p. 783.

- What was the effect of this on the Rangers - men renowned for their toughness and endurance? Halbarad may have felt that he/they had let Aragorn down by allowing the Nazgûl to enter the Shire, while Aragorn himself may have felt guilt at not being there with them.
- Was Halbarad involved in the scouting parties which Elrond sent out after the defeat of the Nazgûl at the Bruinen Ford?
- By 3018-19 had he been put in the picture concerning the Ring, at least being told that it had been found even if he didn't know the full details?

Robert Foster suggests that the name Halbarad means "tall tower"[38] and this seems a fitting interpretation for someone who was certainly a tower of strength to Aragorn at a time of great need.

GENERAL OBSERVATIONS ON ARAGORN AND THE DÚNEDAIN

I finish this chapter with some general observations on Aragorn and the Rangers which emphasise the relationship and the similarities between them:

- In Bree Barliman Butterbur, in answer to Frodo's query as to the identity of the "*strange-looking weather-beaten man*" sitting in the corner at the inn, referred to him just as "*one of the wandering folk - Rangers we call them.*".[39] He went on to refer to Strider's long legs, swiftness and urgency, and the "rare tales" he could tell on the few occasions when he broke his silence. In short he was the epitome of a Ranger.
- Gimli remarked on the similarity between Aragorn and the Grey Company: "*They are a strange company, these newcomers ... Stout men and lordly they are ... grim men of face, worn like weathered rocks for the most part, even as Aragorn himself; and they are silent.*"[40] This was taken up by Legolas who pointed out a further similarity: "*But even as Aragorn they are courteous, if they break their silence*".
- When Éowyn welcomed the Grey Company to Dunharrow: "*... no mightier men had she seen than the Dúnedain ... but on Aragorn most of all her eyes rested.*"[41]
- When the young Aragorn, in the guise of Thorongil (App A.I.iv.1055), served the Steward of Gondor he gained his alias partly from the star brooch he wore on his cloak - similar to those worn by the members of the Grey Company. Murray Smith has suggested that these brooches could have been a symbol of the authority of the king, acting as a secret reminder to the Dúnedain of their allegiance.[42]
- When the sword Andúril was first used in battle (at Helm's Deep), Aragorn's battle-cry was "*Andúril for the Dúnedain!*".[43]
- As Aragorn relaxed, smoking, in the ruins of Isengard with Legolas, Gimli, Merry and Pippin, Pippin exclaimed "*Look! Strider the Ranger has come back!*" Aragorn's reply was "*He has never been away. I am Strider and Dúnadan too, and I belong both to Gondor and the North.*"[44].
- At his coronation it was the Dúnedain - the Rangers of the North - dressed in silver and grey who walked with him to the City Gate (*LotR* 6.5.966).

Regarding the attitude of the Rangers to their Chief, it is stated in *LotR*, as the Grey Company entered the Paths of the Dead, "*Then Aragorn led the way, and such was the strength of his will ... that all the Dúnedain and their horses followed him*"[45], in spite of the terror which gripped them all. There was more to it than strength of will though, as recognised by Éowyn when Aragorn told her that she had no errand to the South (i.e. through

---

38. Op. cit. [21], Foster, 'Halbarad', p. 184.
39. Op. cit. [1], *LotR* 1.9, p. 156.
40. Op. cit., *LotR* 5.2, p. 776.
41. Op. cit., *LotR* 5.2, p. 782.
42. M. Smith, 'Samwise Gamgee SD? Hobbits, heroism and honours', Paper presented at Oxonmoot 2013.
43. Op. cit. [1], *LotR* 3.7, p. 533.
44. Op. cit., *LotR* 3.9, p. 563.
45. Op. cit., *LotR* 5.2, p. 786.

the Paths of the Dead with him). She replied, *"Neither have those others who go with thee. They go only because they would not be parted from thee - because they love thee."*[46] Her view was confirmed by Legolas as he recounted that journey to Merry and Pippin. In answer to Gimli's remark that he was held to the road only by the will of Aragorn, Legolas added, *"And by the love of him also. For all those who come to know him come to love him..."*[47]. Halbarad, himself the supreme example of loyalty and devotion to his Chieftain, was clearly not alone in his feelings and motives. It may be that other members of the Grey Company also lost their lives on the Pelennor Fields, or later at the Morannon. We don't know how many of the thirty survived to attend the coronation and finally experience the reverence they deserved - as indicated by the hush which fell upon the crowd. Aragorn's own feelings are amply illustrated by his words at the joyful meeting with Halbarad on the journey back to the Hornburg: *"My thoughts have often turned to you, and seldom more than tonight..."*[48]. One can feel his yearning for his own people and his relief that they were with him for what lay ahead.

The feelings of the Grey Company implied that they, as well as Halbarad, had maintained a close relationship with Aragorn in spite of their frequent separations. This situation was unique to Aragorn due to his pre-ordained role of defeating Sauron and regaining the kingship of both North and South kingdoms. It was necessary for him to become well-acquainted with the needs and culture of Gondor and to understand the workings of Sauron and the fears and motives of those peoples who were under his sway. As a result his role as Chieftain must of necessity have been devolved to others much of the time. Previous Chieftains - as well as Aragorn's own Rangers - had only had responsibilities in the North. It is quite clear in *LotR* 5.2.774 that Halbarad had not been to Rohan before and the Grey Company as a group were strangers to Théoden and his party. In Chapter 2.6 I refer to the possibility that Denethor, and maybe one or two others, guessed the identity of the young incognito Aragorn during the 2970s, but the people of Gondor in general would not have done. Boromir, at the Council of Elrond, showed that he had been unaware that Isildur's line still survived in the North. It is even possible that the Northern Dúnedain **as a race** were a secret - or at best rumours - as far as their own Southern kin were concerned. After all they (or at least their identity) were a secret in the North too except to Gandalf, the inhabitants of Rivendell and Lothlórien, and presumably Círdan and his people.

Aragorn and his Rangers had gone through a lot together, protecting the inhabitants of the former North Kingdom from evil and danger, and, in more recent years keeping a special guard on the Shire. Their activities were unobtrusive, unnoticed, and unappreciated, as illustrated by Aragorn's remark at the Council of Elrond, *"If simple folk are free from care and fear, simple they will be, and we must be secret to keep them so"*[49], and by Butterbur's admission, after the War of the Ring, *"I don't think we've rightly understood till now what they did for us."*[50].

Gandalf, more picturesquely, likened them to the White Tree sapling found in the hallow on Mount Mindolluin soon after Aragorn's coronation: *"Here it has lain hidden on the mountain, even as the race of Elendil lay hidden in the wastes of the North."*[51].

---

46. Op. cit. [1], *LotR* 5.2, p. 785.
47. Op. cit., *LotR* 5.9, p. 874.
48. Op. cit., *LotR* 5.2, p. 775.
49. Op. cit., *LotR* 2.2, p. 248.
50. Op. cit., *LotR* 6.7, p. 993.
51. Op. cit., *LotR* 6.5, p. 972.

CHAPTER 2.3 - Istari

This chapter on Aragorn's relationship with the Wizards (the Order of the Istari) draws on material from the main narrative of *LotR*, App A.III, App B, *RoP*, *Val* and *UT* 4.2. The main emphasis will obviously be on Gandalf, but I also consider the state of awareness between Aragorn and Saruman and their possible attitudes towards each other. I conclude with brief, speculative comments on the likelihood of Aragorn encountering Radagast and the Blue Wizards, Alatar and Pallando.

First it is necessary to establish who the Istari were. It is clear from the sources mentioned above that they were Maiar sent from the Far West by the Valar to help and unite all those who opposed Sauron. Círdan saw them arrive at the Grey Havens so knew where they had come from. Their arrival coincided with the first reappearance of a "Shadow" in Mirkwood Forest approximately a thousand years into the Third Age. The chief hope for their mission was in the north-west of Middle-earth because that was where the remnants of the Northern Dúnedain and the Eldar lived.

More detail now follows:
- They were "... *sent to contest the power of Sauron, and to unite all those who had the will to resist him...*"[1]
- Their task was to "... *seek to unite in love and understanding all those whom Sauron, should he come again, would endeavour to dominate and corrupt.*"[2]
- *UT* 4.2.508-9 also contains a rough draft of a council held by the Valar to select the various Maiar who were to go to Middle-earth as Istari. The idea was for them to be peers of Sauron (himself a Maia) but also incarnate so as to be able to relate to Elves and Men on equal terms. They were not to use power or try to dominate them by force or fear.

Regarding the general characteristics of the Istari:
- They had "*many powers of mind and hand.*"[3]
- Having mortal bodies they suffered pain, fear and weariness as well as "*the pangs of exile and the deceits of Sauron.*"[4]
- "*Long they journeyed far and wide among Elves and Men, and held converse also with beasts and with birds...*"[5]

GANDALF

(Also called, or known as, Gandalf Greyhame, Gandalf the Grey, Gandalf the White, the Grey Fool, the Grey Messenger, the Grey Pilgrim, the Grey Wanderer, Incánus, Láthspell, Mithrandir, Olórin, Stormcrow, Tharkûn, the White Rider)

In order to reach a full understanding of the relationship between Aragorn and Gandalf it is necessary first

---

1. J.R.R. Tolkien, *The Lord of the Rings,* London, HarperCollins Publishers, 2007, 2nd edition, based on the 50th Anniversary Edition of 2004, App B, p. 1084.
2. C. Tolkien (ed.), *Unfinished Tales of Númenor and Middle-earth*, London, HarperCollins Publishers, 1998, first published in Great Britain by George Allen & Unwin 1980, *UT* 4.2, p. 503.
3. Op. cit. [1], App B, p. 1084.
4. Op. cit. [2], *UT* 4.2, p. 505.
5. C. Tolkien (ed.), *The Silmarillion*, London, HarperCollins Publishers, 1999, first published in Great Britain by George Allen & Unwin 1977, *RoP* p. 360.

to look at Gandalf's origins and history, plus his life and achievements in Middle-earth prior to the start of his friendship with Aragorn. Their relationship can then be studied in context. The following topics are now covered:

- History and mission of Gandalf
- Gandalf's deeds prior to his friendship with Aragorn
- The beginning of the friendship
- The deeds of Gandalf and Aragorn TA 2956-3017
- The deeds of Gandalf and Aragorn during the *LotR* years
- Analysis of their relationship

The two sections on the deeds of the pair are factual summaries with the "meat" of this chapter being in the last section.

History and mission of Gandalf

In *LotR* Faramir quoted to Frodo and Sam some words of Gandalf concerning his names, including the following: *"Olórin I was in my youth in the West that is forgotten..."*[6] In *Val* we learn that *"Wisest of the Maiar was Olórin."*[7] He lived in the garden of Lórien which was the home of Irmo, the Vala of visions and dreams, and his spouse, Estë the healer. Olórin was also linked to Nienna, the Vala who grieved and mourned for the damage done to the world by Morgoth and he learnt pity and patience from her. He also loved the Elves and walked among them unseen or taking their form: *"... they did not know whence came the fair visions or the promptings of wisdom that he put into their hearts. In later days he was the friend of all the Children of Ilúvatar, and took pity on their sorrows; and those who listened to him awoke from despair and put away the imaginations of darkness."*[8]

As stated above *UT* 4.2.508-9 contains a description of the council of the Valar which selected the Istari; this throws further light on Olórin. Initially only two of the Maiar came forward to volunteer: Saruman and one of the Blue Wizards. Manwë then asked where Olórin was. Olórin, who had been sitting at the edge of the Company, objected that he was too weak for such a task and that he feared Sauron. However Manwë declared that that was all the more reason why he should be one of the emissaries to Middle-earth. Christopher Tolkien refers to a note which his father wrote on the identity of Gandalf, possibly around 1972, which put forward the idea that *"... it was believed by many of the 'Faithful' of that time that 'Gandalf' was the last appearance of Manwë himself..."*[9] with the name 'Olórin' being an incognito. However Tolkien himself then went on to say that this interpretation was unlikely.

In *UT* 4.2.504 Gandalf is described as being shorter than the other Istari, more aged-looking and leaning on a staff. However he was recognised by Círdan as the greatest and wisest of the emissaries who arrived at the Grey Havens, with the result that he gave him the Elven ring Narya (the Red Ring) which he himself had possessed up until then. Círdan's speech as he made the gift, recorded in App B, is significant: *"Take this ring, Master, for your labours will be heavy; but it will support you in the weariness that you have taken upon yourself. For this is the Ring of Fire, and with it you may rekindle hearts in a world that grows chill."*[10]

In character Gandalf is depicted as warm and eager, using fire for fun and out of a love of its beauty rather than as a tool of destruction. In *UT* 4.2.505 he is described as merry, kindly (especially to the young and simple) and ready to befriend anyone in need, but quick to anger particularly at foolishness. He lacked pride and was uninterested in praise or power, not wanting to sway people by awe or fear of him. It is also stressed that he had no permanent dwelling (unlike Saruman and Radagast) and no wealth. When the White Council was set up in TA 2463, Galadriel wanted him to lead it, but he refused *"since he would have no ties and no*

---

6. Op. cit. [1], *LotR* 4.5, p. 670.
7. Op. cit. [5], *Val* p. 22.
8. Op. cit., *Val* p. 22.
9. Op. cit. [2], *UT* 4.2, p. 511.
10. Op. cit. [1], App B, p. 1085.

allegiance, save to those who sent him"[11].

As far as friendship and allegiance were concerned Gandalf was the closest of the Istari to the Elves and the Northern Dúnedain. In *HoM-e* XII it is suggested that he may already have visited Middle-earth prior to his appointment as emissary and become acquainted with the Elves and Men there "*... as was possible for one of the Maiar ... but nothing is [>has yet been] said of this.*".[12] He was also the only one who showed any interest in the Hobbits who "*... had been held of small account by Elves and by Men, and neither Sauron nor any of the Wise save Mithrandir had in all their counsels given thought to them.*"[13].

Regarding Gandalf's travels, if we refer again to Faramir's conversation with Frodo and Sam in *LotR* he reported Gandalf as saying "*Many are my names in many countries. Mithrandir among the Elves, Tharkûn to the Dwarves; Olórin I was in my youth in the West that is forgotten, in the South Incánus, in the North Gandalf; to the East I go not.*"[14] *UT* 4.2.514-5, after some discussion, concludes that, though he may have gone as far east as Lake Núrnen in Mordor and as far south as the border between South Gondor and Near Harad in his earlier days in Middle-earth, his main efforts were concentrated further north in Lindon, Eriador and the Vales of Anduin as this was where the Elves, the Dúnedain of the North and the Hobbits were. *LotR* and *The Hobbit*[15] show that Gandalf also went to Mirkwood Forest and the Lonely Mountain, and of course to the Morgul Vale and the Morannon during the War of the Ring. In *LotR* 2.4.296 he told Boromir that he hadn't been in Barad-dûr but had been in Sauron's lesser fortress of Dol Guldur. In *UT* it is stated that "*Gondor attracted his attention less, for the same reason that made it more interesting to Saruman: it was a centre of knowledge and power.*"[16]. It was also an armed threat to Sauron and while its rulers could hold Sauron back by force of arms Gandalf's counsel was not particularly needed. Thus he only became more involved with Gondor during its decline (as Sauron's power increased) when it became clear that it was fighting a losing cause. According to the essay on the Palantíri in *UT* 4.3.525 this involvement only took place after Bilbo found the Ring (2941) and Sauron returned openly to Mordor (2951). In *LotR* it is clearly indicated that Gandalf was a frequent visitor to both Gondor and Rohan during the last years of the Third Age. (For example see *LotR* 3.2.435 and App A.I.iv.1055-6)

Gandalf's deeds prior to his friendship with Aragorn

As stated above, the Istari were sent to Middle-earth around TA 1000 because of concern over the Shadow taking shape in Mirkwood Forest. At this point, due to in-fighting among the King's sons, the North Kingdom of Arnor had already been split into three sub-kingdoms, the chief of which was Arthedain, its King being the senior descendant of Isildur. In addition it was at this time that Hobbits first began to settle in Eriador.

Approximately a hundred years after the arrival of the Istari, it was established that something had set up a seat of power in Dol Guldur in the south of Mirkwood Forest - possibly one of the Nazgûl. This discovery was made by "*The Wise*", namely the Istari, and Eldar such as Galadriel, Elrond and Círdan. *RoP* 360 stresses that it was Gandalf who was most vigilant, and the most suspicious of the activities in Mirkwood. The next event mentioning him is not until the entry for TA 2063 (App B.1087) which states that he went to Dol Guldur because it was feared (correctly) that the power there was actually Sauron. However his action caused Sauron to retreat and hide in the East. During this intervening thousand years the North Kingdom had been destroyed following more than six hundred years of war with the Lord of the Nazgûl - in the guise of the Witch-king of Angmar - whose objective was to destroy the Northern Dúnedain, in particular the line of Isildur. The depleted Dúnedain were now being led by Chieftains rather than Kings.

App B.1087 shows Sauron back in Dol Guldur by 2460, and the formation of the White Council in 2463, its members being Gandalf, Saruman, Elrond, Galadriel, Círdan and other senior Eldar (*RoP* 360-1). Gandalf

---

11. Op. cit. [5], *RoP* p. 361.
12. C. Tolkien (ed.), *The History of Middle-earth*, vol. XII, *The Peoples of Middle-earth*, London HarperColllins Publishers, 2002, first published in Great Britain by HarperCollins Publishers 1996, *HoM-e* XII Part 2, Chapter 13, p. 381.
13. Op. cit. [5], *RoP* p. 364.
14. Op. cit. [1], *LotR* 4.5, p. 670.
15. J.R.R. Tolkien, *The Hobbit*, 3rd edition, London, Allen & Unwin, 1966, 1975 printing.
16. Op. cit. [2], *UT* 4.2, p. 516.

is stated to have helped the Shire folk in the Long Winter of 2758, thus showing that his interest in the Hobbits was established long before Bilbo came on the scene. Indeed it may well have started on his arrival in Middle-earth.

In 2850 Gandalf visited Dol Guldur again and now confirmed the presence of Sauron there uniting the evil things in Mirkwood against the Elves and the Dúnedain. In addition he established that Sauron was gathering all the Rings together, and was also seeking for news of the One Ring **and of the heir of Isildur.** This marked a crucial stage in Gandalf's involvement with the Northern Dúnedain. The war with the Witch-king of Angmar had ended in 1975 with the death of King Arvedui and the destruction of the North Kingdom. The fact that Isildur's line still continued in the Chieftains of the Dúnedain was a closely-guarded secret and Sauron was desperate to find out, one way or the other, whether such a person as the heir of Isildur existed. In 2850 the Chieftainship was in the hands of Argonui - thirteenth Chieftain and Aragorn's great-grandfather. With Sauron's growing power Gandalf's commitment to the Ring and to Aragorn's line - and by implication to the renewal of the kingship in Arnor and Gondor - was firmly established. Also on this visit to Dol Guldur he found the dying Dwarf Thráin (father of Thorin Oakenshield) and obtained from him the key to the secret entrance of the Lonely Mountain. The following year at a meeting of the White Council Gandalf urged an attack on Dol Guldur but was overruled by Saruman who wanted the Ring himself and hoped that it might reveal itself if Sauron were let be for a while. Saruman had found out how, and where, Isildur had died and had started searching the Anduin and its banks in the Gladden Fields area. It was not until 2941, when Saruman realised that Sauron had also learnt of the circumstances of Isildur's death and had sent his own servants to search the Anduin that he supported the White Council in driving him out of Dol Guldur - an event which Sauron had anticipated and included as part of his overall plan to re-establish himself in Mordor.

To put all these activities into context: Arathorn was born in 2873, Bilbo in 2890, Gilraen in 2907 and Aragorn himself in 2931.

App A.III.1077-8 describes Gandalf's involvement with Thorin Oakenshield - also in 2941 - in his quest to retrieve the Dwarves' treasure from the dragon Smaug. Gandalf knew that Sauron was plotting war and had designs on Rivendell. If he were to approach it from the north, only the Dwarves of the Iron Hills stood in his way, plus he would have the advantage of the dragon on the Lonely Mountain. Hence both Gandalf and Thorin wanted Smaug out of the way for their own reasons. Gandalf's foresight made him feel the need to involve Bilbo in order to ensure the success of Thorin's venture, the end result of which was the re-establishment of Dale and of the Dwarf colony in the Lonely Mountain. Since both these peoples were to have a crucial role in the War of the Ring, Gandalf's foresight proved to be accurate. He was later to say that it was all due to his meeting with Thorin in Bree in 2941: "*A chance-meeting, as we say in Middle-earth*"[17]. Of course the other significant outcome of Thorin's venture was that Bilbo came into possession of the One Ring leading to Gollum's emergence from his cave under the Misty Mountains in 2944 desperate to find the thief who had stolen his Precious. Gandalf's friendship with Bilbo continued as shown by his visit to him in the Shire in 2949 accompanied by the Dwarf Balin.

2951 was another key year as far as Gandalf's future relationship with Aragorn was concerned as it was then that Sauron officially declared his presence in Mordor, Gollum began to head towards Mordor, three of the Nazgûl occupied Dol Guldur and Aragorn left Rivendell to take up his role as Chieftain of the Dúnedain. Two years later the last meeting of the White Council took place at which Saruman persuaded his fellow members that the Ring had passed down the Anduin to the sea. He also fortified Isengard, began to spy on Gandalf and sent agents to Bree and the Shire. However the rest of the White Council were oblivious to his treachery.

The following table summarises the events just described.

c. 1000	Istari arrived in Middle-earth. Shadow gathering in Mirkwood. First Hobbits to Eriador.
c. 1100	Discovery of evil power (Nazgûl?) in Dol Guldur.
1975	End of North Kingdom with death of Arvedui. Isildur's line survived in the Chieftains.
2063	Gandalf went to Dol Guldur fearing the power was Sauron. Sauron fled east and hid.

---

17. Op. cit. [1], App A.III, p. 1080.

2460	Sauron back in Dol Guldur.
2463	Formation of White Council.
2758	Gandalf helped the Shire folk in the Long Winter.
2850	Gandalf visited Dol Guldur again. Sauron searching for One Ring and Isildur's heir. Gandalf obtained key to Lonely Mountain from Thráin. Argonui (Aragorn's great-grandfather) was Chieftain of the Dúnedain.
2873	Birth of Arathorn.
2890	Birth of Bilbo.
2907	Birth of Gilraen.
2931	Birth of Aragorn.
2933	Aragorn became Chieftain of the Dúnedain on Arathorn's death. Fostered in Rivendell.
2941	Meeting of Gandalf with Thorin Oakenshield. Destruction of Smaug. Sauron driven out of Dol Guldur by White Council.
2944	Gollum left the Misty Mountains to search for the Ring.
2949	Gandalf and Balin visited Bilbo in the Shire.
2951	Sauron declared himself in Mordor. Gollum headed towards Mordor. Three Nazgûl occupied Dol Guldur. Aragorn left Rivendell.
2953	Last meeting of White Council. Saruman's treachery established but not yet perceived by Gandalf &co.
2956	Beginning of friendship between Gandalf and Aragorn.

The scene was now set for the beginning of the acquaintance between Gandalf and Aragorn.

The beginning of the friendship

In *LotR* Pippin told Beregond, "*Aragorn was the only one of our Company, I think, who really knew him* [Gandalf]."[18]

The relationship between Aragorn and Gandalf was undoubtedly extremely close and long-standing. It was also a relationship of many dimensions ranging from teacher/pupil, supportive colleagues, devoted friends and confidants. Each had complete faith in the other - even if not in himself. In a way the relationship was formed long before Aragorn's birth as Gandalf would clearly have been aware of the prophecies concerning the return of Sauron to power, the finding of the One Ring and the coming of an heir of Isildur who would play a major role in the defeat of Sauron. Also in *UT* 2.4.323 (*The Elessar*), according to one version of the Elessar story, Gandalf actually prophesied to Galadriel that someone would one day possess this green jewel and take its name as his own. [I discuss this in detail in Chapter 1.2.]

Hammond and Scull refer to the entry for the year TA 2956 in App B which marks the beginning of the friendship between Gandalf and Aragorn.[19] They state that Gandalf had visited Rivendell at least twice prior to that date, during Aragorn's fostering there, but that there is no record of them encountering each other. These two visits are identified in the entries for 2941 and 2942 when Gandalf, Bilbo and Thorin Oakenshield's party stayed in Rivendell *en route* for the Lonely Mountain, and then Gandalf and Bilbo stopped there again on their journey back to the Shire. The lack of interaction between Gandalf and Aragorn at that time is not really surprising. Aragorn was only ten/eleven and was being fostered incognito, even to himself. Gandalf must have known this, so was hardly going to make a big issue of becoming acquainted with him at this stage. He would probably have deliberately kept a low profile just treating him the same as any of the Elf children in Rivendell. Aragorn and Gilraen would surely have been aware of the unusual visitors though: presumably this was the first time a Hobbit had been to Rivendell and the first time they had seen one. Dwarves probably didn't go there that often either, and though Gandalf must have been a "frequent" visitor, in the time-scales of the folk

---

18. Op. cit. [1], *LotR* 5.1, p. 760.
19. W.G. Hammond and C. Scull, *The Lord of the Rings: a Reader's Companion,* London, HarperCollins Publishers, 2005, p. 716.

of Rivendell two visits in eight or nine years probably came into that category, so Aragorn may well not have encountered him before - though Gilraen might have done prior to her widowhood. Whatever the situation it seems highly unlikely that the two of them would have missed the experience of being in the Hall of Fire when Gandalf and Bilbo related their adventures.

We don't know how/where Gandalf and Aragorn first met after the latter reached adulthood (Bree? On the road?) but one thing is certain: it would not have been due to pure chance, but rather to *"A chance-meeting, as we say in Middle-earth"*[20]. As part of his mission to encourage, console and unite those opposed to Sauron, Gandalf must have been well-acquainted with the previous Chieftains of the Dúnedain and the Kings of Arthedain before that, as well as with the Dúnedain in general. He would undoubtedly have been interested in the foresight of Aragorn's grandmother Ivorwen with her prophecy of "Hope" being born and her vision of a green stone on the baby Aragorn's breast. This particular Chieftain was exceptional, with an exceptional destiny, and the timing and circumstances of their *"chance-meeting"* would have been planned to a nicety. When Aragorn left Rivendell to be a Ranger at twenty years old he had only just found out who he was, what dangers he would be up against and what would be expected of him. It would have been unrealistic and unproductive for Gandalf to be involved at this stage when Aragorn was raw and vulnerable. By the time the two of them became acquainted Aragorn had been *"de facto"* Chieftain of the Dúnedain for five years and had had a chance to:
- Get used to who he was.
- Get used to being away from Rivendell and living with Men rather than Elves.
- Get to know his own people.
- Get used to being a Ranger and living rough.
- Adjust to being a Chieftain in charge of others.
- Acquire a good knowledge of the lands the Northern Dúnedain guarded and travelled in: for example, east to west from the Misty Mountains to the Blue Mountains, and north to south from the North Downs to Tharbad.

Thus Gandalf was starting with an heir of Isildur who was adult and who had found his feet as a Chieftain among his own people - prerequisites for facing the sort of life and the extra cares his destiny would impose on him.

Gandalf's task was to continue with Aragorn's education and training from the point reached by Elrond, Elladan, Elrohir and Gilraen (plus others in Rivendell who may have been involved in his upbringing). Because of his incognito during childhood and adolescence Aragorn would not have connected the history of Númenor, the Dúnedain, Isildur and the Ring with himself specifically. Also given the short time between being made aware of his true identity and his departure from Rivendell, there would have been no opportunity to address this issue in the required depth. Elrond merely gave him the Shards of Narsil and the Ring of Barahir and intimated that a long and hard struggle lay ahead of him. (App A.I.v.1057). As stated above, the next five years would have been spent learning to be a Ranger and Chieftain. It would then have been left to Gandalf to enlighten him fully as to what would be expected of him thus equipping him to play his part in the struggle to defeat Sauron and renew the kingship in Arnor and Gondor.

This was very much the time of Gandalf as mentor and Aragorn as pupil. Gandalf would have had a vast amount of knowledge and experience to impart and Aragorn's training must have included at least the following areas:
- History of Sauron and of the peoples of Middle-earth who were opposed to him.

As a Maia Gandalf would have witnessed first-hand the evil done by Morgoth in the First Age, the struggles of the Elves against him and his subsequent downfall. He would have known Sauron both prior to, and after, his corruption by Morgoth and been aware of Sauron's seduction of the Númenóreans in the Second Age and of many Men of Middle-earth during the Second and Third Ages. In the Third Age, by the time of

---
20. Op. cit. [1], App A.III, p. 1080.

his first meeting with Aragorn Gandalf had spent nearly two thousand years in Middle-earth investigating the activities of Sauron and his servants, befriending, advising and encouraging those opposed to him, and studying the history and properties of the One Ring. Part of his role would inevitably have involved close liaison with Elrond and Galadriel, and - as indicated earlier - with the Dúnadan Kings and Chieftains and their people.

It would have benefited Aragorn greatly, being now aware of his mission in life, to revisit all this history with such a knowledgeable teacher.

- Awareness of danger.

Aragorn would very likely not have appreciated the real extent of the danger he was in due to Sauron's obsession with searching for Isildur's heir. Gandalf would leave him in no doubt as to what Sauron and the Nazgûl were capable of. In addition he would perhaps have emphasised the aspect of Sauron's character which would make him unable to comprehend that his enemies would want to destroy the Ring - something which would become very important in planning the strategy for the final stages of the War of the Ring.

- Extending his horizons.

Aragorn was striving to regain two kingdoms, but to date he only had personal experience of the (destroyed) northern one. Thus he needed to acquire similar knowledge of Gondor and the surrounding areas, such as Rohan. In addition he would have to learn of the lands which were under Sauron's sway, such as Rhûn (home of the Easterlings), the more southerly lands like Harad and Khand, and the border areas of Mordor itself. Gandalf's intention (as indicated in App A) was to travel with him on "*many perilous journeys*"[21] as a prelude to him making similar journeys alone. Coupled with this would be the need to teach him the lore and customs of places he would be visiting in the future.

- Honing his natural skills.

As a Ranger Aragorn would have been used to living rough in dangerous situations and places, and to dealing with illness and injury both in himself and others. He would also have had knowledge of plants, animals and birds. Gandalf would have helped him to extend his expertise with his own superior understanding in these areas.

- Achieving wisdom.

App A states that Aragorn learnt "*much wisdom*"[22] from Gandalf. Although this phrase is not defined in any detail it could perhaps be taken to include:

- Hints on how to "read" people's character and behaviour - something which was to some degree inherent in Aragorn's own nature.
- The importance of compassion and pity - again something which seems to have been innate in Aragorn.
- The importance of the need to deal with danger by avoiding detection sometimes, rather than facing the threat head on.
- Advice about keeping safe (and sane?) when travelling solo - as opposed to with Rangers or with Gandalf himself.
- Advice on ways of keeping his true identity hidden, such as adopting the language and behaviour of the places he visited.
- Emphasis on the importance of uniting those opposed to Sauron and an awareness of Sauron's policy of stirring up hostility between his opponents.

The result of the wisdom so learnt would perhaps have been the achievement of complete physical and mental self-sufficiency along with some understanding of the way Sauron's mind worked.

- Encouragement and moral support.

Although App A states that "... *hope dwelt ever in the depths of his* [Aragorn's] *heart*..."[23] it is difficult to reconcile this with the seemingly endless burden of danger and hardship he had taken on himself. The young (and indeed the older) Aragorn must have been an obvious candidate to benefit from Gandalf's wielding of Narya with its function of kindling hope.

---
21. Op. cit. [1], App A.I.v, p. 1060.
22. Op. cit., App A.I.v, p. 1060.
23. Op. cit., App A.I.v, p. 1060.

- Possibly chastisement.

There is plenty of evidence of Gandalf's quick temper. Did the young Aragorn get similar treatment to that meted out to Pippin Took if he did something silly? Was it sometimes necessary to use a "cruel to be kind" approach if Aragorn felt tempted to give up on his task?
- Last but not least, Gandalf would surely have passed his love of the Shire and its inhabitants on to Aragorn.

The deeds of Gandalf and Aragorn TA 2956-3017

Aragorn's great journeys are stated as taking place during the period 2957-80, thus starting the year after he and Gandalf became acquainted. Since he went on "*many perilous journeys*" **with** Gandalf and then later travelled "*more often alone*"[24] it seems likely that the early part of this period involved Gandalf expanding Aragorn's horizons nearer to home, perhaps crossing the Misty Mountains to the Anduin and Mirkwood Forest, or travelling further south along the mountain range. Aragorn's service in Rohan and Gondor would thus have taken place later. We know that Gandalf himself was a frequent visitor to these lands during Aragorn's lifetime. For example Aragorn, under his alias of "Thorongil", advised the then Steward of Gondor, Ecthelion II, to welcome the Wizard and his counsel (App A.I.iv.1055), while Éomer referred to Gandalf being a guest in Rohan "*many times in the memory of men*"[25]. In *LotR* 4.5.670 Faramir told Frodo and Sam that Gandalf had made three or four visits to Gondor that he remembered - Faramir was thirty-six when he said this. Taking this into account, Gandalf probably accompanied Aragorn when he first went to Rohan, and introduced him to Thengel King. Also if "Thorongil" had encouraged Ecthelion to welcome Gandalf then Gandalf presumably visited Gondor during Aragorn's service there. Following his time in Gondor, culminating in his defeat of the Corsairs of Umbar, Aragorn was seen setting off alone in the direction of Mordor, so Gandalf clearly was not with him at that point.

After Aragorn's betrothal to Arwen in 2980, we know that he went on further journeys - most likely to Rhûn and Harad and other southern and eastern destinations. There is no real indication that he returned to either Rohan or Gondor until the time of the War of the Ring. As stated earlier, Gandalf's main travels concentrated on the areas further North and West where the Elves and Hobbits were. Aragorn on the other hand had to investigate the threat to Gondor and Rohan and study the lands and peoples who were loyal to Sauron as well as trying to discover the machinations of Sauron himself and his servants. Thus in general he travelled more widely than Gandalf and there must have been long separations between them during the last years of the 2900s.

At the turn of the century when Gandalf began to suspect that Bilbo's ring was in reality Sauron's Ruling Ring, he decided that it was time to share his fears with Aragorn and the two of them began to seek for news of Gollum. The search for him began in earnest in 3009 and was conducted intermittently by both of them in the areas near the Anduin, Mirkwood Forest, Rhovanion and the confines of Mordor until in 3017 Gandalf, in desperation, went to Minas Tirith to read the scroll written by Isildur concerning his appropriation of the Ring, in the hope that it might contain identifying information. While he was doing this Aragorn finally succeeded in capturing Gollum in the Dead Marshes and took him, as pre-arranged, to Thranduil (King of the Elves of Mirkwood) for guarding. He was soon joined there by Gandalf. Clearly both Gandalf and Aragorn must have been liaising with Thranduil regarding the search. In fact as far as Gandalf was concerned the search was a continuation of a much earlier one - during Aragorn's minority - which he had conducted with the Mirkwood Elves but soon abandoned (as he told Frodo in *LotR* 1.2.58).

Both Gandalf and Aragorn would have been keeping an eye on the Shire as a matter of course and by TA 3000 they and the Rangers were guarding it closely. The guard was then doubled as Gandalf's suspicions about Bilbo's ring deepened. It was in 3002 that Bilbo took up residence in Rivendell. In his conversation with Frodo in *LotR* 2.1.231 he said that Gandalf often came to Rivendell. Given how well Aragorn and Bilbo knew each other by this point, it follows that Aragorn too must have been a regular visitor to Rivendell between 3001 and

---

24. Op. cit. [1], App A.I.v, p. 1060.
25. Op. cit., *LotR* 3.2, p. 435.

3018 - when the search for Gollum allowed.

App B.1090 notes that around this same period Saruman began using the Palantír of Orthanc and became ensnared by Sauron using an answering Palantír (the Ithil-stone). Saruman's spies informed him of the close watch being kept on the Shire. (Gandalf and Aragorn were of course unaware of his treachery.) Since the departure of Bilbo from the Shire and the passing of the Ring to Frodo, Gandalf had been making regular visits to Bag End up until 3008 when his visits stopped - this was presumably because of renewed emphasis on the search for Gollum.

The deeds of Gandalf and Aragorn during the *LotR* years

By the time of the events described in *LotR* Aragorn and Gandalf had known each other for over sixty years. The events of TA 3018-9 were, for each of them, the culmination of a lengthy (in the context of their respective lifespans) struggle. There is plenty of insight into the relationship between them, but first I think it is appropriate to summarise their deeds during the final stages of the struggle against Sauron. They were actually separated a good deal of the time during the narrative, so events during these periods are shown in table form so as to view their experiences in parallel. The *LotR* narrative and Appendices (particularly App B) are the main sources, but some of the details of Gandalf's encounters with the Nazgûl between Bree and Rivendell are taken from sections of Marquette Paper 4/2/36 (*The Hunt for the Ring*).[26]

	Gandalf	**Aragorn**
Apr 12 3018	Arrived at Bag End to stay with Frodo	Nothing specific, but in contact with Gandalf
May 1	Meeting with Aragorn at Sarn Ford	Meeting with Gandalf - all well with Frodo, so left on a journey of his own
Late June	Left Bag End as concerned about reports of Nazgûl	On his journey
Mid-year's Day	Met Radagast who confirmed Nazgûl rumours. Night in Bree	On his journey
July 1	Set off to consult Saruman	On his journey
July 10	Imprisoned in Orthanc	On his journey
Sep 18	Rescued from Orthanc by Gwaihir [Nazgûl crossed Fords of Isen]	Now back from journey. Heard news of Nazgûl and of Gandalf's disappearance. Began to watch East Road for Frodo
Sep 19	Reached Edoras	Watching for Frodo
Sep 23	Left Edoras on Shadowfax [Nazgûl entered Shire. Frodo left Shire]	Watching for Frodo
Sep 24	Crossed Fords of Isen	Watching for Frodo
Sep 27	Crossed Greyflood	Watching for Frodo
Sep 28	Reached Sarn Ford	Watching for Frodo
Sep 29	Reached Shire and spoke to Gaffer Gamgee	Met Frodo at Prancing Pony in Bree
Sep 30	[Nazgûl raids at Crickhollow and Bree early hours] Reached Crickhollow then on to Bree in the evening	Left Bree with Frodo and co. that morning
Oct 1	Left Bree	*En route* Bree to Rivendell
Oct 3	Attacked on Weathertop - Nazgûl there already. Fled north followed by four Nazgûl.	*En route* Bree to Rivendell
Oct 6	*En route* to Rivendell via northern route	Attacked on Weathertop by five Nazgûl
Oct 18	Reached Rivendell from north (Ettenmoors)	Met Glorfindel
Oct 20	Added own touches to the Bruinen flood	Crossed Bruinen and reached Rivendell

---

26. Op. cit. [19], reproduced by Hammond and Scull, pp. 166-8.

| Oct 25 | Council of Elrond | Council of Elrond. Set out with scouts. |
| Oct 26-mid-Dec | In Rivendell | Out with scouts searching for Nazgûl |

From mid-December onwards Gandalf and Aragorn were together again in Rivendell. The members of the Fellowship had been chosen and the two of them spent their time planning the route for the journey. Between the Fellowship's departure on December 25th and the abortive attempt to cross the pass of Caradhras on January 11th-12th Aragorn guided the Company, after which Gandalf took over for the journey into Moria until he fell at the Bridge of Khazad-dûm on January 15th.

	Gandalf	**Aragorn**
Jan 15	Fell at the Bridge of Khazad-dûm	Led the Company to Lothlórien
Jan 23	Pursued Balrog to top of Zirakzigil	In Lothlórien
Jan 25	Destroyed Balrog and passed away	In Lothlórien
Feb 15	Returned to life (on Zirakzigil)	In Lothlórien
Feb 16	On Zirakzigil	Left Lothlórien
Feb 17	Carried to Lothlórien by Gwaihir	On the river
Feb 20	*Left Lothlórien. Carried south by Gwaihir	On the river
Feb 25	*Reached Fangorn. Sent Gwaihir to spy out land	On the river
Feb 26	Strove with Barad-dûr from a "*high place*" in Fangorn while Frodo wore the Ring on Amon Hen *	Break-up of Fellowship. Decided to follow the Orcs
Feb 27	In Fangorn. Saw Treebeard **	Following the Orcs
Mar 1	Reunited with Aragorn (and Legolas and Gimli)	Reached Fangorn. Reunited with Gandalf

* Date from Marquette MSS 4/2/18 (Scheme)[27]
** In *LotR* 3.5.499 he told Aragorn, Legolas and Gimli that he had seen Treebeard four days previously. The reunion with Aragorn was, as indicated, on March 1st.

In the conversation following the reunion, Gandalf delivered messages from Galadriel to his three companions, the one to Aragorn clearly referring to the Paths of the Dead and the involvement of Aragorn's Dúnadan kinsfolk in the War of the Ring. [Gandalf and Galadriel had obviously been discussing the members of the Fellowship during his time in Lothlórien.] The four of them then set off to Edoras together, where Gandalf freed Théoden from the hold Saruman had over him through the influence of Gríma Wormtongue. The journey to Helm's Deep and the Battle of the Hornburg followed (*LotR* 3.7.526-42), during which Gandalf left Aragorn, Legolas and Gimli to help Théoden and Éomer while he himself went off to gather those of the Rohirrim who had been scattered after the Battles of the Fords of Isen, and then to seek Treebeard's help in sending Ents and Huorns to dispatch the Orcs at Helm's Deep. The battle was over on the morning of March 4th and in the afternoon the four members of the Fellowship plus Théoden's party set off for Isengard (*LotR* 3.8.543-59). The parley with Saruman took place on March 5th (*LotR* 3.10.576-87) and ended with Gríma throwing the Palantír out of Orthanc. After the incident with Pippin using the Stone, Gandalf presented it to Aragorn then immediately set off for Minas Tirith with Pippin.

Aragorn and Gandalf parted having had a fundamental difference of opinion as to whether it was too soon for Aragorn to use the Orthanc-stone. They would not meet again until after the Battle of the Pelennor Fields on March 15th. Meanwhile Aragorn used the Palantír only a few hours after Gandalf's departure and subsequently embarked on the journey which would take him through the Paths of the Dead, across the southern lands of Gondor to Pelargir and then up the Anduin to the Pelennor Fields. Gandalf arrived in Minas Tirith on March 9th. During the next six days he dealt with an increasingly disturbed Denethor, rescued Faramir from the

---

27. Op. cit. [19], reproduced by Hammond and Scull, p. 396.

Nazgûl, faced the Lord of the Nazgûl at the gates of the City and prevented Faramir from being burned alive by Denethor. His next interaction with Aragorn was when he asked him to come to the Houses of Healing to heal those stricken by the Black Breath of the Nazgûl.

The day after the Battle of the Pelennor Fields, the Last Debate was held to confirm the strategy for the final stage of the war against Sauron. Two days later on March 18th the Army of the West left for the Morannon, arriving there on March 25th. Both Aragorn and Gandalf were involved in the parley with the Mouth of Sauron before the battle took place. At the point when the Ring was destroyed Gandalf organised the rescue of Frodo and Sam from the slopes of Mount Doom, leaving Aragorn in charge at the Morannon (*LotR* 6.4.949).

There now followed a period of healing and recuperation during which Frodo and Sam were honoured on the Field of Cormallen. Aragorn's crowning took place on May 1st (App B.1095) and his wedding to Arwen on Mid-year's Day. Sometime between these two events Gandalf and Aragorn made their ascent to the hallow on Mount Mindolluin and found the sapling of the White Tree representing the continuation of the kingship. Their last recorded conversation took place there. Following the wedding (*LotR* 6.6.974-82) the guests from Lothlórien, Rivendell and Rohan, plus the Fellowship themselves, journeyed to Rohan for Théoden's funeral, then (minus the Rohan party) carried on to Isengard where Gandalf learnt that Treebeard had let Saruman go free. This was the same day (August 22nd) that the Fellowship was finally dissolved with Legolas and Gimli returning (temporarily) to their own lands and Aragorn turning back to Minas Tirith. Aragorn's parting from the Hobbits is described in some detail as is that from Galadriel and Celeborn. This must also have been his final parting from Gandalf - there is no indication that they met again.

Relationship analysis: An overview

By the time of the War of the Ring the relationship between Gandalf and Aragorn was a long-standing, firmly-established one: an alliance, a friendship and generally an equal partnership. The days of teacher/mentor and pupil were largely over. In *UT* Gandalf told Thorin Oakenshield, "*I do not give my love or trust lightly...*"[28] He was referring to Bilbo when he said this, the implication being that he had given his love and trust to the Hobbit. I hope to show that he also gave both of these to Aragorn and that Aragorn reciprocated.

The very first mention of Aragorn in the main narrative of *LotR* occurs long before his meeting with the Hobbits in the Prancing Pony in *LotR* 1.9.156-62. It was made by Gandalf to Frodo as the two of them sat in the study at Bag End discussing the history and nature of Bilbo's ring - now in Frodo's possession. Gandalf referred to Aragorn by his proper name, described him as a friend, called him "*the greatest traveller and huntsman of this age of the world*"[29] and noted that he had endured "*great perils*" in the search for Gollum. He also made the point that this search would have been in vain if it hadn't been for Aragorn's help. There are clear indications here of:

- Affection - Aragorn was a friend.
- Respect - even admiration - for the qualities and deeds in the quoted passages.
- Support for each other - such as carrying out a difficult task together.
- Trust - Aragorn was helping in the search for Gollum because Gandalf had felt able to confide in him about the Ring. Later, at the Council of Elrond he would say "*I opened my heart to Aragorn, the heir of Isildur.*"[30].

There are many more examples which illustrate these mutual aspects of their relationship:
- In *LotR* Gandalf told Frodo, recovering in Rivendell, that "*... we have been saved from disaster, by Aragorn.*"[31]. He then went on to say "*... there are few left in Middle-earth like Aragorn son of Arathorn.*"[32] He valued the Dúnedain in general too, for past services and for the help he would require

---

28. Op. cit. [2], *UT* Part 3, Chapter 3, p. 421.
29. Op. cit. [1], *LotR* 1.2, p. 58.
30. Op. cit., *LotR* 2.2, p. 251.
31. Op. cit., *LotR* 2.1, p. 220.
32. Op. cit., *LotR* 2.1, p. 221.

- from them in the days to come.
- As he gave his report at the Council of Elrond (*LotR* 2.2.263-4) he described the huge relief and delight he had felt on finding out, from Barliman Butterbur, that Frodo had left Bree in the company of "Strider". A little later he told the Council how he had fled north after being attacked by the Nazgûl on Weathertop having no alternative but to trust Aragorn to keep the Hobbits safe. Given Aragorn's anxiety and self-doubt during the journey from Bree to Rivendell it seems that Gandalf had a lot more faith in him than Aragorn had in himself.
- Also in his report Gandalf expressed deep concern about the solitary perils Aragorn had gone through in the search for Gollum. Perhaps also he wished to sing his friend's praises for the benefit of Boromir who was clearly dubious about the prowess and abilities of Aragorn at this stage in the narrative (*LotR* 2.2.253).
- As the Fellowship journeyed down the west side of the Misty Mountains (*LotR* 2.3.284-5) Gandalf showed his respect for Aragorn's ranger-ship: his knowledge of the lands they passed through and his recognition of the unnatural silence in Eregion (Hollin). He subsequently deferred to his advice about curtailing the planned rest period and his order to extinguish the fire.
- In *LotR* 2.4.306 when the Company stood outside Moria, Aragorn was the only one who seemed unperturbed when Gandalf stated that he did not know the password. Later, at a point when Gandalf hesitated about which path to take, Aragorn reassured the others telling them "*I have been with him on many a journey, if never on one so dark ... He will not go astray - if there is any path to find.*"[33] He had complete trust and faith in Gandalf.
- Aragorn's dogged support of Gandalf was shown in *LotR* 2.5.326 on the stairs outside the Chamber of Mazarbul. Initially he refused to obey Gandalf's orders to wait at the bottom of the stairs, only complying when Gandalf shouted at him to obey (one of the few occasions in *LotR* when Gandalf was in "mentor mode" to him). On the Bridge of Khazad-dûm Aragorn only led his companions away from the scene when it was clear that there was nothing else he could do for Gandalf.
- His feelings after Gandalf's fall were eloquently expressed by his words to Éomer: "*It is tidings more grievous than any in this land can understand...*"[34] By these words he recognised the greatness of Gandalf and the seriousness to Middle-earth of his loss, as well as his own resulting grief and fear.
- Aragorn's admiration and reverence for Gandalf were further illustrated after their reunion in Fangorn in the scene where they stood facing each other in silence. Although Aragorn himself appeared as a regal figure, he recognised the power and presence of Gandalf in his new incarnation ("*... a power beyond the strength of kings*"[35]) and referred to him as "*The White Rider*"[36] who had passed through fire and the abyss. He would use this title again at Edoras and the Battle of the Hornburg (*LotR* 3.6.525 and 3.7.541).
- At the door of Meduseld (*LotR* 3.6.511) Gandalf helped Aragorn out in the dispute with Háma over the requirement to leave his sword outside, persuading him to calm down and obey the instruction. He was the only one present (including Théoden inside the hall) who outranked him. This is another example of Gandalf in "mentor mode". Note that prior to reaching Meduseld Gandalf had told his companions, "*Draw no weapon, **speak no haughty word** ... until we are come before Théoden's seat.*"[37] [My emphasis]. Whether justified or not Aragorn had actually disobeyed him.
- In the same incident, Aragorn persuaded Háma to allow Gandalf to take his staff into the hall.
- In *LotR* 3.7.539 Aragorn urged a somewhat doubting Théoden to believe in Gandalf after the Wizard had ridden off towards Isengard (instead of continuing on to Helm's Deep), bidding his companions guard Théoden and "*Await me at Helm's Gate!*"[38] Aragorn showed his trust in Gandalf by urging

---

33. Op. cit. [1], *LotR* 3.4, p. 311.
34. Op. cit., *LotR* 3.2, p. 435.
35. Op. cit., *LotR* 3.5, p. 501.
36. op. cit., *LotR* 3.5, p. 501.
37. Op. cit., *LotR* 3.6, p. 507.
38. Op. cit., *LotR* 3.7, p. 528.

Théoden, "*Do not judge the counsel of Gandalf, until all is over, lord*"[39]. This trust was justified at sunrise approximately twelve hours later when Aragorn stood above Helm's Gate warning the Orcs and Dunlendings of the peril which awaited them. As he rode out of the Hornburg with Théoden the Huorns from Fangorn were seen gathered in the Deeping-coomb and then Gandalf and Erkenbrand appeared over the ridge. Many years previously, while incognito in Gondor, Aragorn had urged the Steward Ecthelion to put his trust in Gandalf (App A.I.iv.1055).

- Further examples of Gandalf's respect for Aragorn relate to the Palantír of Orthanc. In *LotR* 3.11.594 he bowed to him as he presented him with the Stone addressing him as "lord". Later on he told Pippin of his suspicion that Aragorn had used the Palantír to reveal himself to Sauron, praising his boldness and determination and his ability to "*... take his own counsel and dare great risks at need.*"[40]
- At *The Last Debate* in *LotR* 5.9.879 Gandalf showed his appreciation of Aragorn's mental powers with his inference that Aragorn had the strength to wield the One Ring as demonstrated by his successful Palantír confrontation. He also recognised Aragorn's significant action in kicking off the strategy of distracting Sauron: "*As Aragorn has begun, so we must go on.*"[41] Aragorn responded by drawing attention to Gandalf's own lengthy battle against Sauron: "*But for him all would long ago have been lost.*"[42]
- Meanwhile, in *LotR* 5.8.862, Gandalf had shown his regard for Aragorn's healing powers and begged him to enter Minas Tirith to tend the victims of the Black Breath. This is further emphasised in *LotR* 6.4.952,956 where Gandalf acknowledged that it was Aragorn who had healed Frodo and Sam after their ordeal.
- At his coronation Aragorn again gave recognition to Gandalf's struggle with Sauron, stating that he had been "*... the mover of all that has been accomplished, and this is his victory.*"[43]

Throughout this relationship of mutual respect and trust a thread of affection ran as shown by the use of the phrase "my friend" or "dear friend" when addressing each other (for example by each of them at the reunion in Fangorn and by Aragorn at the hallow on Mount Mindolluin).

I now examine the following aspects of the relationship as illustrated in *LotR*:
- Aragorn's dependence on Gandalf
- Gandalf's empathy with Aragorn
- Aragorn's premonition about Moria and the loss of Gandalf
- Interaction between them concerning the Palantír of Orthanc
- How much did Aragorn know/guess about Gandalf's identity?

Relationship analysis: Aragorn's dependence on Gandalf

This was a very significant thread in the relationship which manifested itself as: an emotional dependence such that his confidence increased when Gandalf was around; a tendency to worship Gandalf; and a belief that he couldn't manage without him. For example:
- During the journey from Bree to Rivendell Aragorn clung to the hope of finding Gandalf right up until he reached the summit of Weathertop - he had no alternative plan.
- After Gandalf's fall in Moria his reaction was to despair: "*What hope have we without you?*"[44]. His despair was aggravated by the need to take on Gandalf's role and although this was nothing new (he had been shouldering this burden intermittently since before Frodo left the Shire) it threw him into a state of indecision as he struggled to balance his duty to the Ring-bearer, his duty to the other members

---
39. Op. cit. [1], *LotR* 3.7, p. 539.
40. Op. cit., *LotR* 5.4, p. 815.
41. Op. cit., *LotR* 5.9, p. 880.
42. Op. cit., *LotR* 5.9, p. 880.
43. Op. cit., *LotR* 6.5, p. 968.
44. Op. cit., *LotR* 2.6, p. 333.

of the Fellowship and his own personal yearning to go straight to Minas Tirith.
- He didn't know what Gandalf had intended to do after Lothlórien and, as on Weathertop, he had no plan of his own.
- His low self-esteem was clear from repeated references to Gandalf's loss. For example: *"I am not Gandalf, and though I have tried to bear his part ..."*[45] and *"Now indeed we miss Gandalf most."*.[46] It did not seem to occur to him that he himself was capable of dealing with the situation successfully.
- During the chase across Rohan he referred to himself as being unfit to make decisions and even during the meeting with Éomer he was still running himself down: *"But when the great fall, the less must lead."*[47]
- Aragorn's lack of faith in himself also led to feelings of guilt as illustrated by his breakdown at Parth Galen (*LotR* 3.1.414) where he specifically blamed himself for failing, declaring that Gandalf's trust in him was misplaced. A hint of this trait can also be detected at his first meeting with Frodo in Bree when he seemed to feel guilty about being away on a journey of his own at the point when Gandalf first heard reports about the Nazgûl (*LotR* 1.10.172).
- Aragorn's words at the reunion with Gandalf in Fangorn left no doubt of his joy and relief: *"Beyond all hope you return to us in our need!"*[48]. From then on he displayed the renewed hope and confidence which carried him through the Battle of the Hornburg, the Palantír confrontation, the Paths of the Dead and the Battles of the Pelennor Fields and the Morannon. It was not until his conversation with Gandalf at the hallow on Mount Mindolluin in *LotR* 6.5.971 that we see a return of the old dependence on Gandalf - in fact his behaviour was positively clingy. He knew more than anyone that Gandalf's task in Middle-earth was now complete. In addition, with some supremely impressive achievements to his own credit, he had surely proved beyond doubt even to himself that he was capable of being an able and effective ruler - yet he still felt he couldn't manage without Gandalf. His answer to Gandalf's speech about the passing of the Three Elven Rings, the arrival of the Dominion of Men and the departure of the Elves was *"I know it well, dear friend, but I would still have your counsel."*[49] Gandalf had to resort to the teacher/mentor role to impress on him the fact that the burden was now inescapably his. It is interesting to compare this episode with Gandalf's leave-taking of Frodo and his companions in *LotR* 6.7.995-7. Aragorn, at the hallow on Mount Mindolluin, seemed to be much more uncertain and anxious about the future than the Hobbits were when Gandalf told them they would have to sort out the troubles in the Shire without him. Maybe they didn't realise the full implications (such as Saruman's involvement with the Shire) and that Gandalf would be sailing West. And of course they didn't know or understand Gandalf anything like as well as Aragorn did.

By the time of the *LotR* years Aragorn had supposedly reached the stage of being:
- *"the greatest traveller and huntsman"* of the Third Age.[50]
- *"the most hardy of living Men ... elven-wise ..."* whose gaze few could endure.[51]
- someone capable of making solitary perilous journeys even into the lands ruled by Sauron (App A.I.v.1060).
- someone who was *"... able to take his own counsel and dare great risks..."*.[52]
- someone who was ever hopeful: *"hope dwelt ever in the depths of his heart..."*.[53]

This does not fit with the anxious indecisive man leading the Hobbits to Weathertop and, later, agonising over the right course to take after the Company's departure from Lothlórien. It certainly doesn't fit with the

---
45. Op. cit. [1], *LotR* 2.9, p. 396.
46. Op. cit., *LotR* 2.10, p. 402.
47. Op. cit., *LotR* 3.2, p. 436.
48. Op. cit., *LotR* 3.5, p. 495.
49. Op. cit., *LotR* 6.5, p. 971.
50. Op. cit., *LotR* 1.2, p. 58.
51. Op. cit., App A.I.v, p. 1060.
52. Op. cit., *LotR* 5.4, p. 815.
53. Op. cit., App A.I.v, p. 1060.

weeping figure at Parth Galen overcome with grief and sense of failure, convinced that the breakup of the Fellowship was all his fault. Perhaps the significant hesitancy and dependence on Gandalf which characterise Aragorn in much of *LotR* came on after Gandalf had begun to suspect that Bilbo possessed the One Ring - that is from TA 3001 onwards. This was a momentous development as it was prophesied that the sword of Elendil would be reforged when the Ring was found. (In *RoP* 354-5 Elrond foretold this; also Aragorn referred to it at the Council of Elrond in *LotR* 2.2.247). The culmination of Aragorn's long struggle was approaching - he was seventy in 3001 - bringing with it greatly increased fear, greatly increased danger and later, as he became involved with Frodo, temptation. There was the need to find Gollum, the re-emergence of the Nazgûl and the intensification of Sauron's search - not only for the Ring, but for Isildur's heir as well. Aragorn's earlier years would have been primarily a seemingly endless mental and physical endurance test of hardship and danger. After the identification of the One Ring these would have been compounded by the mounting urgency of the situation. Therefore it is easy to see why his dependence on, and faith in, Gandalf would have become a significant feature of his behaviour in the narrative of *LotR*. His unease would have been greatly exacerbated by Gandalf's unexpected absence at the times when the situation was most crucial and terrifying.

Relationship analysis: Gandalf's empathy with Aragorn

Aragorn's dependence on his friend and mentor was complemented by Gandalf's great empathy with him. In studying this aspect of their relationship I have included a discussion on the similarities between the pair and an examination of Gandalf as a father-figure to Aragorn.

The following passages in *LotR* provide good examples of Gandalf's empathy:
- At the reunion in Fangorn Aragorn gave Gandalf an account of all that had befallen the Fellowship since the events in Moria. When he told him of Boromir's fate, Gandalf said *"You have not said all that you know or guess, Aragorn my friend,"*[54] realising that Aragorn was keeping quiet about Boromir's attempt to seize the Ring from Frodo.
- Later in the same episode, after Aragorn's tale was finished, Gandalf said to him, *"Come, Aragorn son of Arathorn! Do not regret your choice in the valley of the Emyn Muil, nor call it a vain pursuit. You chose amid doubts the path that seemed right: the choice was just, and it has been rewarded. For so we have met in time, who otherwise might have met too late."*[55] It must have been clear to Gandalf that Aragorn was still running himself down, haunted by the events surrounding the breakup of the Fellowship and believing that his decision to follow the Orcs was a *"vain pursuit"* - a phrase he had also used to Legolas and Gimli during the chase (*LotR* 3.2.426). The Wizard's reassurance about the justness of his choice gave him renewed confidence in himself (as Gandalf no doubt intended), as well as convincing him that he hadn't let Gandalf down.
- During the Siege of Gondor Gandalf, while confiding to Pippin his guess that Aragorn had used the Palantír, stated that Aragorn was *"... strong and stern **underneath**..."*[56] [My emphasis], thus implying that he perceived the soft and hesitant side of Aragorn which was often to the fore and understood his tendency to underestimate himself. He knew better than Aragorn himself what he was capable of and in this incident appreciated his courage and initiative. *LotR* 3.11.595 draws attention to Gandalf's doubt about his own ability to use the Palantír especially regarding the difficulty of withdrawing from it. Thus he would have understood the sort of struggle which Aragorn had faced.
- In the Houses of Healing (*LotR* 5.8.864-7) Gandalf took it on himself to silence the Warden and send him off to find someone who had some athelas. He was clearly perceiving the increasing strain Aragorn was under due to the refusal of the healers to take his request for athelas seriously.
- In the same chapter Gandalf helped Aragorn out in a conversation with Éomer by stating, in much stronger and more direct terms, what Aragorn himself hesitated to say. He perceived (as did Aragorn) that Éowyn's suffering was in part due to her yearning to fight alongside the men, instead of helplessly

---
54. Op. cit. [1], *LotR* 3.5, p. 496.
55. Op. cit., *LotR* 3.5, p. 500.
56. Op. cit., *LotR* 5.4, p. 815.

standing by watching Théoden being corrupted by Gríma, and he told Éomer so in no uncertain terms. He realised that it was difficult for Aragorn to talk about this because Éomer thought his sister's grief was all due to her unrequited love for him. Thus he showed his empathy for Aragorn and also for Éowyn.

In *LotR* as Frodo spoke of his growing regard for "Strider" he told Gandalf, "*In fact, he reminds me often of you.*"[57] Later, in the Houses of Healing Pippin spoke of Aragorn and Gandalf thus: "*Was there ever anyone like him [Aragorn]? Except Gandalf, of course. I think they must be related.*"[58] There is no doubt that the similarities between Aragorn and Gandalf - both of character and of circumstances - would have contributed to the rapport between them. Paul Kocher comments "*Like pupils, like master...*"[59] when discussing Frodo's speech quoted above, and Aragorn was clearly greatly influenced by Gandalf, though his similarities of character were largely innate, so that Gandalf's tutelage would have brought out what was there anyway. The following areas of similarity can be identified:

- They both had many names and titles. Gandalf's are given earlier in this chapter. Aragorn had more and I discussed these in Chapter 1.9.
- Their true identities were hidden from the vast majority of people. Only a few of the senior Eldar (such as Círdan, Elrond and Galadriel) would have known for certain who Gandalf was. These same people, along with the Northern Dúnedain and the inhabitants of Rivendell, Lothlórien and probably the Grey Havens, would also have known Aragorn's identity.
- They both appeared to be of more humble station in life than they really were, for example:
  - At the Council of Elrond it was Aragorn, the lean Ranger in his travel-worn clothes, who was the heir to the North and South kingdoms, not Boromir in his rich clothes, fur-lined cloak and silver collar.
  - When the Istari arrived in Middle-earth it was Gandalf, the one who looked old and bent, who was the greatest - as Círdan recognised by giving him Narya.
- On the other hand they both had moments when they underwent impressive transformations. For example Aragorn's response to Éomer's request for his real name on the fields of Rohan (*LotR* 3.2.433) was similar to that of Gandalf to Gríma's insolence in Meduseld (*LotR* 3.6.514): the dramatic uncloaking and the revelation of the power within.
- They both experienced healing and change in Lothlórien:
  - In *LotR* 3.5.502-3 Gandalf told Aragorn how he had been taken there by Gwaihir following his return to life after the battle with the Balrog. He had found healing and was clothed in white, emerging as Gandalf the White instead of Gandalf the Grey.
  - In App A.I.v.1060 it is told how Aragorn was admitted to Lothlórien following an exhausting journey on the borders of Mordor. Galadriel clothed him in silver and white and bound a gem on his brow. He emerged as Arwen's betrothed. On his second visit, with the Fellowship in 3019 (*LotR* 2.7.355), Celeborn urged him to put aside his burden of care for a while. Later his companions saw him briefly transformed into a regal figure as Galadriel presented him with the Elessar (*LotR* 2.8.375).
- They both suffered many years (in proportion to their respective lifespans) of hardship, homelessness and danger.
- They both travelled widely exploring the hearts of those they encountered. *UT* refers to Gandalf in the second millennium of the Third Age as "*... exploring the hearts of Elves and Men who had been and might still be expected to be opposed to Sauron.*"[60] App A states that Aragorn "*... went alone far into the East and deep into the South, exploring the hearts of Men, both evil and good...*"[61]
- They both generally hid their true feelings and personality. *UT* says of Gandalf: "*... his joy, and his swift*

---

57. Op. cit. [1], *LotR* 2.1, p. 220.
58. Op. cit., *LotR* 5.8, p. 870.
59. P. Kocher, *Master of Middle-earth: The Achievement of J. R. R. Tolkien*, London, Pimlico, 2002, first published in Great Britain by Thames & Hudson 1973, Chapter 6, p. 136.
60. Op. cit. [2], *UT* Part 4, Chapter 2, p. 514.
61. Op. cit. [1], App A.I.v, p. 1060.

wrath, were veiled in garments grey as ash, so that only those that knew him well glimpsed the flame that was within."[62] Likewise in *LotR* 5.2.785 only those who knew Aragorn well saw his pain at the parting from Éowyn prior to his journey through the Paths of the Dead.
- Linked with the previous point, Pippin perceived a "*great joy*" and "*fountain of mirth*" in Gandalf.[63] Compare this with App A which says that mirth "*... would arise at times*" from Aragorn's heart "*like a spring from the rock*".[64]
- They both believed in compassion, for example Gandalf's attitude to Gollum, and Aragorn's behaviour to the faint-hearted as the Army of the West made its way to the Morannon.
- They were both self-sacrificing, putting duty or the needs of others before their own wishes or safety, for example Gandalf sacrificing himself in Moria thus enabling his companions to escape, and Aragorn's decision to follow the Orcs who had captured Merry and Pippin ignoring his own yearning to go to Gondor.
- They both had times of self-doubt. This trait in Aragorn has already been discussed in detail. As far as Gandalf was concerned, in *LotR* 5.4.818-19 he admitted to Denethor that he might be outmatched by the Lord of the Nazgûl and as stated earlier, he feared to use the Palantír of Orthanc. However the main example of his self-doubt is the episode in *UT* where, as Olórin, he told Manwë that he was too weak to be his emissary and admitted his fear of Sauron.[65] This surely, above all, explains his empathy with Aragorn's own self-doubt and low self-esteem.

The other significant reason for Gandalf's understanding of Aragorn is his undoubted role of father-figure to him. The following definitions of "father-figure" establish what is involved:
- Chambers 21st Century Dictionary: "*An older man who is respected and admired, who people turn to for help, support, advice, etc.*"[66]
- Oxford Dictionary: "*An older man that somebody respects because he will advise and help them like a father.*"[67]
- http://www.thefreedictionary.com: "*A man (often a powerful or influential man) who arouses emotions usually felt for your real father and with whom you identify psychologically.*"[68]

The first example obviously matches Aragorn's situation - he respected and admired Gandalf and turned to him for help, advice, etc. The second goes further as it actually specifies that the older man in question behaves like a father, while the third emphasises the feelings of the younger person for the older. Paul Kocher, while acknowledging the closeness of the relationship between Aragorn and Gandalf, states that "*Aragorn has sorrows and ambitions of a human kind that the wizard can never know.*"[69] I take this to refer to Aragorn's love for Arwen, a love which Aragorn must have regarded as unrequited for the first twenty-nine years of his wanderings - until their second meeting in Lothlórien. However I feel that Gandalf did in fact have a very good understanding of Aragorn's "*sorrows and ambitions of a human kind*" and hope to demonstrate this in the following discussion of him in the role of father-figure.

Technically Elrond was the one who took on the role of father to Aragorn on the death of Arathorn. He welcomed him into his family at two years old and brought him up as his own son for the next eighteen years. However Elrond was father to a boy who was ignorant of his own identity and destiny. Likewise Elladan and Elrohir were big brothers to a boy who was ignorant of his own identity and destiny. At the point when Elrond told Aragorn who he was Aragorn met and fell in love with Arwen thus putting the relationship with his foster-father under strain in spite of the fact that the affection between them would still endure. Almost immediately

---

62. Op. cit. [2], *UT* Part 4, Chapter 2, p. 505.
63. Op. cit. [1], *LotR* 5.1, p. 759.
64. Op. cit., App A.I.v, p. 1060.
65. Op. cit. [2], *UT* Part 4, Chapter 2, p. 508.
66. Chambers 21st Century Dictionary, http://www.chambers.co.uk.
67. Oxford Learner's Dictionaries, http://www.oxfordlearnersdictionaries.com/?cc=gb.
68. The Free Dictionary by Farlex, http://www.thefreedictionary.com.
69. Op. cit. [59], Kocher, Chapter 6, p. 136.

Aragorn left Rivendell and became a Ranger. There must have been many of his new acquaintances who qualified as older men who were worthy of respect and admiration and were capable of giving him help, support and advice. However as Aragorn was their Chieftain they were all of lower rank than he, a situation which would surely have precluded a totally open relationship. Aragorn may also have had the companionship of Elladan and Elrohir during this period but, as with Elrond, the situation regarding Arwen would perhaps have made full confidence difficult. When, after five years, Aragorn met Gandalf this problem would have ceased to exist as Gandalf was unquestionably much older and of much higher rank. He was also making the acquaintance of a young man who knew who he was and what was expected of him, but who needed someone older and wiser to help him prepare for his destiny. I feel that Gandalf would have slipped automatically into the role of father figure as well as that of mentor and friend. He and Aragorn must have spent a great deal of time together during the early years of their friendship particularly during their *"perilous journeys"*[70], while Aragorn seems to have seen very little, if anything, of Elrond during the twenty-nine years after leaving Rivendell. If any of Gandalf's acquaintances at this period was in need of a father figure it was surely Aragorn! He must have needed all the guidance, advice and encouragement the Wizard could give him. Also given that there were no secrets between him and Gandalf (such as ignorance of name and position) they may well have been closer emotionally than Aragorn had been with Elrond. UT 4.2.503, 508. stresses that the Istari were incarnate so as to be able to relate to Elves and Men on equal terms. Maybe Gandalf found it easier to gel emotionally with Men than Elrond did. Aragorn's crowning, though a formal occasion, had an intimacy to it with Aragorn asking Gandalf to crown him instead of doing what many expected and crowning himself.

To return to Paul Kocher's comment, I find it inconceivable that Gandalf would have failed to appreciate Aragorn's yearning for personal happiness. With his close relationship with both Elrond and Galadriel he must have been well aware of the situation with Arwen from the beginning and have understood what she meant to Aragorn observing how he remained steadfast in his love and perceiving the remote spiritual protection which Arwen wielded. In *LotR* there are little touches which seem to display his fatherly understanding in these areas of romantic attachment:
- In *LotR* 6.5 he clearly understood Aragorn's wish to have the rest of the Fellowship stay in Minas Tirith for his wedding, and also to keep it as a surprise until the actual day. As he said to Frodo, *"Many folk like to know beforehand what is to be set on the table; but those who have laboured to prepare the feast like to keep their secret..."*[71]
- In the same chapter, as the two of them stood at the hallow on Mount Mindolluin, he showed his understanding of Aragorn's impatience for his marriage, his concerns about ensuring the succession and his uneasiness that no sapling could be found to replace the White Tree which was dead - as illustrated by Aragorn's heartfelt question: *"When shall I see a sign that it will ever be otherwise?"*[72]. Gandalf then guided him to the place where the sapling was growing - he must have known or suspected that Isildur or one of the later Kings of Gondor would have planted it there as a safeguard.
- As mentioned earlier in this section, Gandalf was clearly well aware of the conflicting emotions in Aragorn when it came to speaking of Éowyn's distress.

As well as a personal understanding of Aragorn's relationship with Arwen, Gandalf would also have possessed the knowledge, resulting from his position as the emissary of Manwë and/or Ilúvatar, that an Elf/mortal union had been decreed to inject strength into the Kings of Men who would rule in the Fourth Age. Also before leaving Middle-earth he was to be involved with Arwen's plan to allow Frodo to sail West in her place. In a draft letter to Mrs Eileen Elgar of September 1963, Tolkien states that Arwen put a plea to Gandalf using *"... her own renunciation of the right to go West as an argument. Her renunciation and suffering were related to and enmeshed with Frodo's: both were parts of a plan for the regeneration of the state of Men."*[73]

---

70. Op. cit. [1], App A.I.v, p. 1060.
71. Op. cit., *LotR* 6.5, p. 970.
72. Op. cit., *LotR* 6.5, p. 971.
73. H. Carpenter (ed.), *The Letters of J.R.R. Tolkien*, with the assistance of Christopher Tolkien, London, HarperCollins Publishers, 1995. First published in Great Britain by George Allen & Unwin, 1981. Letter. 246, p. 327.

He suggests that Gandalf would have been the authority which accepted her plea - because of his status as emissary and because Círdan had placed himself under Gandalf's command by surrendering the ring Narya to him and therefore would raise no objection to Frodo sailing.

As purely speculative observations:

Did Gandalf perform Aragorn's and Arwen's marriage ceremony? And did he provide fireworks for the occasion? The Elessar, the elanor and niphredil flowers, the White Tree, and the winged crown would all have been suitable subjects. It would have been nice for Aragorn too to see some of Gandalf's "toys". (See *LotR* where Aragorn told the Hobbits "*Gandalf is greater than you Shire-folk know - as a rule you can only see his jokes and toys.*"[74])

Relationship analysis: Aragorn's premonition about Moria and the loss of Gandalf

I feel that the issues surrounding Aragorn's premonition of Gandalf's fall in Moria deserve to be treated in a separate section. A brief history of Moria puts the events of January 3019 in context.

This Dwarf city beneath the Misty Mountains had been in existence since the First Age. In SA 750 (App B.1083) a settlement of Noldorin Elves was established in Eregion close to the western entrance of Moria. Since these Elven craftsmen needed precious stones and metals (including mithril) for their work, friendly relations - and a pooling of skills - grew up between them and the Dwarves of Moria. From SA 1200 onwards Sauron (incognito and still beautiful in appearance) succeeded in seducing the Eregion Elves by teaching them to make, among other things, Rings of Power. This situation lasted until SA 1600 when Sauron forged the One Ring in Mordor leading to the Elves' realisation of his plans to control them. War resulted and Eregion was destroyed by Sauron's forces in SA 1697. The Dwarves meanwhile had shut the west gate of Moria to protect their city. They continued to live and work there until TA 1980 (App B.1087) when, in their continuing search for mithril, they delved deep under Caradhras and disturbed a Balrog which had secreted itself in Moria following the defeat of Morgoth at the end of the First Age. It became known as Durin's Bane as it was responsible for the death of the Dwarf King Durin VI and others. The following year those Dwarves who were still alive fled from Moria. By TA 2480 Sauron was sending his creatures to live there and Orcs were multiplying in the Misty Mountains. Three hundred years later Thrór, the (probably deranged) grandfather of Thorin Oakenshield, entered Moria alone and was killed by Orcs, this incident leading to the War of Dwarves and Orcs during the years 2793-9. Then in TA 2989 Balin made another attempt to recolonise Moria, but this failed six years later with Balin and his company being killed either by Orcs or by the Watcher-in-the-Water.

In *LotR* 2.4.296-7 it is clear that, when the Fellowship went through Moria early in 3019, Balin's fate was unknown. Gimli hoped to find him there; so did Gandalf - though he seems to have feared the worst. Both Aragorn and Gandalf spoke of having been in Moria before - Aragorn specifically only once and Gandalf seemingly only once. Given their ignorance of what had happened to Balin these previous journeys must have been prior to Balin's recolonisation attempt. [I have already discussed Aragorn's earlier visit to Moria in Chapter 1.4.]

Regarding Aragorn's premonition, a chronological approach to this significant aspect of the relationship between him and Gandalf seems to be most appropriate.

Before the Fellowship left Rivendell we are told that "*Aragorn and Gandalf walked together or sat speaking of their road and the perils they would meet*"[75]. Later events would show that the question of whether to travel via the pass of Caradhras (Redhorn Gate) or through the Mines of Moria had been high on their list of issues to be addressed. As the Company drew close to Eregion Gandalf stated that they were making for the Dimrill Gate - which would be reached via the mountain pass - thus implying that the route over Caradhras had been decided on prior to leaving Rivendell. With the appearance of flights of crows over Eregion the first signs of tension between Gandalf and Aragorn regarding the route began to appear with Gandalf's somewhat testy reply to Aragorn's statement that Eregion was being watched: "*And in that case so is the Redhorn Gate, and how we can get over that without being seen, I cannot imagine.*"[76] Later on, following their realisation that

---
74. Op. cit. [1], *LotR* 1.10, p. 172.
75. Op. cit., *LotR* 2.3, p. 277.
76. Op. cit., *LotR* 2.3, p. 285.

more snow than normal was present on the surrounding mountains, it became clear that a major difference of opinion existed between them. Gandalf reminded Aragorn that the weather might actually be more of a danger than the other evils which surrounded them and pointedly asked him what he now thought of his course. Aragorn replied with the rather ambiguous comment, *"I think no good of our course from beginning to end, as you know well, Gandalf,"*[77] implying that previous discussions on the subject must have been somewhat heated. He went on to stress that the mountain crossing must not be delayed as it was too risky to do it further south via the Gap of Rohan now that Saruman's treachery had been discovered. Gandalf's reaction was to suggest an alternative to the pass of Caradhras, *"... the dark and secret way that we have spoken of"*[78] (namely Moria). Aragorn was clearly deeply disturbed, pleading with Gandalf not to speak of it and not to mention it to the rest of the Company unless it came to the point when Moria was their only choice. When Gandalf insisted that they needed to make a decision there and then, Aragorn was still anxious to avoid discussing it with the others, suggesting that they talked while the rest of the Company were sleeping.

This conversation made it very clear that Aragorn was violently opposed to entering Moria and regarded the threatening weather and the risk of being spotted on the mountain as preferable dangers. Once the pass-crossing began the snow quickly became a major problem, but when Gandalf more or less told him "I told you so" saying that this was what he had feared, Aragorn's reply was that he too had feared it, *"... but less than other things."*[79] The attempt on Caradhras nearly proved disastrous as the weather continued to worsen, and the Company escaped to safety by the skin of their teeth largely due to Boromir who initiated the strategy whereby the smaller members of the Company were carried down through the drifting snow.

LotR 2.4.295-6 opens with Gandalf now broaching to the Company the option of going through Moria, making it clear that he himself had wanted to consider that way from the start and stating Aragorn's opposition as the reason for trying the pass of Caradhras first. Aragorn continued to argue against Moria, acknowledging that the road might lead **to** Moria, but querying whether it would actually lead out again the other side. However Gandalf now insisted that it was becoming essential for safety's sake that the Company should "disappear" for a while. He also emphasised the fact that he had been in Moria before and had come out safely. Aragorn then mentioned his own previous visit but made it plain that he didn't want to go there a second time. It was not until Gandalf asked who would accompany him that Aragorn agreed to go, stating as the reason that Gandalf had followed his lead almost to disaster in the snow without uttering a word of blame - so by implication the least he could do was to go with Gandalf now. However he then went on to reveal the real cause of his opposition: *"I will follow your lead now - if this **last** warning does not move you. It is not of the Ring, nor of us others that I am thinking now, **but of you Gandalf**. And I say to you: if you pass the doors of Moria, beware!"*[80] [My emphasis]. This was the first time he had actually mentioned his premonition of evil befalling Gandalf in Moria, but clearly it had been preying on his mind since the planning of the journey in Rivendell. A further indication of the arguments which must have taken place between them is Gandalf's comment when it became clear that Bill the pony would have to be left behind: *"I would have travelled lighter and brought no animal, least of all this one that Sam is fond of, if I had had my way. I feared all along that we should be obliged to take this road."*[81]

Once within the mine, a further reference to Aragorn's premonition appeared in his speech to his companions who were anxious at the unusually long wait while Gandalf decided which path to take: *"Do not be afraid! ... He has led us in here against our fears, but he will lead us out again, **at whatever cost to himself**"*[82] [My emphasis]. The emphasised passage reflects his earlier words quoted in the previous paragraph (*"It is not ... of us others that I am thinking now, but of you Gandalf..."*). His premonition was of harm coming to Gandalf and of Gandalf sacrificing himself to save the rest of the Company. This of course became a reality, beginning outside the Chamber of Mazarbul when Gandalf ordered his companions to go down the stairs, while he used a spell to hold the door against the power on the other side (which it turned out was the Balrog). When Aragorn

---

77. Op. cit. [1], *LotR* 2.3, p. 287.
78. Op. cit., *LotR* 2.3, p. 287.
79. Op. cit., *LotR* 2.3, p. 288.
80. Op. cit., *LotR* 2.4, p. 297.
81. Op. cit., *LotR* 2.4, p. 302.
82. Op. cit., *LotR* 2.4, p. 311.

insisted on staying ("*We cannot leave you to hold the door alone!*") Gandalf turned on him fiercely: "*Do as I say! Swords are no more use here. Go!*"[83] On the Bridge of Khazad-dûm Aragorn, along with Boromir, refused to leave Gandalf in spite of repeated orders to fly, until the Wizard had fallen beyond reach. In his despairing cry at the beginning of *LotR* 2.6 Aragorn reiterated his premonition, bewailing the accuracy of it: "*Did I not say to you: 'if you pass the doors of Moria, beware?' Alas that I spoke true!*"[84]

It is clear that Aragorn's forewarning of disaster to Gandalf had manifested itself prior to the Fellowship's departure from Rivendell. They had had arguments about the route and the desirability of taking a pony, and Aragorn had been vociferous enough to overrule Gandalf on both counts. Still suffering the stress of having to manage without Gandalf in getting Frodo to Rivendell he was driven by his premonition. It clearly influenced his part in planning the Fellowship's journey and his subsequent actions up until the tragedy at the Bridge of Khazad-dûm. It also affected his judgement causing him to under-estimate the dangers of Caradhras so that he was prepared to risk all their lives in the snow. Also, with his wide knowledge of lore and his experience of travelling, he must have been aware of the reputation of "*cruel*" Caradhras (Gimli certainly was in *LotR* 2.3.283) and the risks associated with mountain weather in general - he must have crossed the Misty Mountains numerous times during his journeys. Yet it was left to Boromir to take the initiative in organising their safe retreat from the mountain pass.

Several questions occur to me relating to this premonition:
- When **did** it actually occur? Was it something that had been growing at the back of his mind for a long time, or did it suddenly come over him while planning the journey?
- Aragorn didn't know what the Balrog was (as would be shown by his words to Galadriel and Celeborn in *LotR* 2.7.356) but did he, during his previous visit to Moria, feel the presence of some unknown and overwhelming evil not associated with Orcs or Trolls? The experience of the Dwarf Dáin Ironfoot in TA 2799 (App B.1088) during the Orc/Dwarf war, described in App A.III, would seem to imply such a possibility. Dáin went to the East Doors of Moria to kill the Orc Chieftain Azog, and on emerging afterwards he "*looked grey in the face, as one who has felt great fear*"[85]. He went on to tell Thráin [father of Thorin Oakenshield] that neither of them were going to be entering Khazad-dûm in spite of the victory over the Orcs: "*Only I have looked through the shadow of the Gate. Beyond the shadow it waits for you still: Durin's Bane.*"[86] If Aragorn had sensed this evil it may have triggered his premonition.
- Did his closeness to Gandalf make him more susceptible to premonitions about his fate?

The premonition must have preyed on his mind throughout the journey in Moria, and he must have been observing Gandalf closely. The struggle with the Balrog to hold the door of the Chamber of Mazarbul (*LotR* 2.5.326-7) left the Wizard in a worryingly debilitated state:
- He felt he had met his match and nearly been destroyed. He had sensed it coming into the Chamber of Mazarbul even though he was on the other side of the door.
- He didn't have the strength to provide light for the Company to see by.
- He was nearly broken by the Balrog's counter-spell.
- He was forced to rest in spite of the extreme danger they were all in.

Aragorn must have been very disturbed by his condition. Not only was he dreading something happening to Gandalf, he was also dreading the thought of having to take over from him in that event. His disobedience on the stairs and on the bridge was due to his premonition as well as to love and loyalty. He was hoping beyond hope to be able to retrieve the situation.

I believe that Gandalf was well aware that something momentous and probably disastrous awaited him in Moria. If he didn't know from his **own** foresight he had had enough warnings from Aragorn and he knew and trusted Aragorn well enough to believe these warnings. Yet he was determined to go via Moria and convinced

---

83. Op. cit. [1], *LotR* 2.5, p. 326.
84. Op. cit., *LotR* 2.6, p. 333.
85. Op. cit., App A.III, p. 1075.
86. Op. cit., App A.III, p. 1075.

that that would be the only possible way in the end. He didn't want to bring the pony Sam loved because he knew the animal would have to be abandoned *en route*. His yielding to Aragorn's pressure to go via Caradhras seemed almost like humouring him. Along with this foreknowledge Gandalf was prepared to sacrifice himself if necessary so that his companions could escape.

Gandalf's entry into Moria was subsequently criticised by Celeborn who suggested that he was guilty of folly "... *going needlessly into the net of Moria.*"[87] This was immediately countered by Galadriel: "*Needless were none of the deeds of Gandalf in life. Those that followed him knew not his mind and cannot report his full purpose.*"[88] Also Gimli, referring to the loss of Gandalf, declared that his foresight had failed him. Aragorn's reply was, "*The counsel of Gandalf was not founded on foreknowledge of safety, for himself or for others.*"[89] Had Gandalf felt that it was essential for him to drop out of things to force Aragorn to take on the leadership? Was his purpose (or one of his purposes) to stop Aragorn's dependence on him and make him fulfil his role and potential? Another example of a similar situation had occurred earlier in Rivendell when Gandalf told Frodo that he did not come to him because he had been delayed, adding cryptically "*And yet I am not sure: it may have been better so.*"[90] This could be taken to mean that, because of Gandalf's imprisonment by Saruman, Aragorn had been forced to lead Frodo to Rivendell, coming into contact with the Ring and tackling Nazgûl on the way, which obviously benefited him in the long run. I am well aware that additional motives for Gandalf's absence and sacrifice could be suggested, but this is a study of his relationship with Aragorn. Whether my interpretation of what happened in Moria is correct or not, the result **was** that Aragorn was forced to take on the leadership and he **did** come to realise his full potential - though with considerable grief and suffering along the way. Aragorn made a very good second-in-command to Gandalf, but he needed to be more than that - which Gandalf fully realised.

One factor which would have greatly increased Aragorn's distress at the loss of his beloved friend and mentor was the knowledge that their last (as far as Aragorn knew at the time) hours together had been filled with arguments about the route.

Relationship analysis: Interaction between them concerning the Palantír of Orthanc

HoM-e VIII[91] gives some interesting background to the interaction between Gandalf and Aragorn concerning the Palantír of Orthanc. First I will summarise the final version of the story in *LotR*:
- Gandalf gave the Palantír to Aragorn telling him, "*It is a dangerous charge.*"[92]
- Aragorn was very self-assured - he knew what the Stone was and that it was his by right. He regarded it as a sign that it was time to reveal himself to Sauron.
- Gandalf gave a very pointed warning about the danger of using it prematurely.
- Aragorn disagreed but appeared to yield the argument.
- After Gandalf left he used it against his mentor's advice.
- Gandalf later guessed what he had done and admired him for it.

In *HoM-e* VIII there are two earlier versions of Gandalf's words as he gave the Palantír to Aragorn following Pippin's use of it, namely:

I: "*Take this and guard it, Aragorn. And do not uncover it or handle it yourself, I beg.*"[93]

II: "*It is a dangerous charge, but I can trust you even against yourself.*" Aragorn's reply was "*I know the danger. I will not uncover it, or handle it.*"[94]

---

87. Op. cit. [1], *LotR* 2.7, p. 356.
88. Op. cit., *LotR* 2.7, p. 356.
89. Op. cit., *LotR* 3.2, p. 441.
90. Op. cit., *LotR* 2.1, p. 220.
91. C. Tolkien (ed.), *The History of Middle-earth*, vol. VIII, *The War of the Ring*, London HarperColllins Publishers, 2002, first published in Great Britain by Unwin Hyman 1990, *HoM-e* VIII Part 1, Chapter 6, pp. 68-81.
92. Op. cit. [1], *LotR* 3.11, p. 594.
93. Op. cit. [91], *HoM-e* VIII Part 1, Chapter 6, p. 74.
94. Op. cit., *HoM-e* VIII Part 1, Chapter 6, p. 75.

The emphasis in both versions is purely on finding a trustworthy bearer for the Palantír to keep it out of Pippin's way - in contrast to the final version where Gandalf was returning an important heirloom to Aragorn **in addition** to finding a safe location for it. Later in *HoM-e* VIII.3.2.257 it was Gandalf, **not** Aragorn, who looked into the Palantír and revealed himself to Sauron. This occurred in Minas Tirith during the Siege of Gondor, and Christopher Tolkien states that the incident was the germ of the idea of Denethor using the Anor-stone **and perhaps also of Aragorn revealing himself to Sauron in the Palantír of Orthanc**.

I feel that these passages are interesting as they illustrate the development of Aragorn's role regarding the Palantír and thus also of his character. The early versions of the story show him as Gandalf's trusty second-in-command who would keep the Palantír safe until his mentor needed to use it. The published version of *LotR*, on the other hand, shows him as someone coming into his own with an ancient heirloom in his possession, believing that he had the strength to use it in order to make a momentous contribution to the struggle against Sauron. He knew, from Gandalf's tutelage and his own perception, that it would never enter Sauron's head that anyone would want to destroy the Ring - hence the policy of drawing Sauron out prematurely by implying that he himself had it. He had become his own master, rather than Gandalf's pupil, taking his own decision in spite of his reverence for his mentor's contrary opinion. Gandalf must have been very pleased and proud, not to mention relieved, that Aragorn was finally believing in himself!

Relationship analysis: How much did Aragorn know/guess about Gandalf's identity?

In *RoP* 359-60 it is stated that when the Istari arrived in Middle-earth around TA 1000 only Círdan (who had seen them arrive at the Grey Havens) knew where they had come from and that he only told Galadriel and Elrond. It was only "*afterwards*"[95] that the Elves began to say that they were messengers from Valinor. This vague time "*afterwards*" is also stated in the reference at the beginning of the Third Age section of App B.1084. The purpose of the following observations is to consider how much Aragorn knew or guessed about Gandalf's identity.

Although Aragorn must have seen Gandalf (along with Bilbo and the Dwarves) at Rivendell a couple of times in his childhood he would probably not have attached much significance to this. When he became a Ranger some of his older companions would have known the Wizard and been aware that he had been around for a long time without really appearing to get older. This too would not have made much impact as the same could be said of the Elves - and of the Dúnedain themselves to some extent. However when Aragorn actually met Gandalf himself and was taken under his wing, the truth must have begun to dawn.

Given the nature of Gandalf's role as Aragorn's teacher and supportive friend, as well as the characters of the pair, a bond of trust must soon have been formed. Gandalf's teaching must have revealed his immense knowledge and experience, and it must have become obvious to Aragorn that he was more than an Elf. The *LotR* narrative amply illustrates Aragorn's admiration verging on worship and his awareness that Gandalf was the prime mover in the resistance to Sauron. With the complete trust they had in each other it seems inconceivable that Aragorn didn't have a pretty good idea of who Gandalf was and where he had come from. I feel that the scene in *LotR* 3.5.501 (referred to earlier) after Gandalf's return from death confirms this view. As they faced each other in silence, Aragorn recognised the power and presence of Gandalf in his new incarnation: the White Rider who had passed through fire and the abyss and who displayed "... *a power beyond the strength of kings*"[96]. If he hadn't fully understood Gandalf's identity before there could have been no doubt in his mind now.

These remarks of course relate to Aragorn as he was in *LotR*. There is no indication as to how long it took him to reach this state of realisation - probably it happened gradually over many years of observation and learning. Alternatively, perhaps the time-scale "*afterwards*" referred to above had already come into effect and by Aragorn's lifetime it was common knowledge among the Rivendell folk and senior Dúnedain that Gandalf was an emissary from the West.

There is a similar question-mark over the Three Elven Rings. App B states that "*Throughout the Third Age*

---

95. Op. cit. [5], *RoP* p. 360.
96. Op. cit. [1], *LotR* 3.5, p. 501.

the guardianship of the Three Rings was known only to those who possessed them"[97] (that is Elrond, Galadriel and Gandalf - as well as Círdan who had given Narya to Gandalf). I find it difficult to believe that Aragorn didn't also know, given his close relationship with three of the parties concerned - as well as with Arwen. His rebuke of Frodo in *LotR* for mentioning Galadriel's wielding of the Elven Ring ("*That should not have been said outside Lórien, not even to me*"[98]) does not seem to be the remark of someone who was unaware - or unsuspecting - of the facts.

Relationship analysis: Conclusion

Robert Foster states: "*Gandalf can be said to have been **the person most responsible** for the victory of the West and the downfall of Sauron in the Third Age...*"[99] [My emphasis].

He also says: "*Gandalf was a friend and teacher to Aragorn **seemingly above all other Men**, and the two helped each other greatly.*"[100] [My emphasis].

Given Aragorn's prophesied destiny and his obvious involvement with Sauron and the Ring it is hardly surprising that Gandalf chose to befriend him "*above all other Men*". Gandalf was particularly fitted to mentor him - they were both chosen for crucial roles for the same end - they belonged together naturally. Their relationship started off more as teacher/pupil, even though Aragorn was actually the leader of his own people, but developed into deep friendship, affection and respect. By the time Bilbo's ring had been identified as the One, a situation had developed where Aragorn was someone whom Gandalf trusted completely and could confide in. As a result Aragorn frequently stepped into Gandalf's role. They were partners in the fight against Sauron as indicated by Tolkien himself in a letter of April 1954 to Naomi Mitchison: "*Gandalf's opposite was, strictly, Sauron, in one part of Sauron's operations; as Aragorn was in another.*"[101]

As well as enabling Aragorn to gain the knowledge, experience and wisdom he needed to fulfil his destiny Gandalf also helped him to acquire the necessary psychological independence and self-belief. Returning to my earlier point about Gandalf's absence at crucial points, Hammond and Scull refer to Gandalf removing himself (or being removed) from the story twice, namely early on so that Frodo had to do the journey to Rivendell without the Wizard's support, and later so that Frodo and Sam had to go to Mordor on their own.[102] Gandalf's absences are also extremely relevant for the development of Aragorn for the following reasons:

- He was forced to take on Gandalf's role even prior to Frodo setting out from Bag End.
- Following this he guided Frodo and his companions from Bree until the point where they met Glorfindel.
- After the fall of Gandalf in Moria he took on the leadership of the Company until they became separated at Parth Galen.
- As a side-effect of these periods of enforced leadership Aragorn endured exposure to the Ring, was forced to fight off Nazgûl and gained experience in treating Nazgûl-inflicted wounds.
- Gandalf had also been absent at a crucial stage in the long joint-search for Gollum prior to 3018-9 as he had gone off to Minas Tirith to read the Scroll of Isildur. Thus Aragorn was on his own when he eventually caught up with Gollum, having endured solo the "*deadly perils*"[103] which Gandalf referred to with anxiety at the Council of Elrond.

All these experiences, gained as a result of Gandalf's absence, would have stood Aragorn in very good stead in the light of what was to come. Gandalf's teaching achieved its end on March 6th 3019 when Aragorn disregarded his advice and used the Palantír of Orthanc to initiate the strategy for the final stage in the defeat

---

97. Op. cit. [1], App B, Third Age, p. 1085.
98. Op. cit., *LotR* 2.9, p. 388.
99. 'Gandalf' in R. Foster, *The Complete Guide to Middle-earth: From The Hobbit to The Silmarillion*, London, HarperCollins Publishers, 1993, p. 158. First published in Great Britain by George Allen & Unwin 1978.
100. Op. cit., Foster, p. 159.
101. Op. cit. [73], Letter 144, p. 180.
102. Op. cit. [19], Hammond & Scull, p. 297.
103. Op. cit. [1], *LotR* 2.2, p. 253.

of Sauron. Gandalf could leave Middle-earth knowing that the Fourth Age, the age of Men, would begin with strong leadership and optimism. [In 2009, on my second visit to the Saul Zaentz "*Lord of the Rings*" musical, I was touched by the way Gandalf held out his arms and embraced Aragorn at the curtain-call - this said it all about their relationship really.]

*

As has been stated earlier Aragorn's final parting from the Hobbits, and from Galadriel and Celeborn, at Dol Baran on August 22nd 3019 is described in some detail in *LotR* 6.6.982. However there is no mention at all of what must also have been his last parting from Gandalf. Maybe it was all said in the hallow on Mount Mindolluin - though that meeting was before Aragorn's wedding and it is difficult to believe that they didn't have any further heart-to-heart conversations after that. Whatever the situation their final farewell must have been grievous for both of them. Just over two years later Gandalf sailed into the West with Elrond, Galadriel, Frodo and Bilbo. Is it feasible that Aragorn could have watched the events at the Grey Havens in the Palantír of Minas Tirith?

Regarding the distance involved, *UT* 4.3.534-5 states that prior to the end of the North Kingdom the Palantír of Amon Sûl was used for communication with Gondor. An assessment of the map in *LotR* shows this distance as approximately eight hundred miles in a straight line. There is also a reference to Elendil using the Palantír located in the Tower of Elostirion near the Grey Havens to look into the West, even as far as Tol Eressëa. A further assessment of relevant maps - those in *LotR* and *TSil* along with those of Karen Wynn Fonstad[104], shows this distance as roughly three to four times as far. The distance between the Grey Havens and Minas Tirith is approximately a thousand miles in a direct line - therefore it would seem to be possible for Aragorn to view the events of September 29th 3021 and have a last sight of his friend.

SARUMAN

(Also called, or known as, Curumo, Curunír, Saruman of Many Colours, Saruman Ring-maker, Saruman the White, Saruman the Wise, Sharkey, the White Messenger)

In order to have a meaningful discussion of Aragorn and Saruman in relation to each other it is first necessary to look at Saruman's origin, character and interests as well as his relationship with Gandalf and the development of his treachery. This picture can be built up by studying *RoP*, App B and *UT* 3.4, 4.2, and 4.3.

Saruman [like Sauron] was a Maia close to Aulë, the Vala of the rocks, metals, gems etc. of which the world was made. Like Aulë he was skilled in smith-craft, and his mind was "*... in contrast to Gandalf's always more attracted by artefacts and instruments of power than by persons.*"[105]. Also he found Gondor more interesting than Gandalf did as "*... it was a centre of knowledge and power.*"[106]. Again contrasting with Gandalf, he had a noble bearing and was also renowned for the beauty of his voice. He was generally regarded as the head of the Order of the Istari. App B.1088 states that he settled in Isengard in TA 2759, being given the keys by Beren, the Steward of Gondor at that time. Before that the implication is that he had journeyed mostly in the East, though given that the White Council had been set up in 2463 he must have spent some of his time further West.

It was the White Council which proved one of the triggers for Saruman's ill-will towards Gandalf. As stated earlier Galadriel had wanted Gandalf to lead it but as he refused, the position was given to Saruman who became offended at being second choice. It was at this point that he started studying the lore, making and history of the Rings of Power, an activity which eventually led to the situation described in *RoP*: "*Too long he had studied the ways of Sauron in hope to defeat him, and now he envied him as a rival rather than hated his works.*"[107] *UT* 4.2.504 gives a further reason for Saruman's ill-will namely his discovery, even though Gandalf had kept it secret, that Círdan had given the ring Narya to Gandalf. As the relationship deteriorated Saruman

---
104. KW. Fonstad, *The Atlas of Middle-earth*, Revised Paperback Edition, London, HarperCollins Publishers, 1994, p. 38.
105. Op. cit [2], *UT* 4.3, p. 525.
106. Op. cit., *UT* 4.2, p. 516.
107. Op. cit. [5], *RoP* p. 362.

became increasingly jealous, and also suspicious of his colleague's interest in the Hobbits and the Shire.

RoP 361-2 and App B.1088-9 indicate that Saruman knew about the circumstances surrounding Isildur's death - namely that he was killed by an Orc arrow while attempting to swim across the Anduin near the Gladden Fields, and that his body and the One Ring were then lost in the river. Whether Saruman became aware of all this before or after coming to live in Isengard is not clear. App B.1090 states that he became a traitor to the White Council around TA 3000, that is when he started using the Palantír of Orthanc and thus became ensnared by Sauron who had possession of the Ithil-stone. In fact he had been deceiving and misleading the Council for much longer than that:

- At the Council meeting of 2851 he overruled Gandalf's suggestion of attacking Sauron in his stronghold at Dol Guldur because he wanted to find the Ring himself and hoped that it might reveal itself if Sauron were let be for a while.
- By 2939 he realised that Sauron had also learnt of how/where Isildur had died and had accordingly sent his own servants to search the Anduin. However Saruman kept this information from the rest of the Council. It was not until two years later that he finally agreed to drive Sauron out of Dol Guldur.
- At the last meeting of the Council in 2953, he persuaded his fellow members that the Ring had passed down the Anduin to the sea. Around this time he fortified Isengard, began to spy on Gandalf and sent agents to Bree and the Shire.

UT 3.4.iii.456 states that, nevertheless, Gandalf's report to the Council of Elrond (*LotR* 2.2.257-62) seemed to indicate that he did not seriously suspect Saruman of treachery until his imprisonment in Isengard.

*

The starting point for a study of Aragorn's connection with Saruman, is his period of service in Rohan and Gondor as a young man, somewhere between 2957 and 2980. As just stated, Saruman's secret and potentially treacherous activities were under-estimated by Gandalf and unknown to Elrond, Galadriel and Círdan, all of whom still trusted him right up until the time of the Council of Elrond when Saruman's imprisonment of Gandalf became known. However, strangely, while Aragorn was in Gondor - approximately forty years before the War of the Ring - we learn that he often warned the Steward Ecthelion not to trust Saruman (App A.I.iv.1055). App A.II.1067 holds a possible explanation for young "Thorongil's" apparent superior perception. It states that following the White Council meeting of 2953 Saruman drew his friends and servants from those who hated Gondor and Rohan. In addition, during the reign of Thengel King (and thus during Aragorn's service in Rohan) Saruman supported Rohan's enemies and encroached on its borders. Thus Thorongil may have seen at first-hand why Saruman wasn't to be trusted and subsequently passed on his doubts to Ecthelion. However if this was the case, why did he not make the situation known to Gandalf and Elrond? Did he assume that Gandalf was already aware of Saruman's nature? Or was it possible that he didn't at that stage realise the full significance of Saruman? It would be another 20 years or more before Gandalf would discover the truth about Bilbo's Ring and confide his knowledge in Aragorn. As "Thorongil", in his thirties/forties, Aragorn was still relatively young (for a Dúnadan), and being on affectionate terms with both Gandalf and Ecthelion, may have naturally urged Gandalf's case with the Steward. *UT* 4.3.533 Note 7 makes the point that Saruman's breeding of Orcs didn't start until 2990, by which time Aragorn's service in Gondor and Rohan had come to an end. This activity was no doubt secret at first anyway. Also, in *LotR* 3.2.435, Éomer would tell Aragorn that the trouble with Saruman started after Gandalf's imprisonment in Orthanc and that before that he was regarded as a friend in Rohan. This implied that his activities during Thengel's reign supporting Rohan's enemies were sufficiently discreet not to arouse the suspicion of the Rohirrim. Had he actually visited Rohan in order to appear friendly? Had the young Aragorn been in his presence and, with his gift of heightened perception, sensed something untrustworthy about him?

Looking ahead to *LotR* and the summer of 3018: when Aragorn set off on his unknown journey believing that things were going well and that Gandalf was taking care of Frodo, he obviously wasn't to know that Gandalf would subsequently learn of the reappearance of the Nazgûl and consequently go to seek advice from

Saruman. If Aragorn had been around at that point would alarm bells have rung about turning to Saruman for help?

When Aragorn managed to catch up with Frodo in Bree (*LotR* 1.10.172) he told him that he didn't know of anything other than the Nazgûl, or Sauron himself, which could have hindered Gandalf. Ironically the cause of Gandalf's delay was **Saruman**. Also Aragorn admitted to being initially wary about trusting the Hobbits because the Enemy had set traps for him in the past. By "the Enemy" he obviously meant Sauron - but, again ironically, it had in fact been **Saruman** who had been corrupting people in the Shire (the Bracegirdles and the Sackville-Bagginses) and using Dunlendings to spy on it and channel Shire-produced goods to Isengard (*UT* 3.4.ii.449-50). The squint-eyed southerner was a spy of Saruman until a Nazgûl encounter frightened him into changing his allegiance to Mordor. It was not until the reunion of Aragorn, Legolas and Gimli with Merry and Pippin at Isengard (*LotR* 3.9.575) that the presence of Longbottom Leaf there made Aragorn suspect Saruman of having agents in the Shire. In this same chapter there is another possible link back to "Thorongil". Merry suggested that Saruman did not have much courage in a tight spot without a lot of slaves and machines around him, and that his fame may have been mainly due to his cleverness in settling at Isengard. Aragorn's reply contradicted him: "*Once he was as great as his fame made him. His knowledge was deep, his thought was subtle, and his hands marvellously skilled; and he had a power over the minds of others. The wise he could persuade, and the smaller folk he could daunt. That power he certainly still keeps. There are not many in Middle-earth that I should say were safe, if they were left alone to talk with him, even now when he has suffered a defeat. Gandalf, Elrond, and Galadriel, perhaps, now that his wickedness has been laid bare, but very few others.*"[108] How did he know so much about this? Just from talking to Gandalf? Or from information picked up during his youthful service in Rohan? Or perhaps from recent conversations with Théoden and Éomer?

The parley with Saruman took place on March 5th 3019 (*LotR* 3.10.576-87). Gandalf took Aragorn with him. There was no choice about this as far as Aragorn was concerned - Gandalf just stated that he was to accompany him. No doubt he viewed it as part of Aragorn's education: to see this Wizard at close quarters and test his own response to the Voice. In Aragorn's speech quoted in the previous paragraph he gave his opinion that only Gandalf, Galadriel and Elrond would be immune to the seductive properties of Saruman's voice in a one-to-one conversation with him. What about his own ability in such a situation? His imminent successful confrontation with Sauron in the Palantír of Orthanc would show that he clearly had quite exceptional mental strength and endurance so would perhaps have stood a good chance of being able to withstand Saruman. However it is necessary to take into account the fact that he had certain advantages in the Sauron confrontation which would have been lacking in a one-to-one with Saruman, namely the fact that it was done remotely via a Palantír rather than in person, that the Palantír was his by right and that he had the weapon of shock by being Isildur's heir. Also in *HoM-e* XI[109] (Grey Annals commentary) Christopher Tolkien discusses the successful hypnotism, by the dragon Glaurung, of the First-Age hero Túrin a man who was not easily cowed (see *UT* (Of Mîm the Dwarf): "*few indeed could challenge the eyes of Túrin in set will or in wrath*"[110]). Glaurung appears as "*morally superior and superior in knowledge, his pitiless corruption able to assume an air almost of benevolence, of knowing what is best*". This description is very similar to the effect which Saruman's voice had on some of Théoden's men who were present at the parley. Théoden himself was not taken in by Saruman's voice, but he had suffered great wrong from him and was also in the company of Gandalf and others who staunchly supported him, rather than alone with Saruman. As it turned out Aragorn, on the face of things, seemed to be purely an onlooker at the parley and the text contains no indication at all of any speech or reaction of his. This was no doubt deliberate on his part - he didn't want to draw attention to himself and have Saruman realise who he was, especially given the clear evidence of collusion between Isengard and Mordor. This was obviously a very wise precaution given that the actual means of communication would turn out to be Palantíri, thus creating a real danger of Sauron perceiving Saruman's thoughts and knowledge.

The parley will now be examined from the viewpoint of Saruman and consideration given to the extent of his awareness of Aragorn.

---

108. Op. cit. [1], *LotR* 3.9, p. 567.
109. C. Tolkien (ed.), *The History of Middle-earth*, vol. XI, *The War of the Jewels*, London HarperColllins Publishers, 2002, first published in Great Britain by HarperCollins Publishers 1994, Grey Annals Commentary Section 278-85, p. 143.
110. Op. cit. [2], *UT* Part 1, Chapter 2, p. 127.

Saruman clearly knew some of Gandalf's and Théoden's party. *"Two at least of you I know by name"*[111] he said, meaning Gandalf and Théoden themselves. Also when interruptions were made by Gimli and Éomer he addressed them by name and patronymic. Later he advised Gandalf to *"... leave behind these cut-throats and small rag-tag that dangle at your tail!"*[112] The *"small rag-tag"* were obviously Merry and Pippin who were at the bottom of the stairs, with *"cut-throats"* presumably referring to Aragorn, Legolas and Gimli as they were the only others with Gandalf (or maybe just Aragorn and Legolas - since he had already addressed Gimli by name). At no time during the parley was there any indication that Saruman knew who Aragorn was, knew where he came from, or appreciated his importance. This question of Saruman's knowledge of Aragorn - or lack of it - raises a number of issues:

- There were many sources of information available to Saruman. He had been spying on Gandalf and his activities and associates for well over fifty years, with agents in Bree and the Shire. He must have known about Thorin Oakenshield's expedition to the Lonely Mountain and the resulting destruction of Smaug, followed by the re-establishment of the Kingdom under the Mountain and the rebuilding of Dale and Laketown. In *UT* 3.4.i.437 he is also stated to be spying on Sauron's servants so would have been aware of the messengers sent by Sauron to Dale and the Lonely Mountain asking for information on Hobbits and requesting help in retrieving a ring which one of them had stolen (as recounted by Glóin at the Council of Elrond). He may well have known who Gimli was, and possibly Legolas too, prior to the *LotR* years, though Elves were more difficult to spot and he did not appear to know him during the parley. He obviously knew about the Fellowship as his Orcs were involved in waylaying them at Parth Galen and were the ones who captured Merry and Pippin whom - as Hobbits - Saruman specifically wanted alive.

- Obtaining information about the Dúnedain was a different matter however. They were masters of camouflage, disguise and generally lying low, and Aragorn had always travelled incognito. Very few people knew who he really was. There are hints in *LotR* that Saruman might have been sceptical about the existence of such a person as the heir of Isildur. At the Council of Elrond Gandalf reported the conversation he had had in Orthanc when Saruman had pretended to try and persuade him to join forces with him. He quoted Saruman as saying, *"There is no hope left in Elves or dying Númenor"*[113]. Although these words could have been intended to trick Gandalf into disclosing information about the Elves and the Dúnedain they could simply have implied that Saruman was unaware that Isildur's line still flourished. If he really believed that Númenor was dying, perhaps he just didn't even give a thought to a possible heir of Isildur. His travelling had been mostly in the East and he had been concerned with power, objects and technology rather than people - especially insignificant and downtrodden people. He would have been unlikely to bother himself with the remnants of what Denethor referred to as *"... a ragged house long bereft of lordship and dignity."*[114] Indeed was it partly Saruman's influence which had caused Denethor to hold this view of the Northern Dúnedain? As hinted at the Council of Elrond, in *LotR* 2.2.252 and in App A.I.iv.1055-6, Saruman was generally more welcome and respected in Gondor than Gandalf, particularly by Denethor. Saruman had only bothered himself about the Shire-folk because he was suspicious of Gandalf's interest in them. If he thought about the Northern Dúnedain at all he would perhaps have assumed, from the long war with the Witch-king of Angmar, that Isildur's line had been eradicated. Another reason why he might have such an attitude could lie in Gandalf's words to Merry after the parley, *"... I should say that, at the moment, you and Pippin are more in his thoughts than all the rest of us."*[115]. Saruman was aware that a Hobbit had the Ring. That in itself as far as he was concerned would probably rule out the possibility of an heir of Isildur existing, as such a person would surely have already claimed the Ring. I would not think that Saruman was any more likely than Sauron himself to comprehend that someone would actually want to destroy the Ring - Isildur's heir least of all.

- On the night after the parley, while Gandalf was riding to Minas Tirith with Pippin following the

---

111. Op. cit. [1], *LotR* 5.10, p. 578.
112. Op. cit., *LotR* 5.10, p. 583.
113. Op. cit., *LotR* 2.2, p. 259.
114. Op. cit., *LotR* 5.7, p. 854.
115. Op. cit., *LotR* 3.11, p. 588.

latter's escapade with the Palantír (*LotR* 3.11.599-600), he was worried about the possibility of Sauron finding out Aragorn's identity from Saruman - presumably via Nazgûl sent to check up on what was happening at Isengard now that the Palantír was out of the equation. Gandalf's concerns were based on what had happened on his arrival at Edoras on March 2nd. He had introduced his companions, naming Aragorn as *"Aragorn son of Arathorn, the heir of kings"* who was heading for Minas Tirith (*LotR* 3.6.509). The names were then reported to Théoden, and by implication to Gríma also. Gríma left Edoras for Isengard immediately after the healing of Théoden, **before** Aragorn and Legolas were kitted out in armour - hence Gandalf's remark to Pippin that *"If Wormtongue was not deceived by the armour of Rohan,"* [which Aragorn was wearing at the parley] *"he would remember Aragorn and the title that he claimed."*[116] Although Gríma did not reach Isengard until the morning of March 5th, just a few hours earlier than Gandalf and Théoden and their company (see Pippin's statement in *LotR* 3.9.572-3), the possibility existed that on arrival Gríma had reported the names of Gandalf's companions, and subsequently identified them - Aragorn included - at the parley. This concern of Gandalf's makes one wonder whether it had actually been a wise move to reveal Aragorn's identity given that a cordial welcome in Edoras could not be relied on. Maybe he had felt that drawing attention to the high rank of his companions had been the only way to persuade Théoden to let them in. It is also questionable whether it was wise to let Aragorn go to the parley - though admittedly the decision was made before the discovery of Saruman's Palantír liaison with Sauron.

- As it turned out Gandalf was worrying needlessly because we know that Sauron didn't find out that an heir of Isildur lived until Aragorn himself confronted him in the Palantír. Aragorn specifically stated this to Legolas and Gimli. Because he had seized control of the Palantír from Sauron he was able to perceive his shock and fear at the revelation: *"To know that I lived and walked the earth was a blow to his heart, I deem; **for he knew it not till now**."*[117] [My emphasis]. This was borne out by Sauron's subsequent behaviour which I have described in detail in Chapter 1.6. Thus it can be confirmed that Sauron did not find out about Aragorn from Saruman.
- In addition it can be confirmed that Saruman did not know about Aragorn during the period when he was communicating with Sauron via the Palantír, that is from approximately TA 3000 (App B.1090) until - probably - March 5th 3019 when Gríma threw the Palantír out of Orthanc. If Saruman had possessed such knowledge Sauron would surely have picked it up during their Palantír sessions - after all the subject of Isildur's line was uppermost in his thoughts after the Ring itself. Therefore any knowledge Saruman had could only have been acquired **after** his last use of the Palantír before Gríma deprived him of it. It is not certain when this would have been. In *LotR* 3.9.566, Merry's account of the Ent attack on Isengard on March 2nd stated that a light was gleaming from a high window in the tower of Orthanc when they approached. This probably meant that Saruman was using the Palantír at that point, but there is no other indication of any use of it. However it is possible that he could have used it as late as the interval between Gríma's arrival at Isengard on March 5th and the beginning of the parley. He was clearly drawn to it due to Sauron's hold on it as Gandalf recognised in his conversation with Pippin: *"How long, I wonder, has he* [Saruman] *been constrained to come often to his glass for inspection and instruction...?"*[118]
- The final issue is: How much information, if any, did Saruman actually obtain from Gríma when he joined him in Isengard on March 5th ? There are a number of possible answers to this question:
  - Gríma failed to appreciate Aragorn's title and significance so didn't bother to mention them to Saruman.
  - Gríma failed to pass on information about Aragorn because he had other things on his mind, such as the shock of what the Ents had done at Isengard, fear of Treebeard and terror at the thought of encountering Gandalf and Théoden again. He may also have wanted to keep out of Saruman's way since he would hardly have been very approachable at such a time!
  - Gríma deliberately withheld information due to ill-will towards Saruman - possibly one of his

---

116. Op. cit. [1], *LotR* 3.11, pp. 599-600.
117. Op. cit., *LotR* 5.2, p. 780.
118. Op. cit., *LotR* 3.11, p. 598.

motives for hurling the Palantír out of the window, though a wish to injure Gandalf may also have influenced him. (Compare Aragorn's astute comment: *"The aim was poor, maybe, because he could not make up his mind which he hated more, you or Saruman."*[119])

- Gríma remembered Aragorn's title and reported it to Saruman on March 5th, but then failed to recognise Aragorn at the parley because, contrary to Gandalf's fears, he **was** "*... deceived by the armour of Rohan.*" Saruman may have failed to take such information seriously for the sort of reasons outlined earlier, namely that the Dúnedain were on their last legs with Isildur's line long extinct. The suggestion that the scruffy "*cut-throat*" hanging around with Gandalf was Isildur's heir would probably have struck him as completely absurd.

- Gríma remembered Aragorn's title and reported it to Saruman, either as soon as he arrived in Isengard or at the parley. Thus Saruman knew who Aragorn was, but feigned ignorance because he planned to use the Palantír after the parley to let Sauron have the information, hoping thereby to gain his approval. However the loss of the Palantír made this impossible. By the time Saruman was in a position to tell Sauron by any other means Aragorn had already revealed himself. (If Saruman's last use of the Palantír was **prior** to the parley but **after** Gríma's arrival then Gríma could only have made him aware of Aragorn's identity at the parley itself.)

I suggest that the answer to the question on the extent of Saruman's knowledge of Aragorn lies in Aragorn's own statement to Legolas and Gimli after using the Palantír himself, that *"The eyes in Orthanc did not see through the armour of Théoden..."*[120]. This is potentially ambiguous as it could mean either Saruman's eyes, Gríma's eyes or both. However another interpretation is that Aragorn was referring specifically to Saruman, and was stating, confidently and categorically, that Saruman had not realised who he was. We know that Aragorn had spent many years "*... exploring the hearts of Men, both evil and good...*"[121] and that he would prove capable of perceiving Sauron's fear and shock in the Palantír. Did he also read the nuances of Saruman's words, the subtleties of his mind and the expressions in his eyes and face, and realise that he truly did believe he was looking at some "*cut-throat*" from Rohan rather than Isildur's heir? Was Aragorn, during the parley, conducting his own private confrontation with Saruman and the Voice?

Saruman had of course briefly encountered Aragorn, Legolas and Gimli in Fangorn Forest on the evening of February 30th - the day before Gandalf's reunion with the three friends. He may perhaps have recognised them as Gandalf's "*cut-throats*" at the parley.

*

Saruman's attitude to Aragorn as King was illustrated quite succinctly in his conversation with Gandalf as the remaining members of the Fellowship travelled home through Dunland. Gandalf told him that he would have met the King if he had stayed in Orthanc who "*... would have shown you wisdom and mercy.*" Saruman's reply was, "*... I desire neither of him.... I am seeking a way out of his realm.*"[122]

UT 3.1.358-9 describes the incident where Gimli and Aragorn visited Orthanc during the Fourth Age and searched the heirlooms which Saruman had stolen and hoarded. These included the Elendilmir and Isildur's chain and casket which had borne the One Ring round his neck. Thus the implication was that Isildur's remains had not, as was assumed, been carried down to the sea but had remained in shallow water to be subsequently found by Saruman and robbed of these two precious items. Since no trace had ever been found of Isildur's bones the question was raised as to whether Saruman had removed them and dishonoured them by burning them in one of his furnaces - not something which would have endeared him to King Elessar. Ironically this incident provides a good example of Gandalf's observation to Pippin during the Siege of Gondor (*LotR* 5.4.815) that a traitor may do good he does not intend. Saruman's behaviour enabled Aragorn and Gimli to find

---

119. Op. cit. [1], *LotR* 3.10, p. 584.
120. Op. cit., *LotR* 5.2, p. 780.
121. Op. cit., App A.I.v, p. 1060.
122. Op. cit., *LotR* 6.6, p. 983.

the original Elendilmir, and due to the evidence they uncovered, the story of Isildur was finally able to be set down in its entirety. The same could be said for Gríma's act in throwing the Palantír out of Orthanc as it was this which eventually enabled it to come into the possession of Aragorn. Gandalf's action in preventing Éomer killing Gríma (*LotR* 3.6.520) ensured his survival for the purpose.

RADAGAST

(Also called, or known as, as Aiwendil, Radagast the Bird-tamer, Radagast the Brown, Radagast the Fool, Radagast the Simple)

The accounts of the Istari in *UT* 4.2.509 hint that Saruman, as a Maia of Aulë, was begged/obliged to take Radagast with him as an emissary on account of him being a Maia of Aulë's spouse Yavanna (the Vala of all living things - plants and animals). Radagast subsequently "*... became enamoured of the many beasts and birds that dwelt in Middle-earth, and forsook Elves and Men, and spent his days among the wild creatures.*"[123] He was therefore said to have failed in his mission. This "failure" was compounded by his involvement with Saruman's gathering of spies, particularly birds, which were Radagast's first love. *RoP* states that Radagast assisted Saruman, "*... divining naught of his treachery, and deeming that this was but part of the watch upon the Enemy.*"[124] Gandalf, at the Council of Elrond, reported Saruman's scornful comment regarding Radagast: "*Yet he had just the wit to play the part that I set him*"[125] [that is, lure Gandalf to Isengard].

However Radagast's fondness for animals and birds was in keeping with his role as Yavanna's Maia, and it could be argued that it was his unwitting luring of Gandalf to Isengard which finally uncovered Saruman's treachery. Also he, again unwittingly, enabled Gandalf to escape from Isengard by obeying his instruction to send birds there to report on the Nazgûl's movements - hence the arrival of the eagle Gwaihir in the nick of time to rescue Gandalf.

There is no real evidence either way as to whether a meeting took place between Aragorn and Radagast, although *UT* 4.2.519 Note 4 describes the latter's dwelling, Rhosgobel, as being on the border of Mirkwood Forest between the Carrock and the Old Forest Road, an area which Aragorn must have visited many times on his travels. However all the indications in the *LotR* narrative are vague as to Radagast's whereabouts. When Gandalf spoke of his meeting with him on the Greenway not far from Bree: he said that Radagast had dwelt in Rhosgobel "*at one time,*" but that he had not seen him for "*... many a year.*".[126] Radagast had also stated that he was a stranger in those parts (namely the Bree area) and it was obvious from his conversation that he hadn't visited, or even heard of, the Shire before. Having given Gandalf the news that the Nazgûl were about he rode off "*... as if the Nine were after him.*"[127] It is not clear where he went, but the fact that Gwaihir subsequently went to rescue Gandalf from Orthanc perhaps implies that it was to the area around Rhosgobel - there was a community of eagles not far away from there according to the map in *The Hobbit*. However in *LotR* Elrond's scouts, returning to Rivendell, said that some of them had reached the "*old home of Radagast at Rhosgobel*" and that "*Radagast was not there*"[128]. The word "*old*" implies that he no longer lived there, so perhaps it was the earlier generations of the Northern Dúnedain rather than Aragorn who would have been more likely to encounter him. However it is certainly possible that Aragorn, through his extensive travels, met him somewhere other than at Rhosgobel, possibly without actually knowing who he was.

From the speculative point of view I once came across a piece of Fan-fiction which had Radagast instructing the young Aragorn in communicating with birds. However all the Istari possessed such skills to some extent and Aragorn would very likely have learnt all he needed to know from Gandalf. In addition the Dúnedain themselves were said to have the ability to understand the speech of birds and animals (*LotR* 1.9.149).

---

123. Op. cit. [2], *UT* 4.2, p. 505.
124. Op. cit. [5], *RoP* p. 362.
125. Op. cit. [1], *LotR* 2.2, p. 258.
126. Op. cit., *LotR* 2.2, p. 256.
127. Op. cit., *LotR* 2.2, p. 257.
128. Op. cit., *LotR* 2.3, p. 274.

ALATAR AND PALLANDO

(Also called, or known as, the Blue Wizards, the Ithryn Luin, and Morinehter and Rómestámo)

The Blue Wizards are mentioned indirectly in *LotR* 3.10.583 during the parley at Isengard when Saruman referred to the rods of the Five Wizards. However the main sources of information on them are the essay in *UT* 4.2.502-520 written around 1954, and the somewhat different account in *HoM-e* XII.13.384-5 which contains some of Tolkien's last writings from the early 1970s.

In the 1954 version of their story they are named Alatar and Pallando and are recorded as being Oromë's Maiar, with Pallando accompanying Alatar as a friend rather than as an emissary in his own right. Christopher Tolkien hazards a guess that Oromë, of all the Valar, had the greatest knowledge of the further parts of Middle-earth, and that the Blue Wizards were destined to remain in those regions. Thus when they landed in Middle-earth they went East with Saruman and, unlike him, never returned. In a letter to Rhona Beare written in 1958 Tolkien states that they went East and South *"far out of Númenórean range"*, as *"missionaries to 'enemy-occupied' lands"*.[129] He carries on to suggest that they probably failed in their mission, maybe starting *"secret cults and 'magic' traditions that outlasted the fall of Sauron"*[130]. The only possible link I can see here between Aragorn and the Blue Wizards is that both were travellers in the East and South. Earlier in this chapter I referred to Gandalf going as far east as Lake Núrnen in Mordor, but more as a "one-off" journey rather than regularly. The implication is that the Blue Wizards went further east than that. In App A Aragorn is stated as having travelled *"... far into the East and deep into the South..."*[131], one of his missions being to acquaint himself with the peoples who were in league with Sauron. The Easterlings came from Rhûn, most of which was further east than Mordor in a northerly direction. The people of Khand were also allied to Sauron, and their land was immediately south-east of Mordor. Meanwhile Far Harad extended *"deep into the South"*. Maybe Aragorn encountered one or both of the Blue Wizards on his journeys without knowing who they were. I don't feel that the phrase *"far out of Númenórean range"* rules out such a meeting, as Aragorn was, in Gandalf's words *"... the greatest traveller ... of this age of the world"* [132] and his journeys sometimes **were** *"out of Númenórean range"*. On the other hand what were the time-scales involved here? Like Gandalf, Saruman and Radagast, the Blue Wizards would have been in Middle-earth since approximately TA 1000. By Aragorn's lifetime they could have long disappeared in one way or another if we take the view of them given above in Letter 211, though he might have seen evidence of the *"secret cults and 'magic' traditions"* - assuming these actually existed.

The later account in *HoM-e* XII confirms that the Blue Wizards remained in the East, but instead of coming to Middle-earth in the Third Age, they are said to have arrived around SA 1600, the time of Sauron's forging of the One Ring. Their names are now Morinehter and Rómestámo - meaning Darkness-slayer and East-helper respectively. Their mission was: to help the few tribes of Men in those areas who had not been corrupted by Sauron; to stir up rebellion; and to find out Sauron's hiding-place after his fall in the drowning of Númenor at the end of the Second Age. Although they failed in the third task they seem to have succeeded in the first two, as shown by the following passage: *"They must have had very great influence on the history of the Second Age and Third Age in weakening and disarraying the forces of East ... who would both in the Second Age and Third Age otherwise have ... outnumbered the West."*[133] As suggested to me in feedback from reader José Colón, this new version of their activities perhaps means that Aragorn was more likely to have encountered them.

---

129. Op. cit. [73], Letter 211, p. 280.
130. Op. cit., Letter 211, p. 280.
131. Op. cit. [1], App A.I.v, p. 1060.
132. Op. cit., *LotR* 1.2, p. 58.
133. Op. cit. [12], *HoM-e* XII Chapter 13, p. 385.

CHAPTER 2.4 - Legolas and Gimli

In *LotR* much attention is paid to the close and lasting friendship which developed between Legolas the Elf and Gimli the Dwarf during the course of the narrative. This is understandable due to the enmity between their races and the initial antipathy to each other displayed by the two individuals concerned. However the purpose of this chapter is to study what I consider to be an equally significant relationship, namely that between *Aragorn*, Legolas and Gimli. Although my emphasis is obviously on the threesome, I have found it difficult, and indeed inappropriate in many instances, to avoid detailed discussion about the Legolas/Gimli bond, this being necessary in order to achieve the full picture. The closeness between Legolas and Gimli was to some extent enhanced by their relationship with Aragorn. Likewise their treatment of Aragorn was sometimes influenced by their closeness to each other.

Aragorn, Legolas and Gimli were representatives of three different races who became firmly united by a common enemy and by mutual loyalty, respect and affection. Their bond was given official recognition by Aragorn after the breakup of the Fellowship as he decided that he and his two remaining companions should follow the Orcs who had captured Merry and Pippin: *"We will make such a chase as shall be accounted a marvel among the Three Kindreds: Elves, Dwarves, and Men. Forth the Three Hunters!"*[1].

To examine this friendship in context we need to consider the backgrounds of the three races involved.

The friendship between Legolas and Gimli was remarkable chiefly because there had been a history of enmity between Elves and Dwarves dating back to the First Age when hostility arose between the Elf-king Thingol of Doriath and the Dwarves of the city of Nogrod in the Blue Mountains. As described in *The Silmarillion*[2] Thingol employed some of the craftsmen of Nogrod to set a Silmaril - recovered from Morgoth by Beren and Lúthien - into the Nauglamír, a necklace of Dwarvish make which was in his possession. As the work progressed both parties became consumed by lust for the Silmaril leading to violent quarrels during which Thingol was killed and Doriath plundered. The following battles between the Elves of Doriath and the Dwarves of Nogrod ended with considerable slaughter on both sides and resulted in general hatred between the two races from then on - a notable exception being the friendship between the Dwarves of Moria and the Noldorin Elves of Eregion during the first half of the Second Age.

This brief history from *TSil*, along with the different - and sometimes conflicting - versions of the story of Galadriel and Celeborn in *Unfinished Tales*[3], helps us to understand the attitude to Gimli when the Fellowship entered Lothlórien (*LotR* 2.6.343-8 and 2.7.355-6). Celeborn and Galadriel had both lived in Doriath in the First Age and the assumption is made in *UT* 2.4.301, 303 that they were present at its plundering. In the section *Concerning Galadriel and Celeborn* it is stated that afterwards Celeborn had no liking for Dwarves of any race and never forgave them even though it was only the Nogrod Dwarves who were involved. (In fact *TSil* 22.280 states that the Dwarves from the neighbouring city of Belegost actually advised against continuing the conflict.) His hostility to Gimli in TA 3019 was extended to blaming the Dwarves of Moria for arousing the Balrog, Durin's Bane. Galadriel, on the other hand, had been on good terms with the Dwarves of Moria in the Second Age - who, like Gimli himself, were not of the Nogrod race - and, as a Noldorin Elf, appreciated their craftsmanship. In addition *UT* 2.4.303 states that she realised that the evil in Middle-earth could only be overcome by a union of **all** those opposed to it. To this end she recognised the potential of the Dwarves as warriors. For these reasons she supported Gimli and empathised with his yearning to see Moria.

---

1. J.R.R. Tolkien, *The Lord of the Rings*, London, HarperCollins Publishers, 2007, 2nd edition, based on the 50th Anniversary Edition of 2004, *LotR* 3.1, p. 420.
2. C. Tolkien (ed.), *The Silmarillion*, London, HarperCollins Publishers, 1999, first published in Great Britain by George Allen & Unwin 1977, *TSil* Chapter 22, pp. 277-80.
3. C. Tolkien (ed.), *Unfinished Tales of Númenor and Middle-earth*, London, HarperCollins Publishers, 1998, first published in Great Britain by George Allen & Unwin 1980, *UT* Part 2, Chapter 4, pp. 294-348.

Regarding Legolas's attitude to Dwarves, *UT* 2.4.336 (*Appendix B*) implies that his grandfather Oropher and father Thranduil, who were Sindarin Elves, also originated from Doriath, and it is noted that Thranduil's Mirkwood dwelling in the Third Age resembled a small-scale version of Thingol's palace. It is highly probable that these two also had a lasting dislike of Dwarves on account of the murder of Thingol and ruin of Doriath. For example note Thranduil's attitude to Thorin Oakenshield and company in *The Hobbit*[4]. Legolas would presumably have inherited this hostility. The only problem with this assumption is a statement on the last page of *TH* that after the destruction of the dragon "*... there was friendship in those parts between elves and dwarves and men*"[5], thus implying that relations between the Elves of Mirkwood and the Dwarves of the Lonely Mountain were more cordial at the time of the War of the Ring - even perhaps that Legolas and Gimli might have encountered each other. However, when Tolkien wrote *TH*, *LotR* had not been thought of and there is certainly no indication in the latter work of friendliness or contact between Legolas's folk and Gimli's.

The estrangement between races in Middle-earth at the end of the Third Age was not limited to that between Elves and Dwarves - it also existed between Elves and Men. The Last Alliance of Elves and Men at the end of the Second Age led by Gil-galad and Elendil, which culminated in the overthrow of Sauron and the seizing of the One Ring by Isildur, had been over three thousand years earlier. By the fourth millennium of the Third Age, although Aragorn himself was not estranged from Elves, **most** Men (and Hobbits for that matter) feared them, or doubted their existence, as shown by the scepticism of Ted Sandyman in *LotR* 1.2.45, and the suspicion and wariness of Boromir, Éomer and even Faramir towards the folk of Lothlórien (*LotR* 2.6.338, 3.2.432 and 4.5.667 respectively).

The situation with Dwarves was somewhat different as they had more contact with Men and Hobbits. They were often encountered on the East/West Road journeying to and from the Lonely Mountain and Iron Hills in the East, and the Blue Mountains in the West. This road passed through the Shire, though according to *LotR* 1.2.43 the Dwarves were not very communicative when the Shire-folk asked them for news. In Bree Dwarves visited the Prancing Pony inn - some were there at the same time as Frodo and his companions (*LotR* 1.9.154-5, 161). Also there was clearly considerable contact between the Dwarves of the Lonely Mountain and the Men of Dale as shown by the toys given to the Hobbit children at Bilbo's party - these were of Dwarvish make but had come from Dale (*LotR* 1.1.27).

*

Before carrying out a detailed analysis of this friendship I want firstly to consider the question of whether the three characters would have encountered each other **before** the events of TA 3018-9, and secondly to examine their interaction during the period between the Council of Elrond and the breakup of the Fellowship four months later - that is, the period prior to the formal alliance of the "*Three Hunters*".

Given the extent of Aragorn's travels he must have met Dwarves fairly frequently while in the North - anywhere between the Blue Mountains and the Lonely Mountain and beyond. No doubt too he would have met and observed them in the inn at Bree. However there is no evidence of him actually visiting a Dwarf habitation, though the possibility cannot of course be ruled out. Regarding Gimli himself, a study of *UT* 3.3.425, 435 suggests that he was living in the Blue Mountains (where he was probably born) - but temporarily away from home - at the time when Gandalf and Thorin Oakenshield were there planning the journey to the Lonely Mountain to retrieve the treasure from Smaug. Later he was refused permission to accompany his father Glóin on Thorin's quest because, at sixty-two, he was not considered mature enough (Dwarves could live to two-hundred-and-fifty or older). A reference is made to him travelling on the East Road between his original home and the Lonely Mountain[6], so theoretically he and Aragorn could have passed one another on the road or seen each other in the inn at Bree. However this is pure speculation and even if such an encounter occurred it seems unlikely that either party would have attached any significance to it: names would probably not have been exchanged and the Dwarves would have had no more idea than the Bree-folk of the identity of the Rangers. Any memorable meeting would surely have led to mutual recognition at the Council of Elrond and there is no

---
4. J.R.R. Tolkien, *The Hobbit*, 3rd edition, London, Allen & Unwin, 1966, 1975 printing, *TH* Chapter 9, pp. 182-5.
5. Op. cit., *TH* Chapter 19, p. 317.
6. Op. cit. [3], *UT* Part 3, Chapter 3, p. 425.

evidence of this.

The situation with Legolas is more complex. *UT* 2.4.336 (*Appendix B*) and *LotR* App B.1082 describe how his grandfather and father migrated east of the Blue Mountains at the end of the First Age following the drowning of the lands in the West (including Doriath). Oropher became king of the Silvan Elves of Mirkwood Forest. These Elves had always lived east of the Misty Mountains. They were simpler and more rustic than those who had lived in the West and wished to keep themselves to themselves - an attitude which was adopted by Oropher and Thranduil. Nonetheless they joined the Last Alliance at the end of the Second Age since Oropher recognised the need to unite in destroying Sauron. He was killed in battle leaving Thranduil as king in Mirkwood.

As Thranduil was born during the First Age and lived in Doriath, his mother, as well as his father, was almost certainly a Sindarin Elf. What is not clear is whether he himself married a Sinda - before or after his migration east - or whether his wife was a Silvan Elf of Mirkwood. On the one hand there would be the wish to avoid having mixed blood in the royal family, but on the other, Thranduil and Oropher were keen to integrate themselves into the Silvan values and way of life. Thus there is a possibility that Legolas was half Sinda and half Silvan: although *UT* Index 581 refers to him as a Sindarin Elf this could simply be assigning his father's kindred to him. Assessing the approximate birth-date of Legolas is problematic, but the following evidence offers some suggestions:

- It is clear from *LotR* that he had not seen the sea before. He specifically stated this ("*I have not yet beheld it*"[7]) declaring that the sound of the seagulls at Pelargir prior to the journey up the Anduin to the Pelennor Fields had stirred up the latent sea-longing in him - as Galadriel had predicted it would (*LotR* 3.5.503). Therefore he must have been born after his father and grandfather had migrated east following the drowning of Beleriand. This rules out a birth in the First Age, unless he was only a baby at the time and incapable of remembering the sea. (I feel there would be some reference to this in *LotR* if that were the case). Thus we can assume he was born in Mirkwood during the Second or Third Age.
- *UT* 2.4.334 (*Appendix B*) provides relevant information in a statement that the Mirkwood Elves had lived further to the south of the Forest in the early part of the Second Age, but that Oropher had progressively moved them northwards, partly to increase the distance from Moria and partly because he resented the presence of Galadriel and Celeborn in Lothlórien which lay directly opposite on the west bank of the Anduin. As will be discussed shortly Legolas was a stranger to Lothlórien in *LotR* and did not know Galadriel and Celeborn. This perhaps points to him being only a young child, or not even born at the time when his people were living near them. Thus the field is narrowed slightly to later Second Age or Third Age.
- Legolas is not mentioned as being involved in the Last Alliance (late Second Age), which could mean:
  - That he had not been born then - indicating birth in the Third Age.
  - That he was too young to fight - indicating birth late in the Second Age.
  - That he was deliberately excluded so as to ensure that there was a candidate for the kingship in the event of his father and grandfather being killed - indicating birth around the middle of the Second Age.
  - That Thranduil only married after the death of his father, realising the need to safeguard the succession. Elves did not expect to die and Oropher's death may perhaps have come as a shock to Thranduil. This would also indicate a Third Age birth for Legolas.
- There is also the point made in Tolkien's essay *Laws and Customs among the Eldar*[8] that Elves tended to have children only during times of happiness and peace. There would not have been much of either during the Second Age, as Sauron began to rise again as early as SA 500 (App B.1083) and began building Barad-dûr in SA 1000. If Thranduil was influenced by such considerations then Legolas would probably have been born early in the Third Age - after the apparent defeat of Sauron at the Battle of Dagorlad. However the account in *UT* 2.4.335-6 is not optimistic about Thranduil's state of mind even

---

7. Op. cit. [1], *LotR* 5.9, p. 873.
8. C. Tolkien (ed.), *The History of Middle-earth*, vol. X, *Morgoth's Ring*, London HarperColllins Publishers, 2002, first published in Great Britain by HarperCollins Publishers 1993, *HoM-e* X Part 3, Second Phase, p. 213.

then, stating that he had been lucky to survive the battle and led back only a third of those who had set out. In addition he seems to have been traumatised by the horror of Mordor and to have a premonition that Sauron would arise again.

On balance I would suggest that Legolas was born either around the middle of the Second Age - before the situation with Sauron became too desperate - or early in the Third Age. Thus he would have been somewhere between three thousand and four and a half thousand years old at the time of the War of the Ring.

The *LotR* narrative shows that Legolas was not well-travelled, with most of his knowledge being gleaned from song rather than actual experience. At the Council of Elrond he was referred to as *"a strange Elf"*[9] (presumably meaning "not local" or "not known to the company" rather than peculiar!) and there is nothing particularly to indicate that he had been to Rivendell before. For one thing it was west of the Misty Mountains - which had daunted the Silvan Elves in the First Age and led to them remaining in the East. There is plenty of evidence in *LotR* to show that he had never been to Lothlórien either, as well as other indications of his lack of knowledge of lands beyond northern Mirkwood and the areas bordering it, for example:
- When the Fellowship first came in sight of Lothlórien after their escape from Moria, Legolas gave a very detailed description of the trees there but ended with the words *"So still our songs in Mirkwood say."*[10]
- He knew there was supposed to be a secret power there which protected the land but clearly did not know the nature of the power.
- He did not know whether the people of Lothlórien still lived in trees.
- Later he said that the mallorn trees were *"... of a kind strange to me, save as a name in song."*[11]
- He displayed fear when Haldir called to them (*LotR* 2.6.342). Haldir had heard his voice and recognised the accent as belonging to a Mirkwood Elf, but there was no indication that he actually knew Legolas himself - in fact he stated that their kin from further north were sundered from them. This point, and the following one, are explained by the northward migration of the Silvan Elves mentioned above.
- Later as the Fellowship were presented to Galadriel and Celeborn, Celeborn's greeting to Legolas made no reference to having seen him before - contrary to his greeting to Aragorn (*LotR* 2.7.355).
- Legolas's identification of the Balrog when the Fellowship gave their account of the disaster in Moria (*LotR* 2.7.356) could not be taken to imply that he had actually seen one before, since until the appearance of Durin's Bane it had been assumed that they had all been destroyed in the First Age. His recognition of it would no doubt have been from his father's descriptions and Elven lore - after all it was the greatest Elf-bane apart from Sauron himself.
- Legolas had not been to the Forest of Fangorn prior to the events of *LotR*. Also it is significant that he did not know of the fables concerning it (the subject of a warning from Celeborn) and asked Aragorn for clarification (*LotR* 3.2.442). This respect for Aragorn's travels showed a further indication of his own relative ignorance given his greater lifespan. He had stated that he had heard nothing about the dangers of Fangorn in his own land.
- It is however possible that Legolas fought at the Battle of Five Armies (*TH* 17.286-298).

Although I believe it to be unlikely that Aragorn and Gimli encountered each other prior to *LotR*, it seems extremely probable that meetings occurred between Aragorn and Legolas - particularly in connection with the search for Gollum. *LotR* 1.2.58, 2.2.251-6 and App B.1090, and *UT* 3.4.443-7 all refer to this search which started after Gollum's departure from his cave under the Misty Mountains in TA 2944. Up until 2951 he was tracked by the Mirkwood Elves at Gandalf's request but they failed to catch him. Aragorn could not have been involved at this stage as he was only in his teens at the time and still living in Rivendell. The search was abandoned when Gollum headed away from Mirkwood to the south and was not taken up again until 3001 when Gandalf began to suspect that Bilbo's ring might be the One Ring. He and Aragorn then searched for

---
9. Op. cit. [1], *LotR* 2.2, p. 240.
10. Op. cit., *LotR* 2.6, p. 335.
11. Op. cit., *LotR* 2.6, pp. 341-2.

Gollum intermittently for the next sixteen years, at the end of which Aragorn succeeded in capturing him. He then took him to Mirkwood for safe-keeping as had been agreed with Thranduil and was subsequently joined by Gandalf. This implies that Aragorn stayed with Thranduil and his people, particularly as he had just completed an exhausting, fifty-day, nine-hundred-mile journey from the Dead Marshes with Gollum, on top of the perilous search he had made in the Morgul Vale prior to that. A period of recuperation would have been in order, so, unless Legolas was away from home at the time, he and Aragorn must surely have met during the visit. Indeed, as the King's son, Legolas would probably have been involved in discussions about the care of the captive. The fact that the handing-over of Gollum was pre-arranged perhaps implies previous meetings as well and even some assistance from Thranduil's people. In addition Aragorn's journeys over the years must have taken him to the Anduin, Mirkwood and beyond, so there may well have been other meetings between him and Legolas.

The question of whether Legolas and Gimli might have met before has already been considered and a meeting prior to 3018-9 thought to be unlikely.

*

I will now examine the interactions between Aragorn, Legolas and Gimli prior to the official forming of their bond at Parth Galen following the death of Boromir, the capture of Merry and Pippin and the disappearance of Frodo and Sam.

Between the departure of the Fellowship from Rivendell and the loss of Gandalf in Moria there are a number of indications that the relationship between Legolas and Gimli was initially one of hostility. For example, when the Company tried to light a fire in the snow on Caradhras, one can sense the striving of the pair to be the one whose skills would bring success (*LotR* 2.3.290-92), and then Legolas's indulgent contempt at the clumsiness of his companions in struggling through the snow gave rise to Gimli's emphasis on the ill will of Caradhras to Elves as well as Dwarves. The hostility reached its peak with the Company's arrival at the doors of Moria when Gandalf's reference to the former good relationship between the Elves of Eregion and the Dwarves of Moria sparked an argument between Legolas and Gimli as to which race was responsible for the waning of the friendship. Gandalf's subsequent plea to them to be friends, along with his emphasis on **both** of them being valuable members of the party, perhaps marked the beginning of their future closeness. It is significant that it was Legolas who dragged Gimli away from Balin's tomb when the Orcs arrived, perhaps empathising with his grief at finding his kinsman dead and Moria a place of terror.

From Aragorn's point of view his only involvement with the pair prior to the loss of Gandalf seems to have been his reaction at the Council of Elrond when Legolas gave his report about the escape of Gollum from Mirkwood. Aragorn's abrasive outburst, triggered by anger and frustration on account of his lengthy and gruelling search to find Gollum in the first place, more or less accused the Mirkwood Elves of negligence, and in the ensuing conversation Gimli's father Glóin began to stir up the old hostility between the Elves of Mirkwood and Thorin Oakenshield's company (recounted in *TH* 9.182-5). There is no indication here of any particularly close acquaintance between Aragorn and Legolas - previous meetings would perhaps have been based on business rather than friendship.

It was only after the eight surviving members of the Company had escaped from Moria that the foundation began to be laid for the close relationship which would subsequently develop between Aragorn, Legolas and Gimli. This development became obvious as the Fellowship journeyed towards Lothlórien. Although Gimli had been keen to accompany Gandalf through Moria he displayed no criticism of Aragorn's choice to try the pass of Caradhras first, recognising that if the mountain had been "*less cruel*"[12] the Company would have ended the pass-crossing by descending the Dimrill Stair into the vale where the Mirrormere lay and the source of the Silverlode. It seems that Aragorn must have remembered Gimli's yearning to see the Mirrormere, eloquently expressed to Gandalf prior to the attempt on Caradhras (*LotR* 2.3.283), as he agreed to let the Dwarf visit it briefly in spite of the urgent need to get far away from Moria by nightfall (*LotR* 2.6.334). He then conversed with Gimli about the River Silverlode, and with Legolas about Lothlórien of which both had prior knowledge,

---

12. Op. cit. [1], *LotR* 2.6, p. 333.

Legolas from songs/hearsay and Aragorn from personal experience. The conversation ended with Aragorn confiding in the Elf that his heart would be glad to be in Lothlórien even though it was winter (*LotR* 2.6.335). Sometime later Frodo and Sam, who had both been hurt in Moria and were now unable to keep up any longer with Aragorn's relentless pace, fell further and further behind. This went unnoticed by Aragorn who had even forgotten about their injuries due to to the desperate need for haste, along with the stress of losing Gandalf and having to take on the leadership himself. It was actually Legolas who alerted him to Frodo's and Sam's plight prompting him to hurry back and help them (*LotR* 2.6.335-6). I regard this incident as highly significant as it marks the start of Legolas's role of helping Aragorn at crucial times when grief, indecision or stress threatened to get the better of him. This characteristic of Legolas will become increasingly important. Also, after Aragorn had tended Frodo and Sam, and the Company were on the move again, reference is made to Frodo and Gimli being together at the rear - perhaps indicating an action on Gimli's part to help Aragorn by keeping an eye on Frodo (*LotR* 2.6.337). Both Legolas and Gimli were starting to show more initiative and sense of responsibility.

In *LotR* 2.6.339, it seems to have been the decision of Legolas, rather than Aragorn, that the Company should stop and rest for a while by the River Nimrodel. As he sang of the Elf of the same name, the conversation turned to the evil in Moria and the fact that it was the Dwarves who had awakened it. There was now less hostility between Legolas and Gimli and instead of arguing they began to discuss the different methods of keeping safe: the Dwarves by delving in the ground and the Elves of Lothlórien by living in trees. Gimli's remark that trees would be safer than the ground alerted Aragorn to the fact that they had been sitting by the road for too long and he decided that the Company should follow Gimli's advice and take refuge in the trees for the night. Shortly afterwards they encountered Haldir whose reluctance to allow Gimli to proceed further into Lothlórien was overcome by consultation with Legolas, with both Legolas and Aragorn being held answerable for the Dwarf (*LotR* 2.6.343). Thus it can be seen that Aragorn, Legolas and Gimli were already co-operating with each other. As well as being due to the growing rapport between them, this would have been encouraged by additional factors, for example:
- Their knowledge of Moria and Lothlórien, even if only from hearsay, was greater than that of the others.
- The Hobbits were particularly vulnerable at this point - especially with Frodo and Sam being injured - and were therefore very dependant on their knowledgeable companions.
- Boromir's input to the discussions would have been minimal. As well as being ignorant of the true nature of Lothlórien, his opinion of it was the same as that of the people of Gondor in general, namely he viewed it with deep suspicion and mistrust.

The incident when Haldir proposed to blindfold Gimli for the journey through Lothlórien (*LotR* 2.6.347-8) had the potential to undo the budding friendship and co-operation between Elf and Dwarf and even resulted in weapons being drawn, with Gimli making it clear that he was prepared to fight rather than submit to the indignity of being blindfolded and treated as a possible spy. There was still tension between him and Legolas as shown by the latter's angry reaction when Gimli declared that he would submit if just the Elf shared the blindfolding with him. The matter was resolved by Aragorn's expert handling of the situation: he expressed his sympathy with Gimli's indignation and then gently but firmly used his authority as leader of the Company to decide that in the interests of fairness they should **all** be blindfolded rather than Gimli being singled out. The incident ended with Legolas and Haldir bewailing the estrangement between peoples who should all have been united in opposition to Sauron.

The meeting with Galadriel in *LotR* 2.7.355-6 and her supportive attitude to Gimli removed the last vestige of hostility between him and Legolas. During the following weeks Gimli would often accompany Legolas when he spent time with the Lothlórien Elves. Also they were starting to have more in common with each other through their shared experiences: they were both fascinated by Lothlórien (and by Galadriel in Gimli's case) and they shared the deep-rooted horror of the Balrog, a great Elf-bane to Legolas, and Durin's Bane to Gimli. As preparations took place for the departure of the Fellowship we see Gimli enjoying a cake of lembas and praising its flavour, totally at ease with the Elves. He and Legolas were now "*fast friends*"[13] and as they

---
13. Op. cit. [1], *LotR* 2.8, p. 372.

began the journey down the river, a weeping Gimli opened his heart to Legolas about his feelings for Galadriel. Eight days into the river voyage the Company were attacked by Orcs. When a "winged" Nazgûl also appeared Legolas shot his mount from under him causing the Orcs to flee in dismay. Gimli's whole-hearted praise and admiration further confirmed the warm friendship between him and Legolas (*LotR* 2.9.387).

Nothing more is stated about the development of Aragorn's role in the threesome at this stage. His time in Lothlórien and on the river seems to have been devoted to agonising over the right course to take, both for himself personally and for the Fellowship, now that Gandalf was no longer with them. The conflict between his struggle for the kingship and his duty to the Ring-bearer was very much at the forefront of his mind.

It was during the build-up to the breaking of the Fellowship that further evidence of a bond between a threesome (rather than a twosome) appeared. After nine days on the river the point came when Aragorn decided to carry the boats past the rapids of Sarn Gebir before resuming the river journey (*LotR* 2.9.389-91). He had a heated discussion with Boromir who was strongly opposed to the idea and wished to abandon the boats and turn west towards Minas Tirith. When an old portage-way past the rapids was found during a reconnoitre by Aragorn and Legolas, Gimli reacted indignantly to Boromir's suggestion that this route was only really feasible for the **Men** of the party. His retort was uttered in support of Aragorn and as a protest against what he saw as a slur on his own ability to carry the boats past the rapids. The strained relationship with Boromir was having the effect of drawing Legolas, Gimli and Aragorn closer to each other. I have wondered whether Aragorn and Legolas both going off to reconnoitre was actually a wise decision and the same doubt was expressed at a discussion of the Southampton UK Tolkien Reading Group. Aragorn's instructions, as he and Legolas set off, were that if they hadn't returned within one day then the Company should assume the worst and choose another leader. This raises the issue of whether Boromir would have tried to take the leadership by force - or even tried to take the Ring. On the other hand Boromir would have been the most suitable person to leave behind to deal with any Orc attacks. In fact the wording "It was decided" that Aragorn and Legolas should go and find the portage-way, seems to imply that it was a **group** decision rather than Aragorn's specifically. In any case the outcome might have been roughly the same as it eventually was at Parth Galen, with Boromir succumbing to the Ring and Frodo putting it on and going east followed by Gollum.

Two days later the Company, minus Frodo and Boromir, were sitting on the bank at Parth Galen waiting for Frodo to make his decision as to whether they should now head directly to Mordor or go to Minas Tirith first. Aragorn's uncertainty and hopelessness were clear as he felt that both routes were doomed to failure and his feelings were summed up by his comment that *"Now indeed we miss Gandalf most."*[14] At this point Legolas broke in, agreeing that their loss was grievous, but adding "Y*et we must needs make up our minds without his aid*"[15]. He then suggested that they should try and help Frodo by coming to a decision themselves, kicking off the discussion by stating his own preference. The others joined in and Aragorn did come up with a tentative splitting of the members of the Fellowship so that some would go to Minas Tirith and others direct to Mordor with Frodo - assuming that was what Frodo decided to do. This incident provides another example of Legolas spurring Aragorn to more positive behaviour at times of stress and indecision. Aragorn's suggested division of the Company was that he himself, Gimli and Sam should accompany Frodo to Mordor, while Legolas, Merry and Pippin should go with Boromir to Minas Tirith. However he made the proviso that Legolas could also go to Mordor if he was "... *not willing to leave us*"[16], thus seeming to acknowledge the possibility that Legolas would want to stay with Gimli and perhaps with Aragorn too. Was Aragorn also hinting that he himself would appreciate Legolas's company on a journey to Mordor?

Of course these discussions were overtaken by events with the return of Boromir to the group and the subsequent scattering of the Company. Legolas and Gimli, like the Hobbits, panicked and ran off, ignoring Aragorn's attempts to control the situation. The next time they saw him was when they came upon him weeping over the dead Boromir, convinced that he had let Gandalf down and had failed as leader of the Company, and blaming himself for all that had gone wrong (*LotR* 3.1.414). Legolas's first words implied guilt on his own account that he and Gimli had been elsewhere, particularly as initially he seemed to think that Aragorn too had been fatally wounded - which says much about Aragorn's appearance and demeanour at the time. Thus

---

14. Op. cit. [1], *LotR* 2.10, p. 402.
15. Op. cit., *LotR* 2.10, p. 402.
16. Op. cit., *LotR* 2.10, p. 403.

all three of them shared the uneasy feeling that they had contributed to the death of a comrade by not being around when needed. Again it was Legolas who took the initiative, answering Aragorn's despairing questions with positive suggestions for action: telling him that *"First we must tend the fallen ..."* and then *"... let us do first what we must do,"* [i.e. carry out Boromir's funeral] thus enabling Aragorn to pull himself together and start making his own decisions.[17]

I feel that this was the moment when the bond between the three of them was cemented. Legolas and Gimli had been drawing closer to each other since Gandalf's plea in Moria for them to be friends (*LotR* 2.4.303). The development of their relationship with Aragorn may be less obvious but the signs are there nonetheless. They were the only ones to witness anything of his collapse at Parth Galen - the rest of the Fellowship were absent at this point - and possibly it was a shock to them to see him in this state. On the other hand Legolas at least, with the heightened perception of an Elf, may well have foreseen it. There seems to have been no embarrassment to any of them in the current emotional situation and it occurs to me that this was perhaps the first time that Aragorn had been able to show his true feelings and state of mind to any of the members of the Fellowship.

These feelings and state of mind now need to be examined in detail in order to appreciate the depth of Aragorn's distress and the importance of the alliance which was about to be forged with Legolas and Gimli. I have already covered some of these issues in the narrative approach used in Chapter 1.5, but I feel it is important to give the complete picture here.

Lynn Forest-Hill suggests that by weeping for Boromir Aragorn perhaps fully released his grief for Gandalf at the same time, and that this enabled him to shake off his uncertainty and start making decisions.[18] There is certainly plenty of evidence that his grief for Gandalf had not been fully expressed and he did become more decisive after the episode at Parth Galen. However I feel that his tears were due to more than just suppressed grief, and also that he did not fully regain his confidence until after his reunion with Gandalf. As is usually the case in such situations, Aragorn's behaviour at Parth Galen was the result of a combination of factors building up over time, some of them traceable back to the summer of 3018. I have identified the following in particular:

- Grief
- Shock
- Suppressed fear
- Suppressed worries
- Being thrust into Gandalf's role
- The need to protect others
- Conflicting responsibilities

Grief

After the loss of Gandalf it is true that the Company as a whole had halted and wept immediately after the escape from Moria and that in Lothlórien they had had the opportunity to grieve in peace and safety. However considering Aragorn's case in isolation the picture which emerges is not that of someone who had released his grief and was starting to come to terms with his loss.

At the very end of *LotR* 2.5, after Gandalf had fallen, we are told that the remaining members of the Fellowship "*... wept long: some standing and silent, some cast upon the ground.*"[19] It was Aragorn who called for a premature end to the tears due to their desperate need to get as far away as possible from Moria as quickly as possible - yet he was the person most affected by what had happened, the person who most needed to grieve. The impression here is that he was failing to give full rein to his own grief due to the need to get the Company to safety. He would undoubtedly have been one of those who wept "*standing and silent*" - it was not in his nature to indulge in displays of grief and pain in the presence of others. [For example note the passage in *LotR* 5.2.785 when Éowyn begged in vain to be allowed to accompany him through the Paths of the Dead: his

---

17. Op. cit. [1], *LotR* 3.1, pp. 414-5.
18. L. Forest-Hill, 'Boromir, Byrhtnoth, and Bayard: Finding a language for grief in J. R. R. Tolkien's *The Lord of the Rings*', *Tolkien Studies*, vol. 5, 2008, p. 86.
19. Op. cit. [1], *LotR* 2.5, p. 332.

distress was only apparent to those who were both physically **and** emotionally close to him.]

After the loss of Gandalf Aragorn's grief would have been deeper and more acute than that of his companions due to his long and close friendship with the Wizard, and maybe giving full rein to his feelings would have been embarrassing to himself and disturbing to the others - in particular to the Hobbits. He would have felt it was inappropriate and unwise to let go in front of them - he was the leader and they were depending on him to lead them to safety and calm their fears. There was also his relationship with Boromir to be taken into consideration. Given Boromir's doubts about his [Aragorn's] calibre - made all too obvious at the Council of Elrond - Aragorn would not have felt able to unburden himself in front of him. In Lothlórien he would not have wanted to further diminish his flagging self-esteem by breaking down in front of Galadriel and Celeborn. The healing properties of the place probably did no more than deaden his grief and he would still have felt the need to keep a grip on himself.

Shock

In addition to grief there would have been a shock element from the manner of Gandalf's fall and from Boromir's admission that he had tried to take the Ring. Neither event was wholly unexpected but the shock would have been there nonetheless.

Suppressed fear

There were many issues involved here, some of them long-standing, for example:
- Fear of having to manage without Gandalf.
- Fear of the Nazgûl.
- Fear of failing.
- Fear for Gandalf: when he was missing in summer 3018, and then during the journey through Moria.
- Fear for Frodo due to the influence of the Ring, examples of which Aragorn had witnessed in the inn at Bree and on Weathertop.
- Long-standing fear of premature detection by Sauron, especially given the possibility of having to accompany Frodo to Mordor.

Suppressed worries

The following worries in particular come to mind:
- His premonition about Gandalf coming to grief in Moria. This seems to have arisen during the planning stage of the journey prior to the Fellowship's departure from Rivendell.
- His awareness of Gollum stalking the Company. He had known of Gollum's pursuit throughout the journey in Moria, then as far as the Nimrodel and during the river voyage - though the reader is not made aware of this until a conversation with Frodo in *LotR* 2.9.384.
- Boromir's harassment of Frodo, including warning him against Galadriel. This would have preyed on Aragorn's mind as indicating Boromir's increasing interest in the Ring.
- His own strained relationship with Boromir. This manifested itself in their disagreements about the route and in their widely differing opinions about Galadriel and Lothlórien.

Being thrust into Gandalf's role

As well as taking on the leadership of the Company after Gandalf's fall in Moria, Aragorn had also stepped into Gandalf's shoes during the summer of 3018 when the Wizard had gone missing due to his imprisonment by Saruman. He had taken it on himself to try and guide Frodo and his companions safely to Rivendell. These were the naïve and innocent people he, his Rangers and Gandalf had been guarding over the years, keeping them in ignorance of the dangers which lurked on their borders. In both cases Aragorn had had to take on the Wizard's role at short notice and in circumstances of extreme danger and anxiety.

The need to protect others

Aragorn's task of guiding the Hobbits to Rivendell would have involved:
- Guarding them constantly day and night - except when absences were necessary for matters of urgency, such as searching for athelas plants.
- Protecting them from enemies who instilled terror into the bravest people.
- Protecting them from their own stupidity, ignorance and inexperience.
- Helping them through difficult terrain - such as rocks and marshes.
- Keeping them healthy - he himself may have been used to living rough and have had immunity to illness but they wouldn't have had this advantage.
- Playing down his own fears in order to minimise theirs - fear of the Nazgûl, of what might have happened to Gandalf, of his own identity being discovered.
- Being responsible for a potentially fatally-wounded Frodo who was carrying the One Ring.
- Resisting the pull of the Ring himself.

During the journey with the Fellowship, as well as hiding his own feelings, grief, worries, etc. from the others as best he could, Aragorn frequently stayed awake to keep watch, or shared other people's watches, in times of acute danger. An example of another type of protection was his decision to keep secret Boromir's attempt to seize the Ring thus protecting the reputation of the dead man.

Conflicting responsibilities

After the fall of Gandalf Aragorn became torn between his responsibility to Gondor and his responsibility to the Ring-bearer. The latter conflicted not only with his own desires but with his purpose as well. When the Fellowship had set out from Rivendell he was not **supposed** to be going to Mordor or to be responsible for guiding Frodo; his mission was to go to Gondor and fight Sauron's armies. He reaffirmed this at Parth Galen when he promised the dying Boromir that he would save Minas Tirith. In addition, with the scattering of the Fellowship he gained an extra responsibility for Merry and Pippin.

Summing up these stress factors I emphasise again the time-scale and build-up involved. The state of play at the beginning of TA 3018 was that Aragorn was inured to the constant danger of Sauron searching for an heir of Isildur, he was used to fighting battles and he was adept at working in secret or in disguise to spy on Sauron or to protect the inhabitants of the Shire and Bree. The One Ring had been found some seventeen years earlier and he had successfully captured Gollum so that Gandalf could question him. It had subsequently been decided that Frodo should leave the Shire and make for Rivendell, and at a meeting between Gandalf and Aragorn in May that year it was established that all was well with Frodo and that Gandalf was looking after him. Thus Aragorn went off on a journey of his own. The chain of events which would result in his break-down at Parth Galen began on his return from this journey - probably in the late summer of 3018 - to find that Gandalf was missing and that the Nazgûl had been seen. Aragorn therefore decided that he had to take Gandalf's place and do his best to get Frodo to safety in Rivendell. Thus overnight he had to face a number of totally new challenges and fears:
- It was unheard of for Gandalf to be missing so there was the chilling possibility that he had been captured by the Nazgûl or by Sauron himself.
- The Nazgûl terrified the people of Bree and killed a number of the Dúnedain at Sarn Ford before attacking Frodo on Weathertop.
- Acting as guide to the Hobbits must have been a challenge in itself as indicated above, particularly the urgency of trying to get Frodo to Rivendell before it was too late.
- Aragorn must have been greatly disturbed at witnessing the Ring in action.

When considering Aragorn's burden of worry which got the better of him at Parth Galen, these earlier issues also need to be taken into account, not least because he had had little or no respite from his troubles.

It was not until he arrived in Rivendell that he found out that Gandalf was safe. While the other members of the Fellowship then spent a restful two months in Elrond's house Aragorn would have been lucky to have managed more than a few days' break. In Chapter 1.5 I have shown that he had four days in Rivendell prior to the Council of Elrond, some of which at least was spent on business rather than rest or pleasure. He then joined Elrond's scouts in searching for news of the Nazgûl, only returning shortly before the Fellowship set out. Those last days were spent planning the route with Gandalf and, I believe, developing his uneasy feelings about the risk to Gandalf in Moria. This lack of a chance to "unwind" was combined with a lack of privacy. There was no opportunity for solitude during his journey to Rivendell as he could not leave the Hobbits alone. In Lothlórien the Fellowship's sleeping quarters were communal and he may still have hesitated about going off on his own and leaving Frodo - not least due to Boromir's mistrust of Galadriel and his attempt to influence Frodo against her.

Thus overall, the stress Aragorn experienced during the journey from Moria to Parth Galen was added to an earlier unrelieved burden. His resulting state of mind was manifested by:
- Low self-esteem leading to conviction of his own failure and guilt and his belief that he had let Gandalf, Boromir and Frodo down. For example:
  - *"Now the Company is all in ruin. It is I that have failed. Vain was Gandalf's trust in me."*[20] [Spoken to himself].
  - Also, spoken to Legolas and Gimli: *"Boromir is dead. I am unscathed, for I was not here with him"* and *"... I did not ask him* [Boromir] *if Frodo or Sam were with him: not until it was too late."*[21]
- Inability to make decisions as evidenced by his hesitation in Lothlórien (*LotR* 2.8.367-8) and his words at Parth Galen. For example:
  - *"What shall I do now? Boromir has laid it on me to go to Minas Tirith, and my heart desires it; but where are the Ring and the Bearer? How shall I find them and save the Quest from disaster?"*[22] [Spoken to himself].
  - Then spoken to Legolas and Gimli: *"What is to be done now?"*[23]
- Lapses in concentration, losing touch with what was going on:
  - Forgetting about Frodo and Sam being injured after the escape from Moria (*LotR* 2.6.335).
  - Not noticing they were lagging far behind (*LotR* 2.6.335).
  - Having to be reminded by Gimli of the inadvisability of lingering too long by the Nimrodel (*LotR* 2.6.341).
  - Not noticing Boromir's hints about it being folly to destroy the Ring (*LotR* 2.8.369).
- Hopelessness as evidenced by his cry *"Farewell, Gandalf! .... What hope have we without you?"*[24]
- Finally a belief that fate was against him. For example:
  "Alas! An ill fate is on me this day, and all that I do goes amiss."[25] [Spoken to himself].
  Later, spoken to Legolas and Gimli: *"All that I have done today has gone amiss."*[26]

Without wishing to make light of the appalling strain Frodo was under, it does seem that Aragorn's own situation must have been intolerable.

In *LotR* 3.1.414 following the chaotic scattering of the Fellowship he was finally alone. The death of Boromir was the last straw for him, breaking his self-control and perhaps fully releasing not only his grief for Gandalf but all the fear, stress, worry and uncertainty which he had been bottling up over the previous six months. His tears, along with the support of Legolas and Gimli, would have helped him to clear his mind and given him the relief of actually confiding his feelings to someone. He now took the lead in organising Boromir's funeral.

---

20. Op. cit. [1], *LotR* 3.1, p. 414.
21. Op. cit., *LotR* 3.1, p. 414.
22. Op. cit., *LotR* 3.1, p. 414.
23. Op. cit., *LotR* 3.1, p. 414.
24. Op. cit., *LotR* 2.6, p. 333.
25. Op. cit., *LotR* 3.1, p. 413.
26. Op. cit., *LotR* 3.1, p. 414.

These last acts of farewell to their dead companion would have brought them closer together. Aragorn, having recovered sufficiently to do a full assessment of the situation, including the likely actions and whereabouts of the Hobbits, took it on himself to make the decision to follow the Orcs who had captured Merry and Pippin. Thus the bond between the "*Three Hunters*" was formally declared. He led them, "*... tireless and swift, now that his mind was at last made up.*"[27]

*

During the four-day chase which followed this pact the relationship between Aragorn, Legolas and Gimli was consolidated. Rather than do a chronological study of the relevant chapters (the end of *LotR* 3.1.419-20, *LotR* 3.2.421-43 and 3.5.488-505) it seems more useful to examine the different aspects of the bond between them - a bond which was immediately apparent to Éomer who, on learning of their pursuit of the Orcs, declared "*This deed of the three friends should be sung in many a hall.*"[28]. Some episodes mentioned below appear under more than one of the following headings:
- Mutual respect
- Shared purpose
- Shared suffering
- Mutual support and concern
- Humour
- Aragorn as leader

Mutual respect

- Legolas and Gimli left the tracking to Aragorn as they recognised his superiority in it, which enabled him to spot Pippin's detour from the trail to drop his brooch, and later to work out the Hobbits' movements in Fangorn. According to Gimli Aragorn could obtain useful information from a bent blade of grass.
- Aragorn and Gimli appreciated Legolas's ultra-keen vision: he was able to count the number of Éomer's men long before they drew near and he was the only one who could see the eagle Gwaihir whom Gandalf had asked to reconnoitre the land.
- Legolas turned to Aragorn for information about Fangorn recognising that this well-travelled Man might know more than he did.
- Legolas and Gimli found Aragorn to be someone who pondered things and thought things through from every angle before making a decision.
- Aragorn and Legolas respected the endurance and strength of the Dwarves as displayed by Gimli.

Shared purpose

- All three were single-minded about finding Merry and Pippin: because of the need to prevent Saruman questioning them, and out of compassion and friendship. The emphasis was always on the last two - they didn't want their friends tortured, and their hearts burned at the thought of the Hobbits being "*driven like cattle*"[29] as Legolas put it.

Shared suffering

- The chase began in the evening and they ran throughout the first night. On the second night Aragorn decided that they should stop and sleep - with the result that the Orcs (who had carried on) were too far ahead to be caught. Legolas was particularly unhappy as he had advised against stopping. Aragorn, having been tormented by dreams of galloping horses, spent a long time lying on the ground listening

---
27. Op. cit. [1], *LotR* 3.1, p. 420.
28. Op. cit., *LotR* 3.2, p. 436.
29. Op. cit., *LotR* 3.2, p. 424.

instead of setting off, eventually rising with a pale and drawn face.
- The ever increasing distance between them and the Orcs sapped their optimism and hope, with Aragorn and Gimli in particular becoming weary and dispirited, sleeping only fitfully.
- They were surviving on adrenalin and lembas, eating as they ran.
- An additional cause of exhaustion was the evil influence of Saruman, sensed by Aragorn and Legolas, causing "... *a silence that did not seem to be the quiet of peace.*"[30]. Aragorn recognised that this influence seemed to be encouraging the Orcs to go faster while setting an unseen barrier before him and his companions, leading to an excessive physical weariness which, as a Ranger, he did not expect to feel.
- Their lack of food and rest, in addition to a northerly wind, chilled them so that they sat huddled together with their cloaks wrapped round them while they waited for the Riders of Rohan to approach. Later in Fangorn Gimli lit a fire in spite of the risk and was not prevented by Aragorn.
- Even Legolas, a Wood-elf, felt short of breath by the time they reached Treebeard's stair.
- Overall they were at risk of possible death at Éomer's hands, possible starvation themselves and the potential dangers from Saruman and Fangorn.
- Their stoic acceptance when the horses ran off was perhaps due to a mental numbness rendering them incapable of reacting to any further setback.

Mutual support and concern

- On the first morning of the chase Aragorn was temporarily at a loss when the Orc-trail vanished, but Legolas, by asking pertinent questions, encouraged him to analyse the possible routes the Orcs would have taken and by using his greater knowledge to come up with the right answer.
- At the point where the three of them were discussing whether they should sleep or carry on running through a second night, Gimli and Legolas made Aragorn decide. Perhaps they regarded him as the natural leader with the knowledge and experience to make the best decisions. Or perhaps they were still trying to make him shake off his uncertainty and lack of self-esteem which were patently still plaguing him: "*You give the choice to an ill chooser. Since we passed through the Argonath my choices have gone amiss.*"[31]. The following morning when it appeared that the decision to sleep had enabled the Orcs to get too far ahead, Gimli became concerned that Aragorn may have swooned or fallen asleep again because he lay motionless for so long listening to the ground. In his now familiar role, Legolas chivvied Aragorn into action at this point.
- As the Orcs got further and further ahead Aragorn and Gimli felt the strain, leading to disturbed sleep. Legolas offered encouragement by staying awake predicting that something momentous would happen at sunrise. [They would meet the Rohirrim.]
- Aragorn showed protectiveness towards Legolas and Gimli as the Rohirrim approached, using his knowledge of the land and the people to try and reassure them. Gimli in particular was uneasy but both of them remained sitting in silence as Éomer questioned Aragorn - perhaps paralysed by the scene, afraid to move in case their friend came to harm, or maybe just trusting him to know how to deal with the situation.
- Later Legolas, recognising Gimli's reluctance to mount a horse, invited him to ride with him on Arod.
- As they settled down for the night in Fangorn Aragorn showed concern for Gimli, warning him not to cut any living tree or stray too far in the search for wood. He then expressed his willingness to be woken up if Gimli was worried. This was actually unnecessary as both he and Legolas instantly awoke when Gimli saw the old man who turned out to be Saruman. Aragorn then took over Gimli's watch so he could think things over.
- The following day Gimli felt comforted in his unease in Fangorn by Legolas's statement that he could have been happy there in a time of peace

---

30. Op. cit. [1], *LotR* 3.2, p. 427.
31. Op. cit., *LotR* 3.2, p. 426.

Humour

- In spite of the misfortune of losing the horses, Legolas and Gimli managed to instil some humour into the situation when Aragorn remarked that they had started off on their feet and still had them. Gimli complained that unlike the horses they couldn't eat their feet if the necessity arose, giving rise to Legolas's laughing observation that *"You will make a rider yet"*[32] thinking of his friend's refusal to sit on a horse only a few hours previously. Perhaps it was necessary to make a joke of an incident which could well have proved to be the last straw if they had allowed it to prey on their minds.
- The following morning Aragorn found the fading mallorn leaf and lembas crumbs left by Merry and Pippin along with the cut pieces of cord which had bound their hands and feet. Legolas gave a humorous explanation of the evidence including a suggestion that, following the cutting of their bonds, the Hobbits had sprouted wings and flown away. This produced a smile from Aragorn who then went on to give his own more realistic interpretation. The humour here indicated a glimmer of hope in what was becoming an increasingly futile undertaking.
- During a discussion about Fangorn, Legolas declared that the great age of the Forest made him feel young again - as opposed to feeling old in the company of Aragorn and Gimli whom he referred to as *"you children"*[33].

Aragorn as leader

- Throughout this period Aragorn was unquestionably the leader, in spite of the distressed and indecisive condition his companions had found him in at Parth Galen and the lingering self-doubt which would remain with him until the reunion with Gandalf. Legolas and Gimli clearly regarded him and respected him as the leader They offered help, with pertinent questions and advice, but left it to him to actually make the decisions, which they were prepared to accept even if they did not agree with them.
- In the early stages of the chase Aragorn had looked towards the White Mountains and expressed out loud his yearning to go to Gondor, but then resolutely turned back to the trail. He had made his decision to follow the Orcs and was sticking to it in spite of his own desires.
- He urged his companions on, regardless of whether there was any hope in their undertaking, telling a despairing Gimli at one point that their hope may have come to an end but their toil would not. Indeed his words to them right at the start of the chase contained the same exhortation: *"With hope or without hope we will follow the trail of our enemies."*[34].
- At the meeting with the Rohirrim he showed courageous and diplomatic leadership in dealing with the altercation between Éomer, and Legolas and Gimli on the subject of Galadriel by moving between the protagonists to prevent violence and supporting Legolas and Gimli while at the same time apologising to Éomer thus acknowledging that his anger too was justified. The behaviour of Legolas and Gimli in an already tense atmosphere had after all been undiplomatic to say the least, though no doubt fear and stress had been contributing factors.
- His dramatic revelation of his true identity to win Éomer over and obtain his cooperation left Legolas and Gimli amazed at the transformation in him, with Legolas seeing a vision of a white flame flickering on his brow like a crown.
- As leader Aragorn expected a lot of his companions and of himself, including being prepared to starve to death with Merry and Pippin: *"If that is indeed all we can do, then we must do that."*[35].
- Prior to the realisation that the second "old man" encounter in Fangorn was actually with Gandalf not Saruman, Aragorn displayed moral leadership too, declaring that they could not attack an old man at unawares and unchallenged no matter how frightened or suspicious they were.
- In general Aragorn's leadership throughout the four days showed hints of the strength of will which

---

32. Op. cit. [1], *LotR* 3.2, p. 443.
33. Op. cit., *LotR* 3.5, p. 491.
34. Op. cit., *LotR* 3.1, p. 420.
35. Op. cit., *LotR* 3.5, p. 491.

would become so marked later on during the journey through the Paths of the Dead and beyond. He undoubtedly possessed this quality anyway, but the journey across Rohan with the companionship and support of Legolas and Gimli encouraged and enhanced it.

It appears from studying this episode that Aragorn, Legolas and Gimli complemented and looked after each other, with each contributing to the task at hand in his own way and supporting his companions when necessary. In particular Legolas encouraged Aragorn in his leadership role, perceiving his suffering and lack of self-esteem following the loss of Gandalf. However a less positive aspect to the relationship between the threesome is suggested by Tom Shippey's view that Gimli was consistently negative to Aragorn's decisions following the breaking of the Fellowship, causing tension to build up between them.[36] I therefore decided to look at the contents of *LotR* 3.1, 3.2 and 3.5 with this interpretation in mind.

LotR 3.1
- At Parth Galen, following Legolas's statement that their first task should be to attend to the fallen Boromir, Gimli was anxious to start on the pursuit of the Orcs as soon as possible, even before any investigation had been made as to Frodo's whereabouts. He did not want to spend too much time on tending Boromir, saying "*He would not wish us to linger*"[37], and he objected to the suggestion of building a cairn due to the lack of suitable stones nearby and thus to the labour and time this would involve. When Aragorn then suggested laying Boromir in one of the boats and sending him down the Anduin Gimli showed no objection - presumably because this solution was simpler and quicker. His earlier negativity was in response to Legolas, not Aragorn, as it was he who had suggested both the funeral and the cairn.
- When Aragorn began to search the Orc bodies and ponder their different badges and Saruman's methods of communication Gimli became impatient to get on with the funeral rather than worrying about these "*riddles*"[38]. His attitude here was certainly negative, especially in view of the need to solve the "*riddles*" if they were to take the right course of action. When Aragorn pointed this out Gimli expressed the view that "*Maybe there is no right choice*"[39].
- After Boromir's boat had been sent on its journey down the Anduin, Gimli seemed to accept that it was sensible for Aragorn to try and establish Frodo's whereabouts. However when it became clear that Frodo and Sam must have headed to Mordor together, he became impatient and negative, and in response to the question as to whether they should follow Frodo or pursue the Orcs to rescue Merry and Pippin, declared that "*There is little hope either way. We have already lost precious hours.*"[40] As they set off on the pursuit, he referred again to the delay: "*... it will be a long chase: they have a long start.*"[41]

LotR 3.2
- When the companions came across the dead Orcs Gimli was reluctant to spend time investigating the reason for this saying "*... it needs the light of day, and for that we cannot wait.*"[42]. He also arrived at the worst interpretation of the incident, namely that the Orcs' dispute had not been about choice of route but about Merry and Pippin, perhaps leading to their deaths.
- However soon afterwards all three of them were encouraged by Aragorn's discovery of Pippin's brooch.
- When Aragorn decided that they should stop and rest during the second night of the chase, it was Legolas, not Gimli, who disagreed with him. It was Gimli who was more insistent that Aragorn should take this decision on himself, acknowledging his role as leader and his skill in the chase. His only

---

36. T. Shippey, *Roots and Branches: Selected Papers on Tolkien,* Zollikofen, Walking Tree Publishers, 2007, "Heroes and Heroism" p. 277 (Footnote 4) and "A Fund of Wise Sayings" pp. 314-15.
37. Op. cit. [1], *LotR* 3.1, p. 415.
38. Op. cit., *LotR* 3.1, p. 416.
39. Op. cit., *LotR* 3.1, p. 416.
40. Op. cit., *LotR* 3.1, p. 419.
41. Op. cit., *LotR* 3.1, p. 420.
42. Op. cit., *LotR* 3.2, p. 422.

negative comment at this juncture was that he would have preferred to set out sooner (revisiting his impatience at Parth Galen). Aragorn too was being equally negative by running himself down ("*You give the choice to an ill chooser*"[43]) and referring to their chase as "*a vain pursuit*"[44]. If Aragorn felt irritated by either of his companions at this point it would have been Legolas rather than Gimli: the next morning the Orcs were now too far ahead for there to be any hope of catching them up and the Elf did not mince his words in pointing this out to Aragorn.

- At dusk on the third night, when the Orcs were further ahead than ever, Gimli declared, "*This is a bitter end to our hope and to all our toil!*"[45]. The chase was telling on him by now - and on Aragorn too who was suffering unaccustomed weariness.
- On the fourth night, in answer to Legolas's prediction, "*Rede oft is found at the rising of the Sun*", Gimli responded, "*Three suns already have risen on our chase and brought no counsel*", again displaying a negative attitude to Legolas rather than Aragorn.[46]
- When the Rohirrim came into sight, Gimli again assumed the worst scenario, expecting to get spears rather than news from them.
- As the companions spent the night in Fangorn Forest they were visited briefly by what appeared to be an old man wrapped in a cloak and leaning on a staff. Gimli believed it to be Saruman and after their horses ran off he gave voice to his suspicions finishing with, "*There is more trouble coming to us, mark my words!*"[47] again expecting the worst.

LotR 3.5
- Gimli expressed the view that even if they were to find Merry and Pippin they would no longer be able to do anything except starve to death with them. Aragorn's rejoinder ("*If that is indeed all we can do, then we must do that*"[48]) could perhaps have been due to frustration and irritation as well as noble sentiment.
- Legolas's facetious remark - that the whole Fellowship could have left the river after only two or three days on it, then struck west arriving in Fangorn safely and much earlier - must certainly have struck a raw nerve with Aragorn, while Gimli made the point to Legolas that they had not wanted to come to Fangorn anyway. He was venting his feelings on Legolas rather than Aragorn, while Legolas was also displaying a negative attitude.
- Soon afterwards, at the second confrontation with a dubious-looking old man [Gandalf this time], Gimli reminded Aragorn of his suspicions about Saruman - in an "I told you so" manner - then shouted to Legolas to bend his bow and shoot before a spell was put on them. When Legolas hesitated Gimli hissed at him "*Why are you waiting? What is the matter with you?*"[49] Again it was Legolas rather than Aragorn who was on the receiving end of his ill temper.

From studying the examples given above I concluded that although Gimli was certainly negative this was not specifically about Aragorn's decisions. Also Aragorn and Legolas were negative too in their own way. These conclusions will now be looked at in more detail.

The prime thrust of Gimli's negative attitude seemed to be the **delay** in starting the pursuit of the Orcs, not the decision to do so. There are constant references, before and during the journey, to his impatience to get moving and his fretting at anything which threatened to hold up the chase: even essential things like studying the evidence in order to establish the motives and movements of Frodo and the Orcs, investigating signs *en route*, and even attending to Boromir. Regarding this last-mentioned it occurred to me that he and Boromir had not been on very good terms at their last encounter, when Boromir offended Gimli by casting aspersions on

---

43. Op. cit. [1], *LotR* 3.2, p. 426.
44. Op. cit., *LotR* 3.2, p. 426.
45. Op. cit., *LotR* 3.2, p. 427.
46. Op. cit., *LotR* 3.2, p. 429.
47. Op. cit., *LotR* 3.2, p. 443.
48. Op. cit., *LotR* 3.5, p. 491.
49. Op. cit., *LotR* 3.5, p. 492.

his ability to carry the boats along the portage-way. In addition Boromir's opinion of Galadriel would not have endeared him to the Dwarf. Was Gimli's grief (and that of Legolas), on coming across Aragorn and Boromir at Parth Galen, more on account of the former than the latter given that they initially believed that Aragorn too had been fatally injured?

I feel that the reason for Gimli's urgency may have been because, in spite of his pride in his own strength and endurance ("*Dwarves too can go swiftly, and they do not tire sooner than Orcs*"[50]), he actually felt that he might not be up to the proposed pursuit, which would involve travelling much **faster** than the Orcs if they were to have any chance of catching them up. He would have wanted to live up to Aragorn's answering remark "... *we shall all need the endurance of Dwarves.*"[51] In the event he did indeed struggle physically more than his two companions, as shown by his support for Aragorn's decision to rest during the second night, a decision which, from Aragorn's point of view, was prompted more by the difficulties of tracking in the dark than by his own weariness. Gimli was also perhaps more frightened than the others, as suggested by his obvious unease at the approach of the Rohirrim and his panicky reaction to the appearance of the old man he presumed was Saruman. Later, during the journey through the Paths of the Dead, he would be angry and ashamed on account of the fear he felt and of the fact that Aragorn, Legolas and the Grey Company (i.e. Men and Elves) were coping better than he was. If he had similar feelings (albeit to a lesser degree) during the pursuit of the Orcs this would have been enough to explain his less than positive attitude. His naturally more blunt manner (as illustrated by his abrasive speech to Éomer concerning Galadriel) would have added to the effect.

As shown above, Gimli's negativity was also directed against Legolas sometimes, not solely against Aragorn. Aragorn himself was also negative from the start: running himself down, calling the chase a "*vain pursuit*", and having to be encouraged into action by Legolas. This may well have led to similar feelings of hopelessness in his companions. Legolas too showed negativity, although it took longer to manifest itself, perhaps due to the fact that he experienced less physical suffering than the other two. Also he had been striving, more than Gimli, to encourage positive behaviour in Aragorn. Gimli was perhaps less perceptive regarding Aragorn's mental state than Legolas was.

Shippey observes that all three of them were very close to despair by the time they reached Fangorn Forest.[52] I would suggest that they had reached such a stage earlier on - hence the negative attitudes displayed - though relieved by short periods of hope after finding Pippin's brooch, and following the discovery of the mallorn leaf and lembas crumbs. Overall I feel that some negativity was inevitable in such an ordeal but that there was sufficient mutual regard between the three of them to surmount this. They were sufficiently at ease with each other not to have to hide their feelings.

*

The reunion with Gandalf in *LotR* 3.5.494-505 brought an unexpected resolution to the search for Merry and Pippin, and Aragorn, Legolas and Gimli now followed Gandalf's lead to Edoras. Note Legolas's words to Gandalf, "*Yes, together we will follow you*"[53] meaning he himself, Aragorn and Gimli and echoing Aragorn's commitment to going where Gandalf led. The further development of the friendship between them can be illustrated by numerous incidents in the ensuing days when the Battle of the Hornburg was fought, followed by the journey to Isengard, the reunion with Merry and Pippin and Gandalf's parley with Saruman (*LotR* 3.6-3.10):

- As they drew near to Edoras, Legolas and Gimli listened respectfully while Aragorn spoke and sang of Rohan and Eorl the Young, sharing his knowledge of the history and language of the Rohirrim.
- On their arrival at Meduseld, when Aragorn became involved in an argument with Háma the Doorward due to his reluctance to leave his sword outside, Gimli immediately leapt to his defence. Aragorn had helped Gimli in Lothlórien, and Legolas had sprung to Gimli's aid in the altercation with Éomer. The mutual loyalty between the three was very marked.

---

50. Op. cit. [1], *LotR* 3.1, p. 420.
51. Op. cit., *LotR* 3.1, p. 420.
52. Op. cit. [36], Shippey "A Fund of Wise Sayings", p. 314.
53. Op. cit. [1], *LotR* 3.5, p. 501.

- When Éomer offered to take Gimli on his horse with him, Gimli accepted provided that Legolas rode beside them.
- On arrival at Helm's Deep Legolas felt uneasy near the mountains but was comforted by the presence of Gimli.
- As the battle commenced Legolas and Gimli started an Orc-killing competition with each other. Their rivalry was now unquestionably friendly and the contest perhaps acted as a morale-booster in what appeared to be a very unequal struggle.
- Legolas kept close to Aragorn in the battle as he and Éomer repeatedly rallied and encouraged the men. Due to his proximity to him he was able to help in saving his life at the point when he tripped on the stairs up to the Hornburg and found himself overpowered by Orcs. As the sweating, and no doubt shaken, Aragorn joined him declaring that "*Things go ill, my friends,*" Legolas replied, "*Ill enough, but not yet hopeless, while we have you with us*", thus demonstrating his faith in him[54] particularly as Aragorn's close shave had occurred as a result of him covering the retreat of others before attending to his own safety. Legolas may also have been encouraging him to believe in himself at this vulnerable moment. In return Aragorn tried to allay Legolas's dismay at finding Gimli missing by emphasising the Dwarf's strength and stoutness and expressing the hope that he would make his way to the refuge in the caves. Legolas then referred to the Orc-killing contest raising a laugh from Aragorn. Thus each of them was trying to keep the other's spirits up. As Éomer too could not be accounted for, Legolas now took over his role of accompanying Aragorn as he went round helping and encouraging the men.
- When Gimli reappeared, wounded but the winner of the contest, Legolas admitted his gladness and relief at Gimli's survival relatively unharmed.
- In spite of his head wound Gimli insisted on accompanying Gandalf, Aragorn and Legolas to the parley with Saruman. Aragorn spent the time allocated to resting tending the wound. He knew Gimli would not be gainsaid and he would have wanted to make sure the wound was properly cleansed and treated - for everyone's sake. Did he realise in fact that it was more serious than Gimli was making out?
- As they set off for Isengard, Legolas and Gimli talked of the wonder of Fangorn and the Glittering Caves of Aglarond respectively and made a pact to visit these places together if they were to survive the war. Their differences were still apparent but were now an element of their friendship rather than something which hindered it - even the incident where Legolas, sharing a horse with Gimli, tried to ride into the mysterious forest which had appeared at Helm's Deep while a desperate Gimli demanded to be allowed to dismount.
- In *LotR* 3.9.560-575 the three of them were reunited with Merry and Pippin, enjoying a meal with them, then sitting together in the open air while the Hobbits told their story. It had been intended that Aragorn, Legolas and Gimli should eat with Gandalf, Théoden and the rest of the Rohirrim. That they chose otherwise showed the rapport between all five of them: the three "*hunters*" and the two "*truants*" - as Legolas and Gimli described them. It was perhaps an inevitable choice on the part of Aragorn, Legolas and Gimli after the soul-destroying search for the Hobbits and the subsequent relief of being reunited with them and finding them in good health and spirits.
- When Gandalf proposed that Legolas and Gimli should remain at the bottom of the stairs of Orthanc during the parley with Saruman while he and Aragorn went up, Gimli, speaking for Legolas as well, declared that they would also come up - ostensibly because they wanted to represent their respective races, but maybe also to support Aragorn.
- When Treebeard reacted doubtfully to Legolas's wish to bring Gimli with him on a future visit to Fangorn, Legolas declared "*... while Gimli lives I shall not come to Fangorn alone.*"[55]

Thus it can be seen that during these events surrounding the Battle of the Hornburg the bond between the three of them continued to develop. Legolas's support for Aragorn comes over particularly strongly (he hardly seemed to leave his side) now coloured with increasing respect as shown by his recognition that there was still

---
54. Op. cit. [1], *LotR* 3.7, p. 538.
55. Op. cit., *LotR* 5.10, p. 586.

hope of victory so long as Aragorn was with them. Aragorn was now more self-assured, due partly to Gandalf's presence and partly to being in a role which was familiar to him, namely leading and encouraging men in battle. Also Gimli found a satisfying role for himself in the battle on account of the need for his expertise in blocking the passage of Orcs through the Deeping-stream culvert. Any rivalry between him and Legolas was now good-humoured rather than hostile.

*

The outcome of the parley with Saruman was that Aragorn came into possession of the Palantír of Orthanc of which he was the rightful owner (*LotR* 3.11.594). This was the trigger for the most significant events of his struggle against Sauron, events in which Legolas and Gimli were also to be heavily involved. *LotR* 5.2.773-790 covers their journey back to the Hornburg with Merry and the Rohirrim, the arrival of Halbarad and the Grey Company, Aragorn's use of the Palantír to confront Sauron, and the subsequent journey through the Paths of the Dead and on to Pelargir. The actions and behaviour of the three of them give considerable insight into the nature and development of their relationship:

- As they started out from Dol Baran (the southernmost foothill of the Misty Mountains) where they had spent the night following the parley, Aragorn's mood was dark and pessimistic. He knew it was a momentous time for him ("*An hour long prepared approaches*"[56]), but was full of uncertainty about the route to take ("*... it is dark before me.... I do not yet see the road*"[57]) and lacking in hope ("*Many hopes will wither in this bitter spring*"[58]). Nevertheless Legolas and Gimli announced without hesitation that they were going with him anyway. There was absolutely no question of them splitting up.
- The party arrived back at the Hornburg just before dawn on March 6th, the plan being to rest and take counsel, then leave after the mid-day meal. During a conversation between Legolas, Gimli and Merry prior to the meal, it was clear that Legolas had been keeping an eye on Aragorn and was aware of the "*dark doubt or care*"[59] which was on him, and of the fact that he had had no rest since their arrival, but had gone up to the top of the Hornburg with only Halbarad for company.
- He and Gimli noted the similarity between Aragorn and the other Rangers: worn and weathered, grim and silent, but nonetheless courteous. They worked out that it must have been Galadriel who had sent the message to Rivendell summoning the Dúnedain to ride to Aragorn's aid.
- When Aragorn eventually appeared out of the Hornburg, haggard and exhausted from the Palantír confrontation, Legolas and Gimli were with him, the implication being that they must have been concerned enough to go and investigate his non-appearance.
- As Aragorn bade farewell to Merry following his decision to go through the Paths of the Dead he expressed the hope that Legolas and Gimli would still "*hunt*"[60] with him - obviously referring to the name "*the Three Hunters*" which he had given them all at Parth Galen. Although the bond between them had become close and he craved their company Aragorn's behaviour at this point showed that he did not yet know Legolas and Gimli well enough to judge how they would react to what he had done. When it came to the crunch of using the Palantír it had been, naturally enough, to Halbarad - his kinsman and second-in-command, senior Ranger and long-standing friend and confidant - that he had turned for counsel and support. This would be particularly the case given that the Dúnedain had been sent south specifically to aid their Chieftain. In earlier versions of these events given in *HoM-e* VIII the prophecy stated that an Elf-lord and a Dwarf-lord would also be present to summon the Dead, but this idea was later rejected.[61] Thus Aragorn's desire for the company of Legolas and Gimli would have been based on a wish for their friendship and support. In addition he probably estimated that they would have

---

56. Op. cit. [1], *LotR* 5.2, p. 773.
57. Op. cit., *LotR* 5.2, p. 773.
58. Op. cit., *LotR* 5.2, p. 773.
59. Op. cit., *LotR* 5.2, p. 776.
60. Op. cit., *LotR* 5.2, p. 779.
61. C. Tolkien (ed.), *The History of Middle-earth*, vol. VIII, *The War of the Ring*, London HarperColllins Publishers, 2002, first published in Great Britain by Unwin Hyman 1990, *HoM-e* VIII Part 3, Chapter 4, pp. 300, 305.

the mental and physical stamina to endure the journey, with Legolas unlikely to be distressed by the ghosts of dead mortals and Gimli being well used to travelling in the dark under mountains.

- As he sat in the eating-hall with them, steeling himself to put them in the picture, he was in a very uncomfortable situation: physically ill from the mental exhaustion he was suffering, no doubt struggling to eat, and unable to bring himself to speak to his companions. Eventually Legolas forced the issue by telling him to "*Speak and be comforted, and shake off the shadow!*"[62] thus fulfilling, yet again, his role of encouraging Aragorn at times of stress and need. Aragorn's fears about the reaction he would get were well-founded in Gimli's case, as the Dwarf demanded to know whether he had said anything to Sauron pointing out that even Gandalf had been afraid to use the Palantír. The passage giving Aragorn's reply needs to be quoted in full and analysed:

"'You forget to whom you speak,' said Aragorn sternly, and his eyes glinted. 'What do you fear that I should say to him? Did I not openly proclaim my title before the doors of Edoras? Nay, Gimli,' he said in a softer voice, and the grimness left his face, and he looked like one who has laboured in sleepless pain for many nights. 'Nay, my friends, I am the lawful master of the Stone, and I had both the right and the strength to use it, or so I judged. The right cannot be doubted. The strength was enough - barely.'"[63]

Aragorn's initial outburst in response to Gimli's question showed his anger and indignation at the Dwarf's insolence in suggesting that he might have weakened enough to say something to Sauron, especially as the Stone was his by right. The question would have struck a raw nerve: as discussed in Chapter 1.6 Aragorn believed that because he had the right to use the Palantír he would also have the strength required to break Sauron's hold on it. He did indeed have the strength, but only "*barely*", and in his stressed and exhausted state Gimli's words would really have rubbed salt into the wound. The sudden softening of his attitude would have been due to his acceptance of the fact that the confrontation had been a close-run thing - which he was now prepared to admit - and also from recognising that it was fear and amazement which had prompted Gimli to speak so. This reply as I have quoted it above is taken from the second edition of *LotR*. However Hammond and Scull point out that in the first edition the second sentence was, "*What do you fear that I should say: that I had a rascal of a rebel dwarf here that I would gladly exchange for a serviceable orc?*" They go on to refer to an unpublished letter begun on 22nd September 1963 to Eileen Elgar who had apparently criticised Aragorn's sharp retort in the second half of the sentence.[64] Tolkien's intention was that the words in question were grim humour rather than serious rebuke, but he nevertheless removed them from the second edition of *LotR*, which was first published in 1966. Tom Shippey also comments on the first edition version, his view being that Aragorn's loss of temper was due to continuing tension between him and Gimli as a result of the latter's negativity earlier on and that the text should have remained unchanged.[65] However since the reunion with Gandalf there had been several instances of a far from negative relationship between Aragorn and Gimli, for example:
- Gimli's spirited support of Aragorn when he didn't want to leave his sword outside Meduseld (*LotR* 3.6.511).
- Aragorn's admiration - expressed to Legolas - of Gimli's axe-wielding in battle (*LotR* 3.7.538).
- Aragorn tending Gimli's wound after Helm's Deep, instead of resting (*LotR* 3.8.545).
- The relaxed lunch together following the reunion with Merry and Pippin in Isengard (*LotR* 3.9.560-75).
- On departure from Isengard to return to Helm's Deep Legolas and Gimli had already pledged their company and support even though Aragorn couldn't see his way clearly at that point (*LotR* 5.2.771).

---

62. Op. cit. [1], *LotR* 5.2, p. 780.
63. Op. cit., *LotR* 5.2, p. 780.
64. W.G. Hammond and C. Scull, *The Lord of the Rings: a Reader's Companion*, London, HarperCollins Publishers, 2005, p. 529.
65. Op. cit. [36], Shippey "A Fund of Wise Sayings", pp. 314-5.

- In addition Gandalf's open support for Aragorn's decision to follow the Orcs ("... *the choice was just, and it has been rewarded. For so we have met in time, who otherwise might have met too late*"[66]) must have gone a long way towards resolving any lingering negativity, not just for Gimli, but for all three of them.

I feel that Gimli's reaction to Aragorn's use of the Palantír was due to shock - at the deed itself and the resulting physical state of Aragorn - and fear. After all, he had done something which even Gandalf had doubted his ability to do. [Regarding the two versions of the text in this incident, I came across the following support (though for a different reason) for retaining the original wording: "*I always found it a shame he* [Tolkien] *edited out Aragorn's blackly humorous snap-back at Gimli after his Palantír ordeal*".][67]

- Having restored peace between the three of them, Aragorn went on to tell Legolas and Gimli of the Paths of the Dead and the need to go through them. He made no secret of the potential fear and danger to be encountered and stressed that he only wanted them to go with him of their own free will. However there was no question of these two deserting him now. Gimli had no hesitation in agreeing to accompany him whatever the risks involved (and in fact pledged his support before Legolas did) while Legolas did not fear the ghosts of Men anyway and no doubt hoped that his presence would therefore be of some help to the others. Aragorn's demeanour changed to one of assertiveness and determination once he knew that they were prepared to go with him. Legolas and Gimli must have been very concerned at his condition at this point (in contrast to his generally confident and tireless performance at Helm's Deep) and would have been under no illusion as to the severity of his ordeal. At the same time they would have recognised the courage, self-control and strength of will required to come out the winner in such an encounter.
- Later as Aragorn and the Dúnedain prepared to leave the refuge of Dunharrow to enter the Paths of the Dead, Legolas and Gimli stayed near him and witnessed the incident when Éowyn pleaded to be allowed to go with them. They would have wanted to be close to him for his sake, and for theirs too - they didn't know the Dúnedain and they probably knew less about the Paths of the Dead than their companions who would surely have been aware of the prophecy concerning them. Also Gimli was frightened, as indicated by his later admission that he had not noticed the pain of Aragorn's parting with Éowyn as he had been thinking only of himself at that point.
- On the approach to the Haunted Mountain even Legolas could not long endure the gloom of the black trees there. Perhaps he was not immune to the horror of the place after all. Nevertheless he was sufficiently in command of himself to calm the Rohan horse Arod who, unlike the horses of the Dúnedain, needed special encouragement to enter the Paths.
- As the company proceeded through the mountain, Gimli, to his shame and anger, became almost paralysed by fear, his state of mind aggravated by the fact that an Elf was finding it easier to cope with the underground journey than he. Perhaps there was still a lingering bit of rivalry between him and Legolas. As they went on Gimli marvelled at Aragorn's (apparent) lack of fear when he stopped to examine the remains of Baldor.
- After Aragorn had summoned the Dead at Erech, much emphasis was laid on the desperate haste and weariness of the ride to Pelargir which followed. Only Aragorn had known such a journey before and only his will enabled the others to go on. Among Men the Northern Dúnedain alone could have endured it. Nothing we know of Legolas and Gimli indicates that they would have been accustomed to such journeys and Gimli, being unused to riding, must have found it particularly strenuous and exhausting.

The journey which had begun in the Paths of the Dead ended with their arrival, in the Enemy's black ships, at the Battle of the Pelennor Fields in the nick of time (*LotR* 5.6.847). Most of the emphasis at this point is on

---

66. Op. cit. [1], *LotR* 3.5, p. 500.
67. *The Hall of Fire*, [website], http://www.thehalloffire.net/forum/viewtopic.php?t=1680&postdays=0&postorder=asc&start=80, (accessed 1 August 2010), post number 8.

Aragorn's arrival as King and on his reunion with Éomer, but no doubt Legolas and Gimli were close at hand.

*

The day after the Battle, as told in *LotR* 5.9.872-8, Legolas and Gimli entered Minas Tirith and visited Merry and Pippin in the Houses of Healing where they gave them an account of their journey through the Paths of the Dead. Their behaviour and comments are very enlightening as to their friendship with each other and their feelings towards Aragorn:

- We are told that they "*begged leave*"[68] to go into the City - presumably from Aragorn. Such an interpretation is strengthened by the fact that they subsequently delivered Aragorn's message to Prince Imrahil requesting his and Éomer's presence at the Last Debate. This emphasis on asking leave seems to indicate that Legolas and Gimli now recognised Aragorn as a king as well as being their leader.
- As they walked through the city, they talked of how they would bring some of their own people to make it beautiful again for Aragorn when/if he formally took up the kingship, with Legolas providing songbirds and trees and Gimli bringing stonemasons to improve the walls and streets. This showed both their bond with each other and their shared wish to carry on helping and supporting Aragorn after the war. Strangely Gimli, by the use of the word "when", seemed to assume eventual victory while Legolas said only "if" (*LotR* 5.9.872). Was Gimli perhaps thinking only of Aragorn's impressive qualities of willpower and endurance of war, weariness and danger, while Legolas saw the bigger picture: the true depth of the evil of Sauron, the slender chance of Frodo's mission succeeding and the impossibility of defeating Sauron while the Ring still existed?
- When the pair met Prince Imrahil Legolas pointedly referred to Gimli as his friend and emphasised their connection with the Fellowship and with Aragorn in particular. Merry and Pippin were then also described as "*our friends*"[69].
- During the conversation with the Hobbits Legolas was initially silent, then began to speak of the sea-longing which had been stirred up in him by hearing the gulls at Pelargir. His companions expressed dismay, with Gimli stating that the world would be duller if the Elves were to depart. Legolas now knew that he would not be at peace in Middle-earth again, and was perhaps beginning to understand the effect this would have on his friendships with people of mortal races. The others too realised the implications.
- When pressed by Pippin to talk about the Paths of the Dead Gimli said that if he had known what was before him, he did not think he would have undertaken the journey, "*... not for any friendship...*"[70] He expressed his shame that Elves and Men had coped better than he with the horror of the journey so that the strength of Aragorn's will was the only thing which had kept him going. One gets the impression that it was this shame as much as the horror *per se* which made him so reluctant to talk of the journey - as if he had let himself and his people down.
- Legolas then declared that it was also love for Aragorn which enabled his companions to endure the journey recognising that "*... all those who come to know him come to love him after their own fashion...*"[71] He then spoke of his grief at witnessing the pain at the parting of Aragorn and Éowyn at Dunharrow. Gimli admitted that he had been thinking only of himself at that point.
- The two of them then described the journey to Pelargir emphasising the many qualities displayed by Aragorn: the fact that the Dead obeyed him; his compassion in sending the Dúnedain to comfort the slaves and captives on board the ships; the strength of will which would have made him a "*great and terrible*"[72] lord if he had taken the Ring himself; and the nobility which made him refuse it. "*Not for naught does Mordor fear him*" said Legolas, and "*... mighty indeed was Aragorn that day*" said Gimli.[73]

---

68. Op. cit. [1], *LotR* 5.9, p. 872.
69. Op. cit., *LotR* 5.9, p. 872.
70. Op. cit., *LotR* 5.9, p. 874.
71. Op. cit., *LotR* 5.9, p. 874.
72. Op. cit., *LotR* 5.9, p. 876.
73. Op. cit., *LotR* 5.9, p. 876.

- They also recognised that nothing could diminish the achievement of the journey from the Paths of the Dead to the Pelennor Fields whatever happened afterwards.
- As their account ended, Legolas and Gimli both felt that there was more to come in the war and both hoped to have a part in it, Gimli for the honour of his people of the Lonely Mountain and Legolas for that of his folk in Mirkwood. However Legolas also wanted to take part *"for the love of the Lord of the White Tree."*[74] Then they all became silent, wrapped up in their own thoughts. I have quoted Legolas's comment because I think it sums up the difference between him and Gimli in their feelings for Aragorn. Legolas's realisation that love, as well as will, was a factor in Aragorn's leadership stemmed from personal feelings as well as observation of others. Gimli felt loyalty, affection and friendship for Aragorn, but Legolas loved him. The silence which followed Legolas's statement seems significant: maybe it came as a surprise to the companions - even to Legolas himself.

LotR 5.10.883 describes the departure of the Army of the West for the Morannon, with Legolas and Gimli riding together in the vanguard with Aragorn, Gandalf, the Dúnedain and Elrond's sons. Seven days later they both (along with Pippin) attended the parley with the Mouth of Sauron as representatives of their respective races. Later that day the War of the Ring would come to an end with the destruction of the One Ring.

*

It is clear that the relationship between Aragorn, Legolas and Gimli continued to thrive after the end of the War of the Ring. In fact there are many references which show that Elf and Dwarf returned to Gondor permanently. To get the fullest picture of this friendship post-War-of-the-Ring, it is necessary to study *LotR* 6.4.956, 6.5.968, 970, 6.6.978, 981, App A.III.1079-81, App B.1098, *UT* 3.1.358-9, *HoM-e* XII.1.7.220[75] and the unused Epilogue to *LotR* (*HoM-e* IX.1.11.114-135[76]) which recounts a conversation between Sam and his daughter Elanor some years after the departure of the Ring-bearers:
- As early as the day after the Battle of the Pelennor Fields Legolas and Gimli (as already mentioned) were discussing the work they could do to beautify Minas Tirith. Meanwhile Aragorn, at the same time during the Last Debate, was talking of asking for the help of Gimli's folk in repairing the City Gate (*LotR* 5.9.881).
- At the Field of Cormallen after the honouring of the Ring-bearers Legolas and Gimli (as would be expected) sat at the King's table during the feast. That same evening Legolas stated his intention of asking permission from his father to bring some of the Mirkwood Elves to live in Ithilien.
- In *LotR* 6.5.968, a passage looking forward from the coronation mentions the trees and fountains which would appear in Minas Tirith, its new steel and mithril gates and the white marble paving the streets. It goes on to state that the Folk of the Mountain worked there and the Folk of the Wood rejoiced to go there.
- During the days after his coronation Aragorn became touchingly anxious for all the Fellowship to be with him for his forthcoming wedding.
- When the company departed from Minas Tirith following the wedding celebrations, Legolas and Gimli still rode together on Arod and on arrival at Helm's Deep they visited the Glittering Caves together as agreed between them at the time of the Battle of the Hornburg.
- Later, as the company took their leave of Treebeard, the Fellowship split up, with Legolas and Gimli departing for their own lands via Fangorn Forest - again as previously agreed. The Epilogue states that Legolas now let Arod run free back to Rohan. This was the first time that Legolas and Gimli had been separated from Aragorn since the formation of their bond at Parth Galen, and Aragorn's farewell words expressed his hope that they would soon return to Minas Tirith with the help they had promised. He

---

74. Op. cit. [1], *LotR* 5.9, p. 878.
75. C. Tolkien (ed.), *The History of Middle-earth*, vol. XII, *The Peoples of Middle-earth*, London HarperColllins Publishers, 2002, first published in Great Britain by HarperCollins Publishers 1996, *HoM-e* XII Part 1, Chapter 7, p. 220.
76. C. Tolkien (ed.), *The History of Middle-earth*, vol. IX, *Sauron Defeated*, London HarperColllins Publishers, 2002, first published in Great Britain by HarperCollins Publishers 1992, *HoM-e IX* Part 1, Chapter 11, pp. 114-135.

clearly didn't want the threesome to split up.
- App A gives more detail on Gimli's work stating that he brought south some of the Dwarves of the Lonely Mountain and that they did *"great works"*[77] in both Gondor and Rohan. In the Epilogue Sam told Elanor that Gimli and his folk got used to working in Gondor and settled in the White Mountains near Minas Tirith, with Gimli visiting the Glittering Caves - of which he was now the Master - each year.
- App A.III.1079 also refers to Gimli's compilation - specifically for Aragorn - of the genealogical table of the Dwarves of the Lonely Mountain.
- App B draws attention to the pre-existing friendship with the Lonely Mountain recording the death of Dáin II Ironfoot (who had succeeded Thorin Oakenshield in TA 2941 at the end of *TH*), along with that of King Brand of Dale, in the War of the Ring. The new King under the Mountain, Thorin III Stonehelm, sent an ambassador to Aragorn's coronation. He would maintain a lasting friendship with Gondor, and his kingdom came *"under the crown and protection of the King of the West."*[78]
- UT 3.1.358 tells how Gimli helped Aragorn in excavating the secret places of Orthanc to find the precious heirlooms appropriated by Saruman. (I have given a more detailed account of this incident in Chapter 1.7.)
- In addition to bringing fountains, trees and songbirds to Minas Tirith, Legolas brought some of his people from Mirkwood and founded a settlement in Ithilien. *LotR* records Legolas's appreciation of *"this fair land"*[79] and his stated intention of asking his father's permission to move there. A passage in *HoMe* XII refers to Faramir's new house in the Hills of Emyn Arnen [part of Ithilien] *"whose gardens devised by the Elf Legolas were renowned."*[80].
- Finally, the Epilogue contains Sam's description of the *"wonderful sight"*[81] of companies of Elves and Dwarves travelling south together. Thus it wasn't just Legolas and Gimli as individuals whose friendship deepened through their relationship with Aragorn; their people too became united in friendship as they journeyed to new homes in Aragorn's kingdom.

One further consideration is whether Legolas and Gimli took part in the continuing struggle to subdue Harad and Rhûn after Aragorn became king. As stated in App A.II.1071 this took many years and it would seem to be in character for the Elf and Dwarf to be involved. However I have found no evidence of this. Nevertheless the points noted above clearly illustrate the continuing close friendship - even emotional dependence on each other - between Aragorn, Legolas and Gimli. Their bond was too strong to be dissolved.

Legolas and Gimli perhaps came to know Aragorn better than any of the other members of the Fellowship did, apart from Gandalf. They were thrown together at a crisis in the Ring "Quest" at a point when Aragorn was at a particularly low ebb, and they both matured and developed enormously through their friendship with him. To some extent, regard for Aragorn and their wish to support him strengthened their bond with each other, providing them with a common personal goal in addition to the overall one of uniting against Sauron. For example, in *LotR* when Aragorn was uncertain where to go next, Legolas stated his intention of going anyway, with Gimli immediately adding *"And Gimli with him!"*[82]. Later when Gimli announced that he would accompany Aragorn through the Paths of the Dead Legolas at once followed suit. In both cases they didn't really know or understand the nature of their journey but because Aragorn was going they were going too. The journeys they undertook with him stretched their physical and mental capabilities to the limit, as well as broadening their hitherto somewhat limited view of Middle-earth and its peoples. Legolas, though highly-born, lived with a rustic race of Elves and hardly seems to have been out of his own land and its immediate surroundings before, while Gimli had known only the Dwarf settlements in the Blue Mountains and the Lonely Mountain and the road between the two. Aragorn too benefited from the combination of their unfailing support,

---
77. Op. cit. [1], App A.III, p. 1080.
78. Op. cit., App B, p. 1095.
79. Op. cit., *LotR* 6.4, p. 956.
80. Op. cit. [75], *HoM-e* XII Part 1, Chapter 7, p. 220.
81. Op. cit. [76], *HoM-e* IX, Part 1, Chapter 11, p. 123.
82. Op. cit. [1], *LotR* 5.2, p. 773.

loyalty and respect which developed into admiration and love as he went from strength to strength in his final steps towards the defeat of Sauron and the regaining of the kingship. He remained deeply appreciative of their support throughout.

Inevitably Aragorn's attachment to Legolas and Gimli would have been of a different nature from theirs to him and theirs to each other on account of the depth of the love between him and Arwen. There is no reference to either Legolas or Gimli marrying. It seems that their work and their friendship (with each other and with Aragorn) were enough for them. As discussed earlier, Legolas (in *LotR* 5.9.878) cited his love for Aragorn as one of his reasons for wishing to be involved in the last stage of the War of the Ring. It is not only Legolas's deep feelings for a Dwarf which are noteworthy but also such feelings for a Man. While the attachment to Gimli perhaps originated from the differences between the two of them, the closeness to Aragorn would have stemmed from the latter's natural affinity with Elves due to his upbringing, along with shared traits such as acute perception, foresightedness and an appreciation of nature. Legolas's regard for him is another striking example of the love of an Elf for a Man - just not sexual/romantic love in this case. [Compare the Elf Beleg's deep affection for Túrin in *TSil* 21.238, 243] In addition his feelings seem to have been a blend of protectiveness and respect, with the emphasis being on the former during the early days of their alliance and then increasingly on the latter as time went on. There was also perhaps an element of hero-worship in Legolas's attitude, as for example in his recognition that everyone who knew Aragorn grew to love him, and in the reverence he seemed to feel for his achievements: "*... I looked on Aragorn and thought how great and terrible a lord he might have become in the strength of his will, had he taken the Ring to himself. But nobler is his spirit than the understanding of Sauron...*"[83].

*

The issues of death and immortality are very relevant to a study of the relationship between Aragorn, Legolas and Gimli. There now follows a brief examination of what "death" meant to each of the three races - Dwarves, Elves and Men:

- *TSil* 2.37-42 gives an account of the creation of the Dwarves. Unlike Elves and Men they were not created by Ilúvatar but by the Vala Aulë, who grew impatient waiting for the Children of Ilúvatar (i.e. Elves and Men) to come and so made his own "children" in a hall under the mountains in Middle-earth. Ilúvatar found out, but because Aulë was repentant, he gave independent life to the Dwarves but decreed that they should sleep underground until after the Elves had been brought into existence. The Elves believed that when Dwarves died they "*... returned to the earth and the stone of which they were made...*"[84]. However the Dwarves themselves believed that after death they went to a separate place in the halls of Mandos to await the end of the world at which time Ilúvatar would formally include them among his Children.
- Elves were immortal as long as the world lasted, and by the Fourth Age many of them had left Middle-earth and sailed West to the Undying Lands. If their bodies died - for example through injury or grief - their spirits went to the halls of Mandos until such time as Mandos allowed them to be reborn in their bodies. Legolas was comparatively young for an Elf - as opposed to Elrond, for example, who was born towards the end of the First Age making him between six and seven thousand years old by TA 3018. Many other Elves encountered in *LotR* such as Galadriel, Celeborn, Círdan and Glorfindel would have been much older still. Legolas's journey to Pelargir during the War of the Ring led to him hearing the sound of seagulls, thus awakening his Elvish longing for the Sea and the Undying Lands, hitherto dormant. He expressed his feelings eloquently to Gimli, Merry and Pippin as they sat in the garden of the Houses of Healing: "*Alas! for the gulls. No peace shall I have again under beech or under elm.*"[85]. This had been foreseen by Galadriel whose message had been conveyed to him by the newly-resurrected Gandalf at the reunion in Fangorn Forest:

---

83. Op. cit. [1], *LotR* 5.9, p. 876.
84. Op. cit. [2], *TSil* Chapter 2, p. 39.
85. Op. cit. [1], *LotR* 5.9, p. 873.

> *"If thou hearest the cry of the gull on the shore,*
> *Thy heart shall then rest in the forest no more."*[86]

- Men lived only a short time - even Elros, the first King of Númenor, only lived to be five hundred - and when they died they left the world entirely, for some unknown place and fate.

Thus for the three races there were three types of "death". These fates now need to be considered in the context of their relevance to Aragorn, Legolas and Gimli with the approach of the year FA 120:

- Aragorn, due to his Númenórean lifespan, was now over two hundred years old and had long outlived most (if not all) of his mortal contemporaries from the time of the War of the Ring - apart from Gimli. He had also already lived longer than any of the previous Chieftains of the Dúnedain and longer than many of the Kings in the North prior to them. He knew that after death he would be permanently separated from friends who were not of the race of Men.
- Gimli was, by now, some years older than the average age for a Dwarf. He believed that when he died he would go to a separate place in the halls of Mandos and remain there while the world lasted.
- For the last hundred or more years Legolas had had a longing to leave Middle-earth and live in peace in the Undying Lands - again while the world lasted. As far as he was concerned the question was not **whether** he would sail, but **when**.

This must have been a time of complex and uncertain emotions, with all three friends being aware of Legolas's desire to sail West and of the imminence of death for Aragorn and Gimli. In FA 120 reality hit, with the death of Aragorn on March 1st at the age of two hundred and ten. Later that year Legolas built himself a ship in Ithilien and sailed down the Anduin to the Sea, **taking Gimli with him**.

This highly exceptional incident is referred to in App A.III.1081, which recounts the history of Durin's race of Dwarves to which Gimli belonged, and in App B.1098 where it is recorded in the entry for 1541 (the year of Aragorn's death in Shire Reckoning). The implications need to be examined in some detail. The App A.III account is fuller and gives suggested motives for those involved. Legolas was said to have taken Gimli with him because of their friendship which was greater than any other between an Elf and a Dwarf. This seems to fit with Legolas's behaviour to Gimli in general. For example when the Fellowship had stayed in Lothlórien Legolas had left the Company in order to spend time with the Lórien Elves - however he had taken Gimli with him. Also, in *LotR* 3.10.586, he had been very insistent to Treebeard that he would not visit Fangorn unless he could bring Gimli. Thus, taking him to the Undying Lands seems to fit in with this attitude. Gimli's situation was less straightforward as he would be leaving his beloved mountains and caves to live among Elves. There was also the question of whether he would be welcome in the Undying Lands or even allowed there by the Valar in the first place. The account ends with the assumption that Galadriel may have smoothed over any difficulties because one of Gimli's motives was his attachment to her. On her part Galadriel had been very impressed with his courtesy and lack of greed for gold, and also by his reverence for her gift of the three strands of her hair which he intended to set into imperishable crystal to be a pledge of goodwill between the Dwarves of the Lonely Mountain and the Elves of Lothlórien (*LotR* 2.8.376). Thus the dual motive of friendship with Legolas and regard for Galadriel was perhaps sufficient to explain Gimli's willingness to sail West.

Legolas would have been well aware that Aragorn was content to accept his mortal fate. Indeed as a Númenórean, initiator of the age of Men, and married to Arwen who had renounced her Elvish immortality, Aragorn could not sail West under any circumstances. However at some point it obviously occurred to Legolas that it might be possible for **Gimli** to take ship with him. If no prior permission had been given it seemed an incredibly risky venture to sail West with a Dwarf and expect the Elves and the Valar to accept him in their lands. If there **was** prior permission how was it granted? Given that Galadriel seems to have had a part in Gimli's fate is it conceivable, with her wisdom and foresight, that she had spoken to Legolas on the subject before her own departure from Middle-earth at the end of the Third Age?

In the Epilogue to *LotR*, Sam told Elanor that Legolas would carry on living in Gondor as long as Gimli

---

86. Op. cit. [1], *LotR* 3.5, p. 503.

did but that he would probably go to the Sea one day, thus apparently linking Legolas's long-term plans with the lifespan of Gimli (*HoM-e* IX Part 1, Chapter 11). There appears to be no awareness in this passage of the plan for Gimli to sail, but that could be explained by the fact that this is Sam talking to his daughter only about sixteen years after the destruction of the Ring. Such a plan would undoubtedly have been kept quiet until it became a reality. The Epilogue is also at variance with the evidence in *LotR* from an additional perspective. For example Legolas spoke - perhaps prophetically - of his intention to come and live in Ithilien "*For a while: a month, a life, a hundred years of Men. But Anduin is near, and Anduin leads down to the Sea.*"[87]. The phrase "*a hundred years of Men*" seems to relate to Aragorn rather than Gimli and fits roughly with Legolas's eventual time-scale. Also App A states that "*... when King Elessar gave up his life Legolas followed **at last** the desire of his heart...*"[88] [My emphasis]. The implication here is surely that it was the death of Aragorn which prompted Legolas to sail, that as long as Aragorn was alive he could not bring himself to leave Middle-earth in spite of the call of the Sea. If his plan had just been for Gimli to take ship with him he could have sailed at any time. The longer he waited, the greater was the chance of Gimli dying before this could happen. That Legolas chose not to sail implies that his attachment to Aragorn took priority. Perhaps it was a joint decision between him and Gimli, and perhaps Legolas "knew" that Gimli would outlive Aragorn. [He was two hundred and sixty-two when he sailed.]

All the evidence is that Legolas and Gimli had never left Aragorn from the time of their bonding at Parth Galen, apart from briefly at the end of the War of the Ring while they obtained permission from home to come back to Gondor with some of their folk. In the end it was he who left them. The death of the friend whom they had seen transformed from the despairing and distracted figure at Parth Galen into the revered king and healer must have been a source of unremitting sadness for them, and the journey to the Undying Lands would have been a search for healing of grief as well as a fulfilment of Legolas's sea-longing. With Aragorn's death their bond was broken irrevocably and perhaps they felt there was now nothing left for them in Middle-earth.

Regarding Gimli's ultimate fate, there are several of Tolkien's letters which elaborate on the subject of non-Elves going to the Undying Lands. A letter to Naomi Mitchison of 25th September 1954 specifically mentions Gimli, along with Frodo, Bilbo and Sam, as being one of the exceptions who were allowed to sail into the West because they had "*... played some great part in Elvish affairs*"[89]. Gimli went as a "*... friend of Legolas and 'servant' of Galadriel.*"[90] ['Servant' in this instance referred to the concept of 'courtly love': Gimli became his lady's servant on account of his platonic devotion to her and she gave him a gift in the form of the three strands of her hair.] It is stated that the arrangement was "*only a temporary reward: a healing and redress of suffering*"[91] and that these non-Elves would eventually die and leave the world. A draft letter to Mrs Eileen Elgar of September 1963 hints that Bilbo went to the Undying Lands partly as companion to Frodo as it was difficult to imagine a Hobbit being happy there without one of his own kind.[92] The same could perhaps be said of Gimli being deprived of Dwarvish company, in spite of his great friendship with Legolas. Again the emphasis is on the temporary nature of the arrangement. A third letter to Roger Lancelyn Green dated 17th July 1971 supports this, making it clear that the Valar had no power or right to grant immortality to these non-Elvish folk.[93] Finally the discussion in *Athrabeth Finrod ah Andreth* states that the "*special grace*" granted to some mortals to sail oversea with the Elves enabled them to go "*to a state in which they could acquire greater knowledge and peace of mind, and being healed of all hurts both of mind and body, could at last surrender themselves: die of free will, and even of desire...*".[94]

Thus the implication is that Aragorn, Legolas and Gimli were, in the end, all separated by their individual fates, with Legolas sailing to the Undying Lands, Aragorn leaving the world completely for the unknown fate of Men, and Gimli, after a sojourn in the Undying Lands, going to the place of the Dwarves in the Halls of

---

87. Op. cit. [1], *LotR* 6.4, p. 956.
88. Op. cit., App A.III, p. 1080.
89. H. Carpenter (ed.), *The Letters of J.R.R. Tolkien*, with the assistance of Christopher Tolkien, London, HarperCollins Publishers, 1995. First published in Great Britain by George Allen & Unwin, 1981. Letter. 154, p. 198.
90. Op. cit., Letter. 154, p. 198.
91. Op. cit., Letter. 154, p. 198.
92. Op. cit., Letter 246, p. 328.
93. Op. cit., Letter 325, p. 411.
94. Op. cit. [8], *HoM-e* X Part 4, Author's Note 4, p. 341.

Mandos.

The Fellowship of the Ring had been formed at Rivendell in December TA 3018. Boromir died in February TA 3019, Gandalf and Frodo sailed West in September TA 3021, and Sam in September FA 62. Merry and Pippin retired to Gondor in FA 64 dying a few years later. Aragorn, Legolas and Gimli were thus the last three members of the Fellowship to leave Middle-earth - approximately fifty years later. Their bond was not just a temporary and expedient alliance during the War of the Ring, but a deep and lasting attachment which was only broken by the death of Aragorn one hundred and twenty-two years after the destruction of the Ring.

CHAPTER 2.5 - Hobbits

This chapter examines Aragorn's relationships with the Hobbits: Frodo, Sam, Merry, Pippin and Bilbo. Although Gollum was technically a Hobbit I decided it would be more appropriate to include him in the discussions on Isildur and the Ring in Chapter 2.8.

First it is necessary to trace the history of Dúnadan/Hobbit relations in general prior to the period covered by *LotR*[1].

According to *LotR* Prologue.1-16 the Hobbits' lore suggested that they themselves originated in the vales of the Anduin between the eaves of Greenwood the Great and the Misty Mountains. The first actual record of them is given in the entry for TA 1050 in App B.1085 which states that the Harfoot breed of Hobbits began to migrate westwards at that time. Bree was colonised around TA 1300 during the reign of Malvegil, 6th King of Arthedain (16th of the Northern line), while the crossing of the River Baranduin (the Brandywine) and the settlement of the Shire was in TA 1601 by permission of the reigning King Argeleb II (10th King of Arthedain and 20th of the Northern line). The Shire Hobbits were ruled by their own chieftains and kept themselves to themselves, though they were still officially the King's subjects and under an obligation to keep the roads and bridges in good repair, acknowledge his lordship and let his messengers pass unhindered.

It is clear that, during the time of the Kings, Hobbits and Dúnedain were aware of, and interacting with, each other. The Prologue describes the Dúnadan influence and how the Hobbits learnt writing from them and possibly building and other crafts as well. They also adopted the Common Speech (Westron) which was spoken throughout Arnor and Gondor. In TA 1975 at the end of the six-hundred-year war with the Witch-king of Angmar, the Shire Hobbits sent some archers to the last battle at Fornost. When the North Kingdom ended in the same year the Shire-folk "*... chose... a Thain to hold the authority of the king that was gone,*"[2] and they still attributed all their essential laws to the kings regarding them as ancient and just and declaring that wicked creatures "*... had not heard of the king.*"[3].

The result of the demise of the North Kingdom was that the few Dúnedain who remained became a secret and wandering people ruled by chieftains instead of kings. The Prologue states that the Hobbits were untroubled by wars for a thousand years (that is roughly until the time of the War of the Ring). During this period "*They forgot or ignored what little they had ever known of the Guardians, and of the labours of those that made possible the long peace of the Shire. They were, in fact, sheltered, but they had ceased to remember it.*"[4] The Guardians were obviously the Dúnedain and the implication is that they had begun to develop a protective role towards the Shire right from the days of the first Chieftain. Thus the situation we see in the *LotR* years was long-established, namely that the Dúnedain were protecting the Shire and that its residents were unaware even of their existence, let alone their identity. They had presumably also been guarding Bree all this time as well, where however the situation was different in that the Bree-folk were well aware of the presence of the Rangers but still ignorant of their protective role. The secretiveness was a deliberate policy on the part of the Dúnedain in order to keep their true identity hidden and in particular to conceal the fact that Isildur's line still flourished in the North. It suited their purposes to be seen as scruffy, disreputable, sinister wanderers - or "*mysterious vagabonds*"[5] to use Aragorn's own phrase.

Aragorn and his people would have learnt much about the Shire Hobbits from their secret patrols. Halbarad's words just after Aragorn's Palantír confrontation with Sauron summed up the attitude of the Rangers: "*A little*

---

1. J.R.R. Tolkien, *The Lord of the Rings,* London, HarperCollins Publishers, 2007, 2nd edition, based on the 50th Anniversary Edition of 2004.
2. Op. cit., *LotR* Prologue, p. 5.
3. Op. cit., *LotR* Prologue, p. 9.
4. Op. cit., *LotR* Prologue, p. 5.
5. Op. cit., *LotR* 1.10, p. 164.

people, but of great worth are the Shire-folk. Little do they know of our long labour for the safe-keeping of their borders, and yet I grudge it not."[6]. They would certainly have actually met Hobbits in the Prancing Pony inn at Bree since it was patronised by both Hobbits and Men, who co-existed amicably in the Breeland villages. There were Hobbits in the inn, as customers and staff, on the evening when Aragorn met Frodo. A specific incident is documented in *LotR* 1.10.174 with Aragorn helping Nob, a Hobbit member of staff, to bring the luggage into the parlour after the decision had been made for Frodo and his companions to avoid sleeping in their bedrooms. He was quite prepared to help a small person do a lowly task in a time of danger. Did Halbarad's opinion of the Shire Hobbits apply to those of Bree also? And did the Hobbits of Bree share the same view of the Rangers as the Men of Bree - as exemplified by the suspicious attitude of Barliman Butterbur? The Rangers may also have met Hobbits from Buckland, as Merry told his friends (in *LotR* 1.8.148) that his people went to Bree now and then. In addition Aragorn may have known Farmer Maggot: we know that he knew Tom Bombadil (*LotR* 1.10.163), that Bombadil knew Maggot (*LotR* 1.7.132) and that Maggot was in the communication chain (along with Bombadil himself and Gildor's party) regarding Frodo's predicament in 3018 (*LotR* 1.7.132).

Whatever the answers to these questions the last years of the Third Age would bring about far-reaching changes in Dúnadan-Hobbit relations as summed up in Aragorn's reply to Halbarad's speech just quoted, *"And now our fates are woven together"*[7].

*

Aragorn's first meeting with Frodo and his friends (described in *LotR* 1.9.156-62 and 1.10.163-75) was the culmination of an extremely worrying and frightening few weeks as he became aware of Gandalf's disappearance and subsequently put all his effort into following the movements of the Nazgûl and tracking down the Hobbits. The encounter was fraught with problems and misunderstandings:

- The Hobbits had been very much alarmed by the Black Riders and were not unnaturally afraid and distrustful of the sinister, eavesdropping stranger, twice their height, who was clearly aware of the existence of the Ring and of Frodo's real name and who perhaps bore more than a passing resemblance to their pursuers.
- As I discussed in Chapter 1.5 Aragorn himself must have been as frightened as they were and was also wary on his own part in case Frodo and his friends were not who they appeared to be. His feelings would no doubt have turned to terror after Frodo's use of the Ring followed by Merry's encounter with two of the Nazgûl who had clearly appeared as a result of messages from Bill Ferny and the squint-eyed southerner after witnessing Frodo's mishap.
- The Hobbits' seeming recklessness and gross under-estimation of their danger must initially have led to exasperation and probably contempt on his part - certainly until he established that it was their naïvety and possibly the influence of the Ring which were largely responsible for their behaviour.
- Barliman Butterbur's refusal to allow him to speak to the Hobbits and warn them to lie low instead of socialising in the common-room, had put everyone in greatly increased danger. The innkeeper's general hostility was hardly calculated to help Aragorn gain the trust of the Hobbits.
- Barliman's failure to deliver Gandalf's letter to the Shire three months earlier warning Frodo to leave without delay was of course responsible for the lethal nature of their situation anyway.
- Aragorn was disappointed that it took Gandalf's letter to finally convince Frodo that he was trustworthy, since he had hoped to be accepted by the Hobbits on his own merits.
- He found it necessary to frighten the Hobbits in order to impress upon them the true extent of their danger - again not very conducive to instant trust.

However once trust and respect had been established Aragorn's protectiveness was to the fore with his insistence that he and the Hobbits should all spend the night in the parlour due to the likelihood of the special Hobbit bedrooms being attacked. In addition he himself remained sleepless, sitting up alert and ready to fend

---

6. Op. cit. [1], *LotR* 5.2, p. 779.
7. Op. cit., *LotR* 5.2, p. 780.

off Nazgûl if necessary. Once the companions had got away from Bree, things became more relaxed, with the Hobbits appreciating his knowledge and experience, depending on him for protection and healing, sharing jokes with him (about short-cuts and Trolls), and wondering at the tales he told. They noticed too his grimness and his tendency to want only his own company at times. On his part Aragorn began to give out tentative hints about himself - his connection with Rivendell as a former home and as a place close to his heart, his fluent and passionate telling of the story of Beren and Lúthien - all of which were rather lost on the Hobbits at this stage.

*

"I am Aragorn son of Arathorn; and if by life or death I can save you, I will."[8]

This speech was made by Aragorn, (with a smile that softened his face) to Frodo, Sam and Pippin in the Prancing Pony. The moment marked the acceptance of Aragorn as their guide and protector, and also the beginning of close and lasting friendships with them all. I will now examine Aragorn's relationships with the individual Hobbits: Frodo, Sam, Merry and Pippin - and also with Bilbo. Each one is unique and interesting in its own right.

FRODO BAGGINS

As Gandalf and Frodo sat in the study at Bag End in April 3018 discussing the nature of Bilbo's Ring and the search for Gollum, Gandalf spoke of Aragorn by name (*LotR* 1.2.58). This remark - understandably in the circumstances - seems to have gone over Frodo's head. Later when he read Gandalf's letter of introduction in Bree there would be no indication that he recalled hearing the name Aragorn before.

On September 22nd, at the same time as Frodo was holding his birthday dinner on his last evening in the Shire, Aragorn's Rangers were fighting a losing battle with the Nazgûl at Sarn Ford while Aragorn himself was watching the East Road hoping to find Frodo. Over the following few days a network of communication came into operation - consisting of Tom Bombadil, Farmer Maggot, Gildor Inglorion and Aragorn - in which information about the whereabouts of the Hobbits and the Nazgûl was exchanged. As the Hobbits took leave of Bombadil on September 29th (*LotR* 1.8.147-8) Aragorn was behind the hedge watching and listening. He then followed them to Bree unnoticed. The relationship between him and Frodo had in effect already been established before they had even met, ostensibly on account of the unexplained disappearance of Gandalf three months earlier leading to Aragorn's assumption of the Wizard's role regarding Frodo. However it actually went back even further as shown by Aragorn's words to Frodo in Bree, "*I have often kept watch on the borders of the Shire in the last few years, when he* [Gandalf] *was busy elsewhere.*"[9]. He had in fact been well aware of Frodo's existence and his connection with the Ring since TA 3001 as this was when Gandalf had first shared his concerns with him following Bilbo's party - note his words at the Council of Elrond, "*I opened my heart to Aragorn*"[10].

There is no doubt that Frodo's first feelings towards Aragorn were ones of wariness, discomfort and fear due to the stranger's sinister, weather-beaten appearance and challenging gaze, his apparent ability to read Frodo's thoughts, his "eavesdropping" activities and, above all, his obvious knowledge of the Ring and Frodo's real name. Aragorn, having satisfied himself that the Hobbits were not imposters bribed to entrap him, made it a matter of urgency to bring Frodo to his senses. The "disappearing" incident in the inn (*LotR* 1.9.160) must have been extremely alarming for him, on account of the proximity of the Nazgûl and of the possibility that the Ring itself may have been partly responsible for Frodo's behaviour. It was essential for all their sakes that Frodo should accept him as a guide.

It was not until Frodo read Gandalf's letter (*LotR* 1.10.169-71) that he openly declared his trust in Aragorn. However in reality this trust had been established much sooner, that is once Frodo realised that Aragorn's "reward" for helping him was not money-related, and a satisfactory explanation had been given for the "eavesdropping" which had enabled him to follow the Hobbits to Bree. Frodo said himself that he had trusted

---

8. Op. cit. [1], *LotR* 1.10, p. 171.
9. Op. cit., *LotR* 1.10, p. 172.
10. Op. cit., *LotR* 2.2, p. 251.

(or at least **wanted** to trust) Aragorn **before** reading the letter. In his opinion Aragorn did not act like an enemy. His behaviour in the common-room had merely been aimed at encouraging Frodo to curb Sam's and Pippin's chatter and to try to be more discrete - hardly the action of an enemy. Although he frightened Frodo it was done to make him realise the extent of his danger. Aragorn was genuine, for example: in his appreciation of Frodo answering him back; in his involuntary display of the trauma the Nazgûl induced in him; and in his blunt statement that the level of Frodo's fear of them, great though it was, was nevertheless inappropriately low. He made no attempt to be ingratiating and attractive - which was what Frodo would have expected from a servant of the Enemy. However he had moments of gentleness and, significantly, his smiles had the effect of softening an otherwise grim and stern face. Frodo also noticed the change in Aragorn's voice as he dropped the local Bree accent and began to talk in what was presumably his own natural way of speaking perhaps giving a glimpse of his underlying nobility and goodness. Presumably this change in accent occurred at the point when he felt he could trust the Hobbits - either with a deliberate change of voice or subconsciously as he began to relax in their company. Frodo indeed realised that Aragorn's appearance was a deliberate disguise as illustrated by his opinion that *"you are not really as you choose to look"*, and by his questions: *"Why the disguise? Who are you?"*.[11] It is notable also that Frodo accepted that Butterbur's distrust of Aragorn was due purely to his sinister and ruffianly appearance. Indeed he seemed to doubt the innkeeper's trustworthiness rather than Aragorn's, clearly recognising that he and his friends would have steered clear of the common-room that evening if it hadn't been for Butterbur's refusal to let Aragorn speak to them.

A major delaying factor in Frodo's admittance of trust was his own defensive behaviour. As he took off the Ring in the common-room, Aragorn made the comment, *"You have put your foot in it! Or should I say your finger?"*[12] using grim humour to leave Frodo in no doubt that he knew about the Ring. Frodo reacted by pretending - unconvincingly - that he didn't know what Aragorn was talking about. Then when Aragorn stated his wish to have a private talk with him he acted casual and unconcerned. Later as they talked, he accused him of spying and eavesdropping and deliberately "misunderstood" his hints about Bill Ferny's involvement with the Nazgûl. However, even as early as the "accident" in the common-room the invisible Frodo had crawled away into the corner where Strider was sitting. It could certainly be argued that he would want to find somewhere away from the throng of people before taking off the Ring, but if he had really felt that Strider was an enemy one would think that he would have chosen **any** corner but that one. Did Frodo subconsciously feel that next to Strider was actually the safest place to be at that moment?

To be fair to Frodo, his behaviour was driven by fear and by the knowledge that he had been careless and foolish - even if unintentionally because of the Ring's influence. He wished to exercise a belated common-sense and wariness in not trusting Aragorn too quickly. Gandalf's letter gave him the all-clear he needed to follow his instincts and give his trust openly. Aragorn himself when on the point of telling the Hobbits his own story (at Frodo's request) before being interrupted by the arrival of Butterbur, queried why Frodo should believe what he was about to say if he didn't already trust him.

Once Aragorn had been accepted as Frodo's guide, further evidence of his trustworthiness was provided by his obvious and genuine anxiety about Gandalf which he shared with Frodo and discussed with him on an equal footing. This was also the point where he first drew attention to the Ring as being something which concerned both of them, calling it *"this business of ours"*[13]. When they left Bree the following morning (*LotR* 1.11.180) Frodo walked with him at the head of the group. A few days later as they spent their second night in the Midgewater Marshes the two of them, being the only ones awake, watched and discussed the mysterious flashing lights on the hills in the east. Frodo's naïvety and lack of awareness still showed though, for example in his remark that if he were to get much thinner he would become a wraith, thus filling Aragorn with alarm as Frodo's circumstances meant that becoming a wraith was very much a possibility and certainly not a matter for jesting. As the companions drew near to Weathertop, Aragorn spoke of the Elf-king Gil-galad and the Last Alliance of Elves and Men which had brought about Sauron's downfall at the end of the Second Age. This prompted Sam to recite some verses on the subject which he believed to have been written by Bilbo. Aragorn's statement that the verses were part of an old lay which Bilbo must have translated from an ancient Elvish

---

11. Op. cit. [1], *LotR* 1.10, p. 166.
12. Op. cit., *LotR* 1.9, p. 161.
13. Op. cit., *LotR* 1.10, p. 172.

language passed unnoticed by all the Hobbits. This seems strange as the implication was that Aragorn knew Bilbo quite well and one would have expected Frodo, at least, to wonder how such an acquaintance came about.

The story of Gil-galad was discussed again as they prepared to spend the night in the dell on Weathertop. Aragorn stated that he knew more of the tale than the few verses Sam had recited, and then went on to say, "*So also does Frodo, for it concerns us closely*"[14], thus drawing further attention to the fact that the Ring held great significance for him as well as for Frodo. He was recognising the link which now existed between them, and their shared fate. His role in protecting and supporting Frodo was evident from his continual watchfulness - often while the others slept - and his attempts to reassure Frodo that he was not alone in his struggle.

Frodo's wound from the Lord of the Nazgûl made the Hobbits aware of Aragorn's healing powers, while Aragorn himself began to recognise that Frodo was tougher than he appeared and would be able to resist the evil power of the wound longer than his enemies expected. This would undoubtedly have increased his respect for Frodo and brought them closer. The growing closeness was also evident on Frodo's part from his observation that Aragorn, as well as the Hobbits, was feeling the weariness and strain of the journey, and by his more personal interest in him - for example in his question as to whether he had often been to Rivendell which resulted in Aragorn revealing information about his past. In addition, a greater understanding was developing between the two of them. After the attack on Weathertop Frodo had an increased perception of the danger posed by the Nazgûl and perhaps now appreciated Aragorn's behaviour when speaking of them in the Prancing Pony: why his face had been drawn with pain, his hands had clenched the arms of his chair and he had wiped his brow. Frodo also knew Gandalf better than the other Hobbits did and thus shared Aragorn's alarm and his desperate hope of finding the Wizard. Although Aragorn's anxiety and hesitation had made him careless on Weathertop - even to the point of making their situation more dangerous - this didn't diminish Frodo's trust in him.

Once safely in Rivendell Frodo tried to sum up his feelings about Aragorn in conversation with Gandalf, admitting that he had been afraid of him at first, but had come to regard him with affection in spite of the fact that he was "*... strange, and grim at times*"[15]. He was relieved that Sam's distrust was now a thing of the past and he recognised Aragorn's similarity to Gandalf. He was also well aware of the debt of gratitude he owed to him in getting them to Rivendell: "*We should never have done it without Strider*"[16].

However it is clear that Frodo was still a long way from really understanding Aragorn. This was mainly due to the ignorance which affected all the Shire-folk, both of Men in general and of the Dúnedain in particular. Frodo thought that "*Big People*"[17] as a race were stupid and that Aragorn was "*only a Ranger*"[18], not realising that the Rangers were the descendants of the Númenóreans whom he believed to have long died out. The passage quoted earlier from *LotR* Prologue stating that the Hobbits of the Shire had forgotten about the Guardians who laboured to protect them and maintain peace in their land is certainly illustrated by Frodo's view. Later, after the feast, Frodo would be gently chided by Bilbo for not realising the significance of Aragorn's Sindarin name "Dúnadan" meaning Man of the West. Frodo also failed to perceive the relationship between Aragorn and Arwen even though Bilbo had queried Aragorn's absence from the feast with a pointed observation that Arwen had been there. Shortly afterwards, in spite of Bilbo's hint, Frodo was surprised to see the couple together, talking to each other. Maybe he was distracted by the fact that Arwen turned towards him so that he felt as if the light of her eyes was piercing his heart. Had they been discussing him and the effect of the Ring on him? And was this the beginning of Arwen's idea of Frodo sailing West in her place?

Gandalf had already given Frodo hints as to who Aragorn really was. Nevertheless it was not until the Council of Elrond (*LotR* 2.2.246-7) when Elrond introduced Aragorn to Boromir as Isildur's heir that he fully understood. However his assumption that the Ring therefore belonged to Aragorn and his expectation that he would have to give it up showed that at least the significance of Isildur taking the Ring from Sauron and thenceforward regarding it as an heirloom had been firmly fixed in his mind. With hindsight there were obvious hints of Boromir's interest in the Ring even before his suggestion that it should be used against Sauron rather

---

14. Op. cit. [1], *LotR* 1.11, p. 191.
15. Op. cit., *LotR* 2.1, p. 220.
16. Op. cit., *LotR* 2.1, p. 220.
17. Op. cit., *LotR* 2.1, p. 220.
18. Op. cit., *LotR* 2.1, p. 221.

than destroyed. His eyes had "glinted" as soon as Frodo obeyed Elrond and held it up for the others to see. Then as Elrond declared that the only solution was to "*send the Ring to the Fire*"[19], Boromir stirred and Frodo was clearly aware of this and looked at him. As events progressed both Aragorn and Frodo must inevitably have recalled these incidents.

With the selection of the members of the Fellowship Elrond's choice of Aragorn to accompany the Ring-bearer was partly due to the fact that his route to Gondor would coincide with Frodo's for a large section of the way, but also due to his connection with the Ring as Isildur's heir. Frodo's delight at his inclusion and his words "*I would have begged you to come*"[20] left no doubt of his attachment to Aragorn. With Gandalf also included in the Fellowship, Frodo spent less time than he might otherwise have done being involved in the planning for the journey. He was content to rely on these two wise and trusted guides while he himself spent as much time as possible with Bilbo. It probably did not occur to him that a time would come when he would have to manage without them.

During his time in Rivendell Frodo had matured. His reunion with Bilbo and especially his attendance at the Council of Elrond had given him a greater understanding of events. He now appreciated the full evil of the Ring, the significance of Aragorn as Isildur's heir, and the implications of Sauron's growing power - for the Elves, the people of Gondor and the Dwarves. In other words he now saw the big picture. He was also becoming more perceptive, and more in tune with Aragorn. For example when Aragorn and Gandalf began to argue about the route Frodo overheard them and was aware of Aragorn's intense dismay when Gandalf suggested a "*dark and secret way*"[21] as an alternative to Caradhras. He knew that if **Aragorn** feared it it must be bad and was relieved when the mountain pass was chosen instead. As well as appreciating Aragorn's feelings Frodo also showed his trust in him and respect for his judgement.

On Aragorn's part his pledge to support and protect Frodo was clearly at the forefront of his mind. During the rescue of the Hobbits from the snowdrift (*LotR* 2.3.293) he carried Frodo himself - perhaps even at that stage not wanting to let Boromir get into close contact with the Ring. He praised Frodo's action when he made his first sword-thrust in stabbing the Troll's foot in Moria (*LotR* 2.5.324-5) and he was the one who killed the Orc chieftain who had speared Frodo. He subsequently carried Frodo (whom he presumed to be dead) out of the Chamber of Mazarbul and on finding that he was actually still alive and able to walk expressed amazement at the toughness of Hobbits, stating that he would have spoken more softly in Bree if he had known. His remark could perhaps be interpreted as knowing or jokey, implying that he, as well as Gandalf, suspected there was a good reason why Frodo had survived the spear blow, especially as shortly afterwards an Orc arrow had struck him and sprung back. However, as Aragorn prepared to administer first-aid to Frodo following the Company's escape from Moria, it seemed that he still thought it was purely Hobbit toughness which had saved him. This is evidenced by his words, "*I still marvel that you are alive at all*"[22], his unfeigned wonder at the mithril shirt and his obvious relief that Frodo was protected in this way leading to his advice to keep the shirt on even while he slept.

It is perhaps feasible that, in the horror of the last minutes in Moria, Aragorn missed the incident with the arrow bouncing back after hitting Frodo, especially as subsequently, in his distress and haste, he actually forgot about Frodo's injury altogether. This lapse was compounded by the fact that Frodo, obviously realising the urgency of their need to get to the safety of Lothlórien, kept quiet about the pain and breathlessness he was suffering. There was also the additional factor that he and Bilbo had agreed that the mithril shirt should be a secret just between the two of them. It was this, and not any concern about Aragorn having access to the Ring, which made Frodo uneasy about having his injury tended and his clothes disturbed. His complete trust in Aragorn continued. Right from the start Aragorn had come into close contact with the Ring in his capacity as healer and there was never any hint of Frodo being uneasy about this. It was as if they both knew that Aragorn wasn't going to be tempted by the Ring. This is particularly evident in this episode of the discovery of the mithril shirt. Given that Frodo wore the Ring on a chain round his neck, Aragorn must have had it practically in his grasp.

*

---

19. Op. cit. [1], *LotR* 2.2, p. 267.
20. Op. cit., *LotR* 2.3, p. 276.
21. Op. cit., *LotR* 2.3, p. 287.
22. Op. cit., *LotR* 2.6, p. 336.

On the evening of their escape from Moria the Fellowship reached the outskirts of Lothlórien where they came under the guidance of Haldir for the next two days with much of this time being spent blindfolded. At the point when the blindfolds were removed they had reached the hill of Cerin Amroth, the home of the Elf Amroth in the first half of the Third Age (see *UT* 2.4 (Amroth and Nimrodel)[23]) and, in Haldir's words *"the heart of the ancient realm as it was long ago"*[24]. Frodo's feeling on seeing the two circles of trees at the summit and the profusion of elanor and niphredil flowers dotting the grass was that he was in a timeless, unfading land and also in a vanished world. As he reached the top of the hill a south wind blew bringing with it the sounds of seas and sea-birds which had long ceased to exist. From the flet in the highest tree, he could look south and see the green city of Caras Galadhon - the centre of the power of Galadriel and her Elven Ring - while eastwards he saw the boundary between the light of Lothlórien and the dark shadow of Dol Guldur in southern Mirkwood.

It was Cerin Amroth which provided the setting for a moving and highly significant episode in the relationship between Aragorn and Frodo. Nearly thirty-nine years earlier Aragorn and Arwen had plighted their troth there and as Frodo now descended from the hill he came on Aragorn clearly recalling some beautiful and meaningful experience. Frodo did not know about the betrothal, but he realised at once that he was seeing something from the past as Aragorn appeared to be clothed in white and looked much younger due to the absence of the familiar grimness from his face. He also spoke in Elvish to someone whom Frodo could not see. Frodo was sharing in Aragorn's vision, and when Aragorn returned to the present he was clearly aware of this and did not resent it - on the contrary he showed affection to Frodo and began to hint at the romantic nature of his memories: *"... here my heart dwells ever..."*[25]. He had made similar hints earlier in the narrative by stating that his heart was in Rivendell also, and by his animated account on Weathertop of the story of Lúthien and Beren - but these were never sufficient to make any impact on the naïvety of the Hobbits. It was almost as if he really wanted to confide in them but couldn't bring himself to do so fully.

In the previous paragraph I stated that Frodo realised that he was seeing something from the past. This is based on Tolkien's words, *"... as Frodo looked at him* [Aragorn] *he knew that **he** behold things as they once had been in this same place."*[26] I have interpreted the second "he" (which I have emphasised) as indicating Frodo, but it could also be referring to Aragorn - meaning that Frodo realised that **Aragorn** was seeing something from the past. In practice they were **both** seeing something from the past, with Aragorn reliving his betrothal and Frodo seeing Aragorn as he was then.

The final paragraph of *LotR* 2.6 which concludes this episode needs to be quoted and examined:

"*'Here is the heart of Elvendom on earth,'* he [Aragorn] *said, 'and here my heart dwells ever, unless there be a light beyond the dark roads that we still must tread, you and I. Come with me!' And taking Frodo's hand in his, he left the hill of Cerin Amroth and came there never again as living* man."[27].

Aragorn's first words echoed Haldir's speech about Cerin Amroth being the former heart of the ancient realm and hinted at his personal memories of the place. He then referred to the immediate future and the *"dark roads"* ahead for him and Frodo. This phrase is open to a number of interpretations. Was he using it in a general sense to indicate a dangerous and frightening journey? Did he see his and Frodo's *"dark roads"* as being the same or different? Or was he being more specific and already thinking that he would have to change his plans and go to Mordor instead of Minas Tirith now that Gandalf was no longer there to guide Frodo? Or did he see his own dark road as being the Paths of the Dead? These had not entered the story at this point but Aragorn knew of them and of the prophecies concerning them (as would be made clear in *LotR* 5.2.781-2 when he would give Legolas and Gimli a detailed account of the matter). His words on Cerin Amroth seemed to show foresight but also a fear that the darkness would prevail in the end and his relationship with Arwen be nothing more than the memory of their betrothal in Lothlórien. Whatever interpretation we take, he was sharing his thoughts with Frodo thus creating a personal intimacy between them. There was, in addition, a spiritual intimacy between the pair. Since the attack on Weathertop Frodo's senses had become more acute, for

---

23. C. Tolkien (ed.), *Unfinished Tales of Númenor and Middle-earth*, London, HarperCollins Publishers, 1998, first published in Great Britain by George Allen & Unwin 1980, *UT* 2.4, pp. 310-21.
24. Op. cit. [1], *LotR* 2.6, p. 350.
25. Op. cit., *LotR* 2.6, p. 352.
26. Op. cit., *LotR* 2.6, p. 352.
27. Op. cit., *LotR* 2.6, p. 352.

example his feeling that something evil lurked in the pool before the doors of Moria, his increased ability to see in the dark as the Company went through the mines, and his awareness of Gollum following them. Later on, at the end of the Company's sojourn in Lothlórien (*LotR* 2.7.365-6) Frodo, as a Ring-bearer, was able to sense Galadriel's desire for the One Ring and to see the Elven Ring Nenya (invisible to Sam) on her finger. This increased perception was clearly due in large part to the Ring and the fact that Frodo had actually used it. However there was perhaps some power for the good at work as well, particularly in the scene on Cerin Amroth - maybe the power of Nenya itself, or something higher. Whatever the cause, the increased awareness of Frodo, combined with Aragorn's innate perception and foresightedness, created a strong spiritual bond between them, a bond which was symbolised by the physical contact of Aragorn taking Frodo's hand. Their closeness was enhanced by their shared involvement with the Ring, Frodo as the Ring-bearer and Aragorn because of his heritage and destiny and his pledge to heal the damage done by Isildur. In addition both of them were spiritually closer to Gandalf than their companions were and so would have been more deeply affected by his loss.

Regarding the last sentence in the quoted passage: as Frodo climbed Cerin Amroth we are told that he would still walk there after his return into the outer world. Thus he, as well as Aragorn and Arwen, would himself become part of the "*vanished world*" which he had perceived when his blindfold was removed. However neither Aragorn nor Frodo would actually visit Cerin Amroth again alive. As the Fellowship left Lothlórien we are told, "*To that fair land Frodo never came again*"[28], while Aragorn "... *came there never again as living man.*"[29]. [I have discussed the possibility of him going there again after death in Chapter 2.1.]

On the evening prior to the departure of the Fellowship from Lothlórien Frodo looked in Galadriel's Mirror. It is perhaps significant, and in keeping with the new closeness between him and Aragorn, that one of the future events he saw was Aragorn's ship sailing up the Anduin to the Pelennor Fields with Arwen's banner displayed. There was however another aspect of Aragorn about which all the Hobbits continued to remain in the dark - even Frodo with his developing perceptiveness and empathy - namely the existence of a relationship between him and Arwen. On Cerin Amroth, in spite of the fact that Aragorn had actually spoken Arwen's name during his vision of his betrothal, the significance of this was missed by Frodo. The same lack of recognition occurred during the gift-giving episode immediately prior to the Fellowship's departure from Lothlórien when Arwen's name was again mentioned, in the conversation between Aragorn and Galadriel. This may well have been because the main impression made on everyone at this point was the marked change in Aragorn's appearance when he pinned the Elessar brooch on his breast: he looked tall and kingly with a weight of care removed. Also Frodo's mind was no doubt filled with his own fears and concerns at this time. In the event it would not be until Arwen's arrival in Gondor after Aragorn became King that "the penny would drop" about their relationship.

*

During the period between departure from Lothlórien and the sundering of the Fellowship at Parth Galen I have identified three main aspects of the relationship between Aragorn and Frodo, namely:
- Choice of route
- Closeness and trust
- Protection

Choice of route

As Aragorn told Celeborn in *LotR* 2.8.367, Gandalf had given no indication of his intended route beyond Lothlórien and may not even have had any definite plans. Thus the Fellowship were in a situation where they had to make their own decisions as to which way they should go and when, how far they should go by boat and whether they should stay together or split up. The main burden was on Frodo as Ring-bearer and the only one who was under any obligation to go to Mordor, and on Aragorn who was now leader of the Company and

---

28. Op. cit. [1], *LotR* 2.8, p. 378.
29. Op. cit., *LotR* 2.6, p. 352.

Frodo's chief protector.

Right from the initial discussions which resulted in Celeborn deciding to provide the boats, Boromir insisted that following the west bank of the Anduin to Minas Tirith was the best option, both for himself and the others. However this was not the obvious route to Mordor and Aragorn knew he would be unable to desert Frodo if he refused to go with Boromir. As would be revealed in due course, Frodo himself was convinced that he should head directly to Mordor, and was resigned to going alone due to his unwillingness to take his companions into such danger. But because of his fear he felt unable to actually make the move or to speak out about his decision. Aragorn on the other hand, was unable to make a decision at all apart from to stay with the boats as long as possible (thereby actually delaying a decision) and was waiting for Frodo to speak. Thus both were in a quandary about the route and both kept their concerns to themselves. Frodo was more mentally alert than Aragorn during the discussion on the last evening in Lothlórien (*LotR* 2.8.369), picking up Boromir's mutterings about it being folly to destroy the Ring, and recalling that he had voiced a similar opinion at the Council of Elrond. Aragorn, due to the conflict in his mind between his original mission to go to Gondor with Boromir and his current obligation to Frodo, totally missed the signs of the way Boromir's mind was working at that point. When the Company arrived at Parth Galen and a decision could no longer be postponed, Aragorn finally put the onus on to Frodo, justifying this by the fact that Frodo was the appointed Ring-bearer and must decide his own route. He also declared himself unable to give him advice, seemingly on the grounds of inadequacy as compared with Gandalf. He then concluded by surmising that Gandalf would himself have given the decision to Frodo, adding the words "*Such is your fate*"[30], thus giving the first hint of his feeling that something more than their own decision-making might be at work. It is easy to suggest that he convinced himself of this so as to feel less guilty at putting the burden on Frodo, but he may have been recalling the words of Galadriel on their last evening in Lothlórien: "*Maybe the paths that you each shall tread are already laid before your feet, though you do not see them.*"[31]. In fact this stance was vindicated by subsequent events, during which almost every action of the Company seemed to be illogical and imprudent thus giving the impression that some external power was indeed responsible for their behaviour. For example:

- There were possibly Orcs around, even on the west bank of the river, and Frodo, Aragorn and Sam (at least) were suspicious of Boromir's motives. Yet Frodo asked to be on his own for an hour and Aragorn agreed - though admittedly with the proviso that he should stay close by and within earshot.
- However Frodo seemed to make no attempt to stay close and in earshot. He quickly passed out of sight wandering aimlessly in the wood, then found that "... *his feet were leading him up towards the slopes of the hill.*"[32] [Amon Hen]. Thus Boromir had the opportunity to approach him while he was alone and unprotected.
- The rest of the Company seemed to make no attempt to keep a check on Frodo or to assess how long he was absent. We are told that they "... *remained long by the river-side*"[33] talking of other things, then had their own protracted debate on which route to take.
- No-one (out of six of them!) realised that Boromir had left the group. Even when his absence was eventually noticed (by Sam) it didn't seem to occur to anyone that he might have gone after Frodo.
- During their conversation, in response to Pippin's urging that they should prevent Frodo going to Mordor, Aragorn's answer showed his growing conviction of the role of external powers: "*He is the Bearer, and the fate of the Burden is on him. I do not think that it is our part to drive him one way or the other. Nor do I think that we should succeed, if we tried. There are other powers at work far stronger.*"[34].
- Eventually Aragorn realised that the hour had long passed, and Boromir's return at the same moment finally brought home to them the potential danger to Frodo. At this point "*A sudden panic or madness*"[35] seized them making them run off in different directions, totally ignoring Aragorn's orders to pair up and

---

30. Op. cit. [1], *LotR* 2.10, p. 396.
31. Op. cit., *LotR* 2.8, p. 368.
32. Op. cit., *LotR* 2.10, p. 396.
33. Op. cit., *LotR* 2.10, p. 402.
34. Op. cit., *LotR* 2.10, pp. 403-4.
35. Op. cit., *LotR* 2.10, p. 404.

make a more organised search for Frodo.
- Thus an apparently random, panic-induced separation resulted in Frodo and Sam heading to Mordor together, Boromir dying repentant realising that he was wrong to try and take the Ring, Merry and Pippin on the road which would eventually lead them to Fangorn and Isengard, and Aragorn - accompanied by Legolas and Gimli - making his own circuitous route to Minas Tirith and the kingship.
- After much soul-searching as to whether to follow Frodo or try and rescue Merry and Pippin, Aragorn told Legolas and Gimli,"*My heart speaks clearly at last: the fate of the Bearer is in my hands no longer*"[36], now formally stating that external powers were driving Frodo. Frodo too recognised this, telling Sam as they set off towards Mordor, "*It is plain that we were meant to go together.*"[37].

Closeness and trust

The close and trusting relationship between Aragorn and Frodo continued as strong as ever following the Company's departure from Lothlórien. This was in spite of the problems encountered such as Aragorn's increasing lack of self-esteem, the differences of opinion between him and Boromir, and Boromir's harassment of Frodo as the Ring's influence on him grew. In fact, if anything, these problems drew Aragorn and Frodo closer together.

Due to Aragorn's faulty navigation the Company reached the rapids of Sarn Gebir sooner than anticipated, coming on them suddenly at night and only narrowly escaping. As Aragorn fought to turn their boat round he freely admitted to Frodo that he was out of his reckoning (*LotR* 2.9.386). This lapse failed to reduce Frodo's faith in him. After managing to get clear of the rapids, Aragorn and Boromir had their most serious disagreement over the route as Aragorn wanted to find a portage-way which would enable them to carry the boats past the rapids, while Boromir advocated abandoning the boats there and then and making for Minas Tirith by land. Aragorn won the argument because it was clear that Frodo trusted him implicitly and would go wherever he led them. This trust was further illustrated by Frodo's words to Sam as they prepared to cross to the east bank of the Anduin. As he expressed his hope that the rest of the Company would find a safe road he said, without hesitation, "*Strider will look after them*"[38], thus demonstrating again his complete faith in Aragorn. He obviously did not share the low opinion that Aragorn had of himself. Frodo's trust was the more notable because in general he did not regard Men as trustworthy. While in conversation with Boromir on the slopes of Amon Hen earlier on, he had told him that he mistrusted the strength and truth of Men. As well as his personal reasons for trusting Aragorn he would perhaps have recalled, and recognised the truth of, Gandalf's words in Rivendell that there were few Men like Aragorn still around in Middle-earth.

During these last ten days before the breaking of the Fellowship there are further examples of Frodo's increased empathy and perceptiveness in his relationship with Aragorn. It was Frodo who turned and saw Aragorn briefly transformed into a king returning from exile as the boats sped through the narrow stretch of river at the Argonath (*LotR* 2.9.393). Then, as he reasoned with himself on Amon Hen and made his decision to go alone to Mordor, he included Aragorn as one of the companions whom he regarded as too dear to take with him. The words he spoke aloud to himself ("*Strider, too: his heart yearns for Minas Tirith, and he will be needed there, now Boromir has fallen into evil*"[39]) showed his understanding of Aragorn's own mission and his yearning for his own city as well as the potential self-sacrifice which would make him turn towards Mordor to protect the Ring-bearer. Perhaps Frodo had overheard Aragorn voicing these concerns to himself at the Argonath, or perhaps it was purely the unspoken understanding between them.

There was one moment when Frodo's increased perception and maturity caused him to slip up. As the Company discussed the apparent time discrepancies between Lothlórien and the outside world (*LotR* 2.9.388) he referred to the fact that Galadriel had one of the Three Elven Rings, leading Aragorn to reprimand him. Elrond had indicated at the Council that he was not allowed to disclose the identity of the holders of the Three Rings. If Frodo had forgotten that, then Galadriel's words more recently, addressed specifically to him, should

---

36. Op. cit., *LotR* 3.1, p. 419.
37. Op. cit., *LotR* 2.10, p. 406.
38. Op. cit., *LotR* 2.10, p. 406.
39. Op. cit., *LotR* 2.10, p. 401.

perhaps have reminded him of the sensitivity of the subject and the danger of such information in the wrong hands: "*... it is not permitted to speak of it* [Nenya], a*nd Elrond could not do so* [at the Council]."[40].

Protection

Following the loss of Gandalf, Aragorn's role as Frodo's protector would have assumed an even greater importance than before. Boromir was starting to harass Frodo, by trying to get him to reveal the details of Galadriel's interrogation (*LotR* 2.7.358), then later (*LotR* 2.9.382, 388) by paddling close behind Aragorn's boat to peer at Frodo, and by questioning him eagerly when the winged Nazgûl flew over them. It could not have been accidental that Aragorn and Frodo travelled in the same boat after leaving Lothlórien.

During the episode when Frodo drew his sword after spotting Gollum following the boats down the river, Aragorn was instantly awake. They had both been aware of Gollum's pursuit since the journey through Moria, but had kept quiet about it. Aragorn undoubtedly acted in protective mode, keeping the knowledge to himself rather than worrying the others. Frodo perhaps was not a hundred percent certain about Gollum at first - after the Company's escape from Moria he had mentioned to Gimli that he thought they were being followed by something but the Dwarf had been unable to see or hear anything. When they spent the night in the flet in Lothlórien his suspicions were indeed confirmed but possibly at that stage he didn't want to add to Aragorn's worries, perceiving how much at a loss he was without Gandalf. Thus the protective instinct seems to have been mutual. Later, towards the end of the river journey (*LotR* 2.10.395), when Aragorn was uneasy and wakeful he got up and joined Frodo on his watch rather than leave him alone. Frodo returned the concern by querying Aragorn's wakefulness when it wasn't his watch.

After the scattering of the Company at Parth Galen when Aragorn was torn between trying to rescue Merry and Pippin and going after Frodo, his pledge to protect the latter was clearly uppermost in his mind especially as he may well have blamed himself for failing to notice Boromir slipping away from the Company. It was only when he accepted that Frodo's fate was no longer in his hands and that there was nothing he could actually have done to change things that he was able to reconcile himself to following the Orcs. They would not meet again until after the destruction of the Ring. Nevertheless, as later events would show, Aragorn maintained an awareness of time-scales and Frodo's probable whereabouts and was able to provide timely and crucial distraction for Sauron at the time when Frodo was most exposed.

*

The following table, chiefly based on dates in App B, gives a summary of events after Aragorn and Frodo were separated.

	ARAGORN	FRODO
Feb 26	BREAKING OF THE FELLOWSHIP	BREAKING OF THE FELLOWSHIP
Feb 27	Following Orcs.	Emyn Muil.
Feb 28	Following Orcs.	Emyn Muil.
Feb 29	Following Orcs.	Emyn Muil. Met Gollum.
Feb 30	Following Orcs. Meeting with Éomer.	Between Emyn Muil & Dead Marshes.
Mar 1	Reunion with Gandalf. To Edoras.	Dead Marshes.
Mar 2	Reached Edoras then rode west.	End of Dead Marshes.
Mar 3	Helm's Deep. Battle of the Hornburg.	Between Dead Marshes & the Morannon.
Mar 4	*En route* to Isengard.	Slag mounds near Morannon.

---

40. Op. cit. [1], *LotR* 2.7, p. 365.

Mar 5	Isengard. Acquired Palantír. Judged that Frodo would be getting near to Mordor. Sauron needed to be distracted.	Slag mounds near Morannon. Thought of Aragorn and Gandalf.
Mar 6	Used Palantír. Sauron now aware that an heir of Isildur existed wielding the reforged sword. Set out for Paths of the Dead.	Journeying down west side of Mountains of Shadow. More visible, & in danger of meeting enemy troops.
Mar 7	Reached entrance to Paths of the Dead.	Ithilien. Met Faramir. Faramir's Rangers reported no enemy movement. Sauron distracted.
Mar 8	Paths of the Dead & on to Stone of Erech. Formally summoned the Dead.	Faramir took his leave & told Frodo to take advantage of Sauron's inaction and hasten while he could.
Mar 9	*En route* for Pelargir.	Reached road to Minas Morgul. Sauron began his Darkness - because of Aragorn.
Mar 10	Approximately midway between the Paths of the Dead & Pelargir.	Ascending north wall of Morgul Vale. Witch-king led host out of Minas Morgul. Sensed presence of Ring but carried on marching.
Mar 11	In battle with forces from Umbar & Harad.	Climbed Stairs of Cirith Ungol.
Mar 12	Drove enemy towards Pelargir helped by Dead.	Stung by Shelob.
Mar 13	Captured Corsairs' fleet at Pelargir.	Captured by Orcs of Cirith Ungol. Sauron ignoring reports of intruders on the Stairs.
Mar 14	Sailing up the Anduin to the Pelennor Fields.	Rescued by Sam from Tower of Cirith Ungol.
Mar 15	Battle of the Pelennor Fields.	Began journey along the Morgai. Aware of wind changing causing Sauron's darkness to break too soon.
Mar 16	The Last Debate.	Struggling along Morgai. Sauron thinking only of Aragorn.
Mar 17	Gathering army.	Sauron now aware of intruders - via Shagrat.
Mar 18-24	Heading towards Morgul Vale with army, then to the Morannon.	To Isenmouthe with Orc army, then escaped from Orcs & went east along Barad-dûr road before turning south across plain of Gorgoroth towards Mount Doom. Sauron distracted due to Aragorn & army.
Mar 25	**DESTRUCTION OF RING**	**DESTRUCTION OF RING**

These events will now be discussed.

As shown in the table, between February 26th and March 5th Aragorn had more than enough to occupy him physically and mentally, with the pursuit of the Orcs, the meeting with Éomer, the reunion with Gandalf, then the Battle of the Hornburg and its aftermath - including the journey to Isengard and being present at Gandalf's parley with Saruman on the afternoon of March 5th. On this same date Frodo was in hiding in the slag mounds near the Morannon and his thoughts turned to Aragorn, (and to Gandalf whom he would have assumed to be dead), wondering what to make of Gollum's alternative way into Mordor (*LotR* 4.3.644). Around this time also, the Palantír would have been thrown out of Orthanc by Gríma. By that night it was in the possession of Aragorn (*LotR* 3.11.594). It was at this point that Aragorn knew what he had to do to keep Sauron's attention away from Frodo and his mission. As he would say later at the Last Debate (*LotR* 5.9.879), he believed that the Palantír had come to him for the purpose of revealing himself to Sauron, especially as it was ten days since Frodo had started to head east - the implication being that Frodo would probably have been close to Mordor by then - as indeed is verified in the table. Aragorn used the Palantír early the following morning as Frodo was starting to journey down the west side of the Mountains of Shadow and was thus more exposed than he had been hitherto. Sauron's shock at finding that an heir of Isildur existed rendered him oblivious to the danger at his borders, with all his attention now being concentrated on Aragorn whom he presumed to have the Ring. Thus Frodo was able to travel in comparative safety following his departure from Henneth Annûn due to Sauron's brooding and initial inaction. Then on March 10th the departure of Sauron's army from Minas Morgul under the leadership of the Witch-king coincided with Frodo's climb up the north wall of the Morgul Vale. The Witch-king sensed his presence and possibly that of the Ring also, but continued on his way because "*... at his great Master's bidding he must march with war into the West.*"[41]. That is, Sauron's reaction to Aragorn was such that it took precedence in the Witch-king's mind over his uneasiness about the threat in the Morgul Vale. At the same time Frodo was fighting the urge to put on the Ring by taking hold of the Phial of Galadriel: a collaboration between Aragorn and Frodo (and Galadriel). Aragorn's distraction of Sauron continued - by his actions in battle and by the shock engendered by his revelation of himself. As Shagrat and Gorbag complained (*LotR* 4.10.738), Sauron seemed to be oblivious to reports of intruders on the Stairs of Cirith Ungol. Although by March 16th a search was being made for Frodo along the Morgai it had not been instigated by Sauron but by the Nazgûl in charge of Cirith Ungol (*LotR* 6.2.925). Even when Shagrat took Frodo's mithril shirt to Barad-dûr thus leaving Sauron in no doubt about the presence of intruders Frodo was still able to escape from the Orcs, travel east on the Barad-dûr road and then turn south across the plain of Gorgoroth towards Mount Doom. In *LotR* 6.3.938 we are told that Frodo, at the end of his tether and just desperate to get to the mountain, was no longer bothered about concealment, but this didn't matter any more because of Sauron's brooding and the movement of the Army of the West towards the Morannon - both caused by Aragorn. It was not until Frodo put on the Ring that Sauron realised the truth.

During all this time since their separation Frodo and Aragorn had been striving in parallel, consciously on Aragorn's part, unconsciously on Frodo's. The "*dark roads*" which they had to travel had been first referred to by Aragorn on Cerin Amroth in recognition of their shared suffering to come. This final stage of their struggle was the most crucial part of their alliance, even though they were miles apart with Frodo suspecting that some or all of his former companions were dead (as implied by his conversation with Faramir in *LotR* 4.5.668 on learning of Boromir's fate). In spite of their physical separation there were strange similarities between their journeys, behaviour and experiences:
- Both of them believed that they had made the wrong choices at Parth Galen. Frodo, struggling to find a way through the Emyn Muil and bewailing the fact that he had delayed the parting from his companions, declared, "*All my choices have proved ill*"[42], echoing Aragorn's "*All that I have done today has gone amiss*"[43] after the death of Boromir and his words to Legolas and Gimli in Rohan, "*You give the choice to an ill chooser. Since we passed through the Argonath my choices have gone amiss.*"[44].
- They both had momentous encounters *en route* which would prove to be highly beneficial to them, Aragorn with Éomer and Frodo with Faramir.
- They both underwent apparent transformation at crucial stages in their journey. Aragorn appeared as a regal and impressive figure on revealing his identity to Éomer (*LotR* 3.2.433) while Frodo, during his taming of Sméagol, seemed to be "*... a tall stern shadow, a mighty lord...*"[45]. The result for Aragorn was winning Éomer's friendship and esteem, for Frodo it established a relationship whereby Sméagol was to guide him through the Dead Marshes and thence to Mordor. Aragorn had also shown himself to Sauron in the Palantír as having "*a stern and kingly face*"[46].
- Both recognised the role of fate in their journeys. At Parth Galen Aragorn came to realise that Frodo's fate was not in his hands and that it was not for him to urge a particular action on the Hobbit. As mentioned above, Frodo recognised that he and Sam were "*... meant to go together*" to Mordor, and in the Emyn Muil he told Sam, "*It's my doom, I think, to go to that Shadow yonder, so that a way will be found.*"[47].
- Following on from the previous point: since it was Frodo's doom to go to Mordor he had been willing - indeed intending, before Sam caught up with him - to go there alone. Likewise Aragorn was prepared

---

41. Op. cit. [1], *LotR* 4.8, p. 707.
42. Op. cit., *LotR* 4.1, p. 604.
43. Op. cit., *LotR* 3.1, p. 414.
44. Op. cit., *LotR* 3.2, p. 426.
45. Op. cit., *LotR* 4.1, p. 618.
46. Op. cit., *LotR* 6.2, p. 923.
47. Op. cit., *LotR* 4.1, p. 604.

to go through the Paths of the Dead alone if necessary because it had been prophesied that he was to take that route.

The culmination of Aragorn's pledge to save Frodo was the exhausting and long-drawn-out process of healing him from the effects of his ordeal (*LotR* 6.4.952, 956). This took all Aragorn's power and Frodo did not awake from his healing sleep until April 8th, the day when he and Sam were honoured on the Field of Cormallen. At Parth Galen, when he had made the decision to go to Mordor alone, Frodo had realised that Aragorn yearned for Minas Tirith. He had also seen him transformed into a regal figure at the Argonath. However at Cormallen he did not become aware of the identity of the King he was about to be presented to - the King who had healed him - until he actually drew close enough to recognise Aragorn. At that point he broke with ceremony and ran to meet him. Aragorn's humility in kneeling before the two Hobbits, seating them on his throne and praising them to the gathered crowd left no doubt as to his respect for them and his recognition of their deeds and suffering. This attitude was further emphasised at his coronation by his decision to have Frodo bring the crown to him in token of his role as Ring-bearer.

At the end of *LotR* 6.5.972 Frodo finally came to perceive the relationship between Aragorn and Arwen and to understand the nature of the secret event at which Aragorn wanted the company of his friends. In keeping with the spiritual side of his nature Frodo was struck with wonder at the sight of Arwen, the Evenstar of her people, and felt that with her arrival the night would no longer be full of fear but "*... beautiful and blessed*"[48]. In *LotR* 6.6.974-5 the last recorded conversation between Aragorn and Frodo, at which Arwen was also present, sheds considerable light on the closeness between them:

- Aragorn called Frodo "*dearest friend*".
- Although he understood his desire to go back to the Shire he stressed that there would always be a welcome for him in all the lands of the West.
- He also gave him (and the other Hobbits) permanent freedom of the realm of Gondor (confirming the original pronouncement by Faramir in Ithilien).
- He offered him whatever gifts he wanted, though recognising that no gift could be worthy of his deeds.
- He wanted the Hobbits to be attired as princes when they travelled home.

It was at this point that Arwen offered Frodo the chance to sail into the West in her place if he found he was unable to achieve peace and healing in Middle-earth. She then gave him her white gem to wear round his neck to help him when troubled by his memories. It was observed by the Shire-folk that Frodo "*wore always a white jewel on a chain that he often would finger*"[49] - the Ring had been replaced by Arwen's jewel. Her words as she gave the gift ("*... wear this now in memory of Elfstone and Evenstar with whom your life has been woven!*"[50]) emphasised the bond between Frodo, Aragorn and herself and signified continuing protection of Frodo. They also perhaps implied - by the phrase "*in memory*" - that no further meetings would take place between them after Frodo's return to his home. Aragorn would have understood the significance of Arwen's gifts and must have known he wouldn't see Frodo again. On this assumption the parting at Dol Baran on August 22nd would have been their last one. Just over two years later Frodo rode to the Grey Havens on the same pony which had carried him back to the Shire from Minas Tirith (*LotR* 6.9.1027). It had been renamed "Strider" as a final gesture to the memory of his friend and protector. There is no reference to the pony returning to the Shire with Sam, Merry and Pippin. Did he go in the ship with Frodo, as Shadowfax apparently did with Gandalf according to the unused Epilogue to *LotR* (*HoM-e* IX[51])? Tolkien's letter to Miss A. P. Northey of January 19th 1965 perhaps implies that this was not the case, as Shadowfax had immortal blood [he was descended from the

---

48. Op. cit. [1], *LotR* 6.5, p. 972.
49. Op. cit., *LotR* 6.9, p. 1025.
50. Op. cit., *LotR* 6.6, p. 975.
51. C. Tolkien (ed.), *The History of Middle-earth*, vol. IX, *Sauron Defeated*, London HarperColllins Publishers, 2002, first published in Great Britain by HarperCollins Publishers 1992, *HoM-e* IX Part 1, Chapter 11, p. 123.

horses of the Vala Oromë] and was thus, like Gandalf, "*going home*".[52]

As I suggested in Chapter 2.3, did Aragorn witness the events at the Grey Havens in the Palantír of Minas Tirith?

*

Aragorn's direct involvement with Frodo began with the disappearance of Gandalf in the summer of TA 3018. His role as protector and helper was established immediately, even before they actually met. Once Frodo had placed his trust in Aragorn in Bree their relationship never looked back. It continued after the formation of the Fellowship, becoming increasingly important after the loss of Gandalf. Following the breaking of the Fellowship the two of them became engaged in their joint final struggle to destroy the Ring. Aragorn's healing brought Frodo back from his "dark road" and Arwen's gift of a sojourn in the Undying Lands enabled him to die in peace when the time came.

SAM GAMGEE

In a draft letter to Mrs. Eileen Elgar dated September 1963[53] Tolkien, accepting the fact that some of his readers found Sam irritating and even infuriating (as opposed to lovable and laughable), made a number of observations about him:

- He was "*... a more representative hobbit*" than the others who feature significantly in the story and thus possessed more of a quality which is referred to as "*vulgarity*".[54]
- Vulgarity is then defined as "*... a mental myopia which is proud of itself, a smugness (in varying degrees) and cock-sureness, and a readiness to measure and sum up all things from a limited experience, largely enshrined in sententious traditional 'wisdom'.*"[55]
- He is described as "*deep down a little conceited*"[56] but with his conceit being transformed by his devotion to Frodo and relating solely to his service and loyalty to his master.
- This loyalty, devotion and service had an ingredient of "*pride and possessiveness*" - which Tolkien regarded as "*probably inevitable*" in such a relationship.[57]

These observations are of great relevance in a study of the early stages of the relationship between Sam and Aragorn.

Sam was the only one of the four Hobbits who still withheld his trust from Aragorn when the party left Bree. This was partly because of his limited outlook and his suspicion of anyone outside the Shire and/or of a different race (with the notable exception of the Elves). According to *LotR* 1.3.72 Sam had never been further than twenty miles from Hobbiton. Also in *LotR* 1.1.22 his Gaffer and his next-door neighbour Daddy Twofoot considered the Hobbits of Buckland to be "*queer*" just because they lived on the other side of the Brandywine next to the Old Forest and did supposedly unnatural things like boating. As a "*more representative hobbit*" Sam would have generally shared their views, despite the fact that both he and the Gaffer obviously trusted Frodo (who was half-Brandybuck) and that Sam himself never seemed to have a problem relating to Merry Brandybuck. He had never seen "*Big People*" and was accordingly very wary of them - as became apparent in Bree where he suggested trying to find lodgings with some of the Hobbits there rather than stay in the Prancing Pony with Men. However because of his friendship with Bilbo and Frodo he believed in the existence of Elves (unlike most of his contemporaries) and longed to meet them.

The pursuit of the Hobbits by the Nazgûl was an additional factor which delayed Sam's acceptance of

---

52. H. Carpenter (ed.), *The Letters of J.R.R. Tolkien*, with the assistance of Christopher Tolkien, London, HarperCollins Publishers, 1995. First published in Great Britain by George Allen & Unwin, 1981. Letter. 268, p. 354.
53. Op. cit., Letter 246, pp. 325-333.
54. Op. cit., Letter 246, p. 329.
55. Op. cit., Letter 246, p. 329.
56. Op. cit., Letter 246, p. 329.
57. Op. cit., Letter 246, p. 329.

Aragorn. In *LotR* 1.9.152, on arrival at Bree Sam was struggling to cope with his first encounter with Men and their tall houses - so much so that he pictured black horses in the yard of the inn and imagined Black Riders looking out of the windows. He tended to equate Big People with Black Riders, and the fact that Aragorn, with his height, sinister appearance, dark hair and hooded cloak, probably bore a considerable superficial resemblance to the Nazgûl can only have made a trusting relationship between the pair even more problematical.

Sam's attitude to Aragorn was also influenced by his self-appointed role as Frodo's protector following the meeting with Gildor Inglorion's party of Elves in the Woody End. He had been suspicious of Farmer Maggot at first, even though Pippin knew him as a friend, because the farmer had once beaten Frodo for a youthful misdemeanour. Much later in the story he would be mistrustful of Faramir who, in a desperately perilous situation, needed to cross-question the two members of a previously unencountered species who had turned up in his land, in order to decide whether they posed a danger or not. Ironically Aragorn too, of course, had as his main aim the protection of Frodo. Ironically again, Sam's mistrust of Aragorn, due largely to his determination to protect his master, actually made Frodo's situation far more dangerous, especially when coupled with Barliman Butterbur's attitude. If Frodo had actually heeded Sam's doubts about Aragorn the Hobbits would have been unlikely even to survive the night in Bree as they would have slept in their bedrooms instead of in the parlour.

*

I now follow the development of the interactions between Aragorn and Sam from the first meeting in Bree as far as the party's arrival in Rivendell as narrated in *LotR* 1.9-1.12.

In the common-room at the inn Aragorn's warning to Frodo to "*... stop your young friends from talking too much*"[58] clearly related to Sam as well as Pippin (Merry was not present) as both of them were feeling sufficiently at home to start chatting to the local Hobbits about the doings of the Shire. Although in the event it was Pippin who overstepped the mark by talking about Bilbo's farewell party, Aragorn seemed to regard them both as a potential risk from listening to them. Up to this point it was only Frodo who had had any contact with Aragorn - it wasn't until they were all back in the parlour, having been followed by him, that Sam and Pippin seemed to become aware of the stranger.

Initially it was Frodo who conducted the conversation, with Sam remaining quiet until Aragorn referred indirectly to the Ring as "*... a secret that concerned me and my friends*"[59], at which point both Frodo and Sam immediately reacted, with Frodo merely rising to his feet, but Sam jumping up with a scowl. Frodo calmed down on being reassured by Aragorn, already starting to trust him and actually querying the innkeeper's motives rather than Aragorn's. There was no further indication of Sam's feelings until after Aragorn's involuntary display of pain and fear while talking of the Nazgûl, followed by his appeal to them to accept him as their guide. While Frodo was trying to decide what to do Sam broke in, urging his master forcefully not to give his trust, his main reason apparently being that Aragorn came from the Wild, "*... and I never heard no good of such folk.*"[60]. This is a good example of Sam's "*readiness to measure and sum up all things from a limited experience*" quoted from Letter 246 above.

At this point in the proceedings, Butterbur arrived with Gandalf's letter which put Frodo's (and Pippin's) doubts to rest. Sam, however, still could not bring himself to give his trust, and his tack now changed. He accepted that Gandalf had a friend who fitted Aragorn's description, was known as Strider and was really called Aragorn, but he now cast doubts on whether they were talking to the real Strider or to a "*play-acting spy*" who had "*done in the real Strider and took his clothes.*".[61]

With his gift of perception and his ability to empathise with others Aragorn would certainly have understood that Sam was acting as he was, principally out of concern for Frodo and also partly from ignorance and inexperience. His first recorded words spoken directly to Sam, "*... you are a stout fellow ...*"[62], showed his

---

58. Op. cit. [1], *LotR* 1.9, p. 157.
59. Op. cit., *LotR* 1.10, p. 164.
60. Op. cit., *LotR* 1.10, p. 165.
61. Op. cit., *LotR* 1.10, p. 171.
62. Op. cit., *LotR* 1.10, p. 171.

recognition of Sam's courage. He then used a combination of shock tactics (pretending to be interested in the Ring and making the point that he was strong enough to take it from them and kill them there and then if he wanted to) and gentleness (with his pledge to give his life to save them if necessary). Finally he produced the broken sword, specifically showing it to Sam with the remark that it wasn't much use but explaining that the time was approaching when it would be reforged. This policy of giving information to Sam to try and win his confidence would be used again. When Sam made no reply Aragorn took the opportunity to assume his compliance, perhaps with some irony: "*... with Sam's permission we will call that settled.*"[63]. As would become apparent in the days to come, Aragorn had not yet succeeded in gaining Sam's trust, only in subduing his opposition sufficiently to enable his own acceptance as the Hobbits' guide. This had been essential for everybody's sake.

During the next nineteen days the level of Sam's trust would fluctuate continually, with Aragorn remaining consistently tolerant of his doubts and doing his utmost to calm them.

After they left Bree there appear to have been no further objections from Sam for a while. The Hobbits enjoyed the woodland journey under Aragorn's guidance, they all suffered the marshes together and Sam recited a poem about Gil-galad. However he became mistrustful again after the Nazgûl were spotted from Weathertop, impatiently suggesting to "*Mr. Strider*" that they had better "*clear out quick*".[64] When Aragorn came to the decision that there was nowhere else to go which would prove any safer he specifically addressed his reply to Sam. Sam's mistrust increased at Aragorn's decision to light a fire to try and frighten the Nazgûl off, recognising that such a course of action would also actually draw the Nazgûl's attention to them. Maybe Aragorn's admission of his own carelessness on the top of the hill, due to his anxiety about Gandalf, also increased Sam's wariness - he would have been less empathetic than Frodo to Aragorn's own fears and worries. There was no indication of the other Hobbits doubting their guide, and as the evening wore on they all became engrossed in the stories he told them, with Sam in particular begging for tales about the Elves.

After the wounding of Frodo by the Lord of the Nazgûl things became more precarious again and when Aragorn returned to the scene after searching the area to see if the Nazgûl were still around Sam actually drew his sword on him. After reassuring Sam that he was not a Nazgûl, or in league with them, Aragorn gave Merry and Pippin the task of heating water then took Sam aside for a private talk:
- He spoke of his surprise that only five of the Nazgûl had been present, concluding that they had not expected to be resisted.
- He anticipated that they would return another night, as they believed that Frodo's wound would subdue him to their will.
- He then urged a tearful Sam not to despair and emphasised the necessity of trusting him.
- He gave his opinion that Frodo was proving to be tougher and more resistant than he had expected.
- He promised to do all he could to help and heal him.
- As he hurried off to search for athelas he charged Sam with guarding Frodo.

This episode showed that Aragorn was going to great lengths to win Sam's trust. He displayed patience and gentleness as he reassured Sam that he was not connected with the Nazgûl. He could see his own similarity to the Black Riders and understood Sam's fears. Again he tried to tackle Sam's doubts by sharing information with him, confiding his thoughts and concerns, and leaving Sam in no doubt as to the seriousness of the general situation but at the same time trying to keep his spirits up. In addition his insistent "*You must trust me now*"[65] had more the semblance of an order than a statement, thus providing the necessary firmness in the circumstances. Having one member of their company refusing to trust the leader could only increase their danger. [What if Sam had actually wounded Aragorn instead of merely drawing his sword?] Aragorn's charge to Sam to guard Frodo showed that he recognised and respected Sam's role as Frodo's protector.

There was an undoubted improvement in their relationship from this point. When the companions had to take to the road again after five days of trudging through the pathless lands to the south of it, Sam went with

---
63. Op. cit. [1], *LotR* 1.10, p. 171.
64. Op. cit., *LotR* 1.11, p. 189.
65. Op. cit., *LotR* 1.12, p. 198.

Aragorn to check the road for signs of other travellers. Later he appealed to him for information about Frodo's wound - perhaps trying to comply with Aragorn's instruction to trust him.

The relaxing meal in the sunshine by the stone Trolls a further five days later at which Sam performed his Troll song had all the signs of a gathering of friends who gelled with each other. It was later that day that they met Glorfindel who took over from Aragorn and organised their safe flight to the Bruinen Ford.

During his recovery in Rivendell Frodo told Gandalf that he did not think that Sam had completely trusted Aragorn until the meeting with Glorfindel. There was no glaringly obvious change in Sam's attitude at that meeting - indeed he angrily protested against the Elf's insistence that they must continue their journey through the night, declaring that Frodo needed to rest, though this was only because he initially failed to realise that continuing was now their only option. In retrospect, however, it is easy to see why this encounter finally won Sam over: Glorfindel was an Elf; he had come from Rivendell specifically to help them; he obviously trusted and respected Aragorn and he was the first person to actually address him by his proper name - thus proving that he was "*the real Strider*" to quote Gandalf's letter to Frodo. As Gandalf told Frodo, "*He* [Sam] *has no more doubts now*"[66]. Frodo expressed his relief, on account of his own affection and regard for Aragorn and his wish for someone as loyal as Sam to share these feelings.

*

During the journey of the Fellowship from Rivendell to Parth Galen there are only a few specific references to the relationship between Aragorn and Sam:

- Aragorn joined Sam on his watch in Eregion due to concern about the unusual silence in the place, and when the flock of crows flew over he pulled Sam into the shelter of a bush to try and escape detection (*LotR* 2.3.285).
- After the Company's escape from Moria Aragorn tended the head wound Sam had suffered during the fight with the Orcs and expressed relief that it wasn't infected (*LotR* 2.6.335-6).
- On leaving Lothlórien by river it was natural that Sam should be in the same boat as Aragorn and Frodo (*LotR* 2.8.372).
- During one of his night watches on the river journey Sam spotted Gollum and alerted Frodo. It was Sam who suggested that they should not trouble Strider (and the others) until the morning. Perhaps as their relationship improved he had become more aware of Aragorn's own troubles (*LotR* 2.9.383).
- Later, on their eighth day on the river, Sam gave the first warning that they were dangerously close to the Rapids of Sarn Gebir. He was making up for his lack of expertise in boating by taking his role as lookout seriously, thus probably preventing a disaster by his early awareness of the danger (*LotR* 2.9.385).
- During the passage through the Argonath there seemed to be no real indication that Sam was aware of Aragorn's brief transformation into the image of a returning king even though he was in the same boat (*LotR* 2.9.393). Was this due to the lack of the more spiritual rapport which existed between Frodo and Aragorn, or simply because he was too frightened to notice?

Much more significant interaction between Sam and Aragorn took place at Parth Galen when Frodo had asked for time alone to decide his next move (*LotR* 2.10.396). The rest of the Company (minus Boromir who had slipped off to follow Frodo) sat wondering what his decision would be, trying to work out whether he would choose to go to Mordor and if so whether they should try to stop him or decide who should accompany him. Aragorn, understanding Sam's devotion to his master, knew that he would not be able to bear being parted from Frodo - hence he would have to be one of the ones who went to Mordor if the Company were to split up. It was Sam's analysis of what was going on in Frodo's mind which provided the answer to their uncertainties. He realised that Frodo knew he must go to Mordor, but couldn't quite "screw up" the courage to start off. He also understood Frodo's intention of going alone, not wishing to take any of his friends into such danger. Aragorn must have felt that he ought to have been capable himself of reading Frodo's mind at this time. Perhaps his own

---

66. Op. cit. [1], *LotR* 2.1, p. 220.

troubles had dulled his usual perception and perhaps he felt shamed that it had been Sam - a servant and "*a more representative hobbit*" - who had realised the truth. Nevertheless he wholeheartedly gave Sam the credit and respect for his wisdom: "*I believe you speak more wisely than any of us, Sam*"[67]. Later, after making his decision to follow the Orcs (*LotR* 3.1.419), he would reiterate to Legolas and Gimli that Sam had been right in his assessment of Frodo's intentions.

When the Company panicked after Boromir's return realising that Frodo had been missing for possibly an hour, it was Sam who was the first to run off, ignoring Aragorn's orders. When Aragorn caught him up on Amon Hen he again disobeyed him, failing to remain with him, and taking matters into his own hands by heading for the river where he assumed Frodo was. He might no longer have any doubts about Aragorn, now regarding him as a respected guide, but everything was subordinated to his determination to find Frodo at this point.

*

Sam and Aragorn would not meet again until after the destruction of the Ring, but there are a couple of episodes in the narrative which link them even though they were miles apart:
- In conversation with Faramir (*LotR* 4.5.679-80) Sam waxed lyrical about Galadriel and told Faramir he would need to get hold of Aragorn or Bilbo to sing and write poetry about her. He clearly appreciated Aragorn's musical and literary abilities (perhaps remembering him helping Bilbo to write the song about Eärendil in Rivendell). He also told Faramir of his belief that people took their own peril with them into Lothlórien. He had clearly been influenced in this by Aragorn who had sternly told Boromir, "*There is in her [Galadriel] and in this land no evil, unless a man bring it hither himself.*"[68]
- In *LotR* 6.1.897, while in Cirith Ungol, Sam thought of the rest of the Company and wondered if they were also thinking of him and Frodo. This was March 14th and Aragorn was sailing from Pelargir - obviously thinking of Frodo and Sam as all his actions since the Palantír confrontation had been aimed at diverting Sauron's attention from the Hobbits as well as defeating him in battle. The following day Sam sensed the change in the wind direction, to the south, blowing Aragorn's ships up the Anduin and causing Sauron's darkness to break up.

*

As described in *LotR* 6.4 Frodo and Sam were reunited with Aragorn after their rescue from Mount Doom, though they were unaware of it during the time when Aragorn was actually healing and tending them. When Sam awoke from his long sleep Gandalf told him that the King now awaited him. Sam's reply ("*The King? What king, and who is he?*"[69]) and later his exclamation on the Field of Cormallen ("*Well, if this isn't the crown of all! Strider, or I'm still asleep!*"[70]) showed that he had absolutely no idea of the true significance of Aragorn's struggles. Throughout the narrative, the four Hobbits often used the name "Strider" when addressing and referring to Aragorn, with Sam and Pippin doing so most consistently. It is interesting that although Sam always called Frodo "Mr Frodo" and also used "Mr" when addressing Merry, Pippin and sometimes Gandalf, he nearly always called Aragorn simply "Strider". Was that an indication of Aragorn's ability to empathise and gel with anyone with whom he came into contact? Or was it actually that Sam didn't think of Aragorn as a noble figure? Whatever the reason, Aragorn understood Sam's surprise at Cormallen, gently recalling his difficulty in trusting him in Bree and happily accepting being addressed as "Strider" even though he was now King Elessar. At his humble act of kneeling before them Sam, still seeing himself as very much the servant, felt surprise and great confusion, and was probably still in shock at the revelation of Aragorn's true identity. However Aragorn, as at Parth Galen, had no hesitation in recognising Sam's achievements, declaring that his (and Frodo's) road had been the darkest one. Sam's lowly station in life was irrelevant as far as he was concerned.

---

67. Op. cit. [1], *LotR* 2.10, p. 403.
68. Op. cit., *LotR* 2.7, p. 358.
69. Op. cit., *LotR* 6.4, p. 952.
70. Op. cit., *LotR* 6.4, p. 953.

Sam, along with his three Hobbit companions, attended Aragorn's coronation and wedding and parted from him at Dol Baran on August 22nd TA 3019. None of these episodes related specifically to the relationship between Sam and Aragorn. However, when the Hobbits and Gandalf stopped off in Bree on their return journey they were reunited with Barliman Butterbur. It was Sam who informed the innkeeper of the new King's appreciation of the beer at the Prancing Pony, and Sam who finally told Barliman of the King's identity, thus indicating that all his doubts of Strider were put to rest.

*

There is plenty of evidence in the *LotR* Appendices of Sam's continuing relationship with Aragorn and of the honour in which he and his family were held. For example App A.I.iii.1044 states that when the King came North Sam often stayed at the royal residence in Annúminas. App B.1097 lists several notable events during the first thirty or so years of the Fourth Age. Sam was made a Counsellor of the North Kingdom and his daughter Elanor (his eldest child) was appointed as one of Arwen's maids of honour. This latter event occurred during Aragorn's stay in the North in FA 16. Also during this visit the Star of the Dúnedain was given to Sam. In *UT* 3.1 Note 33 Christopher Tolkien discusses the nature of this award, which is assumed by Robert Foster[71] to be the Elendilmir, the jewel which was worn instead of a crown by the Kings of Arnor. Christopher Tolkien states, *"The Elendilmir is called by several names: the Star of Elendil, the Star of the North, the Star of the North-kingdom; and the Star of the Dúnedain ... is assumed to be yet another.... I have found no other reference to it; but it seems to me to be almost certain that it was not ..."*[72] Personally I have always assumed that "Star of the Dúnedain" referred to the star-shaped brooches worn by the Northern Dúnedain: for example by the Grey Company in *LotR* 5.2.778; by Aragorn when he served in Gondor and Rohan as a young man (which led to him being called "Thorongil", the Eagle of the Star); and by Aragorn when Frodo saw him talking to Arwen in Rivendell (*LotR* 2.1.238). This interpretation was later confirmed by Christopher Tolkien in *HoM-e* VIII 3.iv Note 8[73] following feedback from readers of *UT*.

App B.1097 also states that during FA 22 Sam, Rose and Elanor spent a year in Gondor. In FA 32, a year after Elanor's marriage to Fastred of Greenholm on the Far Downs, the Westmarch (which extended from the Far Downs to the Tower Hills) became part of the Shire by gift of the King. The birth of Elanor's and Fastred's son two years later provided another indication of the mutual regard between Aragorn and Sam's family as the child was named Elfstan - clearly in honour of the King.

The Epilogue to *LotR* (*HoM-e* IX 1.xi.121-133) sheds further light on relations between Aragorn and Sam's family in the years after the War of the Ring. Tolkien originally intended to end *LotR* with this Epilogue, rather than with Sam's return to Bag End after seeing the Ring-bearers sail from the Grey Havens. In the event he was persuaded not to use it, but regretted it, as hinted in a letter to Naomi Mitchison of 25th April 1954[74] and one to Katherine Farrer of 24th October 1955[75]. The version which Tolkien prepared for publication records a conversation between Sam and Elanor fifteen years into the Fourth Age, in which they talked of the imminent visit of King Elessar to his North Kingdom and studied a letter from the King stating his wish to meet the whole family, with each member being mentioned by name and also given an Elvish version of his/her name (*HoM-e* IX 1.xi.126). Sam's Elvish name was *"Master Perhael who should be called Panthael"*, that is *"Samwise who ought to be called Fullwise"*. See App F.1136 which states that the name Samwise means "half-wise", "simple" or "stay-at-home". Aragorn's alternative name was a further indication of his respect for Sam's wisdom.

*

---

71. 'Star of the Dúnedain' in R. Foster, *The Complete Guide to Middle-earth: From The Hobbit to The Silmarillion*, London, HarperCollins Publishers, 1993, p. 364. "Star of the Dúnedain" and "Star of Elendil" entries both relevant. First published in Great Britain by George Allen & Unwin 1978.
72. Op. cit. [23], *UT* 3.1, p. 369.
73 C. Tolkien (ed.), *The History of Middle-earth*, vol. VIII, *The War of the Ring*, London HarperColllins Publishers, 2002, first published in Great Britain by Unwin Hyman 1990, *HoM-e* VIII Part 3, Chapter 4, Note 8, p. 309.
74. Op. cit. [52], Letter 144, p. 179.
75. Op. cit., Letter 173, p. 227.

The rest of the conversation between Elanor and Sam related to various matters recorded in the Red Book (which Sam had been reading aloud to his family). A particular speech of Elanor's led me to compare the Sam/Rose relationship with the Aragorn/Arwen one. To set the scene I now quote two passages from *LotR* followed by the contents of Elanor's speech. I have emphasised the three occurrences of the word "treasure":

- "*Lady, you know all my desire, and long held in keeping the only **treasure** that I seek.*"[76] Aragorn's words to Galadriel in the gift-giving scene in Lothlórien.
- "*Kinsman, farewell! May your doom be other than mine, and your **treasure** remain with you to the end!*"[77] Celeborn's words to Aragorn as he took his leave of him near the Gap of Rohan.
- In the Epilogue Elanor explained to her father that she had recently come to understand what Celeborn had meant when he said goodbye to the King: "*He knew that Lady Arwen would stay, but that Galadriel would leave him. I think it was very sad for him.. And for you, dear Sam-dad. For your **treasure** went too. I am glad Frodo of the Ring saw me, but I wish I could remember seeing him.*"[78]
- Sam then interrupted to mention that Frodo had hinted that he too might be able to sail West at some point.
- Elanor then continued thus: "*... when you're tired, you will go, Sam-dad ....Then I shall go with you. I shall not part with you, like Arwen did with Elrond.*"[79]

The message here is that Celeborn's treasure was Galadriel, Aragorn's treasure was Arwen, but Sam's treasure was Frodo, not Rose. Also Elanor's assertion that she would not be parted from her father seems to imply criticism of Arwen. Admittedly she was only fifteen when she said this and when Sam did eventually sail Elanor stayed in Middle-earth having been married to Fastred for thirty-one years by that time (App B.1097). In his comments on the Epilogue Christopher Tolkien refers to a résumé of *LotR* which his father wrote for Milton Waldman in the early 1950s. In it Tolkien referred to Sam having to "*... choose between love of master and of wife.*"[80] This is apparent throughout *LotR* as well as in the Epilogue:

- Sam was in a romantic relationship with Rose right from the start of the story, but he did not suggest marriage because he knew he would be accompanying Frodo on his mission. Thus he put Frodo first. This is clear from *LotR* 6.9 when he told Frodo that Rose had not liked him going off but because Sam "*hadn't spoken*"[81] she couldn't say so. When he returned she accused him of having wasted a year.
- In *LotR* 6.3 at the point when Sam and Frodo had escaped from the Orc army they had been forced to march with, Sam accepted that his job was now to accompany Frodo to Mount Doom and then die with him. He thought of the Shire: "*... I would dearly like to see Bywater again, and Rosie Cotton and her brothers, and the Gaffer and Marigold and all.*"[82] Admittedly Rose was mentioned first, but was still included in the same sentence as her brothers and Sam's father and sister - there was no particular indication that she meant a great deal more to Sam than the others.
- Even after his return to the Shire Sam could not decide between moving into Bag End with Frodo, and marrying Rose, the problem being resolved by Frodo himself who suggested they made Bag End their marital home - where Rose presumably had to minister to Frodo as well as to Sam. (We are told "*... there was not a hobbit in the Shire that was looked after with such care.*"[83])
- As Frodo prepared to sail from the Grey Havens Sam acknowledged that he couldn't go with him. Frodo agreed but qualified his answer with "*Not yet anyway*" and then suggested that Sam's time might come as he had also been a Ring-bearer, albeit briefly. He then went on to say, "*You cannot be always torn in two. You will have to be one and whole, for many years. You have so much to enjoy and to be, and to do.*"[84]. Frodo was softening Sam's grief at their parting by hinting that he might be able to sail

---

76. Op. cit. [1], *LotR* 2.8, p. 375.
77. Op. cit., *LotR* 6.6, p. 982.
78. Op. cit. [51], *HoM-e* IX Part 1, Chapter 11, pp. 124-125.
79. Op. cit., *HoM-e* IX Part 1, Chapter 11, p. 125.
80. Op. cit., *HoM-e* IX Part 1, Chapter 11, pp. 129, 132.
81. Op. cit. [1], *LotR* 6.9, p. 1024.
82. Op. cit., *LotR* 6.3, p. 934.
83. Op. cit., *LotR* 6.9, p. 1025.
84. Op. cit., *LotR* 6.9, p. 1029.

- To return to the Epilogue: after the conversation with Elanor, Sam spoke affectionately to Rose recalling the day he returned to the Shire [from taking leave of Frodo at the Grey Havens] *"To the most belovedest place in all the world. To my Rose and my garden."*[85] However he was deceiving her because immediately afterwards he heard *"the sigh and murmur of the Sea..."*[86] Although he didn't sail until Rose died it is difficult to avoid the conclusion that in the end Frodo came first. Assuming that mortals had a life after death, Rose was again being forced to wait for a reunion with Sam because of Frodo: a wait determined by however long it took for Frodo to achieve sufficient healing in the Undying Lands to be able to die in peace.
- The Epilogue also illustrates the close relationship between Sam and Elanor. As she left the room at the end of their conversation, to go to bed *"... it seemed to Sam that the fire burned low at her going."*[87] His great rapport with her was because she resembled an Elf. In the Milton Waldman résumé Tolkien stated: *"... in her* [Elanor] *all his love and longing for Elves is resolved and satisfied."*[88] In addition Frodo's hint that Sam might be able to sail one day was a secret between Sam and Elanor, the implication being that Rose was unaware of this plan. She seems to me to have been a definite third in Sam's affections behind Frodo and Elanor.

This is all in stark contrast to the relationship between Aragorn and Arwen:
- Unlike Sam's, Aragorn's wedding was postponed because he had no choice - Elrond had expressly forbidden the marriage until/unless he regained his two kingdoms.
- Aragorn and Arwen came first for each other as witnessed by Arwen's courageous sacrifice: *"I will cleave to you, Dúnadan, and turn from the Twilight"*[89] (spoken at their troth-plighting), and Aragorn's unswerving devotion: *"... from that hour he loved Arwen Undómiel..."*[90] (referring to their first meeting in Rivendell when Aragorn was twenty).
- Arwen was the one person above everyone else who kept Aragorn going and kept him hoping. Although there is no mistaking the affection, joy and male-bonding when Halbarad turned up in Rohan he was bringing the standard made by Arwen and an intimate message from her (*LotR* 5.2.774-5). It was that which rendered Aragorn silent with emotion as he looked to the north. There was no doubt where his priorities lay.
- Aragorn's words to the Hobbits just prior to Arwen's arrival for their wedding were a further illustration of his feelings: *"A day draws near that I have looked for in all the years of my manhood..."*[91].
- Immediately after their wedding we are told that *"... the tale of their long waiting and labours was come to fulfilment."*[92].
- Arwen had sacrificed her immortality for Aragorn and no-one else. When it came to the choice between her father and Aragorn, she chose the man she had fallen in love with. This choice was made when they plighted their troth and she abode by her decision.
- When Rose died Sam sailed to be with Frodo. As Aragorn died he acknowledged his and Arwen's mutual pain: *"... there is no comfort for such pain within the circles of the world"*[93], but exhorted her to believe that they would be together again after death.
- After his death Arwen lost all interest in life and in her family, living alone in a deserted Lothlórien until her own death just under a year later.

Tolkien's own comparison of the two relationships is given in a letter written to Milton Waldman around

---

85. Op. [51], *HoM-e* IX Part 1, Chapter 11, p. 128.
86. Op. cit., *HoM-e* IX Part 1, Chapter 11, p. 128.
87. Op. cit., *HoM-e* IX Part 1, Chapter 11, p. 127.
88. Op. cit., *HoM-e* IX Part 1, Chapter 11, p. 132.
89. Op. cit. [1], App A.I.v, p. 1061.
90. Op. cit., App A.I.v, p. 1058.
91. Op. cit., *LotR* 6.5, p. 970.
92. Op. cit., *LotR* 6.5, p. 973.
93. Op. cit., App A.I.v, p. 1062.

1951[94] where he referred to: *"the highest love-story, that of Aragorn and Arwen"* and *"the simple 'rustic' love of Sam and his Rosie"*.

MERRY BRANDYBUCK

On the evening of the Hobbits' arrival in Bree, Merry decided **not** to join his companions in the common-room at the Prancing Pony. Instead he declared his intention of sitting by the fire in the parlour for a while and then going out for some fresh air. While engaged in the latter pursuit he had an encounter with two Nazgûl. It was only after escaping and fleeing back to the inn that he met Aragorn - that is, **after** the unfortunate incident in the common-room and **after** Frodo, Sam and Pippin had agreed to accept the Ranger as their guide.

Merry was the most practical, organised and street-wise of the four Hobbits. He had masterminded the conspiracy to accompany Frodo from the Shire, and had organised the house move to Crickhollow along with the plan for the departure from there: ponies, food, the decoy role of Fatty Bolger, etc. His home was actually just outside the Shire on the other side of the Brandywine and some of his family had been to Bree before - in fact it was even said that the Brandybucks had some Bree-blood (*LotR* 1.9.150). Therefore he didn't have Sam's inbuilt distrust of everyone who lived beyond the immediate area around Hobbiton. He had been into the Old Forest, he appreciated Maggot's wisdom and knowledge and he also knew about boats (as he would tell Celeborn in *LotR* 2.8.367-8 as the Fellowship prepared for their departure from Lothlórien). Perhaps these characteristics, along with Frodo's evident trust in this *"friend of Gandalf's"*[95], led to Merry trusting Aragorn straightaway. There never seems to have been any question of him doubting Strider - he just accepted his inclusion in their party as a *fait accompli*. Maybe his relatives who had been to Bree had encountered Rangers and described them to Merry. On Aragorn's part his first impression of Merry was of someone who was stout-hearted but foolish, for daring to follow a Nazgûl.

While studying the relationship between Aragorn and Merry I came to the conclusion that it was influenced by two things which happened to Merry before they actually met.

The first was the imprisonment of the Hobbits in the Barrow-downs the previous day by one of the wights which had been roused by the Lord of the Nazgûl (*UT* 3.4.ii.451). Merry - alone of the Hobbits - had experienced a strange awareness of past events. In App A.I.iii.1041 it is suggested that this particular barrow was the burial place of the last Prince of the old northern sub-kingdom of Cardolan who had been killed in TA 1409. While in his trance Merry had experienced the attack on the Dúnedain of Cardolan by the Men of Carn Dûm and had felt the spear which pierced the Prince's heart. The knife which Tom Bombadil subsequently gave him from the hoard in the barrow had been forged by the Dúnedain during the early days of the Third Age when the North Kingdom still existed and its chief enemy was the Witch-king of Angmar (the Lord of the Nazgûl) whose power was centred on Carn Dûm. This knife was the one which Merry would use to help Éowyn slay the Witch-king at the Battle of the Pelennor Fields.

The second incident was Merry's encounter with two of the Nazgûl (already mentioned), during which he felt drawn into following them, then lost consciousness and dreamed that he was falling into deep water. On coming to himself again when roused by Nob, he panicked and fled back to the inn, where he and Nob recounted the details of the attack to the other Hobbits and Aragorn. From his description Aragorn realised that he had been briefly affected by the Black Breath. [Regarding Merry's dream during the first night at Tom Bombadil's, involving water spreading round the house: I am unable to decide whether this was linked to the experience of being trapped in the willow on the bank of the Withywindle, or whether it was in anticipation of the incident with the Nazgûl, or of the flooding of Isengard by the Ents.]

Thus before becoming acquainted with Aragorn, Merry had already had close encounters with the Nazgûl and the Dúnedain. He was being drawn into the ancient prophecy made by Glorfindel that the Witch-king would not be slain by the hand of man. His experience of facing the Nazgûl and his glimpse of the history of Cardolan could be seen as preparation for his part in the destruction of the being whose mission had been to eliminate Aragorn's people and the line of Isildur in particular. This is the context in which I set my analysis of

---

94. Op. cit. [52], Letter 131, pp. 160-1.
95. Op. cit. [1], *LotR* 1.10, p. 173.

the interactions and relationship between Aragorn and Merry. I feel that Merry would have had a subconscious affinity with Aragorn, and with hindsight it is possible to pick up hints of Aragorn's foresight concerning what was to happen to Merry.

From Aragorn's point of view, witnessing the effect of the Nazgûl encounter on Merry gave him some insight into how Hobbits - as opposed to Men - reacted in such circumstances. He had already seen how Harry Goatleaf the gatekeeper had been left *"white and shaking"*[96] when questioned by them and realised how Bill Ferny and some of the travellers from the South were in danger of being driven to evil deeds by them (*LotR* 1.10.174). When Merry explained that it wasn't either courage or foolishness which had made him follow the Nazgûl, but that he had been drawn by them, Aragorn perhaps gained a better understanding of why Frodo had put on the Ring in the common-room. This would also make him appreciate the compulsion Frodo would face on Weathertop. The wonder he felt at Merry's stout heart showed that he was already starting to learn about Hobbit toughness and unexpectedly strong resistance to the Nazgûl - which would also be displayed by Frodo after his wound.

During the journey to Rivendell Merry showed a practical, enquiring approach:
- Accompanying Aragorn and Frodo to the top of Weathertop.
- Being involved in the interpretation of the signs left by Gandalf.
- Asking questions about: the distance to Rivendell; Gil-galad; the names of the rivers; the Nazgûl's senses.
- Having the presence of mind to throw himself to the ground when the Nazgûl were spotted on the East Road.

Significantly it was Merry who was reminded of the Barrow-downs as they walked along the path on the west side of the Weather Hills, and enquired whether there were also barrows there. His experience of Dúnadan burial grounds had clearly made a strong impression on him.

After the attack on Frodo on Weathertop Aragorn gave Merry and Pippin the tasks of heating water, bathing Frodo's wound and keeping him warm while he himself went off to find some athelas. During the following days he demonstrated his appreciation of Merry, taking him with him to reconnoitre the hills north of the East Road. The two of them also investigated the Trolls' cave together. When Merry remonstrated about the effect on Frodo of their exhausting journey, declaring that they could not go any further on that particular day Aragorn took his comments on board while also stressing the need for speed given that there was nothing more he could do to help Frodo where they were. With Frodo injured, Merry was the obvious person for Aragorn to consult, being more detached and knowledgeable than Sam and clearly more mature than Pippin. Aragorn respected Merry's qualities and Merry was confident enough in Aragorn's company to speak his mind.

*

Moving on to the journey of the Fellowship, there are few specific references to the relationship between Aragorn and Merry. However, in *LotR* 2.3.284, it is perhaps significant that Merry was the one who perceived Aragorn's unease at the unusual silence in Eregion and drew attention to it, thus prompting Gandalf to question Aragorn and make the decision to lie low and put out the fire. (Later it was Merry's question about the words on the doors of Moria that eventually put Gandalf on the right track to finding the password.) It was Aragorn who carried Merry during the rescue from the snowdrift on Caradhras. During the journey through the mines, on arrival at the guardroom, Merry and Pippin both charged forward in their relief at finding somewhere more sheltered than the open passageways, causing Gandalf to hold them back so he could investigate first. When the Company entered the room and saw the well in the middle of the floor, Aragorn gave a stark warning to Merry about what might have happened if Gandalf hadn't intervened, emphasising the wisdom of letting the guide go first. He was very much in the role of mentor here indicating that the Hobbits' action had been unwise, perhaps directing his warning to Merry as the elder and more responsible of the two Hobbits who should

---

96. Op. cit. [1], *LotR* 1.10, p. 174.

perhaps - based on past behaviour - have known better. Later, after a temporary victory over the attacking Orcs, the Fellowship seized the opportunity to escape from the Chamber of Mazarbul. In a dramatic scene Aragorn rescued three of the Hobbits simultaneously, picking up the injured Frodo and pushing Merry and Pippin in front of him. (Sam was presumably at Frodo's side anyway).

Between Lothlórien and Parth Galen most of the journey was by boat, with Merry and Pippin travelling with Boromir. *LotR* 2.9.382 describes their uneasiness at Boromir's restlessness, muttering, nail-biting and excessive closeness to Aragorn's boat. Meanwhile Aragorn's mind was being increasingly taken over by a number of concerns: the need to protect Frodo; Boromir's behaviour; Gollum's continuing pursuit of the Company; and the question of which route to choose when the time came to leave the river. Thus there are few direct references to Merry during this part of the narrative. However in *LotR* 2.10.403 he made it very clear that he did not agree with Aragorn's proposed splitting of the Company - which involved Merry and Pippin going to Minas Tirith with Boromir, instead of to Mordor with Frodo. Merry insisted that he had always intended to go wherever Frodo went. However, unlike Sam at this juncture, he failed to realise that Frodo was set on going to Mordor alone and believed that the solution to the problem was to dissuade him from choosing that route.

At Parth Galen Aragorn's initial aim in the panic of the scattering of the Company was to try and find Frodo at all costs, giving Boromir the task of looking after Merry and Pippin: "*Go after those two young hobbits, and guard them at the least, even if you cannot find Frodo.*"[97]. However after the death of Boromir and the evident departure of Frodo and Sam to Mordor, he came to believe that his priority was to follow the Orcs and try to rescue Merry and Pippin, realising that if he went after Frodo and Sam he would be abandoning the younger Hobbits to "*torment and death*"[98]. Note that his emphasis, now and during the ensuing chase, was on saving the Hobbits from being tortured rather than on the danger of them being forced to disclose information if they were taken to Isengard - though the latter was obviously an issue of vital importance. Merry and Pippin were his friends and they were vulnerable, and the need to save them from being cruelly treated was uppermost in his mind (as it was in the minds of Legolas and Gimli too). At the meeting with Éomer Aragorn stated, in answer to Éomer's plea to accompany him there and then to the battle at the Fords of Isen, that he could not desert his friends [i.e. Merry and Pippin] while there was still a slim chance of finding them. Later, when it was clear that the Hobbits had entered Fangorn, Aragorn still would not give up looking for them even though it seemed likely that the only thing they would be able to do if they found them was join them in starving to death. By this stage the Orcs who had captured them were dead so there was now no chance of them being taken to Isengard and interrogated - the search was purely one for lost friends. At the same time as their friends were seeking them, Merry and Pippin were watching the gathering of the Ents for Entmoot and we are told that "*A great longing came over them for the faces and voices of their companions, especially for Frodo and Sam, **and for Strider.***"[99] [My emphasis]. It was abundantly clear that Merry and Pippin returned Aragorn's feelings of friendship. All four Hobbit relationships with Aragorn had come a long way since the first meeting at the Prancing Pony.

To return briefly to the scattering of the Fellowship at Parth Galen, much is made of Aragorn's search of the Orc bodies which resulted in the finding of the knives carried by Merry and Pippin (the ones taken from the Barrow-downs). The blades were shaped like leaves and were damasked in gold and red and Aragorn described them as being "*... work of Westernesse, wound about with spells for the bane of Mordor*"[100] - hence the Orcs' rejection of them. As he took them to keep them safe he stated that he was "*... hoping against hope, to give them back.*"[101]. Did he feel that Merry in particular was destined to do some significant deed with his knife? Or was Aragorn himself being bound into the prophecy as the means whereby Merry would recover this crucial weapon?

*

---

97. Op. cit. [1], *LotR* 2.10, p. 405.
98. Op. cit., *LotR* 3.1, p. 419.
99. Op. cit., *LotR* 3.4, p. 482.
100. Op. cit., *LotR* 3.1, p. 415.
101. Op. cit., *LotR* 3.1, p. 415.

On March 5th 3019, nine days after the breaking of the Fellowship, Aragorn, Legolas and Gimli were reunited with Merry and Pippin in the ruins of Isengard (*LotR* 3.8-3.9.556-575). Legolas and Gimli were torn between fury and delight, with Gimli exchanging friendly insults with the Hobbits. Aragorn remained silent until Gandalf and Théoden's party had gone for their meal. His first words displayed a casual under-reaction: "*Well, well! The hunt is over, and we meet again at last, where none of us ever thought to come*"[102]. He was taking his cue from the Hobbits and following their mood - as were Legolas and Gimli. One can't doubt the depth of his feelings: the relief after the strain of the fruitless chase and the torment of possibly having made the wrong decision, etc. As I suggested in Chapter 1.5 he was now perhaps guarding against a too-emotional reaction which might have embarrassed both him and the Hobbits. All he wanted to do was share a relaxing meal with them and hear their story.

After eating, Merry suggested that they should light up their pipes and pretend "*... that we are all back safe at Bree again, or in Rivendell.*"[103] The Hobbits hadn't actually been, or felt, very safe when they were in Bree, but Merry's words were a recognition that they had in fact been in good hands with Strider looking after them. When Legolas then declared his intention of going out into the fresh air Aragorn suggested that they all join him so that they could "*... sit on the edge of ruin and talk...*"[104] (quoting Gandalf's recent remark to Théoden about the tendency of Hobbits to sit and chat about trivia in the most serious and dangerous situations). This reunion at Isengard provides one of the best examples of how well Aragorn gelled with the Hobbits. It was at this point that he returned the Barrow-down knives to Merry and Pippin with the words, "*Here are some treasures that you let fall*"[105]. Merry exclaimed that he had never expected to see them again and then spoke of how he had marked a few Orcs with his own knife and how Uglúk had thrown them away as if they had burned him. Thus we are given a further hint about the significant properties of these Dúnadan-made knives.

Throughout the ensuing conversation, as the companions told all their news, Merry displayed his usual lively interest in what was going on, for example remarking on the Orc/Man hybrids who resembled the squint-eyed southerner in Bree and expressing his ideas about Saruman. He was more on Aragorn's wavelength intellectually than Pippin or Sam. Although his interpretations were not always correct, he thought things through and tried to understand events in context. That evening, after the parley with Saruman, he plied Gandalf with questions as they rode away from Isengard together on Shadowfax. When Gandalf ran out of patience, declaring that he had too many pressing things on his mind, Merry replied, "*All right, I'll tackle Strider by the camp-fire: he's less testy.*"[106]. He obviously saw Aragorn as a more patient and amenable source of information - at least at that particular moment...

While the party were camped on the slopes of Dol Baran that night Pippin looked into the Palantír of Orthanc. He had become obsessed with it after running to retrieve it when Gríma threw it out of the window. This action would bring about a momentous change in both Merry's and Aragorn's situation. Subsequent events would reveal the depth of their affection and regard for each other, and Merry's affinity with Aragorn was to become much more obvious and intense. I will now examine their relationship during the period between the parley with Saruman and the end of the War of the Ring. I will also consider the relevance of Merry's role in the slaying of the Witch-king and of his relationship with Éowyn.

LotR 3.11 describes a short conversation between Aragorn and Merry which, contrary to Merry's remark to Gandalf just quoted, shows both of them as being distinctly "*testy*". Merry complained, somewhat sarcastically, to Aragorn about the disturbed night and then tactlessly envied Pippin's luck in now being allowed to ride with Gandalf, instead of punished for his misdemeanour by being "*... turned into a stone himself to stand here for ever as a warning.*"[107]. Aragorn, undoubtedly stung by the implication that Merry would prefer to be riding with Gandalf, reprimanded him for his criticism of Pippin, pointing out that he himself might have done worse if he had been the one to inadvertently come into contact with the Palantír. He then returned the sarcasm by telling Merry that he feared it was now his luck to ride with him and ordered him sharply to go and get ready

---

102. Op. cit. [1], *LotR* 3.9, p. 560.
103. Op. cit., *LotR* 3.9, p.562.
104. Op. cit., *LotR* 3.9, p. 563.
105. Op. cit., *LotR* 3.9, p. 564.
106. Op. cit., *LotR* 3.11, p. 589.
107. Op. cit., *LotR* 3.11, p. 596.

immediately.

Clearly both were under great stress at this point thus accounting for their manner to each other. Aragorn now had the Palantír in his possession and was planning to use it to reveal himself to Sauron. It was a momentous time for him, the culmination of a sixty-eight year struggle. Also, having been reunited with Gandalf against all the odds only four days earlier, he was now parted from him again. As for Merry he was separated from Pippin for the first time, and in addition Pippin's behaviour with the Palantír must have alarmed him greatly. While Gandalf had been questioning Pippin, Merry had felt unable to look at his friend, although everyone else had been watching the interrogation intently. He was out of his depth, he didn't fully understand what was going on, he felt that he was a burden on everyone else and he was afraid he would be left behind rather than included in the action. As with Aragorn, **his** time was also drawing near, but unlike Aragorn he was not aware of the fact.

In *LotR* 5.2.773 as the four remaining members of the Fellowship (Aragorn, Merry, Legolas and Gimli) prepared to ride to Helm's Deep with Théoden's party, Merry would have overheard Aragorn's remarks about the way ahead being dark before him and not being able to see the road. He expressed some of his own anxiety to his companions, begging not to be left behind and treated like a piece of baggage. He also referred to Théoden's invitation of the previous day to sit with him and talk of the Shire, prompting Aragorn to say, "*... your road lies with him, I think, Merry*", then adding "*But do not look for mirth at the ending*", thus throwing doubt on what the future held for Théoden.[108] The implication of these remarks seemed to be that Aragorn had some foreknowledge of what lay ahead for Merry (and Théoden). Merry could hardly have failed to notice Aragorn's pessimism and uncertainty.

Their journey was soon interrupted by the arrival of Halbarad's company and Elrond's sons. Merry was riding on the same horse as Aragorn and so would have witnessed the strong emotions generated by the delivery of Arwen's message and gift, and the advice from Elrohir concerning the Paths of the Dead. Such was the depth of Aragorn's feelings that he "*spoke no more while the night's journey lasted*"[109]. Merry's awareness of his frame of mind was clear from his behaviour on waking the following morning when his first words to Legolas and Gimli were, "*Where is Aragorn?*"[110] Aragorn's appearance when he finally emerged from the Hornburg after using the Palantír was clearly a shock to everyone, but the reader sees it chiefly from Merry's viewpoint. He "*... had eyes only for Aragorn, so startling was the change that he saw in him...*"[111] Aragorn's condition must have been deeply worrying for Merry in the same way as Gandalf's condition would have been for Aragorn after the Wizard's initial struggle with the Balrog at the Chamber of Mazarbul. During the Fellowship's journey after the loss of Gandalf, most of the travelling had been by boat, with Merry and Pippin being in the company of Boromir. Merry may therefore have been less aware of the strains on Aragorn at that stage than, say, Frodo who was in the boat with him, or Legolas and Gimli who witnessed his breakdown at Parth Galen. Now, being in close contact with him, Merry would have been shocked to see him so exhausted and apparently vulnerable. He also heard the ensuing discussion between Aragorn, Théoden and Éomer which resulted in Aragorn declaring his decision to go through the Paths of the Dead. Aragorn's farewell to him immediately afterwards ("*I leave you in good hands... Legolas and Gimli will still hunt with me, I hope; but we shall not forget you*"[112]) showed his relief that Merry was with Théoden and was also an attempt to alleviate Merry's anxiety about being left behind. Merry - puzzled, depressed and missing Pippin - could say no more than "*Good-bye!*".

Merry's perplexity was due to lack of information as to what was troubling Aragorn. It is clear from the text of *LotR* 5.2.773-9 that he could not have known that Aragorn had used the Palantír and indeed knew very little about the Palantíri in general, not having had the advantage of a detailed chat with Gandalf on the subject - as Pippin would have on the way to Minas Tirith (*LotR* 3.11.597-9). Legolas and Gimli could not have told him what Aragorn had done because they themselves didn't know until he confided in them in the dining-hall **after** Merry's departure. There was also no reason why Merry would have known that Aragorn even had the Stone in his possession. When Gandalf had put Pippin back into his bed following his misdemeanour, Merry had

---

108. Op. cit. [1], *LotR* 5.2, p. 773.
109. Op. cit., *LotR* 5.2, p. 775.
110. Op. cit., *LotR* 5.2, p. 776.
111. Op. cit., *LotR* 5.2, p. 778.
112. Op. cit., *LotR* 5.2, p. 779.

stayed with his friend so was not present when Aragorn took possession of it. In addition Gandalf had given instructions that its whereabouts should be a secret - particularly from Pippin, and by implication also from Merry who presumably thought that Gandalf had taken it to Minas Tirith with him. He would also have been ignorant of the history and nature of the Paths of the Dead and of the prophecies concerning them. All he had to go on was Elrohir's sinister message from Elrond suggesting that route - which had clearly unsettled Aragorn - and later the reactions of those present when Aragorn informed Théoden and Éomer that he intended to go that way. Théoden trembled and stated that the living could not enter the Paths, but then decided that maybe Aragorn was actually fated to do so. The Riders nearby turned pale, while Éomer assumed that he would not see Aragorn again.

There were several reasons why Aragorn would not have put Merry in the picture:
- He was carrying out Gandalf's instructions to keep the whereabouts of the Palantír secret.
- It was clear to Aragorn that Merry's role was **not** to accompany him through the Paths of the Dead, because of his foresight and because Merry had already been taken into Théoden's service as his esquire.
- The trauma of the Palantír confrontation was very fresh in his mind at this point and he probably felt unable to talk about it - he would not find it easy to tell Legolas and Gimli.
- He would surely not have wanted to burden Merry with the details anyway, or with the subject of the journey through the Paths of the Dead which would be a terrifying undertaking even for the Dúnedain. The Hobbit had his own ordeals to face. Thus there was a strong element of protectiveness towards Merry in his behaviour.

As Merry rode off with Théoden and Éomer, a short, but very revealing, conversation took place between Aragorn and Halbarad. Aragorn said to his kinsman, "*There go three that I love, and the smallest not the least. He knows not to what end he rides; yet if he knew, he still would go on.*"[113]. This speech clearly illustrated the depth of Aragorn's feelings and respect for Merry. It also raised again the issue of his foresight. He **did** know to what end Merry rode.

LotR 5.3.796-7 leaves us in no doubt of the extreme concern Merry felt for Aragorn. As Théoden's party reached Dunharrow they were greeted by Éowyn. Although the reader has seen a fair amount of Éowyn by this point in the story, this was actually Merry's first meeting with her and he suspected at once that she had been crying. The ensuing conversation between her, Théoden and Éomer confirmed that Aragorn had entered the Paths of the Dead to the obvious consternation of all three, with Éomer and Éowyn believing that he was lost for good. Later, during their meal together, Merry finally plucked up the courage to ask his companions about the Paths of the Dead and why Aragorn had gone that way. We are told that the question was "*tormenting*"[114] him. The information he obtained can have done nothing to calm his fears:
- Théoden's tale of Baldor daring to enter the Paths and subsequently being lost.
- Éowyn's mention of rumours that the Dead were gathering as if for a tryst.
- Éomer's view that Merry himself, as Aragorn's friend, would have been more likely to know his purpose.
- Éowyn's comment that she thought that Aragorn was "*Fey ... and like one whom the Dead call*"[115].
- Éomer's lament that a "*fey mood*"[116] should fall on Aragorn in such a crucial time in the war.
- Even Théoden's suggestion that maybe Aragorn was fated to survive the Paths would not have been of any comfort as he **too** believed that he would not see Aragorn again.

Thus Merry's torment on Aragorn's behalf would have continued, his spirits becoming further depressed by Théoden's refusal to let him ride into battle. However, it was after this refusal that Éowyn took him to the armoury tent and provided him with helmet, shield, leather jerkin, belt and knife telling him that she was equipping him for battle at Aragorn's request. This could be taken merely as a wise precaution even if

---
113. Op. cit. [1], *LotR* 5.2, p. 779.
114. Op. cit., *LotR* 5.3, p. 796.
115. Op. cit., *LotR* 5.3, p. 797.
116. Op. cit., *LotR* 5.3, p. 798.

Merry stayed behind in the refuge at Dunharrow. However in that case presumably Théoden himself would have ordered it. Given that the request came from Aragorn, and in the light of earlier hints of Aragorn's foreknowledge of Merry's role, it must surely be yet another example of this. Soon afterwards Merry would ride with the Rohirrim after all, sharing "Dernhelm's" horse and hidden by his companion's cloak.

At the Battle of the Pelennor Fields, as Aragorn sailed up the Anduin in the ships of the Corsairs, Merry carried out his allotted role, piercing the Witch-king in the back of the knee with the sword from the Barrow-downs, thereby disabling him sufficiently to allow Éowyn to strike the death-blow. The sword then "*... burned all away like a piece of wood.*"[117]. Thus the prophecy that the Witch-king would not be slain by the hand of man was fulfilled: "*So passed the sword of the Barrow-downs, work of Westernesse. But glad would he have been to know its fate who wrought it slowly long ago in the North-kingdom when the Dúnedain were young, and chief among their foes was the dread realm of Angmar and its sorcerer king.*"[118].

*

As recounted in *LotR* 5.8.868-71, Merry was reunited with Aragorn in the Houses of Healing that same evening, though he was unaware of it until Aragorn had recalled him from the death-like state brought on by such close contact with the Nazgûl. He had already done the same for Faramir and Éowyn. With the former he was healing someone previously unknown to him; with the latter the situation was delicate due to her unrequited love for him such that he had left the room prior to her regaining consciousness. However with Merry they were close friends who understood each other and for the purpose of this discussion the healing scene needs to be examined in detail.

The atmosphere was much more intimate, for example with Aragorn touching Merry's eyelids and passing his fingers through his hair, rather than the more formal touching, and kissing of the brow as with Faramir and Éowyn. He recognised that Merry's natural resilience and buoyancy would enable him to learn wisdom from his grief rather than be crushed by it. As the Hobbit regained consciousness his immediate request for supper and a pipe confirmed Aragorn's assessment of his personality! Merry then had second thoughts about the smoking as it would bring back memories of Théoden: his politeness, the promised chat about herb-lore which would now never take place and, most of all, their last encounter on the battlefield. Aragorn however encouraged him to go ahead and smoke, knowing that the good memories would help him to deal with his grief as opposed to bottling it up by avoiding thinking of Théoden.

Thus reassured Merry, addressing Aragorn as "Strider", jokingly asked him to provide the pipeweed since his own supply - which he facetiously referred to as "*Saruman's best*"[119] - had been lost with his pack. Aragorn replied in similar vein, declaring that he had not gone through the Paths of the Dead and across Gondor with fire and sword to bring herbs to a careless soldier who had lost his pack (all the while looking at Merry's pack which was by his bed). He then launched into a take-off of the over-talkative Warden of the Houses of Healing, but suddenly ended on a more serious note, drawing attention to his own famished and exhausted state. Merry's immediate reaction was to seize his hand and kiss it, apologising for his frivolity, showing concern for Aragorn's suffering ("*Go at once!*" [that is to eat/rest]) and acknowledging that, "*Ever since that night at Bree we have been a nuisance to you*". He went on to explain that, "*... it is the way of my people to use light words at such times and say less than they mean. We fear to say too much. It robs us of the right words when a jest is out of place.*" Aragorn answered, "*I know that well, or I would not deal with you in the same way. May the Shire live for ever unwithered!*".[120] He then kissed Merry before leaving him and Pippin together.

By kissing Aragorn's hand Merry was undoubtedly expressing gratitude and love/affection, as well as the concern and guilt already mentioned. The gesture also perhaps showed his recognition of Aragorn as the King with the healing hands, along with a realisation that "Strider" was no longer a suitable mode of address. During a conversation with Théoden, Éomer and Éowyn at Dunharrow, he had referred to Aragorn as "Strider" and

---

117. Op. cit. [1], *LotR* 5.8, p. 859.
118. Op. cit., *LotR* 5.6, p. 844.
119. Op. cit., *LotR* 5.8, p. 869.
120. Op. cit., *LotR* 5.8, p. 870.

then hastily changed it to "*the Lord Aragorn*"[121]. The hand-kissing can also be compared with Merry's offering of his service to Théoden in *LotR* 5.2.777, where he kissed the King's hand partly because he was suddenly filled with love for him. His similar gesture to Aragorn showed an even greater spontaneity.

Even leaving aside the traumas of war they had both endured, this acknowledgement of their emotions would have been essential for both of them. Merry must have been extremely relieved to see Aragorn alive as they had last met on the day of his Palantír confrontation with Sauron, and from listening to the talk among the Rohirrim about the Paths of the Dead and being aware of Aragorn's decision to go via that route, Merry may well have assumed that he would never see him again. His emotions at the time were such that he could not find the right words to respond to Aragorn when he took leave of him, being able to answer only "*Good-bye*". Note that Aragorn's arrival at the Pelennor Fields took place **after** the despatch of the Witch-king by which time Merry would have left the battle-field. Aragorn himself had lost Halbarad in the battle, had been very distressed at the state of Éowyn and had come close to losing Merry whom he clearly loved and respected. For both of them too there was the issue of their unexpressed feelings at the reunion in Isengard. I have commented earlier on Aragorn's casual reaction when he, Legolas and Gimli met the Hobbits again after their fruitless search. That episode too is a good example of the Shire-folk using "*light words at such times*" and fearing "*to say too much*", with Aragorn being aware of this and behaving in the same way himself. A further example of Merry's resilience was provided by Aragorn's instructions to the Warden of the Houses of Healing that the Hobbit would probably be fit enough to get up for a while the following day - as opposed to Faramir and Éowyn who would require a longer period of rest.

In *LotR* 5.9.873-8, during a brief reunion with Legolas and Gimli in the Houses of Healing, Merry finally received a detailed account of the journey through the Paths of the Dead.

While the relationship between Merry and Éowyn is largely outside the scope of this study, there are elements of it which **are** relevant and these will now be discussed. Merry first met Éowyn at Dunharrow when she came to greet Théoden on his arrival. The thing which most struck him was that she appeared to have been crying which didn't seem to fit with her stern expression. During the ensuing conversation and later during the evening-meal it became very clear that her distress was due to Aragorn having set out for the Paths of the Dead the previous morning. Merry must have perceived her uneasiness and grief - indeed these must have increased his own concern about Aragorn. It is also possible that he had some inkling of her feelings for Aragorn. Although it would not be until the confrontation with the Witch-king on the Pelennor Fields that he would realise who "Dernhelm" was we know that he was very struck by the face of the "young man" he had seen during the muster who had subsequently offered to take him into the battle, "*... the face of one without hope who goes in search of death.*"[122]. With hindsight he must have put two and two together so that when he and Faramir had their long talk in the Houses of Healing Faramir learnt "*more even than Merry put into words*"[123]. As a friend of Aragorn and as someone concerned for Éowyn Merry was uniquely suited to help Faramir understand the woman with whom he had fallen in love. Perhaps he also helped Faramir to know Aragorn better. He was a link between Aragorn, Éowyn and Faramir.

In *LotR* 5.10.883 as the Army of the West prepared to set off for the Morannon, Merry was overcome by shame at not being included. Sensing this and no doubt remembering Merry's worries about being left behind, Aragorn explained that he had no reason to feel ashamed, pointing out that he had already achieved something momentous in the war and helping him to realise that Pippin should now have his own chance to prove himself. In addition it was essential for Merry to carry on taking things easy after his ordeal. Thus here we see Aragorn as comforter, mentor and healer to his small friend.

Our last view of Merry and Aragorn together in the main narrative of *LotR* is at the feast on the Field of Cormallen where Merry was conspicuous in his role as King Éomer's esquire (*LotR* 6.4.955).

*

The *LotR* Appendices throw some light on later events and on the continuing relationship between the

---

121. Op. cit. [1], *LotR* 5.3, p. 797.
122. Op. cit., *LotR* 5.3, p. 803.
123. Op. cit., *LotR* 6.5, p. 961.

Shire, Rohan and Gondor. Merry in particular had strong connections with all three places. The Introduction to App A.1033 states that he (and Pippin) met Gimli many times in Rohan and Gondor, so he would obviously also have been in touch with both Aragorn and Éomer. In addition the Epilogue to *LotR* (*HoM-e* IX.1.xi.123) refers to Merry visiting Éowyn in Ithilien. Aragorn must have been glad, for Éowyn's sake, of their continuing friendship. App B.1097 records Merry becoming Master of Buckland twelve years into the Fourth Age (presumably on the death of his father) and being made a Counsellor of the North Kingdom by Aragorn two years later.

Merry's intellectual and literary activities, described in *LotR* Prologue.8-9, 14-15, were a significant feature of his life after the War of the Ring. He built up the library at Brandy Hall, actually writing some of the material himself, for example, *Herblore of the Shire*, and *Reckoning of Years* which was about the relation of the calendars of the Shire and Bree to those of Rivendell, Gondor and Rohan. However the library also contained many works on the history of Eriador and Rohan. The latter would have been due to Merry's position as a knight of Rohan, while the former may well have been inspired by a wish to record the history of Aragorn's North Kingdom since Merry himself had played such a decisive role in destroying that kingdom's greatest enemy. He was also involved in putting together *The Tale of Years* (i.e. *LotR* Appendix B) being committed enough to go to Rivendell, on more than one occasion, for assistance from Elladan and Elrohir and others who still remained there after Elrond's sailing.

In FA 64 when Merry was a hundred and two he received a message to say that Éomer wanted to see him. He and Pippin then passed their offices and property to their heirs and left the Shire permanently. They travelled first to Rohan where Merry was able to take farewell of the dying Éomer, then carried on to Gondor where they lived for the remainder of their lives. When they died they were laid in Rath Dínen with the great of Gondor and after Aragorn's death nearly sixty years later the two Hobbits were laid next to him. It is significant that, although he was officially a knight of Rohan, it was in Gondor with Aragorn that Merry chose to spend his last years. By the time he and Pippin died, only Legolas, Gimli and Faramir were still living out of those close to Aragorn during the War of the Ring.

The initial stages of the relationship between Aragorn and Merry were characterised by Aragorn's respect for Merry's "stout heart" and practical common-sense, and Merry's trust and confidence in Aragorn. However as events unfolded the relationship became much more intimate and intense, particularly after Merry's separation from Pippin. There is much emphasis in *LotR* 5.2.773-9, and 5.3.792, 796-7 on Merry's deep concern - almost verging on protectiveness - for Aragorn, starting from the point when Halbarad and Elrohir brought their messages from Rivendell, and greatly increased by Aragorn's sick and exhausted state after using the Palantír and his subsequent departure for the Paths of the Dead. None of the other Hobbits had ever seen him in such a condition. Merry's situation was similar to that of Legolas and Gimli who had witnessed Aragorn's collapse at Parth Galen and had formed an extremely close relationship with him as a result. Merry knew Aragorn's strength and powers of endurance, so he must have realised that he was under some dire stress to be so affected. Even after his return to consciousness in the Houses of Healing his concern was instantly to the fore again when he realised the depth of Aragorn's weariness. It was feelings such as these, in addition to his experience of helping to slay the Witch-king, which led to his greater maturity.

From Aragorn's point of view his regard developed into admiration and love. As a result of Merry's concern he seemed to open up more, both **about** Merry (as shown by his words to Halbarad quoted earlier) and **to** him (as shown during the healing). There were also the emotional implications of the soul-destroying and apparently fruitless search for Merry and Pippin and the subsequent relief of being reunited with them and finding them in good health and spirits. In addition Merry's pre-ordained role in the slaying of the Witch-king provided a subconscious link with Aragorn and his people. Regarding Aragorn's words to Halbarad concerning the Hobbits, "*And now our fates are woven together*"[124], the most natural interpretation is that they refer to Frodo's role, but they could equally well refer to Merry's.

To sum the relationship up: Merry cared for Aragorn greatly and the feeling was reciprocated.

---

124. Op. cit.[1], *LotR* 5.2, p. 780.

PIPPIN TOOK

Pippin, the youngest of Frodo's three companions, was also the one most likely to forget or underestimate the dangerous situation they were in. For example, when Frodo wanted to try and reduce the risk of further Nazgûl encounters by travelling to the Bucklebury Ferry across country rather than openly on the road, Pippin bewailed the fact that this would mean they wouldn't be able to stop for some beer at the Golden Perch. He was also the most likely to act impetuously without thinking of the possible consequences. Some of these actions seemed to be due to forces outside his control, such as visions or "sudden impulses". He also displayed inquisitiveness and awareness about anything apparently odd or magical. Examples of these traits will be emphasised in their context as, put together and with hindsight, they shed light on his relationship with Aragorn.

*

Pippin first came to Aragorn's notice in the inn at Bree (*LotR* 1.9.156-7) because of his unbridled chatter with the Bree-hobbits, first about the collapse of the Town Hole roof in Michel Delving leading to the mayor getting covered in chalk, and then about Bilbo's farewell party. Prompted by Aragorn's fixed stare at his young friend, Frodo realised that "*the ridiculous young Took*"[125] was drawing near to the point of Bilbo's "Disappearance". He was enjoying the attention, as well as the "*... Drink, fire and chance-meeting*"[126] (as Aragorn put it), and seemed oblivious to the danger. It was Frodo's fear that Pippin might even mention the Ring which led to his disastrous attempt to divert attention to himself instead. Any rebuke Aragorn may have been preparing for Pippin was no doubt forgotten by his need to tackle Frodo about his own behaviour which was "*Worse than anything your friends could have said!*"[127] Was Pippin's behaviour really down to the factors just mentioned though? Or was the Ring influencing him too, as well as Frodo?

When the three Hobbits went back to the parlour and found that Aragorn had followed them, Pippin, seeming undaunted, and unintimidated by the stranger's height and sinister appearance, challenged him boldly demanding to know who he was and what he wanted. He did however appear to trust him quite quickly. When Aragorn got to the point of asking the Hobbits to accept him as their guide and Sam spoke up urging Frodo not to give his trust, Pippin became ill at ease. Later his relief on reading Gandalf's letter was very plain.

The first time Pippin was cowed was when he underestimated the extent of Aragorn's travels and hardship by suggesting that they would all look like him after spending days in hedges and ditches. Aragorn erupted, making the point that his appearance was due to **years** - rather than days - of wandering in the Wild and telling Pippin that he would die before he got to that stage, "*unless you are made of sterner stuff than you look to be.*"[128]. He must have been frightened and exasperated at the increased danger of their situation due to Frodo's mishap, and Pippin's naïvety would have been the last straw. (He still had Sam's doubts to deal with too.) Perhaps Aragorn also felt that it was time Pippin was subdued and forced to start taking their predicament much more seriously, as it was clearly his careless conversation in the common-room which had prompted Frodo's unfortunate diversion. Although Aragorn was soon to find out that Hobbits **were** made of sterner stuff than they looked to be, there hadn't at this point been much evidence of it.

Pippin subsided after this incident and the next time he spoke to Aragorn was after the disappearance of their ponies during the Nazgûl attack on the inn in answer to his question as to how much supplies the Hobbits were prepared to carry on their backs. It was Pippin who answered first saying, "*As much as we must,*"[129] though we are told that his heart was sinking. He was undoubtedly reacting to Aragorn's comment just discussed; he didn't want Strider to think he was weak and he was perhaps waking up to the seriousness of their situation.

Once the five of them had left Bree, it was obvious that Pippin was at ease with Aragorn, engaging him in a light-hearted conversation about short-cuts. Later, though, he earned a mild rebuke during the conversation about Gil-galad by referring to Mordor by name rather too loudly for Aragorn's peace of mind. This wasn't

---

125. Op. cit. [1], *LotR* 1.9, p. 157.
126. Op. cit., *LotR* 1.9, p. 157.
127. Op. cit., *LotR* 1.9, p. 161.
128. Op. cit., *LotR* 1.10, p. 171.
129. Op. cit., *LotR* 1.11, p. 178.

an attempt to single out Pippin for mentoring however, as Frodo had also been reprimanded for joking about becoming a wraith if he became much thinner.

After the attack on Weathertop Aragorn instructed Pippin and Merry on how to care for Frodo while he went to find some athelas. This in itself would no doubt have helped to instil some sense of responsibility into Pippin, and the actual attack would certainly have made him appreciate the danger of the Black Riders. A week later the companions crossed to the north side of the East Road, having travelled south of it since the incident on Weathertop. They were now in the old sub-kingdom of Rhudaur which had been destroyed in TA 1409, and Aragorn spoke of the Men who used to live there who had come under the Witch-king's sway. At this point Pippin gave his first sign of curiosity concerning Aragorn's background enquiring as to where he learnt such tales. Five days later they reached the place where Bilbo and Thorin Oakenshield's company had encountered the Trolls seventy-seven years earlier. As they investigated the Troll-hole Pippin recognised it for what it was and wanted to get away quickly, but Aragorn, being aware of the details of Bilbo's journey, knew it was deserted. Pippin was still afraid because he hadn't realised they were at the site of Bilbo's encounter and in fact had never completely believed the story about the Trolls being turned to stone. [This seems slightly odd - one would perhaps think that a Hobbit with Took blood would be more, rather than less, susceptible to such a tale.] However he went on ahead with Merry anyway because he didn't want Aragorn to see his fear. He was still trying to show that he was made of "*sterner stuff*".

*

During the stay in Rivendell Pippin, still undaunted, was reprimanded by Gandalf for referring to Frodo as the Lord of the Ring, and argued forcefully with Elrond when he showed reluctance to include him and Merry in Frodo's party. Pippin's attitude and Gandalf's unexpected support overruled Elrond's counsel.

Although the Pippin who set out as one of the Fellowship was clearly more mature and more aware of the gravity of the undertaking, he still had some way to go. He failed to appreciate the potential danger of the crows which flew over Eregion while the Fellowship were there, being sceptical of Aragorn's insistence that the Company should move on quickly and avoid lighting fires: "*All because of a pack of crows!*"[130]. Along with Merry he pushed ahead into the guardroom in Moria, but instead of becoming more careful after Aragorn's warning about letting the guide go first, he became fascinated by the well there and yielded to a "*sudden impulse*"[131] which made him grope around for a stone and drop it in. However the emphasis here on fascination and "sudden impulse" seems to point to something more than just juvenile irresponsibility. The falling of the stone into the well almost certainly disturbed the Balrog thus leading to Gandalf's fall and forcing his companions to learn to manage without him.

Later as the company prepared to leave Lothlórien it was Pippin who asked the Elves if the cloaks they were giving them were magic. During the river journey, he shared Merry's unease at Boromir's restlessness, muttering, nail-biting and excessive closeness to Aragorn's boat, and also noticed a "*queer gleam*" in Boromir's eye as he "*peered forward gazing at Frodo.*".[132] His interest in the unusual seemed in keeping with his own tendency to exhibit odd behaviour. At Parth Galen Pippin, like Merry, disagreed with Aragorn's proposed splitting of the Company, and also believed that they should prevent Frodo going to Mordor. His insistent "*Stop him! Don't let him go!*"[133] seemed to trigger Aragorn's realisation that some stronger power was driving Frodo and they therefore had no business trying to influence him. As the Company panicked and scattered Pippin and Merry dashed off together.

*

As Pippin regained consciousness in an Orc camp he remembered that he and Merry had run off and

---

130. Op. cit. [1], *LotR* 2.3, p. 285.
131. Op. cit., *LotR* 3.4, p. 313.
132. Op. cit., *LotR* 2.9, p. 382.
133. Op. cit., *LotR* 2.10, p. 403.

taken no notice of *"old Strider"*. *"What had come over them?"*[134] he wondered, evidently realising that something uncanny had been going on as they would not normally have dreamed of disobeying Aragorn in an emergency situation. Strangely, now Aragorn and Pippin were separated, we have the clearest picture yet of an understanding between them with Pippin's unusual tendencies to the fore.

Pippin's initial thought in his predicament was of himself as a piece of luggage, and he hoped that *"... Strider or someone will come and claim us!"*[135] However he then felt that he should not hope for such a thing because that would *"... throw out all the plans."*[136]. Being unaware of the departure of Frodo and Sam alone he must have assumed that Aragorn had gone to Mordor with them. He was starting to think a bit more and wishing he had done so earlier. Like Frodo he had trusted to the competence of Gandalf and Aragorn and hadn't considered the possibility that he would have to manage without them - and even without Frodo himself. As he ran with the Orcs we are told that *"Every now and again there came into his mind **unbidden** a vision of the keen face of Strider bending over a dark trail, and running, running behind."*[137] Then *"A sudden thought **leaped** into Pippin's mind..."*[138] [My emphasis]. There is a clear indication that things were "happening" to him outside his control. That, combined with quick wits, initiative and an understanding of what signs a tracking Ranger would need, led him to run aside briefly from the trail, leaving some of his own footprints unmixed with those of the Orcs, and dropping his Lothlórien brooch as a further sign.

In the previous chapter (*LotR* 3.2) we have already read that Aragorn had found Pippin's brooch and footprints (he knew the prints were his because he was smaller than the other Hobbits). As he showed his find to Legolas and Gimli he said, *"Not idly do the leaves of Lórien fall"*[139]. He perceived exactly what was in Pippin's mind, and Pippin, though he felt that logically Aragorn would have accompanied Frodo to Mordor, knew subconsciously from his vision that he was actually following the Orcs. His perceptive powers showed again when it was he, not Merry, who sensed that the Mordor Orc Grishnákh knew - or guessed - about the Ring.

In *LotR* 3.4.482 while watching the Entmoot Pippin, as well as Merry, longed for the faces and voices of the rest of the Company - Frodo, Sam and Strider in particular. The reunion between Merry and Pippin, and Aragorn, Legolas and Gimli at Isengard (*LotR* 3.9.560-75) has already been discussed in some detail in the section on Merry, but some passages relating specifically to Pippin add extra nuances. After the companions had eaten they went outside to sit and talk. As Aragorn lay back, wrapping his cloak around him to cover the Rohan armour he was wearing, stretching out his legs and smoking, Pippin exclaimed, *"Look! Strider the Ranger has come back!"*[140]. By this stage of the narrative "Strider" was an affectionate nickname as far as the Hobbits were concerned, rather than something scornful and insulting as it had been when used in Bree. Aragorn's reply that *"He* [i.e. Strider] *has never been away"* reassured Pippin that their relationship was still on the same footing in spite of the mail-shirt, Aragorn's recent activities in battle and the esteem with which the Rohirrim regarded him. It was at this point that Pippin received his brooch and Barrow-down knife back. Aragorn praised his action in deliberately dropping the brooch to show the way - and to show that he was still alive: *"One who cannot cast away a treasure at need is in fetters."*[141].

In *LotR* 3.11.591-4, only a few hours after this relaxing scene of reunion, Pippin yielded to his urge to look into the Palantír of Orthanc. This is another example of a situation where his actions seemed to be at least partly due to forces outside his control. One of these forces must have been the Palantír itself due to its corruption by Sauron, but were there other forces - forces which were trying to get it back to its rightful owner? Pippin had been obsessed with it after saving it from falling into a pool. He couldn't sleep for thinking about it and he was desperate to ride with Gandalf (instead of Aragorn) the next day - presumably because he had the Stone and he wanted to ask him about it. When he took it from Gandalf that night as he slept he was *"Driven by some*

---

134. Op. cit. [1], *LotR* 3.3, p. 444.
135. Op. cit., *LotR* 3.3, p. 445.
136. Op. cit., *LotR* 3.3, p. 445.
137. Op. cit., *LotR* 3.3, p. 449.
138. Op. cit., *LotR* 3.3, p. 449.
139. Op. cit., *LotR* 3.2, p. 424.
140. Op. cit., *LotR* 3.9, p. 563.
141. Op. cit., *LotR* 3.9, p. 564.

impulse that he did not understand ..."[142] This impulse then led him on to actually look into it. Once Gandalf had established that fortunately Pippin had escaped being ensnared by Sauron, he told him, "*Wiser ones might have done worse in such a pass.*"[143] Thus we have another example of the strength of Hobbits. This must have been one of the considerations in Aragorn's mind when he subsequently asked how Pippin was. Although he would have been thankful that Pippin hadn't given away information about the Ring, he must also - in spite of Gandalf's reassurance - have been apprehensive wondering whether the Hobbit's escapade would affect his own intended use of the Stone. In the circumstances he must have been very relieved to see Pippin ride off with Gandalf, leaving **him** to travel with the more predictable and sensible Merry.

*

LotR 3.11.596-600 and 5.1.747-51 describe Pippin's ride to Minas Tirith during which Gandalf told him the history of the Palantíri as well as expressing his concern that Saruman and Gríma may have realised who Aragorn was, leading to the possibility of this information reaching Sauron through them. As the journey continued Pippin became drowsy and did not really listen to Gandalf's account of the customs of Gondor, though his curiosity was aroused when he saw the dead White Tree in the Court of the Fountain.

During his time in Minas Tirith Pippin made the acquaintance of Denethor and Faramir and in both cases saw their similarity to Aragorn though for different reasons. With Denethor he was expecting to see a resemblance to Boromir but the Steward's face with its noble bone structure, ivory skin and deep eyes reminded him more of Aragorn's. His first sight of Faramir made a profound impression on him as he realised that he was the sort of person men would follow anywhere out of love - indeed he felt that way himself and went on to name his first son after him. He saw that Faramir had "*an air of high nobility such as Aragorn at times revealed, less high perhaps, yet also less incalculable and remote...*"[144]. This leads one to wonder whether Pippin found Aragorn somewhat intimidating or unapproachable when he had that "*high nobility*" aura about him. Maybe, maybe not. He was certainly entirely at ease with him the next time they met on March 15th at the door of the Houses of Healing, delightedly addressing him as "Strider" in front of Éomer and Imrahil and declaring how "*splendid*" it was to see him. [Had he been encouraged by Aragorn's reassurance at Isengard that he was still the same old Strider?] He continued the conversation by saying, "*Do you know, I guessed it was you in the black ships. But they were all shouting 'corsairs' and wouldn't listen to me. How did you do it?*"[145]. Aragorn, laughing and taking Pippin's hand, seemed equally pleased at this unexpected meeting. This conversation is highly significant in a study of the relationship between Aragorn and Pippin. To understand it fully it is necessary first to backtrack a little and examine the events of the previous ten days, along with various conversations which took place between Gandalf, Pippin and Denethor.

Aragorn and Pippin had last been together at Dol Baran on the night of March 5th-6th just before Pippin was whisked off to Minas Tirith after the horrors of his Palantír encounter. Aragorn was concerned about Pippin and was also mentally preparing to use the Palantír himself. By the time they met again on March 15th he had confronted Sauron, gone through the Paths of the Dead, ridden to Pelargir, captured the Enemy ships and sailed up-river to take part in the Battle of the Pelennor Fields. Pippin had had a four-day journey to Minas Tirith where he had met Denethor and been sworn into his service and then subsequently faced a series of horrors: the siege; seeing Nazgûl at close quarters; Denethor's madness and suicide; and the trauma of seeing his best friend at death's door. In addition Gandalf had shared with him his belief that Aragorn had also looked into the Palantír. Aragorn and Pippin must therefore have been seriously concerned about each other and their overriding emotion at their reunion would have been relief that each had survived their ordeals, particularly the shared ordeal associated with the Palantír. It is not difficult to appreciate why they were so glad to see each other.

The other significant feature of their conversation is Pippin's statement that he guessed it was Aragorn in the

---

142. Op. cit. [1], *LotR* 3.11, p. 591.
143. Op. cit., *LotR* 3.11, pp. 593-4.
144. Op. cit., *LotR* 5.4, p. 810.
145. Op. cit., *LotR* 5.8, p. 863.

black-sailed ships and not the Corsairs of Umbar, thus posing the question: why did he, seemingly alone among those present, hold that view? It is easy to suggest that this was another example of him being influenced by the strange impulses and visions to which he seemed prone, or that it was due to what Christopher Tolkien calls a *"strange presentiment"*[146], or that the idea had occurred to him due to information subconsciously picked up from his meddling with the Palantír and recalled when the ships appeared. However it is also conceivable that his guess was actually an astute one based on logical analysis of various bits of knowledge he had absorbed during his time in Minas Tirith as he strove to become more aware of what was going on, particularly relating to Aragorn's status and destiny. The following points show how this might have come about:

- On March 9th (App B.1093) on their arrival in Minas Tirith Gandalf warned Pippin not to mention Aragorn to Denethor, thus puzzling him as he knew that Aragorn was intending to come to Minas Tirith himself anyway. Gandalf explained that Aragorn's arrival was "*... likely to be in some way that no-one expects, not even Denethor.*"[147]. His next words, referring to Aragorn's intention to claim the kingship filled Pippin with amazement, thus showing his ignorance not only of the history of Gondor but of Aragorn's mission and destiny too. It also indicated that Gandalf's talk during their journey about the possibility of Saruman and Gríma being aware of Aragorn's identity had not made much impression on Pippin. In exasperation Gandalf now told him, "*If you have walked all these days with closed ears and mind asleep, wake up now!*"[148] This was perhaps the push that Pippin needed to make him pay more attention to what was happening around him. Later that day as he talked to Beregond, he observed that only Aragorn out of the Fellowship really knew Gandalf. He was already starting to concentrate more.
- The following day, after Faramir had spoken of his meeting with Frodo and Sam, Gandalf shared his thoughts with Pippin as to why Sauron appeared to have been stirred to action prematurely - with this **not** being due to Frodo. He came to the conclusion that Aragorn may have used the Palantír to confront Sauron and explained that he was capable of taking great risks when necessary (*LotR* 5.4.815).
- In *LotR* 5.7.853 Denethor revealed that he possessed the Palantír of Minas Tirith, telling how he had seen in it the Enemy ships approaching. After the crazed Steward had cremated himself Gandalf explained to Pippin, Beregond and the others present how Sauron was capable of deceiving via the Palantír, making Denethor believe the worst and so fall into despair and madness.

Thus when the black-sailed ships arrived at the Pelennor Fields on March 15th, did Pippin recall Gandalf's words "*it is likely to be in some way that no-one expects*" quoted above? Aragorn hadn't been at the battle up until then, and Pippin must have been wondering when he would appear. He might also have remembered Gandalf saying that Aragorn was capable of taking great risks: seizing the Enemy ships could well have come into that category. Finally there was Denethor's assumption, from using the Palantír, that the Corsairs were approaching, followed by Gandalf's suggestion that Sauron may have been deceiving him. This, more than anything else, could have made Pippin suspect the truth when the ships appeared.

On consideration I feel that Pippin's guess was due to a combination of the factors mentioned. The impulse/vision/Palantír theory fits in with what we know of him, while the analytical theory shows the change which came over him as he made the effort to become better informed and put his undoubted intelligence to good use.

*

Aragorn's healing of Merry (*LotR* 5.8.868-71) has been described in some detail in the previous section as throwing considerable light on their relationship. This episode is also relevant in a study of the Aragorn/Pippin relationship. Prior to healing Merry, Aragorn had been tending Éowyn, but had left the room before she regained consciousness. Pippin stayed at Éowyn's bedside with Gandalf until she awoke and then they went to Merry's room to find Aragorn already there. Initially Pippin thought his friend looked worse and was frightened that he would die, but Aragorn calmed his fears, explaining that he had called him back from the darkness and reassuring Pippin that he would make a full recovery and be the stronger for his experience.

---

146. Op. cit. [73], *HoM-e* VIII Part 3, Chapter 11, p. 391.
147. Op. cit. [1], *LotR* 5.1, p. 753.
148. Op. cit., *LotR* 5.1, p. 754.

Someone as perceptive as Aragorn would have well appreciated the closeness between Merry and Pippin. Once the two Hobbits were alone again Pippin's remark about Aragorn,"*Was there ever any one like him? Except Gandalf, of course*"[149], left no doubt of the esteem in which they both held him. He also pointed out that the pack which Merry had believed lost was by the bed and that Aragorn had seen it all the time. Pippin had clearly appreciated Aragorn's jokey "reprimand" of Merry. The following day he got the answer to his question to Aragorn ("*How did you do it?*"[150]) when Legolas and Gimli gave their account of the journey through the Paths of the Dead and described the seizing of the black-sailed ships.

LotR 5.10.883 describes Pippin setting off for the Morannon in a company of Gondorian soldiers led by Beregond. Aragorn had told a still recuperating Merry that Pippin should have his chance to distinguish himself in battle. Pippin, as well as Merry, had a Dúnadan knife from the Barrow-downs. Did Aragorn feel that his blade too was destined for something significant? In the event Pippin used it to kill a Troll which had stunned Beregond and was about to bite his throat - thus saving Beregond's life. (Unlike Merry's blade, which perished when it pierced the Witch-king at the Pelennor Fields, Pippin's weapon would survive to be used during the Scouring of the Shire when he referred to it as *"this troll's bane"*[151]). We next see Pippin in *LotR* 6.4.955 as King Elessar's esquire at the feast on the Field of Cormallen. During a conversation afterwards we learn from Gimli that Pippin had only got up from his sick-bed the day before. While saving Beregond's life he had come close to losing his own. The implication is surely that he too was healed by Aragorn.

In *LotR* 6.6.982 Aragorn took leave of the four Hobbits at Dol Baran, the hill near Isengard where Pippin had looked in the Palantír. It could be argued that this was merely a convenient spot for him to turn back, but Aragorn must have, consciously or unconsciously, regarded the place as significant. It had been Pippin's meddling with the Palantír which had alerted Gandalf to its nature, resulting in him giving it to Aragorn. If Pippin hadn't become obsessed with it, would it actually have come into Aragorn's possession when it did? Aragorn's remarks at The Last Debate - "*I deemed that the time was ripe, and that the Stone had come to me for just such a purpose*"[152] - showed that he himself regarded his acquiring of the Palantír as a turning-point in his final struggle to defeat Sauron, and Pippin had been instrumental in bringing this about. Certainly the Palantír was uppermost in Pippin's mind too at this farewell scene and he expressed a wish for the Hobbits to have one as well so they could keep in touch with distant friends. Did he still feel the pull of it? Aragorn told him that he was keeping the Orthanc-stone for himself and went on to observe that, "*... you would not wish to see what the Stone of Minas Tirith would show you.*"[153] [Namely Denethor's hands withering in flame.]

With his foresight and heightened perception Aragorn would have realised that Pippin's irresponsible actions often appeared to be due to some external power or influence - the stone thrown into the well in Moria and the incident with the Palantír of Orthanc being the most notable examples. The shared experience of seeing Sauron in the Palantír would have created a bond between them. Also their communication during the Orc chase, resulting in the dropping of Pippin's brooch, showed an understanding between them of a psychic nature. Pippin's ingenuity during this period gained him Aragorn's respect.

*

Pippin remained in close contact with Aragorn for the rest of his life. App A (Introduction.1033), App A.I.iii.1044 and App B.1097-8 give the details. He and Merry often met Gimli in Rohan and Gondor so he must have seen Aragorn as well at these times. In addition he and Sam often stayed with Aragorn at his house in Annúminas when he visited his North Kingdom. Pippin's son Faramir was born in FA 10 and in FA 14 Pippin became Thain (presumably on the death of his father) and was also made a Counsellor of the North Kingdom by Aragorn. The Epilogue to *LotR* has Sam telling Elanor of Pippin's frequent visits to Minas Tirith "*... where he is very highly thought of.*"[154].

---

149. Op. cit. [1], *LotR* 5.8, p. 870.
150. Op. cit., *LotR* 5.8, p. 863.
151. Op. cit., *LotR* 6.8, p. 1005.
152. Op. cit., *LotR* 5.9, p. 879.
153. Op. cit., *LotR* 6.6, p. 982.
154. Op. cit. [51], *HoM-e* IX Part 1, Chapter 11, p. 122.

Like Merry, Pippin spent his last years in Gondor, arriving there in FA 64. He came voluntarily not because he was summoned. Like Merry too, he was laid in Rath Dínen when he died and then, on Aragorn's death, was placed next to him.

*

LotR Prologue.14-15 describes Pippin's work on building up the library at Great Smials during the early years of the Fourth Age. He and his successors collected many manuscripts written by scribes of Gondor, mostly histories and legends relating to Elendil and his heirs. Great Smials was also the only place in the Shire containing extensive material on the history of Númenor and the rising of Sauron. It was probably there too that the *The Tale of Years* (i.e. *LotR* Appendix B.1082-1098) was put together.

Pippin was involved in making the first copy, at Aragorn's request, of the Red Book written by Bilbo and Frodo. This was known as the Thain's book and contained much that was later omitted or lost. When Pippin left the Shire in FA 64 he brought it with him to Minas Tirith where it received annotation and corrections and also, later on, the addition of an abbreviated version of *The Tale of Aragorn and Arwen* describing the aspects of their story which lay outside the main narrative of the War of the Ring. The Thain's book was in turn copied by the Gondorian scribe Findegil in FA 172, probably by request of Pippin's great-grandson. This copy was subsequently kept at Great Smials.

Thus Pippin made amends for his ignorance of Gondorian history - and even of Aragorn's lineage - apparent in much of *LotR*!

BILBO BAGGINS

There is comparatively little in *LotR* referring specifically to Aragorn and Bilbo, but what there is indicates a very obvious rapport between them. The two of them would almost certainly have become acquainted sometime after TA 3002 which was the year when Bilbo took up residence in Rivendell - a year after his dramatic departure from the Shire. However, for completeness, it is necessary to consider the possibility that they knew each other before that.

As I mentioned in Chapters 1.3 and 2.3, *The Hobbit*[155] makes no reference to Aragorn being present during Bilbo's two visits to Rivendell when Aragorn was ten and eleven because *LotR* and Aragorn had not yet been thought of. App B.1089, with the hindsight of *TH*, does record Bilbo's activities during TA 2941 and 2942, but there is no reference to any encounter with Aragorn in Rivendell - although it is difficult to believe that he and his mother were not present on the return visit when Gandalf recounted the adventures of Bilbo and the Dwarves. Given that Aragorn was being raised incognito, if Bilbo noticed him he probably just thought he was one of the Elf children living there. Although what was presumably Aragorn's first sight of a Hobbit must have made a strong impression upon him, he was only a child and it seems unlikely that he would have remembered Bilbo specifically given the many Hobbits he would have seen in later years - particularly in Bree.

There is no evidence of any encounters between Aragorn and Bilbo during the sixty years between Bilbo's return to the Shire in 2942 and his settling in Rivendell in 3002 - or indeed of actual encounters between Aragorn and **any** Shire Hobbit:
- It was the policy of the Northern Dúnedain to work in secret to protect "simple" folk from the fear and horror engendered by Sauron's creatures. The Bree-folk knew the Rangers, but did not know who they were or what their business was; the Shire folk never even saw them, although their borders were well guarded by them.
- We know that Bilbo visited Elves while he was still living in the Shire and that Frodo possibly did too - or at least was seen by Elves when in Bilbo's company (as Gildor told him in *LotR* 1.3)[156]. However there is no indication that Bilbo associated with Rangers. In *LotR* 2.1.232 it is established that he knew

---
155. J.R.R. Tolkien, *The Hobbit*, 3rd edition, London, Allen & Unwin, 1966, 1975 printing.
156. Op. cit. [1], *LotR* 1.3, p. 80.

Aragorn as "*The Dúnadan*" and had never heard him called "*Strider*". If he had known him in his capacity of Ranger he would surely have been aware of the latter alias, as the former one would not have been freely used outside Rivendell.
- If Bilbo had been a friend of Aragorn while he was still living in the Shire then Frodo would surely have known Aragorn as well. However when Frodo first encountered the Ranger in Bree it was quite clear that he had not met anyone like him before. It was equally clear that Aragorn did not know **him** - because he was at great pains to make sure that he wasn't an imposter trying to trap him. We can thus rule out the possibility of a similar situation to that with Gildor as indicated in the previous point: namely with Aragorn recognising Frodo after spotting him in the company of Bilbo, but with Frodo not recognising **him**.

Therefore the only probable scenario is that Bilbo became friendly with Aragorn after settling in Rivendell - during one of Aragorn's visits there. Bilbo's move there of course occurred at the time when Gandalf had begun to have serious suspicions that his ring was Sauron's One Ring and we know that he confided his concerns to Aragorn. Aragorn would therefore have been particularly keen to meet Bilbo, and their relationship would most likely have begun earlier rather than later in the period 3002-3018. Gandalf would presumably have told him all about Bilbo and his exploits, perhaps jogging his memory of the time when Hobbit, Wizard and Dwarves had visited during his childhood. Bilbo would also have made the acquaintance of Arwen around TA 3009 when, according to App B.1090, Elrond sent for her to return from Lothlórien due to the increasing danger of the lands around the Misty Mountains and further east.

*

The first indication of a relationship between Bilbo and Aragorn occurred in *LotR* 1.11.186 as Sam recited part of a Common Speech version of *The Fall of Gil-galad* believing that Bilbo had written it. Aragorn remarked that Bilbo's version must have been a translation of the original which was in an ancient Elvish language. It appears that he knew Bilbo reasonably well to be aware of his intellectual and academic pursuits. However there are two major incidents in *LotR* - both of which took place in Rivendell - which leave no doubt as to the closeness of their friendship.

The first was in *LotR* 2.1 after the feast, at the point when Frodo had just been reunited with Bilbo in the Hall of Fire. Bilbo was lamenting the fact that he hadn't finished a song he was supposed to be writing as part of the evening's entertainment and decided that he needed the help of "*my friend the Dúnadan*"[157]. Elrond sent messengers to find this friend, declaring that the two of them would then have to "*go into a corner*"[158] to finish the song. Meanwhile Bilbo explained to Frodo that he had heard about the trouble caused by the Ring and that, in spite of Gandalf's frequent visits, he had in fact learnt more from "*The Dúnadan*". With Aragorn's eventual arrival - to Frodo's surprise as he had not connected the name Dúnadan with his friend Strider - there was a brief conversation as to why he hadn't been at the feast, followed by the departure of Bilbo and Aragorn "*into a corner*" to finish off Bilbo's song. Later, after the song had been performed Bilbo discussed its reception with Frodo.

This whole incident is very revealing concerning the relationship between Aragorn and Bilbo as the following points illustrate:
- Bilbo's manner of speaking to Aragorn was casual and affectionate, e.g. "my friend", "my dear fellow".
- Bilbo was concerned that Aragorn hadn't been at the feast, particularly as Arwen had been there. His matter-of-fact attitude showed that he obviously knew all about their relationship.
- We have a totally different Aragorn here from the one the other four Hobbits had known up until then - laughing and relaxed.
- Aragorn's kindness and patience were evident: just standing and looking down at Bilbo and Frodo

---

157. Op. cit. [1], *LotR* 2.1, p. 231.
158. Op. cit., *LotR* 2.1, p. 231.

smiling at their chatter rather than announcing himself and interrupting them, and sparing the time to help Bilbo with the song when probably all he wanted to do was be with Arwen.
- Aragorn had talked freely to Bilbo about the Ring - more so than Gandalf had - so obviously regarded him as a trustworthy companion.
- Aragorn and Bilbo felt able to speak their minds to each other. For example Bilbo referred to the completion of his song as being urgent, immediately after Aragorn had been talking about the truly urgent matter of hearing news from Elladan and Elrohir who had returned out of the Wild unexpectedly. During their session on the song, Aragorn told Bilbo that if he had the cheek to write verses about Eärendil in the house of Elrond he should take the consequences.

Overall the incident showed a friendly, bantering relationship between two people who knew each other well, were easy in each other's company and could say what they felt without giving offence. Elrond - whom Bilbo treated in the same familiar way as he did Aragorn - obviously regarded it as an established friendship. The two of them also knew a great deal about each other, although, as a point of interest, Bilbo did not understand Aragorn's insistence in including a reference to a green stone in the song. He probably did not realise that the Elessar had once belonged to Eärendil and was perhaps unaware of the prophecies relating to Aragorn concerning the jewel.

The second incident, which took place at the Council of Elrond (*LotR* 2.2.246-8), lacked the light-hearted element and gave a deeper insight into the relationship. Aragorn had just been introduced to Boromir, by Elrond, as Isildur's heir in possession of the broken Sword of Elendil. Boromir's looks and words made it clear that he was dubious about Aragorn's general appearance and also about his capability of wielding such a sword. At first Bilbo just stirred impatiently next to Frodo but then suddenly shot to his feet in indignation and recited the poem which Tolkien calls *The Riddle of Strider*. This was followed by a dig at Boromir for doubting not only Aragorn, but also the word of Elrond. Then after a scathing remark about Boromir's long journey to find out this information, Bilbo whispered to Frodo that he had composed the poem specifically for Aragorn "*... a long time ago when he first told me about himself*"[159], and expressed his regret that his adventuring days were over thus precluding any chance of accompanying him when his time came. Aragorn, with a smile for Bilbo, then gave a long impassioned speech to Boromir on his own life, travels and struggles.

The implications here are many:
- Bilbo deeply resented Boromir's attitude to his friend.
- He also objected to Boromir's obvious pride in the solitary, one-hundred-and-ten-day journey he had made to get to Rivendell. Knowing Aragorn as well as he did Bilbo would have been aware that Boromir's journey paled in comparison with Aragorn's travels, from the point of view of length, danger and loneliness.
- The poem showed his admiration and respect for Aragorn as well as a knowledge of his history and destiny: the fine character underlying the ragged exterior; the fact that his wanderings had a purpose; that in spite of his long life his strength was undiminished; the prophecies which foresaw the renewal of the kingship and the resurrection of the Dúnedain - and Aragorn himself - from obscurity to glory.

> *"All that is gold does not glitter,*
> *Not all those who wander are lost;*
> *The old that is strong does not wither,*
> *Deep roots are not reached by the frost.*
> *From the ashes a fire shall be woken,*
> *A light from the shadows shall spring;*
> *Renewed shall be blade that was broken:*
> *The crownless again shall be king."*[160]

---
159. Op. cit. [1], *LotR* 2.2, p. 248.
160. Op. cit., *LotR* 2.2, p. 247.

- Bilbo's comment that the poem had been written "*a long time ago*" is a further pointer to an acquaintance with Aragorn being formed soon after he took up residence in Rivendell rather than at a later date.
- Was there also an element of protectiveness in Bilbo's behaviour, seeing a well-loved friend being belittled by a stranger who should have been revering him?
- Aragorn clearly appreciated Bilbo's support as illustrated by his smile of gratitude. The old Hobbit was someone he trusted and had confided in.
- Was Bilbo's speech the trigger which released Aragorn's tirade?

Regarding the name *The Riddle of Strider*, this title could not have been given by Bilbo at the time he wrote his poem as we know that he had never heard Aragorn called Strider until Frodo addressed him thus in October 3018. If Bilbo did give it that name then he must have done so during or after Frodo's stay in Rivendell. Or perhaps the title was given by Frodo when writing his own account of the War of the Ring knowing of the significance of riddles in Bilbo's history.

*

Bilbo was present at the farewell scene when the Fellowship prepared to leave Rivendell. As Aragorn sat with his head bowed we are told that "*only Elrond knew fully what this hour meant to him.*"[161] I have suggested in my discussion of Arwen, that she too would have had a good idea of what Aragorn was going through. Bilbo must also have had some inkling of what was at stake for his friend, though obviously at this juncture his attention would have been mostly on Frodo.

The next reference to Bilbo and Aragorn is not until *LotR* 6.5.970 after the War of the Ring was over and Aragorn was King. The Fellowship remained in Minas Tirith at Aragorn's insistence because he wanted them to be present for his wedding which would soon take place. As he would not reveal the nature of this event, Frodo asked Gandalf what it was - partly because he was anxious to get back to Bilbo and felt that he would be wondering what was delaying their return. Gandalf's reply was that Bilbo knew what was keeping them and was himself waiting for the same day. This conversation showed that Gandalf was well aware of Bilbo's friendship with Aragorn and Arwen.

Sadly, in the event, Bilbo was too old and weary to make the journey south and his last meeting with Aragorn had been that farewell on December 25th 3018 as the Fellowship set off from Rivendell. However Arwen would have seen him more recently - since the destruction of the Ring - probably on May 1st 3019 which was the day she, Elrond and most of their household left for Gondor. She would have seen the condition he was in and she clearly understood the power of the Ring over him answering Frodo's remark about how sad he was not to see Bilbo at the wedding with, "*Do you wonder at that, Ring-bearer? For you know the power of that thing which is now destroyed; and all that was done by that power is now passing away.*"[162]. She knew that Bilbo's life was drawing to its close now that the Ring was no more and recognised that the only long journey he would make now was to death - or, as it turned out, first to the Grey Havens and into the West for healing.

Bilbo's own regrets at not being able to travel to Gondor were brought home to the other four Hobbits when they joined him in Rivendell on September 21st. They found that, out of all their news of their journey and adventures, the only things he showed any real interest in were Aragorn's coronation and wedding. Of the latter he said, "*... I have waited for it long enough.*"[163]. Aragorn's long-awaited success and happiness clearly meant a great deal to him. He must too have felt a similar regard and affection for Arwen. Did he treat her with the same matey familiarity as he did her father, one wonders?

*

It is not difficult to find reasons for the esteem in which Aragorn and Bilbo held each other:
- They were both respected friends of Gandalf.
- They were both well thought of in Rivendell.
- They would have appreciated characteristics such as sensitivity and compassion which they both

---

161. Op. cit. [1], *LotR* 2.3, p. 280.
162. Op. cit., *LotR* 6.6, p. 974.
163. Op. cit., *LotR* 6.6, p. 986.

- possessed.
- They shared intellectual and cultural interests: both were linguists, musicians and poets and had a love of Middle-earth and its inhabitants, landscapes and history. *LotR* Prologue, when talking of the various copies of the Red Book refers to Findegil's copy which also contained Bilbo's three-volume Translations from the Elvish. This is described as "*... a work of great skill and learning in which ... he had used all the sources available to him in Rivendell, both living and written.*"[164]. Had Aragorn been one of the sources, or helped with some of the translation?
- They must both have enjoyed having the company of someone who wasn't an Elf during their time in Rivendell. Happy as he was there, Bilbo missed having Hobbits around (note his remark to Frodo: "*There are no folk like hobbits after all for a real good talk*"[165]) and Aragorn would have given him contact with the non-Elvish world outside. Also it might have been a tonic for Aragorn to hear Bilbo treating Elrond and the Elves in his typical familiar, bordering-on-cheeky manner. Perhaps they shared a similar type of camaraderie to that which Aragorn would later appreciate so much with Merry and Pippin in the ruins of Isengard.
- Of possible significance is the fact that during the years 3002-3009 Arwen was in Lothlórien not Rivendell, and Aragorn may have found it a comfort to talk to someone who knew about their relationship but wasn't actually emotionally involved in the way that Elrond, Elladan and Elrohir were.
- Bilbo would have felt admiration for Aragorn's perseverance in his gruelling journeys and thankless labours, and compassion for his long waiting for Arwen. In his turn Aragorn would have been intrigued and impressed by Bilbo's own adventures and initiative, as well as his intellectual pursuits and his friendships with Elves. Bilbo would probably have been the first non-typical Hobbit he had encountered.
- They both perhaps appreciated each other's mental - as opposed to physical - courage. For example in *TH* as Bilbo went down the tunnel to the chamber where Smaug lay at the heart of the Lonely Mountain, we are told that he stopped when he drew close enough to hear and see the signs of the dragon. Then we are told, "*Going on from there was the bravest thing he ever did. The tremendous things that happened afterwards were as nothing compared to it. He fought the real battle in the tunnel alone...*"[166]. One could say the same of Aragorn's Palantír confrontation, arguably the bravest thing he did and a lone battle, establishing the deceit which made Sauron's defeat possible.

Aragorn's relationships with the four young Hobbits, though all based on mutual regard, friendship and trust, had their own distinctive characteristics: e.g. Frodo - more spiritual; Sam - respected and honoured in spite of his low social status; Merry - affectionate and empathetic; Pippin - slightly psychic. At the start of *LotR* none of them knew Aragorn or anything about him - they found out bit by bit as the narrative progressed. Even his real name and status took a while to sink in.

The situation with Bilbo however was entirely different due to two aspects in particular, namely prior knowledge and age. He had known Aragorn for approximately sixteen years when Frodo arrived in Rivendell in October 3018. He also knew all about him from the start: once he had started living in Rivendell he wouldn't have remained in ignorance for very long, especially given Aragorn's history and connection with the Ring, and his own thirst for learning. He would also have first met Aragorn as his true self - that is not incognito - unlike Frodo and his companions. Bilbo may well have known something of the history of Isildur's line anyway from years of friendship with Gandalf. He was also aware that Aragorn and Arwen were betrothed and that Aragorn would need to regain his kingships before a wedding could take place. The other Hobbits remained in ignorance of all this until Arwen's arrival in Minas Tirith and, in varying degrees, were somewhat slow in the uptake regarding his royal status. They were also very much younger than Aragorn who was eighty-seven when they first met - with Frodo being fifty, Sam thirty-eight, Merry thirty-six and Pippin twenty-eight. Bilbo on the other hand, being born in TA 2890, was nearly forty-one years older than Aragorn (and incidentally seventeen years older than Gilraen). This would no doubt have contributed to his forceful protectiveness at the Council of Elrond and added a fatherly element to his feelings for Aragorn which would have been beneficial

---

164. Op. cit. [1], *LotR* Prologue, p. 15.
165. Op. cit., *LotR* 2.1, p. 238.
166. Op. cit. [155], *TH* Chapter 12, pp. 226-7.

FINAL OBSERVATIONS ON THE HOBBIT RELATIONSHIPS

To finish this chapter on the Hobbits I draw together a number of examples which illustrate the depth of affection and regard between Aragorn and the Hobbits of the Fellowship:

- *LotR* refers to Aragorn's reluctance for the Fellowship to split up following his coronation. This was because, as he told them, "*A day draws near* [his wedding] *that I have looked for in all the years of my manhood, and when it comes I would have my friends beside me.*"[167]. The Hobbits knew they were waiting for some special occasion, but not what it was due to Aragorn's desire to keep it secret until the actual day. (Whether Legolas and Gimli guessed what was going on is another matter). His behaviour here seemed to be almost clingy and vulnerable with his childlike desire to make it all a big surprise and his yearning to have the Fellowship there.
- At the eventual farewell scene at Dol Baran we are told that "*The Hobbits were grieved at this parting; for Aragorn had never failed them and he had been their guide through many perils.*"[168]. Aragorn reminded them, "*... remember, dear friends of the Shire, that my realm lies also in the North, and I shall come there one day.*"[169]
- Aragorn's adoption of "Telcontar", the Quenya version of "Strider", as the name of his royal House showed that he now regarded his Bree-land alias as a mark of affection through its constant use by the Hobbits - rather than the "scornful nickname" he had referred to at the Council of Elrond.
- Frodo, Sam, Merry and Pippin had all been healed by Aragorn. This in itself must have strengthened the relationship between them, bringing healer and healed together.
- *HoM-e* XII[170] describes the making of App A. It tells of the general ignorance of the Hobbits concerning the Kings and Stewards of Gondor, and indeed of anything outside their own lore and wanderings. This changed with the War of the Ring as "*... afterwards all that concerned the King Elessar became of deep interest to them...*"[171]

---

167. Op. cit. [1], *LotR* 6.5, p. 970.
168. Op. cit., *LotR* 6.6, p. 982.
169. Op. cit., *LotR* 6.6, p. 982.
170. C. Tolkien (ed.), *The History of Middle-earth*, vol. XII, *The Peoples of Middle-earth*, London HarperColllins Publishers, 2002, first published in Great Britain by HarperCollins Publishers 1996, *HoM-e* XII Part 1, Chapter 9, pp. 253-289.
171. Op. cit., *HoM-e* XII Part 1, Chapter 9, p. 255.

CHAPTER 2.6 - Gondorians

The relationships to be analysed in this chapter are those with the Steward Ecthelion II (father of Denethor), Denethor himself, Boromir, Faramir, Prince Imrahil of Dol Amroth, Beregond, Ioreth and the Warden of the Houses of Healing. Genealogical Tables 3, 5, 6 and 7 are all relevant.

It is necessary first to summarise the history of Gondor, using material from *LotR* App A.I.iv[1], App B[2], *RoP*[3] and *UT* 3.1[4].

Gondor, along with the northern kingdom of Arnor, was founded in SA 3320 by Elendil the leader of the escapees from the drowning of Númenor and the heir to its royal House. He became the first King of both kingdoms, ruling in Arnor himself and committing the rule of Gondor jointly to his sons Isildur (the elder) and Anárion. Twenty-one years later the Second Age came to an end with the overthrow of Sauron and the deaths of Elendil and Anárion. Thus the Third Age began with Isildur succeeding to Elendil's kingships. Following the pattern set by his father, he committed the rule of Gondor to Anárion's son Meneldil and then set off north intending to rule Arnor himself. When he and his three eldest sons were killed at the Battle of the Gladden Fields on the way, he was succeeded by his youngest son Valandil who, being only a child, was living in Rivendell. Thus the two branches of Elendil's line became separated, with Valandil's (Isildur's) line ruling in Arnor and Meneldil's (Anárion's) line in Gondor.

Nearly two thousand years later (TA 1944) the two lines came close to being reunited following the deaths of Ondoher the thirty-first king of Gondor and his two sons. At this point the kingship of Gondor was claimed by Arvedui, the heir of Araphant, King of the North Kingdom and Isildur's heir. In addition Arvedui was married to Ondoher's daughter Fíriel and was thus claiming on her behalf as well as his own. However his claim failed - largely due to the attitude of the Steward at the time, Pelendur - with the Council of Gondor refusing to recognise inheritance by daughters even though Númenor had had ruling queens as well as kings, and rejecting a claimant of the line of Isildur in spite of the fact that this was the senior branch of Elendil's line. They argued that Isildur had relinquished royal responsibility for Gondor on committing the rule to Anárion's son. The kingship was subsequently given to a more junior (male) member of Anárion's line. Two generations later in TA 2050 that line died out leaving no obvious successor. Many of the lesser members of the royal line of Anárion had married into non-Númenórean families with shorter lifespans thus producing heirs of mixed blood. Since it was just such a situation which had triggered the War of the Kin-strife earlier in the Third Age (approximately 1432 to mid-1800s) no-one was willing to make a claim and risk a repetition of that war. Thus from 2050 onwards Gondor came under the rule of its Stewards, until such time as a King should return. This was still the situation at the time of Aragorn's birth in 2931. [Genealogical Table 3 shows the claim of Arvedui and Fíriel while Table 5 illustrates the extent of the War of the Kin-strife by highlighting relevant kings and events.]

It should be emphasised that the Stewardship had been hereditary since the time of Pelendur, and the line was descended from Húrin of Emyn Arnen, Steward to Gondor's twenty-fifth king Minardil (1621-34). Húrin is described (in App A.I.iv) as being "*... a man of high Númenórean race,*"[5] hence Faramir's statement to

---

1. J.R.R. Tolkien, *The Lord of the Rings,* London, HarperCollins Publishers, 2007, 2nd edition, based on the 50th Anniversary Edition of 2004, App A.I.iv, pp. 1044-57.
2. Op. cit., App B, pp. 1084-90.
3. C. Tolkien (ed.), *The Silmarillion*, London, HarperCollins Publishers, 1999, first published in Great Britain by George Allen & Unwin 1977, *RoP* pp. 348-363.
4. C. Tolkien (ed.), *Unfinished Tales of Númenor and Middle-earth*, London, HarperCollins Publishers, 1998, first published in Great Britain by George Allen & Unwin 1980, *UT* 3.1, pp. 351-7.
5. Op. cit [1], App A.I.iv, p. 1052.

Frodo and Sam, "*We of my house are not of the line of Elendil, though the blood of Númenor is in us.*"[6] [See Genealogical Table 6.]

*

In dealing with Aragorn's Gondorian relationships, App A.I.iv.1055-7 is just as important a source of information as the text of *LotR* itself as it gives significant detail on the background and character of Denethor, Boromir and Faramir as well as Ecthelion. It also covers the young Aragorn's period of service under Ecthelion which is very relevant to the analysis of these relationships. App B.1089-90 is useful throughout for confirming dates and events while *UT* 4.3.521-36 describes the issues surrounding Denethor's use of the Palantír of Minas Tirith. When describing Aragorn's early connections with Gondor in context, I refer to him as "Thorongil" which is the name by which he was known to his contemporaries.

ECTHELION

The starting point is Aragorn's service to Ecthelion, as a young man, incognito, under the alias of "Thorongil". This occurred some time during the years TA 2957-80, which, as stated in App B, were years of "*great journeys and errantries*"[7] for Aragorn. His service in Gondor must have been towards the end of this period as he had already served in Rohan before coming to Gondor and prior to that he had only recently become acquainted with Gandalf and would surely have travelled with him closer to home before venturing south. During 2980 we know (from App A.I.v.1060-1 and App B.1090) that he entered Lothlórien after returning from a gruelling journey in the border areas of Mordor - a journey which seems to have been undertaken immediately after leaving Gondor. Thus the service under Ecthelion was most likely to have taken place during the 2970s, towards the end of Ecthelion's Stewardship (2953-2984), when Thorongil was in his forties. The details are given in the *Stewards* section of App A.I.iv.1052-7 from which quotations for the Ecthelion relationship are taken unless indicated otherwise.

By the late 2900s the Stewards had been ruling in Gondor for over nine hundred years. Nevertheless we are told that many of the people still believed that a king would return at some point, especially as there were rumours that the royal line in the North still continued in secret. [Note the response of some of Faramir's men in *LotR* when Frodo spoke of Aragorn's descent from Isildur: "*The sword of Elendil comes to Minas Tirith! Great tidings!*"[8].] However "*... against such thoughts the Ruling Stewards hardened their hearts.*"[9] The implication here is that the Stewards in general maintained the hostility to Isildur's line which Pelendur had exhibited when rejecting Arvedui's claim, either because they truly believed that that line had no right to the throne of Gondor or (perhaps more likely) because they wanted to keep the royal power for themselves. As will be shown, this attitude is apparent in Denethor and to some extent in Boromir, along with a tendency to regard Gondor and its people as the sole combatant in the struggle against Sauron.

However this was not the case with Ecthelion. The account makes much of his wisdom, his encouragement of men from outside Gondor to enter his service, and his willingness to reward these people if they proved trustworthy. To illustrate the point we are then told that "*In much that he did he had the aid and advice of a great captain whom he loved above all.*"[10] This description of the incognito Aragorn relates to a man whose origin and true name were unknown to his friends and acquaintances in Gondor including the Steward himself. Ecthelion clearly did not have the closed mindset of his son and elder grandson. His acceptance of the mysterious stranger turned out to be amply vindicated by Thorongil's recognition of the threat to Gondor posed by the Corsairs of Umbar and his subsequent defeat of them in a naval battle which would have brought him great honour if he hadn't, at that point, chosen to terminate his service in Gondor and head east towards the borders of Mordor. The phrase "*whom he loved above all*" shows that Ecthelion had a real affection for this captain

---

6. Op. cit. [1], *LotR* 4.5, p. 670.
7. Op. cit., App B, p. 1090.
8. Op. cit., *LotR* 4.5, p. 664.
9. Op. cit., App A.I.iv, p. 1053.
10. Op. cit., App A.I.iv, p. 1055.

and counsellor - in fact more than he seemed to feel for his own son, as we are told that Denethor "... *was ever placed second to the stranger in the hearts of men and the esteem of his father.*"[11] As indicated this affection was clearly also felt by the people of Gondor in general and there seems to have been an overwhelming sense of grief and loss when Thorongil failed to return to Minas Tirith after his victory over the Corsairs. The young Aragorn obviously already possessed that "something" which made others love him. Compare the words of Legolas in *LotR* that "*... all those who come to know him come to love him after their own fashion...*"[12].

Thorongil's ascendancy was certainly not due to being a "yes" man. He appears to have had to make considerable efforts to **persuade** Ecthelion to let him take a fleet to Umbar: "***At last he got leave...***"[13] [My emphasis]. He was also single-minded in urging Ecthelion to put his trust in Gandalf and warning him against Saruman. Overall he showed himself to be determined, persuasive and genuinely committed to the good of Gondor. There is every reason to suppose that he returned Ecthelion's affection, appreciating his wisdom and his readiness to accept counsel - including from those apparently not of Gondorian race or high rank.

Even allowing for Ecthelion's broadmindedness it is perhaps surprising that he was prepared to welcome, trust and honour someone who refused to say who he was or where he came from, though admittedly, since Thorongil came to Minas Tirith fresh from service in Rohan, he may well have been accompanied by a recommendation from Thengel King which would have carried some weight with the Steward. In addition it depends on what Ecthelion really knew or guessed. As will be discussed, there are many hints that Denethor realised who Thorongil was and I find it hard to believe that Ecthelion didn't also guess his identity on account of the mystery surrounding him, his Númenórean appearance (including a strong physical resemblance to Denethor), his connection with Gandalf, the high level of his physical and intellectual skills and the very distinctive "star" brooch on his cloak which, along with his eagle-like swiftness and keen vision, gave rise to his alias. There was also the cryptic and prophetic farewell message he sent to Ecthelion after the victory at Umbar: "*Other tasks now call me, lord, and much time and many perils must pass, ere I come again to Gondor, if that be my fate.*"[14]. Was Ecthelion's suspicion of Thorongil's true identity one of the reasons for his acceptance of, and regard for, this enigmatic character who "*... departed into the shadows whence he came...*"[15]? Was Ecthelion of like temperament to his younger grandson who was to tell Frodo and Sam in *LotR*, "*... I would see the White Tree in flower again in the courts of the kings, and the Silver Crown return ...*"[16]?

The departure of Thorongil from Gondor must have occurred in 2980 or shortly before - depending on the duration of his subsequent journey east. Ecthelion died in 2984 and was succeeded as Steward by Denethor (II).

DENETHOR

A study of the relationship between Thorongil and Ecthelion leaves the reader better prepared to appreciate Denethor's attitude to Gandalf and Aragorn in *LotR*. Not surprisingly, given that Thorongil seemed to have displaced him in his father's affections, Denethor did not share the general warm feeling towards him. The fact that Thorongil had always known his place, acting as befitted a servant of Ecthelion and making no attempt to upstage the Steward's heir, failed to lessen Denethor's jealousy. No doubt his hostility was aggravated by the element of affection - in addition to admiration and respect - in Ecthelion's attitude.

The account in App A.I.iv makes much of the similarity between Thorongil and Denethor with the latter being described as tall, valiant, kingly, wise, far-sighted, learned and "*... as like to Thorongil as to one of nearest kin.*"[17] They were also only a year apart in age with Denethor being born in 2930. As well as bearing a physical resemblance to each other Thorongil and Denethor were also agreed on their counsels to Ecthelion - with the one, very important, exception that Thorongil advised Ecthelion to trust Gandalf, whom Denethor

---

11. Op. cit. [1], App A.I.iv, p.1055.
12. Op. cit., *LotR* 5.9, p. 874.
13. Op. cit., App A.I.iv, p. 1055.
14. Op. cit., App A.I.iv, p. 1055.
15. Op. cit., App A.I.iv, p. 1055.
16. Op. cit., *LotR* 4.5, p. 671.
17. Op. cit., App A.I.iv, p. 1055.

disliked (the feeling seemingly being mutual from a study of their interactions in *LotR*).

App A.I.iv.1055 states that at the time it occurred, Thorongil's unexpected departure was said to be due to his wish to leave Gondor before Denethor became Steward (Ecthelion was now in his nineties), being aware of Denethor's ill-will towards him. However later, with hindsight, it became apparent that Denethor had probably realised who Thorongil actually was and that this was the real reason why the latter left Gondor when he did. The question is: how far did Denethor's suspicions go? Did he believe that Thorongil was directly descended, father-to-son, from Isildur over the last thirty-nine generations with each one being the result of a pure-bred Númenórean marriage? (The continuing long lifespans in the Northern Dúnadan kings and chieftains, mentioned in App A.I.iii.1044, seem to imply that Isildur's line avoided inter-breeding with shorter-lived races.). Or, did Denethor believe that Thorongil was merely one of the Northern Dúnedain with a very distant relationship to Isildur's line and therefore really nothing more than an upstart with no more valid a claim to the throne of Gondor than Denethor himself?

Thorongil's disappearance after the battle at Umbar may well have been for both of the reasons suggested above. There is no doubt that serving under Denethor's stewardship would have been much less pleasant and fulfilling for him than serving Ecthelion. Also, regardless of what Denethor did or didn't know, Thorongil probably felt that the longer he stayed around in Gondor the more likelihood there was of his true identity coming to light, especially now that he had become so renowned - not only in Minas Tirith itself but further south in Pelargir as well. If he had returned to Minas Tirith to the "*great honour*" which awaited him it may have had too much of the aura of a coronation, providing too much publicity. Above all it was obviously imperative that the attention of **Sauron** should not be drawn to Thorongil personally and the danger if this were to happen cannot be overestimated. From the practical point of view it was probably time for him to move on anyway - he must have spent ten years or more in Gondor by now and we know from App A.I.v.1060-61 that his travels were to take him far into the South and East.

UT 4.3.521-36 brings together Tolkien's writings on the Palantíri and includes a discussion of Denethor's use of the Anor-stone, the Palantír of Minas Tirith (524-8). It is suggested that he might have started using it right from the time he succeeded to the Stewardship (TA 2984) with his main motives being jealousy of Thorongil and hostility to Gandalf. He suspected them of wanting to supplant him regarding them as "*usurpers*"[18], and his purpose in using the Anor-stone was to try to surpass them in knowledge and information and keep an eye on them when they were far away.

None of the previous Stewards had dared to use the Palantír, and neither had the last two Kings (not even King Eärnur who had been reckless enough to accept an invitation to meet the Lord of the Nazgûl in single combat - thus bringing the line of the Kings to an end). This wariness was due to the fact that in TA 2002 the Ithil-stone (the Palantír of Minas Ithil) had come into Sauron's possession following the seizure of Minas Ithil (subsequently called Minas Morgul) by the Nazgûl, thus leading to the risk that a King or Steward using the Anor-stone would come into contact with Sauron. The account in *UT* 4.3.526 describes Denethor as being masterful, strong-willed, dauntless and confident in his own strength, as well as more wise and learned than was usual in that age. He believed that he had the strength to use the Anor-stone, and was proved right, to some extent, as he gained much knowledge of people and events far away. What he had **not** bargained for though was the weariness brought on by the struggle to resist Sauron's interference via the Ithil-stone. Although we are told that he probably did not contemplate any confrontation with Sauron, this was ever a threat whether he intended it or not and as time went on he became drawn into just such a situation due to Sauron's continual attempts to wrench the Anor-stone to his own control. It is stated that a grimness in Denethor became apparent to others after the death of his wife, Finduilas, four years after he became Steward. The implication is that Finduilas herself was aware of this change in his character even earlier, thus confirming that Denethor had started using the Palantír as soon as he had taken on the Stewardship.

Unlike Saruman, who began to use the Orthanc-stone some sixteen years later and became corrupted by Sauron, Denethor, as a legitimate user of the Anor-stone due to his position of standing in for the King, was able to maintain his integrity and avoid actually being subjugated to the will of Sauron. Nevertheless Sauron **was** able to influence him by deceit and to control what he saw in the Palantír thus skewing the picture and

---

18. Op. cit. [4], *UT* 4.3, p. 526.

convincing him that his [Sauron's] victory was inevitable. As a result Denethor grew despairing and paranoid, seeing only a single combat between him and Sauron and mistrusting everyone else who resisted the power of Mordor unless they served him [Denethor] alone. Thus by the time of the War of the Ring his attitude to Gandalf and Thorongil/Aragorn and his one-dimensional interpretation of the struggle with Sauron were firmly entrenched.

Whatever Thorongil's motives and Denethor's state of knowledge concerning him the fact remains that Thorongil departed from Gondor around TA 2980. He and Denethor would never meet again. Their last meeting was thus approximately forty years prior to the War of the Ring when Denethor was merely the heir to the Steward of Gondor and Aragorn was the much-respected captain Thorongil.

*

With this background to the relationship between Aragorn and Denethor we can now carry out a more meaningful examination of the main text of *LotR* which contains plenty of evidence that the feelings and doubts stirred up forty years earlier were still present, exacerbated by Denethor's continuing use of the Anor-stone and his resulting grimness and despair brought on by the struggle to resist Sauron.

Owing to the fact that Aragorn and Denethor do not actually meet in *LotR* it is mainly through the Denethor/Gandalf interaction that we see the continuing Denethor/Thorongil relationship. The following aspects will be discussed:
- Denethor's animosity towards Gandalf and the line of Isildur
- Denethor's one-dimensional interpretation of the struggle with Sauron
- Similarities and differences between Denethor and Aragorn
- Wariness of Aragorn and Gandalf towards Denethor
- Denethor's knowledge from using the Anor-stone

Denethor's animosity towards Gandalf and the line of Isildur

This is a dominant thread in *LotR*. For example at the Council of Elrond (*LotR* 2.2.252) Gandalf spoke of his journey to Minas Tirith to search the archives there for any record left by Isildur concerning the One Ring. He had found Denethor unwelcoming and the Steward had only grudgingly allowed him to consult the scrolls and books.

Later, on the arrival of Gandalf and Pippin in Minas Tirith (*LotR* 5.1.757-9), Denethor showed his suspicion of Gandalf by interrogating Pippin in such a manner as to force him to disclose information about Aragorn which Gandalf had felt it best to withhold at that point, thinking it tactless to remind the Steward of a possible claim for the kingship at a time when he was grieving for the death of his heir. Denethor expressed his objection to being "... *made the tool of other men's purposes* ..." stressing that his own purpose was the good of Gondor, "... *and the rule of Gondor, my lord, is mine and no other man's, unless the king should come again.*".[19]

Then in *LotR* 5.7.853 during the last few minutes before his suicide Denethor spoke his mind in no uncertain terms, accusing Gandalf of wanting to supplant him with the "*Ranger of the North*"[20] and to become himself the power behind the throne - not only in Gondor but everywhere else. He then emphasised his own position as Steward of the House of **Anárion** who refused to step down to Aragorn, referring to him as an upstart and disparaging him as being **only** of the line of Isildur "... *even were his claim proved to me...*"[21] [My emphasis]. This wording implies doubt that the claim could actually be proved.

These examples illustrate Denethor's mistrust of Gandalf and his unwillingness to accept Aragorn's right to the kingship of Gondor, as well as emphasising the fact that being of Isildur's line and not Anárion's weakened rather than strengthened his claim. Denethor was clearly of the same view as his ancestor, Pelendur, ignoring the validity of Arvedui's descent from Isildur and disregarding the senior representative of Anárion's line (Fíriel) because she was female. In Chapter 1.7 I referred to a letter Tolkien wrote to Richard Jeffery on

---

19. Op. cit. [1], *LotR* 5.1, p. 758.
20. Op. cit., *LotR* 5.7, p. 853.
21. Op. cit., *LotR* 5.7, p. 854.

Dec 17th 1972[22]. In it he stated that the North kingdom of Arnor, being originally the realm of Elendil, took precedence over the southern realm of Gondor. Thus Denethor was also rejecting a claimant from the senior of the two kingdoms.

The matter of Denethor's reasons for his aversion to Isildur's line is complex with no definite answers. The following points cover a number of possibilities:

- Denethor may really have believed that Isildur's line had no right to the throne of Gondor even though Isildur was the elder son of Elendil who had been the first king of both Arnor and Gondor. If he held such a belief then he would genuinely have viewed Aragorn as a usurper.
- On the other hand he may have convinced himself that Aragorn was a usurper because he wanted to carry on being the ruler of Gondor himself. App A.I.iv states that the Ruling Stewards in general "*hardened their hearts*"[23] against the existence of the royal line in the North. Did Denethor want absolute power too much to accept **any** king? He had many of the qualities of a good ruler, being courageous, confident in his own ability, knowledgeable, far-sighted, strong-minded, and having a genuine love for Gondor. A look through App A.I.iv reveals several other able Stewards in Gondor's history, such as Boromir, Cirion, Beregond and of course Ecthelion II himself.
- He may have rejected the idea of Aragorn's claim to Gondor's kingship purely from personal animosity and continuing jealousy. This feeling may have been increased by information gained from Pippin, particularly if Aragorn came over as a much-respected member/leader of the Fellowship, or as a person who had had disagreements with Boromir.
- The direct influence of Sauron can, I believe, safely be discounted - though the general pessimism he induced would have encouraged Denethor to attribute the worst motives to Gandalf and Aragorn. Sauron didn't know about Aragorn's existence until he was confronted by him in the Palantír of Orthanc in early March 3019. After that he fell into his brooding obsession with Isildur's heir concentrating almost exclusively on him and waiting for his next move. Denethor's attitude to Aragorn and the line of Isildur was firmly entrenched many years before the War of the Ring, very likely even before he began to use the Anor-stone. He probably had the strength to withhold his thoughts about this "usurper" from Sauron, whose chief motives were to try and break down his resistance and to make him believe that he was fighting a lost cause.
- I feel it is more likely that Saruman, rather than Sauron, influenced Denethor's attitude to Aragorn and Isildur's line. According to Gandalf in his report at the Council of Elrond (*LotR* 2.2.252) Saruman had generally been well-received by the rulers of Gondor over the years and Denethor was certainly more favourably disposed towards **him** than he was to Gandalf. Gandalf went on to quote Saruman as declaring that "*There is no hope left in Elves **or dying Númenor***"[24] [My emphasis]. This speech indicates Saruman's opinion (real or feigned) of the state of the descendants of Númenor immediately prior to the outbreak of the War of the Ring. Denethor's words shortly before casting himself into the flames were perhaps an echo of that view, indicating a genuine doubt of the validity of Isildur's line: "*I will not bow to such a one, **last of a ragged house long bereft of lordship and dignity***."[25] [My emphasis].
- In *LotR* 5.4.813-14 Denethor would make it clear that he believed he was entitled to take possession of the Ring and keep it in Minas Tirith, even though the Ring had been seized by Isildur who had subsequently treated it as an heirloom of his House - a House which Denethor regarded as being excluded from making a claim for the kingship of Gondor. This attitude perhaps exemplified his contempt for Isildur's line and his belief in his own superior strength and ability to keep the Ring safe.

A conversation between Faramir, and Frodo and Sam in *LotR* adds further complexity to the matter.

---

22. H. Carpenter (ed.), *The Letters of J.R.R. Tolkien*, with the assistance of Christopher Tolkien, London, HarperCollins Publishers, 1995. First published in Great Britain by George Allen & Unwin, 1981. Letter. 347, p. 428.
23. Op. cit. [1], App A.I.iv, p. 1053.
24. Op. cit., *LotR* 2.2, p. 259.
25. Op. cit., *LotR* 5.7, p. 854.

Faramir, talking of his childhood, told the Hobbits that the young Boromir was displeased that his father was only a steward and not a king. When he had asked Denethor, *"How many hundreds of years needs it to make a steward a king, if the king returns not?"*, Denethor replied that in a place of such royalty as Gondor possessed *"ten thousand years would not suffice."*[26] This advice to Boromir shows an ambiguity in Denethor's stance when seen in parallel with his behaviour elsewhere, thus illustrating the conflict in his mind on the matter of kingship and Isildur's descendants. He seemed to believe deeply in the sanctity of kingship, but at the same time - through personal jealousy, desire for power or genuine conviction - saw in Gandalf and Aragorn only a meddling, power-crazy wizard and an upstart, rather than Ilúvatar's steward striving to achieve his mission, part of which was to restore the kingship and reunite the two branches of Elendil's line. See Gandalf's remarks in *LotR* 5.1: *"I must come to your Lord Denethor, while his stewardship lasts,"* and *"... I also am a steward."*.[27]

Denethor's one-dimensional interpretation of the struggle with Sauron

Denethor's one-dimensional approach was well established by the time of the War of the Ring due to the despair induced by Sauron's deception which made him see the struggle simply as Gondor versus Mordor. He was oblivious to, or distrustful of, people and powers in other parts of Middle-earth who were fighting Sauron in their own way. A number of examples of his attitude occur in *LotR* 5.4. during conversations with Gandalf and Pippin prior to the Siege of Gondor:
- When Pippin told Denethor that the Shire songs he knew would be unsuitable for his halls at such a time, Denethor replied as follows: *"We who have lived long under the Shadow may surely listen to echoes from a land untroubled by it? Then we may feel that our vigil was not fruitless, though it may have been thankless."*[28] This ignored the fact that Pippin's land had only been *"untroubled"* largely because of the vigil of Aragorn's people.
- Later the same day when Denethor criticised Faramir's decision to let Frodo and the Ring go, he declared that he himself would have hidden the Ring in the vaults of the Citadel, only using it in desperate need if Sauron had a victory so final that those in Gondor would not have cared, being dead. Gandalf's reply accused him of thinking only of Gondor *"as is your wont"*[29].
- Then when Pippin cried out in fear, mistakenly thinking that Sauron himself had come to the walls of Minas Tirith, Denethor's reply showed the same Gondor-centred mindset: *"He will not come save only to triumph over **me** when all is won."*[30] [My emphasis].

Gandalf's own view, and by implication Aragorn's, was that the Ring needed to be destroyed to protect not only Gondor there and then, but those elsewhere (Sauron's slaves included), then and in the future. Immediately on arrival in Minas Tirith (*LotR* 5.1.758) he had made it plain that he wouldn't consider that he had completely failed if **anything** fair or fruitful survived the War - even if Gondor itself perished.

Similarities and differences between Denethor and Aragorn

In *LotR* it is natural to compare and contrast Aragorn with Boromir since they are in each other's company a good deal in Book 2 and, despite superficial similarities, have widely differing attitudes to the trials the Fellowship undertake. However a comparison with Denethor is perhaps more logical as they were of the same generation (Boromir was forty-seven years younger than Aragorn) and shared many attributes such as intelligence, learning, mental strength and perception of the minds of others. This section is a brief look at some of the more obvious similarities and differences between Aragorn and Denethor:
- The physical and mental similarity between Denethor and Thorongil observed in App A.I.iv.1055 is borne out in *LotR* 5.1 when Gandalf told Pippin that, by a fluke, the blood of Númenor ran nearly true

---
26. Op. cit. [1], *LotR* 4.5, p. 670.
27. Op. cit., *LotR* 5.1, respectively p. 751 and p. 758.
28. Op. cit., *LotR* 5.4, pp. 806-7.
29. Op. cit., *LotR* 5.4, p. 813.
30. Op. cit., *LotR* 5.4, p. 818.

in Denethor (759), and Pippin, on first meeting Denethor, was reminded of Aragorn because of the Steward's proud bones, ivory skin and deep eyes (754).

- Strangely they both had a scene of mutual appraisal with Gandalf. In *LotR* Pippin, watching as Denethor tried to outstare the Wizard, noted that superficially Denethor appeared more imposing, *"more kingly, beautiful, and powerful; and older"*[31] - even though Gandalf's power was clearly greater. It was Denethor who looked away in the end. A similar scene took place in Fangorn with Legolas and Gimli watching as Aragorn and Gandalf faced each other. Aragorn looked *"... as if some king out of the mists of the sea had stepped upon the shores of lesser men,"* but Gandalf clearly held a power *"... beyond the strength of kings."*.[32] The similarity is obvious; the difference is that Aragorn's emotion was reverence while Denethor's was hostility and scorn. These incidents illustrate their totally different attitudes to Gandalf.
- They also had different attitudes to the struggle with Sauron. In contrast to Denethor's one-dimensional approach Aragorn shared the same mission as Gandalf, wanting to unite those opposed to Sauron, not work in isolation. He was open-minded and saw the overall picture.
- There is a sharp contrast between Denethor's bitterness at Gondor's thankless vigil and the ungrudging protection given to the Shire by Aragorn's Rangers of the North.
- They were both well-versed in the history and lore of Middle-earth, but whereas Aragorn had actually travelled to all the places he had learnt about, mingling with the inhabitants and seeing things for himself at first-hand, Pippin (in *LotR* 5.4.807) reckoned Denethor had not been outside Gondor for many years. Denethor's knowledge came partly from learning and study: for example in *LotR* 5.1.756 he recognised Pippin's Barrow-down blade as being made by the Northern Dúnedain early in the Third Age, and at the Council of Elrond (*LotR* 2.2.246) Boromir made it clear that his father knew that Imladris was the Elvish name for Elrond's dwelling. Denethor's knowledge also came from his use of the Anor-stone - this is discussed in more detail below.
- Both had outstanding perception of the minds of others but used the gift differently, Denethor with scorn, Aragorn with empathy. If Denethor's attitude towards Faramir is anything to go by, it is difficult to imagine him treating the faint-hearted at the Morannon with the compassion meted out to them by Aragorn.
- Aragorn didn't expect others to do things he wouldn't do himself: as at the Morannon and through the Paths of the Dead, he led from the front. Denethor's policy was to lead from the rear - like the Lord of the Nazgûl and Sauron himself - as indicated in the conversation between him, Gandalf and Pippin in *LotR* 5.4.818-19.
- Both had superb mental strength enabling them to resist Sauron in a Palantír, though in different circumstances. Denethor used the Anor-stone over many years and had some success in preventing Sauron from taking over control of it before gradually succumbing to the despair engendered by Sauron's deception, which in the end would unhinge him. His strength came from his own character and also from his right, as the Ruling Steward, to use that particular Palantír. Aragorn, as *de jure* king, had an even stronger right to use any of the Palantíri and, as it turned out, a stronger mind. On taking possession of the Orthanc-stone he succeeded in wrenching it out of Sauron's control, and then carried on to deceive him into thinking that he had the Ring thus sending him into the brooding obsession which would lead to his downfall. Sauron overcame Denethor by deceit, but Aragorn overcame Sauron by deceit.
- Their strength of mind also influenced their attitude to the Ring. Denethor, erroneously in Gandalf's opinion (in *LotR* 5.4.814 he made it very clear that he did not trust Denethor with the Ring), believed that he was strong enough to keep it hidden in Minas Tirith and resist using it. Denethor also believed that Boromir would have brought the Ring to him if it had been he and not Faramir who had met Frodo in Ithilien. Aragorn, on the other hand, knew the Ring would corrupt him if he took possession of it and used his strength to refuse to have anything to do with it. Thus he showed superior wisdom and a willingness to listen to counsel (e.g. of Gandalf and Elrond).

---

31. Op. cit. [1], *LotR* 5.1, p. 757.
32. Op. cit., *LotR* 3.5, p. 501.

- Although both were gifted with great wisdom, Denethor's was impaired by jealousy and his conviction that Sauron's aggression was aimed solely at himself and Gondor.
- Overall Aragorn clung to hope while Denethor succumbed to Sauron-induced despair.

Wariness of Aragorn and Gandalf towards Denethor

As we are told in App A.I.iv.1055, Thorongil aroused the jealousy and suspicion of Denethor during his service to his father. It is inconceivable that someone with Aragorn's perception wouldn't have realised this and as a result his attitude towards Denethor must have been one of extreme wariness, and even fear, due to the increasing risk of his incognito being compromised. These feelings would undoubtedly have gathered momentum over the years, especially with the finding of the Ring and the approach of the time for him to make his claim for the kingship. The possibility of Denethor resisting his claim must have seemed very real and one wonders how he felt when he announced to Boromir at the Council of Elrond, *"I will come to Minas Tirith."*[33]. The thought of encountering Denethor again must have been rather daunting: another hurdle, easily overlooked, which Aragorn believed he would have to face. Gandalf would undoubtedly have shared Aragorn's apprehension, knowing the Steward's attitude to the Ring, his antipathy to Isildur's line and his insular view of the struggle with Sauron.

In *LotR* 5.8.861 after the victory at the Pelennor Fields Aragorn, along with Imrahil and Éomer, reached the walls of Minas Tirith where he took the decision to remain outside in his tents rather than enter the City and claim the kingship. His words to his companions showed his appreciation of the long period of Steward rule in Gondor and his concern to avoid any action which might cause unrest while the outcome of the war with Sauron was unknown. No doubt he was also recalling the last time he had been in Denethor's company and wished to avoid any confrontation at such a time. Imrahil, who knew Denethor well in the capacity of Counsellor, in addition to being his brother-in-law, supported Aragorn in this decision. Ironically Denethor was now actually dead, but Aragorn did not find this out until he received Gandalf's plea to attend the Houses of Healing. On being told that the Steward was a patient in the Houses, Éomer and Imrahil believed that this referred to Denethor until Gandalf enlightened them.

Denethor's knowledge from using the Anor-stone

From *UT* 4.3.526 we know that Denethor probably began using the Anor-stone as soon as he succeeded to the Stewardship in order to keep an eye on Gandalf and Thorongil. No more details are given on this specific motive, but a number of incidents in *LotR* show that he certainly found the Anor-stone a useful source of information:
- In *LotR* 5.1.757 he made it clear to Gandalf that he was already aware of the recent events at Helm's Deep and Isengard.
- In *LotR* 5.4.806-7 Pippin felt that Denethor was aware of what he had said and done the previous day, and later he was amazed at how much the Steward knew about the Rohirrim.
- Denethor also knew, prior to being actually informed, that the Lord of the Nazgûl had ridden out as captain of Sauron's hosts, and that Cair Andros had fallen.

There are also additional issues relating to Denethor's use of the Anor-stone:
- In *LotR* 5.1.757 during a conversation between Gandalf and Denethor about the "Seeing-stones" Pippin noticed that Denethor gave him an odd look as if knew that the Hobbit had looked in one. When Pippin had looked in the Orthanc-stone he had been locked into a confrontation with Sauron. Due to the nature of the Palantíri Denethor would not have been able to eavesdrop on that confrontation because third parties were automatically blocked in such cases. However he could have been using the Anor-stone at the time to look towards Isengard and realised what was going on.
- This begs the question as to whether Denethor knew that Aragorn had used the Orthanc-stone.

---

[33]. Op. cit. [1], *LotR* 2.2, p. 248.

Possibly - though there is no indication either way. Aragorn, like Pippin (though by design rather than accident), would have gone straight into confrontation with Sauron thus again blocking Denethor. After overcoming Sauron, he was able to direct the Stone where he wanted and would certainly have had the strength to avoid any confrontation with Denethor. As in Pippin's case Denethor could only have picked up Aragorn's action via observation.

- The reverse question of course is whether Aragorn realised that Denethor was using the Anor-stone. Again he might have picked this up by observation, especially if he used the Orthanc-stone again after his confrontation with Sauron - say on the journey from the Paths of the Dead to Pelargir and then up the river to the Harlond.
- It is suggested in *UT* 4.3.527-8 that Denethor may have used the Anor-stone to contact Saruman in the Orthanc-stone. As indicated above he was certainly watching events at Isengard and, providing his attempts were not made while Saruman was communicating with Sauron, there seems no reason why he should not have been able to confront Saruman directly. The essay in *UT* goes on to state that he probably did do this - and to his profit. With his superior right to use the Stone he perhaps found the strength to understand Saruman's intentions and was thus forewarned about his treachery.

*

It is clear that, alongside what he saw as a single-handed struggle against Mordor, Denethor's mind was also occupied with the activities of Gandalf and Thorongil/Aragorn and their supposed plot to supplant him. By the time of the War of the Ring thirty-five years into his Stewardship these concerns, along with the struggle to hold off Sauron's attempt to control him via the Anor-stone, had brought his mind to breaking point. Thus, with the battle raging on the Pelennor Fields and Minas Tirith under siege, he was in a state of despair due to a combination of factors:

- The death of Boromir three weeks earlier.
- The apparently imminent death of Faramir, which he saw as a foregone conclusion. Note his words to Pippin that "... ***even** the House of the Stewards has failed*"[34] [My emphasis] which seemed to show beyond doubt that he truly believed Aragorn's claim to be bogus.
- The prospect of Sauron's victory, which he also saw as a foregone conclusion - due to the size of Sauron's armies and the approach of the Corsairs' ships which he had seen in the Anor-stone. In fact when Pippin had suggested that Gandalf might be able to help the wounded Faramir Denethor declared, "*The fool's hope has failed. The Enemy has found it and now his power waxes...*"[35], thus indicating the extent of Sauron's influence on his mind.

As a result he became determined to cremate himself and Faramir on a pyre in the Houses of the Dead, this plan being foiled at the last minute by the intervention of Gandalf. Once Faramir had been removed from the pyre other issues seemed to take precedence in Denethor's mind, as shown by his final conversation with the Wizard. After jeering at Gandalf for continuing to hope for victory, he proceeded to accuse him of wanting to rule in Middle-earth himself, using Pippin as a spy and setting up a spurious claimant for the kingship. He then declared his refusal to submit to an "*upstart*", "*last of a ragged house long bereft of lordship and dignity*"[36], stating that if he could not rule Gondor himself in peace and be succeeded by a son who was uninfluenced by a Wizard then he wanted to have nothing - meaning that he preferred death. When Gandalf accepted his choice but determined that Faramir should be able to make his own decision on the subject, Denethor strode towards his son with a knife - only to be held back by Beregond who came between them. This led to further accusations that Gandalf, having already stolen half Faramir's love, was now working on the servants as well, thus preventing father and son from dying together. It was at this point that Denethor ordered the fire to be lit and jumped into it having broken his Steward's staff.

From Denethor's words and behaviour in this scene, it appears that he now regarded the establishment of

---

34. Op. cit. [1], *LotR* 5.4, p. 824.
35. Op. cit., *LotR* 5.4, pp. 823-4.
36. Op. cit., *LotR* 5.7, p. 854.

the "*Ranger of the North*"[37] in his place as inevitable. Thus his final concern did not seem to be the death of Faramir or the imminent victory of Sauron, both of which he was convinced were going to happen anyway, but fury at the machinations of Gandalf and, by implication, Thorongil who had inadvertently supplanted him in his father's esteem and affection forty years previously and was now (**not** inadvertently) preparing to claim the throne of Gondor. Even an unforeseen victory against Sauron would therefore bring him no joy or satisfaction as he would be replaced by Gandalf's "*upstart*" with the last surviving people of Gondor being ruled by "*mean folk*"[38].

It seems that an accumulation of jealousy and resentment, coupled with the certainty of being "supplanted" was the last straw for a mind already unbalanced.

By the time Aragorn's standard was raised at the Harlond Denethor was dead. If he had lived a few hours longer he would presumably have witnessed the healing of Faramir and realised that Aragorn's healing hands showed him to be the rightful king.

BOROMIR

Boromir was forty years of age in TA 3018 when he arrived in Rivendell in time for the Council of Elrond. In order to understand his general behaviour and his interactions with Aragorn during the journey of the Fellowship it is necessary to consider his family background - in particular the role and influence of Denethor.

App A.I.iv again proves informative. We are told that Boromir was like Denethor in face and pride, "*but in little else*"[39], meaning that he lacked his father's wisdom, perception and love of learning. Instead he resembled the reckless King Eärnur, being physically brave and fearless and concerned only with weapons and warfare. He had no interest in marriage, or in lore - except for tales relating to ancient battles. He also had a high opinion of himself, this opinion being shared by his younger brother Faramir, to whom he acted as helper and protector [a role perhaps encouraged by the untimely death of their mother Finduilas]. The two brothers were very fond of each other in spite of the fact that Denethor openly favoured Boromir over Faramir.

Regarding Denethor's feelings for Boromir it is stated that "*Denethor loved her* [Finduilas], *in his fashion, more dearly than any other,* **unless it were the elder of the sons that she bore him**."[40] [My emphasis]. This was echoed by Gandalf when he spoke of them both to Pippin: "*He loved him greatly: too much perhaps...*"[41]. This excessive love, no doubt increased by the death of Finduilas, may have been coloured by Denethor's experience of being passed over by his own father in favour of Thorongil, possibly - in his view anyway - with the connivance of Gandalf. As discussed earlier Denethor's last conversation with Gandalf prior to cremating himself stated his desire to have a son who was "*no wizard's pupil*"[42], a description which fitted Boromir but not (in Denethor's eyes) Faramir.

Because of Boromir's limited outlook and general lack of perception, he was easily influenced by his father, significantly affecting his relationship with Aragorn in *LotR*. His behaviour and attitude were coloured by Denethor's opinion on two subjects in particular, namely:
- His one-dimensional interpretation of the struggle with Mordor, leading to Boromir's assumption that only Gondor was playing an active and significant role against Sauron.
- His attitude to the Ring. As shown in *LotR* 5.4.813-14 Denethor believed he himself had the strength to resist the Ring, such that he would be able to keep it safe in Minas Tirith, using it only in desperate need. Boromir too would come to believe in his own ability to take possession of the Ring and yet resist its evil.

To put Boromir's life in context a brief chronology follows, based on information in App B.1090-92 and

---
37. Op. cit. [1], *LotR* 5.7, p. 853.
38. Op. cit., *LotR* 5.4, p. 824.
39. Op. cit., App A.I.iv, p. 1056.
40. Op. cit., App A.I.iv, p. 1056.
41. Op. cit., *LotR* 5.1, p. 753.
42. Op. cit., *LotR* 5.7, p. 854.

LotR 2.2.245-6:
- **2978**: Birth of Boromir. Given that Thorongil was possibly still living in Gondor up until 2980, he may well have encountered this one/two-year-old grandson of Ecthelion.
- **2980 approx**: Departure of Thorongil from Gondor.
- **2983**: Birth of Faramir.
- **2984**: Denethor became Steward on the death of Ecthelion.
- **2988**: Death of Finduilas when Boromir was ten years old.
- **3018 (June)**: Attack of Sauron's forces on Osgiliath along with a concurrent attack on the Elves of Mirkwood, the latter effecting the escape of Gollum. Boromir and Faramir were both heavily involved in the battle at Osgiliath. They were also both (but mostly Faramir) troubled by a dream which urged them to seek for the Sword that was Broken in Imladris (Rivendell). The first occurrence of this dream was experienced by Faramir on the eve of the assault on Osgiliath.
- **3018 (July 4th)**: Boromir set out to find Rivendell.
- **3018 (overnight October 24th/25th)**: Boromir arrived in Rivendell after a journey of a hundred and ten days.
- **3018 (October 25th)**: Council of Elrond.
- There is no record of Boromir's activities between the Council and the departure of the Fellowship of the Ring on December 25th, though he presumably spent the time in Rivendell along with Gandalf, the Hobbits, Legolas and Gimli. He then travelled with the Fellowship from December 25th 3018 to February 26th 3019 when he was killed by Orcs at Parth Galen while protecting Merry and Pippin.

I now turn to the main text of *LotR* and examine the Aragorn/Boromir relationship. Most of the material is contained within *LotR* 2.2-2.10 and 3.1.

*

Ignoring any speculative encounter between Thorongil and a two-year-old, Aragorn and Boromir first met at the Council of Elrond. An analysis of their exchanges and interaction at this event highlights the issues which were to shape their relationship, namely:
- Boromir's one-dimensional view of the struggle with Mordor
- Boromir's interest in the Ring
- Boromir's attitude to Aragorn and Isildur's line
- Aragorn's reaction to Boromir

Unless stated otherwise quotations are taken from *LotR* 2.2, beginning with the verse from the dream and *The Riddle of Strider* to help clarify parts of the discussion.

Dream Verse
"Seek for the Sword that was broken:
In Imladris it dwells;
There shall be counsels taken
Stronger than Morgul-spells.
There shall be shown a token
That Doom is near at hand,
For Isildur's Bane shall waken,
And the Halfling forth shall stand."[43]

---
43. Op. cit. [1], *LotR* 2.2, pp. 246-7.

The Riddle of Strider
"All that is gold does not glitter,
Not all those who wander are lost;
The old that is strong does not wither,
Deep roots are not reached by the frost.
From the ashes a fire shall be woken,
A light from the shadows shall spring;
Renewed shall be blade that was broken:
The crownless again shall be king."

Boromir's one-dimensional view of the struggle with Mordor

The first report made to the Council described in *LotR* 2.2 came from Glóin who gave an account of Sauron's threats to the Dwarves of the Lonely Mountain and the people of Dale. After he had finished Elrond told him, "*... you do not stand alone. You will learn that your trouble is but part of the trouble of all the western world*"[44], thus emphasising from the start that the struggle against Sauron was being waged all over the western part of Middle-earth.

Elrond continued with an account of the history of the Ring up to the point where he described the courage of the Lords of Minas Tirith as they continued to maintain the passage of the Anduin against Mordor. He then informed the Council that the Ring had been found and stated his intention of now calling on the relevant people to explain how this had come about. However before anything further could be said Boromir immediately got to his feet and began to proclaim the deeds of Gondor, particularly during Sauron's assault on Osgiliath four months previously. His words clearly showed the influence of Denethor and his belief that Gondor was solely responsible for keeping the West safe: "*By our valour the wild folk of the East are still restrained, and the terror of Morgul kept at bay; and thus **alone** are peace and freedom maintained in the lands behind us, bulwark of the West.*"[45] [My emphasis]. He went on to say that Gondor received much praise but little help from others, apart from the Rohirrim. Not content with extolling his people in general he then spoke of the dream and began to boast about the long solitary journey to Rivendell which he had subsequently taken on himself, against his father's wishes: a journey of one hundred and ten days "*full of doubt and danger*" and "*by roads forgotten...*"[46].

A little later he would give a further indication of his attitude to Gondor's role by misinterpreting the message in the dream, assuming that the Doom which was "*near at hand*" referred to the doom of Minas Tirith rather than that of the western lands in general. Only Gondor was relevant in his mind.

Boromir's attitude was based on ignorance as well as his father's influence. He made assumptions without knowing the facts. It did not occur to him that others might be fighting Sauron in their own way. Even though, as the Council progressed, Elrond and Aragorn gave plenty of evidence that the fight against Sauron was being carried out by others too, Boromir seemed unable to absorb this fact, saying to Elrond almost at the end of the Council, "*It would comfort us to know that others fought also with all the means that they have.*"[47] This was after Galdor had answered his continuing praise of Gondor ("*... even the end of its* [Gondor's] *strength is still very strong*"[48]) by reminding him that Gondor's vigilance could no longer keep back the Nine, and pointing out that Sauron might find other roads unguarded by Gondor. This blindness would continue. Although Elrond answered his concerns by informing him that other powers and realms **were** also playing their part, Boromir's attitude to Lothlórien and Galadriel when the Fellowship arrived there later on displayed little appreciation of what Elrond had said.

---

44. Op. cit. [1], *LotR* 2.2, p. 242.
45. Op. cit., *LotR* 2.2, p. 245.
46. Op. cit., *LotR* 2.2, p. 246.
47. Op. cit., *LotR* 2.2, p. 268.
48. Op. cit., *LotR* 2.2, pp. 266-7.

Boromir's interest in the Ring

Boromir's first recorded contribution at the Council (apart from gazing in wonder at Bilbo and Frodo) occurred prior to the conversations just described, at the point when Elrond recounted how Isildur had cut the One Ring from Sauron's hand and kept it for himself. This was news to Boromir as the story of the fate of the Ring had not penetrated to the South. His words *"Isildur took it! That is tidings indeed"*[49] clearly showed his interest in the Ring right from the start of the proceedings. Elrond answered him by stating that Isildur had regarded the Ring as recompense for the murder of his father and brother by Sauron, but that he had soon been betrayed by it to his death for which reason it became known as Isildur's Bane. He then went on to tell of the dwindling of the kingdoms of Arnor and Gondor and the rise of Sauron again, finishing with the announcement that the Ring had been found after being lost since Isildur's death.

So far Boromir had solved two parts of the dream verse: he had reached Imladris and he knew that Isildur's Bane was the Ring. He had also learnt that the Ring, regarded by Isildur as an heirloom of his House, had been found after being lost for over three thousand years. Since he had not at this point seen the broken sword or become acquainted with Aragorn he must surely have believed that he himself, as the son of Denethor ruler of Gondor, was entitled to claim possession of the Ring. This interpretation is strengthened by considering Faramir's conversation with Frodo in *LotR* 4.5 where Frodo stated that if anyone had a claim to Isildur's Bane it would be Aragorn. Faramir, at that point ignorant of Aragorn's lineage and the nature of the Bane, immediately queried why Boromir, *"prince of the city that the sons of Elendil founded"*[50] had not been the one to claim it.

The production (but not yet the identification) of the broken sword by Aragorn and the subsequent revelation of his descent from Isildur prompted Frodo's exclamation that the Ring therefore belonged to him [Aragorn]. Aragorn immediately disowned it and Gandalf told Frodo to show it to the Council. As Frodo held it up Boromir's eyes glinted. He now thought he understood the meaning of the last four lines of the dream verse, as shown by his words *"The Halfling! Is then the doom of Minas Tirith come at last?"*[51] As far as Boromir was concerned Frodo was clearly the Halfling mentioned, *"Doom"* meant the doom of Minas Tirith alone and the Ring, *"Isildur's Bane"*, was available for him to take back to Gondor to use **against** Sauron. My reasons for arriving at this interpretation are Aragorn's disowning of the Ring, and Boromir's question following his words just quoted, namely *"But why then should we seek a broken sword?"*[52] He had the Ring, *"Isildur's Bane"*, available to him so why should this - as yet unidentified - broken sword, which was in the hands of someone who appeared to be of dubious ability, be of any relevance now? Aragorn answered his question by pointing out that the word "doom" did not specifically apply to Minas Tirith, and by identifying the sword as Elendil's, now about to be reforged since the Ring had been found - in line with the prophecies. Boromir now realised that his interpretation had been incorrect and that *"Isildur's Bane shall waken"* referred to the signal for the reforging of the sword, and *"Seek for the Sword that was broken"* indicated the **House** of Elendil rather than just the **sword** of Elendil. (Later on in *LotR*, it is stated that Aragorn interpreted the message of the dream as being a summons to him, as Elendil's heir, to "... *come forth and strive with Sauron for the mastery.*"[53]).

Later in the Council, at the point when Elrond declared that the Ring must be sent to the Fire, Boromir stirred and fidgeted then eventually asked why they could not use the Ring to defeat Sauron rather than try to destroy it. Elrond's answer, explaining how the Ring corrupted those who tried to possess or use it, the strong and powerful most of all, clearly failed to convince Boromir who just looked doubtful and bowed his head in submission.

Thus there is plenty of evidence that Boromir was falling under the influence of the Ring right from the start, possibly even before actually seeing it. Frodo showed signs of uneasiness at his behaviour (as did Sam according to his words to Faramir in *LotR* 4.5.680) and it is highly improbable that the likes of Aragorn, Gandalf and Elrond failed to perceive Boromir's mind.

---

49. Op. cit. [1], *LotR* 2.2, p. 243.
50. Op. cit., *LotR* 4.5, p. 663.
51. Op. cit., *LotR* 2.2, p. 247.
52. Op. cit., *LotR* 2.2, p. 247.
53. Op. cit., *LotR* 2.8, p. 368.

Boromir's attitude to Aragorn and Isildur's line

Until the point when Aragorn dramatically cast the broken sword on the table Boromir appears not to have actually noticed him, no doubt partly because he was sitting alone in a corner wearing his travelling clothes which would have been camouflaging. Perhaps Aragorn was also overlooked because he appeared to be a person of small importance. Boromir's question, *"And who are you, and what have you to do with Minas Tirith?"*[54] is difficult to interpret. Was it spoken in genuine interest and curiosity, or in indignation and contempt? It is stated that he looked *"in wonder"*[55] at Aragorn's lean face and weather-stained cloak, perhaps comparing the stranger's attire with his own rich clothes, fur-lined cloak and silver collar. He had looked with *"wonder"* at Bilbo and Frodo too, but that would have been because he had not seen Hobbits before and because the verse in the dream had mentioned a Halfling. With Aragorn the wonder was more likely to have been amazement that someone so scruffy and unimposing and bearing a broken sword was considered important enough to be at the Council, and was also somehow connected with Minas Tirith.

When Aragorn asked Boromir if he wanted the House of Elendil to return to Gondor, Boromir's reply was haughty - he was only seeking an answer to the dream not begging for favours - but he reluctantly admitted that the sword of Elendil would be of great help to his people. He then added the words *"if such a thing could indeed return out of the shadows of the past"*[56] - hardly polite or tactful, especially as it was followed up with a doubtful look at Aragorn which made an already twitching Bilbo leap up to defend his friend by reciting *The Riddle of Strider*. Clearly the thoughts behind Boromir's wondering looks were less than complimentary. As Bilbo's speech no doubt intended to show, Boromir was judging Aragorn purely by his appearance and he maintained this attitude even after the extent of Aragorn's own travels and ordeals had been made abundantly clear to him.

When Aragorn declared his intention of reforging the sword and coming to Minas Tirith now that the Ring had been found, Boromir made no direct answer but began to question the truth of this statement (i.e. that the Ring had been found). Now realising that the dream referred to the return of Elendil's line to Gondor he was trying to find an excuse to avoid such a situation by casting doubts on the genuineness of the Ring. His last conversation with Aragorn as the Council drew to a close contained a remark which was insulting in the extreme: *"Mayhap the Sword-that-was-Broken may still stem the tide - **if the hand that wields it has inherited not an heirloom only, but the sinews of the Kings of Men.**"*[57] [My emphasis].

When assessing Boromir's attitude to Aragorn the question arises as to whether his father had spoken to him about a certain "Thorongil". There was nothing particularly in Boromir's behaviour to show that this was the case. His apparent assumption (shared by Faramir) that he himself, as a prince of Gondor, would have a claim to Isildur's Bane seemed to indicate ignorance of the possibility of Isildur's line still surviving in the North. Although his reluctance to welcome Aragorn to Gondor could perhaps have indicated an awareness of Denethor's attitude to the House of Isildur, it was more easily explained by the Steward's desire to carry on ruling Gondor himself - and Boromir's own desire when his turn came. In addition, Denethor's reticence about the words of the dream (all he had told his sons was that Imladris was the Elvish name of Elrond's dwelling in the North) implied that he had probably kept his thoughts of Thorongil's identity to himself. There is no real indication that Boromir shared his father's belief that only members of Anárion's line had the right to claim the throne of Gondor.

Aragorn's reaction to Boromir

Aragorn must have been intensely irritated and annoyed by Boromir's attitude: his arrogance, assumptions, one-sidedness and disrespect. However his initial reaction was merely to provide Boromir with information to help him understand the dream verse. He showed him the broken sword, he recited its ownership and history, and he corrected Boromir's interpretation of the word "Doom". In answer to Boromir's question as to

---

54. Op. cit. [1], *LotR* 2.2, p. 246.
55. Op. cit., *LotR* 2.2, p. 246.
56. Op. cit., *LotR* 2.2, p. 247.
57. Op. cit., *LotR* 2.2, p. 268.

Aragorn's identity it was Elrond who interrupted the proceedings to announce his name and lineage. Following Frodo's exclamation that the Ring thus belonged to Aragorn, Aragorn went on to stress that he did not regard it as belonging to him in spite of the fact that he was Isildur's heir.

It took an actual insult from Boromir and the indignant interruption from Bilbo to release Aragorn's real feelings. He started off quietly, sympathising with Boromir's doubt and agreeing that he did indeed bear little resemblance to the statues of Elendil and Isildur in Minas Tirith. However he then became increasingly vociferous as he regaled Boromir with the history of his people, his own long hard life (thus explaining his ragged and worn appearance), and the range and loneliness of his journeys - journeys which were many times longer and more dangerous than the one Boromir had just undertaken. He emphasised the different type of war - secretive and solitary - which the Northern Dúnedain were waging against Sauron's servants: creatures of Mordor which couldn't be contained by physical barriers, which worked on the mind and spirit inducing terror and despair. Boromir had encountered the Lord of the Nazgûl at Osgiliath, so he should have understood. At the same time Aragorn rode roughshod over Boromir's claim that only Gondor was active in the struggle: *"You know little of the lands beyond your bounds,"* and *"The North would have known them* [i.e. peace and freedom] *little but for us."*.[58] He became increasingly bitter as he described the scorn, ignorance and ingratitude of the people he and his kin were protecting, referring specifically to *"one fat man* [clearly Barliman Butterbur] *who lives within a day's march of foes that would freeze his heart, or lay his little town in ruin, if he were not guarded ceaselessly."*[59]. Then he calmed down and admitted that it was a deliberate policy to keep the activities of the Dúnedain and the nature of the dangers secret in order to prevent those they were guarding from being driven mad with fear. Although he appreciated that the ignorance of the Bree-folk was due to the Dúnedain's own policy, it must really have rankled that the son of the Steward of Gondor had the same misguided perception. He ended his speech by announcing that he would get the broken sword reforged and go to Minas Tirith. He resumed his mild manner for the rest of the Council and even when Boromir raised doubts as to his capability of wielding Elendil's sword, he just answered casually, *"Who can tell? But we will put it to the test one day."*[60] [This must have been no small feat of self-control!]

It is worth noting that by his mention of the statues in Minas Tirith Aragorn was in fact letting Boromir know that he had actually been in Gondor. Likewise, during a discussion as to whether Rohan paid tribute of horses to Mordor, he said, *"It was not so when last I was in that land"*[61], thus making it clear that he had been to Rohan as well.

*

The interaction between Aragorn and Boromir at the Council had not resulted in a very promising start to their relationship, and their feelings would have been ones of mutual wariness and apprehension.

Boromir had made his journey to Rivendell in order to seek an explanation for the dream. This objective had been achieved and he had also gained a valuable weapon for the war against Sauron in the shape of Elendil's sword. However this sword was to be accompanied by its owner who, as the heir of Elendil and Isildur, naturally regarded himself as the rightful King of Gondor. Even assuming that Boromir knew nothing of Thorongil (as seems likely) he must have been well aware of Denethor's attitude to the idea of a returning king - an attitude he himself shared as demonstrated by the remark made by Faramir in *LotR* 4.5.670 [quoted in the section on Denethor] when he told the Hobbits that the young Boromir was displeased that his father was only a steward and not a king.

From Aragorn's point of view he had gained Boromir's theoretical acceptance of his claim and his agreement that he should accompany him to Minas Tirith with Elendil's sword. However he was well aware that although Boromir was glad of the sword he accepted its bearer only reluctantly. At the Council, even after Aragorn's identity, lineage and achievements had been made clear, Boromir did not have the tact to hide his opinion that he lacked the qualities necessary for kingship. Aragorn was being treated with doubt and disrespect by

---

58. Op. cit.[1], *LotR* 2.2, p. 248.
59. Op. cit., *LotR* 2.2, p. 248.
60. Op. cit., *LotR* 2.2, p. 268.
61. Op. cit., *LotR* 2.2, p. 262.

someone who should have been revering him. This situation would undoubtedly cause problems in the event of Aragorn being in a position to actually make a claim for the kingship. He now knew that it was not just Denethor he might have difficulty in winning over, but his heir as well.

Aragorn left Rivendell immediately after the Council to join Elladan, Elrohir and Elrond's scouts in searching for evidence of the Nazgûl following their defeat at the Bruinen Ford. Thus he and Boromir did not meet again until the formation of the Fellowship of the Ring nearly two months later. Neither of them were intending to go all the way to Mordor with Frodo, because Aragorn's mission at this stage was to accompany Boromir to Minas Tirith and go into battle with the sword of Elendil, while Boromir of course was returning to his home. Thus they expected to leave the Company when they reached the Anduin, with Gandalf continuing to lead the other members eastwards. One of Aragorn's worries as preparations got under way for their departure from Rivendell would have been Boromir's attitude to himself as demonstrated at the Council. Boromir's insular view of the war with Mordor and his interest in the Ring were certainly also causes for concern, but not as much as they would be later on.

*

The journey of the Fellowship between the departure from Rivendell and the loss of Gandalf is covered in *LotR* 2.3 to 2.5. A study of these chapters reveals many aspects of Boromir's character and behaviour, both positive and negative. For instance he excelled at activities requiring physical strength and courage (such as face-to-face fighting, and journeying in difficult terrain) displaying fearlessness, loyalty and protectiveness in such situations. On the other hand he could be obstructive, foolish and ignorant, as well as liking his own way and being reluctant to listen to argument and counsel.

I will look at his positive qualities first:
- As the members of the Fellowship were named Boromir's courage was recognised by Aragorn who told Frodo that he was "*a valiant man*"[62]. Aragorn may have formed this opinion of Boromir partly from listening to his outpourings at the Council, but he must also have made it his business over the years to keep himself informed of people and events in Gondor and may have known about the attack on Osgiliath earlier that year. According to Faramir his brother was regarded as the best man in Gondor: "*... no heir of Minas Tirith has for long years been so hardy in toil, so onward into battle, or blown a mightier note on the Great Horn.*"[63]
- During the attempt on the pass of Caradhras Boromir's best qualities were very much in evidence. In fact his strength, courage and mountain know-how probably saved everyone's lives during the blizzard which drove them back. He had travelled in the White Mountains near his home and he was aware that Sauron was supposed to be able to control mountain weather. It was due to his advice that they had taken firewood with them and this was used when the cold became extreme. He was the one who decided when they should turn back and he took the lead in organising the rescue through the snowdrifts. He came over as very protective towards the Hobbits, recognising that they were in danger of freezing to death and removing a hypothermic Frodo from a pile of snow.
The question here is why Aragorn, in spite of his own extensive travels and terrain-awareness, did not take a more pro-active role, but just let himself be guided by Boromir. I believe the reason for this to be his desperate desire to avoid going through Moria owing to his premonition of something dire happening to Gandalf if they were to choose that route. As far as he was concerned the Caradhras route **had** to work and his anxiety led him to underestimate the danger of the blizzard. Boromir of course did not yet know about a possible route through Moria and he would have had no idea of Aragorn's fears for Gandalf. Aragorn's lack of initiative probably only confirmed his general opinion that Isildur's heir lacked some of the necessary qualities for kingship. He did however appreciate his strength during the snow rescue as he referred to them both as "*doughty Men*"[64].

---

62. Op. cit. [1], *LotR* 2.3, p. 276.
63. Op. cit., *LotR* 4.5, p. 679.
64. Op. cit., *LotR* 2.3, p. 292.

- Both Boromir and Aragorn played a significant part during the wolf attack - as was to be expected.
- Boromir was in his element when the Orcs attacked the Company in Moria, fighting the creatures and using his great strength to force doors closed. When the Balrog appeared he blew his horn making it hesitate slightly thus buying the Company a few, maybe vital, seconds. There was no more talk of **him** running away and leaving Gandalf than of Aragorn doing so, though the motives were different with Aragorn being moved by his love of a long-standing friend and mentor in addition to the basic loyalty to a companion in battle. When Aragorn finally led the way out of Moria after Gandalf was beyond help Boromir acted as rearguard.
- Frodo and Sam again benefited from Boromir's strength when they fell behind on the journey to Lothlórien as he and Aragorn carried them to a place where they could rest and have their injuries tended. Boromir co-operated completely with Aragorn in this.

Boromir's negative qualities will now be considered:
- As the Company left Rivendell on December 25th 3018, he blew a loud echoing blast on his horn - simply because he always did that on setting out, not wanting to "... *go forth as a thief in the night.*"[65]. However the Company's hope was in secrecy, and his action earned him a rebuke from Elrond. His ostentatious attitude contrasted sharply with Aragorn's simple Ranger clothing and emphasis on camouflage.
- After the Caradhras route proved impassable and Gandalf raised the possibility of going through Moria Boromir objected because of the evil omens associated with the place. He began to argue that they should travel via the Gap of Rohan instead - the route he had used himself on his journey to Rivendell - no doubt seeing it as a quicker and safer route to Minas Tirith. In the exchange with Gandalf which followed he demonstrated a worrying tunnel-vision. He had been told of Saruman's treachery at the Council yet he still thought it was safe to go to the Gap of Rohan which was within fifty miles of Isengard. He seemed unable to appreciate the different position he was in through being part of the Ring-bearer's Company, as opposed to being a lone traveller, as he had been before. Apart from the increased personal danger, there was the need to keep the Ring as far away as possible from Isengard. It was likely that Boromir's behaviour was already being influenced by his interest in the Ring and that he was driven by a growing determination to take it to Minas Tirith - as no doubt his father would have expected.
Aragorn shared Boromir's wish to go to Minas Tirith and of course carried his own private fear of Moria because of his concern for Gandalf. However he had already agreed to accompany Gandalf into the Mines - from guilt feelings because of the near-disaster on the mountain and probably from a sense of responsibility towards the rest of the Company if his premonition were to prove accurate and they ended up having to manage without Gandalf. He would certainly have appreciated the danger from Saruman's treachery, and, as demonstrated in a conversation at the Council of Elrond, he had an open mind on the subject of the friendship of the Rohirrim given their proximity to Isengard and the rumours that they provided Sauron with horses. Moria was really the only route to take.
- When Boromir couldn't answer Gandalf's arguments he showed his ignorance by likening Moria to Barad-dûr. Gandalf, who had actually been in Moria and in Sauron's lesser stronghold in Dol Guldur, told him in no uncertain terms that he didn't know what he was talking about. It was the arrival of the wolves which persuaded Boromir, as well as everyone else, of the need to get into Moria.
- During the frightening and stressful interval during which Gandalf tried to find the password for the doors of Moria, he and Boromir became quite aggressive to each other, with Boromir making it clear that he didn't trust the Wizard and Gandalf casting aspersions on Boromir's intelligence. This antagonism between them would have been worrying to Aragorn and he must have considered the possibility that Denethor's view of Gandalf had been passed on to his son.
- It was a tense situation with Boromir clearly very ill at ease, even frightened, at the thought of going into Moria and this may have accounted for his stupidity in throwing a stone into the pool. This was a difficult situation for him - being unable to fight a tangible enemy by physical action. Another

---

65. Op. cit. [1], *LotR* 2.3, p. 279.

interpretation is that he was also irritated at not getting his own way as he'd probably always had it before. For example he had told the Council of Elrond that his father had been loth to let him go on the errand to Rivendell, but that he had insisted. This was confirmed by Faramir to Frodo in *LotR*: "... *he would not be stayed*"[66]. Also when Denethor said that Faramir should have gone to Imladris instead of Boromir, Gandalf said, "*Boromir claimed the errand and would not suffer any other to have it. He was a masterful man, and one to take what he desired.*"[67]. Whatever Boromir's motive, Aragorn must have been greatly alarmed by his action and its consequences, especially if he noted, as Gandalf did, that the Watcher-in-the-Water went straight for Frodo. Was Boromir's behaviour caused by the Ring, and did the Watcher want the Ring?

- As the Company reached (temporary) safety inside Moria, Boromir was still complaining that they had entered it against his will, apparently ignoring the fact that there had not actually been any alternative anyway, firstly because of the wolves and secondly because of his own action in rousing the Watcher.

During this part of the journey, from leaving Rivendell on December 25th until the escape from Moria into the Dimrill Dale on January 15th, Boromir seems to have gelled pretty well with the Company, perhaps with the younger Hobbits in particular, so long as he was in a physically demanding, physically protective role. (Later when Pippin was in Gondor and first set eyes on Faramir we are told that he noticed his resemblance to Boromir "... *whom Pippin had liked from the first, admiring the great man's lordly but kindly manner.*"[68]) As for Boromir's relationship with Aragorn the two probably got on best when involved in active struggles together: the mountain rescue; dealing with the wolves; fighting the Orcs in Moria; standing by Gandalf on the Bridge of Khazad-dûm; carrying Frodo and Sam when they lagged behind the others. Boromir was in his element in these situations, doing what he did best and sharing a common goal with Aragorn.

Most of Boromir's negative behaviour at this stage of the journey was connected with his reluctance to go via Moria and his preference for the Gap of Rohan route. Whether or not this meant that he was starting to be influenced by the Ring and looking for ways to get it to Minas Tirith, his behaviour was an indication of what was to come.

*

Aragorn's assumption of the leadership after the fall of Gandalf, and his decision to take the Company to Lothlórien marked the start of a serious deterioration in his relationship with Boromir. All the negative factors which had surfaced so far became much more significant. The Fellowship's journey from the Dimrill Dale to Parth Galen is described in *LotR* 2.6-2.10. I have identified three main issues which influenced the relationship between Aragorn and Boromir during this period:
- Boromir's attitude to Lothlórien
- Disagreement about the onward route
- Influence of the Ring on Boromir

It could be argued that the influence of the Ring was relevant in all three of these issues and the following discussion reflects this. However Boromir's attitude to Lothlórien and the conflicts between him and Aragorn over the route are also significant in their own right and merit their separate headings. The discussion on the influence of the Ring is confined to specific references.

Boromir's attitude to Lothlórien

Aragorn did not know Gandalf's long-term plans for the journey beyond the Misty Mountains (and suspected that the Wizard had not actually had any), but he did know that Gandalf intended to go to Lothlórien, and as this also tied in with his own inclination he accordingly led the Company there. Apart from anything else it was

---

66. Op. cit. [1], *LotR* 4.5, p. 671.
67. Op. cit., *LotR* 5.1, p. 755.
68. Op. cit., *LotR* 5.4, p. 810.

essential that they found somewhere where they could rest and recuperate in safety after the horrors of Moria.

Boromir however was very reluctant to go there, and in answer to Aragorn's question as to what way he would prefer replied, "*A plain road, though it led through a hedge of swords*"[69]. He was convinced that there was something sinister about the Company having journeyed through Moria "*to evil fortune*"[70], still speaking of it as being done against his will and ignoring the fact that it was partly his own action which had forced that route upon them. He was also deeply wary of Lothlórien viewing it as perilous and believing that they were unlikely to get out unscathed - if at all. His attitude was actually that of the Gondorians in general and was shared by the Rohirrim (as demonstrated by Éomer in *LotR* 3.2.432, 437). This was no doubt due to the general estrangement between Elves and Men as the Third Age progressed, aided and abetted by Sauron and his servants. It is possible too that Saruman's influence was a factor: he had long posed as a friend to Gondor, being given the keys to Orthanc by Beren the nineteenth Steward in TA 2759 (App B.1088), and it is made clear at the Council of Elrond that Denethor held him in higher esteem than he did Gandalf. Aragorn was able to persuade Boromir that there was in fact no other way for them to go, at the same time voicing doubts as to the wisdom of the folk of Minas Tirith if they now spoke evil of Lothlórien, and telling Boromir bluntly that the place was only perilous to evil or to people who brought evil with them. He must certainly have come to suspect Boromir of harbouring inappropriate thoughts about the Ring and was now starting to make his suspicions obvious.

Following the meeting with Galadriel and Celeborn, during which the former explored the minds of the Company by reading their thoughts, Boromir displayed an open mistrust of Galadriel personally, specifically warning Frodo against her and casting doubt on her motives. This clearly angered Aragorn who told him to stop speaking ill of her, then emphasised again that evil only existed in Lothlórien if people brought it there themselves - and if they did so, then they should beware. His own attitude was in complete contrast: having rebuked Boromir he then threw himself on to his bed and fell asleep, exhausted by grief and fear and knowing that he was now in a place where he could sleep in safety. It is possible to interpret Boromir's warning to Frodo as indicating that he believed Galadriel herself to be after the Ring. Personally I doubt that he was sufficiently perceptive for this and feel that his attitude was much more likely to be due to him picking up her suspicions of his own motives. [I discuss the question of whether Aragorn suspected Galadriel of being tempted by the Ring in Chapter 2.1.]

Apart from arousing Aragorn's anger, Boromir's attitude to Lothlórien must also have been very distressing for him. Thirty-eight years earlier, with the blessing and connivance of Galadriel, he had taken refuge there after a previous exhausting journey. During that visit he had had a second meeting with Arwen, a meeting which had led to their courtship and betrothal. His attitude towards Galadriel was one of reverence - hence his outspoken defence of her in the face of Boromir's prejudice based on ignorance.

Immediately prior to the departure of the Fellowship from Lothlórien, Celeborn spoke to them of the lands they would pass through, particularly advising against becoming tangled up in Fangorn if Boromir and any of the others decided to leave the river and head off towards Minas Tirith. Boromir complacently dismissed Celeborn's warning as old wives' tales with the amazingly blinkered remark, "*All that lies north of Rohan is now to us so far away that fancy can wander freely there.*"[71]. He then launched again into a description of his journey from Minas Tirith to Rivendell - the long and exhausting nature of it, the loss of his horse, etc. - confidently declaring that he had little doubt that that journey, along with his recent travels with the Fellowship, would equip him to find a way through Rohan and Fangorn too. Celeborn reacted with a loaded acknowledgement that he therefore didn't need to say any more, along with a mild admonition not to dismiss old wives' tales out of hand.

It seems ironic that Boromir had been reassured by Elrond at the Council that, unknown to him [Boromir], other powers besides Gondor were fighting the battle against Sauron in their own way. Lothlórien was clearly one of the powers Elrond had in mind, but Boromir obviously failed to appreciate the fact.

Strangely, as the departing Company rounded a bend in the river after their last sight of Lothlórien we are told that they all had eyes full of tears. By implication this included Boromir, so maybe the leave-taking, with its gifts and sadness, made some sort of favourable impression on him in spite of himself.

---

69. Op. cit. [1], *LotR* 2.6, p. 338.
70. Op. cit., *LotR* 2.6, p. 338.
71. Op. cit., *LotR* 2.8, p. 374.

Disagreement about the onward route

As far as Boromir himself was concerned there was no argument about the route: he was going back home to Minas Tirith. Frodo, as would become evident later, knew he himself had to head direct to Mordor but could not (in Sam's words) "*screw himself up*"[72] to make the decision - partly through fear and partly through reluctance to take his companions with him into such danger. Aragorn, now in the role of Gandalf and thus responsible for supporting the Ring-bearer in the attempt to destroy the Ring, could no longer follow his original intention and simply accompany Boromir, particularly as the obvious road to Mordor was not via Minas Tirith. His resulting indecision as to whether to head east or west - or split the Company - was to lead to conflict with Boromir and a worsening of their relationship, with Boromir chafing with impatience to get back to his home and probably contemptuous of what he saw as Aragorn's lack of decisive leadership. He was clearly not perceptive enough to appreciate his mental turmoil and conflict.

As the Company discussed their route with Celeborn on their last evening in Lothlórien it was Boromir who spoke out, declaring that if they followed **his** advice they would go to Minas Tirith. This was followed by a rather pointed remark aimed at Aragorn, "*But I am not the leader of the Company.*"[73]. Celeborn, seeing the depth of Aragorn's hesitation from his doubtful and troubled expression, agreed to provide the Company with boats so that they could continue travelling for some days before reaching the point where they would have to leave the river and turn either east to Mordor or west to Gondor.

Seven days into the river journey they reached the rapids at Sarn Gebir unexpectedly at night because Aragorn, in his distracted condition, had misjudged the distance. Boromir was vociferous in his criticism, declaring that it was madness to cross the Rapids in the dark, presumably thinking that Aragorn had knowingly tried to do so. It was Boromir who shouted the instructions and encouragement to get the boats into safer waters. This incident resembled the situation on Caradhras with Aragorn misjudging or underestimating the danger and Boromir leaping into action.

Their most serious disagreement over the route occurred the next day. Boromir was becoming much more forceful, wanting to abandon the boats north of Sarn Gebir and head across the Entwash Vale in the direction of Minas Tirith. Meanwhile Aragorn was determined to stay with the boats as long as possible to keep their options open and also to give them the advantage of having the river as a clear path as opposed to the possible problems of fog and fens if Boromir's suggestion were adopted. He was also anxious to visit the lookout hill of Amon Hen above Rauros in a last desperate attempt to see something which might help him decide on the route. This was their most hostile encounter so far with Boromir deprecatingly referring to the "*cockle-boats*"[74] of Lothlórien and sarcastically asking Aragorn if he was going to jump down the Falls of Rauros, while Aragorn angrily chided Boromir for apparently forgetting the significance of the lookout point at the top of Amon Hen during the days of the kings of Gondor. In the end Aragorn won the argument because it was clear that Frodo would go wherever he led. Given that Frodo would by now have been very suspicious of Boromir his unquestioning trust in Aragorn was not really surprising - nevertheless Boromir must have resented it.

In a further argument, on the subject of the portage-way past the Rapids, Gimli also became involved, being angered by Boromir's insinuation that only the Men would be able to manage that route and carry the boats and luggage. Later Boromir sarcastically suggested that Aragorn might want to pass the Argonath (where the river was particularly narrow and fast-flowing) by night, presumably having a dig about his faulty reckoning at the Rapids. He then turned his sarcasm on to an exhausted Gimli.

This last incident occurred late on February 24th. Two days later the Fellowship reached Parth Galen where matters were finally taken out of their hands by the uncanny scattering of the Company.

Influence of the Ring on Boromir

There is no doubt in my mind that by the time the Fellowship were preparing to leave Lothlórien Boromir was determined to ensure that the Ring went to Minas Tirith, hence his arguments in favour of this route for the

---

72. Op. cit. [1], *LotR* 2.10, p. 403.
73. Op. cit., *LotR* 2.8, p. 367.
74. Op. cit., *LotR* 2.9, p. 389.

whole company, even though it would have been a detour for the Ring-bearer. Galadriel had certainly realised, from her reading of his thoughts, that Boromir was *"in peril"*[75] (as reported by Gandalf to Aragorn, Legolas and Gimli). This interpretation fits in with Denethor's statement when he turned on Faramir in the presence of Gandalf for letting the Ring go: "*He* [Boromir] *would have remembered his father's need, and would not have squandered what fortune gave. He would have brought me a mighty gift.*". Gandalf answered: "*In no case would Boromir have brought it to you.... He would have stretched out his hand to this thing, and taking it he would have fallen.*".[76] Even Faramir, who was devoted to his elder brother, was under no illusions about his character and realised that he might have wanted to bring Isildur's Bane - whatever it was - to Minas Tirith, especially if it was some weapon which would have been advantageous in battle. He told Frodo and Sam, "*... I can well believe that Boromir, the proud and fearless, often rash, ever anxious for the victory of Minas Tirith (and his own glory therein), might desire such a thing and be allured by it.*"[77]

As Aragorn was now duty-bound to protect Frodo following the loss of Gandalf Boromir's interest in the Ring was an infinitely more serious problem for him than it had been hitherto. With the spectre of Isildur's fate at the back of his mind and Boromir's increasing harassment of Frodo Aragorn must have felt growing alarm. This harassment began as soon as the Fellowship reached Lothlórien. After Galadriel's interrogation Boromir questioned Frodo persistently and attempted to make him distrust her, perhaps hoping that Frodo would come to believe that it would be foolish to destroy the Ring. Aragorn must have felt the need to be constantly on guard for Frodo and this may explain why he didn't go off and spend time with the Elves as Legolas and Gimli did - though he must surely have wanted to. On the last night in Lothlórien (*LotR* 2.8.369) when the Company were discussing their onward journey Boromir sat with his eyes fixed on Frodo as if trying to read his thoughts. He was so engrossed in this that he began to speak out loud hinting - but not actually saying in so many words - that it would be folly to destroy the Ring. Unfortunately, although Frodo picked up his meaning, Aragorn himself was so wrapped up in his own thoughts that he failed to notice what Boromir was saying.

Later, on the river journey, Boromir became restless, muttering and trying to get close to Frodo's and Aragorn's boat. Further harassment took place after the incident when the Nazgûl flew over the river, with Boromir eagerly questioning Frodo about it and trying to peer into his face. Finally, when the Company arrived at Parth Galen and Frodo left them to seek solitude while he made up his mind which route to take, Boromir watched him intently as he walked away, clearly noting the direction he took. During the discussions which followed he adopted a position at the edge of the group, and when the opportunity arose he was able to slip away unnoticed, follow Frodo and attempt to get the Ring from him - by force when persuasion failed to achieve his objective.

In the scene with Frodo on Amon Hen Boromir was in fact enacting the situation he had originally envisaged at the Council of Elrond, namely that the Ring was destined to come into his possession so that he could take it back to Minas Tirith to use in the war against Sauron. Aragorn had refused it and Boromir saw himself - the rightful owner - driving the hosts of Mordor in battle. His final words which caused Frodo to put on the Ring were "*It should be mine. Give it to me!*"[78].

*

The shock of Frodo's disappearance seemed to bring Boromir to his senses, breaking the hold of the Ring and making him realise the folly of what he had tried to do. Now repentant he wandered alone losing track of the time before finally returning to the rest of the Company at Parth Galen. Aragorn was clearly suspicious of him especially as he would only give the bare outline of where he had been and what he had been doing. However further questioning was prevented by the sudden madness which scattered the Company. The other three Hobbits and Legolas and Gimli all ran off in a panic or followed their own agenda ignoring Aragorn's orders to pair up before starting the search for Frodo. At this point Boromir was the only one who did what Aragorn told him ("*Go after those two young hobbits, and guard them at the least, even if you cannot find*

---

75. Op. cit. [1], *LotR* 3.5, p. 496.
76. Op. cit., *LotR* 5.4, p. 813.
77. Op. cit., *LotR* 4.5, p. 671.
78. Op. cit., *LotR* 2.10, p. 399.

Frodo"[79]) perhaps respecting Aragorn at last. It was also a task he excelled at - guarding the vulnerable from danger - thus giving him the chance to make amends for his error.

His changed attitude was born out by his behaviour when Aragorn found him as he lay dying (*LotR* 3.1.413-4). His first words were a confession that he had tried to take the Ring from Frodo (something he had presumably felt unable to admit in front of the whole Company), followed by an apology and an acknowledgement that he had paid for what he had done. After telling Aragorn that the Halflings had been taken alive by the Orcs, he exhorted him to go and save Minas Tirith. His last words, "*I have failed,*" could be interpreted in several ways. He had succumbed to the lure of the Ring, he had failed to prevent the capture of Merry and Pippin, and he knew he would never now be able to return to his home and save his people. Aragorn responded by taking his hand, kissing his brow and telling him, "*You have conquered. Few have gained such a victory. Be at peace! Minas Tirith shall not fall!*"[80]. By his first two sentences he recognised not only Boromir's military victory over the twenty-plus Orcs he had killed single-handed, but also the more significant psychological one over the Ring at last. The third and fourth sentences were expressions of reassurance to Boromir that he was forgiven and that his city would be saved, while the physical contact provided comfort and even perhaps an element of healing from the mental trauma of yielding to the Ring and the resulting remorse. (In the later healing scenes in *LotR* 5.8.865, 867-70 Aragorn's touch and kiss are significant and clearly part of the healing process.) In addition to respect, compassion and forgiveness, Aragorn also showed discretion and honour by not telling Legolas and Gimli that Boromir had tried to take the Ring ("*The last words of Boromir he long kept secret*"[81]), though on the reunion with Gandalf in *LotR* 3.5.496 his old friend and mentor would read his thoughts and guess the truth.

As I discussed in detail in Chapter 2.4, Aragorn had long been weighed down by stress, fear, indecision and low self-esteem, especially since the loss of Gandalf with its resulting heartache. The death of Boromir was the last straw for him bringing additional grief and also an extra burden, namely guilt: for having let Gandalf down; for the circumstances of Boromir's death; and for the now likely failure of the quest. He had arrived too late to save Boromir; he had not even killed any of the Orcs who had attacked the Company ("*I am unscathed, for I was not here with him*"[82]); and he had failed to ask about the whereabouts of Frodo while Boromir was still able to speak. The reason for his delay was that he had decided to climb up to the Seat of Seeing because he had been unsure what to do. He must also have felt that all these events could have been prevented if he had noticed Boromir slipping away after Frodo in the first place. Thus, he believed, his own inadequacy had brought about Boromir's death and the ruin of the Company.

There was also the question of Boromir's horn. In *LotR* 4.5.666 Faramir explained to Frodo and Sam that the blowing of it **anywhere in Gondor** would summon help. Later on Denethor spoke of the horn to Pippin: "*And in my turn I bore it, and so did each eldest son of our house, far back into the vanished years before the failing of the kings, since Vorondil father of Mardil hunted the wild kine of Araw in the far fields of Rhûn.*"[83] He went on to say that the horn would now "*wind no more*"[84] and questioned Pippin as to why no help came when Boromir blew it. Thus a great heirloom of the Stewards, dating back over a thousand years, had been destroyed, having failed to summon help when Boromir blew it at Parth Galen (the Argonath had marked the boundary of Gondor of old). This destruction of the horn can indeed - as has been argued - be seen as symbolic of the end of the ruling Stewards, with Andúril, reforged, symbolising the imminent return of the kings. However this interpretation was hardly likely to have occurred to Aragorn at this point! As far as he was concerned the events at Parth Galen were caused by his failure, thus greatly increasing his anguish.

With the encouragement of Legolas and Gimli Aragorn pulled himself together sufficiently to organise Boromir's funeral. This was done with respect, sensitivity and an awareness of what was most fitting for the fallen warrior, as shown by the following:

---

79. Op. cit. [1], *LotR* 2.10, p. 405.
80. Op. cit., *LotR* 3.1, p. 414.
81. Op. cit., *LotR* 3.1, p. 419.
82. Op. cit., *LotR* 3.1, p. 414.
83. Op. cit., *LotR* 5.1, p. 755.
84. Op. cit., *LotR* 5.1, p. 755.

- Aragorn's vigil at the bier while Legolas and Gimli went to fetch the boats.
- Lying him in one of the boats and giving him to the Anduin, River of Gondor, which would ensure that his body would not be dishonoured.
- Arranging his own and his enemies' weapons around him, along with his helm and broken horn.
- Caring for his appearance by combing his hair and ensuring that the belt of Lothlórien was round his waist.
- The impromptu lament/eulogy by Aragorn (mostly) and Legolas commemorating Boromir's much-vaunted journey to Rivendell and his last battle at Parth Galen, along with a reference to the Anduin leading to the Sea.
- Above all, the sparing of the time, in a desperately urgent situation, to bid an appropriate farewell to their comrade.

*

The following section looks in more detail at the issues behind the uneasy relationship between Boromir and Aragorn as exemplified by Boromir's ambivalent attitude to Aragorn's leadership of the Company and to his status as Isildur's heir and potential King of Gondor.

In general, although Boromir's behaviour must have added to Aragorn's worries, he did actually observe basic proprieties and principles, accepting decisions even when he didn't agree with them. For example he had wanted to go straight to Minas Tirith from Sarn Gebir and thought it a pointless exercise to carry the boats and luggage past the Rapids, but he did actually co-operate with the task. Also in spite of his ignorance of the significance of Amon Hen and his sarcastic suggestion about Aragorn wanting to pass the Argonath at night, Boromir was actually very respectful when the Company sailed through the Argonath, bowing his head in awe.

He never actually challenged Aragorn's leadership, though that must surely have been partly because he realised that none of the other members of the Company would have supported such a move from him. His dig at Aragorn prior to departure from Lothlórien, when he stated which route he himself would take then pointedly remarked that he was not the leader of the Company, can easily be interpreted as a hint that he would have liked to be the leader because that would have solved his problem of ensuring that the Ring reached Minas Tirith. Indeed the possibility arose of him getting his way when Aragorn and Legolas went off together to find the portage-way. As they left, Aragorn told the rest of the Company to wait for a day after which, if he and Legolas hadn't returned, they should assume that something had happened to them and choose a new leader. Did Boromir think his chance might come? Or did he think that the others would reject his leadership even if Aragorn was no longer there?

Some of the observations made by Faramir and Frodo in *LotR* 4.5.664, 670 shed further light on Boromir's attitude. Note that the conversation took place before Faramir knew the nature of Isildur's Bane:
- When discussing Aragorn's descent from Elendil and Isildur Frodo told Faramir that Boromir had been satisfied that Aragorn's claim was genuine.
  This does seem to have been the case, and in this Boromir differed from his father who persisted in regarding Aragorn as an upstart and usurper. This may well have been because Boromir had heard Elrond's statement, at the Council, of Aragorn's direct descent from Isildur and Elendil.
- Further on in the conversation Faramir spoke of Boromir's dissatisfaction that his father was only a steward and not a king - implying that Boromir would have liked to be a king one day. In fact during the confrontation with Frodo on Amon Hen, while carried away with what he would do if he had the Ring, he had actually seen himself as a king: "... *his talk dwelt on walls and weapons, and the mustering of men .... and he cast down Mordor, and became himself a mighty King, benevolent and wise.*"[85].
  In this he showed a similar attitude to that of Denethor who, while in theory regarding the kingship as sacrosanct, was in practice opposed to the idea of a returning king.
- Frodo answered that, "... *always he* [Boromir] *treated Aragorn with honour*", to which Faramir replied

---
85. Op. cit. [1], *LotR* 2.10, p. 398.

that he did not doubt it and that if Boromir was indeed satisfied with Aragorn's claim then he would "*greatly reverence him.*"[86]

Until the death-scene at Parth Galen I cannot think of any example of Boromir treating Aragorn with honour, or reverencing him! Do we assume that Frodo had witnessed interactions between them which are not described in the narrative? Why did the perceptive Faramir, who must have known of his father's attitude to the kingship, believe that Boromir who was greatly influenced by him would reverence a potential claimant to the throne of Gondor?

- Faramir then went on to explain that, "*... the pinch had not yet come. They had not yet reached Minas Tirith or become rivals in her wars.*"[87]

Faramir now appeared to understand the tensions which would result from Aragorn's arrival in Minas Tirith. He seemed to be contradicting himself, implying that although Boromir was capable of "greatly reverencing" Aragorn he would still regard him as a rival when "*the pinch*" came. Maybe he thought that in the end Boromir would be swayed by Denethor, or merely by resentment at losing his status as "*the best man in Gondor*"[88]. Aragorn himself demonstrated a similar understanding of the tensions as shown by his reluctance to enter the city as king after the Battle of the Pelennor Fields (*LotR* 5.8.861).

Boromir's obsession with the Ring and the influence of his father were clearly major causes of his uneasy relationship with Aragorn. However the differences in the character and attitude of the two of them are also very relevant in this context. Aragorn and Boromir did indeed have many qualities in common - high physical courage, prowess in battle, bodily strength, ability to endure hardship, selfless loyalty and protectiveness towards others in dangerous situations - but the differences between them were much more significant than the similarities. I have identified three main traits of Boromir which illustrate these differences, namely:
- Lack of perceptiveness
- Desire for personal glory
- Antipathy to Gandalf and the Elves

Lack of perceptiveness

In *LotR* Gandalf spoke to Pippin of Denethor thus: "*... by some chance the blood of Westernesse runs nearly true in him* [Denethor]; *as it does in his other son, Faramir,* **and yet did not in Boromir whom he loved best.**"[89] [My emphasis]. Boromir, unlike his father and brother, lacked the characteristics associated with a Númenórean descent - in particular the deep powers of perception inherent in that race. This exemplified the contrast between him and Aragorn - who of course had the Númenórean lineage and qualities to the highest degree. As the following examples show, Boromir displayed little awareness and understanding of the motives, feelings and, to some extent, deeds of others:

- This trait in his character led to him being easily influenced - even brainwashed - by Denethor, with the result that he inherited his father's tunnel-vision concerning the struggle with Sauron, relating it exclusively to Gondor and regarding everything else which went on in the west of Middle-earth as being unimportant.
- In addition - but unlike his father in this respect - he concentrated his energies, interest and sense of value on military matters to the exclusion of all else. This made him oblivious to the concurrent, non-military or less high-profile struggles being operated against Sauron. Even after Aragorn had enlightened him at the Council of Elrond he seemed to have no appreciation of the secret, thankless and dangerous vigil of the Northern Dúnedain, and of Aragorn in particular. His repeated references to his own gruelling and perilous journey from Gondor to Rivendell showed a mental blindness to the appalling danger Aragorn had been in throughout his life simply because of who he was.
- As shown in *LotR* 2.4.296, when he urged the Fellowship to avoid Moria by taking the Gap of Rohan

---

86. Op. cit. [1], *LotR* 4.5, p. 670.
87. Op. cit., *LotR* 4.5, p. 670.
88. Op. cit., *LotR* 4.5, p. 679.
89. Op. cit., *LotR* 5.1, p. 759.

route, Boromir didn't understand that he had been relatively safe during his own solitary journey to Rivendell, but was in increased danger now he was travelling with the Ring-bearer.
- Being spoilt by his father's obsessive love he had too high an opinion of himself which prevented him fully appreciating the merits of others.
- Although he knew the story of Isildur he seemed unable to understand why Aragorn didn't want to use the Ring.
- He did not perceive the psychological aspects of his companions' struggles, particularly Aragorn's feelings of grief and inadequacy on the loss of Gandalf.
- There is no indication as to whether Boromir knew of Aragorn's connection with Arwen. Admittedly he had been in Rivendell for two months prior to the departure of the Fellowship, but Aragorn himself had been absent for most of that time so there would have been no obvious hints of the relationship. Regarding the gift-giving scene in Lothlórien, even Frodo, being wrapped up in his own troubles, missed the hints about Arwen and Aragorn's "treasure", so I think it unlikely that Boromir would have picked anything up. Even if he had it would have failed to register as anything important since he had no interest in affairs of the heart himself.

Desire for personal glory

Faramir (in *LotR* 4.5.671) recognised that Boromir's desire for victory in battle went hand-in-hand with the desire for his own glory. As implied in App A.I.iv.1056-7, he regarded himself as unrivalled in this respect. He wanted people to know who he was and where he came from, and to praise his achievements. With this attitude it is perhaps not surprising that he resented being only the son of a steward rather than of a king.

The following examples highlight the contrast between him and Aragorn in this respect:
- During a discussion of the Southampton UK Tolkien Reading Group in 2010, attention was drawn to the following words spoken by Aragorn as he and the Hobbits prepared to leave Bree: "*But so ends all hope of starting early, and slipping away quietly!* ***We might as well have blown a horn to announce our departure.***"[90] [My emphasis]. This was in fact exactly what Boromir did when the Fellowship left Rivendell in spite of the need for secrecy. The Reading Group observed that this behaviour typifies the difference between the two characters.
- Aragorn's life was one of secrecy, disguise, homelessness and sometimes contemptuous treatment by others, as opposed to Boromir's life of renown, praise, appreciation and luxury. Compare the lean face of Aragorn and his weather-stained cloak with Boromir's rich clothes when they first met at the Council of Elrond.
- Basically we have the scenario of the person who "blows his own trumpet" (or horn?!), shouting out his achievements, as opposed to the person who is quietly doing something just as (or more) vital and praiseworthy behind the scenes but gets no recognition.

Antipathy to Gandalf and the Elves

There are a number of prickly exchanges between Gandalf and Boromir in *LotR*, for example:
- Gandalf's pointed remark at the Council of Elrond that something as significant as the Scroll of Isildur had been overlooked by those in Gondor (*LotR* 2.2.252).
- The difference of opinion between them about the advisability of going via the Gap of Rohan rather than Moria, during which Boromir displayed ignorance and was cut down to size by Gandalf (*LotR* 2.4.296).
- The short-tempered conversation at the doors of Moria while Gandalf was trying to remember the password (*LotR* 2.4.306).

---
90. Op. cit. [1], *LotR* 1.11, p. 178.

These incidents highlight the very different relationship between Boromir and Gandalf compared with that between Aragorn and Gandalf. Aragorn knew Gandalf extremely well and trusted him completely. This was not the case with Boromir who seemed to have absorbed his father's mistrust of the Wizard. (We know from Faramir's conversation with Frodo in *LotR* 4.5.670 that Gandalf had visited Minas Tirith while the brothers were growing up.) Gandalf also seemed to have a personality clash with Boromir - as he did with Denethor. Both these clashes are apparent in *LotR* 5.4 when Gandalf made it plain to Denethor that Boromir would not have brought the Ring to him if he had managed to get hold of it. Denethor's cold reply was, "*You found Boromir less apt to your hand, did you not?*"[91] In addition Boromir's attitude to Aragorn at the Council of Elrond would hardly have endeared him to Gandalf.

It has been suggested (again by the Southampton UK Tolkien Reading Group) that Boromir became more argumentative from Lothlórien onwards due to Aragorn's weakness and because Gandalf was no longer there to keep him in check. This is borne out by the evidence, as Aragorn's behaviour in Lothlórien was generally passive, and later, on the river journey, the arguments between them were mainly due to Aragorn trying to postpone a decision on the route for as long as possible. The loss of Gandalf certainly caused a deterioration in the relationship between Aragorn and Boromir, but the growing influence of the Ring on Boromir cannot be discounted.

In spite of their mutual antipathy, it is noteworthy that Gandalf accepted Boromir's leadership during the rescue on Caradhras. Later, on the Bridge of Khazad-dûm, Boromir's steadfast courage and loyalty were equal to Aragorn's.

Boromir's mistrust extended also to the Elves. When trying to persuade Frodo to accompany him to Minas Tirith he told him, "*... often I doubt if they* [i.e. Elves, Half-elves and Wizards] *are wise and not merely timid*"[92], clearly regarding **himself** as having the strength to use the Ring without being corrupted even if the likes of Elrond were not capable of doing so. At the Council he had been sceptical about Elrond's reasoning as to why the Ring could not be used against Sauron. His doubts about Galadriel were very pronounced, his slurs on her being the only thing which seemed to rouse Aragorn to anger during the time in Lothlórien. He casually dismissed Celeborn's advice about Fangorn as the Fellowship prepared to leave Lothlórien (*LotR* 2.8.374) - clearly implying that after his recent travels and experience even a seven-thousand-year-old (eight thousand?) Elf-lord could have nothing to teach him.

All these people whom Boromir mistrusted - Gandalf, Elrond, Galadriel and Celeborn - were very important to Aragorn personally (as friend and teacher, foster-father, and grandparents to his betrothed), as well as being sources of advice, wisdom and aid. Boromir's doubt and ingratitude, particularly in the case of Galadriel and Celeborn who had offered the Fellowship a safe haven at a supremely dangerous time, must have saddened Aragorn and done nothing to make the relationship easier. Looking at it from Boromir's point of view, the fact that these characters held Aragorn in very high regard and appeared to "side" with him probably increased his negative feelings towards them.

*

As shown by Aragorn's behaviour after the Battle of the Pelennor Fields, he was well aware of the issues surrounding the long stewardship in Gondor. He also knew enough of Denethor's character to understand how he would have influenced Boromir. He would certainly have appreciated the lure of the Ring and empathised with Boromir's struggle with it - both from his own experience and knowledge, and from observation of Frodo and Bilbo.

It is ironic - and sad - that Boromir was at heart a good man. (Even when, under the influence of the Ring, he saw himself as a king it was as a "*benevolent and wise*"[93] one.) He was a potential future Steward to Aragorn, someone Aragorn could have confided in, who could have provided support, advice and a shoulder to cry on after the loss of Gandalf. Unfortunately, due to lack of perception, his father's influence and the lure of the Ring, Boromir merely increased Aragorn's burden with his obstructive, argumentative behaviour and worrying

---

91. Op. cit. [1], *LotR* 5.4, p. 813.
92. Op. cit., *LotR* 2.10, p. 398.
93. Op. cit., *LotR* 2.10, p. 398.

harassment of Frodo. It was not until the last hours of his life when he fully understood the evil of the Ring and realised **why** it had to be destroyed that he appreciated the nature and extent of Aragorn's courage and wisdom and was able (in Faramir's and Frodo's words) to "*reverence*" and "*honour*" him as he should.[94]

FARAMIR

Three meetings between Aragorn and Faramir are described in *LotR*, namely:
- The one in the Houses of Healing when Aragorn healed Faramir from the effects of the Black Breath. Faramir was unconscious for much of the time.
- Aragorn's coronation when Faramir welcomed him to Minas Tirith as King and officiated at his crowning. This was a ceremonial event with crowds of people present and formal language being used.
- Théoden's funeral wake where Faramir's betrothal to Éowyn was announced. No specific interaction between Aragorn and Faramir is recorded and this event in fact has much more significance in a discussion of the Éowyn/Aragorn relationship.

These meetings took place in highly unusual situations, and all occurred near the end of the narrative. The day after healing Faramir Aragorn began preparing for the march to the Morannon for the final desperate stage of the strategy of drawing Sauron's attention away from Frodo. The coronation and the wake both took place after the Ring had been destroyed. Although the healing and coronation meetings shed much light on the characters of Aragorn and Faramir and how they reacted to each other, they cannot be appreciated in isolation. To understand why Aragorn and Faramir behaved as they did on these occasions it is necessary to look at events, interactions and conversations which took place earlier in the story, and to study observations made by other characters, such as Gandalf, Denethor, the Hobbits, Beregond and Éowyn.

First however, the inevitable look at App A.I.iv.1055-7 and App B.1090 establishes Faramir's basic character and his life prior to the events of 3018-19. He is portrayed as being like Boromir in looks, but intellectually superior, with his father's ability to read the minds of others, the difference being that Faramir was more inclined to pity than to scorn. Because he was gentle, loved lore and music and did not seek glory and danger without a good reason, many people mistakenly doubted his courage. He loved Boromir greatly and looked up to him, sharing the high opinion he had of himself! He displeased his father by being on good terms with Gandalf: see *LotR* 5.7 in which Denethor implied that he regarded him as a "*wizard's pupil*"[95]. Any childhood encounter with Thorongil can be ruled out as Faramir was not born until 2983, that is approximately three years after the departure of Thorongil from Gondor and a year before Denethor became Steward. He was only five years old when his mother Finduilas died, but nevertheless - as shown in *LotR* 6.5.961 - he retained a clear impression of her loveliness and the grief he had felt, cherishing her blue mantle with the silver stars which he wrapped around Éowyn as they stood upon the walls of Minas Tirith. Perhaps his gentleness was inherited from Finduilas who had been "*a lady of great beauty and gentle heart*"[96].

To complete the picture of Faramir's background it is necessary to turn to Boromir's report at the Council of Elrond (*LotR* 2.2.245-6). In the run-up to the events of 3018-9, he showed his courage by being present during Sauron's assault on Osgiliath where he and Boromir were two of the four people to survive by swimming across the Anduin to escape, and by his eagerness (mentioned by Boromir at the Council of Elrond) to make the journey to Rivendell following multiple occurrences of the dream - only to be thwarted by Boromir with his single experience of it. As shown by his conversations with Frodo and Sam in Ithilien (*LotR* 4.5.663-4) there was no indication that Faramir had been aware of the possibility of Isildur's line still surviving. This was clear from his assumption that an heirloom of Elendil's House (such as "Isildur's Bane") would automatically belong to Boromir out of those present at the Council - until Frodo enlightened him about the existence and lineage of Aragorn. The implication is that, like Boromir, he was in the dark about his father's acquaintance with Thorongil forty years earlier. After telling Frodo of Boromir's displeasure that he was **only** the son of a steward, he displayed a completely different attitude himself declaring that he would actually welcome the

---
94. Op. cit. [1], *LotR* 4.5, p. 670.
95. Op. cit., *LotR* 5.7, p. 854.
96. Op. cit., App A.I.iv, p. 1056.

return of a king. Thus he showed that he had never aspired to kingship and had also escaped the influence of Denethor which had encouraged Boromir to think so highly of himself - even to the extent of believing himself capable of resisting corruption by the Ring.

*

I believe that the best way to depict the relationship between Aragorn and Faramir is first to draw attention to the ways in which the latter resembled the former, as it was these similarities which brought about the closeness and understanding between them when they eventually met. I have identified the following areas of similarity:
- Character
- Relationship with Gandalf
- Attitude to Elves and Lothlórien
- Attitude to the Ring
- As seen by others

Character

The overriding source of many of their common traits was their Númenórean descent. Gandalf explained to Pippin in *LotR* 5.1.759 that by a fluke, the blood of Númenor ran almost true in Faramir (as well as in his father). The reason this was fluky was because, as Faramir explained to Frodo in *LotR* 4.5.670, his family were not of Elendil's line and therefore his blood was rather dilute compared with Aragorn's. There are many examples illustrating typical Númenórean characteristics in Faramir:
- Like Aragorn he had impressive insight into people's minds and characters as demonstrated in *LotR* 4.5.663-9, as he assessed the trustworthiness of Frodo and Sam with wisdom and perception and read behind Frodo's words to perceive his uneasiness in his dealings with Boromir.
- In the same chapter, as Sam watched him interrogating Frodo, he saw him as stern and commanding with a keen wit behind the searching glance in his grey eyes. Elsewhere Faramir is described as tall and dark haired. Also *HoM-e* XII.7 shows him as being unusually long-lived with his age at death recorded as a hundred and twenty.[97] All these were typical Númenórean physical characteristics as displayed to an even greater degree by Aragorn.
- He showed considerable physical and mental strength, for example being able to function well without sleep and having a high resistance to the presence of Nazgûl. In *LotR* Beregond expressed to Pippin the wish that Faramir would return as "*He would not be dismayed*"[98] (i.e. by the malice and darkness from Mordor). Also he rode to the aid of his men who were being pursued by Nazgûl. Compare this with Aragorn's willingness to stay awake so others could rest, and his stance against the Nazgûl on Weathertop in order to protect Frodo.
- He also had the Númenórean way with animals as pointed out by Beregond: "*... he can master both beasts and men.*"[99] Similarly Aragorn and his Grey Company were able to take their horses through the Paths of the Dead because of the love the animals felt for them.
- Faramir himself was aware of the aura of a true-blooded Númenórean, answering Sam's observation that he reminded him of Gandalf with, "*Maybe you discern from far away the air of Númenor.*"[100].
- Denethor, himself possessing the Númenórean perception though tainted with scorn for Faramir's mild nature, accused him thus: "*Ever your desire is to appear lordly and generous as a king of old, gracious, gentle. That may well befit one of high race, if he sits in power and peace. But in desperate hours gentleness may be repaid with death.*"[101]. Ironically he seemed to be criticising Faramir for getting above

---
97. C. Tolkien (ed.), *The History of Middle-earth*, vol. XII, *The Peoples of Middle-earth*, London HarperColllins Publishers, 2002, first published in Great Britain by HarperCollins Publishers 1996, *HoM-e* XII Part 1, Chapter 7, p. 207.
98. Op. cit. [1], *LotR* 5.4, p. 808.
99. Op. cit., *LotR* 5.4, p. 809.
100. Op. cit., *LotR* 4.5, p. 682.
101. Op. cit., *LotR* 5.4, p. 812.

himself by acting like a benevolent king, while in fact Faramir alone in the family did **not** hanker after kingship. Perhaps Denethor recalled Thorongil displaying similar characteristics and was taking it out on his younger son who undoubtedly resembled the "upstart" from the North in this respect.

Faramir shared many other qualities with Aragorn too, such as:
- Integrity. He regarded his declaration - that he would not take "Isildur's Bane" even if he found it by the roadside - as a vow which he would have honoured regardless, even if he had wanted the Ring. Aragorn showed similar anxiety about keeping his promise to Boromir to save Minas Tirith and he honoured his promise to go to Rohan and help Éomer.
- Sense of duty. This was particularly evident in Faramir's support of Denethor by trying to take Boromir's place in the struggle at Osgiliath. Similarly Aragorn took on the role of leading the Fellowship and looking after Frodo after the loss of Gandalf.
- Initiative. Faramir was prepared to take the law into his own hands if necessary, for example in letting Frodo (and the Ring) go free when he knew Denethor would have expected him to take both to Minas Tirith. Compare this with Aragorn's precipitate use of the Palantír of Orthanc against Gandalf's advice.
- Intellect. Like Aragorn, Faramir was educated, cultured, musical, had a broad understanding and was well-versed in the history of Gondor. For example he referred to the "*Seeing-stones of Númenor*"[102]; he was a leader of Rangers and understood the value of camouflage and secrecy as well as that of open warfare; he appreciated the beauty of the belt and brooch from Lothlórien.
- Pity. This was a quality possessed to a high degree by both men and will be discussed in more detail later.

Relationship with Gandalf

Unlike his father and brother Faramir liked and respected Gandalf, seeking him out on his visits to Gondor and learning from him so that he could read the old documents in the archives of Minas Tirith. In the context of his much shorter acquaintance with the Wizard he appreciated him in much the same way as Aragorn did. He was thirty-six in TA 3019 and had only met Gandalf three or four times, but he came to realise that he was more than a lore-master. He suspected that Boromir's journey to Rivendell may have been doomed as part of a higher purpose of Gandalf's and that this was why Gandalf had not been present in Gondor to explain the dream to them but left them to work it out for themselves.

Attitude to Elves and Lothlórien

From Faramir's conversation with Frodo and Sam he clearly shared Boromir's wariness of the Elves believing it to be "*... perilous now for mortal man wilfully to seek out the Elder People.*"[103] Nevertheless he seemed to revere Lothlórien, knew its old name, Laurelindórenan, and envied the Hobbits for having been there and spoken to Galadriel. He was also able to recognise the elvish air surrounding Frodo as a result of the visit. In general his attitude was nearer to Aragorn's than to Boromir's.

Attitude to the Ring

Like Aragorn Faramir showed wisdom and self-control where the Ring was concerned as demonstrated by his behaviour in Henneth Annûn (*LotR* 4.5.680-1). He had already assured Frodo that he would not take "Isildur's Bane" under any circumstances. When he realised, through Sam's slip-up, that the "Bane" was actually the One Ring he considered himself obliged to abide by what he had said "*Even if I were such a man as to desire this thing...*" He then went on to state that he was not actually such a man, or at least "*... I am wise enough to know that there are some perils from which a man must flee.*".[104] The scene when he pretended to

---
102. Op. cit. [1], *LotR* 4.6, p. 693.
103. Op. cit., *LotR* 4.5, p. 679.
104. Op. cit., *LotR* 4.5, p. 681.

be about to seize the Ring from Frodo, standing towering over him, grey eyes glinting is very reminiscent of the similar scene with Aragorn in the Prancing Pony as he towered over the Hobbits, hand on sword-hilt, eyes gleaming with "*a light, keen and commanding*"[105] as he told them he could have the Ring there and then if he wanted to. I am not convinced that there was any serious danger of either man actually taking the Ring. Both were showing the Hobbits that they were strong enough to take it but chose not to. For Faramir it was a chance to "*show his quality*"[106] which he did by rejecting the Ring, while Aragorn had been trying to convince a doubting Sam that he was genuinely using his strength to help and protect them rather than to try and take the Ring. Like Aragorn Faramir refused to have anything to do with it - even look at it - and with the example of Boromir fresh in his mind he specifically did not want the Ring brought to Minas Tirith.

As seen by others

A very important way in which Faramir resembled Aragorn was in his ability to arouse love and esteem in others as illustrated by the following examples:

- Frodo felt that Faramir looked like his brother, but "*... was a man less self-regarding, both sterner and wiser*"[107] - a description which also fits Aragorn.
- In *LotR* 5.1.766 Beregond sang Faramir's praises to Pippin, stating that he was bolder and more effective in battle than many people thought, often being underestimated simply because he loved learning and music. He finished by describing Faramir as "*Less reckless and eager than Boromir, but not less resolute.*"[108]. The whole conversation echoes Gandalf's remark (also to Pippin) after guessing that Aragorn had used the Palantír to distract Sauron, describing him as being strong and stern underneath, bold and determined and able to take great risks when it was really necessary.
- On arrival in Minas Tirith Gandalf became very anxious at Faramir's non-appearance, pacing up and down. He realised Faramir's potential as he did Aragorn's.
- Pippin's first sight of Faramir as he returned from the east after facing Nazgûl, made a deep impression on him because he realised that he was the sort of person men would follow anywhere out of love, "*even under the shadow of the black wings.*"[109] The parallel with the Grey Company following Aragorn through the Paths of the Dead out of love is unmistakeable. Pippin also saw the similarity between Faramir and Aragorn from the former's "*air of high nobility such as Aragorn at times revealed, less high perhaps, yet also less incalculable and remote...*"[110] Like Aragorn, Faramir also had that "something" which made people love him. Maybe, again as observed by Pippin, it was the touch of the "*wisdom and sadness of the Elder Race*"[111] which both of them exhibited.
- On the following day Faramir set out east a second time taking with him those who "*... **were willing to go** or could be spared.*"[112] [My emphasis]. This is similar to Aragorn's dismissing of the faint-hearted at the Morannon - Faramir knew that some of his men would not be able to cope with further Nazgûl encounters, just as Aragorn understood the terror induced in some of his young soldiers by the desolation near the Morannon. These incidents also illustrate how both men were easily moved to pity.
- Beregond was willing to risk his life for love of Faramir - committing treason (punishable by death) in order to save him. Halbarad knowingly went to his death for love of Aragorn.
- In *LotR* 6.5.959 when Éowyn encountered Faramir for the first time she noticed his pity, sternness and gentleness but also knew that he would be a match for any of her own people in battle. This description applies equally to Aragorn.

*

---

105. Op. cit. [1], *LotR* 1.10, p. 171.
106. Op. cit., *LotR* 4.5, p. 681.
107. Op. cit., *LotR* 4.5, p. 665.
108. Op. cit., *LotR* 5.1, p. 766.
109. Op. cit., *LotR* 5.4, p. 810.
110. Op. cit., *LotR* 5.4, p. 810.
111. Op. cit., *LotR* 5.4, p. 810.
112. Op. cit., *LotR* 5.4, p. 817.

With this background to the relationship between Aragorn and Faramir we are now in a position to appreciate fully the actual encounters between them. The first of these took place in the Houses of Healing and is covered in *LotR* 5.8.863-6.

As the sun set on March 15th 3019, Aragorn, Éomer and Imrahil arrived at the Gate of Minas Tirith after the Battle of the Pelennor Fields. Here Aragorn stated his intention of camping outside the City rather than entering it as King, not wanting to risk unrest among his own people while the war with Sauron was still in the balance. At this point all three of them believed that Denethor was the Steward of Gondor, not realising that he was actually dead. With this in mind it is understandable that Aragorn felt uneasy about entering the City as King and his decision was supported by Imrahil. Later that evening he did actually enter the City, wearing the Elessar but no actual trappings of royalty. This was purely because Gandalf - having clearly now told Aragorn the real situation - had begged him to come and see if he could heal Faramir, Éowyn and Merry. As the two of them reached the Houses of Healing they met Éomer and Imrahil at which point Gandalf informed them that Denethor was dead and the unconscious Faramir now Steward. In answer to Imrahil's suggestion that Aragorn should now rule the City, Aragorn insisted that Imrahil himself should continue to take charge **until Faramir awoke**, with Gandalf providing overall guidance. This shows that he had no wish to enter the City as King while the Steward whose rule he would be replacing lay unconscious.

For clarity I have put the interactions just described into a table:

ARAGORN	ÉOMER & IMRAHIL	GANDALF
Approached City Gate. Believed Denethor to be Steward.	Approached City Gate with Aragorn. Believed Denethor to be Steward.	In Houses of Healing and obviously aware of the real state of things.
Set up camp outside City.	Entered City.	In Houses of Healing, extremely concerned at the condition of Faramir, Éowyn and Merry.
Presumably grieving in tent, especially for the death of Halbarad. (Éomer would later notice that he was "sorrowful".)	Visited Théoden lying in state. Imrahil told Éomer that Éowyn was still alive. Both set off for Houses of Healing.	On hearing Ioreth's "old wives' tale" went to find Aragorn. (This must have occurred roughly at this point.)
Was requested by Gandalf to accompany him to Houses of Healing. Gandalf presumably informed him of Denethor's death and Faramir's Stewardship at this point.	*En route* to Houses of Healing.	Begged Aragorn to come to Houses of Healing. He presumably told him Denethor was dead and Faramir now Steward.
En route to Houses of Healing disguised in Elf-cloak.	*En route* to Houses of Healing.	*En route* to Houses of Healing.
All met at Houses of Healing. Revealed his identity, but insisted he was only there as a healer.	All met at Houses of Healing. Learnt that Denethor was dead and Faramir now Steward. Imrahil wanted Aragorn to rule.	All met at Houses of Healing. Told Éomer and Imrahil that Denethor was dead and Faramir now Steward.
At Aragorn's insistence all agreed that Imrahil should rule the City until Faramir awoke, with Gandalf in overall charge.		

I will now analyse the healing scene in detail.

Faramir was in a fever, deeply unconscious and the closest to death out of the three patients, for all of whom, as Aragorn recognised, time was running out. The situation was such that Aragorn longed for the presence - and healing skills - of Elrond, exhausted and grief-stricken as he was and afraid to spare the time to rest and eat before trying to heal these three. The ensuing conversation at Faramir's bedside showed that he had a much greater understanding of Faramir's condition than Gandalf and Imrahil, both of whom believed that a Nazgûl dart had been responsible for his wound because of the extent of his fever and general severity of his illness even though the wound itself was superficial. Aragorn realised that a wound from a Nazgûl weapon would have killed him the same night (that is forty-eight hours previously) and believed that a Southron arrow was responsible. This was then confirmed by Imrahil who had been present but was misled as to the nature of the arrow due to the seriousness of Faramir's condition. Aragorn had a profound appreciation of what Faramir had been through, realising that the double dose of the Black Breath he had suffered was the really lethal factor. App B.1093. states that Faramir had been rescued from the Nazgûl by Gandalf on March 10th and it was the following day when Denethor sent him out again - while he was still suffering the effects of that first encounter. Aragorn described him as "*a man of staunch will*"[113] and no doubt it was this which had enabled him to resist the Black Breath sufficiently to actually carry on and face the Nazgûl again on March 13th when his wound was received. Aragorn also understood the psychological effect on Faramir of his father's and brother's attitude to him, no doubt realising, from what Gandalf must have told him plus his own knowledge of Denethor and Boromir, that this was not just limited to the current situation but had in fact been going on for years. With his high levels of empathy and perception, along with his own psychological struggles, Aragorn was uniquely suited to relate to Faramir's troubles and to appreciate his outstanding mental strength.

It was Aragorn's voice and touch which played the main role in the healing of Faramir. By holding his hand and laying the other hand on his brow he was able to assess the critical nature of his condition. Then, to recall him from the coma induced by the Black Breath, he placed his hand on his brow again and called to him. The ensuing struggle experienced by Aragorn was clear to the onlookers who watched his face becoming grey from weariness and heard his voice growing fainter as he repeatedly called Faramir's name until it seemed as if the two of them were actually elsewhere with Faramir lost and Aragorn searching for him. When the athelas leaves were eventually brought by the young Bergil, Aragorn comforted the tearful child with the words "*The worst is now over.*"[114] It was the herb which brought Faramir back to consciousness - after Aragorn had breathed on it and then crushed it and steeped it in hot water - but the healing itself had already been effected.

I believe that the athelas had a further purpose in addition to rousing Faramir and lightening the hearts of the onlookers, namely reviving Aragorn himself. We are told that he "*... stood up as one refreshed...*"[115] with a smile in his eyes after infusing the herb. His exhaustion and grief - even **before** the ordeal of the healing - are very evident in this chapter and he would have needed to renew his strength for the further healings ahead of him. One can easily appreciate his words "*Would that Elrond were here*"[116]!

I have already written, in Chapter 2.5, of the atmosphere of intimacy during Merry's healing, with Aragorn touching the Hobbit's eyelids and passing his fingers through his hair. With Faramir he was healing someone previously personally unknown to him, and his behaviour was thus more formal - with a hand on the brow - but none the less tender and gentle for that.

During the healing of Faramir, Boromir must also have been very much in Aragorn's thoughts. He **hadn't** been in time to save **him** and the grief and guilt from the events at Parth Galen must still have been preying on his mind. Ironically he was now in a position where Faramir too needed help in a knife-edge situation. His words on first seeing the Steward's condition - "*Would that I could have been here sooner!*"[117] - amply illustrated his feelings and must have evoked memories of running the mile from Amon Hen to Parth Galen bewailing the ill fate that was on him only to arrive to find Boromir past help. Apart from any other emotions it must have been a huge relief to him when he knew that Faramir would live.

When Faramir opened his eyes, the first thing he saw was Aragorn who was bending over him and we are told that "*... a light of knowledge and love was kindled in his eyes*"[118]. He addressed Aragorn as King: "*My lord, you called me. I come. What does the king command?*"[119] Aragorn's reply reiterated his call to come back from the shadows and showed his appreciation of Faramir's weariness as he exhorted him to rest and eat so as to be ready when needed. Faramir's answer confirmed his understanding of the situation: "*... who would lie idle*

---

113. Op. cit. [1], *LotR* 5.8, p. 864.
114. Op. cit., *LotR* 5.8, p. 865.
115. Op. cit., *LotR* 5.8, p. 865.
116. Op. cit., *LotR* 5.8, p. 863.
117. Op. cit., *LotR* 5.8, p. 864.
118. Op. cit., *LotR* 5.8, p. 866.
119. Op. cit., *LotR* 5.8, p. 866.

when the king has returned?"[120].

Thus it is clear that Faramir was well aware of Aragorn's identity as soon as he saw him and also already regarded him with love. I believe this was due to a combination of reasons:
- He gained this awareness during his delirium, either through dreams or because he subconsciously understood what had happened to him and realised that only a very exceptional person would be able to counter the Black Breath of the Nazgûl.
- The presence of the Elessar on Aragorn's breast must have made a visual impact as he came round (or even before that) and was maybe the first thing he saw - even before Aragorn's face. We know from the gift-giving scene in Lothlórien that the green jewel had the healing property of being able to show Aragorn as kingly in appearance at a time when he was at a very low ebb. It may well have had a similar effect in the Houses of Healing disguising his grey-faced weariness. [I don't believe that Faramir would have recognised the Elessar *per se* as I think knowledge of it would have been restricted to Gandalf and the families and households of Galadriel and Elrond.]
- Apart from that, Aragorn's general appearance was undeniably Númenórean so Faramir would have recognised his lineage.
- There is plenty of evidence in *LotR* that Faramir was prone to memorable and significant dreams, including the one containing the verse which triggered Boromir's journey to Rivendell. In addition, he had often dreamed of the huge wave which destroyed Númenor (as he would tell Éowyn in *LotR* 6.5.962 as they watched the cloud of darkness rising above Mordor at the moment when the Ring was destroyed). The drowning of Númenor had resulted in Elendil and his sons being washed up on the shores of Middle-earth and subsequently establishing the kingdoms of Gondor and Arnor. This begs the question: Did Faramir regard the dreams of Númenor as a foresight experience signifying the return of Elendil's heir from the sea? This had now actually taken place: while Faramir lay in the Houses of Healing Aragorn had arrived at the Pelennor Fields by ship blown by the southerly wind from the sea, displaying the royal standard and wearing the Star of Elendil on his brow. It is perhaps significant that the dark cloud rising above Mordor aroused hope and joy in Faramir rather than fear.
- In addition, when Faramir had met the Hobbits in Ithilien, Frodo had actually told him about Aragorn and said that he was on his way to Minas Tirith. Later in the conversation Faramir had expressed a wish for the king to return. When he finally met Aragorn in the Houses of Healing everything would have fallen into place.

I feel that these considerations, taken together, provide an ample explanation for Faramir's attitude to Aragorn. In the days to come - in spite of Aragorn's absence on the journey to the Morannon - he would get to know him better through his interactions with Éowyn and Merry.

*

During Faramir's convalescence in the Houses of Healing he met and fell in love with Éowyn, being greatly affected by her beauty, courage and obvious unhappiness. At their first meeting on March 20th he asked to carry on seeing her, feeling that it would comfort him in what would very likely be the last few days before Middle-earth came completely under the sway of Sauron. He felt drawn to her because "*you and I have both passed under the wings of the Shadow, and the same hand drew us back.*"[121]. Although Éowyn, at this stage, felt that she was still under the Shadow to some extent, Faramir recognised the bond between them due to both of them having been saved from death by Aragorn against all the odds.

Later that day he also made the acquaintance of Merry after the Warden of the Houses of Healing suggested that the Hobbit might be able to tell him more about Éowyn. As I discussed in Chapter 2.5, Merry not only enabled Faramir to understand Éowyn but also helped him to know Aragorn better. As well as witnessing Éowyn's grief at the apparent loss of Aragorn in the Paths of the Dead Merry was also personally very close

---
120. Op. cit. [1], *LotR* 5.8, p. 866.
121. Op. cit., *LotR* 6.5, p. 960.

to Aragorn himself and it was these factors which led to Faramir learning *"more even than Merry put into words"*[122] during their long talk together.

A later encounter between Faramir and Éowyn during the five-week period between the destruction of the Ring and the coronation throws further light on Faramir's attitude to Aragorn. Faramir was now sure of his own love for Éowyn but she was still torn between her growing regard for him and her feelings for Aragorn which had caused her so much torment. As he helped her to resolve these issues he showed not only the depth of his perception of her own turmoil but also a profound understanding of Aragorn's nature. He realised that Éowyn loved Aragorn because he was *"high and puissant"*[123] and offered her a means of escape from a life which she found degrading being influenced by Saruman (via Gríma) into despising her own people. He also compared her admiration of him with that of a young soldier for a great captain, acknowledging Aragorn's supremacy in that respect. However the chief quality which he identified in Aragorn during this talk with Éowyn - and the one he most revered - was pity, the quality which Éowyn had rejected. He told her *"But when he gave you only understanding and pity* [as opposed to love], *then you desired to have nothing, unless a brave death in battle."*[124] He followed this up by looking her in the eyes and telling her, *"Do not scorn pity that is the gift of a gentle heart, Éowyn!"*.

Athrabeth Finrod ah Andreth[125] in *HoM-e* X, contains a discussion about pity which is very relevant here. The Elf Finrod, in conversation with the wise-woman Andreth, identifies two types of pity: *"... one is of kinship recognized, and is near to love; the other is of difference of fortune perceived, and is near to pride."*[126] It seems that Faramir was making the same distinction and clearly had the first type of pity in mind when speaking of Aragorn - a pity which came not from arrogance but from a gentle heart. This conversation with Éowyn says a lot about Faramir's regard for Aragorn. They had an innate ability to understand each other through their shared gentleness and their ability to feel pity *"near to love"*, as identified by Finrod. Did the gentleness in Aragorn remind Faramir, deep down, of his mother, the *"lady of great beauty and gentle heart"*[127] - a gentleness which he himself had inherited?

*

On Faramir's full recovery, which seems to have occurred soon after the destruction of the Ring, he formally took on the Stewardship of Gondor, *"... although it was only for a little while, and his duty was to prepare for one who should replace him."*[128]. His duty was thus to prepare the City to receive Aragorn as King and to organise what would be a very untypical coronation:
- The line of kings in Gondor had long died out so Aragorn was not succeeding to the kingship in the normal way.
- As Faramir himself was to explain in *LotR* 6.5.967, the normal practice when a new king succeeded had been for the dying king to give the crown to his successor in person. This was clearly impossible in the case of Aragorn. As described in App A.I.iv.1052 the last (childless) King of Gondor, Eärnur, had ridden to Minas Morgul nearly a thousand years earlier after accepting the challenge of the Lord of the Nazgûl to single combat and had never been seen or heard of again.
- If the old king died before being able to pass the crown to his successor it would be placed with him in his tomb from which the new king would then come and take it. This too was not possible in the case of Aragorn even though King Eärnur had placed his crown in the tomb of his own father Eärnil before he had set off to Minas Morgul. Aragorn could not, with propriety, go and retrieve it himself because he was outside the City on his way back from the Field of Cormallen. Also in the circumstances it was

---
122. Op. cit. [1], *LotR* 6.5, p. 961.
123. Op. cit., *LotR* 6.5, p. 964.
124. Op. cit., *LotR* 6.5, p. 964.
125. C. Tolkien (ed.), *The History of Middle-earth*, vol. X, *Morgoth's Ring*, London HarperColllins Publishers, 2002, first published in Great Britain by HarperCollins Publishers 1993, *HoM-e* X Part 4, pp. 301-366.
126. Op. cit., *HoM-e* X Part 4, p. 324.
127. Op. cit. [1], App A.I.iv, p. 1056.
128. Op. cit., *LotR* 6.5, pp. 963-4.

an official requirement for him to be formally invited by the Steward to take on the kingship, with this then being agreed by the assembled people of Gondor.
- Another issue as far as Faramir was concerned was that Denethor had broken his Steward's staff and then cremated it along with himself, thereby signifying his view that the Stewardship, as well as the Kingship, had come to an end.

LotR 6.5.967 makes it clear that Faramir ordered a new rod to be made, thus renewing the Steward's authority which he used to organise the coronation and deal with the potential problems. The text describes the arrival of people from all parts of Gondor, the return of the women and children from the refuges, the musicians, the flowers and the bells. Faramir also had a barrier erected in place of the City Gate which had been destroyed by Sauron's forces. His solution to the issue of the crown was to arrange for it to be taken from Eärnil's tomb and placed in a casket made of black lebethron wood bound with silver. This was then carried ceremonially out of the City by four men in the armour of the Citadel with Faramir himself and Húrin of the Keys leading the way. Lebethron was, as Faramir had told Frodo and Sam, a *"fair tree ... beloved of the woodrights of Gondor"*[129] and no doubt Faramir felt it was very appropriate for carrying the crown of his much-loved king.

Although this was a ceremonial occasion, there are hints of a close rapport between Steward and King amidst the formality. As Faramir went to meet Aragorn he handed him the Steward's rod with the words, *"The last Steward of Gondor begs leave to surrender his office."* Aragorn's response was to return the rod to him saying, *"That office is not ended, and it shall be thine and thy heirs' as long as my line shall last."*.[130] Aragorn had already saved his Steward's life, now he was saving his office as well - for him and his heirs. This exchange was followed by Faramir reciting all Aragorn's titles and qualifications for the kingship: the ones denoting his lineage, those extolling his military victory and not least - for Faramir and for many others - reference to his healing hands which gave him the official name he would bear as King: Elfstone/Elessar after the green jewel with the healing properties.

As Aragorn took the crown from Faramir he held it up and repeated the words spoken by Elendil on his arrival in Middle-earth three thousand years earlier: *"Out of the Great Sea to Middle-earth I am come. In this place will I abide, and my heirs, unto the ending of the world."*[131]. This must have had a special significance for Faramir with his dreams of Númenor as he looked on his newly-crowned King standing *"Tall as the sea-kings of old..."*[132]. Finally the royal banner with the White Tree and the Stars was unfurled upon the Tower of the Citadel replacing the plain white one of the Stewards which had been raised for the last time that morning.

*

Aragorn made Faramir Prince of Ithilien, bidding him live in the hills of Emyn Arnen so as to be in sight of Minas Tirith. Tolkien made some comments about this appointment, in a draft letter[133] to an unknown reader of *LotR* written c.1963, which throw considerable light on Faramir's life under the new régime. This reader had referred to Faramir's new position as a *"market-garden job"*. Tolkien explained that this was far from being the case as the Prince of Ithilien would be the resident march-warden of Gondor in the east, responsible for rehabilitating Ithilien, including Minas Morgul itself, and clearing the area of outlaws and Orcs. He also stated that the Prince of Ithilien was the greatest noble after the Prince of Dol Amroth. Faramir and Imrahil would have a strong military role to play, being the chief commanders under the King with one or other of them acting as military commander at home in the King's absence. Given the considerable amount of fighting in the early days of the new reign this military role was very necessary. Also, as Steward, Faramir would be required to stand in for the King during absence or illness and he would have been the King's chief counsellor in the re-established Great Council of Gondor.

---

129. Op. cit. [1], *LotR* 4.7, p. 694.
130. Op. cit., *LotR* 6.5, p. 967.
131. Op. cit., *LotR* 6.5, p. 967.
132. Op. cit., *LotR* 6.5, p. 968.
133. Op. cit. [22], Letter 244, pp. 323-4.

In fact I feel that the granting of Ithilien to Faramir was very fitting:
- He had been leading Rangers in Ithilien when he met Frodo and Sam and had shown great courage in his attempts to protect Osgiliath both before and during the War of the Ring.
- Aragorn's wish for Faramir to live close to the City seemed to be a precaution until the land further east could be cleaned up and Minas Ithil/Morgul destroyed. There was perhaps also a protectiveness in his attitude - he was more aware than anyone of what Faramir had suffered.
- Faramir himself actually **wanted** to live in Ithilien. In fact the line of the Stewards had originated there being descended from Húrin of Emyn Arnen. In *LotR*, once Faramir knew that Éowyn returned his love, he said to her, "*... let us cross the River and in happier days let us dwell in fair Ithilien and there make a garden.*"[134] [Perhaps this was where the "market garden" image originated in Letter 244.] During the days after the coronation he must have made his wishes known to Aragorn and it is unthinkable that Aragorn wasn't aware of his relationship with Éowyn.
- Faramir was aware that Elves had once lived in Ithilien and though he had never actually seen any at the time he met Frodo and Sam he made it clear that he regarded them with reverence. During Aragorn's reign Legolas would bring a group of his people to live there thus re-establishing the Elves. *HoM-e* XII mentions Faramir's "*... fair new house ... whose gardens devised by the Elf Legolas were renowned.*"[135]

Faramir's position as Prince of Ithilien was a sign of the King's esteem while Ithilien itself had the advantages of proximity to Minas Tirith and congeniality to Faramir and Éowyn. Faramir would undoubtedly have been very happy with his position and its location. There is no doubt either that Faramir, unlike Boromir, was content to be "only" a Steward. He had never wanted the kingship as was confirmed by his laughing reply when Éowyn told him she no longer wanted to be a queen (*"That is well, for I am not a king"*[136]) and by his obvious delight at the thought of marriage to a woman of Rohan not caring that this would seriously dilute the blood of Númenor in the line of the Stewards. In fact, was the return of the king a dream-come-true for Faramir? His words to Frodo and Sam in *LotR* seem to indicate so: *"For myself, I would see the White Tree in flower again ... and the Silver Crown return ..."*[137]

Although Denethor is generally regarded as the last Ruling Steward of Gondor, this title could also be applied to Faramir as he was very briefly in charge of the City in the period between his recovery in the Houses of Healing and the coronation. The first Ruling Steward had been Mardil Voronwë (after whom the stewardship became hereditary) who was referred to by Faramir as *"the good steward"*[138], in App A.I.iv as *"the Good Steward"*[139] and in A.I.ii as *"the Steadfast"*[140]. App A.I.iv.1052 shows his wisdom as well, as he had tried to restrain King Eärnur from responding to the Witch-king's challenge to personal combat, being successful initially, then failing when the challenge was repeated, after which he took on the rule of Gondor himself. Faramir, the last Ruling Steward of Mardil's line, seems to have resembled him in many ways.

The help which Faramir had given to Frodo and Sam must have resulted in a considerable debt of gratitude as far as Aragorn was concerned. In *LotR* 4.6.690 he had used all the authority he had to grant Frodo the freedom of Gondor for a year and a day, hoping that Frodo would be able to come to Minas Tirith during that time, when he [Faramir] would ask Denethor to make the grant lifelong. In *LotR* 6.6.974 Aragorn did just that, also extending the grant to the other Hobbits. In addition Faramir's attitude to the kingship, and his love for the King personally, must have aroused further gratitude in Aragorn as well as relief, particularly after the problems he had encountered with Denethor and Boromir. Adding to this the empathy between the two of them, their many shared characteristics, and the fact that both Faramir and Éowyn owed their lives to the healing hands of Aragorn, it seems safe to assume that they must have become very close friends.

Faramir died in FA 83 at the age of a hundred and twenty, being succeeded as Steward and Prince of Ithilien

---

134. Op. cit. [1], *LotR* 6.5, p. 965.
135. Op. cit. [97], *HoM-e* XII Part 1, Chapter 7, p. 220.
136. Op. cit. [1], *LotR* 6.5, p. 965.
137. Op. cit., *LotR* 4.5, p. 671.
138. Op. cit., *LotR* 4.5, p. 670.
139. Op. cit., App A.I.iv, p. 1052.
140. Op. cit., App A.I.ii, p. 1039.

by his son Elboron. Elboron is mentioned only briefly in Tolkien's writings (in *HoM-e* XII.7.221, 223) and nothing is recorded of any relationship between him and Aragorn. If we assume he was born in the early years of the Fourth Age, he could well have been in his seventies when his father died. Nevertheless if he had a similar lifespan himself he could have still been alive at Aragorn's death thirty-seven years later. However his mother's Rohan (and thus more short-lived) blood could have played a part here in which case he might well have predeceased Aragorn. Thus the Steward and Prince of Ithilien at Aragorn's death may instead have been a grandson of Faramir, possibly Barahir who is mentioned in *LotR* Prologue.15 as being the author of *The Tale of Aragorn and Arwen* written after Aragorn's death. [App A.I.v.1057-63 is a shortened version of this.]

*

I end this section by drawing attention to the role and foresight of Gandalf concerning Faramir:
- As Faramir set out for Osgiliath at Denethor's command Gandalf told him, "*Do not throw your life away rashly or in bitterness. You will be needed here, **for other things than war.***"[141] [My emphasis] What did Gandalf think those things were? To act as the last Ruling Steward to prepare the way for the return of the King? To be instrumental in the healing of Éowyn?
- See also the attitude of the Ranger Mablung in *LotR*. He explained to Frodo and Sam that since the death of Boromir, "*He [Faramir] leads now in all perilous ventures. But his life is charmed, **or fate spares him for some other end.***"[142] [My emphasis]
- Faramir himself realised that there was a higher purpose governing Gandalf's activities, as shown when he told Frodo and Sam that he had come to believe that the Wizard was "*a great mover of the deeds that are done in our time.*"[143] As mentioned earlier, he had suspected that Boromir's journey to Rivendell may have been doomed from the outset.

IMRAHIL, PRINCE OF DOL AMROTH

HoM-e XII.7.220-3 and *UT* 3.2.409 Note 39 refer to the Elven blood in the Princes of Dol Amroth from the marriage (*circa* TA 1981-2) of Imrazôr (a Númenórean faithful to the Eldar whose ancestors had settled in Belfalas prior to the drowning of Númenor) to the Silvan Elf Mithrellas. Mithrellas was one of the companions of Nimrodel whose flight from Lothlórien in TA 1981, when the Balrog first appeared in Moria, is described in the song sung by Legolas after the Fellowship escaped from the Mines (*LotR* 2.6.339-41). Their son Galador was the first Prince of Dol Amroth and Prince Imrahil (the twenty-second Prince) was descended in direct line from him. In *LotR* 5.1.750 Imrahil is referred to as of high blood - presumably meaning Númenórean blood - while *LotR* 5.4.824 records the possibility of his Elvish descent. This is confirmed in *LotR* 5.9.872 where Legolas, on meeting him in Minas Tirith, saw from his appearance that he had Elf blood of Nimrodel's people in him. [See Genealogical Table 7.] The *UT* reference given above indicates some kinship between the Princes of Dol Amroth and Elendil.

As is the case with Denethor, Boromir and Faramir, a proper understanding of the relationship between Imrahil and Aragorn requires consideration of Aragorn's service in Gondor as Thorongil. As nothing is actually recorded of Imrahil's activities during that period it is therefore necessary to look at what is known about other characters and events at the time and come up with some likely conclusions. The reference in *HoM-e* XII mentioned above continues to be useful, along with App A.I.iv.1055-7 and App B.1089-90.

I am assuming that Aragorn/Thorongil was in Gondor from 2970 (or earlier) until about 2980. The reigning Prince of Dol Amroth at the start of this period would have been Imrahil's grandfather Angelimir, then from 2977 onwards his father Adrahil. Imrahil himself did not become Prince until 3010. Being born in 2955 he was twenty-four years younger than Thorongil, thus making him fifteen in 2970 and about twenty-five at Thorongil's departure.

As indicated in Tolkien's draft letter to the unknown reader referred to earlier (Letter 244), the Prince of Dol

---
141. Op. cit. [1], *LotR* 5.4, p. 817.
142. Op. cit., *LotR* 4.4, pp. 659-60.
143. Op. cit., *LotR* 4.5, p. 671.

Amroth was a highly important person in the revived state of Gondor. This importance is also apparent **prior** to the re-establishment of the kingship as shown by Imrahil's presence at Denethor's councils (*LotR* 5.4.808, 816) and at The Last Debate (*LotR* 5.9.878-82), and by the fact that he was in charge in Minas Tirith while Denethor and Faramir were incapacitated. He was actually the most important person after the Steward and his heirs, as emphasised in *HoM-e* XII.7.222 where it is stated that when the line of the Kings ended the Princes of Dol Amroth became virtually independent rulers of Belfalas - though they remained loyal to the Stewards seeing them as representatives of the ancient crown. Thus during Thorongil's time in Gondor, Angelimir and Adrahil in their turn would undoubtedly have been high in the counsels of the Steward and been members of the Council of Gondor. From 2977 - if not before - Imrahil, as his father's heir, must also have been present some of the time for the purpose of learning his future role. He would have been aware of significant events and issues such as the high regard of Ecthelion for Thorongil and the resulting jealousy of Denethor. There was also Thorongil's renowned and impressive defeat of the Corsairs of Umbar around 2979-80 followed by his mysterious disappearance immediately afterwards. Imrahil was in his twenties by then preparing for a time when he would succeed to the princedom and it seems inconceivable that he wouldn't have known of Thorongil's impressive record. Was he present at the debates about the Corsairs? (It seems from the text of App A.I.iv.1055 that Thorongil had to **persuade** Ecthelion to let him take a fleet to Umbar.)

In addition a personal issue linked Imrahil with the Steward's household and perhaps led to an increased presence in Minas Tirith on his part, namely the marriage of his sister Finduilas to Denethor in 2976, followed by the birth of the heir, Boromir, two years later. Was Thorongil at the wedding? It seems likely, given the esteem in which he was held by Ecthelion.

There can be no doubt that Aragorn would have been acquainted with all these people during his service in Gondor: Angelimir, Adrahil, Imrahil and Finduilas. Imrahil was the only one still alive at the time of the War of the Ring and the next area for discussion is to consider how much - if anything - he remembered of Thorongil and whether he recognised him when he arrived at the Battle of the Pelennor Fields in 3019. There seem to be three main issues which, when taken together, suggest a strong possibility of Imrahil recalling Thorongil:

- Fame of Thorongil. Thorongil was clearly a very prominent figure in the Minas Tirith of the 2970s due to his prowess in battle, wisdom as a counsellor, personal charisma, and Númenórean appearance (including a marked resemblance to Denethor). He was also very highly regarded by Ecthelion who loved him "*above all*"[144]. Compare this with Aragorn when he appeared at the Harlond as King in 3019, surrounded by his devoted Grey Company and exhibiting charisma, classic Númenórean appearance and prowess in battle wielding an impressive sword. Imrahil was clearly a person of intelligence and perception and may well have recognised Thorongil during the Battle of the Pelennor Fields where he, Aragorn and Éomer seem to have been very much working together. Note the reference to them riding back exhausted to the City Gate afterwards, unscathed due to fortune and their own skill: "*... few indeed had dared to abide them or look on their faces in the hour of their wrath.*"[145].
- Awareness of the Denethor situation. Imrahil seems to have been very involved with his family members in Minas Tirith. As Denethor's brother-in-law he was well aware of the state of his mind since the death of Boromir and appreciated Aragorn's reluctance to confront him with his claim to the kingship while the war with Sauron was still unresolved. Although it was thirty-nine years since Imrahil had last seen Thorongil, he would have continued to see a great deal of Denethor and could hardly have failed to be aware of his continuing resentment of the stranger from the North who had usurped him in his father's affections and was also, as far as he was concerned, trying to usurp him as ruler of Gondor. From Pippin's first impression of Denethor in *LotR* 5.1.754 the resemblance between him and Aragorn was still apparent, thus increasing the chances that Imrahil would have recognised him in spite of the time lapse since last seeing him. There is also the question of how much he had gleaned from Finduilas while she was alive. For example, had she known/guessed about Denethor's use of the Palantír - especially if it had been used to keep an eye on Gandalf and Thorongil as suggested in *UT*

---

144. Op. cit. [1], App A.I.iv, p. 1055.
145. Op. cit., *LotR* 5.6, p. 849.

4.3.526? Did she tell her brother of her concerns?
- Suspicions of Thorongil's identity. I have already mentioned the possibility of Ecthelion having a good idea of the identity of his favourite captain and counsellor. Following the same theme, did Angelimir and Adrahil also have similar thoughts which they passed on to Imrahil regarding it as good background information for him to have?

My own feeling is that Imrahil would have recognised Thorongil very quickly, perhaps not immediately on his arrival at the Harlond but certainly soon after on witnessing his skill in the battle, while Aragorn's uneasiness about pressing his claim to Denethor could hardly have failed to stir his memory especially if his father or grandfather had raised the issue. There was also the matter of Thorongil's farewell message to Ecthelion c.2980 in App A - "*Other tasks now call me, lord, and much time and many perils must pass, ere I come again to Gondor, if that be my fate*"[146] - which must have made quite an impression at the time.

Whatever the case, there was never any question of Imrahil's loyalty to Aragorn, and his attitude showed a complete acceptance of his claim. He was deferential, sensitive to Aragorn's rank and anxious for him to have the respect he was entitled to. Although he regarded Aragorn's decision to stay outside the City as a wise one, he didn't want him to "*remain like a beggar at the door*"[147]. Later at an unexpected meeting at the Houses of Healing Pippin excitedly, and very informally, addressed Aragorn as "Strider" and was answered in similar vein. Imrahil was clearly taken aback, mainly by the name "Strider" but also perhaps by Aragorn's laughing response to the Hobbit, as it was to Éomer that he voiced his concerns: "*Is it thus that we speak to our kings?*" He then suggested, "*Yet maybe he will wear his crown in some other name!*".[148] His first sentence could be taken to indicate shock or disapproval, but the exclamation mark at the end of his second seems to imply that he was starting to see the funny side of the matter. Aragorn heard him (perhaps not intended - Imrahil probably wasn't aware of his phenomenal hearing) and immediately recited his relevant formal names ("Elessar" and "Envinyatar"), then declared that he would use the Quenya form of "Strider" ("Telcontar") as the name of his royal House - a decision which seems to have been made there and then on the spur of the moment. There is another possible hint as to Imrahil's attitude in App F.II.1133, in a discussion of the familiar and deferential forms of the second-person pronouns in the Common Speech. The deferential form had disappeared in the Shire and thus when Pippin came to Gondor he had used what was, to the Gondorians, the familiar form to everyone, Denethor included. Although Imrahil must have encountered Pippin previously this would have been when he was on his best behaviour in the company of Gandalf or Denethor and he may not have actually heard him speak. In the meeting at the Houses of Healing just described was Pippin, in addition to addressing Aragorn by a rather disrespectful-sounding nickname, also using the familiar form of the second-person pronoun to him? Even if this was justifiable due to the friendship between them it was perhaps inappropriate in the current situation. Maybe Aragorn's response in this incident was a hint to Imrahil that he preferred a more informal approach than was at that time usual in Gondor. The other notable feature of this conversation was the hint of certainty regarding Aragorn's kingship: as far as Imrahil was concerned he **would** wear the crown - it was just the official name which was open to question.

When Imrahil learnt that Denethor was actually dead and that Faramir was seriously ill he again demonstrated his respect for Aragorn's claim by suggesting that he should now take over the rule of the City. Although he had himself been put in charge, by Gandalf, Imrahil was very keen to pass this authority to the King now that the reason for Aragorn's hesitancy was no longer present. It was left to Aragorn to insist that no change should be made until Faramir regained consciousness. It goes without saying that Imrahil must have felt intense gratitude to Aragorn for healing Faramir - the last surviving member of his sister's family.

Imrahil's complete allegiance to Aragorn was illustrated again at The Last Debate during the discussion as to whether a small army should be taken to the Morannon to draw Sauron out. In answer to Aragorn's statement that he did not yet wish to command anyone Imrahil said, "*... the Lord Aragorn I hold to be my liege-lord, whether he claim it or no. His wish is to me a command.*"[149] A few days later during the progress of the Army of

---

146. Op. cit. [1], App A.I.iv, p. 1055.
147. Op. cit., *LotR* 5.8, p. 861.
148. Op. cit., *LotR* 5.8, p. 863.
149. Op. cit., *LotR* 5.9, p. 880.

the West northwards along the Mountains of Shadow Gandalf got the heralds to cry, *"The Lords of Gondor are come!"* However Imrahil suggested that they should cry, *"The King Elessar"*, even though Aragorn had not yet sat upon the throne, because *"... it will give the Enemy more thought..."*.[150] He was, throughout, very prominent in pushing Aragorn's cause and ensuring due respect was given to him.

Looking at Aragorn's attitude to Imrahil, he would surely have remembered the young heir to the princedom of Dol Amroth from his Thorongil days, and he would certainly have made it his business to keep himself informed of events in Gondor after his own departure. He must also have developed a good memory for names and faces. [For example in *LotR* 3.2.438 on first meeting Éomer he told him that he had once been in Rohan and remembered meeting his father Éomund and also Théoden, and he knew that Éomer was too young to have been born at that time.] As with Faramir, Aragorn must have been deeply appreciative of Imrahil's unquestioning acceptance and loyalty - contrasting as they did with the attitude of Denethor and Boromir.

*

Regarding the characters who had bearing on the relationship between Aragorn/Thorongil and Imrahil, the situation on March 15th 3019 was as follows:
- Angelimir. He would have known Thorongil. He had died while the latter was still living in Gondor.
- Ecthelion. He had known Thorongil very well. He had died shortly after the latter's departure.
- Finduilas. She would have encountered him, but was maybe discouraged by Denethor from having too much to do with him. She had died shortly after Thorongil's departure.
- Adrahil. He would have known him. He had died in 3010.
- Boromir. He was barely two years old when Thorongil left Gondor so would not have remembered him. As with Finduilas, Denethor would probably have discouraged any encounters with Thorongil. Boromir had died just under three weeks previously.
- Faramir. He wasn't born until after Thorongil's departure from Gondor.
- Denethor. He had clearly known Thorongil well but had never recognised his right to the kingship of Gondor. He died on March 15th shortly before Aragorn arrived at the Harlond.

Thus Imrahil was the only living link (whom we know by name) in Gondor between Thorongil and King Elessar. [Though see the section on Ioreth.]

Strangely Imrahil, as well as Aragorn, was involved in saving the life of both Faramir and Éowyn. When Faramir was wounded in battle on the way back from Osgiliath on March 13th it was Imrahil's charge which saved him from being hacked to death by the Haradrim as he lay on the ground. Imrahil then lifted his nephew on to his horse and carried him back to Minas Tirith. On March 15th during the Battle of the Pelennor Fields it was Imrahil who, on touching the hand of the apparently dead Éowyn, realised that she was actually still alive. He then proved this by holding his vambrace to her lips resulting in a slight misting on it. Thus both these characters were able to cling to life long enough to receive healing from the hands of Aragorn.

Imrahil died in FA 34 at the age of ninety-nine. He was succeeded as Prince of Dol Amroth by his son Elphir who was in turn succeeded by his own son Alphros. *HoM-e* XII.7.223 shows that Aragorn long outlived both of them.

BEREGOND

Beregond's son Bergil was ten years old at the time of the War of the Ring which probably made Beregond himself somewhere in his thirties, forties or maybe early fifties. He would therefore either have been unborn or a child during Aragorn's time in Gondor as Thorongil. His father Baranor would have been an adult at the time, but we know from Pippin's conversations with both Beregond and Bergil (*LotR* 5.1.762, 770-1) that the family came from the mountain vales in Lossarnach and that Baranor was certainly living there in 3019. Assuming he had always lived there the chances of him knowing Thorongil were perhaps remote, though Lossarnach was close to Minas Tirith according to the *LotR* map and Baranor may have visited the City.

---

150. Op. cit. [1], *LotR* 5.10, p. 885.

In *LotR* there are two recorded meetings between Beregond and Aragorn, namely at the healing of Faramir (*LotR* 5.8.866) - where Bergil was also present for some of the time - and in the scene where Aragorn, as King, pronounced judgement on Beregond for his treason in deserting his post as a Guard of the Citadel and shedding blood in the Houses of the Dead (*LotR* 6.5.968-9).

Apart from these two encounters Beregond is mainly seen through the eyes of Pippin whom he befriended. In *LotR* 5.1.760, 762, 766 and 5.4.808-9 he is portrayed as having a high regard for Gandalf, liking animals and being devoted to Faramir - seeing the strength and courage which lay behind his gentle exterior and artistic temperament. He was also very knowledgeable and perceptive as to what was going on around him. For example he told Pippin, "*This is a great war long-planned, and we are but one piece in it, whatever pride may say.*"[151]. He was aware of Denethor's reputation for being able to read the future and search the thoughts of Sauron, and he knew that the darkness coming from Mordor was a device of Sauron's and not merely exceptionally bad weather.

It was Pippin who first spoke to him of Aragorn, though inadvertently as Gandalf had told him to keep quiet about him. In answer to Beregond's question as to who Aragorn was, Pippin gave a suitably vague reply and then successfully distracted his companion by mentioning Rohan. It was Pippin too who provided the trigger for Beregond's treason by alerting him to Denethor's intention of burning himself and Faramir alive on a pyre in the Houses of the Dead. While Pippin rushed off to find Gandalf Beregond took it on himself to desert his post in the Citadel, kill the resisting porter at the door to Rath Dínen (the Silent Street) and take his keys, and then bar the entrance to the tombs of the Stewards - killing two of the servants in the process - in order to prevent Denethor's servants from going in and lighting the pyre. The result of his actions was that Gandalf was in time to prevent Faramir's death, something which was immediately recognised by Gandalf himself who then appointed him to be guard and servant to Faramir in the Houses of Healing. Thus Beregond was present when Aragorn arrived.

Beregond, keeping watch at the sick-bed, witnessed the recall of Faramir from his deep unconsciousness and experienced the refreshment as Aragorn infused the athelas, after first taking the trouble to reassure Bergil who had come running in with the herb fearful that it would not be fresh enough to be of use and distressed at the sight of Faramir - and by what was perhaps his first experience of serious illness and injury. As Aragorn left the room to go to Éowyn, leaving his Steward conscious and peaceful, we are told that Beregond and his son were "... *unable to contain their joy.*"[152]. Was that joy partly due to the fact that the King had returned as well as the knowledge that Faramir would recover? A few days later as the Army of the West set out for the Morannon, a now more mature Bergil comforted Merry by reminding him that the presence of "*the Lord Elfstone*"[153] - as well as that of his own father - would ensure the return of the men. The army did indeed return, though Beregond only survived because of Pippin's action in killing the Troll-chief who had stunned his friend and was on the point of biting his throat.

As Beregond waited to be taken before his King for judgement he must have been feeling a great mental conflict from the recent events:
- Elation at the defeat of Sauron against all the odds.
- Vulnerability from his recent injuries.
- Gratitude inspired by Aragorn's healing of Faramir. Had Aragorn been involved in healing Beregond as well?
- Awe at the coronation.
- Overall the shadow of the death penalty hanging over him combined with hope of mercy from what he had seen of Aragorn.

In the event his hope of mercy was realised as all penalties were waived due to his bravery in battle, and particularly because, as Aragorn recognised, his treasonable acts had been committed purely for love of Faramir. Having digested this, Beregond was then momentarily plunged into despair when Aragorn told

---
151. Op. cit. [1], *LotR* 5.1, p. 765.
152. Op. cit., *LotR* 5.8, p. 866.
153. Op. cit., *LotR* 5.10, p. 884.

him he must leave the Guard of the Citadel (a post of honour even at the lowest rank) and also depart from Minas Tirith. However his despair was short-lived as Aragorn then explained that he was appointing him to be Captain of Faramir's Guard - the White Company - which would involve him living in Emyn Arnen in Ithilien. Thus Aragorn's "punishment" of removing him from the Citadel Guard and sending him away from the City was really a reward for his willingness to risk his own life to save Faramir. Also it was probably more diplomatic for Beregond to leave Minas Tirith as this would avoid possible repercussions from him coming into contact with relatives and friends of those he had killed.

Beregond had told Pippin when they first met, "*Neither office nor rank nor lordship have I, being but a plain man of arms...*"[154] Thus Aragorn's decision to make him Captain of the White Company must have been more than he could possibly have hoped for, and in addition he would be serving Faramir and living in Ithilien where his own family originally came from. No wonder he departed in "*joy and content*"[155]! Meanwhile Aragorn had the satisfaction of knowing that his Steward had the best possible person to lead his Guard - someone displaying devotion, courage, initiative and selflessness - all qualities which Aragorn would have admired and wished to reward.

IORETH

In *LotR* Ioreth is described as "*an old wife*" and "*the eldest of the women*" serving in the Houses of Healing.[156] If she was, say, in her sixties in 3019 then she would have been in her twenties during Thorongil's time in Gondor. Aragorn at that time was an experienced Ranger of the North and renowned as a military and naval captain in Gondor. He must also have had considerable expertise as a healer due to a natural gift through his lineage and to the training received from Elrond. Thus he may well have been a frequent visitor to the Houses of Healing and if Ioreth had always worked with the healers, then the two of them could have encountered each other. On the other hand it is just as likely that she joined the healers after Thorongil's departure. There is nothing in the text to indicate prior acquaintance between them except perhaps the fact that Aragorn called to her specifically to enquire about the availability of herbs. However this could simply have been due to the fact that she seemed to be the most senior person there. If they **had** met before I feel that Ioreth would have been more likely to recognise Aragorn than the other way round as she herself, if present in the 2970s, would have changed much more over forty years than he with his Númenórean lifespan. Also Thorongil was well-known and probably already had a reputation as a knowledgeable healer so would be more likely to remain in her memory.

What **is** clear is that Ioreth was totally wrapped up in her work with the sick as she was oblivious to any news being talked of in the City, and her only interest in the fighting was her concern that "*those murdering devils*"[157] should not come to the Houses of Healing and disturb her patients. She also thought enough of Faramir to be weeping at his condition and it was her grief for him which made her exclaim, "*Would that there were kings in Gondor, as there were once upon a time, they say!*"[158] She then went on to show her knowledge of old lore as she explained that the rightful king could always be known through his healing hands. It was because of this that Gandalf realised the urgent need to bring Aragorn into the City, telling Ioreth that there was "*hope*"[159] in what she had said - surely a play on Aragorn's childhood name (Estel) and his significance as someone who would bring hope to his people.

Ioreth's knowledge of lore clearly did not extend to the role and properties of athelas in connection with royal healing. When Aragorn - having already heard her account of the problems with errands and deliveries during the siege - asked her if the herb was available in the House he had to listen to her opinion that athelas had little virtue apart from smelling pleasant when bruised, along with an account of a conversation she had had with her sister on the subject, followed by a discussion as to whether "*sweet*" or "*wholesome*" was the

---

154. Op. cit. [1], *LotR* 5.1, p. 767.
155. Op. cit., *LotR* 6.5, p. 969.
156. Op. cit., *LotR* 5.8, p. 860.
157. Op. cit., *LotR* 5.8, p. 861.
158. Op. cit., *LotR* 5.8, p. 860.
159. Op. cit., *LotR* 5.8, p. 860.

more accurate way to describe the aroma of the plant. At this point Aragorn was forced to cut her short, telling her to *"run as quick as your tongue"*[160] and get some, with Gandalf joining in and threatening to take her to the country on Shadowfax if there was no athelas to be found in the City. Ioreth was obviously a talkative and excitable person, but she may also have been reacting to the stress of the situation, and her garrulousness could have been aggravated by being questioned by someone as imposing as Aragorn in such a way as to reveal her ignorance of her trade, just as she was explaining that she and her colleagues naturally did their best to have all the necessary supplies. The delay in obtaining the healing herb must also have increased Aragorn's own stress making him shorter with her than he would otherwise have been.

When Aragorn finally obtained some athelas leaves and steeped them in hot water, Ioreth changed her view of the plant as it now reminded her of the smell of roses from her childhood. After Faramir regained consciousness she was quick to pick up his use of the title "king" when addressing Aragorn, and being the sort of person she was, she soon passed on the information that the king had returned, not forgetting to mention her own role in the matter. It was not long before the news was being passed round the City thus making people aware that help was available to heal their own loved ones who were suffering from exposure to the Black Breath. This would have explained the queue of people waiting to see Aragorn after he finally found time to have a much-needed meal. Ioreth had - albeit unconsciously - greatly eased his acceptance by the people of Minas Tirith.

We next see Ioreth in *LotR* 6.5.966-7 at Aragorn's coronation where she was again in full flow, repeating to her kinswoman the rather exaggerated rumours of the Hobbits' achievements, along with more accurate information - due to being from first-hand knowledge - about Aragorn, calling him *"our Elfstone"*, and *"the Lord Elfstone"* whom she described as *"a marvel"*. She also made the point that he was *"not too soft in his speech"* (no doubt recalling his shortness to her in the Houses of Healing) but had *"a golden heart"* and *"the healing hands"*.[161] Thus she displayed wonder at Aragorn's gifts, affection in her manner of referring to him and recognition of his kindness. She obviously took his shortness with her in good part - she probably knew, herself, that she tended to talk too much! Her further conversation with her kinswoman showed her excitement at her own part in bringing the King into the City and at having spoken with Gandalf and Aragorn: *"And Mithrandir, he said to me..."* and *"... for he [Aragorn] has already entered [the City], as I was telling you; and he said to me ____"*.[162]

Although Faramir was the first person to call Aragorn "king" it was Ioreth who caused the news to be spread - thus between the two of them they obviated the need for Aragorn to actually make a claim for the kingship. Ioreth also provides a good example of Celeborn's advice to Boromir on the subject of old wives' tales: *"But do not despise the lore that has come down from distant years; for oft it may chance that old wives keep in memory word of things that once were needful for the wise to know."*[163]. Ioreth, the old wife, remembered the lore about the hands of the king being the hands of a healer, while Gandalf, one of the wise, listened to her and acted on what she told him. There is little to indicate Aragorn's thoughts about Ioreth apart from his impatience at her chatter, but he appeared to be aware of her regard for Faramir as he prefixed his instruction to run as quick as her tongue with *"if you love the Lord Faramir..."*[164] He would have appreciated, as much as Gandalf and Celeborn did, the wisdom of remembering old lore, and Ioreth's role in facilitating his subjects' acceptance of him must have earned her his gratitude.

THE WARDEN OF THE HOUSES OF HEALING

There is no hint in the text as to the age and history of the Warden/Herb-master of the Houses of Healing, though the fact that he included Ioreth in the "old wives" category seems to point to him being younger than she. There is no hint of any previous encounter between him and Aragorn. He proved to be just as talkative as Ioreth, but whereas she at least had treated Aragorn with respect, the Warden adopted a somewhat patronising

---

160. Op. cit. [1], *LotR* 5.8, p. 864.
161. Op. cit., *LotR* 6.5, p. 966.
162. Op. cit., *LotR* 6.5, pp. 966-7.
163. Op. cit., *LotR* 2.8, p. 374.
164. Op. cit., *LotR* 5.8, p. 864.

attitude to him initially.

First and foremost, he was keen to impress Aragorn with his knowledge of different tongues by citing the name for athelas in various languages - until he realised that Aragorn too knew the Valinorean name which did at least prompt an apology and the recognition that, "*I see you are a lore-master, not **merely** a captain of war.*"[165] [My emphasis]. His general attitude, though, implied that he doubted Aragorn's healing knowledge and was anxious to show that he knew best. Aragorn was only a military man after all and couldn't be expected to have his [the Warden's] expertise in herbs. The fact that he was asking for athelas proved the point. The Houses of Healing were specifically for people who were gravely hurt or ill and would therefore be unlikely to benefit from a herb which was only useful as an air-freshener or an old folk's headache remedy. Therefore there was no athelas available. He also showed that he had no time for old wives' tales, though he was knowledgeable enough about them to be able to quote in full the poem about the power of athelas which ended with the words:

> "*Life to the dying*
> *In the king's hand lying!*"[166]

This he regarded as "*doggrel*" and "*garbled*", a rhyme which the likes of Ioreth repeated without understanding it. Thus he displayed a disparaging attitude to Ioreth as well. Had he in fact come in person to Aragorn partly for the purpose of checking up on Ioreth to see if she had actually got it right about this new healer wanting a herb which, in the Houses of Healing, was generally regarded as pretty useless? It was Gandalf who forced him to start taking Aragorn's request seriously by shouting at him and sending him off to find some old man who had the sense to keep a supply of athelas in his house. Given the Warden's attitude to Aragorn at that point, it probably needed the authority of Gandalf to get things moving.

A little later, after Aragorn had healed Merry, he did a take-off of the Warden's speech for the benefit of Merry and Pippin, substituting pipeweed for athelas and pointing out that it was the Warden himself who didn't understand the old wives' rhymes. This seemed to release his tension as his next conversation with the Warden, when he and Gandalf went to discuss the care of Faramir, Éowyn and Merry, went smoothly. Aragorn had got his frustration out of his system and the Warden was now sufficiently impressed by him to take his instructions very seriously, particularly with regard to Éowyn.

His interaction with Éowyn in the ensuing days will now be examined in detail. The emphasis in quoted passages is mine:
- Before leaving the Houses of Healing to go and eat, Aragorn told the Warden that Éowyn would "*... wish soon to **rise** and depart; but she should not be permitted to do so, if you can in any way restrain her, until **at least ten days** be passed.*"[167]. The date was March 15th. The word "**rise**" indicated that she was supposed to actually stay in bed.
- We are told that Éowyn got up and insisted on being dressed "*When the Captains were **but two days** gone...*"[168] This would have been on March 20th as the Army of the West left for the Morannon on 18th.
- The Warden pointed out that he had been told to tend her with especial care and that she should not have got out of bed for another seven days. The ten days specified by Aragorn would have been up on March 25th. The Warden's seven days from March 20th would have extended her period of bed-rest to 27th.

Did the Warden deliberately add a couple of days to the rest period, to cover himself, or to show how assiduous he was in obeying Aragorn's orders, noting that "*at least*" ten days had been specified? The fact that he **begged** Éowyn to go back to bed could be interpreted as showing that he was frightened at the thought of her having a relapse, both for her sake and his own if he were to be blamed for it. His concerns were eased by Faramir taking on the responsibility for Éowyn's welfare (which involved allowing her to get up and walk

---
165. Op. cit. [1], *LotR* 5.8, p. 865.
166. Op. cit., *LotR* 5.8, p. 865.
167. Op. cit., *LotR* 5.8, p. 870.
168. Op. cit., *LotR* 6.5, p. 958.

in the garden), and we are told that he was "*glad in heart*"[169] to see them both thriving. When Éowyn started failing again in the days after the destruction of the Ring, the Warden went to Faramir with his concerns. It seems significant that once Faramir was assured of Éowyn's love, he made a point of going to the Warden hand-in-hand with her to show that she was well and truly healed. Did he realise the man's nervousness about disobeying Aragorn's instructions? His own advice to Éowyn when he first met her had been to do "*... as the Healer commanded.*"[170] By "*Healer*" he had meant the Warden but in fact the healer in this case was really Aragorn and it was **his** command that Éowyn should rest for a minimum period. Faramir seems to have understood that the Warden needed a higher authority for Éowyn's disregard of his orders. This was fine as far as the Warden was concerned so long as she was continuing to thrive, but once she started to relapse he felt the need to involve Faramir again. If something went wrong, he could argue that the Steward had overruled him.

As indicated earlier, the Warden's attitude to Aragorn changed as a result of his healing of Faramir, Éowyn and Merry on March 15th. The further healings carried out by Aragorn during that night would certainly have confirmed his regard. During his initial conversation with Éowyn on March 20th, when she insisted on getting up, he referred to Aragorn as "*A great lord*" and "*a healer*" and marvelled that healing and military prowess were combined in one person. He went on to state, "*It is not thus in Gondor now, though once it was so, if old tales be true*", showing that his attitude to old wives' tales was also beginning to change.[171] However he still gave no indication of realising that Aragorn was the king - referring to him as merely a captain and a chief. This was in spite of the news going round the City and the fact that Gandalf's angry outburst to him in the Houses of Healing had started with the phrase "*in the name of the king...*"[172]. Maybe he didn't like to admit to himself that Ioreth the "old wife" had been closer to the mark than he had.

OTHER POSSIBLE RELATIONSHIPS

For completeness I consider the following people, mentioned in the main narrative of *LotR*, for potential acquaintance with Aragorn during his service as Thorongil and also from the point of view of Thorongil's knowledge of Gondor as a whole, particularly south of the White Mountains:

- **Anborn**: Ranger of Ithilien
- **Angbor**: Lord of Lamedon; followed the Grey Company to Pelargir with men from Lamedon and Lebennin after Aragorn's dismissal of the Dead Men of Dunharrow. (These men had been held back from going to Minas Tirith due to the presence of the Corsairs at Pelargir - see *LotR* 5.1.765, 770).
- **Damrod**: Ranger of Ithilien
- **Derufin**: son of Duinhir of the Blackroot Vale; fought (and was killed) at the Pelennor Fields
- **Dervorin**: son of the lord of Ringló Vale; fought at the Pelennor Fields
- **Duilin**: son of Duinhir of the Blackroot Vale; fought (and was killed) at the Pelennor Fields
- **Duinhir**: leader of the bowmen of the Blackroot Vale; fought at the Pelennor Fields
- **Forlong** the Fat: Lord of Lossarnach; fought (and was killed) at the Pelennor Fields
- **Golasgil**: Lord of Anfalas; fought at the Pelennor Fields
- **Hirgon**: errand-rider of Denethor who brought the Red Arrow to Théoden symbolising Gondor's request for help and was killed on the return journey with Théoden's response
- **Hirluin of Pinnath Gelin**: fought (and was killed) at the Pelennor Fields
- **Húrin of the Keys**: also called Húrin the Tall and Warden of the Keys
- **Ingold**: leader of the guards at the outwall of the Pelennor Fields when Gandalf, Pippin and Shadowfax arrived there
- **Mablung**: Ranger of Ithilien
- **Targon**: worked in the buttery where Beregond took Pippin

Aragorn's service in Gondor as Thorongil had ended nearly forty years before the events in *LotR*. Therefore

---
169. Op. cit. [1], *LotR* 6.5, p. 961.
170. Op. cit., *LotR* 6.5, p. 960.
171. Op. cit., *LotR* 6.5, p. 958.
172. Op. cit., *LotR* 5.8, p. 865.

any of these people would probably have had to be at least in their late fifties in 3019 to have known him in those days.

The three Rangers of Ithilien - Anborn, Damrod and Mablung - were Dúnedain so could technically have been old enough to remember him due to the longer than average life-span of their race. However Faramir told Frodo, *"We of Gondor do not ever pass east of the Road in these days, and **none of us younger men** has ever done so..."*[173] [My emphasis]. By the words I have emphasised Faramir seems to have been referring to himself and his Rangers. He was in his late thirties in 3019, being born after Thorongil's departure, so if the others were of a similar age any awareness or relationship can be ruled out.

Forlong is described as *"old and grey-bearded"*[174] and also referred to as *"Forlong the old"*[175]. If he was, say, in his sixties in 3019 then he would have been in his twenties during Thorongil's service making it feasible that they could have known each other.

LotR 5.6.846 makes it clear that Húrin was one of the commanders in the Battle of the Pelennor Fields and in *LotR* 6.5.959 the Warden of the Houses of Healing told Éowyn that Húrin was in charge of the Men of Gondor within the City. He also played a very prominent role in officiating at Aragorn's coronation. His name and his obvious high rank implies that he was one of the Dúnedain and therefore long-lived. Thus it is feasible that he and Thorongil knew each other but there is no evidence of this in *LotR*.

The situation is similar for Duinhir, leader of the bowmen from the Blackroot Vale, who brought two adult sons with him to the Pelennor Fields. If he himself was in his fifties or older then he and Thorongil may have met, but again there is no evidence of this.

Dervorin seems to have been the **son** of the lord of Ringló Vale rather than the actual lord (though the wording in *LotR* 5.1.770 is not perfectly clear). This points to him being younger rather than older, though Thorongil could perhaps have encountered his father.

With Angbor, Golasgil, Hirgon, Hirluin, Ingold, and Targon there is no evidence either way. Some of them may have been Dúnedain but, as with the Rangers of Ithilien, this did not necessarily indicate a greater age.

Some of these people came a great distance to fight at the Pelennor Fields: for example parts of Lebennin and Lamedon were about three hundred miles from Minas Tirith, with the western areas of Anfalas and Pinnath Gelin being six hundred miles away. This leads me to consider the question of how much travelling Aragorn, as Thorongil, had done in Gondor as a whole:
- Given the proximity of Ithilien to Mordor he must have known that area well through the necessity of protecting Gondor's eastern border.
- His reputation as a great naval leader and his victory over the Corsairs *circa* 2980 certainly point to him knowing the route from Minas Tirith to Umbar - at least by river and sea.
- Dol Amroth, the chief town of Belfalas, must have been a likely place for Thorongil to have visited due to the prominence of its Princes in the ruling of Gondor.
- One of Thorongil's aims would surely have been to see as much as possible of his potential future southern kingdom, especially as his farewell message to Ecthelion *circa* 2980 implied that he did not intend to return until it was time to make a claim for the kingship.

Aragorn's journey from the Paths of the Dead to Pelargir (March 8th-13th 3019) provides conclusive proof of this last point, showing that his experience of travelling south of the White Mountains must have been extensive. The time-scale required would have left no room for error but he led the way unfalteringly, clearly knowing exactly where he was going. None of his companions (apart from, possibly, Elladan and Elrohir) had been to those lands before - as shown by the words and reactions of Halbarad, Legolas and Gimli in *LotR* 5.2.774, 781-2, 786-90. To cap it all most of the journey was done in the dark as Sauron's Darkness began on the evening of March 9th.

Thorongil had undoubtedly made the most of his time in Gondor.

---

173. Op. cit. [1], *LotR* 4.6, p. 692.
174. Op. cit., *LotR* 5.1, p. 770.
175. Op. cit., *LotR* 5.6, p. 849.

CHAPTER 2.7 - Rohirrim

The main purpose of this chapter is to analyse Aragorn's relationships with Théoden, Éowyn and Éomer. However it is necessary first to look briefly at the history of the Rohirrim in order to understand their close alliance with Gondor, and also to study the young Aragorn's period of service under Théoden's father Thengel. Genealogical Tables 5, 6 and 8 are relevant.

History of the Rohirrim

The following summary is based on information obtained from *LotR*[1] Apps A.I.ii.1038-9, A.I.iv.1044-1057, A.II.1063-1071 and B.1086-8 and from *UT*[2] 3.2.373-414. Aragorn and Faramir also speak of the history of Rohan (*LotR* 3.2.430-1 and *LotR* 4.5.678-9 respectively).

The ancestry of the Rohirrim can be traced back to the first three Houses of Men of the First Age who migrated to the west of Middle-earth and allied themselves with the Eldar in the war against Morgoth. At the beginning of the Second Age, after the defeat of Morgoth by the Valar, some of these people went and lived in Númenor while others stayed in Middle-earth. The people of Rohan were descended from the latter who became known as the Northmen and settled in Rhovanion between Mirkwood Forest and the River Running. By the Third Age, when Númenor was no more, the situation was that friendship existed between the Dúnedain (survivors of Númenor) and the Northmen in recognition of their ancient kinship from way back (*UT* 3.2.i.373-6). Regarding this kinship Aragorn and Faramir seem to have had differing attitudes. Aragorn told Legolas and Gimli that although the Rohirrim had long been friends of the people of Gondor they were "*not akin to them*"[3], going on to stress rather the connection of the Northmen with the Beornings and the Bardings of Dale. Faramir on the other hand when talking to Frodo and Sam, described them as being "*our kin from afar off*"[4]. He also made much of the common descent from the first three Houses of Men, though he regarded this as an affinity rather than actual kinship.

The most striking example of the friendship between these two peoples occurred in the early 1400s of the Third Age when Valacar, who would later become the 20th King of Gondor, married Vidumavi the daughter of Vidugavia King of Rhovanion. On Valacar's death in 1432, the War of the Kin-strife broke out in Gondor due to the objection, of some, to the mixed blood of the new king Eldacar who was half-Dúnadan from his father and half-Northman from his mother. (See Genealogical Table 5.)

UT 3.2.i.374-5 describes the decline of the Northmen following an outbreak of plague in TA 1636. More than two hundred years later, in the 1850s, attacks by the Wainriders (Easterlings) from the area south and east of the Sea of Rhûn further diminished the Northman population at which point a remnant broke away as a separate people - the Éothéod - settling in the Vales of Anduin between the Carrock and the Gladden Fields where they mingled with the Beornings and the people in the west eaves of Mirkwood. However their leaders continued to stress their descent from the Kings of Rhovanion and thus also claimed kinship with the kings of Gondor who were descended from the Dúnadan-X-Northman King Eldacar. Maybe it was actually this kinship which Faramir was referring to in his comment to Frodo and Sam (quoted earlier).

In TA 1977, after the defeat of the Witch-king of Angmar, the Éothéod moved further north to the lands he had ruled, driving away the remnants of his people. This was partly to get away from the Shadow in Dol Guldur and also because their population - both human and equine - had increased and they needed more space.

---

1. J.R.R. Tolkien, *The Lord of the Rings,* London, HarperCollins Publishers, 2007, 2nd edition, based on the 50th Anniversary Edition of 2004.
2. C. Tolkien (ed.), *Unfinished Tales of Númenor and Middle-earth*, London, HarperCollins Publishers, 1998, first published in Great Britain by George Allen & Unwin 1980.
3. Op. cit. [1], *LotR* 3.2, pp. 430-31.
4. Op. cit., *LotR* 4.5, p. 678.

By the third millennium of the Third Age the size of their population was again becoming a problem. It was in 2510 that the Battle of the Field of Celebrant took place in which Eorl the Young, the leader of the Éothéod, responded to a request from Gondor's Ruling Steward Cirion for help in dealing with invasions by wild men from the north-east and Orcs from the Misty Mountains. It was Eorl's cavalry charge which saved the day and as a reward for his aid Cirion gave him and his people Calenardhon (the thinly-populated part of Gondor between the rivers Anduin and Isen) to live in. Thus Eorl became the first King of the Mark and his people called themselves the Eorlingas. Gondor called them the Rohirrim and their land Rohan. *"There the Rohirrim lived afterwards as free men under their own kings and laws, but in perpetual alliance with Gondor."*[5]

Aragorn's service in Rohan

Information on this period of Aragorn's life can be found in Apps A.I.iv.1055-6, A.I.v.1060, A.II.1069-70 and B.1090, *UT* 3.5.460-84, *HoM-e* XII[6] and *LotR* 3.2.438.

For the purpose of this discussion I have assumed that Aragorn's service in Rohan - which we know to be **prior** to that in Gondor - took place roughly between 2960 and 2970. See App A: *"He came to Ecthelion from Rohan, where he had served the King Thengel..."*[7] and App B for 2957-80 where it is stated that during this period: *"As Thorongil he serves in disguise both Thengel of Rohan and Ecthelion II of Gondor."*[8] I have also assumed, using the second of these references, that he was known as "Thorongil" in Rohan as well as in Gondor even though the account in App A.I.iv seems to imply that the name was not given to him until he went to Gondor (*"Thorongil men called him in Gondor"*[9]). This is partly for convenience and partly for another reason which will become clear shortly.

An interesting point is that, although the evidence points to a single block of service in Rohan prior to the events in *LotR*, Aragorn actually told Éomer, *"... I have been in this land before, **more than once...**"*[10] [My emphasis]. Later in the same conversation he made the point that Éomer was too young for him to have known him previously. As Éomer was born in 2991 any subsequent visit to Rohan must have been prior to that, though I can find no reference to one. Maybe Aragorn's service with Thengel King was split into two parts with a journey elsewhere in the middle, or possibly he spent time in Rohan again on his way back from his journey in the border areas of Mordor which took place around 2980 after the completion of his service in Gondor. [This was when he was intending to go straight to Rivendell but became drawn into Lothlórien on the way (App A.I.v.1060).] The problem with such a suggestion is that 2980 was the year of Théoden's accession as King of Rohan and since Thorongil's service is stated to have been under Thengel we can probably rule out such a visit at this time - unless Thorongil knew that Thengel was failing and wished to see him again before he died.

There is little additional information about Aragorn's time in Rohan except for a further statement to Éomer, *"... I have spoken with Éomund your father, and with Théoden son of Thengel."* Thus there is specific evidence that Aragorn knew Thengel, Théoden and Éomund during this period of his life. From this we can infer that he must also have known a number of other characters referred to in the account of the history of the Rohirrim (App A.II.1069-70). I will now examine the evidence for and against his acquaintance with the various members of the Rohan royal family of that period. This serves two purposes, namely to give a fuller picture of Aragorn's service in Rohan as a thirty-something-year-old, and to give a more meaningful background to the relationship analyses for Théoden, Éowyn and Éomer.

The following table gives details of the characters most relevant to the discussion. Most of the information comes from App A.II.

---

5. Op. cit. [1], App A.II, p. 1064.
6. C. Tolkien (ed.), *The History of Middle-earth*, vol. XII, *The Peoples of Middle-earth*, London HarperColllins Publishers, 2002, first published in Great Britain by HarperCollins Publishers 1996, *HoM-e* XII Part 1, Chapter 7, p. 206 & Part 1, Chapter 9.iii, p. 274.
7. Op. cit. [1], App A.I.iv, p. 1055.
8. Op. cit., App B, p. 1090.
9. Op. cit., App A.I.iv, p. 1055.
10. Op. cit., *LotR* 3.2, p. 438.

TURGON	Born 2855*	Died 2953	Steward of Gondor 2914-2953.
ECTHELION II	Born 2886*	Died 2984	Son of Turgon. Steward of Gondor 2953-2984.
FENGEL	Born 2870	Died 2953	King of Rohan 2903-2953.
THENGEL	Born 2905	Died 2980	Son of Fengel. King of Rohan 2953-2980. Married Morwen of Lossarnach (related to Prince Imrahil) in 2943.
MORWEN	Born c. 2922	Died ?	Married Thengel in 2943.
THÉODEN	Born 2948	Died 3019	Son of Thengel and Morwen. King of Rohan 2980-3019. Married Elfhild (of Eastfold**).
ELFHILD	Born ?	Died 2978	Married Théoden
THÉODRED	Born 2978	Died 3019	Son of Théoden and Elfhild.
THÉODWYN	Born 2963	Died 3002	Sister of Théoden. Married Éomund of Eastfold in 2989.
ÉOMUND	Born ?	Died 3002	Married Théodwyn in 2989.
ÉOMER	Born 2991	Died FA 64	Son of Éomund and Théodwyn. Théoden's "sister son"
ÉOWYN	Born 2995	Died ?	Daughter of Éomund and Théodwyn. Théoden's "sister daughter".

* According to *HoM-e* XII.7.206 **According to *HoM-e* XII.9.iii.274 Note 4

Fengel King appears to have been a rather unpleasant character, being greedy and falling out with his marshals and his children. As a result Thengel - his heir - went to live in Gondor when he reached adulthood, only returning to Rohan on his father's death in 2953 when he became King himself. This no doubt explained his marriage to a Gondorian woman, Morwen of Lossarnach, in 2943. Three of their five children - two daughters and the future king Théoden - were born in Gondor. From App A.II we learn that Thengel "... *won honour in the service of Turgon*"[11] who was Steward of Gondor at the time and father of Ecthelion and grandfather of Denethor. As shown in the table, 2953 was the year when Ecthelion became Steward of Gondor on the death of Turgon, and Thengel succeeded Fengel as King of Rohan. A few years later Aragorn, probably approaching thirty years old, arrived in Rohan and "... *rode in the host of the Rohirrim...*"[12]. My belief that Aragorn acquired the name Thorongil in Rohan rather than in Gondor arises from Thengel's lengthy (it must have been over twenty years) sojourn in the latter place. App A.II tells us that on Thengel's return to Rohan "*the speech of Gondor*"[13] was spoken in his house. This could mean Common Speech which was the language of Gondor, but it could also mean Sindarin which was spoken by the elite - and certainly by the Southern Dúnedain as shown in *LotR* 4.4.659 where Faramir's Rangers, Mablung and Damrod spoke an Elvish language (presumably Sindarin as Quenya tended to be a more academic language rather than one for everyday speech). Thengel would certainly have known Sindarin even if it wasn't actually spoken in his house in Rohan, so he may well have coined the Sindarin name Thorongil.

There is no indication of the circumstances surrounding Aragorn's acceptance into Thengel's service. (Did Gandalf perhaps have a role in it?) App A.I.v.1060 implies that he won renown there and this seems to be born out by his later acceptance for service under Ecthelion. Thengel and Ecthelion must have known each other well after all their years together in Gondor and it seems very natural and probable that Thorongil arrived in Gondor bearing Thengel's specific recommendation.

Thengel, being born in 2905, was twenty-six years older than Thorongil - and thus aged fifty-five in 2960, with his son Théoden being twelve. Thengel and Morwen had two more daughters in Rohan, the younger, Théodwyn, being born during Thorongil's period of service. Thus, as well as remembering a young Théoden, Aragorn would no doubt also have recalled his four sisters along with the celebrations at the birth of the youngest one. It stands to reason that he would also have been acquainted with Morwen.

We know that Théoden married Elfhild and that their son Théodred was born in 2978, an event which led to Elfhild's death in childbirth. Thorongil would have been in Gondor at the time, where the news would surely have been reported. He left Gondor two years later, and as a repeat visit to Rohan on his way back west in 2980

---

11. Op. cit. [1], App A.II, p. 1069.
12. Op. cit., App A.I.v, p. 1060.
13. Op. cit., App A.II, p. 1069.

is purely speculation on my part, it seems unlikely that he would ever have encountered Théodred - who was to die in 3019 at the First Battle of the Fords of Isen on February 25th, that is the day before the breaking of the Fellowship and the death of Boromir. Regarding Elfhild, there is no record of her year of birth or the date of her marriage, though the latter event presumably took place a year or two prior to the birth of Théodred. If she was in her twenties at the time, this points to a birth-date in the 2950s so Thorongil may well have encountered her. *HoM-e* XII Part 1.9.iii.274 Note 4 refers to her as Elfhild of Eastfold thus perhaps implying kinship with Éomund of Eastfold.

Théodwyn married Éomund in 2989 at the age of twenty-six. As already mentioned Thorongil may have been aware of her as a child of perhaps seven years old at the time when he left for Gondor. There is no record of Éomund's age at marriage, so it is not clear in what capacity Aragorn remembered him. If Éomund was, say, ten years older than his wife he would have been seventeen at Thorongil's departure from Rohan. He is described in App A.II as hating Orcs and often riding out against them "*... in hot anger, unwarily and with few men.*"[14] Thus Thorongil perhaps knew him as a hot-headed youngster! In 3002 Éomund's recklessness led him to pursue a small band of Orcs to the Emyn Muil where he was taken by surprise by a much bigger force hiding in the rocks and killed in the ensuing battle. Soon afterwards Théodwyn became ill and died, leaving Éomer and Éowyn as orphans. They had been born in 2991 and 2995 respectively, thus they were too young for Thorongil to have known them.

For completeness the following Rohirrim, mentioned in the main narrative of *LotR*, should also be considered for potential acquaintance with Thorongil:
- **Ceorl**: the rider who met Théoden and company as they rode towards Helm's Deep and brought news of the second defeat at the Fords of Isen on March 2nd 3019 (*LotR* 3.7.527)
- **Déorwine**: chief of the knights of Théoden's household
- **Dúnhere**: Lord of Harrowdale, nephew of Erkenbrand
- **Elfhelm**: a marshal of Rohan
- **Erkenbrand**: Master of Westfold and the Hornburg
- **Gálmód**: father of Gríma
- **Gamling**: one of the leaders at the Battle of The Hornburg
- **Gléowine**: Théoden's minstrel
- **Gríma/Wormtongue**
- **Grimbold**: a junior marshal under Théodred
- **Guthláf**: Théoden's standard-bearer
- **Háma**: Théoden's Door-ward
- **Widfara**: The rider who sensed the coming south wind as the Rohirrim approached Minas Tirith

Erkenbrand is referred to in *UT* 3.5.478 Appendix (i) as if his youth were long past by 3019, an impression strengthened by the fact that his nephew, Dúnhere, is described as a valiant captain (474) and thus perhaps not likely to be in the first flush of youth himself. Gamling, in *LotR*, is described as "*an old man*" and "*Gamling the Old*".[15] In these cases it depends on what is meant by old. Someone of sixty in 3019 would have been twenty-eight years younger than Aragorn and thus, at the end of Thorongil's Rohan service when he was around forty, would have been only twelve years old. These two would have had to be aged around seventy for Thorongil to have encountered them as adults, though he may have been aware of them as children.

Gríma is described, in *LotR*, as being "*wizened*"[16] which could imply age, but it could also be an indication of his twisted character being reflected in his appearance - perhaps even caused by Saruman. In fact Pippin observed that he "*looked a queer twisted sort of creature*"[17]. There is no evidence in the main narrative of *LotR* of any sort of previous awareness between Aragorn and Gríma thus suggesting that the latter's wizened look was not due to age. Thorongil may well have encountered Gríma's father Gálmód though, assuming he held

---
14. Op. cit. [1], App A.II, p. 1070.
15. Op. cit., *LotR* 3.7, p. 530 and *LotR* 3.8, p. 543 respectively.
16. Op. cit., *LotR* 3.6, p. 512.
17. Op. cit., *LotR* 3.9, p. 573.

some sort of position in Thengel's court or household.

With the other characters in the list - Ceorl, Déorwine, Elfhelm, Gléowine, Grimbold, Guthláf, Háma and Widfara - there is no indication either way. Most of them were in positions of responsibility but they could easily have attained these as relatively young men. If they were in their forties or fifties in 3019 they would either have been born after Thorongil left Rohan or else have been young children during his service - in which case **he** may have remembered **them** but not the other way round.

In *LotR* 5.6.849, the lament composed by a minstrel of Rohan to commemorate those who fell at the Battle of the Pelennor Fields includes some Rohirrim not mentioned elsewhere, namely Fastred, Harding, Herefara, Herubrand and Horn. There is no indication as to the age of these people.

Connected with this speculation is the question of whether Thengel had any suspicion of Thorongil's true identity. There is nothing to suggest this in Apps A.I.iv, A.I.v and B where Thorongil's service in Rohan is only briefly described in the three short passages I have already quoted. He would have had a lower profile than later on in Gondor, being younger and less experienced and just one of the Riders - as opposed to the military and naval captain and wise counsellor whom Ecthelion came to know and respect. Also the question of the ancient kingship in Gondor would not have been such a significant issue in Rohan. However it is possible that Thengel came to suspect something in later years through communication with Ecthelion during Thorongil's service in Gondor.

*

There are many indications in the *LotR* narrative that Aragorn had absorbed the culture and values of Rohan and that he had found his service there enjoyable and rewarding:
- In *LotR* 3.2.430 he described the Rohirrim to Legolas and Gimli as being bold, proud and wilful but also true-hearted and generous - as well as wise in spite of their lack of learning, being more inclined to song than writing. He made it clear that he valued their long friendship with Gondor.
- He was suspicious at the lack of any signs of life as they crossed the Eastemnet of Rohan as he remembered there being studs and herds there, along with herdsmen living in tents - even in winter.
- He also stated that he didn't believe they supplied horses to Sauron. When he met Éomer shortly afterwards he was quick to assure him that he and his companions meant no harm to Rohan neither to man **nor horse** - thus showing his appreciation of the Rohirrim's regard for their horses. Earlier, at the Council of Elrond, he had given his reaction to this rumour: "*... it grieves me more than many tidings that might seem worse to learn that Sauron levies such tribute.*"[18].
- In *LotR* 3.6.507 as Aragorn, Legolas and Gimli - now accompanied by Gandalf - drew near to Edoras they passed the burial mounds of the Rohirrim. Aragorn remarked on the fact that there were nine mounds in the right-hand line (these were for the first nine Kings of Rohan from Eorl to Helm) and seven in the left-hand line. Was he thinking to himself that the last time he had been in Rohan there were only six on the left? Thengel, the King he had served as Thorongil, had since died.
- He showed his awareness of the language and history of Rohan explaining how their speech was now sundered from that of their Northern forebears, and chanting the ancient poem describing Eorl ("*Where now the horse and the rider?... etc.*"[19]), first in Rohirric then translating it into Common Speech. He also recounted the story of Eorl, later pointing out the tapestry in the hall of Meduseld which depicted him at the Battle of the Field of Celebrant.
- Also when Théoden announced that he was ready to ride to battle even if it led to his death, Aragorn declared: "*Then even the defeat of Rohan will be glorious in song*"[20], thus further indicating his awareness of the importance of song in Rohan's culture.
- In *LotR* 5.2.787, during the journey through the Paths of the Dead, the Company came upon the bones of Baldor lying as if he had been trying to claw his way through a closed stone door when he died. He had been the heir of Eorl's son Brego and potentially the third King of Rohan, and had entered the Paths after making a drunken vow to do so. Aragorn stopped to examine his remains, referring again to

---

18. Op. cit. [1], *LotR* 2.2, p. 262.
19. Op. cit., *LotR* 3.6, p. 508.
20. Op. cit., *LotR* 3.6, p. 518.

the nine and seven burial mounds, lamenting the absence [i.e. in the Paths] of the white symbelmynë flowers which covered them, and wondering why Baldor was trying to get through the door. He was obviously aware of the story - from his general knowledge of the history and lore of Middle-earth and from his time as Thorongil in Rohan. Murray Smith has likened Aragorn's behaviour to Baldor to his attitude to the dying Boromir: taking the time to show compassion even in a situation of grave urgency and danger.[21]

Aragorn's sojourn in Rohan clearly made a deep impression on him. In addition to becoming acquainted with the people and their culture he would have learnt much about the structure of their armed forces, and gained experience of being part of a cavalry force. Although he would obviously have learnt horsemanship in his earlier life, this would not have been as a member of an organised cavalry. Also as a Ranger, working in secret, tracking and stalking, much of his travelling would have been on foot. Overall his time in Rohan enabled him to become well-acquainted with Gondor's closest ally prior to moving on to Gondor itself.

THÉODEN

Théoden would have been about twelve years old at the beginning of Thorongil's service to his father and approximately twenty-two when Thorongil left for Gondor. Aragorn remembered him, as he told Éomer when they met (*LotR* 3.2.438). He also remembered a very different Rohan from that of 3019, one where it would have been unthinkable for its ruler to try and force him to abandon his pursuit of the Orcs who had captured his friends - as Éomer was now trying to do acting on Théoden's orders. This situation was due to the sinister influence of Saruman and of those people "*... close to the king's ear, that speak craven counsels...*"[22] as Éomer explained. Éomer himself was in potential danger of imprisonment, even death, from his own uncle for riding against these same Orcs without permission. Gandalf had recently had a hostile reception in Rohan resulting in Théoden telling him to take any horse and go, whereupon the Wizard took Shadowfax and apparently rendered him untameable - to Théoden's fury. The situation was summed up by Gandalf when he told Aragorn, Legolas and Gimli, "*There is war in Rohan, and worse evil: it goes ill with Théoden.*"[23]. When they reached the gates of Edoras Gandalf lost his temper when it became clear that orders were actually coming from Gríma rather than Théoden. All this must have been in stark contrast with Aragorn's earlier experience of Rohan.

Théoden's situation in March 3019 was that his health was failing. *UT* states that his malady had begun around 3014 when he was sixty-six, and that it may have been due to natural causes or else brought on - or aggravated - by Gríma administering "*subtle poisons*".[24] Théoden was deeply under the influence of Gríma (and thus Saruman) who had persuaded him that Éomer was not to be trusted and was pursuing his own agenda by drawing men away from the defence of Edoras. In practice of course the immediate threat to Rohan at that time, as Éomer realised, was not Mordor or Dunland but Saruman. In addition Théoden's son (and only child) Théodred had been killed in battle with Saruman's forces at the Fords of Isen on February 25th a week before the arrival of Gandalf, Aragorn, Legolas and Gimli at Edoras. There is no indication that Théoden remembered or recognised Aragorn, either at their first encounter in Meduseld or later.

*

Aragorn was an onlooker rather than a participant during the meeting with Théoden, as the main purpose at this stage was for Gandalf to free Théoden from the influence of Saruman. However prior to actually entering the hall of Meduseld Aragorn was involved in a potentially dangerous argument with Háma the Door-ward because he didn't want to leave his sword, Andúril, outside the hall. In the event Gandalf persuaded him to comply with the instruction but not before Háma had barred Aragorn's way pointing his sword toward him and Gimli had threatened Háma with his axe in support of his friend. Aragorn's behaviour, on the face of it, seemed

---

21. M. Smith, 'Princes Fictional and Real', Paper presented at Oxonmoot 2008.
22. Op. cit. [1], *LotR* 3.2, p. 436.
23. Op. cit., *LotR* 3.5, p. 500.
24. Op. cit. [2], *UT* 3.5, p. 460.

to be directly at variance with Gandalf's earlier instruction to *"speak no haughty word..."*[25]. This episode needs to be looked at in detail, examining the reasons for Aragorn's seemingly arrogant behaviour and addressing the question as to whether it had been normal policy during his time as Thorongil for weapons to be left outside the hall.

There is a reasonable amount of evidence pointing to the likelihood of the ban on weapons being a recent order from Théoden under Gríma's influence:
- The guards were initially doubtful that Théoden would be willing to receive his visitors and when his agreement came it was only on condition that they left their weapons outside. The actual wording was: "*... any weapon that you bear, **be it only a staff**...*"[26] [My emphasis]. Gríma, working secretly with Saruman and responsible for persuading Théoden to mistrust Gandalf, would have realised the importance of preventing Gandalf's **staff** from entering Meduseld and undoing all Saruman's work. Thus the implication was that the ban on weapons was down to this treacherous servant of Théoden.
- In addition Gandalf's own behaviour during the altercation with Háma implied that the instruction was unexpected. His words, "*A king will have his way in his own hall, be it folly or wisdom*"[27] seemed very much a "let's humour him" type of attitude, acknowledging that the order was unnecessary but realising that Théoden was "not himself".
- It could also be argued that if this policy had always been in operation then Aragorn would have expected Háma's instruction and presumably complied without making an issue of the matter.

However, looking at it from a different angle, even if such a policy **had** been in existence in the past, Aragorn may still have found it difficult to accept it in 3019:
- When he had been in Rohan as Thorongil he had been a young man and incognito **as a subordinate**. The situation was now different as he had revealed his true identity to Éomer and he had been introduced by Gandalf as "*Aragorn son of Arathorn, the heir of Kings*"[28] who was on his way to Minas Tirith. Being now revealed as potential King of Gondor (and thus superior in standing to the King of Rohan) he may well have found it deeply insulting to be told to leave his weapon outside, as illustrated by his questioning the propriety of Théoden's wishes taking precedence over his own.
- During his previous time in Rohan it had been a place of safety and friendship for him. In 3019 it was obviously much more dangerous. He, Legolas and Gimli would have already been imprisoned if Éomer hadn't disobeyed orders when they met at the edge of Fangorn and allowed them to go free. It was not at all clear what sort of situation they were going to find inside the hall and therefore it would have been logical for him to want to be armed. Gandalf was not worried about leaving his own sword outside as his staff gave him all the protection he needed.

There is also another consideration, namely that of the sword itself. As Aragorn made clear, he would have been happy to obey the instruction of **any** house-owner, however lowly, and leave **any** other sword outside. The difference in this incident was that the sword was Andúril - special for many reasons:
- It had originally been forged in the First Age by Telchar the greatest Dwarf smith.[29]
- There was its impressive history: the sword which had been broken in the struggle between Elendil and Sauron, but which had nevertheless had its hilt used by Isildur to cut the One Ring from Sauron's hand.
- Coupled with this was the aura of the prophecy relating to it, namely that it would be reforged when the One Ring was found, the sign for an heir of Elendil to come to the fore again and either defeat Sauron or perish along with the rest of his race. Even prior to the finding of the Ring, the prophecies had marked Aragorn out as the heir of Elendil in question. [This issue is covered in Elrond's conversations with the

---

25. Op. cit., [1], *LotR* 3.6, p. 507.
26. Op. cit., *LotR* 3.6, p. 509.
27. Op. cit., *LotR* 3.6, p. 511.
28. Op. cit., *LotR* 3.6, p. 509.
29. C. Tolkien (ed.), *The Silmarillion*, London, HarperCollins Publishers, 1999, first published in Great Britain by George Allen & Unwin 1977, *TSil* Chapter 10, p. 103.

twenty-year-old Aragorn in App A.I.v.1057, 1059]
- The One Ring had now been found and the sword had just been reforged.
- Galadriel had given Aragorn a sheath for it which would prevent the blade being stained or broken even in defeat.
- According to Aragorn's words to Háma there was a spell or prophecy relating to the sword which would bring about the death of anyone who drew it, apart from Elendil's heir: *"Death shall come to any man that draws Elendil's sword save Elendil's heir."*[30]

Being considered fit to carry and wield such a sword was a tremendous responsibility. The prophecy concerning it was in the process of being realised after three thousand years of watching and waiting - on the part of people like Gandalf, Galadriel and Elrond as well as the Dúnedain themselves. Aragorn himself too had come so far, having waited for nearly seventy years for this to happen. So much depended on this sword - his destiny and the rescue of Middle-earth from Sauron, not to mention his personal happiness - and if something had gone wrong due to him letting it out of his sight the failure would have been overwhelming. Thus it is not hard to understand his anxiety about Andúril being handled by someone else, from the point of view of harm coming to the sword and to the person concerned - neither of which was worth risking. He was not taking any chances and when he eventually agreed to leave it he placed it against the wall himself and gave Háma strict instructions not to let anyone else touch it. Maybe he was using scare tactics to frighten Háma, but there was clearly a valid reason for doing so.

In a discussion of this incident by the Southampton UK Tolkien Reading Group in 2010, it was suggested that Aragorn's behaviour may have been aimed at diverting attention from Gandalf's staff. By causing a scene about Andúril and with Gandalf willingly giving up his own sword it was easier to make the case for letting a 'walking stick' pass. It could certainly be argued that there are some of the hallmarks of a deliberate strategy here:
- It wasn't the **swords** which were the chief danger as far as Gríma (and Saruman) was concerned, but Gandalf's staff, and Aragorn would have realised that. Therefore he would have had a motive for making the opposite appear to be the case to throw Háma off his guard.
- The fact that the staff was referred to as a stick and a support by both Aragorn and Gandalf could even suggest that the whole scene was a put-up job between the two of them.
- When Aragorn, apparently persuaded by Gandalf, finally agreed to leave his sword he made a point of letting Háma know that this weapon was the *"Blade that was Broken"*[31], was wrought by Telchar and was only to be used by Elendil's heir. This speech had a striking effect on Háma who stepped back in amazement, becoming deferential and addressing him as "lord". Then when Gandalf pretended to take offence at being asked to give up his staff, Aragorn broke the tension by laughing and appealing to Háma to let the old man keep his support. Thus prompted, Háma used his own judgement and, believing them to be *"... friends and folk worthy of honour, who have no evil purpose"*[32], let Gandalf take his staff into the hall, thereby disobeying the orders he had been given. His behaviour resembled that of Éomer in *LotR* 3.2.434, who was similarly awestruck by Aragorn, his ancestry and his sword, and was thus persuaded by him to do what he believed to be right rather than blindly obeying twisted orders.

On balance I feel that Aragorn's reluctance to leave his sword outside was more likely to have been caused by the weighty and awesome responsibility of possessing such a weapon rather than by intentional manipulation. The end result - namely ensuring that Gandalf went into Meduseld with the means of effecting Théoden's cure - was the same whatever interpretation is put on the events which led up to it.

*

---

30. Op. cit. [1], *LotR* 3.6, p. 511.
31. Op. cit., *LotR* 3.6, p. 511.
32. Op. cit., *LotR* 3.6, p. 511.

Once Théoden was healed the relationship between him and Aragorn was characterised by a mutual regard and by Aragorn's role as champion and protector of the king. As Théoden recovered, Aragorn, addressing him as "lord", pledged his support in any ensuing battle. He also made the - perhaps pointed - remark that he and his companions had not brought their weapons merely to have them rest against Théoden's wall, maybe still smarting from being asked to leave his sword outside the hall. However in general a study of *LotR* 3.6 and 3.7 (pp. 506-542) shows a marked contrast between Aragorn's demeanour at the door of Meduseld and his respectful attitude subsequently, even though Théoden was actually his vassal, and therefore not entitled to give him orders or overrule him. This lends weight to the interpretation that his earlier behaviour was not due to any kind of arrogance or pulling rank, but rather to anxiety about leaving Andúril (or else to a ruse to facilitate the acceptance of Gandalf's staff).

At the Battle of the Hornburg he was true to his pledge, fighting alongside Éomer, helping and encouraging the men and urging a now somewhat doubtful Théoden to keep trusting in Gandalf in spite of the seemingly hopeless state of their fortunes. During this conversation he repeatedly addressed Théoden as "lord", with Théoden calling him "Aragorn" and later "son of Arathorn". When Théoden decided that he would not give in to Saruman's forces without a fight, he asked Aragorn to accompany him when he rode out from the Hornburg hoping to make a glorious end if nothing else. This was a request not an order and was readily accepted by Aragorn. Their action, carried out at sunrise, coincided with the arrival of the Huorns in the Deeping-coomb, and that of Gandalf and Erkenbrand.

Aragorn's role in the battle was made the more impressive by the fact that he was wielding Andúril. Its stirring effect was celebrated by the Rohirrim as he and Éomer drew their swords together: "*Andúril goes to war. The Blade that was Broken shines again!*"[33]. The Rohirrim clearly knew all about this legendary weapon as was made clear by Éomer's reaction on first meeting Aragorn. Andúril is described as "*gleaming with **white fire***", and we are told that "*... three times Andúril **flamed** in a desperate charge that drove the enemy from the wall.*"[34] The words I have emphasised reflect the meaning of its name, "Flame of the West". In addition to arousing the Rohirrim its fiery appearance instilled terror into the Enemy following the breach of the Deeping Wall, enabling Aragorn to hold them off long enough for the men to take refuge in the Hornburg. In doing this he barely escaped with his own life, being saved only by an opportune arrow from Legolas and a boulder hurled from above on to the pursuing Orcs.

When Théoden, Gandalf, Aragorn and their companions arrived at Isengard two days after the battle, Aragorn was perfectly happy for Théoden to be considered as one of "*the great ones*" who had gone to "*discuss high matters*" (in the words of Legolas) while he himself enjoyed an informal meal and smoke in the company of Elf, Dwarf and Hobbits.[35]

*

In *LotR* 5.2.774-5 as Théoden's company made their way back to the Hornburg after the parley with Saruman, Aragorn maintained his role as protector of the King. When a group of unknown horsemen came up behind them he immediately dismounted and stood by Théoden's stirrup with his sword drawn. The "strangers" were in fact Halbarad and the Grey Company along with Elladan and Elrohir. Aragorn continued his deferential manner toward Théoden making a point of asking his leave for the Dúnedain to ride with them. He continued to call him "*lord*" in this chapter, but Théoden now started addressing **him** as "*my lord Aragorn*". The obvious reason for this change is that Théoden felt admiration and gratitude on account of Aragorn's performance at Helm's Deep. However there was also the matter of the Orthanc-stone. Théoden had witnessed the aftermath of Pippin's meddling with this Palantír and would have realised that he had encountered Sauron in it. He had watched Gandalf present it to Aragorn, bowing as he did so and calling him "lord", but also warning him to be wary about using the Stone prematurely. There had then been a difference of opinion between them with Aragorn believing that the time had actually come to abandon secrecy. Théoden had only been freed from Saruman's influence three days earlier and during that time he had ridden to Helm's Deep, been involved in

---

33. Op. cit. [1], *LotR* 3.7, p. 534.
34. Op. cit., *LotR* 3.7, p. 534 and p. 535 respectively.
35. Op. cit., *LotR* 5.9, p. 560.

a nearly-disastrous battle, witnessed the amazing sight of Ents and Huorns and taken part in a parley with Saruman which had ended with the company acquiring a mysterious black globe which had apparently been used to communicate with Sauron. This hectic activity, both physical and mental, would not have left much opportunity for contemplation, particularly for someone who was, on his own admission, genuinely feeling the frailty of advancing years. The incident concerning the Palantír and Gandalf's deferential attitude to Aragorn perhaps brought home to him the true significance and awe-inspiring destiny of the man who had acquitted himself so impressively at Helm's Deep.

From this point the relationship between Aragorn and Théoden took on a more sombre quality characterised by a mixture of premonition and uncertainty.

Following the departure of Gandalf and Pippin for Minas Tirith the rest of the Company prepared to travel back to Helm's Deep. Aragorn was full of pessimism and doubt, telling Legolas, Gimli and Merry, "... *it is dark before me ... I do not yet see the road.*"[36]. When Merry begged not to be left behind Aragorn told him he thought his road lay with Théoden, but that there would be no happy ending, telling him, "*It will be long, I fear, ere Théoden sits at ease again in Meduseld. Many hopes will wither in this bitter Spring.*"[37] In fact Théoden would never sit at ease again in Meduseld, so this was only a partial premonition.

Aragorn used the Orthanc-stone to confront Sauron early the following morning. When he realised that he had no hope of reaching Pelargir in time to intercept the ships of the Corsairs of Umbar if he carried on journeying with the Rohirrim he told Théoden that he was going through the Paths of the Dead. Théoden at first trembled at the mention of the Paths, but then acknowledged that it might be Aragorn's doom to go that way, and made no attempt to change his mind even though he was grieved by their separation and recognised that it weakened his force. Aragorn's parting words from him urging him to "*Ride unto great renown!*"[38] seemed to indicate foreknowledge. This was the last time he would see Théoden alive.

Théoden's reaction to Aragorn's decision differed from that of the other Riders nearby who turned pale, with Éomer openly assuming that Aragorn was going to his death. Their behaviour was clearly influenced by what had happened to Baldor in TA 2570. In *LotR* 5.3.793-8 Théoden's party - which included Merry - joined Éowyn at Dunharrow. Mainly to answer Merry's questions, Théoden gave a full account of Baldor's boast that he would go through the Paths of the Dead and his subsequent loss there. As before, he suggested that Aragorn "*was called*" to go that way and went on to recount a further story of Baldor, saying how he had gone with his father, Brego, to the door of the Paths of the Dead at the time when the Rohirrim first settled in their new land. There they encountered an aged withered man who told them the door was shut "*until the time comes*", then died before answering Baldor's question as to when that time would be. [No doubt it was this strange incident which originally sparked Baldor's curiosity and led to his reckless dare during the "house-warming" celebrations for the Hall of Meduseld.] In order to comfort Éowyn, Théoden went on to suggest that maybe the time which had been foretold had now actually come and Aragorn would be permitted to go through the Paths. This was of course the case and in fact it was Aragorn who finally found out - over four-hundred years after the event - what had happened to Baldor. As well as feeling that Aragorn had been called, Théoden also believed that he would not see him again while at the same time acknowledging that he was "*... a kingly man of high destiny.*"[39] The implication is therefore that he was predicting his own death rather than Aragorn's. (When Éowyn regained consciousness in the Houses of Healing she would tell Éomer, "*He* [Théoden] *is dead* **as he foresaw**"[40] [My emphasis].) Immediately after this conversation Hirgon, an errand-rider from Gondor, arrived bearing the Red Arrow as a token of war and as a request for Rohan to come to Gondor's aid.

Further light can be shed on the relationship between Théoden and Aragorn by considering the regard which both men had for Merry. When Théoden took the Hobbit under his wing and accepted his service Aragorn was clearly relieved, acknowledging that he was in good hands. Although Théoden was obviously fond of Merry he did admit that he had received him as swordthain for his safe-keeping. Was this partly as a favour to Aragorn, a "thank you" for his deeds at Helm's Deep? Or because he realised that Merry could not possibly go with

---

36. Op. cit. [1], *LotR* 5.2, p. 773.
37. Op. cit., *LotR* 5.2, p. 773.
38. Op. cit., *LotR* 5.2, p. 779.
39. Op. cit., *LotR* 5.3, p. 797.
40. Op. cit., *LotR* 5.8, p. 868.

the Grey Company through the Paths of the Dead? Or as a safeguard in case Aragorn did come to grief on his journey?

After Théoden's death on the Pelennor Fields Aragorn arranged for him to be laid in a tomb in the Hallows among the Kings of Gondor. Referring to him as *"Théoden the Renowned"*[41], he offered Éomer the choice of letting him stay there or else taking him back to Rohan. Éomer chose the latter course and, after the celebrations following Aragorn's wedding, this was done. *LotR* specifically states that *"the kings of Gondor and Rohan"*[42] went to the tombs and carried Théoden away on a bier, passing through the City and then laying the bier on a wain. The implication is certainly that Aragorn and Éomer personally carried out these tasks.

*

It was Gandalf who healed Théoden freeing him from the insidious influence of Saruman and Gríma. This healing was in effect a struggle between two members of the Order of the Istari and as such would not have been achievable by Aragorn. However Aragorn's selfless support for Théoden at Helm's Deep coupled with the respect he showed him must have cheered and encouraged him in his new-found vigour. He specifically wanted Aragorn beside him as he rode out from the Hornburg, determined to take a brave stand against all the odds.

The following quotations sum up the regard the two of them had for each other:

"If these kinsmen be in any way like to yourself, my Lord Aragorn, thirty such knights will be a strength that cannot be counted by heads."[43]

Théoden, in answer to Aragorn's request that the Grey Company should ride with them.

"There go three that I love..."[44].

Aragorn to Halbarad, referring to Théoden, Éomer and Merry.

"... he [Théoden] was a gentle heart and a great king and kept his oaths; and he rose out of the shadows to a last fair morning."[45].

Aragorn to Merry in the Houses of Healing. [Note Aragorn's appreciation of Théoden's gentleness.]

ÉOWYN

Éowyn was twenty-four in TA 3019. She had lost her parents, Éomund and Théodwyn in TA 3002 when she was seven and she and Éomer had subsequently been taken in by Théoden who had doted on Théodwyn (his youngest sister). Théoden had long been a widower and his only child was his son and heir Théodred who was twenty-four at the time. *UT* states that, prior to the intervention of Saruman and Gríma, Théoden was *"vigorous and of martial spirit, and a great horseman"*[46], while Théodred and Éomer are described as *"vigorous men, devoted to the King, and high in his affections"*[47]. There is no reason to assume that Éowyn felt, or was treated, any differently, and with Théodred being seventeen years older, she may well have looked up to and admired him.

Her upbringing in an all-male household - brother, uncle and cousin - along with her natural strength, ability and courage, would have made it easy for her to gain the martial and riding skills and experience which she clearly possessed in *LotR*. However it would also have increased her dissatisfaction at the domestic role which

---

41. Op. cit. [1], *LotR* 6.5, p. 969.
42. Op. cit., *LotR* 6.6, p. 975.
43. Op. cit., *LotR* 5.2, p. 775.
44. Op. cit., *LotR* 5.2, p. 779.
45. Op. cit., *LotR* 5.8, p. 869.
46. Op. cit. [2], *UT* 3.5, p. 476.
47. Op. cit., *UT* 3.5, p. 460.

was repeatedly assigned to her rather than one of active military defence of her people. This was clearly a lifelong issue for her which, as time went on, led to feelings of desperation and suffocation. The unhappiness which both Aragorn and Gandalf perceived in her during their time in Edoras in 3019 was aggravated by a number of additional factors which had their origin in Saruman's hold on Théoden using Gríma as his means of achieving this:

- The death of Théodred at the First Battle of the Fords of Isen had occurred on February 25th, just a week prior to Aragorn's arrival in Edoras. *UT* 3.5.460-1 makes it clear that this was specifically engineered by Saruman.
- Théoden had become completely reliant on Gríma as a counsellor, refusing to take any stand against Saruman, and being poisoned against Éomer.
- Éowyn herself was being stalked by Gríma, the unpleasantness of which must have been greatly increased by the dread of being forcibly married to him if Saruman were to prove victorious. (This was hinted at by Gandalf in *LotR* 3.6.520) In addition Théoden was failing to recognise what was going on, so she was without support.
- Gríma's influence was acting on her, as well as on Théoden, causing her to start despising her own people - as exemplified by the condition of Théoden and her role of waiting on him, powerlessly watching his decline. Gandalf told Éomer "... *her* [Éowyn's] *part seemed to her more ignoble than that of the staff he leaned on.*"[48]

This situation had been going on for approximately five years - since she was nineteen.

*

Before analysing the relationship between Aragorn and Éowyn I want to draw attention to the fact that Tolkien's earlier treatment of their story, as portrayed in *HoM-e* VII[49] and VIII[50], was very different from the final version in *LotR*. Briefly the development was as follows:

- It was originally intended that Aragorn would return Éowyn's love and that they would marry. There are a number of examples of them behaving like a couple, such as riding together from Isengard to Dunharrow and generally choosing to be in each other's company.
- Later the story changed to have Éowyn dying at the Battle of the Pelennor Fields.
- Finally the idea of Aragorn returning her love was rejected.

I will now look at each stage in the Aragorn/Éowyn relationship as published in *LotR*.

First meeting

(*LotR* 3.6.506-25) During the encounter following the arrival of Gandalf, Aragorn, Legolas and Gimli in Meduseld Éowyn was at first totally involved in looking after Théoden. After her uncle's healing she helped him outside into the fresh air, whereupon Gandalf asked her to leave him in his care. As she returned to the hall she stopped on the threshold and looked back with a grave and thoughtful expression on her face, regarding Théoden with "*cool pity*". It was at this point that she and Aragorn first saw each other properly in full daylight. Physically she combined fair-haired beauty and slenderness with strength and a steel-like sternness, and we are told that Aragorn "*thought her fair, fair and cold, like a morning of pale spring that is not yet come to womanhood.*"[51] [The coldness of Éowyn will be discussed in more detail later on.] Éowyn on her

---
48. Op. cit. [1], *LotR* 5.8, p. 867.
49. C. Tolkien (ed.), *The History of Middle-earth*, vol. VII, *The Treason of Isengard*, London HarperColllins Publishers, 1993, first published in Great Britain by Unwyn Hyman 1989, *HoM-e* VII Chapter 26, pp. 445, 447-8.
50. C. Tolkien (ed.), *The History of Middle-earth*, vol. VIII, *The War of the Ring*, London HarperColllins Publishers, 2002, first published in Great Britain by Unwin Hyman 1990, *HoM-e* VIII Part 1, Chapter 6, pp. 70, 79; Part 3, Chapter 2(ii), pp 242-3, 246; Part 3, Chapter 2, Notes, p. 267; Part 3, Chapter 5, p. 318; Part 3, Chapter 8, p. 359; Part 3, Chapter 10, pp. 380, 383.
51. Op. cit. [1], *LotR* 3.6, p. 515.

part immediately perceived his age and wisdom and sensed the innate and awe-inspiring power in him. Then she quickly turned back and went into the hall - perhaps realising that she had been staring.

Later, when she took the farewell cup of wine round at the departure of Théoden and his party for Helm's Deep her eyes shone when she came close to Aragorn and looked at him. He responded by smiling down at her "*fair face*" but when their hands accidentally met on the cup he knew that hers trembled. Suddenly perceiving the nature of her feelings he stopped smiling and "... *his face now was troubled* ..."[52] Soon afterwards, as Théoden handed over to Éowyn the responsibility for leading the people to Dunharrow in his absence, she told him that each day until his return would feel like a year. However she was actually looking at Aragorn as she spoke. Aragorn, with a flash of foresight told her, "*The king shall come again. Fear not! Not West but East does our doom await us*"[53], maintaining the pretence that her words had been addressed to Théoden. This was an immediate attempt to indicate that romance was out of the question, trying to nip the idea in the bud right from the outset. As the company departed, leaving Éowyn at the house, Aragorn looked back at her and saw her standing there with her sword, clothed in mail and shining in the sun. She herself remained still and alone watching them until they were far off over the plain.

Apart from the speech just quoted, the only words spoken between them were formal greetings at the drinking of the wine, namely: "*Hail Aragorn son of Arathorn!*" and "*Hail Lady of Rohan!*".[54]

Paul Kocher[55] is particularly anxious to disprove the idea that Aragorn flirted with Éowyn in this first encounter, stating that none of Aragorn's behaviour suggested "love-liking" on his part, though it may have implied admiration or compassion. If he had returned Éowyn's feelings he wouldn't have been "*troubled*".

This word "*troubled*" is very significant when we consider how the story of Aragorn and Éowyn was developed. In the original version of the story in which their feelings were mutual, the scene where Éowyn gave the wine to Aragorn (*HoM-e* VII.26.447) closely resembles the one in *LotR*, but when their hands met on the cup hers did not tremble and his face was not "*troubled*". The encounter ended with Aragorn promising to return if he survived the coming battle and suggesting that they might then ride together. The reference to Aragorn's face being "*troubled*" in *LotR* shows that Éowyn's feelings were a cause for concern to him. Her falling in love with him was the last thing he wanted and after her hand trembled he gave her no further encouragement. As for Kocher's suggestion that Aragorn felt admiration or compassion, future developments would show that both were true.

Paul Kocher also suggests[56] that Éowyn's feelings towards Aragorn created a special relationship between them whether he liked it or not. I think this was the case. Being the sort of person he was, he would have felt obliged to try and discourage her and he would have wanted to do it gently. As he would make clear later, he was aware of her unhappiness as soon as he first saw her. While his backward glance at her could be regarded as being due to attraction, with hindsight it was much more likely to have been prompted by concern and pity. Seeing her in battle dress, he may perhaps have realised that this was how she wanted to be, not staying behind in a domestic role. This was part of the process of coming to understand her.

Nevertheless I think it is possible that Éowyn may have been - albeit very briefly - justified in believing that her feelings might be reciprocated. We are told that when Aragorn first saw her he "*thought her fair*". This was not surprising: she was young, slim, attractive, sexually innocent, physically strong - and unhappy - a combination which would subsequently be irresistible to Faramir. I feel that by smiling at her "*fair face*" and shining eyes Aragorn may have - completely unintentionally - led her on just for a few seconds. In App A, in a description of the effect of Aragorn's hardships on his appearance, we are told that "... *he became somewhat grim to look upon, **unless he chanced to smile**...*"[57] [My emphasis], implying that his smile could transform his appearance. Thus his unguarded smile may have instantly captivated her. Whatever the case, this first encounter was a prelude to a period of considerable distress for both of them with Éowyn becoming

---

52. Op. cit. [1], *LotR* 3.6, pp. 522-3.
53. Op. cit., *LotR* 3.6, p. 523.
54. Op. cit., *LotR* 3.6, p. 523.
55. P. Kocher, *Master of Middle-earth: The Achievement of J. R. R. Tolkien*, London, Pimlico, 2002, first published in Great Britain by Thames & Hudson 1973, Chapter 6, pp. 152-4.
56. Op. cit., Kocher, Chapter 6, p. 154.
57. Op. cit. [1], App A.I.v, p. 1060.

determined to die in battle due to this unrequited love, and Aragorn being tormented by feelings of guilt and pity on account of his inability to return her feelings. In addition Éowyn couldn't, or wouldn't, comprehend the hints he gave out precluding a relationship between them.

Meeting and parting at Dunharrow

(*LotR* 5.2.773-790) The encounter just described took place on March 2nd. The next meeting between Aragorn and Éowyn was in the evening of March 7th on his arrival at the refuge at Dunharrow with the Grey Company, Elladan, Elrohir, Legolas and Gimli. During the intervening days Éowyn had led her people to this refuge while Aragorn had fought at the Battle of Helm's Deep, attended Gandalf's parley with Saruman, acquired the Palantír of Orthanc, confronted Sauron in it and subsequently decided to travel through the Paths of the Dead which began at Dunharrow.

If Aragorn had hoped that Éowyn had thought things over and accepted that he was not romantically interested in her, his hopes were soon to be dashed. She was clearly very impressed with the Grey Company, no doubt perceiving in them a similar wisdom, power and lineage to those displayed by Aragorn, and her eyes shone at the description of the battle at Helm's Deep, giving further indication of her preference for warfare rather than domesticity. However we are told that "... *on Aragorn most of all her eyes rested.*"[58] [The account of the battle must have been given by Aragorn, Legolas and Gimli since they were the only ones of the company who had been there.]

Aragorn's rejection of her offer of better accommodation the following day due to the urgency of his journey prompted her to smilingly assume (or pretend to assume) that he had made a detour in order to see her: "... *it was kindly done, lord, to ride so many miles out of your way to bring tidings to Éowyn ...*"[59] Her assumption was understandable to some extent as the only road out of Dunharrow was through the Paths of the Dead and it naturally wouldn't have occurred to her that he was going there. She would have expected him to take the normal road to Gondor from Edoras - which would have precluded turning aside to Dunharrow. In the circumstances she could perhaps be excused for convincing herself that he had come specifically to see her. However Aragorn's reply, although polite and complimentary, left no doubt that his presence at Dunharrow was totally unrelated to visiting her, and her realisation of this and the resulting hurt she felt were clear from her response that he was therefore astray and had better go back the way he had come. He sternly pointed out that he had travelled in Rohan before she was even born, thus insinuating that she had no business questioning his knowledge of the place. This was the only time he was actually sharp with her, no doubt irritated at this young woman presuming to tell him he didn't know his way around. His heart must have sunk to find that she was as infatuated as ever and his coolness was a further attempt to get through to her. He then stated his intention of taking the Paths of the Dead the following morning.

Éowyn's reaction indicated the shock she felt at this statement, as she turned white and stared speechlessly at Aragorn for a long time while everyone sat in silence. Note that this was taking place at the supper table in the presence of the Dúnedain, Elladan, Elrohir, Legolas and Gimli. Up to this point the conversation had been conducted in a formal manner with Éowyn addressing Aragorn as "lord" and him addressing her as "lady". When she eventually recovered from her shock sufficiently to be able to speak she addressed him as "Aragorn" for the first time, telling him bluntly that he would be seeking death on such a route. When he argued that he might actually be able to take that path safely and reiterated his intention to go that way, she declared that his behaviour was madness, and berated him for taking people of the calibre of the Dúnedain into such danger when he should be leading them directly to war. Her message then became more personal as she urged him to stay and ride with her brother, thus giving them all some hope. Aragorn, still addressing her as "lady", denied the accusation of madness explaining that he himself was going "*on a path appointed*"[60], but emphasising that those who went with him should only go of their own free will. If any of his company wanted to stay and ride with the Rohirrim then they could do so.

Her criticisms were apparently hitting home, perhaps making him realise what he was actually expecting of

---

58. Op. cit. [1], *LotR* 5.2, p. 782.
59. Op. cit., *LotR* 5.2, p. 783.
60. Op. cit., *LotR* 5.2, p. 783.

his companions. Prior to this conversation with Éowyn there had been no indication of him offering the Grey Company the option of riding with the Rohirrim or emphasising that they were to go with him only of their own free will (although such a choice had been offered to Legolas and Gimli). Probably this attitude was due to the significance- to the Dúnedain - of the prophecy of Malbeth the Seer and the words of Galadriel's message concerning it:

> ***Where now are the Dúnedain**, Elessar, Elessar?*
> *Why do thy kinsfolk wander afar?*
> *Near is the hour when the Lost should come forth,*
> ***And the Grey Company ride from the North**.*
> *But dark is the path **appointed** for thee:*
> *The Dead watch the road that leads to the Sea.*[61] [My emphasis]

Galadriel had also sent a message to Elrond that Aragorn needed his kindred, obviously meaning for the journey through the Paths of the Dead. Aragorn would therefore have assumed that his kinsfolk were all going via that route, while Galadriel's words and his knowledge of the prophecy convinced him that his path was "*appointed*". He now told Éowyn that he undertook to do the journey alone if necessary - thus presumably implying that Legolas and Gimli too could back out of their agreement to go with him. This was a new development and his announcement of his intention silenced Éowyn's arguments. For the rest of the meal she couldn't take her eyes off him and her distress was clear for everyone else to see. [Perhaps fortunately she was unaware that the brothers of Aragorn's betrothed were among those present.]

Later, as Aragorn went to his sleeping-quarters, she followed him dressed in white and her eyes "*on fire*". In answer to her single question, "*Aragorn, why will you go on this deadly road?*"[62] he tried to make her understand that he had no choice if he were to have any hope of doing his part in the war against Sauron. He went on to tell her that he did not **choose** such a perilous route and that if it were up to **him** where he went he would now be in Rivendell. At this point he was desperately trying to drive home to her two things: namely that he was going through the Paths of the Dead whatever argument she put up because he could see no other way to do his duty, and that there was no question of a relationship between them because he was in love with another woman. Perhaps it was the emotion of the occasion which made him lapse into the informality of addressing her as "Éowyn" for the first time.

He must have been dismayed when, having finally seemed to accept that he must take that route, her next tack was to lay her hand on his arm and beg to be allowed to go with him - seeing a chance to escape at last from her trammelled existence and perhaps achieve the action and renown she yearned for. His response, that her duty was to stay with her people, unleashed her bitterness and resentment causing her to speak her mind: "*... am I not of the House of Eorl, a shieldmaiden and not a dry-nurse?*"[63] He reminded her again of her duty, pointing out that she had accepted the charge to govern her people until Théoden returned. When she bewailed the fact that she was being deprived of the renown won by the men, he told her that a time was likely to come when no-one would return from battle and those left behind in the homes would have to make a last defence, requiring valour **without** renown, but their deeds being none the less valiant for that. She retorted that what he really meant was that, as a woman, it was her job to stay at home while all the men won honour dying in battle after which she would be allowed to die defending the homes. Again she drew attention to her lineage stressing that she was not a serving-woman, but one who could ride and use a sword, and who was unafraid of pain and death. When Aragorn asked her what she **did** fear she told him "*A cage*"[64], clearly referring to her present restricted life. She went on to explain that she dreaded becoming inured to such an existence through habit and age until she had lost the ability, and even the desire, to seek valour and renown. In the heat and stress of the situation Éowyn had actually opened her heart to Aragorn, something which she had not done to anyone before if Éomer's ignorance of her feelings - which would be made clear in the Houses of Healing

---

61. Op. cit. [1], *LotR* 3.5, p. 503.
62. Op. cit., *LotR* 5.2, p. 784.
63. Op. cit., *LotR* 5.2, p. 784.
64. Op. cit., *LotR* 5.2, p. 784.

(*LotR* 5.8.866-8) - was anything to go by.

Aragorn picked up on her wish to be exposed to danger by querying why she was counselling **him** to **avoid** the Paths of the Dead because they were dangerous. Her answer indicated that she still hadn't accepted that this journey was "appointed" to him and she returned to her tactic of trying to persuade him to ride straight to battle using his sword to bring him renown and victory. Her final words were, "*I would not see a thing that is high and excellent cast away needlessly.*" His reply was "*Nor would I*", thus spelling out the reason why she should stay and not accompany him, and also showing his genuine regard and admiration for her.[65] He continued, "*For you have no errand to the South.*" Her reply was that his companions hadn't either: "*They go only because they would not be parted from **thee** - because they love **thee**.*".[66] [My emphasis]. As Paul Kocher states[67], this was close to being an outright declaration of love, emphasised by the fact that she had started using the familiar form of the second-person singular when speaking to him. [Arwen's message to Aragorn, delivered by Halbarad earlier in this same chapter, also addressed him using "thee" - as would be expected from the woman who was betrothed to him.]

Early the following morning Éowyn came to take leave of Aragorn and his companions, bringing the cup of wine for the parting drink. This ceremony was carried out in formal manner, with Aragorn addressing her as "Lady of Rohan" and drinking to the fortunes of her House, herself and her people. He then bade her tell Éomer, showing another glimpse of foresight, "*... beyond the shadows we may meet again!*"[68] At this point she was in tears - to the distress of Legolas and Gimli who found such behaviour hard to cope with in the context of her generally stern and proud demeanour. (They presumably hadn't overheard the conversation the previous evening). She then lapsed into using his first name and the familiar form of address again, making a last fruitless attempt to turn him from his purpose and then pleading to be allowed to accompany him. She was dressed as a Rider and armed with her sword at this encounter - as opposed to the white garments of the night before - ready to ride with him at a moment's notice if necessary. When Aragorn explained that he could not grant her request without the consent of her uncle and brother - impossible to obtain in the urgent time-scale he was working to - she went down on her knees and begged him. He remained polite, firm and formal throughout, addressing her as "lady", studiously avoiding the familiar form, and saying only what was necessary to make it clear that he was not going to change his mind. Then he raised her from her knees, kissed her hand, mounted his horse and rode off without looking back, "*... and only those who knew him well and were near to him saw the pain that he bore.*"[69] This must have been a deeply upsetting scene even for those who were not close enough to witness Aragorn's feelings.

Fleming Rutledge[70] emphasises the guilt he must have felt at this juncture. He had made it clear the previous night that his companions must only go through the Paths of the Dead of their own free will, but Éowyn was now insisting that they were doing it purely out of love for him. Thus in effect, by going himself, he was forcing **them** to go, therefore he couldn't throw off the responsibility for them by saying that they were led by free will. (In *LotR* 5.9.874 Gimli attributed the successful passing through the Paths of the Dead to the strength of Aragorn's will, with Legolas adding that it was also due to the love they all felt for him.)

Éowyn, standing still as stone with hands clenched, watched until the company disappeared into the shadows under the Haunted Mountain, after which she went back to her lodging stumbling like a blind person. She alone out of the people in Dunharrow had got up to take leave of him and his companions - everyone else had been too frightened, believing the strangers were "*Elvish wights*"[71] who should go into the dark places where they belonged and never return. Her love for Aragorn and desire to be with him had overridden her fear. This too was recognised by Legolas and recounted to Merry and Pippin in *LotR* 5.9.874 along with his admission of the grief he had felt on witnessing the parting of Aragorn and Éowyn.

---

65. Op. cit. [1], *LotR* 5.2, p. 785.
66. Op. cit., *LotR* 5.2, p. 785.
67. Op. cit. [55], Kocher, Chapter 6, p. 155.
68. Op. cit. [1], *LotR* 5.2, p. 785.
69. Op. cit., *LotR* 5.2, p. 785.
70. F. Rutledge, *The Battle for Middle-earth: Tolkien's Divine Design in The Lord of the Rings*, Grand Rapids Michigan and Cambridge UK, Wm. B. Eerdmans Publishing Co., 2004, Book V, pp. 263-4.
71. Op. cit. [1], *LotR* 5.2, p. 785.

It is stressed in this encounter that Aragorn specifically **did not** look back as he rode away - in contrast to his behaviour when leaving Edoras with Théoden. The situation had become too painful. It was also essential to cut the whole proceedings short due to his urgent need for speed. Éowyn's troubles had to be put second. Was Aragorn afraid that if he looked back he would either spend more time trying to calm her, or else relent and allow her to go with him for fear of what would happen to her if he left her behind? On the other hand he must have dreaded the possibility of her perhaps dying of terror - strong though she was - if he let her accompany him. It is much in his favour that he spared time for her even in the light of the serious delay she was causing to his journey.

At this point I want to refer to an early draft of this parting in *HoM-e* VIII Part 3 Chapter 12, where Legolas is telling Merry and Pippin about the Paths of the Dead. He states that Éowyn wept and actually threw her arms round Aragorn begging him not to go down the Paths, while Aragorn "... *stood there unmoved, stern as stone...*" Then Gimli says, "*But do not think that he was not moved. Indeed, I think Aragorn himself was so deeply grieved that he went through all perils after like a man that can feel little more.*"[72] I think this subsequently rejected speech of Gimli's probably sums up Aragorn's state of mind very well when considering his situation:
- He must still have been recovering from the horrific struggle with Sauron in the Palantír.
- He was steeling himself to go through the Paths of the Dead.
- He was aware of the momentous nature of the task before him: the fulfilling of the prophecies that an heir of Isildur would summon the Men of Dunharrow again - it was three thousand years since Isildur had cursed them. Perhaps because of this both Éowyn and Éomer thought that he looked "fey".
- He also knew what sort of journey lay ahead if the Paths of the Dead were successfully conquered.
- He was terrified of not being in time to save Minas Tirith.

To now have to deal with Éowyn's grief and despair and her implied declaration of love must have been almost unbearable - as if he didn't have enough on his mind. Unwanted love can be a huge burden if the person experiencing it is naturally inclined to compassion and has a lively conscience. One cannot help wondering if some of Aragorn's companions, loving him as they did, felt less than charitable towards Éowyn, perhaps harbouring a desire to forcibly remove her from the scene, or at least utter a blunt order to her to stop tormenting him at such a time.

Éowyn herself was suffering no less:
- The death of Théodred was still very recent.
- She must have feared for Théoden as he prepared for battle.
- The behaviour of Gríma was wearing her down: stalking her and subtly persuading her to despise her own people.
- Her lifelong frustration at being "caged" was reaching crisis point in the light of the urgent need for action.
- Capping all of this was her love for Aragorn (which she must by now have known was not returned), her grief as he set off on a journey which she assumed would lead to his death, and her despair at his refusal to let her go with him.

During these painful scenes at Dunharrow she seemed to have no sense of dignity, propriety or modesty, being unable, or unwilling, to control her feelings at the supper-table, then at Aragorn's departure weeping and pleading - even to the point of going down on her knees - and making her love so obvious by touching him, by choice of words and familiarity in speech. She had also lost her ability to think of the consequences of her actions. For instance: What would have happened if she had gone with Aragorn? Had she told anyone of her plans? She was the only one of the Rohirrim who had got up early to see the departure of the Grey Company. Surely someone else would have been around if they had had any inkling of her intentions. Her frame of mind would have further added to Aragorn's own grief and disquiet, particularly in the light of his genuine

---
72. Op. cit. [50], *HoM-e* VIII, Part 3, Chapter 12, p. 406.

Dernhelm

(*LotR* 5.3.791-805) Aragorn had left Dunharrow at daybreak on March 8th. On the evening of March 9th Théoden, Éomer and Merry arrived there and were met by Éowyn. Her grief was obvious to Merry who thought that she had been crying and shared the feelings of Legolas that this didn't fit with the sternness of her face. It was clear that Aragorn had given her news of Théoden's timescales as she had been ready to receive him. He too was aware of her grief and the cause of it, confirmed by her words, "*... he has passed into the shadow from which none have returned. I could not dissuade him. He is gone.*"[73]

Later, at the evening meal Théoden, by way of enlightening Merry as to the nature of Aragorn's journey, told the story of Baldor. He then continued by speaking of the rumour that, although the Dead Men did not allowing the living to pass, they did themselves occasionally come out of the Haunted Mountain thereby frightening the people of Harrowdale who would shut their doors and windows. This happened apparently "*... only at times of great unquiet and coming death.*"[74] Éowyn herself then took up the story saying that only recently "*a great host in strange array*"[75] had been seen going into the mountain as if to keep a tryst. She also revealed that when she had seen Aragorn the previous day she found him "*Greatly changed ... grimmer, older. Fey ...* **like one whom the Dead call.**"[76] [My emphasis] Picking up on this, perhaps in an attempt to comfort her, Théoden suggested that maybe Aragorn had actually been called. Nevertheless subsequent events implied that Éowyn still believed that Aragorn **had** gone to his death.

The following morning (March 10th) as the Riders prepared to set out for Edoras and then to war Éowyn was present when Théoden told Merry that he was to stay behind with her in Dunharrow. When Merry protested Théoden agreed to let him carry on to Edoras. At this point Éowyn intervened and took Merry off to the armoury explaining that Aragorn had asked her to arm him for battle. This raises the issue of Aragorn's foresight again. Before taking leave of Éowyn, Aragorn had told her that she had no errand to the South, which could be interpreted as foreknowledge of her presence at the Battle of the Pelennor Fields. His request that Merry should be armed begs the question: Did he also foresee a similar role for Merry? Fleming Rutledge[77] takes up this incident in the context of Éowyn thinking that Aragorn had gone to his death, suggesting that she was achieving some comfort by carrying out what she believed to be one of his last requests. Rutledge also remarks that being close to Merry - Aragorn's friend - made her feel closer to Aragorn. I agree with this: as Aragorn's friend, Merry was deeply concerned about him not just because he had gone through the Paths of the Dead, but also because he had witnessed - as Éowyn had not - Aragorn's mental and physical condition prior to, and immediately after, using the Palantír of Orthanc. Thus Merry and Éowyn would have drawn close together because of the strong feelings of affection and anxiety they **both** had for Aragorn.

I now continue to follow the sequence of events in *LotR* 5.3.

As Éowyn took her leave of Merry she exhorted him to bear his weapons and armour to good fortune before suggesting that maybe they would meet again. On the face of it this seems like an example of foresight, but I believe that Éowyn was now beginning to formulate her plan of riding to battle and also taking Merry with her. She had heard Merry's protests to Théoden about being left behind and Théoden's kindly (but not serious) remark about taking him with him on Snowmane. She would obviously have empathised completely with Merry's feelings. Shortly afterwards as Théoden left Dunharrow to journey to Edoras we are told that he had said farewell to Éowyn. As Merry rode behind the King past the long line of Riders he became aware of a young "man" near the end who made a point of catching his eye, "his" face that "*of one without hope who goes in search of death.*"[78] This seems to confirm that Éowyn was unconvinced by Théoden's suggestion

---

73. Op. cit. [1], *LotR* 5.3, p. 796.
74. Op. cit., *LotR* 5.3, p. 797.
75. Op. cit., *LotR* 5.3, p. 797.
76. Op. cit., *LotR* 5.3, p. 797.
77. Op. cit. [70], Rutledge, Book V, p. 268.
78. Op. cit. [1], *LotR* 5.3, p. 803.

that Aragorn *"was called"*[79] to go through the Paths of the Dead. On arrival at Edoras Théoden reiterated his command that Merry was to go no further. As Merry retreated out of Théoden's sight Éowyn, incognito as "Dernhelm", approached him and invited him to ride on her horse hidden under her cloak. After taking leave of Théoden in Dunharrow she must have donned her disguise and joined the back of the line of Riders in the éored of the Marshal Elfhelm who, it would become apparent, was colluding in her arrangements.

Éowyn's quest for death and renown in war was to lead her to the Battle of the Pelennor Fields where she and Merry would despatch the Lord of the Nazgûl, thus bringing her the renown, but not the death, she craved. Her next encounter with Aragorn would be at the Houses of Healing, though she herself was unconscious throughout.

Physical healing

(*LotR* 5.8.858-871) The account of Aragorn's healing of Éowyn in the Houses of Healing further develops some of the aspects of their relationship which have been touched on so far. For the purpose of the discussion it is necessary to quote some passages in full as they provide considerable insight into his feelings about Éowyn and illustrate the depth of his understanding and compassion.

As Aragorn carried out an initial medical assessment on Éowyn he recognised that her broken left arm had been properly treated and would mend in time, **provided** that she had the strength to live. However her sword-arm was lifeless in spite of being apparently undamaged. He then made the following speech:

> *"Alas! For she was pitted against a foe beyond the strength of her mind or body. And those who will take a weapon to such an enemy must be sterner than steel, if the very shock shall not destroy them. It was an evil doom that set her in his path. For she is a fair maiden, fairest lady of a house of queens. And yet I know not how I should speak of her. When I first looked on her and perceived her unhappiness, it seemed to me that I saw a white flower standing straight and proud, shapely as a lily, and yet knew that it was hard, as if wrought by elf-wrights out of steel. Or was it, maybe, a frost that had turned its sap to ice, and so it stood, bitter-sweet, still fair to see, but stricken, soon to fall and die? Her malady begins far back before this day, does it not, Éomer?"*[80]

With his knowledge of the mental and physical effects of Nazgûl on anyone who came into contact with them, he was under no illusions as to the severity of her condition. This was not in any way belittling her courage: his own Rangers had been unable to face the Nine at Sarn Ford the previous September (*UT* 3.4.i.441). In addition she had actually used a weapon on the Lord of the Nazgûl, something which required the utmost mental strength to endure. She was indeed still alive, but Aragorn was doubtful as to her chance of survival knowing that dying of shock was a real possibility. He was clearly disturbed at the thought of this lovely, noble and innocent young woman being put in such a situation and he railed at the evil fate which had brought it about. He must surely have known of Glorfindel's prophecy from a thousand years earlier, *"Far off yet is his doom, and not by the hand of man will he fall."*[81]. He then went on to consider his changing perception of her by pointing out that he had seen her unhappiness the first time he had looked at her, likening her to a white flower, upright and shapely, but hard as steel. The implication here seems to be that he had initially thought she possessed the steel-like sternness necessary in facing a Nazgûl, but then he went on to soften the simile so that the flower became more fragile, its sap turned to ice by frost, rendering it delicate and short-lived. In this context it is interesting to consider a comment Aragorn would make about Merry shortly afterwards when he told Pippin that his friend had sustained a similar affliction to that suffered by Éowyn because he too had used a blade on the Lord of the Nazgûl. However he then went on to say that *"... these evils can be amended, so strong and gay a spirit is in him."*[82]. Merry, with his natural Hobbit's resilience and a life where he had had

---

79. Op. cit. [1], *LotR* 5.3, p. 797.
80. Op. cit., *LotR* 5.8, p. 866.
81. Op. cit., App A.I.iv, p. 1051.
82. Op. cit., *LotR* 5.8, p. 869.

freedom and a chance to fulfil his desire for adventure, was better equipped than Éowyn to make a mental recovery from his Nazgûl encounter.

Aragorn's last sentence in the passage quoted above showed his appreciation of all these issues, unlike Éomer whose reply indicated that he had picked up his sister's feelings for Aragorn but had been largely unaware of her more long-standing troubles. Aragorn had clearly seen much more deeply into Éowyn's character and unhappiness than her brother had, and in addition Éowyn had actually opened her heart to him on the subject in a way which she obviously hadn't done to Éomer (as just indicated), or to Théoden given his degenerate condition in recent years. She had told him during their conversation at Dunharrow how she hated being confined, unable to have the freedom to fight for her people, dreading that she would reach a stage when she no longer cared. As for the effect on her of Gríma's influence and the decline of the House of Eorl, Aragorn would have realised all this anyway. In the event it was Gandalf who actually voiced Éowyn's long-term problems at this point, stepping in perhaps to help Aragorn out in a difficult situation and telling Éomer quite forthrightly about his sister's grief at seeming to be aiding Théoden's decline, her frustration at not being able to fight, and her harassment by Gríma and being forced to listen to his poisonous words.

Aragorn realised that Éowyn's love for him, which he was unable to return, was the last straw which had tipped her over into despair. He spoke to Éomer himself at this point showing how deeply he felt about not being able to reciprocate Éowyn's love. He told him:

> "Few other griefs ... have more bitterness and shame for a man's heart than to behold the love of a lady so fair and brave that cannot be returned. Sorrow and pity have followed me ever since I left her desperate in Dunharrow and rode to the Paths of the Dead; and no fear upon that way was so present as the fear for what might befall her."[83]

As well as his fear for Éowyn, this speech indicates his feeling of guilt at the pain he had caused her and also his admiration for her beauty and courage. What did he fear "*might befall*" her? Had he foreseen her participation in the Battle of the Pelennor Fields and thought that she might die as a result? Had he even foreseen her role regarding the Lord of the Nazgûl? Was he afraid that she would actually kill herself, either in cold blood, or by deliberate rashness in a battle situation? Or would her despair bring on a depression and physical decline, in its turn leading to suicide at a later date? There was also the issue of what would happen to her if Sauron won the war, especially if she was in a prominent position in the battle. He must have known the story of Morgoth's "*evil lust*"[84] for Lúthien, and he would certainly have known how Celebrían had suffered when she was captured by Orcs (App A.I.iii.1043). Also the Lord of the Nazgûl himself gave Éowyn some indication of what she could expect to happen to her in Barad-dûr: "*... thy flesh shall be devoured, and thy shrivelled mind be left naked to the Lidless Eye.*"[85]. Aragorn's own frame of mind at this period was certainly conducive to exaggerating his fears and causing his imagination to work overtime, leading him to expect the worst outcome. His old enemy, guilt, was also to the fore again, making him feel personally responsible for what happened to Éowyn. As at Parth Galen, he was undoubtedly being too hard on himself. Looked at from another perspective, maybe his concern for Éowyn numbed his fear of the Paths of the Dead.

As Aragorn turned to the task of recalling Éowyn from her deep unconsciousness he once again expressed doubts as to her future:

> "I have, maybe, the power to heal her body, and to recall her from the dark valley. But to what she will awake: hope, or forgetfulness, or despair, I do not know. And if to despair, then she will die, unless other healing comes which I cannot bring. Alas! for her deeds have set her among the queens of great renown"[86]

The insertion of the word "*maybe*" in the first sentence shows that it was not just the mental healing which

---

83. Op. cit. [1], *LotR* 5.8, p. 867.
84. Op. cit. [29], *TSil* Chapter 19, p. 212.
85. Op. cit. [1], *LotR* 5.6, p. 841.
86. Op. cit., *LotR* 5.8, p. 867.

was in question here: he even seemed unsure of his ability to heal her physically. His last sentence indicated admiration, even reverence, for her and also grief at the likelihood of a tragic outcome. From the description of Éowyn at this stage it is almost as if she were already dead, as her face "... *was indeed white as a lily, cold as frost, and hard as graven stone.*"[87] Compare this with the scene when she was found on the battle-field in *LotR* 5.6.845 and everyone thought she was dead because she was cold and did not appear to be breathing. It had been Prince Imrahil who had detected a barely perceptible amount of breath coming from her in spite of her cold face and lips. Now, in the Houses of Healing, as Aragorn kissed her brow and called to her she began to breathe normally again. This was followed by using an infusion of athelas leaves to bathe her brow and her cold, nerveless right arm. At this point we are told that a wind blew through the window, unscented but "... *wholly fresh and clean and young, as if it had not before been breathed by any living thing and came new-made from snowy mountains high beneath a dome of stars, or from shores of silver far away washed by seas of foam.*"[88]. In the text it is suggested that this may have been due to some Númenórean power which Aragorn was able to wield over the athelas, or else that it was his words about Éowyn which had the effect. However, as Hammond and Scull point out[89], the wind could have been due to the intervention of the Vala Manwë, as the description of the mountains and the dome of stars seem to relate to his home on Taniquetil and the silver shores recall the Elven beaches in the Undying Lands. When Aragorn called to Éowyn to awake and held her right hand, it was warm. He then called her again, "*Awake! The shadow is gone and all darkness is washed clean!*"[90]. At this point he laid her hand in Éomer's and quietly left the room leaving her brother to call her back to consciousness. This sensitive and tactful move was best for everyone in the circumstances - including himself.

On regaining consciousness Éowyn told Éomer that she had believed the House of Eorl had "*sunk in honour less than any shepherd's cot*"[91], thus proving the accuracy of Gandalf's surmise. [Maybe Aragorn was nearer to the truth than he realised when he said he would obey the owner of the house and leave any sword but Andúril outside if Meduseld was only a woodman's cot.] Éowyn also confirmed Aragorn's doubts as to her mental recovery by telling Gandalf that she may have returned to health but hope was not so likely. Her main thought was of getting back into the saddle and into battle.

As with the healing of Faramir and Merry, Aragorn had actually recalled Éowyn from the Shadow **before** using the athelas. It was his kiss which enabled her to breathe normally again. What is not clear is whether she was aware in her unconsciousness that it was Aragorn who was calling her back - this appeared to have been the case during Faramir's healing as he immediately knew who Aragorn was when he woke up.

As Aragorn left the Houses after healing Merry he spoke to the Warden to give instructions for the care of his patients. He knew Éowyn well enough to realise that she would want to get up and leave as soon as possible, but he also knew the extent of her physical and mental exhaustion and told the Warden that he must do his utmost to keep her in bed for at least ten days. Aragorn's next action was to get a much-needed meal before spending most of the night healing others, with the help of Elladan and Elrohir. The next morning the Last Debate was held, followed by two days of preparation before leaving for the Morannon on March 18th. It is therefore unlikely that he would have been back to the Houses of Healing in that time. Indeed his act of giving guidance to the Warden would seem to indicate that he had no intention of doing so. Thus he would not see Éowyn again until his coronation on May 1st.

I finish this section by giving further consideration to the many "cold" references in connection with Éowyn, particularly in the healing episode but also in the earlier encounters with Aragorn:
- At their first meeting she had looked at Théoden with "*cool pity*", and Aragorn had "*thought her fair, fair and cold, like a morning of pale spring that is not yet come to womanhood.*".[92] A steel-like sternness was also noted in her.

---

87. Op. cit. [1], *LotR* 5.8, p. 867.
88. Op. cit., *LotR* 5.8, p.868.
89. W.G. Hammond and C. Scull, *The Lord of the Rings: a Reader's Companion,* London, HarperCollins Publishers, 2005, p. 582.
90. Op. cit. [1], *LotR* 5.8, p. 868.
91. Op. cit., *LotR* 5.8, p. 868.
92. Op. cit., *LotR* 3.6, p. 515.

- When Legolas spoke to Merry and Pippin of the journey through the Paths of the Dead, he said that everyone who knew Aragorn came to love him in his/her own way, "... *even the cold maiden of the Rohirrim*"[93] [My emphasis].
- At different points in the story, first Legolas and Gimli (*LotR* 5.2.785), then Merry (*LotR* 5.3.795), became disturbed by evidence of Éowyn weeping because it seemed inconsistent with her stern demeanour. However it could also be viewed as an indication of the breaking-down of her coldness.
- At Dunharrow when she followed Aragorn to his sleeping-quarters, she was dressed in white as befitted her coldness but this made her appear "*as a glimmer in the night*" and her eyes were "*on fire*" - presumably from the strength of her emotions.[94]
- The scene in the Houses of Healing described above brings together Éowyn's bodily chill due to the Black Breath of the Nazgûl and Aragorn's perception of the combination of steely hardness and icy vulnerability which made up her mental chilliness.

I feel that her coldness stemmed from a combination of the stress of her physically restricted existence, unexpressed emotions and immaturity. She resented not being able to enjoy the same freedom as the men to ride and do battle. In addition there was the frustration which went with this, in view of the fact that her spirit and courage were at least equal to her brother's (as Gandalf pointed out in *LotR* 5.8.867). The female role she was obliged to adopt caused her to feel caged or trammelled like a wild creature in a hutch (again using some of Gandalf's words). When Saruman and Gríma began preying on Théoden her situation was made worse because she was powerless to do anything about it with her uncle totally under the influence of his treacherous servant. When Gríma's poison also began to be directed at **her** she grew to despise not only the House of Eorl but herself, and her role in powerlessly standing by and watching Théoden decline. None of these feelings were expressed openly until her conversation with Aragorn at Dunharrow when she gave vent to at least some of them. Up until then she had dealt with them by bottling them up and masking them with a proud and steely coldness.

Regarding Éowyn's coldness being also due to immaturity, she wasn't actually that young at twenty-four but there is no indication of any previous romantic interest in her life. Paul Kocher, referring to Legolas's description of Éowyn as cold, supposes that this was "*in the sense ... of interest in martial prowess at the expense of a gentler femininity*"[95]. However Aragorn's first impression, likening her coldness to "*a morning of pale spring that is not yet come to womanhood*"[96], seems to me to imply sexual immaturity or inexperience. Assuming this interpretation, she would have found it much more difficult to cope with Gríma's stalking than if she had been older and more worldly-wise. There was also the fear that his behaviour might at any time become more than simply stalking her. Her uncle was too decrepit to support her in such a situation and she would have been afraid to involve Éomer as any threat he made to Gríma may well have brought punishment on himself. Issues such as these would also have been hidden behind her cold exterior.

Mental healing

(*LotR* 6.5.958-73 and 6.6.974-88) As Aragorn had anticipated, Éowyn insisted on getting up far too soon - after only five days instead of the ten which he had specified - thereby greatly worrying the Warden of the Houses of Healing as evidenced by his words, "... *I was commanded to tend you **with especial care**.*"[97] The words I have emphasised show Aragorn's anxiety that she should get the rest she needed to maximise her chance of a full recovery. As far as Éowyn was concerned her body was healing and her main aim was to continue her involvement in the war as soon as possible. Her conversation with the Warden and at her first meeting with Faramir revealed her continuing desire for death in battle - which was what Aragorn had feared would be the case:

---

93. Op. cit. [1], *LotR* 5.9, p. 874.
94. Op. cit., *LotR* 5.2, pp. 783-4.
95. Op. cit. [55], Kocher, Chapter 6, p. 153.
96. Op. cit. [1], *LotR* 3.6, p. 515.
97. Op. cit., *LotR* 6.5, p. 958.

- When the Warden begged her to go back to bed she countered his arguments with: "*... it is not always good to be healed in body. Nor is it always evil to die in battle, even in bitter pain. Were I permitted, in this dark hour I would choose the latter.*"[98]
- When the Warden took her to Faramir she told him, "*... I cannot lie in sloth, idle, caged. I looked for death in battle. But I have not died, and battle still goes on.*"[99]
- Later she told him, "*I wish to ride to war like my brother Éomer, or better like Théoden the king, for he died and has both honour and peace.*"[100]

Her yearning for death in battle, **combined with the renown this would bring**, is traceable as follows:
- To some extent she had always had a yearning for battle and renown. She had the courage and ability to fight and she wanted to do something noble to help her people, and be praised and remembered for it - as the men could do, without it being questioned.
- This yearning would naturally have increased during the years of Gríma's ascendancy.
- Her situation in March 3019 was that her love was unrequited, Aragorn was going to his death (she believed) and she was not allowed to accompany him and die with him. Thus her yearning for renown in battle became a yearning for renown **and death** in battle. Note Merry's observation when he first saw "Dernhelm": "his" face was that of *"one without hope who goes in search of death."*[101]. It was not a purely suicidal tendency in that she simply wanted to kill herself; she did want to die, but she also wanted to die in a way which would bring her renown.

During their first conversation together Faramir reminded her that death in battle might yet come to all of them whether they went to war or not, thereby echoing Aragorn's words to her at Dunharrow (when he told her that her duty was to stay with her people but that a brave stance might still be required - no less brave for being unsung). As Faramir spoke he was aware that "*something in her softened, as though a bitter frost were yielding at the first faint presage of spring. A tear sprang in her eye and fell down her cheek, like a glistening rain-drop.*"[102] Éowyn had been unable to handle such a remark from Aragorn but now she accepted it from Faramir - probably because Faramir indicated acceptance of such a scenario for himself. Her coldness was breaking down further. However there was still some way to go: when Faramir told her that it would help him if he could carry on seeing her due to them both being healed by Aragorn, she answered, "*Shadow lies on me still. Look not to me for healing! I am a shieldmaiden and my hand is ungentle.*"[103].

For the next five days Éowyn and Faramir spent time together in the garden of the Houses of Healing. The fifth day - March 25th - was cold and Faramir had wrapped his mother's mantle around Éowyn. At the moment the Ring was destroyed they were standing on the walls of the City with their hands clasped and she had drawn close to him. When they realised that the Shadow had departed, he kissed her brow and their hair mingled in the wind. Yet a few moments prior to this, Éowyn had looked northwards in the direction of the Morannon, judging that Aragorn must now have arrived there and remarking that it was seven days since he had left Minas Tirith. Thus even though she was starting to fall in love with Faramir, she still seemed to have Aragorn uppermost in her mind. This was borne out by her decline in health over the next few days when, according to Faramir's guess, she was torn between grief that only her brother, and not Aragorn, had invited her to attend the celebrations at the Field of Cormallen and her wish to stay in the City to be near him [Faramir]. She still insisted that it was **Aragorn**'s love she wanted, and she clearly resented the fact that he only gave her his pity.

At this point it is necessary to examine in more detail the nature of Éowyn's attachment to Aragorn. Both Aragorn and Faramir give their views on this in *LotR*:
- Aragorn to Éomer in the Houses of Healing: "*And yet, Éomer, I say to you that she loves you more truly than me; for you she loves and knows; but in me she loves only a shadow and a thought: a hope of glory*

---

98. Op. cit. [1], *LotR* 6.5, pp. 958-9.
99. Op. cit., *LotR* 6.5, p. 959.
100. Op. cit., *LotR* 6.5, p. 960.
101. Op. cit., *LotR* 5.3, p. 803.
102. Op. cit., *LotR* 6.5, p. 960.
103. Op. cit., *LotR* 6.5, p. 961.

and great deeds, and lands far from the fields of Rohan."[104]

Aragorn stressed the fact that Éowyn couldn't really love him because she didn't know him. She loved the image of him which she had built in her mind and believed he offered her what she craved: military action and glory, and escape from her present restricted life.

- Faramir to Éowyn herself: *"You desired to have the love of the Lord Aragorn. Because he was high and puissant, and you wished to have renown and glory and to be lifted far above the mean things that crawl on the earth. And as a great captain may to a young soldier he seemed to you admirable. For so he is, a lord among men, the greatest that now is. But when he gave you only understanding and pity, then you desired to have nothing, unless a brave death in battle."*[105]

Faramir expressed the same ideas but with different emphasis, due to the different circumstances. For instance he made much of Aragorn's impressive qualities which had attracted Éowyn (which obviously Aragorn wouldn't have done when talking to Éomer out of modesty and sensitivity). He was more outspoken about the life which Éowyn wanted to escape (clearly Aragorn would not have described the situation in Rohan as *"mean things that crawl on the earth"* when talking to Éomer!). Also he added an extra dimension by referring to Éowyn's attitude to the understanding and pity shown her by Aragorn. She had wanted his love or nothing - hence her desire for death in battle.

Faramir helped Éowyn to understand why she had fallen for Aragorn and the nature of her feelings for him. Like her brother she perceived Aragorn's inherent power and wisdom, but in her case this was also coupled with a vision of escape from what she saw as her ignominious life [including the unpleasantness of Gríma's attentions]. Also, in her immature way, there must have been a romantic element. Thus her feelings were partly the hero-worship of a young soldier and partly a crush on an older charismatic figure. Perhaps she **needed** someone to look up to (as she may have done to Théodred).

As well as helping her to understand herself better, Faramir also made her see that the pity offered her by Aragorn was not something to be despised: *"Do not scorn pity that is the gift of a gentle heart, Éowyn!"*[106]. Thus he was able to give her the mental healing which Aragorn knew he himself wasn't able to provide. She next saw Aragorn on May 1st as she stood at the City Gate with Elfhelm watching Faramir officiate at the coronation. A week later she and Éomer left to set affairs in order in Rohan, so she would not have been present at Aragorn's wedding to Arwen on Mid-year's Day. However according to App B.1095 she and her brother would have met Arwen and her escort at Edoras when she arrived there on June 14th *en route* to Gondor.

The last encounter between Aragorn and Éowyn described in the main narrative of *LotR* took place at Théoden's funeral wake on August 10th. During this event Éomer officially announced the betrothal of his sister to Faramir, emphasising this extra bond in the friendship between Gondor and Rohan. Aragorn then made a joking remark about Éomer's generosity in giving the fairest thing in his realm to Gondor - in other words paying Éowyn a teasing compliment, something he would never have dreamed of doing before! Éowyn then looked into his eyes with the words, *"Wish me joy, my liege-lord and healer!"* Aragorn's reply was, *"I have wished **thee** joy ever since first I saw **thee**. It heals my heart to see **thee** now in bliss."*[107] [My emphasis]. This short exchange demonstrated how relaxed they now were with each other. He had addressed her as "thee" knowing he could safely do so without her misinterpreting his meaning. He was using the familiar form as between two people who loved and respected each other as friends and had each other's welfare at heart. I feel too that his words spoke volumes of relief.

Paul Kocher says that: *"... Aragorn's manner of perceiving and rejecting her* [Éowyn's] *love reveals an intimate side of his nature that appears nowhere else..."*[108] Although I don't necessarily agree with the last four words in this passage, Kocher's statement is certainly borne out by the tenderness, understanding and compassion with which Aragorn treated Éowyn, combined with the insight we get into his own suffering as a result of this relationship. Although it was Faramir who provided Éowyn with mental healing and helped her to

---

104. Op. cit. [1], *LotR* 5.8, p. 867.
105. Op. cit., *LotR* 6.5, p. 964.
106. Op. cit., *LotR* 6.5, p. 964.
107. Op. cit., *LotR* 6.6, p. 977.
108. Op. cit. [55], Kocher, Chapter 6, pp. 152-3.

know herself, it was her relationship with Aragorn which first released her suppressed frustration, resentment and emotions and triggered the chain of events which took her to glory in battle, near-death and finally healing and happiness.

*

When Tolkien eventually rejected the idea of Aragorn returning Éowyn's love, the reason he gave was that he was too old, lordly and grim for her (*HoM-e* VII.26.448), and it is easy to see why he decided this. Éowyn was twenty-four and Aragorn eighty-eight when they met and even allowing for Aragorn's Dúnadan life-span with its extended period of vigorous manhood, this was a big age-gap. Regarding him being too lordly, his Elvish and Númenórean lineage alone provide adequate evidence of this, but it is quite clear that, even for a Númenórean, Aragorn was something special - as recognised/prophesied by the likes of Elrond, Gandalf, Galadriel, Arwen and Ivorwen. Aragorn's grimness and the reasons for it are well-documented in App A.I.v.1060-1, as well as in the main text of *LotR*. His suffering and trials, both mental and physical, would have killed a lesser man due to their severity and length. In the aftermath of his struggles and with the burden of kingship ahead he needed a wife like Arwen with her Elven wisdom and perception, and the strength and fidelity to forsake her people and her immortality for him, someone capable of helping him to achieve his own mental healing. The Aragorn/Éowyn relationship was inherently untenable.

Tolkien provides further information on this subject in a draft written around 1963 to an unknown reader who appears to have criticised some aspects of the Éowyn/Faramir relationship. He says:

> *"It is possible to love more than one person (of the other sex) at the same time, but in a different mode and intensity. I do not think that Éowyn's feelings for Aragorn really changed much; and when he was revealed as so lofty a figure, in descent and office, she was able to go on **loving** and admiring him. He was **old** ... when not accompanied by any physical decay age can be alarming or awe-inspiring"*[109] [Tolkien's emphasis].

*

As Éowyn accepted and returned Faramir's love she renounced a number of things:
- Her wish to be a queen.
- Her "shieldmaiden" role.
- Her wish to compete with the Riders.
- Her love of battle songs to the exclusion of others.

Instead she declared her intention of becoming a healer and loving "*all things that grow and are not barren*"[110].

This sudden change in her could be seen as rejecting her previous spirited independent ways and yielding at last to the dominant male culture, accepting her role as a woman, etc. However I should like to offer a different interpretation, namely that she was emulating Aragorn in those areas where his chief renown lay, as a healer and a renewer, the "renewer" aspect being indicated by the passage I have just quoted. Through Faramir's love and influence, she had come to understand Aragorn better, realising that his prowess in battle was not necessarily his finest quality, though it was the one she had originally admired. Perhaps too she had seen that he did not crave renown and battle for their own sake. Above all she had learnt that his healing and compassion were worthy of admiration and reverence. In other words she was coming to know **him** rather than the "*shadow*" and the "*thought*" which Aragorn had referred to in the Houses of Healing. Also of course Aragorn had been responsible for saving not only her own life, but that of the man she was in love with as well. Therefore it was quite logical that Éowyn should now want to be a healer. When the Warden of the Houses of

---

109. H. Carpenter (ed.), *The Letters of J.R.R. Tolkien*, with the assistance of Christopher Tolkien, London, HarperCollins Publishers, 1995. First published in Great Britain by George Allen & Unwin, 1981. Letter. 244, p. 323.
110. Op. cit. [1], *LotR* 6.5, p. 965.

Healing discharged her from his care she told him, "*Yet now that I have leave to depart, I would remain. For this House has become to me of all dwellings the most blessed.*"[111]. She accordingly remained there until Éomer arrived from the Field of Cormallen, perhaps occupying herself with learning the skills of a healer.

ÉOMER

Éomer was four years older than his sister, being eleven when his parents died and twenty-eight in TA 3019. Like Éowyn he had been taken into the household of his widowed uncle Théoden King and had grown up with his older cousin Théodred.

From 3014 onwards Éomer too became badly affected by Gríma's hold on Théoden. In addition he was infuriated by the man's stalking of Éowyn to the extent that he had considered killing him (see *LotR* 3.6.520). The main thrust of Gríma's policy - on behalf of Saruman - is described in *UT* 3.5.460-1 where three aims are specified:
- To turn Théoden against Théodred and Éomer.
- To get rid of Théodred and Éomer.
- To turn Théodred and Éomer against each other.

The last aim proved impossible as Éomer clearly looked up to Théodred, with *UT* stating that "*... his love and respect for Théodred ... was only second to his love of his foster-father.*"[112] In addition we are told that Éomer was "*not an ambitious man*"[113], no doubt partly because he was the equivalent of the younger son and didn't expect to become King given the existence of Théodred. Also, as quoted earlier (F47), both Théodred and Éomer were "*devoted to the King, and high in his affections*" and their loyalty to Théoden did not waver even when his condition deteriorated.

The second aim partly succeeded with the death of Théodred at the First Battle of the Fords of Isen. Saruman's orders had been that Théodred must be eliminated at all costs and this was duly carried out.

The first aim too was partially successful with Gríma changing his tactics so that, rather than turning Théoden against Théodred **and** Éomer, he just persuaded him that Éomer was eager to increase his own authority and was therefore acting without consulting the King or his heir. This worked in that it made Théoden ignore Éomer's advice which led to Éomer **actually** acting independently and even disobeying orders since this was the only way he could get anything done. The best example of this occurred at the end of February 3019 when he rode out, without permission, against a party of Orcs who had been reported as entering Rohan from the Emyn Muil, these Orcs being in fact the ones who had captured Merry and Pippin at Parth Galen. Éomer's action was to lead to the annihilation of the Orcs at the edge of Fangorn Forest thus enabling the Hobbits to escape, and to his first meeting with Aragorn which took place on February 30th as he headed back to Edoras. There follows an analysis of this encounter between Aragorn and Éomer described in *LotR* 3.2.430-9.

When Aragorn drew attention to himself by standing up in the grasslands of Rohan and asking for news, Éomer's Riders reacted by wheeling round from the course they were following, then enclosing Aragorn, Legolas and Gimli in a diminishing moving circle before halting with their weapons pointing at them, Éomer's spear being within a foot of Aragorn's breast. No word had been spoken during this procedure and it was obviously a well-practised manoeuvre which they used when encountering strangers. When Aragorn gave his name as "Strider" and said that he came from the North and was hunting Orcs, Éomer dismounted, drew his sword and stood facing him, "*surveying him keenly, and not without wonder.*"[114] This "*wonder*", as will be seen, was very different from that displayed by Boromir at the Council of Elrond.

Éomer was in an uncomfortable situation:
- By being where he was, he was blatantly disregarding orders.

---

111. Op. cit. [1], *LotR* 6.5, p. 965.
112. Op. cit. [2], *UT* Part 3, Chapter 5, p. 460.
113. Op. cit., *UT* Part 3, Chapter 5, p. 460.
114. Op. cit. [1], *LotR* 3.2, p. 432.

- He was aware that strangers were not allowed to wander free in Rohan without the King's permission.
- He was worried about the threat from Saruman.
- He was also very dubious about Aragorn and his companions. How had they escaped the Riders' sight? Why had Aragorn given an obviously false name? Were they Elvish? Had they sprung out of the grass? What were the strange clothes they were wearing?

Therefore he had to be wary - he couldn't risk anything going wrong.

Aragorn, for his part, knew the general nature and character of the Rohirrim from his service with them forty to fifty years previously: they were proud and wilful but true-hearted and generous, bold but not cruel, wise but unlearned. However things had changed since then:
- There was a different King.
- He didn't know Éomer.
- There were rumours that Rohan might be in league with Sauron or Saruman - being stuck between the threat of these two.
- Although he didn't actually believe that Rohan was having any dealings with Mordor he still had to be careful - especially about giving his real name. He would have been in a very dangerous situation if such a link **did** exist - for example as an agreement to supply horses.
- In addition he was surrounded by a forest of weapons: spears, bows and swords.

He had a number of objectives at this point:
- He was desperate for news of the Orcs who had captured Merry and Pippin.
- He was anxious to minimise delay so he could carry on the search for them as a matter of urgency.
- He needed to know for certain whether Rohan - and Éomer himself - could be trusted.
- He would have felt responsible for the safety of Legolas and Gimli who remained sitting still and silent in the grass leaving their friend to deal with the situation.

Initially business was conducted peacefully, with Aragorn standing firm in the face of all the weapons and calmly answering Éomer's questions. It was the mention of Lothlórien which nearly led to disaster as Éomer was clearly hostile to the Golden Wood, to the Lady who lived in it, and now also to these strangers who had been there. In addition he **voiced** his hostility, suggesting that the three companions might also be "*net-weavers and sorcerers*"[115] themselves, and then looking coldly at Legolas and Gimli demanding to know why they didn't speak. Nevertheless he reacted relatively mildly to Gimli's subsequent aggressive response (with hand on axe) and his insistence that he [Éomer] should give his name first. He only became angry when Gimli, infuriated by what he saw as a slur on Galadriel, started insulting his intelligence, but his behaviour still fell short of violence. His statement that he would cut off Gimli's head if it stood a little higher from the ground implied that he had no intention of actually carrying out the deed. It was the Riders closing in, with their spears at the ready, followed by Legolas fitting an arrow to his bow which threatened to cause actual bloodshed and it was only at this point that Éomer raised his sword. The situation was saved by Aragorn's courage and diplomacy, as he leaped between them with his hand raised and succeeded in pacifying both parties. He immediately apologised to Éomer but at the same time made it clear that Legolas and Gimli were justified in their anger. He showed that he realised Éomer's derogatory comments about Galadriel and Lothlórien were due to lack of knowledge rather than, as Gimli had said, to "*little wit*"[116]. Aragorn went on to assure Éomer that they intended no harm to Rohan, "*neither to man nor to horse*"[117] thus indicating that he understood and empathised with Éomer's concern and realised how important their horses were to them. He finished by appealing to him to listen to their story before deciding to use weapons on them, thus softening the aggression which had angered Éomer in the behaviour of Legolas and Gimli. However before telling their story he had to confirm that he could really trust Éomer, especially in the light of his demand to know his real name, before they went any further. Having reassured himself that Rohan was not in any way allied to Mordor and was just struggling to maintain

---

115. Op. cit. [1], *LotR* 3.2, p. 432.
116. Op. cit., *LotR* 3.2, p. 432.
117. Op. cit., *LotR* 3.2, p. 433.

its freedom and self-sufficiency subject to no *"foreign lord"*, he spoke passionately of his own independence (*"I serve no man"*), his mission of pursuing the servants of Sauron, and his determination to follow these particular ones who had captured his friends even though he was ill-equipped and hopelessly outnumbered.[118] This stirring speech not only disproved Éomer's initial assumption of Aragorn's ignorance of Orcs but led on to a dramatic and awe-inspiring revelation of his true identity which amazed Legolas and Gimli and stunned Éomer into physically stepping back from him.

An examination of this scene illustrates how Aragorn's manner had changed completely from appealing and pacifying, to a show of power and authority. As he threw back his Elf-cloak in a very Gandalf-like manner, drew his sword and recited his names and titles, we are told that *"... in his living face they* [Legolas and Gimli] *caught a brief vision of the power and majesty of the kings of stone"* and *"... it seemed to the eyes of Legolas that a white flame flickered on the brows of Aragorn like a shining crown."*.[119] The names and titles he used all had their own relevance for the situation, namely:

- Firstly he cried out *"Elendil!"* as a battle-cry as he drew the sword in order to indicate that it truly had belonged to Elendil and thus was the weapon which had robbed Sauron of the One Ring.
- Regarding *"Aragorn son of Arathorn"*, Éomer, as would be shown, was knowledgeable and may well have been aware that the "Ar" prefix indicated nobility, such as a king or chieftain.
- *"Elessar"* and *"Elfstone"* were the Quenya and Common Speech versions of the royal name which had been prophesied for him.
- *"Dúnadan"* indicated his Númenórean lineage.
- He also stressed his descent from Elendil and Isildur thus illustrating his claim to the throne of Gondor.
- Finally he referred to *"the Sword that was Broken"* which had now been reforged.

He finished with the abrupt question, *"Will you aid me or thwart me?"* followed by the command to *"Choose swiftly!"*[120]

The effect on Éomer was instantaneous. He immediately became awestruck and deferential, addressing Aragorn as *"lord"*. His request for the meaning of the dream verse which had prompted Boromir's journey north showed that he was well aware of the "dreams and legends" which were now "springing to life out of the grass" as he put it, and so was under no illusion as to the significance of Aragorn's revelations. Aragorn on his part, having acted according to his rank initially to make the necessary impact to achieve Éomer's co-operation, now dropped this show of authority and **asked for**, rather than demanded, help and tidings. It was also at this point that he first stated his intention of going to Théoden.

Although Éomer himself had no doubts about Aragorn, being deeply affected by his majesty and charisma, the rest of the Riders were not so impressed, with Éothain in particular becoming rude, and suggesting that Aragorn, Legolas and Gimli should be taken prisoner. He was clearly sceptical about their story, but his manner may also have been due to anxiety, knowing that Éomer was defying orders and that the sooner they returned to Edoras the better. Éomer's reaction was to tell him to move away and prepare the éored to ride, so that he himself could talk to Aragorn in private. He knew he was telling the truth, but realised he was holding back and he needed more information in order to decide what to do.

Left to themselves both were able to speak more freely and Aragorn described his journey to date, and how he came to lead the Company after the loss of Gandalf, explaining that *"... when the great fall, the less must lead"*[121]. There was no need at this juncture to carry on his show of authority and he reverted to a more self-deprecating mode of expression. Éomer made it clear that he knew Gandalf and the history of his relations with Rohan. He also thought well of him, in spite of the very different opinion held by Théoden, and regarded his loss in Moria as *"heavy tidings"*[122]. He was grieved too at the death of Boromir, again understanding the impact this would have. The four-day journey on foot which Aragorn, Legolas and Gimli had made in pursuit of the

---

118. Op. cit. [1], *LotR* 3.2, pp. 433-4.
119. Op. cit., *LotR* 3.2, pp. 433-4.
120. Op. cit., *LotR* 3.2, p. 433.
121. Op. cit., *LotR* 3.2, p. 436.
122. Op. cit., *LotR* 3.2, p. 435.

Orcs was a real eye-opener as far as Éomer was concerned, leading him to give Aragorn the name "Wingfoot" in recognition of his achievement and to declare that *"This deed of the three friends should be sung in many a hall"*[123] - a great compliment as the Rohirrim were not a literate people, instead commemorating their heroes in song.

Éomer now began to confide in Aragorn telling him of his worries about Saruman whom he recognised as being currently the main problem for the Rohirrim, gathering armies of Orcs, wolf-riders and Men to harry them so that they were hemmed in on the west as well as the east. He also realised that Saruman had his spies within Rohan itself - obviously hinting at the activities of Gríma. At this point he began to pile on the pressure to get Aragorn to go back with him to Edoras: *"Do I hope in vain that you have been **sent to me** for a help in doubt and need?"*[124] [My emphasis]. When Aragorn said he would come when he could, Éomer repeated his request stressing that battle with Saruman's troops was taking place there and then in the Westemnet. Then he told Aragorn of his pursuit, against orders, of the Orcs who had entered Rohan from the Emyn Muil, some wearing Saruman's badges, thus confirming his worst fear, namely the existence of a league between Orthanc and Barad-dûr. He again repeated his plea to Aragorn to go back with him, now trying to win over Legolas and Gimli as well, assuring them that there would be opportunities for them to use their weapons and apologising for his comments about Galadriel, explaining that, *"I spoke only as do all men in my land, and I would gladly learn better."*[125] There is a great deal of underlying anxiety and fear here: of Saruman's influence over his uncle, and of what would happen to the Rohirrim and to him personally. In addition there seems to be an indication that he believed this meeting with Aragorn to be fated (see the words I have emphasised above).

When Aragorn stated his determination to carry on with the search for Merry and Pippin *"while hope remains"*[126] Éomer turned on further pressure by trying to convince him that the search was in fact hopeless. However Aragorn clinched the argument by countering Éomer's conviction that nothing could have escaped the Riders' encirclement of the Orc party by pointing out that the Elf cloaks Merry and Pippin were wearing would have hidden them from view - as they had done with himself, Legolas and Gimli. (Éomer hadn't noticed them until Aragorn stood up and called to him even though the Riders had passed right next to them as they sat in the grass.) Éomer now reluctantly accepted that Aragorn was going to carry on with his search and that there was still a possibility of it having a successful outcome. He was now nervous about going back without them as it was against the current law in Rohan to let strangers wander at will unless given leave by the King. Although he trusted Aragorn completely and wanted to let him go free, he would be risking trouble for himself by doing so, being duty-bound to take them back as prisoners or kill them. Maybe he had thought that by taking Aragorn back with him Théoden would come round and realise the danger of his and Rohan's situation.

Aragorn now pulled out all the stops to break down Éomer's resistance by:
- Arguing that the law in question was not intended for such as the current situation.
- Adding that he was not in fact a stranger as he had been in Rohan before and had actually known Éomer's father as well as Théoden himself.
- Stressing that during his earlier time in Rohan it would have been unthinkable for one of its lords to have forced someone to abandon a search like his.
- Emphasising that his duty was clearly to go on.
- Encouraging Éomer to make his choice.
- Finally stressing that if Éomer attempted to use force on him and his two companions they would resist, thereby reducing the number of Riders who would return to Edoras.

This had the desired effect as Éomer agreed to let them go and even lend them horses to help their search. Perhaps this was prompted by Aragorn's earlier remark, *"... a man that has no horse will go on foot"*[127].

Aragorn's speech and demeanour during the encounter constituted a mixture of persuasion, exercise of

---

123. Op. cit. [1], *LotR* 3.2, p. 436.
124. Op. cit., *LotR* 3.2, p. 437.
125. Op. cit., *LotR* 3.2, p. 437.
126. Op. cit., *LotR* 3.2, p. 437.
127. Op. cit., *LotR* 3.2, p. 433.

authority, appeal to Éomer's better judgement, encouragement to use his initiative rather than following the law to the letter, plus an element of threat. Éomer would also have appreciated Aragorn's determination, sense of duty, and the loyalty and affection which inspired him to carry on looking for his friends. Also he was well aware of the alliance between Rohan and Gondor and of the superior rank of Aragorn, were he to become King, over the King of Rohan. All these issues would have swayed him in making his decision. Nevertheless he was in a dangerous position, with his life very likely being dependent on Aragorn keeping faith and coming to Rohan himself, to fight and to return the horses he had borrowed.

Éomer was becoming used to "sticking his neck out" and risking the disapproval of Théoden - or more accurately Gríma - but his actions in response to this first encounter with Aragorn surely exceeded anything he had done hitherto, as indicated by the "*dark and doubtful glances*"[128] of his men, particularly Éothain who having already expressed his uneasiness and scepticism by doubting the existence of Hobbits and ignoring Aragorn when he spoke, now took exception to a Dwarf being given a horse of Rohan. There are several possible reasons for Éomer's belief in Aragorn as opposed to the attitude of his companions:
- He had had the advantage of a private conversation with him and thus realised the significance of this meeting more than they did.
- He also seems to have been a knowledgeable and astute young man. As well as being a good judge of character he was well aware of Saruman's doings and motives and knew all about the history of Gondor, the significance of the Sword that was Broken, and Boromir's journey - including the message of the dream verse.
- In addition he had fallen very much under Aragorn's spell at this first meeting, as Éowyn would do, perceiving his inherent greatness and power. There was an element of reverence and hero-worship in his behaviour; he was very much younger than Aragorn, and this was someone he could look up to, particularly needed in the light of Théoden's deterioration. Later - when the War of the Ring was over - he would tell Aragorn that he had loved him since their first meeting.

As the two parties took their leave of each other, Éomer joked with Gimli on the subject of Galadriel thus reinforcing his efforts to make friends with Aragorn's companions.

*

When Gandalf, Aragorn, Legolas and Gimli arrived at Edoras two days later (March 2nd) Éomer was being held prisoner on account of the case Gríma had brought against him as described in *UT* 3.5.476-7 Appendix (i). There were three elements to this case:
- He had disobeyed Théoden by taking uncommitted forces from Edoras thus leaving it insufficiently defended.
- He had known of the disaster at the Fords of Isen and the death of Théodred **before** he set out to pursue the Orcs.
- He had disobeyed general orders and allowed strangers to go free, even lending them horses.

Regarding taking uncommitted forces from Edoras:
Éomer knew that Edoras was insufficiently defended and had acknowledged it to Aragorn - hence his hurry to get back. His actions had however been necessary in order to destroy the Orcs, recognising as he did the serious danger caused by the alliance between Mordor and Isengard which clearly existed as shown by the presence of both Mordor Orcs and Isengard Orcs in the party.

Regarding his supposed prior knowledge of the death of Théodred at the Fords of Isen:
The following timetable is based on dates given in App B.1092-3 supplemented by information in *UT* 3.5.460-478.

---

128. Op. cit. [1], *LotR* 3.2, p. 439.

Feb 25: Death of Théodred.

Feb 26: Éomer heard reports from his scouts of Orcs coming down from the Emyn Muil. On the same date Erkenbrand heard the news of the defeat at the Fords and the death of Théodred. He sent errand-riders to Edoras to tell Théoden of Théodred's last words and to suggest that Éomer should be sent westwards without delay.

Feb 27: Erkenbrand's errand-riders arrived in Edoras around noon. Éomer set out to pursue the Orcs around midnight, hence the thrust of Gríma's accusation - but see Feb 30.

Feb 28: Éomer overtook the Orcs at the edge of Fangorn Forest.

Feb 29: His éored destroyed the Orcs at sunrise.

Feb 30: Éomer met Aragorn on his return journey. His statement, made during the ensuing conversation, that *"There is battle even now upon the Westemnet, and I fear that it may go ill for us"*[129] implies that he was unaware of the defeat at the Fords and the death of Théodred at this point. This interpretation is strengthened by the mention of Gríma's delaying tactics (*UT* 3.5.466) stating that he deliberately caused delays in sending aid west and in fact this wasn't done until after Gandalf's healing of Théoden on March 2nd. In addition he presumably failed to inform Éomer of the errand-riders' message. By insisting that Éomer knew about the death of Théodred before riding unbidden against the Orcs was Gríma making out that Éomer now regarded himself as Théoden's heir and was taking the law into his own hands even more than hitherto?

Mar 2: Arrival of Gandalf, Aragorn, Legolas and Gimli at Edoras.

Regarding allowing strangers to go free and lending them horses:

Éomer had obviously done this. At the point when Aragorn arrived at Edoras it is stated (in *LotR* 3.6.509) that Gríma had given orders two days previously (February 30th) - ostensibly from Théoden - that no strangers were to be admitted. He was presumably hoping to prevent Aragorn keeping his promise to come to Théoden and return the horses, thereby discrediting Éomer completely and thus ensuring his continuing imprisonment and maybe even his death. Éomer's fear that his life might depend on Aragorn keeping his promise was probably not unfounded. The dismay of Aragorn, Legolas and Gimli in *LotR* 3.2.443 when the borrowed horses were frightened off by Saruman was clearly because they were now deprived of a speedy means of travel and so at increased risk of running out of food. However Aragorn must also have believed that part at least of his promise to Éomer - namely to return the horses - was now broken.

*

The events following the arrival of Gandalf, Aragorn, Legolas and Gimli are covered in *LotR* 3.6.506-525. Théoden himself added a further reason for Éomer's imprisonment when he told Gandalf that, as well as rebelling against his commands, Éomer had threatened to kill Gríma in the hall of Meduseld itself - an act which was forbidden.

A question which arises at this juncture is: How much had Éomer told Théoden when he got back to Edoras after his meeting with Aragorn? It is clear from the conversation between Gandalf, Théoden and Gríma in Meduseld that he had reported on Gandalf's fall in Moria and had mentioned that Aragorn, Legolas and Gimli had visited Lothlórien. There is, however, nothing to indicate that he had passed on the information concerning Aragorn's identity and the reforging of Elendil's sword, even though the impression given in *LotR* 3.2.437-9 is that he would have regarded such information as justification for letting Aragorn and his companions go free. However Gríma seemed to have disregarded Gandalf's introduction of his three companions as he referred to them as *"Three ragged wanderers in grey"*[130]. He may similarly have decided to ignore Éomer's news of Aragorn's identity, and also have prevented Éomer from speaking directly to Théoden.

During Gandalf's healing of Théoden, leading to the exposure of Gríma in his true colours and the restoration of Éomer to Théoden's affection and trust, Aragorn was an onlooker. However he was clearly very aware of his promise to Éomer that the two of them should draw swords together and wanted to carry it out to the letter.

---

129. Op. cit. [1], *LotR* 3.2, p. 437.
130. Op. cit., *LotR* 3.6, p. 513.

He therefore insisted that he, Legolas and Gimli should ride west with the Rohirrim immediately, refusing Théoden's offer of a place to rest after their long ride from Fangorn. Éomer, for his part, was still serious about killing Gríma, and since business was being conducted outside at this point rather than in the hall, would have carried this out if Gandalf had not stepped in to prevent him. Although Éomer was well aware that Gríma had been stalking Éowyn, he did not seem to realise the full extent to which he was in Saruman's power until Gandalf enlightened him. As the company set out to ride to Helm's Deep Éomer continued cementing his friendship with Legolas and Gimli by taking Gimli on his horse and having Aragorn and Legolas ride on either side of them. He no doubt recognised the extremely close relationship between this Man, Elf and Dwarf, and in loyalty to Aragorn if for no other reason, would have wanted to be on good terms with all three.

LotR 3.7 illustrates the very evident bond between Aragorn and Éomer at the Battle of the Hornburg, with Legolas and Gimli also being drawn into this partnership:
- When taking leave of Aragorn at the edge of Fangorn Éomer had said, "*... let our swords hereafter shine together!*"[131]. This now took place as they fought alongside each other - thus Aragorn's promise was fulfilled. Éomer's choice of words here seemed to indicate his greater enthusiasm for fighting compared with Aragorn. The sight of the Sword that was Broken now being used in battle cheered the Rohirrim who were clearly aware of the significance of the weapon.
- Aragorn and Éomer repeatedly rallied and encouraged the men.
- Aragorn also offered encouragement to Éomer and Gamling urging them to keep hoping.
- Aragorn was dismayed when Éomer didn't manage to reach the Hornburg after the Deeping Wall was breached. He subsequently rode out from the Hornburg with Théoden thus supporting the King himself and also taking on Éomer's role which he wasn't there to carry out.
- Legolas and Gimli played their own part, with Gimli swiftly decapitating two Orcs who attacked Éomer, as well as directing the blocking of the culvert, and Legolas joining Aragorn in encouraging the men when Éomer was forced to retreat into the caves.

The Battle of the Hornburg took place overnight on March 3rd- 4th and was followed by the journey to Isengard for the parley with Saruman on March 5th. Éomer showed complete resistance to the power of Saruman's voice, calling him "*an old liar with honey on his forked tongue*"[132] and urging Théoden to remember the deaths of Théodred and Háma and not be taken in by him. This reaction was hardly surprising given the damage caused by Gríma's activities over the previous five years, especially as Éomer now appreciated the full extent of Saruman's involvement in this.

During the return journey to Helm's Deep, along with the rest of Théoden's company, Éomer would have learnt of Pippin's meddling with the Orthanc-stone at Dol Baran and watched Gandalf's deferential presentation of the Stone to Aragorn. When they passed into Rohan again and were overtaken by the Grey Company in the early hours of March 6th (*LotR* 5.2.774) it was Éomer who was the first to speak to Halbarad and he was close by at the joyful meeting between Aragorn and his kinsman. The next day he was the one who noticed Aragorn's absence from the midday meal and when Théoden told him to send word to him that it was time to leave, it seemed that Éomer was sufficiently uneasy to go himself rather than just send a message as he was actually accompanying Aragorn when he finally emerged from the Hornburg with Halbarad following his use of the Orthanc-stone.

Maybe Éomer had been aware of Aragorn's uncertainty as to his next step, expressed to Legolas, Gimli and Merry as they prepared to depart from Dol Baran. Certainly he would have been concerned at his appearance and perhaps came to the conclusion that he must have used the Palantír. He was clearly very disturbed when he found out that Aragorn was intending to lead the Grey Company through the Paths of the Dead. He had been assuming that the two of them would continue fighting together (something which Éowyn would urge Aragorn to do when they met at Dunharrow the following evening), but the chief cause of his anxiety was that he was convinced that Aragorn was going to certain death (from his knowledge of Baldor's experience).

---
131. Op. cit. [1], *LotR* 3.2, p. 439.
132. Op. cit., *LotR* 3.10, p. 579.

Neither Théoden's understanding that Aragorn might have to "... *tread strange paths that others dare not*"[133], or Aragorn's own words, "... *in battle we may yet meet again, though all the hosts of Mordor should stand between*"[134], made any impact on his pessimism. Aragorn must have realised this because two days later, on taking leave of Éowyn at Dunharrow, he would tell her to repeat the message to her brother no doubt wanting to give him hope and encouragement. Now as he watched Théoden, Éomer and Merry ride away through the mountain roads his words to Halbarad, "*There go three that I love...*"[135], left no doubt of his regard for Éomer. On arrival at Dunharrow on March 9th to find that Aragorn had indeed taken the Paths of the Dead the previous day Éomer's despair was confirmed: "*Then our paths are sundered. He is lost. We must ride without him, and our hope dwindles.*"[136]. In the ensuing conversation Éowyn declared that she had thought Aragorn fey as if called by the Dead and Théoden suggested that perhaps he **had** actually been called and would be able to pass safely. However this did nothing to change Éomer's mood: after freely admitting his own fear of the Paths such that he would rather face Sauron's hosts alone than risk such a journey, he lamented, "*Alas that a fey mood should fall on a man so greathearted in this hour of need!*"[137] He did not seem to hold Aragorn to blame, just assumed that something outside his control had called him to his death.

Éomer's views would undergo a dramatic change at the Battle of the Pelennor Fields six days later. Following his mad and furious grief at seeing Éowyn apparently dead on the battle-field, and driven by the strength of these feelings, by the kingship newly-thrust upon him by the death of Théoden, and by his battle fervour, he ended up only a mile from the Harlond where a great press of Sauron's troops were amassed between him and the haven. Meanwhile new foes were cutting him off behind. He was on the point of organising a shield-wall and fighting to the death when he realised that the approaching ships contained Aragorn and his company and not the Corsairs of Umbar. There followed a glad and unexpected (by Éomer anyway) meeting comparable with that between Aragorn and Halbarad, with Aragorn repeating his words of hope: "*Thus we meet again, though all the hosts of Mordor lay between us. Did I not say so at the Hornburg?*"[138]. Éomer's explanation for his scepticism was that hope could deceive, and also that he had not realised that Aragorn was foresighted. The end of the battle found them - along with Imrahil - too weary to feel either sorrow or joy. They were however physically unharmed due to luck/fate, their skill and weapons, and the aspect they presented to the Enemy such that few were actually prepared to stand against them. As shown at Helm's Deep Aragorn and Éomer functioned very well together in battle.

*

LotR 5.8.861-2 describes Aragorn, Éomer and Imrahil reaching the City Gate where Aragorn insisted on staying outside in his tents while the war with Sauron was still going on, rather than making a formal claim for the kingship. Éomer pointed out that he had already revealed himself as king, by his battle standard and by wearing the Star of Elendil, and expressed concern that these might be challenged. Aragorn, supported by Imrahil, had to explain that he was trying to avoid civil unrest which may have arisen if he had entered the City at that point. Aragorn and Imrahil both knew Denethor (whom they assumed to be still alive) well enough to realise that a claim for the kingship at that point would be like a red rag to a bull to him. Since Éomer did not have this specific knowledge he seems to have viewed the situation more simplistically, assuming that because he himself was satisfied with the validity of Aragorn's claim the Steward of Gondor would be too. It seems unlikely that he had been to Gondor or encountered Denethor, especially as, with hindsight, most of Denethor's knowledge of other lands had come from using the Palantír of Minas Tirith.

While Aragorn went to his tents Éomer and Imrahil entered the City and went up to the Citadel where Théoden was lying in state. It was here while in conversation with Imrahil that Éomer found out that Éowyn was still alive. Imrahil had of course known and assumed that Éomer also knew. The two of them immediately

---

133. Op. cit. [1], *LotR* 5.2, p. 779.
134. Op. cit., *LotR* 5.2, p. 779.
135. Op. cit., *LotR* 5.2, p. 779.
136. Op. cit., *LotR* 5.3, p. 796.
137. Op. cit., *LotR* 5.3, p. 798.
138. Op. cit., *LotR* 5.6, p. 848.

headed for the Houses of Healing where Gandalf, accompanied by a heavily cloaked Aragorn, informed them that Denethor was dead and Faramir the new Steward was lying injured.

Now that Éomer knew Éowyn was alive, but critically ill, he was thrown into a state of extreme anxiety as opposed to the grief and acceptance while he had thought she was dead. After Aragorn had made a preliminary assessment of his three patients he sighed and acknowledged that he would need all his healing power and skill in order to save them. He then expressed a wish that Elrond were there. At this Éomer, "*seeing that he was both sorrowful and weary*"[139], suggested that he should rest and eat before taking on the task of healing. In spite of the fact that it was his own sister - whom he undoubtedly loved - who was at the point of death, he showed an acute awareness of Aragorn's own suffering. He perhaps realised that Aragorn was grieving at the loss of Halbarad in particular, as he had witnessed the joyful meeting between them and would have known that Halbarad was the only one to accompany him during the sleepless night in the Hornburg. Also Aragorn's wish for Elrond's presence made it clear that he doubted his own ability to do the task which lay ahead. This would perhaps have been the first time Éomer had seen him in self-doubting mode.

During the healing of Éowyn it became clear that Aragorn had seen much more deeply into her troubles than her brother had, having perceived her unhappiness from their first meeting. He tried to explain this in his eloquent speech comparing her with an ice-cold flower, at the same time avoiding the issue of Éowyn's feelings for himself. When he ended his speech with the rhetorical question: "*Her malady begins far back before this day, does it not, Éomer?*"[140] he seemed to be assuming corroboration from Éomer. However Éomer's answer indicated that as far as he was concerned Éowyn had simply shared his own worries during Théoden's bewitchment by Gríma and had become increasingly unhappy only recently, when she fell in love with Aragorn. Éomer had perhaps realised at once that this love was unrequited. It is significant that he did not blame Aragorn in any way ("*... I hold you blameless in this matter, as in all else...*"[141]) and certainly did not appear to think that he had been encouraging her.

It needed a tirade from Gandalf to make Éomer see that his sister's problems were actually much deeper and more long-standing. I quote this in full in view of the need to discuss its likely impact on Éomer and Aragorn.

> "*My friend, you had horses, and deeds of arms, and the free-fields; but she, born in the body of a maid, had a spirit and courage **at least** the match of yours.* [My emphasis] *Yet she was doomed to wait upon an old man, whom she loved as a father, and watch him falling into a mean dishonoured dotage; and her part seemed to her more ignoble than that of the staff he leaned on.*
> *Think you that Wormtongue had poison only for Théoden's ears? 'Dotard! What is the house of Eorl but a thatched barn where brigands drink in the reek, and their brats roll on the floor among their dogs?' Have you not heard those words before? Saruman spoke them, the teacher of Wormtongue. Though I do not doubt that Wormtongue at home wrapped their meaning in terms more cunning. My lord, if your sister's love for you, and her will still bent to her duty, had not restrained her lips, you might have heard even such things as these escape them. But who knows what she spoke to the darkness, alone, in the bitter watches of the night, when all her life seemed shrinking, and the walls of her bower closing in about her, a hutch to trammel some wild thing in?*"[142]

Éomer reacted by looking at Éowyn in silence, and Aragorn took the opportunity to tell him, "*I saw also what you saw, Éomer. Few other griefs ... have more bitterness and shame for a man's heart than to behold the love of a lady so fair and brave that cannot be returned.*"[143] He went on to describe how he had thought of her with sorrow and pity as he went through the Paths of the Dead, his fear of that journey being submerged by the fear of what might happen to her. In addition he made Éomer see that Éowyn's sisterly love for him was greater

---

139. Op. cit. [1], *LotR* 5.8, p. 863.
140. Op. cit., *LotR* 5.8, p. 866.
141. Op. cit., *LotR* 5.8, p. 866.
142. Op. cit., *LotR* 5.8, p. 867.
143. Op. cit., *LotR* 5.8, p. 867.

than her supposed love for himself because it was a love for someone she knew - as opposed to love for what he called "*a shadow*", "*a thought*" and "*a hope of glory and great deeds*".[144]

In Chapter 2.3 I have suggested that Gandalf's input at this juncture was aimed at helping Aragorn out in an uncomfortable situation. Aragorn was finding it difficult to talk about Éowyn's feelings for him and he also wanted to refer to the **underlying** causes of her unhappiness to her brother, being perhaps taken aback that Éomer had not actually been aware of these issues. Gandalf, as well as his concern for Aragorn, would also have recognised the importance of Éomer reaching a full understanding of his sister, and by virtue of his greater power and authority could get away with stating the situation much more bluntly than Aragorn would have felt able to do. Éomer's subsequent silence, as well as being due to him trying to absorb what Gandalf had said, may also have been caused by him feeling cowed by the Wizard and ashamed for being so imperceptive as to be unaware of the issues. In addition Gandalf had been pretty outspoken regarding the relative courage of the siblings: the words "*at least*" which I have emphasised above could be taken to imply that Éowyn actually outshone him in courage and spirit. (A good example can be seen in Éomer's attitude to the Paths of the Dead - that he would not go that way even if he was alone with the hosts of Mordor with no other escape - compared with that of Éowyn who, alone of the folk at Dunharrow, had got up to take leave of the Grey Company and had actually been prepared to go with them.) Éomer was perhaps relieved that Aragorn showed no sign of having any less regard for him following Gandalf's words. From Aragorn's own point of view he now felt able to unburden himself to Éomer and talk about his relationship with Éowyn for the first time. As a result of this conversation at Éowyn's bedside a huge amount of previously unexpressed feeling was now out in the open, to the benefit of all concerned.

When Aragorn had broken the hold of the Black Breath on Éowyn he went out of the room leaving a grateful and tearful Éomer to be the one to call her back to consciousness.

The following day (March 16th) Éomer was present at the Last Debate where, if he hadn't already realised, he learnt that Aragorn had used the Palantír of Orthanc to confront Sauron thus initiating the strategy of drawing his attention away from Mordor in order to increase Frodo's chance of avoiding detection. When it was proposed by Gandalf that this strategy should continue in the form of a small army at the Morannon acting as a bait to draw Sauron out, Aragorn gave his whole-hearted support but emphasised that he was not actually **ordering** anyone else to follow suit. Éomer's reaction was simply, "... *I have little knowledge of these deep matters; but I need it not ... it is enough, that as my friend Aragorn succoured me and my people, so I will aid him when he calls*"[145], thus demonstrating complete faith in Aragorn, as well as affection and an appreciation of the significance of the Gondor/Rohan alliance.

*

Although we know that Éomer led the Rohirrim to the Morannon and was present at the celebrations surrounding the honouring of the Ring-bearers at the Field of Cormallen, there is no mention of any further specific encounter between him and Aragorn until their very affectionate meeting after the newly-crowned King Elessar had passed his judgements. After they had embraced each other Aragorn stated, "*Between us there can be no word of giving or taking, nor of reward; for we are brethren*", with Éomer declaring, "*Since the day when you rose before me out of the green grass of the downs I have loved you, and that love shall not fail.*".[146] From Aragorn's remark to Halbarad mentioned above ("*There go three that I love...*"[147]) it is quite clear that he returned Éomer's affection.

Initially it had been mainly Aragorn's military prowess and his powerful charisma which had aroused Éomer's love and esteem, but by the end of the War of the Ring he knew a great deal more about him than at that first meeting. As well as someone who had fought alongside him at Helm's Deep and the Pelennor Fields, Éomer now knew Aragorn as a healer who alone had had the ability to save the life of his sister, as someone who had a level of mental strength which had enabled him to wrest the Palantír of Orthanc out of Sauron's

---

144. Op. cit. [1], *LotR* 5.8, p. 867.
145. Op. cit., *LotR* 5.9, p. 880.
146. Op. cit., *LotR* 6.5, p. 969.
147. Op. cit., *LotR* 5.2, p. 779.

control, and as someone gifted with remarkable foresight. In addition he would have come to appreciate Aragorn's wisdom and compassion having witnessed his behaviour to the faint-hearted at the Morannon. He had in general followed a similar path to that of Éowyn and, like her, had come to realise that prowess in battle was not necessarily Aragorn's finest quality, though it was the one he had originally admired.

Another non-military aspect of Aragorn's character which Éomer would have come to appreciate was the tolerance and friendship he showed to other races, for example:
- Aragorn was obviously friendly with Elves as shown by his close companionship with Legolas and his reverence for Lothlórien. This was very different from Éomer's hostility to the "*Lady in the Golden Wood*", and indeed to Legolas even before the altercation about Galadriel.
- Aragorn's similar closeness to Gimli indicated his willingness to be friendly with Dwarves, another race regarded with suspicion by Éomer and probably by the Rohirrim in general. This seems to have dated back prior to the founding of Rohan around TA 2000 when Fram of the Éothéod slew the dragon Scatha and seized his hoard which was also claimed by the Dwarves. Owing to the fact that Fram wouldn't give them anything except the teeth of the dragon made into a necklace one assumes the Dwarves felt a similar hostility - as shown by the suggestion that they killed Fram for this insult (App A.II.1064-5).
- Éomer's hostility to the Dunlendings was illustrated at the Battle of the Hornburg where he described their voices as "*the scream of birds and the bellowing of beasts*"[148]. Although he did not actually witness Aragorn's warning to them of the danger from the approaching Huorns, he must have heard about it and realised that Aragorn shared the attitude of Gamling, and later Erkenbrand, in realising that these people were fighting Rohan because Saruman had stirred up the old hostility between the two races. (This was due to the Dunlendings being driven west when Rohan was established.)
- During the meeting with Ghân-buri-Ghân in *LotR* 5.5.832-3 Éomer's manner to him was somewhat sceptical and patronising. It was also indicated that the Rohirrim sometimes hunted the Drúedain for sport. Aragorn's behaviour to them after the War of the Ring was to give the Forest of Drúadan to Ghân-buri-Ghân's people in perpetuity with other races only entering it with their leave.

Aragorn's acceptance of different races, even if physically unattractive by general standards, must have been a good example to the young and rather inexperienced Éomer. In general Aragorn must have helped him to prepare for a kingship he had not expected to hold before the death of Théodred. Did he recall his own feelings as a young man when Elrond had told him of his true identity?

The final encounters between Aragorn and Éomer in the main text of *LotR* are centred on the burial and funeral of Théoden. When pronouncing his judgements Aragorn had offered Éomer the choice of taking Théoden back to rest in Rohan or leaving him permanently in a tomb among the Kings of Gondor. Éomer had chosen the former, and in *LotR* 6.6.975 the two of them personally (this is certainly implied) carried his bier from the Houses of the Dead to the wain which would take it to Rohan. At the funeral wake when Éomer announced the betrothal of Éowyn to Faramir, he expressed his joy at this new bond between Gondor and Rohan. Aragorn's answer was, "*No niggard are you, Éomer, to give thus to Gondor the fairest thing in your realm!*"[149]

Also covered in *LotR* 6.6.975 is Éomer's settlement with Gimli regarding the beauty of Galadriel. App B.1095 states that Éomer returned to Minas Tirith on July 18th after spending approximately two and a half months restoring order in Rohan (and thus not being present at Aragorn's wedding). A feast was held at which he encountered Arwen and Galadriel - among others from Rivendell and Lothlórien - and he subsequently called for Gimli to say that he thought that Arwen, not Galadriel, was the fairest lady living, although he would have put Galadriel first if he had not also seen Arwen. Gimli accepted this. Although the implication here seems to be that this was the first time Éomer had seen Galadriel and Arwen, a study of App B.1095 shows that Arwen's escort (which included Galadriel) had stayed at Edoras between June 14th and 16th, a time when Éomer and Éowyn would have been there. However Gimli of course had not been present on that occasion,

---

148. Op. cit. [1], *LotR* 3.7, p. 536.
149. Op. cit., *LotR* 6.6, p. 977.

hence the matter not being raised until mid-July. I only mention this incident to show that Éomer had now formally made his peace with Gimli (and by implication with Legolas) after his *faux pas* regarding the Lady of Lothlórien - an incident which had had the potential to make that first encounter at the edge of Fangorn turn out very differently. In practice the peace had been made long back.

*

I finish this study of Aragorn and Éomer with a further look at the alliance between Rohan and Gondor and, more specifically, at its forming by Cirion, the twelfth Steward of Gondor, and Eorl the Young in TA 2510 as described in *UT* 3.2.iii.388-398.

The two characteristics of the alliance which stand out are perpetuity and mutuality as expressed in Aragorn's words to Éomer: "*In happy hour did Eorl ride from the North, and never has any league of peoples been more blessed, so that neither has ever failed the other, nor shall fail.*"[150] Denethor had been the twenty-sixth Steward.

After the Battle of the Field of Celebrant, Cirion gave the area of Gondor called Calenardhon to Eorl and his people during a ceremony on the holy mountain Halifirien - the most westerly of the beacon hills of Gondor along the line of the White Mountains. Afterwards they climbed to the hallow on the summit where Elendil's tomb was situated, set there by Isildur in what was then the mid-point of Gondor. Here Eorl held the blade of his sword on the mound and swore an oath of friendship to Gondor for himself and his heirs in perpetuity along with a promise of aid in battle "... *to the utmost end of our strength.*"[151]. Any failure on the part of his descendants in the upholding of the oath would lead to them being accursed. Cirion then, with one hand on the tomb and the other raising the white wand of the Stewards, vowed that Gondor would be bound by an identical oath and promise of aid. He then declared that the oath was sworn in memory of Númenor and Elendil, calling to witness the Valar and Eru himself. We are told that "*Such an oath had not been heard in Middle-earth since Elendil himself had sworn alliance with Gil-galad King of the Eldar.*"[152] As stated in Note 44 to *UT* 3.2.iii.410-11, the law had been that only the King of Númenor could call on Eru to witness an oath. However Elendil, being descended from a King of Númenor, had therefore regarded himself as having the requisite authority. Cirion too, being the Ruling Steward of Gondor acting on behalf of a line of kings descended from Elendil, could reasonably claim the same right.

The account stresses that, as well as being wise policy, the actions of Cirion and Eorl were driven by the general friendship between the two peoples and between the two men themselves. "*On the part of Cirion the love was that of a wise father, old in the cares of the world, for a son in the strength and hope of his youth; while in Cirion Eorl saw the highest and noblest man of the world that he knew, and the wisest, on whom sat the majesty of the Kings of Men of long ago.*"[153]. It is difficult not to see a parallel with Aragorn and Éomer here. Aragorn may well have felt fatherly towards Éomer who was so much younger than he, and Éomer could easily have regarded Aragorn as a father-figure - more so on the loss of Théoden - recognising his own youth and inexperience. We are told that Cirion was "... *a man of little pride and of great courage and generosity of heart, the noblest of the Stewards of Gondor*"[154], thus further emphasising the similarity to Aragorn. In addition, as Cirion stood up to speak his oath, "... *the sun went down in flame in the West and his white robe seemed to be on fire...*"[155] Compare this with the image of Aragorn at his parting from the Hobbits in *LotR* 6.6.982.

Following the gifting of Calenardhon Cirion removed Elendil's burial casket from the mound and placed it in the Hallows in Minas Tirith. The mound on Halifirien was no longer the mid-point of Gondor, but was on the border between Gondor and Rohan - Calenardhon had been relinquished permanently on oath.

UT 3.2.410 Note 44 also tells us that Aragorn and Éomer renewed the bond of Cirion and Eorl in the Hallow on Halifirien, with Aragorn using the same oath as Cirion, i.e. invoking the memory of Númenor and Elendil and calling on the Valar and Eru as witnesses. App A.II.1071 also gives an account of this incident emphasising

---

150. Op. cit. [1], *LotR* 6.5, p. 969.
151. Op. cit. [2], *UT* 3.2.iii, p. 394.
152. Op. cit., *UT* 3.2.iii, p. 395.
153. Op. cit., *UT* 3.2.iii, pp. 392-3.
154. Op. cit., *UT* 3.2.iii, p. 398.
155. Op. cit., *UT* 3.2.iii, p. 395.

the renewal of the gift of the land of Calenardhon/Rohan as well as the retaking of the oaths. Clearly, as with Cirion and Eorl, the close relationship between Gondor and Rohan was also due to the deep personal affection between Éomer and Aragorn.

In the first part of his reign Aragorn had many uprisings to deal with in the lands East and South, where Sauron's influence still prevailed, before a full and lasting peace was obtained. The closing paragraph of App A.II sums up quite movingly the relationship between him and Éomer during the early years of the Fourth Age:

> "... wherever King Elessar went with war King Éomer went with him; and beyond the Sea of Rhûn and on the far fields of the South the thunder of the cavalry of the Mark was heard, and the White Horse upon Green flew in many winds until Éomer grew old."[156]

Éomer died in FA 64 at the age of ninety-three and was succeeded by his son, Elfwine the Fair. Aragorn survived Éomer by fifty-seven years but I can find no reference to any dealings between him and Elfwine. Indeed in view of the timescales involved Aragorn would almost certainly have outlived Elfwine too. Éomer married Elfwine's mother Lothíriel in the first year of the Fourth Age when he was about thirty. Even if as much as ten years elapsed before Elfwine was born, which perhaps seems unlikely, he would have been fifty-three when Éomer died and if he had then survived Aragorn he would have been a hundred and ten. This also seems unlikely given that the Rohirrim did not have the extended lifespan of the Dúnedain - unless the smidgeon of Silvan Elf blood in Lothíriel (as the daughter of Prince Imrahil) played a part here, resulting in a longer life as well as the beauty and the friendship for Elves implied by her son's name and epithet.

OBSERVATIONS ON THE GONDOR/ROHAN ALLIANCE IN TA 3019

There are many indications in *LotR* that Aragorn, Théoden, Éomer and Éowyn were fully committed to the alliance between Gondor and Rohan:
- The first use of Andúril in war (as opposed to dealing with the wolves in Eregion and the Orcs in Moria) was actually in Rohan not Gondor. By fighting at the Battle of the Hornburg, Aragorn was in effect acting on behalf of Gondor in helping Rohan.
- Théoden, even before the arrival of the Red Arrow representing Denethor's plea for help, was committed to riding to Gondor's aid. This applied to his nephew and niece as well: note Imrahil's words on seeing Éowyn on the battlefield at the Pelennor Fields, "*Have even the women of the Rohirrim come to war in our need?*"[157]
- UT 3.2.i.376 compares the Ride of the Rohirrim in 3019 with the one led by Eorl at the Battle of the Field of Celebrant in 2510.
- Aragorn found the remains of Baldor in the Paths of the Dead. Thus, four hundred and fifty years after his disappearance, the Rohirrim found out what had happened to him.
- After the War of the Ring was over the alliance was further cemented by the marriages of Faramir and Éowyn, and Éomer and Lothíriel.

There are also a number of references specifically relating to the significance of oaths:

"*My lord* [i.e. Denethor] *does not issue any command to you, he begs you only to remember old friendship and oaths long spoken...*"[158]
Hirgon to Théoden on presenting the Red Arrow to him.

"*Oaths ye have taken: now fulfil them all, to lord and land and league of friendship!*"[159]
Théoden as the Rohirrim drew close to the Pelennor Fields.

---
156. Op. cit. [1], App A.II, p. 1071.
157. Op. cit., *LotR* 5.6, p. 845.
158. Op. cit., *LotR* 5.3, p. 799.
159. Op. cit., *LotR* 5.5, p. 836.

(As quoted earlier in this chapter)
"... *he* [Théoden] *was a gentle heart and a great king and kept his oaths ...*"[160]
Aragorn to Merry in the Houses of Healing.

---

160. Op. cit. [1], *LotR* 5.8, p. 869.

CHAPTER 2.8 - Ancestors, The Ring and Gollum

This chapter has three purposes:
- **To look at the effect which certain of Aragorn's ancestors had on his life, destiny and struggles.**
- **To analyse Aragorn's attitude to the One Ring and the effect it had on him. This also involves discussion of his attitude to the Nazgûl.**
- **To examine Aragorn's relationship with Gollum.**

As well as the main text of *LotR*[1] information is taken from *The Silmarillion*[2] *Ak* and *RoP*, *UT*[3] 3.1, 3.2 and 3.4, and Apps A.I.iv, A.I.v and B. *HoM-e* XII[4] has also been used to establish approximate birth and death dates in some cases.

In order to set the context for these discussions it is necessary to give a brief history of Sauron's activities in the Second and Third Ages and to summarise the role of Elendil's family in opposing him. *Ak*, *RoP* and App B are the chief sources.

After the defeat of Morgoth at the end of the First Age Sauron, his greatest servant, took up residence incognito in Middle-earth where he began building his fortress of Barad-dûr in Mordor and set about corrupting and enslaving Men and Elves. He was still able, during this period, to adopt the appearance of being fair and trustworthy and as a result found Men easy to win over - as opposed to the Elves who were generally much more suspicious of him. For example, Elrond and the Elf-king Gil-galad mistrusted him even though they did not know who he actually was. However by mid-way through the Second Age (1200-1500), under the name of Annatar (Lord of Gifts), he succeeded in winning over the Elven jewel-smiths of Eregion (the area to the west of Moria) who were led by Celebrimbor, grandson of Fëanor. He offered them gifts and shared his creativity and his deep knowledge of smith-craft with them, including teaching them to make Rings of Power. Eventually Celebrimbor achieved such skill that he was able to forge the Three Elven Rings - Nenya, Vilya and Narya - unaided by Sauron. At this point Sauron returned to Mordor and, around SA 1600, forged the One Ring in Mount Doom, letting a great deal of his strength and will pass into it. Barad-dûr was then completed using the power of the Ring. Sauron's intention was to use the One Ring to rule all the others, and although this worked in most cases, he was not able to ensnare the Three Elven Rings. As soon as he put on the One, Celebrimbor realised who he was and what his aims were, so he hid the Three and the names of their bearers were kept secret. The relationship between Sauron and the Elves was obviously now hostile and during the 1690s Sauron waged war on Eregion eventually laying waste to it and then taking over Eriador before being defeated in 1701 by the combined efforts of Gil-galad's Elves from Lindon and an army which arrived by ship from Númenor.

Although the Three Rings were safe, Sauron had seized all the other Rings of Power which he now used for the purpose of enslavement. In particular there were the Seven Rings given to Dwarves and the Nine Rings given to Men who were in positions of power. The Dwarves had considerable resistance to such attempts at dominance - they did however develop an overwhelming greed for gold. The owners of the Nine Rings initially became great kings, sorcerers or warriors achieving wealth and glory but eventually succumbed to Sauron. They obtained apparently unending life, as well as the ability to be invisible and to see things in worlds

---

1. J.R.R. Tolkien, *The Lord of the Rings,* London, HarperCollins Publishers, 2007, 2nd edition, based on the 50th Anniversary Edition of 2004.
2. C. Tolkien (ed.), *The Silmarillion*, London, HarperCollins Publishers, 1999, first published in Great Britain by George Allen & Unwin 1977.
3. C. Tolkien (ed.), *Unfinished Tales of Númenor and Middle-earth*, London, HarperCollins Publishers, 1998, first published in Great Britain by George Allen & Unwin 1980.
4. C. Tolkien (ed.), *The History of Middle-earth*, vol. XII, *The Peoples of Middle-earth*, London HarperColllins Publishers, 2002, first published in Great Britain by HarperCollins Publishers 1996.

which were invisible to mortal Men. However these visions were mostly delusions and phantoms created by Sauron and as they grew more in thrall to him, they found life intolerable. In the end The Nine became permanently invisible - unless clothed - and became Sauron's most terrifying servants. App B.1083 gives SA 2251 as the approximate date of their first appearance as the Nazgûl. For them to have reached this state of permanent invisibility following on from an abnormally long life-span the Rings must have been given to them several hundred years earlier, from 1600 onwards. *Ak* 320 states that three of the Nazgûl were thought to have originally been great lords of Númenórean race and since Númenóreans began to establish dominions on the coasts of Middle-earth during the 1800s it was probably some of those settling around the Bay of Belfalas whom Sauron chose to enslave.

Following his defeat in Eregion and Eriador, Sauron concentrated his efforts on extending his power in the East, and on seducing and enslaving Men rather than Elves. Eventually, towards the end of the Second Age, his growing power caused Ar-Pharazôn, King of Númenor, to come and challenge him, sailing to Umbar with a massive fleet. Sauron yielded to Ar-Pharazôn's command to swear fealty to him and agreed to be taken as a hostage to Númenor where he soon won over the King along with most of his people. The climax of this corruption occurred in SA 3319 when Ar-Pharazôn, spurred on by Sauron, attempted to invade Valinor and demand immortality. This resulted in the destruction and drowning of Númenor from which only Elendil and his sons Isildur and Anárion - along with their supporters, families and households - escaped by ship. Sauron's body was destroyed in the wreck of Númenor, but his spirit survived and made its way in secret back to Mordor where he took up the One Ring again and became strong enough to appear incarnate once more. However he was no longer able to look fair and his new guise was *"an image of malice and hatred made visible"*[5] which few could endure. Meanwhile Elendil's ships were driven to the Grey Havens on the coast of Lindon which was ruled by Gil-galad, while Isildur and Anárion were blown south and eventually sailed up the Anduin. The kingdoms of Arnor in the North and Gondor in the South were founded in SA 3320 by these three who had resisted the wiles of Sauron and remained faithful to the Valar and the Eldar. Elendil now left his sons to rule in Gondor, while he ruled in Arnor. However he was himself overall king of both kingdoms. In a letter to Robert Murray written in November 1954 Tolkien says that Elendil, Isildur and Anárion *"... established a kind of diminished memory of Númenor in Exile on the coasts of Middle-earth – inheriting the hatred of Sauron, the friendship of the Elves, the knowledge of the True God and (less happily) the yearning for longevity, and the habit of embalming and the building of splendid tombs..."*[6]

Just over a hundred years later Sauron, now making his presence known, prepared for war and captured Isildur's dwelling at Minas Ithil just west of the Mountains of Shadow. Isildur and his wife and children managed to escape down the Anduin into the Bay of Belfalas and from there sailed north to join Elendil. The following year the Last Alliance of Elves and Men was formed defeating Sauron at the Battle of Dagorlad (near the Morannon) and subsequently besieging Barad-dûr. Six years into the siege Anárion was killed when a stone cast from Barad-dûr hit him crushing his helmet. The following year the siege came to an end when Sauron himself came out and wrestled with Gil-galad and Elendil who succeeded in bringing him down but were themselves killed in the struggle. The Scroll of Isildur, quoted by Gandalf in *LotR* 2.2.253 suggests that Gil-galad was burnt to death by the heat of Sauron's hand. Was it the same for Elendil? As Elendil fell, his sword Narsil broke in two beneath him, at which point Isildur seized its hilt-shard and used it to cut the One Ring from Sauron's hand thus completing the destruction of Sauron's body and causing Barad-dûr to crumble. This marked the end of the Second Age. However Sauron's spirit still survived and fled away into hiding. The actual foundations of Barad-dûr remained in place, their existence tied to that of the Ring - as explained by Elrond at the Council in *LotR* 2.2.244.

Both Elrond and Círdan were present at the final battle with Sauron and when they realised that Isildur had taken possession of the Ring they urged him to destroy it by taking it to Mount Doom and throwing it into the fiery chasm where it had been forged. However their efforts were of no avail as Isildur was determined to keep it as recompense for the deaths of Elendil and Anárion.

The Third Age began with Isildur succeeding his father as overall King of both Arnor and Gondor. Also, with

---

5. Op. cit. [2], *Ak*, p. 336.
6. H. Carpenter (ed.), *The Letters of J.R.R. Tolkien*, with the assistance of Christopher Tolkien, London, HarperCollins Publishers, 1995. First published in Great Britain by George Allen & Unwin, 1981. Letter. 156, p. 206.

Anárion dead, he was now sole King in Gondor. Following the pattern set by his father, he committed the rule of Gondor to Anárion's son Meneldil and set off north intending to rule Arnor himself. He was accompanied by his guard of two hundred men and his three eldest sons, Elendur, Aratan and Ciryon. On the banks of the Anduin near the Gladden Fields they were taken by surprise by a host of Orcs and the ensuing struggle left only three survivors, namely Isildur's esquire Ohtar with his companion who between them safely conveyed the Shards of Narsil to Rivendell, and Elendur's esquire Estelmo, found alive under Elendur's body. Isildur himself first tried to escape by putting on the Ring and swimming across the river, but the Ring came off and was lost in the water leaving him now visible and a target for the Orcs. His body was also lost in the river, though according to hints given in *UT* 3.1.359 it was eventually found and dishonoured by Saruman. The Ring itself was found over two thousand years later by a Hobbit called Déagol during a fishing trip with his friend Sméagol. Sméagol, overcome by the lure of the Ring, murdered Déagol and took the Ring for himself, subsequently becoming increasingly sneaky and malicious until his grandmother turned him out of the family home. A few years later his wanderings resulted in him burrowing his way beneath the Misty Mountains where he and the Ring remained until Bilbo's arrival nearly five hundred years later - as described in *The Hobbit*[7].

The following table summarises these events.

SA 1-c.1500	Sauron lived incognito in Middle-earth corrupting Men.
SA 1500s	Sauron succeeded in ingratiating himself with the Elves of Eregion. Rings of Power were made.
SA c.1590	The Three Elven Rings were forged by Celebrimbor - untouched by Sauron.
SA 1600	The One Ring was forged by Sauron in Mount Doom. The Elves perceived his treachery and identity. Barad-dûr was completed.
SA 1600-1680s	Hostility now existed between Sauron and the Elves of Eregion.
SA 1690s	Sauron waged war on Eregion, laying it waste and taking over Eriador. Celebrimbor killed.
SA 1700	Sauron was defeated by the Elves of Lindon and a fleet from Númenor.
SA 1701	Sauron was driven out of Eriador. The Three Rings were safe, but all the others had been seized by Sauron. Sauron returned to Mordor to concentrate on seducing/enslaving Men in eastern areas, partly by giving them Rings of Power.
SA 2251	Approximate date of the first appearance of the Nazgûl.
SA 3262	Sauron was taken to Númenor as Ar-Pharazôn's prisoner. He soon corrupted him along with most of the Númenóreans.
SA 3299	Birth of Isildur's eldest son Elendur (*UT* 3.1.362 Note 11).
SA 3319	Ar-Pharazôn sailed to Valinor to demand immortality from the Valar. Númenor was destroyed. Elendil, Isildur and Anárion escaped from the drowning of Númenor to Middle-earth. Sauron's spirit escaped from Númenor and flew back to Mordor and the One Ring.
SA 3320	The Kingdoms of Arnor and Gondor were founded by Elendil, Isildur and Anárion.
SA 3429	Sauron captured Minas Ithil (Isildur's dwelling in Gondor). Isildur escaped down the Anduin and sailed to Elendil in Arnor.
SA 3430	The Last Alliance of Elves and Men was formed against Sauron. Birth of Isildur's youngest son Valandil (*HoM-e* XII.7.192).
SA 3434	Sauron was defeated at the Battle of Dagorlad - near the Morannon. Beginning of siege of Barad-dûr.
SA 3440	Death of Anárion in year six of the siege.

---

7. J.R.R. Tolkien, *The Hobbit*, 3rd edition, London, Allen & Unwin, 1966, 1975 printing. Chapter 5, pp. 79-100.

SA 3441	Sauron was overthrown by Gil-galad and Elendil who both died in the struggle. Isildur cut the One Ring from Sauron's hand using Elendil's broken sword. Isildur refused to destroy the Ring. Sauron's spirit went into hiding. **END OF THE SECOND AGE**
TA 2	Isildur was killed by Orcs on his way north with the One Ring. The Ring was lost in the Anduin.
TA 2463	Déagol found the Ring while fishing in the Anduin. He was murdered by Sméagol/Gollum who took the Ring for himself.
TA 2470	Gollum took up residence underneath the Misty Mountains.
TA 2850	Sauron's presence in Dol Guldur in Mirkwood Forest was confirmed.
TA 2941	Bilbo, fleeing Orcs in passages under the mountains, found the Ring and met Gollum. Sauron was driven out of Dol Guldur by the White Council and returned to Mordor in secret.
TA 2951	Sauron declared himself in Mordor and began rebuilding Barad-dûr.
TA 3001	Bilbo's 111th birthday party took place, after which the Ring came into Frodo's possession.

ANCESTORS

This discussion features Elendil, Isildur and Anárion in particular, but inevitably involves other family members, namely:
- Elendil's father Amandil
- Isildur's eldest and youngest sons (Elendur and Valandil respectively)
- Anárion's son Meneldil
- Elendil's namesake, Tar-Elendil fourth King of Númenor, and his daughter Silmarien from whom Elendil, Isildur, Anárion, and eventually Aragorn himself were directly descended
- Arvedui, the last King of the North Kingdom in the Third Age, and his wife Fíriel, Princess of Gondor, who made a joint claim for the throne of Gondor in TA 1944

These relationships are depicted in Genealogical Tables 2, 3 and 4.

I now look at the significance of Elendil, Isildur and Anárion individually before discussing their combined influence on Aragorn's life.

Elendil

Elendil, son of Amandil, was the most senior member of the royal line of Númenor to survive the Downfall, tracing his descent back to his namesake Tar-Elendil (also the son of an Amandil) the Fourth King of Númenor via his eldest child Silmarien. At the time of Tar-Elendil's reign, Númenórean laws of succession had not yet begun to recognise descent via the female line and it had been Silmarien's younger brother who had succeeded to the crown. His line become extinct in SA 3319 when Númenor was destroyed, leaving Elendil as the obvious royal successor. Silmarien had married Elatan of Andúnië and became the fore-mother of the dynasty of the Lords of Andúnië, the eighteenth Lord being Elendil's father Amandil. It had been Amandil who, knowing of Ar Pharazôn's intention of sailing to Valinor, had instigated the plan for his son and grandsons to escape from Númenor in the event of disaster, a plan which was wholeheartedly taken on by Elendil. Amandil himself had then attempted to sail for Valinor hoping to be able to intercede with the Valar - at least on behalf of those who had remained faithful and not fallen under the sway of Sauron. He was never heard of again, though there is a hint in *Ak* 335 that maybe he did reach Valinor and plead the case of the Faithful, given that Elendil and his sons survived. Thus it is perhaps Amandil who should ultimately take the credit for the survival of the line which produced Aragorn forty-one generations later.

The Númenóreans were great mariners and it was during Tar-Elendil's reign that they had first begun to make voyages to Middle-earth where the presence of Sauron cast a shadow over the inhabitants. *Ak* 314-5 describes how in these early years the Númenóreans took pity on Middle-earth bringing help in the form of crops, wine and instruction in agriculture, wood-craft and building. As a result they were revered as *"tall Sea-kings"* and *"kindly kings"*[8] and regarded as gods - a situation which became just a memory as the Second Age progressed and corruption set in, leading some Númenóreans to actually settle in Middle-earth, felling trees for ship-building, helping themselves to resources, taking tribute from the people and dominating them rather than helping and teaching. Since those who remained uncorrupted did not take part in these activities, the arrival of Elendil and his sons in Middle-earth no doubt recalled the era of the *"kindly"* kings rather than the dominant ones. It is significant that Aragorn, on accepting the crown of Gondor, decided to repeat Elendil's own words on his landing in Lindon over three thousand years earlier: *"Out of the Great Sea to Middle-earth I am come. In this place will I abide, and my heirs, unto the ending of the world."*[9]. At this moment Aragorn is described as being *"Tall as the sea-kings of old"*[10].

Elendil is called variously *"the Tall"* by Elrond[11], *"the Fair"* by Faramir[12] and *"the Faithful"* in *UT* 3.2.iii.394 - that is faithful to the Eldar and the Valar, refusing to listen to the lies of Sauron. A description of Elendil's eldest grandson Elendur in *UT* is, by implication, a description of Elendil himself: *"... in his strength and wisdom, and his majesty without pride, one of the greatest, the fairest of the seed of Elendil, **most like to his grandsire**."*[13] [My emphasis]

Elendil was the ancestor whom Aragorn was expected to strive to emulate, as Elrond made clear to him shortly after learning of his feelings for Arwen: *"A great doom awaits you, either to rise above the height of all your fathers since the days of Elendil, or to fall into darkness..."*[14]. It is clear in *LotR* that he succeeded in this task, and in *RoP* it is stated that he turned out to be *"... more like to Elendil than any before him."*[15] To return to Elendur: *UT* 3.1.367-8 (Note 26) also states that Elrond (among others with elvish lifespans), having known Elendur **and** Aragorn, was struck by the great similarity between them, both physically and mentally. Galadriel too recognised Aragorn's potential as she presented him with the Elessar brooch prior to the Fellowship's departure from Lothlórien, saying to him, *"In this hour take the name that was foretold for you, Elessar, **the Elfstone of the House of Elendil!**"*[16] [My emphasis]. She seemed to be recognising him as a precious jewel of the House of Elendil.

Although it had been Isildur who had cut the Ring from Sauron's hand, this only happened after Elendil and Gil-galad had wrestled with him and thrown him down. Also the sword Isildur used to do the deed was actually Elendil's. This sword became a legend in its own right, and a treasured heirloom of the Kings and Chieftains in the North. There are many examples in *LotR* of the awe and respect felt for this weapon:
- *LotR* 2.2.247, 268: Boromir, at the Council of Elrond, appreciated the potential of the Sword even if he had doubts about its bearer.
- *LotR* 2.8.374: Galadriel regarded it as sufficiently special to give it a sheath which would prevent it being stained or broken - even in defeat.
- *LotR* 3.2.437-8: Éomer was suitably awestruck by it.
- *LotR* 3.6.511: So was Háma in Meduseld.
- *LotR* 3.7.534: The Rohirrim were delighted to have it (and its bearer) at Helm's Deep.
- *LotR* 4.5.664: When Frodo told Faramir of Aragorn's lineage and his possession of Elendil's sword some of his men rejoiced at the thought of the weapon coming to Gondor.
- *LotR* 5.2.780: After confronting Sauron in the Palantír Aragorn told Legolas and Gimli *"Sauron has not forgotten Isildur **and the sword of Elendil**."* [My emphasis].
- *LotR* 5.6.848: At the Battle of the Pelennor Fields the sword is described as *"... the Flame of the West,*

---

8. Op. cit. [2], *Ak*, p. 314 and p. 328 respectively.
9. Op. cit. [1], *LotR* 6.5, p. 967.
10. Op. cit., *LotR* 6.5, p. 968.
11. Op. cit., *LotR* 2.2, p. 242.
12. Op. cit., *LotR* 4.5, p. 678.
13. Op. cit. [3], *UT* 3.1, p. 355.
14. Op. cit. [1], App A.I.v, p. 1059.
15. Op. cit. [2], *RoP*, p. 364.
16. Op. cit. [1], *LotR* 3.8, p. 375.

Andúril like a new fire kindled, Narsil re-forged as deadly as of old".
- *LotR* 6.5.967: One of the titles Faramir gave to Aragorn at his coronation was "*wielder of the Sword Reforged*".

Aragorn himself used the name "Elendil" as a battle-cry on at least three occasions:
- *LotR* 2.5.331 on the Bridge of Khazad-dûm.
- *LotR* 3.1.413 at Parth Galen.
- *LotR* 3.2.433 at the meeting with Éomer who made it clear that the presence of the heir of Elendil in battle would be extremely welcome to the Rohirrim.
- No doubt he used it at the Pelennor Fields and the Morannon as well - it just isn't recorded!

Another heirloom connected with Elendil was the white gem which the kings wore in Arnor instead of a crown. As well as being known as the Star of the North and the Star of the North Kingdom it was also called the Star of Elendil or the Elendilmir. This jewel had descended to Elendil through Silmarien. In addition there was the Rod of Andúnië which Elendil brought with him from Númenor and which subsequently became the chief symbol of royalty in the North Kingdom as the Sceptre of Annúminas. Likewise the Ring of Barahir also survived the drowning of Númenor through being in Elendil's possession. This too had come to him from Silmarien who had been given it by her father. One cannot help wondering if some foresight had been at play here on the part of Tar-Elendil and Silmarien herself.

In addition, *UT* 2.3.293 Note 16 refers to a further legacy of Elendil, namely that he was the author of the account of the drowning of Númenor, *Akallabêth* (see *Ak* 309-338). It also says that he was responsible for the preservation of the story in *UT* concerning the troubled marriage of Aldarion, sixth King of Númenor, and his wife Erendis, which is described as '*one of the few detailed histories preserved from Númenor*'[17]. The first of these would naturally have been a highly important element of Aragorn's history lessons, while the second contains a letter from Gil-galad written sometime in SA 800s to Aldarion's father, Meneldur (fifth King of Númenor), expressing his belief that a servant of Morgoth was giving rise to a new Shadow in the East, and begging help from Númenor.

There seems no reason to doubt that Aragorn's feelings towards Elendil would have been those of unadulterated reverence, an attitude apparently shared by Isildur who, as described in *UT* 3.2.iv.398-401, went to great trouble to ensure the sanctity and secrecy of the hallow on the summit of Mount Eilenaer (Halifirien) where his father's remains were buried.

Isildur

Aragorn's attitude to Isildur was much more ambivalent and complex.

On the simplistic level Isildur's failure to destroy the Ring weighed heavily on Aragorn as foreseen by Elrond in TA 2850 on hearing Gandalf's report that an increasing Shadow in Dol Guldur was actually Sauron: "*In the hour that Isildur took the Ring and would not surrender it, this doom was wrought, that Sauron should return.*"[18]. Righting this wrong was Isildur's legacy to Aragorn. He had inherited Isildur's guilt and it was his duty to atone for it. It was clear that he realised this when he told the Council of Elrond his reason for helping in the search for Gollum: "*... it seemed fit that Isildur's heir should labour to repair Isildur's fault*"[19]. He felt a personal responsibility for making amends for his ancestor's weakness.

However there are other significant aspects of Isildur's legacy to him characterised by an element of foresight in each case and these will now be discussed.

The Shards of Narsil

When Isildur became aware of the Orcs attacking at the Gladden Fields he realised that the Enemy not

---
17. Op. cit. [3], *UT* 2.3, p. 293.
18. Op. cit. [2], *RoP*, p. 361.
19. Op. cit. [1], *LotR* 2.2, p. 251.

only greatly outnumbered his party, but also had the advantage of being able to attack from above due to approaching from the top of the sloping river bank. We are told that *"A shadow of foreboding fell upon his heart"*[20] at this point. His reaction was to give the Shards of Narsil to Ohtar his esquire and order him and his companion to save them at whatever cost, even at the risk of being regarded as cowards and deserters. He must have known subconsciously that the Orcs were being drawn by the Ring and would not be driven away easily. Perhaps, suspecting that his end might be near, a flash of foresight told him how crucial his father's broken sword would become in the future.

Ohtar and his companion did eventually get the Shards of Narsil safely to Rivendell where Elrond foretold that the sword would not be reforged *"until the Ruling Ring should be found again and Sauron should return"*[21]. Aragorn himself referred to this prophecy at the Council of Elrond. The legendary Sword that was Broken became a cherished heirloom for Isildur's line and it was the dominant element in the dream verse which prompted Boromir's journey to Rivendell to *"Seek for the Sword that was broken"*[22]. It also featured in Bilbo's *The Riddle of Strider* poem which he wrote for Aragorn: *"Renewed shall be blade that was broken"*[23].

The White Tree

In *LotR* 6.5.971 Gandalf pointed Aragorn to the location of a sapling of the White Tree growing in the hallow at the snow-line on Mount Mindolluin. This sapling was subsequently planted in the Court of the Fountain in the Citadel of Minas Tirith replacing the dead tree which had stood there since the death of the Steward Belecthor II in TA 2872. Aragorn was thus reassured that the line of the White Tree was still going strong and with it the line of Kings - in accordance with the prophecy of Tar-Palantir, twenty-fourth King of Númenor. Gandalf explained to him that a fruit must have been planted there before the kings failed in Gondor or the tree withered. He went on to say, *"though the fruit of the Tree comes seldom to ripeness, yet the life within may then lie sleeping through many long years, and none can foretell the time in which it will awake. Remember this. For if ever a fruit ripens, it should be planted, lest the line die out of the world."*[24]

It was in fact Isildur, more than anyone else, who was responsible for the survival of the White Tree, being himself clearly aware of the significance of Tar-Palantir's prophecy:
- As described in *Ak* 326-7, sometime during the period SA 3262-3319 (that is in the reign of Ar-Pharazôn prior to the downfall of Númenor) he risked his life by going in disguise to the King's court one autumn night, slipping past the guards of the White Tree and taking a fruit from it. At this point he was spotted, but in spite of being wounded he managed to fight his way out and take the fruit to his grandfather (Amandil) who planted it and blessed it. In the spring a sapling started to grow and Isildur, who had been near death from his wounds during the winter, was healed. He had carried out this action because Amandil had explained to his family that Sauron was trying to persuade Ar-Pharazôn to destroy the tree. Soon afterwards this did actually happen.
- When Isildur and his father and brother escaped from the drowning of Númenor he took the sapling in his ship. On establishment of the kingdoms in exile it was planted in front of his home of Minas Ithil.
- In SA 3429 one of Sauron's actions following his seizure of Minas Ithil was to kill the White Tree. When Isildur subsequently escaped down the Anduin and sailed into the North to his father he obviously must have taken a seedling with him as, after the downfall of Sauron, we learn that he planted one in Minas Anor in memory of Anárion. He had obviously taken the precaution of following the advice which Gandalf would give to Aragorn in *LotR* 6.5.972.

According to App B.1086 it seems that this tree survived until TA 1636 when Gondor's King Telemnar died in an outbreak of plague along with his immediate family. The entry for that year states that the White Tree

---

20. Op. [3], *UT* 3.1, p. 353.
21. Op. cit. [2], *RoP*, p. 355.
22. Op. cit. [1], *LotR* 2.2, p. 246.
23. Op. cit., *LotR* 2.2, p. 247.
24. Op. cit., *LotR* 6.5, p. 972.

died too and also that Telemnar's nephew Tarondor, who succeeded him, found a sapling. It is not clear **where** he found it. Was it in the same hallow on Mount Mindolluin and had it too been planted by Isildur? It seems likely given his record of obsessive care for safeguarding the line of the Tree. However it could equally well have been planted by any of the kings in between Isildur and Tarondor.

The same questions can be asked about Aragorn's sapling itself. Had that one also been put there by Isildur? This is possible if we assume that the one Tarondor found was obtained elsewhere. However if Tarondor got his sapling from the hallow on Mount Mindolluin then the one Gandalf and Aragorn found there in 3019 could not have been put there by Isildur - unless he planted two of them, which seems unlikely from Gandalf's reference to the rarity of a ripening fruit. There is a very good case for King Tarondor being responsible for the one found in the hallow in 3019 given his own experience of a dying Tree. It could also have been any king who came after him or indeed, presumably, one of the Stewards who happened to be favourably disposed to the idea of the Kings returning one day.

What is clear is that the fruit which eventually produced Aragorn's sapling in 3019 must have been picked and planted prior to the death of Belecthor II as the tree died at the same time and remained in place, dead, until Aragorn became King. The fact that App B.1088 states that no sapling could be found after Belecthor died indicates that Aragorn's sapling must still have been in its "fruit" state and *"sleeping through many long years"* and therefore undetectable by anyone visiting the hallow. In *LotR* 6.5.971 Aragorn stated that his sapling was less than seven years old - therefore it must have first become visible to a searcher around 3013. I think we can safely assume that Denethor would not have made such a search!

To sum this up, I feel that there would probably have been only the one hallow in Minas Tirith where a White Tree fruit would have been planted as this was where Gandalf took Aragorn in 3019. Assuming this, although the sapling which King Tarondor found could well have been put there by Isildur, the one which Gandalf and Aragorn found could not - except in the unlikely situation of Isildur planting two fruits. Whatever the case, Isildur undoubtedly took it on himself to do all in his power to ensure the survival of the Tree and thus the line of the Kings. He had a similar attitude to the preservation of his father's remains as described in some detail in *UT* 3.2.iv.398-401 During the brief time that he was sole King of Gondor he left instructions to be passed down from king to king about ensuring the secrecy and sacred nature of the hallow on the summit of Eilenaer/Halifirien where Elendil's remains were buried - in the central point of Gondor. Only an heir of Elendil was to be allowed to go there, along with those invited by him. This arrangement lasted until the creation of Rohan under the rule of the Steward Cirion who exchanged oaths of friendship with Eorl. With Eilenaer being now on the border with Rohan and no longer central, Elendil's remains were taken to the tombs of the Kings in Minas Tirith. The Stewards, acting on behalf of the heirs of Elendil, continued to maintain the sanctity and secrecy of the hallow. Isildur's actions regarding the preservation of the White Tree and of the hallow on Mount Mindolluin were in keeping with this. Even if he could not continue to protect the tree himself, he would certainly have left specific instructions for planting a fruit as soon as it ripened, emphasising the importance of secrecy and sanctity.

The next section will emphasise Isildur's foresight, something which I feel must also have been a factor in his actions regarding the Tree. He, not Elendil or Anárion, was the one who took on the responsibility for its survival.

The Paths of the Dead

On March 6th 3019 Aragorn decided to make the journey through the Paths of the Dead. When he told Legolas and Gimli of his decision he answered their questions by reciting the prophecy of Malbeth the Seer who had lived during the time of Kings Araphant and Arvedui of the North Kingdom (TA 1800s-1900s). Malbeth had foreseen a situation where the Dead Men of Dunharrow, who had been cursed by Isildur for failing to keep their oath to fight against Sauron, would be given another chance to fulfil it. They would be called again by *"The heir of him to whom the oath they swore"*[25] who would come from the North driven by need. The words *"... him to whom the oath they swore"* applied of course to Isildur, as Aragorn went on to

---

25. Op. cit. [1], *LotR* 5.2, p. 781.

explain to his friends, telling them how the King of the Mountains had sworn allegiance to Isildur at the time when the kingdom of Gondor was established (i.e. SA 3320). This oath had been taken on the Hill of Erech, the site of a spherical black stone said to have been brought from Númenor by Isildur (though an alternative theory of its origin - also given in *LotR* 5.2 - states that it looked "*Unearthly ... as though it had fallen from the sky, as some believed*"[26]). However prior to the existence of Gondor the Men of the Mountains had supported Sauron, and when Isildur summoned them to fulfil their oath - presumably in SA 3430 when the Last Alliance was formed - they refused. Isildur's reply to their king, as recited by Aragorn to Legolas and Gimli, was as follows: "*Thou shalt be the last king. And if the West prove mightier than thy Black Master, this curse I lay upon thee and thy folk: to rest never until your oath is fulfilled. For this war will last through years uncounted, and **you shall be summoned once again ere the end**.*"[27] [My emphasis]. Such was his wrath and the power of his curse that they were too frightened to actually fight for Sauron, instead fleeing to live in secret places in the mountains until they dwindled and died, becoming the "*Sleepless Dead*"[28] unable to find peace.

This speech of Isildur's shows that he had considerable foresight. He knew that the present King of the Mountains would be the last king, and that the war with Sauron had "*years uncounted*"[29] still to run. Also - most significant as far as Aragorn was concerned - he knew the Men would be summoned again and given a second chance to fulfil their oath. Approximately a hundred and ten years had elapsed between the swearing of the oath and Isildur's summons; Aragorn's summons would not come for another three thousand and thirty years. It must be stressed that this example of Isildur's foresight occurred prior to the downfall of Sauron and the seizing of the Ring. Thus ironically, by taking possession of the Ring, Isildur ensured the accuracy of his own prophecy.

Another issue relating to Aragorn's summoning of the Dead is the matter of the horn he used for the purpose. It appears to have been brought specifically from Rivendell as Elrohir produced it when the Grey Company reached Erech. This suggests that it had either been made specially for the occasion, or had actually belonged to Isildur and been left by him in Rivendell until it was time for the prophecy to be fulfilled. The words of Malbeth on the subject support these interpretations as shown by the words I have emphasised in the following quotation from his prophecy as recited by Aragorn in *LotR* 5.2.781:

> .... *The Dead awaken;*
> *for the hour is come for the oathbreakers:*
> *at the Stone of Erech they shall stand again*
> *and **hear there a horn in the hills ringing.***
> ***Whose shall the horn be?** Who shall call them*
> *from the grey twilight, the forgotten people?*
> ***The heir of him to whom the oath they swore.***

There were other horns available to Aragorn - Halbarad had one for instance - but Elrond had clearly seen the necessity for this particular one to be used.

*

Consideration of some of the similarities and differences between Isildur and Aragorn helps us to understand the latter's ambivalent attitude towards this particular ancestor.

UT refers to Isildur as "*... a man of strength and endurance that few even of the Dúnedain of that age could equal*"[30]. Aragorn too had outstanding strength and endurance - but the Dúnedain in the Third Age did not have the stature of their forebears from Númenor. Hammond & Scull refer to a note written by Tolkien around 1969

---

26. Op. cit. [1], *LotR* 5.2, p. 789.
27. Op. cit., *LotR* 5.2, p. 782.
28. Op. cit., *LotR* 5.2, p. 782.
29. Op. cit., *LotR* 5.2, p. 782.
30. Op. cit. [3], *UT* 3.1, p. 356.

stating that Elendil and Isildur were both seven feet tall - as opposed to Aragorn's six foot six.[31] Lifespans too had dwindled over the centuries: Elendil was about three hundred and twenty-two when he died and Isildur about two hundred and thirty-three - and both were killed prematurely while still in their prime. Compare this with Aragorn giving up his life at two hundred and ten because he knew his mind and body were beginning to fail.

Isildur is also described as "... *a man of great pride and vigour*"[32]. With this went self-belief and self-confidence as shown by his willingness to take on his father's dual kingship of Arnor and Gondor, his tireless efforts to protect heirlooms, his preservation of the sanctity of the White Tree and his father's burial place, not to mention his support of his father at the final battle with Sauron and his quick reaction of cutting the Ring from Sauron's hand. However his pride led him to reject the advice of Elrond and Círdan. He believed himself entitled to keep the Ring, partly as recompense for the death of his father and brother and partly because he was the one who had actually dealt Sauron his death blow - by depriving him of the Ring. He had confidence in his ability to wield the Ring and was complacent enough to think his troubles were now all over. *RoP* states that as he stopped for the night at the Gladden Fields on his way north he was "*heedless and set no guard, deeming that all his foes were overthrown.*"[33] Generally in *LotR* Aragorn did not appear to think highly of himself and displayed a distinct lack of complacency - except perhaps in underestimating the strength required to confront Sauron in the Palantír of Orthanc. In many ways it was Boromir rather than Aragorn who resembled Isildur.

Aragorn often blamed himself for things going wrong - as exemplified particularly by his demeanour at Parth Galen on the breakup of the Fellowship. There is no indication of this tendency in Isildur until his realisation that he was not strong enough to wield the Ring. In *UT* we are told that he intended to go to Rivendell on the way to Arnor as he had "*an urgent need for the counsel of Elrond.*"[34] When battle ensued at the Gladden Fields he told his son Elendur he dreaded the pain of touching the Ring and admitted that he hadn't found the strength to bend it to his will, recognising that, "*It needs one greater than I now know myself to be. My pride has fallen. It should go to the Keepers of the Three.*"[35] Like Boromir would, he realised he had done wrong by succumbing to the lure of the Ring and, like Boromir, he was big enough to admit it - albeit too late. He was prepared to eat humble pie and seek help from Elrond.

These comparisons help to explain Aragorn's feelings about Isildur. Part of his *raison d'être* was to atone for Isildur's weakness, yet on the other hand he revered his illustrious ancestor, as illustrated by his words at the Council of Elrond, "*Little do I resemble the figures of Elendil and Isildur as they stand carven in their majesty in the halls of Denethor. I am but the heir of Isildur, not Isildur himself.*"[36]. Also when the Fellowship passed the Argonath his reverence for the place was clear: "*Long have I desired to look upon the likenesses of Isildur and Anárion, my sires of old.*"[37]. Leaving the Ring issue aside Isildur had been a great king, so while Aragorn strove to make amends for his ancestor's weakness in succumbing to the Ring, he also strove to emulate his greatness and courage. In addition Isildur - by his foresight regarding the Paths of the Dead and his care for the White Tree - had given Aragorn plenty to be grateful for.

As it turned out Aragorn was stronger - mentally - than Isildur as shown by his resistance of the Ring, his psychological battle with Sauron in the Palantír, his journey through the Paths of the Dead and his tireless healing after Pelennor Fields: all mental struggles. He defeated Sauron by deceiving and frightening him and making him act foolishly. Isildur may have defeated Sauron's bodily form, but Aragorn defeated his mind, because his own mind/will proved stronger than Sauron's - and stronger than Isildur's because he refused to consider trying to take the Ring.

*

---

31. W.G. Hammond and C. Scull, *The Lord of the Rings: a Reader's Companion,* London, HarperCollins Publishers, 2005, p. 272, (referring to the Tolkien Papers, Bodleian Library, Oxford).
32. Op. cit. [3], *UT* 3.1, p. 351.
33. Op. cit. [2], *RoP*, p. 354.
34. Op. cit. [3], *UT* 3.1, p. 351.
35. Op. cit., *UT* 3.1, p. 354.
36. Op. cit. [1], *LotR* 2.2, p. 248.
37. Op. cit., *LotR* 2.9, p. 393.

I now examine the significance of two of Isildur's sons, Elendur and Valandil, to Aragorn's inheritance.

Elendur

Elendur was the eldest of Isildur's four sons and, along with the second and third sons, was with his father in the South, went to battle with him as part of the Last Alliance, and accompanied him as he set off for the North in TA 2. As described in *UT* 3.1.353-4 he was completely in Isildur's confidence regarding the Ring, and at the Gladden Fields when it became clear that the Orcs were going to be victorious he suggested to his father that he use the Ring to overcome them. Isildur explained that he was not strong enough to wield it and only wanted to get it to Rivendell. By now the two younger sons were fatally injured and Elendur commanded Isildur to escape with the Ring even if it meant abandoning his few surviving men - just as Isildur himself had commanded Ohtar to get the Shards of Narsil to safety. It is clear from their conversation that Isildur knew the Ring was going to cause not only his own death but also that of his three eldest sons and all his men (bar the two who took the Shards of Narsil and the one who happened to be hidden by Elendur's dead body): "*Forgive me, and my pride that has brought you to this doom.*"[38] It is clear too that Elendur's love and support for his father were such that he willingly accepted his doom.

To quote from *UT* again: "*So perished Elendur, who should afterwards have been King .... one of the greatest, the fairest of the seed of Elendil, most like to his grandsire.*"[39] This was the man whom Elrond recalled nearly three thousand years later while watching Aragorn grow up, noting the similarity between them in looks and character: "*So long was it before he* [Elendur] *was avenged.*"[40]. Thus the implication is that Aragorn avenged the death of Elendur which was caused by Isildur's decision to keep the Ring.

Valandil

Valandil was Isildur's fourth and youngest son, and was living safely in Rivendell during the final struggle with Sauron at the end of the Second Age. App A.I.ii.1038 states that he was actually born there. His namesake was Valandil, son of Silmarien, who became the First Lord of Andúnië. By choosing this name Isildur emphasised the high lineage of his line.

HoM-e XII.7.192 gives Valandil's birth-date as SA 3430, the year after Sauron's attack on Minas Ithil which led to Isildur, his wife and their children escaping down the Anduin and sailing north. Valandil would therefore have been conceived either just before the escape or after his parents' arrival in the North. Since full-scale war was now imminent with the formation of the Last Alliance it was only wise for mother and child to be in the safety of Elrond's refuge. In the event it was Valandil who ensured the continuation of Isildur's line as after the events at the Gladden Fields he was the only surviving son (and surviving child? there is no reference to any daughters), being thirteen when his father died.

Valandil was also significant as the first possessor of the Shards of Narsil after their safe conveyance to Rivendell, and the first King to wear the replacement Elendilmir made by the Elven-smiths of Rivendell. The original one which Elendil brought from Númenor was lost with Isildur's body in the Anduin and would not be found until early in the Fourth Age.

Anárion

It is clear from Aragorn's reaction to the images at the Argonath - referred to earlier - that his reverence applied equally to Anárion. When Minas Ithil was attacked by Sauron, and Isildur escaped down the river, it was Anárion who held Osgiliath against Sauron and even drove him back for the time being. It was his realisation that this respite was only temporary which led to the decision to form the Last Alliance. During the siege of Barad-dûr Anárion appears to have been in the thick of things and the stone which killed him may well have been specifically aimed at him.

---

38. Op. cit. [3], *UT* 3.1, p. 355.
39. Op. cit., *UT* 3.1, p. 355.
40. Op. cit., *UT* 3.1, p. 368 (Note 26).

Anárion played a less visible role in shaping Aragorn's destiny partly because the direct male descent was via Isildur's line and partly because, being already dead by the time of the final showdown with Sauron, he had no involvement with his elder brother's decision to keep the Ring. However *UT* contains information on Anárion's son, Meneldil, which gives some scope for speculation on the relationship between the families of Isildur and Anárion and on the long-term implications for the kingship in Gondor. Before Isildur departed for the North, he handed over the rule of Gondor to Meneldil, and his nephew politely wished him all the best for his journey. Meneldil is described as "... *a man of courtesy, but far-seeing and he did not reveal his thoughts.*"[41] The note also states that he was glad to see the back of Isildur and his sons and hoped that they would be long occupied with affairs in the North Kingdom.

Meneldil's courtesy and at least **some** of his hidden thoughts are clearly illustrated here, but there are a number of questions and implications arising from this note, for example:
- What did he foresee?
- Did he anticipate evil repercussions from his uncle's decision to keep the Ring?
- Was it fear of being caught up in these repercussions which made him wish to have Isildur's family out of the way?
- Or was it just that he found Isildur overbearing and wanted to be his own boss?
- Had Isildur been overbearing to Anárion too?
- What additional thoughts was Meneldil keeping hidden?

It is tempting to see here the first stirrings of the hostility displayed by Gondor to Isildur's line. This hostility would later manifest itself in the rejection of the claim of Arvedui and Fíriel to the throne of Gondor in TA 1944 following the deaths of the King (Ondoher) and his two sons. Although Arvedui was directly descended from Isildur (being at this time heir apparent to the North Kingdom) and his wife Fíriel was directly descended from Anárion (being now the dead king's only surviving child), the Steward Pelendur and the Council of Gondor preferred a male claimant from a junior branch of Anárion's line. When this junior line died out two generations later, Gondor was ruled by Stewards rather than an approach being made to the line of Isildur. This attitude was exemplified by Denethor II in *LotR* when he said to Gandalf, "*I am Steward **of the House of Anárion** .... Even were his* [Aragorn's] *claim proved to me, still he comes **but of the line of Isildur.**"*[42] [My emphasis].

Further to the question of Meneldil's attitude, his hope that Isildur and his sons would find plenty to occupy them in Arnor implied that he recognised Isildur's position as high king of both kingdoms and thought it possible that he might come back south at some point. Such an attitude actually supported Arvedui's later claim and counteracted the argument put forward by Pelendur that Isildur had given up his claim to Gondor when he handed over to Meneldil.

Whatever the arguments for and against, the lines of Isildur and Anárion did become separated and the attempt by Arvedui and Fíriel to unite them again failed due - at least in part - to hostility to Isildur's line. In *UT* Isildur is described as "*second King of all the Dúnedain, lord of Arnor and Gondor*"[43]. The next such king didn't succeed until over three thousand years later in the person of Aragorn.

*

I now look at the significance, in *LotR*, of Aragorn's "heir of ..." titles and how the mode of addressing him varies according to circumstances and the desired effect. For example when it came to validating his claim to the kingship of Gondor it was necessary to stress his descent from Elendil rather than Isildur in certain situations, while sometimes referring to him as the heir of Isildur was more appropriate/relevant. In other situations it was a combination of titles which best fitted requirements.

---

41. Op. cit. [3], *UT* 3.1, p. 362 (Note 10).
42. Op. cit. [1], *LotR* 5.7, pp. 853-4.
43. Op. cit. [3], *UT* 3.1, p. 357.

"Heir of Elendil"

As a general observation, Elendil was indisputably the first king of both kingdoms and ultimately the one on whom Aragorn's joint claim depended. This was confirmed by Gandalf quoting from the Scroll of Isildur at the Council of Elrond: *"The Great Ring shall go now to be an heirloom of the North Kingdom; but records of it shall be left in Gondor, where also dwell the heirs of Elendil"*[44]. Thus Aragorn's descent from Elendil tended to be stressed whenever it was necessary to show him as having a valid claim to Gondor (there was no question-mark over his claim to Arnor), or alternatively where the context indicated an heirloom of Elendil's House. For example:

- At the Council of Elrond Aragorn put much emphasis on the House of Elendil, partly to stress to Boromir his right to the kingship of Gondor, and partly because Boromir had come to investigate a dream concerning Elendil's sword.
- Later (*LotR* 2.8.368) as the Fellowship prepared to leave Lothlórien we are told that Aragorn believed that the dream meant that the time was near when the heir of Elendil should come forward and strive with Sauron - Elendil was the one who had actually striven with Sauron.
- At Meduseld when Aragorn was reluctant to leave his sword outside, he queried with Háma as to whether Théoden's will should take precedence over that of *"Elendil's heir of Gondor"* then, on eventually agreeing to leave the sword, he predicted death *"... to any man that draws Elendil's sword save Elendil's heir"*.[45] The dual emphasis in this incident was on his descent from Elendil rather than Isildur thus stressing the right to the throne of Gondor, and on the fact that the subject being discussed was Elendil's sword.
- In *LotR* 5.1.753 a description of the livery of the Guards of the Citadel makes it clear that this livery was that of the heirs of Elendil.
- Similarly, after the Battle of the Pelennor Fields (*LotR* 5.8.861), Éomer referred to the tokens of Elendil's House, meaning the sword and the Elendilmir.

"Heir of Isildur"

On some occasions, even in the context of kingship in Gondor, it is descent from Isildur which is particularly relevant:

- When Aragorn formally summoned the Dead Men of Dunharrow at the Stone of Erech, he raised the standard of Gondor and announced himself as *"Elessar, Isildur's heir of Gondor."*[46] This was essential to enact the prophecy and let the Dead know his identity. It was Isildur who had cursed them for not fulfilling their oath to support him against Sauron - and he had been King of Gondor at the time.
- Similarly, during the ride to Pelargir accompanied by the Dead, he bade Angbor of Lamedon gather his men and follow him saying, *"At Pelargir the Heir of Isildur will have need of you"*[47]. When the black ships of the Corsairs had been taken with the assistance of the Dead, Aragorn dismissed them with the following words: *"Hear now the words of the Heir of Isildur! Your oath is fulfilled ... Depart and be at rest!"*[48]
- A further quality of the title "Isildur's heir" was its significance for Sauron, indicating as it did someone (who might, or might not, exist) descended from the Man responsible for robbing him of the Ring. The "heir of Isildur" was Sauron's obsession, and the reason for his relentless war on the North Kingdom during the second millennium of the Third Age.

---

44. Op. cit. [1], *LotR* 2.2, p. 252.
45. Op. cit., *LotR* 3.6, pp. 510-11.
46. Op. cit., *LotR* 5.2, p. 789.
47. Op. cit., *LotR* 5.9, p. 875.
48. Op. cit., *LotR* 5.9, p. 876.

"Heir of Anárion"

Aragorn was in fact also directly descended from Anárion but via the female line which Gondor failed to recognise. So although he never used the title "heir of Anárion" it would in fact have been a perfectly valid one.

"Heir of Valandil"

At the Council of Elrond Aragorn addressed the following speech to Boromir: "*For here* [in the North] *the heirs of Valandil have ever dwelt in long line unbroken from father unto son for many generations. Our days have darkened, and we have dwindled; but ever the Sword has passed to a new keeper.*"[49] The reference to Valandil is because he was the first owner of the Shards of Narsil after Isildur sent them north, and Aragorn, as his heir, was the current owner. Boromir was seeking the Sword that was Broken.

Combination

Very often two or more of Aragorn's ancestors needed to be referenced:
- In *LotR* Elrond introduced him to Boromir as "*Aragorn son of Arathorn*", the descendant of "*Isildur Elendil's son of Minas Ithil*".[50] The descent from Elendil as well as that from Isildur was emphasised: even if the Stewards of Gondor were reluctant to consider an heir of Isildur, the descent from Elendil was more difficult to ignore seeing as Elendil had been indisputably recognised as King of both kingdoms. Also Elrond's linking of Isildur with Minas Ithil emphasised Isildur's own connection with Gondor: his home, when ruling jointly with Anárion, had been in Minas Ithil.
- When the Fellowship passed through the Argonath during their river voyage Aragorn referred to Isildur and Anárion (represented by the statues) as "*my sires of old*", then proclaimed himself, "*Elessar, the Elfstone son of Arathorn of the House of Valandil Isildur's son, heir of Elendil*".[51] Elendil, Isildur, Valandil and - by implication - Anárion were all referred to as his ancestors, thus leaving no doubt as to his right to pass the old northern boundary of Gondor.
- At Aragorn's first encounter with Éomer he referred to himself, among other titles, as "*the heir of Isildur Elendil's son of Gondor*"[52] simultaneously sweeping out his sword, thus drawing attention to his descent from Elendil as the owner of his sword and stressing Isildur's connection with Gondor rather than with the North Kingdom.
- During his confrontation with Sauron in the Palantír (*LotR* 5.2.780), he revealed himself as Isildur's heir wielding the sword of Elendil. It was Isildur, using the sword of Elendil, who had taken the One Ring from Sauron's hand at the end of the Second Age.
- During the Battle of the Pelennor Fields (*LotR* 5.6.847) he sailed up the Anduin as King wearing the Star of the North Kingdom (the Elendilmir) on his brow and displaying the standard of the King of Gondor. It was necessary for him to proclaim to Sauron's armies the presence of Isildur's descendant, with a claim to the **two** kingdoms, thus completing what was begun in the Palantír confrontation.
- At Aragorn's coronation Faramir proclaimed the full list of his titles: "*Here is Aragorn son of Arathorn, chieftain of the Dúnedain of Arnor, Captain of the Host of the West, bearer of the Star of the North, wielder of the Sword Reforged, victorious in battle, whose hands bring healing, the Elfstone, Elessar of the line of Valandil, Isildur's son, Elendil's son of Númenor.*"[53] This speech emphasised Aragorn's descent from Elendil via Isildur and Valandil, drew attention to the heirlooms (the sword and the Elendilmir) and stressed Elendil's Númenórean lineage - as well as Aragorn's by reference to his chieftainship of the Dúnedain.

---

49. Op. cit. [1], *LotR* 2.2, p. 248.
50. Op. cit., *LotR* 2.2, p. 246.
51. Op. cit., *LotR* 2.9, p. 393.
52. Op. cit., *LotR* 3.2, p. 433.
53. Op. cit., *LotR* 6.5, p. 967.

It is noteworthy that when Narsil was reforged as Andúril the device on it included emblems for all three of Aragorn's most significant ancestors, consisting of seven stars - the sign of Elendil - between a crescent moon representing Isildur and a rayed sun representing Anárion (*LotR* 2.3.276). Also when Arwen's standard was unfurled at the Pelennor Fields it too depicted the Seven Stars of Elendil along with a crown representing his high kingship of both kingdoms - in addition to the White Tree of Gondor.

THE RING

This section analyses Aragorn's attitude to the One Ring and also to the Nazgûl.

The Last Alliance was so called because it was the last time Elves and Men joined together to fight Sauron. The two races were still generally on friendly terms at the end of the Second Age and there was particular friendship between Elendil and Gil-galad. *RoP* 348 describes how Gil-galad befriended Elendil when he landed at the Grey Havens after escaping the destruction of Númenor. It is also suggested that it was Gil-galad who had the three towers built for his friend on the Tower Hills. A Palantír (the Elendil-stone) was placed in the tallest tower so that Elendil could look West "*when the yearning of exile was upon him*"[54]. *UT* 3.2.iii.395 refers to the oath of alliance they swore. In the end they died together sacrificing themselves to bring down Sauron. Isildur finished off what they achieved by depriving Sauron of the Ring and thus dealing the "*death-blow*"[55] as he himself referred to it in *RoP*. However he then let himself and everyone else down by refusing to destroy the Ring.

Estrangement between Elves and Men set in during the Third Age, ostensibly because the Elves decreased in number due to many of them leaving Middle-earth, while Men in general multiplied - though the population of the Dúnedain themselves decreased. However it does also seem that the estrangement was partly caused by Isildur's behaviour. Did this add to Aragorn's feeling of personal responsibility for his ancestor's weakness? Did he feel he had to prove to the Elves who had reared, protected and supported him in his youth that a Man could resist the Ring? It was imperative that he found the strength to do this as well as striving to emulate Elendil.

Aragorn must have learnt about Isildur and the Ring as part of his education while growing up in Rivendell ignorant of his own identity. Once he knew who he was he would also have been made aware of the prophecies concerning his own role in defeating Sauron which would only be realised with the finding of the Ring followed by the reforging of the sword of Elendil. His adult life would have been spent waiting for the Ring to be found.

App B.1089 states that in TA 2953 Saruman told a meeting of the White Council that he had discovered that the Ring had been washed down the Anduin and out to sea and was therefore now inaccessible while the world lasted. The friendship between Gandalf and Aragorn began three years later, but it was not until 3001 that Gandalf became seriously suspicious of the nature of Bilbo's ring and confided his fears to Aragorn. At the Council of Elrond when talking of his earlier concerns about this ring he specifically said, "*But I spoke yet of my dread to none*", then went on to make it clear that he only "*opened my heart to Aragorn, the heir of Isildur*" after Bilbo's party.[56] Thus Aragorn would have been ignorant of Gandalf's initial vague uneasiness and of the theories voiced by Saruman at the White Council, theories which Gandalf could never have really believed, especially if he trusted the prophecies about the One Ring and their relevance to the sword and Aragorn's doom. As described in *LotR* Prologue.5, the Shire had been guarded by Rangers since the days of the first Chieftain of the Dúnedain - that is from around TA 1975 - so that activity in itself wouldn't have rung any alarm bells for Aragorn. However after Gandalf started to believe that Bilbo actually had the One Ring, the guard on the Shire was doubled. When speaking to Halbarad about the Hobbits, Aragorn said, "*And now our fates are woven together*"[57]. He must have begun to feel that when Gandalf first confided in him about the Ring.

It was in 3002 that Bilbo settled in Rivendell and Aragorn probably became acquainted with him soon afterwards as there are indications in *LotR* that they were long-standing friends by the time of the War of the Ring. He would undoubtedly have perceived the effect the Ring had had on Bilbo, for example his extremely

---

54. Op. cit. [2], *RoP*, p. 350.
55. Op. cit., *RoP*, p. 354.
56. Op. cit. [1], *LotR* 2.2, p. 251.
57. Op. cit., *LotR* 5.2, p. 780.

long life and - at least at the time of his arrival in Rivendell - youthful appearance, as well as the psychological effects from being deprived of it. The other significant outcome of Gandalf's revelations about the Ring was that Aragorn spent much time between 3001-3017 searching for Gollum, sometimes with Gandalf, sometimes alone. In 3017, alone on this occasion, he succeeded in capturing him and taking him to the Elf-king Thranduil in Mirkwood Forest. During this journey he would have seen a far more extreme example of the effects of the Ring, illustrated not least by the fact that Gollum was still alive and physically strong, at over five hundred years old. (The average life-span for a Hobbit seems to have been around ninety to a hundred.) At the far end of the spectrum were the Nazgûl, former possessors of the Nine Rings. They were now well over four thousand years old, permanently invisible and so much under the sway of Sauron that they would have taken the One Ring straight to him if they were to obtain it (as stated in *UT* 3.4.ii.443).

By the time Aragorn met Frodo he must have been steeped in theoretical knowledge about the Ring, having witnessed the effects of it and of being deprived of it. However he lacked any direct exposure to it and this was only acquired because Gandalf went missing during the summer and early autumn of 3018 leaving Aragorn to take on the task of protecting Frodo and guiding him to Rivendell. As a result Aragorn had to get used to the idea, at very short notice, of coming into close contact with the Ring. As he followed the Hobbits to Bree after witnessing their parting from Tom Bombadil he knew that he was building up to his first such encounter. He could not have known how he himself would react to being in such close proximity to the Ring and must have been extremely apprehensive of such a situation, not to mention frightened at the possibility of succumbing to its power.

Before considering Aragorn's practical experience of the Ring, I give a brief listing, for the purpose of discussion and comparison, of the effect of the Ring on some of the other characters in *LotR*, as shown by specific encounters with it or by general attitudes held:

- Bilbo had possessed it for sixty years and only gave it up with Gandalf's help. During a confrontation with Gandalf Bilbo accused him of wanting the Ring for himself (*LotR* 1.1.34) prompting a display of power on Gandalf's part to make the Hobbit see the sense of parting with it. This occurred before either party knew the true nature of Bilbo's ring.
- In *LotR* 1.2.61 Frodo asked Gandalf to take the Ring. The Wizard reacted violently ordering Frodo not to tempt him. By this stage he knew what the Ring was and realised that even if he took it only to keep it safe the temptation to use it would be too much for him.
- Frodo offered the Ring to Galadriel. She freely admitted that she had long wanted it but when it came to the crunch she refused it because, as she told Sam when he urged her to take it and make folk pay for their dirty work, "*That is how it would begin. But it would not stop with that, alas!*"[58].
- Boromir tried to take the Ring from Frodo by force, believing he would be able to wield it to save Gondor from Sauron. He later realised he was wrong and repented (*LotR* 2.10.399-400).
- In *LotR* 4.5 Faramir found out unexpectedly - due to Sam letting the information slip - that "Isildur's Bane" which Frodo carried was in fact Sauron's One Ring. He reacted by speaking softly "*with a strange smile*", then sprang to his feet, eyes glinting, as if about to try and take the Ring, then sat down again and "*began to laugh quietly*"[59]. There must have been an element of shock here from the suddenness of the revelation coupled with the realisation that Frodo and Sam were totally at his mercy so that he could easily take the Ring from them. The fact that he had already made a promise (before he knew what it was) that he wouldn't take "Isildur's Bane" even if he found it by the roadside, along with his appreciation of the inherent evil in the Ring as exemplified by what had happened to Boromir, enabled him to resist it.
- Denethor believed himself capable of keeping the Ring safe in the vaults of the citadel in Minas Tirith and only using it in direst need. Gandalf knew the Steward would not be able to resist using it (*LotR* 5.4.814).
- Sam took the Ring in Cirith Ungol when he thought Frodo was dead intending to carry on the quest,

---
58. Op. cit. [1], *LotR* 2.7, p. 366.
59. Op. cit., *LotR* 4.5, pp. 680-1.

then used it to help him rescue Frodo (*LotR* 4.10.732-3). His love for Frodo enabled him to resist its corruption, but he was nevertheless reluctant to hand it back even though he had only had it briefly (*LotR* 6.1.911-12).
- Gollum possessed the Ring for four hundred and seventy-eight years. By the time of the War of the Ring he had been deprived of it for seventy-seven years, and was desperate to track down the "thief" who had taken it (App B.1087, 1089).
- Elrond would have had close contact with the Ring while healing Frodo's Nazgûl-inflicted wound. In addition some of his people put the Ring on a chain for Frodo. The Elves - and Elrond in particular - were well aware of the damage done in the Second Age by the Elves of Eregion putting their trust in Sauron, and more recently of the repercussions of Isildur keeping the Ring. Thus the chances of them yielding to temptation - or even being tempted in the first place - were slim.
- The members of the Fellowship were obviously in close contact with the Ring while they were travelling with Frodo:
  - Of these Boromir, the Man, would prove most vulnerable.
  - The Hobbits were held from serious temptation by their general nature and their regard for Frodo.
  - Legolas, as an Elf and now fully aware of the evil in the Ring from his attendance at the Council, would not have been easily tempted.
  - Gimli, as well as benefiting from the knowledge at the Council, had witnessed the harassment of his own folk by Sauron's servants as they attempted to recover the Ring. In addition his Dwarvish nature gave him a high resistance to corruption anyway.
  - Gandalf had already admitted to being tempted by the Ring in *LotR* 1.2.61 when Frodo asked him to take it at Bag End. On being reunited with Aragorn, Legolas and Gimli and learning that Frodo, Sam and the Ring were on the way to Mordor, he expressed relief that *"We can no longer be tempted to use the Ring."*[60]. He had actually been with Frodo very little during his journey from the Shire to Parth Galen - just from Rivendell to Moria - and there is no indication of close physical contact between him and Frodo such as experienced by Aragorn while healing.

*

Aragorn first saw the Ring in action when Frodo put it on in the bar of the Prancing Pony (*LotR* 1.9.160-1). During the private conversation which took place afterwards between him and the Hobbits he told them that he could take the Ring there and then if he wanted to, standing towering over them with his hand on his sword-hilt. This could be interpreted as evidence that he was being tempted by the Ring, but I believe that in this scene he was merely making a desperate attempt to convince the Hobbits that they must accept him as their guide. His wry comment a few minutes later, about the sword he had been handling not being much use because it was broken, just serves to emphasise the point. Barliman Butterbur had been advising the Hobbits not to take up with a Ranger, and Sam was persisting in his distrust even though Frodo and Pippin had been won over. Aragorn had to make them (Sam in particular) see that even though he was strong enough to take the Ring, and must have been feeling the pull of it, he chose not to because he was trying to help them.

In *LotR* 1.11.189 as he and the Hobbits reached Weathertop he told Frodo that the Nazgûl were drawn towards them because of the Ring. He would have acquired such knowledge from sources such as Elrond or Gandalf, but it was not until the attack on Weathertop that he actually witnessed such an event. The gathering of the available Nazgûl and Frodo's yielding to the pressure to put on the Ring followed by the physical attack on Frodo by the Lord of the Nazgûl must have been just as traumatic for Aragorn as for the Hobbits. It was one thing knowing the theory, quite another to actually have to put theory into practice in a life/death situation. In the event it seems that the urgent need to protect Frodo and the Ring overcame his fear sufficiently for him to drive the Nazgûl off with flaming brands.

Although, unlike with Gandalf and Galadriel, Frodo did not actually offer Aragorn the Ring, an incident at the Council of Elrond amounted to an indirect offer which he rejected. This occurred when Boromir queried

---

60. Op. cit. [1], *LotR* 3.5, p. 500.

the identity of the Ranger with the lean face and weather-stained cloak who had just deposited a broken sword on the table. In response to Elrond's introduction of Aragorn as the direct heir of Isildur, Frodo exclaimed, "*Then it* [the Ring] *belongs to you, and not to me at all!*" leaping to his feet "*as if he expected the Ring to be demanded at once.*"[61]. Aragorn's reply was that it did not belong to either of them but that it had been ordained that Frodo should hold it for a while. He then went on to refer to the prophecy which stated that Elendil's sword would be reforged when the Ring was found. The implication of the prophecy was that the sword, in the hands of the heir of the House of Elendil, would now finish the job it had started but which had failed because Isildur had kept the Ring. Isildur had regarded the Ring as an heirloom of his House (as shown in his Scroll cited by Gandalf at the Council). As far as Aragorn was concerned it was most definitely **not** an heirloom and did not belong to him any more than it did to Frodo. This was Aragorn's official rejection of the Ring, made publicly in front of the members of the Council. Although the Council would debate the matter for a while yet Aragorn, being in the confidence of Gandalf and with the example of Isildur before him, must have known all along that the only solution was to destroy the Ring in Mount Doom where it had been forged - this being the advice which Isildur had ignored.

In general the Ring was very much "in Aragorn's face" while he travelled with Frodo, particularly during times of close physical contact when tending wounds, as exemplified by two main incidents, namely the aftermath of the Nazgûl attack on Weathertop, and the dressing of Frodo's wounds after the escape from Moria involving the removal of clothing on Frodo's upper body. In the first of these it would have been easy for Aragorn to take the Ring with only the terrified Hobbits to withstand him. In the second it would have been much more difficult with the other members of the Fellowship being present, but the temptation would have been greater because Frodo was wearing the Ring on a chain around his neck and Aragorn could therefore hardly have avoided touching it. In fact Frodo appeared to be more worried about his mithril shirt being discovered than about any imaginary threat to the Ring. There was also the ten-day river journey spent in close contact with Frodo and Sam in a small boat.

When the Fellowship started out from Rivendell, the intention had been for Aragorn and Boromir to leave the Company at the River Anduin and make for Minas Tirith together. Instead, due to the loss of Gandalf, Aragorn ended up leading the Company and by the time they reached Parth Galen had accepted that he would probably have to accompany Frodo into Mordor. In the event everything turned out differently due to Boromir's attempt to take the Ring, followed by the uncanny scattering of the Fellowship. Aragorn would have no further exposure to the Ring.

*

Overall Aragorn seemed to display a remarkable resistance to the Ring, either because he really felt no temptation or because his self-control and his commitment to its destruction were sufficient to prevent any weakness. The following observations are also relevant:
- He was eighty-seven in TA 3018 and his mission in life of undoing the evil caused by Isildur's failure to destroy the Ring must have long been deeply ingrained in his psyche.
- He knew what the Ring could do - even to his illustrious ancestor who was, after all, one of the Faithful of Númenor who realised the evil that Sauron was doing. He must have known very well that he had nothing to gain from seizing the Ring. Isildur's case must have greatly strengthened his resolve - just as Faramir's would be strengthened by his knowledge of what had happened to Boromir.
- He had also now witnessed the effect of the Ring on Frodo. As well as the shock of seeing him disappear in such a dramatic fashion the implication that the Ring itself may have been partly or wholly responsible for Frodo's behaviour in the inn and on Weathertop must have been extremely disturbing.
- He held Elrond, Gandalf and Galadriel in the highest regard, affection and trust. Succumbing to the lure of the Ring would have been a complete betrayal of these people who loved him and believed in him and had themselves refused to wield the Ring.
- At his betrothal to Arwen (described in App A.I.v) nearly forty years earlier, she had told him that she

---
61. Op. cit. [1], *LotR* 2.2, p. 247.

rejoiced in spite of the darkness of the Shadow because she knew that he would be "... *among the great whose valour will destroy it.*". Although he could not foresee this himself, he was buoyed up by her hope telling her, "... *the Shadow I utterly reject*"[62]. More than anything else the depth of Arwen's faith in him would have strengthened his will to resist the Ring.

Thus Aragorn, more than anyone, had the strongest of motives **not** to take the Ring. Nevertheless it is difficult to believe that its sudden unexpected proximity did not impose an additional burden of stress on him.

His reaction to the Nazgûl was similar. He demonstrated a considerable ability to withstand them, including being apparently immune to their Black Breath, but this was not achieved without considerable suffering on his part, as shown at his first meeting with Frodo and his companions where he displayed hatred, fear and pain. For example his eyes were "*cold and hard*" as he spoke of them and he described them as "*terrible*" before clutching the arms of his chair, eyes unseeing and face "*drawn as if with pain*". When he recovered he made it clear to the Hobbits that they were underestimating the danger of the creatures: "*You fear them, but you do not fear them enough, yet.*"[63]. At this point in the story he was afraid that the Nazgûl might have been responsible for Gandalf's disappearance, an indication of the level of danger with which he associated them. His hatred of the Nazgûl would have been triggered partly by the fear they invoked in others: even the Dúnedain at Sarn Ford had not been able to withstand them when they were all together (*UT* 3.4.i.441), and weaker characters were easily driven to evil by such fear. Was his hatred also due to the fact that the Nazgûl, like Isildur, had succumbed to Sauron even though some of them had originally been great Númenóreans? Was hatred a factor in spurring him on during the attack on Weathertop?

The Lord of the Nazgûl would have aroused particularly strong emotions in him as he was the one who had been chiefly responsible for the devastating effect on the Rangers and it was he who dealt Frodo his wound. Also for six hundred years, as the Witch king of Angmar, he had pursued his master's savage vendetta on the Northern Dúnedain with the chief aim of wiping out Isildur's line.

In Chapter 1.4 I raised the possibility of Aragorn encountering Nazgûl in their "unclothed" state during his travels prior to mid-3018. Although such experiences would have given him an idea of what he was up against they would also have served to increase his dread of future encounters.

*

Returning to Aragorn's ancestors: we know very well how Isildur reacted to the Ring, but how would Elendil, Elendur and Anárion have reacted to it?

With Anárion there is only pure speculation to go on as he died before the last physical combat with Sauron, though maybe his son's anxiety to get Isildur and his family out of Gondor indicated misgivings about that branch of the family and perhaps pointed to Anárion as being someone who would have been more likely to take the advice of Elrond and Círdan concerning the Ring. There doesn't seem to be much information about Anárion's character apart from the fact that he clearly had the prowess and courage to drive Sauron back from Osgiliath following the attack on Minas Ithil and to take on a prominent role in the Battle of Dagorlad and the following Siege of Barad-dûr.

Regarding Elendur there is more to go on, namely in his last conversation with his father at the Gladden Fields (described in *UT* 3.1.354-5). Knowing that Isildur had the Ring, he made the obvious suggestion that it should be used to control and overcome the Orcs who were attacking their party. When Isildur explained his dread of the pain from wearing the Ring and his realisation that it needed someone greater than he to wield it, Elendur accepted what he said. From then on his only concerns were that the Ring should be taken to safety and his father relieved of his burden. Thus he told him to leave the battle and get himself and the Ring to Rivendell, freely accepting his own death as the price for this. This does not seem to be the behaviour of someone who would have ignored the advice of Elrond and Círdan, though such an assessment of Elendur is perhaps coloured by the fact that Aragorn was later considered to resemble him. It is also possible that Elendur

---

62. Op. cit. [1], App A.I.v, p. 1061.
63. Op. cit., *LotR* 1.10, p. 165.

may only have arrived at this state of wisdom through seeing someone of his father's calibre and self-assurance being brought down to the level of admitting to pain and weakness, and realising that the Ring was responsible. There is also the question of what Isildur and Elendur actually expected to happen in the event of the Ring reaching Rivendell. Isildur certainly knew that the original advice had been to destroy it, but it is not clear whether Elendur knew this. Did he/they think it could be kept safely in Rivendell? Did they think Elrond would have the strength and willingness to use it? Or was their only concern, as seems most likely, that Isildur should get rid of his burden by passing it on to someone else?

Regarding Elendil himself I feel he would have been most unlikely to have taken possession of the Ring, partly due to the mutual friendship and respect between him and Gil-galad. As Elrond was Gil-galad's herald at the Battle of Dagorlad and the one to whom he gave the Elven ring Vilya before he died I find it difficult to believe that Elendil would have ignored his advice along with that of such an ancient and venerable Elf as Círdan. Círdan too must have been a friend of Elendil since he was the guardian of the Palantír which Elendil used in order to look into the West. In addition, the fact that Elendil was held up as someone for Aragorn to emulate really precludes him being prey to the sort of over-confidence and arrogance displayed by Isildur. To return to Isildur's recognition that wielding the Ring needed "... *one greater than I now know myself to be*"[64]: this greater one of course turned out to be Aragorn who showed his superior greatness by using his strength not to wield this particular "heirloom", but to disown it.

As well as having the potential to rule the Three, the Seven and the Nine, the One Ring ruled Aragorn's destiny. As Elrond said to Frodo when selecting the members of the Fellowship, *"For men you shall have Aragorn son of Arathorn, **for the Ring of Isildur concerns him closely**."*[65] [My emphasis]

GOLLUM

This section examines Aragorn's relationship with Gollum.

Although Gollum was actually a Hobbit I have included him in this chapter, rather than in the Hobbit one, because of his obvious connection with the Ring. There is also his connection with Isildur in Aragorn's mind such that the search for him - in order to find out more about the ring his ancestor had once possessed - became part of the atonement for Isildur's error. Aragorn became involved in this search as a result of Gandalf confiding in him about his suspicions of Bilbo's ring following the farewell party - i.e. when it appeared that the One Ring had been found.

The search

Most of the details about the search for Gollum along with his capture - first by Sauron then by Aragorn - are described in *UT* 3.4.436-459 in which Christopher Tolkien cites several of his father's manuscript writings on the subject. There is also additional information in *LotR* 2.2.251-6 from discussion at the Council of Elrond, and in App B.1089-91. In the introduction to *UT*[66] Christopher Tolkien refers to date discrepancies between *UT* 3.4 and App B, which he attributes to the fact that the manuscripts involved were written **after** the publication of the first volume of *LotR*, but **prior** to that of Volume Three which contained the Appendices. Therefore, where this is an issue, I have followed the dates in App B as being the later - and published - version of the events.

Combining the three sources we learn that at some time between 3009-17 Gollum, (who had been conducting his own search for the Ring - and for the "thief" who had stolen it - since 2944) ventured close to Mordor and was captured and taken to Barad-dûr for interrogation. The account in *UT* 3.4.i.436 states that Sauron did not trust Gollum because he realised there was something indomitable in him. Being aware of the depth of his malice towards those who had robbed him he released him as soon as he had finished questioning him assuming he would carry on his search for the "thief" and thus inadvertently lead the spies of Barad-dûr to the Ring. However this plan was foiled by Gollum's recapture by Aragorn almost immediately. App B.1090 gives

---

64. Op. cit. [3], *UT* 3.1, p. 354.
65. Op. cit. [1], *LotR* 2.3, p. 276.
66. Op. cit. [3], *UT* Introduction, p. 16.

the date of his release and of his recapture as 3017 while *UT* 3.4.ii.444 specifies that Aragorn caught Gollum on February 1st.

The search for Gollum was conducted jointly by Gandalf and Aragorn during 3001-4. It then stalled for a while as during 3004-8 Gandalf is recorded as visiting Frodo at intervals and we know (by combining information from App A.I.v.1061 and App B.1090) that Aragorn was in the North during late 3006 visiting his mother who died early in 3007. The entry for 3009 in App B.1090 states that both of them then renewed the hunt at intervals over the next eight years, searching in the Anduin vales, Mirkwood and the rest of Rhovanion down to the borders of Mordor. By early 3017 Gandalf despaired of being able to find Gollum, but then had the idea of travelling to Minas Tirith to look in the archives there to see if Isildur had left any record of the secret markings which were supposed to be on the One Ring, in the hope of being able to make a positive identification of Bilbo's ring. Aragorn carried on searching alone until he also gave up in despair and began the homeward journey. However it was at this point that he found Gollum's trail at the edge of the Dead Marshes and succeeded in capturing him soon afterwards. Meanwhile Gandalf had read the Scroll of Isildur which contained a copy of the inscription on the Ring.

The account in *UT* 3.4.ii.444-5 gives details of Aragorn's journey after the capture:
- He drove Gollum through the north end of the Emyn Muil.
- He crossed the Anduin just above Sarn Gebir, tying his captive to a log and swimming across with him.
- Staying as far west as possible he went through the skirts of Fangorn, then crossed the Rivers Limlight, Nimrodel and Silverlode and went through the eaves of Lothlórien.
- Avoiding Moria and the Dimrill Dale, he crossed the River Gladden then carried on until he drew near to the Carrock where the Beornings helped him cross the Anduin again.
- He then entered Mirkwood Forest reaching Thranduil's residence on March 21st 3017.

This route was chosen to reduce the chance of being detected by Sauron's spies. Two days after he reached Thranduil, Gandalf arrived there too. He had been on his way back from reading the Scroll of Isildur, when he received the news of Gollum's capture by Aragorn via messengers from Lothlórien.

*

The moment of Gollum's capture is described by Aragorn as he gave his report to the Council of Elrond: "*And then, by fortune, I came suddenly on what I sought: the marks of soft feet beside a muddy pool... Along the skirts of the Dead Marshes I followed it, and then I had him. Lurking by a stagnant mere, **peering in the water as the dark eve fell, I caught him, Gollum. He was covered with green slime.***"[67] [My emphasis]. A bit further on in his account he described the handing over of Gollum to Thranduil with the words, "*I was glad to be rid of his company, **for he stank**.*"[68] [My emphasis]. There is a passage in *LotR* 4.2 which also seems to relate to Gollum's capture - though this is not actually stated. During the journey of Frodo, Sam and Gollum through the Dead Marshes Sam saw dead faces in the pools and, realising that the bodies couldn't really be there, queried whether it was some devilry from Mordor which was responsible. Gollum's answer was, "*You cannot reach them, you cannot touch them. **We tried once**, yes, precious. **I tried once**; but you cannot reach them.*"[69] [My emphasis]. A little further on, a lot of attention is given to the smell of the marshes and of the Hobbits themselves: "*Often they floundered, stepping or falling hands-first into waters as noisome as a cesspool, **till they were slimed and fouled** almost up to their necks and stank in one another's nostrils.*"[70] [My emphasis]. These passages must surely be linked. Gollum tried once to get to the faces, and while his attention was thus engaged Aragorn was able to take him unawares.

Aragorn had more to say to the Council on his travels with Gollum: "*... he bit me, and I was not gentle ... I*

---
67. Op. cit. [1], *LotR* 2.2, p. 253.
68. Op. cit., *LotR* 2.2, p. 253.
69. Op. cit., *LotR* 4.2, p. 628.
70. Op. cit., *LotR* 4.2, p. 628.

deemed it the worst part of all my journey ... watching him day and night, making him walk before me with a halter on his neck, gagged, until he was tamed by lack of drink and food ..."[71]. It is noteworthy that the usual compassion one associates with Aragorn appears to be lacking here and it is perhaps not surprising that the only thing he ever got from Gollum's mouth was the marks of his teeth - it being left to Gandalf to cajole/threaten information out of him. However there are a number of factors which explain, and even excuse, his attitude. In many ways it is difficult to see how he could have treated Gollum any differently in the circumstances:

- He did not have the advantage which Frodo later had of being able to use the presence of the Ring to persuade Gollum to cooperate.
- The trauma of the search should not be underestimated, with its foulness, risk and protracted nature in some of the most dangerous places Aragorn had travelled in. Gandalf, at the Council of Elrond, voiced considerable concern for him, particularly on account of the solitary nature of his journey at that point: *"Into what deadly perils he had gone alone, I dared not guess."*[72] Although Aragorn brushed the concern aside making out that the hardship he had suffered was only to be expected in the circumstances, his outburst about Gollum just quoted came immediately afterwards. Given that the search had continued on and off for sixteen years he was probably at the end of his tether by the time he actually found Gollum.
- Gollum had bitten him after grubbing around in the cesspit-like filth of the Dead Marshes, thus no doubt incurring a high risk of infection in his victim. We know Aragorn was tough but he was at a particularly low ebb at this point.
- According to *UT* 3.4.ii.444 the journey from the Dead Marshes to Thranduil's residence was nine hundred miles and took fifty days. The only way for Aragorn to get any semblance of rest during this time without the risk of being throttled in his sleep would have been to tie Gollum up. (Like Sauron, Aragorn recognised the malice in Gollum and the physical strength this gave him.) Aragorn of course, unlike Frodo, did not have the advantage of a loyal companion to alternate watch and sleeping periods with him.
- Also it would have been necessary to prevent Gollum making a noise - hence the gagging. In spite of Aragorn's precautions the two of them **were** seen and followed towards the end of the journey by Sauron's spies from Dol Guldur (*UT* 3.4.ii.444). As described in the account he gave to the Council of Elrond (*LotR* 2.2.253) Gandalf would hear the news of Aragorn's capture of Gollum from the folk of Lothlórien, thus implying that they had been looking out for Aragorn and possibly protecting him as well during his passage through the eaves of their land. However Aragorn would not have been aware of this, and even if he had been he would still have regarded himself as being in the utmost danger with an urgent need of speed and secrecy.
- Although Aragorn's greatest ordeal began with the disappearance of Gandalf and the entry of the Nazgûl into the Shire in the summer of 3018, he must in fact have been under tremendous pressure ever since Gandalf confided in him, in 3001, that Bilbo almost certainly had the One Ring and the search for Gollum actually began. By the time he eventually found him, right at the point of giving up hope, he must have been experiencing extreme antagonism towards both Isildur and Gollum. Any sort of cordial relationship between him and the latter would have been doomed from the start due to the circumstances.

Legolas's news at the Council, that Gollum had escaped, must have been the last straw which no doubt explained Aragorn's angry reaction. This, and the apparent lack of pity he displayed in his speech about the capture of Gollum, may also have been aggravated by ill humour at Boromir's arrogance and thinly-disguised contempt throughout the Council. However it is notable that, in answer to Boromir's question as to what "doom" had been meted out to Gollum, Aragorn did acknowledge the considerable suffering, torment and fear which Gollum had experienced.

*

---

71. Op. cit. [1], *LotR* 2.2, p. 253.
72. Op. cit., *LotR* 2.2, p. 253.

As recounted in *UT* 3.4.444-447, when Sauron learnt that Gollum had been taken captive by a Man, and that Gandalf and the Elves of Mirkwood were both involved, he planned a simultaneous attack on Thranduil and Gondor aiming to kill/capture Gollum and also to seize the bridge at Osgiliath so that the Nazgûl could cross the river and start searching for the Ring in earnest. These actions took place in June 3018, but although the bridge was successfully taken Gollum eluded both the Orcs who recaptured him and the Elves who pursued them. Eventually he swam across to the west bank of the Anduin and ended up taking refuge in Moria through fear of the Nazgûl. Thus when the Fellowship arrived there in January 3019 he was able to start following them.

There were no further meetings between Aragorn and Gollum after the latter had been delivered to the care of Thranduil - just glimpses, after Gollum started trailing the Fellowship through Moria, past Lothlórien and down the Anduin. When it became clear to Aragorn that Frodo too had been aware of Gollum's pursuit he told him how he had tried to catch him with the intention of making him useful, but having failed in this he felt that they must try to lose him. There was no talk of killing him even though he regarded him as dangerous. Maybe he appreciated the effect of the Ring better by now, having seen what it could do to Frodo. Perhaps he also knew of Gandalf's wish to show pity to Gollum or even of the Wizard's feeling that the creature might have a part to play - though I throw some doubt on this last supposition below.

Similarities between Aragorn and Gollum

Strange as it may seem, Aragorn and Gollum did actually have many characteristics and experiences in common:

- They were both adept at tracking and finding paths, which was the reason why Aragorn was uniquely suited to stalk and capture Gollum. In the Prancing Pony he told the Hobbits, "*I have hunted many wild and wary things...*"[73], no doubt thinking of Gollum in particular as he said it, given that the search would have been pretty fresh in his mind at that point. Gollum's skills in these areas can be illustrated by his pursuit of the Fellowship and by his guidance of Frodo and Sam through the Dead Marshes where, as described in *LotR* 4.2.626, he used eyes, ears and feet to work out a safe passage, testing the ground and listening with one ear pressed to the earth. Aragorn had led the Hobbits through the Midgewater Marshes on the journey to Rivendell, and his tracking of the Orcs across Rohan earned him the wondering admiration of Éomer.
- Both had travelled widely, gathering knowledge and meeting different peoples. This was of course Aragorn's main business during his adulthood prior to the War of the Ring. Gollum's activities are illustrated by his long journeys in pursuit of the Ring and the "thief", and also by the conversation where he told Frodo and Sam that he had spoken with Orcs and "*to many peoples*"[74]. He also seemed to have a pretty shrewd knowledge of the way Sauron's mind worked. In addition he had built up a working relationship with Shelob.
- Both were good at dealing with water travel, being skilled with boats and at swimming. Aragorn led the Fellowship's boats down the Anduin and had also had experience of ships and naval battles during his service in Gondor as a young man, while Gollum had spent his "Hobbit" life fishing and boating. After capturing Gollum Aragorn tied him to a log and swam across the Anduin pushing him. Later, when following the Company, Gollum used a log as a boat and a disguise rather than swimming. Aragorn praised Gollum's skill to Frodo explaining his dashed hope that the river voyage would have put an end to his pursuit of the Fellowship: "*... he is too clever a waterman.*"[75]
- In *LotR* 4.2.630-1 Frodo was feeling the weight of the Ring and the Eye of Sauron searching for it. Gollum too was aware of the Eye and also felt the pressure from the proximity of the Ring. Aragorn must have felt a similar pressure while travelling with Frodo, particularly on Weathertop.
- At the Council of Elrond, Aragorn said of Gollum, "*His malice is great and gives him **a strength hardly***

---

73. Op. cit. [1], *LotR* 1.10, p. 163.
74. Op. cit., *LotR* 4.3, p. 642.
75. Op. cit., *LotR* 2.9, p. 384.

to be believed in one so lean and withered."[76] [My emphasis]. Gollum's strength is also illustrated by his ability to survive in Moria from autumn 3018 until the arrival of the Fellowship in mid-January 3019. Aragorn too was lean and haggard-looking but with exceptional strength and endurance, "*the most hardy of living Men*"[77]. The only difference was that Aragorn's leanness was due to a combination of his Númenórean blood and (probably) insufficient food combined with innate bodily and mental strength, rather than to the Ring, though it does seem that Gollum was naturally physically strong anyway, at least compared with his friend Déagol (*LotR* 1.2.53).

- Most significantly they both had the mental strength to overcome their fear of Sauron sufficiently to be able to deceive him. This point will now be expanded.

Gollum's deception was that, when Sauron questioned him about the whereabouts of the Hobbits' land, he pretended to believe that it was near his own old home on the banks of the River Gladden. The account in *UT* describes Gollum as "*Ultimately indomitable ... except by death*" because of his Hobbit nature and because of his hatred of Sauron which was greater than his terror of him, "*seeing in him truly his greatest enemy and rival*".[78] It was Gollum's hatred and his determination to prevent Sauron regaining the Ring which enabled him to carry out this deception. The force of his feelings is illustrated in *LotR* when he told Frodo and Sam that he was ordered to seek for the Precious and had indeed done so, "*But not for the Black One*"[79]. This in fact added disobedience to the deception. Sauron obviously did not appreciate any of this as he had released Gollum believing that he would lead his spies to the Ring.

Aragorn's deception was of course via the Palantír confrontation which led Sauron to think that Isildur's heir was the one who had the Ring. It is certainly feasible that hatred was one of the feelings which overrode Aragorn's fear during this incident, but determination to right the wrong done by Isildur by ensuring the destruction of the Ring would have been by far the dominant motive, entailing as it did all the associated issues of protecting Frodo, achieving his kingship and winning the hand of Arwen, not to mention the overall goal of saving Middle-earth. He would certainly have seen Sauron as his greatest rival, as the defeat of Sauron was his *raison d'être*.

Thus we can establish that Aragorn and Gollum were both capable of deceiving Sauron and both were able to conquer their fear to achieve this deception. However Aragorn failed to realise that Gollum had this ability. Like Sauron he had not perceived the "*indomitable*" quality in Gollum. To be fair he did not know that he himself had the ability to deceive Sauron until he faced him in the Palantír - approximately three weeks **after** his last sighting of Gollum as he followed the Fellowship down the Anduin. By the time Aragorn looked into the Palantír Gollum was leading Frodo and Sam into Ithilien. Aragorn also failed to appreciate the sense of rivalry Gollum felt towards Sauron, assuming that he was under orders from Sauron to lead his servants to the Ring and was therefore powerless to disobey him. Thus he also assumed that Gollum's purpose was to spy on the Fellowship and betray them to Sauron via any Orcs who happened to be around. That this was not the case was made very clear to Frodo and Sam, when Gollum shook his fist at the East crying, "*We won't! ... Not for you*"[80], clearly meaning that he had no intention of letting Sauron get the Ring.

The following examples confirm Aragorn's view of Gollum's motives:
- He told the Council of Elrond that Gollum's malice was such that "*He could work much mischief still, if he were free.*"[81].
- A few minutes later, on learning of Gollum's escape from the Elves, he declared, "*That is ill news indeed. We shall all rue it bitterly, I fear.*"[82]
- In *LotR* 2.9.385 during the seventh day of the Company's river voyage he lay awake (they travelled by

---

76. Op. cit. [1], *LotR* 2.2, p. 255.
77. Op. cit., App A.I.v, p. 1060.
78. Op. cit. [3], *UT* 3.4.i, p. 436.
79. Op. cit. [1], *LotR* 4.3, p. 643.
80. Op. cit., *LotR* 4.1, p. 616.
81. Op. cit., *LotR* 2.2, p. 255.
82. Op. cit., *LotR* 2.2, p. 255.

night so this was a rest period) watching the birds circling above and wondering if Gollum had passed news of their voyage to Sauron's servants. However his view - expressed to Frodo the previous night - that Gollum was capable of *"murder by night"*[83] was certainly reasonable.
- As the Company waited for Frodo to return to them with a decision on their route he stated, *"It is now more hopeless than ever for the Company to go east, since we have been tracked by Gollum, and must fear that the secret of our journey is already betrayed."*[84]

The misunderstandings indicated here are rather strange in the light of Aragorn's considerable foresight and his ability to perceive the feelings and motives of others. It is almost as if the something *"indomitable"* in Gollum prevented the exercise of these qualities. It seems that Gandalf's belief that Gollum would have a part to play before the end had only been shared with Frodo and that such a possibility had not occurred to Aragorn. It also did not occur to Aragorn that Gollum could be following any will except Sauron's. He regarded him as a servant of Sauron rather than as a Hobbit who still had a spark of good in him (as recognised by Gandalf and later by Frodo) and a mind of his own, in spite of being tormented and corrupted by the Ring for so long.

Gollum's attitude to Aragorn

Unsurprisingly Gollum's feelings towards Aragorn were ostensibly those of malice and hatred. His attitude is illustrated in *LotR* 4.3.643 by a conversation between him and Frodo while the latter tried to decide whether he should take Gollum's alternative route into Mordor (via Cirith Ungol) now that the Morannon had been proved to be impassable. The conversation hinged on Gollum's claim to have escaped from Mordor via that route and Frodo's doubt as to whether he had **genuinely** escaped or, as Aragorn had thought, had been *"permitted"* to escape. It was Frodo's identification of "Aragorn" as being the person who had caught him in the Dead Marshes which aroused Gollum's hostility, leading to *"an evil light"* appearing in his eyes and accusations that Aragorn was a liar. As already stated Aragorn had been right in his assumption, as Sauron was hoping that Gollum at large would lead his servants to the Ring. Also in *LotR* 4.10.738 Shagrat told Gorbag that Gollum had been to Mordor before and that when he left, orders had been given to let him pass. However Frodo realised that Gollum genuinely believed that he had escaped through his own skill, having *"all the injured air of a liar suspected when for once he has told the truth, or part of it."*[85] This was apparently in spite of the fact that Gollum insisted he had escaped *"all by my poor self"*[86] and then contradicted himself by saying that he had been told to seek for the Precious!

The mention of Aragorn put Gollum into a sulk to the extent that he now refused to give Frodo and Sam a clear answer as to whether Cirith Ungol was guarded or not. His ill-feeling towards Aragorn would clearly have been linked to the gagging, starving into submission and tethering he had endured, as well as to the slur on his truthfulness.

A couple of points are worth raising here, namely:
- In both *LotR* 4.3.643 and 4.10.738 Gollum's *"escape"* from Mordor is said - by Gollum himself and Shagrat respectively - to have occurred *"years ago"*. This seems strange given that Gollum was let out of Mordor in 3017 according to App B.1090 - only two years previously.
- As indicated in *LotR* 4.2.625 Gollum's capture by Sauron's servants had taken place near the Morannon. *LotR* 4.3.643 makes it clear that when he left Mordor - through his own skill as far as he was concerned - it was via Cirith Ungol. Thus he became familiar with both access routes to/from Mordor.

*

A moving and ironical twist to the conversation just described was that the young Gollum had heard tales

---
83. Op. cit. [1], *LotR* 2.9, p. 384.
84. Op. cit., *LotR* 2.10, p. 402.
85. Op. cit., *LotR* 4.3, p. 643.
86. Op. cit., *LotR* 4.3, p. 643.

about the Men from Númenor with shining eyes, the silver crown, the White Tree of the Kings of Gondor, and the building of the silver-white Tower of the Moon (Minas Ithil) in Isildur's time. He was aware too of Isildur's deed in cutting the Ring from Sauron's hand and Sauron's resulting hatred of Minas Ithil. He recalled these stories with obvious pleasure and nostalgia referring to them as "*wonderful tales*" told " ... *in the evening, sitting by the banks of the Great River, in the willow-lands* ..." and weeping as he remembered it all.[87]

This scenario is moving in that it shows how Gollum was once able to appreciate goodness and beauty - even that of Minas Ithil with its image of the Moon, the "White Face" which he was later to fear and hate. It is also ironical in that Aragorn, whom he hated, represented the ancient beauty of the "*wonderful tales*". Aragorn's wry comment at the Council of Elrond, "*He will never love me, I fear...*"[88], alas proved only too true. Legolas's comment about Aragorn, "*... all those **who come to know him** come to love him...*"[89] [My emphasis], found an exception in Gollum, though perhaps the significance lies in the words I have emphasised. Gollum did **not** come to know Aragorn as Aragorn did **not** come to know **him**. There is an intrinsic sadness in this situation because both characters played a vital role in bringing about the Ring's destruction.

---

87. Op. cit. [1], *LotR* 4.3, p. 641.
88. Op. cit., *LotR* 2.2, p. 253.
89. Op. cit., *LotR* 5.9, p. 874.

CHAPTER 2.9 - Miscellaneous Relationships

In *LotR*[1] Gandalf told Frodo of his friend Aragorn who was the greatest traveller of the Third Age, a statement borne out by the fact that Aragorn, in his sixty-eight-year "apprenticeship", seems to have journeyed over a wider area of Middle-earth than anyone else in *LotR*. Thus he must have formed many more relationships than the ones I have analysed so far. The purpose of this chapter is to examine the less obvious associations, mainly with races rather than individuals (though there are a few of these as well), looking at what we know of Aragorn, the lands he visited and the people he would have encountered. Some of it is inevitably based on inference, assumption or speculation.

As an introduction to this study I find it helpful to summarise the situation regarding the languages of Middle-earth during the Third Age, using information in App F.1127-32 which also gives an idea of the different races of Men living at the time plus some indication of their history.

The widely-used Common Speech (Westron) had its roots in the language of the three Houses of Men who had been allies of the Elves in the First Age. This language was subsequently developed by the Númenóreans during the Second Age, being known as Adûnaic. As the Second Age progressed, an increasing number of Númenóreans settled in Middle-earth, particularly at Pelargir near the Mouths of the Anduin. It was here that the Common Speech first came into existence, being a mixture of Adûnaic and the languages used by the natives of the area. When the exiled Númenórean survivors (the Dúnedain) arrived in Middle-earth after the Downfall of Númenor they too adopted this common language.

Since most of the existing inhabitants of the north-west of Middle-earth were also descended from the same three Houses of Men their languages were related to Adûnaic and bore varying degrees of similarity to the new Common Speech. The most similar were the languages of the Beornings, the Woodmen of Western Mirkwood and the Men of Lake-town and Dale. The people living between the River Gladden and the Carrock, from whom the Rohirrim were descended, maintained their own ancestral language. The speech of the Drúedain (Ghân-buri-Ghân's people) was "*Wholly alien*"[2] to Adûnaic, while that of the race who were subsequently known as the Dunlendings was "*only remotely akin*"[3] to it. During the Third Age, the Common Speech became the actual native language of most people (excluding the Elves) who lived within the original boundaries of Gondor and Arnor. These boundaries constituted all the coastline from Umbar round to the Bay of Forochel, inland as far as the Misty Mountains and the Mountains of Shadow, and included the land south of the Gladden Fields between the Misty Mountains and the Anduin. The Dúnedain also spoke the Elvish languages, Sindarin and (in the case of the wisest and most educated) Quenya. The Rohirrim continued to use their own language but their ruling classes also spoke the Common Speech extremely well. The other use of Common Speech in *LotR* was between different species of Orcs who did not know each other's dialects. Some of them also had it as their native language. The Black Speech devised by Sauron, which had been used for the inscription on the One Ring, was now only used in Barad-dûr itself and by Mordor's captains.

With this linguistic background I now consider the following races/individuals in the context of relationships or associations with Aragorn:
- Bree-men, Dunlendings and the Dead Men of Dunharrow
- Beornings and Woodmen of Western Mirkwood
- Men of Dale and Lake-town (Esgaroth)

---

1. J.R.R. Tolkien, *The Lord of the Rings*, London, HarperCollins Publishers, 2007, 2nd edition, based on the 50th Anniversary Edition of 2004, *LotR* 1.2, p. 58.
2. Op. cit., App F.I, p. 1129.
3. Op. cit., App F.I, p. 1129.

- Drúedain
- Lossoth
- The Enemy's slaves
- Tom Bombadil
- Treebeard and the Ents
- The Enemy
  - Men of Harad: Haradrim of Near Harad, Corsairs of Umbar, Inhabitants of Far Harad
  - Men of the East
  - Variags of Khand
  - Orcs
  - Trolls
  - Balrogs
  - Shelob and her offspring
  - Dragons
- Nature: animals, birds, plants, the land itself

BREE-MEN, DUNLENDINGS AND THE DEAD MEN OF DUNHARROW

As described in App F these three races shared a common ancestry - hence the reason for grouping them together. They had originated in the northern valleys of the White Mountains "*in ages past*"[4] which I take to mean in the First Age since we are told that in the Dark Years (indicated as being the Second Age in App B.1082) some of them migrated, settling in the southern dales of the Misty Mountains, or in some cases going further north even as far as the Barrow-downs. The Men of Bree were descended from these last-mentioned, and when Elendil and his sons founded the North Kingdom of Arnor the Bree-men became their subjects and adopted the Common Speech. As indicated in *LotR* 1.9.149, at the time of the War of the Ring the villages of Bree, Staddle, Combe and Archet together formed a small inhabited region of farmland and woodland surrounded by empty lands. This was the most westerly settlement of Men at the time.

Of those who remained in their original home some became absorbed into Elendil's South Kingdom of Gondor, including the group who subsequently became the Dead Men of Dunharrow. With the cession of the White Mountain valley area to the new kingdom of Rohan in TA 2510, the remainder of the native people were pushed further west into the most southerly valleys of the Misty Mountains where some of their ancestors had settled. The Rohirrim called this area Dunland and the people Dunlendings. They were the only ones of their race to retain their original language and primitive way of life.

Bree-men

I have already looked at Aragorn's encounters with Bree-**hobbits** in Chapter 2.5. The emphasis here is specifically on the **Men** of Bree and the people of Bree in general. *LotR* 1.9 and 1.10 provide the relevant information for much of this section on the Bree-folk.

By the time of the War of the Ring the Bree-folk were aware of the presence of the few surviving Dúnedain of the North but ignorant of their identity and origin, because by now the memory of the kings had long ago "*faded into the grass*"[5]. They were known merely as mysterious wanderers who came from further east and, on their rare visits to the Prancing Pony inn, brought news from afar and told "*strange forgotten tales*"[6] which were eagerly listened to. However in spite of their interest in the tales the Bree-folk were not disposed to make friends of these people whom they called "Rangers". This was no doubt partly due to the fact that they were taller, darker, leaner and grimmer than the Men of Bree (probably considerably so given that the Bree-men are described as "*brown-haired, broad, and rather short, cheerful and independent*"[7]) and must have been

---
4. Op. cit. [1], App F.I, pp. 1129-30.
5. Op. cit., *LotR* 1.9, p. 149.
6. Op. cit., *LotR* 1.9, p. 149.
7. Op. cit., *LotR* 1.9, p. 149.

somewhat sinister and off-putting in appearance due to their harsh and nomadic lifestyle. They must also have carried weapons with them which would have been a matter for concern, and maybe the fact that they *"were believed to have strange powers of sight and hearing"*[8] added to the wariness of their reception. Their long life-spans could also have been disturbing with, for example, the same Ranger being known to two or even three generations of Bree-folk.

These attitudes are epitomised by looking at the case of Aragorn himself. He obviously stood out, even among the Rangers, as being exceptionally tall and swift, hence the name "Strider" which was given to him in Bree (as he told Bilbo in *LotR* 2.1.232). The extended travels, danger and hardship he endured (that is, over and above those of his kinsmen) must have made him appear particularly grim, like a *"mysterious vagabond..."* with a *"rascally look"* to use his own words about himself.[9] As Frodo found out, he would sit semi-camouflaged in a corner listening to what was being said around him and he seemed to have an uncanny ability to read the thoughts of others and hear whispered conversations from across a crowded bar. In addition he could quell people simply by looking at them giving him what must have been an unnerving aura of authority when necessary: for example it was thus that he was able to silence most of those who shouted rude remarks and names as he and the Hobbits set out from Bree. All these characteristics would have encouraged the wariness and unease of the Breelanders.

If the Bree-folk were wary, so was Aragorn. As Barliman Butterbur told Frodo, *"He seldom talks"* - even for a Ranger presumably - though he too was capable of telling *"a rare tale when he has the mind."*.[10] As well as being on the lookout for threats to the people of Bree he was also aware of his own personal danger, having run into traps himself in the past. This explained his care in making sure that Frodo and his companions were not imposters. In addition there was the risk of the Bree-folk being drawn into Sauron's spy network.

Like the Shire, Bree had long been protected by the Dúnedain as Aragorn eloquently stated at the Council of Elrond describing how, working in secret, they drove off the *"dark things"* issuing from *"houseless hills"* and *"sunless woods"*.[11] Thus the naïve and trusting folk of the Shire and Bree were able to live in peace and without fear by being kept in ignorance of the horrors around them, some of which even the tough and hardened Dúnedain would prove unable to face (as demonstrated when the Nazgûl overcame them at Sarn Ford). The secrecy practised by Aragorn and his people was necessary for this policy to succeed. However it also meant that their deeds were unappreciated by those they were protecting. In the case of the Shire this secrecy was achieved by ensuring that they weren't detected. They were masters of camouflage and concealment and they didn't actually enter the Shire, they just guarded the borders: in effect the line of the Brandywine and up towards the North Downs. (The Elves' land of Lindon formed the western border.) The east border of the Shire at the Brandywine Bridge was the best part of a hundred miles west of Bree. Although the East/West Road actually went through the Shire, it was only used by Dwarves going to the Blue Mountains (who were sometimes seen by the Hobbits) and by Elves going to the Grey Havens (who were rarely spotted). No Men would have reason to be travelling on that section of the road.

With Bree, the situation was very different due to its nature and location. It was situated at a major road junction, namely that of the East/West and North/South roads - although the latter was little used by the later years of the Third Age. For generations the Prancing Pony inn had been a hub for news and information, a meeting-place for the locals of Bree - both Men and Hobbits - and for a variety of travellers and wanderers from all directions. These could be Dwarves, Hobbits, various races of Men, or Gandalf. It was neither possible nor desirable for Aragorn and his people to avoid detection - hence the need to integrate to some extent by being merely another category of the miscellaneous people/travellers/wanderers who passed through for business or any other reasons. Quite apart from providing the Dúnedain with brief recuperation in the shape of a decent meal, beer, washing facilities and warm bed, "The Pony" would have been important as a rendezvous (for example with each other, or with Gandalf) and for absorbing information, identifying trouble (such as Bill Ferny's activities) or new dangers, and assessing whether their protection strategy was working. During his years of watchfulness Aragorn came to know Bree and its surroundings very well as demonstrated by his

---

8. Op. cit. [1], *LotR* 1.9, p. 149.
9. Op. cit., *LotR* 1.10, p. 164.
10. Op. cit., *LotR* 1.9, p. 156.
11. Op. cit., *LotR* 2.2, p. 248.

statement to the Hobbits in *LotR* 1.10.172 that he knew other ways out of the village apart from via the main road, and by the devious and intricate route he took through the Chetwood in order to throw any pursuers off their track.

An additional issue for Aragorn in his dealings with Bree and its people was that it was absolutely essential, for his own safety, to keep his identity a secret. Bree was surrounded by wild lands which, in the years leading up to the War of the Ring, were becoming increasingly infiltrated by Sauron's creatures, with the accompanying risk of Bree-folk being drawn into his spy network. This need for secrecy along with the requirement for concealing the nature of the Dúnedain's "Guardian" activities, sat uncomfortably with having to integrate with the community. Perhaps it was not really surprising that Aragorn chose to adopt the guise of a *"mysterious vagabond"*, going to some trouble to perfect this image as shown by his demonstration of his *"rascally look"* to Frodo. However this was in stark contrast to his emotional words to the Hobbits shortly afterwards: "... *I hoped you would take to me for my own sake. A hunted man sometimes wearies of distrust and longs for friendship. But there, I believe my looks are against me.*"[12]

*

Aragorn must certainly have found out a great deal about the various personalities in Bree and three in particular are given enough prominence in *LotR* to justify discussion on an individual basis, namely Barliman Butterbur, Bill Ferny and Harry Goatleaf.

Barliman Butterbur

As the innkeeper of the Prancing Pony Barliman was regarded as an important person in the Bree-land due to the role of the inn as a major meeting-place for both locals and travellers. Moreover his family had run the inn for generations, so his high profile also had an inherited element. In addition he was considered to be very knowledgeable - for instance when Frodo pretended to be writing a book about Hobbits from outside the Shire Barliman was referred to as being a chief source of information. Given that Aragorn had been a Ranger for nearly seventy years at the time of the War of the Ring he must have known more than one generation of the Butterbur family. The landlord of the inn would have been Barliman's father or grandfather when Aragorn first went there and Barliman himself had probably not even been born. Aragorn must have watched him growing up and the young Barliman would presumably have been used to seeing him about the place. He told Frodo that "Strider" was in the habit of disappearing *"for a month, or a year"*[13] then turning up again. Barliman was referred to, by Aragorn, Frodo and the Bree-folk in the inn, as "Old Butterbur" or "Old Barliman", which perhaps indicated that he was not a young man, though maybe he was middle-aged rather than actually elderly.

Aragorn knew that Barliman was trustworthy, both from his own observations and from Gandalf's faith in the man. When Frodo expressed doubt about him due to him encouraging the Hobbits to join the company in the bar Aragorn reassured him that there was no ulterior motive. However Barliman clearly distrusted the Rangers, and "Strider" in particular, as the events at the inn on the evening of September 29th 3018 would show. Ironically, in spite of his basic decency and integrity, Barliman put Aragorn and the Hobbits at greatly increased risk by his very evident antipathy to the former. The relationship between Aragorn and the innkeeper at this juncture was particularly fraught, the tension between them being aggravated by Aragorn's inability to show his true character and by the extremely stressful (for both men) events during those last few days of September.

By the time Aragorn invited himself into the Hobbits' parlour in the inn, his anxiety and fear must have reached fever pitch on account of:
- The continuing unexplained absence of Gandalf.
- The proximity of the Nazgûl, which would have increased his dread of his own identity being discovered.
- Being forced into close contact with the Ring for the first time and then actually seeing it in action

---

12. Op. cit. [1], *LotR* 1.10, p. 170.
13. Op. cit., *LotR* 1.9, p. 156.

during the recent disturbing episode in the bar.
- The realisation that the incident had probably been reported to the Nazgûl by people from Bree.

In addition he now had to persuade the Hobbits to accept him, a task which would be hindered by the obstructive behaviour of Barliman. The innkeeper's attitude greatly exacerbated their danger and resulted in Aragorn's suppressed exasperation and bitterness boiling over during the course of the evening. For example Barliman:
- Had refused to let him speak to the Hobbits beforehand so he could warn them to stay in their private parlour, and then didn't even bother to introduce him in the bar.
- Had forgotten to deliver Gandalf's letter, which Frodo should have received three months previously.
- Told Frodo about the two black Men asking for Baggins, then referred to "Strider's" request to speak to him almost in the same breath, clearly regarding him and the Nazgûl as equals in the potential danger stakes.
- Used a disrespectful mode of speech to Aragorn: *"You! You're always popping up. What do you want now?"*[14] (Their earlier conversation had obviously been a fraught one.)
- Displayed continuing hostility even after it was obvious that Aragorn was trying to help the Hobbits: *"... if I was in your plight, I wouldn't take up with a Ranger."*[15]
- Gave *"... another doubtful look at Strider and a shake of his head"*[16] as he left the room, in spite of taking Aragorn seriously when he told him that the Nazgûl came from Mordor, and accepting that he himself [Barliman] would be unable to protect the Hobbits. He would subsequently tell Gandalf that Aragorn had *"got at"*[17] the Hobbits in spite of his efforts to prevent him.

The advice to the Hobbits (quoted above) not to take up with a Ranger would have been the last straw as far as Aragorn was concerned. Barliman's action in keeping him away from them earlier on had indirectly caused the episode in the bar: they would not have been there if Aragorn had managed to speak to them beforehand. In addition the failure to deliver the letter to Frodo was wholly responsible for Frodo's *"plight"*: if it had been delivered in July, as Gandalf intended, Frodo would have had a chance to get to Rivendell long before the arrival of the Nazgûl. Now, just as Aragorn was succeeding in winning Frodo's trust, Barliman was casting further slurs on his character and it was this which caused Aragorn's angry outburst, *"Then who would you take up with? A fat innkeeper who only remembers his own name because people shout it at him all day?"*[18] Superficially his speech was a personally insulting reference to Barliman's girth and absent-mindedness. But this was a "life and death" situation with a greater risk of the latter if the Hobbits were to heed Barliman's advice about not taking up with a Ranger. Deep down Aragorn was expressing a growing build-up of exasperation, anger, offence and fear. He would revisit these feelings at the Council of Elrond a month later while telling Boromir of the thankless labours of the Northern Dúnedain, referring in particular to *"... one fat man* [clearly Barliman] *who lives within a day's march of foes that would freeze his heart, or lay his little town in ruin, if he were not guarded ceaselessly."*[19]. Although the fact that Barliman was fat may seem trivial, Aragorn referred to it twice, perhaps contrasting this with his own leanness which must have been due to insufficient food as well as natural physique. He and his people were living on short rations so that Barliman and his ilk could be well-fed and free of fear. At that point in the Council Boromir too, dressed in rich clothing, was displaying distrust of Aragorn's leanness and shabbiness, as well as a lack of appreciation of his crucial and dangerous activities in fighting Mordor. Thus he triggered Aragorn's still festering bitterness at Barliman's attitude and behaviour.

From Barliman's point of view, there were several issues which could have influenced and/or explained his attitude to Aragorn:

---

14. Op. cit. [1], *LotR* 1.10, p. 168.
15. Op. cit., *LotR* 1.10, p. 168.
16. op. cit., *LotR* 1.10, p. 169.
17. op. cit., *LotR* 2.2, p. 263.
18. op. cit., *LotR* 1.10, p. 168.
19. Op. cit., *LotR* 2.2, p. 248.

- Although Aragorn had good reason for his disguise, Barliman was suspicious of his disreputable appearance, perhaps understandably in his position as landlord of a presumably respectable inn.
- Also, as a responsible landlord, he would have been concerned for the welfare of his customers which no doubt partly explained his refusal to let Aragorn in to see the Hobbits even before they had had "*bite or sup*"[20]. He must have been twice their height and thus would have appeared threatening for that reason alone. Aragorn's urgency was of course due to the danger of the situation but Barliman would not have known that.
- After Frodo's disappearing act, Barliman told him that the people in Bree were a bit suspicious of anything "*out of the way*" or "*uncanny*"[21]. Note that three days earlier he had been visited by two Nazgûl, an experience which he also found "*Uncanny*"[22] as the dogs were yammering, the geese screaming and the Hobbit servant Nob's hair was standing on end. This incident too would have influenced his reaction to Aragorn's request to speak to Frodo, especially as the Nazgûl had been asking for a Hobbit.
- Barliman seemed to be unnerved by the way Aragorn kept "popping up". He told Frodo that he [Aragorn] "*disappears for a month, or a year, and then he **pops up** again.*"[23]. Then there was his outburst quoted earlier: "*You! You're always **popping up**.*" [My emphasis].
- Aragorn's habit of sitting in the corners and shadows, camouflaged, eavesdropping on conversations (with his enhanced hearing) would have had the same effect. Barliman's accusation of "*popping up*" was triggered by his realisation that Aragorn had been standing in the shadows unobserved all the time that he [Barliman] had been apologising for his failure to deliver Gandalf's letter and also incidentally complaining about Aragorn's behaviour in trying to get in to speak to the Hobbits.

The following year when Gandalf and the Hobbits returned to Bree after the War of the Ring, almost Barliman's first words were that he had never expected to see any of the Hobbits again after "*... going off into the Wild with that Strider, and all those Black Men about.*"[24]. However, later that evening he admitted that the Breelanders had just begun to realise what the Rangers had done for them, protecting them from things that were "*worse than robbers ... Wolves ... dark shapes in the woods, dreadful things that it makes the blood run cold to think of.*"[25] Compare this description with Aragorn's outburst, quoted earlier, at the Council of Elrond where he spoke of "*dark things*" and "*foes that would freeze his* [Barliman's] *heart*". There seems to be a contradiction here in that Barliman still thought Aragorn was sinister and disreputable even though he was now grateful to the Rangers in general. When the conversation turned to the subject of the new King it was clear, from the missed hints given out by Gandalf and Sam about the King's regard for Bree and his appreciation of the beer at "The Pony", that it had never entered Barliman's mind that Aragorn could be the King in question, even though he now realised what Bree owed to the Rangers and was, presumably, aware that "Strider" was their chief.

Another anomaly was Barliman's high regard for Gandalf: "*A wizard they say he is, but he's a good friend of mine, whether or no*"[26]. This was a strange friendship for someone who was wary of anything "*uncanny*" or "*out of the way*" and also it was inconsistent with Barliman's suspicious attitude to Aragorn, as Gandalf was close friends with him and well-disposed towards the Dúnedain in general. One possible explanation is that Gandalf could afford to be friendly and ingratiating towards Barliman, praising his beer, showing that he trusted him, etc. He didn't have Aragorn's problem of having to keep his identity secret: Sauron knew very well who Gandalf was. Aragorn couldn't afford to compromise himself by being too nice and approachable. Also by September 29th 3018, he must have been near the limits of his endurance physically and mentally and this would have been reflected in his looks and manner. As a result it does seem that he was regarded with particular hostility by Barliman, this hostility being based on appearance rather than on anything more

---

20. op. cit. [1], *LotR* 1.10, p. 168.
21. Op. cit., *LotR* 1.9, p. 162.
22. op. cit., *LotR* 1.10, p. 168.
23. op. cit., *LotR* 1.9, p. 156.
24. Op. cit., *LotR* 6.7, p. 990.
25. op. cit., *LotR* 6.7, p. 993.
26. op. cit., *LotR* 1.10, p. 167.

concrete. It could of course be argued that Barliman was not in fact aware of the closeness between Gandalf and Aragorn since they may well have thought it wise to hide their friendship. This argument holds, up until the point when Gandalf arrived in Bree on the evening of September 30th 3018 (Aragorn and the Hobbits had left that morning). In his report at the Council of Elrond Gandalf recounted in detail how delighted and relieved he had been when Barliman told him that the Hobbits were with Aragorn, shouting out loud with joy, embracing the innkeeper and putting a seven-year enchantment of excellence on his beer. Whether or not Barliman had been aware of their friendship before, he could hardly have failed to appreciate it after that. However he still regarded Aragorn with suspicion and believed that the Hobbits would have come to grief after going off with him.

Bill Ferny

Bill Ferny is described as *"swarthy"* and after Frodo's mishap in the bar he looked at Sam and Pippin *"with a knowing and half-mocking expression"*.[27] Aragorn himself referred to him as a *"swarthy sneering fellow"*[28]. Although he was clearly in the pay of the Nazgûl in September 3018 he later become a chief supporter of Saruman and was responsible for letting his thugs into Bree early the following year.

There is no indication of his age in 3018. However even if he had been as old as in his sixties (which seems unlikely), he would still have been unborn when Aragorn first became a Ranger. Therefore there is the same assumption as with Barliman Butterbur, that Aragorn must have known his parents or grandparents and known Bill himself as a child. This begs the question: Had the Fernys always been a problem? It is not clear whether Bill had been got at by Sauron's spies because he - and perhaps his family in general - was not a particularly nice person, or whether he had been perfectly pleasant before, but possibly weak or short of money and therefore easily led. Certainly in *LotR* 1.9.160, 1.10.165, 173-4 and 1.11.179-82 he is portrayed as rather a "nasty piece of work" as shown by the following observations:

- He and a friend - an Orc/Dunlending hybrid referred to as the *"squint-eyed southerner"*[29] - reported back to the Nazgûl following Frodo's use of the Ring in the inn. They had left the inn together immediately after the incident and later the two Nazgûl encountered by Merry were seen outside Ferny's house. That night the Hobbits' bedrooms were attacked by these Nazgûl.
- He was possibly implicated in the escape of the horses and ponies during the attack on the inn.
- He sold a half-starved pony to the Hobbits taking advantage of their desperate situation to charge three times its value.
- He was cruel to animals as demonstrated by the condition of the pony.
- Aragorn suspected Bill of following them as he and the Hobbits left Bree and was worried that he would report their direction of travel to others - meaning the Nazgûl.
- He was exceptionally rude to Aragorn. At the Council of Elrond Aragorn would refer to the scornful name of Strider which he had to put up with in Bree. However Bill Ferny's repertoire was much more insulting, not to mention slanderous. As Aragorn and the Hobbits left Bree he called him *"Longshanks"* and *"Stick-at-naught Strider"*[30], then hinted that there were *"other names not so pretty"*[31] and warned the Hobbits to watch out that night. He also referred sarcastically to Aragorn's lack of friends. He was certainly not in awe of him - in fact he treated him with contempt.
- When Aragorn warned the Hobbits that some folk in Bree weren't to be trusted he mentioned Bill in particular, telling them that he had an evil name in the Bree-land, that *"queer folk"*[32] called at his house, and that he would do anything for money and enjoyed making mischief.
- Aragorn was clearly not alone in his opinion. Barliman Butterbur, who actually paid for the pony, found being cheated by Bill Ferny hard to bear and Bob the stable-man/hobbit also had the same view.

---

27. Op. cit. [1], *LotR* 1.9, p. 160.
28. Op. cit., *LotR* 1.10, p. 165.
29. Op. cit., *LotR* 1.9, p. 160.
30. Op. cit., *LotR* 1.11, p. 181.
31. Op. cit., *LotR* 1.11, p. 181.
32. Op. cit., *LotR* 1.10, p. 165.

Further consideration of these points shows that Aragorn and Bill knew a lot about each other.

Aragorn must have known of other cases of Bill ill-treating animals as he overruled Frodo's concern that the pony they had bought would betray them to him as its former owner by saying that he couldn't imagine any animal wanting to go back to him once it had got away. He was proved right by the pony's improvement in health and happiness even on the hard road it had to travel with him and the Hobbits, and later with the Fellowship. His awareness of Bill's dubious business practices and love of mischief-making also implied that he knew him pretty well. The unpleasantness of Bill's behaviour to Aragorn as he left Bree indicated a deep hostility. Had Aragorn had cause to take him to task about cheating, ill-treatment of animals, etc.?

Bill's bad reputation was clearly long-standing and he appears to have been generally disliked by the Bree-folk as well as by Aragorn. Therefore this could not have been due solely to his liaison with the Nazgûl who had only been around the Shire and Bree for a week. These considerations give rise to some important issues. When Aragorn left Bree and led the Hobbits into the Chetwood he suspected Bill of noting where they turned off the road but didn't think he would follow them because Bill knew he that he was not a match for him in a wood. For Bill to know that he wasn't a match for Aragorn he must have been in the habit of spying on him and stalking him, and for Aragorn to be aware that Bill recognised his own inferior ability he must in turn have been keeping a very close eye on **him** and knew he was able to throw him off his track. The depth of mutual awareness implies that this state of affairs must have been long-standing.

Had Ferny been in communication with Sauron's spies for some time? Had he been told to report on Rangers, and Aragorn in particular as their Chief? Regarding Aragorn's statement to the Hobbits that the Enemy had set traps for him in the past, had this been with the assistance of Bill Ferny or of someone else in the Breeland, possibly from the same family? This would explain his and Bill's knowledge of each other. Also the fact that Aragorn realised what Bill was up to, and why, would have increased Bill's hostility. The infiltration of Sauron's spy network into the naïve, good-natured Breelanders who would be unaware of the full implications of their actions made Aragorn's personal situation more dangerous because it increased the risk of Sauron finding out that he was Isildur's heir. Aragorn told Frodo of his fears regarding the Nazgûl: "... *their power is in terror, and already some in Bree are in their clutch. They will drive these wretches to some evil work...*"[33]. He was referring particularly to Bill, some of the strangers (from the South) and maybe the gatekeeper Harry Goatleaf.

Harry Goatleaf

Harry was the gatekeeper at the West-gate of Bree. As with Barliman Butterbur and Bill Ferny there is the question of how old he was and the likelihood of Aragorn knowing other generations of the family during his time as a Ranger.

Harry's first appearance in the narrative is in *LotR* 1.9.151 when Frodo and his companions arrived at the West-gate on the evening of September 29th. His reception of them was suspicious and unfriendly, with him questioning them gruffly as to their names and business and telling them that others were also likely to be asking questions as "*There's queer folk about.*"[34] Frodo didn't like his look or tone of voice. On the face of it the "*queer folk*" could have applied to some of the more dubious travellers from the South, in particular the squint-eyed southerner. It could also have applied to Aragorn. It is true that Aragorn climbed over the West-gate undetected by Harry after the Hobbits had passed through, but he had actually been around and in and out of Bree for several days prior to the Hobbits' arrival. This was made clear later that evening when Aragorn enlightened Frodo and his friends as to the cause of Harry's demeanour. He told them that he himself had been near the West-gate three days earlier and had seen Nazgûl talking to Harry, an encounter which had left the gatekeeper "*white and shaking*"[35]. If Harry had also seen Aragorn around at that time he probably tarred him with the same brush - as Barliman had - thus emphasising the case for Aragorn being included in the "*queer folk*" category. It was this incident which made Aragorn suspect Harry of being in the "*clutch*"[36] of the Nazgûl and involved with Bill Ferny. This was confirmed early the next year when he joined Bill in letting Saruman's

---

33. Op. cit. [1], *LotR* 1.10, p. 174.
34. Op. cit., *LotR* 1.9, p. 151.
35. Op. cit., *LotR* 1.10, p. 174.
36. Op. cit., *LotR* 1.10, p. 174.

thugs into Bree.

Aragorn's description of Harry's condition following his encounter with the Nazgûl showed his understanding of the effect it had on him. There is a definite element of compassion in his account, in spite of the danger which would result. He understood that fear was the main element in turning a susceptible character to evil. Perhaps Bill Ferny's case was similar, although he did seem to have a pronounced tendency towards criminal and anti-social activities anyway.

Hammond and Scull state[37] that in editions of *LotR* prior to 2004 Harry was included with Bill Ferny and the squint-eyed southerner when they left the inn following Frodo's disappearing incident. This reference was removed in post-2004 editions on the advice of Christopher Tolkien.

Aragorn and the Bree-folk in general

In App A.I we are told that during his years of wandering Aragorn "*... seemed to Men worthy of honour, as a king that is in exile, **when he did not hide his true shape**.*"[38] [My emphasis]. In Bree he very much did hide his true shape - hence the wariness and sometimes hostility which he and his people encountered there. As stated earlier I believe he adopted this approach because he felt it was the best way to give the Bree-folk protection and peace of mind, and to ensure his own personal safety. An examination of the behaviour and attitude of Barliman Butterbur and Bill Ferny shows that Aragorn himself probably suffered more at their hands than the Rangers in general did, as illustrated by Barliman's eventual appreciation (in *LotR* 6.7.990, 993) of what the Rangers had done for Bree but coupled with a continuing distrust of Aragorn. Some of the Bree-folk just laughed at the talk of the King returning and only began to be convinced of the truth of the story when they saw the impressive attire of Gandalf and the Hobbits, namely Gandalf in his blue and silver mantle over his white clothes and the Hobbits with their mail, helms and weapons. Was their scepticism because the King was said to be Strider, the most disreputable-looking of the Rangers?

The attitude of the Breelanders to Aragorn can however be approached from a different angle. We only know Bill Ferny and Barliman Butterbur in any detail and both of them caused Aragorn a lot of grief and trouble in spite of the fact that, ironically, the latter was trusted by Aragorn himself and by Gandalf. Bill was very clearly not a typical Bree-man, and perhaps Barliman wasn't either being, as innkeeper, more likely to be drawn into a confrontational situation with Aragorn than the average Breelander - especially during late September 3018. He may also have influenced others to adopt his own attitude. Although Aragorn's bitter words to Boromir at the Council of Elrond ("*Travellers scowl at us, and countrymen give us scornful names. 'Strider' I am ...*"[39]) appear to indicate the Bree-folk in general he was actually referring specifically to Barliman in this speech. I now consider whether in fact the average Breelander **did** treat Aragorn with active hostility and contempt. The following points perhaps suggest a different **general** attitude:

- Although the name "Strider" seems at this stage to have been regarded as disrespectful by Aragorn himself it was in fact merely a reference to his long pace and swiftness and was used by people who had no idea what his real name was. It seems to have been Bill Ferny who made it insulting by adding the epithet "Stick-at-naught". In the end of course, due to Frodo, Sam, Merry and Pippin using it as an affectionate name, Aragorn became fond enough of it to adopt its Quenya translation as the name of his House when he became King. If he had hated it that much while in Bree he would surely have asked his Hobbit friends to stop using it.
- When Aragorn and the Hobbits left the inn most of the inhabitants of the Bree-land came to watch their departure. We are told that "*Not all the faces were friendly, nor all the words that were shouted.*"[40]. The implication here is that presumably some of the faces and words **were** friendly. It was big news that Aragorn had joined the Hobbits and mere curiosity must have been a very significant motive for the interest shown.
- Most of the Bree-folk were in awe of Aragorn which implied respect rather than contempt. Those who

---

37. W.G. Hammond and C. Scull, *The Lord of the Rings: a Reader's Companion,* London, HarperCollins Publishers, 2005, pp. 157-8..
38. Op. cit. [1], App A.I.v, p. 1060.
39. op. cit., *LotR* 2.2, p. 248.
40. Op. cit., *LotR* 1.11, p. 180.

- shouted rude remarks after him and the Hobbits were quickly reduced to silence by a look from him.
- There is no indication of the **Hobbits** of Bree being particularly unfriendly to Aragorn. Notably Nob showed no unease in his presence: indeed Aragorn accompanied him to help carry the luggage from the Hobbit bedrooms into the parlour. They left and returned together thus implying that Aragorn was present when Nob did his decoy job with the bolsters and mat. (Did he help him?!)
- Regarding Gandalf and the Hobbits bringing the news of the return of the King, it clearly wasn't **all** the Breelanders who were sceptical, as the wording is "***Even** those who had laughed at all the talk about the King...*"[41] [My emphasis] which perhaps implies that the doubters were in the minority.

Only Bill and Barliman are shown to have been consistently hostile, with the latter clearly managing to overrule Aragorn when he asked to speak to Frodo immediately after his arrival. Aragorn's need to avoid appearing unduly agitated or aggressive may perhaps have reduced the impact of his request thus making it easier for the inn-keeper to quash him. Bill's rudeness and Barliman's suspicious attitude would have developed from their close contact with him, Barliman from dealing with him as a customer of the inn and Bill from his spying activities. Barliman's outright hostility during the events of late-September 3018, would have been fuelled by fear of the Nazgûl. Nevertheless his behaviour was clearly hurtful, humiliating and insulting to Aragorn.

*

Barliman Butterbur, on hearing the news of the new King, the proposed rebuilding of the town of Fornost Erain and the re-population of the waste-lands, became concerned at the possibility of an influx of strangers into Bree and the surrounding area. Gandalf reassured him by telling him that the King would leave Bree alone because "*He knows it and loves it*"[42]. This statement seems somewhat strange in the light of the unpleasantness Aragorn had faced in Bree just over a year earlier, and perhaps provides further evidence that the general treatment he received from the Breelanders was not unmitigated hostility.

So why did Aragorn love Bree? It can't just have been because of Barliman's beer (see Sam's comment: "*... he says your beer is always good*"[43]).

I suggest that his feelings for Bree were similar to his feelings for the Shire, namely protective, and appreciative of the simplicity and peacefulness of a generally hard-working, unambitious community with low crime levels. Did he actually enjoy regaling his fellow inn patrons with the "*strange forgotten tales*"[44] which they listened to so eagerly? In spite of the bitterness and exasperation which got the better of him in September and October 3018, deep down he understood why Barliman mistrusted his vagabond-like appearance and he empathised with Harry Goatleaf's terror of the Nazgûl. He realised that it was primarily fear which led Bill Ferny to evil. The generous words spoken by Halbarad about the Shire-folk could also sum up Aragorn's attitude to the Bree-folk: "*Little do they know of our long labour for the safekeeping of their borders, and yet I grudge it not.*"[45]

In addition Aragorn would have liked the cosmopolitan nature of Bree, with Hobbits and Men peacefully co-existing and Dwarves visiting the inn. It was important to him that the Free Peoples, all of whom were involved in fighting Sauron, should be on friendly terms with each other as was shown by the situation in Fourth Age Minas Tirith where Men, Elves, Dwarves and Hobbits were all welcome and happy.

We know that King Elessar visited his North Kingdom, including the Shire borders. He must also have visited Bree if he liked it and its inn so much. Did he still go to the Prancing Pony? And was there a subsidiary Butterbur brewery in Minas Tirith?!

---

41. Op. cit. [1], *LotR* 6.7, p. 995.
42. Op. cit., *LotR* 6.7, p. 994.
43. Op. cit., *LotR* 6.7, p. 994.
44. op. cit., *LotR* 1.9, p. 149.
45. op. cit., *LotR* 5.2, p. 779.

Dunlendings

LotR contains little in the way of specific encounters between Aragorn and the Dunlendings. It is therefore necessary to assess his likely attitude to them - and theirs to him - by looking at their history and general nature, fitting these with what we know of Aragorn's character and travels.

As well as *LotR* itself and App F, there is information on the Dunlendings in *UT*[46] 3.4.ii.449-50, 3.5.460-75 and *UT* 3.5.App ii.479-84.

App F states that the Dunlendings were *"a secret folk, unfriendly to the Dúnedain, hating the Rohirrim."*[47] This was due to a number of events which occurred during the Second and Third Ages:

- In the Second Age their ancestors who had moved away from their original habitation in the White Mountains into Enedwaith further west were the victims of extensive forest clearance by the Númenóreans. Their hostility was thus aroused and Sauron found them useful as spies against the Númenóreans.
- As far as those who remained in the White Mountain vales were concerned some became citizens of Gondor when that kingdom was formed at the end of the Second Age, but others found themselves pushed further west. They were too few to trouble the people of Gondor and too much in awe of them to oppose them seriously, but that didn't prevent their hostility.
- As Gondor's power waned in the mid-Third Age, the Men of the Mountains ceased to regard themselves as subject to it but nevertheless began to drift back eastwards. When this part of Gondor became Rohan the Rohirrim drove them back again into the area which they subsequently called Dunland. Thus the hatred of the Dunlendings for Rohan began.
- Approximately a hundred and thirty-five years later the Dunlendings began to filter back into Rohan again and the resulting hostilities continued unabated until the War of the Ring.
- A specific incident which aggravated this ill-feeling occurred in the reign of Helm, Ninth King of Rohan. As described in App A.II.1065-6 a man called Freca, who claimed to be related to the royal House of Rohan but also had Dunlending blood, asked for the hand of Helm's daughter in marriage for his son. Helm took offence at his impudence (as he saw it) and killed him.
- At one point (prior to Saruman taking up residence there) the Dunlendings took over Isengard - which actually belonged to Gondor - overruling the small hereditary guard there. Therefore there was now increased hostility with Gondor as well.

Thus it can be seen that after Saruman took over Isengard and began to follow his treacherous path, the stage was set for his use of the Dunlendings in war (particularly at the two Battles of the Fords of Isen and the Battle of the Hornburg), as agents for spying on Gandalf and the Shire, and for finding out about the One Ring.

One of the most unpleasant actions of Saruman was the cross-breeding of Dunlendings and Orcs, a specific example being the squint-eyed southerner encountered in Bree. There were also many such people in his army at Helm's Deep - in fact according to Merry in *LotR* 3.9.566 these were actually more Orc-like than the squint-eyed southerner, perhaps being the result of cross-breeding Orcs with the hybrids rather than with pure Dunlendings. The squint-eyed southerner is the only individual Dunlending mentioned in the main text of *LotR*. *UT* 3.4.ii.449-50 has more information on him describing him as one of Saruman's most trusted servants and stating that he was actually an outlaw driven out of Dunland on account of his supposed Orc blood (which incidentally suggests that the Dunlendings were no more enamoured of the Orcs than the people of Rohan or Gondor were). He became an agent for Saruman for the purpose of obtaining pipeweed supplies and for spying on the Shire due to Saruman's belief that this would help him to track down the Ring. Accordingly he had maps and other information which made him of particular interest when he was intercepted by the Nazgûl while travelling between the Shire and Dunland. Out of sheer terror of the Nazgûl he betrayed Saruman and was then sent on to Bree as an agent of Sauron - hence his appearance at the Prancing Pony in the company of Bill Ferny on September 29th 3018. The following morning Frodo spotted him lurking in Bill's house.

---

46. C. Tolkien (ed.), *Unfinished Tales of Númenor and Middle-earth*, London, HarperCollins Publishers, 1998, first published in Great Britain by George Allen & Unwin 1980.
47. Op. cit. [1], App F.I, p. 1130.

LotR 1.9.153, 155 and 1.10.165 contain references to travellers coming from the South to the Bree area looking for somewhere else to settle due to troubles in their own land. Some of these were genuine refugees seeking peace and safety, while others were in the pay of Saruman or Sauron. Some at least must have been Dunlendings and the squint-eyed southerner is mentioned specifically. Although the Bree-folk were less than welcoming to these travellers they were in fact of similar descent.

Dunland bordered the old kingdom of Arnor on the south-east. It also, as discussed, bordered Rohan and thus had to be traversed to reach it if travelling from the west. There is evidence of some interbreeding between the Dunlendings and the Rohirrim - see the example of Freca described above. Also *UT* 3.5.472 Note 4 refers to the land between the rivers Isen and Adorn beyond the Gap of Rohan which was technically part of Rohan. However in practice most of the inhabitants were of mixed blood and tended to side with Saruman. In a similar way, though probably further back, there must surely have been interbreeding with the people of Arnor and also Gondor.

Because of Dunland's location it would have been included in Aragorn's travels by default, but he must also have lingered there long enough to absorb the culture of its people, using his wisdom and perception to assess their fears and attitudes as well as the risk they posed to Rohan and Gondor. In *LotR* Merry described the Dunlendings he had seen as "*... rather tall and dark-haired, and grim but not particularly evil-looking*"[48] - in other words not that dissimilar to Aragorn who would no doubt have been able to integrate with them without too much difficulty.

The only specific encounter in *LotR* between Aragorn and Dunlendings occurred during the Battle of the Hornburg and is described in *LotR* 3.7.536-40. As dawn approached Aragorn, Éomer and Gamling took a brief rest from the fighting. Gamling, who understood the speech of the Dunlendings in Saruman's army, knew that they were referring to the Rohirrim as "*Strawheads*" and "*robbers of the North*", and he spoke of how Saruman had stirred up their old hatred of Rohan.[49] Soon afterwards Aragorn stood up on the Deeping Wall to parley, warning the enemy of the imminent danger awaiting them. He knew of the planned sortie of Théoden from the Hornburg. Did he also sense/foresee the presence of the Huorns, and the arrival of Erkenbrand and Gandalf? The Orcs in Saruman's army jeered at him, but many of the Dunlendings were awed by the "*power and royalty*"[50] he displayed. Large numbers of them gave themselves up when the afore-mentioned perils descended on them. *UT* 3.5.469 states that in spite of their hatred of the Rohirrim they were afraid of meeting them face to face as they were less skilled in warfare and less well armed. They were subsequently amazed at the mercy shown to them by Erkenbrand, his terms being that they were to help in the repairs and burials at Helm's Deep then take an oath of loyalty and go home free. Their dead were put in their own burial mound. Saruman had told them that the Rohirrim burnt their captives alive.

Although Erkenbrand was acting autonomously his actions were in the same merciful vein as Aragorn's stance on the Deeping Wall - at great danger to himself - to warn the Dunlendings of their own danger. This lends weight to the theory that Aragorn had been among them and come to appreciate their character and fears. Erkenbrand was well aware that they had been misled by Saruman, and Aragorn himself, with his long experience of seeing people corrupted and deceived by Sauron, must certainly have understood what the Dunlendings had gone through - both recently and in their history. He was also aware of the steady stream of them seeking refuge in Bree and realised that some of them were susceptible to the influence of the Nazgûl. His words to the Hobbits concerning the Nazgûl, "*They will drive these wretches to some evil work*"[51], referred to "*some of the strangers*"[52] as well as to Bill Ferny and Harry Goatleaf.

Whatever the nature and extent of Aragorn's contact with the Dunlendings he would have understood their hostility to Rohan and Gondor on account of having - as they would have seen it - their lands usurped by these stronger powers and as a result being continually pushed further west. Such a situation would not have fitted with his desire to unite the different races and species. *LotR* 6.5.968 tells of his first days as King when he received an embassy from Dunland. This seems to have been a promising further step towards permanent

---

48. Op. cit. [1], *LotR* 3.9, p. 566.
49. Op. cit., *LotR* 3.7, pp. 536-7.
50. Op. cit., *LotR* 3.7, p. 540.
51. Op. cit., *LotR* 1.10, p. 174.
52. Op. cit., *LotR* 1.10, p. 174.

reconciliation which had been initiated by Aragorn himself at Helm's Deep as he warned the Dunlendings of impending danger, and furthered by Erkenbrand's mercy and understanding.

Dead Men of Dunharrow

UT describes the Dunlendings as "*a sullen folk, akin to the ancient inhabitants of the White Mountain valleys whom Isildur cursed*"[53], thus establishing the common origin of the Dunlendings and the Dead Men of Dunharrow.

During the "dark years" (App B.1082) of the Second Age this group of mountain people, who would become the ghostly inhabitants of the Paths of the Dead in *LotR*, had worshipped Sauron, but when the kingdom of Gondor was established in SA 3320 the current King of the Mountains swore allegiance to Isildur at the Stone of Erech. However when Isildur summoned them to keep their oath and actually fight against Sauron - probably when the Last Alliance was formed in SA 3430 or maybe earlier - they refused. Isildur's response was to curse them so that they would be unable to rest until they had fulfilled their oath which, at some unspecified time in the future, they would be given another chance to do. Being now too frightened to support Sauron openly they fled and lived in secret places in the White Mountains where they dwindled and died out - there were no further kings - becoming sleepless ghosts unable to rest with the curse of Isildur hanging over them. The Stone of Erech was said to be a trysting-place for them.

The Dead took up residence in the Haunted Mountain close to what would become the refuge of Dunharrow used by the Rohirrim. They were aware that they would be summoned again when the time was right, but meanwhile they would not allow any living person to pass through their mountain. The only one to attempt this was Baldor son of Brego (second king of Rohan) in TA 2570 (App B.1087), following a drunken vow to go through the Paths of the Dead. That was the last his people saw of him.

*

Three thousand and thirty years after Isildur's curse, in fulfilment of the prophecies of Isildur himself and Malbeth the Seer and backed by the advice of Galadriel and Elrond, Aragorn entered the Paths of the Dead and gave the Men of the Mountains a second chance to keep their oath. Isildur's last dealings with these people had been, understandably, characterised by extreme anger. In fact it was his wrath which had so terrified them that they fled and hid rather than join Sauron's forces. As will be shown Aragorn's attitude was very different and much more complex. His encounter with the Dead and its related issues is described in *LotR* 5.2.773-790 with further detail in *LotR* 5.9.874-8 where Legolas and Gimli give their own account to Merry and Pippin, and in *LotR* 5.3.795-8 via a conversation between Théoden and Éowyn.

For clarity I now give a brief timetable and summary of this episode before analysing it. App B.1093 is helpful for confirming dates (in TA 3019).

Mar 6: Following the sighting of the ships of the Corsairs of Umbar in the Palantír of Orthanc Aragorn came to realise that a short-cut via the Paths of the Dead gave him the only possible chance of being able to intercept the ships before they could attack Minas Tirith. Accordingly he and his companions set out (from Helm's Deep).

Mar 7: They reached Dunharrow and the Haunted Mountain in the evening.

Mar 8: They entered the Paths of the Dead at dawn. The Dead followed them. Aragorn found the remains of Baldor. He ordered the Dead to let his company pass and then follow them to the Stone of Erech. After emerging from the mountain they rode across the Blackroot Vale and reached Erech just before midnight. Aragorn summoned the Dead with a horn-call and commanded them to follow him to Pelargir.

Mar 9: They rode from Erech, passed Tarlang's Neck into Lamedon and on to Calembel. Sauron's Darkness began that night.

Mar 10: The Dawnless Day. They crossed the River Ringló.

---

53. Op. cit. [46], *UT* 3.5, pp. 479-80.

Mar 11: They reached Linhir where enemy forces were contesting the fords at the mouth of the River Gilrain.

Mar 12: They drove the enemy across Lebennin and towards Pelargir.

Mar 13: They reached Pelargir and captured the enemy fleet with the help of the Dead. The Dead were then released.

Mar 14: The ships set off up the Anduin.

Mar 15: They arrived at the Battle of the Pelennor Fields.

A detailed examination of the behaviour of Aragorn and the Dead during these few days shows much of interest concerning their motives and their attitude to each other.

Aragorn's knowledge of the prophecies was matched by that of the Dead who had taken Isildur's words seriously when he spoke of a second summons to fulfil their oath. He had also told them that the war with Sauron would last for "*years uncounted*"[54] and this had clearly come about. The conversation between Théoden and Éowyn adds an extra dimension to their awareness. As stated by Théoden in answer to Merry's anxious questions, the Dead usually stayed inside the Haunted Mountain but occasionally, at times of "*great unquiet and coming death*"[55], they would come out and terrorise the people living nearby. Such a time was clearly at hand as Éowyn continued the conversation by speaking of "*a great host in strange array*" who, "*but little while ago*", were said to have made their way into the Haunted Mountain "*as if they went to keep a tryst.*"[56]. This conversation took place on March 9th and Aragorn had entered the Paths of the Dead on the morning of 8th. The implication is that the Dead, being more than usually restless, had been out in the valleys but for some reason had decided, *en masse*, to go back into the mountain. Their unrest was no doubt due to a feeling that the war with Sauron was approaching some sort of climax, but it is difficult to escape the interpretation that they must have sensed some sort of call or urgency, somehow knowing that their moment of reckoning was approaching. When Aragorn and his company entered the Haunted Mountain the Dead obeyed his command to let them pass then followed him through the mountain and all the way to the Stone of Erech. It was only here that he actually announced himself by blowing the silver horn which Elrohir gave him (was it the one Isildur had used for the original summons?), gave his name and title as Elessar, Isildur's heir of Gondor and told Halbarad to unfurl the standard. However the Dead had clearly been convinced of his identity as soon as he entered the mountain as they had let him and his companions pass.

Both parties had their own desperate motive in this encounter but these motives complemented each other. The Paths of the Dead were the only route which would enable Aragorn and his companions to **intercept** the Corsairs of Umbar in the time-scale available and the Dead themselves were the only people who would be able to help him **defeat** them. He told Legolas and Gimli, "*... that way I must go, since there are none **living** to help me.*"[57] [My emphasis]. His company was pathetically small. Halbarad had stated that he had brought thirty of the Northern Dúnedain with him - all that he could gather in the time available. He himself made thirty-one, while Elladan and Elrohir made thirty-three with Legolas, Gimli and Aragorn himself thirty-six. Numbers were not the issue - he had told Éowyn he would go alone if necessary - it was purely about arousing the Dead to fulfil their oath. As far as the Dead were concerned only Aragorn could absolve them from their oath-breaking and give them peace as he was the destined descendant of Isildur referred to in the prophecies. By doing for him what they had pledged themselves to do for Isildur - namely fighting against Sauron - they would redeem their crime.

Because of this joint commitment to help each other complete cooperation was obtained. Combined with Aragorn's qualities of leadership, courage and compassion this cooperation would assume a cohesive and gathering momentum. In fact the two companies - the Dúnedain and the ghostly remnant of the Men of the White Mountains - seemed to gel into one. As they rode towards Erech, the people in the surrounding hamlets were terrified and the universal cry was, "*The King of the Dead is come upon us!*"[58]. Then we are told that "...

---

54. Op. cit. [1], *LotR* 5.2, p. 782.
55. Op. cit., *LotR* 5.3, p. 797.
56. Op. cit., *LotR* 5.3, p. 797.
57. Op. cit., *LotR* 5.2, p. 782.
58. Op. cit., *LotR* 5.2, p. 789.

all men fled before the face of Aragorn"[59]. The leader of the ghosts was the King of the Dead, but Aragorn too was the King of the Dead as the leader of both companies and the descendant of Isildur, the King of Gondor who had originally summoned them to fight against Sauron. Perhaps it is not surprising that readers of *LotR* (including me at one stage) sometimes get confused by the name "*Grey Company*" and think that it refers to the Dead rather than the Dúnedain!

Legolas's account in *LotR* 5.9.874-5 shows the single-mindedness of the Dead as they became fired up by the urgency of the dual mission, appearing stronger and more terrifying in Sauron's Darkness, with their great speed, gleaming eyes and their attempt to sweep round and overtake the Dúnedain. Aragorn too was concerned only with speed and getting the Dead to fulfil their oath - he was not interested in their secrets, such as what had happened to Baldor or why he had been clawing at the locked door. [Hammond and Scull refer to a note in a later work of Tolkien's which suggests that the door in question was the entrance to an evil temple hall.[60] When Baldor came to it the door was shut in his face, following which his legs were broken and he was left to die in the dark.]

In his treatment of the Dead Aragorn displayed firm but compassionate leadership with no sign of the anger which had so terrified them in Isildur. As always he was understanding of weakness, and well aware of the power of Sauron to terrorise, dominate and deceive. In his dealings with these ghostly subjects he showed appreciation of their yearning for peace. As he stood at the Stone of Erech he asked them why they had come and they told him, "*To fulfil our oath and have peace.*" Aragorn's reply, "*The hour is come* **at last**" [My emphasis], showed his recognition of their long wait.[61] He then ordered them to follow him to Pelargir explaining that he would consider their oath fulfilled when that area was clean of Sauron's servants, adding that then "*... ye shall have peace and depart for ever.*" Gimli's account describes the events at Pelargir, the fulfilment of the oath and the resulting release of the Dead, Aragorn's last words to them being, "*Depart and be at rest!*"[62]

The firmness which accompanied his compassion was evident in the incident where the Dead tried to get past the Dúnedain and go in front of them. Aragorn forbade this, causing Legolas to observe that "*Even the shades of Men are obedient to his will*"[63], and from then on they followed his orders without question, driving the enemy forces away from the fords at Linhir and then on to Pelargir. Here, as related by Gimli, they hung back - perhaps sensing that this was the crucial moment. Then at Aragorn's command they "*came up like a grey tide, sweeping all away before it*"[64] thus bringing about the defeat of the enemy and the capture of the Corsairs' ships. Aragorn had expected them to do what was necessary to redeem themselves and in the end they saved the day because, when they were loosed against Sauron's forces, Gimli's concerns as to whether their weapons would still function were groundless: the fear they invoked was all that was needed to overcome the enemy who either fled south to their own lands or leaped into the river and drowned. Thus ironically "*wraiths of fear and darkness*"[65] were used **against** Mordor rather than by it, giving rise to Gimli's exclamation, "*With its own weapons was it worsted!*"[66] As Aragorn finally released the Dead to peace and rest, their King stepped forward, broke his spear and cast it down on the ground before bowing low to him. Then he turned away and the whole host "*vanished like a mist that is driven back by a sudden wind*"[67].

By the action of bowing, the King of the Dead displayed respect and gratitude to Aragorn who, while unquestionably regal and commanding, had treated them with justice and compassion. Though he had expected them to atone for their oath-breaking he understood the torment of their three millennia of unrest. In addition Aragorn in his turn must have felt respect and gratitude to them as without their actions at Pelargir the enemy ships would have reached Minas Tirith, the Battle of the Pelennor Fields would have been lost and Sauron's overall victory would have been a certainty.

---

59. Op. cit. [1], *LotR* 5.2, p. 789.
60. Op. cit. [37], p. 534, referring to The Rivers and Beacon-hills of Gondor, reproduced in Vinyar Tengwar 42 (July 2001)
61. Op. cit. [1], *LotR* 5.2, p. 789.
62. Op. cit., *LotR* 5.9, p. 876.
63. Op. cit., *LotR* 5.9, p. 875.
64. Op. cit., *LotR* 5.9, p. 876.
65. Op. cit., *LotR* 5.9, p. 876.
66. Op. cit., *LotR* 5.9, p. 876.
67. Op. cit., *LotR* 5.9, p. 877.

When Legolas said, "*Great deed was the riding of the Paths of the Dead...*"[68] he was no doubt referring to the achievement of the living participants but perhaps the Dead Men of Dunharrow should also share in the credit.

BEORNINGS AND WOODMEN OF WESTERN MIRKWOOD

As stated in App A.II.1063, the Beornings and the Woodmen of Western Mirkwood both came from the upper vales of the Anduin and both were akin to the forefathers of the Rohirrim (the Éothéod) from the days when they had lived between the Carrock and the River Gladden.

Beornings

The only individual Beorning to play a part in Tolkien's works is Beorn whom Gandalf, Bilbo and the Dwarves encountered in *The Hobbit*[69] receiving shelter and assistance from him. Being huge, strong and able to adopt the form of a bear he played a major part in bringing about victory for Men, Elves and Dwarves in the Battle of Five Armies. He also had a great rapport with animals. In *TH* we are told that he became "*... a great chief afterwards in those regions and ruled a wide land between the mountains and the wood*"[70].

At some point after the events of *TH* (TA 2941-2) Beorn was succeeded by his son Grimbeorn as indicated by Glóin in *LotR* 2.1.228 when Frodo met him in Rivendell in 3018. Glóin also told Frodo of the valour and trustworthiness of the Beornings pointing out that it was only through their efforts that Orcs and wolves were held at bay and the passage between Rivendell and Dale kept open. This included the High Pass and the Ford of Carrock used by Bilbo and the Dwarves. However they charged sizeable tolls for this service and were still (as in *TH*) not very fond of Dwarves. *TH* 18.307 states that Beorn's male descendants were, for many generations, also able to take on a bear's shape, though Tolkien's letter to Naomi Mitchison of April 25th 1954[71] seems to emphasise the relative normality of Beorn by stating that he was only a Man with a normal lifespan in spite of being a skin-changer, and says nothing about this being a general characteristic of this people.

Aragorn was of course only a ten/eleven-year-old child living in Rivendell during the events related in *TH*, so any contact he may have had with Beorn could only have taken place at least ten years later when he became a Ranger. We don't actually know the date of Beorn's death and the succession of Grimbeorn, so if these events occurred prior to 2951 Aragorn would not have known Beorn himself at all. However the quotation from *TH* given above perhaps implies a longer than ten-year rule as a "*great chief*". This would still allow for Grimbeorn being old enough to be called "*the Old*" (which Glóin does) in 3018. Therefore we can state definitely that Aragorn as a Ranger co-existed with Grimbeorn and we can probably assume that he co-existed with Beorn as well.

The only documented encounter between Aragorn and the Beornings is described in *UT* 3.4.ii.444 in the account of his capture of Gollum and his subsequent long journey with him to Thranduil's dwelling in Mirkwood. As Aragorn came near the Carrock the Beornings helped him to cross the Anduin with his captive. *TH* describes this crossing as being a ford "*of huge flat stones*"[72] over which the Dwarves had to carry Bilbo. The implication is that the Beornings had known of Aragorn's errand through the Elves of Mirkwood and presumably knew Aragorn as a friend of Gandalf even though they must certainly have been ignorant of his true identity. Since the capture of Gollum took place only a year before the events of *LotR* it would have been Grimbeorn who was the chief when this episode occurred.

Given the extent of Aragorn's travels during his adult life there must have been many other meetings between him and Beorn's (or Grimbeorn's) people. It is not clear whether Beorn's understanding of animals

---

68. Op. cit. [1], *LotR* 5.9, p. 877.
69. J.R.R. Tolkien, *The Hobbit*, 3rd edition, London, Allen & Unwin, 1966, 1975 printing, *TH* Chapter 7, pp. 122-150 and Chapter 18 302, 305-7.
70. Op. cit., *TH* Chapter 18, p. 307.
71. H. Carpenter (ed.), *The Letters of J.R.R. Tolkien*, with the assistance of Christopher Tolkien, London, HarperCollins Publishers, 1995. First published in Great Britain by George Allen & Unwin, 1981. Letter. 144, p. 178.
72. Op. cit. [69], *TH* Chapter 7, pp. 123, 125.

was a characteristic of his people as a whole. If it was it would have been a shared trait with Aragorn and the Dúnedain in general.

The Beornings were affected by the attacks on Mirkwood Forest by Sauron's armies of Easterlings during the War of the Ring. When Frodo looked out from Amon Hen he saw their land aflame (*LotR* 2.10.400).

On a lighter note, the Beornings were well-known for their baking, especially their honey-cakes. In *LotR* 2.8.369-70 Gimli declared that lembas was actually better than the honey-cakes which was high praise indeed. He went on to say that the Beornings were reluctant to give out their cakes to travellers but maybe Aragorn was favoured with them especially if he was in the company of Gandalf.

Woodmen of Western Mirkwood

TH 6.112 mentions woodmen coming from further south and settling near the area west of the Carrock near where Gandalf, Bilbo and the Dwarves were trapped by Wargs. Presumably these were some of the Woodmen of Western Mirkwood and presumably it was the growing presence of the Necromancer [Sauron] in the south of the forest which led to this migration. They are referred to as brave and well-armed so that the Wargs did not dare to attack them if it was daylight or if there was a large number of them.

There is no reference to any encounter between Aragorn and these people, though on his journey to hand Gollum over to Thranduil - and on any other journeys he made in that area - he must inevitably have met them. They were clearly courageous and trustworthy and in fact *UT* 3.1.357 refers to their role three thousand years previously during the battle between Isildur and the Orcs at the Gladden Fields. We are told that the Woodmen, becoming aware of what was happening, sent runners to inform Thranduil and also organised an ambush against the Orcs. Although they were too late to help in the battle they were in time to prevent the Orcs mutilating the bodies. Aragorn may have been aware of this piece of his history.

*

The Beornings and Woodmen are referred to almost as one people in some contexts. During Aragorn's first days as King we are told, in *LotR* 6.5.968, that he received embassies from the borders of Mirkwood which seems to mean the Beornings and the Woodmen. After the War of the Ring, as indicated in App B.1094, Thranduil and Celeborn divided up Mirkwood Forest (renamed Eryn Lasgalen), with Thranduil taking the area from the Mountains of Mirkwood northwards and Celeborn taking the part south of the Narrows (the indentation in the eastern border of the forest - see *UT* 3.2.402, 404 Notes 3 and 13). The whole of the area in between, which appears to be the largest part on the *LotR* maps, was given to the Beornings and the Woodmen. There is no indication as to how it would be divided - maybe they mingled and co-existed amicably.

MEN OF DALE AND LAKE-TOWN

These Men were also known as Bardings. In *LotR* 3.2.431 Aragorn told Legolas and Gimli that the Rohirrim were akin to the Bardings of Dale (as well as with the Beornings and the Woodmen as indicated in App A.II.1063).

App B.1088-9 and *TH* 10.201-13 are the best sources of information about Dale and Lake-town. The town of Dale was situated just south of the Lonely Mountain, while Lake-town was built on a wooden platform on the Long Lake approximately twenty-five miles away. Dale was destroyed in TA 2770 by the dragon Smaug, with its Lord, Girion, being killed. However his wife and son escaped down the River Running, thus ensuring the survival of the line. At the time of the events in *TH* (TA 2941-2) Dale was still a ruin and the descendants of its people lived in Lake-town, including Bard, the heir of Girion's line. It seems that Lake-town had been destroyed and rebuilt at some time in the past because reference is made to the remains of a larger town which appeared in the water when the level was low. By the end of *TH* Lake-town was again a ruin, but after the death of Smaug at the hands of Bard, and victory against the Orcs in the Battle of Five Armies, both Dale and Lake-town were rebuilt with Bard ruling them as King along with an extended area around them - hence the name Bardings. This was the situation when Gandalf and Balin visited Bilbo at Bag End in 2949.

In the conversation between Frodo and Glóin in Rivendell, referred to earlier in this chapter (*LotR* 2.1.229), Glóin sang the praises of the people of Dale who were now ruled (in 3018) by Brand the grandson of Bard. App B.1090 tells us that Brand had become king in 3007, on the death of his father Bain who had succeeded Bard in 2977. Glóin described the Bardings as good people who were very friendly to the Dwarves, with Brand being a strong king.

There is no record of any specific encounters between Aragorn and the Bardings. However he would certainly have been aware of their history and culture, and, as with the other races living between the Misty Mountains and Mirkwood Forest and beyond, he must inevitably have met and interacted with them on numerous occasions during his journeys. Perhaps he detected the weakness and fear in King Brand, strong king though he was, which Glóin referred to at the Council of Elrond when voicing his concern that Brand might yield to the demands of Sauron's messengers and pass on information about Bilbo - particularly as Sauron was clearly making war preparations against Dale.

The most interesting issue relating to Aragorn and the Men of Dale is the discussion in John D Rateliff's description of Bard as a prototype Aragorn: "*A dispossessed heir, he lives to achieve unexpected victory over the surpassingly strong hereditary foe who had destroyed his homeland, re-establishes the kingship, and founds a dynasty that renews alliances with nonhuman neighbors and helps bring renewed prosperity to the region. In short, he is a precursor of Strider (Aragorn) ...*"[73] There are many passages in *TH* which show some similarity between Bard and Aragorn:

- In conversation with Bilbo Smaug, referring to the line of Girion of Dale, asked "*... where are his sons' sons that dare approach me? .... I laid low the warriors of old and their like is not in the world today.*"[74] This is comparable with Sauron destroying many of the Northern Dúnedain through the war waged by the Witch-king of Angmar. However Smaug, depending on the interpretation of the quoted passage, either thought that Girion's line had ended or else that his descendants were not of the same calibre as their forefathers. Sauron on the other hand was haunted by the thought that Isildur's line might still exist, regarding such a situation with extreme trepidation.
- In *TH* 12.240 we are told that the Men of Dale had once understood the language of thrushes, using these birds to take messages to the Men of the Lake and elsewhere. Bilbo felt that there weren't any Lake-men left who knew thrush language, but it turned out that Bard did. In *LotR* 1.9.149 it is suggested that the Northern Dúnedain understood the languages of birds and animals.
- *TH* contains many details about Bard's appearance and character:
  - He is described as "*grim-voiced*", "*grim-faced*" and dark-haired.[75] Although he was accused of being gloomy the people knew of his worth and courage. He was also fore-sighted ("*always foreboding gloomy things*"[76]), knowledgeable, sensible and quick to take action when needed. This description also fits Aragorn quite well.
  - During the struggle when Smaug descended on Lake Town Bard held his ground, standing alone in the end after even his company of archers gave up the fight. He is described as running to and fro encouraging the archers and urging the Master to give orders. This behaviour is very similar to that of Aragorn at Helm's Deep.
  - The Black Arrow he used to kill Smaug was an heirloom of his House in the same way as Aragorn's sword Narsil/Andúril was an heirloom of the House of Elendil.
  - Like Aragorn, Bard proved to be more than a "mere fighting man" (to use a phrase of the Master of Lake-town), organising the care of the sick and wounded after the battle was over and approaching the Elvenking for help for the homeless people. In particular compare this description of Bard with the statement made by the Warden of the Houses of Healing about Aragorn: "*A great lord is that, and a healer; and it is a thing passing strange to me that the healing hand should also wield the*

---

73. J.D. Rateliff, *The History of The Hobbit, Part Two: Return to Bag-End*, London, HarperCollins Publishers, 2007 (2008 printing), Chapter 13.i, p. 557.
74. Op. cit. [69], *TH* Chapter 12, p. 238.
75. Op. cit., *TH* Chapter 14, pp. 261, 263.
76. Op. cit., *TH* Chapter 14, p. 258.

- In *TH* 14.263, when the people of Lake-town shouted for Bard to be king the Master of the town objected, with comments about Girion being lord of Dale not king of Lake-town. There is a similarity here to Denethor's objection to Isildur's line due to his insistence that only Anárion's descendants had a valid claim to the kingship of Gondor.
- Bard emerged from the lake following the death of Smaug proclaiming, "*Bard is not lost! He dived from Esgaroth, when the enemy was slain. I am Bard, of the line of Girion; I am the slayer of the dragon!*"[78] Although the speech and behaviour here seem to me to resemble Boromir, Bard's announcement of his lineage fits with Aragorn.
- In *TH* 19.316-17, following the Battle of Five Armies Bard took up the kingship of Dale and Lake-town, rebuilding both places and encouraging friendship between Elves, Dwarves and Men. The similarity to Minas Tirith under King Elessar is clear.

App B.1095 describes how King Brand was killed in 3019 in the War of the Ring alongside Dáin II (Ironfoot) King under the Mountain. Simultaneously with sending armies to Minas Tirith Sauron had also sent a force of Easterlings against the folk of Dale and the Lonely Mountain. Brand was succeeded by Bard II who sent an ambassador to Aragorn's coronation. Thereafter Dale maintained a lasting friendship with Gondor, coming "*under the crown and protection of the King of the West.*"[79]

DRÚEDAIN

The Drúedain are also referred to in various contexts as Wild Men (of the Woods), Woses, and Púkel-men. Those who feature in *LotR* lived in the Drúadan Forest (the Grey Wood) in Anórien and their role, under the leadership of Ghân-buri-Ghân, was to lead Théoden and his army through their land by a secret path, enabling him to avoid the Orc army on the main road to Gondor. Thus the Riders of Rohan were able to reach Minas Tirith safely and participate in the Battle of the Pelennor Fields.

The relevant chapters in *LotR* are 5.3.794 and 5.5.830-6, but *UT* 4.1.487-501 contains a large amount of information about these people put together by Christopher Tolkien from what he calls (in the relevant section of *UT* Introduction): "*a long, discursive, and unfinished essay concerned primarily with the interrelations of the languages of Middle-earth*"[80] which his father had written. The following summary of this is an attempt to establish the origin and nature of Ghân-buri-Ghân's ancestors in order to see him and his people in context and obtain insight into Aragorn's likely attitude to them.

There is considerable detail about their physical appearance and skills/gifts. They are described as being short, stumpy and broad, with heavy buttocks, short thick legs, wide faces and mouths, flat noses, little or no facial hair and deep-set eyes with heavy brows. Their eyes were black - rendering their pupils indistinguishable - but glowed red when they were angry. Their voices were deep and guttural and their laughter infectious. They were very gifted trackers of all living creatures making them secret and silent hunters. They had great knowledge of plants - their names and whether or not they were poisonous - and could carve life-like figures out of wood and stone. In addition they had the ability to sit still and silent for days on end and for this reason were revered as watchmen.

Tolkien was anxious to stress that they weren't related to Hobbits: they were taller (about 4 feet), heavier and stronger, with only sparse hair and none on their legs and feet - or even chins as a rule. Unlike Hobbits they ate little and drank only water. They were also more grim and ruthless - in fact they generally resembled Dwarves rather than Hobbits but, unlike Dwarves, were only short-lived.

Regarding the origin of these people, it is helpful to look at the three ages of Middle-earth in turn:
- First Age. There are two main threads here. The Drúedain appear to have originated in lands south of

---

77. Op. cit. [1], *LotR* 6.5, p. 958.
78. Op. cit. [69], *TH* Chapter 14, p. 263.
79. Op. cit. [1], App B, p. 1095.
80. Op. cit. [46], *UT* Introduction.17, p. 17.

what eventually became Mordor, then moved west and north into what would later (i.e. in the Third Age) be called Ithilien. From there they crossed the Anduin and settled in the vales of the White Mountains, occupying both sides of the range in fact. However it is also stated that a small breakaway group attached themselves to the forest-dwelling People of Haleth (one of the races of early Men who were allies of the Elves in their battles against Morgoth) and went west with them into Beleriand. There they lived among them in the Forest of Brethil in a similar set-up to that later found in Bree where Men and Hobbits lived in harmony.

- Second Age. After the defeat of Morgoth at the end of the First Age it is suggested that some of the Drúedain who had lived with the People of Haleth accompanied them to Númenor, though these were said to have died out or to have returned to Middle-earth by the time of the Downfall of Númenor. They are recorded as being foresighted, particularly regarding the voyages to Middle-earth by Aldarion, sixth King of Númenor, believing (rightly as it eventually turned out) that no good would come of them. Also during the Second Age there is a reference to the people of Enedwaith fleeing from the Númenóreans who had sailed to Middle-earth, but avoiding the lands (called the Drúwaith Iaur) between the Rivers Isen and Lefnui because of the "Púkel-men" who had always lived there. They were known as secret and silent hunters who used poisoned arrows.

- Third Age. *UT* 4.1.496 states that by the Third Age the Drúedain only survived in Anórien, in the Drúadan Forest, but that the people of Anfalas believed that some still existed in Drúwaith Iaur. In fact they were shown to be right by a further statement that after the Battles of the Fords of Isen in TA 3019 the Drúedain of Drúwaith Iaur came out of their caves and attacked Saruman's fleeing forces which were being driven southwards (*UT* 4.1.500 Note 13). There is also a reference to "Wild Men" on the coasts of Enedwaith who were fishers and fowlers and who were supposed to be akin to the Drúedain in race and speech.

The Drúedain suffered a long history of persecution, beginning in the First Age and prompting their original move west. However after settling in the vales of the White Mountains they suffered further torment from later arrivals of Men who were under the influence of Sauron. Even in the Third Age there is evidence, from Ghân-buri-Ghân's reference to being hunted as if they were beasts (*LotR* 5.5.833), that the Rohirrim didn't really recognise the Drúedain (or the "Woses" or "Wild Men of the Woods" as they called them) as human.

Continuing with the study of *UT* 4.1.488-90, 499, it was not in the nature of the Drúedain to rejoice in victory, even over Orcs for whom they felt extreme hatred. This hatred was demonstrated by their use of poisoned arrows against them - a weapon which they used against nothing/no-one else. They often carved Orc figures designed to look as if they were fleeing in terror and placed them at their borders. They also put images of themselves at the entrance to trails or at turns in paths, and these 'watch-stones' were feared by the Orcs as they believed them to be filled with the hostility of their makers. In the Third Age the statues which Merry saw on the way to Dunharrow were recognised by Gondor as being carvings of, and by, the Drúedain. *LotR* 5.3.794 states that they were located at each turn of the road and describes their huge clumsy limbs, squatting position, stumpy feet and fat bellies. This chapter goes on to refer to Dunharrow as being "*the work of long-forgotten men*"[81] during the time before the Númenóreans began to sail to Middle-earth. These men had now vanished, leaving the statues but no memory of the purpose of the refuge. Although the Men concerned were clearly Drúedain the Rohirrim (according to *UT* 4.1.496) did not realise the connection between Ghân-buri-Ghân's people in the Grey Wood in Anórien and the statues at Dunharrow which they referred to as "Púkel-men", paying them scant attention and regarding them as harmless. "Púkel" is based on the Anglo-Saxon word "púcel" meaning goblin or demon (*UT* 4.1.500-1 Note 14) and perhaps sums up the attitude of the Rohirrim to the Drúedain.

By the time of the War of the Ring the few surviving Drúedain in Anórien maintained their implacable hatred of Orcs but did not dare to actually go to war against Sauron. The account of Ghân-buri-Ghân's assistance to Théoden in mid-March 3019 is given in *LotR* 5.5.831-2, starting with Merry's awareness of the drumbeats by which the Drúedain communicated with each other. In answer to Merry's questions the knowledgeable Elfhelm

---

81. Op. cit. [1], *LotR* 5.3, p. 795.

spoke of the inhabitants of the Drúadan Forest as being a remnant of an older time, secretive, and wild and wary as animals. They had never fought Gondor or Rohan and Elfhelm realised that they were now troubled by Sauron's darkness and dreaded the return of the Dark Years (i.e. the period prior to the establishment of Arnor and Gondor) - hence their offer to help Théoden. Elfhelm knew too that they used poisoned arrows and that their wood-craft was exceptional. As soon as Merry saw Ghân-buri-Ghân sitting in front of Théoden he recognised the similarity between him and the Púkel-men, the images of Ghân's ancestors. The description of the "Wild Man's" deep guttural voice, halting rendering of the Common Speech and hatred of Orcs match the account of his race in *UT* 4.1.488 and the comments in App F.1129 about the Drúedain having their own language far removed from the Common Speech.

Ghân-buri-Ghân was very conscious of his own dignity and lineage as shown by his reminder that his people had been living in the Drúadan Forest before Gondor even existed, and by his obvious sense of offence when Éomer became sceptical about his ability to help, underestimating the Drúedain's powers of sight, hearing and assessment of numbers. In the event it was only due to the leadership of Ghân-buri-Ghân through the Stonewain Valley, thus avoiding the Orcs on the road, that the Rohirrim were able to reach Minas Tirith at all. He was also the first to detect the change in wind direction to the southerly breeze which would send Aragorn's ships up the Anduin. He proved to be faithful, true and totally reliable, giving Théoden permission to have him killed if he failed in his pledge to lead them safely. When he took his leave of them, all the Rohirrim were firmly convinced of the trustworthiness of his people, *"strange and unlovely though they might appear."*[82]

*

In *LotR* 6.6.976 following Aragorn's and Arwen's wedding celebrations the departing guests, along with Théoden's funeral cortège, left Minas Tirith. On the way to Rohan the party rode through Anórien and as they entered the Drúadan Forest they heard the drums of the Drúedain beating. At this point Aragorn ordered trumpets to be blown and the heralds announced the presence of King Elessar. They went on to say that the King formally gave the Forest to Ghân-buri-Ghân and his people in perpetuity, and that no-one was now allowed to enter it without their leave. The drums rolled again in acknowledgement and thus the only recorded encounter between Aragorn and Ghân-buri-Ghân ended.

When Théoden had promised Ghân-buri-Ghân *"rich reward"* and *"the friendship of the Mark for ever"* if he were to lead them faithfully, Ghân had replied that his people just wanted to be left alone in the woods and not be hunted as if they were wild animals.[83] Thus, by the action just described, Aragorn granted this request on behalf of Théoden and Éomer and undoubtedly on his own behalf too. His own gratitude for the part the Drúedain had played in the War of the Ring surely goes without saying. His treatment of them was very similar to his actions regarding the Shire and Bree, namely giving them protection and freedom from harassment, along with autonomy. In spite of Tolkien's anxiety to show that the Drúedain were not akin to Hobbits Aragorn seems to have viewed them in a similar way, as simple, unassuming folk whose gifts and desire to live life in their own way he respected.

Aragorn would surely have encountered the Drúedain during his travels prior to becoming King. He must have known all the lands between Rohan and Gondor extremely well - including Dunharrow and the Drúadan Forest. With his exceptional tracking ability, perception, powers of observation and long experience of living in the Wild he would have sensed the worth of these people and appreciated their bond with nature. Aragorn too was the last person to judge others by their outward appearance (*"All that is gold does not glitter... etc."*) and he would have realised (as did the Elves and the Edain in the First Age) that the integrity of the Drúedain shone through their superficial "unloveliness". He would also have pitied their history of persecution and understood their long-standing hatred of Sauron's creatures (and Morgoth's before that).

Presumably he must also have come across the Drúedain of Drúwaith Iaur and the "Wild Men" of Enedwaith during his journeys.

---

82. Op. cit. [1], *LotR* 5.5, p. 835.
83. Op. cit., *LotR* 5.5, p. 833.

Two previous versions of the encounter between Aragorn and Ghân-buri-Ghân in *HoM-e* IX[84] are worthy of attention. In the first, Ghân-buri-Ghân and two of his headmen actually came to Minas Tirith after Aragorn became King and humbled themselves before him by laying their foreheads on his feet, whereupon Aragorn raised them up and blessed them before granting them the Drúadan Forest. In the second, a similar meeting took place in the Forest itself. Perhaps the published version fits more with what we know of Ghân-buri-Ghân: his dignity and pride in his own rank, along with his, and his people's, desire to keep themselves to themselves. His liaison with Théoden during the journey of the Rohirrim to Minas Tirith in March 3019 was clearly a most unusual occurrence.

LOSSOTH

The Lossoth were also known as Snowmen. They are recorded, in App A.I.iii, as being the remnant of the Forodwaith who were the inhabitants of the frozen north of Middle-earth in the First Age. During the Third Age they lived mainly on the Cape of Forochel situated north-west of the Bay of that name, but sometimes camped on the south shores of the Bay at the feet of the Blue Mountains. They are referred to as *"strange"* and *"unfriendly"*.[85] Nothing is recorded of Aragorn having any contact with these people. However they had become caught up in the final stage of the war with the Witch-king of Angmar, through their contact with Arvedui last King of the North Kingdom. These events too are recounted in App A.I.iii.1041-2, and also partly in App A.I.iv.1049-51, and have some bearing on Aragorn's inheritance.

In TA 1974, after waging war on the Dúnedain for approximately six hundred years, the Witch-king of Angmar captured Fornost, the chief town of the North Kingdom, and drove most of the inhabitants - including the king's sons - westward over the River Lune. King Arvedui himself held out until the end and then escaped northwards on horse-back with some of his guard. After hiding in the tunnels of some old Dwarf-mines in the far north of the Blue Mountains, he was driven by hunger to request aid from some of the Lossoth who were camping nearby. The Lossoth only helped him reluctantly, partly because they placed no value on the few jewels he was able to offer them in payment, and partly because of their fear of the Witch-king whom they believed capable of controlling the weather. In the end it was a mixture of pity for Arvedui and fear of the weapons he and his men carried which led them to provide food and build some snow-huts for them. Thus they were clearly not servants of Sauron.

These events must have occurred during winter as we are told that in March 1975 a ship was sent north by Círdan who had been informed by Arvedui's elder son Aranarth of his father's escape and approximate whereabouts. Arvedui's hosts were by now friendlier toward him and used sleighs to take his company far enough across the ice for a boat to be sent from the ship to pick them up. However at this point the Lossoth became uneasy, sensing the approach of bad weather, and they begged Arvedui to ask for food and supplies from the ship for everyone and then stay with them until the summer, saying of the Witch king, *"... in summer his power wanes; but now his breath is deadly, and his cold arm is long."*[86]. The Lossoth had been living in fear of the Witch-king for generations by this time and had become wise to his pattern of behaviour. For reasons not specified Arvedui rejected his hosts' counsel. Maybe he was just desperate to escape from the frozen north and return to his own family and people, or maybe he didn't take the Lossoth's forebodings seriously. Perhaps, with his knowledge of the prophecy of Malbeth the Seer (namely that he would be the last king of the North Kingdom) along with the failure of his attempt to claim the kingship of Gondor and reunite the two branches of Elendil's line, he was now prepared to accept his fate. Whatever his reasons, he boarded the ship and subsequently it was driven on to the ice and wrecked by a fierce storm from the north. All on board perished and, in addition, the Palantíri of Annúminas and Amon Sûl were lost in the sea.

Later that same year Eärnur, son of King Eärnil II of Gondor, arrived by sea at the Grey Havens with a huge army. He and Círdan's army of Men and Elves went into battle against the Witch-king. On the arrival of a new force from Rivendell, led by Glorfindel, the Witch-king was finally defeated and disappeared from the

---

84. C. Tolkien (ed.), *The History of Middle-earth*, vol. IX, *Sauron Defeated*, London HarperColllins Publishers, 2002, first published in Great Britain by HarperCollins Publishers 1992, first version Part 1, Chapter 6, p. 56, second version Part 1, Chapter 7 pp. 61-2, 67-8.
85. Op. cit. [1], App A.I.iii, p. 1041.
86. Op. cit., App A.I.iii, p. 1042.

North. This was of course too late to save Arvedui. The Dúnedain of the North were now too few to constitute a kingdom and Aranarth took the title of Chieftain of the Dúnedain. We are told that it wasn't until *"long afterwards"*[87] that news of the shipwreck was learnt from the Lossoth so presumably Aranarth organised a search for his father, only taking the new title after Arvedui was confirmed dead.

A significant aspect of this account is that, before Arvedui boarded the ship at the Bay of Forochel, he gave the Ring of Barahir to the chief of the Lossoth explaining how valuable an heirloom it was to the Dúnedain and telling him that in case of need he would be able to ransom it *"with great store of all that you desire."*[88]. This was subsequently done, though I cannot find any reference as to when. Arvedui's action in saving the Ring of Barahir from destruction gives further weight to the suggestion that he knew the game was up and accepted that his end was near. Once ransomed the Ring was kept in Rivendell along with the other heirlooms of the House of Isildur until Elrond gave it to Aragorn on his coming of age. Aragorn gave it to Arwen in TA 2980 on their betrothal (App B.1090).

I find it hard to believe that Aragorn wouldn't have made contact with these folk who had helped his ancestor at a crucial point and who had been instrumental in preserving an important heirloom of Isildur's line. (If Arvedui had kept the ring with him it would have been lost along with the two Palantíri.) In addition the south shores of the Bay of Forochel were only just over the northern border of the old kingdom of Arnor, so any Lossoth camping there were in fact close neighbours and it would have made sense to investigate them and be aware of their allegiance. Also Forochel was the habitat of the White Wolves who occasionally featured in the history of Middle-earth in the Third Age (for example some of them threatened Bree in the winter of 3018-19) thus providing an additional reason for the Dúnedain to monitor that area.

THE ENEMY'S SLAVES

In this section I am interpreting the term "slave" as someone actually owned by Sauron (or Saruman) and therefore forced to work for him whether willing or not - as opposed to a "servant", who in theory had some choice in the matter. However the two words are not always used consistently in *LotR* and are sometimes interchangeable. The word "servant" is used freely to indicate those working for, or serving, Sauron, Saruman, Denethor and Imrahil - to give a few examples - and also to describe Sam Gamgee, and Nob from the Prancing Pony. The Nazgûl are also referred to as servants throughout the work, but in *LotR* 6.3.938 they are called slaves. They did indeed have characteristics of both, as did the Orcs, because although they seemed to have a certain amount of autonomy, in practice they were quite incapable of acting against their master's wishes.

In *LotR* 6.5.968 we are told that, after becoming King, Aragorn released the slaves of Mordor and gave them all the lands around Lake Núrnen (in the south of Mordor) to be their own. There are two issues here, namely the identity of the slaves in question and the location and nature of Lake Núrnen.

Identity of the slaves

Although the slaves in this instance seem to be Men (as opposed to any other species), in particular the ones from *"... the great slave-worked fields"*[89] in southern Mordor, the word is used in many different contexts in *LotR*:
- *LotR* 3.8.553-4 mentions Saruman's slaves who tilled part of the vale round Isengard and states that workers, servants, slaves and warriors were housed around the inner wall. These slaves were presumably a mixture of Orcs and Dunlendings along with some hybrids of the two.
- In *LotR* 4.2 Frodo, Sam and Gollum came to the desolation which lay before Mordor: *"the lasting monument to the dark labour of its slaves"*[90]. Here "slaves" is used in a general sense encompassing all species.
- *LotR* 4.9.724 refers to Orcs as being useful slaves.

---
87. Op. cit. [1], App A.I.iii, p. 1042.
88. Op. cit., App A.I.iii, p. 1042.
89. Op. cit., *LotR* 6.2, p. 923.
90. Op. cit., *LotR* 4.2, p. 631.

- Denethor voiced his opinion that the Ring should be kept beyond Sauron's grasp, except in the case of a victory so final that they would all be dead anyway and not bothered about it. In reply Gandalf reminded him that there were other people to come after them who should be considered, adding, "*And for me, I pity **even** his slaves.*"[91] [My emphasis]. This perhaps implies that he meant Orc slaves; if he was thinking of slaves who were Men he surely wouldn't have said "even".
- In the same chapter Gandalf stated that the Lord of the Nazgûl "*... rules ... from the rear, driving his slaves in madness on before.*"[92] This implies both Orcs and Men.
- Gimli's account of the battle against the Corsairs of Umbar in *LotR* 5.9.876-7 referred to their ships being manned by slaves. These were later identified as Men. There were also prisoners on board some of whom were people of Gondor who had been seized in raids. This may have applied to the oarsmen as well.
- It is stated that Sauron "*had few servants but many slaves of fear...*"[93]
- *LotR* tells of "*the great roads that ran away east and south* [from Mordor] *to tributary lands*"[94] along which new slaves (among other 'goods') were brought. The slaves in question seem to have been Men, as fresh supplies came in from east and south, meaning presumably from Harad, Khand or Rhûn. As in Gimli's account referred to above, those from Harad may have been people of Gondor taken by the Corsairs.
- As Frodo and Sam made their way towards Mount Doom we are told that "*Of all the slaves of the Dark Lord, only the Nazgûl could have warned him* [Sauron]"[95] of their approach.
- Later in *LotR* 6.3.946 Sauron's slaves were said to quail when Frodo put on the Ring. In this context we are talking about the members of his army - a mixture of Orcs, Men and Trolls. Presumably it was only the Orcs and Trolls who quailed as the Men would still have been capable of independent action even after Sauron's power was removed.
- Tolkien himself made a further suggestion in the letter to Naomi Mitchison of April 25th 1954[96] when he hinted that, back in the Second Age, Sauron might have captured some of the Entwives from their dwellings in the Brown Lands and taken them to Mordor as slaves in order to use their cultivation skills for the system of "*industrialized and militarized agriculture*" he had created to provide food for his armies. Although the Entwives themselves were no more, their expertise had survived. This fits with Treebeard's words to Merry and Pippin in *LotR* 3.4.476 when he told them how the Entwives had taught their crafts to Men and were held in high honour by them.

By the time of Aragorn's inauguration as King, the Nazgûl had of course been destroyed. The same applies to most of the Orcs and Trolls from Enemy armies, any survivors no doubt being rigorously hunted down. Regarding Men such as Easterlings, Haradrim or Dunlendings who had fought for Sauron/Saruman: Aragorn had made peace with their lands and they would have returned to their homes. The same would have applied to any slaves who were Gondorians. Therefore the slaves to whom Aragorn gave the lands around Lake Núrnen must have been Men (rather than any other species), who for some reason either had no specific place to go back to, or actually chose to carry on living where they were since the area was clearly fertile. Had there been generations of slaves there?

Nature of Lake Núrnen

During a discussion held by the Southampton UK Tolkien Reading Group a participant wondered - on account of the rather dubious descriptions in *LotR* of Lake Núrnen - why the ex-slaves would have wanted to live near it. *LotR* 6.2.923 refers to "*the dark sad waters*" of the lake and *LotR* 4.3.636 calls it a "*bitter inland*

---

91. Op. cit. [1], *LotR* 5.4, p. 814.
92. Op. cit., *LotR* 5.4, p. 819.
93. Op. cit., *LotR* 6.1, p. 900.
94. Op. cit., *LotR* 6.2, p. 923.
95. Op. cit., *LotR* 6.3, p. 938.
96. Op. cit. [71], Letter 144, p. 179.

sea". A look at the *LotR* map shows that four rivers, all with their sources in either the Mountains of Shadow or the Ash Mountains, drained into the lake which had no outlet. Hammond and Scull[97] discuss the meaning of the name Núrnen, referring to Tolkien's unfinished index which glosses it as 'sad-water'. They also point out that an older meaning of 'sad' was dark-coloured, particularly an unpleasant colour, while 'bitter' could also mean 'sad', but alternatively could mean 'unpalatable'. Overall there is the impression that the lake and thus the area surrounding it were unwholesome.

It seems to me that 'sad' in the conventional sense is fitting due to the lake's location in Mordor and the fact that the land around it was worked by slaves. Also, unpalatable and discoloured water is not necessarily unwholesome or harmful: for example water flowing through peat landscapes is dark brown and water with iron in it has a taste which certainly requires getting used to. The slaves probably **were** used to it. The water which Sam and Frodo drank as it trickled down from the Morgai tasted *"bitter and oily"*[98] but didn't seem to harm them. In fact the only warning they received about Mordor water was given by Faramir who had told them not to drink any water which flowed **out** of the Morgul Vale (*LotR* 4.7.694). The north-western part of Mordor, where Mount Doom, Barad-dûr, the Morannon, Cirith Ungol and Minas Morgul were located, is described as *"waterless"*[99], hence the presence of tanks along the road to Barad-dûr, one of which Frodo and Sam drank from. This water obviously came from elsewhere, presumably from the south of Mordor. It is notable that the four rivers flowing into Lake Núrnen in fact all originated in the southern or eastern parts of the two mountain ranges - there is nothing from the north-west where the greatest danger of pollution lay. From an examination of the *LotR* map, along with Karen Wynn Fonstad's maps of the area[100], it can be seen that their sources were between a-hundred-and-fifty and three-hundred-and-sixty miles from Barad-dûr and Mount Doom.

All this is to say that I cannot imagine Aragorn giving the area to the newly-freed slaves if it didn't have the potential to be a safe and pleasant place to live. Being well away from the pollution of the northern part of Mordor it would, of necessity, have had to be fertile to support Sauron's vast armies and gangs of workers, and perhaps something of the Entwives' teaching (if any had indeed gone there) had passed down over the centuries. In addition the removal of Sauron would obviously have given it a completely different atmosphere.

*

Turning to the *LotR* map again, it appears to be possible to get into Mordor from the east - either approaching from the south via Khand or from the north via the Sea of Rhûn area - as there is no mountain range on that border. Since we know from App A that Aragorn's travels took him *"far into the East"*[101] he may have actually entered Mordor from that direction and seen the plight of the slaves at first hand. He may also have become aware of their treatment prior to their arrival in Mordor, for example by observing their capture by the Corsairs or seeing them being transported. Out of pity, if from nothing else, he would have made it a high priority to redress the sufferings of these people if he were to regain his kingship. Such a compassionate attitude features in Gimli's account, in *LotR* 5.9.876, of the events at Pelargir when the Grey Company and the Dead defeated the Corsairs of Umbar. Since the slaves manning the ships were chained to their oars they, along with the prisoners on board, were not able to flee from the terror inflicted by the Dead. However Aragorn sent the Dúnedain round the ships to offer comfort and reassurance, and to free them all. Thus encouraged, the ex-captives worked in order to enable the Dúnedain to take some much-needed rest and when the fleet set off up-river to the Pelennor Fields *"The oars were now wielded by free men"*[102].

TOM BOMBADIL

In *LotR* 1.10.163 Aragorn told Frodo and his friends that he had been hiding behind the hedge on the East

---

97. Op. cit. [37], Hammond & Scull, p. 457.
98. Op. cit. [1], *LotR* 6.2, p. 921.
99. Op. cit., *LotR* 6.3, p. 936.
100. KW. Fonstad, *The Atlas of Middle-earth*, Revised Paperback Edition, London, HarperCollins Publishers, 1994, pp. 92-3.
101. Op. cit. [1], App A.I.v, p. 1060.
102. Op. cit., *LotR* 5.9, p. 877.

Road and had witnessed their parting from Tom Bombadil, casually referring to him as "*old Bombadil*". This showed that he recognised Tom and perhaps indicated that he was reasonably well acquainted with him. There is no other direct reference to such an acquaintance but a study of *LotR* 1.7 and 1.8 is quite revealing on the subject.

Soon after the arrival of the Hobbits at Tom's house Tom told them that he and Goldberry had had news of their predicament and later he made it clear that he had had dealings with the Elves and had received news of Frodo's flight via Gildor Inglorion in some way, with further information reaching him from Farmer Maggot. Since we know that Aragorn had been in contact with Gildor, it would seem logical that he had also been involved in the chain of communication. He certainly didn't seem to find it particularly surprising that the Hobbits were in Tom's company when he eventually tracked them down, and maybe it was no accident that he happened to be behind the hedge on that particular stretch of the East/West Road.

As Tom prepared to take leave of the Hobbits after he had escorted them safely away from the Barrow-downs he recommended that they walk on to Bree and spend the night at the Prancing Pony Inn. He knew - or knew **of** - Barliman Butterbur as he mentioned him by name and referred to him as "worthy". When the Hobbits asked him to come and have a drink with them at the inn he refused saying "*Tom's country ends here:* [i.e. at the East Road] *he will not pass the borders.*"[103]. Therefore the question is: How did he know the inn, and even the inn-keeper, well enough to make his recommendation? One answer could be that Farmer Maggot had talked about them as he and Tom seemed to know each other well. Maggot's farm was admittedly well over fifty miles from Bree - rather a long way to regard the Prancing Pony as a "local" - but since he evidently visited Tom he may have visited the inn as well. However another possibility is that it was the Dúnedain - or Aragorn in particular - who recommended the inn and that Tom specifically advised the Hobbits to go there so that they would have a chance of meeting Aragorn. My reason for arguing this is that I believe Tom had some affinity with the Dúnedain.

I have already mentioned that Aragorn seemed to know Tom and that he was possibly involved in the business of letting Tom and Goldberry know about Frodo's situation. Also, in *LotR* 2.2.265 at the Council, Elrond referred to some other names by which Tom was known, including "Orald" which was used by Northern Men. It is not clear what era Elrond was talking about, but Tom was obviously well known - or had been at some point - by "Northern Men" which could well include the Dúnedain among other races. Aragorn must have travelled extensively in the Old Forest, over the Downs and along the River Withywindle, and this adds to the case for him knowing Tom reasonably well. However the chief reason for my belief in Tom's affinity with the Dúnedain is that he was very aware of, and clearly moved by, the history of the North Kingdom as shown by the following observations from *LotR* 1.8.135-48:

- His sadness when leading the Hobbits over the border of the old sub-kingdom of Cardolan.
- His description of the depredations of the Witch-king of Angmar.
- His knowledge of those who were buried in the barrow where the Hobbits were trapped, including the last prince of Cardolan who was killed in TA 1409 (suggested in App A.I.iii.1041).
- His action in taking the blue brooch for Goldberry to wear so that its former owner (presumably a princess of Cardolan), whom he remembered as being beautiful, should not be forgotten.
- His selection of the knives for the Hobbits to use as swords, knowing that they had been forged long before by the Dúnedain. Did he actually have some foresight that one of these blades would destroy the Witch-king?
- Finally there was his wistful remark about the Witch-king's victims: "*Few now remember them, yet still some go wandering, sons of forgotten kings walking in loneliness, guarding from evil things folk that are heedless.*"[104] As he spoke these words the Hobbits saw a vision of the Chieftains of the Dúnedain over the centuries, the last of whom wore a star on his brow. They were, unknowingly, seeing Aragorn before actually meeting him - Aragorn as the returning king as shown by the presence of the star (the Elendilmir).

---

103. Op. cit. [1], *LotR* 1.8, p. 148.
104. Op. cit., *LotR* 1.8, p. 146.

These points seem to me to illustrate Tom's personal and emotional interest in Aragorn and his people, both at the time of the War of the Ring and earlier, along with an awareness of the prophecies regarding Aragorn's destiny. On a more mundane level, if he communicated with the Dúnedain he would have known of their patronage and appreciation of the Prancing Pony. [As an aside, it has been suggested to me that the Prancing Pony was actually named after Bombadil's own pony Fatty Lumpkin. The pony on the inn's signboard, rearing up on its hind legs, was fat and white. Fatty Lumpkin was, as his name suggested, fat but nevertheless more agile than would be expected from his girth and therefore capable of prancing. However his colour is not specified. The inn had presumably had its name for many years - or even centuries - so subscribing to this theory would mean that Fatty Lumpkin could not have been an ordinary "mortal" animal - which he probably wasn't.]

On the assumption that such a friendship existed between Aragorn and Tom other issues arise, such as:
- Had Aragorn also sat in the house on the edge of the Barrow-downs listening to Tom's tales of nature and Goldberry's singing, and enjoying the cream and honey and the clear drink which had gone to the Hobbits' hearts like wine?
- Had he received advice from Tom on dealing with Old Man Willow?
- Had he received tuition from Tom on the subject of the wights in the burial mounds? From a practical angle he needed to be aware of the danger, and from the personal viewpoint those were his own people lying there in the mounds, destroyed by the Witch-king who was himself responsible for the presence of the wights.

TREEBEARD AND THE ENTS

A study of *LotR* 3.2.440-43 and 3.5.488-500 shows that although Aragorn seemed to know a reasonable amount about the Forest of Fangorn he displayed a surprising ignorance and even scepticism regarding the Ents themselves.

The following observations, some of which arose in *LotR* 3.2 during a discussion between Aragorn, Legolas and Gimli as to why Celeborn (in *LotR* 2.8.373-4) had warned the Fellowship about Fangorn, illustrate his knowledge of the actual forest:
- He had learnt from Elrond that Fangorn was as old as the Old Forest and much bigger, with both being strongholds of the huge forests of the First Age before the existence of Men.
- He knew that Fangorn held some secret of its own.
- He knew too that it was supposed to be dangerous to cut twigs and branches from living trees there, urging Gimli to let the fire go out if necessary and to wake him if he was frightened.
- Nevertheless two years earlier he had travelled via the skirts of Fangorn on his journey from the Dead Marshes to the north of Mirkwood with the captured Gollum. He had presumably regarded it as preferable to going any nearer to Dol Guldur (*UT* 3.4.ii.444).
- Aragorn also stated that he was familiar with the many tales about the forest told in Gondor and elsewhere, emphasising that if it hadn't been for Celeborn's warning he would have regarded them merely as fables which over time had replaced actual knowledge. Legolas then referred to the songs sung in his own land which referred to the Onodrim, or Ents, living in Fangorn in the distant past.

The actual nature of the danger in Fangorn was not specified as was apparent in the wording of Celeborn's warning: "*That is a strange land, and is now little known*"[105]. The impression given was that Celeborn himself was not really clear as to the risks. Also, in a conversation with Merry and Pippin in *LotR* 3.4.467, Treebeard revealed that he himself would have given a similar warning about Lothlórien. The sum total of Legolas's knowledge was from the songs referred to above.

Aragorn's ignorance of Ents was made clear when he told Gandalf that he had not heard of Treebeard,

---
105. Op. cit. [1], *LotR* 2.8, pp. 373-4.

and then, on being enlightened, expressed amazement that Ents still existed, exclaiming *"I thought they were only a memory of ancient days, if indeed they were ever more than a legend of Rohan"*[106]. Indeed by the latter description, he even cast doubt as to whether Ents had **ever** existed, prompting a highly indignant reaction from Legolas. His ignorance was rather surprising given that the Ents had featured in the history of the First Age. *The Silmarillion*[107] refers to their origin as the Shepherds of the Trees at the instigation of the Vala Yavanna whose thought had summoned spirits to live in trees and act as protectors of plants. This coincided with the awakening of the Elves in Middle-earth and, as Treebeard told Merry and Pippin in *LotR* 3.4.468, it was the Elves who had taught the Ents to speak. *TSil* 22.282 relates the involvement of the Shepherds of the Trees at the sacking of Doriath in order to drive off the Dwarves of Nogrod who had attacked Thingol and his people. Treebeard also told Merry and Pippin of the estrangement between the Ents and Entwives during the First Age resulting in the latter travelling east and crossing the Anduin where they made gardens and taught their skills to Men. The gardens were subsequently destroyed by Sauron sometime during the Second Age and the area became known as the Brown Lands. As the Fellowship passed that way on their journey down the river we are told that *"even Aragorn"*[108] didn't know what deed of the Enemy had caused the destruction.

It is true that there does seem to have been a veil of obscurity over the whole issue of Fangorn and the threat within, but one would have expected someone with Aragorn's level of education and knowledge to have been much more aware of the Ents and their history or at least to have known that they (had) really existed.

*

Aragorn and Treebeard did not actually meet until after the parley with Saruman (*LotR* 3.10.585) when Gandalf introduced them. There is however a hint about a possible awareness of Aragorn on Treebeard's part stemming from a conversation with Merry and Pippin about Lothlórien with Treebeard telling them, *"I am surprised that you ever got out, but much more surprised that you ever got in: **that has not happened to strangers for many a year**."*[109] [My emphasis] This raises the question of whether he had been aware of Aragorn being drawn into that land nearly forty years earlier, though without knowing who he was.

Regarding the meeting at Isengard it is clear from the context that Gandalf had already spoken to Treebeard about Aragorn, Legolas and Gimli and this presumably involved giving him an account of the identity and significance of Aragorn. No doubt Merry and Pippin too had spoken to Treebeard of the other members of the Fellowship. By this time Aragorn was of course well aware of Treebeard's role in the defeat of Saruman and of the well-timed actions of the Huorns at Helm's Deep. There is no indication of what was said at this first encounter, just that Treebeard looked *"long and searchingly"*[110] at Aragorn and his two companions and spoke to them in turn.

Their second encounter (the only other recorded) also took place at Isengard when Aragorn, as King, accompanied his guests on the first part of their journey to their respective homes. By this time Treebeard had given further cause for gratitude by leading the Ents to the Wold of Rohan to destroy the Orc army which had invaded Rohan from the north. After praising the achievements of all his visitors he referred to this latest deed of his people explaining that the Orcs they destroyed had not heard of Ents before, then adding *"though that might be said also of better folk"*[111], a gentle dig at Aragorn and Éomer among others. Aragorn was well aware of what he owed to the Ents and told Treebeard that their deeds would never be forgotten by Gondor and Rohan, a speech which gave rise to the Ent's observation that *"**Never** is too long a word even for me. Not while your kingdoms last, you mean; but they will have to last long indeed to seem long to Ents."*[112] However Gandalf pointed out to Treebeard that the kingdoms of Men might well outlast him.

---

106. Op. cit. [1], *LotR* 3.5, p. 499.
107. C. Tolkien (ed.), *The Silmarillion*, London, HarperCollins Publishers, 1999, first published in Great Britain by George Allen & Unwin 1977, *TSil* Chapter 2, pp. 40-41.
108. Op. cit. [1], *LotR* 2.9, p. 380.
109. Op. cit., *LotR* 3.4, p. 467.
110. Op. cit., *LotR* 3.10, p. 585.
111. Op. cit., *LotR* 6.6, p. 979.
112. Op. cit., *LotR* 6.6, p. 979.

This meeting also involved Aragorn retaking possession of Orthanc (which actually belonged to Gondor), giving the Ents free rein to plant trees in the surrounding valley in return for ensuring that no unauthorised person entered it [Orthanc]. At this point it became clear that Treebeard had managed to get the keys from Saruman before letting him go and the Ent Quickbeam came forward and presented them to Aragorn. Still trying to assure Treebeard of his gratitude Aragorn now expressed the wish for his forest to grow in peace and gave him leave to take over the land west of the Misty Mountains as well, "*where once you walked long ago.*"[113] When Treebeard pointed out that the Ents would dwindle and therefore not need to spread, Aragorn suggested that there might be more hope in the search for the Entwives now that the lands to the east were open again. This idea was also rejected by Treebeard on the grounds of the eastern areas being too far away and there being too many Men there.

The impression I get from this encounter is of Aragorn being ashamed of his former ignorance of the Ents and now trying to make up for it by repeated expressions of gratitude and by exhibiting his (obviously) newly-acquired knowledge of their history - hence his references to the Entwives and to the fact that the Ents had once roamed over a much wider area. Treebeard would have seen through this and it is difficult to escape the feeling that he must have regarded Aragorn as rather ignorant, though he would undoubtedly have appreciated his role in the defeat of Sauron and Saruman.

Two other possible links between Treebeard and Aragorn are worthy of mention:
- In a letter to Fr. Douglas Carter dated June 1972 on the subject of whether the Ents and Entwives ever found each other again, Tolkien raised the possibility of them sharing "*... the hope of Aragorn that they were 'not bound for ever to the circles of the world and beyond them is more than memory'*"[114] (quoting Aragorn's dying words in App A.I.v.1063).
- The second link is more tenuous. In *LotR* 3.4.470 the blending of the two lights - one gold and one green - from Treebeard's lamps is said to resemble the summer sun shining through a roof of young leaves. There is a similar description when Galadriel presented Aragorn with the Elessar brooch: "*... the gem flashed like the sun shining through the leaves of spring.*"[115]. The Elessar had healing properties and so did the river of Fangorn, the Entwash, as illustrated by the effects of the Ent-draughts on Merry and Pippin.

THE ENEMY

App A.I.v contains a number of statements concerning the nature of Aragorn's travels and activities during his adult life prior to the War of the Ring. He:
- "*... seemed to Men worthy of honour ... when he did not hide his true shape*"[116]
- "*... went in many guises, and won renown under many names*"[117]
- "*... went alone far into the East and deep into the South, exploring the hearts of Men, both evil and good, and uncovering the plots and devices of the servants of Sauron*"[118]
- "*... became ... skilled in their* [Men's] *crafts and lore*"[119]

These observations have been seen to be relevant when considering Aragorn's relations with the "good" people of Middle-earth - which is where the "relationship" discussions have chiefly been concentrated. For example: he seemed "*worthy of honour*" when incognito in Rohan and Gondor, but not in Bree where he hid his "*true shape*" by appearing to be a "*mysterious vagabond*"[120]; he had the ability to empathise with others and

---
113. Op. cit. [1], *LotR* 6.6, p. 980.
114. Op. cit. [71], Letter 338, p. 419.
115. Op. cit. [1], *LotR* 2.8, p. 375.
116. Op. cit., App A.I.v, p. 1060.
117. Op. cit., App A.I.v, p. 1060.
118. Op. cit., App A.I.v, p. 1060.
119. Op. cit., App A.I.v, p. 1060.
120. Op. cit., *LotR* 1.10, p. 164.

was well-versed in the history and customs of the Rohirrim. However my main purpose in this section is to use the quoted passages as the basis of a discussion of Aragorn's dealings and associations with the "evil" peoples, the "*servants of Sauron*", the enemies of the Elves, Dwarves, Hobbits, Ents and Men of Gondor, Arnor, Rohan, etc. Also relevant is Aragorn's ability to adapt his manner of speaking to that of his companions and associates as described in App F.II.1133-4 and observed by Frodo in Bree (*LotR* 1.10.166) where "Strider" initially spoke like the locals but then changed his voice once he began to trust the Hobbits.

The following races are covered:
- Men of Harad: Haradrim of Near Harad, Corsairs of Umbar, Inhabitants of Far Harad
- Men of the East
- Variags of Khand
- Orcs
- Trolls
- Balrogs
- Shelob and her offspring
- Dragons

Orcs and Trolls as races supported Sauron, being bred or warped by him and thus delighting in evil as part of their psyche. Men, on the other hand, were neither inherently evil nor bred by Sauron and therefore had to be "persuaded" to support him. *HoM-e* X.5[121], in an essay on the origins of Orcs, describes Sauron's corruption of Men, comparing him with Morgoth: "*And he [Sauron] proved even more skilful than his Master also in the corruption of Men who were beyond the reach of the Wise, and in reducing them to a vassalage, in which they would march with the Orcs, **and vie with them in cruelty and destruction**.*" [My emphasis]. The three races of Men in the list above were "*beyond the reach of the Wise*" due to their physical location (South and East, closer to Mordor, etc.) and came under Sauron's sway during the Second and Third Ages. As a result they were subjected to such intense corruption and mental enslavement that they attained a level of evil comparable with that of the Orcs, though without losing their independence of action. This perhaps explains the determination of some of them to fight on regardless which is notable in the battle accounts in *LotR* - particularly of the Battle of the Morannon where the Orcs and Trolls fled once Sauron's power had been removed by the destruction of the Ring (*LotR* 6.4.949) - and the equal determination of the leaders of the West to destroy or subdue them.

Men of Harad

As indicated this heading includes three sub-categories, which are now described and then discussed in the context of the quoted passages at the beginning of this section.

Haradrim of Near Harad (also called Southrons or Swertings)
Near Harad was immediately south of Mordor and its people had been under Sauron's sway on and off during the Second and Third Ages. In *LotR*, as the Rangers of Ithilien prepared to ambush a regiment of them who were on their way to the Morannon, Damrod summed up the general feeling of Gondor towards them: he cursed them, being particularly irate that they were marching on roads built by Gondor, briefly referred to periods in their history when they had been on friendly terms with Gondor [for example in the reign of Ciryaher in the eleventh and twelfth centuries as described in App A.I.iv.1045] but then stated that "*the Enemy has been among them, and they are gone over to Him, or back to Him - they were ever ready to his will*"[122]. Gollum thought that they appeared to be "*very cruel wicked Men*"[123], while Faramir called them "*cruel Haradrim*"[124]. *LotR* describes those who were present at the Battle of the Pelennor Fields as "*bold men and grim, and fierce

---
121. C. Tolkien (ed.), *The History of Middle-earth*, vol. X, *Morgoth's Ring*, London HarperColllins Publishers, 2002, first published in Great Britain by HarperCollins Publishers 1993, *HoM-e* X, Part 5, Myth Transformed, p.420.
122. Op. cit. [1], *LotR* 4.4, p. 659.
123. Op. cit., *LotR* 4.3, p. 646.
124. Op. cit., *LotR* 4.5, p. 678.

in despair"[125]; they were wiped out and the only news their homeland received of them consisted of tales and rumours. A further contingent was sent to the Battle of the Morannon. Following the destruction of the Ring most of them fled eastward, some sued for mercy and some gathered for a desperate last stand, the remnant of these being eventually subdued during the ensuing days. Although *LotR* 6.5.968 states that Aragorn, in his first days as King, received embassies from the South and made peace with Harad it was in fact many years before a full peace was achieved as Sauron's legacy of hatred remained. App A.II.1071 refers to Éomer, even as an old man, helping Aragorn to deal with anti-Gondor risings in the South.

In *LotR* 4.3.646 Gollum described the Haradrim as being much bigger than Orcs with black eyes and long black hair, wearing red cloaks, gold earrings and red paint on their cheeks. The one which Sam saw killed in the ambush carried out by Faramir's Rangers was brown-skinned, wore a golden collar and had his black hair in plaits braided with gold. It seems to me, reading these details, that it would have been relatively easy for Aragorn to appear to be one of the Haradrim since his build and hair colouring fitted and no doubt he would have been sun-tanned after living in what must have been a warmer climate than further north. Suitable clothing, appropriate hair-style, face-paint and jewellery would have completed the outfit while his mastery of accent and language and his ability to adopt "*many guises*" and "*hide his true shape*" could have enabled a pretty successful integration. The Common Speech was presumably adopted by the Haradrim in the Second Age when contact first began between the Númenóreans and the natives. Given that Aragorn seems to have spent a considerable time in these hostile lands it probably became second nature to adopt the semblance of cruelty, and hatred of Gondor when required. The more he was able to achieve this the better understanding he would have had of Sauron's influence over these people.

Corsairs of Umbar

Umbar was a great natural haven south of the Bay of Belfalas (*UT* Index 607). More information is contained in App A.I.iv.1044-8, 1052 and App B.1085-6. Two-thirds of the way through the Second Age it was made into a fortress of the Númenóreans being a stronghold of "King's Men", that is those who became corrupted, sought power and mastery in Middle-earth, believed they were entitled to the immortality of the Elves and hated "The Faithful" (the followers of Elendil and his ancestors who had remained faithful to the Elves and the Valar). It was there that Ar-Pharazôn landed to challenge Sauron towards the end of that age. In the Third Age the rebel ('Black') Númenóreans gradually intermarried with the neighbouring Haradrim with many of them becoming pirates known as the Corsairs of Umbar. As with the Haradrim in general the Common Speech would have been adopted following the arrival of the Númenóreans and the merging of the Adûnaic and native languages. During the War of the Kin-strife (approximately TA 1400s-1800s - see Genealogical Table 5) Umbar became the centre for the supporters of Castamir the Usurper and his descendants. Although it was retaken by Gondor several times this was only temporarily and the two powers remained at war with each other, with the Corsairs being an increasing threat as the Third Age progressed and Sauron's power grew again. The culmination of their activities was the threatened attack on Minas Tirith in TA 3019 which was foiled by Aragorn's Grey Company and the Dead Men of Dunharrow. It was not until after Aragorn became King that Umbar was completely subdued.

As far as the Corsairs were concerned it was Aragorn's time in Gondor serving the Steward Ecthelion under the alias of "Thorongil", coupled with his undoubted knowledge of the history of Númenor and Gondor, which led to his awareness of the activities of these people. He would have known of their alliance with the Haradrim (by blood and politically), their role in supporting the rebels during the Kin-strife, the death of a King of Gondor at their hands (Minardil in 1634) and the massive attack in 2758 when three large fleets attacked Gondor all along its coastline as far as the mouth of the River Isen. With this knowledge Aragorn, during his service as Thorongil in approximately TA 2970-80, was especially suspicious and vigilant and put pressure on Ecthelion to allow him to take a fleet to Umbar. His suspicions were proved right and with his small fleet he defeated the Corsairs with little loss on his own side - an exploit for which he received great renown. Maybe he had already been to Umbar - either openly or in secret, by land or by river/sea - prior to entering Ecthelion's service so that he had observed the activity there in person and realised the danger of leaving it unchecked.

---

125. Op. cit. [1], *LotR* 5.6, p. 848.

These events were of course the reason why he honed in on Umbar with the Palantír of Orthanc in 3019 once he had managed to wrest it from Sauron's control - he knew what was likely to be happening. Any visit to Umbar after his "Thorongil" days would of necessity have had to be in disguise as he could not have risked being recognised.

Inhabitants of Far Harad

The inhabitants of Far Harad are only mentioned as being present at the Battle of the Pelennor Fields. They are described as "*black men like half-trolls with white eyes and red tongues*" and as "*troll-men ... that hated the sunlight*".[126] One wonders whether Sauron had been creating hybrids similar to Saruman's Orc-X-Dunlending ones. Presumably those present in the battle were all destroyed like their counterparts of Near Harad. There seems to be no indication that any of them were at the Battle of the Morannon.

At the Council of Elrond Aragorn stated that he had been to Rhûn and Harad "*where the stars are strange.*"[127]. There is also the quotation from App A given above that he had travelled "***alone** ... deep into the South*" [My emphasis]. These points are taken up in *UT* where Christopher Tolkien quotes his father's comment on the subject which says that "*The 'strange stars' apply strictly only to the Harad, and must mean that Aragorn travelled **or voyaged** some distance into the southern hemisphere.*"[128] [My emphasis]. The *LotR* map - as far as it goes - shows Far Harad as extending an unspecified distance further south than Umbar but there is no indication of where the Equator would be. Karen Wynn Fonstad's maps of the southern lands[129] are based on Tolkien's earliest world maps (in *HoM-e* IV.5)[130] and the implication is that Far Harad extended south indefinitely - Harad, after all, means South - and that in fact the area we see in the *LotR* map was all north of any Equator. Therefore we can only guess at the extent of Aragorn's travels if he had actually gone into the Southern Hemisphere. What is clear though, is that he must certainly have observed these people of Far Harad at first hand, though he may have had to acquire some knowledge of their language if they hadn't adopted the Common Speech. It is also clear that it would have been difficult for him to appear as one of them, thus any observation must have been done from a distance or secretly - unless he was able to come up with a convincing reason for being among them. Perhaps there are some clues in the three words I have emphasised above: he was alone, and/or he travelled at least some of the way by sea.

Men of the East

The account of the history of Gondor in the Third Age, in App A.I.iv.1044-6, 1048-9, 1053, indicates that - in addition to the Corsairs and the Haradrim - various races of Men from the East were a frequent threat. Some of these were from the area just east of Mirkwood Forest but generally "the East" indicates the land named as Rhûn on the *LotR* map, east of the Sea of that name. The first attack seems to have been in TA 400s by "*wild men out of the East*"[131]. In TA 1800-1900s further attacks were made by a confederacy of peoples from the East, stronger and better-armed than before, who travelled in wains while their chieftains fought in chariots. These were known as the Wainriders and it is stated that they had been stirred up by emissaries of Sauron. Around 1940 it became clear that Sauron was co-ordinating attacks on Gondor and Arnor. For example the Haradrim and the Men of Khand were also attacking Gondor in the South and the War with the Witch-king of Angmar had been going on in the North for over five-hundred years by then.

A similar situation occurred in the 2500s during the Stewardship of Cirion when attacks were made by the Balchoth who lived in the area between Mirkwood Forest and the River Running. They are stated to have been "*wholly under the shadow of Dol Guldur*"[132] and their numbers were continually increased by similar people

---

126. Op. cit. [1], *LotR* 5.6, pp. 846, 848.
127. Op. cit., *LotR* 2.2, p. 248.
128. Op. cit. [46], *UT* 4.2, Note 10, p. 520.
129. Op. cit. [100], Fonstad, p. 53.
130. C. Tolkien (ed.), *The History of Middle-earth*, vol. IV, *The Shaping of Middle-earth*, London HarperColllins Publishers, 2002, first published in Great Britain by George Allen & Unwin (Publishers) Ltd, 1986, *HoM-e* IV, Chapter 5, pp. 248-51.
131. Op. cit. [1], App A.I.iv, p. 1044.
132. Op. cit., App A.I.iv, p. 1053.

who came from further east. At the same time Cirion was also being assailed by the Corsairs of Umbar, thus indicating again the influence of Sauron in co-ordinating these attacks.

Although the Wainriders and the Balchoth appear to have been wiped out during their eventual defeats by Gondor more Men from the East were involved in the War of the Ring. Damrod's remarks about the Haradrim quoted earlier were applied also to the Easterlings, namely that *"the Enemy has been among them, and they are gone over to Him, or back to Him - they were ever ready to his will"*. Faramir called them *"wild Easterlings"*[133]. As far as their appearance was concerned Ingold referred to *"countless companies of Men of a new sort that we have not met before. Not tall, but broad and grim, bearded like dwarves, wielding great axes. Out of some savage land in the wide East they come, we deem."*[134] At Pelennor Fields they showed themselves as *"strong and war-hardened and asked for no quarter"*[135] and kept rallying. There were also some in the force which blocked the road between Rohan and Gondor forcing Théoden and the Rohirrim to use the secret Stonewain Valley route guided by Ghân-buri-Ghân (*LotR* 5.5.832). On being scattered they took over the island of Cair Andros in the Anduin until the faint-hearted, whom Aragorn dismissed at the desolation at the north-west border of Mordor, were sent to recover it. Easterlings were also part of the force (along with Orcs) which attempted to ambush the Army of the West in Ithilien as it made its way to the Morannon (*LotR* 5.10.885). This ambush was foiled and its participants killed or driven eastwards into the foothills of the Mountains of Shadow. At the Battle of the Morannon, after the destruction of the Ring, some Easterlings gathered for a desperate last stand while a greater number fled eastward and some sued for mercy. As with the Haradrim the remnants were eventually subdued. *LotR* 6.5.968 tells of Aragorn's first days as King when he received embassies from the East. He pardoned the Easterlings who had given themselves up sending them away free. However, as with Harad, it was in fact many years before a full peace was achieved and the elderly Éomer accompanied Aragorn into battle in the East as well as in the South.

Another, totally different, connection between Gondor and the East concerned the horn carried by Boromir in *LotR*. Denethor stated that this was made from the horn of a wild ox caught by Vorondil father of Mardil (the first Ruling Steward of Gondor) who was in the habit of hunting these creatures *"in the far fields of Rhûn"*[136]. They were supposedly descended from *"the wild kine of Araw"*[137], Araw being a name for the Vala Oromë. Vorondil died in TA 2029 and the eldest son of the Steward carried the horn from then on until it was broken at Parth Galen in 3019 during Boromir's final battle with the Orcs.

In *LotR* 2.2.248 at the Council of Elrond Aragorn told Boromir that he had been to Rhûn. Also App A states that he went *"far into the East"*[138]. On the *LotR* map Rhûn clearly lies east of the Sea of Rhûn and seems to extend roughly from the Iron Hills in the north down to the eastern border of Mordor in the south. Therefore Aragorn's travels there could have taken in any, or all, of that area, including an approach to Mordor from the east. *"Far into the East"* is even more open-ended as we don't know how far east Rhûn went or what was beyond it. The far eastern range of the Red Mountains (the Orocarni) is shown on Tolkien's first maps (*HoM-e* IV.5.249, 256), and also on one of Karen Wynn Fonstad's First Age maps[139], but they appear to have been destroyed in a seismic upheaval at the end of the First Age as they don't appear on the *LotR* map and I can find no reference to them existing in the later Ages. In Chapter 2.3 I have discussed the possibility of Aragorn visiting the same areas as the Blue Wizards whom we know to have travelled only in the far East and South (*UT* 4.2.504, 518).

As regards mingling with the Easterlings, Aragorn, being tall and lean rather than short and broad, would have had difficulty in passing for one of them. Therefore his role must have been more that of observing/spying rather than integrating unless he could find a convincing reason for mixing with them. Given that these people were serving in multi-race armies they must have spoken some dialect of Common Speech, though what language they used in private is not clear. Aragorn would no doubt have picked up sufficient for his needs.

---

133. Op. cit. [1], *LotR* 4.5, p. 678.
134. Op. cit., *LotR* 5.4, p. 821.
135. Op. cit., *LotR* 5.6, p. 848.
136. Op. cit., *LotR* 5.1, p. 755.
137. Op. cit., *LotR* 5.1, p. 755.
138. Op. cit., App A.I.v, p. 1060.
139. Op. cit. [100], Fonstad, p. 5.

After the War of the Ring he showed mercy, justice and wisdom in his dealings with the Easterlings, pardoning and making peace - as opposed to attempting to wipe them out which seems to have been the norm in the past with the Wainriders and the Balchoth.

Variags of Khand

On the *LotR* map Khand is situated immediately to the south-east of Mordor bordered by the south-eastern range of the Mountains of Shadow. Near Harad lies to its south and Rhûn to its north. Khand is mentioned in the account of Gondor's history in App A.I.iv.1049 as being allied with the people of Near Harad and the Wainriders during the attacks on Gondor in TA 1900s. Thus the implication is that it had long been under the sway of Sauron, with its location being an added reason for this assumption.

The only mention of the Variags of Khand in *LotR* is at the Battle of the Pelennor Fields (*LotR* 5.6.846, 848), and apart from the fact that they hated the sunlight we know no more about them. It is possible that they resembled the people of neighbouring Near Harad and perhaps spoke the Common Speech. However their dislike of the sunlight seems to fit more with the Troll-like people of Far Harad and they may instead have resembled them. This interpretation could also explain their apparent absence at the Battle of the Morannon as the Far Harad people are also not mentioned as being there. They were perhaps all destroyed on the Pelennor Fields and no further contingents were sent to the later battle. How heavily populated was Khand? And Far Harad?

Although we don't know how far south Khand extended there is no doubt that its location in general fitted easily within the range of Aragorn's journeys and that he was able to assess the nature, fears and loyalties of the inhabitants by associating with them, or observing them secretly, depending on which approach was most fitting.

Orcs

"Orc" is used in *LotR* as the general Common Speech term for all varieties of Orc. "Goblin" is also sometimes used, particularly by the Hobbits. The Elvish word for Orc was "Orch", plural "Yrch" (used by Legolas and the Elves of Lothlórien) with a further Elvish word "Glamhoth" appearing in *UT* Index 570. Ghân-buri-Ghân's people called Orcs "Gorgûn". The terms "Uruk" and "Uruk-hai" were used to denote a larger breed of Orc.

App F.I.1131 states that Orcs were originally bred by Morgoth in the First Age while *TSil* 3.47 states that they were bred from captured and corrupted Elves. However *HoM-e* X Part Five, Sections VIII, IX and X 408-24 contain a selection of late essays on Orcs and their nature and origins, some of which suggest that they originated from Men rather than Elves. Whatever the case, after the defeat of Morgoth Sauron carried on breeding them throughout the Second and Third Ages. In the Third Age Saruman also bred them. Unlike Men, once the Ring was destroyed the Orcs in Sauron's army were unable to function without their master's will driving them - hence they fled unable to attempt a last stand.

From App B.1087-90 we can see that Orc activity increased during the third millennium of the Third Age following the discovery of the One Ring by Déagol in TA 2463. They made strongholds in the Misty Mountains causing all the passes to become dangerous and over the next few hundred years parties of them attacked Rohan, Ithilien and Eriador - even the Shire. In addition there was the Dwarf/Orc War in 2793-9 and then in 2941 the Battle of Five Armies (described in *TH* Chapter 17 286-98) after which Orc activity died down for a while. However, as indicated in *LotR* 1.2.43-4 and App B.1090, the Orcs began multiplying again in the Misty Mountains from about 3009 onwards.

Orcs can be classified in several different ways in *LotR*, some of which overlap:
- By location. There were Orcs of the Misty Mountains some of whom had taken up residence in Moria. (These attacked the Fellowship when they arrived there in January 3019). There were also the Orcs of Mordor, breaking down into the groups from Minas Morgul, Barad-dûr and Cirith Ungol. In addition there were the Orcs of Isengard and no doubt there were many other groups in lands such as Eriador and Mirkwood Forest.

- By physical characteristics. Many Orcs seem to have been smaller than Men as illustrated by the Hobbits being able to fight them successfully in Moria (*LotR* 2.5.324-5). Also Denethor queried why Boromir died at Parth Galen with "*... only orcs to withstand him*"[140], implying that the likes of the Dúnedain should be able to deal with Orcs easily. However the Orc-chieftain encountered in Moria was tall enough and strong enough to push Boromir over and quick enough to dodge Aragorn. In fact there were large Orcs among the ones killed by Boromir at Parth Galen too. The general physical appearance of Orcs included features such as yellow fangs, black skin, black blood, long arms hanging almost to the ground (for example Grishnákh in *LotR* 3.3.455), claws, bow legs, hairy ears, eyes like coals, red tongues, foul breath and unpleasant personal habits.
- By type. Orcs were sometimes designated specific roles, such as tracker or soldier. Most of the soldier Orcs were Uruk-hai. They were much bigger and stronger, and also black-skinned, and according to App A.I.iv.1053 first appeared out of Mordor in TA 2470s. There were black Uruks present when the Fellowship was attacked in Moria - the Orc-chieftain mentioned above was presumably one. Saruman also bred them, for example Uglúk, "*a large black Orc*"[141] who was the leader of the Isengard Orcs who captured Merry and Pippin. There were also Orc/Man hybrids, for example the squint-eyed southerner encountered by the Hobbits in Bree (*LotR* 1.11.180) who was half Orc and half Dunlending (see also *LotR* 1.9.155, 160). Many similar characters, even more Orc-like, were present at the Battle of Helm's Deep (*LotR* 3.9.566).

Regarding Orc speech App F.I.1131 states that they didn't have their own language but perverted others to fit their requirements, with each settlement having its own dialect. Since these dialects were incomprehensible to other tribes the Common Speech was used in inter-tribal communication. App E.II.1118 makes it clear that they could read and write after a fashion. They also had some skill in healing and first-aid as indicated by the efficacy of the draughts and ointment used on Merry and Pippin in *LotR* 3.3.448.

*

In *LotR* 3.2.432-3, at the first encounter between Aragorn and Éomer, the following words were exchanged:
Ar: "*I am called Strider. I came out of the North. I am hunting Orcs.*"
Eo: "*... you know little of Orcs, if you go hunting them in this fashion.*"
A little later as Éomer insisted on knowing more about this stranger who had entered Rohan, Aragorn told him "*There are few among mortal Men who know more of Orcs*".

I now consider Orcs in the light of Aragorn's attitude to them and his knowledge of them.

When it became clear to the Fellowship that they were about to be attacked by Orcs, Aragorn grimly declared, "*We will make them fear the Chamber of Mazarbul!*"[142] as he felt the edge of his sword. He was as good as his word as he was the one who eventually succeeded in despatching the Orc-chieftain who had managed to floor Boromir and, initially, avoid Aragorn himself. As Andúril split the chieftain's helmet, along with his head, his followers fled howling. A little later, after the fall of Gandalf, the Fellowship reached the East Gate of Moria but found a guard of Orcs barring their way. An enraged and grief-stricken Aragorn brought down the captain so forcefully that the remaining Orcs "*fled in terror of his wrath.*"[143]

Aragorn and his people clearly had good reason to feel hatred for the Orcs as these creatures were steeped in the unadulterated evil of their Master who had ruthlessly attempted to destroy the Northern Dúnedain. However there were perhaps additional factors which further explained his attitude:
- It was Orcs from the Misty Mountains who had helped to bring about the escape of Gollum from his prison in Mirkwood (as described by Legolas in *LotR* 2.2.255) after Aragorn's lengthy and gruelling

---
140. Op. cit. [1], *LotR* 5.1, p. 755.
141. Op. cit., *LotR* 3.3, p. 447.
142. Op. cit., *LotR* 2.5, p. 324.
143. Op. cit., *LotR* 2.5, p. 331.

search for him.
- Orcs had been in the habit of plundering Moria and taking mithril to Sauron (*LotR* 2.4.317).
- As the Fellowship discovered for themselves, it was Orcs of the mountains who had been responsible for destroying Balin's people in Moria (*LotR* 2.5.321-2).
- Although Aragorn, prior to the last stage of the War of the Ring, did not know of Treebeard and the activities of the Orcs in Fangorn (such as destroying trees and wounding Ents as documented in *LotR* 3.4.473-5) he would have been aware of the general destruction of nature carried out by Orcs.
- *LotR* 3.2.436 refers to Orcs raiding Rohan's horses on behalf of Sauron.
- Aragorn also had more personal reasons for his hatred of Orcs, such as his awareness of their attack on Celebrían (Elrond's wife, and daughter of Galadriel and Celeborn) which had so traumatised her that she had left Middle-earth altogether taking ship into the West. Although this had occurred five hundred years previously (App B.1087) the incident was very much alive in the behaviour of Elladan and Elrohir who had waged a relentless and vengeful personal war against Orcs ever since. Aragorn's own father, Arathorn II, had been killed by an Orc arrow in the eye while accompanying Elladan and Elrohir on such a foray (App A.I.v.1057). Isildur too had been killed by Orcs at the Battle of the Gladden Fields along with all but three of his companions.

Thus in addition to the natural hatred which the Dúnedain would have felt towards the creatures of Sauron, Aragorn's attitude to Orcs was also influenced by historical and personal issues.

Regarding Aragorn's knowledge of Orcs, spelt out in no uncertain terms to Éomer, there is plenty of hard evidence in *LotR*:
- In *LotR* 2.6.334 as the Fellowship made their escape from Moria to Lothlórien, Aragorn showed his awareness of the Orcs' inability to tolerate daylight, assuming that they would not come out of Moria until after dusk but wisely not counting on this. In addition he knew that the Moon was about to set so that the resulting dark night would give the Orcs a further advantage.
- In the same chapter Aragorn dressed Sam's wound realising that it was not infected and recognising this as unusual since Orc weapons were normally poisoned.
- At Parth Galen after the Orcs had carried off Merry and Pippin, Aragorn knew that they would be afraid to keep the Hobbits' knives, telling Legolas and Gimli that these were "*work of Westernesse, wound about with spells for the bane of Mordor.*"[144]
- He recognised Misty Mountain Orcs among those whom Boromir had killed as well as the Mordor Orcs. His experienced eye also picked out others of a breed he had not come across before: "goblin-soldiers", bigger than the norm, with different weapons from standard Orc ones, and bearing a "white hand" device and an "S" rune. Aware that Sauron's Orcs of Barad-dûr used the "red eye" device and recalling Gandalf's account at the Council of Elrond of Saruman's treachery he now guessed that these new Orcs were Saruman's.
- As he decided that he, Legolas and Gimli should follow the Orcs he knew that they were in for an exceptional chase due to the speed and tirelessness of the creatures.
- In *LotR* 3.2.422 he showed his awareness of the propensity of Orcs to quarrel with each other, especially if different tribes were present. Later he voiced his concern that the Orcs they were chasing had behaved untypically by continuing to journey by daylight.
- Further on in the chase, Aragorn told Legolas and Gimli that neither Sauron nor Saruman would have risked actually mentioning the Ring to Orcs since they weren't to be trusted (*LotR* 3.5.490). [It does however appear, in *LotR* 3.3.455-6, that the Mordor Orc Grishnákh knew more than he should have done.]

We can add to these specific examples by considering what we know of Aragorn's education and travels. As well as the fate of Isildur, he must also have learnt about the War between the Orcs of the Misty Mountains

---
144. Op. cit. [1], *LotR* 3.1, p. 415.

and the Dwarves of Moria, TA 2793-9 (App A.III.1073-6 and App B.1088), and later of the Battle of Five Armies during which Elves, Dwarves and Men united against the Orcs (*TH* 17.286-98). The area to the north of the White Mountains too had suffered from invasions, both before and after the granting of that land to the Rohirrim. This is without mentioning the depredations which must have been carried out by Orcs in the North Kingdom - they even got as far as the Northfarthing of the Shire in TA 2747.

Aragorn's personal experience prior to the War of the Ring must have included many encounters with Orcs, both in forays with his Rangers and presumably actually in battle during his service as "Thorongil" in Rohan and Gondor. However we know that much of his travelling was done alone, in which case he could not have relied on being able to defeat his adversaries unless he encountered them in suitably small numbers. There must have been very many situations when his only option was to avoid them, especially in the obvious "risk" areas like the Misty Mountains and the lands bordering Mordor - or Mordor itself. He was of course an exemplary tracker which would have enabled him to become aware of Orcs before **they** became aware of **him**. As he told the Hobbits he had keen hearing, had hunted "*many wild and wary things*"[145] and could usually avoid being seen - he must have been a master of camouflage. Orcs too had excellent trackers among them, who clearly used scent as a method of creeping up on prey. For example Orcs are described as "*keen as hounds on a scent*"[146] as it became clear that they had followed the Fellowship into Lothlórien. Haldir too referred to them picking up a scent, and in *LotR* 6.2.925 the tracker Orc who was attempting to follow Frodo and Sam along the Morgai complained about losing the scent. During the chase across Rohan (*LotR* 2.2.426) Aragorn woke Gimli early one morning telling him to hurry because the scent was growing cold thus implying that he himself used scent when trying to detect the presence of Orcs. It was clearly absolutely crucial, when travelling alone, for him to take measures to prevent Orcs finding him through scent, either by trying to ensure that he remained downwind of them or by disguising his own scent. Certain plants could perhaps be used to create a neutralising effect, or else a less pleasant option may have been to make himself smell like an Orc.

The point of this discussion is to show that Aragorn could well have been in far more danger from Orcs when on his own using avoiding tactics than in a confrontation situation, the risk being even more acute if for some reason he needed to actually track the creatures for the purpose of spying on them as opposed to merely avoiding them. As well as constant vigilance and concentration such activities would have required some understanding of Orc speech. As stated earlier Orcs knew the Common Speech but only tended to speak it when in multi-tribe company, using their own specific dialect within their own group. Aragorn must therefore have acquired knowledge of some of these dialects, including possibly the Black Speech spoken by the Orcs of Barad-dûr.

Clearly Aragorn had more than enough knowledge and experience of Orcs to justify his words to Éomer. However these words actually specified that there were "*few **among mortal Men***" [My emphasis] who knew more of Orcs. Among non-mortals Gandalf must inevitably have taught him a certain amount, especially in the early days of their friendship, but perhaps Elladan and Elrohir should receive the greatest credit for giving Aragorn his grounding in Orc know-how. App A describes him, as a twenty-year-old, returning to Rivendell "*after great deeds in the company of the sons of Elrond*"[147]. These "*great deeds*" must surely have involved confrontations with Orcs.

It is worth noting that Aragorn's words of warning to Saruman's army at Helm's Deep - on account of the approaching Huorns and the imminent arrival of Gandalf and Erkenbrand - were addressed to the Orcs as well as the Dunlendings (*LotR* 3.7.540). While the Dunlendings were impressed by his majesty and took his warning seriously the Orcs just jeered at him. This was perhaps what he had expected from his knowledge of them.

Trolls

In *HoM-e* X part 5, section 8, 409, 412, it is stated that the implication in *LotR* is that Trolls had always existed in their own right but were "*tinkered*" with by Morgoth. In addition (in Note 3) it is suggested that

---

145. Op. cit. [1], *LotR* 1.10, p. 163.
146. Op. cit., *LotR* 2.6, p. 345.
147. Op. cit., A.I.v, p. 1057.

Stone-trolls may have been counterfeits, a point taken up by Treebeard in *LotR* 3.4.486 when he gave his opinion that Trolls in general were made by Morgoth in mockery of Ents. App F.I.1132 describes the original Trolls as being dull and lumpish with no proper language until Sauron took them over, teaching them wicked ways and honing their limited intelligence.

Several different types of Troll are mentioned in *LotR*:
- Stone-trolls. These were presumably of the type encountered in *TH* 2.37-54 and, in their stone form, in *LotR* 1.12.204-8.
- Cave-trolls. One of these was encountered by the Fellowship in Moria in *LotR* 2.5.324. It had greenish scales, flat toeless feet and black blood which smoked on the floor. Its body was able to turn and notch Boromir's sword-blade.
- Hill-trolls. Some of these had captured and killed Aragorn's grandfather Arador in the Coldfells in TA 2930 (App A.I.v.1057 and App B.1089). *LotR* 1.12.200, 203 also cites the Ettenmoors and Ettendales, located (like the Coldfells) to the north-west of Rivendell, as areas where these Trolls lived.
- Olog-hai. App F tells us that these came into being at the end of the Third Age in southern Mirkwood and the mountain borders of Mordor. They were bred by Sauron, were bigger and more powerful than other Trolls and were *"filled with the evil will of their master: a fell race, strong, agile, fierce and cunning, but harder than stone."*[148] They could also cope with sunlight so long as Sauron's will was guiding them. Their actual make-up was in fact uncertain: some folk believed they were giant Orcs rather than Trolls, but others noted that they were totally unlike even large Orcs both physically and mentally. The Mountain-trolls who wielded Grond at the Siege of Gondor in *LotR* 5.4.828 were perhaps Olog-hai. Also *LotR* 5.10.892 refers to the Trolls present at the Battle of the Morannon who were taller and broader than Men, roared like beasts, wore a close-fitting mesh of horny scales, and wielded heavy hammers. They also had black blood and were in the habit of biting the throats of those they felled - as almost happened to Beregond. Although the text calls these creatures *"hill-trolls out of Gorgoroth"*[149] the description seems to fit that of the Olog-hai.

Like the Orcs, once the Ring was destroyed the Trolls fled, unable to function without Sauron's will driving them.

There is little specifically relating to Aragorn and Trolls in *LotR* but there are a few references which throw some light on his knowledge of them.
- In general he would certainly have made it his business to be aware of the nature, distribution and characteristics of these creatures, for example the developments described in *LotR* which refer to Trolls which were *"no longer dull-witted, but cunning and armed with dreadful weapons."*[150]
- In *LotR* 1.12.204-6 it is clear that he knew there were now no Trolls actually living in the area where Bilbo had encountered them in *TH* 37-54 - just the stone versions left over from then. He knew that Trolls didn't build, the ruined towers being relics of the old North Kingdom. He was also clearly aware of Bilbo's adventures and of the inability of Trolls to survive in sunlight.
- *LotR* 1.11.190 states that Trolls sometimes strayed down from the northern valleys of the Misty Mountains, so he must have seen or encountered them during the years of his travels.
- Nevertheless as he and the Hobbits made their circuitous way towards the Bruinen Ford he realised that they had gone too far north and knew that they had to change their course to avoid going near the Ettendales. That area, he said, was *"troll-country, and little known to me."*[151]

App F.I.1132 states that Trolls had learnt language from the Orcs, thus there would have been a mixture of dialects involved, from the debased Common Speech used by the Stone-trolls in the West, to the Black Speech

---
148. Op. cit. [1], App F.I, p. 1132.
149. Op. cit., *LotR* 1.10, p. 892.
150. Op. cit., *LotR* 1.2, p. 44.
151. Op. cit., *LotR* 1.12, p. 203.

spoken by the Olog-hai. As with the Orcs, some grasp of the dialects involved would have aided Aragorn in any spying activity, though the evidence points more to complete avoidance, his scant knowledge of the "*troll-country*" north of Rivendell seeming slightly strange given the wide-ranging nature of his travels in general. Perhaps he deliberately gave the area a wide berth because of the fate of his grandfather.

Balrogs

Balrogs were Maiar who were corrupted by Morgoth during the First Age. *Val* describes them as "*demons of terror*"[152] while *TSil* 3 states that "*... their hearts were of fire, but they were cloaked in darkness, and terror went before them; they had whips of flame.*"[153] Morgoth used them in his war with the Eldar until, at the end of the Age, he was defeated by a host of the Valar leading to the Balrogs being destroyed, "*... save some few that fled and hid themselves in caverns inaccessible at the roots of the earth...*"[154] In TA 1980 one of these escapees was disturbed in Moria as the Dwarves delved deep for mithril (App B.1087). It became known as Durin's Bane after killing Durin VI and by the following year the Dwarves had fled from Moria. When it attacked the Fellowship in TA 3019 Legolas wailed and identified it as a Balrog while Gandalf muttered, "*A Balrog*"[155]. Aragorn obviously missed both these statements as shown by his words to Celeborn and Galadriel in Lothlórien: "*An evil of the Ancient World it seemed, such as I have never seen before ... It was both a shadow and a flame, strong and terrible.*"[156] Although ignorant of its name he rightly connected the Balrog with the "Ancient World" thereby linking it to Morgoth and the First Age. He was familiar with Sauron's creatures and had been able to withstand even Nazgûl to some extent, but the Balrog was a different matter. It had apparently destroyed Gandalf, and the Orcs themselves were terrified of it. Gandalf had felt its presence in the Chamber of Mazarbul even though he was on the other side of the door, and the battle between them to put spells on the door had sent the Wizard into a state of exhaustion. When he saw it and actually identified it as a Balrog he shouted to his companions to "*Fly! This is a foe beyond any of you.*"[157].

I have suggested in Chapter 2.3 that, on Aragorn's first visit to Moria which must have occurred somewhere between 2951 (when he became a Ranger) and 2989 (the year of Balin's ill-fated attempt to recolonise the Mines), he felt the presence of some great terror lurking there, thus accounting for his description of the memory as being "*very evil*". If this was indeed the case then all would have become clear to him after witnessing the events on the Bridge of Khazad-dûm in 3019. I also referred to the experience of Dáin Ironfoot in TA 2799 who certainly sensed something deeply horrible and frightening when he approached the East Gate of Moria. His words to Thráin [father of Thorin Oakenshield] afterwards were, "*Only I have looked through the shadow of the Gate. Beyond the shadow it waits for you still: Durin's Bane.* **The world must change and some other power than ours must come before Durin's Folk walk again in Moria.**"[158] Perhaps a natural interpretation of the passage I have emphasised is that the "*other power*" was Gandalf and that with his defeat of the Balrog Moria would have been safe following the fall of Sauron. However Hammond and Scull[159] point out that in the Epilogue to *LotR* (*HoM-e* IX 11.122) Sam expressed doubt (fifteen years into the Fourth Age) that the Dwarves had returned to Moria: "*Maybe the foretelling about Durin is not for our time.*" He felt that it would still take "*a lot of trouble and daring deeds*" to remove the evil there, commenting that there were still many Orcs left in such places. However if it was only Orcs who were making it dangerous then it should have been relatively straightforward to deal with the problem. A more sinister interpretation of Sam's words is that there was a possibility that another Balrog was secreted under the Misty Mountains. The passage from *TSil* which I quoted at the beginning of this section ("*... save **some few** that fled and hid themselves in caverns inaccessible at the roots of the earth*" [My emphasis]) certainly implies that more than one survived - in which case it is difficult

---

152. Op. cit. [107], *Val*, p. 23.
153. Op. cit., *TSil* Chapter 3, p. 43.
154. Op. cit., *TSil* Chapter 24, p. 302.
155. Op. cit. [1], *LotR* 2.5, p. 330.
156. op. cit., *LotR* 2.7, p. 356.
157. Op. cit., *LotR* 2.5, p. 330.
158. Op. cit., App A.III, p. 1075.
159. Op. cit. [37], Hammond & Scull, p. 707.

to visualise Moria ever being recolonised given the departure of beings like Gandalf and Glorfindel who might have been able to destroy the creature(s).

Shelob and her offspring

I include Shelob in this "Enemy" section although she was not actually a servant of Sauron or a creation of Morgoth, but a totally independent being who moved into her lair in the north wall of the Morgul Vale prior to Sauron's arrival in Mordor (and therefore sometime during the Second Age). Her descent in fact can be traced back to Ungoliant, one of the Maiar, who took the form of a huge spider and helped Morgoth to destroy the Two Trees of Valinor in the First Age (*TSil* 8.76-81). She also founded a whole race of spider-like creatures some of which Beren encountered during his wanderings prior to meeting Lúthien (*TSil* 19.192). Shelob herself is described as the "*last child of Ungoliant to trouble the unhappy world*"[160]. Her own offspring included the spiders found in Mirkwood Forest as described in *TH* 8.166-76.

When Frodo was wondering whether to follow Gollum's alternative route into Mordor we are told that, "*Its name was Cirith Ungol, a name of dreadful rumour.* **Aragorn could perhaps have told them that name and its significance...**"[161] [My emphasis]. With Sindarin being one of his native languages Aragorn would certainly have known that Cirith Ungol meant pass of the Spider.

This leaves the questions as to how much he actually knew about Cirith Ungol and whether he ever encountered Shelob.

We know that he had travelled in the Morgul Vale at least once - notably in the search for Gollum - and he must have picked up the name, and the rumours concerning it, from overhearing Orc conversations. Apart from the occasional prisoner sent by Sauron, the Orcs were the only prey available to Shelob by the time of the War of the Ring since Elves and Men had ceased living in the border areas of Mordor. The conversation between Shagrat and Gorbag in *LotR* 4.10.736-41 indicated the risk she posed to their people. There seemed to be an unspoken agreement between her and Sauron that she acted as a last guard against intruders who managed to bypass Minas Morgul. This would imply that she spent all her time in her lair and the tunnel leading to it. Thus I think it unlikely that Aragorn would have encountered her. Assuming he was aware of the location of the entrance to her pass he must have realised/suspected that it would be possible to enter Mordor that way and consequently avoided it. A confrontation with Shelob would have drawn far too much attention to him and put him at high risk of being captured. If Shelob did ever stray out into the Morgul Vale (there is no indication that she did so) then it is possible that Aragorn might have seen her, in which case I feel that avoidance rather than confrontation would have been his chosen option.

I do think it very likely that he would have encountered the Mirkwood spiders during his travels, generally having the skills to avoid them but able to despatch them easily if necessary.

Dragons

As implied in *TSil* 13.132-3 the dragons were originally bred by Morgoth during the First Age. Although they still existed in the Third Age there is no indication of any direct connection between them and Sauron. Nevertheless they certainly remained hostile to Elves, Men and Dwarves as illustrated by the account in *TH* of Thorin Oakenshield's undertaking to destroy Smaug and regain his kingdom in the Lonely Mountain. Also Gandalf recognised the potential of dragons to ally themselves with Sauron as shown in *UT* 3.3.416 where he anticipated the role which Smaug could play if Sauron were to invade Rivendell from the north-east, something which Gandalf believed very possible given that the kingdom of Dale had been destroyed and only the Dwarves of the Iron Hills would be available to provide resistance. This explained his own involvement in Thorin's mission: both of them had compelling reasons for getting rid of the dragon.

Aragorn, being only ten years old and living in Rivendell at the time of these events, would not have witnessed them, though he no doubt heard of them during the visit of Gandalf and Bilbo in TA 2942 as they

---

160. Op. cit. [1], *LotR* 4.9, p. 723.
161. Op. cit., *LotR* 4.3, p. 644.

travelled back to the Shire. However there was in theory a possibility of him encountering dragons during his long years of journeying prior to the War of the Ring as Gandalf's words to Frodo could be interpreted as meaning that some still existed: "*It has been said that dragon-fire could melt and consume the Rings of Power, but **there is not now any dragon left on earth in which the old fire is hot enough***"[162]. This interpretation is backed by Tolkien himself in a letter to Naomi Mitchison of 25th April 1944 where he says, "*Have I said anything to suggest the final ending of dragons? If so it should be altered.*" He then quotes the passage I have emphasised and adds, "*But that implies, I think, that there are still dragons, if not of full primeval stature.*"[163]. The map in *TH* shows the Grey Mountains and the Withered Heath about fifty miles to the north of Mirkwood Forest as being the area where the dragons of the Third Age originated. There is nothing to indicate one way or another whether Aragorn travelled to that area, so any suggestion that he encountered dragons by sight, sound or smell must remain speculation.

*

Over his many years of travelling, incognito and often disguised, Aragorn set about "*... exploring the hearts of Men ... and uncovering the plots and devices of the servants of Sauron*"[164]. He did this either by integrating himself totally into the communities (as perhaps was possible with the Haradrim for example) or else by observations and spying where integration was dangerous or impossible (as must have been the case with the Troll-men of Far Harad). He would have been aided in this work by his mastery of languages and accents. As a result he would have acquired a very significant understanding of the motives and fears of the races whom Sauron had enslaved. Above all he gained an appreciation of Sauron's ability to control people and force them to his will - hence his mercy in victory at the end, and his efforts to bring about peace.

NATURE

I round off these "relationship" discussions by considering Aragorn and nature.

LotR states that the Northern Dúnedain were believed "*to understand the languages of beasts and birds.*"[165] On the face of it this seems rather an exaggerated claim for which there is no concrete evidence. Certainly there are examples in *LotR* of birds as messengers (and even transport), and the horse Shadowfax appeared to understand speech, but the bird messengers are used by Maiar (Gandalf, Saruman and Radagast) not by humans, Shadowfax had horses of Valinor among his ancestors (App A.II.1065) and the Eagle Gwaihir was one of Manwë's Eagles and thus not a real "mortal" bird. *TH* has Beorn's animals who wait on him at table (*TH* 7.125-144), the example of Bard and the thrush being able to talk to each other (*TH* 14.261), and the speaking raven Roäc (*TH* 15.268-71) who incidentally was a hundred and fifty three years old - many times a normal raven lifespan. However *LotR* is written in a different vein with examples of special powers being more understated. If we interpret the quoted passage as indicating that the Dúnedain were able to read the behaviour of animals and birds, then there is more room for discussion, along with plenty of evidence of Aragorn's rapport with, and understanding of, all aspects of the natural world.

Animals

Aragorn, and the Dúnedain in general, certainly had an affinity with horses. In *UT* 2.1.218-19 we read about how the Númenóreans could summon a favourite horse at need by thought alone if horse and rider loved each other enough, and this trait survived into the Third Age. In *LotR* 5.2.786 the horses of the Grey Company allowed themselves to be led into the Paths of the Dead, partly because of the strength of Aragorn's will and partly because of the depth of the love they felt for their riders. The bond between Aragorn and his own horse, Roheryn, given to him by Arwen and brought from the North by Halbarad, must have been particularly strong.

---

162. Op. cit. [1], *LotR* 1.2, p. 61.
163. Op cit. [71], Letter 144, p. 177.
164. Op. cit. [1], App A.I.v, p. 1060.
165. Op. cit., *LotR* 1.9, p. 149.

In an earlier incident, in *LotR* 1.11.179, he showed an appreciation of the mind of Bill the pony, telling the Hobbits that he couldn't imagine any animal wanting to go back to Bill Ferny once it had escaped from him - thus dispelling Frodo's worry that the pony would betray them or run off with their luggage. Also from his words at the Council of Elrond (*LotR* 2.2.262) it clearly grieved him to think that the Rohirrim might be paying tribute of horses to Sauron.

Apart from horses he must have been very familiar with the usual farm and domestic animals (there were dogs at the Prancing Pony and Bob had a cat) and with the common wild animals such as foxes, squirrels, rabbits, badgers and deer, as well as river and pond life. On the subject of hostile animals, it was clear in *LotR* 2.4.297-9 that he was used to dealing with Wargs/Wolves, and was also aware of their distribution as he exclaimed in shock that the particular ones who attacked the Fellowship had come west of the mountains - presumably something he hadn't been expecting. When he travelled further afield did he encounter creatures such as the white wolves of the North which had attacked the Shire in TA 2911 (App B.1089), bears, big cats, primates and snakes? Did some of these sightings provide the subject matter for a *"rare tale"*[166] told in the Prancing Pony?

Birds

Aragorn's familiarity with the bird-life of Middle-earth is shown in *LotR* 2.3.284-5 as the Fellowship passed through Eregion. He knew the place well and immediately became uneasy due to the unaccustomed silence all around them. Normally there were plenty of wild creatures there, especially birds, but now the only sounds were the voices of his companions. Soon afterwards a flock of crows flew over, further increasing his suspicions because he knew they were not native to the area but came from Fangorn and Dunland. It was because of this incident that the Company decided to move on earlier than intended. *LotR* 2.9.381, 385 has further examples of Aragorn's awareness of birds as the Fellowship journeyed down the river, namely his study of the Eagle flying overhead and his observation that the swans who flew over at one point were black. However no indication is given as to whether or not he thought these were spies of Sauron.

In *LotR* 4.4.656 Frodo and Sam were aware of Faramir and his Rangers using bird calls to summon each other, thus indicating knowledge of different birds and their sounds. The Northern Dúnedain must have had similar ways of communicating.

Although Aragorn, as a mortal, was not able to liaise with Manwë's Eagles as Gandalf did, eagles did have some significance for him. The Sindarin name which he was given during his youthful service in Rohan and Gondor was Thorongil because he was swift and keen-eyed as an eagle and wore a star on his cloak: Thoron=eagle, gil=star. In addition the silver brooch in which the Elessar was set, given to him by Galadriel in Lothlórien, was shaped like an eagle with outspread wings. It is interesting that the name Thorongil pre-dated the giving of the Elessar by approximately fifty years.

Plants

The most significant plant one associates with Aragorn is of course athelas. As he explained to the Hobbits in *LotR* it had been brought to Middle-earth by the Númenóreans and grew only near places where they had lived or camped *"of old"*[167]. Those places would have been mainly further south as it was generally at Pelargir and Umbar that the Númenórean ships landed during the Second Age and Aragorn went on to say that the plant was not known in the North *"except to some of those who wander in the Wild"*[168]. The athelas he managed to find to treat Frodo on Weathertop had been growing south of the East Road and since it was dark he had detected it by the smell of its leaves. Some of these leaves were still in his herb-pouch when the Fellowship escaped from Moria in *LotR* 2.6.336. Even though they were withered by then, he knew they would still be effective and he used them to treat Frodo's and Sam's injuries. This was also the case in the Houses of Healing (*LotR* 5.8.865): when Bergil came running in with two-week-old leaves anxious in case they were not fresh

---

166. Op. cit. [1], *LotR* 1.9, p. 156.
167. Op. cit., *LotR* 1.12, p. 198.
168. Op. cit., *LotR* 1.12, p. 198.

enough, Aragorn reassured him knowing that they would still serve his purpose. He also made it clear that he knew the different names for the plant, using the colloquial "kingsfoil" to Ioreth when he realised that she did not know the name "athelas" and interrupting the Warden who wanted to show that he knew the Valinorean name "asëa aranion".

In general Aragorn would have had to know the nature of the various plants he encountered: whether they were poisonous, safe, good to eat, medicinal, etc., and where to find them. This must have been more difficult when he journeyed further afield among unfamiliar vegetation and would have necessitated familiarising himself with the local plant knowledge and lore.

The land itself

In addition to animals, birds and plants Aragorn would have had immense experience of negotiating all the different types of terrain in Middle-earth: farmland, hills and downs, forests, mountains, moorlands, marshes, grasslands, rivers, lakes, coastal areas, the volcanic desolation around Mordor, and no doubt deserts in the far south, and frozen areas around the Bay of Forochel if we assume he went there. In addition he had an awareness of altitude, latitude, climate and the stars. A few examples illustrate the breadth of his experience:
- In *LotR* 1.11.181-2 he demonstrated his impressive forest-craft when he guided the Hobbits through the Chetwood by circuitous paths to throw any pursuers off their track.
- He clearly knew the Midgewater marshes well and had the necessary skill to lead the Hobbits safely across them. He had also tracked Gollum along the edges of the Dead Marshes as discussed at the Council of Elrond (*LotR* 2.2.253).
- In *LotR* 1.12.200, when he and the Hobbits encountered signs of rain as they approached the Bridge of Mitheithel he judged that it had fallen two days previously.
- His statement that the stars "*were strange*"[169] in the far south indicated his general familiarity with the constellations.
- *LotR* 2.3.281 refers to him knowing the lands around Rivendell and down the west side of the Misty Mountains even in the dark.
- As the Fellowship began to make their way up towards the pass of Caradhras (*LotR* 2.3.288) he knew that the snow-fall was unusually heavy for the altitude they were at, observing that the paths were generally open all winter. With his obvious familiarity with the mountains he must have become adept at negotiating steep, narrow or precipitous paths.
- In *LotR* 2.9.381 he showed his awareness of the surrounding geography as the Fellowship journeyed down the Anduin, pointing out where Rohan was and comparing their current latitude and climate with that of the Bay of Belfalas much further south of Rohan.
- Aragorn's experience of travelling by water is very evident in *LotR* as indicated by the journey down the Anduin with the Fellowship and then the capture of the ships of the Corsairs of Umbar prior to sailing up-river to Minas Tirith. In addition App A refers to him as a great leader "*by land or by sea*"[170] before going on to describe his earlier exploits against the Corsairs which involved sea rather than river travel.

Significance of Aragorn's rapport with nature

Aragorn's knowledge and experience were prerequisites for the self-sufficiency, tracking and navigation which were vital elements of his travels, particularly when he was alone, but also in situations where his companions lacked experience and were thus dependent on his know-how. For example:
- His healing expertise, apart from being essential in the event of his own injuries and illness, also enabled him to keep Frodo alive after the Nazgûl attack on Weathertop.
- When food was starting to run short during the journey from Bree, for obvious reasons of speed he told the Hobbits they would just have to tighten their belts and look forward to the meals they would get in

---
169. Op. cit. [1], *LotR* 2.2, p. 248.
170. Op. cit., App A.I.v, p. 1060.

Rivendell. However he made it clear that if it was a case of imminent starvation he was able to hunt and knew of berries, roots and herbs which could provide food if necessary (*LotR* 1.11.190). Hunting would presumably have included fishing.
- His tracking ability acquired from reading the terrain - scents, footprints, "*a bent blade* [of grass]"[171] (to quote Gimli), listening to the ground - enabled him to find Gollum, and to lead Legolas and Gimli across Rohan in pursuit of the Orcs.
- Navigating by the Sun, Moon, stars, landmarks, and no doubt memory in some instances, enabled him to travel across country rather than just following roads and paths.
- His riding, sailing and rowing expertise gave him the options of travelling on horseback or by boat if such opportunities arose.

The depth of Aragorn's understanding of Middle-earth, its terrain, geography and its non-speaking inhabitants is perhaps best summed up by Gandalf who called him "*the greatest traveller and huntsman of this age of the world*"[172] and by the observation in App A that he became "*the most hardy of living Men*"[173].

---

171. Op. cit. [1], *LotR* 3.5, p. 488.
172. Op. cit., *LotR* 1.2, p. 58.
173. Op. cit., App A.I.v, p. 1060.

CONCLUSION

As I stated in Chapter 1.5, Tolkien's draft letter to Michael Straight from early 1956 describes *LotR*[1] as "*hobbito-centric*", giving this as the reason for Aragorn's story prior to TA 3018-9 being confined to an appendix. Although it was an essential element of the tale, "*it could not be worked into the main narrative without destroying its* [hobbito-centric] *structure*".[2] Meanwhile Paul Kocher refers to Aragorn as being "*unquestionably the leading man*"[3] in *LotR*. These quotations prompt the following questions:
- Did Tolkien make *LotR* "*hobbito-centric*" because readers of *TH* were asking for more about Hobbits and their adventures? (*LotR* Foreword.xxii.)
- By "man" does Kocher mean "Man" as a species (as opposed to Hobbits, Elves, Dwarves, etc.)? If so it is difficult to argue that Aragorn **wasn't** the leading "Man" in *LotR*.
- On the other hand does "man" just mean male character? In which case Kocher appears to be saying that Aragorn is actually the leading character in *LotR*.

Whatever the answers, it is true that the "hobbito-centricity" of *LotR* obscures the personality and crucial role of Aragorn, especially for first-time readers and for those who take the most obvious interpretation that Frodo and Sam have the central role in saving Middle-earth.

I now sum up Aragorn's role and importance, both in 3018-9 and in the wider context. This exercise has the dual purpose of providing a conclusion to the book and setting out the evidence for Aragorn being the leading character in *LotR* - an interpretation not necessarily contradicted by Tolkien, as will be seen.

*

A list of his achievements in *LotR* now follows:
- When Gandalf disappeared in the summer of 3018 (being imprisoned by Saruman) it was Aragorn who assumed the responsibility for tracking down Frodo and his companions and making contact with them in Bree where he took it on himself to guide and protect them.
- He saved their lives by preventing them sleeping in the Hobbit bedrooms in the inn and then guided them most of the way to Rivendell through inhospitable country, driving off Nazgûl and using his healing powers to keep Frodo alive until they met Glorfindel.
- When the Fellowship set out from Rivendell, even though Gandalf was the leader, it was Aragorn who actually guided them for the first seventeen days until they were defeated by the pass of Caradhras and the decision was made to go through Moria - where Aragorn's role became the dangerous one of rearguard instead.
- In Moria one of his deeds was to despatch the Orc chieftain who attacked Frodo. Then after Gandalf fell from the Bridge of Khazad-dûm it was Aragorn who led the Company safely out of the Mines by killing another Orc chieftain who confronted them at the exit thus causing the rest of the Orcs to flee.
- He then led his companions to the safety of Lothlórien.
- Following their departure from Lothlórien, he guided them down the River Anduin to the Falls of Rauros.
- After the breakup of the Fellowship he led Legolas and Gimli across Rohan and into Fangorn in pursuit of the Orcs who had captured Merry and Pippin. Although the chase itself proved fruitless, it led to the

---

1 J.R.R. Tolkien, *The Lord of the Rings,* London, HarperCollins Publishers, 2007, 2nd edition, based on the 50th Anniversary Edition of 2004.
2. H. Carpenter (ed.), *The Letters of J.R.R. Tolkien*, with the assistance of Christopher Tolkien, London, HarperCollins Publishers, 1995. First published in Great Britain by George Allen & Unwin, 1981. Letter. 181, p. 237.
3. P. Kocher, *Master of Middle-earth: The Achievement of J. R. R. Tolkien*, London, Pimlico, 2002, first published in Great Britain by Thames & Hudson 1973, Chapter 6, p. 130.

reunion with Gandalf, the journey to Edoras and a major role in the Battle of The Hornburg.
- Following his acquisition of the Palantír of Orthanc Aragorn used it to confront Sauron leading him to believe that Isildur's Heir was in possession of the Ring. Thus Aragorn initiated the strategy whereby Sauron's attention was to be diverted from the presence of Frodo at his borders. This confrontation alone, in my opinion, puts his achievements at least on a level with those of Gandalf, Frodo, and Sam.
- He also acquired information from the Palantír which led to his journey through the Paths of the Dead and the defeat of the Corsairs of Umbar thus enabling him to reach the Battle of the Pelennor Fields in time to secure a victory.
- After the battle he spent most of the night healing victims of the Black Breath.
- A few days later the journey to the Morannon, culminating in the battle there, provided the concluding act of distraction for Sauron, with Aragorn and his small Army of the West managing to keep Sauron's attention firmly northward until the final moments when the Ring was destroyed.
- When Frodo and Sam were brought from Mount Doom by the Eagles, they were only saved from death by Aragorn's healing powers.
- Aragorn was always ready to administer first aid, reassure, keep watch, or sort out disputes.
- In spite of coming into extremely close contact with the Ring he resisted the pull of it.

There was also a strong element of self-sacrifice in his behaviour, for example:
- Staying awake so others could sleep.
- Searching for signs and whereabouts of the Nazgûl instead of resting in Rivendell for two months.
- Being prepared to give up his own personal goal of going to Minas Tirith to fight Sauron and claim his kingship. Following the loss of Gandalf he accepted that his first duty was to Frodo and was prepared to accompany him to Mordor. After the breaking of the Fellowship when Frodo took matters out of his hands by setting off for Mordor with Sam, he turned his attention instead to the rescuing of Merry and Pippin from the Orcs in spite of his yearning for his own City.
- Drawing Sauron's attention on to himself in order to give Frodo a slim chance of destroying the Ring.
- Generally disregarding his own physical and psychological needs. Many of the actions listed were carried out at times when he himself was at a very low ebb. For example: from the loss of Gandalf until the scattering of the Fellowship he was verging on a breakdown; after the Battle of the Pelennor Fields he was starving, exhausted and grieving but nevertheless put further pressure on himself by hours of healing.
- Overall he was prepared to die to help the Ring-bearer. At his first meeting with the Hobbits in Bree, he told them, "*I am Aragorn son of Arathorn; and if by life or death I can save you, I will.*"[4]. He fulfilled that promise many times over.

Aragorn's presence and actions were absolutely essential for the successful completion of Frodo's mission. From Frodo's departure from Hobbiton until the destruction of the Ring, he was effectively being guided and/ or protected by Aragorn, either in person, or remotely by misleading Sauron. Although from the reader's (and Frodo's) point of view Aragorn does not come into the narrative until the meeting at Bree in the ninth chapter, he was directly committed to Frodo's protection from the time he realised that Gandalf was missing - probably one to two months before Frodo left the Shire. Indeed, we can go further and state that, either personally or through his Rangers, he had been protecting Frodo ever since Bilbo's party seventeen years earlier (in TA 3001) as this was the point at which Gandalf confided his concerns about the Ring and the secret guard on the Shire was doubled. The role of Aragorn and his people is emphasised by Gandalf's words to Frodo as he described his anxiety for the Hobbit's welfare: "*... even when I was far away there has never been a day when the Shire has not been guarded by watchful eyes.*"[5] This was confirmed by Aragorn himself when he first met Frodo in Bree: "*I have often kept watch on the borders of the Shire in the last few years...*"[6]. Also during these years he was helping in the search for Gollum. It was Aragorn himself who eventually succeeded in capturing

---

4. Op. cit. [1], *LotR* 1.10, p. 171.
5. Op. cit., *LotR* 1.2, p. 60.
6. Op. cit., *LotR* 1.10, p. 172.

him, thus enabling Gandalf to question him and establish his part in the history of the Ring.

As I have shown in this book, it has been necessary to delve a bit to put together a full picture of Aragorn. For example it is only when one reads between the lines that one can appreciate his crucial contribution to the struggle to destroy the Ring. This is in contrast to the more obvious and visible roles of the other main characters:
- Frodo, as the Ring-bearer.
- Gandalf, the one master-minding the mission and co-ordinating the opposition to Sauron.
- Sam, Frodo's close companion, without whose courage and dogged support Frodo would not have survived once the pair entered Mordor.
- Gollum, long connected with the Ring and ultimately the one who destroyed it.

Holly A. Crocker[7] believes that Aragorn's feats are not as important as Frodo's, while Jennifer Neville[8] states that it is not the heroic Aragorn *"... who has the power to defeat Sauron; rather it is Frodo, a Hobbit, someone even smaller and weaker than the average man, who must do the deed."* She goes on to say that *"Great heroes merely serve as a diversion."* In answer to the last point my reaction is: Yes, but what a diversion! Frodo, Sam and Gollum between them physically destroyed the Ring but Aragorn actually made it possible for them to do so by his effective - and total - deception of Sauron as to the Ring's whereabouts. The Hobbits succeeded precisely because Aragorn **did** have *"the power to defeat Sauron"* - psychologically - via the Palantír, thereby creating a **crucial** *"diversion"*, hence my opinion that this "feat" was certainly as important as Frodo's. Frodo said to Gandalf, on waking up in Rivendell, *"We should never have done it without Strider."*[9]. He was of course referring to the journey from Bree to Rivendell. However it would have been just as applicable if he had said it on Mount Doom as Gollum overbalanced into the fire taking the Ring with him.

Tolkien's own view of Aragorn's importance is given in *HoM-e* XII.9.ii[10] in an earlier and fuller version of App A.I.v entitled *The Tale of Aragorn and Arwen* - as opposed to **Part** *of the Tale of Aragorn and Arwen* [My emphasis] which is the title in the published version. Instead of covering Aragorn's role in *LotR* in a couple of sentences, it gives an account of what Christopher Tolkien calls Aragorn's *"commanding significance"*[11] in the War of the Ring. He also quotes his father as saying: *"It was the part of Aragorn, as Elrond foresaw, to be the chief Captain of the West, and by his wisdom yet more than his valour to redress the past and the folly of his forefather Isildur."*[12] To quote from the Tale itself:

> *"It was not his [Aragorn's] task to bear the burden of the Ring, but to be a leader in those battles by which the Eye of Sauron was turned far from his own land and from the secret peril which crept upon him in the dark. Indeed, it is said that Sauron believed that the Lord Aragorn, heir of Isildur, had found the Ring and had taken it to himself, even as his forefather had done, and arose now to challenge the tyrant of Mordor and set himself in his place.*
> *But it was not so, and in this most did Aragorn reveal his strength; for though the Ring came indeed within his grasp, he took it not, and refused to wield its evil power, but surrendered it to the judgement of Elrond and to the Bearer whom he appointed."*[13]

Looking beyond *LotR*, Aragorn's significance extends backwards three thousand years to Isildur's failure to destroy the Ring, and forward to the Fourth Age with the kingship restored and the North and South kingdoms

---

7. H.A. Crocker, 'Masculinity', in R. Eaglestone (ed.), *Reading The Lord of the Rings: New Writings on Tolkien's Classic*, London, New York, Continuum, 2005, pp. 119-120.
8. J. Neville, 'Women', in R. Eaglestone (ed.), *Reading The Lord of the Rings: New Writings on Tolkien's Classic*, London, New York, Continuum, 2005, p. 108.
9. Op. cit. [1], *LotR* 2.1, p. 220.
10. C. Tolkien (ed.), *The History of Middle-earth*, vol. XII, *The Peoples of Middle-earth*, London HarperColllins Publishers, 2002, first published in Great Britain by HarperCollins Publishers 1996, *HoM-e* XII.9.ii, pp. 262-70.
11. Op. cit., *HoM-e* XII.9.ii, p. 267.
12. Op. cit., *HoM-e* XII.9.ii, p. 266.
13. Op. cit., *HoM-e* XII.9.ii, pp. 266-7.

reunited. As indicated throughout this work, and in the passage just quoted, Aragorn had been prophesied for such a role, a role which, in the eyes of Gandalf, Elrond, Galadriel and the Dúnedain, would have been a supremely important one. During the writing of this book I came to view Aragorn as the thread linking the whole saga of *LotR* together as well as linking it to the past and the future. Everything and everybody relates to him in some way:

- Through his destiny as the one prophesied to undo the damage done by Isildur and defeat Sauron
- Through his diverse roles:
  - Senior representative of the exiled Númenóreans
  - Chieftain of the Northern Dúnedain
  - King-in-waiting
  - Heir of Elendil and Isildur
  - Gandalf's deputy
  - Military and naval captain
  - Leader and guide
  - Healer
  - Faithful lover to Arwen
- Through his associated tasks:
  - Maintaining what was left of the old North Kingdom
  - Getting to know his subjects and allies - their lore, languages, motives and fears
  - Getting to know the Enemy and his allies - their plots, motives and fears
  - Redeeming Isildur's mistake by resisting the Ring
  - Taking on Gandalf's role when necessary
  - Searching for and finding Gollum
  - Guiding and protecting the Ring-bearer, even when they were separated
  - Fighting battles - not just military, but emotional and psychological - and developing physical and mental endurance
- Through his relationships. He had a relationship - or potential, or inferred, relationship - with practically all the characters and races in the story.

Aragorn's legacy

As Ivorwen foresaw, although her grandson grew up to display "*Kingly Valour*" his **chief** renown was as a healer and a renewer.[14] He brought healing to Middle-earth by the part he played in the defeat of Sauron and his actions as King, making peace with his enemies and cleansing those lands defiled by Sauron. Through his healing hands he brought healing to his people. In restoring the kingship in Arnor and Gondor he reunited the two branches of Elendil's line (Isildur's and Anárion's), and by his marriage to Arwen he also reunited the two branches of the Half-elven (the line of Elrond and the line of Elros) which had been sundered at the end of the First Age. He renewed the glory of Númenor: in his own person and in the work he did in his Reunited Kingdom. He also founded a new dynasty: the House of Telcontar.

In keeping with the bitter-sweet nature of Aragorn's story it seems fitting to end with the following passage from *HoM-e* XII.8.244-5:

> "*Of Eldarion son of Elessar it was foretold that he should rule a great realm, and that it should endure for a hundred generations of Men after him, that is until a new age brought in again new things; and from him should come the kings of many realms in long days after. But if this foretelling spoke truly, none now can say, for Gondor and Arnor are no more; and even the chronicles of the House of Elessar and all their deeds and glory are lost.*"

---

14. Op. cit. [10], *HoM-e* XII.Foreword.xii, p. xii.

APPENDICES

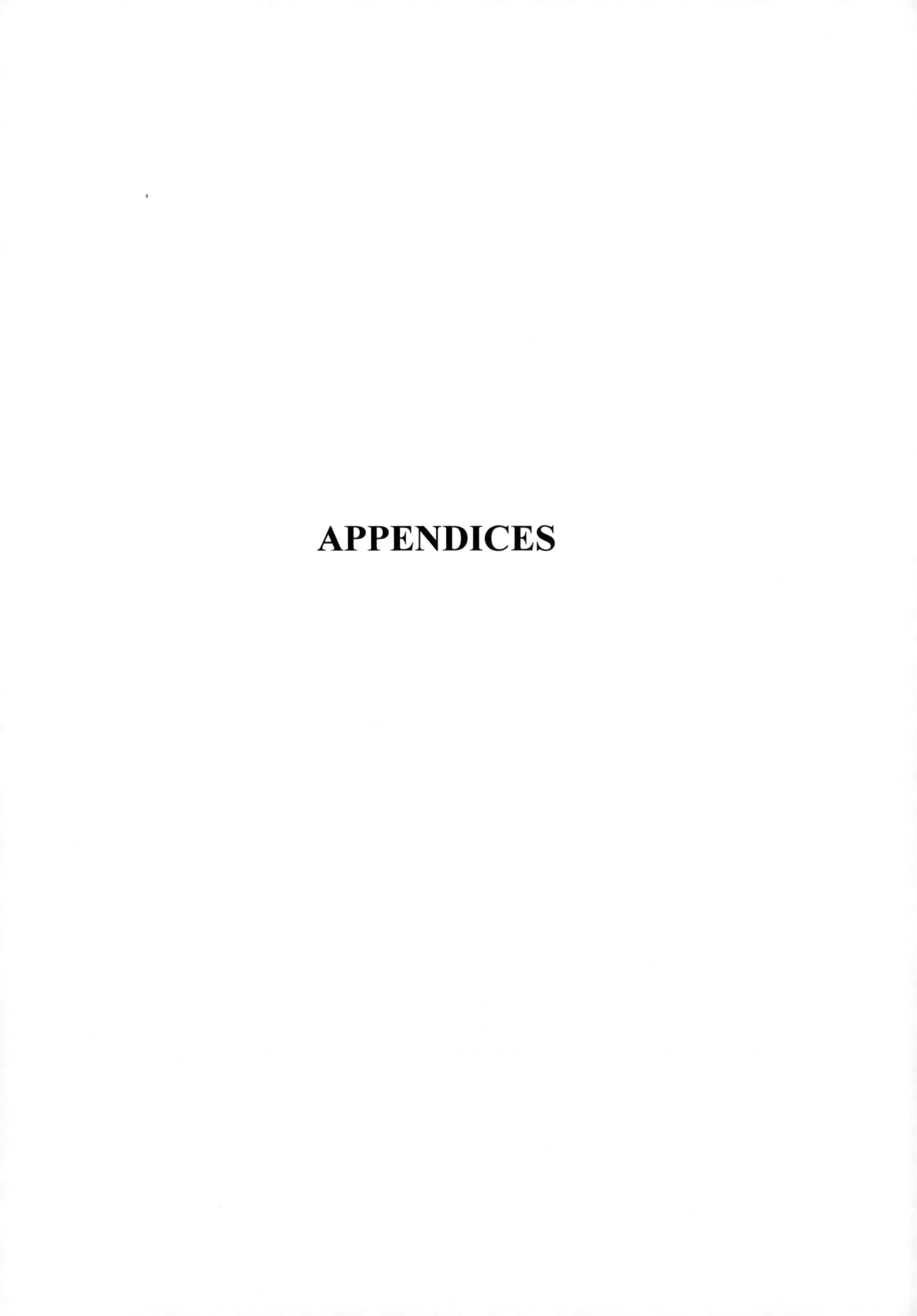

GENEALOGICAL TABLES

TABLE 1: OVERVIEW OF ARAGORN'S ANCESTRY FROM FIRST TO THIRD AGES
[V=Vanyar N=Noldor T=Teleri S=Sindar B=House of Bëor H=Houses of Haladin and Hador]

```
                                    3 BROTHERS
                                   /     |      \
   FINWË = INDIS          OLWË    ELMO    ELWË/THINGOL = MELIAN [Maia]
   [Elf N]  [Elf V]       [Elf T] [Elf S] [Elf S]
        |                           |
        |                        GALADHON            BEREN = LÚTHIEN TINÚVIEL
        |                        [Elf S]             [Man B] [Elf S-X-Maia:chose mortality]
   FINGOLFIN    FINARFIN = EÄRWEN    |
   [Elf N]      [Elf N]    [Elf T]   |
        |            |               |
   TURGON = ELENWË   GALADRIEL = CELEBORN  GALATHIL
   [Elf N]  [Elf V]  [Elf N]    [Elf S]   [Elf S]
        |                |                     |
                                           NIMLOTH = DIOR ELUCHÍL
                                           [Elf S]   [Half-elven:mortal]
   IDRIL CELEBRINDAL = TUOR [Man H:                        |
   [Elf N]              Sailed West.                       |
                        [Immortal?]]                [Died in childhood]
        |                                                  |
   EÄRENDIL ========================== ELWING   ELURÉD   ELURÍN
   [Half-elven:chose to be Elf]     [Half-elven:chose to be Elf]

   ELROS            CELEBRÍAN =================== ELROND
   [Half-elven:chose to be mortal]  [Elf S]       [Half-elven:chose to be Elf]
   [First King of Númenor]

   Kings/Queens of Númenor (Second Age)
   Lords of Andúnië (Second Age)
   Kings of Gondor (Third Age)
   Kings of Arnor and its sub-kingdoms (Third Age)
   Chieftains of the Dúnedain (Third Age)

   ARAGORN ==================== ARWEN              ELLADAN    ELROHIR
   [63rd generation from Elros] [Half-elven:chose mortality]  [Half-elven:choice unknown]

            Kings/Queens of Fourth Age
```

TABLE 2: ARAGORN'S NÚMENÓREAN ANCESTRY

[Dates are Second Age unless indicated otherwise. K=King, Q=Queen.]

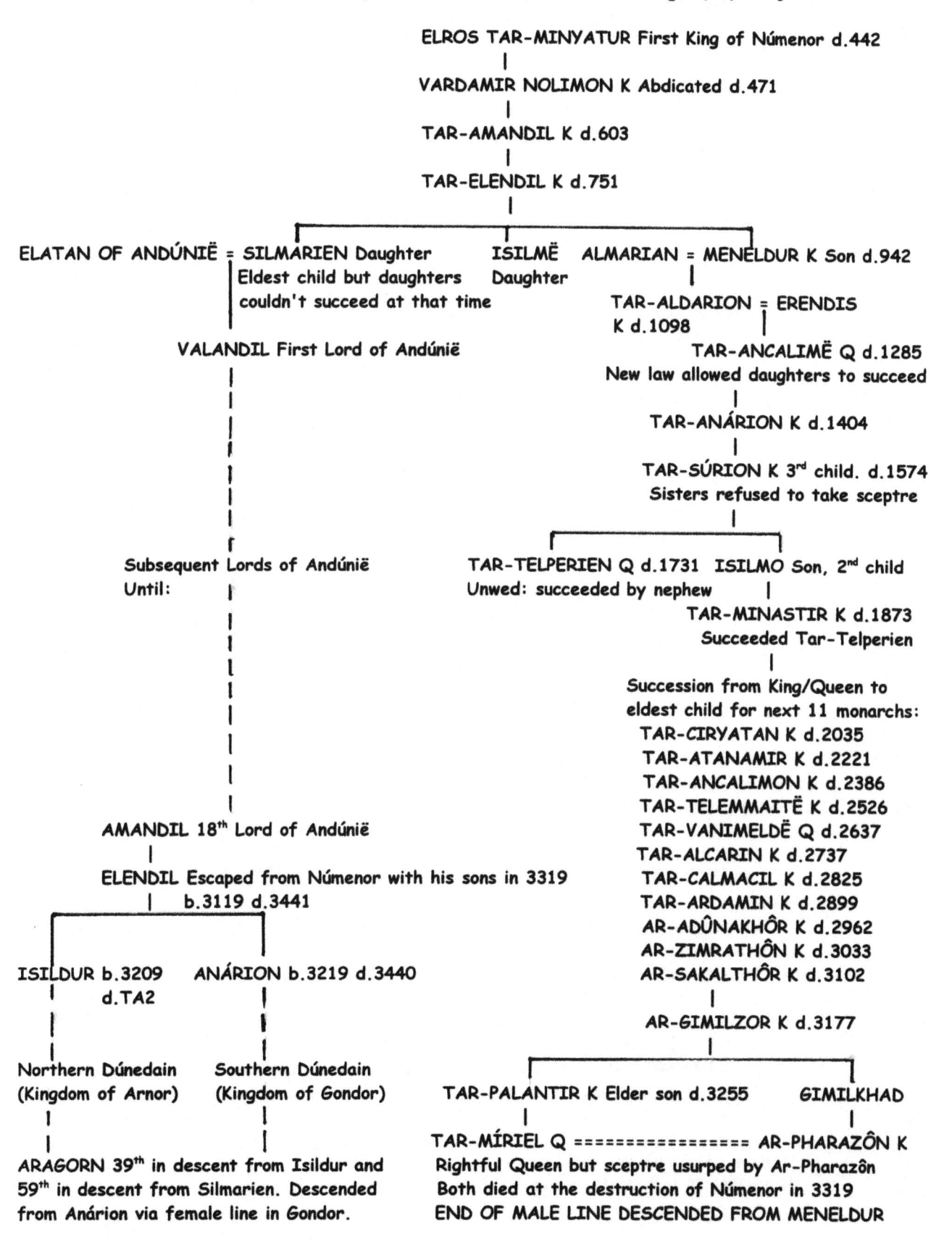

```
                              ELROS TAR-MINYATUR First King of Númenor d.442
                                                    |
                              VARDAMIR NOLIMON K Abdicated d.471
                                                    |
                              TAR-AMANDIL K d.603
                                                    |
                              TAR-ELENDIL K d.751
                                                    |
    ┌───────────────────────────────┬──────────────┬────────────────────────────┐
ELATAN OF ANDÚNIË = SILMARIEN Daughter   ISILMË    ALMARIAN = MENELDUR K Son d.942
                    Eldest child but daughters   Daughter              |
                    couldn't succeed at that time           TAR-ALDARION = ERENDIS
                                                            K d.1098   |
           VALANDIL First Lord of Andúnië            TAR-ANCALIMË Q d.1285
                    |                                 New law allowed daughters to succeed
                    |                                              |
                    |                                 TAR-ANÁRION K d.1404
                    |                                              |
                    |                                 TAR-SÚRION K 3rd child. d.1574
                    |                                 Sisters refused to take sceptre
                    |                                              |
    Subsequent Lords of Andúnië    ┌────────────────────────────┴──────────────────┐
    Until:                   TAR-TELPERIEN Q d.1731   ISILMO Son, 2nd child
                             Unwed: succeeded by nephew            |
                                                         TAR-MINASTIR K d.1873
                                                         Succeeded Tar-Telperien
                                                                   |
                                                         Succession from King/Queen to
                                                         eldest child for next 11 monarchs:
                                                           TAR-CIRYATAN K d.2035
                                                           TAR-ATANAMIR K d.2221
                                                           TAR-ANCALIMON K d.2386
                                                           TAR-TELEMMAITË K d.2526
                                                           TAR-VANIMELDË Q d.2637
    AMANDIL 18th Lord of Andúnië                           TAR-ALCARIN K d.2737
                    |                                      TAR-CALMACIL K d.2825
    ELENDIL Escaped from Númenor with his sons in 3319     TAR-ARDAMIN K d.2899
            | b.3119 d.3441                                AR-ADÛNAKHÔR K d.2962
    ┌───────┴────────┐                                     AR-ZIMRATHÔN K d.3033
ISILDUR b.3209   ANÁRION b.3219 d.3440                     AR-SAKALTHÔR K d.3102
        d.TA2                                                        |
    |                 |                                    AR-GIMILZOR K d.3177
    |                 |                                              |
Northern Dúnedain   Southern Dúnedain                     ┌──────────┴──────────┐
(Kingdom of Arnor)  (Kingdom of Gondor)          TAR-PALANTIR K Elder son d.3255   GIMILKHAD
    |
ARAGORN 39th in descent from Isildur and          TAR-MÍRIEL Q ================ AR-PHARAZÔN K
59th in descent from Silmarien. Descended         Rightful Queen but sceptre usurped by Ar-Pharazôn
from Anárion via female line in Gondor.           Both died at the destruction of Númenor in 3319
                                                  END OF MALE LINE DESCENDED FROM MENELDUR
```

TABLE 3: ARAGORN'S ARNOR AND GONDOR ANCESTRY
[Dates are Third Age unless indicated otherwise]

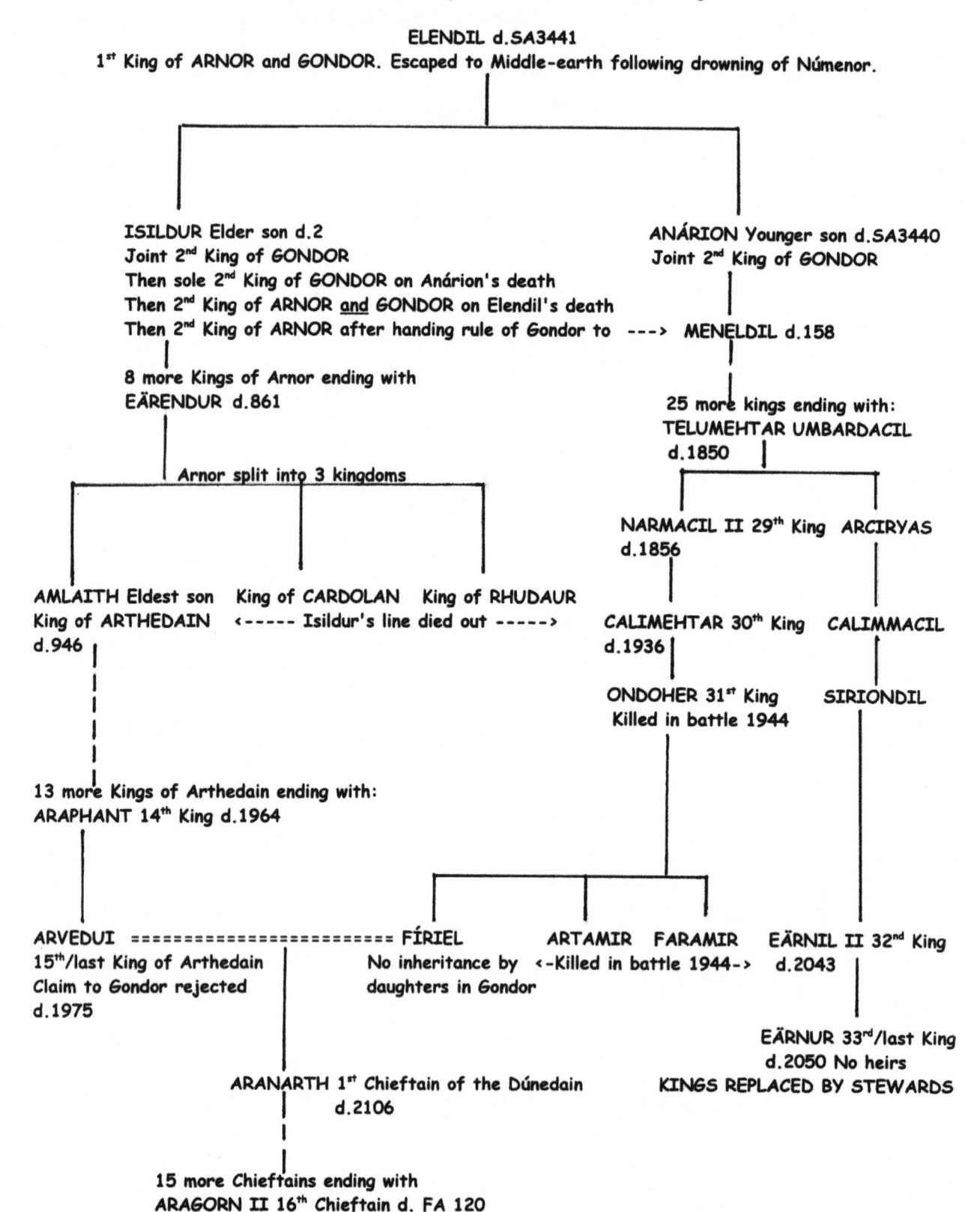

ELENDIL d.SA3441
1st King of ARNOR and GONDOR. Escaped to Middle-earth following drowning of Númenor.

ISILDUR Elder son d.2
Joint 2nd King of GONDOR
Then sole 2nd King of GONDOR on Anárion's death
Then 2nd King of ARNOR and GONDOR on Elendil's death
Then 2nd King of ARNOR after handing rule of Gondor to --->

ANÁRION Younger son d.SA3440
Joint 2nd King of GONDOR

MENELDIL d.158

8 more Kings of Arnor ending with
EÄRENDUR d.861

25 more kings ending with:
TELUMEHTAR UMBARDACIL d.1850

Arnor split into 3 kingdoms

AMLAITH Eldest son
King of ARTHEDAIN
d.946

King of CARDOLAN   **King of RHUDAUR**
<----- Isildur's line died out ----->

NARMACIL II 29th King   **ARCIRYAS**
d.1856

CALIMEHTAR 30th King   **CALIMMACIL**
d.1936

ONDOHER 31st King   **SIRIONDIL**
Killed in battle 1944

13 more Kings of Arthedain ending with:
ARAPHANT 14th King d.1964

ARVEDUI ========================= **FÍRIEL**   **ARTAMIR FARAMIR**   **EÄRNIL II 32nd King**
15th/last King of Arthedain   No inheritance by   <-Killed in battle 1944->   d.2043
Claim to Gondor rejected   daughters in Gondor
d.1975

ARANARTH 1st Chieftain of the Dúnedain
d.2106

EÄRNUR 33rd/last King
d.2050 No heirs
KINGS REPLACED BY STEWARDS

15 more Chieftains ending with
ARAGORN II 16th Chieftain d. FA 120

TABLE 4: KINGS OF ARNOR/ARTHEDAIN AND CHIEFTAINS OF THE DÚNEDAIN
[Dates are Third Age unless indicated otherwise. Ordinal numbers indicate kings.]

ELENDIL 1st d. SA3441

ISILDUR 2nd b. SA3209 Killed at Battle of the Gladden Fields TA2

ELENDUR d.2 (b. SA3299), ARATAN d.2, CIRYON d.2 — All three killed at Battle of the Gladden Fields

VALANDIL 3rd b. SA3430 Took up kingship TA10 d.249

SUCCESSION FROM FATHER TO ELDEST SON UNTIL EÄRENDUR
- ELDACAR 4th d.339
- ARANTAR 5th d.435
- TARCIL 6th d.515
- TARONDOR 7th d.602
- VALANDUR 8th d.652
- ELENDUR 9th d.777
- EÄRENDUR 10th d.861

Arnor split into 3 kingdoms 861

AMLAITH [Eldest son] 1st King of Arthedain d.946

Kings of CARDOLAN Destroyed c. 1670

Kings of RHUDAUR Destroyed c. 1409 — ISILDUR'S LINE DIED OUT HERE

SUCCESSION FROM FATHER TO ELDEST SON UNTIL ARVEDUI
- BELEG 2nd d.1029
- MALLOR 3rd d.1110
- CELEPHARN 4th d.1191
- CELEBRINDOR 5th d.1272
- MALVEGIL 6th d.1349
- ARGELEB I 7th d.1356
- ARVELEG I 8th d.1409
- ARAPHOR 9th d.1589
- ARGELEB II 10th d.1670
- ARVEGIL 11th d.1743
- ARVELEG II 12th d.1813
- ARAVAL 13th d.1891
- ARAPHANT 14th d.1964 - renewed contact/alliance with Gondor's King ONDOHER
- ARVEDUI 15th d.1974 = FÍRIEL of Gondor   ARTHEDAIN DESTROYED BUT ISILDUR'S LINE SURVIVED

ARANARTH 1st Chieftain of the Dúnedain d.2106

SUCCESSION FROM FATHER TO ELDEST SON UNTIL ARATHORN II:
- ARAHAEL 2nd d.2177
- ARANUIR 3rd d.2247
- ARAVIR 4th d.2319
- ARAGORN I 5th d.2327
- ARAGLAS 6th d.2455
- ARAHAD I 7th d.2523
- ARAGOST 8th d.2588
- ARAVORN 9th d.2654
- ARAHAD II 10th d.2719
- ARASSUIL 11th d.2784
- ARATHORN I 12th d.2848
- ARGONUI 13th d.2912
- ARADOR 14th d.2930
- ARATHORN II 15th d.2933 ======================== GILRAEN THE FAIR d.3007

IVORWEN = DÍRHAEL

ARAGORN II 16th and last Chieftain of the Dúnedain. First King of the Reunited Kingdom. Died FA 120

TABLE 5: KINGS OF GONDOR

[Dates are Third Age unless indicated otherwise. Ordinal numbers indicate kings. ___ = KIN-STRIFE]

ELENDIL 1st d.SA3441   SUCCESSION FROM FATHER TO SON UNTIL SIRIONDIL:
ISILDUR d.2 & ANÁRION d.SA3440 Joint 2nd
[ISILDUR Sole 2nd]
MENELDIL 3rd d.158 (b.SA3318 - Anárion's fourth child, last man born in Númenor)
CEMENDUR 4th d.238
EÄRENDIL 5th d.324
ANARDIL 6th d.411
OSTOHER 7th d.492
RÓMENDACIL I (TAROSTAR) 8th d.541
TURAMBAR 9th d.667
ATANATAR I 10th d.748
SIRIONDIL 11th d.830

BERÚTHIEL = TARANNON FALASTUR 12th d.913   TARCIRYAN,
Childless   SUCCESSION FROM FATHER TO SON UNTIL ATANATAR II:
                                                   EÄRNIL I 13th d.936
                                                   CIRYANDIL 14th d.1015
                                                   HYARMENDACIL I (CIRYAHER) 15th d.1149
                                                   ATANATAR II ALCARIN 16th d.1226

NARMACIL I 17th d.1294   CALMACIL 18th d.1304
Childless

VIDUGAVIA King of Rhovanion   MINALCAR/RÓMENDACIL II 19th d.1366 Built the Argonath   CALIMEHTAR

VIDUMAVI ================ VALACAR 20th Mixed marriage d.1432   Unnamed Son

ELDACAR/VINITHARYA 21st Mixed blood d.1490   CASTAMIR THE USURPER 22nd Killed by Eldacar 1447
                                               Sons and other kin became focus for King's enemies at
                                               Pelargir until early 1800s

ORNENDIL Killed by Castamir   ALDAMIR 23rd d.1540

                                   HYARMENDACIL II (VINYARION) 24th d.1621

                                   MINARDIL 25th d.1634   great-grandsons
                                   Slain by Corsairs of Umbar led by ----> ANGAMAITE & SANGAHYANDO

TELEMNAR 26th d.1636   MINASTAN
He and his children died in plague
White Tree also died   TARONDOR 27th d.1798 Planted White Tree sapling

TELUMEHTAR UMBARDACIL 28th d.1850. Got Umbar back briefly. End of Castamir's line

NARMACIL II 29th d.1856   ARCIRYAS

CALIMEHTAR 30th d.1936   CALIMMACIL

ONDOHER 31st d.1944 (in battle)   SIRIONDIL
Steward Pelendur ruled for a year until succession agreed
                                                   EÄRNIL II 32nd d 2043

[Claim not recognised]   [Both d.1944 in battle]
FÍRIEL=ARVEDUI OF ARTHEDAIN   ARTAMIR   FARAMIR EÄRNUR 33rd Last King d.2050

TABLE 6: STEWARDS OF GONDOR: House of Húrin (Númenórean race)
[Dates are Third Age. Ordinal numbers indicate Ruling Stewards.]

HÚRIN of Emyn Arnen Steward to King MINARDIL (1621-34)
From then on Stewards were chosen from his descendants

PELENDUR d.1998
Ruled for a year after death of King ONDOHER (1944) until succession agreed
Responsible for rejecting Arvedui's claim and supporting Eärnil's
Stewardship now became hereditary

VORONDIL THE HUNTER d.2029 (Made the horn of Boromir)

MARDIL VORONWË the Steadfast d.2080
First Ruling Steward

SUCCESSION FROM FATHER TO SON UNLESS INDICATED OTHERWISE:

ERADAN 2nd d.2116
HERION 3rd d.2148
BELEGORN 4th d.2204
HÚRIN I 5th d 2244
TÚRIN I 6th d.2278
HADOR 7th d.2395
BARAHIR 8th d.2412
DIOR 9th d.2435 (Childless)
DENETHOR I 10th d.2477 (Son of Dior's sister)
BOROMIR 11th d.2489
CIRION 12th d.2567 (Eorl's folk to Calenardhon, i.e. Rohan)
HALLAS 13th d.2605
HÚRIN II 14th d.2628
BELECTHOR I 15th d.2655
ORODRETH 16th d.2685
ECTHELION I 17th d.2698 (Childless)
EGALMOTH 18th d.2743 (Grandson of Orodreth's sister)
BEREN 19th d.2763 (Gave the keys of Orthanc to Saruman)
BEREGOND 20th d.2811
BELECTHOR II 21st d.2872 (The White Tree died at his death)
THORONDIR 22nd d.2882

ADRAHIL PRINCE OF DOL AMROTH

TÚRIN II 23rd d.2914
TURGON 24th d.2953
ECTHELION II 25th d.2984

IMRAHIL   FINDUILAS ======= DENETHOR II 26th d.3019 Last Ruling Steward (See *)
          d.2988

BOROMIR d.3019   ÉOWYN === FARAMIR 27th d.FA83 Last Ruling Steward (See *)
                                     Steward to King Elessar

ELBORON

BARAHIR (Wrote *The Tale of Aragorn and Arwen*)

* This title could apply to both Denethor and Faramir, albeit only briefly in the latter's case

TABLE 7: ANCESTRY OF THE PRINCES OF DOL AMROTH

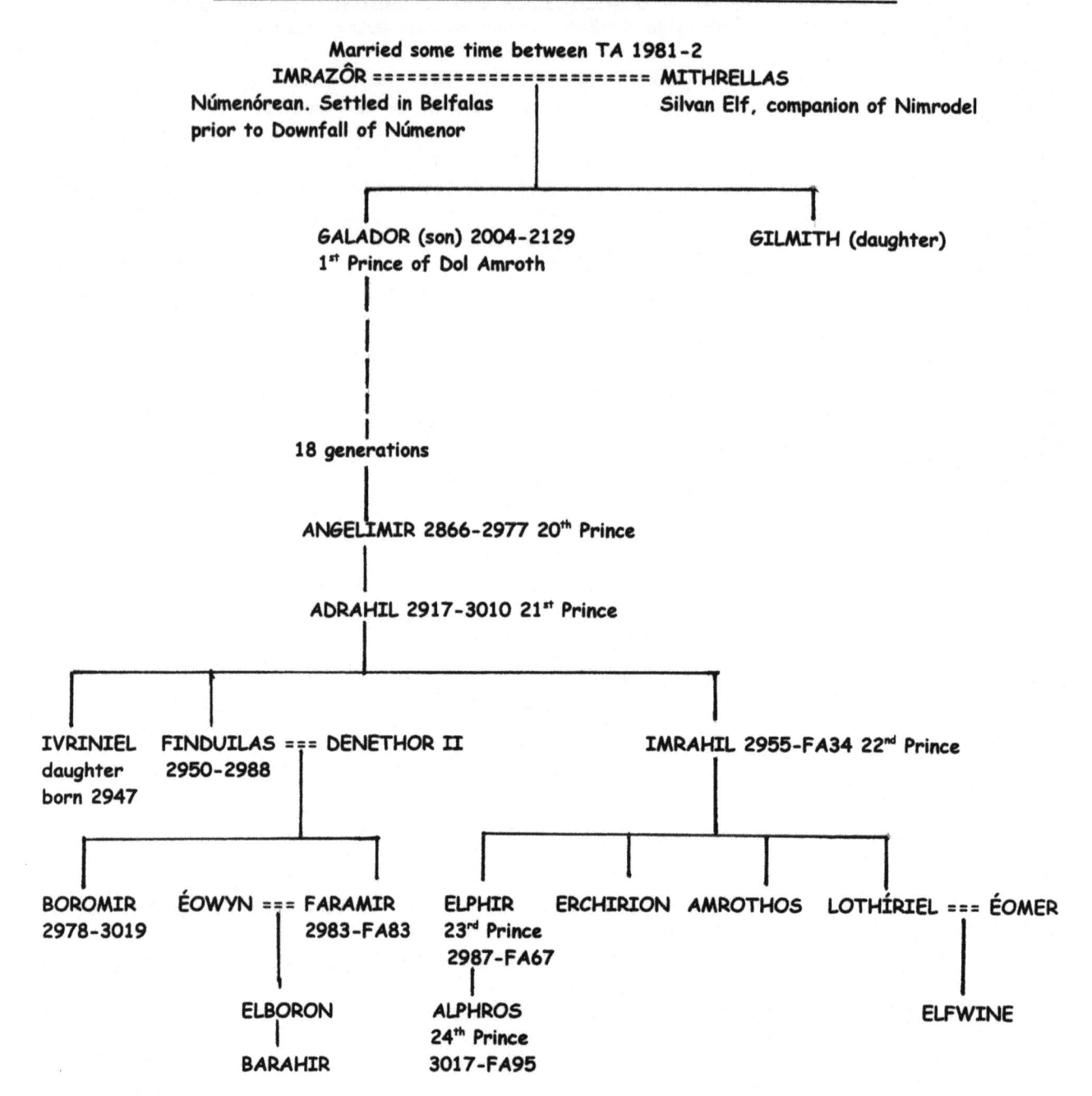

Married some time between TA 1981-2

IMRAZÔR ========================= **MITHRELLAS**

Númenórean. Settled in Belfalas prior to Downfall of Númenor — Silvan Elf, companion of Nimrodel

- **GALADOR** (son) 2004-2129 — 1st Prince of Dol Amroth
- **GILMITH** (daughter)

⋮ 18 generations

ANGELIMIR 2866-2977 20th Prince

ADRAHIL 2917-3010 21st Prince

Children of Adrahil:
- **IVRINIEL** daughter born 2947
- **FINDUILAS** 2950-2988 === **DENETHOR II**
- **IMRAHIL** 2955-FA34 22nd Prince

Children of Finduilas and Denethor II:
- **BOROMIR** 2978-3019
- **ÉOWYN** === **FARAMIR** 2983-FA83
  - **ELBORON**
    - **BARAHIR**

Children of Imrahil:
- **ELPHIR** 23rd Prince 2987-FA67
  - **ALPHROS** 24th Prince 3017-FA95
- **ERCHIRION**
- **AMROTHOS**
- **LOTHÍRIEL** === **ÉOMER**
  - **ELFWINE**

TABLE 8: KINGS OF ROHAN: THIRD AGE
[Dates indicate birth and death]

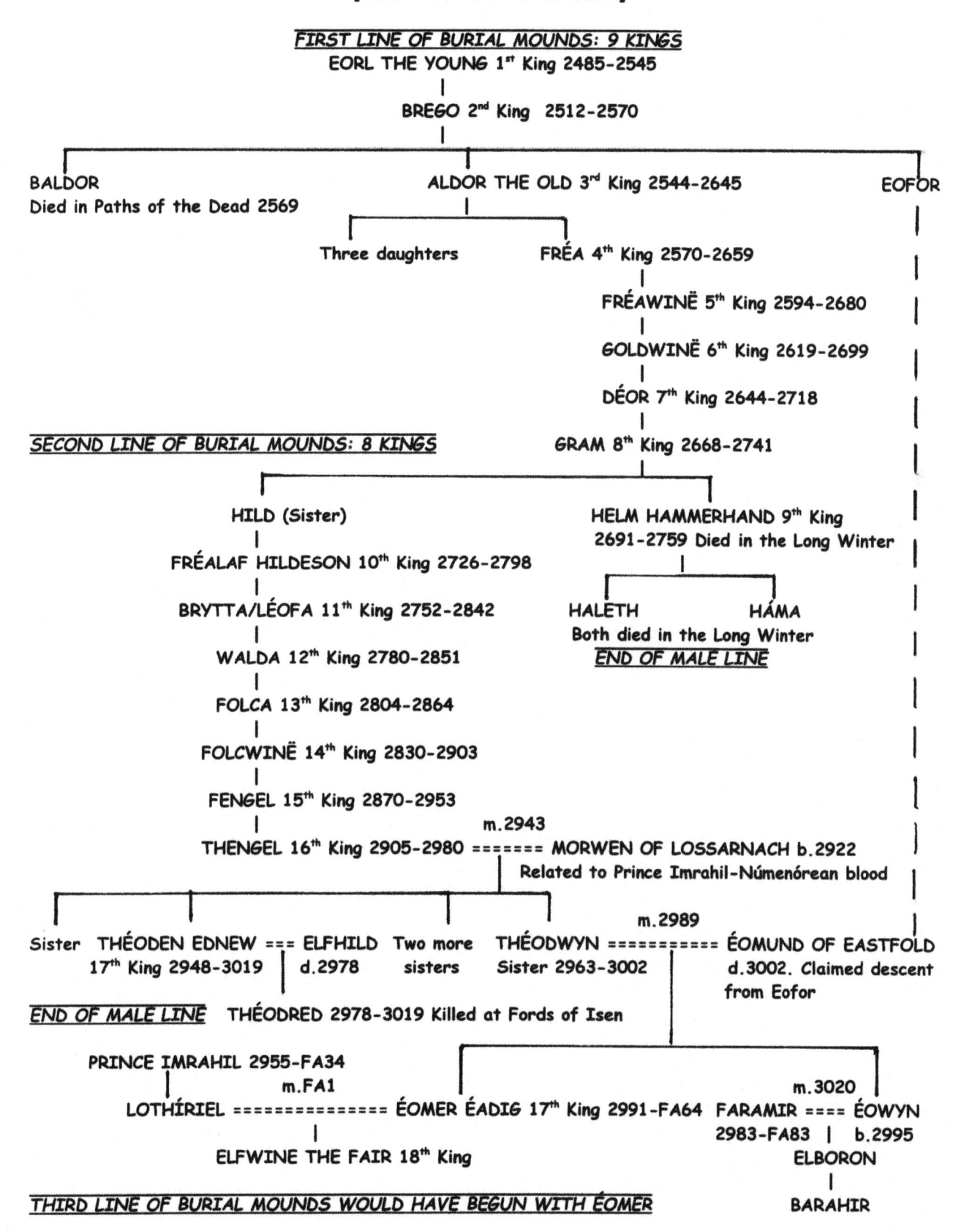

FIRST LINE OF BURIAL MOUNDS: 9 KINGS
EORL THE YOUNG 1st King 2485-2545

BREGO 2nd King 2512-2570

- BALDOR — Died in Paths of the Dead 2569
- ALDOR THE OLD 3rd King 2544-2645
  - Three daughters
  - FRÉA 4th King 2570-2659
    - FRÉAWINË 5th King 2594-2680
      - GOLDWINË 6th King 2619-2699
        - DÉOR 7th King 2644-2718
          - GRAM 8th King 2668-2741
- EOFOR

SECOND LINE OF BURIAL MOUNDS: 8 KINGS

- HILD (Sister)
  - FRÉALAF HILDESON 10th King 2726-2798
    - BRYTTA/LÉOFA 11th King 2752-2842
      - WALDA 12th King 2780-2851
        - FOLCA 13th King 2804-2864
          - FOLCWINË 14th King 2830-2903
            - FENGEL 15th King 2870-2953
              - THENGEL 16th King 2905-2980 ======= MORWEN OF LOSSARNACH b.2922
                m.2943
                Related to Prince Imrahil-Númenórean blood
- HELM HAMMERHAND 9th King 2691-2759 Died in the Long Winter
  - HALETH   HÁMA
    Both died in the Long Winter
    END OF MALE LINE

Children of Thengel and Morwen:
- Sister
- THÉODEN EDNEW 17th King 2948-3019 === ELFHILD d.2978
- Two more sisters
- THÉODWYN Sister 2963-3002 ========== ÉOMUND OF EASTFOLD d.3002. Claimed descent from Eofor (m.2989)

END OF MALE LINE — THÉODRED 2978-3019 Killed at Fords of Isen

PRINCE IMRAHIL 2955-FA34
m.FA1
LOTHÍRIEL =============== ÉOMER ÉADIG 17th King 2991-FA64

ELFWINE THE FAIR 18th King

m.3020
FARAMIR ==== ÉOWYN
2983-FA83 | b.2995
ELBORON
BARAHIR

THIRD LINE OF BURIAL MOUNDS WOULD HAVE BEGUN WITH ÉOMER

THE SILMARILLION: CHIEF NAMES AND CONCEPTS USED

The following notes list the chief names and concepts from *The Silmarillion* which have been used in this book.

Eru/Ilúvatar: equivalent of God, The One, Father of All.

Eä: the world. Created by Ilúvatar.

Ainur (singular **Ainu**): the Powers, divine beings.

Valar (singular **Vala**, female plural **Valier**): those of the Ainur who descended into the world and took up residence there.

The following are mentioned in the book: Aulë, Estë, Irmo/Lórien, Manwë, Námo/Mandos, Nienna, Oromë, Ulmo, Vana, Varda/Elbereth, Yavanna.

Also Melkor who, in the First Age, rebelled against his fellow Valar and against Ilúvatar. Called Morgoth (the Black Enemy) by the Elves.

Maiar (singular **Maia**): lesser Powers, divine beings.

The following are mentioned in the book: Alatar, Melian, Olórin (Gandalf), Pallando, Radagast, Saruman, Sauron, Ungoliant. Sauron was Morgoth's chief servant. Balrogs were also Maiar.

Valinor: the home of the Valar and Maiar, across the Sea in the West. Some Elves lived there too.

Beleriand: Area west of the Blue Mountains during the First Age. Flooded by the sea at the end of that age leaving only the land of Lindon (Harlindon and Forlindon on the north-west corner of the *LotR* map).

Eldar (singular **Elda**): Elves who completed (or started) the journey West to Valinor in the First Age. The name also applied to their descendants.

The Elf kindreds who completed the journey to Valinor were the Vanyar, the Noldor and the Teleri. Some of the Teleri, who made the decision to stay in Beleriand and not go over Sea, became known as the Sindar or Grey Elves.

Some Elves refused the journey to Valinor, or abandoned it very early on. Among their number were Silvan Elves from Mirkwood Forest and Lothlórien.

Elves were immortal for as long as the world lasted, but they could die of grief or be killed in battle, in which circumstances their spirits went to the Halls of Mandos in Valinor. Their bodies could subsequently be reincarnated.

Elves mentioned in the book are: Aegnor, Beleg, Celeborn, Celebrimbor, Círdan, Eärwen, Elmo, Elwë/Thingol, Erestor, Fëanor, Finduilas, Finrod Felagund, Finwë, Galadriel, Gil-galad, Gildor Inglorion, Glorfindel, Gwindor, Haldir, Idril Celebrindal, Indis, Legolas, Lindir, Lúthien Tinúviel, Mithrellas, Nimloth, Nimrodel, Olwë, Oropher, Thranduil, Turgon.

Tol Eressëa: an island between Middle-earth and Valinor where some Elves settled at the end of the First Age.

The Undying Lands: applied to Valinor and Tol Eressëa.

The Two Trees of Valinor (Telperion and Laurelin): Created by Yavanna and Nienna when Valinor first came into existence to provide light to the Undying Lands. Destroyed by Morgoth and Ungoliant. What was left of them was fashioned into the Moon and the Sun. Descendants of Telperion survived.

The Silmarils: Three jewels made by the Elf Fëanor prior to the destruction of the Two Trees and capturing their light. Seized by Morgoth thus causing the war of the Eldar against him.

Elvish languages: Quenya - formal, Sindarin - less formal.

Edain (singular **Adan**): Men who journeyed West in the First Age and became allies of the Eldar. The name also applied to their descendants.
There were three Houses: the House of Bëor, the Haladin (also called the People of Haleth) and the House of Hador.
Men lived only a short time in Middle-earth then died leaving the world completely.
First Age heroes mentioned in the book are: Barahir, Beren, Huor, Húrin, Tuor, Túrin.

Númenor: an island between Middle-earth and Tol Eressëa created at the beginning of the Second Age as a home for those Edain who had assisted the Eldar in the war against Morgoth in the First Age. Its inhabitants were the Númenóreans.

Dúnedain (singular **Dúnadan**): the Third Age survivors of Númenor (and their descendants) following its downfall and drowning at the end of the Second Age.

Elf/Mortal (i.e. Elda/Adan) marriages of the First Age: Lúthien to Beren, Idril to Tuor.

Half-elven: the offspring of these unions and their descendants, namely Dior, Elwing, Eärendil, Elrond, Elros, Elladan, Elrohir, Arwen.

Children of Ilúvatar: Elves (the Elder Children) and Men (the Younger Children).

BIBLIOGRAPHY

Works by J.R.R. Tolkien

The Hobbit, 3rd edition, London, Allen & Unwin, 1966 (1975 printing).

The History of Middle-earth. Edited by Christopher Tolkien.
- Volume III, *The Lays of Beleriand*. Paperback edition. London: HarperCollins Publishers 2002. First published in Great Britain by George Allen & Unwin (Publishers) Ltd. 1985.
- Volume IV, *The Shaping of Middle-earth*. Paperback edition. London: HarperCollins Publishers 2002. First published in Great Britain by George Allen & Unwin (Publishers) Ltd. 1986.
- Volume V, *The Lost Road*. Paperback edition. London: HarperCollins Publishers 2002. First published in Great Britain by Unwin Hyman 1987.
- Volume VI, *The Return of the Shadow*. Paperback edition. London: HarperCollins Publishers 2002. First published in Great Britain by Unwin Hyman 1988.
- Volume VII, *The Treason of Isengard*. Paperback edition. London: HarperCollins Publishers 1993. First published in Great Britain by Unwin Hyman 1989.
- Volume VIII, *The War of the Ring*. Paperback edition. London: HarperCollins Publishers 2002. First published in Great Britain by Unwin Hyman 1990.
- Volume IX, *Sauron Defeated*. Paperback edition. London: HarperCollins Publishers 2002. First published in Great Britain by HarperCollins Publishers 1992.
- Volume X, *Morgoth's Ring*. Paperback edition. London: HarperCollins Publishers 2002. First published in Great Britain by HarperCollins Publishers 1993.
- Volume XI, *The War of the Jewels*. Paperback edition. London: HarperCollins Publishers 2002. First published in Great Britain by HarperCollins Publishers 1994.
- Volume XII, *The Peoples of Middle-earth*. Paperback edition. London: HarperCollins Publishers 2002. First published in Great Britain by HarperCollins Publishers 1996.

The Letters of J. R. R. Tolkien. Selected and edited by Humphrey Carpenter with the assistance of Christopher Tolkien. London: HarperCollins Publishers 1995. First published in Great Britain by George Allen & Unwin 1981.

The Lord of the Rings. 2nd edition. London: HarperCollins Publishers 2007 (based on the 50th Anniversary Edition of 2004).

Marquette Papers 4/2/18 (Scheme). Quoted by Wayne G. Hammond and Christina Scull in *The Lord of the Rings: A Reader's companion*.

Marquette Papers 4/2/36 (Hunt for the Ring). Quoted by Wayne G. Hammond and Christina Scull in *The Lord of the Rings: A Reader's companion*.

The Road Goes Ever On: A Song Cycle. Poems by J.R.R. Tolkien, music by Donald Swann. Boston: Houghton Mifflin, 1967. Referred to by Wayne G. Hammond and Christina Scull in *The Lord of the Rings: A Reader's companion*.

The Silmarillion. Edited by Christopher Tolkien. Paperback edition. London: HarperCollins Publishers 1999. First published in Great Britain by George Allen & Unwin 1977.

Unfinished Tales of Númenor and Middle-earth. Edited by Christopher Tolkien. Paperback edition. London: HarperCollins Publishers 1998. First published in Great Britain by George Allen & Unwin 1980.

Words, Phrases and Passages in various tongues in 'The Lord of the Rings'. Edited by Christopher Gilson. *Parma Eldalamberon* XVII. Mythopoeic Society 2007.

Works by other authors

Armstrong, Helen. 'There are Two People in this Marriage'. *Mallorn 36* (November 1998), pp. 5-12.

Arvidsson, Håken. 'Aragorn: Tales of the heir of Isildur, Part 1 - the evolution of the man'. *Mallorn 44* (August 2006), pp. 47-59.

Blackwelder, Richard E. *A Tolkien Thesaurus*. New York: Garland 1990. Referred to by Richard C. West in *The Lord of the Rings 1954-2004: Scholarship in Honor of Richard E. Blackwelder*. Edited by Wayne G. Hammond and Christina Scull.

Bridoux, Denis. 'Re-readings and Re-interpretations 1: *The Tale of Aragorn and Arwen*'. *Amon Hen 250* (November 2014), pp. 14-16.

Cass-Beggs, Rosemary. 'They're only characters in a book - why do they seem so real?' Paper presented at Oxonmoot 2008.

Crabbe, Katharyn W. *J. R. R. Tolkien*. Revised and expanded edition. New York: Continuum 1988. Quoted from by Wayne G. Hammond and Christina Scull in *The Lord of the Rings: A Reader's companion*.

Crocker, Holly A. 'Masculinity'. *Reading The Lord of the Rings: New Writings on Tolkien's Classic*. Edited by Robert Eaglestone. London, New York: Continuum 2005, pp. 111-123.

Encyclopedia of Arda, <http://www.glyphweb.com/arda/default.asp>.

Fonstad, Karen Wynn. *The Atlas of Middle-earth*. Revised paperback edition. London: HarperCollins Publishers 1994.

Forest-Hill, Lynn. 'Boromir, Byrhtnoth, and Bayard: finding a language for grief in J. R. R. Tolkien's *The Lord of the Rings*'. *Tolkien Studies* Volume V (2008), pp. 73-97.

Foster, Robert. *The Complete Guide to Middle-earth: From The Hobbit to The Silmarillion*. Paperback edition. London: HarperCollinsPublishers 1993. First published in Great Britain by George Allen & Unwin 1978.

Hammond, Wayne G. & Scull, Christina. *The Lord of the Rings: a Reader's Companion*. London: HarperCollins Publishers 2005.

Hawes, Rachel C. A. M. 'Aragorn: Not a Laudable Lord'. *Amon Hen 60* (February 1983), p. 17.

Kocher, Paul. *Master of Middle-earth: The Achievement of J. R. R. Tolkien*. London: Pimlico 2002. First published in Great Britain by Thames & Hudson 1973.

Neville, Jennifer. 'Women'. Reading *The Lord of the Rings: New Writings on Tolkien's Classic*. Edited by Robert Eaglestone. London, New York: Continuum 2005, pp. 101-110.

Petty, Anne. *One Ring to bind them all: Tolkien's mythology*. Tuscaloosa and London: The University of Alabama Press 2002. First published 1979.

Rateliff, John D. *The History of The Hobbit, Part Two: Return to Bag-End*. London: HarperCollinsPublishers 2007 (2008 printing).

'*Rómenna Meeting Report*, 26 October 1986, p.3. Quoted from by Wayne G. Hammond and Christina Scull in *The Lord of the Rings: A Reader's companion*.

Rutledge, Fleming. *The Battle for Middle-earth: Tolkien's Divine Design in The Lord of the Rings*. Grand Rapids, Michigan and Cambridge UK: Wm. B. Eerdmans Publishing Co. 2004.

Salo, David. Reference to possible location of the dwellings of the Dúnedain. Posted on <http://www.bornofhope.com/QA.html> Source: microfilms at Marquette University, Series 3, Box 9, Folder 3.

Shippey, Tom A. *J. R. R. Tolkien: Author of the Century*. Paperback edition. London: HarperCollins Publishers 2001.

Shippey, Tom A. *Roots and Branches: Selected Papers on Tolkien*. Walking Tree Publishers 2007.

Sleith, Valerie M. 'In Defence of Aragorn'. *Amon Hen 62* (July 1983), pp. 14-15.

Smith, Murray. 'Princes Fictional and Real'. Paper presented at Oxonmoot 2008.

Smith, Murray. 'Samwise Gamgee SD? Hobbits, heroism and honours.' Paper presented at Oxonmoot 2013

Stephen, Elizabeth M. *Hobbit to Hero: The Making of Tolkien's King*. Moreton in Marsh: ADC Publications Ltd. 2012.

West, Richard C. '"*Her Choice was made and her Doom appointed*": Tragedy and Divine Comedy in the Tale of Aragorn and Arwen'. *The Lord of the Rings 1954-2004: Scholarship in Honor of Richard E. Blackwelder*. Edited by Wayne G. Hammond and Christina Scull. Marquette University Press 2006, pp. 317-329.

INDEX

This index covers the people, places, events and objects mentioned in the book. As many of them have more than one name "See" references are used to group related names together, thus making searches easier and quicker. In some cases, if the alternative names are significant in their own right, "See also" references are used. For example this is done with "Narsil" and "Andúril": both refer to the same sword but indicate two significant states of it, namely broken and reforged.

Regarding Aragorn himself, it would be unhelpful just to index every page-reference to him. Therefore the following approach has been adopted:

- His interactions and relationships with other characters and races are indexed under the people concerned.
- In addition the book's chapter headings are generally self-explanatory as far as identifying groups of relationships and the various stages of Aragorn's life.
- His own index entry is confined to aspects of him (chiefly related to his character and struggles) which are not easily searchable via the first two methods.

All battles are indexed under "Battle of <name>".

The following sections of the book are not indexed:
- Footnotes
- Genealogical Tables
- *The Silmarillion*: Chief Names and Concepts Used
- Bibliography

A

Abbreviations used ii
Adorn, River 374
Adrahil, Prince of Dol Amroth 21;
    Relationship with Aragorn 288-291
Adûnaic 363, 393
Aegnor 132
Aglarond, Glittering Caves of 79, 197, 202-203
Aiwendil - See Radagast
Akallabêth 342
Alatar (Blue Wizard) 148; Relationship with Aragorn 179
Aldarion 138, 342, 382
Amandil 61, 77, 83, 340, 343
Amin - See Aragorn: Early names
Amon Hen 43-44, 157, 216-217, 226, 271-272, 274, 283, 371; Hill of Sight 43; Seat of Seeing 44, 273
Amon Lhaw 43; Hill of Hearing 43
Amon Sûl, Palantír of - See Palantír: Palantír of Amon Sûl
Amroth 102, 214
Anárion 9, 61, 75-76, 94, 106, 251, 255, 265, 338-340, 343-344, 346-348, 350-351, 355, 381, 410;
    Influence on Aragorn 347-348;
    Heir of Anárion (title) 350

Anborn 296-297
Andreth 4, 86, 119, 123, 132, 206, 285
Anduin, River 20, 43-44, 48-49, 54, 57, 65, 68, 77-78, 87, 94, 96, 113, 128, 150-151, 155, 157, 173, 182, 184, 194, 205-206, 208, 215-217, 219, 226, 236, 263, 267, 274, 278, 298-299, 338-340, 343, 347, 350-351, 354, 357, 359-360, 363, 376, 378, 382-383, 390, 395, 405, 407
Andúnië, Lords of 77, 340, 347
Andúnië, Rod of - See Annúminas, Sceptre of
Andúril 46-48, 92, 95, 146, 273, 303-306, 318, 335, 342, 351, 380, 397; Flame of the West 306, 341;
    Sword Reforged 92, 97, 342, 350;
    See also Narsil
Anfalas 296-297, 382
Angbor of Lamedon 96, 296-297, 349;
    See also Lamedon
Angelimir, Prince of Dol Amroth 21;
    Relationship with Aragorn 288-291
Annatar - See Sauron
Annúminas, Palantír of - See Palantír: Palantír of Annúminas
Annúminas 64, 79-81, 227, 244. 384
Annúminas, Sceptre of 12, 16-17, 57, 77, 122, 342;
    Rod of Andúnië 77, 342; Sceptre of Arnor 85

Anor-stone - See Palantír: Palantír of Minas Tirith
Anórien 381-383
Ar-Pharazôn 9, 13, 77, 83, 85, 338-339, 343, 393
Arador 15, 400; Relationship with Aragorn 137-138
Araglas 18
Aragorn:
Character
2, 31-57 *passim*, 61, 65, 71-74, 78-81, 93-98, 111, 114, 117, 119, 122, 132, 160-162, 164, 185-204 *passim*, 210, 224-226, 236-237, 246-249, 252-253, 257-259, 265-268, 270, 273, 275-279, 280-282, 287, 289, 292-294, 303-306, 310-314, 316-321, 324-329, 332-333, 346, 358-359, 366, 376-377, 407-409;
Coronation
56, 77-79, 81, 113, 125-126, 143, 158, 165-166, 221, 227, 248, 278, 285-286, 332, 341;
Death/Immortality Issues
8-9, 17-19, 21, 81-83, 85-87, 91, 99-102, 107, 112, 114, 117-118, 120, 122-123, 127, 129-132, 139, 165, 201, 204-207, 215, 229, 322;
Disguise/Camouflage/Transformation
1, 18-19, 24-25, 32-34, 37, 42-43, 46, 48, 55-57, 64, 93-99, 103-107, 124, 132, 163, 175, 189, 193, 206, 208, 211, 215, 217, 220-221, 225, 265, 268, 276, 282, 299, 310, 364-366, 368, 391-396, 399, 403;
Early Names
4, 92-93;
Education/Skills
12, 15-16, 18, 20, 24, 30, 35-36, 39, 43-47, 51-52, 64, 82-84, 98, 105-106, 120-121, 128, 130, 153-155, 168, 174, 191, 194, 196, 209-210, 226, 241, 246, 248-249, 253, 258, 289-290, 293, 295, 302-303, 330-331, 342, 351, 359, 366, 370, 380, 383, 388-393, 398-399, 402-406, 410;
Fear
3, 17, 19, 23, 30-35, 40-41, 45-46, 50-51, 62, 104, 124, 159, 162, 167, 187-190, 193, 199, 209-210, 213-214, 223-224, 239, 259, 267-268, 270, 272-273, 314, 317, 319, 331, 352-353, 355, 360, 366-367, 370;
Foresight
19, 40-41, 49-51, 55, 111-112, 114-115, 119-121, 137, 140, 160, 166-168, 188, 204, 214-215, 230-232, 234-236, 244, 267-268, 307, 310, 313, 315, 317, 330, 333, 361, 374;
Healing
1, 10, 16, 27, 35-36, 41, 49, 51-56, 63-64, 74, 76-77, 80-81, 89-92, 97-98, 102, 105, 111-112, 115, 118, 121-122, 124-125, 127-128, 130, 138, 145, 158, 160, 162-163, 197, 206, 210, 212-213, 215, 221-222, 224, 226, 236-238, 243-244, 250, 259, 261, 273, 278, 282-284, 286-287, 290-296, 316-323, 331-332, 346, 350, 353, 380, 391, 404-405, 407-408, 410;
Hope/Despair
11, 15, 17, 19, 41, 43-46, 49, 52-53, 55, 65, 73, 76, 86, 90, 92, 96, 111-113, 115-118, 120-121, 123-127, 138, 140-144, 153-154, 160-161, 168, 175, 186-187, 190, 192-198, 206, 212, 232, 234, 256, 259-260, 293, 306-307, 312, 326, 330, 355, 357, 361, 391;
Identity/Role/Incognito Issues
1-3, 7, 11, 15-19, 20-21, 23-25, 30-31, 34, 37, 41, 46, 48, 52, 54, 64-65, 74, 80-81, 87-91, 93-98, 100, 103-107, 114, 120, 125, 128, 130-131, 139-143, 146-147, 151-155, 160, 163-164, 169-171, 173, 175-177, 181, 186-189, 193-194, 198, 208, 210, 212, 218, 220-223, 226-227, 231, 241, 243, 245, 249-250, 252-254, 259, 265-267, 271, 280, 282-284, 290, 300, 302, 304, 306, 324-325, 328, 333, 341, 349, 351, 354, 362, 364, 366, 368, 376-378, 390-396, 403, 407-410;
Marriage
21, 27, 45, 55-57, 77-78, 82-83, 107, 112-120, 122, 125-127, 129-130, 132-134, 139-140, 142-143, 145, 158, 165-166, 172, 202, 205, 227, 229, 248-250, 308, 321, 333, 383, 410;
Mental Strength and Mental Suffering
7, 16-19, 31-33, 35-38, 40-49, 51-52, 60, 62-64, 73-74, 82-83, 104, 111, 115-116, 118, 122, 127, 129, 141, 143-146, 154, 159-162, 164, 168-169, 171, 174, 185-196, 198-199, 201, 216-217, 219-220, 234, 237-238, 242, 249, 257-259, 268, 270-274, 276, 279, 283, 294, 307, 310-311, 313-315, 317, 321-322, 331-332, 341, 346, 355, 360, 366-368, 372, 408-410;
Perception/Empathy
33, 42, 52, 54-55, 64, 81, 98-100, 106, 111-112, 116, 142, 170, 173, 176-177, 204, 214-215, 223, 226, 241, 244, 249, 257-259, 264, 277, 279, 283, 287, 289, 309-310, 316-317, 319, 324, 361, 372, 374, 377, 383, 391;
Physical Endurance and Physical Suffering
7, 16, 19, 33, 35, 37, 39, 41, 46-47, 49-52, 62-65, 73-74, 100, 102-104, 107, 111, 120-121, 126-127, 142, 144, 146, 154, 158, 162-163, 169, 171, 191-192, 195, 198-201, 234, 236, 238, 253, 275, 279-280, 315, 322, 331, 341, 345, 358, 360, 365, 367-368, 408, 410;
Pity/Compassion
51, 54-55, 80, 111, 154, 164, 191, 201, 248, 258, 273, 280-281, 285, 303, 310-311, 314, 316-317, 320-322, 331, 333, 358-359, 371, 376-377, 387, 395;
Relationships - See relevant individuals or races;
Renewer
10-12, 79-80, 85, 90, 97, 138, 151, 153, 247, 263, 322, 334-335, 343, 380, 410;
Ring, Connection with
1, 11-12, 14, 22-23, 31-33, 35-36, 40-41, 44-45, 48, 51, 54-55, 60, 62, 64-65, 67-69, 71-74, 76, 86, 94, 96, 98, 104, 107, 115, 128, 142, 151-155, 158, 160, 162, 167, 169-171, 173, 175-176, 183-184, 186, 188-190, 201, 204, 209-213, 215, 217, 219, 222-224, 231, 239, 242, 246-247, 249, 257-259, 264-266, 271-273, 276-277, 281, 304-305, 325, 337-338, 342-343, 346-347, 349-361, 366-367, 408-410;
Sea, Connection with
18, 20, 25, 49-51, 56, 64-65, 67-68, 74, 77, 82-83, 86, 126, 252-253, 258, 284, 286, 289, 297, 302, 312, 341, 359, 393-394, 405;
Travels/Journeys
18-23, 25, 28-31, 43, 45-46, 63, 65, 80-84, 86, 92, 102-103, 107, 115, 119-121, 124, 127-128, 134-135, 137, 141, 147, 153-156, 158-159, 161, 163, 165-166, 168, 173, 178-179, 181, 183-185, 189, 191, 200, 239, 247, 249, 252-254, 258, 265-267, 270, 296-297, 299-301, 303, 311, 324, 352, 355, 357-359, 363, 365, 373-374, 378-380, 383, 385, 387-389, 391-396, 398-399, 400-406

Aragorn Elfstone son of Arathorn Tarkil - See Aragorn: Early names
Aragorn son of Aramir - See Aragorn: Early names
Aragorn son of Celegorn - See Aragorn: Early names
Aragorn son of Kelegorn - See Aragorn: Early names
Aranarth 76, 135, 138, 384-385
Araphant 75, 135, 251, 344
Araphor 135
Aratan 339
Arathorn II 11, 15, 18, 90, 128, 139-140, 143, 151-152, 164, 398;
  Relationship with Aragorn 137-138
Araw - See Oromë
Archet 364
Argeleb II 208
Argonath 3, 43, 46, 94-95, 101, 106, 192, 217, 220-221, 225, 271, 273-274, 346-347, 350
Argonui 151-152
Armstrong, Helen 17
Arnor 1, 9, 12-14, 21, 25-26, 35, 55-57, 61, 75-78, 83, 85, 89, 92, 97, 115, 123, 125, 135, 137, 150-151, 153, 208, 227, 251, 256, 264, 284, 338-339, 342, 346, 348-350, 363-364, 374, 383, 385, 392, 394, 410
Arnor, Sceptre of - See Annúminas, Sceptre of
Arod 192, 200, 202
Arthedain 9, 75, 88, 150, 153, 208
Arvedui 9, 12-13, 75-76, 102, 135-136, 151, 251-252, 255, 340, 344, 348, 384-385
Arveleg I 135
Arvidsson, Håken 2
Arwen 1, 3, 8, 12, 15-19, 21-23, 25-26, 38, 41-42, 44-45, 49-51, 55-57, 77-79, 81-83, 85-91, 93-94, 96, 101, 106-107, 112, 119-144 *passim*, 155, 158, 163-166, 171, 204-205, 212, 214-215, 221-222, 227-230, 234, 245-249, 270, 276, 288, 313, 321-322, 333, 341, 351, 354-355, 360, 383, 385, 403, 409-410;
  Evenstar 38, 89, 116, 118, 221; Undómiel 21, 132, 229; Relationship with Aragorn 112-119
Asëaaranion - See Athelas
Ash Mountains 387
AtanatarAlcarin 77
Athelas 35-36, 41, 51-53, 162, 189, 224, 231, 240, 283, 292-295, 318, 404-405; Asëa aranion 405; Kingsfoil 405
Athrabeth Finrod Ah Andreth 4, 86, 119, 123, 132, 206, 285
Auden W. H. 1
Aulë 172, 178, 204

B

Bag End 22, 27-30, 58, 94, 156, 158, 171, 210, 227-228, 354, 379-380
Baggins, Bilbo 4, 10-11, 15, 22, 24, 32, 37-38, 80, 82, 86, 88-90, 94, 106, 113, 116-117, 121, 123, 134, 137, 142, 150-153, 155, 156, 158, 162, 170-173, 181, 183, 206, 208, 210-213, 222-223, 226, 239-240, 245, 264-266, 277, 339-340, 343, 351-352, 356-358, 365, 378-380, 400, 402, 408;
  Relationship with Aragorn 245-249
Baggins, Frodo 1, 3-4, 13-14, 22-26, 27-45 *passim*, 47-48, 51, 53-56, 58-59, 60-61, 65-73 *passim*, 80, 82, 86-92, 94-96, 99-107, 112-113, 115-118, 121, 126, 129, 133-135, 137, 146, 149-150, 155-163, 165-166, 168-169, 171-174, 181, 184-186, 188-190, 194-195, 201, 206-207, 208-210, 222-232 *passim*, 234, 238-241, 243, 245-250, 252-253, 256-258, 264-281 *passim*, 284, 286-288, 297-298, 332, 340-341, 352-361, 363, 365-373, 378-380, 385-388, 392, 399, 402-405, 407-409;
  Underhill (Frodo's alias in Bree) 32;
  Relationship with Aragorn 210-222
Bain 380
Balchoth - See Easterlings
Baldor 200, 235, 302-303, 307, 315, 329, 335, 375, 377
Balin 22, 151-152, 166, 184, 379, 398, 401
Balrogs 22, 133, 157, 163, 166-168, 180, 183, 185, 234, 240, 268, 288, 364, 392; Durin's Bane 22, 166, 168, 180, 183, 185, 401; Elf-bane 183, 185; Relationship with Aragorn 401-402
Barad-dûr 9, 17, 61-63, 65, 67-70, 123, 150, 157, 182, 219-220, 268, 317, 326, 337-340, 347, 355-356, 363, 387, 396, 398-399;
  Lugbúrz 68-69
Barad-dûr, Siege of 9, 67, 338-339, 347, 355
Barahir (author of *The Tale of Aragorn and Arwen*) 288
Barahir (First Age hero) 12, 77, 132;
  See also Ring of Barahir
Baranduin - See Brandywine
Baranor 291
Bard I 379-380, 403; Comparison with Aragorn 380-381
Bard II 79, 381
Bardings of Dale 298;
  Relationship with Aragorn 379-380
Barrow-downs 36, 58-59, 230-233, 236, 241, 244, 258, 264, 388-389
Barrow-wight 13, 58, 230, 389
Battle of Dagorlad 55, 77, 182, 338-339, 355-356; See also Dagorlad
Battle of Five Armies 183, 378-379, 381, 396, 399
Battle of the Field of Celebrant 129, 299, 302, 334-335
Battle of the Gladden Fields 9, 77-78, 173, 251, 339, 342, 346-347, 355, 379, 398
Battle of the Hornburg 47, 60, 62-63, 157, 159, 161, 196-197, 202, 218-219, 301, 306, 329, 333, 336, 373-374, 408
Battle of the Morannon 54-55, 60, 69-73, 78, 80, 82, 87, 91, 97, 101, 116, 128, 130, 147, 158, 161, 164, 202, 219-220, 237, 244, 258, 278, 281, 284, 290, 292, 295, 318, 320, 332, 342, 392-396, 400, 408
Battle of the Pelennor Fields 48, 51-52, 63, 65, 68, 73, 76, 78, 80, 82-83, 87, 96, 102, 116, 128, 130, 143, 145, 147, 157-158, 161, 200, 202, 215, 219, 230, 236-237, 242-244, 259-260, 275, 277, 282, 284, 289, 291, 296-297, 302, 308-309, 315-317, 330, 332, 335, 341-342, 346, 349-351, 376-377, 381, 387, 392, 394-396, 408
Battles of the Fords of Isen 157, 232, 301, 303, 309, 323, 327, 373, 382
Beare, Rhona 179
Bearer of the Star of the North (title of Aragorn) 91, 97, 350; Derivation 91
"Behold!", use of 86-87, 116
Belecthor II 14, 56, 343-344
Beleg (First Age Elf) 204
Beleriand 8-9, 36, 125, 182, 382

Belfalas 288-289, 297
Belfalas, Bay of 338, 393, 405
Bëor, House of 8, 86, 100, 102, 123; See also Edain Beorn 378, 403
Beornings 298, 357, 363, 379;
    Relationship with Aragorn 378-379
Beregond 64-65, 78, 152, 243-244, 251, 260, 278-279, 281, 296, 400;
    Relationship with Aragorn 291-293
Beregond, (Steward of Gondor) 256
Beren (First Age hero) 8, 12, 35-36, 54, 77, 86-87, 99, 112-114, 118, 120, 122-124, 132, 139-140, 181, 210, 214, 402
Beren (Steward of Gondor) 172, 270
Bergil 89, 283, 291-292, 404
Berúthiel, Queen 39
Bill (pony) 167, 369-370, 404
BlackArrow 380
Black Breath 10, 30, 52-53, 63, 97, 104, 130, 158, 160, 230, 278, 283-284, 294, 319, 332, 355, 408
Black One, The - See Sauron
Black Riders - See Nazgûl
Black Speech 364, 399, 400
Blackroot Vale 296-297, 375
Blackwelder, Richard E. 87
Blade that was Broken - See Narsil
Blue Mountains 20, 153, 180-182, 203, 365, 384
Blue Wizards (Ithryn Luin) 148-149, 395; Relationship with Aragorn 179; See also Alatar, Pallando, Morinehtar, Rómestámo
Bob 369, 404
Bolger, Fatty 58, 230
Bombadil, Tom 13, 28, 30, 34, 58, 105-106, 209-210, 230, 352; Orald 388;
    Relationship with Aragorn 387-389
Boromir 12, 21, 37-45, 47, 57-58, 72-73, 89, 94, 101-106, 121, 124, 126-127, 147, 150, 159, 162-163, 167-168, 181, 184-190, 194-196, 207, 212-213, 216-218, 220, 225-226, 232, 234, 240, 242, 247, 251-252, 256-260, 278-281, 283-284, 287-289, 291, 294, 301, 303, 323, 325, 327, 341, 343, 346, 349-350, 352-354, 358, 367, 371, 381, 395, 397-398, 400;
    Relationship with Aragorn 261-278
Boromir (Steward of Gondor) 256
Bracegirdles 174
Brand 203, 380-381
Brandy Hall 238
Brandybuck, Merry 1, 13, 32, 36, 45-53, 56, 58, 62, 77, 79-80, 82, 87, 90, 95, 102, 104-105, 122, 124, 128, 144-147, 164, 175-176, 180, 184, 186, 189, 191, 193-199, 201, 204, 207-210, 217-218, 221-224, 226, 240-245, 249-250, 262, 273, 282-285, 292, 295-296, 307-308, 313-316, 318-320, 323-324, 326, 329, 330, 336, 369, 371, 373-376, 382-383, 386, 389-391, 397-398, 407-408;
    Relationship with Aragorn 230-238
Brandybucks 222, 230
Brandywine Bridge 58, 81, 137, 365
Brandywine, River 208, 222, 230, 365; Baranduin 208
Bree/Bree-land 1, 19, 22-24, 27-31, 34-38, 40, 45, 56, 58, 72, 81, 88, 90, 94, 98, 100, 105-6, 121, 134, 137, 146, 151, 153, 156, 159-161, 171, 173-175, 178, 181, 188-189, 208-209, 196, 200-201, 208-211, 213, 222-224, 226-227, 230, 233, 236, 238-239, 241, 245-246, 250, 276, 352, 364-374, 382-383, 385, 388, 391-392, 397, 405, 407-409
Bree-folk (Breelanders, Bree-men, Bree-hobbits) 31, 37, 90, 181, 208-209, 245, 266, 374;
    Relationships with Aragorn 364-372
Brego 302, 307, 375
Brethil, Forest of 382
Bridge of Khazad-dûm - See Khazad-dûm, Bridge of
Bridoux, Denis 118
Brodda the Easterling 100
Broken Sword - See Narsil
Brown Lands 386, 390
Bruinen, Ford 35, 59, 72, 89, 133, 146, 225, 267, 400
Bruinen, River 137, 156
Bucklebury Ferry 58, 239
Butterbur, Barliman 28, 30, 32-34, 37, 58, 79, 81, 102-106, 142, 146-147, 159, 209, 211, 223, 227, 266, 353, 365, 369-372, 388;
    Relationship with Aragorn 366-369

C

Cair Andros 54-56, 70, 259, 395
Calembel 375
Calenardhon 14, 299, 334-335
Campbell, Roy 104
Captain of the Host of the West (title of Aragorn) 91, 97, 350; Derivation 97
Caradhras 22, 38-40, 129, 157, 166-169, 184, 213, 231, 267-268, 271, 277, 405, 407
Caras Galadhon 40, 214
Cardolan 31, 230, 388
Carn Dûm 230
Carrock 178, 298, 357, 363, 378-379
Carter, Fr. Douglas 391
Cass-Beggs, Rosemary 3
Castamir (the Usurper) 97, 393
Cave-trolls - See Trolls
Celeborn 8-9, 22, 40, 42, 57, 82, 102-103, 112, 114, 119, 122, 124, 128, 132, 158, 163, 168-169, 172, 180, 182-183, 188, 204, 215-216, 228, 230, 270-271, 277, 294, 379, 389, 398, 401;
    Relationship with Aragorn 126-127
Celeborn (tree) 13
Celebrían 8, 10, 18, 42, 114-115, 119, 123, 125, 129-130, 317, 398
Celebrimbor 10, 337, 339
Ceorl 301-302
Cerin Amroth 21, 41-42, 106, 113, 118, 214-215, 220
Chamber of Mazarbul 159, 167-168, 213, 232, 234, 397, 401
Chetwood 35, 366, 370, 405
Chieftain of the Dúnedain 9, 12-16, 18, 75-78, 88-89, 120, 128, 135-139, 141, 145, 147, 150-154, 205, 208, 254, 325, 341, 351, 385, 388;
    Title of Aragorn 1, 9, 15-16, 18, 20, 24-25, 75, 89, 97-98, 128, 130-131, 137, 141, 143, 147, 151-153, 165, 198, 350, 388, 410
Círdan 64, 94, 102, 112, 147-150, 163, 166, 170-173, 204,

338, 346, 355-356, 384;
  Relationship with Aragorn 135-136
Cirion 14, 79, 256, 299, 334-335, 344, 394-395
Cirith Gorgor 54-55
Cirith Ungol 65-69, 71, 73, 219-220, 226, 352, 361, 387, 396, 402
Ciryaher Hyarmendacil 20, 392
Ciryandil 20
Ciryon 339
Coldfells 137, 400
Combe 364
Common Speech 47, 88-89, 97, 209, 246, 290, 300, 302, 325, 363-364, 383, 393-397, 399-400;
  Westron 208, 364
Cormallen, Field of 1, 55-56, 90, 106, 116, 158, 202-221, 226, 237, 244, 285, 320, 323, 332
Corsairs of Umbar 20, 23, 25, 48-51, 60, 64-65, 67, 73, 87, 96, 155, 219, 236, 242-243, 252-253, 260, 289, 296-297, 307, 330, 349, 375-377, 386-387, 394-395, 405, 408;
  Relationship with Aragorn 393-394; See also Umbar
Cotton, Rose 80, 227-229
Council of Elrond 1, 18, 22-23, 28, 37-38, 58, 90, 94, 98, 103-106, 127, 130, 135, 147, 157-159, 162-163, 171, 173, 175, 178, 181, 183-184, 188, 190, 210, 212-213, 216, 247, 249-250, 255-256, 258-259, 261-262, 268-270, 272, 275-278, 302, 323, 341-343, 346, 349-351, 353, 356-360, 362, 365, 367-369, 371, 380, 394-395, 398, 404-405
Council of Gondor - See Gondor, Council of
Counsellor of the North Kingdom 79, 227, 238, 244
Crabbe, Katharyn W. 52-53
Cracks of Doom 55, 71
Crickhollow 58, 156, 230
Crocker, Holly A. 60, 409
Curumo - See Saruman
Curunír - See Saruman

D

Dagorlad 23; See also Battle of Dagorlad
Dáin II (Ironfoot) 168, 203, 381, 401
Dale 78-79, 151, 175, 181, 203, 263, 299, 364, 378-381, 402
Damrod 101, 296-297, 300, 392
Dark Lord - See Sauron
Dead Marshes 22-23, 65, 127, 155, 184, 218, 220, 357-359, 361, 389, 405
Dead Men of Dunharrow 12, 48, 65, 67, 91, 96, 116, 296, 315, 344, 349, 363-364, 393;
  Relationship with Aragorn 375-378
Dead, Paths of - See Paths of the Dead
Déagol 87, 339-340, 360, 396
Deeping Wall 306, 329, 374
Deeping-coomb 160, 306
Deeping-stream 198
Denethor II 14, 21, 25, 61-62, 64, 73, 76, 78-79, 87, 96-97, 101, 103, 106, 147, 157-158, 164, 170, 175, 242-244, 251-253, 261-270, 272-275, 277-280, 282-283, 286-292, 296, 300, 330-331, 334-335, 344, 346, 348, 352, 381, 385-386, 395, 397;
  Relationship with Aragorn 253-261
Déorwine 301-302, 336
Dernhelm - See Éowyn
Derufin 296
Dervorin 296-297
Dimrill Dale 39, 53, 269, 357
Dimrill Gate 22, 166
Dimrill Stair 184
Dior 8-9
Dírhael 15, 137, 143; Relationship with Aragorn 138-139
Dol Amroth 54, 297
Dol Amroth, Princes of 21, 286, 288-289, 291; See also Imrahil, Adrahil, Angelimir, Galador
Dol Baran 57, 82, 122, 172, 198, 221, 227, 233, 242, 244, 250, 329
Dol Guldur 12, 15, 17, 23, 57, 123, 127, 150-152, 173, 214, 268, 298, 340, 342, 358, 389, 394
Doriath 103, 118, 123-124, 180-182, 390
Dragons 364, 392; Relationship with Aragorn 402-403; See also Smaug
Drúadan Forest 78, 381-384, 424-427;
  Grey Wood 381-382
Drúedain 333, 363-364; Púkel-men 381-383;
  Wild Men of the Woods 382-383;
  Woses 381-382;
  Relationship with Aragorn 381-384
Drúwaith Iaur 382-383
Du-finnion - See Aragorn: Early names
Duilin 296
Duinhir (of the Blackroot Vale) 296-297
Dúnadan 13, 15, 19, 22, 49, 95, 97, 100-101, 128, 137-139, 144, 154, 157, 173, 208-209, 231, 233, 244, 254, 298, 322;
  Name of Aragorn (also The Dúnadan) 1, 24, 88-89, 95, 115, 121, 134, 137, 146, 212, 229, 246, 325; Derivation 89, 95, 137, 212, 325
Dúnedain 3, 9, 11-14, 17-18, 24-25, 30-31, 34-37, 40, 49-51, 58, 72, 75-76, 78-79, 82-85, 89-90, 94, 96-97, 99, 101-103, 111, 116, 119-121, 123, 126, 128, 130-131, 133-135, 148, 150-151, 153, 158, 163, 170, 175, 177-178, 189, 198, 200-202, 208, 212, 227, 230, 235-236, 245, 247, 254, 258, 266, 275, 297-298, 300, 305-306, 311-312, 335, 345, 348, 351, 355, 363-368, 373, 376-377, 379-380, 384-385, 387-389, 397-398, 403-404, 410;
  Men of the West 9, 89, 137, 212;
  Men of Westernesse 13;
  Relationship with Aragorn 137-147;
  See also Rangers, Grey Company, Chieftain of the Dúnedain, Star of the Dúnedain
Dunharrow 49-50, 63, 66, 86, 102, 104, 113, 130, 145-146, 200-201, 235-237, 307, 309-311, 313-317, 319-320, 329-330, 332, 375, 382-383; Men of 12, 314
Dunharrow, Dead Men of - See Dead Men of Dunharrow
Dúnhere 301
Dunland 78, 177, 303, 364, 373-374, 404
Dunlendings 3, 20, 24, 47, 160, 174, 333, 364, 375, 385-386, 399;
  Relationship with Aragorn 373-375
Durin I 205
Durin VI 166, 401

Durin's Bane - See Balrogs
Dwarves (in general) 4, 15, 22, 41-42, 54, 69, 80-81, 94-95, 100, 111, 150-152, 166, 168, 170, 174, 180-181, 184-185, 191, 196, 198-199, 203-206, 213, 245-246, 263, 304, 327, 333, 337, 353, 365, 372, 378-381, 384, 390, 392, 395-396, 399, 401-402, 407;
   Relationship with Aragorn 180-181
Dwimorberg - See Haunted Mountain

E

Eagle and Child (public house) 104
Eärendil 8, 10-11, 114, 130, 133-134, 226, 247
Eärnil I 20
Eärnil II 76-77, 87, 135, 285-286, 384
Eärnur 76, 133, 135, 254, 261, 285, 287, 384
Eärwen 8
Eastemnet - See Rohan
Easterlings 19, 55, 70, 78-79, 154, 179, 298, 379, 381, 386, 395-396; Balchoth 394-396; Men of the East 364, 392; Wainriders 298, 394-396;
   Relationship with Aragorn 394-396
Ecthelion II 19-21, 25, 155, 160, 173, 251-254, 256, 262, 289-291, 297, 299-300, 302, 393;
   Relationship with Aragorn 252-253
Edain (in general) 99-100, 112, 124, 142, 383;
   See also Bëor/Hador/Haladin, House of;
   See also Haleth, People of
Edoras 47, 49, 57, 65, 91, 95, 122, 156-157, 159, 176, 196, 199, 218, 302-303, 309, 311, 314-316, 321, 323, 325-328, 333, 408
Eilenaer - See Halifirien
Elanor (flower) 118, 166, 214
Elanor (Sam's daughter) - See Gamgee, Elanor
Elatan of Andúnië
Elbereth 59, 135
Elboron 288
Eldacar 97, 298
Eldakar - See Aragorn:Earlynames
Eldamir - See Aragorn: Early names
Eldar (in general) 13, 17, 61, 112, 114, 119, 124-125, 148, 150, 163, 288, 298, 334, 338, 341, 401;
   See also Noldor, Sindar, Teleri, Vanyar, Elves
Eldarion 83, 85-86, 131, 410
Eldavel - See Aragorn:Earlynames
Eledon - See Aragorn: Early names
Elendil 8-9, 11-13, 20, 24-25, 44, 51, 55, 61, 72-73, 75-77, 80, 83, 85, 91, 94-95, 97, 102, 106, 116, 120-121, 136-137, 145, 172, 181, 245, 251, 256, 264, 266, 274, 284, 286, 288, 304, 325, 334, 337-340, 344, 346-351, 355-356, 364, 393;
   Battle-cry 325, 342;
   Influence on Aragorn 340-342;
   Heir of Elendil (title) 8, 47, 73, 91, 94, 123, 266, 304-305, 342, 344, 349-350, 410;
   Derivation 91, 348-350;
   House/Line of 10-12, 57, 89, 94, 123-124, 137, 147, 252, 257, 264-265, 278-279, 347, 354, 380, 384, 410;
   Sword of Elendil - See Narsil
Elendil-stone See Palantír: Palantír of the Tower Hills
Elendilmir 12-13, 77-79, 81, 91, 125-126, 128, 177-178, 227, 342, 347, 349-350, 388; Star of Elendil 12, 51, 77, 125, 227, 284, 330, 342; Star of the North 12, 77, 91, 96-97, 125, 227, 342, 350; Star of the North Kingdom 12, 77, 96, 125, 227, 342, 350
Elendur 11, 339-341, 346-347, 355-356
Elessar (jewel) 10, 24, 42, 52, 64, 70, 89-90, 94, 97, 106, 113, 115-116, 123-126, 152, 163, 166, 215, 247, 282, 284, 286, 341, 391, 404
Elessar (name of Aragorn) 1, 10, 11, 24, 42, 70, 75, 80-81, 89-90, 94-97, 115-116, 123-125, 138, 152, 177, 206, 226-227, 244, 250, 286, 290-291, 312, 325, 332, 335, 341, 349-350, 372, 376, 381, 383, 410; Derivation 89
Elf-bane - See Balrogs
Elf-friend - See Aragorn: Early names
Elfhelm - See Aragorn: Early names
Elfhelm (of Rohan) 301-302, 316, 321, 382-383
Elfhild 300-301
Elfmere - See Aragorn: Early names
Elfspear - See Aragorn: Early names
Elfstan - See Aragorn: Early names
Elfstan (Fairbairn) 227
Elfstone, or The Elfstone (name of Aragorn) 1, 10, 24, 42, 52, 80, 90, 94-95, 97, 115-116, 124-126, 138, 144, 221, 286, 292, 294, 325, 341, 350; Derivation 89
Elfstone (jewel) 10, 24, 42, 52, 94, 97, 115, 124-125, 286, 341
Elfstone son of Elfhelm - See Aragorn: Early names
Elfwine the Fair 335
Elfwold - See Aragorn: Early names
Elgar, Eileen 63, 118, 165, 199, 206, 222
Elladan 8, 18, 20, 24-25, 38, 42, 49, 53-54, 78, 82, 100-101, 112, 122, 131, 134, 137, 153, 164-165, 238, 247, 249, 267, 295, 306, 311, 318, 376, 398, 399;
   Sons of Elrond 128-130, 399;
   Relationship with Aragorn 128-131
Elmo 8
Elostirion, Tower of 61, 64, 83, 135, 172
Elrohir 8, 12, 18, 20, 23-25, 38, 42, 49, 50, 52, 54, 78, 82, 100-101, 112, 122, 131, 134, 137, 153, 164-165, 234-235, 238, 247, 249, 267, 297, 306, 311, 318, 345, 376, 398-399;
   Sons of Elrond 128-130, 399;
   Relationship with Aragorn 128-131
Elrond 3-4, 8, 11-12, 14-19, 21, 24-26, 36-38, 42, 44, 49, 52, 54, 56-57, 59, 72, 77, 82-83, 86, 89-90, 94, 100-101, 107, 112-117, 119, 124, 126-144 passim, 146, 150, 153-154, 162-165, 170-174, 178, 190, 204, 212-213, 217-218, 228-229, 235, 238, 240, 246-249, 258, 263-268, 270, 274, 277, 282-284, 293, 304-305, 312, 322, 331, 333, 337-338, 341- 343, 345-347, 350, 353-356, 375, 385, 388-389, 398, 409-410;
   Relationship with Aragorn 119-122;
   See also Council of Elrond
Elros 8, 83, 112, 130-131, 205, 410
Elves (in general) 3-4, 8-9, 11, 13, 16, 18, 29, 31, 53, 55, 57-59, 61, 63, 67, 81-83, 85-86, 94, 99, 101-102, 111, 139, 148-151, 153, 155, 161, 163, 165-166, 170, 175, 178, 180-185, 196, 201-206, 211, 213, 222-224, 229, 240, 245, 249, 256, 262, 270, 272, 275-277, 279-280, 287, 333, 335, 337- 339, 351, 353, 359-360, 363, 365, 372, 378, 381-384, 388, 390, 392-393, 396, 399, 402,

407;
   Relationship with Aragorn 112-136;
   See also Eldar, Noldor, Sindar, Teleri, Vanyar, Silvan Elves
Elwë - See Thingol
Elwing 8, 130
Emyn Arnen 203, 251, 286-287, 293
Emyn Muil 46, 65, 162, 218, 220, 301, 323, 326, 328, 357
Encyclopedia of Arda 60
Enedwaith 373, 382-383
Ent-draught 391
Entmoot 232, 241
Ents 79, 157, 176, 230, 232, 307, 364, 392, 398, 400;
   Onodrim 389; Shepherds of the Trees 390;
   Relationship with Aragorn 389-391
Entwash, River 43, 271, 391
Entwives 386-387, 390-391
Envinyatar (name of Aragorn) 11, 90, 97, 138, 290;
   Derivation 90
Éomer 21, 24, 45-47, 49-52, 54, 65, 76, 79, 82, 88-92, 95-98, 106, 130, 144-145, 155, 157, 159, 161-163, 173-175, 178, 181, 191-193, 196-197, 201, 218-220, 232, 234-236, 238, 242, 259, 270, 280, 282, 289-291, 298-309, 313-321, 335, 342, 349-350, 359, 374, 383, 390, 393, 395, 397-399;
   Relationship with Aragorn 323-335
Éomund 21, 291, 299-301, 308
Eorl (the Young) 14, 47, 79, 129-130, 196, 299, 302, 312, 317- 319, 331, 334-335, 344
Eorlingas 299
Éothain 325, 327
Éothéod 298-299, 333, 378
Éowyn 47, 49-53, 57, 63, 65, 77, 79-80, 82, 86, 100, 102, 104, 113, 122, 128, 145-146, 163-164, 187, 200-201, 230, 233, 235-238, 243, 278, 281-282, 284-285, 287-288, 291-292, 295-301, 307, 323, 327, 329-333, 335, 375-376;
   As Dernhelm 237, 315-316, 320;
   Relationship with Aragorn 308-323
Erech 66, 142, 129, 200, 345, 375-376;
   Stone of 50, 66, 91, 96, 116, 145, 219, 349, 375-377;
   Hill of 345
Eregion 39, 159, 166, 180, 184, 225, 231, 240, 335, 337-339, 353, 404; Hollin 39, 159
Erendis 342
Erestor 134
Eriador 22, 141, 150-151, 238, 337-339, 396
Erkenbrand - See Aragorn: Early names
Erkenbrand (of Rohan) 47, 160, 301, 306, 328, 333, 374, 399
Eru 334; See also Ilúvatar
Eryn Lasgalen - See Mirkwood Forest
Estë 53, 149
Estel (meaning Hope) 86, 142, 293
Estel (name of Aragorn) 11, 15-17, 24-25, 86, 92, 115, 117, 120, 128, 142, 293; Derivation 90
Estelmo 339
Ethelion - See Aragorn: Early names
Ettendales 400
Ettenmoors 156, 400
Evenstar - See Arwen

F

Faithful, The 149, 340-341, 354, 393
Falls of Rauros - See Rauros, Falls of
Fangorn, Forest of 27, 41, 45-47, 49, 127, 157, 159-162, 177, 183, 191-193, 195-197, 202, 204-205, 217, 232, 258, 270, 277, 304, 323, 328-329, 334, 357, 389-391, 398, 404, 407
Far Downs 79, 227
Far Harad 179, 364, 392, 394, 396, 403
Faramir 12, 14, 21, 23, 41, 52-54, 56-57, 66-67, 71-73, 76-80, 82-83, 86-87, 89, 91-92, 96-98, 101-102, 104, 122, 128, 149-150, 155, 157-158, 181, 203, 219-221, 223, 226, 236-238, 242-244, 251-252, 256-258, 260-262, 264-267, 269, 272-278, 288-298, 300, 310, 318-322, 331, 333, 335, 341-342, 350, 352, 354, 387, 392-393, 395, 404;
   Prince of Ithilien 78-79, 286-288;
   Relationship with Aragorn 278-288
Farmer Maggot - See Maggot
Farrer, Katherine 227
Fastred of Greenholm 227-228
Fastred of Rohan 302
Fatty Lumpkin 389
Fëanor 61-62, 337
Fellowship (of the Ring) 3, 10, 22, 31, 38-40, 42-45, 47, 53, 57, 65, 79, 82, 88-89, 94, 101-103, 106, 112-113, 115-116, 121, 124, 126-128, 157-159, 161-163, 165-166, 175, 177, 180-181, 183-187, 189-190, 194-195, 201-203, 205, 207, 213-215, 217-218, 222, 225, 230-234, 240, 243, 248, 250, 256-257, 261-263, 267, 270-272, 275-277, 280, 288, 301, 346, 349-350, 353-354, 356, 359-360, 370, 389-390, 396-401, 404-405, 407-408
Fengel 300
Ferny, Bill 32, 34-35, 90, 209, 211, 231, 365-366, 370-374, 404;
   Relationship with Aragorn 369-370
Field of Cormallen - See Cormallen, Field of
Findegil 245, 249
Finduilas (First Age Elf) 140
Finduilas (of Dol Amroth) 21, 254, 261-262, 278, 289, 291
Finrod Felagund 4, 12, 77, 86, 119, 123, 132, 206, 285
Finwë 8
Fíriel 75-76, 251, 255, 340, 348
Flame of the West - See Andúril
Fonstad, Karen Wynn 172, 387, 394-395
Fords of Isen - See Isen, Fords of
Forest of Brethil - See Brethil, Forest of
Forest-Hill, Lynn 2, 187
Forlong the Fat 296-297
Fornost Erain 78, 135, 208, 372, 384
Forochel 12, 135, 363, 384-385, 405
Forodwaith 384
Foster, Robert 60, 141, 146, 171, 227
Fram (of the Éothéod) 333
Freca 373-374

G

Gaffer, The - See Gamgee, Hamfast
Galador, Prince of Dol Amroth 288

Galadriel 1, 4, 8, 10-12, 14, 24, 40-42, 46-47, 49, 57, 72, 82-83, 86-87, 89, 94, 101, 106, 112-119, 122, 126-128, 132, 144, 149-150, 152, 154, 157-158, 163, 165, 168-174, 180, 182-183, 185-186, 188, 190, 193, 196, 198, 204- 206, 214-217, 220, 226, 228, 263, 270, 272, 277, 280, 284, 305, 312, 322, 324, 326-327, 333, 341, 352-354, 375, 391, 398, 401, 404, 410;
   Phial of 115, 220;
   Relationship with Aragorn 123-126
Galathilion 13
Galdor 94, 135, 263
Gálmód 301
Gamgee, Elanor 79-80, 130, 202-203, 205, 227-229, 244
Gamgee, Hamfast (The Gaffer) 30, 58, 156, 222, 228
Gamgee, Marigold 228
Gamgee, Rose - See Cotton, Rose
Gamgee, Sam 1, 13-14, 23, 33, 36-37, 39, 41-42, 44-45, 47, 53-56, 61, 65-73, 79-82, 86, 90-92, 94-95, 105-107, 115, 130, 134, 149-150, 155, 158, 160, 167, 169, 171, 184-186, 190, 194, 202-203, 205-207, 210-212, 215-217, 219-221, 230-233, 239, 241, 243-244, 246, 249-250, 252-253, 256, 264, 268-269, 272-273, 278-281, 286-288, 298, 352-354, 357, 359-361, 368-369, 371, 385-387, 393, 399, 401, 404, 407-409;
   Relationship with Aragorn 222-230
Gamling 301, 329, 333, 374
Gandalf
   Relating to Aragorn 1, 3, 18-20, 22-25, 28-31, 33-41, 43-49, 52, 54-57, 60-63, 67-73, 81-83, 88, 90-95, 97, 99, 102-103, 105-106, 111, 113, 120, 122, 127-128, 134-136, 142-144, 147, 173-174, 176-178, 183-190, 193-199, 202-203, 209-219, 222-226, 230-231, 233-235, 239, 241-244, 246-248, 252-261, 264, 267-269, 271-273, 276-283, 289, 291-296, 300, 302-307, 317, 322, 325, 327-329, 331-332, 343-344, 348, 351-359, 363, 365-369, 371-372, 374, 378-379, 389-390, 397-399, 406-410;
   Relationship with Aragorn 148-172;
   Relating to Bree 28, 30, 33, 58, 79, 88, 102-103, 105, 209, 223, 227, 367-369, 371-372;
   Relating to the Dúnedain 14, 148, 150-151, 153-154, 157-158, 170, 175, 188, 202, 365, 408;
   Relating to Dwarves 15, 151-152, 158, 170, 181, 184, 187, 193, 195-197, 202, 245-246, 272, 302-303, 327-328, 353, 378-379, 390, 402;
   Relating to Elves 4, 10-12, 23, 42, 49, 82, 123, 126, 135-136, 144, 149-155, 157, 163, 165-166, 169-172, 175, 183-184, 187, 193, 195-197, 202, 204, 240, 272, 284, 302-303, 327-328, 342, 353, 357-359, 390;
   Relating to Gondor 23, 52, 54-55, 61-62, 67-69, 76-77, 97, 101, 105, 127, 149-150, 155, 157-160, 162, 164, 173, 175, 242-243, 253-262, 264, 267-270, 272, 275-283, 288-296, 307, 331-332, 338, 348-349, 352, 354, 357, 386;
   Relating to Hobbits 1, 4, 15, 22-23, 27-31, 36, 38, 48, 55-56, 58, 60-62, 65-67, 73, 82, 86-88, 91-92, 94, 99, 102, 105-106, 127, 133-134, 142, 150-152, 155-156, 158, 161-165, 170-172, 175-177, 183-184, 189, 207, 209-217, 219, 223, 225-227, 231, 233-235, 239-249, 255, 257-261, 264, 275, 279-282, 290, 292, 296, 307, 351-353, 356-359, 361, 367-369, 371-373, 378-379, 402-403, 407-409;
   Relating to Maiar/Valar 19, 22, 28, 31, 34, 57-59, 63, 67-70, 72-73, 149-154, 156-158, 160, 163-165, 167-176, 178-179, 188-189, 191, 196-197, 199-200, 219, 221, 240, 243, 256, 258, 270, 303, 308, 311, 342, 351, 373, 386, 401-404, 407, 409;
   Relating to Rohan 47-48, 60, 88, 91, 95, 150, 155, 157, 159-160, 162, 173-176, 178, 196-197, 233, 282, 295, 300, 302-306, 308-309, 317-319, 325, 327-329, 331-332, 374, 399, 408;
   Gandalf Greyhame 148; Gandalf the Grey 148, 163; Gandalf the White 148, 163; Grey Fool 148; Grey Messenger 148; Grey Pilgrim 148; Grey Wanderer 148; Incánus 148, 150; Láthspell 148; Mithrandir 148, 150, 294; Olórin 10, 42, 52, 90, 148-150, 164; Stormcrow 148; Tharkûn 148, 150; White Rider 148, 159, 170
Gap of Rohan 167, 228, 268-269, 275-276, 374
Ghân-buri-Ghân 78, 333, 363, 395-396;
   Relationship with Aragorn 381-384
Gil-galad 9, 72-73, 133, 181, 211-212, 224, 231, 239, 246, 334, 337-338, 340-342, 351, 356
Gildor Inglorion 27, 29-30, 57-58, 112, 134, 209-210, 223, 245-246, 388;
   Relationship with Aragorn 134-135
Gilraen 11, 15-16, 24-25, 82, 90, 129, 137-139, 151-153, 249;
   Relationship with Aragorn 139-143
Gilrain, River 376
Gilson, C. 88-89
Gimli 12, 38, 42-51, 57, 60, 62-65, 67, 71, 74, 78-80, 82, 86, 91, 94-95, 103-104, 106, 112, 129, 144-147, 157-158, 162, 166, 168-169, 174-177, 214, 217-218, 220, 226, 232-235, 237-238, 241, 244, 250, 258, 262, 271-274, 297-298, 302-304, 307, 309, 311-314, 319, 323-329, 333-334, 341, 344-345, 353, 375-377, 379, 386-387, 389-390, 398-399, 406-407;
   Relationship with Aragorn 180-207;
   Lord of the Glittering Caves of Aglarond 79, 197
Girdle of Melian - See Melian, Girdle of
Girion 379-381
Gladden Fields 151, 298, 346, 360, 363, 379;
   See also Battle of the Gladden Fields
Gladden, River 357, 360, 363, 378
Glamhoth - See Orcs
Glaurung 174
Gléowine 301-302
Glittering Caves of Aglarond - See Aglarond, Glittering Caves of
Glóin 22, 94, 175, 181, 184, 263, 378, 380
Glorfindel 34-36, 51, 59, 72, 89, 92-93, 102, 112, 135, 156, 171, 204, 225, 230, 316, 384, 402, 407;
   Relationship with Aragorn 133-134
Goatleaf, Harry 30, 34, 58, 105, 231, 366, 370, 372, 374;
   Relationship with Aragorn 370-371
Goblins - See Orcs
Golasgil, Lord of Anfalas 296-297
Goldberry 388-389
Golden Perch 239
Golden Wood - See Lothlórien
Gollum 1, 15, 17, 22, 23, 25, 37, 39, 40, 43, 54-55, 57, 61, 65-67, 71, 73, 94, 103-104, 106, 127, 142, 151-152,

155-156, 158-159, 162, 164, 171, 183-184, 186, 188-189, 208, 210, 215, 218-219, 225, 232, 262, 337, 340, 342, 352-353, 378-379, 385, 389, 392-393, 397, 402-406, 408-410; Sméagol 220, 339-340;
Relationship with Aragorn 356-362
Gondolin 10-11, 114, 133
Gondor 1, 4, 9, 13-14, 18-21, 24-26, 37, 39, 45, 48, 50-51, 55-57, 61, 63-67, 75-80, 82-85, 87, 91-92, 94-97, 103, 106, 111, 115-116, 119-123, 125, 129, 133, 135, 137, 145-147, 150-151, 153-155, 157, 160, 164-165, 172-173, 175, 185, 189, 193, 202-203, 205-208, 213, 215-216, 221, 227, 236, 238, 242-245, 248, 250, 298-304, 307-308, 311, 321, 325, 327, 330, 332-335, 338-341, 343-346, 348-352, 355, 359, 362-364, 373-377, 381-384, 386, 389-396, 399, 404, 410
Gondor, Council of 75, 251, 286, 289, 348
Gondor, People of 14, 19, 21, 24, 37, 55-56, 66, 75-76, 78, 80, 89, 91, 94, 111, 121, 147, 155, 160, 173, 175, 185, 202-203, 205-207, 213, 216, 227, 238, 244-245, 298-300, 302, 307-308, 321, 330, 334-335, 340-341, 344, 348-349, 352, 355, 373-374, 381-382, 384, 386, 389-393, 395; Relationships with Aragorn 251-297
Gondor, Siege of 162, 170, 177, 242, 257, 260, 293, 400
Gondor, Stewards/Stewardship 9, 14, 19, 21, 25, 56, 61, 75-76, 78-79, 87, 94, 96-97, 101, 146, 155, 160, 172-173, 242-243, 250-260, 262, 265-266, 270, 273-274, 276-278, 282-283, 285-289, 292-293, 296, 299-300, 330-331, 334, 343-344, 348, 350, 352, 393-395
Gorbag 67-68, 220, 361, 402
Gorgoroth, Plain of 65, 70, 219-220, 400
Gorgûn - See Orcs
Great Council of Gondor - See Gondor, Council of
Great Smials 245
Green, Roger Lancelyn 206
Greenway 28, 58, 178
Greenwood the Great - See Mirkwood Forest
Grey Company 12, 20, 49, 65, 91, 96, 103, 121, 126, 128, 130, 134, 137, 143-147, 196, 198, 227, 279, 281, 289, 296, 306, 308, 311-312, 314, 329, 332, 345, 377, 387, 393, 403;
See also Rangers, Dúnedain
Grey Fool - See Gandalf
Grey Havens 61, 82, 117, 133, 135-136, 148-149, 163, 170, 172, 221-222, 227-229, 248, 338, 351, 365, 384
Grey Messenger - See Gandalf
Grey Pilgrim - See Gandalf
Grey Wanderer - See Gandalf
Grey Wood - See Drúadan Forest
Gríma Wormtongue 48, 52, 58, 60, 157, 163, 176-178, 219, 233, 242-243, 285, 301, 303-305, 308-309, 314, 317, 319, 323, 326-329, 331
Grimbeorn 378
Grimbold 301-302
Grishnákh 241, 397-398
Guthláf 301-302
Guthrond 80
Gwaihir 55, 156-157, 163, 178, 191, 403
Gwindor 140

H

Hador, House of 8; See also Edain
Haladin, House of the 8; See also Edain
Halbarad 3, 20, 25, 49-50, 65, 72, 78, 82, 89, 96, 116, 122, 126, 128, 130, 134, 138, 147, 198, 229, 235, 237-238, 281-282, 297, 306, 308, 313, 329-332, 345, 351, 372, 376, 403;
Relationship with Aragorn 143-146
Haldir 42, 124, 183, 185, 214, 399
Haleth, People of 382; See also Edain
Halifirien 334, 342, 344; Eilenaer 342, 344
Hall of Fire 106, 153, 246
Háma (Doorward) 47, 95, 159, 196, 301-305, 329, 341, 349
Hammond, Wayne G. 3, 22, 28, 36, 52, 57, 69, 87, 102, 118, 125, 135, 152, 156-157, 171, 199, 318, 345-346, 371, 377, 387, 401
Harad 21, 25, 67, 78-79, 154-155, 203, 219, 364, 386, 392-395
Haradrim 19, 66, 291, 364, 386, 393-395, 403;
Southrons 55, 392; Swertings 392;
Relationship with Aragorn 392-393
Harding 302
Harfoot 208
Harlond 51, 68, 260-261, 289-291, 330
Harondor - See South Gondor
Harrowdale 301, 315
Hastings, Peter 131-132
Haunted Mountain 12, 50-51, 74, 200, 313, 315, 375-376
Hawes, Rachel C. A. M. 93, 96-97
Heir of Anárion - See Anárion
Heir of Elendil - See Elendil
Heir of Isildur - See Isildur
Heir of Kings (title of Aragorn) 91, 95, 176, 304;
Derivation 91
Heir of Valandil - See Valandil
Helm, Ninth King of Rohan 302, 373
Helm's Deep 47-49, 57, 60, 65, 79, 96, 145-146, 157, 159, 197, 199-200, 202, 218, 234, 259, 301, 306-308, 310-311, 329-330, 332, 341, 473-375, 380, 390, 397, 399;
See also Battle of the Hornburg
Helm's Gate 159-160
Henneth Annûn 83, 219, 280
Herefara 302
Herubrand 302
Hill of Erech - See Erech
Hill of Hearing - See Amon Lhaw
Hill of Sight - See Amon Hen
Hill-trolls - See Trolls
Hirgon 296-297, 307, 335
Hirluin of Pinnath Gelin 296-297
Hobbits (in general) 4, 31, 34, 80-81, 92, 111, 144, 150-151, 155, 173, 175, 181, 208-209, 212-213, 222-223, 231, 233, 238-239, 242, 245, 249-250, 265, 327, 351-352, 364-366, 372, 381-383, 392, 407;
Relationship with Aragorn 208-209
Hollin - See Eregion
Horn (Boromir's) 44, 267-268, 273-274, 307;
History of 273, 395
Horn (Halbarad's) 145, 345
Horn (man of Rohan) 302

Horn (used at Erech) 12, 129, 345, 375-376
Hornburg 47, 49, 73, 116, 144-145, 147, 160, 197-198, 234, 301, 306, 308, 329, 330-331, 374;
   See also Battle of the Hornburg
House of Bëor - See Bëor
House of Elendil - See Elendil
House of Hador - See Hador
House of the Haladin - See Haladin
Houses of Healing 27, 49, 51-53, 76, 89, 97, 102, 105, 115, 122, 127-128, 145, 158, 162-163, 201, 204, 236-238, 242, 259, 278, 282, 284, 287, 290, 292-296, 307-308, 312, 316, 318-320, 322, 331, 336, 404;
   See also Warden of the Houses of Healing
Houses of the Dead 78, 87, 260, 292, 333
Huor 139
Huorns 47, 157, 160, 306-307, 333, 374, 390, 399
Húrin (First Age hero) 139
Húrin of Emyn Arnen (founder of House of Stewards) 251, 287; House of Húrin 76
Húrin of the Keys 286, 296-297
Húrin, House of - See Húrin of Emyn Arnen

I

Idril Celebrindal 8, 10-11, 112, 114, 120, 133
Ilúvatar 9, 53, 85, 124, 132, 140, 149, 165, 204, 257;
   See also Eru
Imladris - See Rivendell
Imrahil, Prince of Dol Amroth 21, 51, 54, 76, 79, 82, 87, 90, 96-97, 105, 201, 242, 259, 282-283, 286, 300, 318, 330, 335, 385;
   Relationship with Aragorn 288-291
Imrazôr 288
Incánus - See Gandalf
Indis 8
Ingold - See Aragorn: Early names
Ingold (man of Gondor) 296-297, 395
Ingold son of Ingrim - See Aragorn: Early names
Ioreth 52, 76, 80, 89, 97, 127, 282, 291, 294-296, 405;
   Relationship with Aragorn 293-294
Iron Hills 151, 181, 395, 402
Isen, Fords of 30, 57, 156-157;
   See also Battles of the Fords of Isen
Isen, River 58, 209, 374, 382, 392
Isengard 27-28, 47-49, 57-58, 60, 65, 72-73, 79, 95-96, 126, 146, 151, 157-159, 172-174, 176-179, 196-197, 199, 217-219, 230, 232-233, 237, 241-242, 244, 249, 259-260, 268, 306, 309, 327, 329, 373, 385, 390, 396-397
Isenmouthe 65, 70, 219
Isildur 1, 9, 11-13, 15-16, 19, 31, 35, 48, 51, 53, 61, 66-67, 69, 71-78, 88-89, 91-98, 102-103, 106, 121, 123, 129, 132-133, 135, 138-139, 141-142, 145, 147, 150-152, 162, 165, 173-178, 181, 208, 212-213, 215, 230, 247, 249, 251-252, 254-257, 259, 262, 264-267, 272, 274, 276, 278, 280, 304, 314, 325, 334, 338-342, 347-358, 360, 362, 370, 375-377, 379-381, 385, 398, 408-410;
   Heir of Isildur 1, 9, 15, 17, 31, 62, 64-65, 72, 86, 91, 95-96, 116, 120, 136-137, 151-152, 158, 175-176, 189, 219, 314, 346, 348-351, 354, 409;
   Derivation 91, 348-350;
   Influence on Aragorn 342-347
Isildur, Scroll of 23, 155, 171, 276, 338, 349, 354, 357
Isildur's Bane - See Ring
Isildur's chain 177
Istari Relationship with Aragorn 148-179
Ithil-stone - See Palantír: Palantír of Minas Ithil
Ithilien 3, 61, 70-71, 78-79, 202-203, 205-206, 219, 221, 238, 258, 278, 284, 286-287, 293, 297, 360, 382, 395-396
Ithilien, Prince of - See Faramir
Ithilien, Rangers of 66, 96, 101, 219, 280, 287-288, 296-297, 300, 392-393, 404
Ithryn Luin - See Blue Wizards
Ivorwen 10-11, 15, 24, 52, 80, 85, 88, 90, 140, 143, 153, 322, 410;
   Relationship with Aragorn 138-139

J

Jackson, Peter 2, 60
Jeffery, Richard 76, 88, 255

K

Khamûl 30, 57-59
Khand 21, 154, 179, 364, 386-387, 392, 394, 396
Khazad-dûm - See Moria
Khazad-dûm, Bridge of 39-40, 157, 159, 168, 269, 277, 342, 401, 407
Kin-strife, War of the 97, 251, 298, 393
King of Gondor (title of Aragorn) 25, 76, 91, 95-96, 106, 274, 304, 350; Derivation 91
King of the Dead (title of Aragorn) 91, 377; Derivation 91
King of the Dead (leader of the Dead Men of Dunharrow) 91, 376-377; King of the Mountains 345, 375
King of the Elder Days (title of Aragorn) Derivation 91
King of the Mountains - See King of the Dead
King of the Númenóreans (title of Aragorn) Derivation 91
King of the Reunited Kingdom (title of Aragorn) 92, 117; Derivation 92
King of the West (title of Aragorn) 57, 79, 92, 203, 381; Derivation 92
Kings of Númenor - See Númenor, Kings of
Kingsfoil - See Athelas
Kocher, Paul 1-2, 37, 65, 72, 80-81, 83, 111, 113, 132, 163-165, 310, 313, 319, 321, 407

L

Lake Núrnen - See Núrnen
Lake-town 363, 379, 381
Lamedon 296-297, 375; See also Angbor of Lamedon
Languages 15-16, 18, 47, 88, 154, 196, 212, 246, 278, 295, 300, 302, 363-364, 380-381, 383, 393-395, 397, 400, 402-403, 410
Last Alliance (of Elves and Men) 9, 31, 55, 67, 181-182, 211, 338-339, 345, 347, 351, 375
Last Debate 51, 54, 68, 71-72, 74, 80, 96-97, 128-129, 158, 160, 201-202, 219, 244, 289-290, 318, 332
Láthspell - See Gandalf
Laurelindórenan - See Lothlórien
Lebennin 296-297, 376

Lefnui, River 382
Legolas 12, 22, 37-39, 42, 44-51, 57, 60, 62-65, 71, 74, 79, 82, 86, 91-92, 94-95, 100, 102-104, 106, 111-112, 117, 144-147, 157-158, 162, 174-177, 214, 217, 220, 226, 232-235, 237-238, 241, 244, 250, 253, 258, 262, 272-274, 287-288, 297-298, 302-304, 306-307, 309, 311-315, 319, 323-329, 333-334, 341, 344-345, 353, 358, 362, 375-379, 389-390, 396-398, 401, 406-407; Relationship with Aragorn 180-207
Lembas 185, 192-193, 196, 379
Limlight, River 357
Lindir 134
Lindon 135-136, 150, 337-339, 341, 365
Linhir 67, 376-377
Lonely Mountain 15, 54, 78-80, 94, 150-152, 175, 181, 202-203, 205, 249, 263, 379, 381, 402
Long Lake 379
LongWinter 151-152
Longbottom Leaf 174
Longshanks (name of Aragorn) 90, 369; Derivation 90
Lord of the Dúnedain (title of Aragorn) 89, 93; Derivation 89
Lord of the Glittering Caves of Aglarond - See Gimli
Lord of the Nazgûl 4, 9, 30-31, 35-36, 51, 57, 66-68, 72-73, 76, 87, 150, 158, 164, 212, 224, 230, 254, 258-259, 266, 285, 316-317, 353, 355, 386; Witch-king (of Angmar) 4, 9, 12, 31-32, 35-36, 68, 72, 76, 103, 133, 135, 150-151, 175, 208, 219-220, 230, 233, 236-238, 240, 244, 287, 298, 355, 380, 384, 388-389, 394; Relationship with Aragorn 355; See also Nazgûl
Lord of the Western Lands (title of Aragorn) 92, 106; Derivation 92
Lord of the White Tree (title of Aragorn) 92, 202; Derivation 92; See also White Tree
Lords of Andúnië - See Andúnië, Lords of
Lórien - See Lothlórien
Lórien (Valinor) 149
Lossarnach 54, 291, 296, 300
Lossoth 12, 364; Snowmen 384; Relationship with Aragorn 384-385
Lothíriel 79, 335
Lothlórien 1, 10, 16, 21-24, 27, 39-43, 47, 57, 64, 89, 103, 106, 112-116, 118, 120-121, 123-129, 131, 141, 147, 157-158, 161, 163-164, 180-188, 190, 196, 205, 213-218, 225-226, 228-230, 232, 240-241, 246, 249, 252, 263, 268-272, 274, 276-277, 279-280, 284, 288-289, 324, 328, 333-334, 341, 349, 357-359, 389-390, 396, 398-399, 401, 404, 407; Golden Wood 123, 224, 333; Laurelindórenan 280; Lórien 42, 127, 171, 205, 241
Lugbúrz - See Barad-dûr
Lune, River 135, 348
Lúthien 8-9, 35-36, 54, 87, 112-114, 116, 118, 120, 122-125, 131-132, 139-140, 180, 210, 214, 317, 402; Tinúviel 8, 35, 112, 114, 118, 124

M

Mablung 101, 288, 296-297, 300
Maggot, Farmer 27, 34, 58, 209-210, 223, 230, 388
Maiar 8-9, 51, 63, 99, 103, 107, 112, 114-115, 122-123, 137, 148-150, 153, 172, 178-179, 401-403
Malbeth (The Seer) 12-13, 76, 123, 135, 138, 312, 344-345, 375, 384
Mallorn (tree) 183, 193, 196
Malvegil, 6th King of Arthedain 208
Mandos 114, 204-205, 207
Manwë 8, 130, 149, 164-165, 318, 403-404
Mardil Voronwë 273, 287, 395
Marquette Papers 57, 69, 88, 156-157
Mazarbul, Chamber of - See Chamber of Mazarbul
Meduseld 47, 95, 98, 159, 163, 196, 199, 302-307, 309, 318, 328, 341, 349
Melian 8, 53-54, 63, 99, 112, 117, 122-124, 132
Melian, Girdle of 123
Men (as a race) 1, 4, 8-9, 11-13, 19, 30, 37, 48, 50-51, 53, 55, 63-65, 67, 72, 76, 81, 83, 85-87, 89, 91, 93, 95-96, 98-103, 107, 111-112, 116-117, 119, 121, 123, 132-133, 135, 137, 146-148, 150, 153, 155, 161, 163, 165, 171-172, 177-181, 186, 191, 196, 200-201, 204-206, 209, 211-212, 217, 222-223, 230-231, 233, 236, 240, 258, 265, 267, 270-271, 280, 296-299, 314-316, 321, 326, 329, 334, 337-339, 344-345, 349, 351, 353, 356, 359-360, 362-365, 367-368, 371-373, 375-386, 388-397, 399-400, 402-403, 406-407, 409-410
Men of Dunharrow - See Dunharrow
Men of the East - See Easterlings
Men of the West - See Dúnedain
Men of Westernesse - See Dúnedain
Meneldil 9, 75, 251, 339-340, 348
Meneldur 342
Meneltarma 83
Merry - See Brandybuck, Merry
Michel Delving 239
Midgewater Marshes 35, 211, 359, 405
Minardil 251, 393
Minas Anor 3, 43, 343; See also Minas Tirith
Minas Ithil 61, 79, 94, 254, 287, 338-339, 343, 347, 350, 355, 362; See also Minas Morgul
Minas Ithil, Palantír of - See Palantír: Palantír of Minas Ithil
Minas Morgul 54, 57, 61, 64-67, 69-70, 76, 219, 254, 285-287, 387, 396, 402; See also Minas Ithil
Minas Tirith 3, 14, 20, 23, 27, 39, 41-45, 47-49, 51-52, 54, 56-57, 61-62, 64-65, 67, 73, 75, 78-79, 81, 87, 91, 94-96, 102, 105, 116, 122, 127-128, 131, 134, 155, 157-158, 160-161, 165, 170-172, 175-176, 186, 189-190, 201-203, 214-217, 221, 232, 234-235, 242-245, 248-249, 252-261, 263-275, 277-278, 280-282, 284, 286-289, 291, 293-294, 296-297, 301, 304, 307, 314, 320, 333-334, 343-344, 352, 354, 357, 372, 375, 377, 381, 383-384, 393, 405, 408; See also Minas Anor
Minas Tirith, Palantír of - See Palantír: Palantír of Minas Tirith
Mindolluin - See Mount Mindolluin
Mirkwood Forest 12, 17, 20, 23, 38, 44, 57, 78, 127, 133, 148, 150-151, 155, 178, 181-184, 202-203, 214, 262, 298, 340, 352, 357, 359, 363, 378-380, 389, 394, 396-397, 400, 402-403; Eryn Lasgalen 379; Greenwood the Great 207
Mirrormere 184

Misty Mountains 15, 20, 35, 39-40, 44, 115, 129, 151-153, 155, 159, 166, 168, 182-183, 198, 208, 246, 269, 299, 339-340, 363-364, 380, 391, 396-401, 405
Mitchison, Naomi 53, 171, 206, 227, 278, 386, 403
Mitheithel, Bridge 35, 59, 134, 405
Mitheithel, River 137
Mithrandir - See Gandalf
Mithrellas 288
Mithril 77, 79, 81, 116, 145, 166, 202, 398, 401
Mithril shirt 41, 69, 213, 220, 354
Mithrim 139
Morannon 23, 27, 37, 54-55, 63, 66, 69-73, 82, 91, 97, 147, 150, 158, 164, 202, 218-220, 237, 244, 258, 278, 281, 284, 290, 292, 295, 318, 320, 332-333, 338-339, 361, 387, 392, 395, 408; See also Battle of the Morannon
Mordor 3, 15, 17, 21, 23, 36, 39-41, 44-45, 48, 50-51, 54-55, 58-59, 63, 65-70, 78-79, 84, 86, 96, 103, 106, 120, 123, 129, 132, 150-152, 154-155, 163, 166, 171, 174, 179, 183, 186, 188-189, 194, 201, 214-217, 219-221, 225, 232, 239-241, 252, 255, 257, 260-263, 266-267, 271-272, 274, 279, 284, 292, 297, 299, 303, 324, 327, 330, 332, 337-340, 353-354, 356-357, 361, 363, 367, 377, 382, 385-387, 392, 395-400, 402, 405, 408-409
Morgai 65, 69, 71, 115, 219, 220, 387, 399
Morgoth 9, 11-13, 85, 99, 114, 123, 132, 139, 149, 153, 166, 180, 298, 317, 337, 342, 382-383, 392, 396, 399-402
Morgul Vale 21, 23, 37, 63, 66, 71, 73, 86, 150, 184, 219-220, 387, 402
Morgul-knife 36, 53, 134
Moria 22, 27, 36, 38-41, 51, 53, 157, 159-160, 162, 164, 166-169, 171, 180, 182-185, 187-188, 190, 213-215, 218, 225, 231, 240, 244, 267-270, 275-276, 288, 325, 328, 335, 337, 353-354, 357, 359-360, 396-402, 404, 407;
    Khazad-dûm 168
Morinehter (Blue Wizard) 179;
    Relationship with Aragorn 179
Mortensen, Viggo 2
Morwen (First Age, mother of Túrin) 100-101, 139-140
Morwen of Lossarnach (mother of Théoden) 300
Mount Doom 55, 65, 70-71, 158, 219-220, 226, 228, 337-339, 354, 386-387, 408-409
Mount Mindolluin 56, 82-83, 113, 147, 158, 160-161, 165, 172, 343-344
Mountain-trolls - See Trolls
Mountains of Shadow 20, 54, 65-66, 71, 219, 291, 338, 363, 387, 395-396
Mouth of Sauron 55, 70-71, 101, 158, 202
Murray, Robert 86, 338
Muster of Rohan 49, 65, 237

N

Narsil 9, 338, 342, 351, 380; Blade that was Broken 12, 95, 247, 263, 305-306, 343; Broken Sword 31, 33, 37, 94, 121, 224, 247, 264-266, 340, 343, 354; Shards of Narsil 9, 12, 16, 30-31, 77, 92, 105, 153, 339, 342-343, 347, 350; Sword of Elendil 9, 11-12, 14, 17, 31, 33, 37-38, 61-62, 65, 67, 76, 95-98, 120-121, 162, 247, 252, 264-267, 328, 340-341, 349-351, 354;
    Sword that was Broken 12, 262, 264-265, 325, 327, 329, 343, 350;
    See also Andúril
Narya (the Red Ring) 149, 154, 163, 166, 171-172, 337
Nauglamir 180
Nazgûl 3-4, 10, 17, 23, 27-38, 45, 52, 54-55, 61, 63, 65, 67-73, 86, 97, 105, 121, 123, 128, 130, 133-134, 137, 142-143, 145-146, 150-152, 154, 156-159, 161-162, 169, 171, 173-174, 176, 178, 186, 188-190, 209-212, 218, 220, 222-224, 230-231, 236, 239, 242, 254, 267, 272, 279, 281-284, 316-317, 319, 337-339, 351-354, 358-359, 365-374, 385-386, 401, 405, 407-408;
    Black Riders 1, 4, 23, 209, 223-224, 240;
    The Nine 4, 34-35, 178, 263, 316, 338;
    Table of activities 57-59;
    Relationship with Aragorn 355;
    See also Lord of the Nazgûl
Near Harad 150, 364, 392, 394, 396
Necromancer - See Sauron
Nenya (the White Ring) 123, 125-126, 215, 218, 337
Neville, Jennifer 409
Nienna 149
Nimloth (First Age Elf) 8-9
Nimloth (tree) 13
Nimrodel (Elf) 113, 236, 321
Nimrodel, River 185, 188, 190, 357
Nine, The - See Nazgûl
Nine Rings 67, 337, 352
Niphredil 118, 166, 214
Nob 34, 209, 230, 368, 372, 385
Nogrod 180, 390
Noldor/Noldorin 8, 125, 134, 166, 180;
    See also Eldar, Elves
North Downs 20, 153, 365
Northey, A. P. 221
Northfarthing 399
Númenor 8-9, 12-13, 24, 52-53, 56, 61, 63, 75, 77, 80, 83, 85, 97, 99, 107, 110, 117, 119, 125, 138, 153, 175, 179, 205, 245, 251, 256-257, 279, 284, 286-288, 298, 334, 337-340, 342-343, 345, 347, 350-351, 354, 363, 382, 393, 457;
    Westernesse 232, 236, 275, 398
Númenor, Kings of 9, 77, 97, 117, 125
Númenor, Sceptre of 77
Númenóreans (including characteristics) 9, 13, 20, 50, 53, 75-77, 82-83, 85-87, 89, 91, 95, 99-103, 107, 112, 119, 136-137, 153, 179, 205, 212, 251, 253-254, 275, 279, 284, 288-289, 293, 318, 322, 325, 338-341, 350, 355, 360, 363, 373, 382, 393, 403-404, 410
Núrnen, Lake 78, 150, 179, 385-387

O

Ohtar 339, 343, 347
Old Forest 58, 222, 230, 388-389
Old Forest Road (Mirkwood Forest) 178
Old Man Willow 389
Olog-hai - See Trolls
Olórin - See Gandalf
Olwë 8
Ondoher 75, 251, 348
One Ring - See Ring
Onodrim - See Ents

Orald - See Bombadil, Tom
Orch - See Orcs
Orcs 4, 9, 12, 15, 18, 20, 22, 24, 39-41, 43-47, 66-70, 73, 77-78, 91, 100, 102-103, 128-130, 137, 142, 157, 160, 162, 164, 166, 168, 173, 175, 180, 184, 186, 191-200, 213, 216, 218-220, 225-226, 228, 232-233, 240-241, 244, 262, 268-269, 273, 286, 299, 301, 303, 306, 317, 323-329, 335, 339-340, 342-343, 347, 355, 359-360, 363-364, 369, 373-374, 378-379, 381-383, 385-386, 390, 392-395, 400-402, 406-408;
    Glamhoth 396; Goblins 382, 396, 398; Gorgûn 396; Orch 396; Uruk-hai 69, 396-397; Uruks 396-397; Yrch 396; Relationship with Aragorn 396-399
Orocarni - See Red Mountains
Oromë 179, 222, 395; Araw 273, 395
Oropher 181-182
Orthanc 50, 54, 64-65, 68-69, 72, 87-90, 172-173, 191, 193-196, 218, 224, 243, 300, 363, 435
Orthanc, Palantír of - See Palantír: Palantír of Orthanc
Orthanc-stone - See Palantír: Palantír of Orthanc
Osgiliath 56-57, 262-263, 266-267, 278, 280, 287-288, 291, 347, 355, 359
Our King (title of Aragorn) 81, 92; Derivation 92

P

Padathir - See Aragorn: Early names
Palantír (plural Palantíri) 4, 45, 135, 144, 174, 234, 242, 258-259; Seeing-stones 4, 61, 259; Stones 4, 61, 64;
    History and nature of 61-64;
    Palantír of Amon Sûl 35, 64, 172, 384-385;
    Palantír of Annúminas 64, 384-385;
    Palantír of Minas Ithil (Ithil-stone) 22, 61, 72, 156, 173, 254;
    Palantír of Minas Tirith (Anor-stone) 61, 64, 79, 170, 172, 222, 243, 252, 254-256, 258-260, 289, 330;
    Palantír of Orthanc (Orthanc-stone) 4, 20, 22, 31, 47-48, 54, 57, 60-65, 68, 70-73, 79, 82, 86, 95-98, 102, 104, 106, 115-116, 128, 131, 143-144, 156-157, 160-162, 164, 169-171, 173-174, 176-178, 198-200, 208, 219-220, 226, 233-235, 237-238, 241-244, 249, 254, 256, 258-260, 280-281, 306-307, 311, 314-315, 329, 332, 341, 346, 350, 360, 375, 394, 408-409;
    Palantír of the Tower Hills (Elendil-stone) 61, 64, 83, 135-136, 172, 351, 356;
    Analysis of Aragorn's use of the Palantír of Orthanc 60-74
Pallando (Blue Wizard) 148;
    Relationship with Aragorn 179
Parth Galen 27, 43-46, 161-162, 171, 175, 184, 186-187, 189-190, 193-196, 198, 202, 206, 215-216, 218, 220-221, 225-226, 232, 234, 238, 240, 262, 269, 271-275, 283, 317, 323, 342, 346, 353-354, 395, 397-398
Paths of the Dead 12, 30, 41, 48-52, 55, 63, 65-66, 73-74, 78, 82, 95-96, 102, 113, 116, 121-123, 126, 128-130, 140, 144-147, 157, 161, 164, 187, 194, 196, 198, 200-203, 214, 219, 221, 234-238, 242, 244, 258, 260, 279, 281, 284, 297, 302, 307-308, 311-317, 319, 329-332, 335, 375-376, 378, 403, 408;
    History of 344-347
Pelargir 20, 30, 48-52, 63-67, 74, 77, 96, 102, 128, 157, 182, 198, 200-201, 204, 219, 226, 242, 254, 260, 296-297, 307, 349, 363, 375-377, 387, 404
Pelendur 75, 251-252, 255, 348
Pelennor Fields 27, 48, 51-52, 65, 68, 182;
    See also Battle of the Pelennor Fields
People of Haleth - See Haleth
Petty, Anne 38, 42, 50
Phial of Galadriel - See Galadriel, Phial of
Pinnath Gelin 297
Pippin - See Took, Pippin
Plague 56, 298, 343
Plain of Gorgoroth - See Gorgoroth, Plain of
Prancing Pony 1, 28, 30, 32, 37, 81, 93, 101, 104-106, 145, 156, 158, 181, 209-210, 212, 222, 227, 230, 232, 281, 353, 359, 364-366, 372-373, 385, 388-389, 404
Precious - See Ring
Prince of Ithilien - See Faramir
Princes of Dol Amroth - See Dol Amroth, Princes of
Púkel-men - See Drúedain

Q

Qendemir - See Aragorn: Early names
Quenya 10, 88-90, 97, 250, 290, 300, 325, 363, 371
Quickbeam 79, 391

R

Radagast 28, 148-149, 156, 179, 403;
    Aiwendil 178; Radagast the Bird-tamer 178; Radagast the Brown 178; Radagast the Fool 178; Radagast the Simple 178;
    Relationship with Aragorn 178
Rangers 1, 18-20, 22, 24-25, 29-33, 35, 37, 39, 46, 49, 58, 77, 81, 84, 94-95, 105, 114, 120, 126, 128, 130, 134, 137, 141, 143-147, 153-155, 159, 163, 165, 170, 181, 188, 192, 198, 208-210, 212, 230, 241, 245-246, 255, 258, 261, 268, 293, 298, 303, 316, 351, 353-355, 364-371, 378, 399, 401, 404, 408;
    See also Dúnedain, Grey Company;
    See also Ithilien, Rangers of
Rateliff, John D. 380
Rath Dínen (Silent Street) 238, 245, 292
Rauros, Falls of 43, 69, 271, 407
Red Arrow 296, 307, 335
Red Book 80, 228, 245, 249
Red Eye 398
Red Mountains (Orocarni) 395
Redhorn Gate 166
Renewer (title of Aragorn) 10-11, 80, 85, 90, 97, 138, 322, 410
Rhosgobel 178
Rhovanion 155, 298, 357
Rhudaur 31, 240
Rhûn 25, 154-155, 179, 203, 273, 298, 386, 394-396
Rhûn, Sea of 21, 79, 335, 387, 395
Rían 139-140
Riddle of Strider, The 11-12, 80, 247-248, 262-263, 265, 343
Riders of Rohan 46, 100, 192, 235, 307, 315-316, 322-326, 381

Rimbedir - See Aragorn: Early names
Ring 1, 9, 11-12, 14, 22-23, 27, 31-33, 35-36, 41-42, 44-45, 48, 51, 54-60, 62-65, 67-74, 76-78, 86-87, 94, 96, 98, 102, 104-107, 115-117, 121, 123, 126, 128, 134-135, 142, 146, 150-158, 160, 162, 166, 169, 170-171, 173, 175-177, 179, 181, 183, 186, 188-190, 201-204, 206-213, 215-224, 226, 231, 239, 241-242, 246-249, 259, 261-281, 284-285, 287, 289, 296, 304-305, 320, 325, 337-343, 345-350, 357-364, 366, 369, 373, 386, 392-393, 395-396, 398, 400, 408-410;
   Isildur's Bane 74, 86, 262, 264-265, 272, 274, 278, 280, 352; One Ring 1, 9, 14-15, 22, 31, 42, 67, 72, 77-78, 87, 96, 123, 134, 142, 151-152, 154, 160, 162, 166, 173, 177, 179, 181, 183, 189, 202, 215, 246, 255, 264, 280, 304-305, 325, 337-340, 350-352, 356-358, 363, 373, 396;
   Precious 15, 151, 360-361;
   Ruling Ring 11, 155, 343;
   Aragorn's attitude to the One Ring 351-356
Ring of Barahir 12, 16, 77, 153, 342, 385; History of 12;
   See also Barahir (First Age hero)
Ring-bearers 4, 31, 44-45, 54, 58-59, 69, 116, 121, 160, 186, 189-190, 202, 213, 215-217, 221, 227-228, 248, 268, 271-272, 276, 332, 408-410
Ringló, River 375
Ringló Vale 296-297
Rings Of Power 166, 172, 403;
   Forging and history 337-339
Rivendell 3, 9, 11-12, 15-19, 21, 24, 27, 29-31, 33-42, 45, 55, 57-59, 77-78, 82, 87, 89-90, 101, 103-104, 106, 112-116, 119-122, 124, 126-131, 133-135, 137-143, 145, 147, 151-153, 155-160, 163, 165-171, 178, 183-184, 188-190, 198, 207, 210, 212-214, 217, 223, 225-227, 229, 231, 233, 238, 240, 245-249, 251, 261-263, 266-270, 274-276, 278, 280, 284, 288, 299, 312, 333, 339, 343, 345-347, 351-356, 359, 367, 378, 380, 384-385, 399-402, 405-409;
   Imladris 137, 258, 262, 264-265, 269
Roäc 403
Rod of Andúnië - See Annúminas, Sceptre of
Rohan 3, 14, 19-21, 24-25, 43-50, 54, 57, 65, 73, 78-79, 82, 84, 88, 91, 95, 100, 102-103, 116, 119-120, 126, 128, 130, 134, 143-145, 147, 150, 154-155, 158, 161, 163, 167, 173-174, 176-177, 192, 194, 196, 200, 202-203, 220, 227-229, 238, 241, 244, 252-253, 266, 268-270, 275-276, 280, 287-288, 291-292, 298, 344, 359, 364, 373-375, 381, 383, 390-392, 395-399, 404-407;
   Eastemnet 302; Westemnet 326, 328; Wold 390
Rohan, Gap of - See Gap of Rohan
Rohan, Muster of - See Muster of Rohan
Rohan, Riders of - See Riders of Rohan
Roheryn 50, 116, 144, 403
Rohirric 302
Rohirrim 3, 18, 45-47, 50, 65, 79, 91, 95, 97, 145, 157, 173, 192-193, 195-198, 236-237, 241, 259, 263, 268, 270, 341-342, 363-364, 373-375, 378-379, 382-384, 392, 395, 399, 404;
   Relationships with Aragorn 298-336
Rómenna Meeting Report 52
Rómestámo (Blue Wizard) 179;
   Relationship with Aragorn 179
Royal Standard 116, 121-122, 124, 284

Ruling Ring - See Ring
Running, River 298, 379, 394
Rutledge, Fleming 65, 96, 143, 313, 315

S

Sackville-Bagginses 174
Salo, David 137
Sandyman, Ted 181
Sarn Ford 27-32, 58, 72, 143, 145, 156, 189, 210, 316, 355, 365
Sarn Gebir, 43, 186, 217, 225, 271, 274, 357
Saruman 15, 19-20, 22, 27-28, 31, 34, 45-48, 57-58, 60-62, 64-65, 72-73, 78, 95, 104, 143, 148-152, 156-158, 161, 167, 169, 178-179, 188, 191-198, 203, 219, 233, 236, 242-243, 253-254, 256, 260, 268, 270, 285, 301, 303-309, 311, 319, 323-324, 326-329, 331, 333, 339, 351, 369-370, 373-374, 382, 385-386, 390-391, 394, 396-399, 403, 407; Curumo 172; Curunír 172; Saruman of Many Colours 172; Saruman Ring-maker 172; Saruman the White 172; Saruman the Wise 172; Sharkey 172; White Messenger 172; Relationship with Aragorn 172-178
Sauron 1, 4, 7, 9, 12-26, 31, 34, 37, 39, 41, 43, 45, 48-49, 51-52, 54-55, 57, 59, 78-80, 82, 84-86, 89-93, 96-98, 101, 103-104, 106-107, 112-116, 120-121, 123, 127-133, 135, 142-144, 147-156, 158, 160-164, 166, 169-177, 179, 181-183, 185, 188-189, 198-199, 201-204, 208, 211-213, 218-220, 226, 234, 237, 241-246, 249, 251-252, 254-264, 266-268, 270, 272, 275, 277-278, 281-282, 284, 286, 289-290, 292, 297, 302, 304-307, 311-312, 314, 317, 324-325, 330, 332, 335, 337-362 passim, 363, 365-366, 368-370, 372-377, 379-387, 390-396, 398, 400-404, 408-410; Annatar 337; Black One 360; Dark Lord 17, 22, 55, 70, 73, 80, 123, 386; Necromancer 379;
   History of 337-340;
   Palantír confrontation with Aragorn 60-74
Scatha 333
Sceptre of Annúminas - See Annúminas, Sceptre of
Sceptre of Arnor - See Annúminas, Sceptre of
Sceptre of Númenor - See Númenor, Sceptre of
Scouring of the Shire 244
Scroll of Isildur - See Isildur, Scroll of
Scull, Christina 3, 22, 28, 36, 52, 57, 69, 102, 118, 125, 135, 152, 171, 199, 318, 345, 371, 377, 387, 401
Sea of Rhûn - See Rhûn, Sea of
Seat of Seeing - See Amon Hen
Seeing-stones - See Palantír
Seven Rings 337, 356
Seven Stars 116, 351
Shadowfax 61, 156, 221, 233, 294, 296, 303, 403
Shagrat 67-69, 219-220, 361, 402
Shards of Narsil - See Narsil
Sharkey - See Saruman
Shelob 23, 67-69, 115, 219, 359, 392;
   Relationship with Aragorn 402
Shepherds of the Trees - See Ents
Shippey, Tom A. 65, 194, 196, 199
Shire/Shire-folk 4, 19, 22-25, 27-29, 31, 37, 52, 58, 79-81, 92, 134, 137, 144-147, 151-152, 155-156, 160-

161, 166, 173-175, 178, 181, 189, 205, 208-210, 212, 221-223, 227-230, 234, 236-238, 244-246, 250, 257-258, 290, 351, 353, 358, 365-366, 370, 372-373, 383, 396, 399, 403-404, 408
Siege of Barad-dûr - See Barad-dûr, Siege of
Siege of Gondor - See Gondor, Siege of
Silent Street - See Rath Dínen
Silmarien 75-77, 340, 342, 347
Silmarils 12, 123, 132, 146, 180, 199
Silvan Elves 182-183, 288, 335; See also Elves
Silverlode, River 184, 357
Sindar/Sindarin 8-9, 181-182; See also Eldar, Elves
Sindarin (language) 20, 89-91, 212, 300, 363, 402, 404
Sleith, Valerie M. 93
Smaug 15, 151-152, 175, 181, 249, 379-381, 402; See also Dragons
Sméagol - See Gollum
Smith, Murray 146, 303
Snaga 69
Snowmane 315
Snowmen - See Lossoth
Sons of Elrond - See Elladan, Elrohir
South Gondor 150
Southrons - See Haradrim
Spells 36, 53, 95, 114, 116, 167-168, 195, 232, 262, 305, 327, 398, 401
Squint-eyed southerner 57, 174, 209, 233, 369-371, 373-374, 397
Staddle 364
Star of Elendil - See Elendilmir
Star of the Dúnedain 79, 227
Star of the North - See Elendilmir
Star of the North Kingdom - See Elendilmir
Stephen, Elizabeth 89
Stewards/Stewardship (Gondor) - See Gondor, Stewards/Stewardship
Stick-at-naught Strider (name of Aragorn) 90, 369, 371; Derivation 90
Stone of Erech - See Erech
Stone-trolls - See Trolls
Stones - See Palantír
Stonewain Valley 383, 395
Stormcrow - See Gandalf
Straight, Michael 27, 407
Strider (name of Aragorn) 1, 11-12, 24, 27, 29-30, 32-36, 56, 80, 84, 88, 90, 93-95, 97, 100, 104, 106, 134, 146, 159, 163, 211-212, 217, 223-227, 230, 232-233, 236, 239, 241-242, 246-248, 250, 262-263, 265, 290, 323, 343, 365-369, 371, 380, 392, 397, 409; Derivation 90
Strider (pony) 221
Swann, Donald 135
Swertings - See Haradrim
Sword of Elendil - See Narsil
Sword Reforged - See Andúril
Sword that was Broken - See Narsil
Symbelmynë 303

T

Tale of Aragorn and Arwen, The 15, 88, 113, 245, 288, 409
Taniquetil 318

Tar-Elendil 340, 342
Tar-Palantir 13, 56, 113, 143, 343
Tarannon Falastur 20, 39
Tarantar - See Aragorn: Early names
Targon 296-297
Tarlang's Neck 375
Tarondor 344
Tasarinan 125
Telchar 95, 304-305
Telcontar (name of Aragorn) 90, 93, 97, 250, 290, 410; Derivation 90
Telemnar 56, 343-344
Teleri/Telerin 8-9; See also Eldar, Elves
Telperion 13
Tharbad 20, 153
Tharkûn - See Gandalf
Thengel 19-21, 25, 155, 173, 253; Relationship with Aragorn 299-302
Théoden 3, 21, 25, 47-49, 57, 60, 65, 78, 88, 90, 95-96, 144-145, 147, 157-160, 163, 174-177, 197, 233-237, 282, 291, 296, 299-302, 308-310, 312, 314-321, 323, 325-331, 333-336, 349, 374-376, 381-385; Relationship with Aragorn 303-308
Théodred 300-301, 303, 308-309, 314, 321, 323, 327-329, 333
Théodwyn 300-301, 308
Thingol (Elwë) 8, 103, 120, 123, 139, 180-181, 390
Thorin II (Oakenshield) 15, 123, 151-152, 158, 166, 168, 175, 181, 184, 203, 240, 401-402
Thorin III (Stonehelm) 79, 203
Thorongil (name of Aragorn) 20-21, 24-25, 77, 83, 91, 96, 100-101, 146, 155, 173-174, 227, 252-255, 257, 259-262, 265-266, 278, 280, 288-291, 293, 296-297, 299-304, 393-394, 399, 404; Derivation 91
Thráin II 151-152, 168, 401
Thranduil 23, 37, 155, 181-182, 184, 352, 357-359, 378-379
Three Elven Rings (Three Rings) 10, 126, 161, 170-171, 217, 337, 339, 356
Thrór 166
Tinúviel - See Lúthien
Tol Eressëa 13, 64, 83, 136, 172
Tolkien, Christopher 2, 4, 8-10, 23, 28-29, 79-80, 88, 102, 104, 149, 170, 174, 179, 227-228, 243, 371, 381, 394, 409
Tolkien, J. R. R. 1-4, 9, 11, 15, 27, 38, 53, 60, 63, 69, 76, 79, 86-89, 92, 100, 102, 104, 118-119, 125, 131-133, 135, 138, 141-142, 149, 165, 171, 179, 181-182, 199-200, 206, 214, 221-222, 227-229, 247, 254-255, 286, 288, 309, 322, 338, 345, 377-378, 381, 383, 386-387, 391, 394-395, 403, 407, 409
Tolkien, Michael 118
Tom Bombadil - See Bombadil, Tom
Took, Faramir 271
Took, Pippin 1, 13, 24, 32-33, 36, 45-51, 56-57, 60-65, 67, 73, 79-82, 87, 90, 95, 97, 100-101, 105, 124, 146-147, 152, 155, 157, 160, 162-164, 169-170, 174-177, 180, 184, 186, 189, 191, 193-197, 199, 201-202, 204, 207, 210-211, 216-218, 221-224, 226, 230-238, 249-250, 255-262, 269, 273, 275, 279, 281, 289-293, 295-296, 301, 306-307, 313-314, 316, 319, 323-324, 326, 329,

353, 369, 371, 375, 386, 389-391, 397-398, 407-408;
Relationship with Aragorn 238-245
Torfir - See Aragorn: Early names
Tower Hills 79, 83, 135, 227, 351
Tower Hills, Palantír of the - See Palantír: Palantír of the Tower Hills
Tower of Elostirion - See Elostirion, Tower of
Translations from the Elvish 249
Treebeard 57, 79, 124-125, 157-158, 176, 192, 197, 202, 205, 386, 398, 400;
Relationship with Aragorn 389-391
Trolls 35, 137-138, 168, 210, 225, 231, 240, 244, 292, 386, 392, 394, 396, 403;
Cave-trolls 400; Hill-trolls 400; Mountain-trolls 400; Olog-hai 400; Stone-trolls 35, 400;
Relationship with Aragorn 399-401
Trotter - See Aragorn: Early names
Tuor 8-9, 11, 99, 112, 120, 133, 139
Turgon (of Gondolin) 10-11, 114, 120
Turgon (Steward of Gondor) 300
Túrin 100-101, 103, 139-140, 155, 174, 204
Two Trees of Valinor 62, 402
Twofoot, Daddy 222

U

Uglúk 233, 397
Ulmo 11, 112
Umbar 25, 49, 67, 219, 253-254, 289, 297, 338, 393-395, 404; See also Corsairs of Umbar
Underhill - See Baggins, Frodo
Undómiel - See Arwen
Undying Lands 61, 83, 85-86, 112, 115, 117-118, 123, 129, 132, 136, 204-206, 222, 229, 318
Ungoliant 402
Uruk-hai - See Orcs
Uruks - See Orcs

V

Valacar 298
Valandil, First Lord of Andúnië 347
Valandil (son of Isildur) 9, 78, 89, 91, 94, 97, 251, 339, 350; Heir of Valandil (title) 91, 347;
Influence on Aragorn 347
Valar 9, 11, 13, 53, 59, 83, 86, 112, 114, 117, 130, 133, 135, 148-149, 172, 178-179, 204-206, 222, 298, 318, 334, 338-341, 347, 390, 393, 395, 401
Valinor 8-11, 13, 62, 85, 117, 133, 170, 338-340, 402-403
Vana 53
Vanyar 8; See also Eldar, Elves
Variags of Khand 392;
Relationship with Aragorn 396
Vidugavia, King of Rhovanion 298
Vidumavi 298
Vilya (the Blue Ring) 337, 356
Vorondil 273, 395

W

Wainriders - See Easterlings
Waldman, Milton 101, 119, 228-229
War of the Kin-strife - See Kin-strife, War of the
War of the Ring 20, 23, 54, 61, 74-75, 77-80, 82, 115-116, 122, 125-126, 130, 132, 137, 145, 147, 150-151, 154-155, 157-158, 173, 181, 183, 202-208, 227, 233, 238, 245, 248, 250, 255-257, 260, 287, 289, 291, 327, 332-333, 335, 351, 353, 359, 364, 366, 368, 373, 379, 381-383, 389, 391, 395-396, 398-399, 402-403, 409
Warden of the Houses of Healing 80, 162, 236-237, 284, 297, 318-320, 322, 380, 405;
Relationship with Aragorn 294-296;
See also Houses of Healing
Wargs 379, 404
Watcher-in-the-Water 166, 269
Weather Hills 231
Weathertop 32, 35-36, 39, 51, 53, 58-59, 72, 113, 118, 124, 134, 156, 159, 160-161, 188-189, 211-212, 214, 224, 231, 240, 279, 353-355, 359, 404-405
West, Richard C. 87
Westemnet - See Rohan
Westernesse - See Númenor
Westernesse, Men of - See Dúnedain
Westmarch 79, 227
Westron - See Common Speech
White Company 293
White Council 15, 22, 94, 123, 149-152, 172-173, 340, 351
White Hand 398
White Messenger - See Saruman
White Mountains 193, 203, 267, 296-297, 334, 364, 373, 375-376, 382, 399
White Rider - See Gandalf
White Tree 13-14, 56, 81, 113, 116-117, 143, 145, 147, 158, 165-166, 242, 253, 286-287, 346, 351, 362; History of 343-344;
See also Lord of the White Tree
White Wolves 385, 404
Whitfoot, Will 105
Widfara 301-302
Wielder of the Sword Reforged (title of Aragorn) 92, 97, 342, 350; Derivation 92
Wild Men of the Woods - See Drúedain
Wingfoot (name of Aragorn) 91, 326; Derivation 91
Witch-king (of Angmar) - See Lord of the Nazgûl
Withywindle, River 230, 38
Wold - See Rohan
Woodmen of Western Mirkwood 363; Relationship with Aragorn 379
Woody End 223
Woses - See Drúedain

Y

Yavanna 13, 53, 117, 178, 390
Yrch - See Orcs